Thomas Mann

Thomas **Mann**

Death in Venice

Tristan

Tonio Kröger

Doctor Faustus

Mario and the Magician

A Man and His Dog

The Black Swan

Confessions of Felix Krull, Confidence Man

Secker & Warburg / Octopus

Death in Venice first published as *Der Tod in Venedig* 1913
Translated by H. T. Lowe-Porter
and first published in Great Britain by Martin Secker 1928
Translation © H. T. Lowe-Porter 1928

Tristan first published 1903
Translated by H. T. Lowe-Porter
and first published in Great Britain by Martin Secker 1928
Translation © H. T. Lowe-Porter 1928

Tonio Kröger first published 1903
Translated by H. T. Lowe-Porter
and first published in Great Britain by Martin Secker 1928
Translation © H. T. Lowe-Porter 1928

Doctor Faustus first published 1947
© Thomas Mann 1947
Translated by H. T. Lowe-Porter
and first published in Great Britain by Martin Secker & Warburg Limited 1949
Translation © Martin Secker & Warburg Limited

Mario and the Magician first published as *Mario und der Zauberer* 1930
Translated by H. T. Lowe-Porter
and first published in Great Britain by Martin Secker 1930
Translation © Martin Secker & Warburg Limited

A Man and His Dog first published as *Herr und Hund* 1919
Translated by H. T. Lowe-Porter
and first published in Great Britain in *Stories of Three Decades*
by Martin Secker & Warburg Limited 1936
Translation © Martin Secker & Warburg Limited

The Black Swan first published as *Die Betrogene* 1953
Translated by Willard R. Trask
and first published in Great Britain by Martin Secker & Warburg Limited 1954
Translation © Martin Secker & Warburg Limited 1954

Confessions of Felix Krull, Confidence Man
first published as *Beckenntnisse des Hochstaplers Felix Krull* 1954
© Thomas Mann 1954
Translated by Denver Lindley
and first published in Great Britain by Martin Secker & Warburg Limited 1955
Translation © Martin Secker & Warburg Limited 1955

This edition first published in Great Britain in 1979 by
Martin Secker & Warburg Limited
54 Poland Street
London W1
in association with
Octopus Books Limited
59 Grosvenor Street
London W1

ISBN 0 905712 38 2

Printed in the United States

Contents

Death
in
Venice

TRANSLATED FROM THE GERMAN BY

H.T. Lowe-Porter

Gustave Aschenbach – or von Aschenbach, as he had been known officially since his fiftieth birthday – had set out alone from his house in Prince Regent Street, Munich, for an extended walk. It was a spring afternoon in that year of grace 19–, when Europe sat upon the anxious seat beneath a menace that hung over its head for months. Aschenbach had sought the open soon after tea. He was overwrought by a morning of hard, nerve-taxing work, work which had not ceased to exact his uttermost in the way of sustained concentration, conscientiousness, and tact; and after the noon meal found himself powerless to check the onward sweep of the productive mechanism within him, that *motus animi continuus* in which, according to Cicero, eloquence resides. He had sought but not found relaxation in sleep – though the wear and tear upon his system had come to make a daily nap more and more imperative – and now undertook a walk, in the hope that air and exercise might send him back refreshed to a good evening's work.

May had begun, and after weeks of cold and wet a mock summer had set in. The English Gardens, though in tenderest leaf, felt as sultry as in August and were full of vehicles and pedestrians near the city. But towards Aumeister the paths were solitary and still, and Aschenbach strolled thither, stopping awhile to watch the lively crowds in the restaurant garden with its fringe of carriages and cabs. Thence he took his homeward way outside the park and across the sunset fields. By the time he reached the North Cemetery, however, he felt tired, and a storm was brewing above Föhring; so he waited at the stopping-place for a train to carry him back to the city.

He found the neighbourhood quite empty. Not a wagon in sight, either on the paved Ungererstrasse, with its gleaming tram-lines stretching off towards Schwabing, nor on the Föhring highway. Nothing stirred behind the hedge in the stonemason's yard, where crosses, monuments, and commemorative tablets made a supernumerary and untenanted graveyard opposite the real one. The mortuary chapel, a structure in Byzantine style, stood facing it, silent in the gleam of the ebbing day. Its façade was adorned with Greek crosses and tinted hieratic designs, and displayed a symmetrically arranged selection of scriptural texts in gilded letters, all of them with a bearing upon the future life, such as: 'They are entering into the House of the Lord' and 'May the Light Everlasting shine upon them'. Aschenbach beguiled some minutes of his waiting with reading these formulas and letting his mind's eye lose itself in their mystical meaning. He was brought back to reality by the sight of a man standing in the portico, above the two apocalyptic beasts that guarded the staircase, and something not quite usual in this man's appearance gave his thoughts a fresh turn.

Whether he had come out of the hall through the bronze doors or mounted unnoticed from outside, it was impossible to tell. Aschenbach casually inclined to the first idea. He was of medium height, thin, beardless, and strikingly snub-nosed; he belonged to the red-haired type and possessed its milky, freckled skin. He was obviously not Bavarian; and the broad, straight-brimmed straw hat he had on even made him look distinctly exotic. True, he had the indigenous rucksack buckled on his back, wore a belted suit of yellowish woollen stuff, apparently frieze, and carried a grey mackintosh cape across his left forearm, which was propped against his waist. In his right hand, slantwise to the ground, he held an ironshod stick, and braced himself against its crook, with his legs crossed. His chin was up, so that the Adam's apple looked very bald in the lean neck rising from the loose shirt: and he stood there sharply peering up into space out of colourless, red-lashed eyes, while two pronounced perpendicular furrows showed on his forehead in curious contrast to his little turned-up nose. Perhaps his heightened and heightening position helped out the impression Aschenbach received. At any rate, standing out as though at survey, the man had a bold and domineering, even a ruthless, air, and his lips completed the picture by seeming to curl back, either by reason of some deformity or else because he grimaced, being blinded by the sun in his face; they laid bare the long, white, glistening teeth to the gums.

Aschenbach's gaze, though unawares, had very likely been inquisitive and tactless; for he became suddenly conscious that the stranger was returning it, and indeed so directly, with such hostility, such plain intent to force the withdrawal of the other's eyes, that Aschenbach felt an unpleasant twinge, and turning his back, began to walk along the hedge, hastily resolving to give the man no further heed. He had forgotten him the next minute. Yet whether the pilgrim air the stranger wore kindled his fantasy or whether some other physical or psychical influence came in play, he could not tell; but he felt the most surprising consciousness of a widening of inward barriers, a kind of vaulting unrest, a youthfully ardent thirst for distant scenes – a feeling so lively and so new, or at least so long ago outgrown and forgot, that he stood there rooted to the spot, his eyes on the ground and his hands clasped behind him, exploring these sentiments of his, their bearing and scope.

True, what he felt was no more than a longing to travel; yet coming upon him with such suddenness and passion as to resemble a seizure, almost a hallucination. Desire projected itself visually: his fancy, not quite yet lulled since morning, imaged the marvels and terrors of the manifold earth. He saw. He beheld a landscape, a tropical marshland, beneath a reeking sky, steaming, monstrous, rank – a kind of primeval wilderness-world of islands, morasses, and alluvial channels. Hairy palm-trunks rose near and far out of lush brakes of fern, out of bottoms of crass vegetation, fat, swollen, thick with incredible bloom. There were trees, mis-shapen as a dream, that dropped their naked roots straight through the air into the ground or into water that was stagnant and shadowy and glassy-green, where mammoth milk-white blossoms floated, and strange high-shouldered birds with curious bills stood gazing sidewise without sound or stir. Among the knotted joints of a bamboo thicket the eyes of a crouching tiger gleamed – and he felt his heart throb with terror, yet with a longing inexplicable. Then the vision vanished. Aschenbach, shaking his head, took up his march once more along the hedge of the stonemason's yard.

He had, at least ever since he commanded means to get about the world at will, regarded travel as a necessary evil, to be endured now and again willy-nilly for the sake of one's health. Too busy with the tasks imposed upon him by his own ego and the European soul, too laden with the care and duty to create, too preoccupied to be an amateur of the gay outer world, he had been content to know as much of the earth's surface as he could without stirring far outside his own sphere – had, indeed, never even been tempted to leave Europe. Now more than ever, since his life was on the wane, since he could no longer brush aside as fanciful his artist fear of not having done, of not being finished before the works ran down, he had confined himself to close range, had hardly stepped outside the charming city which he had made his home and the rude country house he had built in the mountains, whither he went to spend the rainy summers.

And so the new impulse which thus late and suddenly swept over him was speedily made to conform to the pattern of self-discipline he had followed from his youth up. He had meant to bring his work, for which he lived, to a certain point before leaving for the country, and the thought of a leisurely ramble across the globe, which should take him away from his desk for months, was too fantastic and upsetting to be seriously entertained. Yet the source of the unexpected contagion was known to him only too well. This yearning for new and distant scenes, this craving for freedom, release, forgetfulness – they were, he admitted to himself, an impulse towards flight, flight from the spot which was the daily theatre of a rigid, cold, and passionate service. That service he loved, had even almost come to love the enervating daily struggle between a proud, tenacious, well-tried will and this growing fatigue, which no one must suspect, nor the finished product betray by any faintest sign that his inspiration could ever flag or miss fire. On the other hand, it seemed the part of common sense not to span the bow too far, not to suppress summarily a need that so unequivocally asserted itself. He thought of his work, and the place where yesterday and again today he had been forced to lay it down, since it would not yield either to patient effort or a swift *coup de main*. Again and again he had tried to break or untie the knot – only to retire at last from the attack with a shiver of repugnance. Yet the difficulty was actually not a great one; what sapped his strength was distaste for the task, betrayed by a fastidiousness he could no longer satisfy. In his youth, indeed, the nature and inmost essence of the literary gift had been, to him, this very scrupulosity; for it he had bridled and tempered his sensibilities, knowing full well that feeling is prone to be content with easy gains and blithe half-perfection. So now, perhaps, feeling, thus tyrannized, avenged itself by leaving him, refusing from now on to carry and wing his art and taking away with it all the ecstasy he had known in form and expression. Not that he was doing bad work. So much, at least, the years had brought him, that at any moment he might feel tranquilly assured of mastery. But he got no joy of it – not though a nation paid it homage. To him it seemed his work had ceased to be marked by that fiery play of fancy which is the product of joy, and more, and more potently, than any intrinsic content, forms in turn the joy of the receiving world. He dreaded the summer in the country, alone with the maid who prepared his food and the man who served him; dreaded to see the familiar mountain peaks and walls that would shut him up again with his heavy discontent. What he needed was a break, an interim existence, a means of passing time, other air and a new stock of blood, to make the summer tolerable and productive. Good, then, he would go a journey. Not far – not all the way to the tigers. A night in a *wagon-lit*, three or four weeks of lotus-eating at some one of the gay world's playgrounds in the lovely south...

So ran his thoughts, while the clang of the electric tram drew nearer down the Ungererstrasse; and as he mounted the platform he decided to devote the evening to a study of maps and railway guides. Once in, he bethought him to look back after the man in the straw hat, the companion of this brief interval which had after all been so fruitful. But he was not in his former place, nor in the tram itself, nor yet at the next stop; in short, his whereabouts remained a mystery.

Gustave Aschenbach was born at L–, a country town in the province of Silesia. He was the son of an upper official in the judicature, and his forbears had all been officers, judges, departmental functionaries – men who lived their strict, decent, sparing lives in the service of king and state. Only once before had a livelier mentality – in the quality of a clergyman – turned up among them; but swifter, more perceptive blood had in the generation before the poet's flowed into the stock from the mother's side, she being the daughter of a Bohemian musical conductor. It was from her he had the foreign traits that betrayed themselves in his appearance. The union of dry, conscientious officialdom and ardent, obscure impulse, produced an artist – and this particular artist; author of the lucid and vigorous prose epic on the life of Frederick the Great; careful, tireless weaver of the richly patterned tapestry entitled *Maia*, a novel that gathers up the threads of many human destinies in the warp of a single idea; creator of that powerful narrative *The Abject*, which taught a whole grateful generation that a man can still be capable of moral resolution even after he has plumbed the depths of knowledge; and lastly – to complete the tale of works of his mature period – the writer of that impassioned discourse on the theme of Mind and Art whose ordered force and antithetic eloquence led serious critics to rank it with Schiller's *Simple and Sentimental Poetry*.

Aschenbach's whole soul, from the very beginning, was bent on fame – and thus, while not precisely precocious, yet thanks to the unmistakable trenchancy of his personal accent he was early ripe and ready for a career. Almost before he was out of high school he had a name. Ten years later he had learned to sit at his desk and sustain and live up to his growing reputation, to write gracious and pregnant phrases in letters that must needs be brief, for many claims press upon the solid and successful man. At forty, worn down by the strains and stresses of his actual task, he had to deal with a daily post heavy with tributes from his own and foreign countries.

Remote on one hand from the banal, on the other from the eccentric, his genius was calculated to win at once the adhesion of the general public and the admiration, both sympathetic and stimulating, of the connoisseur. From childhood up he was pushed on every side to achievement, and achievement of no ordinary kind; and so his young days never knew the sweet idleness and blithe *laissez aller* that belong to youth. A nice observer once said of him in company – it was at the time when he fell ill in Vienna in his thirty-fifth year: 'You see, Aschenbach has always lived like this' – here the speaker closed the fingers of his left hand to a fist – 'never like this' – and he let his open hand hang relaxed from the back of his chair. It was apt. And this attitude was the more morally valiant in that Aschenbach was not by nature robust – he was only called to the constant tension of his career, not actually born to it.

By medical advice he had been kept from school and educated at home. He had grown up solitary, without comradeship; yet had early been driven to see that he belonged to those whose talent is not so much out of the common as is the physical basis on which talent relies for its fulfilment. It is a seed that gives early of its fruit, whose powers seldom reach a ripe old age. But his favourite motto was 'Hold fast'; indeed, in his novel on the life of Frederick the Great he envisaged nothing else than the apotheosis of the old hero's word of command, '*Durchhalten*', which seemed to him the epitome of fortitude under suffering. Besides, he deeply desired to live to a good old age, for it was his conviction that only the artist to whom it has been granted to be fruitful on all stages of our human scene can be truly great, or universal, or worthy of honour.

Bearing the burden of his genius, then, upon such slender shoulders and resolved to go so far, he had the more need of discipline – and discipline, fortunately, was his native inheritance from the father's side. At forty, at fifty, he was still living as he had commenced to live in the years when others are prone to waste and revel, dream high thoughts and postpone fulfilment. He began his day with a cold shower over chest and back; then, setting a pair of tall wax candles in silver holders at the head of his manuscript, he sacrificed to art, in two or three hours of almost religious fervour, the powers he had assembled in sleep. Outsiders might be pardoned for believing that his *Maia* world and the epic amplitude revealed by the life of Frederick were a manifestation of great power working under high pressure, that they came forth, as it were, all in one breath. It was the more triumph for his morale; for the truth was that they were heaped up to greatness in layer after layer, in long days of work, out of hundreds and hundreds of single inspirations; they owed their excellence, both of mass and detail, to one thing and one alone; that their creator could hold out for years under the strain of the same piece of work, with an endurance and a tenacity of purpose like that which had conquered his native province of Silesia, devoting to actual composition none but his best and freshest hours.

For an intellectual product of any value to exert an immediate influence which shall also be deep and lasting, it must rest on an inner harmony, yes, an affinity, between the personal destiny of its author and that of his contemporaries in general. Men do not know why they award fame to one work of art rather than another. Without being in the faintest connoisseurs, they think to justify the warmth of their commendations by discovering in it a hundred virtues, whereas the real ground of their applause is inexplicable – it is sympathy. Aschenbach had once given direct expression – though in an unobtrusive place – to the idea that almost everything conspicuously great is great in despite: has come into being in defiance of affliction and pain, poverty, destitution, bodily weakness, vice, passion, and a thousand other obstructions. And that was more than observation – it was the fruit of experience, it was precisely the formula of his life and fame, it was the key to his work. What wonder, then, if it was also the fixed character, the outward gesture, of his most individual figures?

The new type of hero favoured by Aschenbach, and recurring many times in his works, had early been analysed by a shrewd critic: 'The conception of an intellectual and virginal manliness, which clenches its teeth and stands in modest defiance of the swords and spears that pierce its side.' That was beautiful, it was *spirituel*, it was exact, despite the suggestion of too great passivity it held. Forbearance in the face of fate, beauty constant under torture, are not merely passive. They are a positive achievement, an explicit triumph; and the figure of Sebastian is the most beautiful symbol, if not of art as a whole, yet certainly of the art we speak of here. Within that world of Aschenbach's creation were exhibited many phases of this theme: there was the aristocratic self-command that is eaten out within and for as long as it can conceals its biologic decline from the eyes of the world; the sere and ugly outside, hiding the embers of smouldering fire – and having power to fan them to so pure a flame as to challenge supremacy in the domain of beauty itself; the pallid languors of the flesh, contrasted with the fiery ardours of the spirit within, which can fling a whole proud people down at the foot of the Cross, at the feet of its own sheer self-abnegation; the gracious bearing preserved in the stern, stark service of form; the unreal, precarious existence of the born intrigant with its swiftly enervating alternation of schemes and desires – all these human fates and many more of their like one read in Aschenbach's pages, and reading them might doubt the existence of any other kind of heroism than the heroism born of weakness. And, after all, what kind could be truer to the spirit of the times? Gustave Aschenbach was the poet-spokesman of all those who labour at the edge of exhaustion; of the over-burdened, of those who are already worn out but still hold themselves upright; of all our modern moralizers of accomplishment, with stunted growth and scanty resources, who yet contrive by skilful husbanding and prodigious spasms of will to produce, at least for a while, the effect of greatness. There are many such, they are the heroes of the age. And in Aschenbach's pages they saw themselves; he justified, he exalted them, he sang their praise – and they, they were grateful, they heralded his fame.

He had been young and crude with the times and by them badly counselled. He had taken false steps, blundered, exposed himself, offended in speech and writing against tact and good sense. But he had attained to honour, and honour, he used to say, is the natural goal towards which every considerable talent presses with whip and spur. Yes, one might put it that his whole career had been one conscious and overweening ascent to honour, which left in the rear all the misgivings or self-derogation which might have hampered him.

What pleases the public is lively and vivid delineation which makes no demands on the intellect; but passionate and absolutist youth can only be enthralled by a problem. And Aschenbach was an absolute, as problematist, as any youth of them all. He had done homage to intellect, had overworked the soil of knowledge and ground up her seed-corn; had turned his back on the 'mysteries', called genius itself in question, held up art to scorn – yes, even while his faithful following revelled in the characters he created, he, the young artist, was taking away the breath of the twenty-year-olds with his cynic utterances on the nature of art and the artist life.

But it seems that a noble and active mind blunts itself against nothing so quickly as the sharp and bitter irritant of knowledge. And certain it is that the youth's constancy of purpose, no matter how painfully conscientious, was shallow beside the mature resolution of the master of his craft, who made a right-about-face, turned his back on the realm of knowledge, and passed it by with averted face, lest it lame his will or power of action, paralyse his feelings or his passions, deprive any of these of their conviction or utility. How else interpret the oft-cited story of *The Abject* than as a rebuke to the excesses of a psychology-ridden age, embodied in the delineation of the weak and silly fool who manages to lead fate by the nose; driving his wife, out of sheer innate pusillanimity, into the arms of a beardless youth, and making this disaster an excuse for trifling away the rest of his life?

With rage the author here rejects the rejected, casts out the outcast – and the measure of his fury is the measure of his condemnation of all moral shilly-shallying. Explicitly he renounces sympathy with the abyss, explicitly he refutes the flabby humanitarianism of the phrase: '*Tout comprendre c'est tout pardonner.*' What was here unfolding, or rather was already in full bloom, was the 'miracle of regained detachment', which a little later became the theme of one of the author's dialogues, dwelt upon not without a certain oracular emphasis. Strange sequence of thought! Was it perhaps an intellectual consequence of this rebirth, this new austerity, that from now on his style showed an almost exaggerated sense of beauty, a lofty purity, symmetry, and simplicity, which gave his productions a stamp of the classic, of conscious and deliberate mastery? And yet: this moral fibre, surviving the hampering and disintegrating effect of knowledge, does it not result in its turn in a dangerous simplification, in a tendency to equate the world and the human soul, and thus to strengthen the hold of the evil, the forbidden, and the ethically impossible? And has not form two aspects? Is it not moral and immoral at once; moral in so far as it is the expression and result of discipline, immoral – yes, actually hostile to morality – in that of its very essence it is indifferent to good and evil, and deliberately concerned to make the moral world stoop beneath its proud and undivided sceptre?

Be that as it may. Development is destiny; and why should a career attended by applause and adulation of the masses necessarily take the same course as one which does not share the glamour and the obligations of fame? Only the incorrigible bohemian smiles or scoffs when a man of transcendent gifts outgrows his carefree prentice stage, recognizes his own worth and forces the world to recognize it too and pay it homage, though he puts on a courtly bearing to hide his bitter struggles and his loneliness. Again, the play of a developing talent must give its possessor joy, if of a wilful, defiant kind. With time, an official note, something almost expository, crept into Gustave Aschenbach's method. His later style gave up the old sheer audacities, the fresh and subtle nuances – it became fixed and exemplary, conservative, formal, even formulated. Like Louis XIV – or as tradition has it of him – Aschenbach, as he went on in years, banished from his style every common word. It was at this time that the school authorities adopted selections from his works into their text-books. And he found it only fitting – and had not thought but to accept – when a German prince signalized his accession to the throne by conferring upon the poet-author of the life of Frederick the Great on his fiftieth birthday the letters-patent of nobility.

He had roved about for a few years, trying this place and that as a place of residence, before choosing, as he soon did, the city of Munich for his permanent home. And there he lived, enjoying among his fellow-citizens the honour which is in rare cases the reward of intellectual eminence. He married young, the daughter of a university family; but after a brief term of wedded happiness his wife had died. A daughter, already married, remained to him. A son he never had.

Gustave von Aschenbach was somewhat below middle height, dark and smooth-shaven, with a head that looked rather too large for his almost delicate figure. He wore his hair brushed back; it was thin at the parting, bushy and grey on the temples, framing a lofty, rugged, knotty brow – if one may so characterize it. The nose-piece of his rimless gold spectacles cut into the base of his thick, aristocratically hooked nose. The mouth was large, often lax, often suddenly narrow and tense; the cheeks lean and furrowed, the pronounced chin slightly cleft. The vicissitudes of fate, it seemed, must have passed over his head, for he held it, plaintively, rather on one side; yet it was art, not the stern discipline of an active career, that had taken over the office of modelling these features. Behind this brow were born the flashing thrust and parry of the dialogue between Frederick and Voltaire on the theme of war; these eyes, weary and sunken, gazing through their glasses, had beheld the blood-stained inferno of the hospitals in the Seven Years'

War. Yes, personally speaking too, art heightens life. She gives deeper joy, she consumes more swiftly. She engraves adventures of the spirit and the mind in the faces of her votaries; let them lead outwardly a life of the most cloistered calm, she will in the end produce in them a fastidiousness, an over-refinement, a nervous fever and exhaustion, such as a career of extravagant passions and pleasures can hardly show.

Eager though he was to be off, Aschenbach was kept in Munich by affairs both literary and practical for some two weeks after that walk of his. But at length he ordered his country home put ready against his return within the next few weeks, and on a day between the middle and the end of May took the evening train for Trieste, where he stopped only twenty-four hours, embarking for Pola the next morning but one.

What he sought was a fresh scene, without associations, which should yet be not too out-of-the-way; and accordingly he chose an island in the Adriatic, not far off the Istrian coast. It had been well known some years, for its splendidly rugged cliff formations on the side next the open sea, and its population, clad in a bright flutter of rags and speaking an outlandish tongue. But there was rain and heavy air; the society at the hotel was provincial Austrian, and limited; besides, it annoyed him not to be able to get at the sea – he missed the close and soothing contact which only a gentle sandy slope affords. He could not feel this was the place he sought; an inner impulse made him wretched, urging him on he knew not whither; he racked his brains, he looked up boats, then all at once his goal stood plain before his eyes. But of course! When one wanted to arrive overnight at the incomparable, the fabulous, the like-nothing-else-in-the-world, where was it one went? Why, obviously; he had intended to go there, what ever was he doing here? A blunder. He made all haste to correct it, announcing his departure at once. Ten days after his arrival on the island a swift motor-boat bore him and his luggage in the misty dawning back across the water to the naval station, where he landed only to pass over the landing-stage and on to the wet decks of a ship lying there with steam up for the passage to Venice.

It was an ancient hulk belonging to an Italian line, obsolete, dingy, grimed with soot. A dirty hunchbacked sailor, smirkingly polite, conducted him at once belowships to a cavernous, lamplit cabin. There behind a table sat a man with a beard like a goat's; he had his hat on the back of his head, a cigar-stump in the corner of his mouth; he reminded Aschenbach of an old-fashioned circus-director. This person put the usual questions and wrote out a ticket to Venice, which he issued to the traveller with many commercial flourishes.

'A ticket for Venice,' he repeated, stretching out his arm to dip the pen into the thick ink in a tilted ink-stand. 'One first-class to Venice! Here you are, *signore mio.*' He made some scrawls on the paper, strewed bluish sand on it out of a box, thereafter letting the sand run off into an earthen vessel, folded the paper with bony yellow fingers, and wrote on the outside. 'An excellent choice,' he rattled on. 'Ah, Venice! What a glorious city! Irresistibly attractive to the cultured man for her past history as well as her present charm.' His copious gesturings and empty phrases gave the odd impression that he feared the traveller might alter his mind. He changed Aschenbach's note, laying the money on the spotted table-cover with the glibness of a croupier. 'A pleasant visit to you, signore,' he said, with a melodramatic bow. 'Delighted to serve you.' Then he beckoned and called out: 'Next' as though a stream of passengers stood waiting to be served, though in point of fact there was not one. Aschenbach returned to the upper deck.

He leaned an arm on the railing and looked at the idlers lounging along the quay to watch the boat go out. Then he turned his attention to his fellow-passengers. Those of the second class, both men and women, were squatted on their bundles of luggage on the forward deck. The first cabin consisted of a group of lively youths, clerks from Pola, evidently, who had made up a pleasure excursion to Italy and were not a little thrilled at the prospect, bustling about and laughing with satisfaction at the stir they made. They leaned over the railings and shouted, with a glib command of epithet, derisory remarks at such of their fellow-clerks as they saw going to business along the quay; and these in turn shook their sticks and shouted as good back again. One of the party, in a dandified buff suit, a rakish panama with a coloured scarf, and a red cravat, was loudest of the loud: he outcrowed all the rest. Aschenbach's eye dwelt on him, and he was shocked to see that the apparent youth was no youth at all. He was an old man, beyond a doubt, with wrinkles and crow's-feet round eyes and mouth; the dull carmine of the cheeks was rouge, the brown hair a wig. His neck was shrunken and sinewy, his turned-up moustaches and small imperial were dyed, and the unbroken double row of yellow teeth he showed when he laughed were but too obviously a cheapish false set. He wore a seal ring on each forefinger, but the hands were those of an old man. Aschenbach was moved to shudder as he watched the creature and his association with the rest of the group. Could they not see he was old, that he had no right to wear the clothes they wore or pretend to be one of them? But they were used to him, it seemed; they suffered him among them, they paid back his jokes in kind and the playful pokes in the ribs he gave them. How could they? Aschenbach put his hand to his brow, he covered his eyes, for he had slept little, and they smarted. He felt not quite canny, as though the world were suffering a dreamlike distortion of perspective which he might arrest by shutting it all out for a few minutes and then looking at it afresh. But instead he felt a floating sensation, and opened his eyes with unreasoning alarm to find that the ship's dark sluggish bulk was slowly leaving the jetty. Inch by inch, with the to-and-fro motion of her machinery, the strip of iridescent dirty water widened, the boat manoeuvred clumsily and turned her bow to the open sea. Aschenbach moved over to the starboard side, where the hunchbacked sailor had set up a deck-chair for him, and a steward in a greasy dress-coat asked for orders.

The sky was grey, the wind humid. Harbour and island dropped behind, all sight of land soon vanished in mist. Flakes of sodden, clammy soot fell upon the still undried deck. Before the boat was an hour out a canvas had to be spread as a shelter from the rain.

Wrapped in his cloak, a book in his lap, our traveller rested; the hours slipped by unawares. It stopped raining, the canvas was taken down. The horizon was visible right round: beneath the sombre dome of the sky stretched the vast plain of empty sea. But immeasurable unarticulated space weakens our power to measure time as well: the time-sense falters and grows dim. Strange, shadowy figures passed and repassed – the elderly coxcomb, the goat-bearded man from the bowels of the ship – with vague gesturings and mutterings through the traveller's mind as he lay. He fell asleep.

At midday he was summoned to luncheon in a corridor-like saloon with the sleeping-cabins giving off it. He ate at the head of the long table; the party of clerks, including the old man, sat with the jolly captain at the other end, where they had been carousing since ten o'clock. The meal was

wretched, and soon done. Aschenbach was driven to seek the open and look
at the sky – perhaps it would lighten presently above Venice.

He had not dreamed it could be otherwise, for the city had ever given him
a brilliant welcome. But sky and sea remained leaden, with spurts of fine,
mistlike rain; he reconciled himself to the idea of seeing a different Venice
from that he had always approached on the landward side. He stood by the
foremast, his gaze on the distance, alert for the first glimpse of the coast. And
he thought of the melancholy and susceptible poet who had once seen the
towers and turrets of his dreams rise out of these waves; repeated the
rhythms born of his awe, his mingled emotions of joy and suffering – and
easily susceptible to a prescience already shaped with him, he asked his own
sober, weary heart if a new enthusiasm, a new preoccupation, some late
adventure of the feelings could still be in store for the idle traveller.

The flat coast showed on the right, the sea was soon populous with
fishing-boats. The Lido appeared and was left behind as the ship glided at
half speed through the narrow harbour of the same name, coming to a full
stop on the lagoon in sight of garish, badly built houses. Here it waited for
the boat bringing the sanitary inspector.

An hour passed. One had arrived – and yet not. There was no conceivable
haste – yet one felt harried. The youths from Pola were on deck, drawn
hither by the martial sound of horns coming across the water from the
direction of the Public Gardens. They had drunk a good deal of Asti and
were moved to shout and hurrah at the drilling *bersaglieri*. But the young-old
man was a truly repulsive sight in the condition to which his company with
youth had brought him. He could not carry his wine like them: he was
pitiably drunk. He swayed as he stood – watery-eyed, a cigarette between his
shaking fingers, keeping upright with difficulty. He could not have taken a
step without falling and knew better than to stir, but his spirits were
deplorably high. He buttonholed anyone who came within reach, he
stuttered, he giggled, he leered, he fatuously shook his beringed old
forefinger; his tongue kept seeking the corner of his mouth in a suggestive
motion ugly to behold. Aschenbach's brow darkened as he looked, and there
came over him once more a dazed sense, as though things about him were
just slightly losing their ordinary perspective, beginning to show a distortion that might merge into the grotesque. He was prevented from dwelling
on the feeling, for now the machinery began to thud again, and the ship took
up its passage through the Canal di San Marco which had been interrupted
so near the goal.

He saw it once more, that landing-place that takes the breath away, that
amazing group of incredible structures the Republic set up to meet the awe-
struck eye of the approaching seafarer: the airy splendour of the palace and
Bridge of Sighs, the columns of lion and saint on the shore, the glory of the
projecting flank of the fairy temple, the vista of gateway and clock. Looking,
he thought that to come to Venice by the station is like entering a palace by
the back door. No one should approach, save by the high seas as he was doing
now, this most improbable of cities.

The engines stopped. Gondolas pressed alongside, the landing-stairs
were let down, customs officials came on board and did their office, people
began to go ashore. Aschenbach ordered a gondola. He meant to take up his
abode by the sea and needed to be conveyed with his luggage to the landing-
stage of the little steamers that ply between the city and the Lido. They
called down his order to the surface of the water where the gondoliers were
quarrelling in dialect. Then came another delay while his trunk was worried

down the ladder-like stairs. Thus he was forced to endure the importunities of the ghastly young-old man, whose drunken stare obscurely urged him to pay the stranger the honour of a formal farewell. 'We wish you a very pleasant sojourn,' he babbled, bowing and scraping. 'Pray keep us in mind. *Au revoir, excusez et bon jour, votre Excellence.*' He drooled, he blinked, he licked the corner of his mouth, the little imperial bristled on his elderly chin. He put the tips of two fingers to his mouth and said thickly: 'Give her our love, will you, the p-pretty little dear' – here his upper plate came away and fell down on the lower one . . . Aschenbach escaped. 'Little sweety-sweety-sweetheart' he heard behind him, gurgled and stuttered, as he climbed down the rope stair into the boat.

Is there anyone but must repress a secret thrill, on arriving in Venice for the first time – or returning thither after long absence – and stepping into a Venetian gondola? That singular conveyance, come down unchanged from ballad times, black as nothing else on earth except a coffin – what pictures it calls up of lawless, silent adventures in the plashing night; or even more, what visions of death itself, the bier and solemn rites and last soundless voyage! And has anyone remarked that the seat in such a bark, the arm-chair lacquered in coffin-black, and dully black-upholstered, is the softest, most luxurious, most relaxing seat in the world? Aschenbach realized it when he had let himself down at the gondolier's feet, opposite his luggage, which lay neatly composed on the vessel's beak. The rowers still gestured fiercely; he heard their harsh, incoherent tones. But the strange stillness of the water-city seemed to take up their voices gently, to disembody and scatter them over the sea. It was warm here in the harbour. The lukewarm air of the sirocco breathed upon him, he leaned back among his cushions and gave himself to the yielding element, closing his eyes for very pleasure in an indolence as unaccustomed as sweet. 'The trip will be short,' he thought, and wished it might last forever. They gently swayed away from the boat with its bustle and clamour of voices.

It grew still and stiller all about. No sound but the splash of the oars, the hollow slap of the wave against the steep, black, halbert-shaped beak of the vessel, and one sound more – a muttering by fits and starts, expressed as it were by the motion of his arms, from the lips of the gondolier. He was talking to himself, between his teeth. Aschenbach glanced up and saw with surprise that the lagoon was widening, his vessel was headed for the open sea. Evidently it would not do to give himself up to sweet *far niente*; he must see his wishes carried out.

'You are to take me to the steamboat landing, you know,' he said, half turning round towards it. The muttering stopped. There was no reply.

'Take me to the steamboat landing,' he repeated, and this time turned quite round and looked up into the face of the gondolier as he stood there on his little elevated deck, high against the pale grey sky. The man had an unpleasing, even brutish face, and wore blue clothes like a sailor's, with a yellow sash; a shapeless straw hat with the braid torn at the brim perched rakishly on his head. His facial structure, as well as the curling blond moustache under the short snub nose, showed him to be of non-Italian stock. Physically rather undersized, so that one would not have expected him to be very muscular, he pulled vigorously at the oar, putting all his body-weight behind each stroke. Now and then the effort he made curled back his lips and bared his white teeth to the gums. He spoke in a decided, almost curt voice, looking out to sea over his fare's head: 'The signore is going to the Lido.'

Aschenbach answered: 'Yes, I am. But I only took the gondola to cross over to San Marco. I am using the *vaporetto* from there.'

'But the signore cannot use the *vaporetto*.'

'And why not?'

'Because the *vaporetto* does not take luggage.'

It was true. Aschenbach remembered it. He made no answer. But the man's gruff, overbearing manner, so unlike the usual courtesy of his countrymen towards the stranger, was intolerable. Aschenbach spoke again: 'That is my own affair. I may want to give my luggage in deposit. You will turn round.'

No answer. The oar splashed, the wave struck dull against the prow. And the muttering began anew, the gondolier talked to himself, between his teeth.

What should the traveller do? Alone on the water with this tongue-tied, obstinate, uncanny man, he saw no way of enforcing his will. And if only he did not excite himself, how pleasantly he might rest! Had he not wished the voyage might last forever? The wisest thing – and how much the pleasantest! – was to let matters take their own course. A spell of indolence was upon him; it came from the chair he sat in – this low, black-upholstered arm-chair, so gently rocked at the hands of the despotic boatman in his rear. The thought passed dreamily through Aschenbach's brain that perhaps he had fallen into the clutches of a criminal; it had not power to rouse him to action. More annoying was the simpler explanation: that the man was only trying to extort money. A sense of duty, a recollection, as it were, that this ought to be prevented, made him collect himself to say:

'How much do you ask for the trip?'

And the gondolier, gazing out over his head, replied: 'The signore will pay.'

There was an established reply to this; Aschenbach made it, mechanically:

'I will pay nothing whatever if you do not take me where I want to go.'

'The signore wants to go to the Lido.'

'But not with you.'

'I am a good rower, signore, I will row you well.'

'So much is true,' thought Aschenbach, and again he relaxed. 'That is true, you row me well. Even if you mean to rob me, even if you hit me in the back with your oar and send me down to the kingdom of Hades, even then you will have rowed me well.'

But nothing of the sort happened. Instead, they fell in with company: a boat came alongside and waylaid them, full of men and women singing to guitar and mandolin. They rowed persistently bow for bow with the gondola and filled the silence that had rested on the waters with their lyric love of gain. Aschenbach tossed money into the hat they held out. The music stopped at once, they rowed away. And once more the gondolier's mutter became audible as he talked to himself in fits and snatches.

Thus they rowed on, rocked by the wash of a steamer returning citywards. At the landing two municipal officials were walking up and down with their hands behind their backs and their faces turned towards the lagoon. Aschenbach was helped on shore by the old man with a boat-hook who is the permanent feature of every landing-stage in Venice; and having no small change to pay the boatman, crossed into the hotel opposite. His wants were supplied in the lobby, but when he came back his possessions were already on a hand-car on the quay, and gondola and gondolier were gone.

'He ran away, signore,' said the old boatman. 'A bad lot, a man without a licence. He is the only gondolier without one. The others telephoned over, and he knew we were on the look-out, so he made off.'

Aschenbach shrugged.

'The signore has had a ride for nothing,' said the old man, and held out his hat. Aschenbach dropped some coins. He directed that his luggage be taken to the Hôtel des Bains and followed the hand-cart through the avenue, that white-blossoming avenue with taverns, booths, and pensions on either side it, which runs across the island diagonally to the beach.

He entered the hotel from the garden terrace at the back and passed through the vestibule and hall into the office. His arrival was expected, and he was served with courtesy and dispatch. The manager, a small, soft, dapper man with a black moustache and a caressing way with him, wearing a French frock-coat, himself took him up in the lift and showed him his room. It was a pleasant chamber, furnished in cherrywood, with lofty windows looking out to sea. It was decorated with strong-scented flowers. Aschenbach, as soon as he was alone, and while they brought in his trunk and bags and disposed them in the room, went up to one of the windows and stood looking out upon the beach in its afternoon emptiness, and at the sunless sea, now full and sending long, low waves with rhythmic beat upon the sand.

A solitary, unused to speaking of what he sees and feels, has mental experiences which are at once more intense and less articulate than those of a gregarious man. They are sluggish, yet more wayward, and never without a melancholy tinge. Sights and impressions which others brush aside with a glance, a light comment, a smile, occupy him more than their due; they sink silently in, they take on meaning, they become experience, emotion, adventure. Solitude gives birth to the original in us, to beauty unfamiliar and perilous – to poetry. But also, it gives birth to the opposite: to the perverse, the illicit, the absurd. Thus the traveller's mind still dwelt with disquiet on the episodes of his journey hither: on the horrible old fop with his drivel about a mistress, on the outlaw boatman and his lost tip. They did not offend his reason, they hardly afforded food for thought; yet they seemed by their very nature fundamentally strange, and thereby vaguely disquieting. Yet here was the sea; even in the midst of such thoughts he saluted it with his eyes, exulting that Venice was near and accessible. At length he turned round, disposed his personal belongings and made certain arrangements with the chambermaid for his comfort, washed, and was conveyed to the ground floor by the green-uniformed Swiss who ran the lift.

He took tea on the terrace facing the sea and afterwards went down and walked some distance along the shore promenade in the direction of Hôtel Excelsior. When he came back it seemed to be time to change for dinner. He did so, slowly and methodically as his way was, for he was accustomed to work while he dressed; but even so he found himself a little early when he entered the hall, where a large number of guests had collected – strangers to each other and affecting mutual indifference, yet united in expectancy of the meal. He picked up a paper, sat down in a leather arm-chair, and took stock of the company, which compared most favourably with that he had just left.

This was a broad and tolerant atmosphere, of wide horizons. Subdued voices were speaking most of the principal European tongues. That uniform of civilization, the conventional evening dress, gave outward conformity to the varied types. There were long, dry Americans, large-familied Russians,

English ladies, German children with French *bonnes*. The Slavic element predominated, it seemed. In Aschenbach's neighbourhood Polish was being spoken.

Round a wicker table next to him was gathered a group of young folk in charge of a governess or companion – three young girls, perhaps fifteen- to seventeen years old, and a long-haired boy of about fourteen. Aschenbach noticed with astonishment the lad's perfect beauty. His face recalled the noblest moment of Greek sculpture – pale, with a sweet reserve, with clustering honey-coloured ringlets, the brow and nose descending in one line, the winning mouth, the expression of pure and godlike serenity. Yet with all this chaste perfection of form it was of such unique personal charm that the observer thought he had never seen, either in nature or art, anything so utterly happy and consummate. What struck him further was the strange contrast the group afforded, a difference in educational method, so to speak, shown in the way the brother and sisters were clothed and treated. The girls, the eldest of whom was practically grown up, were dressed with an almost disfiguring austerity. All three wore half-length slate-coloured frocks of cloister-like plainness, arbitrarily unbecoming in cut, with white turn-over collars as their only adornment. Every grace of outline was wilfully suppressed; their hair lay smoothly plastered to their heads, giving them a vacant expression, like a nun's. All this could only be by the mother's orders; but there was no trace of the same pedagogic severity in the case of the boy. Tenderness and softness, it was plain, conditioned his existence. No scissors had been put to the lovely hair that (like the Spinnario's) curled about his brows, above his ears, longer still in the neck. He wore an English sailor suit, with quilted sleeves that narrowed round the delicate wrists of his long and slender though still childish hands. And this suit, with its breast-knot, lacings, and embroideries, lent the slight figure something 'rich and strange', a spoilt, exquisite air. The observer saw him in half profile, with one foot in its black patent leather advanced, one elbow resting on the arm of his basket-chair, the cheek nestled into the closed hand in a pose of easy grace, quite unlike the stiff subservient mien which was evidently habitual to his sisters. Was he delicate? His facial tint was ivory-white against the golden darkness of his clustering locks. Or was he simply a pampered darling, the object of a self-willed and partial love? Aschenbach inclined to think the latter. For in almost every artist nature is inborn a wanton and treacherous proneness to side with the beauty that breaks hearts, to single out aristocratic pretensions and pay them homage.

A waiter announced, in English, that dinner was served. Gradually the company dispersed through the glass doors into the dining-room. Late-comers entered from the vestibule or the lifts. Inside, dinner was being served; but the young Poles still sat and waited about their wicker table. Aschenbach felt comfortable in his deep arm-chair, he enjoyed the beauty before his eyes, he waited with them.

The governess, a short, stout, red-faced person, at length gave the signal. With lifted brows she pushed back her chair and made a bow to the tall woman, dressed in palest grey, who now entered the hall. This lady's abundant jewels were pearls, her manner was cool and measured; the fashion of her gown and the arrangement of her lightly powdered hair had the simplicity prescribed in certain circles whose piety and aristocracy are equally marked. She might have been, in Germany, the wife of some high official. But there was something faintly fabulous, after all, in her appearance, though lent it solely by the pearls she wore: they were well-nigh priceless, and consisted of ear-rings and a three-stranded necklace, very long, with gems the size of cherries.

The brother and sisters had risen briskly. They bowed over their mother's hand to kiss it, she turning away from them, with a slight smile on her face, which was carefully preserved but rather sharp-nosed and worn. She addressed a few words in French to the governess, then moved towards the glass door. The children followed, the girls in order of age, then the governess, and last the boy. He chanced to turn before he crossed the threshold, and as there was no one else in the room, his strange, twilit grey eyes met Aschenbach's, as our traveller sat there with the paper on his knee, absorbed in looking after the group.

There was nothing singular, of course, in what he had seen. They had not gone in to dinner before their mother, they had waited, given her a respectful salute, and but observed the right and proper forms on entering the room. Yet they had done all this so expressly, with such self-respecting dignity, discipline, and sense of duty that Aschenbach was impressed. He lingered still a few minutes, then he, too, went into the dining-room, where he was shown to a table far off from the Polish family, as he noted at once, with a stirring of regret.

Tired, yet mentally alert, he beguiled the long, tedious meal with abstract, even with transcendent matters: pondered the mysterious harmony that must come to subsist between the individual human being and the universal law, in order that human beauty may result; passed on to general problems of form and art, and came at length to the conclusion that what seemed to him fresh and happy thoughts were like the flattering inventions of a dream, which the waking sense proves worthless and insubstantial. He spent the evening in the park, that was sweet with the odours of evening – sitting, smoking, wandering about; went to bed betimes, and passed the night in deep, unbroken sleep, visited, however, by varied and lively dreams.

The weather next day was no more promising. A land breeze blew. Beneath a colourless, overcast sky the sea lay sluggish, and as it were shrunken, so far withdrawn as to leave bare several rows of long sand-banks. The horizon looked close and prosaic. When Aschenbach opened his window he thought he smelt the stagnant odour of the lagoons.

He felt suddenly out of sorts and already began to think of leaving. Once, years before, after weeks of bright spring weather, this wind had found him out; it had been so bad as to force him to flee from the city like a fugitive. And now it seemed beginning again – the same feverish distaste, the pressure on his temples, the heavy eyelids. It would be a nuisance to change again; but if the wind did not turn, this was no place for him. To be on the safe side, he did not entirely unpack. At nine o'clock he went down to the buffer, which lay between the hall and the dining-room and served as breakfast-room.

A solemn stillness reigned here, such as it is the ambition of all large hotels to achieve. The waiters moved on noiseless feet. A rattling of tea-things, a whispered word – and no other sounds. In a corner diagonally to the door, two tables off his own, Aschenbach saw the Polish girls with their governess. They sat there very straight, in their stiff blue linen frocks with little turn-over collars and cuffs, their ash-blonde hair newly brushed flat, their eyelids red from sleep, and handed each other the marmalade. They had nearly finished their meal. The boy was not there.

Aschenbach smiled. 'Aha, little Phaeax,' he thought. 'It seems you are privileged to sleep yourself out.' With sudden gaiety he quoted:

'Oft veränderten Schmuck und warme Bäder und Ruhe.'

He took a leisurely breakfast. The porter came up with his braided cap in
his hand, to deliver some letters that had been sent on. Aschenbach lighted a
cigarette and opened a few letters and thus was still seated to witness the
arrival of the sluggard.

He entered through the glass doors and walked diagonally across the room
to his sisters at their table. He walked with extraordinary grace – the carriage
of the body, the action of the knee, the way he set down his foot in its white
shoe – it was all so light, it was at once dainty and proud, it wore an added
charm in the childish shyness which made him twice turn his head as he
crossed the room, made him give a quick glance and then drop his eyes. He
took his seat, with a smile and a murmured word in his soft and blurry
tongue; and Aschenbach, sitting so that he could see him in profile, was
astonished anew, yes, startled, at the godlike beauty of the human being.
The lad had on a light sailor suit of blue and white striped cotton, with a red
silk breast-knot and a simple white standing collar round the neck – a not
very elegant effect – yet above this collar the head was poised like a flower, in
incomparable loveliness. It was the head of Eros, with the yellowish bloom
of Parian marble, with fine serious brows, and dusky clustering ringlets
standing out in soft plenteousness over temples and ears.

'Good, oh, very good indeed!' thought Aschenbach, assuming the
patronizing air of the connoisseur to hide, as artists will, their ravishment
over a masterpiece. 'Yes,' he went on to himself, 'if it were not that sea and
beach were waiting for me, I should sit here as long as you do.' But he went
out on that, passing through the hall, beneath the watchful eye of the
functionaries, down the steps and directly across the board walk to the
section of the beach reserved for the guests of the hotel. The bathing-master,
a barefoot old man in linen trousers and sailor blouse, with a straw hat,
showed him the cabin that had been rented for him, and Aschenbach had
him set up table and chair on the sandy platform before it. Then he dragged
the reclining-chair through the pale yellow sand, closer to the sea, sat down,
and composed himself.

He delighted, as always, in the scene on the beach, the sight of sophisticated society giving itself over to a simple life at the edge of the element. The
shallow grey sea was already gay with children wading, with swimmers, with
figures in bright colours lying on the sand-banks with arms behind their
heads. Some were rowing in little keelless boats painted red and blue, and
laughing when they capsized. A long row of *capanne* ran down the beach,
with platforms, where people sat as on verandas, and there was social life,
with bustle and with indolent repose; visits were paid, amid much chatter,
punctilious morning toilettes hob-nobbed with comfortable and privileged
dishabille. On the hard wet sand close to the sea figures in white bath-robes
or loose wrappings in garish colours strolled up and down. A mammoth
sand-hill had been built up on Aschenbach's right, the work of children,
who had stuck it full of tiny flags. Vendors of sea-shells, fruit, and cakes
knelt beside their wares spread out on the sand. A row of cabins on the left
stood obliquely to the others and to the sea, thus forming the boundary of
the enclosure on this side; and on the little veranda in front of one of these a
Russian family was encamped; bearded men with strong white teeth, ripe,
indolent women, a Fräulein from the Baltic provinces, who sat at an easel
painting the sea and tearing her hair in despair; two ugly but good-natured
children and an old maidservant in a head-cloth, with the caressing, servile

manner of the born dependent. There they sat together in grateful enjoyment of their blessings: constantly shouting at their romping children, who paid not the slightest heed; making jokes in broken Italian to the funny old man who sold them sweetmeats, kissing each other on the cheeks – no jot concerned that their domesticity was overlooked.

'I'll stop,' thought Aschenbach. 'Where could it be better than here?' With his hands clasped in his lap he let his eyes swim in the wideness of the sea, his gaze lose focus, blur, and grow vague in the misty immensity of space. His love of the ocean had profound sources: the hard-worked artist's longing for rest, his yearning to seek refuge from the thronging manifold shapes of his fancy in the bosom of the simple and vast; and another yearning, opposed to his art and perhaps for that very reason a lure, for the unorganized, the immeasurable, the eternal – in short, for nothingness. He whose preoccupation is with excellence longs fervently to find rest in perfection; and is not nothingness a form of perfection? As he sat there dreaming thus, deep, deep into the void, suddenly the margin line of the shore was cut by a human form. He gathered up his gaze and withdrew it from the illimitable, and lo, it was the lovely boy who crossed his vision coming from the left along the sand. He was barefoot, ready for wading, the slender legs uncovered above the knee, and moved slowly, yet with such a proud, light tread as to make it seem he had never worn shoes. He looked towards the diagonal row of cabins; and the sight of the Russian family, leading their lives there in joyous simplicity, distorted his features in a spasm of angry disgust. His brow darkened, his lips curled, one corner of the mouth was drawn down in a harsh line that marred the curve of the cheek, his frown was so heavy that the eyes seemed to sink in as they uttered beneath the black and vicious language of hate. He looked down, looked threateningly back once more; then giving it up with a violent and contemptuous shoulder-shrug, he left his enemies in the rear.

A feeling of delicacy, a qualm, almost like a sense of shame, made Aschenbach turn away as though he had not seen; he felt unwilling to take advantage of having been, by chance, privy to this passionate reaction. But he was in troth both moved and exhilarated – that is to say, he was delighted. This childish exhibition of fanaticism, directed against the good-naturedest simplicity in the world – it gave to the godlike and inexpressive the final human touch. The figure of the half-grown lad, a masterpiece from nature's own hand, had been significant enough when it gratified the eye alone; and now it evoked sympathy as well – the little episode had set it off, lent it a dignity in the onlooker's eyes that was beyond its years.

Aschenbach listened with still averted head to the boy's voice announcing his coming to his companions at the sand-heap. The voice was clear, though a little weak, but they answered, shouting his name – or his nickname – again and again. Aschenbach was not without curiosity to learn it, but could make out nothing more exact than two musical syllables, something like Adgio – or, often still, Adjiu, with a long-drawn-out *u* at the end. He liked the melodious sound, and found it fitting; said it over to himself a few times and turned back with satisfaction to his papers.

Holding his travelling-pad on his knees, he took his fountain-pen and began to answer various items of his correspondence. But presently he felt it too great a pity to turn his back, and the eyes of his mind, for the sake of mere commonplace correspondence, to this scene which was, after all, the most rewarding one he knew. He put aside his papers and swung round to the sea; in no time, beguiled by the voices of the children at play, he had turned his head and sat resting it against the chair-back, while he gave himself up to contemplating the activities of the exquisite Adgio.

His eyes found him at once, the red breast-knot was unmistakable. With some nine or ten companions, boys and girls of his own age and younger, he was busy putting in place an old plank to serve as a bridge across the ditches between the sand-piles. He directed the work by shouting and motioning with his head, and they were all chattering in many tongues – French, Polish, and even some of the Balkan languages. But his was the name oftenest on their lips, he was plainly sought after, wooed, admired. One lad in particular, a Pole like himself, with a name that sounded something like Jaschiu, a sturdy lad with brilliantined black hair, in a belted linen suit, was his particular liegeman and friend. Operations at the sand-pile being ended for the time, the two walked away along the beach, with their arms round each other's waists, and once the lad Jaschiu gave Adgio a kiss.

Aschenbach felt like shaking a finger at him. 'But you, Critobulus,' he thought with a smile, 'you I advise to take a year's leave. That long, at least, you will need for complete recovery.' A vendor came by with strawberries, and Aschenbach made his second breakfast of the great luscious, dead-ripe fruit. It had grown very warm, although the sun had not availed to pierce the heavy layer of mist. His mind felt relaxed, his senses revelled in this vast and soothing communion with the silence of the sea. The grave and serious man found sufficient occupation in speculating what name it could be that sounded like Adgio. And with the help of a few Polish memories he at length fixed on Tadzio, a shortened form of Thaddeus, which sounded, when called, like Tadziu or Adziu.

Tadzio was bathing. Aschenbach had lost sight of him for a moment, then descried him far out in the water, which was shallow a very long way – saw his head, and his arm striking out like an oar. But his watchful family were already on the alert; the mother and governess called from the veranda in front of their bathing-cabin, until the lad's name, with its softened consonants and long-drawn u-sound, seemed to possess the beach like a rallying-cry; the cadence had something sweet and wild: 'Tadziu! Tadziu!' He turned and ran back against the water, churning the waves to a foam, his head flung high. The sight of this living figure, virginally pure and austere, with dripping locks, beautiful as a tender young god, emerging from the depths of sea and sky, outrunning the element – it conjured up mythologies, it was like a primeval legend, handed down from the beginning of time, of the birth of form, of the origin of the gods. With closed lids Aschenbach listened to this poesy hymning itself silently within him, and anon he thought it was good to be here and that he would stop awhile.

Afterwards Tadzio lay on the sand and rested from his bathe, wrapped in his white sheet, which he wore drawn underneath the right shoulder, so that his head was cradled on his bare right arm. And even when Aschenbach read, without looking up, he was conscious that the lad was there; that it would cost him but the slightest turn of the head to have the rewarding vision once more in his purview. Indeed, it was almost as though he sat there to guard the youth's repose; occupied, of course, with his own affairs, yet alive to the presence of that noble human creature close at hand. And his heart was stirred, it felt a father's kindness: such an emotion as the possessor of beauty can inspire in one who has offered himself up in spirit to create beauty.

At midday he left the beach, returned to the hotel, and was carried up in the lift to his room. There he lingered a little time before the glass and looked at his own grey hair, his keen and weary face. And he thought of his fame, and how people gazed respectfully at him in the streets, on account of his unerring gift of words and their power to charm. He called up all the worldly successes his genius had reaped, all he could remember, even his patent of nobility. Then went to luncheon down in the dining-room, sat at his little table and ate. Afterwards he mounted again in the lift, and a group of young folk, Tadzio among them, pressed with him into the little compartment. It was the first time Aschenbach had seen him close at hand, not merely in perspective, and could see and take account of the details of his humanity. Someone spoke to the lad, and he, answering, with indescribably lovely smile, stepped out again, as they had come to the first floor, backwards, with his eyes cast down. 'Beauty makes people self-conscious,' Aschenbach thought, and considered within himself imperatively why this should be. He had noted, further, that Tadzio's teeth were imperfect, rather jagged and bluish, without a healthy glaze, and of that peculiar brittle transparency which the teeth of chlorotic people often show. 'He is delicate, he is sickly,' Aschenbach thought. 'He will most likely not live to grow old.' He did not try to account for the pleasure the idea gave him.

In the afternoon he spent two hours in his room, then took the *vaporetto* to Venice, across the foul-smelling lagoon. He got out at San Marco, had his tea in the Piazza, and then, as his custom was, took a walk through the streets. But this walk of his brought about nothing less than a revolution in his mood and an entire change in all his plans.

There was a hateful sultriness in the narrow streets. The air was so heavy that all the manifold smells wafted out of houses, shops, and cook-shops – smells of oil, perfumery, and so forth – hung low, like exhalations, not dissipating. Cigarette smoke seemed to stand in the air, it drifted so slowly away. Today the crowd in these narrow lanes oppressed the stroller instead of diverting him. The longer he walked, the more was he in tortures under that state, which is the product of the sea air and the sirocco and which excites and enervates at once. He perspired painfully. His eyes rebelled, his chest was heavy, he felt feverish, the blood throbbed in his temples. He fled from the huddled, narrow streets of the commercial city, crossed many bridges, and came into the poor quarter of Venice. Beggars waylaid him, the canals sickened him with their evil exhalations. He reached a quiet square, one of those that exist at the city's heart, forsaken of God and man; there he rested awhile on the margin of a fountain, wiped his brow, and admitted to himself that he must be gone.

For the second time, and now quite definitely, the city proved that in certain weathers it could be directly inimical to his health. Nothing but sheer unreasoning obstinacy would linger on, hoping for an unprophesiable change in the wind. A quick decision was in place. He could not go home at this stage, neither summer nor winter quarters would be ready. But Venice had not a monopoly of sea and shore: there were other spots where these were to be had without the evil concomitants of lagoon and fever-breeding vapours. He remembered a little bathing-place not far from Trieste of which he had had a good report. Why not go thither? At once, of course, in order that this second change might be worth the making. He resolved, he rose to his feet and sought the nearest gondola-landing, where he took a boat and was conveyed to San Marco through the gloomy windings of many canals, beneath balconies of delicate marble traceries flanked by carven lions; round slippery corners of wall, past melancholy façades with ancient business shields reflected in the rocking water. It was not too easy to arrive at his destination, for his gondolier, being in league with various lace-makers and glass-blowers, did his best to persuade his fare to pause, look, and be tempted to buy. Thus the charm of this bizarre passage through the heart of Venice, even while it played upon his spirit, yet was sensibly cooled by the predatory commercial spirit of the fallen queen of the seas.

Once back in his hotel, he announced at the office, even before dinner, that circumstances unforeseen obliged him to leave early next morning. The management expressed its regret, it changed his money and receipted his bill. He dined, and spent the luke-warm evening in a rocking-chair on the rear terrace, reading the newspapers. Before he went to bed, he made his luggage ready against the morning.

His sleep was not of the best, for the prospect of another journey made him restless. When he opened his window next morning, the sky was still overcast, but the air seemed fresher – and there and then his rue began. Had he not given notice too soon? Had he not let himself be swayed by a slight and momentary indisposition? If he had only been patient, not lost heart so quickly, tried to adapt himself to the climate, or even waited for a change in the weather before deciding! Then, instead of the hurry and flurry of departure, he would have before him now a morning like yesterday's on the beach. Too late! He must go on wanting what he had wanted yesterday. He dressed and at eight o'clock went down to breakfast.

When he entered the breakfast-room it was empty. Guests came in while he sat waiting for his order to be filled. As he sipped his tea he saw the Polish girls enter with their governess, chaste and morning-fresh, with sleep-reddened eyelids. They crossed the room and sat down at their table in the window. Behind them came the porter, cap in hand, to announce that it was time for him to go. The car was waiting to convey him and other travellers to the Hôtel Excelsior, whence they would go by motor-boat through the company's private canal to the station. Time pressed. But Aschenbach found it did nothing of the sort. There still lacked more than an hour of train-time. He felt irritated at the hotel habit of getting the guests out of the house earlier than necessary; and requested the porter to let him breakfast in peace. The man hesitated and withdrew, only to come back again five minutes later. The car could wait no longer. Good, then it might go, and take his trunk with it, Aschenbach answered with some heat. He would use the public conveyance, in his own time; he begged them to leave the choice of it to him. The functionary bowed. Aschenbach pleased to be rid of him, made a leisurely meal, and even had a newspaper of the waiter. When at length he rose, the time was grown very short. And it so happened that at that moment Tadzio came through the glass doors into the room.

To reach his own table he crossed the traveller's path, and modestly cast down his eyes before the grey-haired man of the lofty brows – only to lift them again in that sweet way he had and direct his full soft gaze upon Aschenbach's face. Then he was past. 'For the last time, Tadzio,' thought the elder man. 'It was all too brief!' Quite unusually for him, he shaped a farewell with his lips, he actually uttered it, and added: 'May God bless you!' Then he went out, distributed tips, exchanged farewells with the mild little manager in the frock-coat, and, followed by the porter with his hand-luggage, left the hotel. On foot as he had come, he passed through the white-blossoming avenue, diagonally across the island to the boat-landing. He went on board at once – but the tale of his journey across the lagoon was a tale of woe, a passage through the very valley of regrets.

It was the well-known route: through the lagoon, past San Marco, up the

Grand Canal. Aschenbach sat on the circular bench in the bows, with his elbow on the railing, one hand shading his eyes. They passed the Public Gardens, once more the princely charm of the Piazzetta rose up before him and then dropped behind, next came the great row of palaces, the canal curved, and the splendid marble arches of the Rialto came in sight. The traveller gazed – and his bosom was torn. The atmosphere of the city, the faintly rotten scent of swamp and sea, which had driven him to leave – in what deep, tender, almost painful draughts he breathed it in! How was it he had not known, had not thought, how much his heart was set upon it all! What this morning had been slight regret, some little doubt of his own wisdom, turned now to grief, to actual wretchedness, a mental agony so sharp that it repeatedly brought tears to his eyes, while he questioned himself how he could have foreseen it. The hardest part, the part that more than once it seemed he could not bear, was the thought that he should never more see Venice again. Since now for the second time the place had made him ill, since for the second time he had had to flee for his life, he must henceforth regard it as a forbidden spot, to be forever shunned; senseless to try it again, after he had proved himself unfit. Yes, if he fled it now, he felt that wounded pride must prevent his return to this spot where twice he had made actual bodily surrender. And this conflict between inclination and capacity all at once assumed, in this middle-aged man's mind, immense weight and importance; the physical defeat seemed a shameful thing, to be avoided at whatever cost; and he stood amazed at the ease with which on the day before he had yielded to it.

Meanwhile the steamer neared the station landing; his anguish of irresolution amounted almost to panic. To leave seemed to the sufferer impossible, to remain not less so. Torn thus between two alternatives, he entered the station. It was very late, he had not a moment to lose. Time pressed, it scourged him onward. He hastened to buy his ticket and looked round in the crowd to find the hotel porter. The man appeared and said that the trunk had already gone off. 'Gone already?' 'Yes, it has gone to Como.' 'To Como?' A hasty exchange of words – angry questions from Aschenbach, and puzzled replies from the porter – at length made it clear that the trunk had been put with the wrong luggage even before leaving the hotel, and in company with other trunks was now well on its way in precisely the wrong direction.

Aschenbach found it hard to wear the right expression as he heard this news. A reckless joy, a deep incredible mirthfulness shook him almost as with a spasm. The porter dashed off after the lost trunk, returning very soon, of course, to announce that his efforts were unavailing. Aschenbach said he would not travel without his luggage; that he would go back and wait at the Hôtel des Bains until it turned up. Was the company's motor-boat still outside? The man said yes, it was at the door. With his native eloquence he prevailed upon the ticket-agent to take back the ticket already purchased; he swore that he would wire, that no pains should be spared, that the trunk would be restored in the twinkling of an eye. And the unbelievable thing came to pass; the traveller, twenty minutes after he had reached the station, found himself once more on the Grand Canal on his way back to the Lido.

What a strange adventure indeed, this right-about face of destiny – incredible, humiliating, whimsical as any dream! To be passing again, within the hour, these scenes from which in profoundest grief he had but now taken leave forever! The little swift-moving vessel, a furrow of foam at its prow, tacking with droll agility between steamboats and gondolas, went like a shot to its goal; and he, its sole passenger, sat hiding the panic and thrills of a truant schoolboy beneath a mask of forced resignation. His breast still heaved from time to time with a burst of laughter over the contretemps. Things could not, he told himself, have fallen out more luckily. There would be the necessary explanations, a few astonished faces – then all would be well once more, a mischance prevented, a grievous error set right; and all he had thought to have left forever was his own once more, his for as long as he liked ... And did the boat's swift motion deceive him, or was the wind now coming from the sea?

The waves struck against the tiled sides of the narrow canal. At Hôtel Excelsior the automobile omnibus awaited the returned traveller and bore him along by the crisping waves back to the Hôtel des Bains. The little mustachioed manager in the frock-coat came down the steps to greet him.

In dulcet tones he deplored the mistake, said how painful it was to the management and himself; applauded Aschenbach's resolve to stop on until the errant trunk came back; his former room, alas, was already taken, but another as good awaited his approval. 'Pas de chance, monsieur,' said the Swiss lift-porter, with a smile, as he conveyed him upstairs. And the fugitive was soon quartered in another room which in situation and furnishings almost precisely resembled the first.

He laid out the contents of his hand-bag in their wonted places; then, tired out, dazed by the whirl of the extraordinary forenoon, subsided into the arm-chair by the open window. The sea wore a pale-green cast, the air felt thinner and purer, the beach with its cabins and boats had more colour, notwithstanding the sky was still grey. Aschenbach, his hands folded in his lap, looked out. He felt rejoiced to be back, yet displeased with his vacillating moods, his ignorance of his own real desires. Thus for nearly an hour he sat, dreaming, resting, barely thinking. At midday he saw Tadzio, in his striped sailor suit with red breast-knot, coming up from the sea, across the barrier and along the board walk to the hotel. Aschenbach recognized him, even at this height, knew it was he before he actually saw him, had it in mind to say to himself: 'Well, Tadzio, so here you are again too!' But the casual greeting died away before it reached his lips, slain by the truth in his heart. He felt the rapture of his blood, the poignant pleasure, and realized that it was for Tadzio's sake the leavetaking had been so hard.

He sat quite still, unseen at his high post, and looked within himself. His features were lively, he lifted his brows; a smile, alert, inquiring, vivid, widened the mouth. Then he raised his head, and with both hands, hanging limp over the chair-arms, he described a slow motion, palms outward, a lifting and turning movement, as though to indicate a wide embrace. It was a gesture of welcome, a calm and deliberate acceptance of what might come.

Now daily the naked god with cheeks aflame drove his four fire-breathing steeds through heaven's spaces; and with him streamed the strong east wind that fluttered his yellow locks. A sheen, like white satin, lay over all the idly rolling sea's expanse. The sand was burning hot. Awnings of rust-coloured canvas were spanned before the bathing-huts, under the ether's quivering silver-blue; one spent the morning hours within the small, sharp square of shadow they purveyed. But evening too was rarely lovely: balsamic with the breath of flowers and shrubs from the near-by park, while overhead the constellations circled in their spheres, and the murmuring of the night-girded sea swelled softly up and whispered to the soul. Such nights as these contained the joyful promise of a sunlit morrow, brim-full of sweetly ordered idleness, studded thick with countless precious possibilities.

The guest detained here by so happy a mischance was far from finding the return of his luggage a ground for setting out anew. For two days he had suffered slight inconvenience and had to dine in the large salon in his travelling clothes. Then the lost trunk was set down in his room, and he hastened to unpack, filling presses and drawers with his possessions. He meant to stay on – and on; he rejoiced in the prospect of wearing a silk suit for the hot morning hours on the beach and appearing in acceptable evening dress at dinner.

He was quick to fall in with the pleasing monotony of this manner of life, readily enchanted by its mild soft brilliance and ease. And what a spot it is, indeed! – uniting the charms of a luxurious bathing-resort by a southern sea with the immediate nearness of a unique and marvellous city. Aschenbach was not pleasure-loving. Always, wherever and whenever it was the order of the day to be merry, to refrain from labour and make glad the heart, he would soon be conscious of the imperative summons – and especially was this so in his youth – back to the high fatigues, the sacred and fasting service that consumed his days. This spot and this alone had power to beguile him, to relax his resolution, to make him glad. At times – of a forenoon perhaps, as he lay in the shadow of his awning, gazing out dreamily over the blue of the southern sea, or in the mildness of the night, beneath the wide starry sky, ensconced among the cushions of the gondola that bore him Lido-wards after an evening on the Piazza, while the gay lights faded and the melting music of the serenades died away on his ear – he would think of his mountain home, the theatre of his summer labours. There clouds hung low and trailed through the garden, violent storms extinguished the lights of the house at night, and the ravens he fed swung in the tops of the fir trees. And he would feel transported to Elysium, to the ends of the earth, to a spot most carefree for the sons of men, where no snow is, and no winter, no storms or downpours of rain; where Oceanus sends a mild and cooling breath, and days flow on in blissful idleness, without effort or struggle, entirely dedicate to the sun and the feasts of the sun.

Aschenbach saw the boy Tadzio almost constantly. The narrow confines of their world of hotel and beach, the daily round followed by all alike, brought him in close, almost uninterrupted touch with the beautiful lad. He encountered him everywhere – in the salons of the hotel, on the cooling rides to the city and back, among the splendours of the Piazza, and besides all this in many another going and coming as chance vouchsafed. But it was the regular morning hours on the beach which gave him his happiest oppor-tunity to study and admire the lovely apparition. Yes, this immediate happiness, this daily recurring boon at the hand of circumstance, this it was that filled him with content, with joy in life, enriched his stay, and lingered out the row of sunny days that fell into place so pleasantly one behind the other.

He rose early – as early as though he had a panting press of work – and was among the first on the beach, when the sun was still benign and the sea dazzling white in its morning slumber. He gave the watchman a friendly good-morning and chatted with the barefoot, white-haired old man who prepared his place, spread the awning, trundled out the chair and table on to the little platform. Then he settled down; he had three or four hours before the sun reached its height and the fearful climax of its power; three or four hours while the sea went deeper and deeper blue; three or four hours in which to watch Tadzio.

He would see him coming up, on the left, along the margin of the sea; or from behind, between the cabins; or, with a start of joyful surprise, would discover that he himself was late, and Tadzio already down, in the blue and white bathing-suit that was now his only wear on the beach; there and engrossed in his usual activities in the sand, beneath the sun. It was a sweetly idle, trifling, fitful life, of play and rest, of strolling, wading, digging, fishing, swimming, lying on the sand. Often the women sitting on the platform would call out to him in their high voices: 'Tadziu! Tadziu!' and he would come running and waving his arms, eager to tell them what he had found, what caught – shells, seahorses, jelly-fish, and sidewards-running crabs. Aschenbach understood not a word he said; it might be the sheerest commonplace, in his ear it became mingled harmonies. Thus the lad's foreign birth raised his speech to music; a wanton sun showered splendour on him, and the noble distances of the sea formed the background which set off his figure.

Soon the observer knew every line and pose of this form that limned itself so freely against sea and sky; its every loveliness, though conned by heart, yet thrilled him each day afresh; his admiration knew no bounds, the delight of his eye was unending. Once the lad was summoned to speak to a guest who was waiting for his mother at their cabin. He ran up, ran dripping wet out of the sea, tossing his curls, and put out his hand, standing with his weight on one leg, resting the other foot on the toes; as he stood there in a posture of suspense the turn of his body was enchanting, while his features wore a look half shamefaced, half conscious of the duty breeding laid upon him to please. Or he would lie at full length, with his bath-robe around him, one slender young arm resting on the sand, his chin in the hollow of his hand; the lad they called Jaschiu squatting beside him, paying him court. There could be nothing lovelier on earth than the smile and look with which the playmate thus singled out rewarded his humble friend and vassal. Again, he might be at the water's edge, alone, removed from his family, quite close to Aschenbach; standing erect, his hands clasped at the back of his neck, rocking slowly on the balls of his feet, day-dreaming away into blue space, while little waves ran up and bathed his toes. The ringlets of honey-coloured hair clung to his temples and neck, the fine down along the upper vertebrae was yellow in the sunlight; the thin envelope of flesh covering the torso betrayed the delicate outlines of the ribs and the symmetry of the breast-structure. His armpits were still as smooth as a statue's, smooth the glistening hollows behind the knees, where the blue network of veins suggested that the body was formed of some stuff more transparent than mere flesh. What discipline, what precision of thought were expressed by the tense youthful perfection of this form! And yet the pure, strong will which had laboured in darkness and succeeded in bringing this godlike work of art to the light of day – was it not known and familiar to him, the artist? Was not the same force at work in himself when he strove in cold fury to liberate from the marble mass of language the slender forms of his art which he saw with the eye of his mind and would body forth to men as the mirror and image of spiritual beauty?

Mirror and image! His eyes took in the proud bearing of that figure there at the blue water's edge; with an outburst of rapture he told himself that what he saw was beauty's very essence; form as divine thought, the single and pure perfection which resides in the mind, of which an image and likeness, rare and holy, was here raised up for adoration. This was very frenzy – and without a scruple, nay, eagerly, the ageing artist bade it come.

His mind was in travail, his whole mental background in a state of flux. Memory flung up in him the primitive thoughts which are youth's inheritance, but which with him had remained latent, never leaping up into a blaze. Has it not been written that the sun beguiles our attention from things of the intellect to fix it on things of the sense? The sun, they say, dazzles; so bewitching reason and memory that the soul for very pleasure forgets its actual state, to cling with doting on the loveliest of all the objects she shines on. Yes, and then it is only through the medium of some corporeal being that it can raise itself again to contemplation of higher things. Amor, in sooth, is like the mathematician who in order to give children a knowledge of pure form must do so in the language of pictures; so, too, the god, in order to make visible the spirit, avails himself of the forms and colours of human youth, gilding it with all imaginable beauty that it may serve memory as a tool, the very sight of which then sets us afire with pain and longing.

Such were the devotee's thoughts, such the power of his emotions. And the sea, so bright with glancing sunbeams, wove in his mind a spell and summoned up a lovely picture: there was the ancient plane-tree outside the walls of Athens, a hallowed, shady spot, fragrant with willow-blossom and adorned with images and votive offerings in honour of the nymphs and Achelous. Clear ran the smooth-pebbled stream at the foot of the spreading tree. Crickets were fiddling. But on the gentle grassy slope, where one could lie yet hold the head erect, and shelter from the scorching heat, two men reclined, an elder with a younger, ugliness paired with beauty and wisdom with grace. Here Socrates held forth to youthful Phaedrus upon the nature of virtue and desire, wooing him with insinuating wit and charming turns of phrase. He told him of the shuddering and unwonted heat that comes upon him whose heart is open, when his eye beholds an image of eternal beauty; spoke of the impious and corrupt, who cannot conceive beauty though they see its image, and are incapable of awe; and of the fear and reverence felt by the noble soul when he beholds a godlike face or a form which is a good image of beauty: how as he gazes he worships the beautiful one and scarcely dares to look upon him, but would offer sacrifice as to an idol or a god, did he not fear to be thought stark mad. 'For beauty, my Phaedrus, beauty alone, is lovely and visible at once. For, mark you, it is the sole aspect of the spiritual which we can perceive through our senses, or bear so to perceive. Else what should become of us, if the divine, if reason and virtue and truth, were to speak to us through the senses? Should we not perish and be consumed by love, as Semele aforetime was by Zeus? So beauty, then, is the beauty-lover's way to the spirit – but only the way, only the means, my little Phaedrus.' . . . And then, sly arch-lover that he was, he said the subtlest thing of all: that the lover was nearer the divine than the beloved; for the god was in the one but not in the other – perhaps the tenderest, most mocking thought that ever was thought, and source of all the guile and secret bliss the lover knows.

Thought that can emerge wholly into feeling, feeling that can merge wholly into thought – these are the artist's highest joy. And our solitary felt in himself at this moment power to command and wield a thought that thrilled with emotion, an emotion as precise and concentrated as thought: namely, that Nature herself shivers with ecstasy when the mind bows down in homage before beauty. He felt a sudden desire to write. Eros, indeed, we are told, loves idleness, and for idle hours alone was he created. But in this crisis the violence of our sufferer's seizure was directed almost wholly towards production, its occasion almost a matter of indifference. News had reached him on his travels that a certain problem had been raised, the

intellectual world challenged for its opinion on a great and burning question
of art and taste. By nature and experience the theme was his own: and he
could not resist the temptation to set it off in the glistering foil of his words.
He would write, and moreover he would write in Tadzio's presence. This
lad should be in a sense his model, his style should follow the lines of this
figure that seemed to him divine; he would snatch up this beauty into the
realms of the mind, as once the eagle bore the Trojan shepherd aloft. Never
had the pride of the word been so sweet to him, never had he known so well
that Eros is in the word, as in those perilous and precious hours when he sat
at his rude table, within the shade of his awning, his idol full in his view and
the music of his voice in his ears, and fashioned his little essay after the
model Tadzio's beauty set: that page and a half of choicest prose, so chaste,
so lofty, so poignant with feeling, which would shortly be the wonder and
admiration of the multitude. Verily it is well for the world that it sees only
the beauty of the completed work and not its origins nor the conditions
whence it sprang; since knowledge of the artist's inspiration might often but
confuse and alarm and so prevent the full effect of its excellence. Strange
hours, indeed, these were, and strangely unnerving the labour that filled
them! Strangely fruitful intercourse this, between one body and another
mind! When Aschenbach put aside his work and left the beach he felt
exhausted, he felt broken – conscience reproached him, as it were after a
debauch.

Next morning on leaving the hotel he stood at the top of the stairs leading
down from the terrace and saw Tadzio in front of him on his way to the
beach. The lad had just reached the gate in the railings, and he was alone.
Aschenbach felt, quite simply, a wish to overtake him, to address him and
have the pleasure of his reply and answering look; to put upon a blithe and
friendly footing his relations with this being who all unconsciously had so
greatly heightened and quickened his emotions. The lovely youth moved at
a loitering pace – he might be easily overtaken; and Aschenbach hastened his
own step. He reached him on the board walk that ran behind the bathing-
cabins, and all but put out his hand to lay it on shoulder or head, while his
lips parted to utter a friendly salutation in French. But – perhaps from the
swift pace of his last few steps – he found his heart throbbing unpleasantly
fast, while his breath came in such quick pants that he could only have
gasped had he tried to speak. He hesitated, sought after self-control, was
suddenly panic-stricken lest the boy notice him hanging there behind him
and look round. Then he gave up, abandoned his plan, and passed him with
bent head and hurried step.

'Too late! Too late!' he thought as he went by. But was it too late? This
step he had delayed to take might so easily have put everything in a lighter
key, have led to a sane recovery from his folly. But the truth may have been
that the ageing man did not want to be cured, that his illusion was far too
dear to him. Who shall unriddle the puzzle of the artist nature? Who
understands that mingling of discipline and licence in which it stands so
deeply rooted? For not to be able to want sobriety is licentious folly.
Aschenbach was no longer disposed to self-analysis. He had no taste for it;
his self-esteem, the attitude of mind proper to his years, his maturity and
single-mindedness, disinclined him to look within himself and decide
whether it was constraint or puerile sensuality that had prevented him from
carrying out his project. He felt confused, he was afraid someone, if only the
watchman, might have been observing his behaviour and final surrender –
very much he feared being ridiculous. And all the time he was laughing at

himself for his serio-comic seizure. 'Quite crestfallen,' he thought. 'I was like the gamecock that lets his wings droop in the battle. That must be the Love-God himself, that makes us hang our heads at sight of beauty and weighs our proud spirits low as the ground.' Thus he played with the idea – he embroidered upon it, and was too arrogant to admit fear of an emotion.

The term he had set for his holiday passed by unheeded; he had no thought of going home. Ample funds had been sent him. His sole concern was that the Polish family might leave and a chance question put to the hotel barber elicited the information that they had come only very shortly before himself. The sun browned his face and hands, the invigorating salty air heightened his emotional energies. Heretofore he had wont to give out at once, in some new effort, the powers accumulated by sleep or food or outdoor air; but now the strength that flowed in upon him with each day of sun and sea and idleness he let go up in one extravagant gush of emotional intoxication.

His sleep was fitful; the priceless, equable days were divided one from the next by brief nights filled with happy unrest. He went, indeed, early to bed, for at nine o'clock, with the departure of Tadzio from the scene, the day was over for him. But in the faint greyness of the morning a tender pang would go through him as his heart was minded of its adventure; he could no longer bear his pillow and rising, would wrap himself against the early chill and sit down by the window to await the sunrise. Awe of the miracle filled his soul new-risen from its sleep. Heaven, earth, and its waters yet lay enfolded in the ghostly, glassy pallor of dawn; one paling star still swam in the shadowy vast. But there came a breath, a winged word from far and inaccessible abodes, that Eos was rising from the side of her spouse, and there was that first sweet reddening of the farthest strip of sea and sky that manifests creation to man's sense. She neared, the goddess, ravisher of youth, who stole away Cleitos and Cephalus and, defying all the envious Olympians, tasted beautiful Orion's love. At the world's edge began a strewing of roses, a shining and a blooming ineffably pure; baby cloudlets hung illuminated, like attendant amoretti, in the blue and blushful haze; purple effulgence fell upon the sea, that seemed to heave it forward on its welling waves; from horizon to zenith went quivering thrusts like golden lances, the gleam became a glare; without a sound, with godlike violence, glow and glare and rolling flames streamed upwards, and with flying hoof-beats the steeds of the sun-god mounted the sky. The lonely watcher sat, the splendour of the god shone on him, he closed his eyes and let the glory kiss his lids. Forgotten feelings, precious pangs of his youth, quenched long since by the stern service that had been his life and now returned so strangely metamorphosed – he recognized them with a puzzled, wondering smile. He mused, he dreamed, his lips slowly shaped a name; still smiling, his face turned sea-wards and his hands lying folded in his lap, he fell asleep once more as he sat.

But that day, which began so fierily and festally, was not like other days; it was transmuted and gilded with mythical significance. For whence could come the breath, so mild and meaningful, like a whisper from higher spheres, that played about temple and ear? Troops of small feathery white clouds ranged over the sky, like grazing herds of the gods. A stronger wind arose, and Poseidon's horses ran up, arching their manes, among them too the steers of him with the purpled locks, who lowered their horns and bellowed as they came on; while like prancing goats the waves on the farther strand leaped among the craggy rocks. It was a world possessed, peopled by Pan, that closed round the spellbound man, and his doting heart conceived the most delicate fancies. When the sun was going down behind Venice, he would sometimes sit on a bench in the park and watch Tadzio, white-clad, with gay-coloured sash, at play there on the rolled gravel with his ball; and at such times it was not Tadzio whom he saw, but Hyacinthus, doomed to die because two gods were rivals for his love. Ah, yes, he tasted the envious pangs that Zephyr knew when his rival, bow and cithara, oracle and all forgot, played with the beauteous youth; he watched the discus, guided by torturing jealousy, strike the beloved head; paled as he received the broken body in his arms, and saw the flower spring up, watered by that sweet blood and signed for evermore with his lament.

There can be no relation more strange, more critical, than that between two beings who know each other only with their eyes, who meet daily, yes, even hourly, eye each other with a fixed regard, and yet by some whim or freak of convention feel constrained to act like strangers. Uneasiness rules between them, unslaked curiosity, a hysterical desire to give rein to their suppressed impulse to recognize and address each other; even, actually, a sort of strained but mutual regard. For one human being instinctively feels respect and love for another human being so long as he does not know him well enough to judge him; and that he does not, the craving he feels is evidence.

Some sort of relationship and acquaintanceship was perforce set up between Aschenbach and the youthful Tadzio; it was with a thrill of joy the older man perceived that the lad was not entirely unresponsive to all the tender notice lavished on him. For instance, what should move the lovely youth, nowadays when he descended to the beach, always to avoid the board walk behind the bathing-huts and saunter along the sand, passing Aschenbach's tent in front, sometimes so unnecessarily close as almost to graze his table or chair? Could the power of an emotion so beyond his own so draw, so fascinate its innocent object? Daily Aschenbach would wait for Tadzio. Then sometimes, on his approach, he would pretend to be preoccupied and let the charmer pass unregarded by. But sometimes he looked up, and their glances met; when that happened both were profoundly serious. The elder's dignified and cultured mien let nothing appear of his inward state; but in Tadzio's eyes a question lay – he faltered in his step, gazed on the ground, then up again with that ineffably sweet look he had; and when he was past, something in his bearing seemed to say that only good breeding hindered him from turning round.

But once, one evening, it fell out differently. The Polish brother and sisters, with their governess, had missed the evening meal, and Aschenbach had noted the fact with concern. He was restive over their absence, and after dinner walked up and down in front of the hotel, in evening dress and a straw hat; when suddenly he saw the nunlike sisters with their companion appear in the light of the arc-lamps, and four paces behind them Tadzio. Evidently they came from the steamer-landing, having dined for some reason in Venice. It had been chilly on the lagoon, for Tadzio wore a dark-blue reefer-jacket with gilt buttons, and a cap to match. Sun and sea air could not burn his skin, it was the same creamy marble hue as at first – though he did look a little pale, either from the cold or in the bluish moonlight of the arc-lamps. The shapely brows were so delicately drawn, the eyes so deeply dark – lovelier he was than words could say, and as often the thought visited Aschenbach, and brought its own pang, that language could but extol, not reproduce, the beauties of the sense.

The sight of that dear form was unexpected, it had appeared unhoped-for, without giving him time to compose his features. Joy, surprise, and admiration might have painted themselves quite openly upon his face – and just at this second it happened that Tadzio smiled. Smiled at Aschenbach, unabashed and friendly, a speaking, winning, captivating smile, with slowly parting lips. With such a smile it might be that Narcissus bent over the mirroring pool, a smile profound, infatuated, lingering, as he put out his arms to the reflection of his own beauty; the lips just slightly pursed, perhaps half-realizing his own folly in trying to kiss the cold lips of his shadow – with a mingling of coquetry and curiosity and a faint unease, enthralling and enthralled.

Aschenbach received that smile and turned away with it as though entrusted with a fatal gift. So shaken was he that he had to flee from the lighted terrace and front gardens and seek out with hurried steps the darkness of the park at the rear. Reproaches strangely mixed of tenderness and remonstrance burst from him: 'How dare you smile like that! No one is allowed to smile like that!' He flung himself on a bench, his composure gone to the winds, and breathed in the nocturnal fragrance of the garden. He leaned back, with hanging arms, quivering from head to foot, and quite unmanned he whispered the hackneyed phrase of love and longing – impossible in these circumstances, absurd, abject, ridiculous enough, yet sacred too, and not unworthy of honour even here: 'I love you!'

In the fourth week of his stay on the Lido, Gustave von Aschenbach made certain singular observations touching the world about him. He noticed, in the first place, that though the season was approaching its height, yet the number of guests declined and, in particular, that the German tongue had suffered a rout, being scarcely or never heard in the land. At table and on the beach he caught nothing but foreign words. One day at the barber's – where he was now a frequent visitor – he heard something rather startling. The barber mentioned a German family who had just left the Lido after a brief stay, and rattled on in his obsequious way: 'The signore is not leaving – he has no fear of the sickness, has he?' Aschenbach looked at him. 'The sickness?' he repeated. Whereat the prattler fell silent, became very busy all at once, affected not to hear. When Aschenbach persisted he said he really knew nothing at all about it, and tried in a fresh burst of eloquence to drown the embarrassing subject.

That was one forenoon. After luncheon, Aschenbach had himself ferried across to Venice, in a dead calm, under a burning sun; driven by his mania, he was following the Polish young folk, whom he had seen with their companion, taking the way to the landing-stage. He did not find his idol on the Piazza. But as he sat there at tea, at a little round table on the shady side, suddenly he noticed a peculiar odour, which, it seemed to him now, had been in the air for days without his being aware: a sweetish, medicinal smell, associated with wounds and disease and suspect cleanliness. He sniffed and pondered and at length recognized it; finished his tea and left the square at the end facing the cathedral. In the narrow space the stench grew stronger. At the street corners placards were stuck up, in which the city authorities warned the population against the danger of certain infections of the gastric system, prevalent during the heated season; advising them not to eat oysters or other shell-fish and not to use the canal waters. The ordinance showed every sign of minimizing an existing situation. Little groups of people stood about silently in the squares and on the bridges; the traveller moved among them, watched and listened and thought.

He spoke to a shopkeeper lounging at his door among dangling coral necklaces and trinkets of artificial amethyst, and asked him about the disagreeable odour. The man looked at him, heavy-eyed, and hastily pulled himself together. 'Just a formal precaution, signore,' he said, with a gesture. 'A police regulation we have to put up with. The air is sultry – the sirocco is not wholesome, as the signore knows. Just a precautionary measure, you understand – probably unnecessary . . .' Aschenbach thanked him and passed on. And on the boat that bore him back to the Lido he smelt the germicide again.

On reaching his hotel he sought the table in the lobby and buried himself in the newspapers. The foreign-language sheets had nothing. But in the German papers certain rumours were mentioned, statistics given, then officially denied, then the good faith of the denials called in question. The departure of the German and Austrian contingent was thus made plain. As for other nationals, they knew or suspected nothing – they were still undisturbed. Aschenbach tossed the newspapers back on the table. 'It ought to be kept quiet,' he thought, aroused. 'It should not be talked about.' And he felt in his heart a curious elation at these events impending in the world about him. Passion is like crime: it does not thrive on the established order and the common round; it welcomes every blow dealt the bourgeois structure, every weakening of the social fabric, because therein it feels a sure hope of its own advantage. These things that were going on in the unclean alleys of Venice, under cover of an official hushing-up policy – they gave Aschenbach a dark satisfaction. The city's evil secret mingled with the one in the depths of his heart – and he would have staked all he possessed to keep it, since in his infatuation he cared for nothing but to keep Tadzio here, and owned to himself, not without horror, that he could not exist were the lad to pass from his sight.

He was no longer satisfied to owe his communion with his charmer to chance and the routine of hotel life; he had begun to follow and waylay him. On Sundays, for example, the Polish family never appeared on the beach. Aschenbach guessed they went to mass at San Marco and pursued them thither. He passed from the glare of the Piazza into the golden twilight of the holy place and found him he sought bowed in worship over a prie-dieu. He kept in the background, standing on the fissured mosaic pavement among the devout populace, that knelt and muttered and made the sign of the cross; and the crowded splendour of the oriental temple weighed voluptuously on his sense. A heavily ornate priest intoned and gesticulated before the altar, where little candle-flames flickered helplessly in the reek of incense-breathing smoke; and with that cloying sacrificial smell another seemed to mingle – the odour of the sickened city. But through all the glamour and glitter, Aschenbach saw the exquisite creature there in front turn his head, seek out and meet his lover's eye.

The crowd streamed out through the portals into the brilliant square thick with fluttering doves, and the fond fool stood aside in the vestibule on the watch. He saw the Polish family leave the church. The children took ceremonial leave of their mother, and she turned towards the Piazzetta on her way home, while his charmer and the cloistered sisters, with their governess, passed beneath the clock tower into the Merceria. When they were a few paces on, he followed – he stole behind them on their walk through the city. When they paused, he did so too; when they turned round, he fled into inns and courtyards to let them pass. Once he lost them from view, hunted feverishly over bridges and in filthy *culs-de-sac*, only to confront them suddenly in a narrow passage whence there was no escape, and experience a moment of panic fear. Yet it would be untrue to say he suffered. Mind and heart were drunk with passion, his footsteps guided by the daemonic power whose pastime it is to trample on human reason and dignity.

Tadzio and his sisters at length took a gondola. Aschenbach hid behind a portico or fountain while they embarked and directly they pushed off did the same. In a furtive whisper he told the boatman he would tip him well to follow at a little distance the other gondola, just rounding a corner, and fairly sickened at the man's quick, sly grasp and ready acceptance of the go-between's role.

Leaning back among soft, black cushions he swayed gently in the wake of the other black-snouted bark, to which the strength of his passion chained him. Sometimes it passed from his view, and then he was assailed by an anguish of unrest. But his guide appeared to have long practice in affairs like these; always, by dint of short cuts or deft manoeuvres, he contrived to overtake the coveted sight. The air was heavy and foul, the sun burnt down through a slate-coloured haze. Water slapped gurgling against wood and stone. The gondolier's cry, half warning, half salute, was answered with singular accord from far within the silence of the labyrinth. They passed little gardens high up the crumbling wall, hung with clustering white and purple flowers that sent down an odour of almonds. Moorish lattices showed shadowy in the gloom. The marble steps of a church descended into the canal, and on them a beggar squatted, displaying his misery to view, showing the whites of his eyes, holding out his hat for alms. Farther on a dealer in antiquities cringed before his lair, inviting the passer-by to enter and be duped. Yes, this was Venice, this the fair frailty that fawned and that betrayed, half fairy-tale, half snare; the city in whose stagnating air the art of painting once put forth so lusty a growth, and where musicians were moved to accords so weirdly lulling and lascivious. Our adventurer felt his senses wooed by this voluptuousness of sight and sound, tasted his secret knowledge that the city sickened and hid its sickness for love of gain, and bent an even more unbridled leer on the gondola that glided on before him.

It came at last to this – this his frenzy left him capacity for nothing else but to pursue his flame; to dream of him absent, to lavish, loverlike, endearing terms on his mere shadow. He was alone, he was a foreigner, he was sunk deep in this belated bliss of his – all which enabled him to pass unblushing through experiences well-nigh unbelievable. One night, returning late from Venice, he paused by his beloved's chamber door in the second storey, leaned his head against the panel, and remained there long, in utter drunkenness, powerless to tear himself away, blind to the danger of being caught in so mad an attitude.

And yet there were not wholly lacking moments when he paused and reflected, when in consternation he asked himself what path was this on which he had set his foot. Like most other men of parts and attainments, he had an aristocratic interest in his forbears, and when he achieved a success he liked to think he had gratified them, compelled their admiration and regard. He thought of them now, involved as he was in this illicit adventure, seized of these exotic excesses of feeling; thought of their stern self-command and decent manliness, and gave a melancholy smile. What would they have said? What, indeed, would they have said to his entire life, that varied to the point of degeneracy from theirs? This life in the bonds of art, had not he himself, in the days of his youth and in the very spirit of those bourgeois forefathers, pronounced mocking judgement upon it? And yet, at bottom, it had been so like their own! It had been a service, and he a soldier, like some of them; and art was war – a grilling, exhausting struggle that nowadays wore one out before one could grow old. It had been a life of self-conquest, a life against odds, dour, steadfast, abstinent; he had made it symbolical of the kind of over-strained heroism the time admired, and he was entitled to call it manly, even courageous. He wondered if such a life might not be somehow specially pleasing in the eyes of the god who had him in his power. For Eros had received most countenance among the most valiant nations – yes, were we not told that in their cities prowess made him flourish exceedingly? And many heroes of olden time had willingly borne his yoke, not counting any humiliation such as if it happened by the god's decree; vows, prostrations, self-abasements, these were no source of shame to the lover; rather they reaped him praise and honour.

Thus did the fond man's folly condition his thoughts; thus did he seek to hold his dignity upright in his own eyes. And all the while he kept doggedly on the traces of the disreputable secret the city kept hidden at its heart, just as he kept his own – and all that he learned fed his passion with vague, lawless hopes. He turned over newspapers at cafés, bent on finding a report on the progress of the disease; and in the German sheets, which had ceased to appear on the hotel table, he found a series of contradictory statements. The deaths, it was variously asserted, ran to twenty, to forty, to a hundred or more; yet in the next day's issue the existence of the pestilence was, if not roundly denied, reported as a matter of a few sporadic cases such as might be brought into a seaport town. After that the warnings would break out again, and the protests against the unscrupulous game the authorities were playing. No definite information was to be had.

And yet our solitary felt he had a sort of first claim on a share in the unwholesome secret; he took a fantastic satisfaction in putting leading questions to such persons as were interested to conceal it, and forcing them to explicit untruths by way of denial. One day he attacked the manager, that small, soft-stepping man in the French frock-coat, who was moving about among the guests at luncheon, supervising the service and making himself socially agreeable. He paused at Aschenbach's table to exchange a greeting, and the guest put a question, with a negligent, casual air: 'Why in the world are they forever disinfecting the city of Venice?' 'A police regulation,' the adroit one replied; 'a precautionary measure, intended to protect the health of the public during this unseasonably warm and sultry weather.' 'Very praiseworthy of the police.' Aschenbach gravely responded. After a further exchange of meteorological commonplaces the manager passed on.

It happened that a band of street musicians came to perform in the hotel gardens that evening after dinner. They grouped themselves beneath an iron stanchion supporting an arc-light, two women and two men, and turned their faces, that shone white in the glare, up towards the guests who sat on the hotel terrace enjoying this popular entertainment along with their coffee and iced drinks. The hotel lift-boys, waiters, and office staff stood in the doorway and listened; the Russian family displayed the usual Russian absorption in their enjoyment – they had their chairs put down into the garden to be nearer the singers and sat there in a half-circle with gratitude painted on their features, the old serf in her turban erect behind their chairs.

These strolling players were adepts at mandolin, guitar, harmonica, even compassing a reedy violin. Vocal numbers alternated with instrumental, the younger woman, who had a high, shrill voice, joining in a love-duet with the sweetly falsettoing tenor. The actual head of the company, however, and incontestably its most gifted member, was the other man, who played the guitar. He was a sort of baritone buffo; with no voice to speak of, but possessed of a pantomime gift and remarkable burlesque *élan*. Often he stepped out of the group and advanced towards the terrace, guitar in hand, and his audience rewarded his sallies with bursts of laughter. The Russians in their parterre seats were beside themselves with delight over this display of southern vivacity; their shouts and screams of applause encouraged him to bolder and bolder flights.

Aschenbach sat near the balustrade, a glass of pomegranate-juice and soda-water sparkling ruby-red before him, with which he now and then moistened his lips. His nerves drank in thirstily the unlovely sounds, the vulgar and sentimental tunes, for passion paralyses good taste and makes its victim accept with rapture what a man in his senses would either laugh at or turn from with disgust. Idly he sat and watched the antics of the buffoon with his face set in a fixed and painful smile, while inwardly his whole being was rigid with the intensity of the regard he bent on Tadzio, leaning over the railing six paces off.

He lounged there, in the white belted suit he sometimes wore at dinner, in all his innate, inevitable grace, with his left arm on the balustrade, his legs crossed, the right hand on the supporting hip; and looked down on the strolling singers with an expression that was hardly a smile, but rather a distant curiosity and polite toleration. Now and then he straightened himself and with a charming movement of both arms drew down his white blouse through his leather belt, throwing out his chest. And sometimes – Aschenbach saw it with triumph, with horror, and a sense that his reason was tottering – the lad would cast a glance, that might be slow and cautious, or might be sudden and swift, as though to take him by surprise, to the place where his lover sat. Aschenbach did not meet the glance. An ignoble caution made him keep his eyes in leash. For in the rear of the terrace sat Tadzio's mother and governess; and matters had gone so far that he feared to make himself conspicuous. Several times, on the beach, in the hotel lobby, on the Piazza, he had seen, with a stealing numbness, that they called Tadzio away from his neighbourhood. And his pride revolted at the affront, even while conscience told him it was deserved.

The performer below presently began a solo, with guitar accompaniment, a street song in several stanzas, just then the rage all over Italy. He delivered it in a striking and dramatic recitative, and his company joined in the refrain. He was a man of slight build, with a thin, undernourished face; his shabby felt hat rested on the back of his neck, a great mop of red hair sticking out in front; and he stood there on the gravel in advance of his troupe, in an impudent, swaggering posture, twanging the strings of his instrument and flinging a witty and rollicking recitative up to the terrace, while the veins on his forehead swelled with the violence of his effort. He was scarcely a Venetian type, belonging rather to the race of Neapolitan jesters, half bully, half comedian, brutal, blustering, an unpleasant customer, and entertaining to the last degree. The words of his song were trivial and silly, but on his lips, accompanied with gestures of head, hands, arms, and body, with leers and winks and the loose play of the tongue in the corner of his mouth, they took on meaning; an equivocal meaning, yet vaguely offensive. He wore a white sports shirt with a suit of ordinary clothes, and a strikingly large and naked-looking Adam's apple rose out of the open collar. From that pale, snub-nosed face it was hard to judge of his age; vice sat on it, it was furrowed with grimacing, and two deep wrinkles of defiance and self-will, almost of desperation, stood oddly between the red brows, above the grinning mobile mouth. But what more than all drew upon him the profound scrutiny of our solitary watcher was that this suspicious figure seemed to carry with it its own suspicious odour. For whenever the refrain occurred and the singer, with waving arms and antic gestures, passed in his grotesque march immediately beneath Aschenbach's seat, a strong smell of carbolic was wafted up to the terrace.

After the song he began to take up money, beginning with the Russian family, who gave liberally, and then mounting the steps to the terrace. But here he became as cringing as he had before been forward. He glided between the tables, bowing and scraping, showing his strong white teeth in a servile smile, though the two deep furrows on the brow were still very marked. His audience looked at the strange creature as he went about collecting his livelihood, and their curiosity was not unmixed with disfavour. They tossed coins with their finger-tips into his hat and took care not to touch it. Let the enjoyment be never so great, a sort of embarrassment always comes when the comedian oversteps the physical distance between himself and respectable people. This man felt it and sought to make his peace by fawning. He came along the railing to Aschenbach, and with him came that smell no one else seemed to notice.

'Listen!' said the solitary, in a low voice, almost mechanically; 'they are disinfecting Venice – why?' The mountebank answered hoarsely: 'Because of the police. Orders, signore. On account of the heat and the sirocco. The sirocco is oppressive. Not good for the health.' He spoke as though surprised that anyone could ask, and with the flat of his hand he demonstrated how oppressive the sirocco was. 'So there is no plague in Venice?' Aschenbach asked the question between his teeth, very low. The man's expressive face fell, he put on a look of comical innocence. 'A plague? What sort of plague? Is the sirocco a plague? Or perhaps our police are a plague? You are making fun of us, signore! A plague! Why should there be? The police make regulations on account of the heat and the weather...' He gestured. 'Quite,' said Aschenbach, once more, soft and low; and dropping an unduly large coin into the man's hat dismissed him with a sign. He bowed very low and left. But he had not reached the steps when two of the hotel servants flung themselves on him and began to whisper, their faces close to his. He shrugged, seemed to be giving assurances, to be swearing he had said nothing. It was not hard to guess the import of his words. They let him go at last and he went back into the garden, where he conferred briefly with his troupe and then stepped forward for a farewell song.

It was one Aschenbach had never to his knowledge heard before, a rowdy air, with words in impossible dialect. It had a laughing-refrain in which the other three artists joined at the top of their lungs. The refrain had neither words not accompaniment, it was nothing but rhythmical, modulated, natural laughter, which the soloist in particular knew how to render with most deceptive realism. Now that he was farther off his audience, his self-assurance had come back, and this laughter of his rang with a mocking tone. He would be overtaken, before he reached the end of the last line of each stanza; he would catch his breath, lay his hand over his mouth, his voice would quaver and his shoulders shake, he would lose power to contain himself longer. Just at the right moment each time, it came whooping, bawling, crashing out of him, with a verisimilitude that never failed to set his audience off in profuse and unpremeditated mirth that seemed to add gusto to his own. He bent his knees, he clapped his thigh, he held his sides, he looked ripe for bursting. He no longer laughed, but yelled, pointing his finger at the company there above as though there could be in all the world nothing so comic as they; until at last they laughed in hotel, terrace, and garden, down to the waiters, lift-boys, and servants – laughed as though possessed.

Aschenbach could no longer rest in his chair, he sat poised for flight. But the combined effect of the laughing, the hospital odour in his nostrils, and the nearness of the beloved was to hold him in a spell; he felt unable to stir. Under cover of the general commotion he looked across at Tadzio and saw that the lovely boy returned his gaze with a seriousness that seemed the copy of his own; the general hilarity, it seemed to say, had no power over him, he kept aloof. The grey-haired man was overpowered, disarmed by this docile, childlike deference; with difficulty he refrained from hiding his face in his hands. Tadzio's habit, too, of drawing himself up and taking a deep sighing breath struck him as being due to an oppression of the chest. 'He is sickly, he will never live to grow up,' he thought once again, with that dispassionate vision to which his madness of desire sometimes so strangely gave way. And compassion struggled with the reckless exultation of his heart.

The players, meanwhile, had finished and gone; their leader bowing and scraping, kissing his hands and adorning his leavetaking with antics that grew madder with the applause they evoked. After all the others were outside, he pretended to run backwards full tilt against a lamp-post and slunk to the gate apparently doubled over with pain. But there he threw off his buffoon's mask, stood erect, with an elastic straightening of his whole figure, ran out his tongue impudently at the guests on the terrace, and vanished in the night. The company dispersed. Tadzio had long since left the balustrade. But he, the lonely man, sat for long, to the waiters' great annoyance, before the dregs of pomegranate-juice in his glass. Time passed, the night went on. Long ago, in his parental home, he had watched the sand filter through an hour-glass – he could still see, as though it stood before him, the fragile, pregnant little toy. Soundless and fine the rust-red streamlet ran through the narrow neck and made, as it declined in the upper cavity, an exquisite little vortex.

The very next afternoon the solitary took another step in pursuit of his fixed policy of baiting the outer world. This time he had all possible success. He went, that is, into the English travel bureau in the Piazza, changed some money at the desk, and posing as the suspicious foreigner, put his fateful question. The clerk was a tweed-clad young Britisher, with his eyes set close together, his hair parted in the middle, and radiating that steady reliability which makes his like so strange a phenomenon in the *gamin*, agile-witted south. He began: 'No ground for alarm, sir. A mere formality. Quite regular in view of the unhealthy climatic conditions.' But then, looking up, he chanced to meet with his own blue eyes the stranger's weary, melancholy gaze, fixed on his face. The Englishman coloured. He continued in a lower voice, rather confused: 'At least, that is the official explanation, which they see fit to stick to. I may tell you there's a bit more to it than that.' And then, in his good, straightforward way, he told the truth.

For the past several years Asiatic cholera had shown a strong tendency to spread. Its source was the hot, moist swamps of the delta of the Ganges, where it bred in the mephitic air of that primeval island-jungle, among whose bamboo thickets the tiger crouches, where life of every sort flourishes in rankest abundance, and only man avoids the spot. Thence the pestilence had spread throughout Hindustan, ranging with great violence; moved eastwards to China, westward to Afghanistan and Persia; following the great caravan routes, it brought terror to Astrakhan, terror to Moscow. Even while Europe trembled lest the spectre be seen striding westward across country, it was carried by sea from Syrian ports and appeared simultaneously at several points on the Mediterranean littoral; raised its head in Toulon and Malaga, Palermo and Naples, and soon got a firm hold in Calabria and Apulia. Northern Italy had been spared – so far. But in May the horrible vibrios were found on the same day in two bodies: the emaciated, blackened corpses of a bargee and a woman who kept a greengrocer's shop. Both cases were hushed up. But in a week there were ten more – twenty, thirty in different quarters of the town. An Austrian provincial, having come to Venice on a few days' pleasure trip, went home and died with all the symptoms of the plague. Thus was explained the fact that the German-language papers were the first to print the news of the Venetian outbreak. The Venetian authorities published in reply a statement to the effect that the state of the city's health have never been better; at the same time instituting the most necessary precautions. But by that time the food supplies – milk, meat, or vegetables – had probably been contaminated, for death unseen and unacknowledged was devouring and laying waste in the narrow streets, while a brooding, unseasonable heat warmed the waters of the canals and encouraged the spread of the pestilence. Yes, the disease seemed to flourish and wax strong, to redouble its generative powers. Recoveries were rare. Eighty out of every hundred died, and horribly, for the onslaught was of the extremest violence, and not infrequently of the 'dry' type, the most malignant form of the contagion. In this form the victim's body loses power to expel the water secreted by the blood-vessels, it shrivels up, he passes with hoarse cries from convulsion to convulsion, his blood grows thick like pitch and he suffocates in a few hours. He is fortunate indeed, if, as sometimes happens, the disease, after a slight *malaise*, takes the form of a profound unconsciousness, from which the sufferer seldom or never rouses. By the beginning of June the quarantine buildings of the *ospedale civico* had quietly filled up, the two orphan asylums were entirely occupied, and there was a hideously brisk traffic between the *Nuovo Fundamento* and the island of San Michele, where the cemetery was. But the city was not swayed by high-minded motives or regard for international agreements. The authorities were more actuated by fear of being out of pocket, by regard for the new exhibition of paintings just opened in the Public Gardens, or by apprehension of the large losses the hotels and the shops that catered to foreigners would suffer in case of panic and blockade. And the fears of the people supported the persistent official policy of silence and denial. The city's first medical officer, an honest and competent man, had indignantly resigned his office and been privily replaced by a more compliant person. The fact was known; and this corruption in high places played its part, together with the suspense as to where the walking terror might strike next, to demoralize the baser elements in the city and encourage those antisocial forces which shun the light of day. There was intemperance, indecency, increase of crime. Evenings one saw many drunken people, which was unusual. Gangs of men in surly mood made the streets unsafe, theft and assault were said to be frequent, even murder; for in two cases persons supposedly victims of the plague were proved to have been poisoned by their own families. And professional vice was rampant, displaying excesses heretofore unknown and only at home much farther south and in the east.

Such was the substance of the Englishman's tale. 'You would do well,' he concluded, 'to leave today instead of tomorrow. The blockade cannot be more than a few days off.'

'Thank you,' said Aschenbach, and left the office.

The Piazza lay in sweltering sunshine. Innocent foreigners sat before the cafés or stood in front of the cathedral, the centre of clouds of doves that, with fluttering wings, tried to shoulder each other away and pick the kernels of maize from the extended hand. Aschenbach strode up and down the spacious flags, feverishly excited, triumphant in possession of the truth at last, but with a sickening taste in his mouth and a fantastic horror at his heart. One decent, expiatory course lay open to him; he considered it. Tonight, after dinner, he might approach the lady of the pearls and address her in words which he precisely formulated in his mind: 'Madame, will you permit an entire stranger to serve you with a word of advice and warning which self-interest prevents others from uttering? Go away. Leave here at once, without delay, with Tadzio and your daughters. Venice is in the grip of pestilence.' Then might he lay his hand in farewell upon the head of that instrument of a mocking deity; and thereafter himself flee the accursed morass. But he knew that he was far indeed from any serious desire to take such a step. It would restore him, would give him back himself once more; but he who is beside himself revolts at the idea of self-possession. There crossed his mind the vision of a white building with inscriptions on it, glittering in the sinking sun – he recalled how his mind had dreamed away into their transparent mysticism; recalled the strange pilgrim apparition that had wakened in the ageing man a lust for strange countries and fresh sights. And these memories again brought in their train the thought of returning home, returning to reason, self-mastery, an ordered existence, to the old life of effort. Alas! the bare thought made him wince with a revulsion that was like physical nausea. 'It must be kept quiet,' he whispered fiercely. 'I will not speak!' The knowledge that he shared the city's secret, the city's guilt – it put him beside himself, intoxicated him as a small quantity of wine will a man suffering from brain-fag. His thoughts dwelt upon the image of the desolate and calamitous city, and he was giddy with fugitive, mad, unreasoning hopes and visions of a monstrous sweetness. That tender sentiment he had a moment ago evoked, what was it compared with such images as these? His art, his moral sense, what were they in the balance beside the boons that chaos might confer? He kept silence, he stopped on.

That night he had a fearful dream – if dream be the right word for a mental and physical experience which did indeed befall him in deep sleep, as a thing quite apart and real to his senses, yet without his seeing himself as present in it. Rather its theatre seemed to be his own soul, and the events burst in from outside, violently overcoming the profound resistance of his spirit; passed him through and left him, left the whole cultural structure of a life-time trampled on, ravaged, and destroyed.

The beginning was fear; fear and desire, with a shuddering curiosity. Night reigned, and his senses were on the alert; he heard loud, confused noises from far away, clamour and hubbub. There was a rattling, a crashing, a low dull thunder; shrill halloos and a kind of howl with a long-drawn *u*-sound at the end. And with all these, dominating them all, flute-notes of the cruellest sweetness, deep and cooing, keeping shamelessly on until the listener felt his very entrails bewitched. He heard a voice, naming, though darkly, that which was to come: 'The stranger god!' A glow lighted up the surrounding mist and by it he recognized a mountain scene like that about his country home. From the wooded heights, from among the tree-trunks and crumbling moss-covered rocks, a troop came tumbling and raging down, a whirling rout of men and animals, and overflowed the hillside with flames and human forms, with clamour and the reeling dance. The females stumbled over the long, hairy pelts that dangled from their girdles; with heads flung back they uttered loud hoarse cries and shook their tambourines high in air; brandished naked daggers or torches vomiting trails of sparks. They shrieked, holding their breasts in both hands; coiling snakes with quivering tongues they clutched about their waists. Horned and hairy males, girt about the loins with hides, drooped heads and lifted arms and thighs in unison, as they beat on brazen vessels that gave out droning thunder, or thumped madly on drums. There were troops of beardless youths armed with garlanded staves; these ran after goats and thrust their staves against the creatures' flanks, then clung to the plunging horns and let themselves be borne off with triumphant shouts. And one and all the mad rout yelled that cry, composed of soft consonants with a long-drawn *u*-sound at the end, so sweet and wild it was together, and like nothing ever heard before! It would ring through the air like the bellow of a challenging stag, and be given back many-tongued; or they would use it to goad each other on to dance with wild excess of tossing limbs – they never let it die. But the deep, beguiling notes of the flute wove in and out and over all. Beguiling too it was to him who struggled in the grip of these sights and sounds, shamelessly awaiting the coming feast and the uttermost surrender. He trembled, he shrank, his will was steadfast to preserve and uphold his own god against this stranger who was sworn enemy to dignity and self-control. But the mountain wall took up the noise and howling and gave it back manifold; it rose high, swelled to a madness that carried him away. His senses reeled in the steam of panting bodies, the acrid stench from the goats, the odour as of stagnant waters – and another, too familiar smell – of wounds, uncleanness, and disease. His heart throbbed to the drums, his brain reeled, a blind rage seized him, a whirling lust, he craved with all his soul to join the ring that formed about the obscene symbol of the godhead, which they were unveiling and elevating, monstrous and wooden, while from full throats they yelled their rallying-cry. Foam dripped from their lips, they drove each other on with lewd gesturings and beckoning hands. They laughed, they howled, they thrust their pointed staves into each other's flesh and licked the blood as it ran down. But now the dreamer was in them and of them, the stranger god was his own. Yes, it was he who was flinging himself upon the animals, who bit and tore and swallowed smoking gobbets of flesh – while on the trampled moss there now began the rites in honour of the god, an orgy of promiscuous embraces – and in his very soul he tasted the bestial degradation of his fall.

The unhappy man woke from this dream shattered, unhinged, powerless in the demon's grip. He no longer avoided men's eyes nor cared whether he exposed himself to suspicion. And anyhow, people were leaving; many of the bathing-cabins stood empty, there were many vacant places in the dining-room, scarcely any foreigners were seen in the streets. The truth seemed to have leaked out; despite all efforts to the contrary, panic was in the air. But the lady of the pearls stopped on with her family; whether because the rumours had not reached her or because she was too proud and fearless to heed them. Tadzio remained; and it seemed at times to Aschenbach, in his obsessed state, that death and fear together might clear the island of all other souls and leave him there alone with him he coveted. In the long mornings on the beach his heavy gaze would rest, a fixed and reckless stare, upon the lad; towards nightfall, lost to shame, he would follow him through the city's narrow streets where horrid death stalked too, and at such time it seemed to him as though the moral law were fallen in ruins and only the monstrous and perverse held out a hope.

Like any lover, he desired to please; suffered agonies at the thought of failure, and brightened his dress with smart ties and handkerchiefs and other youthful touches. He added jewellery and perfumes and spent hours each day over his toilette, appearing at dinner elaborately arrayed and tensely excited. The presence of the youthful beauty that had bewitched him filled him with disgust of his own ageing body; the sight of his own sharp features and grey hair plunged him in hopeless mortification; he made desperate efforts to recover the appearance and freshness of his youth and began paying frequent visits to the hotel barber. Enveloped in the white sheet, beneath the hands of that garrulous personage, he would lean back in the chair and look at himself in the glass with misgiving.

'Grey,' he said, with a grimace.

'Slightly,' answered the man. 'Entirely due to neglect, to a lack of regard for appearances. Very natural, of course, in men of affairs, but, after all, not very sensible, for it is just such people who ought to be above vulgar prejudice in matters like these. Some folk have very strict ideas about the use of cosmetics; but they never extend them to the teeth, as they logically should. And very disgusted other people would be if they did. No, we are all as old as we feel, but no older, and grey hair can misrepresent a man worse than dyed. You, for instance, signore, have a right to your natural colour. Surely you will permit me to restore what belongs to you?'

'How?' asked Aschenbach.

For answer the oily one washed his client's hair in two waters, one clear and one dark, and lo, it was as black as in the days of his youth. He waved it with the tongs in wide, flat undulations, and stepped back to admire the effect.

'Now if we were just to freshen up the skin a little,' he said.

And with that he went on from one thing to another, his enthusiasm waxing with each new idea. Aschenbach sat there comfortably; he was incapable of objecting to the process – rather as it went forward it roused his hopes. He watched it in the mirror and saw his eyebrows grow more even and arching, the eyes gain in size and brilliance, by dint of a little application below the lids. A delicate carmine glowed on his cheeks where the skin had been so brown and leathery. The dry, anaemic lips grew full, they turned the colour of ripe strawberries, the lines round eyes and mouth were treated with a facial cream and gave place to youthful bloom. It was a young man who looked back at him from the glass – Aschenbach's heart leaped at the sight. The artist in cosmetic at last professed himself satisfied; after the manner of such people, he thanked his client profusely for what he had done himself. 'The merest trifle, the merest, signore,' he said as he added the final touches. 'Now the signore can fall in love as soon as he likes.' Aschenbach went off as in a dream, dazed between joy and fear, in his red neck-tie and broad straw hat with its gay striped band.

A lukewarm storm-wind had come up. It rained a little now and then, the air was heavy and turbid and smelt of decay. Aschenbach, with fevered cheeks beneath the rouge, seemed to hear rushing and flapping sounds in his ears, as though storm-spirits were abroad – unhallowed ocean harpies who follow those devoted to destruction, snatch away and defile their viands. For the heat took away his appetite and thus he was haunted with the idea that his food was infected.

One afternoon he pursued his charmer deep into the stricken city's huddled heart. The labyrinthine little streets, squares, canals, and bridges, each one so like the next, at length quite made him lose his bearings. He did not even know the points of the compass; all his care was not to lose sight of the figure after which his eyes thirsted. He slunk under walls, he lurked behind buildings or people's backs; and the sustained tension of his senses and emotions exhausted him more and more, though for a long time he was unconscious of fatigue. Tadzio walked behind the others, he let them pass ahead in the narrow alleys, and as he sauntered slowly after, he would turn his head and assure himself with a glance of his strange, twilit grey eyes that his lover was still following. He saw him – and he did not betray him. The knowledge enraptured Aschenbach. Lured by those eyes, led on the leading-string of his own passion and folly, utterly lovesick, he stole upon the footsteps of his unseemly hope – and at the end found himself cheated. The Polish family crossed a small vaulted bridge, the height of whose archway hid them from sight, and when he climbed it himself they were nowhere to be seen. He hunted in three directions – straight ahead and on both sides of the narrow, dirty quay – in vain. Worn quite out and unnerved, he had to give over the search.

His head burned, his body was wet with clammy sweat, he was plagued by intolerable thirst. He looked about for refreshment, of whatever sort, and found a little fruit-shop where he bought some strawberries. They were overripe and soft; he ate them as he went. The street he was on opened out into a little square, one of those charmed, forsaken spots he liked; he recognized it as the very one where he had sat weeks ago and conceived his abortive plan of flight. He sank down on the steps of the well and leaned his head against its stone rim. It was quiet here. Grass grew between the stones and rubbish lay about. Tall, weather-beaten houses bordered the square, one of them rather palatial, with vaulted windows, gaping now, and little iron balconies. In the ground floor of another was an apothecary's shop. A waft of carbolic acid was borne on a warm gust of wind.

There he sat, the master: this was he who had found a way to reconcile art and honours; who had written *The Abject*, and in a style of classic purity renounced bohemianism and all its works, all sympathy with the abyss and the troubled depths of the outcast human soul. This was he who had put knowledge underfoot to climb so high; who had outgrown the ironic pose and adjusted himself to the burdens and obligations of fame; whose renown had been officially recognized and his name ennobled, whose style was set for a model in the schools. There he sat. His eyelids were closed, there was only a swift, sidelong glint of the eyeballs now and again, something between a question and a leer; while the rouged and flabby mouth uttered single words of the sentences shaped in his disordered brain by the fantastic logic that governs our dreams.

'For mark you, Phaedrus, beauty alone is both divine and visible; and so it is the sense's way, the artist's way, little Phaedrus, to the spirit. But, now tell me, my dear boy, do you believe that such a man can ever attain wisdom and true manly worth, for whom the path to the spirit must lead through the senses? Or do you rather think – for I leave the point to you – that it is a path of perilous sweetness, a way of transgression, and must surely lead him who walks in it astray? For you know that we poets cannot walk the way of beauty without Eros as our companion and guide. We may be heroic after our fashion, disciplined warriors of our craft, yet are we all like women, for we exult in passion, and love is still our desire – our craving and our shame. And from this you will perceive that we poets can be neither wise nor worthy citizens. We must needs be wanton, must needs rove at large in the realm of feeling. Our magisterial style is all folly and pretence, our honourable repute a farce, the crowd's belief in us is merely laughable. And to teach youth, or the populace, by means of art is a dangerous practice and ought to be forbidden. For what good can an artist be as a teacher, when from his birth up he is headed direct for the pit? We may want to shun it and attain to honour in the world; but however we turn, it draws us still. So, then, since knowledge might destroy us, we will have none of it. For knowledge, Phaedrus, does not make him who possesses it dignified or austere. Knowledge is all-knowing, understanding, forgiving; it takes up no position, sets no store by form. It has compassion with the abyss – it *is* the abyss. So we reject it, firmly, and henceforward our concern shall be with beauty only. And by beauty we mean simplicity, largeness, and renewed severity of discipline; we mean a return to detachment and to form. But detachment, Phaedrus, and preoccupation with form lead to intoxication and desire, they may lead the noblest among us to frightful emotional excesses, which his own stern cult of the beautiful would make him the first to condemn. So they too, they too, lead to the bottomless pit. Yes, they lead us thither, I say, us who are poets – who by our natures are prone not to excellence but to excess. And now, Phaedrus, I will go. Remain here; and only when you can no longer see me, then do you depart also.'

A few days later, Gustave Aschenbach left his hotel rather later than usual in the morning. He was not feeling well and had to struggle against spells of giddiness only half physical in their nature, accompanied by a swiftly mounting dread, a sense of futility and hopelessness – but whether this referred to himself or to the outer world he could not tell. In the lobby he saw a quantity of luggage lying strapped and ready; asked the porter whose it was, and received in answer the name he already knew he should hear – that of the Polish family. The expression of his ravaged features did not change; he only gave that quick lift of the head with which we sometimes receive the uninteresting answer to a casual query. But he put another: 'When?' 'After luncheon,' the man replied. He nodded, and went down to the beach.

It was an unfriendly scene. Little crisping shivers ran all across the wide stretch of shallow water between the shore and the first sand-bank. The whole beach, once so full of colour and life, looked now autumnal, out of season; it was nearly deserted and not even very clean. A camera on a tripod stood at the edge of the water, apparently abandoned; its black cloth snapped in the freshening wind.

Tadzio was there, in front of his cabin, with the three or four playfellows still left him. Aschenbach set up his chair some halfway between the cabins and the water, spread a rug over his knees, and sat looking on. The game this time was unsupervised, the elders being probably busy with the packing, and it looked rather lawless and out-of-hand. Jaschiu, the sturdy lad in the belted suit, with the black, brilliantined hair, became angry at a handful of sand thrown in his eyes; he challenged Tadzio to a fight, which quickly ended in the downfall of the weaker. And perhaps the coarser nature saw here a chance to avenge himself at last, by one cruel act, for his long weeks of subserviency: the victor would not let the vanquished get up, but remained kneeling on Tadzio's back, pressing Tadzio's face into the sand – for so long a time that it seemed the exhausted lad might even suffocate. He made spasmodic efforts to shake the other off, lay still and then began a feeble twitching. Just as Aschenbach was about to spring indignantly to the rescue, Jaschiu let his victim go. Tadzio, very pale, half sat up, and remained so, leaning on one arm, for several minutes, with darkening eyes and rumpled hair. Then he rose and walked slowly away. The others called him, at first gaily, then imploringly; he would not hear. Jaschiu was evidently overtaken by swift remorse; he followed his friend and tried to make his peace, but Tadzio motioned him back with a jerk of one shoulder and went down to the water's edge. He was barefoot and wore his striped linen suit with the red breast-knot.

There he stayed a little, with bent head, tracing figures in the wet sand with one toe; then stepped into the shallow water, which at its deepest did not wet his knees; waded idly through it and reached the sand-bar. Now he paused again with his face turned seaward; and next began to move slowly leftwards along the narrow strip of sand the sea left bare. He paced there, divided by an expanse of water from the shore, from his mates by his moody pride; a remote and isolated figure with floating locks, out there in sea and wind, against the misty inane. Once more he paused to look: with a sudden recollection, or by an impulse, he turned from the waist up, in an exquisite movement, one hand resting on his hip, and looked over his shoulder at the shore. The watcher sat just as he had sat that time in the lobby of the hotel when first the twilit grey eyes had met his own. He rested his head against the chair-back and followed the movements of the figure out there, then lifted it, as it were in answer to Tadzio's gaze. It sank on his breast, the eyes looked out beneath their lids, while his whole face took on the relaxed and brooding expression of deep slumber. It seemed to him the pale and lovely Summoner out there smiled at him and beckoned; as though with the hand he lifted from his hip, he pointed outward as he hovered on before into an immensity of richest expectation.

Some minutes passed before anyone hastened to the aid of the elderly man sitting there collapsed in his chair. They bore him to his room. And before nightfall a shocked and respectful world received the news of his decease.

1911

Tristan

TRANSLATED FROM THE GERMAN BY

H.T. Lowe-Porter

Einfried, the sanatorium. A long, white retilinear building with a side wing, set in a spacious garden pleasingly equipped with grottoes, bowers, and little bark pavilions. Behind its slate roofs the mountains tower heavenwards, evergreen, massy, cleft with wooded ravines.

Now as then Dr Leander directs the establishment. He wear a two-pronged black beard as curly and wiry as horsehair stuffing; his spectacle-lenses are thick, and glitter; he has the look of a man whom science has cooled and hardened and filled with silent, forebearing pessimism. And with this beard, these lenses, this look, and in his short, reserved, pre-occupied way, he holds his patients in his spell; holds those sufferers who, too weak to be laws unto themselves, put themselves into his hands that his severity may be a shield unto them.

As for Fräulein von Osterloh, hers it is to preside with unwearying zeal over the housekeeping. Ah, what activity! How she plies, now here, now there, now upstairs, now down, from one end of the building to the other! She is queen in kitchen and storerooms, she mounts the shelves of the linen-presses, she marshals the domestic staff; she ordains the bill of fare, to the end that the table shall be economical, hygienic, attractive, appetizing, and all these in the highest degree; she keeps house diligently, furiously; and her exceeding capacity conceals a constant reproach to the world of men, to no one of whom has it yet occurred to lead her to the altar. But ever on her cheeks there glows, in two round, carmine spots, the unquenchable hope of one day becoming Frau Dr Leander.

Ozone, and stirless, stirless air! Einfried, whatever Dr Leander's rivals and detractors may choose to say about it, can be most warmly recom-mended for lung patients. And not only these, but patients of all sorts, gentlemen, ladies, even children, come to stop here. Dr Leander's skill is challenged in many different fields. Sufferers from gastric disorders come, like Frau Magistrate Spatz – she has ear trouble into the bargain – people with defective hearts, paralytics, rheumatics, nervous sufferers of all kinds and degrees. A diabetic general here consumes his daily bread amid continual grumblings. There are several gentlemen with gaunt, fleshless faces who fling their legs about in that uncontrollable way that bodes no good. There is an elderly lady, a Frau Pastor Höhlenrauch, who has brought fourteen children into the world and is now incapable of a single thought, yet has not thereby attained to any peace of mind, but must go roving spectre-like all day long up and down through the house, on the arm of her private attendant, as she has been doing this year past.

Sometimes a death takes place among the 'severe cases', those who lie in their chambers, never appearing at meals or in the reception-rooms. When this happens no one knows of it, not even the person sleeping next door. In the silence of the night the waxen guest is put away and life at Einfried goes tranquilly on, with its massage, its electric treatment, douches, baths; with its exercises, its steaming and inhaling, in rooms especially equipped with all the triumphs of modern therapeutics.

Yes, a deal happens hereabouts – the institution is in a flourishing way. When new guests arrive, at the entrance to the side wing, the porter sounds the great gong; when there are departures, Dr Leander, together with Fräulein von Osterloh, conducts the traveller in due form to the waiting carriage. All sorts and kinds of people have received hospitality at Einfried. Even an author is here stealing time from God Almighty – a queer sort of man, with a name like some kind of mineral or precious stone.

Lastly there is, besides Dr Leander, another physician, who takes care of the slight cases and the hopeless ones. But he bears the name of Müller and is not worth mentioning.

At the beginning of January a business man named Klöterjahn – of the firm of A. C. Klöterjahn & Co. – brought his wife to Einfried. The porter rang the gong, and Fräulein von Osterloh received the guests from a distance in the drawing-room on the ground floor, which, like nearly all the fine old mansion, was furnished in wonderfully pure Empire style. Dr Leander appeared straightway. He made his best bow, and a preliminary conversation ensued, for the better information of both sides.

Beyond the windows lay the wintry garden, the flower-beds covered with straw, the grottoes snowed under, the little temples forlorn. Two porters were dragging in the guests' trunks from the carriage drawn up before the wrought-iron gate – for there was no drive up to the house.

'Be careful, Gabriele, *doucement, doucement*, my angel, keep your mouth closed.' Herr Klöterjahn had said as he led his wife through the garden; and nobody could look at her without tender-heartedly echoing the caution – though, to be sure, Herr Klöterjahn might quite as well have uttered it all in his own language.

The coachman who had driven the pair from the station to the sanatorium was an uncouth man, and insensitive; yet he sat with his tongue between his teeth as the husband lifted down his wife. The very horses, steaming in the frosty air, seemed to follow the procedure with their eyeballs rolled back in their heads out of sheer concern for so much tenderness and fragile charm.

The young wife's trouble was her trachea; it was expressly so set down in the letter Herr Klöterjahn had sent from the shores of the Baltic to announce their impending arrival to the director of Einfried – the trachea, and not the lungs, thank God! But it is a question whether, if it had been the lungs, the new patient could have looked any more pure and ethereal, any remoter from the concerns of this world, than she did now as she leaned back pale and weary in her chaste white-enamelled arm-chair, beside her robust husband, and listened to the conversation.

Her beautiful white hands, bare save for the simple wedding-ring, rested in her lap, among the folds of a dark, heavy cloth skirt; she wore a close-fitting waist of silver-grey with a stiff collar – it had an all-over pattern of arabesques in high-pile velvet. But these warm, heavy materials only served to bring out the unspeakable delicacy, sweetness, and languor of the little head, to make it look more than ever touching, exquisite and unearthly. Her light-brown hair was drawn smoothly back and gathered in a knot low in her neck, but near the right temple a single lock fell loose and curling, not far from the place where an odd little vein branched across one well-marked eyebrow, pale blue and sickly amid all that pure, well-nigh transparent spotlessness. That little blue vein above the eye dominated quite painfully the whole fine oval of the face. When she spoke, it stood out still more; yes, even when she smiled – and lent her expression a touch of strain, if not actually of distress, that stirred vague fear in the beholder. And yet she spoke, and she smiled: spoke frankly and pleasantly in her rather husky voice, with a smile in her eyes – though they again were sometimes a little difficult and showed a tendency to avoid a direct gaze. And the corner of her eyes, both sides of the base of the slender little nose, were deeply shadowed. She smiled with her mouth too, her beautiful wide mouth, whose lips were so pale and yet seemed to flash – perhaps because their contours were so exceedingly pure and well-cut. Sometimes she cleared her throat, then carried her handkerchief to her mouth and afterwards looked at it.

'Don't clear your throat like that, Gabriele,' said Herr Klöterjahn. 'You know, darling, Dr Hinzpeter expressly forbade it, and what we have to do is to exercise self-control, my angel. As I said, it is the trachea,' he repeated. 'Honestly, when it began, I thought it was the lungs, and it gave me a scare, I do assure you. But it isn't the lungs – we don't mean to let ourselves in for that, do we, Gabriele, my love, eh? Ha ha!'

'Surely not,' said Dr Leander, and glittered at her with his eye-glasses.

Whereupon Herr Klöterjahn ordered coffee, coffee and rolls; and the speaking way he had of sounding the *c* far back in his throat and exploding the *b* in 'butter' must have made any soul alive hungry to hear it.

His order was filled; and rooms were assigned to him and his wife, and they took possession with their things.

And Dr Leander took over the case himself, without calling in Dr Müller.

The population of Einfried took unusual interest in the fair new patient; Herr Klöterjahn, used as he was to see homage paid her, received it all with great satisfaction. The diabetic general, when he first saw her, stopped grumbling a minute; the gentlemen with the fleshless faces smiled and did their best to keep their legs in order; as for Frau Magistrate Spatz, she made her her oldest friend on the spot. Yes, she made an impression, this woman who bore Herr Klöterjahn's name! A writer who had been sojourning a few weeks in Einfried, a queer sort, he was, with a name like some precious stone or other, positively coloured up when she passed him in the corridor, stopped stock-still and stood there as though rooted to the ground, long after she had disappeared.

Before two days were out, the whole little population knew her history. She came originally from Bremen, as one could tell by certain pleasant small twists in her pronunciation; and it had been in Bremen that, two years gone by, she had bestowed her hand upon Herr Klöterjahn, a successful businessman, and become his life-partner. She had followed him to his native town on the Baltic coast, where she had presented him, some ten months before the time of which we write, and under circumstances of the greatest difficulty and danger, with a child, a particularly well-formed and vigorous son and heir. But since that terrible hour she had never fully recovered her strength – granting, that is, that she had ever had any. She had not been long up, still extremely weak, with extremely impoverished vitality, when one day after coughing she brought up a little blood – oh, not much, an insignificant quantity in fact; but it would have been much better to be none at all; and the suspicious thing was, that the same trifling but disquieting incident recurred after another short while. Well, of course, there were things to be done, and Dr Hinzpeter, the family physician, did them. Complete rest was ordered, little pieces of ice swallowed; morphine administered to check the cough, and other medicines to regulate the heart action. But recovery failed to set in; and while the child, Anton Klöterjahn, junior, a magnificent specimen of a baby, seized on his place in life and held it with prodigious energy and ruthlessness, a low, unobservable fever seemed to waste the young mother daily. It was, as we have heard, an affection of the trachea – a word that in Dr Hinzpeter's mouth sounded so soothing, so consoling, so reassuring, that it raised their spirits to a surprising degree. But even though it was not the lungs, the doctor presently found that a milder climate and a stay in a sanatorium were imperative if the cure was to be hastened. The reputation enjoyed by Einfried and its director had done the rest.

Such was the state of affairs; Herr Klöterjahn himself related it to all and sundry. He talked with a slovenly pronunciation, in a loud, good-humoured voice, like a man whose digestion is in as capital order as his pocket-book; shovelling out the words pell-mell, in the broad accents of the northern coast-dweller; hurtling some of them forth so that each sound was a little explosion, at which he laughed as at a successful joke.

He was of medium height, broad, stout, and short-legged; his face full and red, with watery blue eyes shaded by very fair lashes; with wide nostrils and humid lips. He wore English side-whiskers and English clothes, and it enchanted him to discover at Einfried an entire English family, father, mother and three pretty children with their nurse, who were stopping here for the simple and sufficient reason that they knew not where else to go. With this family he partook of a good English breakfast every morning. He set great store by good eating and drinking and proved to be a connoisseur both of food and wines, entertaining the other guests with the most exciting accounts of dinners given in his circle of acquaintance back home, with full descriptions of the choicer and rarer dishes; in the telling his eyes would narrow benignly, and his pronunciation take on certain palatal and nasal sounds, accompanied by smacking noises at the back of his throat. That he was not fundamentally averse to earthly joys of another sort was evinced upon an evening when a guest of the cure, an author by calling, saw him in the corridor trifling in not quite permissible fashion with a chambermaid – a humorous little passage at which the author in question made a laughably disgusted face.

As for Herr Klöterjahn's wife, it was plain to see that she was devotedly attached to her husband. She followed his words and movements with a smile: not the rather arrogant toleration the ailing sometimes bestow upon the well and sound, but the sympathetic participation of a well-disposed invalid in the manifestations of people who rejoice in the blessing of abounding health.

Herr Klöterjahn did not stop long in Einfried. He had brought his wife hither, but when a week had gone by and he knew she was in good hands and well looked after, he did not linger. Duties equally weighty – his flourishing child, his no less flourishing business – took him away; they compelled him to go, leaving her rejoicing in the best of care.

Spinell was the name of that author who had been stopping some weeks at Einfried – Detlev Spinell was his name, and his looks were quite out of the common. Imagine a dark man at the beginning of the thirties, impressively tall, with hair already distinctly grey at the temples, and a round, white, slightly bloated face, without a vestige of beard. Not that it was shaven – that you could have told; it was soft, smooth, boyish, with at most a downy hair here and there. And the effect was singular. His bright, doe-like brown eyes had a gentle expression, the nose was thick and rather too fleshy. Also, Herr Spinell had an upper lip like an ancient Roman's, swelling and full of pores; large, carious teeth, and feet of uncommon size. One of the gentlemen with the rebellious legs, a cynic and ribald wit, had christened him 'the dissipated baby'; but the epithet was malicious, and not very apt. Herr Spinell dressed well, in a long black coat and a waistcoat with coloured spots.

He was unsocial and sought no man's company. Only once in a while he might be overtaken by an affable, blithe, expansive mood; and this always happened when he was carried away by an aesthetic fit at the sight of beauty, the harmony of two colours, a vase nobly formed, or the range of mountains lighted by the setting sun. 'How beautiful!' he would say, with his head on one side, his shoulders raised, his hands spread out, his lips and nostrils curled and distended. 'My God! look, how beautiful!' And in such moments of ardour he was quite capable of flinging his arms blindly round the neck of anybody, high or low, male or female, that happened to be near.

On his table, for anybody to see who entered his room, there always lay the book he had written. It was a novel of medium length, with a perfectly bewildering drawing on the jacket, printed on a sort of filter-paper. Each letter of the type looked like a Gothic cathedral. Fräulein von Osterloh had read it once, in a spare quarter-hour, and found it 'very cultured' – which was her circumlocution for inhumanly boresome. Its scenes were laid in fashionable salons, in luxurious boudiors full of chioce *objets d'art*, old furniture, gobelins, rare porcelains, priceless stuffs, and art treasures of all sorts and kinds. On the description of these things was expended the most loving care; as you read you constantly saw Herr Spinell, with distended nostrils, saying: 'How beautiful! My God! look, how beautiful!' After all, it was strange he had not written more than this one book; he so obviously adored writing. He spent the greater part of the day doing it, in his room, and sent an extraordinary number of letters to the post, two or three nearly every day – and that made it more striking, even almost funny, that he very seldom received one in return.

Herr Spinell sat opposite Herr Klöterjahn's wife. At the first meal of which the new guests partook, he came rather later into the dining-room, on the ground floor of the side wing, bade good-day to the company generally in a soft voice, and betook himself to his own place, whereupon Dr Leander perfunctorily presented him to the newcomers. He bowed, and self-consciously began to eat, using his knife and fork rather affectedly with the large, finely shaped white hands that came out from his very narrow coat-sleeves. After a little he grew more at ease and looked tranquilly first at Herr Klöterjahn and then at his wife, by turns. And in the course of the meal Herr Klöterjahn addressed to him sundry queries touching the general situation and climate of Einfried; his wife, in her charming way, added a word or two, and Herr Spinell gave courteous answers. His voice was mild, and really agreeable; but he had a halting way of speaking that almost amounted to an impediment – as though his teeth got in the way of his tongue.

After luncheon, when they had gone into the salon, Dr Leander came up to the new arrivals to wish them *Mahlzeit*, and Herr Klöterjahn's wife took occasion to ask about their *vis-à-vis*.

'What was the gentleman's name?' she asked. 'I did not quite catch it. Spinelli?'

'Spinell, not Spinelli, madame. No, he is not an Italian; he only comes from Lemberg, I believe.'

'And what was it you said? He is an author, or something of the sort?' asked Herr Klöterjahn. He had his hands in the pockets of his very easy-fitting English trousers, cocked his head towards the doctor, and opened his mouth, as some people do, to listen the better.

'Yes ... I really don't know,' answered Dr Leander. 'He writes ... I believe he has written a book, some sort of novel. I really don't know what.'

By which Dr Leander conveyed that he had no great opinion of the author and declined all responsibility on the score of him.

'But I find that most interesting,' said Herr Klöterjahn's wife. Never before had she met an author face to face.

'Oh, yes,' said Dr Leander obligingly. 'I understand he has a certain amount of reputation,' which closed the conversation.

But a little later, when the new guests had retired and Dr Leander himself was about to go, Herr Spinell detained him in talk to put a few questions for his own part.

'What was their name?' he asked. 'I did not understand a syllable, of course.'

'Klöterjahn,' answered Dr Leander, turning away.

'What's that?' asked Herr Spinell.

'*Klöterjahn* is their name,' said Dr Leander, and went his way. He set no great store by the author.

Have we got as far on as where Herr Klöterjahn went home? Yes, he was back on the shore of the Baltic once more, with his business and his babe, that ruthless and vigorous little being who had cost his mother great suffering and a slight weakness of the trachea; while she herself, the young wife, remained in Einfried and became the intimate friend of Frau Spatz. Which did not prevent Herr Klöterjahn's wife from being on friendly terms with the rest of the guests – for instance with Herr Spinell, who, to the astonishment of everybody, for he had up to now held communion with not a single soul, displayed from the very first an extraordinary devotion and courtesy, and with whom she enjoyed talking, whenever she had any time left over from the stern service of the cure.

He approached her with immense circumspection and reverence, and never spoke save with his voice so carefully subdued that Frau Spatz, with her bad hearing, seldom or never caught anything he said. He tiptoed on his great feet up to the arm-chair in which Herr Klöterjahn's wife leaned, fragilely smiling; stopped two paces off, with his body bent forward and one leg poised behind him, and talked in his halting way, as though he had an impediment in his speech; with ardour, yet prepared to retire at any moment and vanish at the first sign of fatigue or satiety. But he did not tire her; she begged him to sit down with her and the Rätin; she asked him questions and listened with curious smiles, for he had a way of talking sometimes that was so odd and amusing, different from anything she had ever heard before.

'Why are you in Einfried, really?' she asked. 'What cure are you taking, Herr Spinell?'

'Cure? Oh, I'm having myself electrified a bit. Nothing worth mentioning. I will tell you the real reason why I am here, madame. It is a feeling for style.'

'Ah?' said Herr Klöterjahn's wife; supported her chin on her hand and turned to him with exaggerated eagerness, as one does to a child who wants to tell a story.

'Yes, madame. Einfried is perfect Empire. It was once a castle, a summer residence, I am told. This side wing is a later addition, but the main building is old and genuine. There are times when I cannot endure Empire, and then times when I simply must have it in order to attain any sense of well-being. Obviously, people feel one way among furniture that is soft and comfortable and voluptuous, and quite another among the straight lines of these tables, chairs and draperies. This brightness and hardness, this cold, austere simplicity and reserved strength, madame – it has upon me the ultimate effect of an inward purification and rebirth. Beyond a doubt, it is morally elevating.'

'Yes, that is remarkable,' she said. 'And when I try I can understand what you mean.'

Whereto he responded that it was not worth her taking any sort of trouble, and they laughed together. Frau Spatz laughed too and found it remarkable in her turn, though she did not say she understood it.

The reception-room was spacious and beautiful. The high white folding doors that led to the billiard-room were wide open, and the gentlemen with the rebellious legs were disporting themselves within, others as well. On the opposite side of the room a glass door gave on the broad veranda and the garden. Near the door stood a piano. At a green-covered folding table, the diabetic general was playing whist with some other gentlemen. Ladies sat reading or embroidering. The rooms were heated by an iron stove, but the chimney-piece, in the purest style, had coals pasted over with red paper to simulate a fire, and chairs were drawn up invitingly.

'You are an early riser, Herr Spinell,' said Herr Klöterjahn's wife. 'Two or three times already I have chanced to see you leaving the house at half past seven in the morning.'

'An early riser? Ah, with a difference, madame, with a vast difference. The truth is, I rise early because I am such a late sleeper.'

'You really must explain yourself, Herr Spinell.' Frau Spatz too said she demanded an explanation.

'Well, if one is an early riser, one does not need to get up so early. Or so it seems to me. The conscience, madame, is a bad business. I, and other people like me, work hard all our lives to swindle our consciences into feeling pleased and satisfied. We are feckless creatures, and aside from a few good hours we go around weighted down, sick and sore with the knowledge of our own futility. We hate the useful; we know it is vulgar and unlovely, and we defend this position, as a man defends something that is absolutely necessary to his existence. Yet all the while conscience is gnawing at us, to such an extent that we are simply one wound. Added to that, our whole inner life, our view of the world, our way of working, is of a kind – its effect is frightfully unhealthy, undermining, irritating, and this only aggravates the situation. Well, then, there are certain little counter-irritants, without which we would most certainly not hold out. A kind of decorum, a hygienic regimen, for instance, becomes a necessity for some of us. To get up early, to get up ghastly early, take a cold bath, and go out walking in a snowstorm – that may give us a sense of self-satisfaction that lasts as much as an hour. If I were to act out my true character, I should be lying in bed late into the afternoon. My getting up early is all hypocrisy, believe me.'

'Why do you say that, Herr Spinell? On the contrary, I call it self-abnegation.' Frau Spatz, too, called it self-abnegation.

'Hypocrisy or self-abnegation – call it what you like, madame, I have such a hideously downright nature –'

'Yes, that's it. Surely you torment yourself far too much.'

'Yes, madame, I torment myself a great deal.'

The fine weather continued. Rigid and spotless white the region lay, the mountains, house and garden, in a windless air that was blinding clear and cast bluish shadows; and above it arched the spotless pale-blue sky, where myriads of bright particles of glittering crystals seemed to dance. Herr Klöterjahn's wife felt tolerably well these days: free of fever, with scarce any cough, and able to eat without too great distaste. Many days she sat taking her cure for hours on end in the sunny cold on the terrace. She sat in the snow, bundled in wraps and furs, and hopefully breathed in the pure icy air to do her trachea good. Sometimes she saw Herr Spinell, dressed like herself, and in fur boots that made his feet a fantastic size, taking an airing in the garden. He walked with tentative tread through the snow, holding his arms in a certain careful pose that was stiff yet not without grace; coming up to the terrace he would bow very respectfully and mount the first step or so to exchange a few words with her.

'Today on my morning walk I saw a beautiful woman – good Lord! how beautiful she was!' he said; laid his head on one side and spread out his hands.

'Really, Herr Spinell. Do describe her to me.'

'That I cannot do. Or, rather, it would not be a fair picture. I only saw the lady as I glanced at her in passing. I did not actually see her at all. But that fleeting glimpse was enough to rouse my fancy and make me carry away a picture so beautiful that – good Lord! how beautiful it is!

She laughed. 'Is that the way you always look at beautiful women, Herr Spinell? Just a fleeting glance?'

'Yes, madame; it is a better way than if I were avid of actuality, stared them plump in the face, and carried away with me only a consciousness of the blemishes they in fact possess.'

'"Avid of actuality" – what a strange phrase, a regular literary phrase, Herr Spinell; no one but an author could have said that. It impresses me very much, I must say. There is a lot in it that I dimly understand; there is something free about it, and independent, that even seems to be looking down on reality though it is so very respectable – is respectability itself, as you might say. And it makes me comprehend, too, that there is something else besides the tangible, something more subtle –'

'I know only one face,' he said suddenly, with a strange lift in his voice, carrying his closed hands to his shoulders as he spoke and showing his carious teeth in an almost hysterical smile. 'I know only one face of such lofty nobility that the mere thought of enhancing it through my imagination would be blasphemous; at which I could wish to look, on which I could wish to dwell, not minutes and not hours, but my whole life long; losing myself utterly therein, forgotten to every earthly thought...'

'Yes, indeed, Herr Spinell. And yet don't you find Fräulein von Osterloh has rather prominent ears?'

He replied only by a profound bow; then, standing erect, let his eyes rest with a look of embarrassment and pain on the strange little vein that branched pale-blue and sickly across her pure translucent brow.

An odd sort, a very odd sort. Herr Klöterjahn's wife thought about him sometimes; for she had much leisure for thought. Whether it was that the change of air began to lose its effect or some positively detrimental influence was at work, she began to go backward, the condition of her trachea left much to be desired, she had fever not infrequently, felt tired and exhausted, and could not eat. Dr Leander most emphatically recommended rest, quiet, caution, care. So she sat, when indeed she was not forced to lie, quite motionless, in the society of Frau Spatz, holding some sort of sewing which she did not sew, and following one or another train of thought.

Yes, he gave her food for thought, this very odd Herr Spinell; and the strange thing was she thought not so much about him as about herself, for he had managed to rouse in her a quite novel interest in her own personality. One day he had said, in the course of conversation:

'No, they are positively the most enigmatic facts in Nature – women, I mean. That is a truism, and yet one never ceases to marvel at it afresh. Take some wonderful creature, a sylph, an airy wraith, a fairy dream of a thing, and what does she do? Goes and gives herself to a brawny Hercules at a country fair, or maybe to a butcher's apprentice. Walks about on his arm, even leans her head on his shoulder and looks round with an impish smile as if to say: "Look on this, if you like, and break your heads over it." And we break them.'

With this speech Herr Klöterjahn's wife had occupied her leisure again and again.

Another day, to the wonderment of Frau Spatz, the following conversation took place:

'May I ask, madame – though you may very likely think me prying – what your name really is?'

'Why, Herr Spinell, you know my name is Klöterjahn!'

'H'm. Yes, I know that – or, rather, I deny it. I mean your own name, your maiden name, of course. You will in justice, madame, admit that anybody who calls you Klöterjahn ought to be thrashed.'

She laughed so hard that the little blue vein stood out alarmingly on her brow and gave the pale sweet face a strained expression disquieting to see.

'Oh, no! Not at all, Herr Spinell! Thrashed, indeed! Is the name Klöterjahn so horrible to you?'

'Yes, madame. I hate the name from the bottom of my heart. I hated it the first time I heard it. It is the abandonment of ugliness; it is grotesque to make you comply with the custom so far as to fasten your husband's name upon you; it is barbarous and vile.'

'Well, and how about Eckhof? Is that any better? Eckhof is my father's name.'

'Ah, you see! Eckhof is quite another thing. There was a great actor named Eckhof. Eckhof will do nicely. You spoke of your father – Then is your mother – ?'

'Yes, my mother died when I was little.'

'Ah! Tell me a little more of yourself, pray. But not if it tires you. When it tires you, stop, and I will go on talking about Paris, as I did the other day. But you could speak very softly, or even whisper – that would be more beautiful still. You were born in Bremen?' He breathed, rather than uttered, the question with an expression so awed, so heavy with import, as to suggest that Bremen was a city like no other on earth, full of hidden beauties and nameless adventures, and ennobling in some mysterious way those born within its walls.

'Yes, imagine,' said she involuntarily. 'I was born in Bremen.'

'I was there once,' he thoughtfully remarked.

'Goodness me, you have been there, too? Why, Herr Spinell, it seems to me you must have been everywhere there is between Spitsbergen and Tunis!'

'Yes, I was there once,' he repeated. 'A few hours, one evening. I recall a narrow old street, with a strange, warped-looking moon above the gabled roofs. Then I was in a cellar that smelled of wine and mould. It is a poignant memory.'

'Really? Where could that have been, I wonder? Yes, in just such a grey old gabled house I was born, one of the old merchant houses, with echoing wooden floor and white-painted gallery.'

'Then your father is a business man?' he asked hesitatingly.

'Yes, but he is also, and in the first place, an artist.'

'Ah! In what way?'

'He plays the violin. But just saying that does not mean much. It is *how* he plays, Herr Spinell – it is that that matters! Sometimes I cannot listen to some of the notes without the tears coming into my eyes and making them burn. Nothing else in the world makes me feel like that. You won't believe it –'

'But I do. Oh, very much I believe it! Tell me, madame, your family is old, is it not? Your family has been living for generations in the old gabled house – living and working and closing their eyes on time? –'

'Yes. Tell me why you ask.'

'Because it not infrequently happens that a race with sober, practical bourgeois traditions will towards the end of its days flare up in some form of art.'

'Is that a fact?'

'Yes.'

'It is true, my father is surely more of an artist than some that call themselves so and get the glory of it. I only play the piano a little. They have forbidden me now, but at home, in the old days, I still played. Father and I played together. Yes, I have precious memories of all those years; and especially of the garden, our garden, behind the house. It was dreadfully wild and overgrown, and shut in by crumbling mossy walls. But it was just that that gave it such charm. In the middle was a fountain with a wide border of sword-lilies. In summer I spent long hours there with my friends. We all sat round the fountain on little camp-stools –'

'How beautiful!' said Herr Spinell, and flung up his shoulders. 'You sat there and sang?'

'No, we mostly crocheted.'

'But still –'

'Yes, we crotcheted and chattered, my six friends and I –'

'How beautiful! Good Lord! think of it, *how beautiful*!' cried Herr Spinell again, his face quite distorted with emotion.

'Now, what is it you find so particularly beautiful about that, Herr Spinell?'

'Oh, there being six of them besides you, and your being not one of the six, but a queen among them ... set apart from your six friends. A little gold crown showed in your hair – quite a modest, unostentatious little crown, still it was there –'

'Nonsense, there was nothing of the sort.'

'Yes, there was; it shone unseen. But if I had been there, standing among the shrubbery, one of those times I should have seen it.'

'God knows what you would have seen. But you were not there. Instead of that, it was my husband who came out of the shrubbery one day, with my father. I was afraid they had been listening to our prattle –'

'So it was there, then, madame, that you first met your husband?'

'Yes, there it was I saw him first,' she said, in quite a glad, strong voice; she smiled, and as she did so the little blue vein came out and gave her face a constrained and anxious expression. 'He was calling on my father on business, you see. Next day he came to dinner, and three days later he proposed for my hand.'

'Really? It all happened as fast as that?'

'Yes. Or, rather, it went a little slower after that. For my father was not very much inclined to it, you see, and consented on condition that we wait a long time first. He would rather I had stopped with him, and he had doubts in other ways too. But —'

'But?'

'But I had set my heart on it,' she said, smiling; and once more the little vein dominated her whole face with its look of constraint and anxiety.

'Ah, so you set your heart on it.'

'Yes, and I displayed great strength of purpose, as you see —'

'As I see. Yes.'

'So that my father had to give way in the end.'

'And so you forsook him and his fiddle and the old house with the overgrown garden, and the fountain and your six friends, and clave unto Herr Klöterjahn —'

'"And clave unto" — you have such a strange way of saying things, Herr Spinell. Positively biblical. Yes, I forsook all that; Nature has arranged things that way.'

'Yes, I suppose that is it.'

'And it was a question of my happiness —'

'Of course. And happiness came to you?'

'It came, Herr Spinell, in the moment when they brought little Anton to me, our little Anton, and he screamed so lustily with his strong little lungs — he is very, very strong and healthy, you know —'

'This is not the first time, madame, that I have heard you speak of your little Anton's good health and great strength. He must be quite uncommonly healthy?'

'That he is. And looks so absurdly like my husband!'

'Ah! . . . So that was the way of it. And now you are no longer called by the name of Eckhof, but a different one, and you have your healthy little Anton, and are troubled with your trachea.'

'Yes. And you are a perfectly enigmatic man, Herr Spinell, I do assure you.'

'Yes, God knows you certainly are,' said Frau Spatz, who was present on this occasion.

And that conversation, too, gave Herr Klöterjahn's wife food for reflection. Idle as it was, it contained much to nourish those secret thoughts of hers about herself. Was this the baleful influence which was at work? Her weakness increased and fever often supervened, a quiet glow in which she rested with a feeling of mild elevation, to which she yielded in a pensive mood that was a little affected, self-satisfied, even rather self-righteous. When she had not to keep her bed, Herr Spinell would approach her with immense caution, tiptoeing on his great feet; he would pause two paces off, with his body inclined and one leg behind him, and speak in a voice that was hushed with awe, as though he would lift her higher and higher on the tide of his devotion until she rested on billowy cushions of cloud where no shrill sound nor any earthly touch might reach her. And when he did this she would think of the way Herr Klöterjahn said: 'Take care, my angel, keep your mouth closed, Gabriele,' a way that made her feel as though he had struck her roughly though well-meaningly on the shoulder. Then as fast as she could she would put the memory away and rest in her weakness and elevation of spirit upon the clouds which Herr Spinell spread out for her.

One day she abruptly returned to the talk they had had about her early life. 'Is it really true, Herr Spinell,' she asked, 'that you would have seen the little gold crown?'

Two weeks had passed since that conversation, yet he knew at once what she meant, and his voice shook as he assured her that he would have seen the little crown as she sat among her friends by the fountain – would have caught its fugitive gleam among her locks.

A few days later one of the guests chanced to make a polite inquiry after the health of little Anton. Herr Klöterjahn's wife gave a quick glance at Herr Spinell, who was standing near, and answered in a perfunctory voice:

'Thanks, how should he be? He and my husband are quite well, of course.'

There came a day at the end of February, colder, purer, more brilliant than any that had come before it, and high spirits held sway at Einfried. The 'heart cases' consulted in groups, flushed of cheek, the diabetic general carolled like a boy out of school, and the gentlemen of the rebellious legs cast aside all restraint. And the reason for all these things was that a sleighing party was in prospect, an excusion in sledges into the mountains, with cracking whips and sleigh-bells jingling. Dr Leander had arranged this diversion for his patients.

The serious cases, of course, had to stop at home. Poor things! The other guests arranged to keep it from them; it did them good to practise this much sympathy and consideration. But a few of those remained at home who might very well have gone. Fräulein von Osterloh was of course excused, she had too much on her mind to permit her even to think of going. She was needed at home, and at home she remained. But the disappointment was general when Herr Klöterjahn's wife announced her intention of stopping away. Dr Leander exhorted her to come and get the benefit of the fresh air – but in vain. She said she was not up to it, she had a headache, she felt too weak – they had to resign themselves. The cynical gentleman took occasion to say:

'You will see, the dissipated baby will stop at home too.'

And he proved to be right, for Herr Spinell gave out that he intended to 'work' that afternoon – he was prone thus to characterize his dubious activities. Anyhow, not a soul regretted his absence; nor did they take more to heart the news that Frau Magistrate Spatz had decided to keep her young friend company at home – sleighing made her feel sea-sick.

Luncheon on the great day was eaten as early as twelve o'clock, and immediately thereafter the sledges drew up in front of Einfried. The guests came through the garden in little groups, warmly wrapped, excited, full of eager anticipation. Herr Klöterjahn's wife stood with Frau Spatz at the glass door which gave on the terrace, while Herr Spinell watched the setting-forth from above, at the window of his room. They saw the little struggles that took place for the best seats, amid joking and laughter; and Fräulein von Osterloh, with a fur boa round her neck, running from one sleigh to the other and shoving baskets of provisions under the seats; they saw Dr Leander, with his fur cap pulled low on his brow, marshalling the whole scene with his spectacle-lenses glittering, to make sure everything was ready. At last he took his own seat and gave the signal to drive off. The horses started up, a few of the ladies shrieked and collapsed, the bells jingled, the short-shafted whips cracked and their long lashes trailed across the snow; Fräulein von Osterloh stood at the gate waving her handkerchief until the train rounded a curve and disappeared; slowly the merry tinkling died away. Then she turned and hastened back through the garden in pursuit of her duties; the two ladies left the glass door, and almost at the same time Herr Spinell abandoned his post of observation above.

Quiet reigned at Einfried. The party would not return before evening. The serious cases lay in their rooms and suffered. Herr Klöterjahn's wife took a short turn with her friend, then they went to their respective chambers. Herr Spinell kept to his, occupied in his own way. Towards four o'clock the ladies were served with half a litre of milk apiece, and Herr Spinell with a light tea. Soon after, Herr Klöterjahn's wife tapped on the wall between her room and Frau Spatz's and called:

'Shan't we go down to the salon, Frau Spatz? I have nothing to do up here.'

'In just a minute, my dear,' answered she. 'I'll just put on my shoes – if you will wait a minute. I have been lying down.'

The salon, naturally, was empty. The ladies took seats by the fireplace. The Frau Magistrate embroidered flowers on a strip of canvas; Herr Klöterjahn's wife took a few stitches too, but soon let her work fall in her lap and, leaning on the arm of her chair, fell to dreaming. At length she made some remark hardly worth the trouble of opening her lips for; the Frau Magistrate asked what she said, and she had to make the effort of saying it all over again, which quite wore her out. But just then steps were heard outside, the door opened, and Herr Spinell came in.

'Shall I be disturbing you?' he asked mildly from the threshold, addressing Herr Klöterjahn's wife and her alone; bending over her, as it were, from a distance, in the tender, hovering way he had.

The young wife answered:

'Why should you? The room is free to everybody – and besides, why should it be disturbing us? On the contrary, I am convinced that I am boring Frau Spatz.'

He had no ready answer, merely smiled and showed his carious teeth, then went hesitatingly up to the glass door, the ladies watching him, and stood with his back to them looking out. Presently he half turned round, still gazing into the garden, and said:

'The sun has gone in. The sky clouded over without our seeing it. The dark is coming on already.'

'Yes, it is all overcast,' replied Herr Klöterjahn's wife. 'It looks as though our sleighing party would have some snow after all. Yesterday at this hour it was still broad daylight, now it is already getting dark.'

'Well,' he said, 'after all these brilliant weeks a little dullness is good for the eyes. The sun shines with the same penetrating clearness upon the lovely and the commonplace, and I for one am positively grateful to it for finally going under a cloud.'

'Don't you like the sun, Herr Spinell?'

'Well, I am no painter ... when there is no sun one becomes more profound ... It is a thick layer of greyish-white cloud. Perhaps it means thawing weather for tomorrow. But, madame, let me advise you not to sit there at the back of the room looking at your embroidery.'

'Don't be alarmed; I am not looking at it. But what else is there to do?'

He had sat down on the piano-stool, resting one arm on the lid of the instrument.

'Music,' he said. 'If we could only have a little music here. The English children sing darky songs, and that is all.'

'And yesterday afternoon Fräulein von Osterloh rendered "Cloister Bells" at top speed,' remarked Herr Klöterjahn's wife.

'But you play, madame!' said he, in an imploring tone. He stood up. 'Once you used to play every day with your father.'

'Yes, Herr Spinell, in those old days I did. In the time of the fountain, you know.'

'Play for us today,' he begged. 'Just a few notes – this once. If you knew how I long for some music –'

'But our family physician, as well as Dr Leander, expressly forbade it, Herr Spinell.'

'But they aren't here – either of them. We are free agents. Just a few bars –'

'No, Herr Spinell, it would be no use. Goodness knows what marvels you expect of me – and I have forgotten everything I knew. Truly. I know scarcely anything by heart.'

'Well, then, play that scarcely anything. But there are notes here too. On top of the piano. No, that is nothing. But there is some Chopin.'

'Chopin?'

'Yes, the Nocturnes. All we have to do is to light the candles –'

'Pray don't ask me to play, Herr Spinell. I must not. Suppose it were to be bad for me –'

He was silent; standing there in the light of the two candles, with his great feet, in his long black tail-coat, with his beardless face and greying hair. His hands hung down at his sides. 'Then, madame, I will ask no more,' he said at length, in a low voice. 'If you are afraid it will do you harm, then we shall leave the beauty dead and dumb that might have come alive beneath your fingers. You were not always so sensible; at least not when it was the opposite question from what it is today, and you had to decide to take leave of beauty. Then you did not care about your bodily welfare; you showed a firm and unhesitating resolution when you left the fountain and laid aside the little gold crown. Listen,' he said, after a pause, and his voice dropped still lower; 'if you sit down and play as you used to play when your father stood behind you and brought tears to your eyes with the tones of his violin – who knows but the little gold crown might glimmer once more in your hair...'

'Really,' said she, with a smile. Her voice happened to break on the word, it sounded husky and barely audible. She cleared her throat and went on: 'Are those really Chopin's Nocturnes you have there?'

'Yes, here they are open at the place; everything is ready.'

'Well, then, in God's name, I will play one,' said she. 'But only one – do you hear? In any case, one will do you, I am sure.'

With which she got up, laid aside her work, and went to the piano. She seated herself on the music-stool, on a few bound volumes, arranged the lights and turned over the notes. Herr Spinell had drawn up a chair and sat beside her, like a music-master.

She played the Nocturne in E major, opus 9, number 2. If her playing had really lost very much then she must originally have been a consummate artist. The piano was mediocre, but after the first few notes she learned to control it. She displayed a nervous feeling for modulations of timbre and a joy in mobility of rhythm that amounted to the fantastic. Her attack was at once firm and soft. Under her hands the very last drop of sweetness was wrung from the melody; the embellishments seemed to cling with slow grace about her limbs.

She wore the same frock as on the day of her arrival, the dark, heavy bodice with the velvet arabesques in high relief, that gave her head and hands such an unearthly fragile look. Her face did not change as she played but her lips seemed to become more clear-cut, the shadows deepened at the corners of her eyes. When she finished she laid her hands in her lap and went on looking at the notes. Herr Spinell sat motionless.

She played another Nocturne, and then a third. Then she stood up, but only to look on the top of the piano for more music.

It occurred to Herr Spinell to look at the black-bound volumes on the piano-stool. All at once he uttered an incoherent exclamation, his large white hands clutching at one of the books.

'Impossible! No, it cannot be,' he said. 'But yes, it is. Guess what this is – what was lying here! Guess what I have in my hands.'

'What?' she asked.

Mutely he showed her the title-page. He was quite pale; he let the book sink and looked at her, his lips trembling.

'Really? How did that get here? Give it me,' was all she said; set the notes on the piano and after a moment's silence began to play.

He sat beside her, bent forward, his hands between his knees, his head bowed. She played the beginning with exaggerated and tormenting slow-ness, with painfully long pauses between the single figures. The *Sehnsuchtsmotiv*, roving lost and forlorn like a voice in the night, lifted its trembling question. Then silence, a waiting. And lo, an answer: the same timorous, lonely note, only clearer, only tenderer. Silence again. And then, with that marvellous muted *sforzando*, like mounting passion, the love-motif came in; reared and soared and yearned ecstatically upward to its consummation, sank back, was resolved; the cellos taking up the melody to carry it on with their deep, heavy notes of rapture and despair.

Not unsuccessfully did the player seek to suggest the orchestral effects upon the poor instrument at her command. The violin runs of the great climax rang out with brilliant precision. She played with a fastidious reverence, lingering on each figure, bringing out each detail, with the self-forgotten concentration of the priest who lifts the Host above his head. Here two forces, two beings, strove towards each other, in transports of joy and pain; here they embraced and became one in delirious yearning after eternity and the absolute ... The prelude flamed up and died away. She stopped at the point where the curtains part, and sat speechless, staring at the keys.

But the boredom of Frau Spatz had by now reached that pitch where it distorts the countenance of man, makes the eyes protrude from the head, and lends the features a corpse-like and terrifying aspect. More than that, this music acted on the nerves that controlled her digestion, producing in her dyspeptic organism such *malaise* that she was really afraid she would have an attack.

'I shall have to go up to my room,' she said weakly. 'Good-bye; I will come back soon.'

She went out. Twilight was far advanced. Outside the snow fell thick and soundlessly upon the terrace. The two tapers cast a flickering, circumscribed light.

'The Second Act,' he whispered, and she turned the pages and began.

What was it dying away in the distance – the ring of a horn? The rustle of leaves? The rippling of a brook? Silence and night crept up over grove and house; the power of longing had full sway, no prayers or warnings could avail against it. The holy mystery was consummated. The light was quenched, with a strange clouding of the timbre the death-motif sank down: white-veiled desire, by passion driven, fluttered towards love as through the dark it groped to meet her.

Ah, boundless, unquenchable exultation of union in the eternal beyond! Freed from torturing error, escaped from fettering space and time, the Thou and the I, the Thine and the Mine at one forever in a sublimity of bliss! The day might part them with deluding show; but when night fell, then by the power of the potion they would see clear. To him who has looked upon the night of death and known its secret sweets, to him day never can be aught but vain, nor can he know a longing save for night, eternal, real, in which he is made one with love.

O night of love sink downwards and enfold them, grant them the oblivion they crave, release them from this world of partings and betrayals. Lo, the last light is quenched. Fancy and thought alike are lost, merged in the mystic shade that spread its wings of healing above their madness and despair. 'Now when deceitful daylight pales, when my raptured eye grows dim, then all that from which the light of day would shut my sight, seeking to blind me with false show, to the stanchless torments of my longing soul – then, ah, then, O wonder of fulfilment, even then I am the world!' Followed Brangäne's dark notes of warning, and then those soaring violins so higher than all reason.

'I cannot understand it all, Herr Spinell. Much of it I only divine. What does it mean, this "even then I am the world"?'

He explained, in a few low-toned words.

'Yes, yes. It means that. How is it you can understand it all so well, yet cannot play it?'

Strangely enough, he was not proof against this simple question. He coloured, twisted his hands together, shrank into his chair.

'The two things seldom happen together,' he wrung from his lips at last. 'No, I cannot play. But go on.'

And on they went, into the intoxicated music of the love-mystery. Did love ever die? Tristan's love? The love of thy Isolde, and of mine? Ah, no, death cannot touch that which can never die – and what of him could die, save what distracts and tortures love and severs united lovers? Love joined the two in sweet conjunction, death was powerless to sever such a bond, save only when death was given to one with the very life of the other. Their voices rose in mystic unison, rapt in the wordless hope of that death-in-love, of endless oneness in the wonder-kingdom of the night. Sweet night! Eternal night of love! And all-encompassing land of rapture! Once envisaged or divined, what eye could bear to open again on desolate dawn? Forfend such fears, most gentle death! Release these lovers quite from need of waking. Oh, tumultuous storm of rhythms! Oh, glad chromatic upward surge of metaphysical perception! How find, how bind this bliss so far remote from parting's torturing pangs? Ah, gentle glow of longing, soothing and kind, ah, yielding sweet-sublime, ah, raptured sinking into the twilight of eternity! Thou Isolde, Tristan I, yet no more Tristan, no more Isolde...

All at once something startling happened. The musician broke off and peered into the darkness with her hand above her eyes. Herr Spinell turned round quickly in his chair. The corridor door had opened, a sinister form appeared, leant on the arm of a second form. It was a guest of Einfried, one of those who, like themselves, had been in no state to undertake the sleigh-ride, but had passed this twilight hour in one of her pathetic, instinctive rounds of the house. It was that patient who had borne fourteen children and was no longer capable of a single thought; it was Frau Pastor Höhlenrauch, on the arm of her nurse. She did not look up; with groping step she paced the dim background of the room and vanished by the opposite door, rigid and still, like a lost and wandering soul. Stillness reigned once more.

'That was Frau Pastor Höhlenrauch,' he said.

'Yes, that was poor Frau Höhlenrauch,' she answered. Then she turned over some leaves and played the finale, played Isolde's song of love and death.

How colourless and clear were her lips, how deep the shadows lay beneath her eyes! The little pale-blue vein in her transparent brow showed fearfully plain and prominent. Beneath her flying fingers the music mounted to its unbelievable climax and was resolved in that ruthless, sudden *pianissimo* which is like having the ground slide from beneath one's feet, yet like a sinking too into the very deeps of desire. Followed the immeasurable plenitude of that vast redemption and fulfilment; it was repeated, swelled into a deafening, unquenchable tumult of immense appeasement that wove and welled and seemed about to die away, only to swell again and weave the *Sehnsuchtsmotiv* into its harmony; at length to breathe an outward breath and die, faint on the air, and soar away. Profound stillness.

They both listened, their heads on one side.

'Those are bells,' she said.

'It is the sleighs,' he said. 'I will go now.'

He rose and walked across the room. At the door he halted, then turned and shifted uneasily from one foot to the other. And then, some fifteen or twenty paces from her, it came to pass that he fell upon his knees, both knees, without a sound. His long black coat spread out on the floor. He held his hands clasped over his mouth, and his shoulders heaved.

She sat there with hands in her lap, leaning forward, turned away from the piano, and looked at him. Her face wore a distressed, uncertain smile, while her eyes searched the dimness at the back of the room, searched so painfully, so dreamily, she seemed hardly able to focus her gaze.

The jingling of sleigh-bells came nearer and nearer, there was the crack of whips, a babel of voices.

The sleighing party had taken place on the twenty-sixth of February, and was talked of for long afterwards. The next day, February twenty-seventh, a day of thaw, that set everything to melting and dripping, splashing and running, Herr Klöterjahn's wife was in capital health and spirits. On the twenty-eighth she brought up a little blood – not much, still it was blood, and accompanied by far greater loss of strength than ever before. She went to bed.

Dr Leander examined her, stony-faced. He prescribed according to the dictates of science – morphia, little pieces of ice, absolute quiet. Next day, on account of pressure of work, he turned her case over to Dr Müller, who took it on in humility and meekness of spirit and according to the letter of his contract – a quiet, pallid, insignificant little man, whose unadvertised activities were consecrated to the care of the slight cases and the hopeless ones.

Dr Müller presently expressed the view that the separation between Frau Klöterjahn and her spouse had lasted overlong. It would be well if Herr Klöterjahn, in case his flourishing business permitted, were to make another visit to Einfried. One might write him – or even wire. And surely it would benefit the young mother's health and spirits if he were to bring young Anton with him – quite aside from the pleasure it would give the physicians to behold with their own eyes this so healthy little Anton.

And Herr Klöterjahn came. He got Herr Müller's little wire and arrived from the Baltic coast. He got out of the carriage, ordered coffee and rolls, and looked considerably aggrieved.

'My dear sir,' he asked, 'what is the matter? Why have I been summoned?'

'Because it is desirable that you should be near your wife,' Dr Müller replied.

'Desirable! Desirable! But is it *necessary*? It is a question of expense with me – times are poor and railway journeys cost money. Was it imperative I should take this whole day's journey? If it were the lungs that are attacked, I should say nothing. But as it is only the trachea, thank God –'

'Herr Klöterjahn,' said Dr Müller mildly, 'in the first place the trachea is an important organ . . .' He ought not to have said 'in the first place', because he did not go on to the second.

But there also arrived at Einfried, in Herr Klöterjahn's company, a full-figured personage arrayed all in red and gold and plaid, and she it was who carried on her arm Anton Klöterjahn, junior, that healthy little Anton. Yes, there he was, and nobody could deny that he was healthy even to excess. Pink and white and plump and fragrant, in fresh and immaculate attire, he rested heavily upon the bare red arm of his bebraided body-servant, consumed huge quantities of milk and chopped beef, shouted and screamed, and in every way surrendered himself to his instincts.

Our author from the window of his chamber had seen him arrive. With a peculiar gaze, both veiled and piercing, he fixed young Anton with his eye as he was carried from the carriage into the house. He stood there a long time with the same expression on his face.

Herr Spinell was sitting in his room 'at work'.

His room was like all the others at Einfried – old-fashioned, simple, and distinguished. The massive chest of drawers was mounted with brass lions' heads; the tall mirror on the wall was not a single surface, but made up of many little panes set in lead. There was no carpet on the polished blue paved floor, the stiff legs of the furniture prolonged themselves on it in clear-cut shadows. A spacious writing-table stood at the window, across whose panes the author had drawn the folds of a yellow curtain, in all probability that he might feel more retired.

In the yellow twilight he bent over the table and wrote – wrote one of those numerous letters which he sent weekly to the post and to which, quaintly enough, he seldom or never received an answer. A large, thick quire of paper lay before him, in whose upper left-hand corner was a curious involved drawing of a landscape and the name Detlev Spinell in the very latest thing in lettering. He was covering the page with a small, painfully neat, and punctiliously traced script.

'Sir:' he wrote, 'I address the following lines to you because I cannot help it; because what I have to say so fills and shakes and tortures me, the words come in such a rush, that I should choke if I did not take this means to relieve myself.'

If the truth were told, this about the rush of words was quite simply wide of the fact. And God knows what sort of vanity it was made Herr Spinell put it down. For his words did not come in a rush; they came with such pathetic slowness, considering the man was a writer by trade, you would have drawn the conclusion, watching him, that a writer is one to whom writing comes harder than to anybody else.

He held between two finger-tips one of those curious downy hairs he had on his cheek, and twirled it round and round, whole quarter-hours at a time, gazing into space and not coming forwards by a single line; then wrote a few words, daintily, and stuck again. Yet so much was true: that what had managed to get written sounded fluent and vigorous, though the matter was odd enough, even almost equivocal, and at times impossible to follow.

'I feel,' the letter went on, 'an imperative necessity to make you see what I see; to show you through my eyes, illuminated by the same power of language that clothes them for me, all the things which have stood before my inner eye for weeks, like an indelible vision. It is my habit to yield to the impulse which urges me to put my own experiences into flamingly right and unforgettable words and to give them to the world. And therefore hear me.

'I will do no more than relate what has been and what is: I will merely tell a story, a brief, unspeakable touching story, without comment, blame, or passing of judgement; simply in my own words. It is the story of Gabriele Eckhof, of the woman whom you, sir, call your wife – and mark you this: it is your story, it happened to you, yet it will be I who will for the first time lift it for you to the level of an experience.

'Do you remember the garden, the old, overgrown garden behind the grey patrician house? The moss was green in the crannies of its weather-beaten wall, and behind the wall dreams and neglect held sway. Do you remember the fountain in the centre? The pale mauve lilies leaned over its crumbling rim, the little stream prattled softly as it fell upon the riven paving. The summer day was drawing to its close.

'Seven maidens sat circlewise round the fountain; but the seventh, or rather the first and only one, was not like the others, for the sinking sun seemed to be weaving a queenly coronal among her locks. Her eyes were like troubled dreams, and yet her pure lips wore a smile.

'They were singing. They lifted their little faces to the leaping streamlet and watched its charming curve droop earthward – their music hovered round it as it leaped and danced. Perhaps their slim hands were folded in their laps the while they sang.

'Can you, sir, recall the scene? Or did you ever see it? No, you saw it not. Your eyes were not formed to see it nor your ears to catch the chaste music of their song. You saw it not, or else you would have forbidden your lungs to breathe, your heart to beat. You must have turned aside and gone back to your own life taking with you what you had seen to preserve it in the depth of your soul to the end of your earthly life, a sacred and inviolable relic. But what did you do?

'That scene, sir, was an end and culmination. Why did you come to spoil it, to give it a sequel, to turn it into the channels of ugly and commonplace life? It was a peaceful apotheosis and a moving, bathed in a sunset beauty of decadence, decay, and death. An ancient stock, too exhausted and refined for life and action, stood there at the end of its days; its late manifestations were those of art: violin notes, full of that melancholy understanding which is ripeness for death ... Did you look into her eyes – those eyes where tears so often stood, lured by the dying sweetness of the violin? Her six friends may have had souls that belonged to life; but hers, the queen's and sister's, death and beauty had claimed for their own.

'You saw it, that deathly beauty; saw, and coveted. The sight of that touching purity moved you with no awe or trepidation. And it was not enough for you to see, you must possess, you must use, you must desecrate ... It was the refinement of a choice you made – you are a gourmand, sir, a plebeian gourmand, a peasant with taste.

'Once more let me say that I have no wish to offend you. What I have just said is not an affront; it is a statement, a simple, psychological statement of your simple personality – a personality which for literary purposes is entirely uninteresting. I make the statement solely because I feel an impulse to clarify for you your own thoughts and actions; because it is my inevitable task on this earth to call things by their right names, to make them speak, to illuminate the unconscious. The world is full of what I call the unconscious type, and I cannot endure it; I cannot endure all these unconscious types! I cannot bear all this dull, uncomprehending, unperceiving living and behaving, this world of maddening *naïveté* about me! It tortures me until I am driven irresistibly to set it all in relief, in the round, to explain, express and make self-conscious everything in the world – so far as my powers will reach – quite unhampered by the result, whether it be for good or evil, whether it brings consolation and healing or piles grief on grief.

'You, sir, as I said, are a plebeian gourmand, a peasant with taste. You stand upon an extremely low evolutionary level; your own constitution is coarse-fibred. But wealth and a sedentary habit of life have brought about in you a corruption of the nervous system, as sudden as it is unhistoric; and this corruption has been accompanied by a lascivious refinement in your choice of gratifications. It is altogether possible that the muscles of your gullet began to contract, as at the sight of some particularly rare dish, when you conceived the idea of making Gabriele Eckhof your own.

'In short, you lead her idle will astray, you beguile her out of that moss-grown garden into the ugliness of life, you give her your own vulgar name and make of her a married woman, a housewife, a mother. You take that deathly beauty – spent, aloof, flowering in lofty unconcern of the uses of this world – and debase it to the service of common things, you sacrifice it to that stupid, contemptible, clumsy graven image we call "Nature" – and not the faintest suspicion of the vileness of your conduct visits your peasant soul.

'Again. What is the result? This being, whose eyes are like troubled dreams, she bears you a child; and so doing she endows the new life, a gross continuation of its author's own, with all the blood, all the physical energy she possesses – and she dies. She dies, sir! And if she does not go hence with your vulgarity upon her head; if at the very last she has lifted herself out of the depths of degradation, and passes in an ecstasy, with the deathly kiss of beauty on her brow – well, it is I, sir, who have seen to that! You, meanwhile, were probably spending your time with chambermaids in dark corners.

'But your son, Gabriele Eckhof's son, is alive; he is living and flourishing. Perhaps he will continue in the way of his father, become a well-fed, trading, tax-paying citizen; a capable, philistine pillar of society; in any case, a tone-deaf, normally functioning individual, responsible, sturdy, and stupid, troubled by not a doubt.

'Kindly permit me to tell you, sir, that I hate you. I hate you and your child, as I hate the life of which you are the representative: cheap, ridiculous, but yet triumphant life, the everlasting antipodes and deadly enemy of beauty. I cannot say I despise you – for I am honest. You are stronger than I. I have no armour for the struggle between us, I have only the Word, avenging weapon of the weak. Today I have availed myself of this weapon. This letter is nothing but an act of revenge – you see how honourable I am –

and if any word of mine is sharp and bright and beautiful enough to strike home, to make you feel the presence of a power you do not know, to shake even a minute your robust equilibrium, I shall rejoice indeed. – DETLEV SPINELL.'

And Herr Spinell put this screed into an envelope, applied a stamp and a many-flourished address, and committed it to the post.

Herr Klöterjahn knocked on Herr Spinell's door. He carried a sheet of paper in his hand covered with neat script and he looked like a man bent on energetic action. The post office had done its duty, the letter had taken its appointed way: it had travelled from Einfried to Einfried and reached the hand for which it was meant. It was now four o'clock in the afternoon.

Herr Klöterjahn's entry found Herr Spinell sitting on the sofa reading his own novel with the appalling cover-design. He rose and gave his caller a surprised and inquiring look, though at the same time he distinctly flushed.

'Good afternoon,' said Herr Klöterjahn. 'Pardon the interruption. But may I ask if you wrote this?' He held up in his left hand the sheet inscribed with fine clear characters and struck it with the back of his right and made it crackle. Then he stuffed that hand into the pocket of his easy-fitting trousers, put his head on one side, and opened his mouth, in a way some people have, to listen.

Herr Spinell, curiously enough, smiled; he smiled engagingly, with a rather confused, apologetic air. He put his hand to his head as though trying to recollect himself, and said:

'Ah! – yes, quite right, I took the liberty –'

The fact was, he had given in to his natural man today and slept nearly up to midday, with the result that he was suffering from a bad conscience and a heavy head, was nervous and incapable of putting up a fight. And the spring air made him limp and good-for-nothing. So much we must say in extenuation of the utterly silly figure he cut in the interview which followed.

'Ah? Indeed! Very good!' said Herr Klöterjahn. He dug his chin into his chest, elevated his brows, stretched his arms, and indulged in various other antics by way of getting down to business after his introductory question. But unfortunately he so much enjoyed the figure he cut that he rather overshot the mark, and the rest of the scene hardly lived up to this preliminary pantomime. However, Herr Spinell went rather pale.

'Very good!' repeated Herr Klöterjahn. 'Then permit me to give you an answer in person; it strikes me as idiotic to write pages of letter to a person when you can speak to him any hour of the day.'

'Well, idiotic . . .' Herr Spinell said, with his apologetic smile. He sounded almost meek.

'Idiotic!' repeated Herr Klöterjahn, nodding violently in token of the soundness of his position. 'And I should not demean myself to answer this scrawl; to tell the truth, I should have thrown it away at once if I had not found in it the explanation of certain changes – however, that is no affair of yours, and has nothing to do with the thing anyhow. I am a man of action, I have other things to do than to think about your unspeakable visions.'

'I wrote "*indelible vision*",' said Herr Spinell, drawing himself up. This was the only moment at which he displayed a little self-respect.

'Indelible, unspeakable,' responded Herr Klöterjahn, referring to the text. 'You write a villainous hand, sir; you would not get a position in my office, let me tell you. It looks clear enough at first, but when you come to study it, it is full of shakes and quavers. But that is your affair, it's no business of mine. What I have come to say to you is that you are a tomfool – which you probably know already. Furthermore, you are a cowardly sneak; I don't suppose I have to give the evidence for that either. My wife wrote me once that when you meet a woman you don't look her square in the face, but just give her a side squint, so as to carry away a good impression, because you are afraid of the reality. I should probably have heard more of the same sort of stories about you, only unfortunately she stopped mentioning you. But this is the kind of thing you are: you talk so much about "beauty"; you are all chicken-livered hypocrisy and cant – which is probably at the bottom of your impudent allusion to out-of-the-way corners too. That ought to crush me, of course, but it just makes me laugh – it doesn't do a thing but make me laugh! Understand? Have I clarified your thoughts and actions for you, you pitiable object, you? Though of course it is not my invariable calling –'

'"*Inevitable*" was the word I used,' Herr Spinell said; but he did not insist on the point. He stood there, crestfallen, like a big, unhappy, chidden, grey-haired schoolboy.

'Invariable or inevitable, whichever you like – anyhow you are a contemptible cur, and that I tell you. You see me every day at table, you bow and smirk and say good-morning – and one fine day you send me a scrawl full of idiotic abuse. Yes, you've a lot of courage – on paper! And it's not only this ridiculous letter – you have been intriguing behind my back. I can see that now. Though you need not flatter yourself it did any good. If you imagine you put any ideas into my wife's head you never were more mistaken in your life. And if you think she behaved any differently when we came from what she always does, then you just put the cap onto your own foolishness. She did not kiss the little chap, that's true, but it was only a precaution, because they have the idea now that the trouble is with her lungs, and in such cases you can't tell whether – though that still remains to be proved, no matter what you say with your "She dies, sir," you silly ass!'

Here Herr Klöterjahn paused for breath. He was in a furious passion; he kept stabbing the air with his right forefinger and crumpling the sheet of paper in his other hand. His face, between the blond English mutton-chops, was frightfully red and his dark brow was rent with swollen veins like lightnings of scorn.

'You hate me,' he went on, 'and you would despise me if I were not stronger than you. Yes, you're right there! I've got my heart in the right place, by God, and you've got yours mostly in the seat of your trousers. I would most certainly hack you into bits if it weren't against the law, you and your gabble about the "Word", you skulking fool! But I have no intention of putting up with your insults; and when I show this part about the vulgar name to my lawyer at home, you will very likely get a little surprise. My name, sir, is a first-rate name, and I have made it so by my own efforts. You know better than I do whether anybody would ever lend you a penny piece on yours, you lazy lout! The law defends people against the kind you are! You are a common danger, you are enough to drive a body crazy! But you're left this time, my master! I don't let individuals like you get the best of me so fast! I've got my heart in the right place –'

Herr Klöterjahn's excitement had really reached a pitch. He shrieked, he bellowed, over and over again, that his heart was in the right place.

'"They were singing." Exactly. Well, they weren't. They were knitting. And if I heard what they said, it was about a recipe for potato pancakes; and when I show my father-in-law that about the old decayed family you'll probably have a libel suit on your hands. "Did you see the picture?" Yes, of course I saw it; only I don't see why that should make me hold my breath and run away. I don't leer at women out of the corner of my eye; I look at them square, and if I like their looks I go for them. I have my heart in the right place –'

Somebody knocked. Knocked eight or ten times, quite fast, one after the other – a sudden, alarming little commotion that made Herr Klöterjahn pause; and an unsteady voice that kept tripping over itself in its haste and distress said:

'Herr Klöterjahn, Herr Klöterjahn – oh, is Herr Klöterjahn there?'

'Stop outside,' said Herr Klöterjahn, in a growl ... 'What's the matter? I'm busy talking.'

'Oh, Herr Klöterjahn,' said the quaking, breaking voice, 'you must come! The doctors are there too – oh, it is all so dreadfully sad –'

He took one step to the door and tore it open. Frau Magistrate Spatz was standing there. She had her handkerchief before her mouth, and great egg-shaped tears rolled into it, two by two.

'Herr Klöterjahn,' she got out. 'It is so frightfully sad ... She has brought up so much blood, such a horrible lot of blood ... She was sitting up quite quietly in bed and humming a little snatch of music ... and there it came ... my God, such a quantity you never saw ...'

'Is she dead?' yelled Herr Klöterjahn. As he spoke he clutched the Rätin by the arm and pulled her to and fro on the sill. 'Not quite? Not dead; she can see me, can't she? Brought up a little blood again, from the lung, eh? Yes, I give in, it may be from the lung. Gabriele!' he suddenly cried out, and his eyes filled with tears; you could see what a burst of good, warm, honest human feeling came over him. 'Yes, I'm coming,' he said, and dragged the Rätin after him as he went with long strides down the corridor. You could still hear his voice, from quite a distance, sounding fainter and fainter: 'Not quite, eh? From the lung?'

Herr Spinell stood still on the spot where he had stood during the whole of Herr Klöterjahn's rudely interrupted call and looked out of the open door. At length he took a couple of steps and listened down the corridor. But all was quiet, so he closed the door and came back into the room.

He looked at himself awhile in the glass, then he went up to the writing-table, took a little flask and a glass out of a drawer, and drank a cognac – for which nobody can blame him. Then he stretched himself out on the sofa and closed his eyes.

The upper half of the window was down. Outside in the garden birds were twittering; those dainty, saucy little notes held all the spring, finely and penetratingly expressed. Herr Spinell spoke once: '*Invariable calling,*' he said, and moved his head and drew in the air through his teeth as though his nerves pained him violently.

Impossible to recover any poise or tranquillity. Crude experiences like this were too much – he was not made for them. By a sequence of emotions, the analysis of which would lead us too far afield, Herr Spinell arrived at the decision that it would be well for him to have a little out-of-doors exercise. He took his hat and went downstairs.

As he left the house and issued into the mild, fragrant air, he turned his head and lifted his eyes, slowly, scanning the house until he reached one of the windows, a curtained window, on which his gaze rested awhile, fixed and sombre. Then he laid his hands on his back and moved away across the gravel path. He moved in deep thought.

The beds were still straw-covered, the trees and bushes bare; but the snow was gone, the path was only damp in spots. The large garden with its grottoes, bowers and little pavilions lay in the splendid colourful afternoon light, strong shadow and rich, golden sun, and the dark network of branches stood out sharp and articulate against the bright sky.

It was about that hour of the afternoon when the sun takes shape, and from being a formless volume of light turns to a visibly sinking disk, whose milder, more saturated glow the eye can tolerate. Herr Spinell did not see the sun, the direction the path took hid it from his view. He walked with bent head and hummed a strain of music, a short phrase, a figure that mounted wailingly and complainingly upward – the *Sehnsuchtsmotiv* ... But suddenly, with a start, a quick, jerky intake of breath, he stopped, as though rooted to the path, and gazed straight ahead of him, with brows fiercely gathered, staring eyes, and an expression of horrified repulsion.

The path had curved just here, he was facing the setting sun. It stood large and slantwise in the sky, crossed by two narrow strips of gold-rimmed cloud; it set the tree-tops aglow and poured its red-gold radiance across the garden. And there, erect in the path, in the midst of the glory, with the sun's mighty aureola above her head, there confronted him an exuberant figure, all arrayed in red and gold and plaid. She had one hand on her swelling hip, with the other she moved to and fro the graceful little perambulator. And in this perambulator sat the child – sat Anton Klöterjahn, junior, Gabriele Eckhof's fat son.

There he sat among his cushions, in a woolly white jacket and large white hat, plump-cheeked, well cared for, and magnificent; and his blithe unerring gaze encountered Herr Spinell's. The novelist pulled himself together. Was he not a man, had he not the power to pass this unexpected, sun-kindled apparition there in the path and continue on his walk? But Anton Klöterjahn began to laugh and shout – most horrible to see. He squealed, he crowed with inconceivable delight – it was positively uncanny to hear him.

God knows what had taken him; perhaps the sight of Herr Spinell's long, black figure set him off; perhaps an attack of sheer animal spirits gave rise to his wild outburst of merriment. He had a bone teething-ring in one hand and a tin rattle in the other; and these two objects he flung aloft with shoutings, shook them to and fro, and clashed them together in the air, as though purposely to frighten Herr Spinell. His eyes were almost shut. His mouth gaped open till all the rosy gums were displayed; and as he shouted he rolled his head about in excess of mirth.

Herr Spinell turned round and went thence. Pursued by the youthful Klöterjahn's joyous screams he went away across the gravel, walking stiffly, yet not without grace; his gait was the hesitating gait of one who would disguise the fact that, inwardly, he is running away.

1902

Tonio Kröger

TRANSLATED FROM THE GERMAN BY

H.T. Lowe-Porter

The winter sun, poor ghost of itself, hung milky and wan behind layers of cloud above the huddled roofs of the town. In the gabled streets it was wet and windy and there came in gusts a sort of soft hail, not ice, not snow.

School was out. The hosts of the released streamed over the paved court and out at the wrought-iron gate, where they broke up and hastened off right and left. Elder pupils held their books in a strap high on the left shoulder and rowed, right arm against the wind, towards dinner. Small people trotted gaily off, splashing the slush with their feet, the tools of learning rattling amain in their walrus-skin satchels. But one and all pulled off their caps and cast down their eyes in awe before the Olympian hat and ambrosial beard of a master moving homewards with measured stride...

'Ah, there you are at last, Hans,' said Tonio Kröger. He had been waiting a long time in the street and went up with a smile to the friend he saw coming out of the gate in talk with other boys and about to go off with them ... 'What?' said Hans, and looked at Tonio. 'Right-oh! We'll take a little walk, then.'

Tonio said nothing and his eyes were clouded. Did Hans forget, had he only just remembered that they were to take a walk together today? And he himself had looked forward to it with almost incessant joy.

'Well, good-bye, fellows,' said Hans Hansen to his comrades. 'I'm taking a walk with Kröger.' And the two turned to their left, while the others sauntered off in the opposite direction.

Hans and Tonio had time to take a walk after school because in neither of their families was dinner served before four o'clock. Their fathers were prominent business men, who held public office and were of consequence in the town. Hans's people had owned for some generations the big wood-yards down by the river, where powerful machine-saws hissed and spat and cut up timber; while Tonio was the son of Consul Kröger, whose grain-sacks with the firm's name in great black letters you might see any day driven through the streets; his large, old ancestral home was the finest house in all the town. The two friends had to keep taking off their hats to their many acquaintances; some folk did not even wait for the fourteen-year-old lads to speak first, as by rights they should.

Both of them carried their satchels across their shoulders and both were well and warmly dressed: Hans in a short sailor jacket, with the wide blue collar of his sailor suit turned out over shoulders and back, and Tonio in a belted grey overcoat. Hans wore a Danish sailor cap with black ribbons, beneath which streamed a shock of straw-coloured hair. He was uncommonly handsome and well built, broad in the shoulders and narrow in the hips, with keen, far-apart, steel-blue eyes; while beneath Tonio's round fur cap was a brunette face with the finely chiselled features of the south; the dark eyes, with delicate shadows and too heavy lids, looked dreamily and a little timorously on the world. Tonio's walk was idle and uneven, whereas the other's slim legs in the black stockings moved with an elastic, rhythmic tread.

Tonio did not speak. He suffered. His rather oblique brows were drawn together in a frown, his lips were rounded to whistle, he gazed into space with his head on one side. Posture and manner were habitual.

Suddenly Hans shoved his arm into Tonio's, with a sideways look – he knew very well what the trouble was. And Tonio, though he was silent for the next few steps, felt his heart soften.

'I hadn't forgotten, you see, Tonio,' Hans said, gazing at the pavement. 'I only thought it wouldn't come off today because it was so wet and windy. But I don't mind that at all, and it's jolly of you to have waited. I thought you had gone home, and I was cross...'

Everything in Tonio leaped and jumped for joy at the words.

'All right; let's go over the wall,' he said with a quaver in his voice. 'Over the Millwall and the Holstenwall, and I'll go as far as your house with you, Hans. Then I'll have to walk back alone, but that doesn't matter; next time you can go round my way.'

At bottom he was not really convinced by what Hans said; he quite knew the other attached less importance to this walk than he did himself. Yet he saw Hans was sorry for his remissness and willing to be put in a position to ask pardon, a pardon that Tonio was far indeed from withholding.

The truth was, Tonio loved Hans Hansen, and had already suffered much on his account. He who loves the more is the inferior and must suffer; in this hard and simple fact his fourteen-year-old soul had already been instructed by life; and he was so organized that he received such experiences consciously, wrote them down as it were inwardly, and even, in a certain way, took pleasure in them, though without ever letting them mould his conduct, indeed, or drawing any practical advantage from them. Being what he was, he found this knowledge far more important and far more interesting than the sort they made him learn in school; yes, during his lesson hours in the vaulted Gothic classrooms he was mainly occupied in feeling his way about among these intuitions of his and penetrating them. The process gave him the same kind of satisfaction as that he felt when he moved about in his room with his violin – for he played the violin – and made the tones, brought out as softly as ever he knew how, mingle with the plashing of the fountain that leaped and danced down there in the garden beneath the branches of the old walnut tree.

The fountain, the old walnut tree, his fiddle, and away in the distance, the North Sea, within sound of whose summer murmurings he spent his holidays – these were the things he loved, within these he enfolded his spirit, among these things his inner life took its course. And they were all things whose names were effective in verse and occurred pretty frequently in the lines Tonio Kröger sometimes wrote.

The fact that he had a notebook full of such things, written by himself, leaked out through his own carelessness and injured him no little with the masters as well as among his fellows. On the one hand, Consul Kröger's son found their attitude both cheap and silly, and despised his schoolmates and his masters as well, and in his turn (with extraordinary penetration) saw through and disliked their personal weaknesses and bad breeding. But then, on the other hand, he himself felt his verse-making extravagant and out of place and to a certain extent agreed with those who considered it an unpleasing occupation. But that did not enable him to leave off.

As he wasted his time at home, was slow and absent-minded at school, and always had bad marks from the masters, he was in the habit of bringing home pitifully poor reports, which troubled and angered his father, a tall, fastidiously dressed man with thoughtful blue eyes, and always a wild flower in his buttonhole. But for his mother, she cared nothing about the reports – Tonio's beautiful black-haired mother, whose name was Consuelo, and who was so absolutely different from the other ladies in the town, because father had brought her long ago from some place far down on the map.

Tonio loved his dark, fiery mother, who played the piano and mandolin so wonderfully, and he was glad his doubtful standing among men did not distress her. Though at the same time he found his father's annoyance a more dignified and respectable attitude and despite his scoldings understood him very well, whereas his mother's blithe indifference always seemed just a little wanton. His thoughts at times would run something like this: 'It is true enough that I am what I am and will not and cannot alter: heedless, self-willed, with my mind on things nobody else thinks of. And so it is right they should scold and punish me and not smother things all up with kisses and music. After all, we are not gypsies living in a green wagon; we're respectable people, the family of Consul Kröger.' And not seldom he would think: 'Why is it I am different, why do I fight everything, why am I at odds with the masters and like a stranger among the other boys? The good scholars, and the solid majority – they don't find the masters funny, they don't write verses, their thoughts arc all about things that people do think about and can talk about out loud. How regular and comfortable they must feel, knowing that everybody knows just where they stand! It must be nice! But what is the matter with me, and what will be the end of it all?'

These thoughts about himself and his relation to life played an important part in Tonio's love for Hans Hansen. He loved him in the first place because he was handsome; but in the next because he was in every respect his own opposite and foil. Hans Hansen was a capital scholar, and a jolly chap to boot, who was head at drill, rode and swam to perfection, and lived in the sunshine of popularity. The masters were almost tender with him, they called him Hans and were partial to him in every way; the other pupils curried favour with him; even grown people stopped him in the street, twitched the shock of hair beneath his Danish sailor cap, and said: 'Ah, here you are, Hans Hansen, with your pretty blond hair! Still head of the school? Remember me to your father and mother, that's a fine lad!'

Such was Hans Hansen; and ever since Tonio Kröger had known him, from the very minute he set eyes on him, he had burned inwardly with a heavy, envious longing. 'Who else has blue eyes like yours, or lives in such friendliness and harmony with all the world? You are always spending your time with some right and proper occupation. When you have done your prep you take your riding-lesson, or make things with a fret-saw; even in the holidays, at the seashore, you row and sail and swim all the time, while I wander off somewhere and lie down in the sand and stare at the strange and mysterious changes that whisk over the face of the sea. And all that is why your eyes are so clear. To be like you . . .'

He made no attempt to be like Hans Hansen, and perhaps hardly even seriously wanted to. What he did ardently, painfully want was that just as he was, Hans Hansen should love him; and he wooed Hans Hansen in his own way, deeply, lingeringly, devotedly, with a melancholy that gnawed and burned more terribly than all the sudden passion one might have expected from his exotic looks.

And he wooed not in vain. Hans respected Tonio's superior power of putting certain difficult matters into words; moreover, he felt the lively presence of an uncommonly strong and tender feeling for himself; he was grateful for it, and his response gave Tonio much happiness – though also many pangs of jealousy and disillusion over his futile efforts to establish a communion of spirit between them. For the queer thing was that Tonio, who after all envied Hans Hansen for being what he was, still kept on trying to draw him over to his own side; though of course he could succeed in this at most only at moments and superficially...

'I have just been reading something so wonderful and splendid...' he said. They were walking and eating together out of a bag of fruit toffees they had bought at Iverson's sweetshop in Mill Street for ten pfennigs. 'You must read it, Hans, it is Schiller's *Don Carlos* ... I'll lend it you if you like...'

'Oh, no,' said Hans Hansen, 'you needn't, Tonio, that's not anything for me. I'll stick to my horse books. There are wonderful cuts in them, let me tell you. I'll show them to you when you come to see me. They are instantaneous photography – the horse in motion; you can see him trot and canter and jump, in all positions, that you never can get to see in life, because they happen so fast...'

'In all positions?' asked Tonio politely. 'Yes, that must be great. But about *Don Carlos* – it is beyond anything you could possibly dream of. There are places in it that are so lovely they make you jump ... as though it were an explosion –'

'An explosion?' asked Hans Hansen. 'What sort of an explosion?'

'For instance, the place where the king has been crying because the marquis betrayed him ... but the marquis did it only out of love for the prince, you see, he sacrifices himself for his sake. And the word comes out of the cabinet into the antechamber that the king has been weeping. "Weeping? The king has been weeping?" All the courtiers are fearfully upset, it goes through and through you, for the king has always been so frightfully stiff and stern. But it is so easy to understand why he cried, and I feel sorrier for him than for the prince and the marquis put together. He is always so alone, nobody loves him, and then he thinks he has found one man, and then *he* betrays him...'

Hans Hansen looked sideways into Tonio's face, and something in it must have won him to the subject, for suddenly he shoved his arm once more into Tonio's and said:

'How had he betrayed him, Tonio?'

Tonio went on.

'Well,' he said, 'you see all the letters for Brabant and Flanders –'

'There comes Irwin Immerthal,' said Hans.

Tonio stopped talking. If only the earth would open and swallow Immerthal up! 'Why does he have to come disturbing us? If he only doesn't go with us all the way and talk about the riding-lessons!' For Irwin Immerthal had riding-lessons too. He was the son of the bank president and lived close by, outside the city wall. He had already been home and left his bag, and now he walked towards them through the avenue. His legs were crooked and his eyes like slits.

''lo, Immerthal,' said Hans. 'I'm taking a little walk with Kröger...'

'I have to go into town on an errand,' said Immerthal. 'But I'll walk a little way with you. Are those fruit toffees you've got? Thanks, I'll have a couple. Tomorrow we have our next lesson, Hans.' He meant the riding-lesson.

'What larks!' said Hans. 'I'm going to get the leather gaiters for a present, because I was top lately in our papers.'

'You don't take riding-lessons, I suppose, Kröger?' asked Immerthal, and his eyes were only two gleaming cracks.

'No...' answered Tonio, uncertainly.

'You ought to ask your father,' Hans Hansen remarked, 'so you could have lessons too, Kröger.'

'Yes...' said Tonio. He spoke hastily and without interest; his throat had suddenly contracted, because Hans had called him by his last name. Hans seemed conscious of it too, for he said by way of explanation: 'I call you Kröger because your first name is so crazy. Don't mind my saying so, I can't do with it at all. Tonio – why, what sort of name is that? Though of course I know it's not your fault in the least.'

'No, they probably called you that because it sounds so foreign and sort of something special,' said Immerthal, obviously with intent to say just the right thing.

Tonio's mouth twitched. He pulled himself together and said:

'Yes, it's a silly name – Lord knows I'd rather be called Heinrich or Wilhelm. It's all because I'm named after my mother's brother Antonio. She comes from down there, you know...'

There he stopped and let the others have their say about horses and saddles. Hans had taken Immerthal's arm; he talked with a fluency that *Don Carlos* could never have roused in him ... Tonio felt a mounting desire to weep pricking his nose from time to time; he had hard work to control the trembling of his lips.

Hans could not stand his name – what was to be done? He himself was called Hans, and Immerthal was called Irwin; two good, sound, familiar names, offensive to nobody. And Tonio was foreign and queer. Yes, there was always something queer about him, whether he would or no, and he was alone, the regular and usual would none of him; although after all he was no gypsy in a green wagon, but the son of Consul Kröger, a member of the Kröger family. But why did Hans call him Tonio as long as they were alone and then feel ashamed as soon as anybody else was by? Just now he had won him over, they had been close together, he was sure. 'How had he betrayed him, Tonio?' Hans asked, and took his arm. But he had breathed easier directly Immerthal came up, he had dropped him like a shot, even gratuitously taunted him with his outlandish name. How it hurt to have to see through all this! ... Hans Hansen did like him a little, when they were alone, that he knew. But let a third person come, he was ashamed, and offered up his friend. And again he was alone. He thought of King Philip. The king had wept ...

'Goodness, I have to go,' said Irwin Immerthal. 'Good-bye and thanks for the toffee.' He jumped upon a bench that stood by the way, ran along it with his crooked legs, jumped down and trotted off.

'I like Immerthal,' said Hans, with emphasis. He had a spoilt and arbitrary way of announcing his likes and dislikes, as though graciously pleased to confer them like an order on this person and that ... He went on talking about the riding-lessons where he had left off. Anyhow, it was not very much farther to his house; the walk over the walls was not a long one. They held their caps and bent their heads before the strong, damp wind that rattled and groaned in the leafless trees. And Hans Hansen went on talking,

Tonio throwing in a forced yes or no from time to time. Hans talked eagerly, had taken his arm again; but the contact gave Tonio no pleasure. The nearness was only apparent, not real; it meant nothing...

They struck away from the walls close to the station, where they saw a train puff busily past, idly counted the coaches, and waved to the man who was perched on top of the last one bundled in a leather coat. They stopped in front of the Hansen villa on the Lindenplatz, and Hans went into detail about what fun it was to stand on the bottom rail of the garden and let it swing on its creaking hinges. After that they said good-bye.

'I must go in now,' said Hans. 'Good-bye, Tonio. Next time I'll take you home, see if I don't.'

'Good-bye, Hans,' said Tonio. 'It was a nice walk.'

They put out their hands, all wet and rusty from the garden gate. But as Hans looked into Tonio's eyes, he bethought himself, a look of remorse came over his charming face.

'And I'll read *Don Carlos* pretty soon, too,' he said quickly. 'That bit about the king in his cabinet must be nuts.' Then he took his bag under his arm and ran off through the front garden. Before he disappeared he turned and nodded once more.

And Tonio went off as though on wings. The wind was at his back; but it was not the wind alone that bore him along so lightly.

Hans would read *Don Carlos*, and then they would have something to talk about, and neither Irwin Immerthal nor another could join in. How well they understood each other! Perhaps – who knew? – some day he might even get Hans to write poetry! ... No, no, that he did not ask. Hans must not become like Tonio, he must stop just as he was, so strong and bright, everybody loved him as he was, and Tonio most of all. But it would do him no harm to read *Don Carlos* ... Tonio passed under the squat old city gate, along by the harbour, and up the steep, wet, windy, gabled street to his parents' house. His heart beat richly: longing was awake in it, and a gentle envy; a faint contempt, and no little innocent bliss.

Ingeborg Holm, blonde little Inge, the daughter of Dr Holm, who lived on Market Square opposite the tall old Gothic fountain with its manifold spires – she it was Tonio Kröger loved when he was sixteen years old.

Strange how things come about! He had seen her a thousand times; then one evening he saw her again; saw her in a certain light, talking with a friend in a certain saucy way, laughing and tossing her head; saw her lift her arm and smooth her back hair with her schoolgirl hand, that was by no means particularly fine or slender, in such a way that the thin white sleeve slipped down from her elbow; heard her speak a word or two, a quite indifferent phrase, but with a certain intonation, with a warm ring in her voice; and his heart throbbed with ecstasy, far stronger than that he had once felt when he looked at Hans Hansen long ago, when he was still a little stupid boy.

That evening he carried away her picture in his eye: the thick blonde plait, the longish, laughing blue eyes, the saddle of pale freckles across the nose. He could not go to sleep for hearing that ring in her voice; he tried in a whisper to imitate the tone in which she had uttered the commonplace phrase, and felt a shiver run through and through him. He knew by experience that this was love. And he was accurately aware that love would surely bring him much pain, affliction, and sadness, that it would certainly destroy his peace, filling his heart to overflowing with melodies which would be no good to him because he would never have the time or tranquillity to give them permanent form. Yet he received this love with joy, surrendered himself to it, and cherished it with all the strength of his being; for he knew that love made one vital and rich, and he longed to be vital and rich, far more than he did to work tranquilly on anything to give it permanent form.

Tonio Kröger fell in love with merry Ingeborg Holm in Frau Consul Hustede's drawing-room on the evening when it was emptied of furniture for the weekly dancing-class. It was a private class, attended only by members of the first families; it met by turns in the various parental houses to receive instruction from Knaak, the dancing-master, who came from Hamburg expressly for the purpose.

François Knaak was his name, and what a man he was! '*J'ai l'honneur de me vous représenter,*' he would say, '*mon nom est Knaak* ... This is not said during the bowing, but after you have finished and are standing up straight again. In a low voice, but distinctly. Of course one does not need to introduce oneself in French every day in the week, but if you can do it correctly and faultlessly in French you are not likely to make a mistake when you do it in German.' How marvellously the silky black frock-coat fitted his chubby hips! His trouser-legs fell down in soft folds upon his patent-leather pumps with their wide satin bows, and his brown eyes glanced about him with languid pleasure in their own beauty.

All this excess of self-confidence and good form was positively over-powering. He went trippingly – and nobody tripped like him, so elastically, so weavingly, rockingly, royally – up to the mistress of the house, made a bow, waited for a hand to be put forth. This vouchsafed, he gave murmurous voice to his gratitude, stepped buoyantly back, turned on his left foot, swiftly drawing the right one backwards on its toe-tip and moved away with his hips shaking.

When you took leave of a company you must go backwards out at the door; when you fetched a chair, you were not to shove it along the floor or clutch it by one leg; but gently by the back, and set it down without a sound. When you stood you were not to fold your hands on your tummy or seek with your tongue the corners of your mouth. If you did, Herr Knaak had a way of showing you how it looked that filled you with disgust for that particular gesture all the rest of your life.

This was deportment. As for dancing, Herr Knaak was, if possible, even more of a master at that. The salon was emptied of furniture and lighted by a gas-chandelier in the middle of the ceiling and candles on the mantel-shelf. The floor was strewn with talc, and the pupils stood about in a dumb semi-circle. But in the next room, behind the portières, mothers and aunts sat on plush-upholstered chairs and watched Herr Knaak through their lorgnettes, as in little springs and hops, curtsying slightly, the hem of his frock-coat held up on each side by two fingers, he demonstrated the single steps of the mazurka. When he wanted to dazzle his audience completely he would suddenly and unexpectedly spring from the ground, whirling his two legs about each other with bewildering swiftness in the air, as it were trilling with them, and then, with a subdued bump, which nevertheless shook everything within him to its depths, returned to earth.

'What an unmentionable monkey!' thought Tonio Kröger to himself. But he saw the absorbed smile on jolly little Inge's face as she followed Herr Knaak's movements; and that, though not that alone, roused in him something like admiration of all this wonderfully controlled corporeality. How tranquil, how imperturbable was Herr Knaak's gaze! His eyes did not plumb the depth of things to the place where life becomes complex and melancholy; they knew nothing save that they were beautiful brown eyes. But that was just why his bearing was so proud. To be able to walk like that, one must be stupid; then one was loved, then one was lovable. He could so well understand how it was that Inge, blonde, sweet little Inge, looked at Herr Knaak as she did. But would never a girl look at him like that?

Oh, yes, there would, and did. For instance, Magdalena Vermehren, Attorney Vermehren's daughter, with the gentle mouth, and the great, dark, brilliant eyes, so serious and adoring. She often fell down in the dance; but when it was 'ladies' choice' she came up to him; she knew he wrote verses and twice she had asked him to show them to her. She often sat at a distance, with drooping head, and gazed at him. He did not care. It was Inge he loved, blonde, jolly Inge, who most assuredly despised him for his poetic effusions . . . he looked at her, looked at her narrow blue eyes full of fun and mockery, and felt an envious longing; to be shut away from her like this, to be forever strange – he felt it in his breast, like a heavy, burning weight.

'First couple *en avant*,' said Herr Knaak; and no words can tell how marvellously he pronounced the nasal. They were to practise the quadrille, and to Tonio Kröger's profound alarm he found himself in the same set with Inge Holm. He avoided her where he could, yet somehow was forever near her; kept his eyes away from her person and yet found his gaze ever on her. There she came, tripping up hand-in-hand with red-headed Ferdinand Matthiessen; she flung back her braid, drew a deep breath, and took her place opposite Tonio. Herr Heinzelmann, at the piano, laid bony hands upon the keys. Herr Knaak waved his arm, the quadrille began.

She moved to and fro before his eyes, forwards and back, pacing and swinging; he seemed to catch a fragrance from her hair or the folds of her thin white frock, and his eyes grew sadder and sadder. 'I love you, dear, sweet Inge,' he said to himself, and put into his words all the pain he felt to see her so intent upon the dance with not a thought for him. Some lines of an exquisite poem by Storm came into his mind: 'I would sleep, but thou must dance.' It seemed against all sense, and most depressing, that he must be dancing when he was in love . . .

'First couple *en avant*,' said Herr Knaak; it was the next figure. '*Compliment! Moulinet des dames! Tour de main!*' and he swallowed the silent *e* in the '*de*', with quite indescribable ease and grace.

'Second couple *en avant!*' This was Tonio Kröger and his partner. '*Compliment!*' And Tonio Kröger bowed. '*Moulinet des dames!*' And Tonio Kröger, with bent head and gloomy brows, laid his hand on those of the four ladies, on Ingeborg Holm's hand, and danced the *moulinet*.

Roundabout rose a tittering and laughing. Herr Knaak took a ballet pose conventionally expressive of horror. 'Oh, dear! Oh, dear!' he cried. 'Stop! Stop! Kröger among the ladies! *En arrière*, Fräulein Kröger, step back, *fi donc!* Everybody else understood it but you. Shoo! Get out! Get away!' He drew out his yellow silk handkerchief and flapped Tonio Kröger back to his place.

Everyone laughed, the girls and the boys and the ladies beyond the portières; Herr Knaak had made something too utterly funny out of the little episode, it was as amusing as a play. But Herr Heinzelmann at the piano sat and waited, with a dry, business-like air, for a sign to go on; he was hardened against Herr Knaak's effects.

Then the quadrille went on. And the intermission followed. The parlourmaid came clinking in with a tray of wine-jelly glasses, the cook followed in her wake with a load of plum-cake. But Tonio Kröger stole away.

He stole out into the corridor and stood there, his hands behind his back, in front of a window with the blind down. He never thought that one could not see through the blind and that it was absurd to stand there as though one were looking out.

For he was looking within, into himself, the theatre of so much pain and longing. Why, why was he here? Why was he not sitting by the window in his own room, reading Storm's *Immensee* and lifting his eyes to the twilight garden outside, where the old walnut tree moaned? That was the place for him? Others might dance, others bend their fresh and lively minds upon the pleasure in hand! ... But no, no, after all, his place was here, where he could feel near Inge, even although he stood lonely and aloof, seeking to distinguish the warm notes of her voice amid the buzzing, clattering and laughter within. Oh, lovely Inge, blonde Inge of the narrow, laughing blue eyes! So lovely and laughing as you are one can only be if one does not read *Immensee* and never tries to write things like it. And that was just the tragedy!

Ah, she *must* come! She *must* notice where he had gone, must feel how he suffered! She must slip out to him, even pity must bring her, to lay her hand on his shoulder and say: 'Do come back to us, ah, don't be sad – I love you, Tonio.' He listened behind him and waited in frantic suspense. But not in the least. Such things did not happen on this earth.

Had she laughed at him too, like all the others? Yes, she had, however gladly he would have denied it for both their sakes. And yet it was only because he had been so taken up with her that he had danced the *moulinet des dames*. Suppose he had – what did that matter? Had not a magazine accepted a poem of his a little while ago – even though the magazine had failed before his poem could be printed? The day was coming when he would be famous, when they would print everything he wrote; and *then* he would see if that made any impression on Inge Holm! No, it would make no impression at all; that was just it. Magdalena Vermehren, who was always falling down in the dances, yes, she would be impressed. But never Ingeborg Holm, never blue-eyed, laughing Inge. So what was the good of it?

Tonio Kröger's heart contracted painfully at the thought. To feel stirring within you the wonderful and melancholy play of strange forces and to be aware that those others you yearn for are blithely inaccessible to all that moves you – what a pain is this! And yet! He stood there aloof and alone, staring hopelessly at a drawn blind and making, in his distraction, as though he could look out. But yet he was happy. For he lived. His heart was full; hotly and sadly it beat for thee, Ingeborg Holm, and his soul embraced thy blonde, simple, pert, commonplace little personality in blissful self-abnegation.

Often after that he stood thus, with burning cheeks, in lonely corners, whither the sound of the music, the tinkling of glasses and fragrance of flowers came but faintly, and tried to distinguish the ringing tones of thy voice amid the distant happy din; stood suffering for thee – and still was happy! Often it angered him to think that he might talk with Magdalena Vermehren, who always fell down in the dance. She understood him, she laughed or was serious in the right places; while Inge the fair, let him sit never so near her, seemed remote and estranged, his speech not being her speech. And still – he was happy. For happiness, he told himself, is not in being loved – which is a satisfaction of the vanity and mingled with disgust. Happiness is in loving and perhaps in snatching fugitive little approaches to the beloved object. And he took inward note of this thought, wrote it down in his mind; followed out all its implications and felt it to the depths of his soul.

'Faithfulness,' thought Tonio Kröger. 'Yes, I will be faithful, I will love thee, Ingeborg, as long as I live!' He said this in the honesty of his intentions. And yet a still small voice whispered misgivings in his ear: after all, he had forgotten Hans Hansen utterly, even though he saw him every day! And the hateful, the pitiable fact was that this still, small, rather spiteful voice was right: time passed and the day came when Tonio Kröger was no longer so unconditionally ready as once he had been to die for the lively Inge, because he felt in himself desires and powers to accomplish in his own way a host of wonderful things in this world.

And he circled with watchful eye the sacrificial altar, where flickered the pure, chaste flame of his love; knelt before it and tended and cherished it in every way, because he so wanted to be faithful. And in a little while, unobservably, without sensation or stir, it went out after all.

But Tonio Kröger still stood before the cold altar, full of regret and dismay at the fact that faithfulness was impossible upon this earth. Then he shrugged his shoulders and went his way.

He went the way that go he must, a little idly, a little irregularly, whistling to himself, gazing into space with his head on one side; and if he went wrong, it was because for some people there is no such things as a right way. Asked what in the world he meant to become, he gave various answers, for he was used to say (and had even already written it) that he bore within himself the possibility of a thousand ways of life, together with the private conviction that they were all sheer impossibilities.

Even before he left the narrow streets of his native city, the threads that bound him to it had gently loosened. The old Kröger family gradually declined, and some people quite rightly considered Tonio Kröger's own existence and way of life as one of the signs of decay. His father's mother, the head of the family, had died, and not long after his own father followed, the tall, thoughtful, carefully dressed gentleman with the field-flower in his buttonhole. The great Kröger house, with all its stately tradition, came up for sale, and the firm was dissolved. Tonio's mother, his beautiful, fiery mother, who played the piano and mandolin so wonderfully and to whom nothing mattered at all, she married again after a year's time; married a musician, moreover, a virtuoso with an Italian name, and went away with him into remote blue distances. Tonio Kröger found this a little irregular, but who was he to call her to order, who wrote poetry himself and could not even give an answer when asked what he meant to do in life?

And so he left his native town and its tortuous, gabled streets with the damp wind whistling through them; left the fountain in the garden and the ancient walnut tree, familiar friends of his youth; left the sea too, that he loved so much, and felt no pain to go. For he was grown up and sensible and had come to realize how things stood with him; he looked down on the lowly and vulgar life he had led so long in these surroundings.

He surrendered utterly to the power that to him seemed the highest on earth, to whose service he felt called, which promised him elevation and honours: the power of intellect, the power of the Word, that lords it with a smile over the unconscious and inarticulate. To this power he surrendered with all the passion of youth, and it rewarded him with all it had to give, taking from him inexorably, in return, all that it is wont to take.

It sharpened his eyes and made him see through the large words which puff out the bosoms of mankind; it opened for him men's souls and his own, made him clairvoyant, showed him the inwardness of the world and the ultimate behind men's words and deeds. And all that he saw could be put in two words: the comedy and the tragedy of life.

And then, with knowledge, its torment and its arrogance, came solitude; because he could not endure the blithe and innocent with their darkened understanding, while they in turn were troubled by the sign on his brow. But his love of the Word kept growing sweeter and sweeter, and his love of form; for he used to say (and had already said it in writing) that knowledge of the soul would unfailingly make us melancholy if the pleasures of expression did not keep us alert and of good cheer.

He lived in large cities and in the south, promising himself a luxuriant ripening of his art by southern suns; perhaps it was the blood of his mother's race that drew him thither. But his heart being dead and loveless, he fell into adventures of the flesh, descended into the depths of lust and searing sin, and suffered unspeakably thereby. It might have been his father in him, that tall, thoughtful, fastidiously dressed man with the wild flower in his buttonhole, that made him suffer so down there in the south; now and again he would feel a faint, yearning memory of a certain joy that was of the soul; once it had been his own, but now, in all his joys, he could not find it again.

Then he would be seized with disgust and hatred of the senses; pant after purity and seemly peace, while still he breathed the air of art, the tepid, sweet air of permanent spring, heavy with fragrance where it breeds and brews and burgeons in the mysterious bliss of creation. So for all result he was flung to and fro forever between the two crass extremes: between icy intellect and scorching sense, and what with his pangs of conscience led an exhausting life, rare, extraordinary, excessive, which at bottom he, Tonio Kröger, despised. 'What a labyrinth!' he sometimes thought. 'How could I possibly have got into all these fantastic adventures? As though I had a wagonful of travelling gypsies for my ancestors!'

But as his health suffered from these excesses, so his artistry was sharpened; it grew fastidious, precious, *raffiné*, morbidly sensitive in questions of tact and taste, rasped by the banal. His first appearance in print elicited much applause; there was joy among the elect, for it was a good and workmanlike performance, full of humour and acquaintance with pain. In no long time his name – the same by which his masters had reproached him, the same he had signed to his earliest verses on the walnut tree and the fountain and the sea, those syllables compact of the north and the south, that good middle-class name with the exotic twist to it – became a synonym for excellence; for the painful thoroughness of the experiences he had gone through, combined with a tenacious ambition and a persistent industry, joined battle with the irritable fastidiousness of his taste and under grinding torments issued in work of a quality quite uncommon.

He worked, not like a man who works that he may live; but as one who is bent on doing nothing but work; having no regard for himself as a human being but only as a creator; moving about grey and unobtrusive among his fellows like an actor without his make-up, who counts for nothing as soon as he stops representing something else. He worked withdrawn out of sight and sound of the small fry, for whom he felt nothing but contempt, because to them a talent was a social asset like another; who, whether they were poor or not, went about ostentatiously shabby or else flaunted startling cravats, all the time taking jolly good care to amuse themselves, to be artistic and charming without the smallest notion of the fact that good work only comes out under pressure of a bad life; that he who lives does not work; that one must die to life in order to be utterly a creator.

'Shall I disturb you?' asked Tonio Kröger on the threshold of the *atelier*. He held his hat in his hand and bowed with some ceremony, although Lisabeta Ivanovna was a good friend of his, to whom he told all his troubles.

'Mercy on you, Tonio Kröger! Don't be so formal,' answered she, with her lilting intonation. 'Everybody knows you were taught good manners in your nursery.' She transferred her brush to her left hand, that held the palette, reached him her right, and looked him in the face, smiling and shaking her head.

'Yes, but you are working,' he said. 'Let's see. Oh, you've been getting on,' and he looked at the colour-sketches leaning against chairs at both sides of the easel and from them to the large canvas covered with a square linen mesh, where the first patches of colour were beginning to appear among the confused and schematic lines of the charcoal sketch.

This was in Munich, in a back building in Schellingstrasse several storeys up. Beyond the wide window facing the north were blue sky, sunshine, birds twittering; the young sweet breath of spring streaming through an open pane mingled with the smells of paint and fixative. The afternoon light, bright golden, flooded the spacious emptiness of the atelier; it made no secret of the bad flooring or the rough table under the window, covered with little bottles, tubes, and brushes; it illuminated the unframed studies on the unpapered walls, the torn silk screen that shut off a charmingly furnished little living-corner near the door; it shone upon the inchoate work on the easel, upon the artist and the poet there before it.

She was about the same age as himself – slightly past thirty. She sat there on a low stool, in her dark-blue apron, and leant her chin in her hand. Her brown hair, compactly dressed, already a little grey at the sides, was parted in the middle and waved over the temples, framing a sensitive, sympathetic, dark-skinned face, which was Slavic in its facial structure, with flat nose, strongly accentuated cheek-bones, and little bright black eyes. She sat there measuring her work with her head on one side and her eyes screwed up; her features were drawn with a look of misgiving, almost of vexation.

He stood beside her, his right hand on his hip, with the other furiously twirling his brown moustache. His dress, reserved in cut and a soothing shade of grew, was punctilious and dignified to the last degree. He was whistling softly to himself, in the way he had, and his slanting brows were gathered in a frown. The dark-brown hair was parted with severe correctness, but the laboured forehead beneath showed a nervous twitching, and the chiselled southern features were sharpened as though they had been gone over again with a graver's tool. And yet the mouth – how gently curved it was, the chin how softly formed! ... After a little he drew his hand across his brow and eyes and turned away.

'I ought not to have come,' he said.

'And why not, Tonio Kröger?'

'I've just got up from my desk, Lisabeta, and inside my head it looks just the way it does on this canvas. A scaffolding, a faint first draft smeared with corrections and a few splotches of colour; yes, and I come up here and see the same thing. And the same conflict and contradiction in the air,' he went on, sniffing, 'that has been torturing me at home. It's extraordinary. If you are possessed by an idea, you find it expressed everywhere, you even *smell* it. Fixative and the breath of spring; art and – what? Don't say Nature,

Lisabeta, "Nature" isn't exhausting. Ah, no, I ought to have gone for a walk, though it's doubtful if it would have made me feel better. Five minutes ago, not far from here, I met a man I know, Adalbert, the novelist. "God damn the spring!" says he in the aggressive way he has. "It is and always has been the most ghastly time of the year. Can you get hold of a single sensible idea, Kröger? Can you sit still and work out even the smallest effect, when your blood tickles till it's positively indecent and you are teased by a whole host of irrelevant sensations that when you look at them turn out to be unworkable trash? For my part, I am going to a café. A café is neutral territory, the change of the seasons doesn't affect it; it represents, so to speak, the detached and elevated sphere of the literary man, in which one is only capable of refined ideas." And he went into the café . . . and perhaps I ought to have gone with him.'

Lisabeta was highly entertained.

'I like that, Tonio Kröger. That part about the indecent tickling is good. And he is right too, in a way, for spring is really not very conducive to work. But now listen. Spring or no spring, I will just finish this little piece – work out this little effect, as your friend Adalbert would say. Then we'll go into the "salon" and have tea, and you can talk yourself out, for I can perfectly well see you are too full for utterance. Will you just compose yourself somewhere – on that chest, for instance, if you are not afraid for your aristocratic garments –'

'Oh, leave my clothes alone, Lisabeta Ivanovna! Do you want me to go about in a ragged velveteen jacket or a red waistcoat? Every artist is as bohemian as the deuce inside! Let him at least wear proper clothes and behave outwardly like a respectable being. No. I am not too full for utterance,' he said as he watched her mixing her paints. 'I've told you, it is only that I have a problem and a conflict that sticks in my mind and disturbs me at my work . . . Yes, what was it we were just saying? We were talking about Adalbert, the novelist, that stout and forthright man "Spring is the most ghastly time of the year," says he, and goes into a café. A man has to know what he needs, eh? Well, you see he's not the only one; the spring makes me nervous, too; I get dazed with the triflingness and sacredness of the memories and feelings it evokes; only that I don't succeed in looking down on it; for the truth is it makes me ashamed; I quail before its sheer naturalness and triumphant youth. And I don't know whether I should envy Adalbert or despise him for his ignorance . . .

'Yes, it is true; spring is a bad time for work; and why? Because we are feeling too much. Nobody but a beginner imagines that he who creates must feel. Every real and genuine artist smiles at such naïve blunders as that. A melancholy enough smile, perhaps, but still a smile. For what an artist talks about is never the main point; it is the raw material, in and for itself indifferent, out of which, with bland and serene mastery, he creates the work of art. If you care too much about what you have to say, if your heart is too much in it, you can be pretty sure of making a mess. You get pathetic, you wax sentimental; something dull and doddering, without roots or outlines, with no sense of humour – something tiresome and banal grows under your hand, and you get nothing out of it but apathy in your audience and disappointment and misery in yourself. For so it is, Lisabeta; feeling, warm, heartfelt feeling, is always banal and futile; only the irritations and icy ecstasies of the artist's corrupted nervous system are artistic. The artist must be unhuman, extra-human; he must stand in a queer aloof relationship to our humanity; only so is he in a position, I ought to say only so would he be tempted, to represent it, to present it, to portray it to good effect. The very gift of style of form and expression, is nothing else than this cool and fastidious attitude towards humanity; you might say there has to be this impoverishment and devastation as a preliminary condition. For sound natural feeling, say what you like, has no taste. It is all up with the artist as soon as he becomes a man and begins to feel. Adalbert knows that; that's why he betook himself to the café, the neutral territory – God help him!'

'Yes, God help him, Batuschka,' said Lisabeta, as she washed her hands in a tin basin. 'You don't need to follow his example.'

'No, Lisabeta, I am not going to; and the only reason is that I am now and again in a position to feel a little ashamed of the springtime of my art. You see sometimes I get letters from strangers, full of praise and thanks and admiration from people whose feelings I have touched. I read them and feel touched myself at these warm if ungainly emotions I have called up; a sort of pity steals over me at this naïve enthusiasm; and I positively blush at the thought of how these good people would freeze up if they were to get a look behind the scenes. What they, in their innocence, cannot comprehend is that a properly constituted, healthy, decent man never writes, acts, or composes – all of which does not hinder me from using his admiration for my genius to goad myself on; nor from taking it in deadly earnest and aping the airs of a great man. Oh, don't talk to me, Lisabeta. I tell you I am sick to death of depicting humanity without having any part or lot in it . . . Is an artist a male, anyhow? Ask the females! It seems to me we artists are all of us something like those unsexed papal singers . . . we sing like angels; but –'

'Shame on you, Tonio Kröger. But come to tea. The water is just on the boil, and here are some *papyros*. You were talking about singing soprano, do go on. But really you ought to be ashamed of yourself. If I did not know your passionate devotion to your calling and how proud you are of it –'

'Don't talk about "calling", Lisabeta Ivanovna. Literature is not a calling, it is a curse, believe me! When does one begin to feel the curse? Early, horribly early. At a time when one ought by rights to be living in peace and harmony with God and the world. It begins by your feeling yourself set apart, in a curious sort of opposition to the nice, regular people; there is a gulf of ironic sensibility, of knowledge, scepticism, disagreement, between you and the others; it grows deeper and deeper, you realize that you are alone; and from then on any *rapprochement* is simply hopeless! What a fate! That is, if you still have enough heart, enough warmth of affections, to feel how frightful it is! . . . Your self-consciousness is kindled, because you among thousands feel the sign on your brow and know that everyone else sees it. I once knew an actor, a man of genius, who had to struggle with a morbid self-consciousness and instability. When he had no role to play, nothing to represent, this man, consummate artist but impoverished human being, was overcome by an exaggerated consciousness of his ego. A genuine artist – not one who has taken up art as a profession like another, but artist foreordained and damned – you can pick out, without boasting very sharp perceptions, out of a group of men. The sense of being set apart and not belonging, of being known and observed, something both regal and incongruous shows in his face. You might see something of the same sort on the features of a prince walking through a crowd in ordinary clothes. But no civilian clothes are any good here, Lisabeta. You can disguise yourself, you can dress up like an attaché or a lieutenant of the guard on leave; you hardly need to give a glance or speak a word before everyone knows you are not a human being, but something else: something queer, different, inimical.

'But what is it, to be an artist? Nothing shows up the general human dislike of thinking, and man's innate craving to be comfortable, better than his attitude to this question. When these worthy people are affected by a work of art, they say humbly that that sort of thing is a "gift". And because in their innocence they assume that beautiful and uplifting results must have beautiful and uplifting causes, they never dream that the "gift" in question is a very dubious affair and rests upon extremely sinister foundations. Everybody knows that artists are "sensitive" and easily wounded; just as everybody knows that ordinary people, with a normal bump of self-confidence, are not. Now you see, Lisabeta, I cherish at the bottom of my soul all the scorn and suspicion of the artist gentry – translated into terms of the intellectual – that my upright old forbears there on the Baltic would have felt for any juggler or mountebank that entered their houses. Listen to this. I know a banker, a grey-haired business man, who has a gift for writing stories. He employs this gift in his idle hours, and some of his stories are of the first rank. But despite – I say despite – this excellent gift his withers are by no means unwrung: on the contrary, he has had to serve a prison sentence, on anything but trifling grounds. Yes, it was actually first *in prison* that he became conscious of his gift, and his experiences as a convict are the main theme in all his works. One might be rash enough to conclude that a man has to be at home in some kind of jail in order to become a poet. But can you escape the suspicion that the source and essence of his being an artist had less to do with his life in prison than they had with the reasons that *brought him there*? A banker who writes – that is a rarity, isn't it? But a banker who isn't a criminal, who is irreproachably respectable, and yet writes – he doesn't exist. Yes, you are laughing, and yet I am more than half serious. No problem, none in the world, is more tormenting than this of the artist and his human aspect. Take the most miraculous case of all, take the most typical and therefore the most powerful of artists, take such a morbid and profoundly equivocal work as *Tristan and Isolde*, and look at the effect it has on a healthy young man of thoroughly normal feelings. Exaltation, encouragement, warm, downright enthusiasm, perhaps incitement to "artistic" creation of his own. Poor young dilettante! In us artists it looks fundamentally different from what he wots of, with his "warm heart" and "honest enthusiasm". I've seen women and youths go mad over artists . . . and I *knew* about them . . . ! The origins, the accompanying phenomena, and the conditions of the artist life – good Lord, what I haven't observed about them, over and over!'

'Observed, Tonio Kröger? If I may ask, only "observed"?'

He was silent, knitting his oblique brown brows and whistling softly to himself.

'Let me have your cup, Tonio. The tea is weak. And take another cigarette. Now, you perfectly know that you are looking at things as they do not necessarily have to be looked at . . .'

'That is Horatio's answer, dear Lisabeta. "'Twere to consider too curiously, to consider so."'

'I mean, Tonio Kröger, that one can consider them just exactly as well from another side. I am only a silly painting female, and if I can contradict you at all, if I can defend your own profession a little against you, it is not by saying anything new, but simply by reminding you of some things you very well know yourself: of the purifying and healing influence of letters, the subduing of the passions by knowledge and eloquence; literature as the guide to understanding, forgiveness and love, the redeeming power of the

word, literary art as the noblest manifestation of the human mind, the poet
as the most highly developed of human beings, the poet as saint. Is it to
consider things not curiously enough, to consider them so?'

'You may talk like that, Lisabeta Ivanovna, you have a perfect right. And
with reference to Russian literature, and the works of your poets, one can
really worship them; they really come close to being that elevated literature
you are talking about. But I am not ignoring your objections, they are part of
the things I have in mind today ... Look at me, Lisabeta. I don't look any
too cheerful, do I? A little old and tired and pinched, eh? Well, now to come
back to the "knowledge". Can't you imagine a man, born orthodox, mild-
mannered, well-meaning, a bit sentimental, just simply overstimulated by his
psychological clairvoyance, and going to the dogs? Not to let the sadness of
the world unman you; to read, mark, learn, and put to account even the most
torturing things and to be of perpetual good cheer, in the sublime
consciousness of moral superiority over the horrible invention of existence –
yes, thank you! But despite all the joys of expression once in a while the thing
gets on your nerves. *"Tout comprendre c'est tout pardonner."* I don't know
about that. There is something I call being sick of knowledge, Lisabeta:
when it is enough for you to see through a thing in order to be sick to death of
it, and not in the least in a forgiving mood. Such was the case of Hamlet the
Dane, that typical literary man. He knew what it meant to be called to
knowledge without being born to it. To see things clear, if even through
your tears, to recognize, notice, observe – and have to put it all down with a
smile, at the very moment when hands are clinging, and lips meeting, and
the human gaze is blinded with feeling – it is infamous, Lisabeta, it is
indecent, outrageous – but what good does it do to be outraged?

'Then another and no less charming side of the thing, of course, is your
ennui, your indifferent and ironic attitude towards truth. It is a fact that
there is no society in the world so dumb and hopeless as a circle of literary
people who are hounded to death as it is. All knowledge is old and tedious to
them. Utter some truth that it gave you considerable youthful joy to conquer
and possess – and they will all chortle at you for your *naïveté*. Oh, yes,
Lisabeta, literature is a wearing job. In human society, I do assure you, a
reserved and sceptical man can be taken for stupid, whereas he is really only
arrogant and perhaps lacks courage. So much for "knowledge". Now for the
"Word". It isn't so much a matter of the "redeeming power" as it is of
putting your emotions on ice and serving them up chilled! Honestly, don't
you think there's a good deal of cool cheek in the prompt and superficial way
a writer can get rid of his feelings by turning them into literature? If your
heart is too full, if you are overpowered with the emotions of some sweet or
exalted moment – nothing simpler! Go to the literary man, he will put it all
straight for you *instanter*. He will analyse and formulate your affair, label it
and express it and discuss it and polish it off and make you indifferent to it
for time and eternity – and not charge you a farthing. You will go home
quite relieved, cooled off, enlightened; and wonder what it was all about and
why you were so mightily moved. And will you seriously enter the list
in behalf of this vain and frigid charlatan? What is uttered, so runs
this *credo*, is finished and done with. If the whole world could be expressed,
it would be saved, finished and done ... Well and good. But I am not a
nihilist –'

'You are not a –' said Lisabeta ... She was lifting a teaspoonful of tea to her
mouth and paused in the act to stare at him.

'Come, come, Lisabeta, what's the matter? I say I am not a nihilist, with respect, that is, to lively feeling. You see the literary man does not understand that life may go on living, unashamed, even after it has been expressed and therewith finished. No matter how much it has been redeemed by becoming literature, it keeps right on sinning – for all action is sin in the mind's eye –

'I'm nearly done, Lisabeta. Please listen. I love life – this is an admission. I present it to you, you may have it. I have never made it to anyone else. People say – people have even written and printed – that I hate life, or fear or despise or abominate it. I liked to hear this, it has always flattered me; but that does not make it true. I love life. You smile; and I know why, Lisabeta. But I implore you not to take what I am saying for literature. Don't think of Caesar Borgia or any drunken philosophy that has him for a standard-bearer. He is nothing to me, your Caesar Borgia. I have no opinion of him, and I shall never comprehend how one can honour the extraordinary and daemonic as an ideal. No, life as the eternal antimony of mind and art does not represent itself to us as a vision of savage greatness and ruthless beauty; we who are set apart and different do not conceive it as, like us, unusual; it is the normal, respectable, and admirable that is the kingdom of our longing: life, in all its seductive banality! That man is very far from being an artist, my dear, whose last and deepest enthusiasm is the *raffiné*, the eccentric and satanic; who does not know a longing for the innocent, the simple, and the living, for a little friendship, devotion, familiar human happiness – the gnawing, surreptitious hankering, Lisabeta, for the bliss of the commonplace...

'A genuine human friend. Believe me, I should be proud and happy to possess a friend among men. But up to now all the friends I have had have been daemons, kobolds, impious monsters, and spectres dumb with excess of knowledge – that is to say, literary men.

'I may be standing upon some platform, in some hall in front of people who have come to listen to me. And I find myself looking round among my hearers, I catch myself secretly peering about the auditorium, and all the while I am thinking who it is that has come here to listen to me, whose grateful applause is in my ears, with whom my art is making me one ... I do not find what I seek, Lisabeta, I find the herd. The same old community, the same old gathering of early Christians, so to speak: people with fine souls in uncouth bodies, people who are always falling down in the dance, if you know what I mean; the kind to whom poetry serves as a sort of mild revenge on life. Always and only the poor and suffering, never any of the others, the blue-eyed ones, Lisabeta – they do not need mind...

'And, after all, would it not be a lamentable lack of logic to want it otherwise? It is against all sense to love life and yet bend all the powers you have to draw it over to your own side, to the side of finesse and melancholy and the whole sickly aristocracy of letters. The kingdom of art increases and that of health and innocence declines on this earth. What there is left of it ought to be carefully preserved; one ought not to tempt people to read poetry who would much rather read books about the instantaneous photography of horses.

'For, after all, what more pitiable sight is there than life led astray by art? We artists have a consummate contempt for the dilettante, the man who is leading a living life and yet thinks he can be an artist too if he gets the chance. I am speaking from personal experience, I do assure you. Suppose I am in a company in a good house, with eating and drinking going on, and plenty of conversation and good feeling; I am glad and grateful to be able to lose myself among good regular people for a while. Then all of a sudden – I am thinking of something that actually happened – an officer gets up, a lieutenant, a stout, good-looking chap, whom I could never have believed guilty of any conduct unbecoming his uniform, and actually in good set terms asks the company's permission to read some verses of his own composition. Everybody looks disconcerted, they laugh and tell him to go on, and he takes them at their word and reads from a sheet of paper he has up to now been hiding in his coat-tail pocket – something about love and music, as deeply felt as it is inept. But I ask you: a lieutenant! A man of the world! He surely did not need to ... Well, the inevitable result is long faces, silence, a little artificial applause, everybody thoroughly uncomfortable. The first sensation I am conscious of is guilt – I feel partly responsible for the disturbance this rash youth has brought upon the company; and no wonder, for I, as a member of the same guild, am a target for some of the unfriendly glances. But next minute I realize something else: this man for whom just now I felt the greatest respect has suddenly sunk in my eyes. I feel a benevolent pity. Along with some other brave and good-natured gentlemen I go up and speak to him. "Congratulations, Herr Lieutenant," I say, "that is a very pretty talent you have. It was charming." And I am within an ace of clapping him on the shoulder. But is that the way one is supposed to feel towards a lieutenant – benevolent? ... It was his own fault. There he stood, suffering embarrassment for the mistake of thinking that one may pluck a single leaf from the laurel tree of art without paying for it with his life. No, there I go with my colleague, the convict banker – but don't you find, Lisabeta, that I have quite a Hamlet-like flow of oratory today?'

'Are you done, Tonio Kröger?'

'No. But there won't be any more.'

'And quite enough too. Are you expecting a reply?'

'Have you one ready?'

'I should say. I have listened to you faithfully, Tonio, from beginning to end, and I will give you the answer to everything you have said this afternoon and the solution of the problem that has been upsetting you. Now: the solution is that you, as you sit there, are, quite simply, a bourgeois.'

'Am I?' he asked a little crestfallen.

'Yes; that hits you hard, it must. So I will soften the judgement just a little. You are a bourgeois on the wrong path, a bourgeois *manqué*.'

Silence. Then he got up resolutely and took his hat and stick.

'Thank you, Lisabeta Ivanovna; now I can go home in peace. I am expressed.'

Towards autumn Tonio Kröger said to Lisabeta Ivanovna: 'Well, Lisabeta, I think I'll be off. I need a change of air. I must get away, out into the open.'

'Well, well, well, little Father! Does it please your Highness to go down to Italy again?'

'Oh, get along with your Italy, Lisabeta. I'm fed up with Italy, I spew it out of my mouth. It's a long time since I imagined I could belong down there. Art, eh? Blue-velvet sky, ardent wine, the sweets of sensuality. In short, I don't want it – I decline with thanks. The whole *bellezza* business makes me nervous. All those frightfully animated people down there with their black animal-like eyes; I don't like them either. These Romance peoples have no soul in their eyes. No, I'm going to take a trip to Denmark.'

'To Denmark?'

'Yes. I'm quite sanguine of the results. I happen never to have been there, though I lived all my youth so close to it. Still I have always known and loved the country. I suppose I must have this northern tendency from my father, for my mother was really more for the *bellezza*, in so far, that is, as she cared very much one way or the other. But just take the books that are written up there, that clean, meaty whimsical Scandinavian literature, Lisabeta, there's nothing like it, I love it. Or take the Scandinavian meals, those incomparable meals, which can only be digested in strong sea air (I don't know whether I can digest them in any sort of air); I know them from my home too, because we ate that way up there. Take even the names, the given names that people rejoice in up north; we have a good many of them in my part of the country too: Ingeborg, for instance, isn't it the purest poetry – like a harp-tone? And then the sea – up there it's the Baltic! . . . In a word, I am going, Lisabeta. I want to see the Baltic again and read the books and hear the names on their native heath; I want to stand on the terrace at Kronberg, where the ghost appeared to Hamlet, bringing despair and death to that poor, noble-souled youth . . .'

'How are you going, Tonio, if I may ask? What route are you taking?'

'The usual one,' he said, shrugging his shoulders, and blushed perceptibly. 'Yes, I shall touch my – my point of departure, Lisabeta, after thirteen years, and that may turn out rather funny.'

She smiled.

'That is what I wanted to hear, Tonio Kröger. Well, be off, then, in God's name. Be sure to write to me, do you hear? I shall expect a letter full of your experiences in – Denmark.'

And Tonio Kröger travelled north. He travelled in comfort (for he was wont to say that anyone who suffered inwardly more than other people had a right to a little outward ease); and he did not stay until the towers of the little town he had left rose up in the grey air. Among them he made a short and singular stay.

The dreary afternoon was merging into evening when the train pulled into the narrow, reeking shed, so marvellously familiar. The volumes of thick smoke rolled up to the dirty glass roof and wreathed to and fro there in long tatters, just as they had, long ago, on the day when Tonio Kröger, with nothing but derision in his heart, had left his native town. – He arranged to have his luggage sent to his hotel and walked out of the station.

There were the cabs, those enormously high, enormously wide black cabs drawn by two horses, standing in a rank. He did not take one, he only looked at them, as he looked at everything: the narrow gables, and the pointed towers peering above the roofs close at hand; the plump, fair, easy-going populace, with their broad yet rapid speech. And a nervous laugh mounted in him, mysteriously akin to a sob. – He walked on, slowly, with the damp wind constantly in his face, across the bridge, with the mythological statues on the railings and some distance along the harbour.

Good Lord, how tiny and close it all seemed! The comical little gabled streets were climbing up just as of yore from the port to the town! And on the ruffled waters the smoke-stacks and masts of the ships dipped gently in the wind and twilight. Should he go up that next street, leading, he knew, to a certain house? No, tomorrow. He was too sleepy. His head was heavy from the journey, and slow, vague trains of thought passed through his mind.

Sometimes in the past thirteen years, when he was suffering from indigestion, he had dreamed of being back home in the echoing old house in the steep, narrow street. His father had been there too, and reproached him bitterly for his dissolute manner of life, and this, each time, he had found quite as it should be. And now the present refused to distinguish itself in any way from one of those tantalizing dream-fabrications in which the dreamer asks himself if this be delusion or reality and is driven to decide for the latter, only to wake up after all in the end ... He paced through the half-empty streets with his head inclined against the wind, moving as though in his sleep in the direction of the hotel, the first hotel in the town, where he meant to sleep. A bow-legged man, with a pole at the end of which burned a tiny fire, walked before him with a rolling, seafaring gait and lighted the gas-lamps.

What was at the bottom of this? What was it burning darkly beneath the ashes of his fatigue, refusing to burst out into a clear blaze? Hush, hush, only no talk. Only don't make words! He would have liked to go on so, for a long time, in the wind, through the dusky, dreamily familiar streets – but everything was so little and close together here. You reached your goal at once.

In the upper town there were arc-lamps, just lighted. There was the hotel with the two black lions in front of it; he had been afraid of them as a child. And there they were, still looking at each other as though they were about to sneeze; only they seemed to have grown much smaller. Tonio Kröger passed between them into the hotel.

As he came on foot, he was received with no great ceremony. There was a porter, and a lordly gentleman dressed in black, to do the honours; the latter, shoving back his cuffs with his little fingers, measured him from the crown of his head to the soles of his boots, obviously with intent to place him, to assign him to his proper category socially and hierarchically speaking and then mete out the suitable degree of courtesy. He seemed not to come to any clear decision and compromised on a moderate display of politeness. A mild-mannered waiter with yellow-white side-whiskers, in a dress suit shiny with age, and rosettes on his soundless shoes, led him up two flights into a clean old room furnished in patriarchal style. Its windows gave on to a twilit view of courts and gables, very medieval and picturesque, with the fantastic bulk of the old church close by. Tonio Kröger stood awhile before this window; then he sat down on the wide sofa, crossed his arms, drew down his brows and whistled to himself.

Lights were brought and his luggage came up. The mild-mannered waiter laid the hotel register on the table, and Tonio Kröger, his head on one side, scrawled something on it that might be taken for a name, a station, and a place of origin. Then he ordered supper and went on gazing into space from his sofa-corner. When it stood before him he let it wait long untouched, then took a few bites and walked up and down an hour in his room, stopping from time to time and closing his eyes. Then he very slowly undressed and went to bed. He slept long and had curiously confused and ardent dreams.

It was broad day when he woke. Hastily he recalled where he was and got up to draw the curtains; the pale-blue sky, already with a hint of autumn, was streaked with frayed and tattered cloud; still, above his native city the sun was shining.

He spent more care than usual upon his toilette, washed and shaved and made himself fresh and immaculate as though about to call upon some smart family where a well-dressed and flawless appearance was *de rigueur*; and while occupied in this wise he listened to the anxious beating of his heart.

How bright it was outside! He would have liked better a twilight air like yesterday's, instead of passing through the streets in the broad sunlight, under everybody's eye. Would he meet people he knew, be stopped and questioned and have to submit to be asked how he had spent the last thirteen years? No, thank goodness, he was known to nobody here; even if anybody recognized him, it was unlikely he would be recognized – for certainly he had changed in the meantime! He surveyed himself in the glass and felt a sudden sense of security behind his mask, behind his work-worn face, that was older than his years . . . He sent for breakfast, and after that he went out; he passed under the disdainful eye of the porter and the gentleman in black, through the vestibule and between the two lions, and so into the street.

Where was he going? He scarcely knew. It was the same as yesterday. Hardly was he in the midst of this long-familiar scene, this stately conglomeration of gables, turrets, arcades, and fountains, hardly did he feel once more the wind in his face, that strong current wafting a faint and pungent aroma from far-off dreams, than the same mistiness laid itself like a veil about his senses . . . The muscles of his face relazed, and he looked at men and things with a look grown suddenly calm. Perhaps right there, on that street corner, he might wake up after all . . .

Where was he going? It seemed to him the direction he took had a connexion with his sad and strangely rueful dreams of the night . . . He went to Market Square, under the vaulted arches of the Rathaus, where the butchers were weighing out their wares red-handed, where the tall old Gothic fountain stood with its manifold spires. He paused in front of a house, a plain narrow building, like many another, with a fretted baroque gable; stood there lost in contemplation. He read the plate on the door, his eyes rested a little while on each of the windows. Then slowly he turned away.

Where did he go? Towards home. But he took a roundabout way outside the walls – for he had plenty of time. He went over the Millwall and over the Holstenwall, clutching his hat, for the wind was rushing and moaning through the trees. He left the wall near the station, where he saw a train puffing busily past, idly counted the coaches, and looked after the man who sat perched upon the last. In the Lindenplatz he stopped at one of the pretty villas, peered long into the garden and up at the windows, lastly conceived the idea of swinging the gate to and fro upon its hinges till it creaked. Then he looked awhile at his moist, rust-stained hand and went on, went through the squat old gate, along the harbour, and up the steep, windy street to his parents' house.

It stood aloof from its neighbours, its gable towering above them; grey and sombre, as it had stood these three hundred years; and Tonio Kröger read the pious, half-illegible motto above the entrance. Then he drew a long breath and went in.

His heart gave a throb of fear, lest his father might come out of one of the doors on the ground floor, in his office coat, with the pen behind his ear, and take him to task for his excesses. He would have found the reproach quite in order; but he got past unchidden. The inner door was ajar, which appeared to him reprehensible though at the same time he felt as one does in certain broken dreams, where obstacles melt away of themselves, and one presses onward in marvellous favour with fortune. The wide entry, paved with great square flags, echoed to his tread. Opposite the silent kitchen was the curious projecting structure, of rough boards, but cleanly vanished, that had been the servants' quarters. It was quite high up and could only be reached by a sort of ladder from the entry. But the great cupboards and carven presses were gone. The son of the house climbed the majestic staircase, with his hand on the white-enamelled, fret-work balustrade. At each step he lifted his hand, and put it down again with the next as though testing whether he could call back his ancient familiarity with the stout old railing . . . But at the landing of the entresol he stopped. For on the entrance door was a white plate; and on it in black letters he read: 'Public Library'.

'Public Library?' thought Tonio Kröger. What were either literature or the public doing here? He knocked . . . heard a 'Come in', and obeying it with gloomy suspense gazed upon a scene of most unhappy alteration.

The storey was three rooms deep, and all the doors stood open. The walls were covered nearly all the way up with long rows of books in uniform bindings, standing in dark-coloured bookcases. In each room a poor creature of a man sat writing behind a sort of counter. The farthest two just turned their heads, but the nearest got up in haste and, leaning with both hands on the table, stuck out his head, pursed his lips, lifted his brows, and looked at the visitor with eagerly blinking eyes.

'I beg pardon,' said Tonio Kröger without turning his eyes from the bookshelves. 'I am a stranger here, seeing the sights. So this is your Public Library? May I examine your collection a little?'

'Certainly, with pleasure,' said the official, blinking still more violently. 'It is open to everybody . . . Pray look about you. Should you care for a catalogue?'

'No, thanks,' answered Tonio Kröger, 'I shall soon find my way about.' And he began to move slowly along the walls, with the appearance of studying the rows of books. After a while he took down a volume, opened it, and posted himself at the window.

This was the breakfast-room. They had eaten here in the morning instead of in the big dining-room upstairs, with its white statues of gods and goddesses standing out against the blue walls . . . Beyond there had been a bedroom, where his father's mother had died – only after a long struggle, old as she was, for she had been of a pleasure-loving nature and clung to life. And his father too had drawn his last breath in the same room: that tall, correct, slightly melancholy and pensive gentleman with the wild flower in his buttonhole . . . Tonio had sat at the foot of his death-bed, quite given over to unutterable feelings of love and grief. His mother had knelt at the bedside, his lovely, fiery mother, dissolved in hot tears; and after that she had withdrawn with her artist into the far blue south . . . And beyond still, the small third room, likewise full of books and presided over by a shabby man – that had been for years on end his own. Thither he had come after school and a walk – like today's; against that wall his table had stood with the drawer where he kept his first clumsy heart-felt attempts at verse . . . The walnut tree . . . a pang went through him. He gave a sideways glance out at the window. The garden lay desolate, but there stood the old walnut tree where it used to stand, groaning and creaking heavily in the wind. And Tonio Kröger let his gaze fall upon the book he had in his hands, an excellent piece of work, and very familiar. He followed the black lines of print, the paragraphs, the flow of words that flowed with so much art, mounting in the ardour of creation to a certain climax and effect and then as artfully breaking off . . .

'Yes, that was well done,' he said; put back the book and turned away. Then he saw that the functionary still stood bolt-upright, blinking with a mingled expression of zeal and misgiving.

'A capital collection, I see,' said Tonio Kröger. 'I have already quite a good idea of it. Much obliged to you. Good-bye.' He went out; but it was a poor exit, and he felt sure the official would stand there perturbed and blinking for several minutes.

He felt no desire for further researches. He had been home. Strangers were living upstairs in the large rooms behind the pillared hall; the top of the stairs was shut off by a glass door which used not to be there, and on the door was a plate. He went away, down the steps, across the echoing corridor, and left his parental home. He sought a restaurant, sat down in a corner, and brooded over a heavy, greasy meal. Then he returned to his hotel.

'I am leaving,' he said to the fine gentleman in black. 'This afternoon.' And he asked for his bill, and for a carriage to take him down to the harbour where he should take the boat for Copenhagen. Then he went up to his room and sat there stiff and still, with his cheek on his hand, looking down on the table before him with absent eyes. Later he paid his bill and packed his things. At the appointed hour the carriage was announced and Tonio Kröger went down in travel array.

At the foot of the stairs the gentleman in black was waiting.

'Beg pardon,' he said, shoving back his cuffs with his little fingers . . . 'Beg pardon, but we must detain you just a moment, Herr Seehaase, the proprietor, would like to exchange two words with you. A matter of form . . . He is back there . . . If you will have the goodness to step this way . . . It is only Herr Seehaase, the proprietor.'

And he ushered Tonio Kröger into the background of the vestibule . . . There, in fact, stood Herr Seehaase. Tonio Kröger recognized him from old time. He was small, fat, and bow-legged. His shaven side-whisker was white, but he wore the same old low-cut dress coat and little velvet cap embroidered in green. He was not alone. Beside him, at a little high desk fastened into the wall, stood a policeman in a helmet, his gloved right hand resting on a document in coloured inks; he turned towards Tonio Kröger with his honest, soldierly face as though he expected Tonio to sink into the earth at his glance.

Tonio Kröger looked at the two and confined himself to waiting.

'You came from Munich?' the policeman asked at length in a heavy, good-natured voice.

Tonio Kröger said he had.

'You are going to Copenhagen?'

'Yes, I am on the way to a Danish seashore resort.'

'Seashore resort? Well, you must produce your papers,' said the policeman. He uttered the last word with great satisfaction.

'Papers . . . ?' He had no papers. He drew out his pocketbook and looked into it; but aside from notes there was nothing there but some proof-sheets of a story which he had taken along to finish reading. He hated relations with officials and had never got himself a passport . . .

'I am sorry,' he said, 'but I don't travel with papers.'

'Ah!' said the policeman. 'And what might be your name?'

Tonio replied.

'Is that a fact?' asked the policeman, suddenly erect, and expanding his nostrils as wide as he could . . .

'Yes, that is a fact,' answered Tonio Kröger.

'And what are you, anyhow?'

Tonio Kröger gulped and gave the name of his trade in a firm voice. Herr Seehaase lifted his head and looked him curiously in the face.

'H'm,' said the policeman. 'And you give out that you are not identical with an individdle named' – he said 'individdle' and then, referring to his document in coloured inks, spelled out an involved, fantastic name which mingled all the sounds of all the races – Tonio Kröger forgot it next minute –

'of unknown parentage and unspecified means,' he went on, 'wanted by the Munich police for various shady transactions, and probably in flight towards Denmark?'

'Yes, I give out all that, and more,' said Tonio Kröger, wriggling his shoulders. The gesture made a certain impression.

'What? Oh, yes, of course,' said the policeman. 'You say you can't show any papers –'

Herr Seehaase threw himself into the breach.

'It is only a formality,' he said pacifically, 'nothing else. You must bear in mind the official is only doing his duty. If you could only identify yourself somehow – some document...'

They were all silent. Should he make an end of the business by revealing to Herr Seehaase that he was no swindler without specified means, no gypsy in a green wagon, but the son of the late Consul Kröger, a member of the Kröger family? No, he felt no desire to do that. After all, were not these guardians of civic order within their right? He even agreed with them – up to a point. He shrugged his shoulders and kept quiet.

'What have you got, then?' asked the policeman. 'In your portfoly, I mean?'

'Here? Nothing. Just a proof-sheet,' answered Tonio Kröger.

'Proof-sheet? What's that? Let's see it.'

And Tonio Kröger handed over his work. The policeman spread it out on the shelf and began reading. Herr Seehaase drew up and shared it with him. Tonio Kröger looked over their shoulders to see what they read. It was a good moment, a little effect he had worked out to a perfection. He had a sense of self-satisfaction.

'You see,' he said, 'there is my name. I wrote it, and it is going to be published, you understand.'

'All right, that will answer,' said Herr Seehaase with decision, gathered up the sheets and gave them back. 'That will have to answer, Petersen,' he repeated crisply, shutting his eyes and shaking his head as though to see and hear no more. 'We must not keep the gentleman any longer. The carriage is waiting. I implore you to pardon the little inconvenience, sir. The officer has only done his duty, but I told him at once he was on the wrong track...'

'Indeed!' thought Tonio Kröger.

The officer seemed still to have his doubts; he muttered something else about individdle and document. But Herr Seehaase, overflowing with regrets, led his guest through the vestibule, accompanied him past the two lions to the carriage, and himself, with many respectful bows, closed the door upon him. And then the funny, high, wide old cab rolled and rattled and bumped down the steep, narrow street to the quay.

And such was the manner of Tonio Kröger's visit to his ancestral home.

Night fell and the moon swam up with silver gleam as Tonio Kröger's boat reached the open sea. He stood at the prow wrapped in his cloak against a mounting wind, and looked beneath into the dark going and coming of the waves as they hovered and swayed and came on, to meet with a clap and shoot erratically away in a bright gush of foam.

He was lulled in a mood of still enchantment. The episode at the hotel, their wanting to arrest him for a swindler in his own home, had cast him down a little, even although he found it quite in order – in a certain way. But after he came on board he had watched, as he used to do as a boy with his father, the lading of goods into the deep bowels of the boat, amid shouts of mingled Danish and Plattdeutsch; not only boxes and bales, but also a Bengal tiger and a polar bear were lowered in cages with stout iron bars. They had probably come from Hamburg and were destined for a Danish menagerie. He had enjoyed these distractions. And as the boat glided along between flat river-banks he quite forgot Officer Petersen's inquisition; while all the rest – his sweet, sad, rueful dreams of the night before, the walk he had taken, the walnut tree – had welled up again in his soul. The sea opened out and he saw in the distance the beach where he as a lad had been let listen to the ocean's summer dreams; saw the flashing of the lighthouse tower and the lights of the Kurhaus where he and his parents had lived . . . The Baltic! He bent his head to the strong salt wind; it came sweeping on, it enfolded him, made him faintly giddy and a little deaf; and in that mild confusion of the senses all memory of evil, of anguish and error, effort and exertion of the will, sank away into joyous oblivion and were gone. The roaring, foaming, flapping, and slapping all about him came to his ears like the groan and rustle of an old walnut tree, the creaking of a garden gate . . . More and more the darkness came on.

'The stars! Oh, by the Lord, look at the stars!' a voice suddenly said, with a heavy sing-song accent that seemed to come out of the inside of a tun. He recognized it. It belonged to a young man with red-blond hair who had been Tonio Kröger's neighbour at dinner in the salon. His dress was very simple, his eyes were red, and he had the moist and chilly look of a person who has just bathed. With nervous and self-conscious movements he had taken unto himself an astonishing quantity of lobster omelet. Now he leaned on the rail beside Tonio Kröger and looked up at the skies, holding his chin between thumb and forefinger. Beyond a doubt he was in one of those rare and festal and edifying moods that cause the barriers between man and man to fall; when the heart opens even to the stranger, and the mouth utters that which otherwise it would blush to speak . . .

'Look, by dear sir, just look at the stars. There they stahd and glitter; by goodness, the whole sky is full of theb! And I ask you, when you stahd ahd look up at theb, ahd realize that bany of theb are a huddred tibes larger thad the earth, how does it bake you feel? Yes, we have idvehted the telegraph and the telephode and all the triuphs of our bodern tibes. But whed we look up there, after all we have to recogdize and uhderstad that we are worbs, biserable worbs, ahd dothing else. Ab I right, sir, or ab I wrog? Yes, we are worbs,' he answered himself and nodded meekly and abjectly in the direction of the firmament.

'Ah, no, he has no literature in his belly,' thought Tonio Kröger. And he recalled something he had lately read, an essay by a famous French writer on cosmological and psychological philosophies, a very delightful *causerie*.

He made some sort of reply to the young man's feeling remarks, and they went on talking, leaning over the rail, and looking into the night with its movement and fitful lights. The young man, it seemed, was a Hamburg merchant on his holiday.

'Y'ought to travel to Copedhagen on the boat, thigks I, and so here I ab, and so far it's been fide. But they shouldn't have given us the lobster obelet, sir, for it's going to be storby – the captain said so hibself – and that's do joke with indigestible food like that in your stobach . . .'

Tonio Kröger listened to all this engaging artlessness and was privately drawn to it.

'Yes,' he said, 'all the food up here is too heavy. It makes one lazy and melancholy.'

'Belancholy?' repeated the young man, and looked at him, taken aback. Then he asked, suddenly: 'You are a stradger up here, sir?'

'Yes, I come from a long way off,' answered Tonio Kröger vaguely, waving his arm.

'But you're right,' said the youth; 'Lord, kdows you are right about the belancholy. I am dearly always belancholy, but specially on evedings like this when there are stars in the sky.' And he supported his chin again with thumb and forefinger.

'Surely this man writes verses,' thought Tonio Kröger; 'business man's verses, full of deep feeling and single-mindedness.'

Evening drew on. The wind had grown so violent as to prevent them from talking. So they thought they would sleep a bit, and wished each other good night.

Tonio Kröger stretched himself out on the narrow cabin bed, but he found no repose. The strong wind with its sharp tang had power to rouse him; he was strangely restless with sweet anticipations. Also he was violently sick with the motion of the ship as she glided down a steep mountain of wave and her screw vibrated as in agony, free of the water. He put on all his clothes again and went up to the deck.

Clouds raced across the moon. The sea danced. It did not come on in full-bodied, regular waves; but far out in the pale and flickering light the water was lashed, torn, and tumbled; leaped upwards like great licking flames; hung in jagged and fantastic shapes above dizzy abysses, where the foam seemed to be tossed by the playful strength of colossal arms and flung upward in all directions. The ship had a heavy passage; she lurched and stamped and groaned through the welter; and far down in her bowels the tiger and the polar bear voiced their acute discomfort. A man in an oilskin, with the hood drawn over his head and a lantern strapped to his chest, went straddling painfully up and down the deck. And at the stern, leaning far out, stood the young man from Hamburg suffering the worst. 'Lord!' he said, in a hollow, quavering voice, when he saw Tonio Kröger. 'Look at the uproar of the elebents, sir!' But he could say no more – he was obliged to turn hastily away.

Tonio Kröger clutched at a taut rope and looked abroad into the arrogance of the elements. His exultation outvied storm and wave; within himself he chanted a song to the sea, instinct with love of her: 'O thou wild friend of my youth. Once more I behold thee –' But it got no further, he did not finish it. It was not fated to receive a final form or in tranquillity to be welded to a perfect whole. For his heart was too full . . .

Long he stood; then stretched himself out on a bench by the pilot-house and looked up at the sky, where stars were flickering. He even slept a little. And when the cold foam splashed his face it seemed in his half-dreams like a caress.

Perpendicular chalk-cliffs, ghostly in the moonlight, came in sight. They were nearing the island of Möen. Then sleep came again, broken by salty showers of spray that bit into his face and made it stiff . . . When he really roused, it was broad day, fresh and palest grey, and the sea had gone down. At breakfast he saw the young man from Hambug again, who blushed rosy-red for shame of the poetic indiscretions he had been betrayed into by the dark, ruffled up his little red-blond moustache with all five fingers, and called out a brisk and soldierly good morning – after that he studiously avoided him.

And Tonio Kröger landed in Denmark. He arrived in Copenhagen, gave tips to everybody who laid claim to them, took a room at a hotel, and roamed the city for three days with an open guide-book and the air of an intelligent foreigner bent on improving his mind. He looked at the king's New Market and the 'Horse' in the middle of it, gazed respectfully up the columns of the Frauenkirch, stood long before Thorwaldsen's noble and beautiful statuary, climbed the round tower, visited castles, and spent two lively evenings in the Tivoli. But all this was not exactly what he saw.

The doors of the houses – so like those in his native town, with open-work gables of baroque shape – bore names known to him of old; names that had a tender and precious quality, and withal in their syllables an accent of plaintive reproach, of repining after the lost and gone. He walked, he gazed, drawing deep, lingering draughts of moist sea air; and everywhere he saw eyes as blue, hair as blond, faces as familiar, as those that had visited his rueful dreams the night he had spent in his native town. There in the open street it befell him that a glance, a ringing word, a sudden laugh would pierce him to his marrow.

He could not stand the bustling city for long. A restlessness, half memory and half hope, half foolish and half sweet, possessed him; he was moved to drop this role of ardently inquiring tourist and lie somewhere, quite quietly, on a beach. So he took ship once more and travelled under a cloudy sky, over a black water, northwards along the coast of Seeland towards Helsingör. Thence he drove, at once, by carriage, for three-quarters of an hour, along and above the sea, reaching at length his ultimate goal, the little white 'bath-hotel' with green blinds. It stood surrounded by a settlement of cottages, and its shingled turret tower looked out on the beach and the Swedish coast. Here he left the carriage, took possession of the light room they had ready for him, filled shelves and presses with his kit, and prepared to stop awhile.

It was well on in September; not many guests were left in Aalsgaard. Meals were served on the ground floor, in the great beamed dining-room, whose lofty windows led out upon the veranda and the sea. The landlady presided, an elderly spinster with white hair and faded eyes, a faint colour in her cheek and a feeble twittering voice. She was forever arranging her red hands to look well upon the table-cloth. There was a short-necked old gentleman, quite blue in the face, with a grey sailor beard; a fish-dealer he was, from the capital, and strong at the German. He seemed entirely congested and inclined to apoplexy; breathed in short gasps, kept putting his beringed first finger to one nostril, and snorting violently to get a passage of air through the other. Notwithstanding, he addressed himself constantly to the whisky bottle, which stood at his place at luncheon and dinner, and breakfast as well. Besides him the company consisted only of three tall American youths with their governor or tutor, who kept adjusting his glasses in unbroken silence. All day long he played football with his charges, who had narrow, taciturn faces and reddish-yellow hair parted in the middle. 'Please pass the *wurst*,' said one. 'That's not *wurst*, it's *schinken*,' said the other, and this was the extent of their conversation, as the rest of the time they sat there dumb, drinking hot water.

Tonio Kröger could have wished himself no better table-companions. He revelled in the peace and quiet, listened to the Danish palatals, the clear and the clouded vowels in which the fish-dealer and the landlady desultorily conversed; modestly exchanged views with the fish-dealer on the state of the barometer, and then left the table to go through the veranda and on to the beach once more, where he had already spent long, long morning hours.

Sometimes it was still and summery there. The sea lay idle and smooth, in stripes of blue and russet and bottle-green, played all across with glittering silvery lights. The seaweed shrivelled in the sun and the jelly-fish lay steaming. There was a faintly stagnant smell and a whiff of tar from the fishing-boat against which Tonio Kröger leaned, so standing that he had before his eyes not the Swedish coast but the open horizon and in his face the pure, fresh breath of the softly breathing sea.

Then grey, stormy days would come. The waves lowered their heads like bulls and charged against the beach; they ran and ramped high up the sands and left them strewn with shining wet sea-grass, driftwood and mussels. All abroad beneath an overcast sky extended ranges of billows, and between them foaming valleys palely green; but above the spot where the sun hung behind the cloud a patch like white velvet lay on the sea.

Tonio Kröger stood wrapped in wind and tumult, sunk in the continual dull, drowsy uproar that he loved. When he turned away it seemed suddenly warm and silent all about him. But he was never unconscious of the sea at his back; it called, it lured, it beckoned him. And he smiled.

He went landward, by lonely meadow-paths, and was swallowed up in the beech-groves that clothed the rolling landscape near and far. Here he sat down on the moss against a tree, and gazed at the strip of water he could see between the trunks. Sometimes the sound of surf came on the wind – a noise like boards collapsing at a distance. And from the tree-tops over his head a cawing – hoarse, desolate, forlorn. He held a book on his knee, but did not read a line. He enjoyed profound forgetfulness, hovered disembodied above space and time; only now and again his heart would contract with a fugitive pain, a stab of longing and regret, into whose origin he was too lazy to inquire.

Thus passed some days. He could not have said how many and had no desire to know. But then came one on which something happened; happened while the sun stood in the sky and people were about; and Tonio Kröger, even, felt no vast surprise.

The very opening of the day had been rare and festal. Tonio Kröger woke early and suddenly from his sleep, with a vague and exquisite alarm; he seemed to be looking at a miracle, a magic illumination. His room had a glass door and balcony facing the sound; a thin white gauze curtain divided it into living- and sleeping-quarters, both hung with delicately tinted paper and furnished with an airy good taste that gave them a sunny and friendly look. But now to his sleep-drunken eyes it lay bathed in a serene and roseate light, an unearthly brightness that gilded walls and furniture and turned the gauze curtain to radiant pink cloud. Tonio Kröger did not at once understand. Not until he stood at the glass door and looked out did he realize that this was the sunrise.

For several days there had been clouds and rain; but now the sky was like a piece of pale-blue silk, spanned shimmering above sea and land, and shot with light from red and golden clouds. The sun's disk rose in spendour from a crisply glittering sea that seemed to quiver and burn beneath it. So began the day. In a joyous daze Tonio Kröger flung on his clothes, and breakfasting in the veranda before everybody else, swam from the little wooden bath-house some distance out into the sound, then walked for an hour along the beach. When he came back, several omnibuses were before the door, and from the dining-room he could see people in the parlour next door where the piano was, in the veranda, and on the terrace in front; quantities of people sitting at little tables enjoying beer and sandwiches amid lively discourse.

There were whole families, there were old and young, there were even a few children. At second breakfast – the table was heavily laden with cold viands, roast, pickled, and smoked – Tonio Kröger inquired what was going on. 'Guests,' said the fish-dealer. 'Tourists and ball-guests from Helsingör. Lord help us, we shall get no sleep this night! There will be dancing and music, and I fear me it will keep up till late. It is a family reunion, a sort of celebration and excursion combined; they all subscribe to it and take advantage of the good weather. They came by boat and bus and they are having breakfast. After that they go on with their drive but at night they will all come back for a dance here in the hall. Yes, damn it, you'll see we shan't get a wink of sleep.'

'Oh, it will be a pleasant change,' said Tonio Kröger.

After that there was nothing more said for some time. The landlady arranged her red fingers on the cloth, the fish-dealer blew through his nostril, the Americans drank hot water and made long faces. Then all at once a thing came to pass: *Hans Hansen and Ingeborg Holm walked through the room.*

Tonio Kröger, pleasantly fatigued after his swim and rapid walk, was leaning back in his chair and eating smoked salomn on toast; he sat facing the veranda and the ocean. All at once the door opened and the two entered hand-in-hand – calmly and unhurried. Ingeborg, blonde Inge, was dressed just as she used to be at Herr Knaak's dancing-class. The light flowered frock reached down to her ankles and it had a tulle fichu draped with a pointed opening that left her soft throat free. Her hat hung by its ribbons over her arm. She, perhaps, was a little more grown up than she used to be, and her wonderful plait of hair was wound round her head; but Hans Hansen was the same as ever. He wore his sailor overcoat with gilt buttons, and his wide blue sailor collar lay across his shoulders and back; the sailor cap with its short ribbons he was dangling carelessly in his hand. Ingeborg's narrow eyes were turned away; perhaps she felt shy before the company at table. But Hans Hansen turned his head straight towards them and measured one after another defiantly with his steel-blue eyes; challengingly, with a sort of contempt. He even dropped Ingeborg's hand and swung his cap harder than ever, to show what manner of man he was. Thus the two, against the silent, blue-dyed sea, measured the length of the room and passed through the opposite door into the parlour.

This was at half past eleven in the morning. While the guests of the house were still at table the company in the veranda broke up and went away by the side door. No one else came into the dining-room. The guests could hear them laughing and joking as they got into the omnibuses, which rumbled away one by one . . . 'So they are coming back?' asked Tonio Kröger.

'That they are,' said the fish-dealer. 'More's the pity. They have ordered music, let me tell you – and my room is right above the dining-room.'

'Oh, well, it's a pleasant change,' repeated Tonio Kröger. Then he got up and went away.

That day he spent as he had the others, on the beach and in the wood, holding a book on his knee and blinking in the sun. He had but one thought; they were coming back to have a dance in the hall, the fish-dealer had promised they would, and he did nothing but be glad of this, with a sweet and timorous gladness such as he had not felt through all these long dead years. Once he happened, by some chance association, to think of his friend Adalbert, the novelist, the man who had known what he wanted and betaken himself to the café to get away from the spring. Tonio Kröger shrugged his shoulders at the thought of him.

Luncheon was served earlier than usual, also supper, which they ate in the parlour because the dining-room was being got ready for the ball, and the whole house flung in disorder for the occasion. It grew dark; Tonio Kröger sitting in his room heard on the road and in the house the sounds of approaching festivity. The picnickers were coming back; from Helsingör, by bicycle and carriage, new guests were arriving; a fiddle and a nasal clarinet might be heard practising down in the dining-room. Everything promised a brilliant ball . . .

Now the little orchestra struck up a march; he could hear the notes, faint but lively. The dancing opened with a polonaise. Tonio Kröger sat for a while and listened. But when he heard the march-time go over into a waltz he got up and slipped noiselessly out of his room.

From his corridor it was possible to go by the side stairs to the side entrance of the hotel and thence to the veranda without passing through a room. He took this route, softly and stealthily as though on forbidden paths, feeling along through the dark, relentlessly drawn by this stupid jigging music, that now came up to him loud and clear.

The veranda was empty and dim, but the glass door stood open into the hall, where shone two large oil lamps, furnished with bright reflectors. Thither he stole on soft feet; and his skin prickled with the thievish pleasure of standing unseen in the dark and spying on the dancers there in the brightly lighted room. Quickly and eagerly he glanced about for the two whom he sought . . .

Even though the ball was only half an hour old, the merriment seemed in full swing; however, the guests had come hither already warm and merry, after a whole day of carefree, happy companionship. By bending forward a little, Tonio Kröger could see into the parlour from where he was. Several old gentlemen sat there smoking, drinking, and playing cards; others were with their wives on the plush-upholstered chairs in the foreground watching the dance. They sat with their knees apart and their hands resting on them, puffing out their cheeks with a prosperous air; the mothers, with bonnets perched on their parted hair, with their hands folded over their stomachs and their heads on one side, gazed into the whirl of dancers. A platform had been erected on the long side of the hall, and on it the musicians were doing their utmost. There was even a trumpet, that blew with a certain caution, as though afraid of its own voice, and yet after all kept breaking and cracking. Couples were dipping and circling about, others walked arm-in-arm up and down the room. No one wore ballroom clothes; they were dressed as for an outing in the summertime: the men in countrified suits which were obviously their Sunday wear: the girls in light-coloured frocks with bunches of field-flowers in their bodices. Even a few children were there, dancing with each other in their own way, even after the music stopped. There was a long-legged man in a coat with a little swallow-tail, a provincial lion with an eye-glass and frizzed hair, a post-office clerk or some such thing; he was like a comic figure stepped bodily out of a Danish novel; and he seemed to be the leader and manager of the ball. He was everywhere at once, bustling, perspiring, officious, utterly absorbed; setting down his feet in shiny, pointed, military half-boots, in a very artificial and involved manner, toes first; waving his arms to issue an order, clapping his hands for the music to begin; here, there, and everywhere, and glancing over his shoulder in pride at his great bow of office, the streamers of which fluttered grandly in his rear.

Yes, there they were, those two, who had gone by Tonio Kröger in the broad light of day; he saw them again – with a joyful start he recognized them almost at the same moment. Here was Hans Hansen by the door, quite close; his legs apart, a little bent over, he was eating with circumspection a large piece of sponge-cake, holding his hand cupwise under his chin to catch the crumbs. And there by the wall sat Ingeborg Holm, Inge the fair; the post-office clerk was just mincing up to her with an exaggerated bow and asking her to dance. He laid one hand on his back and gracefully shoved the other into her bosom. But she was shaking her head in token that she was a little out of breath and must rest awhile, whereat the post-office clerk sat down by her side.

Tonio Kröger looked at them both, these two for whom he had in the past suffered love – at Hans and Ingeborg. They were Hans and Ingeborg not so much by virtue of individual traits and similarity of costume as by similarity of race and type. This was the blond, fair-haired breed of the steel-blue eyes, which stood to him for the pure, the blithe, the untroubled in life; for a virginal aloofness that was at once both simple and full of pride . . . He looked at them. Hans Hansen was standing there in his sailor suit, lively and well built as ever, broad in the shoulders and narrow in the hips; Ingeborg was laughing and tossing her head in a certain high-spirited way she had; she carried her hand, a schoolgirl hand, not at all slender, not at all particularly aristocratic, to the back of her head in a certain manner so that the thin sleeve fell away from her elbow – and suddenly such a pang of home-sickness shook his breast that involuntarily he drew farther back into the darkness lest someone might see his features twitch.

'Had I forgotten you?' he asked. 'No, never. Not thee, Hans, not thee, Inge the fair! It was always you I worked for; when I heard applause I always stole a look to see if you were there . . . Did you read *Don Carlos*, Hans Hansen, as you promised me at the garden gate? No, don't read it! I do not ask it any more. What have you to do with a king who weeps for loneliness? You must not cloud your clear eyes or make them dreamy and dim by peering into melancholy poetry . . . To be like you! To begin again, to grow up like you, regular like you, simple and normal and cheerful, in conformity and understanding with God and man, beloved of the innocent and happy. To take you, Ingeborg Holm, to wife, and have a son like you, Hans Hansen – to live free from the curse of knowledge and the torment of creation, live and praise God in blessed mediocrity! Begin again? But it would do no good. It would turn out the same – everything would turn out the same as it did before. For some go of necessity astray, because for them there is no such thing as a right path.'

The music ceased; there was a pause in which refreshments were handed round. The post-office assistant tripped about in person with a trayful of herring salad and served the ladies; but before Ingeborg Holm he even went down on one knee as he passed her the dish, and she blushed for pleasure.

But now those within began to be aware of a spectator behind the glass door; some of the flushed and pretty faces turned to measure him with hostile glances; but he stood his ground. Ingeborg and Hans looked at him too, at almost the same time, both with that utter indifference in their eyes that looks so like contempt. And he was conscience, too, of a gaze resting on him from a different quarter; turned his head and met with his own the eyes that had sought him out. A girl stood not far off, with a fine, pale little face – he had already noticed her. She had not danced much, she had few partners, and he had seen her sitting there against the wall, her lip closed in a bitter line. She was standing alone now too; her dress was a thin light stuff, like the others, but beneath the transparent frock her shoulders showed angular and poor, and the thin neck was thrust down so deep between those meagre shoulders that as she stood there motionless she might almost be thought a little deformed. She was holding her hands in their thin mitts across her flat breast, with the finger-tips touching; her head was dropped, yet she was looking up at Tonio Kröger with black swimming eyes. He turned away . . .

Here, quite close to him, were Ingeborg and Hans. He had sat down beside her – she was perhaps his sister – and they ate and drank together surrounded by other rosy-cheeked folk; they chattered and made merry, called to each other in ringing voices, and laughed aloud. Why could he not go up and speak to them? Make some trivial remark to him or her, to which they might at least answer with a smile? It would make him happy – he longed to do it; he would go back more satisfied to his room if he might feel he had established a little contact with them. He thought out what he might say; but he had not the courage to say it. Yes, this too was just as it had been: they would not understand him, they would listen like strangers to anything he was able to say. For their speech was not his speech.

It seemed the dance was about to begin again. The leader developed a comprehensive activity. He dashed hither and thither, adjuring everybody to get partners; helped the waiters to push chairs and glasses out of the way, gave orders to the musicians, even took some awkward people by the shoulders and shoved them aside . . . What was coming? They formed squares of four couples each . . . A frightful memory brought the colour to Tonio Kröger's cheeks. They were forming for a quadrille.

The music struck up, the couples bowed and crossed over. The leader called off; he called off – Heaven save us – in French! And pronounced the nasals with great distinction. Ingeborg Holm danced close by, in the set nearest the glass door. She moved to and fro before him, forwards and back, pacing and turning; he caught a waft from her hair or the thin stuff of her frock and it made him close his eyes with the old, familiar feeling, the fragrance and bitter-sweet enchantment he had faintly felt in all these days, that now filled him utterly with irresistible sweetness. And what was the feeling? Longing, tenderness? Envy? Self-contempt? . . . *Moulinet des dames*. 'Did you laugh, Ingeborg the blonde, did you laugh at me when I disgraced myself by dancing the *moulinet*? And would you still laugh today even after I have become something like a famous man? Yes, that you would, and you would be right to laugh. Even if I in my own person had written the nine symphonies and *The World as Will and Idea* and painted the Last Judgement, you would still be eternally right to laugh . . .' As he looked at her he thought of a line of verse once so familiar to him, now long forgotten: 'I would sleep, but thou must dance.' How well he knew it, that melancholy northern mood it evoked – its heavy inarticulateness. To sleep . . . To long to be allowed to live the life of simple feeling, to rest sweetly and passively in feeling alone, without compulsion to act and achieve – and yet to be forced to dance, dance the cruel and perilous sword-dance of art; without even being allowed to forget the melancholy conflict within oneself; to be forced to dance, the while one loved . . .

A sudden wild extravagance had come over the scene. The sets had broken up, the quadrille was being succeeded by a galop, and all the couples were leaping and gliding about. They flew past Tonio Kröger to a maddeningly quick *tempo*, crossing, advancing, retreating, with quick, breathless laughter. A couple came rushing and circling towards Tonio Kröger; the girl had a pale, refined face and lean, high shoulders. Suddenly, directly in front of him, they tripped and slipped and stumbled ... The pale girl fell, so hard and violently it almost looked dangerous; and her partner with her. He must have hurt himself badly, for he quite forgot her, and, half rising, began to rub his knee and grimace; while she, quite dazed, it seemed, still lay on the floor. Then Tonio Kröger came forward, took her gently by the arms, and lifted her up. She looked dazed, bewildered, wretched; then suddenly her delicate face flushed pink.

'*Tak, O, mange tak!*' she said, and gazed up at him with dark, swimming eyes.

'You should not dance any more, Fräulein,' he said gently. Once more he looked round at *them*, at Ingeborg and Hans, and then he went out, left the ball and the veranda and returned to his own room.

He was exhausted with jealousy, worn out with the gaiety in which he had had no part. Just the same, just the same as it had always been. Always with burning cheeks he had stood in his dark corner and suffered for you, you blond, you living, you happy ones! And then quite simply gone away. Somebody *must* come now! Ingeborg *must* notice he had gone, must slip after him, lay a hand on his shoulder and say: 'Come back and be happy. I love you!' But she came not at all. No, such things did not happen. Yes, all was as it had been, and he too was happy, just as he had been. For his heart was alive. But between that past and this present what had happened to make him become that which he now was? Icy desolation, solitude: mind, and art, forsooth!

He undressed, lay down, put out the light. Two names he whispered into his pillow, the few chaste northern syllables that meant for him his true and native way of love, of longing and happiness; that meant to him life and home, meant simple and heartfelt feeling. He looked back on the years that had passed. He thought of the dreamy adventures of the senses, nerves, and mind in which he had been involved; saw himself eaten up with intellect and introspection, ravaged and paralysed by insight, half worn out by the fevers and frosts of creation, helpless and in anguish of conscience between two extremes, flung to and fro between austerity and lust; *raffiné*, impoverished, exhausted by frigid and artificially heightened ecstasies; erring, forsaken, martyred, and ill – and sobbed with nostalgia and remorse.

Here in his room it was still and dark. But from below life's lulling, trivial waltz-rhythm came faintly to his ears.

Tonio Kröger sat up in the north, composing his promised letter to his friend Lisabeta Ivanovna.

'Dear Lisabeta down there in Arcady, whither I shall shortly return,' he wrote: 'here is something like a letter but it will probably disappoint you, for I mean to keep it rather general. Not that I have nothing to tell; for indeed, in my way, I have had experiences; for instance, in my native town they were even going to arrest me ... but of that by word of mouth. Sometimes now I have days when I would rather state things in general terms than go on telling stories.

'You probably still remember, Lisabeta, that you called me a *bourgeois*, *a bourgeois manqué*? You called me that in an hour when, led on by other confessions I had previously let slip, I confessed to you my love of life, or what I call life. I ask myself if you were aware how very close you came to the truth, how much of my love of "life" is one and the same thing as my being a *bourgeois*. This journey of mine has given me much occasion to ponder the subject.

'My father, you know, had the temperament of the north: solid, reflective, puritanically correct, with a tendency to melancholia. My mother, of indeterminate foreign blood, was beautiful, sensuous, naïve, passionate and careless at once, and, I think, irregular by instinct. The mixture was no doubt extraordinary and bore with it extraordinary dangers. The issue of it, a *bourgeois* who strayed off into art, a bohemian who feels nostalgic yearnings for respectability, an artist with a bad conscience. For surely it is my *bourgeois* conscience makes me see in the artist life, in all irregularity and all genius, something profoundly suspect, profoundly disreputable; that fills me with this lovelorn *faiblesse* for the simple and good, the comfortably normal, the average unendowed respectable human being.

'I stand between two worlds. I am at home in neither, and I suffer in consequence. You artists call me a *bourgeois*, and the *bourgeois* try to arrest me . . . I don't know which makes me feel worse. The *bourgeois* are stupid; but you adorers of the beautiful, who call me phlegmatic and without aspirations, you ought to realize that there is a way of being an artist that goes so deep and is so much a matter of origins and destinies that no longing seems to it sweeter and more worth knowing than longing after the bliss of the commonplace.

'I admire those proud, cold beings who adventure upon the paths of great and daemonic beauty and despise "mankind"; but I do not envy them. For if anything is capable of making a poet of a literary man, it is my *bourgeois* love of the human, the living and usual. It is the source of all warmth, goodness, and humour; I even almost think it is itself that love of which it stands written that one may speak with the tongues of men and of angels and yet having it not is as sounding brass and tinkling cymbals.

'The work I have so far done is nothing or not much – as good as nothing. I will do better, Lisabeta – this is a promise. As I write, the sea whispers to me and I close my eyes. I am looking into a world unborn and formless, that needs to be ordered and shaped; I see into a whirl of shadows of human figures who beckon to me to weave spells to redeem them: tragic and laughable figures and some that are both together – and to these I am drawn. But my deepest and secretest love belongs to the blond and blue-eyed, the fair and the living, the happy, lovely, and commonplace.

'Do not chide this love, Lisabeta; it is good and fruitful. There is longing in it, and a gentle envy; a touch of contempt and no little innocent bliss.'

1903

Doctor Faustus

TRANSLATED FROM THE GERMAN BY

H.T. Lowe-Porter

Doctor Faustus

Lo *giorno se n'andava e l'aere bruno*
toglieva gli animai che sono in terra
dalle fatiche loro, ed io sol uno
m'apparecchiava a sostener la guerra
sì del cammino e sì della pietate,
che ritrarrà la mente que non erra.
O Muse, o alto ingegno, or m'aiutate,
o mente che scrivesti ciò ch'io vidi,
qui si parrà la tua nobilitate.
    'Dante: *Inferno*, Canto II'

Translator's Note

'Les traductions sont comme les femmes: lorsqu'elles sont belles, elles ne sont pas fidèles, et lorsqu'elles sont fidèles, elles ne sont pas belles.' From a more familiar source we are instructed that 'to have honesty coupled to beauty is to have honey a sauce to sugar'. And on the highest authority of all we know that the price of a virtuous woman, with no mention of other charm, is above rubies. All things considered, what remains to hope is only that the English version of *Doctor Faustus* here presented may at least not conjure up the picture of a femme ni belle ni fidèle.

It is to be feared. The author himself has feared it. I venture to quote on this point, lifting them from their context in the Epilogue, some words of the narrator, who here surely speaks for the author himself: 'In actual fact I have sometimes pondered ways and means of sending these pages to America, in order that they might first be laid before the public in an English translation ... True, there comes the thought of the essentially foreign impression my book must make in that cultural climate; and coupled with it the dismaying prospect that its translation into English must turn out, at least in some all too radically German parts, to be an impossibility.'

Grievous difficulties do indeed confront anyone essaying the role of copyist to this vast canvas, this cathedral of a book, this woven tapestry of symbolism. Translations deal with words; and in two fields at least the situation is unsatisfactory (I do not include in the list the extended musical discussion and critique, since music, and talk about it, uses an exact and international language). But dialect cannot be translated, it can only be got round by a sort of trickery which is usually unconvincing. Again, there are chapters resorting to archaic style and spelling. The English-speaking world boasts no Luther in the history of its language; and the vocabulary of Wycliffe, Tindale, Thomas More can scarcely evoke for us the emotions of the literate German in so far as these are summoned up by the very words themselves which Luther used. On the other hand this archaic style is employed only in a few chapters, as a device to suggest an element that is indicated by other means as well. And the final difficulty is hardly a linguistic one, but rather a matter of the 'cultural climate' of which the author speaks: that knotted and combined association, symbolism, biography, and autobiography which might make even German readers be glad of a key to unlock its uttermost treasure.

So, after all, these difficulties are seen to be a matter of degree. Against them, far outweighing them, is the fact that this *Monstrum aller Romane* is addressed not only to Germans, not only to Europeans, but equally to ourselves. All that our world has lived through in this past quarter-century has forced us to enter this climate and to recognize that these are our proper stresses. Readers of *Faustus* will and must be involved, with shudders, in all three strands of the book: the German scene from within and its broader, its universal origins; the depiction of an art not German alone but vital to our whole civilization; music as one instance of the arts and the state in which the arts find themselves today; and, finally, the invocation of the daemonic. It is necessary for us to read *Faustus*, even in a version which cannot lay claim to being beautiful, though in very intent it is deeply faithful.

The translator wishes to express warm and heartfelt thanks to the scholars who have been so helpful in certain chapters: especially to Dr Mosco Carner, conductor and musicologist, adviser to the Musical Staff of the B.B.C.; and Mr Graham Orton, of the University of Durham, England, who has been indefatigably resourceful and suggestive in the medieval portions. Other scholars in various fields, notably Professor R. D. Welch, head of the Music Department of Princeton University, and Mrs Welch, have helped the translator with comments and suggestions in ways too numerous to specify in detail. That they have done so is a tribute to the author of *Faustus*.

Chapter One

I wish to state quite definitely that it is by no means out of any wish to bring my own personality into the foreground that I preface with a few words about myself and my own affairs this report on the life of the departed Adrian Leverkühn. What I here set down is the first and assuredly very premature biography of that beloved fellow-creature and musician of genius, so afflicted by fate, lifted up so high, only to be so frightfully cast down. I intrude myself, of course, only in order that the reader – I might better say the future reader, for at this moment there exists not the smallest prospect that my manuscript will ever see the light unless, by some miracle, it were to leave our beleagured European fortress and bring to those without some breath of the secrets of our prison-house – to resume: only because I consider that future readers will wish to know who and what the author is do I preface these disclosures with a few notes about myself, indeed, my mind misgives me that I shall only be awakening the reader's doubt whether he is in the right hands: whether, I mean, my whole existence does not disqualify me for a task dictated by my heart rather than by any true competence for the work.

I read over the above lines and cannot help remarking in myself a certain discomfort, a physical oppression only too indicative of the state of mind in which I sit down today in my little study, mine these many years, at Freising on the Isar, on the the 27th of May, 1943, three years after Leverkühn's death (three years, that is, after he passed from deep night into the deepest night of all), to make a beginning at describing the life of my unhappy friend now resting – oh, may it be so – now resting in God. My words, I say, betray a state of mind in anguished conflict between a palpitating impulse to communicate and a profound distrust of my own adequacy. I am by nature wholly moderate, of a temper, I may say, both healthy and humane, addressed to reason and harmony; a scholar and *conjuratus* of the 'Latin host', not lacking all contact with the arts (I play the viola d'amore) but a son of the Muses in that academic sense which by preference regards itself as descended from the German humanists of the time of the 'Poets'.

Heir of a Reuchlin, a Crotus of Dornheim, of Mutianus and Eoban of Hesse, the daemonic, little as I presume to deny its influence upon human life, I have at all times found utterly foreign to my nature. Instinctively I have rejected it from my picture of the cosmos and never felt the slightest inclination rashly to open the door to the powers of darkness: arrogantly to challenge, or if they of themselves ventured from their side, even to hold out my little finger to them. To this attitude I have made my sacrifices, not only ideally but also to my practical disadvantage: I unhesitatingly resigned my beloved teaching profession, and that before the time when it became evident that it could not be reconciled with the spirit and claims of our historical development. In this respect I am content with myself. But my self-satisfaction or, if you prefer, my ethical narrow-mindedness can only strengthen my doubt whether I may feel myself truly called to my present task.

Indeed, I had scarcely set my pen in motion when there escaped it a word which privately gave me a certain embarrassment. I mean the word 'genius': I spoke of the musical genius of my departed friend. Now this word 'genius', although extreme in degree, certainly in kind has a noble, harmonious, and humane ring. The likes of me, however far from claiming for my own person a place in this lofty realm, or ever pretending to have been blest with the *divinis influxibus ex alto*, can see no reasonable ground for shrinking, no reason for not dealing with it in clear-eyed confidence. So it seems. And yet it cannot be denied (and has never been) that the daemonic and irrational have a disquieting share in this radiant sphere. We shudder as we realize that a connexion subsists between it and the nether world, and that the reassuring *epitheta* which I sought to apply: 'sane, noble, harmonious, humane', do not for that reason quite fit, even when – I force myself, however painfully, to make this distinction – even when they are applied to a pure and genuine, God-given, or shall I say God-inflicted genius, and not to an acquired kind, the sinful and morbid corruption of natural gifts, the issue of a horrible bargain ...

Here I break off, chagrined by a sense of my artistic short-comings and lack of self-control. Adrian himself could hardly – let us say in a symphony – have let such a theme appear so prematurely. At the most he would have allowed it to suggest itself afar off, in some subtly disguised, almost imperceptible way. Yet to the reader the words which escaped me may seem but a dark, distrustable suggestion, and to me alone like a rushing in where angels fear to tread. For a man like me it is very hard, it affects him almost like wanton folly, to assume the attitude of a creative artist to a subject which is dear to him as life and burns him to express; I know not how to treat it with the artist's easy mastery. Hence my too hasty entry into the distinction between pure and impure genius, a distinction the existence of which I recognize, only to ask myself at once whether it has a right to exist at all. Experience has forced me to ponder this problem so anxiously, so urgently, that at times, frightful to say, it has seemed to me that I should be driven beyond my proper and becoming level of thought, and myself experience an 'impure' heightening of my natural gifts.

Again I break off, in the realization that I came to speak of genius, and the fact that it is in any case daemonically influenced, only to air my doubt whether I possess the necessary affinity for my task. Against my conscientious scruples may the truth avail, which I always have to bring into the field against them, that it was vouchsafed me to spend many years of my life in close familiarity with a man of genius, the hero of these pages; to have known him since childhood, to have witnessed his growth and his destiny and shared in the modest role of adjuvant to his creative activity. The libretto from Shakespeare's comedy *Love's Labour's Lost*, Leverkühn's exuberant youthful composition, was my work; I also had something to do with the preparation of the texts for the grotesque opera suite *Gesta Romanorum* and the oratorio *The Revelation of St John the Divine*. And perhaps there was this, that, and the other besides. But also I am in possession of papers, priceless sketches, which in days when he was still in health, or if that is saying too much, then in comparatively and legally sound ones, the deceased made over to me, to me and to no other; on these I mean to base my account, yes, I intend to select and include some of them direct. But first and last –

and this justification was always the most valid, if not before men, then before God – I loved him, with tenderness and terror, with compassion and devoted admiration, and but little questioned whether he in the least returned my feeling.

That he never did – ah, no! In the note assigning his sketches and journals there is expressed a friendly, objective, I might almost say a gracious confidence, certainly honourable to me, a belief in my conscientiousness, loyalty, and scrupulous care. But love? Whom had this man loved? Once a woman, perhaps. A child, at the last, it may be. A charming trifler and winner of hearts, whom then, probably just because he inclined to him, he sent away – to his death. To whom had he opened his heart, whomever had he admitted into his life? With Adrian that did not happen. Human devotion he accepted, I would swear, often unconsciously. His indifference was so great that he was hardly ever aware what went on about him, what company he was in. The fact that he very seldom addressed by name the person he spoke with makes me conjecture that he did not know the name, though the man had every reason to suppose he did. I might compare his absentness to an abyss, into which one's feeling towards him dropped soundless and without a trace. All about him was coldness – and how do I feel, using this word, which he himself, in an uncanny connexion, once also set down? Life and experience can give to single syllables an accent utterly divorcing them from their common meaning and lending them an aura of horror, which nobody understands who has not learned them in that awful context.

Chapter Two

My name is Serenus Zeitblom, PH.D. I deplore the extraordinary delay in introducing myself, but the literary nature of my material has prevented me from coming to the point until now. My age is sixty, for I was born A.D. 1883, the eldest of four brothers and sisters, at Kaisersaschern on the Saale, in the district of Merseburg. In the same town it was that Leverkühn too spent his school-days; thus I can postpone a more detailed description until I come to them. Since altogether my personal life was very much interwoven with that of the Meister, it will be well to speak of them both together, to avoid the error of getting ahead of my story – which, when the heart is full, tends to be the case.

Only so much must be set down for the nonce, that it was in the modest rank of a semi-professional middle class that I came into the world. My father, Wohlgemut Zeitblom, was an apothecary, though the first in the town, for the other pharmacy in Kaisersaschern never enjoyed the same public confidence as the Zeitblom shop of the 'Blessed Messengers' and had at all times a hard struggle against it. Our family belonged to the small Catholic community of the town, the majority of its population of course being of the Lutheran confession. In particular my mother was a pious daughter of the Church, punctually fulfilling her religious duties, whereas my father, probably from lack of time, was laxer in them, without in the least denying his solidarity, which indeed had also its political bearing, with the community of his faith. It was remarkable that besides our priest Eccl Councillor Zwilling, the rabbi of the place, Dr Carlebach by name, used also to visit us in our home above the shop and laboratory, and that, in Protestant houses, would not have been easy. The man of the Roman Church made the better appearance. But I have retained the impression, based principally, I suppose, upon things my father said, that the little long-bearded, cap-wearing Talmudist far surpassed his colleague of another faith in learning and religious penetration. It may be the result of his youthful experience, but also because of the keen-scented receptivity of Jewish circles for Leverkühn's work; but I have never, precisely in the Jewish problem and the way it has been dealt with, been able to agree fully with our Führer and his paladins; and this fact was not without influence on my resignation from the teaching staff here. Certainly specimens of the race have also crossed my path – I need only think of the private scholar Breisacher in Munich, on whose dismayingly unsympathetic character I propose in the proper place to cast some light.

As for my Catholic origin, it did of course mould and influence my inner man. Yet that lifelong impress never resulted in any conflict with my humanistic attitude in general, my love of the 'liberal arts' as one used to call them. Between these two elements of my personality there reigned an unbroken harmony, such as is easily preserved if like me one has grown up within the frame of 'old-world' surroundings whose memories and monuments reach back into pre-schismatic times, back into a world of unity in Christ. True, Kaisersaschern lies in the midst of the native home of the Reformation, in the heart of Lutherland. It is the region of cities with the names of Eisleben, Wittenberg, Quedlinburg, likewise Grimma, Wolfenbüttel and Eisenach – all, again, rich with meaning for the inner life of the Lutheran Leverkühn and linked with the direction his studies originally took, the theological one. But I like to compare the Reformation to a bridge, which leads not only from scholastic times to our world of free thought, but also and equally back into the Middle Ages, or perhaps even further, as a Christian-Catholic tradition of a serene love of culture, untouched by churchly schism. For my part I feel very truly at home in that golden sphere where one called the Holy Virgin *Jovis alma parens*.

But to continue with the most indispensable facts in my *vita*: my parents allowed me to attend our gymnasium, the same school where, two forms below me, Adrian was taught. Founded in the second half of the fifteenth century, it had until very recently borne the name of 'School of the Brethren of the Common Life', finally changed out of embarrassment at the too historical and for the modern ear slightly comic sound of this name. They now called themselves after the neighbouring Church of St Boniface. When I left school, at the beginning of the present century, I turned without hesitation to the study of the classic tongues, in which the schoolboy had already shown a certain proficiency. I applied myself to them at the universities of Giessen, Jena, Leipzig and from 1904–6 at Halle, at the same time – and that not by chance – as Leverkühn also studied there.

Here, as so often, I cannot help dwelling on the inward, the almost mysterious connexion of the old philological interest with a lively and loving sense of the beauty and dignity of reason in the human being. The bond is expressed in the fact that we give to the study of the ancient tongues the name of the *humaniora*; the mental coordination of language and the passion for the humanities is crowned by the idea of education, and thus the election of a profession as the shaper of youth follows almost of itself out of having chosen philology as a study. The man of the sciences and practical affairs can of course be a teacher too; but never in the same sense or to the same extent as his fellow of the *bonae literae*. And that other, perhaps more intense, but strangely inarticulate language, that of tones – if one may so designate music – does not seem to me to be included in the pedagogic-humanistic sphere, although I well know that in Greek education and altogether in the public life of the *polis* it played an ancillary role. Rather, it seems to me, in all its supposedly logical and moral austerity, to belong to a world of the spirit for whose absolute reliability in the things of reason and human dignity I would not just care to put my hand in the fire. That I am even so heartily affected to it is one of those contradictions which, for better or worse, are inseparable from human nature.

This is a marginal note. And yet not so marginal; since it is very pertinent to my theme, indeed only too much so, to inquire whether a clear and certain line can be drawn between the noble pedagogic world of the mind and that world of the spirit which one approaches only at one's peril. What sphere of human endeavour, even the most unalloyed, the most dignified and benevolent, would be entirely inaccessible to the influence of the powers of the underworld, yes, one must add, quite independent of the need of fruitful contact with them? This thought, not unbecoming even in a man whose personal nature lies remote from everything daemonic, has remained to me from certain moments of that year and a half spent by me in visiting Italy and Greece, my good parents having made the journey possible after I had passed my state examinations. When from the Acropolis I looked down upon the Sacred Way on which the initiates marched, adorned with the saffron band, with the name of Iacchus on their lips; again, when I stood at the place of initiation itself, in the district of Eubulus at the edge of the Plutonian cleft overhung by rocks, I experienced by divination the rich feeling of life which expressed itself in the initiate veneration of Olympic Greece for the deities of the depths; often, later on, I explained to my pupils that culture is in very truth the pious and regulating, I might say propitiatory, entrance of the dark and uncanny into the service of the gods.

Returned from this journey, the twenty-five-year-old man found a position in the high school of his native town, where he had received his own education. There, for some years, I assumed by modest stages the teaching in Latin, Greek, and also history, until, that is, the twelfth year of the present century, at which time I entered the service of the Bavarian Department of Education and moved to Friesing. I took up my abode there as professor in the gymnasium and also as docent in the theological seminary, in the two fields, and for more than two decades enjoyed a satisfying activity.

Quite early, soon after my appointment at Kaisersaschern, I married: need for regularity and desire for a proper establishment in life led me to the step. Helene, born Oelhafen, my excellent wife, who still accompanies my declining years, was the daughter of an older colleague at Zwickau in Saxony. At the risk of making the reader smile I will confess that the Christian name of the budding girl, Helene, those beloved syllables, played not the least considerable role in my choice. Such a name means a consecration; to its pure enchantment one cannot fail to respond, even though the outward appearance of the bearer corresponds to its lofty claims only to a modest middle-class extent and even that but for a time, since the charms of youth are fleeting. And our daughter, who long since married a good man, manager at the Regensburg branch of the Bavarian Securities and Exchange Bank, we also called Helene. Besides her my dear wife presented me with two sons, so that I have enjoyed the due to humanity of the joys and sorrows of paternity, if within moderate limits. None of my children ever possessed a childhood loveliness even approaching that of little Nepomuk Schneidewein, Adrian's nephew and later idol – I myself would be the last to say so. Today my two sons serve their Führer, the one in civil life, the other with the armed forces; as my position of aloofness *vis-à-vis* the authorities of the Fatherland has made me somewhat isolated, the relations of these two young men with the quiet paternal home must be called anything but intimate.

Chapter Three

The Leverkühns came of a stock of superior hand-workers and small farmers, which flourished partly in the Schmalkalden region and partly in the province of Saxony, along the Saale. Adrian's own family had been settled for several generations at Buchel, a farm belonging to the village community of Oberweiler, near Weissenfels, whence one was fetched by wagon after a three-quarters-hour journey by train from Kaisersaschern. Buchel was a property of a size corresponding to the ownership of a team and cattle; it was a good fifty acres of meadow and ploughed land, with communal rights to the adjoining mixed woodland and a very comfortable wood and frame dwelling-house on a stone foundation. With the lofts and stalls it formed an open square in the centre of which stood a never-to-be forgotten ancient linden tree of a mighty growth. It had a circular green bench round it and in June it was covered with gloriously fragrant blossoms. The beautiful tree may have been a little in the way of the traffic in the courtyard: I have heard that each heir in turn in his young years, on practical grounds, always maintained against his father's veto that it ought to be cut down; only one day, having succeeded to the property, to protect it in the same way from his own son.

Very often must the linden tree have shaded the infant slumbers and childhood play of little Adrian, who was born, in the blossom-time of 1885, in the upper storey of the Buchel house, the second son of the Leverkühn pair, Jonathan and Elsbeth. His brother, George, now long since the master of Buchel, was five years his senior. A sister, Ursel, followed after an equal interval. My parents belonged to the circle of friends and acquaintances of the Leverkühns in Kaisersaschern and the two families had long been on particularly cordial terms. Thus we spent many a Sunday afternoon in the good time of year at the farm, where the town-dwellers gratefully partook of the good cheer of the countryside with which Frau Leverkühn regaled them: the grainy dark bread with fresh butter, the golden honey in the comb, the delicious strawberries in cream, the curds in blue bowls sprinkled with black breadcrumbs and sugar. In Adrian's early childhood – he was called Adri then – his grandparents sat with us still, though now retired, the business being entirely in the hands of the younger generation. The old man, while most respectfully listened to, took part only at the evening meal and argued with his toothless mouth. Of these earlier owners, who died at about this time, I have little memory. So much the more clearly stands before my eyes the picture of their children Jonathan and Elsbeth Leverkühn, although it too has seen its changes and in the course of my boyhood, my schoolboy, and my student years glided over, with that imperceptible effectiveness time knows so well, from the youthful phase into one marked by the passiveness of age.

Jonathan Leverkühn was a man of the best German type, such as one seldom sees now in our towns and cities, certainly not among those who today, often with blatant exaggeration, represent our German manhood. He had a cast of features stamped as if it were in an earlier age, stored up in the country and come down from the time before the Thirty Years War. That idea came into my head when as a growing lad I looked at him with eyes already halfway trained for seeing. Unkempt ash-blond hair fell on a domed brow strongly marked in two distinct parts, with prominent veins on the temples; hung unfashionably long and thick in his neck and round the small, well-shaped ears, to mingle with the curling blond beard that covered the chin and the hollow under the lip. This lower lip came out rather strong and full under the short, slightly drooping moustache, with a smile which made a most charming harmony with the blue eyes, a little severe, but a little smiling too, their gaze half absent and half shy. The bridge of the nose was thin and finely hooked, the unbearded part of the cheeks under the cheekbones shadowed and even rather gaunt. He wore his sinewy throat uncovered and had no love for 'city clothes', which did not suit his looks, particularly not his hands, those powerful, browned and parched, rather freckled hands, one of which grasped the crook of his stick when he went into the village to town meetings.

A physician might have ascribed the veiled effort in his gaze, a certain sensitiveness at the temples, to migraine; and Jonathan did in fact suffer from headaches, though moderately, not oftener than once a month and almost without hindrance to his work. He loved his pipe, a half-length porcelain one with a lid, whose odour of pipe tobacco, peculiar to itself and far pleasanter than the stale smoke of cigar or cigarette, pervaded the atmosphere of the lower rooms. He loved too as a night-cap a good mug of Merseburg beer. On winter evenings, when the land of his fathers lay under snow, you saw him reading, preferably in a bulky family Bible, bound in pressed pigskin and closed with leather clasps; it had been printed about 1700 under the ducal licence in Brunswick, and included not only the '*Geistreichen*' prefaces and marginal comments of Dr Martin Luther but also all sorts of summaries, *locos parallelos*, and historical-moralizing verses by a Herr David von Schweinitz explaining each chapter. There was a legend about this volume; or rather the definite information about it was handed down, that it had been the property of that Princess of Brunswick-Wolfenbüttel who married the son of Peter the Great. Afterwards they gave out that she had died, and her funeral took place, but actually she escaped to Martinique and there married a Frenchman. How often did Adrian, with his keen sense of the ridiculous, laugh with me later over this tale, which his father, lifting his head from his book, would relate with his mild, penetrating look and then, obviously unperturbed by the slightly scandalous provenance of the sacred text, return to the versified commentaries of Herr von Schweinitz or the 'Wisdom of Solomon to the Tyrants'.

But alongside the religious cast his reading took another direction, which in certain times would have been characterized as wanting to 'speculate the elements'. In other words, to a limited extent and with limited means, he carried on studies in natural science, biology, even perhaps in chemistry and physics, helped out occasionally by my father with material from our laboratory. But I have chosen that antiquated and not irreproachable description for such practices because a tinge of mysticism was perceptible in them, which would once have been suspect as a leaning to the black arts. But I will add, too, that I have never misunderstood this distrust felt by a religious and spiritual-minded epoch for the rising passion to investigate the mysteries of nature. Godly fear must see in it a libertine traffic with forbidden things, despite the obvious contradiction involved in regarding the Creation, God, Nature and Life as a morally depraved field. Nature itself is too full of obscure phenomena not altogether remote from magic – equivocal moods, weird, half-hidden associations pointing to the unknown – for a disciplined piety not to see therein a rash overstepping of ordained limits.

When Adrian's father opened certain books with illustrations in colour of exotic lepidoptera and sea creatures, we looked at them, his sons and I, Frau Leverkühn as well, over the back of his leather-cushioned chair with the ear-rests; and he pointed with his forefinger at the freaks and fascinations there displayed in all the colours of the spectrum, from dark to light, mustered and modelled with the highest technical skill: genus Papilio and genus Morpho, tropical insects which enjoyed a brief existence in fantastically exaggerated beauty, some of them regarded by the natives as evil spirits bringing malaria. The most splendid colour they displayed, a dreamlike lovely azure, was, so Jonathan instructed us, no true colour at all, but produced by fine little furrows and other surface configurations of the scales on their wings, a miniature construction resulting from artificial refraction of the light rays and exclusion of most of them so that only the purest blue light reached the eyes.

'Just think,' I can still hear Frau Leverkühn say, 'so it is all a cheat?'

'Do you call the blue sky a cheat?' answered her husband looking up backwards at her. 'You cannot tell me the pigment it comes from.'

I seem as I write to be standing with Frau Elsbeth, George, and Adrian behind their father's chair, following his finger across the pictured pages. Clearwings were there depicted which had no scales on their wings, so that they seemed delicately glassy and only shot through with a net of dark veins. One such butterfly, in transparent nudity, loving the duskiness of heavy leafage, was called *Hetaera esmeralda*. Hetaera had on her wings only a dark spot of violet and rose; one could see nothing else of her, and when she flew she was like a petal blown by the wind. Then there was the leaf butterfly, whose wings on top are a triple chord of colour, while underneath with insane exactitude they resemble a leaf, not only in shape and veining but in the minute reproduction of small imperfections, imitation drops of water, little warts and fungus growths and more of the like. When this clever creature alights among the leaves and folds its wings, it disappears by adaptation so entirely that the hungriest enemy cannot make it out.

Not without success did Jonathan seek to communicate to us his delight in this protective imitation that went so far as to copy blemishes. 'How has the creature done it?' he would ask. 'How does Nature do it through the creature? For one cannot ascribe the trick to its own observation and calculation. Yes, yes, Nature knows her leaf precisely: knows not only its perfection but also its small usual blunders and blemishes; mischieviously or benevolently she repeats its outward appearance in another sphere, on the under side of this her butterfly, to baffle others of her creatures. But why is it just this one that profits by the cunning? And if it is actually on purpose that when resting it looks just like a leaf, what is the advantage, looked at from the point of view of its hungry pursuers, the lizards, birds, and spiders, for which surely it is meant for food? Yet when it so wills, however keen their sight they cannot make it out. I am asking that in order that you may not ask me.'

This butterfly, then, protected itself by becoming invisible. But one only needed to look further on in the book to find others which attained the same end by being strikingly, far-reachingly visible. Not only were they exceptionally large but also coloured and patterned with unusual gorgeousness; and Father Leverkühn told us that in this apparently challenging garb they flew about in perfect security. You could not call them cheeky, there was something almost pathetic about them; for they never hid, yet never an animal – not ape or bird or lizard – turned its head to look at them. Why? Because they were revolting. And because they advertised the fact by their striking beauty and the sluggishness of their flight. Their secretions were so foul to taste and smell that if ever any creature mistakenly thought one of them would do him good he soon spat it out with every sign of disgust. But all nature knows they are inedible, so they are safe – tragically safe. We at least, behind Jonathan's chair, asked ourselves whether this security had not something disgraceful about it, rather than being a cause for rejoicing. And what was the consequence? That other kinds of butterfly tricked themselves out in the same forbidding splendour and flew with the same heavy flight, untouchable although perfectly edible.

I was infected by Adrian's mirth over this information; he laughed till he shook his sides, and tears squeezed out of his eyes, and I had to laugh too, right heartily. But Father Leverkühn hushed us; he wished all these matters to be regarded with reverence, the same awe and sense of mystery with which he looked at the unreadable writing on the shells of certain mussels, taking his great square reading-glass to help him and letting us try too. Certainly the look of these creatures, the sea-snails and salt-water mussels, was equally remarkable, at least when one looked at their pictures under Jonathan's guidance. All these windings and vaultings, executed in splendid perfection, with a sense of form as bold as it was delicate, these rosy openings, these iridescent faience splendours – all these were the work of their own jelly-like proprietors. At least on the theory that Nature makes itself, and leaving the Creator out. The conception of Him as an inspired craftsman and ambitious artist of the original pottery works is so fantastic that the temptation lies close to hand – nowhere closer – to introduce an intermediate deity, the Demiurge. Well, as I was saying, the fact that these priceless habitations were the work of the very mollusc which they sheltered was the most astonishing thing about them.

'As you grew,' said Jonathan to us, 'and you can easily prove it by feeling your elbows and ribs, you formed in your insides a solid structure, a skeleton which gives your flesh and muscles stability, and which you carry round inside you – unless it be more correct to say it carries you around. Here it is just the other way: these creatures have put their solid structure outside, not as frame-work but as house, and that it is an outside and not an inside must be the very reason for its beauty.'

We boys, Adrian and I, looked at each other, half-smiling, half taken aback at such remarks from his father as this about the vanity of appearances.

Sometimes it was even malignant, this outward beauty: certain conical snails, charmingly asymmetric specimens bathed in a veined pale rose or white-spotted honey brown, had a notoriously poisonous sting. Altogether, according to the master of Buchel, a certain ill fame, a fantastic ambiguity, attached to this whole extraordinary field. A strange ambivalence of opinion had always betrayed itself in the very various uses to which the finest specimens were put. In the Middle Ages they had belonged to the standing inventory of the witches' kitchen and alchemist's vault: they were considered the proper vessels for poisons and love potions. On the other hand, and at the same time, they had served as shrines and reliquaries and even for the Eucharist. What a confrontation was there! – poison and beauty, poison and magic, even magic and ritual. If we did not think of all that ourselves, yet Jonathan's comments gave us a vague sense of it.

As for the hieroglyphs which so puzzled him, these were on a middle-sized shell, a mussel from New Caledonia: slightly reddish-brown characters on a white ground. They looked as though they were made with a brush, and round the rim became purely ornamental strokes; but on the larger part of the curved surface their careful complexity had the most distinct look of explanatory remarks. In my recollection they showed strong resemblance to ancient Oriental writing, for instance the old Aramaic *ductus*. My father had actually brought archaeological works from the not ill-provided town library of Kaisersaschern to give his friend the opportunity for comparison and study. There had been, of course, no result, or only such confusion and absurdity as came to nothing. With a certain melancholy Jonathan admitted it when he showed us the riddling reproduction. 'It has turned out to be impossible,' he said, 'to get at the meaning of these marks. Unfortunately, my dears, such is the case. They refuse themselves to our understanding, and will, painfully enough, continue to do so. But when I say refuse, that is merely the negative of reveal – and that Nature painted these ciphers, to which we lack the key, merely for ornament on the shell of her creature, nobody can persuade me. Ornament and meaning always run alongside each other; the old writings too served for both ornament and communication. Nobody can tell me that there is nothing communicated here. That it is an inaccessible communication, to plunge into this contradiction, is also a pleasure.'

Did he think, if it were really a case of secret writing, that Nature must command a language born and organized out of her own self? For what man-invented one should she choose, to express herself in? But even as a boy I clearly understood that Nature, outside of the human race, is fundamentally illiterate – that in my eyes is precisely what makes her uncanny.

Yes, Father Leverkühn was a dreamer and speculator, and I have already said that his taste for research – if one can speak of research instead of mere dreamy contemplation – always leaned in a certain direction – namely, the mystical or an intuitive half-mystical, into which, as it seems to me, human thinking in pursuit of Nature is almost of necessity led. But the enterprise of experimenting on Nature, of teasing her into manifestations, 'tempting' her, in the sense of laying bare her workings by experiment; that all this had quite close relations with witchcraft, yes, belonged in that realm and was itself a work of the 'Tempter', such was the conviction of earlier epochs. It was a decent conviction, if you were to ask me. I should like to know with what eyes one would have looked on the man from Wittenberg who, as we heard from Jonathan, a hundred and some years before had invented the experiment of visible music, which we were sometimes permitted to see. To the small amount of physical apparatus which Adrian's father had at his command belonged a round glass plate, resting only on a peg in the centre and revolving freely. On this glass plate the miracle took place. It was strewn with fine sand and Jonathan, by means of an old cello bow which he drew up and down the edge from top to bottom made it vibrate, and according to its motion the excited sand grouped and arranged itself in astonishingly precise and varied figures and arabesques. This visible acoustic, wherein the simple and the mysterious, law and miracle, so charmingly mingled, pleased us lads exceedingly; we often asked to see it, and not least to give the experimenter pleasure.

A similar pleasure he found in ice crystals, and on winter days when the little peasant windows of the farmhouse were frosted, he would be absorbed in their structure for half an hour, looking at them both with the naked eye and with his magnifying glass. I should like to say that all that would have been good and belonging to the regular order of things if only the phenomena had kept to a symmetrical pattern, as they ought, strictly regular and mathematical. But that they did not. Impudently, deceptively, they imitated the vegetable kingdom: most prettily of all, fern fronds, grasses, the calyxes and corollas of flowers. To the utmost of their icy ability they dabbled in the organic; and that Jonathan could never get over, nor cease his more or less disapproving but also admiring shakes of the head. Did, he inquired, these phantasmagorias prefigure the forms of the vegetable world, or did they imitate them? Neither one nor the other, he answered himself, they were parallel phenomena. Creatively dreaming Nature dreamed here and there the same dream: if there could be a thought of imitation, then surely it was reciprocal. Should one put down the actual children of the field as the pattern because they possessed organic actuality, while the snow crystals were mere show? But their appearance was the result of no smaller complexity of the action of matter than was that of the plants. If I understood my host aright, then what occupied him was the essential unity of animate and so-called inanimate nature, it was the thought that we sin against the latter when we draw too hard and fast a line between the two fields, since in reality it is pervious and there is no elementary capacity which is reserved entirely to the living creature and which the biologist could not also study on an inanimate subject.

We learned how bewilderingly the two kingdoms mimic each other, when Father Leverkühn showed us the 'devouring drop', more than once giving it its meal before our eyes. A drop of any kind, paraffin, volatile oil – I no longer feel sure what it was, it may have been chloroform – a drop, I say, is not animal, not even of the most primitive type, not even an amoeba; one does not suppose that it feels appetite, seizes nourishment, keeps what suits it, rejects what does not. But this was what our drop did. It hung by itself in a glass of water, wherein Jonathan had submerged it, probably with a dropper. What he did was as follows: he took a tiny glass stick, just a glass thread, which he had coated with shellac, between the prongs of a little pair of pincers and brought it close to the drop. That was all he did; the rest the drop did itself. It threw up on its surface a little protuberance, something like a mount of conception, through which it took the stick into itself, lengthwise. At the same time it got longer, became pear-shaped in order to get its prey all in, so that it should not stick out beyond, and began, I give you my word for it, gradually growing round again, first by taking on an egg-shape, to eat off the shellac and distribute it in its body. This done, and returned to its round shape, it moved the stick, licked clean, crosswise to its own surface and ejected it into the water.

I cannot say that I enjoyed seeing this, but I confess that I was fascinated, and Adrian probably was too, though he was always sorely tempted to laugh at such displays and suppressed his laughter only out of respect for his father's gravity. The devouring drop might conceivably strike one as funny. But no one, certainly not myself, could have laughed at certain other phenomena, 'natural', yet incredible and uncanny, displayed by Father Leverkühn. He had succeeded in making a most singular culture; I shall never forget the sight. The vessel of crystallization was three-quarters full of slightly muddy water – that is, dilute water-glass – and from the sandy bottom there strove upwards a grotesque little landscape of variously coloured growths: a confused vegetation of blue, green, and brown shoots which reminded one of algae, mushrooms, attached polyps, also moss, then mussels, fruit pods, little trees or twigs from trees, here and there of limbs. It was the most remarkable sight I ever saw, and remarkable not so much for its appearance, strange and amazing though that was, as on account of its profoundly melancholy nature. For when Father Leverkühn asked us what we thought of it and we timidly answered him that they might be plants: 'No,' he replied, 'they are not, they only act that way. But do not think the less of them. Precisely because they do, because they try as hard as they can, they are worthy of all respect.'

It turned out that these growths were entirely unorganic in their origin; they existed by virtue of chemicals from the apothecary's shop, the 'Blessed Messengers'. Before pouring the water-glass, Jonathan had sprinkled the sand at the bottom with various crystals; if I mistake not potassium chromate and sulphate of copper. From this sowing, as the result of a physical process called 'osmotic pressure', there sprang the pathetic crop for which their producer at once and urgently claimed our sympathy. He showed us that these pathetic imitations of life were light-seeking, helio-tropic, as science calls it. He exposed the aquarium to the sunlight, shading three sides against it, and behold, towards that one pane through which the light fell, thither straightway slanted the whole equivocal kith and kin: mushrooms, phallic polyp-stalks, little trees, algae, half-formed limbs. Indeed, they so yearned after warmth and joy that they actually clung to the pane and stuck fast there.

'And even so they are dead,' said Jonathan, and tears came in his eyes, while Adrian, as of course I saw, was shaken with suppressed laughter.

For my part, I must leave it to the reader's judgement whether that sort of thing is matter for laughter or tears. But one thing I will say: such weirdnesses are exclusively Nature's own affair, and particularly of nature arrogantly tempted by man. In the high-minded realms of the *humaniora* one is safe from such impish phenomena.

Chapter Four

Since the foregoing section has swollen out of all conscience, I shall do well to begin a new one, for it is my purpose now to do honour to the image of the mistress of Buchel, Adrian's dear mother. Gratitude for a happy childhood, in which the good things she gave us to eat played no small part may add lustre to my picture of her. But truly in all my life I have never seen a more attractive woman than Elsbeth Leverkühn. The reverence with which I speak of her simple, intellectually altogether unassuming person flows from my conviction that the genius of the son owed very much to his mother's vigour and bloom.

Jonathan Leverkühn's fine old-German head was always a joy to my eyes; but they rested with no less delight on his wife's figure, so altogether pleasant it was, so individual and well proportioned. She was born near Apolda, and her type was that brunette one which is sometimes found amongst us, even in regions where there is no definite ground to suspect Roman blood. The darkness of her colouring, the black hair, the black eyes with their quiet, friendly gaze, might have made me take her for an Italian were it not for a certain sturdiness in the facial structure. It was a rather short oval, this face, with somewhat pointed chin, a not very regular nose, slightly flat and a little tilted, and a tranquil mouth, neither voluptuous nor severe. The hair half covered the ears, and as I grew up it was slowly silvering; it was drawn tightly back, as smooth as glass, and the parting above the brow laid bare the whiteness of the skin beneath. Even so, not always, and so probably unintentionally some loose strands hung charmingly down in front of the ears. The braid, in our childhood still a massive one, was twined peasant-fashion round the back of the head and on feast-days it might be wound with a gay embroidered ribbon.

City clothes were as little to her liking as to her husband's: the lady-like did not suit her. On the other hand, the costume of the region, in which we knew her, became her to a marvel: the heavy home-made skirt and a sort of trimmed bodice with a square opening leaving bare the rather short, sturdy neck and the upper part of the breast, where hung a simple gold ornament. The capable brown hands with the wedding ring on the right one were neither coarse nor fastidiously cared for; they had, I would say, something so humanly right and responsible about them that one enjoyed the sight of them, as well as the shapely feet, which stepped out firmly, neither too large nor too small, in the easy, low-heeled shoes and the green or grey woollen stockings which spanned the neat ankles. All this was pleasant indeed. But the finest thing about her was her voice, in register a warm mezzo-soprano, and in speaking, though with a slight Thuringian inflection, quite extra-ordinarily winning. I do not say flattering, because the word seems to imply intention. The vocal charm was due to an inherently musical temperament, which, however, remained latent, for Elsbeth never troubled about music, never so to speak 'professed' it. She might quite casually strum a few chords on the old guitar that decorated the living-room wall; she might hum this or that snatch of song. But she never committed herself, never actually sang, although I would wager that there was excellent raw material there.

In any case, I have never heard anyone speak more beautifully, though what she said was always of the simplest and most matter-of-fact. And this native, instinctive taste, this harmony, was from the first hour Adrian's lullaby. To me that means something, it helps to explain the incredible ear which is revealed in his work – even though the objection lies to hand that his brother George enjoyed the same advantage without any influence upon his later life. George looked more like his father too, while Adrian physically resembled the mother – though again there is a discrepancy, for it was Adrian, not George, who inherited the tendency to migraine. But the general habit of my deceased friend, and even many particular traits: the brunette skin, the shape of eye, mouth, and chin, all that came from the mother's side. The likeness was plain so long as he was smooth-shaven, before he grew the heavy beard. That was only in his latter years; it altered his looks very much. The pitch-black of the mother's eyes had mingled with the father's azure blue to a shadowy blue-grey-green iris with little metallic sprinkles and a rust-coloured ring round the pupils. To me it was a moral certainty that the contrast between the eyes of the two parents, the blending of hers into his, was what formed his taste in this respect or rather made it waver. For never, all his life long, could he decide which, the black or the blue, he liked better. Yet always it was the extreme that drew him: the very blue, or else the pitch-black gleam between the lashes.

Frau Elsbeth's influence on the hands at Buchel – not very numerous save at harvest-time, and then the neighbours came in to help – was of the very best; if I am right, her authority among them was greater than her husband's. I can still see the figures of some of them; for instance, that of Thomas, the ostler, who used to fetch us from Weissenfels and bring us back: a one-eyed, extraordinarily long and bony man, with a slight hump, on which he used to let little Adrian ride; it was, the Meister often told me later, a most practical and comfortable seat. And I recall the cowgirl Hanne, whose bosoms flapped as she walked and whose bare feet were always caked with dung. She and the boy Adrian had a close friendship, on grounds still to be gone into in detail. Then there was the dairywoman Frau Luder, a widow in a cap. Her face was set in an expression of exaggerated dignity, probably due to her renown as a mistress of the art of making liqueurs and caraway cheese. It was she, if not Elsbeth herself, who took us to the cow-stalls, where the milkmaid crouched on her stool, and under her fingers there ran into our glasses the lukewarm foaming milk, smelling of the good and useful animal that gave it.

All this detail, these memories of our country world of childhood in its simple setting of wood and meadow, pond and hill – I would not dwell upon them but that just they formed the early surroundings of Adrian up to his tenth year. This was his parental home, his native heath, the scene where he and I so often came together. It was the time in which our *du* was rooted, the time when he too must have called me by my Christian name. I hear it no more, but it is unthinkable that at six or eight years he should not have called me Serenus or simply Seren just as I called him Adri. The date cannot be fixed, but it must certainly have been in our early schooldays that he ceased to bestow it on me and used only my last name instead, though it would have seemed to me impossibly harsh to do the same. Thus it was – though I would not have it look as though I wanted to complain. Yet it seemed to me worth mention that I called him Adrian; he on the other hand, when he did not altogether avoid all address, called me Zeitblom. – Let us not dwell on the odd circumstance, which became second nature to me, but drop it and return to Buchel.

His friend, and mine too, was the yard dog, Suso. The bearer of this singular name was a rather mangy setter. When one brought her her food she used to grin across her whole face, but she was by no means good-natured to strangers, and led the unnatural life of a dog chained all day to its kennel and only let free to roam the court at night. Together Adrian and I looked into the filthy huddle in the pigsty and recalled the old wives' tales we had heard about these muddy sucklings with the furtive white-eyelashed little blue eyes and the fat bodies so like in colour to human flesh: how these animals did sometimes actually devour small children. We forced our vocal chords to imitate the throaty grunt of their language and watched the rosy snouts of the litter at the dugs of the sow. Together we laughed at the hens behind the wire of the chicken-house: they accompanied their fatuous activities by a dignified gabbling, breaking out only now and then into hysterical squawks. We visited the beehives behind the house, but kept our distance, knowing already the throbbing pain caused by these busy creatures when one of them blundered against your nose and defended itself with its sting.

I remember the kitchen garden and the currant bushes whose laden stems we drew through our lips; the meadow sorrel we nibbled; certain wild-flowers from whose throats we sucked the drop of fine nectar; the acorns we chewed, lying on our backs in the wood; the purple, sun-warmed black-berries we ate from the wayside bushes to quench our childish thirst with their sharp juice. We were children – ah, it is not on my own account but on his that I am moved as I look back, at the thought of his fate, and how from that vale of innocence he was to mount up to inhospitable, yes, awful heights. It was the life of an artist; and because it was given to me, a simple man, to see it all so close by, all the feelings of my soul for human lot and fate were concentrated about this unique specimen of humanity. Thanks to my friendship with Adrian, it stands to me for the pattern of how destiny shapes the soul, for the classic, amazing instance of that which we call becoming, development, evolution – and actually it may be just that. For though the artist may all his life remain closer, not to say truer, to his childhood than the man trained for practical life, although one may say that he, unlike the latter, abides in the dreamy, purely human and playful childlike state, yet his path out of his simple, unaffected beginnings to the undivined later stages of his course is endlessly farther, wilder, more shattering to watch than that of the ordinary citizen. With the latter, too, the thought that he was once a child is not nearly so full of tears.

I beg the reader to put down entirely to my own account the feelings here expressed and not ascribe them to Leverkühn. I am an old-fashioned man who has stuck by certain romantic notions dear to me, one of which is the highly subjectivizing contrast I feel between the nature of the artist and that of the ordinary man. Adrian – if he had found it worth the trouble – would have coldly contradicted such a view. He had extremely neutral views about art and artists; he reacted so witheringly to the 'romantic tripe' which the world in its folly had been pleased to utter on the subject that he even disliked the words 'art' and 'artist', as he showed in his face when he heard them. It was the same with the word 'inspiration'. It had to be avoided in his company and 'imagination' used, if necessary, instead. He hated the word, he jeered at it – and when I think of that hatred and those jeers, I cannot help lifting my hand from the blotter over my page to cover my eyes. For his hatred and mockery were too tormented to be a merely objective reaction to the intellectual movements of the time. Though they were objective too; I recall that once, even as a student, he said to me that the nineteenth century must have been an uncommonly pleasant epoch, since it had never been harder for humanity to tear itself away from the opinions and habits of the previous period than it was for the generation now living.

I referred above to the pond which lay only ten minutes away from the house, surrounded by pasture. It was called the Cow Trough, probably because of its oblong shape and because the cows came there to drink. The water, why I do not know, was unusually cold, so that we could only bathe in it in the afternoon when the sun had stood on it a long time. As for the hill, it was a favourite walk of half an hour: a height called, certainly from old days and most inappropriately, Mount Zion. In the winter it was good for coasting, but I was seldom there. In summer, with the community bench beneath the oak trees crowning its summit, it was an airy site with a good view, and I often enjoyed it with the Leverkühn family before supper on Sunday afternoons.

And now I feel constrained to comment as follows: the house and its surroundings in which Adrian later as a mature man settled down when he took up permanent quarters with the Schweigestills at Pfeiffering near Waldshut in Oberbayern – indeed, the whole setting – were a most extraordinary likeness and reproduction of his childhood home; in other words, the scene of his later days bore a curious resemblance to that of his early ones. Not only did the environs of Pfeiffering (or Pfeffering, for the spelling varies) have a hill with a community bench, though it was not called Mount Zion, but the Rohmbühel; not only was there a pond, at somewhat the same distance from the house as the Cow Trough, here called the Klammer pond, the water of which was strikingly cold. No, for even the house, the courtyard, and the family itself were all very like the Buchel setting. In the yard was a tree, also rather in the way and preserved for sentimental reasons – not a linden tree, but an elm. True, characteristic differences existed between the structure of the Schweigestill house and that of Adrian's parents, for the former was an old cloister, with thick walls, deep-vaulted casements, and rather dank passages. But the odour of pipe tobacco pervaded the air of the lower rooms as it did at Buchel; and the owner and his wife, Herr and Frau Schweigestill, were a father and a mother too; that is, they were a long-faced rather laconic, quiet, and contemplative farmer and his no longer young wife, who had certainly put on flesh but was well-proportioned, lively, energetic, and capable, with hair smoothed tightly back and shapely hands and feet. They had a grown son and heir, Gereon (not George), a young man very progressive in agricultural matters, always thinking about new machinery, and a later-born daughter named Clementine. The yard dog in Pfeiffering could laugh, even though he was not called Suso, but Kaschperl – at least originally. For the boarder had his own ideas about this 'originally' and I was a witness of the process by which under his influence the name Kaschperl became slowly a memory and the dog himself answered better to Suso. There was no second son, which rather strengthened the case than otherwise, for who would this second son have been?

I never spoke to Adrian about this whole singular and very obvious parallel. I did not do so in the beginning, and later I no longer wanted to. I never cared for the phenomenon. This choice of a place to live, reproducing the earlier one, this burying oneself in one's earliest, outlived childhood, or at least in the outer circumstances of the same – it might indicate attachment, but in any case it is psychologically disturbing. In Leverkühn it was the more so since I never observed that his ties with the parental home were particularly close or emotional, and he severed them early without observable pain. Was that artificial 'return' simply a whim? I cannot think so. Instead it reminds me of a man of my acquaintance who, though outwardly robust and even bearded, was so highly strung that when he was ill – and he inclined to illnesses – he wished to be treated only by a child-specialist. Moreover the doctor to whom he went was so small in person that a practice for grown people would obviously not have been suitable and he could only have become a physician for children. I ought to say at once that I am aware of digressing in telling this anecdote about the man with the child-specialist, in so far as neither of them will appear in this narrative. If that is an error, and while without doubt it was an error to yield to the temptation to bring in Pfeiffering and the Schweigestills before their time, I would implore the reader to attribute such irregularities to the excitement which has possessed me since I began this biography, and to tell the truth not only as I write. I have been working now for several days on these pages, but though I try to keep my sentences balanced and find fitting expression for my thoughts, the reader must not imagine that I do not feel myself in a state of permanent excitement, which even expresses itself in a shakiness in my handwriting, usually so firm. I even believe, not only that those who read me will in the long run understand this nervous perturbation, but also that they themselves will in time not be strange to it.

I forgot to mention that there was in the Schweigestill courtyard, Adrian's later home, and certainly not surprisingly, a stable-girl, with bosoms that shook as she ran and bare feet caked with dung; she looked as much like Hanne of Buchel as one stable-girl does look like another, and in the reproduction was named Waltpurgis. Here, however, I am not speaking of her but of her prototype Hanne, with whom little Adrian stood on a friendly footing because she loved to sing and used to do little exercises with us children. Oddly enough, though Elsbeth Leverkühn, with her lovely voice, refrained, in a sort of chaste reserve, from song, this creature smelling of her animals made free with it, and sang to us lustily, of evenings on the bench under the linden tree. She had a strident voice, but a good ear; and she sang all sorts of popular tunes, songs of the army and the street; they were mostly either gruesome or mawkish and we soon made tunes and words of our own. When we sang with her, she accompanied us in thirds, and from there went down to the lower fifth and lower sixth and left us in the treble, while she ostentatiously and predominantly sang the second. And probably to fix our attention and make us properly value the harmonic enjoyment, she used to stretch her mouth and laugh just like Suso the dog when we brought her her food.

By we, I mean Adrian, myself, and George, who was already thirteen when his brother and I were eight and ten years old. Little sister Ursel was too small to take part in these exercises, and moreover, of us four probably one was superfluous in the kind of vocal music to which Hanne elevated our lusty shoutings. She taught us, that is, to sing rounds – of course, the ones that children know best: *O, wie wohl ist mir am Abend, Es tönen die Lieder*, and the one about the cuckoo and the ass; and those twilight hours in which we enjoyed them remain in my memory – or rather the memory of them later took on a heightened significance because it was they, so far as I know, that first brought my friend into contact with a 'music' somewhat more artistically organized than that of mere unison songs. Here was a succession of interweaving voices and imitative entries, to which one was roused by a poke in the ribs from the stable-girl Hanne when the song was already in progress; when the tune had got to a certain point but was not yet at the end. The melodic components presented themselves in different layers, but no jangle or confusion ensued, for the imitation of the first phrase by the second singer fitted itself very pleasantly point for point to the continuation sung by the first. But if this first part – in the case of the piece *O, wie wohl ist mir am Abend* – had reached the repeated '*Glocken läuten*' and begun the illustrative '*Ding-dang-dong*', it now formed the bass not only to '*Wenn zur Ruh*', which the second voice was just then singing, but also the beginning '*O wie wohl*', with which, consequent on a fresh nudge in the ribs, the third singer entered, only to be relieved, when he had reached the second stage of the melody, by the first starting again at the beginning, having surrendered to the second as the fundamental bass the descriptive '*Ding-dang-dong*' – and so on. The fourth singer inevitably coincided with one of the others, but he tried to enliven the doubling by roaring an octave below, or else he began before the first voice, so to speak before the dawn with the fundamental bell-figure and indefatigably and cheerfully carried on with it or the fa, la, la that gaily plays round the earlier stages of the melody during the whole duration of the song.

In this way we were always separate from each other in time, but the melodic presence of each kept together pleasantly with that of the others and what we produced made a graceful web, a body of sound such as unison singing did not; a texture in whose polyphony we delighted without inquiring after its nature and cause. Even the eight- or nine-year-old Adrian probably did not notice. Or did the short laugh, more mocking than surprised, which he gave when the last 'Ding-dong' faded on the air and which I came later to know so well – did it mean that he saw through the device of these little songs, which quite simply consists in that the beginning of the melody subsequently forms the second voice and that the third can serve both as bass? None of us was aware that here, led by a stable-girl, we were moving on a plane of musical culture already relatively very high, in a realm of imitative polyphony, which the fifteenth century had had to discover in order to give us pleasure. But when I think back at Adrian's laugh, I find in retrospect that it did have in it something of knowledge and mocking initiate sense. He kept it as he grew up; I often heard it, sitting with him in theatre or concert-hall, when he was struck by some artful trick, some ingenious device within the musical structure, noticed only by the few; or by some fine psychological allusion in the dialogue of a drama. In the beginning it was unsuitable for his years, being just as a grown person would have laughed: a slight expulsion of air from nose and mouth, with a toss of the head at the same time, short, cool, yes, contemptuous, or at most as though he would say: 'Good, that; droll, curious, amusing!' But his eyes were taking it in, their gaze was afar and strange, and their darkness, metal-sprinkled, had put on a deeper shade.

Chapter Five

The chapter just finished is also, for my taste, much too extended. It would seem only too advisable to inquire how the reader's patience is holding out. To myself, of course every word I write is of burning interest; but what care must I take not to see this as a guarantee of the sympathy of the detached reader. And certainly I must not forget that I am writing for posterity; not for the moment, nor for readers who as yet know nothing of Leverkühn and so cannot long to know more about him. What I do is to prepare these pages for a time when the conditions for public interest will be quite different, and certainly much more favourable; when curiosity about the details of so thrilling an existence, however well or ill presented, will be more eager and less fastidious.

That time will come. Our prison, so wide and yet so narrow, so suffocatingly full of foul air, will some day open, I mean when the war now raging will have found, one way or the other, its end – and how I shudder at this 'one way or the other', both for myself and for the awful impasse into which fate has crowded the German soul! For I have in mind only one of the two alternatives: only with this one do I reckon, counting upon it against my conscience as a German citizen. The never-ending public instruction has impressed on us in all its horrors the crushing consequences of a German defeat; we cannot help fearing it more than anything else in the world. And yet there is something else – some of us fear it at moments which seem to us criminal, but others quite frankly and steadily – something we fear more than German defeat, and that is German victory. I scarcely dare ask myself to which of these groups I belong. Perhaps to still a third, in which one yearns indeed, steadily and consciously, for defeat, yet also with perpetual torments of conscience. My wishes and hopes must oppose the triumph of German arms, because in it the work of my friend would be buried, a ban would rest upon it for perhaps a hundred years, it would be forgotten, would miss its own age and only in a later one receive historic honour. That is the special motivation of my criminal attitude; I share it with a scattered number of men who can easily be counted on the fingers of my two hands. But my mental state is only a variant of that which, aside from cases of ordinary self-interest or extraordinary stupidity, has become the destiny of a whole people; and this destiny I am inclined to consider in the light of a unique and peculiar tragedy, even while I realize that it has been before now laid on other nations, for the sake of their own and the general future, to wish for the downfall of their state. But considering the decency of the German character, its confidingness, its need for loyalty and devotion, I would fain believe that in our case the dilemma will come to a unique conclusion as well; and I cannot but cherish a deep and strong resentment against the men who have reduced so good a people to a state of mind which I believe bears far harder on it than it would on any other, estranging it beyond healing for itself. I have only to imagine that my own sons, through some unlucky chance, became acquainted with the contents of these pages and in Spartan denial of every gentler feeling denounced me to the secret police – to be able to measure, yes, actually with a sort of patriotic pride, the abysmal nature of this conflict.

I am entirely aware that with the above paragraph I have again regrettably overweighted this chapter, which I had quite intended to keep short. I would not even suppress my suspicion, held on psychological grounds, that I actually seek digressions and circumlocutions, or at least welcome with alacrity any occasion for such, because I am afraid of what is coming. I lay before the reader a testimony to my good faith in that I give space to the theory that I make difficulties because I secretly shrink from the task which, urged by love and duty, I have undertaken. But nothing, not even my own weakness, shall prevent me from continuing to perform it – and I herewith resume my narrative, with the remark that it was by our singing of rounds with the stable-girl that, so far as I know, Adrian was first brought into contact with the sphere of music. Of course I know that as he grew older he went with his parents to Sunday service in the village church at Oberweiler, where a young music student from Weissenfels used to prelude on the little organ and accompany the singing of the congregation, even attending its departure with timid improvisations. But I was almost never with them, since we usually went to Buchel only after morning church and I can but say that I never heard from Adrian a word to indicate that his young mind was any way moved by the offerings of that youthful adept; or – that being scarcely likely – that the phenomenon of music itself had ever struck him. So far as I can see, even at that time and for years afterwards he gave it no attention and kept concealed from himself that he had anything to do with the world of sound. I see in that a mental reserve; but a physiological explanation is also possible, for actually it was at about his fourteenth year, at the time of beginning puberty, and so at the end of the period of childhood, in the house of his uncle at Kaisersaschern, that he began of his own motion to experiment on the piano. And it was at this time that the inherited migraine began to give him bad days.

His brother George's future was conditioned by his position as heir, and he had always felt in complete harmony with it. What should become of the second son was for the parents an open question, which must be decided according to the tastes and capacities he might show; and it was remarkable how early the idea was fixed in his family's head and in all of ours that Adrian was to be a scholar. What sort of scholar remained long in doubt; but the whole bearing of the lad, his way of expressing himself, his clear definition, even his look, his facial expression, never left a doubt, in the mind of my father for instance, that this scion of the Leverkühn stock was called to 'something higher'; that he would be the first scholar of his line.

The decisive confirmation of this idea came from the ease, one might say the superior facility, with which Adrian absorbed the instruction of the elementary school. He received it in the paternal home, for Jonathan Leverkühn did not send his children to the village school, and the chief factor in this decision was, I believe, not so much social ambition as the earnest wish to give them a more careful education than they could get from instruction in common with the cottage children of Oberweiler. The schoolmaster, a still young and sensitive man, who never ceased to be afraid of the dog Suso, came over to Buchel afternoons when he had finished his official duties, in winter fetched by Thomas in the sleigh. By the time he took young Adrian in hand he had already given the thirteen-year-old George all the necessary foundation for his further training as agronomist. But now he, schoolmaster Michelson, was the very first to declare, loudly and with a certain vehemence, that the boy must 'in God's name', go to high school and the university, for such a learning head and lightning brain, he, Michelson, had never seen, and it would be a thousand pities if one did not do everything to open to this young scholar the way to the heights of knowledge. Thus or something like it, certainly rather like a seminarist, did he express himself, speaking indeed of *ingenium*, of course in part to show off with the word, which sounded droll enough applied to such childish achievements. Yet obviously it came from an awed and astonished heart.

I was never present at these lesson-hours and know only by hearsay about them; but I can easily imagine that the behaviour of my young Adrian must sometimes have been a little hard on a preceptor himself young, and accustomed to drive his learning with whip and spurs into dull and puzzled or rebellious heads. 'If you know it all already,' I once heard him say to the boy, 'then I can go home.' Of course it was not true that the pupil 'knew it all already', but his manner did suggest the thought, simply because here was a case of that swift, strangely sovereign and anticipatory grasp and assimilation, as sure as easy, which soon dried up the master's praise, for he felt that such a head meant a danger to the modesty of the heart and betrayed it easily to arrogance. From the alphabet to syntax and grammar, from the progression of numbers and the first rules to the rule of three and simple sums in proportion, from the memorizing of little poems (and there was no memorizing, the verses were straightway and with the utmost precision grasped and possessed) to the written setting down of his own train of

thought on themes out of the geography – it was always the same: Adrian gave
it his ear, then turned round with an air that seemed to say: 'Yes, good, so
much is clear, all right, go on!' To the pedagogic temperament there is something revolting about that. Certainly the young schoolmaster was tempted
again and again to cry: 'What is the matter with you? Take some pains!' But
why, when obviously there was no need to take pains?

As I said, I was never present at the lessons; but I am compelled to
conclude that my friend received the scientific data purveyed by Herr
Michelson fundamentally with the same mien, so hard to characterize, with
which under the lime tree he had accepted the fact that if a horizontal melody
of nine bars is divided into three sections of three bars each, they will still
produce a harmonically fitting texture. His teacher knew some Latin; he
instructed Adrian in it and then announced that the lad – he was now ten
years old – was ready if not for the fifth, then certainly for the fourth form.
His work was done.

Thus Adrian left his parents' house at Easter 1895 and came to town to
attend our Boniface gymnasium, the school of the Brethren of the Common
Life. His uncle, Nikolaus Leverkühn, his father's brother, a respected
citizen of Kaisersaschern, declared himself ready to receive the lad into his
house.

Chapter Six

And as for Kaisersaschern, my native town on the Saale, the stranger should
be informed that it lies somewhat south of Halle, towards Thuringia. I had
almost said it *lay*, for long absence has made it slip from me into the past. Yet
its towers rise as ever on the same spot, and I would not know whether its
architectural profile has suffered so far from the assaults of the air-war. In
view of its historic charm that would be in the highest degree regrettable. I
can add this quite calmly, since I share with no small part of our population,
even those hardest hit and homeless, the feeling that we are only getting
what we gave, and even if we must suffer more frightfully than we have
sinned, we shall only hear in our ears that he who sows the wind must reap
the whirlwind.

Neither Halle itself, the industrial town, nor Leipzig, the city of Bach the
cantor of St Thomas, nor Weimar, nor even Dessau nor Magdeburg is far
distant; but Kaisersaschern is a junction, and with its twenty-seven
thousand inhabitants entirely self-sufficient; feeling itself like every
German town a centre of culture, with its own historical dignity and
importance. It is supported by several industries: factories and mills for the
production of machinery, leather goods, fabrics, arms, chemicals, and so on.
Its museum, besides a roomful of crude instruments of torture, contains a
very estimable library of twenty-five thousand volumes and five thousand
manuscripts, among the latter two books of magic charms in alliterative
verse; they are considered by some scholars to be older than those in
Merseburg. The charms are perfectly harmless: nothing worse than a little
rain-conjuring, in the dialect of Fulda. The town was a bishopric in the tenth
century, and again from the beginning of the twelfth to the fourteenth. It has
a castle, and a cathedral church where you may see the tomb of Kaiser Otto

III, son of Adelheid and husband of Theophano, who called himself Emperor of the Romans, also Saxonicus; the latter not because he wanted to be a Saxon but in the sense in which Scipio called himself Africanus, because he had conquered the Saxons. He was driven out of his beloved Rome, and died in misery in the year 1002; his remains were brought to Germany and buried in the cathedral in Kaisersaschern – not at all what he would have relished himself, for he was a prize specimen of German self-contempt and had been all his life ashamed of being German.

As for the town – which I refer to by choice in the past tense, since after all I am speaking of the Kaisersaschern of our youth – there is this to be said of it, that in atmosphere as well as in outward appearance it had kept a distinctly medieval air. The old churches, the faithfully preserved dwelling-houses and warehouses, buildings with exposed and jutting upper storeys; the round towers in the wall, with their peaked roofs; the tree-studded squares with cobblestones; the Town Hall of mixed Gothic and Renaissance architecture, with a bell-tower on the high roof, loggias underneath, and two other pointed towers forming bays and continuing the façade down to the ground – all these gave a sense of continuity with the past. More, even, the place seemed to wear on its brow that famous formula of timelessness, the scholastic *nunc stans*. Its individual character, which was the same as three hundred, nine hundred years ago, asserted itself against the stream of time passing over it, constantly making changes in many things, while others, decisive for the picture, were preserved out of piety; that is to say, out of a pious defiance of time and also out of pride in them, for the sake of their value and their memories.

This much of the scene itself. But something still hung on the air from the spiritual constitution of the men of the last decades of the fifteenth century: a morbid excitement, a metaphysical epidemic latent since the last years of the Middle Ages. This was a practical, rational modern town – Yet no, it was not modern, it was old; and age is past as presentness, a past merely overlaid with presentness. Rash it may be to say so, but here one could imagine strange things: as for instance a movement for a children's crusade might break out; a St Vitus's dance; some wandering lunatic with communistic visions, preaching a bonfire of the vanities; miracles of the Cross, fantastic and mystical folk-movements – things like these, one felt, might easily come to pass. Of course they did not – how should they? The police, acting in agreement with the times and the regulations, would not have allowed them. And yet what all in our time have the police not allowed – again in agreement with the times, which might readily, by degrees, allow just such things to happen again now? Our time itself tends, secretly – or rather anything but secretly; indeed, quite consciously, with a strangely complacent consciousness, which makes one doubt the genuineness and simplicity of life itself and which may perhaps evoke an entirely false, unblest historicity – it tends, I say, to return to those earlier epochs; it enthusiastically re-enacts symbolic deeds of sinister significance, deeds that strike in the face the spirit of the modern age, such, for instance, as the burning of the books and other things of which I prefer not to speak.

The stamp of old-world, underground neurosis which I have been describing, the mark and psychological temper of such a town, betrays itself in Kaisersaschern by the many 'originals', eccentrics, and harmlessly half-mad folk who live within its walls and, like the old buildings belong to the picture. The pendant to them is formed by the children, the 'young 'uns', who pursue the poor creatures, mock them, and then in superstitious panic run away. A certain sort of 'old woman' used always in certain epochs without more ado to be suspected of witchcraft, simply because she looked 'queer', though her appearance may well have been, in the first place, nothing but the result of the suspicion against her, which then gradually justified itself till it resembled the popular fancy: small, grey, bent, with a spiteful face, rheumy eyes, hooked nose, thin lips, a threatening crook. Probably she owned cats, an owl, a talking bird. Kaisersaschern harboured more than one such specimen; the most popular, most teased and feared was Cellar-Lise, so called because she lived in a basement in Little Brassfounder's Alley – an old woman whose figure had so assimilated itself to popular prejudice that even the most unaffected could feel an archaic shudder at meeting her, especially when the children were after her and she was putting them to flight by spitting curses. Of course, quite definitely there was nothing wrong with her at all.

Here let me be bold enough to express an opinion born of the experiences of our own time. To a friend of enlightenment the word and conception 'the folk' has always something anachronistic and alarming about it; he knows that you need only tell a crowd they are 'the folk' to stir them up to all sorts of reactionary evil. What all has not happened before our eyes – or just not quite before our eyes – in the name of 'the folk', though it could never have happened in the name of God or humanity or the law. But it is the fact that actually the folk remain the folk, at least in a certain stratum of its being, the archaic; and people from Little Brassfounder's Alley and round about, people who voted the Social-Democratic ticket at the polls, are at the same time capable of seeing something daemonic in the poverty of a little old woman who cannot afford a lodging above-ground. They will clutch their children to them when she approaches, to save them from the evil eye. And if such an old soul should have to burn again today, by no means an impossible prospect, were even a few things different, 'the folk' would stand and gape behind the barriers erected by the Mayor, but they would probably not rebel – I speak of the folk; but this old, folkish layer survives in us all, and to speak as I really think, I do not consider religion the most adequate means of keeping it under lock and key. For that, literature alone avails, humanistic science, the ideal of the free and beautiful human being.

To return to those oddities of kaisersaschern; there was a man of indefinite age who, if suddenly called to on the street, had a compulsion to execute a sort of twitching dance with his legs drawn up. His face was both ugly and sad, but as though he were begging pardon, he would smile at the urchins bawling at his heels. Then there was a woman named Mathilde Spiegel, dressed in the fashion of a bygone time: she wore a train trimmed with ruffles, and a *fladus* – a ridiculous corruption of the French *flute douce*, originally meaning flattery, but here used for a curious coiffure with curls and ornaments. She wore rouge too, but was not immoral, being far too witless; she merely rambled through the streets with her nose in the air, accompanied by pug dogs with satin saddle-cloths – A small rentier was another such freak; he had a bulbous purple nose, and a big seal ring on his fore-finger. His real name was Schnalle, but he was called Tootle-oo, because he had a habit of adding this senseless chirrup to everything he said. He liked to go to the railway station, and when a freight train pulled out would lift his finger and warn the man sitting on the roof of the last car: 'Don't fall off, don't fall off, tootle-oo!'

It may be that these grotesque memories are unworthy of inclusion here – I am inclined to believe it. Yet all these figures were, in a way, public institutions, uncommonly characteristic of the psychological picture of my native town, Adrian's setting till he went to the university, for nine years of his young life. I spent them at his side, for though by age I was two forms beyond him, we kept together, apart from our respective classmates, during the recesses in the walled courtyard, and also met each other in the afternoons, in our little studies: either he came over to the shop or I went to him in the house of his uncle at Parochialstrasse 15, where the mezzanine storey was occupied by the well-known Leverkühn musical-instruments firm.

Chapter Seven

It was a quiet spot, removed from the business section of Kaisersaschern, the Market Street, or Gritsellers' Row: a tiny street without a pavement, near the Cathedral; Nikolaus Leverkühn's house stood out as the most imposing one in it. It had three storeys, not counting the lofts of the separate roof, which was built out in bays; and in the sixteenth century it had been the dwelling-house of an ancestor of the present owner. It had five windows in the first storey above the entrance door and only four, with blinds, in the second, where, instead of in the first, the family living-rooms lay. Outside, the foundation storey was unwhitewashed and unadorned; only above it did the ornamental woodwork begin. Even the stairs widened only after the beginning of the mezzanine, which lay rather high above the stone entry, so that visitors and buyers – many of these came from abroad, from Halle and even Leipzig – had not too easy a climb to the goal of their hopes, the instrument warehouse. But as I mean to show forthwith, it was certainly worth a steep climb.

Nikolaus, a widower – his wife died young – had up to Adrian's coming lived alone in the house with an old-established housekeeper, Frau Butze, a maid, and a young Italian from Brescia, named Luca Cimabue (he did actually bear the family name of the thirteenth-century painter of Madonnas), who was his assistant and pupil at the trade of violin-making; for Uncle Leverkühn also made violins. He was a man with untidy ash-coloured hair hanging loose about his beardless, sympathetically moulded face, prominent cheekbones, a hooked, rather drooping nose, a large, expressive mouth, and brown eyes with good-heartedness and concern as well as shrewdness in their gaze. At home one always saw him in a wrinkled fustian smock closed to the throat. I think it pleased the childless man to receive a young kinsman in his far too spacious house. Also I have heard that he let his brother in Buchel pay the school fees, but took nothing himself for board and lodging. Altogether he treated Adrian, on whom he kept an indefinitely expectant eye, like his own son, and greatly enjoyed having this family addition to his table, which for so long had had round it only the above-mentioned Frau Butze and, in patriarchal fashion, Luca, his apprentice.

That this young Italian, a friendly youth speaking a pleasantly broken German, had found his way to Kaisersaschern and to Adrian's uncle, when he surely must have had opportunity at home to improve himself in his trade, was perhaps surprising, but indicated the extent of Nikolaus Leverkühn's business connexions, not only with German centres of instrument-making, like Mainz, Braunschweig, Leipzig, Barmen, but also with foreign firms in London, Lyons, Bologna, even New York. He drew his symphonic merchandise from all quarters and had a reputation for a stock-in-trade not only first-class as to quality but also gratifyingly complete and not easily obtainable elsewhere. Thus there only needed to be anywhere in the kingdom a Bach festival in prospect, for whose performance in classic style an oboe d'amore was needed, the deeper oboe long since disappeared from the orchestra, for the old house in Parochialstrasse to receive a visit from a client, a musician who wanted to play safe and could try out the elegiac instrument on the spot.

The warerooms in the mezzanine often resounded with such rehearsals, the voices running through the octaves in the most varied colours. The whole place afforded a splendid, I might say a culturally enchanting and alluring sight, stimulating the aural imagination till it effervesced. Excepting the piano, which Adrian's foster-father gave over to that special industry, everything was here spread out: all that sounds and sings, that twangs and crashes, hums and rumbles and roars – even the keyboard instruments, in the form of the celesta, the lovely *Glockenklavier*, were always represented. There hung behind glass, or lay bedded in receptacles which like mummy cases were made in the shape of their occupants, the charming violins, varnished some yellower and some browner, their slender bows with silver wire round the nut fixed into the lid of the case; Italian ones, the pure, beautiful shapes of which would tell the connoisseur that they came from Cremona; also Tirolese, Dutch, Saxon, Mittenwald fiddles, and some from Leverkühn's own workshop. The melodious cello, which owes its perfect form to Antonio Stradivari, was there in rows; likewise its predecessor, the six-stringed viola da gamba, in older works still honoured, next to it; the viola and that other cousin of the fiddle, the viola alta, were always to be found, as well as my own viola d'amore on whose seven strings I have all my life enjoyed performing. My instrument came from the Parochialstrasse, a present from my parents at my confirmation.

There were several specimens of the violone, the giant fiddle, the unwieldy double-bass, capable of majestic recitative, whose pizzicato is more sonorous than the stroke of the kettle-drum, and whose harmonics are a veiled magic of almost unbelievable quality. And there was also more than one of its opposite number among the wood-wind instruments, the contra-bassoon, sixteen-foot likewise – in other words, sounding an octave lower than the notes indicate – mightily strengthening the basses, built in twice the dimensions of its smaller brother the humorous bassoon, to which I give that name because it is a bass instrument without proper bass strength, oddly weak in sound, bleating, burlesque. How pretty it was, though, with its carved mouthpiece, shining in the decoration of its keys and levers! What a charming sight altogether, this host of shawms in their highly developed stage of technical perfection, challenging the passion of the virtuoso in all of their forms: as bucolic oboe, as cor anglais well versed in tragic ways; the many-keyed clarinet, which can sound so ghostly in the deep chalumeau register but higher up can gleam in silvery blossoming harmony, as basset horn and bass clarinet.

All of these, in their velvet beds, offered themselves in Uncle Leverkühn's stock; also the transverse flute, in various systems and varied execution, made of beechwood, granadilla, or ebony, with ivory head-pieces, or else entirely of silver; next their shrill relative the piccolo, which in the orchestral tutti piercingly holds the treble, dancing in the music of the will-o'-the wisp and the fire-magic. And now the shimmering chorus of the brasses, from the trim trumpet, visible symbol of the clear call, the sprightly song, the melting cantilena, through that darling of the romantics, the voluted valve-horn, the slender and powerful trombone, and the cornet-à-pistons, to the weighty bass tuba. Rare museum pieces such as a pair of beautifully curved bronzed lurer turned right and left, like steer-horns, were also to be found in Leverkühn's warehouse. But in a boy's eyes, as I see it again in retrospect, most gay and glorious of all was the comprehensive display of percussion instruments – just because the things that one had found under the Christmas tree, the toys and dream-possessions of childhood, now turned up in this dignified grown-up display. The side-drum, how different it looked here from the ephemeral painted thing of wood, parchment, and twine we thumped on as six-year-olds! It was not meant to hang round your neck. The lower membrane was stretched with gut strings; it was screwed fast for orchestral use, in conveniently slanting position, on a metal trivet, and the wooden sticks, also much nicer than ours, stuck invitingly into rings at the sides. There was the glockenspiel; we had had a childhood version of it, on which we practised *Kommt ein Vogel geflogen*. Here, in an elegant locked case, lying in pairs on cross-bars and free to swing, were the metal plates, so meticulously tuned, with the delicate little steel hammers belonging to them and kept in the lined lid of the case. The xylophone which seems made to conjure up a vision of a dance of skeletons – here it was with its numerous wooden bars, arranged in the chromatic scale. There was the giant-studded cylinder of the bass drum, with a felt-covered stick to beat it; and the copper kettle-drum, sixteen of which Berlioz still included in his orchestra. He did not know the pedal drum as represented here, which the drummer can with his hand easily adapt to a change of key. How well I remember the pranks we practised on it. Adrian and I – no, it was probably only I – making the sticks roll on the membrane while the good Luca tuned it up and down, so that a thudding and thumping in the strangest glissando ensued. And then there were the extraordinary cymbals, which only the Turks and the Chinese know how to make, because they have preserved the secret of hammering molten bronze. The performer, after clashing them, holds up their inner sides in triumph towards the audience. The reverberating gong, the tambourine beloved the gypsies, the triangle with its open end, sounding brightly under the steel stick; the cymbals of today, the hollow castanets clacking in the hand. Consider all this splendid feast of sound, with the golden, gorgeous structure of the Érard pedal harp towering above it – and how easy it is to feel the fascination that Uncle's warehouse had for us, this silent paradise, which yet in hundreds of forms heralded sweetest harmony!

For us? No, I shall do better to speak only of myself, my own enchantment, my own pleasure – I scarcely dare to include my friend when I speak of those feelings. Perhaps he wanted to play the son of the house, to whom the warerooms were commonplace everyday; perhaps the coolness native to him in general might thus express itself; for he maintained an almost shoulder-shrugging indifference to all these splendours, replying to my admiring exclamations with his short laugh and a 'Yes, very nice' or 'Funny stuff' or 'What all don't people think of!' or 'More fun to sell this than groceries.' Sometimes – I repeat that it was at my wish, not his – we would descend from his attic, which gave a pleasant view over the roofs of the town, the castle pond, the old water-tower, and invade the showrooms. They were not forbidden to us; but young Cimabue came too, partly, I suspect, to keep guard, but also to play cicerone in his pleasant way. From him we learned the history of the trumpet: how once it had to be put together out of several metal tubes with a ball connexion before we learned the art of bending brass tubes without splitting them, by first filling them with pitch and resin, then with lead, which was melted again in the fire. And then he could explain the assertion of the *cognoscenti* that it made no difference what material, whether wood or metal, an instrument was made of, it sounded according to its family shape and proportions. A flute might be made of wood or ivory, a trumpet of brass or silver, it made no difference. But his master, he said, Adrian's *zio*, disputed that. He knew the importance of the material, the sort of wood and varnish used, and engaged to be able to tell by listening to a flute what it was made of. He, Luca, would do the same. Then with his small, shapely Italian hands he would show us the mechanism of the flute, which in the last one hundred and fifty years, since the famous virtuoso Quantz, saw such great changes and developments: the mechanism of Boehm's cylindrical flute, more powerful than the old conical, which sounds sweeter. He showed us the system of fingering on the clarinet and the seven-holed bassoon with its twelve closed and four open keys, whose sound blends so readily with that of the horns; instructed us about the compass of the instruments, the way to play them and more such matters.

There can now be no doubt that Adrian, whether he was aware of it or not, followed these demonstrations with at least as much attention as I – and with more profit than it was given me to draw from them. But he betrayed nothing, not a gesture indicated that all this concerned or ever would concern him. He let me ask Luca the questions, yes, he moved away, looked at something else than the thing under discussion, and left me alone with the assistant. I will not say that he was shamming, and I do not forget that at that time music had hardly any reality to us other than that of the purely material objects in Nikolaus Leverkühn's storerooms. We were indeed brought into cursory contact with chamber music, for every week or so there was a performance in Adrian's uncle's house, but only occasionally in my presence and by no means always in his. The players were our Cathedral organist, Herr Wendell Kretschmar, a stutterer, who was later to become Adrian's teacher, and the singing-master from the Boniface gymnasium; Adrian's uncle played with them, quartets by Haydn and Mozart, he himself playing first violin, Luca Cimabue second, Herr Kretschmar cello, and the singing-master the viola. These were masculine evenings, with the beer-glass on the floor beside the chair, a cigar in the mouth, and frequent bursts of talk, strange, dry interruptions in the middle of the language of music; tapping of the bow and counting back of the bars when the players got out, which was almost always the fault of the singing-master. A real concert, a symphony orchestra, we had never heard, and whoever likes may find therein an explanation of Adrian's obvious indifference to the world of instruments. At any rate he seemed to think it must be sufficient, and so considered it himself. What I mean is he hid himself behind it, hid himself from the music: very long with instinctive persistence, he hid himself from his destiny.

Anyhow, nobody for a long time thought of connecting young Adrian in any way with music. The idea that he was destined to be a scholar was fixed in their minds and continually strengthened by his brilliant performance in school, his rank in his form, which began slightly to waver only in the upper forms, say from the fifth on, when he was fifteen. This was on account of the migraine, which from then on hindered him in the little preparation he had to do. Even so he easily mastered the demands made on him – though the word 'mastered' is not well chosen, for it cost him nothing to satisfy them. And if his excellence as a pupil did not earn for him the affection of his masters, for it did not, as I often observed – one saw instead a certain irritation, a desire to trap him – it was not so much that they found him conceited, though they did. They did not, however, think him proud of his achievements; the trouble was, he was not proud enough, just therein lay his arrogance. He obviously looked down on all this that was so easy for him: that is, the subject-matter of the lessons, the various branches of study, the purveying of which made up the dignity and the livelihood of the masters. It was only too natural that they should not enjoy seeing these things so competently and carelessly dismissed.

For my own part I had much more cordial relations with them – no wonder, since I was soon to join their number and had even seriously announced my intention. I too might call myself a good pupil; but I was, and might call myself so, only because my reverent love for my chosen field, especially the ancient tongues and the classic poets and writers, summoned and stimulated what powers I had, while he on every occasion made it clear – to me he made no secret of it and I fear it was not one to the masters either – how indifferent and so to speak unimportant to him the whole of his education was. This often distressed me, not on account of his career, which thanks to his facility was not endangered, but because I asked myself what was not indifferent and unimportant to him. I did not see the 'main thing', and really it was not there to see. In those years school life is life itself, it stands for all that life is, school interests bound the horizon that every life needs in order to develop values, through which, however relative they are, the character and the capacities are sustained. They can, however, do that, humanly speaking, only if the relativeness remains unrecognized. Belief in absolute values, illusory as it always is, seems to me a condition of life. But my friend's gifts measured themselves against values the relative character of which seemed to lie open to him, without any visible possibility of any other relation which would have detracted from them as values. Bad pupils there are in plenty. But Adrian presented the singular phenomenon of a bad pupil as the head of the form. I say that it distressed me, but how impressive, how fascinating, I found it too! How it strengthened my devotion to him, mingling with it – can one understand why? – something like pain, like hopelessness!

I will make one exception to this uniform ironic contempt which he presented to what the school offered him and the claims it made upon him. That was his apparent interest in a discipline in which I myself did not shine – mathematics. My own weakness in this field, which was only tolerably made good by joyful application in philology, made me realize that excellence in performance is naturally conditioned by sympathy with the subject and thus it was a real boon to me to see this condition – at least here – fulfilled by my friend too. *Mathesis*, as applied logic, which yet confines itself to pure and lofty abstractions, holds a peculiar middle position between the humanistic and the practical sciences, and from the explanations which Adrian gave me of the pleasure he took in it, it appeared that he found this middle position at once higher, dominating, universal, or, as he expressed it, 'the true'. It was a genuine pleasure to hear him describe anything as 'the true', it was an anchor, a hold, not quite in vain did one inquire about 'the main thing'. 'You are a lout,' he said, 'not to like it. To look at the relations between things must be the best thing, after all. Order is everything. Romans xiii: "For there is no power but of God: the powers that be are ordained of God." ' He reddened, and I looked at him large-eyed. It turned out that he was religious.

With him everything had first to 'turn out', one had to take him by surprise, catch him in the act, get behind the words; then he would go red and one would have liked to kick oneself for not having seen it before. He went further than necessary in his algebra, played with the logarithmic tables for sheer amusement, sat over equations of the second class before he had been asked to identify unknown quantities raised to a higher power. I caught him at all that by mere chance, and even then he spoke mockingly of them before he made the above admissions. Another discovery, not to say unmasking, had preceded this: I have already mentioned his self-taught and secret exploration of the keyboard, the chord, the compass, the tonality, the cycle of fifths, and how he, without knowledge of notes and fingering, used this harmonic basis to practise all sorts of modulations and to build up melodic pictures rhythmically undefined. When I discovered all this, he was in his fifteenth year. I had sought him in vain one afternoon in his room, and found him before a little harmonium which stood rather unregarded in the corridor of the family rooms. For a moment I had listened, standing at the door, but not quite liking this I went forward and asked him what he was doing. He let the bellows rest, took his hands from the manuals, blushed and laughed. 'Idleness,' he said, 'is the mother of all vice. I was bored. When I am bored I sometimes poke about down here. The old treadlebox stands here pretty forlorn; but for all its simpleness it has the meat of the matter in it. Look, it is curious – that is, of course, there is nothing curious about it, but when you make it out the first time for yourself it is curious how it all hangs together and leads round in a circle.'

And he played a chord: all black keys, F sharp, A sharp, C sharp, added an E, and so unmasked the chord, which had looked like F-sharp major, as belonging to B major, as its dominant. 'Such a chord,' he said, 'has of itself no tonality. Everything is relation, and the relation forms the circle.' The A, which, forcing the resolution into G sharp, leads over from B major to E major, led him on, and so via the keys of A, D, and G he came to C major and to the flat keys, as he demonstrated to me that on each one of the twelve notes of the chromatic scale one could build a fresh major or minor scale.

'But all that is an old story,' he said. 'That struck me a long time ago. Now look how you can improve on it!' And he began to show me modulations between more distant keys, by using the so-called relation of the third, the Neapolitan sixth.

Not that he would have known how to name these things; but he repeated: 'Relationship is everything. And if you want to give it a more precise name, it is ambiguity.' To illustrate the meaning of the word, he played me chord-progressions belonging to no definite key; demonstrated for me how such a progression fluctuates between C major and G major, if one leaves out the F, that in G major turns into F sharp; how it keeps the ear uncertain as to whether that progression is to be understood as belonging to C major or F major if one avoids the B, which in F major is flattened to B flat.

'You know what I find?' he asked. 'That music turns the equivocal into a system. Take this or that note. You can understand it so or respectively so. You can think of it as sharpened or flattened, and you can, if you are clever, take advantage of the double sense as much as you like.' In short, in principle he showed himself aware of enharmonic changes and not unaware of certain tricks by which one can by-pass keys and use the enharmonic change for modulations.

Why was I more than surprised, namely moved and a little startled? His cheeks were hot, as they never were in school, not even over his algebra. I did indeed ask him to improvise for me a little, but felt something like relief when he put me off with a 'Nonsense, nonsense!' What sort of relief was that? It might have taught me how proud I was of his general indifference, and how clearly I felt that in his 'It is curious' indifference became a mask. I divined a budding passion – a passion of Adrian's! Should I have been glad? Instead, I felt at once ashamed and anxious.

I knew now that he, when he thought himself alone, worked on his music; indeed, in the exposed position of the old instrument that could not long remain a secret. One evening his foster-father said to him:

'Well, nephew, from what I heard today you were not practising for the first time.'

'What do you mean, Uncle Niko?'

'Don't be so innocent! You were making music.'

'What an expression!'

'It has had to serve for worse. How you got from F major to A major, that was pretty clever. Does it amuse you?'

'Oh, Uncle!'

'Well, of course, I'll tell you something: We'll put the old box up in your room, nobody sees it down her anyhow. Then you'll have it at hand, to use when you feel like it.'

'You're frightfully good, Uncle, but surely it is not worth the trouble.'

'It's so little trouble that even so the pleasure might be greater. And anyhow, nephew, you ought to have piano lessons.'

'Do you think so, Uncle Niko? I don't know, it sounds like a girls' high school.'

'Might be higher and still not quite girls'! If you go to Kretschmar, it will be something like. He won't skin us alive, because of our old friendship, and you will get a foundation for your castles in the air. I'll speak to him.'

Adrian repeated this conversation to me literally, in the school court. From now on he had lessons twice a week from Wendell Kretschmar.

Chapter Eight

Wendell Kretschmar, at that time still young, at most in the second half of his twenties, was born in the state of Pennsylvania of German-American parentage. He had got his musical education in his country of origin; but he was early drawn back to the old world whence his grandparents had once migrated, and where his own roots lay and those of his art. In the course of his wanderings, the stages and sojourns of which seldom lasted more than a year or so, he had become our organist in Kaisersaschern. It was only an episode, preceded by others (he had worked as conductor in small state theatres in the Reich and Switzerland) and followed certainly by others still. He had even appeared as composer and produced an opera, *The Statue*, which was well received and played on many stages.

Unpretentious in appearance, a short, thickset, bullet-headed man with little clipped moustache and brown eyes prone to laughter, with now a musing and now a pouncing look, he might have meant a real boon to the cultural life of Kaisersaschern if there had been any such life to begin with. His organ-playing was expert and excellent, but you could count on the fingers of one hand the number of those in the community able to appreciate it. Even so, a considerable number of people were attracted by his free afternoon concerts, in which he regaled us with organ music by Michael Pretorious, Froberger, Buxtehude, and of course Sebastian Bach, also all sorts of curious genre compositions from the time between Handel's and Haydn's highest periods. Adrian and I attended the concerts regularly. A complete failure, on the other hand, at least to all appearance, were the lectures which he had held indefatigably throughout a whole season in the hall of the Society of Activities for the Common Weal, accompanied by illustrations of the piano and demonstrations on a blackboard. They were a failure in the first place because our population had on principle no use for lectures; and secondly because his themes were not popular but rather capricious and out of the ordinary; and in the third place because his stutter made listening to them a nerve-racking occupation, sometimes bringing your heart into your mouth, sometimes tempting you to laughter, and altogether calculated to distract your attention from the intellectual treat in anxious expectation of the next convulsion.

His stutter was of a particularly typical and developed kind – tragic, because he was man gifted with great and urgent riches of thought, passionately addicted to giving out information. And his little bark would move upon the waters by stretches swift and dancing, with a suspicious ease that might make one forget and scout his affliction. But inevitably, from time to time, while constantly and only too justifiably awaited, came the moment of disaster; and there he stood with red, swollen face on the rack; whether stuck on a sibilant, which he weathered with wide-stretched mouth, making the noise of an engine giving off steam; or wrestling with a labial, his cheeks puffed out, his lips launched into a crackling quick-fire of short, soundless explosions; or finally, when with his breathing in helpless disorder, his mouth like a funnel, he would gasp for breath like a fish out of water; laughing with tears in his eyes, for it is a fact that he himself seemed to treat the thing as a joke. Not everybody could take that consoling view; the public was really not to be blamed if it avoided the lectures with that degree of unanimity that in fact several times not more than half a dozen hearers occupied the seats: my parents, Adrian's uncle, young Cimabue, the two of us, and a few pupils from the girls' high school, who did not fail to giggle when the speaker stuttered.

Kretschmar would have been ready to defray out of his own pocket such expenses for hall and lighting as were not covered by the ticket money. But my father and Nikolaus Leverkühn had arranged in committee to have the society make up the deficit, or rather relinquish the charge for the hall, on the plea that the lectures were important for culture and served the common good. That was a friendly gesture; the effect on the common weal was doubtful, since the community did not attend them, in part, as I said, because of the all too specialized character of the subjects treated. Wendell Kretschmar honoured the principle, which we repeatedly heard from his lips, first formed by the English tongue, that to arouse interest was not a question of the interest of others, but of our own; it could only be done, but then infallibly was, if one was fundamentally interested in a thing oneself, so that when one talked about it one could hardly help drawing others in, infecting them with it, and so creating an interest up to then not present or dreamed of. And that was worth a great deal more than catering to one already existent.

It was a pity that our public gave him almost no opportunity to prove his theory. With us few, sitting at his feet in the yawning emptiness of the old hall with the numbered chairs, he proved it conclusively, for he held us charmed by things of which we should never have thought they could so capture our attention; even his frightful impediment did in the end only affect us as a stimulating and compelling expression of the zeal he felt. Often did we all nod at him consolingly when the calamity came to pass, and one or the other of the gentlemen would utter a soothing 'There, there!' or 'It's all right,' or 'Never mind!' Then the spasm would relax in a merry, apologetic smile and things would run on again in almost uncanny fluency, for a while.

What did he talk about? Well, the man was capable of spending a whole hour on the question: Why did Beethoven not write a third movement to the Piano Sonata opus III? It is without doubt a matter worth discussing. But think of it in the light of the posters outside the hall of activities for the Common Weal, or inserted in the Kaisersaschern *Railway Journal*, and ask yourself the amount of public interest it could arouse. People positively did not want to know why op. III has only two movements. We who were present at the explanation had indeed an uncommonly enriching evening, and this although the sonata under discussion was to that date entirely unknown to us. Still it was precisely through these lectures that we got to know it, and as a matter of fact very much in detail; for Kretschmar played it to us on the inferior cottage piano that was all he could command, a grand piano not being granted him. He played it capitally despite the rumbling noise the instrument made: analysing its intellectual content with great impressiveness as he went, describing the circumstances under which it – and two others – were written and expatiating with caustic wit upon the master's own explanation of the reason why he had not done a third movement corresponding to the first. Beethoven, it seems, had calmly answered this question, put by his famulus, by saying that he had not had time and therefore had somewhat extended the second movement. No time! And he had said it 'calmly', to boot. The contempt for the questioner which lay in such an answer had obviously not been noticed, but it was justified contempt. And now the speaker described Beethoven's condition in the year 1820, when his hearing, attacked by a resistless ailment, was in progressive decay, and it had already become clear that he could no longer conduct his own works. Kretschmar told us about the rumours that the famous author was quite written out, his productive powers exhausted, himself incapable of larger enterprises, and busying himself like the old Haydn with writing down Scottish songs. Such reports had continually gained ground, because for several years no work of importance bearing his name had come on the market. But in the late autumn, returning to Vienna from Mödling, where he had spent the summer, the master had sat down and written these three compositions for the piano without, so to speak, once looking up from the notes, all in one burst, and gave notice of them to his patron, the Count of Brunswick, to reassure him as to his mental condition. And then Kretschmar talked about the Sonata in C minor, which indeed it was not easy to see as a well-rounded and intellectually digested work, and which had given his contemporary critics, and his friends as well, a hard aesthetic nut to crack. These friends and amirers, Kretschmar said, simply could not follow the man they revered beyond the height to which at the time of his maturity he had brought the symphony, the piano sonata, and the classical string quartet. In the works of the last period they stood with heavy hearts before a process of dissolution or alienation, of a mounting into an air no longer familiar or safe to meddle with: even before a *plus ultra*, wherein they had been able to see nothing else than a degeneration of tendencies previously present, an excess of introspection and speculation, and extravagance of minutiae and scientific musicality – applied sometimes to such simple material as the arietta theme of the monstrous movement of variations which forms the second part of this sonata. The theme of this movement goes through a hundred vicissitudes, a hundred worlds of rhythmic contrasts, at length outgrows itself, and is finally lost in giddy heights that one might call other-worldly or abstract. And in just that very way Beethoven's art had outgrown itself, risen out of the habitable regions of tradition, even before the startled gaze of human eyes, into spheres of the entirely and utterly and nothing-but personal – an ego painfully isolated in the absolute, isolated too from sense by the loss of his hearing; lonely prince of a realm of spirits, from whom now only a chilling breath issued to terrify his most willing contemporaries, standing as they did aghast at these communications of which only at moments, only by exception, they could understand anything at all.

So far, so good, said Kretschmar. And yet again, good or right only conditionally and incompletely. For one would usually connect with the conception of the merely personal, ideas of limitless subjectivity and of radical harmonic will to expression, in contrast to polyphonic objectivity (Kretschmar was concerned to have us impress upon our minds this distinction between harmonic subjectivity and polyphonic objectivity) and this equation, this contrast, here as altogether in the masterly late works, would simply not apply. As a matter of fact, Beethoven had been far more 'subjective', not to say far more 'personal', in his middle period than in his last, had been far more bent on taking all the flourishes, formulas, and conventions, of which music is certainly full, and consuming them in the personal expression, melting them into the subjective dynamic. The relation of the later Beethoven to the conventional, say in the last five piano sonatas, is, despite all the uniqueness and even uncanniness of the formal language, quite different, much more complaisant and easy-going. Untouched, untransformed by the subjective, convention often appeared in the late works, in a baldness, one might say exhaustiveness, an abandonment of self, with an effect more majestic and awful than any reckless plunge into the personal. In these forms, said the speaker, the subjective and the conventional assumed a new relationship, conditioned by death.

At this word Kretschmar stuttered violently; sticking fast at the first sound and executing a sort of machine-gun fire with his tongue on the roof of his mouth, with jaw and chin both quivering, before they settled on the vowel which told us what he meant. But when we had guessed it, it seemed hardly proper to take it out of his mouth and shout it to him, as we sometimes did, in jovial helpfulness. He had to say it himself and he did. Where greatness and death come together, he declared, there arises an objectivity tending to the conventional, which in its majesty leaves the most domineering subjectivity far behind, because therein the merely personal – which had after all been the surmounting of a tradition already brought to its peak – once more outgrew itself, in that it entered into the mythical, the collectively great and supernatural.

He did not ask if we understood that, nor did we ask ourselves. When he gave it as his view that the main point was to hear it, we fully agreed. It was in the light of what he had said, he went on, that the work he was speaking of in particular, Sonata op III, was to be regarded. And then he sat down at the cottage piano and played us the whole composition out of his head, the first and the incredible second movement, shouting his comments into the midst of his playing and in order to make us conscious of the treatment demonstrating here and there in his enthusiasm by singing as well; altogether it made a spectacle partly entrancing, partly funny; and repeatedly greeted with merriment by his little audience. For as he had a very powerful attack and exaggerated the *forte*, he had to shriek extra loud to make what he said halfway intelligible and to sing with all the strength of his lungs to emphasize vocally what he played. With his lips he imitated what the hands played. 'Tum-tum, tum-tum tum-tr-r!' he went, as he played the grim and startling first notes of the first movement; he sang in a high falsetto the passages of melodic loveliness by which the ravaged and tempestuous skies of the composition are at intervals brightened as though by faint glimpses of light. At last he laid his hands in his lap, was quiet a moment, and then said: 'Here it comes!' and began the variations movement, the '*adagio molto semplice e cantabile*'.

The arietta theme, destined to vicissitudes for which in its idyllic innocence it would seem not to be born, is presented at once, and announced in sixteen bars, reducible to a motif which appears at the end of its first half, like a brief soul-cry – only three notes, a quaver, a semiquaver, and a dotted crotchet to be scanned as, say: 'heav-en's blue, lov-ers' pain, fare-thee well, on a-time, mead-ow-land' – and that is all. What now happens to this mild utterance, rhythmically, harmonically, contrapuntally, to this pensive, subdued formulation; with what its master blesses and to what condemns it; into what black nights and dazzling flashes, crystal spheres wherein coldness and heat, repose and ecstasy are one and the same, he flings it down and lifts it up; all that one may well call vast, strange, extravagantly magnificent, without thereby giving it a name, because it is quite truly nameless: and with labouring hands Kretschmar played us all those enormous transformations, singing at the same time with the greatest violence, 'Dim-dada!' and mingling his singing with shouts. 'These chains of trills!' he yelled. 'These flourishes and cadenzas! Do you hear the conventions that are left in? Here – the language – is no longer – purified of the flourishes – but the flourishes – of the appearance – of their subjective – domination – the appearance – of art is thrown off – at last – art always throws off the appearance of art. Dim-dada! Do listen, how here – the melody is dragged down by the centrifugal weight of chords! It becomes static, monotonous – twice D, three times D, one after the other – the chords do it – dim-dada! Now notice what happens here –'

It was extraordinarily difficult to listen to his shouts and to the highly complicated music both at once. We all tried. We strained, leaning forward, hands between knees, looking by turn at his hands and his mouth. The characteristic of the movement of course is the wide gap between bass and treble, between the right and the left hand, and a moment comes, an utterly extreme situation, when the poor little motif seems to hover alone and forsaken above a giddy yawning abyss – a procedure of awe-inspiring unearthliness, to which then succeeds a distressful making-of-itself-small, a start of fear as it were, that such a thing could happen. Much else happens before the end. But when it ends and while it ends, something comes, after so much rage, persistence, obstinacy, extravagance: something entirely unexpected and touching in its mildness and goodness. With the motif passed through many vicissitudes, which takes leave and so doing becomes itself entirely leave-taking, a parting wave and call, with this D G G occurs a slight change, it experiences a small melodic expansion. After an introductory C, it puts a C sharp before the D, so that it no longer scans 'heav-en's blue', 'mead-owland', but 'O-thou heaven's blue', 'Greenest meadowland', 'Fare-thee well for aye'; and this added C sharp is the most moving, consolatory, pathetically reconciling thing in the world. It is like having one's hair or cheek stroked, lovingly, understandingly, like a deep and silent farewell look. It blesses the object, the frightfully harried formulation, with overpowering humanity, lies in parting so gently on the hearer's heart in eternal farewell that the eyes run over. 'Now for-get the pain,' it says. 'Great was – God in us.' ''Twas all – but a dream.' 'Friendly – be to me.' Then it breaks off. Quick, hard triplets hasten to a conclusion with which any other piece might have ended.

Kretschmar did not return from the piano to his desk. He sat on his revolving stool with his face turned towards us, in the same position as ours, bent over, hands between his knees, and in a few words brought to an end his lecture on why Beethoven had not written a third movement to op. III. We had only needed, he said, to hear the piece to answer the question ourselves. A third movement? A new approach? A return after this parting – impossible! It had happened that the sonata had come, in the second, enormous movement, to an end, an end without any return. And when he said 'the sonata', he meant not only this one in C minor, but the sonata in general, as a species, as traditional art-form; it itself was here at an end, brought to its end, it had fulfilled its destiny, reached its goal, beyond which there was no going, it cancelled and resolved itself, it took leave – the gesture of farewell of the D G G motif, consoled by the C sharp, was a leave-taking in this sense too, great as the whole piece itself, the farewell of the sonata form.

With this Kretschmar went away, accompanied by thin but prolonged applause, and we went too, not a little reflective, weighted down by all these novelties. Most of us, as usual, as we put on our coats and hats and walked out, hummed bemusedly to ourselves the impression of the evening, the theme-generating motif of the second movement, in its original and its leave-taking form, and for a long time we heard it like an echo from the remoter streets into which the audience dispersed, the quiet night streets of the little town: 'Fare – thee well,' 'fare thee well for aye,' 'Great was God in us.'

That was not the last time we heard the stutterer on Beethoven. He spoke again soon, this time on 'Beethoven and the Fugue'. This lecture too I remember quite clearly, and see the announcement before me, perfectly aware that it, as little as the other, was likely to produce in the hall of the 'Common Weal' any crowd so large as to endanger life and limb. But our little group got from this evening too the most positive pleasure and profit. Always, we were told, the opponents and rivals of the bold innovator asserted that Beethoven could not write a fugue, 'That he just cannot,' they said, and probably they knew what they were talking about, for this respectable art-form stood at the time in high honour, and no composer found favour in the high courts of music or satisfied the commands of the potentates and great gentlemen who issued them if he did not stand his man in the perfection of the fugue. Prince Esterházy was an especial friend of this master art, but in the Mass in C which Beethoven wrote for him, the composer, after unsuccessful attempts, had not arrived at a fugue; even socially considered, that was a discourtesy, but artistically it had been an unpardonable lack, and the oratorio *Christ on the Mount of Olives* altogether lacked any fugue form, although it would have been most proper there. Such a feeble effort as the fugue in the third quartet of op. 59 was not calculated to counteract the view that the great man was a bad contrapuntist – in which the opinion of the authoritative musical world could only have been strengthened by the passages in fugue form in the funeral march in the 'Eroica' and the Allegretto of the A major Symphony. And now the closing movement of the Cello Sonata in D, op. 102, superscribed 'Allegro fugato'! The outcry, the fist-shaking, had been great, Kretschmar told us. Unclear to the point of unenjoyableness, that was what they taxed the whole with being; but at least for twenty bars long, they said, there reigned such scandalous confusion – principally in consequence of too strongly coloured modulations – that after it one could close the case for the incapacity of this man to write in the 'strict style'.

I interrupt myself in my reproduction to remark that the lecturer was talking about matters and things in the world of art, situations that had never come within our horizon and only appeared now on its margin in shadowy wise through the always compromised medium of his speech. We were unable to check up on it except through his own explanatory performances on the cottage piano, and we listened to it all with the dimly excited fantasy of children hearing a fairy-story they do not understand while their tender minds are none the less in a strange, dreamy, intuitive way enriched and advantaged. Fugue, counterpoint, 'Eroica', 'confusion in consequence of too strongly coloured modulations', 'strict style' – all that was just magic spells to us, but we heard it as greedily, as large-eyed, as children always hear what they do not understand or what is even entirely unsuitable – indeed, with far more pleasure than the familiar, fitting, and adequate can give them. Is it believable that this is the most intensive, splendid, perhaps the very most productive way of learning: the anticipatory way, learning that spans wide stretches of ignorance? As a pedagogue I suppose I should not speak in its behalf; but I do know that it profits youth extraordinarily. And I believe that the stretches jumped over fill in of themselves in time.

Beethoven, then, so we heard, was reputed not to be able to write a fugue; and now the question was how far this malicious criticism was true. Obviously he had taken pains to refute it. Several times he had written fugues into his later piano music, and indeed in three voices: in the 'Hammerklavier' Sonata as well as the one in A major. Once he had added 'with some liberties' (*'mit einigen Freiheiten'*), in token that the rules he had offended against were well known to him. Why he ignored them, whether arbitrarily or because he had not managed it, remained a vexed question. And then had come the great fugue overture, op. 124, and the majestic fugues in the Gloria and the Credo in evidence at last that in the struggle with this angel the great wrestler had conquered, even though thereafter he halted on his thigh.

Kretschmar told us a frightful story, impressing upon our minds an unforgettable and awful picture of the sacred trials of this struggle and the person of the afflicted artist. It was in high summer of the year 1819, at the time when Beethoven was working on the *Missa solemnis* in the Haffner house at Mödling, in despair because each movement turned out much longer than he had anticipated, so that the date of completion, March of the following year, in which the installation of the Archduke Rudolf as Bishop of Olmütz was to take place, could not possibly be kept to. It was then that two friends and professional colleagues visited him one afternoon and found an alarming state of things. That same morning the master's two maids had made off: for the night before, at about one o'clock, there had been a furious quarrel, rousing the whole house from slumber. The master had wrought late into the night, on the Credo, the Credo with the fugue, without a thought of the meal that stood waiting on the hearth; while the maids, yielding to nature, had at last fallen asleep. When the master, between twelve and one, demanded something to eat, he found the maids asleep, the food burnt and dried up. He had burst into the most violent rage, sparing the nightly rest of the house the less because he could himself not hear the noise he made. 'Could you not watch one hour with me?' he kept thundering. But it had been five or six hours, and the outraged maidservants had fled at dawn, leaving such an ill-tempered master to himself, so that he had had no midday meal either – nothing at all since the middle-day before. Instead he worked in his room on the Credo, the Credo with the fugue – the young ones heard him through the closed door. The deaf man sang, he yelled and stamped above the Credo – it was so moving and terrifying that the blood froze in their veins as they listened. But as in their great concern they were about to retreat, the door was jerked open and Beethoven stood there – in what guise? The very most frightful! With clothing dishevelled, his features so distorted as to strike terror to the beholders; the eyes dazed, absent, listening, all at once; he had stared at them, they got the impression that he had come out of a life-and-death struggle with all the opposing hosts of counterpoint. He had stammered something unintelligible, and then burst out complaining and scolding at the fine kind of housekeeping he had, and how everybody had run away and left him to starve. They had tried to pacify him, one of them helped him to put his clothing to rights, the other ran to the inn to get him some solid food ... Only three years later was the Mass finished.

Thus Kretschmar, on *Beethoven and the Fugue*; and certainly it gave us matter for talk on the way home – ground too for being silent together and for vague and silent reflection upon the new, the far, and the great, which sometimes glibly running on, sometimes appallingly impeded, had penetrated into our souls. I say into ours, but it is of course only Adrian's that I have in mind. What I heard, what I took in, is quite irrelevant.

What principally impressed him, as I heard while we were walking home, and also next day in the school courtyard, was Kretschmar's distinction between cult epochs and cultural epochs, and his remark that the secularization of art, its separation from divine service, bore only a superficial and episodic character. The pupil of the upper school appeared to be struck by the thought, which the lecturer had not expressed at all but had kindled in him, that the separation of art from the liturgical whole, its liberation and elevation into the individual and culturally self-purposive, had laden it with an irrelevant solemnity, an absolute seriousness, a pathos of suffering, which was imaged in Beethoven's frightful apparition in the doorway, and which did not need to be its abiding destiny, its permanent intellectual constitution. Hearken to the youth! Still almost without any real or practical experience in the field of art, he speculated in the void and in precocious language on the probably imminent retreat from its present role to a more modest, happier one in the service of a higher union, which did not need to be, as it once was, the Church. What it would be he could not say. But that the cultural idea was a historically transitory phenomenon, that it could lose itself again in another one, that the future did not inevitably belong to it, this thought he had certainly singled out from Kretschmar's lecture.

'But the alternative,' I threw in, 'to culture is barbarism.'

'Permit me,' said he. 'After all, barbarism is the opposite of culture only within the order of thought which it gives us. Outside of it the opposite may be something quite different or no opposite at all.'

I imitated Luca Cimabue, saying '*Santa Maria!*' and crossing myself. He gave his short laugh. Another time he asserted:

'For a cultural epoch, there seems to me to be a spot too much talk about culture in ours, don't you think? I'd like to know whether epochs that possessed culture knew the word at all, or used it. *Naïveté*, unconsciousness, taken-for-grantedness, seems to me to be the first criterion of the constitution to which we give this name. What we are losing is just this *naïveté*, and this lack, if one may so speak of it, protects us from many a colourful barbarism which altogether perfectly agreed with culture, even with very high culture. I mean: our state is that of civilization – a very praiseworthy state no doubt, but also neither was there any doubt that we should have to become very much more barbaric to be capable of culture again. Technique and comfort – in that state one talks about culture but one has not got it. Will you prevent me from seeing in the homophone-melodic constitution of our music a condition of musical civilization – in contrast to the old contrapuntal polyphone culture?'

In such talk, with which he teased and irritated me, there was much that was merely imitative. But he had a way of adapting what he picked up and giving it a personal character which took from his adaptations anything that might sound ridiculous, if not everything boyish and derivative. He commented a good deal too – or we commented in lively exchange – on a lecture of Kretschmar's called *Music and the Eye* – likewise an offering which deserved a larger audience. As the title indicates, our lecturer spoke of his art in so far as – or rather, also as – it appeals to the sense of sight, which, so he developed his theme, it does in that one puts down, through the notation, the tonal writing which – since the days of the old neumes, those arrangements of strokes and points, which had more or less indicated the flow of sound – had been practised with growing care and pains. His demonstration became very diverting and, likewise flattering, since it assumed in us a certain apprentice and brush-washer intimacy with music. Many a turn of phrase in musician's jargon came not from the acoustic but the visual, the note-picture: for instance, one speaks of *occhiali* because the broken drum-basses, half-notes that are coupled by a stroke through their necks, look like a pair of spectacles; or as one calls 'cobbler's patches' (*rosalia*) certain cheap sequences one after another in stages at like intervals (he wrote examples for us on the blackboard). He spoke of the mere appearance of musical notation, and assured us that a knowledgeable person could get from one look at the notation a decisive impression of the spirit and value of a composition. Thus it had once happened to him that a colleague, visiting his room where an uninspired work submitted to him by a dilettante was spread out on the desk, had shouted: 'Well, for heaven's sake, what sort of tripe is that you've got there?' On the other hand he sketched for us the enchanting pleasure which even the visual picture of a score by Mozart afforded to the practised eye; the clarity of the texture, the beautiful disposition of the instrumental groups, the ingenious and varied writing of the melodic line. A deaf man, he cried, quite ignorant of sound, could not but delight in these gracious visions. 'To hear with eyes belongs to love's fine wit,' he quoted from a Shakespeare sonnet, and asserted that in all time composers had secretly nested in their writing things that were meant more for the reading eye than for the ear. When, for instance, the Dutch masters of polyphony in their endless devices for the crossing of parts had so arranged them contrapuntally that one part had been like another when read backwards; that could not be perceived by the way they actually sounded, and he would wager that very few people would have detected the trick by ear, for it was intended rather for the eye of the guild. Thus Orlandus Lassus in the *Marriage at Cana* used six voices to represent the six water-jugs, which could be better perceived by seeing the music than by hearing it; and in the St John Passion by Joachim von Burck 'one of the servants', who gave Jesus a slap in the face, has only one note, but on the '*zween*' (two) in the next phrase, 'with him two others', there are two.

He produced several such Pythagorean jests, intended more for the eye than the ear, which music had now and again been pleased to make and came out roundly with the statement that in the last analysis he ascribed to the art a certain inborn lack of the sensuous, yes an antisensuality, a secret tendency to asceticism. Music was actually the most intellectual of all the arts, as was evident from the fact that in it, as in no other, form and content are interwoven and absolutely one and the same. We say of course that music 'addresses itself to the ear'; but it does so only in a qualified way, only in so far, namely, as the hearing, like the other senses, is the deputy, the instrument, and the receiver of the mind. Perhaps, said Kretschmar, it was music's deepest wish not to be heard at all, nor even seen, nor yet felt: but only – if that were possible – in some Beyond, the other side of sense and sentiment, to be perceived and contemplated as pure mind, pure spirit. But bound as she was to the world of sense, music must ever strive after the strongest, yes, the most seductive sensuous realization: she is a Kundry, who wills not what she does and flings soft arms of lust round the neck of the fool. Her most powerful realization for the senses she finds in orchestral music, where through the ear she seems to affect all the senses with her opiate wand and to mingle the pleasures of the realm of sound with those of colour and scent. Here, rightly, she was the penitent in the garb of the seductress. But there was an instrument – that is to say, a musical means of realization – through which music, while becoming audible to the sense of hearing, did so in a half-sensuous, an almost abstract way, audible, that is, in a way peculiarly suited to its intellectual nature. He meant the piano, an instrument that is not an instrument at all in the sense of the others, since all specialization is foreign to it. It can indeed, like them, be used in a solo performance and as a medium of virtuosity; but that is the exceptional case and speaking very precisely a misuse. The piano, properly speaking, is the direct and sovereign representative of music itself in its intellectuality, and for that reason one must learn it. But piano lessons should not be – or not essentially and not first and last – lessons in a special ability, but lessons in m-m –

'Music!' cried a voice from the tiny audience, for the speaker could simply not get the word out, often as he had used it before, but kept on mumbling the *m*.

'Yes, of course,' said he, released and relieved. Took a swallow of water and went on his way.

But perhaps I may be pardoned for letting him appear once more. For I am concerned with a fourth lecture which he gave us, and I would have left out one of the others if necessary, rather than this, since no other – not to speak of myself – made such a deep impression on Adrian.

I cannot recollect its exact title. It was 'The Elemental in Music' or 'Music and the Elemental' or 'The Elements of Music' or something like that. In any case the elemental, the primitive, the primeval beginning, played the chief role in it, as well as the idea that among all the arts it was precisely music that – whatever the richly complicated and finely developed and marvellous structure she had developed into in the course of the centuries – had never got rid of a religious attitude towards her own beginnings; a pious proneness to call them up in solemn invocation – in short, to celebrate her elements. She thus celebrates, he said, her cosmic aptitude for allegory; for those elements were, as it were, the first and simplest materials of the world, a parallelism of which a philosophizing artist of a day not long gone by – it was Wagner again of whom he spoke – had shrewdly, perhaps with somewhat too mechanical, too ingenious cleverness, made use, in that in his cosmogonic myth of the *Ring* he made the basic elements of music one with those of the world. To him the beginning of all things had its music; the music of the beginning was that, and also the beginning of music; the E-flat major triad of the flowing depths of the Rhine, the seven primitive chords, out of which, as though out of blocks of Cyclopean masonry, primeval stone, the 'Götterburg' arose. Surpassingly brilliant, in the grand style, he presented the mythology of music at the same time with that of the world; in that he bound the music to the things and made them express themselves in music, he created an apparatus of sensuous simultaneity – most magnificent and heavy with meaning, if a bit too clever after all, in comparison with certain revelations of the elemental in the art of the pure musicians, Beethoven and Bach; for example, in the prelude to the cello suite of the latter – also an E-flat major piece, built up in primitive triads. And he spoke of Anton Bruckner, who loved to refresh himself at the organ or piano by the simple succession of triads. 'Is there anything more heartfelt, more glorious,' he would cry, 'than such a progression of mere triads? It is not like a purifying bath for the mind?' This saying too, Kretschmar thought, was a piece of evidence worth thinking about, for the tendency of music to plunge back into the elemental and admire herself in her primitive beginnings.

Yes, the lecturer cried, it lay in the very nature of this singular art that it was at any moment capable of beginning at the beginning, of discovering itself afresh out of nothing, bare of all knowledge of its past cultural history, and of creating anew. It would then run through the same primitive stages as in its historical beginnings and could on one short course, apart from the main massif of its development, alone and unheeded by the world, reach most extraordinary and singular heights. And now he told us a story which in the most fantastic and suggestive way fitted into the frame of his present theme.

At about the middle of the eighteenth century there had flourished in his native home in Pennsylvania a German community of pious folk belonging to the Baptist sect. Their leading and spiritually most respected members lived celibate lives and had therefore been honoured with the name of Solitary Brethren and Sisters; but the majority of them reconciled with the married state an exemplarily pure and godly manner of life, strictly regulated, hard-working and dietetically sound, full of sacrifice and self-discipline. Their settlements had been two: one called Ephrata, in Lancaster County, the other in Franklin County, called Snowhill; and they had all looked up reverently to their head shepherd and spiritual father, the founder of the sect, a man named Beissel, in whose character fervent devotion to God mingled with the qualities of leadership, and fanatic religiosity with a lively and blunt-spoken energy.

Johann Conrad Beissel had been born of very poor parents at Eberbach in the Palatinate and early orphaned. He had learned the baker's trade and as a roving journeyman had made connexions with Pietists and devotees of the Baptist confession, which had awakened in him the slumbering inclinations towards an explicit service of the truth and a freely arising conviction of God. All this had brought him dangerously near to a sphere regarded in his country as heretical, and the thirty-year-old man decided to flee from the intolerance of the Old World and emigrate to America. There, in various places, in Germantown and Conestoga, he worked for a while as a weaver. Then a fresh impulse of religious devotion came over him and he had followed his inward voice, leading as a hermit in the wilderness an entirely solitary and meagre life, fixed only upon God. But as it will happen that flight from mankind sometimes only involves the more with humanity the man who flees, so Beissel had soon seen himself surrounded by a troop of admiring followers and imitators of his way of life, and instead of being free of the world, he had unexpectedly become, in the turning of a hand, the head of a community, which quickly developed into an independent sect, the Seventh-Day Anabaptists. He commanded them the more absolutely in that, so far as he knew, he had never sought the leadership, but was rather called to it against his intention and desire.

Beissel had never enjoyed any education worth mentioning; but in his awakened state he had mastered by himself the skills of reading and writing, and as his mind surged like the sea, tumultuous with mystical feelings and ideas, the result was that he filled his office chiefly as writer and poet and fed the souls of his flock: a stream of didactic prose and religious songs poured from his pen to the edification of the brethren in their silent hours and to the enrichment of their services. His style was high-flown and cryptic, laden with metaphor, obscure Scriptural allusions, and a sort of erotic symbolism. A tract on the Sabbath, *Mystyrion Anomalias*, and a collection of ninety-nine *Mystical and Very Secret Sayings* were the beginning. A series of hymns followed on, which were to be sung to well-known European choral melodies, and appeared in print under such titles as *Songs for God's Love and Praise, Jacob's Place of Struggle and Elevation, Zionist Hill of Incense*. It was these little collections that a few years later, enlarged and improved, became the official song-book of the Seventh-Day Baptists of Ephrata, with the sweetly mournful title 'Song of the Lonely and Forsaken Turtle Dove, the Christian Church'. Printed and reprinted, further enriched by the emulative members of the sect, single and married, men and even more women, the standard work changed its title and also appeared once as *Miracle Play in Paradise*. It finally contained not less than seven hundred and seventy hymns, among them some with an enormous number of stanzas.

The songs were meant to be sung, but they lacked music. They were new texts to old tunes and were so used for years by the community. But now a new inspiration visited Johann Conrad Beissel. The spirit commanded him to take to himself in addition to the role of poet and prophet that of composer.

There had been a young man staying at Ephrata, a young adept of the art of music, who held a singing-class; Beissel loved to attend and listen to the instruction. He must thus have made the discovery that music afforded possibilities for the extension and realization of the kingdom of the spirit, in a way of which young Herr Ludwig never dreamed. The extraordinary man's resolve was swiftly formed. No longer of the youngest, already far on in the fifties, he applied himself to work out a musical theory of his own, suited to his special requirements. He put the singing-teacher aside and took things firmly in his own hands – with such success that before long he had made music the most important element in the religious life of the community.

Most of the chorals, which had come over from Europe, seemed to him much too forced, complicated, and artificial to serve for his flock. He wanted to do something new and better and to inaugurate a music better answering to the simplicity of their souls and enabling them by practice to bring it to their own simple perfection. An ingenious and practical theory of melody was swiftly and boldly resolved on. He decreed that there should be 'masters' and 'servants' in every scale. Having decided to regard the common chord as the melodic centre of any given key, he called 'masters' the notes belonging to this chord, and the rest of the scale 'servants'. And those syllables of a text upon which the accent lay had always to be presented by a 'master', the unaccented by a 'servant'.

As for the harmony, he made use of a summary procedure. He made chord-tables for all possible keys, with the help of which anybody could write out his tunes comfortably enough, in four or five parts; and thus he caused a perfect rage for composition in the community. Soon, there was no longer a single Seventh-Day Baptist, whether male or female, who, thus assisted, had not imitated the master and composed music.

Rhythm was now the part of theory which remained to be dealt with by this redoubtable man. He accomplished it with consummate success. He painstakingly followed with the music the cadence of the words, simply by providing the accented syllables with longer notes, and giving the unaccented shorter ones. To establish a fixed relation between the values of the notes did not occur to him; and just for that reason he preserved considerable flexibility for his metre. Like practically all the music of his time it was written in recurrent metres of like length – that is to say, in bars – but he either did not know this or did not trouble about it. This ignorance or unconcern, however, was above all else to his advantage; for the free, fluctuating rhythm made some of his compositions, particularly his setting of prose, extraordinarily effective.

This man cultivated the field of music, once he had entered it, with the same persistence with which he had pursued all of his other aims. He put together his thoughts on theory and published them as a preface to the book of the *Turtle Dove*. In uninterrupted application he provided with musical settings all the poems in the *Mount of Incense*, some of them with two or three, and set to music all the hymns he had himself ever written, as well as a great many by his pupils. Not satisfied with that, he wrote a number of more extended chorals, with texts taken direct from the Bible. It seemed as though he was about to set to music according to his own receipt the whole of the Scriptures; certainly he was the man to conceive such a plan. If it did not come to that, it was only because he had to devote a large part of his time to the performance of what he had done, the training in execution and instruction in singing – and in this field he now achieved the simply extraordinary.

The music of Ephrata, Kretschmar told us, was too unusual, too amazing and arbitrary, to be taken over by the world outside, and hence it had sunk into practical oblivion when the sect of the German Seventh-Day Baptists ceased to flourish. But a faint legend had persisted down the years, sufficient in fact to make known how utterly peculiar and moving it had been. The tones coming from the choir had resembled delicate instrumental music and evoked an impression of heavenly mildness and piety in the hearer. The whole had been sung falsetto, and the singers had scarcely opened their mouths or moved their lips – with wonderful acoustic effect. The sound, that is, had thus been thrown up to the rather low ceiling of the hall, and it had seemed as though the notes, unlike any familiar to man, and in any case unlike any known church music, floated down thence and hovered angelically above the heads of the assemblage.

His own father, Kretschmar said, had often heard these sounds as a young man, and in his old age, when he talked to his family about it, his eyes had always filled with tears. He had spent a summer near Snowhill and on a Friday evening, the beginning of the Sabbath, had once ridden over as an onlooker at the house of worship of those pious folk. After that he had gone again and again: every Friday, as the sun set, driven by a resistless urge, he had saddled his horse and ridden the three miles to listen. It had been quite indescribable, not to be compared with anything in this world. He had, so the elder Kretschmar had said, sat in English, French, and Italian opera houses; that had been music for the ear, but Beissel's rang deep down into the soul and was nothing more nor less than a foretaste of heaven.

'A great art,' so our reporter said in closing, 'which, as it were aloof from time and time's great course, could develop a little private history of this kind, and by forgotten side-paths lead to such exceptional beatitudes.'

I recall as though it were yesterday how I went home with Adrian after this lecture. Although we did not talk much, we were unwilling to separate; and from his uncle's house, whither I accompanied him, he went back with me to the shop, and then I back with him to Parochialstrasse. Though of course we often did that. We both made merry over the man Beissel, this backwoods dictator with his droll thirst for action, and agreed that his music reform reminded us very much of the passage in Terence: 'to behave stupidly with reason'. But Adrian's attitude to the curious phenomenon differed from mine in what was after all so distinctive a way that it soon occupied me more than the subject itself. I mean that even while he mocked he set store by preserving the right to appreciate: set store by the right, not to say the privilege of keeping a distance, which includes in itself the possibility of good-natured acceptance, of conditioned agreement, half-admiration, along with the mockery and laughter. Quite generally this claim to ironic remoteness, to an objectivity which surely is paying less honour to the thing than to the freedom of the person has always seemed to me a sign of uncommon arrogance. In so young a person as Adrian was then, the presumption of this attitude, it must be admitted, is disquieting; it was calculated to cause one concern for the health of his soul. Of course it is also very impressive to a companion with a simpler mental constitution, and since I loved him, I loved his arrogance as well – perhaps I loved him for its sake. Yes, that is how it was: this arrogance was the chief motive of the fearful love which all my life I cherished for him in my heart.

'Leave me alone,' said he, as with our hands in our overcoat pockets we went to and fro between our two dwellings, in the wintry mist that wrapped the gas-lamps, 'leave me in peace with my old codger, I can do with him. At least he had a sense of order and even a silly order is better than none at all.'

'Surely,' I answered him, 'you won't defend such a ridiculous and dogmatic arrangement, such childish rationalism as this invention of masters and servants. Imagine how these Beissel hymns must have sounded, in which every accented syllable had to have one note of the chord fall on it!'

'In any case not sentimental,' he responded, 'rather rigidly conforming to the law, and that I approve. You can console yourself that there was plenty of play for the fancy you put high above the law, in the free use of the servant notes.'

He had to laugh at the word, bent over as he walked, and laughed down upon the wet pavement.

'Funny, it's very funny,' he said. 'But one thing you will admit. Law, every law, has a chilling effect, and music has so much warmth anyhow, stable warmth, cow warmth, I'd like to say, that she can stand all sorts of regulated cooling off – she has even asked for it.'

'There may be some truth in that,' I admitted. 'But our Beissel isn't after all any very striking example of it. You forget that his rhythm, quite unregulated and abandoned to feeling, at least balanced the rigidity of his melody. And then he invented a singing style for himself – up to the ceiling and then floating down in a seraphic falsetto – it must have been simply ravishing and certainly gave back to music all the bovine warmth that it had previously taken away through the pedantic cooling off.'

'Ascetic, Kretschmar would say,' he answered, 'the ascetic cooling off. In that Father Beissel was very genuine. Music always does penance in advance for her retreat into the sensual. The old Dutchmen made her do the rummest sort of tricks, to the glory of God; and it went harder and harder on her from all one hears, with no sense appeal, excogitated by pure calculation. But then they had these penitential practices sung, delivered over to the sounding breath of the human voice, which is certainly the most stable-warm imaginable thing in the world of sound ...'

'You think so?'

'Why not? No unorganic instrumental sound can be compared with it. Abstract it may be, the human voice – the abstract human being, if you like. But that is a kind of abstraction more like that of the naked body – it is after all more a pudendum.' I was silent, confounded. My thoughts took me far back in our, in his past.

'There you have it,' said he, 'your music.' I was annoyed at the way he put it, it sounded like shoving music off on me, as though it were more my affair than his. 'There you have the whole thing, she was always like that. Her strictness, or whatever you like to call the moralism of her form, must stand for an excuse for the ravishments of her actual sounds.'

For a moment I felt myself the older, more mature.

'A gift of life like music,' I responded, 'not to say a gift of God, one ought not to explain by mocking antinomies, which only bear witness to the fullness of her nature. One must love her.'

'Do you consider love the strongest emotion?' he asked.

'Do you know a stronger?'

'Yes, interest.'

'By which you presumably mean a love from which the animal warmth has been withdrawn.'

'Let us agree on the definition!' he laughed. 'Good night!'

We had got back to the Leverkühn house, and he opened his door.

Chapter Nine

I will not look back, I will take care not to count the pages I have covered between the last Roman numeral and this one I have just written down. The evil – in any case quite unanticipated – has come to pass and it would be useless to expend myself in excuses or self-accusations. The question whether I might and should have avoided it by giving a chapter to each one of Kretschmar's lectures I must answer in the negative. Each separate division of a work needs a certain body, a definite volume sufficient to add to the significance of the whole, and this weight, this volume of significance, pertains to the lectures only collectively (in so far as I have reported them) and not to the single ones.

But why do I ascribe such significance to them? Why have I seen myself induced to reproduce them in such detail? I give the reason, not for the first time. It is simply this: that Adrian heard these things then, they challenged his intelligence, made their deposit in the vessel of his feelings, and gave matter to feed or to stimulate his fancy. And for the fancy, food and stimulant are one and the same. The reader must perforce be made a witness of the process; since no biography, no depiction of the growth and development of an intellectual life, could properly be written without taking its subject back to the pupil stage, to the period of his beginnings in life and art, when he listened, learned, divined, gazed and ranged now afar, now close at hand. As for music in particular, what I want to strive to do is to make the reader see it as Adrian did; to bring him in touch with music, precisely as it happened to my departed friend. And to that end everything his teacher said seems to me not only not a negligible means but even an indispensable one.

And so, half jestingly, I would address those who in that last monstrous chapter have been guilty of some skipping: I would remind them of how Laurence Sterne once dealt with an imaginary listener who betrayed that she had not always been paying attention. The author sent her back to an earlier chapter to fill in the gaps in her knowledge. After having informed herself, the lady rejoins the group of listeners and is given a hearty welcome.

The passage came to my mind because Adrian as a top-form student, at a time when I had already left for the University of Giessen, studied English outside the school courses, and after all outside the humanistic curriculum, under the influence of Wendell Kretschmar. He read Sterne with great pleasure. Even more enthusiastically he read Shakespeare, of whom the organist was a close student and passionate admirer. Shakespeare and Beethoven together formed in Kretschmar's intellectual heaven a twin constellation outshining all else, and he dearly loved calling his pupil's attention to remarkable similarities and correspondences in the creative principles and methods of the two giants – an instance of the stutterer's far-reaching influence on my friend's education, quite aside from the piano lessons. As a music-teacher, of course, he had to give Adrian the childish beginnings; but on the other hand, and in strange contrast, he gave him at the same time and almost in passing his earliest contact with greatness. He opened to him the ample page of world literature; whetting his appetite by small foretastes, he lured him into the broad expanses of the Russian, English, and French novel, stimulated him to read the lyrical poems of Shelley and Keats, Hölderlin and Novalis; gave him Manzoni and Goethe, Schopenhauer and Meister Eckehart. Through Adrian's letters, as well as by word of mouth when I came home in the holidays, I shared in these conquests, and I will not deny that sometimes, despite my knowledge of his facility, I was concerned for his strength. After all, these acquirements were premature, they must have burdened his young system, in addition to the preparations for his finals. About the latter, indeed, he spoke contemptuously. He often looked pale, and that not only on days when the hereditary migraine laid him low. Obviously he had too little sleep, for his reading was done in the night hours. I did not refrain from confessing my concern to Kretschmar and asking him if he did not see in Adrian, as I did, a nature that in the intellectual field should rather be held back than urged forwards. But the musician, although so much older than I, proved to be a thorough-going partisan of impatient youth avid of knowledge, unsparing of his strength. Indeed, the man showed in general a certain ideal harshness and indifference to the body and its 'health', which he considered a right philistine, not to say cowardly value.

'Yes, my dear friend,' said he (I omit the hitches which detracted from his impressiveness), 'if it is healthiness you are after – well, with mind and art it has not got much to do, it even in a sort of way opposes them, and anyhow they have never troubled much about each other. To play the family doctor who warns against premature reading because it was always premature to him all his life – I'm no good for that. And besides, I find nothing more tactless and barbarous than nailing a gifted youth down to his "immaturity" and telling him in every other word: "That is nothing for you yet." Let him judge for himself! Let him see how he comes on! That the time will be long to him till he can crawl out of the shell of this sleepy old place is only too easy to understand.'

So there I had it – and Kaisersaschern too. I was vexed, for the standards of the family doctor were certainly not mine either. And besides that, I saw not only that Kretschmar was not content to be a piano-teacher and trainer in a special technique, but that music itself, the goal of his teaching, if it were pursued one-sidedly and without connexion with other fields of form, thought, and culture, seemed to him a stunting specialization, humanly speaking. As a matter of fact, from all that I heard from Adrian, the lesson-hours in Kretschmar's medieval quarters in the Cathedral were a good half of the time taken up with talks on philosophy and poetry. Despite that, so long as I was still in school with him, I could follow his progress literally from day to day. His self-won familiarity with keyboard and keys accelerated of course the first steps. He practised conscientiously, but a lesson-book, so far as I know, was not used; instead Kretschmar simply let him play set chorals and – however strange they sounded on the piano – four-part psalms by Palestrina consisting of pure chords with some harmonic tensions and cadenzas: then somewhat later little preludes and fuguettes of Bach, two-part inventions also by him, the Sonata Facile of Mozart, one-movement sonatas by Scarlatti. Kretschmar did not hesitate to write little pieces himself, marches and dances, partly for playing solo, partly as duets in which the musical burden lay in the second part, while the first, for the pupil, was kept quite simple so that he had the satisfaction of sharing in the performance of a production which as a whole moved on a higher plane of technical competence than his own.

All in all it was a little like the education of a young prince. I remember that I used the word teasingly in talk with my friend; remember too how he turned away with the odd short laugh peculiar to him, as though he would have pretended not to hear. No doubt he was grateful to his teacher for a kind of instruction taking cognizance of the pupil's general mental development, which did not belong to the childish stage of his present and rather tardy musical beginnings. Kretschmar was not unwilling, in fact he rather preferred, to have this youth, plainly vibrating with ability, hurry on ahead in music too and concern himself with matters that a more pedantic mentor would have forbidden as time-wasting. For Adrian scarcely knew the notes when he began to write and experiment with chords on paper. The mania he then developed of thinking out musical problems, which he solved like chess problems, might make one fear lest he thought this contriving and mastering of technical difficulties was already composition. He spent hours in linking up, in the smallest possible space, chords that together contained all the notes of the chromatic scale, without their being chromatically side-slipped and without producing harshnesses in their progression. Or he amused himself by writing very sharp dissonances and finding all possible re-solutions for them, which, however, just because the chord contained so many discordant notes, had nothing to do with each other, so that the acid chord, like a magic formula, created relations between the remotest chords and keys.

One day the beginner in the theory of harmony brought to Kretschmar, to the latter's amusement, the discovery he had himself made of double counterpoint. That is, he gave to his teacher to read two parts running simultaneously, each of which could form the upper or the lower part and thus were interchangeable. 'If you have got the triple counterpoint,' said Kretschmar, 'keep it to yourself. I don't want to hear about your rashness.'

He kept much to himself, sharing his speculations with me only in moments of relaxation, and then especially his absorption in the problem of unity, interchangeability, identity of horizontal and vertical writing. He soon possessed what was in my eyes an uncanny knack of inventing melodic lines which could be set against each other simultaneously, and whose notes telescoped into complex harmonies — and, on the other hand, he invented chords consisting of note-clusters that were to be projected into the melodic horizontal.

In the schoolyard, between a Greek and a trigonometry class, leaning on the ledge of the glazed brick wall, he would talk to me about these magic diversions of his idle time: of the transformation of the horizontal interval into the chord, which occupied him as nothing else did; that is, of the horizontal into the vertical, the successive into the simultaneous. Simultaneity, he asserted, was here the primary element; for the note, with its more immediate and more distant harmonics, was a chord in itself, and the scale only the analytical unfolding of the chord into the horizontal row.

'But with the real chord, consisting of several notes, it is after all something different. A chord is meant to be followed up by another, and so soon as you do it, carry it over into another, each one of its component notes becomes a voice-part. I find that in a chordal combination of notes one should never see anything but the result of the movement of voices and do honour to the part as implied in the single chord-note – but not honour the chord as such, rather despise it as subjective and arbitary, so long as it cannot prove itself to the the result of part-writing. The chord is no harmonic narcotic but polyphony in itself, and the notes that form it are parts. But I assert they are that the more, and the polyphonic character of the chords is the more pronounced, the more dissonant it is. The degree of dissonance is the measure of its polyphonic value. The more discordant a chord is, the more notes it contains contrasting and conflicting with each other, the more polyphonic it is, and the more markedly every single note bears the stamp of the part already in the simultaneous sound-combination.'

I looked at him for some time, nodding my head with half-humorous fatalism.

'Pretty good! You're a wonder!' said I, finally.

'You mean that for me?' he said, turning away as he so often did. 'But I am talking about music, not about myself – some little difference.'

He insisted upon this distinction, speaking of music always as a strange power, a phenomenon amazing but not touching him personally, talking about it with critical detachment and a certain condescension; but he talked about it, and had more to say, because in these years, the last I spent with him at school, and my first semesters as a university student, his knowledge of the world's musical literature rapidly broadened, so that soon, indeed, the difference between what he knew and what he could do lent to the distinction he emphasized a sort of strikingness. For while as pianist he was practising such things as Schumann's *Kinderscenen* and the two little sonatas of Beethoven, op. 45, and as a music pupil dutifully harmonizing choral themes so that the theme came to lie in the centre of the chord; he was at the same time, and with an excessive, even headlong acceleration of pace, gaining a comprehensive view, incoherent indeed, but with extensive detail, of preclassic, classic, romantic, late-romantic and modern production, all this of course through Kretschmar, who was himself too much in love with everything – just everything – made of notes not to burn to introduce to a pupil who knew how to listen as Adrian did this world of shapes and figures, inexhaustibly rich in styles, national characteristics, traditional values, and charms of personality, historic and individual variations of the ideal beauty.

I need scarcely say that opportunities to listen to music were, for a citizen of Kaisersaschern, extraordinarily few. Aside from the evenings of chamber music at Nikolaus Leverkühn's and the organ concerts in the Cathedral we had almost no opportunity at all, for seldom indeed would a touring virtuoso or an orchestra with its conductor from some other city penetrate into our little town. Now Kretschmar had flung himself into the breach, and with his vivid recitals had fed, if only temporarily and by suggestion, a partly unconscious, partly unconfessed yearning of my young friend for culture. Indeed, the stream was so copious that I might almost speak of a cataract of musical experience flooding his youthful receptivity. After that came years of disavowal and dissimulation, when he had far less music than at the time I speak of, although the circumstances were much more favourable.

It began, very naturally, with the teacher demonstrating for him the structure of the sonata in works by Clementi, Mozart, and Haydn. But before long he went on to the orchestra sonata, the symphony, and performed (in the piano-abstraction) to the watching listener sitting with drawn brows and parted lips the various chronological and personal variations of this richest manifestation of creative musical art, speaking most variedly to senses and mind. He played instrumental works by Brahms and

Bruckner, Schubert, Robert Schumann; then by the later and the latest, Tchaikovsky, Borodin, and Rimsky-Korsakov; by Anton Dvořák, Berlioz, César Franck, and Chabrier, constantly challenging his pupil's power of imagination with loud explanations, to give orchestral body and soul to the insubstantial piano version: 'Cello cantilena! You must think of that as drawn out. Bassoon solo! And the flutes give the flourishes to it! Drum-roll! There are the trombones! Here the violins come in! Follow it on the score! I have to leave out the little fanfare with the trumpets, I have only two hands!'

He did what he could with those two hands, often adding his voice, which crowed and cracked, but never badly; no, it was all even ravishing, by reason of its fervid musicality and enthusiastic rightness of expression.

Dashing from one thing to another, or linking them together, he heaped them up – first because he had endless things in his head, and one thing led on to the next; but in particular because it was his passion to make comparisons and discover relations, display influences, lay bare the interwoven connexions of culture. It pleased him to sharpen his young pupil's sense; hours on hours he spent showing him how French had influenced Russians, Italians Germans, Germans French. He showed him what Gounod had from Schumann, what César Franck from Liszt, how Debussy based on Mussorgsky and where D'Indy and Chabrier wagnerized. To show how sheer contemporaneity set up mutual relations between such different natures as Tchaikovsky and Brahms, that too belonged to these lesson-hours. He played him bits from the works of the one that might well be by the other. In Brahms, whom he put very high, he demonstrated the reference to the archaic, to old church modes, and how this ascetic element in him became the means of achieving a sombre richness and gloomy grandeur. He told his pupil to note how, in this kind of romanticism, with a noticeable reference to Bach, the polyphonic principle seriously confronted the harmonic colour and made it retreat. But true independence of parts, true polyphony, that was not: and had already not been with Bach, in whom one does indeed find the contrapuntal devices peculiar to the vocal polyphony of an older period, but who by blood had been a harmonist and nothing else – already as the man to use the tempered scale, this premise for all the later art of modulation, and his harmonic counterpoint had at bottom no more to do with the old vocal polyphony than Handel's harmonic alfresco style.

It was precisely such remarks as these for which Adrian's ear was so peculiarly keen. In conversations with me he went into it.

'Bach's problem,' he said, 'was this: how is one to write pregnant polyphony in a harmonic style? With the moderns the question presents itself somewhat differently. Rather it is: how is one to write a harmonic style that has the appearance of polyphony? Remarkable, it looks like bad conscience – the bad conscience of homophonic music in face of polyphony.'

It goes without saying that by so much listening he was led to the enthusiastic reading of scores, partly from his teacher's, partly from the town library. I often found him at such studies and at written instrumentation. For information about the compass of the individual orchestral instruments (instruction which the instrument-dealer's foster-son hardly needed) also flowed into the lessons, and Kretschmar had begun giving him to orchestrate short classical pieces, single piano movements from Schubert and Beethoven, also the piano accompaniments of songs: studies whose weaknesses and slips he then pointed out and corrected. This was the beginning of Adrian's acquaintance with the glorious period of the

German lied, which after fairly jejune beginnings bursts out wonderfully in
Schubert, to celebrate its incomparable national triumphs with Schumann,
Robert Franz, Brahms, Hugo Wolf, and Mahler. A glorious conjunction! I
was happy to be present and share all this. A jewel and miracle like
Schumann's *Mondnacht*, with the lovely, delicate seconds in the accompaniment! Other Eichendorff compositions of the same master, like that piece
involving all the romantic perils and threats to the soul, which ends with the
uncannily moral warning: '*Hüte dich, sei wach und munter!*' a masterly
invention like Mendelssohn's *Auf Flügeln des Gesanges*, the inspiration of a
musician whom Adrian used to extol very highly to me, calling him the most
gifted of all in his use of different metres – ah, what fruitful topics for
discussion! In Brahms as a song-writer my friend valued above all else the
peculiarly new and austere style in the *Four Serious Songs* written for Bible
texts, expecially the religious beauty of '*O Tod, wie bitter bist Du!*' But
Schubert's always twilit genius, death-touched, he liked above all to seek
where he lifts to the loftiest expression a certain only half-defined but
inescapable destiny of solitude, as in the grandly self-tormenting '*Ich komme
vom Gerbirge her*' from the Smith of Lübeck and that '*Was vermeid' ich die
Wege, wo die andern Wandrer gehn?*' from the *Winterreise*, with the perfectly
heart-breaking stanza beginning:

> *Hab' ja doch nichts begangen*
> *Das ich Menschen sollte scheu'n.*

These words, and the following:

> *Welch ein törichtes Verlangen*
> *Treibt mich in die Wüstenei'n?*

I have heard him speak to himself, indicating the musical phrasing, and to
my unforgettable amazement I saw the tear spring to his eyes.

Of course his instrumental writing suffered from a lack of experience
through actual hearing and Kretschmar set himself to remedy the defect. In
Michaelmas and Christmas holidays they went (with Uncle Niko's permission) to operas and concerts in near-by cities: Merseburg, Erfurt, even
Weimar, in order that he might realize in actual sound what he had received
in the abstract and seen at most on paper. Thus he could take in the childlike
solemnity and esoteric mystery of *The Magic Flute*, the formidable charm of
Figaro, the daemony of the low clarinets in Weber's glorious transmuted
operetta *Der Freischütz*; similar figures of painful and sombre solitude like
those of *Hans Heiling* and *The Flying Dutchman*; finally the lofty humanity
and brotherhood of *Fidelio*, with the great Overture in C, played before the
final scene. This last, of course, was the most impressive, the most
absorbing, of all that his young receptive mind came in contact with. For
days after that evening he kept the score of No. 3 by him and read it
constantly.

'My friend,' he said, 'probably they haven't been waiting for me to say so;
but that is a perfect piece of music. Classicism – yes, it isn't sophisticated at
all, but it is great. I don't say: *for* it is great, because there is such a thing as
sophisticated greatness; but this is at bottom much more intimate. Tell me,
what do you think about greatness? I find there is something uncomfortable
about facing it eye to eye, it is a test of courage – can one really look it in the
eye? You can't stand it, you give way. Let me tell you, I incline more and
more to the admission that there is something very odd indeed about this
music of yours. A manifestation of the highest energy – not at all abstract,

but without an object, energy in a void, in pure ether – where else in the universe does such a thing appear? We Germans have taken over from philosophy the expression "in itself", we use it every day without much idea of the metaphysical. But here you have it, such music is energy itself, yet not as idea, rather in its actuality. I call your attention to the fact that that is almost the definition of God. *Imitatio Dei* – I am surprised that it is not forbidden. Perhaps it is. Anyhow that is a very nice point – in more than one sense of the word. Look: the most powerful, most varied, most dramatic succession of events and activities, but only in time, consisting only of time articulated, filled up, organized – and all at once almost thrust into the concrete exigencies of the plot by the repeated trumpet-signals from without. All that is most elegantly and grandly conceived, kept witty and rather objective, even in the high spots – neither scintillating nor all too splendid, nor even very exciting in colour, only just masterly beyond words. How all that is brought in and transformed and put before you, how one theme is led up to and another left behind, taken apart; yet in the process something new is getting ready, so that there is no empty or feeble passage; how flexibly the rhythm changes, a climax approaches, takes in tributaries from all sides, swells like a rising torrent, bursts out in roaring triumph, triumph itself, triumph "in and for itself" – I do not like to call it beautiful, the word "beauty" has always been half offensive to me, it has such a silly face, and people feel wanton and corrupt when they say it. But it is good, good in the extreme it could not be better, perhaps it ought not to be better ...'

Thus Adrian. It was a way of talking that in its mixture of intellectual self-criticism and slight feverishness affected me as indescribably moving. Moving because he felt the feverishness in it and found it offensive, was unpleasantly aware of the tremble in his still boyishly thin voice and turned away, flushing.

A great advance in musical knowledge and enthusiastic participation took place at that time in his life, only to get no further for years – at least to all appearance.

Chapter Ten

During his last year at school, in the highest form, Leverkühn in addition to everything else began the study of Hebrew, which was not obligatory and which I did not pursue. Thus he betrayed the direction of his plans for a profession: it 'turned out' (I purposely repeat the expression I used to describe the moment when by a chance word he betrayed his religious inner life), it turned out that he intended to study theology. The approach of the final examinations demanded a decision, the election of a faculty, and he declared his choice: declared it in answer to his uncle, who raised his brows and said 'Bravo!' – declared it of his own accord to his parents at Buchel, who received the news even better pleased; and had already told me earlier, confessing at the same time that he did not envisage his choice as preparation for taking a parish and assuming a cure of souls, but as an academic career.

That should have been a kind of reassurance to me; indeed, it was that, for it went against me to imagine him as a candidate for the office of preacher or

pastor, or even as councillor of the consistory or other high office. If only he
had been a Catholic, as we were! His easily imaginable progress up to the
stages of the hierarchy, to a prince of the Church, would have seemed to me a
happier, more fitting prospect. But the very resolve was itself something of a
shock and I think I changed colour when he told me. Why? I could hardly
have said what he should else have chosen. Actually, to me there was nothing
good enough for him; that is, the civilian, empirical side of any calling did
not seem to me worthy of him, and I should have looked round in vain for
another in the practical, professional performance of which I could properly
imagine him. The ambition I cherished on his account was absolute. And yet
a shudder went through me when I divined – divined very clearly – that he
had made his choice out of arrogance.

We had on occasion agreed, of course, or more correctly we had both
espoused the general view, that philosophy was the queen of the sciences.
Among them, we had affirmed, she took a place like that of the organ among
instruments: she afforded a survey; she combined them intellectually, she
ordered and refined the issues of all the fields of research into a universal
picture, an overriding and decisive synthesis comprehending the meaning of
life, a scrutinizing determination of man's place in the cosmos. My
consideration of my friend's future, my thoughts about a 'profession' for
him, had always led me to similar conclusions. The many-sidedness of his
activities, while they made me anxious for his health, his thirst for
experience, accompanied as it was by a critical attitude, justified such
dreams. The most universal field, the life of a masterly polyhistor and
philosopher seemed to me just right for him – and further my powers of
imagination had not brought me. Now I was to learn that he on his side had
privately gone much further. Without giving a sign – for he expressed his
decision in very quiet, unassuming words – he had outbid and put to shame
the ambitions of his friend for him.

But there is, if you like, a discipline in which Queen Philosophy becomes
the servant, the ancillary science, academically speaking a subsidiary branch
of another; and that other is theology. Where love of wisdom lifts itself to
contemplation of the highest essence, the source of being, the study of God
and the things of God: there, one might say, is the peak of scientific dignity,
the highest and noblest sphere of knowledge, the apex of all thinking; to the
inspired intellect its most exalted goal is here set. The most exalted because
here the profane sciences, for instance my own, philology, as well as history
and the rest, become a mere tool for the service of knowledge of the divine –
and again, the goal to be pursued in the profoundest humility, because in the
words of the Scriptures it is 'higher than all reason' and the human spirit
thereby enters into a more pious, trusting bond than that which any other of
the learned professions lays upon him.

This went through my mind when Adrian told me of his decision. If he
had made it out of an instinct of spiritual self-discipline, out of the wish to
hedge in by a religious profession that cool and ubiquitous intellect of his,
which grasped everything so easily and was so spoilt by its own superiority –
then I should have agreed. I would not only have tranquillized my indefinite
concern, always present, albeit silently; and moreover it would have touched
me deeply, for the *sacrificium intellectus*, which of necessity contemplation
and knowledge of the other world carries with it, must be esteemed the more
highly, the more powerful the intellect that makes it. But I did not at bottom
believe in my friend's humility. I believed in his pride, of which for my part I
was proud too, and could not really doubt that it was the source of his

decision. Hence the mixture of joy and concern, the grounds of the shudder than went through me.

He saw my conflict and seemed to ascribe it to a third person, his music-teacher.

'You mean, of course, Kretschmar will be disappointed,' he said. 'Naturally, I know he would have liked me to give myself to Polyhymnia. Strange, people always want you to follow the same path they do. One can't please everybody. But I'll remind him that through liturgy and her history music plays very strongly into the theological; more practically and artistically, indeed, than into the mathematical and physical, or into acoustics.'

In announcing his purpose of saying as much to Kretschmar, he was really, as I well knew, saying it to me; and when I was alone I thought of it again and again. Certainly, in relation to theology and the service of God, music – of course like all the arts, and also the secular sciences, but music in particular – took on ancillary, auxiliary, character. The thought was associated in my mind with certain discussions which we had had on the destiny of art, on the one hand very conducive, but on the other sadly hampering; we referred to her emancipation from cult, her cultural secularization. It was all quite clear to me: his choice had been influenced by his personal desire and his professional prospects, the wish to reduce music again to the position that once, in times he considered happier, she had held in the union of cults. Like the profane disciplines, so likewise music: he would see them all beneath the sphere to which he would dedicate himself as adept. And I got a strange vision, a sort of allegory of his point of view: it was like a baroque painting, an enormous altarpiece, whereon all the arts and sciences in humble and votive posture paid their devotions to theology enthroned.

Adrian laughed loudly at my vision when I told him about it. He was in high spirits at that time, much inclined to jest – and quite understandably. The moment of taking flight, when freedom dawns, when the school gate shuts behind us, the shell breaks, the chrysalis bursts, the world lies open – is it not the happiest, or the most exciting, certainly the most expectant in all our lives? Through his musical excursions with Wendell Kretschmar to the larger near-by cities, Adrian had tasted the outer world a few times; now Kaisersaschern, the place of witches and strangelings, of the instrument warehouse and the imperial tomb in the Cathedral, would finally loose its hold on him, and only on visits would he walk its streets, smiling like one aware of other spheres.

Was that true? Had Kaisersaschern ever released him? Did he not take her with him wherever he went and was he not conditioned by her whenever he thought to decide? What is freedom? Only the neutral is free. The characteristic is never free, it is stamped, determined, bound. Was it not 'Kaisersaschern' that spoke in my friend's decision to study theology? Adrian Leverkühn and Kaisersaschern: obviously the two together yielded theology. I asked myself further what else I had expected. He devoted himself later to musical composition. But if it was very bold music he wrote, was it after all 'free' music, world music? That it was not. It was the music of one who never escaped; it was, into its most mysterious, inspired, bizarre convolution, in every hollow breath and echo it gave out, characteristic music, music of Kaisersaschern.

He was, I said, in high spirits at that time – and why not? Dispensed from oral examination on the basis of the maturity of his written work, he had taken leave of his teachers, with thanks for all they had done; while on their side respect for the profession he had chosen repressed the private annoyance they had always felt at his condescending facility. Even so, the worthy director of the School of the Brethren of the Common life, a Pomeranian named Dr Stoientin, who had been Adrian's master in Greek, Middle High German, and Hebrew, did not fail at their private leave-taking to utter a word of warning.

'*Vale,*' he said, 'and God be with you, Leverkühn. – The parting blessing comes from my heart, and whether you are of that opinion or not, it seems to me you may need it. You are a person richly gifted and you know it – as why should you not? You know too that He above, from whom all comes, gave you your gifts, for to Him you now offer them. You are right: natural merits are God's merits in us, not our own. It is His foe who, fallen through pride himself, would teach us to forget. He is evil to entertain, a roaring lion who goes about seeking whom he may devour. You are among those who have reason to be on guard against his wiles. It is a compliment I am paying you, or rather to what you are from God. Be it in humility, my friend, not in defiance or with boasting; and be ever mindful that self-satisfaction is like a falling away and unthankfulness against the Giver of all mercies!'

Thus our honest schoolmaster, under whom later I served as teacher in the gymnasium. Adrian reported it smiling, on one of the many walks we took through field and forest, in that Eastertide at Buchel. For he spent several weeks of freedom there after leaving school, and his good parents invited me to bear him company. Well I remember the talks we had as we strolled, about Stoientin's warning, especially about the expression 'native merit' which he had used in his farewell. Adrian pointed out that he took it from Goethe, who enjoyed using it, and also 'inborn merits', seeking in the paradoxical combination to divorce from the word 'merit' its moral character, and, conversely, to exalt the natural and inborn to a position of extra-moral, aristocratic desert. That was why he was against the claims of modesty which were always put forward by those disadvantaged by nature, and declared that 'Only good-for-nothings are modest.' But Director Stoientin had used Goethe's words more in Schiller's sense, to whom everything had depended on freedom, and who therefore distinguished in a moral sense between talent and personal merit, sharply differentiating merit and fortune, which Goethe considered to be inextricably interwoven. The director followed Schiller, when he called Nature God and native talent the merit of God in us, which we were to wear in humility.

'The Germans,' said the new undergraduate, a grass blade in his mouth, 'have a two-track mind and an inexcusable habit of combination; they always want one thing and the other, they want to have it both ways. They are capable of turning out great personalities with antithetic principles of thought and life. But then they muddle them, using the coinage of the one in the sense of the other; mixing everything all up and thinking they can put freedom and aristocracy, idealism and natural childlikeness under one hat. But that probably does not do.'

'But they have both in themselves,' I retorted, 'otherwise they could not have exhibited both of them. A rich nation.'

'A confused nation,' he persisted, 'and bewildering for the others.'

But on the whole we philosophized thus but little, in these leisurely country weeks. Generally speaking, he was more inclined to laughter and pranks than to metaphysical conversation. His sense of the comic, his fondness for it, his proneness to laughter, yes, to laughing till he cried, I have

already spoken of, and I have given but a false picture of him if the reader has
not seen this kind of abandon as an element in his nature. Of humour I would
not speak; the word sounds for my ear too moderate, too good-natured to fit
him. His love of laughter was more like an escape, a resolution, slightly
orgiastic in its nature, of life's manifold sternness; a product of extraordinary gifts, but to me never quite likeable or healthy. Looking back upon
the school life now ending, he gave this sense of the comic free rein, recalling
droll types among pupils and teachers, or describing his last cultural
expedition and some small-town opera performance, whose improvisations
could not fail to be a source of mirth, though without detriment to the
seriousness of the work performed. Thus a paunchy, knock-kneed King
Heinrich in *Lohengrin* was the butt of much laughter; Adrian was like to split
over the round black mouth-hole in a beard like a woolly rug, out of which
there poured his thundering bass. That was but one instance, perhaps too
concrete, of the occasions he found for his paroxysms. Oftener there was no
occasion at all, it was the purest silliness, and I confess that I always had
certain difficulties in seconding him. I do not love laughter so much, and
when he abandoned himself to it I was always compelled to think of a story
which I knew only from him. It was from St Augustine's *De civitate Dei* and
was to the effect that Ham, son of Noah and father of Zoroaster the magian,
had been the only man who laughed when he was born – which could only
have happened by the help of the Devil. It came inevitably to my mind
whenever the occasion arose; but probably it was only an accompaniment to
other inhibitions I had; for instance, I realize that the look that I inwardly
directed upon him was too serious, not free enough from anxious suspense,
for me to follow him whole-heartedly in his abandon. And perhaps my own
nature has a certain stiffness and dryness that makes me inapt.

Later he found in Rüdiger Schildknapp, a writer and Anglophile whose
acquaintance he made in Leipzig, a far better partner in such moods –
wherefore I have always been a little jealous of the man.

Chapter Eleven

At Halle Theological and philological educational traditions are interwoven
in many ways; and first of all in the historical figure of August Hermann
Francke, patron saint of the town, so to speak: that pietistic pedagogue who
at the end of the seventeenth century – in other words, soon after the
foundation of the university – formed in Halle the famous Francke
Foundation of schools and orphanages, and in his own person and by its
influence united the religious interest with the humanistic and linguistic.
And then the Castein Bible Institute, first authority for the revision of
Luther's language work, it too establishes a link between religion and textual
criticism. Also there was active in Halle at that time an outstanding Latinist,
Heinrich Osiander, at whose feet I ardently desired to sit; and more than
that, as I heard from Adrian, the course in Church history given by
Professor Hans Kegel, D.D., included an extraordinary amount of material
for a student of profane history, which I wished to avail myself of, as I
intended to select history as my subsidiary course.

Thus there was good intellectual justification when, after studying for two semesters in Jena and Giessen, I decided to draw my further nourishment from the breast of Alma Mater Hallensis. And my imagination saw an advantage in the fact that it was identical with the University of Wittenberg, the two having been united when they were reopened after the Napoleonic Wars. Leverkühn had matriculated there a half-year before I joined him, and of course I do not deny that his presence had played a weighty, yes, a decisive part in my choice. Shortly after his arrival, and obviously out of some feeling of loneliness and forsakenness, he had even proposed to me to join him; and though some months would have to pass before I answered his call, I was at once ready, yes, probably would not have needed the invitation. My own wish to be near him, to see how he went on, what progress he made and how his talents unfolded in the air of academic freedom, this wish to live in daily intercourse with him, to watch over him, to have an eye on him from near by, would very likely have been enough of itself to take me to him. And there were besides, as I said, sufficing intellectual grounds.

Of course in these pages I can only picture in a foreshortened form, just as I did with his schooldays, the two years of our youth that I spent at Halle with my friend; the course of them interrupted, indeed, by holidays in Kaisersaschern and at his father's farm. Were they happy years? Yes, they were, in the sense that they were the core of a period when with my senses at their freshest I was freely seeing, searching, and gathering in. Happy too in that I spent them at the side of a childhood companion to whom I clung, yes, whose life-problem, his being and becoming, at bottom interested me more than my own. For my own was simple, I did not need to spend much thought on it, only to ensure by faithful work the postulates for its prescribed solution. His was higher and in a sense more puzzling, a problem upon which the concern about my own progress always left me much time and mental energy to dwell. If I hesitate to describe those years by the epithet 'happy' – always a questionable word – it is because by association with him I was drawn much more effectively into his sphere of studies than he into mine, and the theological air did not suit me. It was not canny, it choked me; besides, it put me in an inward dilemma. The intellectual atmosphere there had been for centuries full of religious controversy, of those ecclesiastical brawls which have always been so detrimental to the humanistic impulse to culture. In Halle I felt a little like one of my scientific forebears, Crotus Rubeanus, who in 1530 was canon at Halle, and whom Luther called nothing else than 'the Epicurean Crotus' or 'Dr Kröte, lickspittle of the Cardinal at Mainz'. He even said 'the Divel's sow, the Pope', and was in every way an intolerable boor, although a great man. I have always sympathized with the embarrassment that the Reformation caused to spirits like Crotus, because they saw in it an invasion of subjective arbitrariness into the objective statutes and ordinances of the Church. Crotus had the scholar's love of peace; he gladly leaned to reasonable compromise, was not against the restitution of the Communion cup – and was indeed put after that in a painfully awkward position, through the detestable harshness with which his superior, Archbishop Albrecht, punished the enjoyment of the Communion at Halle in both kinds.

So goes it with tolerance, with love of culture and peace, between the fires of fanaticism. – It was Halle that had the first Lutheran superintendent: Justus Jonas, who went thither in 1541 and was one of those who, like Melanchthon and Hutten, to the distress of Erasmus, had gone over from the humanistic camp to the reformers. But still worse in the eyes of the sage of Rotterdam was the hatred that Luther and his partisans brought down upon classical learning – Luther had personally little enough of it – as the source of the spiritual turmoil. But what went on then in the bosom of the Universal Church, the revolt of subjective wilfulness, that is, against the objective bond, was to repeat itself a hundred and some years later, inside Protestantism itself, as a revolution of pious feelings and inner heavenly joy against a petrified orthodoxy from which not even a beggar would any longer want to accept a piece of bread: as pietism, that is, which at the foundation of the University of Halle manned the whole theological faculty. It too, whose citadel the town now long remained, was, as formerly Lutheranism, a renewal of the Church, a reform and reanimation of the dying religion, already fallen into general indifference. And people like me may well ask themselves whether these recurrent rescues of a hope already declining to the grave are from a cultural point of view to be welcomed; whether the reformers are not rather to be regarded as backsliding types and bringers of evil. Beyond a doubt, endless blood-letting and the most horrible self-laceration would have been spared the human race if Martin Luther had not restored the Church.

I should be sorry, after what I have said, to be taken for an utterly irreligious man. That I am not, for I go with Schleiermacher, another Halle theologian, who defined religion as 'feeling and taste for the Infinite' and called it 'a pertinent fact', present in the human being. In other words, the science of religion has to do not with philosophical theses, but with an inward and given psychological fact. And that reminds me of the ontological evidence for the existence of God, which has always been my favourite, and which from the subjective idea of a Highest Being derives His objective existence. But Kant has shown in the most forthright words that such a thesis cannot support itself before the bar of reason. Science, however, cannot get along without reason; and to want to make a science out of a sense of the infinite and the eternal mysteries is to compel two spheres fundamentally foreign to each other to come together in a way that is in my eyes most unhappy and productive only of embarrassment. Surely a religious sense, which I protest is in no way lacking in me, is something other than positive and formally professed religion. Would it not have been better to hand over that 'fact' of human feeling for the infinite to the sense of piety, the fine arts, free contemplation, yes, even to exact research, which as cosmology, astronomy, theoretical physics, can serve this feeling with entirely religious devotion to the mystery of creation – instead of singling it out as the science of the spirit and developing on it structures of dogma, whose orthodox believers will then shed blood for a copula? Pietism, by virtue of its overemotional nature, would indeed make a sharp division between piety and science, and assert that no movement, no change in the scientific picture, can have any influence on faith. But that was a delusion, for theology has at all times willy-nilly let itself be determined by the scientific currents of the epoch, has always wanted to be a child of its time, although the time (in greater or less degree) made that difficult for it and drove it into an anachronistic corner. Is there another discipline at whose mere name we feel ourselves in such a degree set back into the past, into the sixteenth, the twelfth century? There is here no possibility of adaptation, of concession to scientific critique. What these display is a hybrid half-and-half of science and belief in revelation, which lies on the way to self-surrender. Orthodoxy itself committed the blunder of letting reason into the field of religion, in that she sought to prove the positions of faith by the test of reason. Under the pressure of the Enlightenment, theology had almost nothing to do but defend herself against the intolerable contradictions which were pointed out to her: and only in order to get round them she embraced so much of the anti-revelation spirit that it amounted to an abandonment of faith. That was the time of the 'reasonable worship of God', of a generation of theologians in whose name Wolff declared at Halle: 'Everything must be proved by reason, as on the philosophers' stone': a generation which pronounced that everything in the Bible which did not serve 'moral betterment' was out of date, and gave out that the history and teaching of the Church were in its eyes only a comedy of errors. Since this went a little too far, there arose an accommodation theology, which sought to uphold a conservative middle ground between orthodoxy and a liberalism already by virtue of its reasonableness inclined to demoralization. But the two ideas 'preserving' and 'abandoning' have since then conditioned the life of 'the science of religion' – ideas both of which have something provisional about them, for theology therewith prolonged its life. In its conservative form, holding to revelation and the traditional exegesis, it sought to save what was to be saved of the elements of Bible religion; on the other hand it liberally accepted the historicocritical methods of the profane science of history and abandoned to scientific criticism its own most important contents: the belief in miracles, considerable portions of Christology, the bodily resurrection of Jesus, and what not besides. But what sort of science is that, which stands in such a forced and precarious relation to reason, constantly threatened with destruction by the very compromises that she makes with it? In my view 'liberal theology' is a '*contradictio in adjecto*', a contradiction in terms. A proponent of culture, ready to adapt itself to the ideals of bourgeois society, as it is, it degrades the religious to a function of the human; the ecstatic and paradoxical elements so essential to the religious genius it waters down to an ethical progressiveness. But the religious cannot be satisfied in the merely ethical, and so it comes about that scientific thought and theological thought proper part company again. The scientific superiority of liberal theology, it is now said, is indeed incontestable, but its theological position is weak, for its moralism and humanism lack insight into the daemonic character of human existence. Cultured indeed it is, but shallow; of the true understanding of human nature and the tragic nature of life the conservative tradition has at bottom preserved far more; for that very reason it has a profounder, more significant relation to culture than has progressive bourgeois ideology.

Here one sees clearly the infiltration of theological thinking by irrational currents of philosophy, in whose realm, indeed, the non-theoretic, the vital, the will or instinct, in short the daemonic, have long since become the chief theme of theory. At the same time one observes a revival of the study of Catholic medieval philosophy, a turning to Neo-Thomism and Neo-Scholasticism. On these lines theology, grown sickly with liberalism, can take on deeper and stronger, yes, more glowing hues; it can once more do justice to the ancient aesthetic conceptions which are involuntarily associated with its name. But the civilized human spirit, whether one calls it bourgeois or merely leaves it at civilized, cannot get rid of a feeling of the uncanny. For theology, confronted with that spirit of the philosophy of life which is irrationalism, is in danger, by its very nature, of becoming daemonology.

I say all this only in order to explain the discomfort caused in me at times by my stay in Halle and my participation in Adrian's studies, the lectures that I followed as a guest hearer in order to hear what he heard. I found in him no understanding for my uneasiness. He liked to talk over with me the theological problems touched on in the lectures and debated in the seminar; but he avoided any discussion that would have gone to the root of the matter and have dealt with the problematic position of theology among the sciences, and thus he evaded precisely the point which to my easily aroused anxiety was more pressing than all the rest. And so it was in the lectures as well: and so it went in association with his fellow-students, the members of the Christian Students' Union Winfried, which he had joined on external grounds and whose guest I sometimes was. Of that perhaps more later. Here I will only say that some of these young people were the pale-complexioned 'candidate' type, some robust as peasants, some also distinguished figures who obviously came from good academic circles. But they were all theologians, and conducted themselves as such with a decent and godly cheerfulness. How one can be a theologian, how in the spiritual climate of the present day one comes on the idea of choosing this calling, unless, indeed, it were simply by the operation of family tradition, they did not say, and for my part it would have been tactless and prying to cross-examine them. A forthright question on the subject could at most have been in place and had any chance of results in the course of a students' evening jollification, when tongues and brains were loosened and livened by drink. But of course the members of Winfried were superior; they condemned not only duelling but also 'boozing', and so they were always sober – that is, they were inaccessible to questions they might not like to answer. They knew that State and Church needed ghostly officers, and they were preparing themselves for that career. Theology was to them something given – and something historically given it certainly is.

I had to put up with it too, when Adrian took it in the same way, although it pained me that regardless of our friendship, rooted in early days as it was, he no more permitted the question than did his comrades. That shows how little he let one approach him; what fixed bounds he set to intimacy. But did I not say that I had found his choice of a profession significant and characteristic? Have I not explained it with the word 'Kaisersaschern'? Often I called the thought to my aid when the problem of Adrian's field of study plagued me. I said to myself that both of us had shown ourselves true children of that corner of German antiquity where we had been brought up, I as humanist and he as theologian. And when I looked round in our new circle I found that our theatre had indeed broadened but not essentially changed.

Chapter Twelve

Halle was, if not a metropolis, at least a large city, with more than two hundred thousand inhabitants. Yet despite all the modern volume of its traffic, it did not, at least in the heart of the town, where we both lived, belie its lofty antiquity. My 'shop', as we students said, was in the Hansastrasse, a narrow lane behind the Church of St Moritz, which might well have run its anachronistic course in Kaisersaschern. Adrian had found an alcoved room in a gabled dwelling-house in the Market Square, renting from the elderly widow of an official during the two years of his stay. He had a view of the square, the medieval City Hall, the Gothic Marienkirche, whose domed towers were connected by a sort of Bridge of Sighs; the separate 'Red Tower', a very remarkable structure, also in Gothic style; the statue of Roland and the bronze statue of Handel. The room was not much more than adequate, with some slight indication of middle-class amenity in the shape of a red plush cover on the square table in front of the sofa, where his books lay and he drank his breakfast coffee. He had supplemented the arrangements with a rented cottage piano always strewn with sheets of music, some written by himself. On the wall above the piano was an arithmetical diagram fastened with drawing-pins, something he had found in a second-hand shop: a so-called magic square, such as appears also in Dürer's *Melancolia*, along with the hour-glass, the circle, the scale, the polyhedron, and other symbols. Here as there, the figure was divided into sixteen Arabic-numbered fields, in such a way that number one was in the right-hand lower corner, sixteen in the upper left; and the magic, or the oddity, simply consisted in the fact that the sum of these numerals, however you added them, straight down, crosswise, or diagonally, always came to thirty-four. What the principle was upon which this magic uniformity rested I never made out, but by virtue of the prominent place Adrian had given it over the piano, it always attracted the eye, and I believe I never visited his room without giving a quick glance, slanting up or straight down and testing once more the invariable, incredible result.

Between my quarters and Adrian's there was a going to and fro as once between the Blessed Messengers and his uncle's house: evenings after theatre, concert, or a meeting of the Winfried Verein, also in the mornings when one of us fetched the other to the university and before we set out we compared our notebooks. Philosophy, the regular course for the first examination in theology, was the point at which our two programmes coincided, and both of us had put ourselves down with Kolonat Nonnenmacher, then one of the luminaries of the University of Halle. With great brilliance and *élan* he discussed the pre-Socratic, the Ionian natural philosophers, Anaximander, and more extendedly Pythagoras, in the course of which discussion a good deal of Aristotle came in, since it is almost entirely through the Stagirite that we learn of the Pythagorean theory of the universe. We listened, we wrote down; from time to time we looked up into the mildly smiling face of the white-maned professor, as we heard this early cosmological conception of a stern and pious spirit, who elevated his fundamental passion, mathematics, abstract proportion, number, to the principle of the origin and existence of the world; who, standing opposite All-Nature as an initiate, a dedicated one, first addressed her with a great gesture as 'Cosmos', as order and harmony, as the interval-system of the spheres sounding beyond the range of the senses. Number, and the relation of numbers, as constituting an all-embracing concept of being and moral value: it was highly impressive, how the beautiful, the exact, the moral, here, solemnly flowed together to comprise the idea of authority which animated the Pythagorean order, the esoteric school or religious renewal of life, of silent obedience, and strict subjection under the '*Autós*' *épha*. I must chide myself for being tactless, because involuntarily I glanced at Adrian at such words, to read his look. Or rather it became tactless simply because of the discomfort, the red, averted face, with which he met my gaze. He did not love personal glances, he altogether refused to entertain them or respond to them, and it is hard to understand why I, aware though I was of this peculiarity, could not always resist looking at him. By so doing I threw away the possibility of talking objectively afterwards, without embarrassment, on topics to which my wordless look had given a personal reference.

So much the better when I had resisted such temptation and practised the discretion he exacted. How well, for instance, we talked, going home after Nonnenmacher's class, about that immortal thinker, influential down the millennia, to whose meditation and sense of history we owe our knowledge of the Pythagorean conception of the world! Aristotle's doctrine of matter and form enchanted us; matter as the potential, possible, that presses towards form in order to realize itself; form as the moving unmoved, that is mind and soul, the soul of the existing that urges it to self-realization, self-completion in the phenomenon; thus of the entelechy, which, a part of eternity, penetrates and animates the body, manifests itself shapingly in the organic and guides its motive-power, knows its goal, watches over its destiny. Nonnenmacher had spoken beautifully and impressively about these intuitions, and Adrian appeared extraordinarily impressed thereby. 'When,' he said, 'theology declares that the soul is from God, that is philosophically right, for as the principle which shapes the single manifestations, it is a part of the pure form of all being, comes from the eternally self-contemplating contemplation which we call God.... I believe I understand what Aristotle meant by the word "entelechy". It is the angel of the individual, the genius of his life, in whose all-knowing guidance it gladly confides. What we call prayer is really the statement of this confidence, a notice-giving or invocation. But prayer it is correctly called, because it is at bottom God whom we thus address.'

I could only think: May thine own angel prove himself faithful and wise!

How I enjoyed hearing this course of lectures at Adrian's side! But the theological ones, which I – though not regularly – attended on his account, were for me a more doubtful pleasure; and I went to them only in order not to be cut off from what occupied him. In the curriculum of a theology student in the first years the emphasis is on history and exegesis, history of the Church and of dogma, Assyriology and a variety of special subjects. The middle years belong to systematics; that is to say, to the philosophy of religion, ethics, and apologetics. At the end come the practical disciplines, the science of preaching, catechesis, the care of souls, Church law, and the science of Church government. But academic freedom leaves much room for personal preference, and Adrian made use of it to throw over the regular order, devoting himself from the first to systematics, out of general intellectual interest, of course, which in this field comes most to account; but also because its professor, Ehrenfried Kumpf, was the 'meatiest' lecturer in the whole university and had altogether the largest attendance from students of all years, not only theological ones. I said indeed that we both heard Church history from Kegel, but those were comparatively dull hours, and the tedious Kegel could by no means vie with Kumpf.

The latter was very much what the students called a 'powerful personality'; even I could not forgo a certain admiration for his temperament, though I did not like him in the least and have never been able to believe that Adrian was not at times unpleasantly impressed by his crude heartiness, though he did not make fun of him openly. Powerful he certainly was, in his physical person; a big, full-bodied, massive man with hands like cushions, a thundering voice, and an underlip that protruded slightly from much talking and tended to spit and sputter. It is true that Kumpf usually read his lecture from a printed textbook, his own production; but his glory was the so-called 'extra-punches' which he interpolated, delivered with his fists thrust into his vertical trouser-pockets past the flung-back frock coat, as he stamped up and down on his platform. Thanks to their spontaneity, bluntness, coarse and hearty good humour, and picturesquely archaic style, they were uncommonly popular with the students. It was his way – to quote him – to say a thing 'in good round terms, no mealy-mouthing' or 'in good old German, without mincing matters'. Instead of 'gradually' he said 'by a little and a little'; instead of 'I hope' he said 'I hope and trow'; he never spoke of the Bible otherwise than as Godes Boke. He said 'There's foul work' instead of 'There's something wrong.' Of somebody who, in his view, was involved in scientific error, he said 'He's in the wrong pew;' of a vicious man: 'he spends his life like the beasts of the field.' He loved expressions like: 'He that will eat the kernel must crack the nut;' or 'It pricketh betimes that will be a sharp thorn.' Medieval oaths like 'Gogs wownds', by 'Goggys bodye', even 'by the guts of Goliath' came easily to his lips and – especially the last – were received by the students with lusty tramplings.

Theologically speaking, Kumpf was a representative of that middle-of-the-road conservatism with critical and liberal traits to which I have referred. As a student he was, as he told us in his peripatetic extempores, dead set on classical literature and philosophy, and boasted of having known by heart all of Schiller's and Goethe's 'weightier' works. But then something had come over him, connected with the revival movement of the middle of the previous century, and the Pauline gospel of sin and justification made him turn away from aesthetic humanism. One must be a born theologian to estimate properly such spiritual destinies and Damascus experiences. Kumpf had convinced himself that our thinking too is a broken reed and needs justification, and precisely this was the basis of his liberalism, for it led him to see in dogmatism an intellectual form of phariseeism. Thus he had arrived at criticism of dogma by a route opposite to that of Descartes, to whom, on the contrary, the self-certainty of the consciousness, the *cogitare*, seemed more legitimate than all scholastic authority. Here we have the difference between theological and philosophical sanctions. Kumpf had found his in a blithe and hearty trust in God, and reproduced it before us hearers 'in good old German words'. He was not only anti-pharisaic, anti-dogmatic, but also anti-metaphysical, with a position addressed entirely to ethics and theoretic knowledge, a proponent of the morally based ideal of personality and mightily opposed to the pietistic divorce of world and religion; secularly religious, indeed, and ready for healthy enjoyment, an affirmer of culture, especially of German culture, for on every occasion he showed himself to be a nationalist of the Luther stamp, out of whole cloth. He could say of a man nothing worse than he thought he taught like a 'flatulent furriner'. Red as a turkey-cock with rage, he might add: 'And may the Divel shit on him, Amen!' – which again was greeted with loud stampings of applause.

His liberalism, that is, was not based on humanistic distrust of dogma, but on religious doubt of the reliability of our thinking. It did not prevent him from believing stoutly in revelation, nor indeed from being on a very familiar footing with the Devil, if also, of course, the reverse of a cordial one. I cannot and would not inquire how far he believed in the personal existence of the Great Adversary. I only say to myself that wherever theology is, and certainly in so 'meaty' a personality as Ehrenfried Kumpf, there too the Devil belongs to the picture and asserts his complementary reality to that of God. It is easy to say that a modern theologian takes him 'symbolically'. In my view theology cannot be modern – one may reckon that to its advantage, of course – and as for symbolism, I cannot see why one should take hell more symbolically than heaven. The people have certainly never done so. Always the crass, obscenely comic figure of the 'Divel' has been nearer to them than the Eternal Majesty; and Kumpf, in hs way, was a man of the people. When he spoke with relish of the 'everlasting fire and brimstone' and of 'hell's bottomless pit', that picturesque form, while slightly comic, at least carried more conviction than ordinary words would have done. One did not at all get the impression that he was speaking symbolically, but rather that this was 'good plain German, with nothing mealy-mouthed about it'. It was the same with Satan himself. I did say that Kumpf, as a scholar and man of science, made concessions to criticism in the matter of literal faith in the Bible, and at least by fits and starts 'abandoned' much, with a great air of intellectual respectability. But at bottom he saw the Arch-Deceiver, the Wicked Fiend capitally at work on the reason itself and seldom referred to him without adding: '*Si Diabolus non esset mendax et homicida!*' He appeared reluctant to name him straight out, preferring to say 'Divel' or 'Debble'; sometimes 'the great old Serpent', or, with literary relish, 'Timothy Tempter'. But just this half-jesting, half-shrinking avoidance had something of a grim and reluctant recognition about it. And he had at command still other pithy and forgotten epithets, some homely and some classic, such as: Old Blackie, Abaddon, Belial, also Master Dicis-et-non-facis, Black Kaspar, the old Serpent and the Father of Lies. They did, in a half-humorous way, express his highly personal and intimate animosity to the Great Adversary.

After Adrian and I had paid our formal call, we were now and again invited by Kumpf to his house, and took supper with him, his wife, and their two daughters, who had glaringly red cheeks and hair first wet and then so tightly plaited that it stuck straight out from their heads. One of them said grace while the rest of us bowed our heads discreetly over our plates. Then the master of the house, expatiating the while on God and the world, the Church, the university, politics, and even art and the theatre, in unmistakable imitation of Luther's *Table Talk*, laced powerfully into the meat and drink, as an example to us and in token that he had nothing against the healthy and cultured enjoyment of the good things of this world. He repeatedly urged us to fall to, not to despise the good gifts of God, the leg of mutton, the elder-blossom Moselle. After the sweet, to our horror, he took a guitar from the wall, pushed away from the table, flung one leg across the other, and sang in his booming voice, to the twanging of the strings: 'To Wander is the Miller's Joy', 'Lutzow's Wild Reckless Ride', 'The Lorelei', '*Gaudeamus Igitur*', 'Wine, Women, and Song'. Yes, it had to come, and it came. He shouted it out, and before our faces he took his plump wife round the waist. Then with his fat forefinger he pointed to a dark corner where the rays of the shaded lamp over the supper-table did not fall – 'Look!' he cried. 'There he stands in the corner, the mocking-bird, the make-bate, the malcontent, the sad, bad guest, and cannot stand it to see us merry in God with feasting and song. But he shall not harm us, the arch-villain, with his sly fiery arrows! *Apage!*'' he thundered, seized a roll and flung it into the dark corner. After this he took his instrument again and sang: 'He who the world will joyous rove.'

All this was pretty awful, and I take it Adrian must have thought so too, though his pride prevented him from exposing his teacher. However, when we went home after that fight with the Devil, he had such a fit of laughter in the street that it only gradually subsided with the diversion of his thoughts.

Chapter Thirteen

But I must devote a few words to another figure among our teachers; the equivocal nature of this man intrigued me, so that I remember him better than all the rest. He was Privat-docent Eberhard Schleppfuss, who for two semesters at this time lectured at Halle among the *venia legendi* and then disappeared from the scene, I know not whither. Schleppfuss was a creature of hardly average height, puny in figure, wrapped in a black cape or mantle instead of an overcoat, which closed at the throat with a little metal chain. With it he wore a sort of soft hat with a brim turned up at the sides, rather like a Jesuit's. When we students greeted him on the street he would take it off with a very sweeping bow and say: 'Your humble servant!' It seemed to me that he really did drag one foot, but people disputed it; I could not always be sure of it when I saw him walk, and would rather ascribe my impression to a subconscious association with his name. It was not in any case so far-fetched, considering the nature of his two-hour lectures. I do not remember precisely how they were listed. In matter certainly they were a little vague, they might have been called lectures on the psychology of religion – and very probably were. The material was 'exclusive' in its nature, not important for examinations, and only a handful of intellectual and more or less revolutionary-minded students, ten or twelve, attended it. I wondered, indeed, that there were no more, for Schleppfuss's offering was interesting enough to arouse a more extended curiosity. But the occasion went to prove that even the piquant forfeits its popularity when accompanied by demands on the intellect.

I have already said that theology by its very nature tends and under given circumstances always will tend to become daemonology. Schleppfuss was a good instance of the thing I mean, of a very advanced and intellectual kind, for his daemonic conception of God and the universe was illuminated by psychology and thus made acceptable, yes, even attractive, to the modern scientific mind. His delivery contributed to the effect, for it was entirely calculated to impress the young. It was impromptu, well expressed, without effort or break, smooth as though prepared for the press, with faintly ironical turns of phrase; and he spoke not from the platform but from somewhere at one side, half-sitting on the balustrade, the ends of his fingers interlaced in his lap, with the thumbs spread out, and his parted little beard moving up and down. Between it and the twisted moustaches one saw his pointed teeth like tiny splinters. Professor Kumpf's good out-and-out ways with the Devil were child's play compared to the psychological actuality with which Schleppfuss invested the Destroyer, that personified falling-away from God. For he received, if I may so express myself, dialectically speaking, the blasphemous and offensive into the divine and hell into the empyrean; declared the vicious to be a necessary and inseparable concomitant of the holy, and the holy a constant satanic temptation, an almost irresistible challenge to violation.

He demonstrated this by instances from the Christian Middle Ages, the classical period of religious rule over the life and spirit of man, and in particular from its ultimate century; thus from a time of complete harmony between ecclesiastical judge and delinquent, between inquisitor and witch on the fact of the betrayal of God, of the alliance with the Devil, the frightful partnership with demons. The provocation of vice proceeding from the sacrosanct was the essential thing about it, it was the thing itself, betrayed for instance in the characterization by apostates of the Virgin as 'the fat woman', or by extraordinarily vulgar interpolations, abominable filthinesses, which the Devil made them mutter to themselves at the celebration of the Mass. Dr Schleppfuss, with his fingers interlaced, repeated them word for word; I refrain from doing so myself, on grounds of good taste, but am not reproaching him for paying scientific exactitude its due. It was odd, all the same, to see the students conscientiously writing that sort of thing down in their notebooks. According to Schleppfuss all this – evil, the Evil One himself – was a necessary emanation and inevitable accompaniment of the Holy Existence of God, so that vice did not consist in itself but got its satisfaction from the defilement of virtue, without which it would have been rootless; in other words, it consisted in the enjoyment of freedom, the possibility of sinning, which was inherent in the act of creation itself.

Herein was expressed a certain logical incompleteness of the All-powerfulness and All-goodness of God; for what He had not been able to do was to produce in the creature, in that which He had liberated out of Himself and which was now outside Him, the incapacity for sin. That would have meant denying to the created being the free will to turn away from God – which would have been an incomplete creation, yes, positively not a creation at all, but a surrender on the part of God. God's logical dilemma had consisted in this: that He had been incapable of giving the creature, the human being and the angel, both independent choice, in other words free will, and at the same time the gift of not being able to sin. Piety and virtue, then, consisted in making a good use, that is to say no use at all, of the freedom which God had to grant the creature as such – and that, indeed, if you listened to Schleppfuss, was a little as though this non-use of freedom meant a certain existential weakening, a diminution of the intensity of being, in the creature outside of God.

Freedom. How extraordinary the word sounded, in Schleppfuss's mouth! Yes, certainly it had a religious emphasis, he spoke as a theologian, and he spoke by no means with contempt. On the contrary, he pointed out the high degree of significance which must be ascribed by God to this idea, when He had preferred to expose men and angels to sin rather than withhold freedom from them. Good, then freedom was the opposite of inborn sinlessness, freedom meant the choice of keeping faith with God, or having traffic with demons and being able to mutter beastlinesses at the Mass. That was a definition suggested by the psychology of religion. But freedom has before now played a role, perhaps of less intellectual significance and yet not lacking in seriousness in the life of the peoples of the earth and in historical conflicts. It does so at this moment – as I write down this description of a life – in the war now raging, and as I in my retreat like to believe, not least in the souls and thoughts of our German people, upon whom, under the domination of the most audacious licence, is dawning perhaps for the first time in their lives a notion of the importance of freedom. Well, we had not got so far by then.

The question of freedom was, or seemed, in our student days, not a burning one, and Dr Schleppfuss, might give to the word the meaning that suited the frame of his lecture and leave any other meanings on one side. If only I had had the impression that he did leave them on one side; that absorbed in his psychology of religion he was not mindful of them! But he was mindful of them; I could not shake off the conviction. And his theological definition of freedom was an apologia and a polemic against the 'more modern', that is to say more insipid, more ordinary ideas, which his hearers might associate with them. See, he seemed to say, we have the word too, it is at our service, don't think that it only occurs in your dictionaries and that your idea of it is the only one dictated by reason. Freedom is a very great thing, the condition of creation, that which prevented God making us proof against falling away from Him. Freedom is the freedom to sin, and piety consists in making no use of it out of love for God, who had to give it.

Thus he developed his theme: somewhat tendentiously, somewhat maliciously, if I do not deceive myself. In short, it irritated me. I don't like it when a person wants the whole show; takes the word out of his opponent's mouth, turns it round, and confuses ideas with it. That is done today with the utmost audacity; it is the main ground of my retirement. Certain people should not speak of freedom, reason, humanity; on grounds of scrupulosity, they should leave such words alone. But precisely about humanity did Schleppfuss speak, just that – of course in the sense of the 'classic centuries of belief' on whose spiritual constitution he based his psychological discussion. Clearly it was important to him to make it understood that humanity was no invention of the free spirit, that not to it alone did this idea belong, for that it had always existed. For example, the activities of the Inquisition were animated by the most touching humanity. A woman, he related, had been taken, in that 'classic' time, tried and reduced to ashes, who for full six years had had knowledge of an incubus, at the very side of her sleeping husband, three times a week, preferably on holy days. She had promised the Devil that after seven years she would belong to him body and soul. But she had been lucky: for just before the end of the term God in His loving-kindness made her fall into the hands of the Inquisition, and even under a slight degree of the question she had made a full and touchingly penitent confession, so that in all probability she obtained pardon from God. Willingly indeed did she go to her death, with the express declaration that even if she were freed she would prefer the stake, in order to escape from the power of the Demon, so repugnant had her life become to her through her subjection to her filthy sin. But what beautiful unanimity of culture spoke in this harmonious accord between the judge and the delinquent and what warm humanity in the satisfaction at snatching through fire his soul from the Devil at the very last minute and securing for it the pardon of God!

Schleppfus drew our attention to this picture, he summoned us to observe not only what else humanity could be but also what it actually was. It would have been to no purpose to bring in another word from the vocabulary of the free-thinker and to speak of hopeless superstition. Schleppfuss knew how to use this word too, in the name of the 'classic' centuries, to whom it was far from unknown. That woman with the incubus had surrendered to senseless superstition and to nothing else. For she had fallen away from God, fallen away from faith, and that was superstition. Superstition did not mean belief in demons and incubi, it meant having to do with them for harm, inviting the pestilence and expecting from them what is only to be expected from God. Superstition meant credulity, easy belief in the suggestions and instigations of the enemy of the human race, the conception covered all the chants, invocations, and conjuring formulae, all the letting oneself in with the black arts, the vices and crimes, the *flagellum haereticorum fascinariorum,* the *illusiones daemonum.* Thus might one define the word 'superstition', thus it had been defined, and after all it was interesting to see how man can use words and what he can get out of them.

Of course the dialectic association of evil with goodness and holiness played an important role in the theodicy, the vindication of God in view of the existence of evil, which occupied much space in Schleppfuss's course. Evil contributed to the wholeness of the universe, without it the universe would not have been complete; therefore God permitted it, for He was consummate and must therefore will the consummate – not in the sense of the consummately good but in the sense of All-sidedness and reciprocal enlargement of life. Evil was far more evil if good existed; good was far more good if evil existed; yes, perhaps – one might disagree about this – evil would not be evil at all if not for the good, good not good at all if not for evil. St Augustine, at least, had gone so far as to say that the function of the bad was to make the good stand out more strongly; that it pleased the more and was the more lovely, the more it was compared with the bad. At this point indeed Thomism had intervened with a warning that it was dangerous to believe that God wanted evil to happen. God neither wanted that nor did He want evil not to happen, rather He permitted, without willing or not willing, the rule of evil, and that was advantageous to the completeness of the whole. But it was aberration to assert that God permitted evil on account of the good; for nothing was to be considered good except it corresponded to the idea 'good' in itself, and not by accident. Anyhow, said Schleppfuss, the problem of the absolute good and beautiful came up here, the good and beautiful without reference to the evil and ugly – the problem of quality without comparison. Where comparison falls away, he said, the measure falls away too, and one cannot speak of heavy or light, of large or small. The good and beautiful would then be divested of all but being, unqualitied, which would be very like not-being, and perhaps not preferable to it.

We wrote that down in our notebooks, that we might go home more or less cheered. The real vindication of God, in view of the pains of creation, so we added, to Schleppfuss's dictation, consisted in His power to bring good out of evil. This characteristic certainly demanded, to the glory of God, practical use, and it could not reveal itself if God had not made over the creature to sin. In that case the universe would be deprived of that good which God knew how to create out of sin, suffering, and vice, and the angels would have had less occasion for songs of praise. Now indeed arose, the other way round, as history continually teaches, out of good much evil, so that God, to prevent it, had also to prevent the good, and altogether might not let the world alone. Yet this would have contradicted His existence as creator; and therefore He had to create the world as it is – namely, saturated with evil – that is to say, to leave it open in part to daemonic influences.

It never became quite clear whether these were actually Schleppfuss's own dogmas which he delivered to us, or whether he was simply concerned with familiarizing us with the psychology of the classic centuries of faith. Certainly he would not have been a theologian without showing himself sympathetic with such a psychology. But the reason I wondered why more young men were not attracted to his lectures was this: that whenever the subject was the power of demons over human life, sex always played a prominent role. How could it have been otherwise? The daemonic character of this sphere was a chief appurtenance of the 'classical psychology', for there it formed the favourite arena of the demons, the given point of attack for God's adversary, the enemy and corrupter. For God had conceded him greater magic power over the venereal act than over any other human activity; not only on account of the outward indecency of the commission of this act, but above all because the depravity of the first father passed over as original sin to the whole human race. The act of procreation, characterized by aesthetic disgustingness, was the expression and the vehicle of original sin – what wonder that the Devil had been left an especially free hand in it? Not for nothing had the angel said to Tobias: 'Over them who are given to lewdness the demon wins power.' For the power of the demons lay in the loins of man, and these were meant, where the Evangelist said: 'When a strong man armed watcheth his palace his goods remain in peace.' That was of course to be interpreted sexually; such a meaning was always to be deduced from enigmatic sayings, and keen-eared piety always heard it in them.

But it was astonishing how lax the angelic watch had always been in the case of God's saints, at least so far as 'peace' came in question. The book of the Holy Fathers was full of accounts to the effect that even while defying all fleshly lust, they have been tempted by the lust after women, past the bounds of belief. 'There was given to me a thorn in the flesh, the messenger of Satan, to buffet me.' That was an admission, made to the Corinthians, and though the writer possibly meant something else by it, the falling sickness or the like, in any case the godly interpreted it in their own way and were probably right after all, for their instinct very likely did not err when it darkly referred to the demon of sex in connexion with the temptations that assailed the mind. The temptation that one withstood was indeed no sin; it was merely a proof of virtue. And yet the line between temptation and sin was hard to draw, for was not temptation already the raging of sin in the blood, and in the very state of fleshly desire did there not lie much concession to evil? Here again the dialectical unity of good and evil came out, for holiness was unthinkable without temptation, it measured itself against the frightfulness of the temptation, against a man's sin-potential.

But from whom came the temptation? Who was to be cursed on its account? It was easy to say that it came from the Devil. He was its source, but the curse had to do with its object. The object, the *instrumentum* of the Tempter, was woman. She was also, and by that token, indeed, the instrument of holiness, since holiness did not exist without raging lust for sin. But the thanks she got had a bitter taste. Rather the remarkable and profoundly significant thing was that though the human being, both male and female, was endowed with sex, and although the localization of the daemonic in the loins fitted the man better than the woman, yet the whole curse of fleshliness, of slavery to sex, was laid upon the woman. There was even a saying: 'A beautiful woman is like a gold ring in the nose of the sow.' How much of that sort of thing, in past ages, has not been said and felt most profoundly about woman! It had to do with the concupiscence of the flesh in general; but was equated with that of the female, so that the fleshliness of the man was put down to her account as well. Hence the words: 'I found the woman bitterer than death, and even a good woman is subject to the covetousness of the flesh.'

One might have asked: and the good man too? And the holy man quite especially so? Yes, but that was the influence of the woman, who represented the collective concupiscence of the world. Sex was her domain, and how should she not, who was called *femina*, which came half from *fidus* and half from *minus* – that is, of lesser faith – why should she not be on evil and familiar footing with the obscene spirits who populated this field, and quite particularly suspect of intercourse with them, of witchcraft? There was the instance of that married woman who next to her trusting, slumbering spouse had carried on with an incubus, and that for years on end. Of course there were not only incubi but also succubi, and in fact an abandoned youth of the classical period lived with an idol, whose diabolic jealousy he was in the end to experience. For after some years, and more on practical grounds than out of real inclination, he had married a respectable woman, but had been prevented from consummating his marriage because the idol had always come and lain down between them. Then the wife in justifiable wrath had left him, and for the rest of his life he had seen himself confined to the unaccommodating idol.

Even more telling, Schleppfuss thought, for the psychological situation, was the restriction imposed upon a youth of that same period: it had come upon him by no fault of his own, through female witchcraft, and tragic indeed had been the means of his release. As a comment upon the studies I pursued in common with Adrian I will briefly recount the tale, on which Privat-docent Schleppfuss dwelt with a considerable wit and relish.

At Merseburg near Constance, towards the end of the fifteenth century, there lived an honest young fellow, Heinz Klöpfgeissel by name and cooper by calling, quite sound and well-built. He loved and was loved by a maiden named Bärbel, only daughter of a widowed sexton and wished to marry her, but the young couple's desire met with her father's opposition, for Klöpfgeissel was poor, and the sexton insisted on a considerable setting-up in life, and that he should be a master in his trade before he gave him his daughter. But the desires of the young people had proved stronger than their patience and the couple had prematurely become a pair. And every night, when the sexton went to ring the bell, Klöpfgeissel slipped in to his Bärbel and their embraces made each find the other the most glorious thing on earth.

Thus things stood when one day the cooper and some lively companions went to Constance to a church dedication and they had a good day and were a bit beyond themselves, so they decided to go to some women. It was not Klöpfgeissel's mind, he did not want to go with them. But the others jeered at him for an old maid and egged him on with taunts against his honour and hints that all was not right with him; and as he could not stand that, and had drunk just as much beer as the others besides, he let himself be talked round, said: 'Ho-ho, I know better than that,' and went up with the others into the stews.

But now it came about that he suffered such frightful chagrin that he did not know what sort of face to put on. For against all expectation things went wrong with him with the slut, a Hungarian woman it was, he could give no account of himself at all, he was just not there, and his fury was unbounded, his fright as well. For the creature not only laughed at him, but shook her head and gave it as her view that there must be something wrong, it certainly had a bad smell, when a fine lusty chap like him all of a sudden was just not up to it, he must be possessed, somebody must have given him something – and so on. He paid her a goodly sum so that she would say nothing, and went home greatly cast down.

As soon as he could, though not without misgiving, he made a rendezvous with his Bärbel, and while the sexton was ringing his bell they had a perfect hour together. He found his manly honour restored and should have been well content. For aside from the one and only he cared for no one, and why should he care about himself save only for her? But he had been uneasy in his mind ever since that one failure; it gnawed at him, he felt he must make another test: just once and never again, play false to his dearest and best. So he sought secretly for a chance to test himself – himself and her too, for he could cherish no misgiving about himself that did not end in slight, even tender, yet anxious suspicion of her upon whom his soul hung.

Now, it so fell out that he had to tighten the hoops of two casks in the wine-cellar of the inn landlord, a sickly pot-belly, and the man's wife, a comely wench, still pretty fresh, went down with him to watch him work. She patted his arm, put hers beside it to compare, and so demeaned herself that it would have been impossible to repulse her, save that his flesh, in all the willingness of his spirit, was entirely unable, and he had to say he was not in the humour, and he was in a hurry, and her husband would be coming downstairs, and then to take to his heels, hearing her scornful laughter behind him and owing her a debt which no stout fellow should ever refuse to pay.

He was deeply injured and bewildered about himself, but about himself not only; for the suspicion that even after the first mishap had lodged in his mind now entirely filled him, and he had no more doubt that he was indeed 'possessed'. And so, because the healing of a poor soul and the honour of his flesh as well were at stake, he went to the priest and told him everything in his ear through the little grating; how he was bewitched, how he was unable, how he was prevented with everybody but one, and how about all that and had the Church any maternal advice to give against such injury.

Now, at that time, and in that locality the pestilence of witchcraft, accompanied by much wantonness, sin, and vice instigated by the enemy of the human race, and abhorrent to the Divine Majesty, had been gravely widespread, and stern watchfulness had been made the duty of all shepherds of souls. The priest, all too familiar with this kind of mischief, and men being tampered with in their best strength, went to the higher authorities with Klöpfgeissel's confession. The sexton's daughter was arrested and examined, and confessed, truly and sincerely that in the anguish of her heart over the faithfulness of the young man, lest he be filched from her before he was hers before God and man, she had procured from an old bath-woman a specific, a salve, said to be made of the fat of an infant dead unbaptized, with which she had anointed her Heinz on the back while embracing him, tracing a certain figure thereon, only in order to bind him to herself. Next the bathing-woman was interrogated, who denied it stoutly. She had to be brought before the civil authorities for the application of methods for questioning which did not become the Church; and under some pressure the expected came to light. The old woman had in fact a compact with the Devil, who appeared to her in the guise of a monk with goat's feet and persuaded her to deny with frightful curses the Godhead and the Christian faith, in return for which he gave her directions for making not only that love unction but also other shameful panaceas, among them a fat, smeared with a piece of wood would instantly rise with the sorcerer into the air. The ceremonies by which the Evil One had sealed his pact with the one crone came out bit by bit under repeated pressure, and were hair-raising.

Everything now depended upon the question: how far was the salvation of the deceived one involved by her receiving and using the unholy preparation? Unhappily for the sexton's daughter the old woman deposed that the Dragon had laid upon her to make many converts. For every human being she brought to him by betraying it to the use of his gifts, he would make her somewhat more secure against the everlasting flames; so that after assiduous marshalling of converts she would be armed with an asbestos buckler against the flames of hell. – This was Bärbel's undoing. The need to save her soul from eternal damnation, to tear her from the Devil's claws by yielding her body to the flames, was perfectly apparent. And since on account of the increasing ravages of corruption an example was bitterly needed, the two witches, the old one and the young, were burned at the stake, one beside the other on the open square. Heinz Klöpfgeissel, the bewitched one, stood in the throng of spectators with his head bared, murmuring prayers. The shrieks of his beloved, choked by smoke and unrecognizable with hoarseness, seemed to him like the voice of the Demon, croaking as against his will he issued from her. From that hour the vile inhibition was lifted from him, for no sooner was his love reduced to ashes than he recovered the sinfully alienated free use of his manhood.

I have never forgotten this revolting tale, so characteristic of the tone of Schleppfuss's course, nor have I ever been able to be quite cool about it. Among us, between Adrian and me, as well as in discussions in Winfried it was much talked about; but neither in him, who was always taciturn about his teachers and what they said, nor in his theological fellow-students did I succeed in rousing the amount of indignation which would have satisfied my own anger at the anecdote, especially against Klöpfgeissel. Even today in my thoughts I address him breathing vengeance and call him a prize ass in every sense of the word. Why did the donkey have to tell? Why had he to test himself on other women when he had the one he loved, loved obviously so much that it made him cold and 'impotent' with others? What does 'impotent' mean in this connexion, when with the one he loved he had all the potency of love? Love is certainly a kind of noble selectiveness of sexuality, and if it is natural that sexual activity should decline in the absence of love, yet it is nothing less than unnatural if it does so in the presence and face of love. In any case, Bärbel had fixed and 'restricted' her Heinz – not by means of any devil's hocus-pocus but by the charm she had for him and the will by which she held him as by a spell against other temptations. That this protection in its strength and influence on the youth's nature was psychologically reinforced by the magic salve and the girl's belief in it, I am prepared to accept, though it does seem to me simpler and more correct to look at the matter from his side and to make the selective feeling given by his love responsible for the inhibition over which he was so stupidly upset. But this point of view too includes the recognition of a certain natural wonder-working of the spiritual, its power to affect and modify the organic and corporeal in a decisive way – and this so to speak magic side of the thing it was, of course, that Schleppfuss purposely emphasized in his comments on the Klöpfgeissel case.

He did it in a quasi-humanistic sense, in order to magnify the lofty idea which those supposedly sinister centuries had had of the choice constitution of the human body. They had considered it nobler than all other earthly combinations of matter, and in its power of variation through the spiritual had seen the expression of its aristocracy, its high rank in the hierarchy of bodies. It got cold or hot through fear or anger, thin with affliction; blossomed in joy; a mere feeling of disgust could produce a physiological reaction like that of bad food, the mere sight of a dish of strawberries could make the skin of an allergic person break out; yes, sickness and death could follow purely mental operations. But it was only a step – though a necessary one – from this insight into the power of the mind to alter its own and accompanying physical matter, to the conviction, supported by ample human experience, that mind, whether wilfully or not, was able, that is by magic, to alter another person's physical substance. In other words, the reality of magic, of daemonic influence and bewitchment, was corroborated; and phenomena such as the evil eye, a complex of experience concentrated in the saga of the death-dealing eye of the basilisk, were rescued from the realm of so-called superstition. It would have been culpable inhumanity to deny that an impure soul could produce by a mere look, whether deliberate or not, physically harmful effects in others, for instance in little children, whose tender substance was especially susceptible to the poison of such an eye.

Thus Schleppfuss in his exclusive course – exclusive because it was both intellectual and questionable. Questionable: a capital word, I have always ascribed a high philological value to it. It challenges one both to go in to and to avoid; anyhow to a very cautious going-in; and it stands in the double light of the remarkable and the disreputable, either in a thing – or in a man.

In our bow to Schleppfuss when we met him in the street or in the corridors of the university we expressed all the respect with which the high intellectual plane of his lectures inspired us hour by hour; but he on his side took off his hat with a still deeper flourish than ours and said: 'Your humble servant.'

Chapter Fourteen

Mystic numbers are not much in my line; I had been concerned to see that they fascinated Adrian, whose interest in them had been for a long time clearly though silently in evidence. But I feel a certain involuntary approval of the fact that the number thirteen, so generally considered unlucky, stands at the head of the foregoing chapter. I am almost tempted to think that there is more than chance at work here. But seriously speaking, it was chance after all; for the reason that this whole complex of Halle University life, just as in the earlier case of the Kretschmar lectures, does form a natural unity, and it was only out of consideration for the reader, who justly expects divisions and caesuras and places where he can draw breath, that I divided into several chapters matter which in the author's real and candid opinion has no claim to such articulation. If I had the say, we should still be in Chapter Eleven, and only my tendency to compromise has got Dr Schleppfuss his number Thirteen. I wish him joy of it; yes, I would willingly have given the unlucky numeral to the whole corpus of memories of our student years at Halle; for as I said before, the air of that town, the theological air, did not suit me, and my guest visits to Adrian's courses were a sacrifice which, with mixed feelings, I made to our friendship.

To ours? I might better say to mine; for he did not in the least lay stress on my keeping at his side when we went to hear Kumpf or Schleppfuss; or think that I might be neglecting my own programme. I did it of my own free will, only out of the imperative desire to hear what he heard, know what he learned, *to 'keep track' of him* – for that always seemed to me highly necessary, though at the same time futile. A peculiarly painful combination that: necessity and futility. I was clear in my own mind that this was a life which one might indeed watch over, but not change, not influence; and my urge to keep a constant eye on my friend, not to stir from his side, had about it something like a premonition of the fact that it would one day be my task to set down an account of the impressions that moulded his early life. Certainly so much is clear, that I did not go into the matters dealt with above just in order to explain why I was not particularly comfortable in Halle. My reason was the same as that which made me so explicit on the subject of Wendell Kretschmar's Kaisersaschern lectures: namely, because I do and must stress the importance of making the reader a witness of Adrian's experiences in the world of intellect and spirit.

On the same ground I invite him to accompany us young sons of the Muses on the excursions we made in company, in the better times of the year, from Halle. As Adrian's childhood intimate, and of course because, although not a theologian, I seemed to display a decided interest in the field of religious study, I was welcomed into the guest circle of the Christian Society Winfried and permitted to share in the excursions made by the group in order to enjoy the beauty of God's green creation.

They took place more frequently than we shared them. For I need hardly say that Adrian was no very zealous participant and his membership was more a matter of form than of punctual performance of activities. Out of courtesy and to show his good will towards the organization, he had let himself be persuaded; but under various pretexts, mostly on account of his headaches, he stopped away this or that time from the gatherings which took the place of the student 'beer evenings'. Even after a year or more he had got so little upon the '*frère et cochon*' footing with the seventy members that he did not manage to call them all by their right names or address them 'in the singular'. But he was respected among them. The shouts that greeted him, when I must almost say on rare occasions, he appeared at a session in the smoke-filled private room in Mütze's tavern, did contain a little fun at the expense of his supposed misanthropy; but they expressed genuine pleasure as well. For the group esteemed the part he played in their theological and philosophical debates, to which, without leading them, he would often throw in a remark and give an interesting turn. They were particularly pleased with his musical gift, which was useful because he could accompany the customary glees better than the others who tried it, with more animation and a fuller tone. Also he would oblige the assembly with a solo, a toccata of Bach, a movement of Beethoven or Schumann, at the instance of the leader, Baworinski, a tall dark lean person, with dropping lids and mouth puckered as though to whistle. Sometimes Adrian would even sit down unasked in the society's room at the piano, whose dull flat tone was strongly reminiscent of the inadequate instrument on which Wendell Kretschmar had imparted his knowledge to us in the hall of the Common Weal, and lose himself in free, experimental play. This especially happened before the beginning of a sitting, whilst the company were gathering. He had a way, I shall never forget it, of coming in, casually greeting the company, and then, sometimes without taking off his hat and coat, his face drawn with concentration, going straight to the piano, as though that alone were his goal. With a strong attack, bringing out the transition notes, with lifted brows, he would try chords, preparations, and resolutions which he may have excogitated on the way. But this rushing at the piano as though for refuge: it looked as though the place and its occupants frightened him; as though he sought shelter – actually within himself – from a bewildering strangeness into which he had come.

Then if he went on playing, dwelling on a fixed idea, changing and loosely shaping it, some one of those standing round, perhaps little Probst, a typical student, blond, with half-long, oily hair, would ask:

'What is that?'

'Nothing,' answered the player, with a short shake of the head, more like the gesture with which one shakes off a fly.

'How can it be nothing,' the other answered back, 'since you are playing it?'

'He is improvising,' explained the tall Baworinski sensibly.

'Improvising!' cried Probst, honestly startled, and peered with his pale blue eyes at Adrian's forehead as though he expected it to be glowing with fever.

Everybody burst out laughing, Adrian as well, letting his closed hands rest on the keyboard and bowing his head over them.

'Oh, Probst, what an ass you are!' said Baworinski. 'He is making up, can't you understand? He just thought of that this very minute.'

'How can he think up so many notes right and left at once,' Probst defended himself, 'and how can he say "It is nothing" of something he is actually playing? One surely cannot play what is not?'

'Oh, yes,' said Baworinski mildly. 'One can play what does not yet exist.'

I can still hear a certain Deutschlin, Konrad Deutschlin, a robust fellow with hair hanging in strings on his forehead, adding: 'And everything was once nothing, my good Probst, and then became something.'

'I can assure you,' said Adrian, 'that it really was nothing, in every sense of the word.'

He had been bent over with laughter, but now he lifted his head and you could see by his face that it was no easy matter: that he felt exposed. I recall that there now ensued a lengthy discussion on the creative element, led by Deutschlin and by no means uninteresting. The limitations were debated, which this conception had to tolerate, by virtue of culture, tradition, imitation, convention, pattern. Finally the human and creative element was theologically recognized, as a far, reflected splendour of divinely existent powers; as an echo of the first almighty summons to being, and the productive inspiration as in any case coming from above.

Moreover, and quite in passing, it was pleasant to me that I too, admitted from the profane faculty, could contribute when asked to the entertainment with my viola d'amore. For music was important in this circle, if only in a certain way, rather vaguely and as it were on principle: it was thought of as an art coming from God, one had to have 'relations' with it, romantic and devout, like one's relations with nature. Music, nature, and joyous worship, these were closely related and prescribed ideas in the Winfried. When I referred to 'sons of the Muses', the phrase, which to some perhaps would seem hardly suitable for students of theology, none the less found its justification in this combination of feeling, in the free and relaxed spirit, the clear-eyed contemplation of the beautiful, which characterized these tours into the heart of nature to which I now return.

Two or three times in the course of our four terms at Halle they were undertaken *in corpore*, and Baworinski summoned up all the seventy members of Winfried. Adrian and I never joined these mass enterprises. But single groups, more intimately connected, also made similar excursions and these we repeatedly joined, in company with a few of the better sort. There was our leader himself; the sturdy Deutschlin; then a certain Dungersheim, Carl von Teutleben, and some others, named respectively Hubmeyer,

Matthaeus Arzt, and Schappeler. I recall their names and to some extent their faces; it were superfluous to describe them.

The neighbourhood of Halle is a sandy plain, admittedly without charm. But a train conveys you in a few hours up the Saale into lovely Thuringia, and there, mostly at Naumburg or Apolda (the region where Adrian's mother was born), we left the train and set out with rucksacks and capes, on shank's mare, in all-day marches, eating in village inns or sometimes camping at the edge of a wood and spending the night in the hayloft of a peasant's yard, waking in the grey dawn to wash and refresh ourselves at the long trough of a running spring. Such an interim form of living, the entry of city folk, brain workers, into the primitive countryside and back to mother earth, with the knowledge, after all, that we must – or might – soon return to our usual and 'natural' sphere of middle-class comfort: such voluntary screwing down and simplification has easily, almost necessarily something artificial, patronizing, dilettante about it; of this we were humorously aware, and knew too that it was the cause of the good-natured, teasing grin with which many a peasant measured us on our request for his hayloft. But the kindly permission we got was due to our youth; for youth, one may say, makes the only proper bridge between the bourgeois and the state of nature; it is a pre-bourgeois state from which all student romance derives, the truly romantic period of life. To this formula the ever intellectually lively Deutschlin reduced the subject when we discussed it in our loft before falling asleep, by the wan light of the stable lantern in the corner. We dealt with the matter of our present mode of existence; and Deutschlin protested that it was poor taste for youth to explain youth: a form of life that discusses and examines itself thereby dissolves as form, and only direct and unconscious being has true existence.

The statement was denied, Hubmeyer and Schappeler contradicted it and Teutleben too demurred. It might be still finer, they ironically said, if only age were to judge youth and youth could only be the subject of outside observation, as though it had no share of objective mind. But it had, when it concerned itself too, and must be allowed to speak as youth about youth. There was something that one called a feeling of life, which came near to being consciousness of self, and if it were true that thereby the form of life was abrogated, then there was no sense of life possible at all. Mere dull unconscious being, ichthyosaurus-being, was no good, and today one must consciously not be wanting, one must assert one's specific form of life with an articulate feeling of self. It had taken a long time for youth to be so recognized.

'But the recognition has come more from pedagogy, that is from the old,' Adrian was heard to say, 'rather than from youth itself. It found itself one day presented, by an era that also talks about the century of the child and has invented the emancipation of woman, all in all a very compliant era, with the attribute of an independent form of life; of course it eagerly agreed.'

'No, Leverkühn,' said Hubmeyer and Schappeler, and the others supported them. He was wrong, they said, at least for the most part. It had been the feeling of life in youth itself that by dint of becoming conscious had asserted itself against the world, whether or no the latter had not been quite undecided for recognition.

'Not in the least,' said Adrian. 'Not at all undecided. I suppose one only needed to say to the era: "I have this and this sense of life," and the era just made it a low bow. Youth knocked on an open door.' Moreover there was nothing to say against it, provided youth and its time understood each other.

'Why are you so supercilious, Leverkühn? Don't you find it good that today youth gets its rights in bourgeois society and that the values peculiar to the period of development are recognized?'

'Oh, certainly,' said Adrian. 'But I started, you started – that is, we started – with the idea –'

He was interrupted by a burst of laughter. I think it was Matthaeus Arzt who said: 'That was perfect Leverkühn. You led up to a climax. First you leave us out altogether, then you leave yourself out, then you manage to say "we", but you obviously find it very difficult, you hard-boiled individualist!'

Adrian rejected the epithet. It was quite false, he said, he was no individualist, he entirely accepted the community.

'Theoretically, perhaps,' answered Arzt, 'and condescendingly, with Adrian Leverkühn excepted. He talks of youth condescendingly too, as though he were not young himself; as though he were incapable of including himself and fitting in; as far as humility goes he knows very little about it.'

'But we were not talking about humility,' Adrian parried, 'rather, on the contrary, of a conscious sense of life.' Deutschlin suggested that they should let Adrian finish what he had to say.

'That was all,' said the latter. 'We started with the idea that youth has closer relations with nature than the mature man in a bourgeois society – something like woman, to whom also has been ascribed, compared with man, a greater nearness to nature. But I cannot follow. I do not find that youth stands on a particularly intimate footing with nature. Rather its attitude towards her is shy and reserved, actually strange. The human being comes to terms with his own natural side only with the years and only slowly gets accommodated to it. It is precisely youth, I mean more highly developed youth, that is more likely to shrink or be scornful, to display hostility. What do we mean by nature? Woods, meadows, mountains, trees, lakes, beauty of scenery? For all that, in my opinion, youth has much less of an eye than has the older, more tranquil man. The young one is by no means so disposed to see and enjoy nature. His eye is directed inwards, mentally conditioned, disinclined to the senses, in my opinion.'

'*Quod demonstramus*,' said somebody, very likely Dungersheim – 'we wanderers lying here in our straw, marching through the forests of Thuringia to Eisenach and the Wartburg.'

'"In my opinion", you always say,' another voice interjected. 'You probably mean: "in my experience".'

'You were just reproaching me,' retorted Adrian, 'for speaking condescendingly about youth and not including myself. Now all of a sudden you tell me I am making myself stand for it.'

'Leverkühn,' Deutschlin commented, 'has his own thoughts about youth; but obviously he too regards it as a specific form of life, which must be respected as such; and that is the decisive factor. I only spoke against youth's discussion of itself in so far as that disintegrates the immediacy of life. But as consciousness of self it also strengthens life, and in this sense – I mean also to this extent – I call it good. The idea of youth is a prescriptive right and prerogative of our people, the German people; the others scarcely know it; youth as consciousness of self is as good as unknown to them. They wonder at the conscious bearing of German youth, to which the elder sections of the population give their assent, and even at their unbourgeois dress. Let them! German youth, precisely as youth, represents the spirit of the people itself, the German spirit, which is young and filled with the future: unripe, if you like, but what does unripe mean? German deeds were always done out of a certain mighty immaturity, and not for nothing are we the people of the Reformation. That too was a work of immaturity. Mature, that was the Florentine citizen of the Renaissance, who before he went to church said to his wife: "Well, let us now make our bow to popular error!" But Luther was unripe enough, enough of the people, of the German people, to bring in the new, the purified faith. Where would the world be if maturity were the last word? We shall in our unripeness vouchsafe it still some renewal, some revolution.'

After these words of Deutschlin we were silent for a while. Obviously there in the darkness each young man turned over in his mind the feelings of personal and national youthfulness, mingling as one. The phrase 'mighty immaturity' had certainly a flattering ring for the most.

'If I only knew,' I can hear Adrian say, breaking the silence, 'how it is we are so unripe, so young as you say we are, I mean as a people. After all, we have come as far as the others, and perhaps it is only our history, the fact that we were a bit late getting together and building up a common consciousness, which deludes us into the notion of our uncommon youthfulness.'

'But it is probably something else,' responded Deutschlin. 'Youth in the ultimate sense has nothing to do with political history, nothing to do with history at all. It is a metaphysical endowment, an essential factor, a structure, a conditioning. Have you never heard of German Becoming, of German Wandering, of the endless migratings of the German soul? Even foreigners know our word *"Wanderlust"*. If you like, the German is the eternal student, the eternal searcher, among the peoples of the earth –'

'And his revolutions,' Adrian interpolated, with his short laugh, 'are the puppet-shows of world history.'

'Very witty, Leverkühn. But yet I am surprised that your Protestantism allows you to be so witty. It is possible, if necessary, to take more seriously what I mean by youth. To be young means to be original, to have remained nearer to the sources of life; it means to be able to stand up and shake off the fetters of an outlived civilization, to dare – where others lack the courage – to plunge again into the elemental. Youthful courage, that is the spirit of dying and becoming, the knowledge of death and rebirth.'

'Is that so German?' asked Adrian. 'Rebirth was once called *rinascimento* and went on in Italy. And "back to Nature", that was first prescribed in French.'

'The first was a cultural renewal,' answered Deutschlin, 'the second a sentimental pastoral play.'

'Out of the pastoral play,' persisted Adrian, 'came the French Revolution, and Luther's Reformation was only an offshoot and ethical bypath of the Renaissance, its application to the field of religion.'

'The field of religion, there you are. And religion is always something besides archaeological revival and an upheaval in social criticism. Religiosity, that is perhaps youth itself, it is the directness, the courage and depth of the personal life, the will and the power, the natural and daemonic side of being, as it has come into our consciousness again through Kierkegaard, to experience it in full vitality and to live through it.'

'Do you consider the feeling for religion a distinctively German gift?' asked Adrian.

'In the sense I mean, as soulful youth, as spontaneity, as faith, and Düreresque knighthood between Death and Devil – certainly.'

'And France, the land of cathedrals, whose head was the All-Christian

King, and which produced theologians like Bossuet and Pascal?'
'That was long ago. For centuries France has been marked out by history
as the European power with the anti-Christian mission. Of Germany the
opposite is true, and that you would feel and know, Leverkühn, if you were
not Adrian Leverkühn – in other words, too cool to be young, too clever to be
religious. With cleverness one may go a long way in the Church, but scarcely
in religion.'

'Many thanks, Deutschlin,' laughed Adrian. 'In good old German words,
as Ehrenfried Kumpf would say, you have given it to me straight, without
any mealy-mouthing. I have a feeling that I shan't go very far in the Church
either; but one thing is certain, that I should not have become a theologian
without her. I know of course that it is the most talented among you, those
who have read Kierkegaard, who place truth, even ethical truth, entirely in
the subjective, and reject with horror everything that savours of herd
existence. But I cannot go with you in your radicalism – which certainly will
not long persist, as it is a student licence – I cannot go with you in your
separation, after Kierkegaard, of Church and Christianity. I see in the
Church, even as she is today, secularized and reduced to the bourgeois, a
citadel of order, an institution for objective disciplining, canalizing,
banking-up of the religious life, which without her would fall victim to
subjectivist demoralization, to a chaos of divine and daemonic powers, to a
world of fantastic uncanniness, an ocean of daemony. To separate Church
and religion means to give up separating the religious from madness.'

'Oh, come!' from several voices. But:

'He is right,' Matthaeus Arzt declared roundly. The others called him the
Socialist, because the social was his passion. He was a Christian Socialist and
often quoted Goethe's saying that Christianity was a political revolution
which, having failed, became a moral one. Political, he said now, it must
again become, that is to say social: that was the true and only means for the
disciplining of the religious element, now in danger of a degeneration which
Leverkühn had not so badly described. Religious socialism, religiosity
linked with the social, that was it: for everything depended on finding the
right link, and the theonomic sanction must be united with the social, bound
up with the God-given task of social fulfilment. 'Believe me,' he said, 'it all
depends on the development of a responsible industrial population, an
international nation of industry, which some day can form a right and
genuine European economic society. In it all shaping impulses will lie, they
lie in the germ even now, not merely for the technical achievement of a new
economic organization, not only to result in a thorough sanitation of the
natural relations of life, but also to found new political orders.'

I repeat the ideas of these young people as they were uttered, in their own
terminology, a sort of learned lingo, quite unaware how pompous they
sounded, flinging about the stilted and pretentious phrases with artless
virtuosity and self-satisfaction. 'Natural relations of life', 'theonomic
sanctions', such were their preciosities. Certainly they could have put it all
more simply, but then it would not have been their scientific-theological
jargon. With gusto they propounded the 'problem of being', talked about
'the sphere of the divine', 'the political sphere', or 'the academic sphere';
about the 'structural principle', 'condition of dialectic tension', 'existential
correspondences', and so on. Deutschlin, with his hands clasped behind his
head, now put the 'problem of being' in the sense of the genetic origin of
Arzt's economic society. That was nothing but economic common sense,
and nothing but this could ever be represented in the economic society. 'But

we must be clear on this point, Matthaeus,' said he, 'that the social idea of an economic social organization comes from autonomous thinking in its nature enlightening, in short from a rationalism which is still by no means grasped by the mighty forces either above or below the rational. You believe you can develop a just order out of the pure insight and reason of man, equating the just and the socially useful, and you think that out of it new political forms will come. But the economic sphere is quite different from the political, and from economic expediency to historically related political consciousness there is no direct transition. I don't see why you fail to recognize that. Political organization refers to the State, a kind and degree of control not conditioned by usefulness; wherein other qualities are represented than those known to representatives of enterprises and secretaries of unions; for instance, honour and dignity. For such qualities, my dear chap, the inhabitants of the economic sphere do not contribute the necessary existential correspondences.'

'Ach, Deutschlin, what are you talking about?' said Arzt. 'As modern sociologists we very well know that the State too is conditioned by utilitarian functions. There is the administration of justice and the preservation of order. And then after all we live in an economic age, the economic is simply the historical character of this time, and honour and dignity do not help the State one jot, if it does not of itself have a grasp of the economic situation and know how to direct it.'

Deutschlin admitted that. But he denied that useful functions were the *essential* objects and *raisons d'être* of the State. The legitimacy of the State resided, he said, in its elevation, its sovereignty, which thus existed independent of the valuations of individuals, because it – very much in contrast to the shufflings of the Contrat Social – was there *before* the individual. The supra-individual associations had, that is, just as much original existence as the individual human beings, and an economist, for just that reason, could understand nothing of the State, because he understood nothing of its transcendental foundation.

To which Teutleben added:

'I am of course not without sympathy for the socio-religious combination that Arzt is speaking for, it is anyhow better than none at all, and Matthaeus is only too right when he says that everything depends on finding the right combination. But to be right, to be at once political and religious, it must be of the people, and what I ask myself is: can a new nationality rise out of an economic society? Look at the Ruhr: there you have your assembly centres of men, yet no new national cells. Travel in the local train from Leuna to Halle. You will see workmen sitting together, who can talk very well about tariffs; but from their conversation it does not appear that they had drawn any national strength from their common activity. In economics the nakedly finite rules more and more.'

'But the national is finite too,' somebody else said, it was either Hubmeyer or Schappeler, I don't know which. 'As theologians we must not admit that the folk is anything eternal. Capacity for enthusiasm is very fine and a need for faith very natural to youth; but it is a temptation too, and one must look very hard at the new groupings, which today, when liberalism is dying off, are everywhere being presented, to see whether they have genuine substance, and whether the thing creating the bond is itself something real or perhaps only the product of, let us say, structural romanticism, which creates for itself ideological connexions in a nominalistic not to say fictionalistic way. I think, or rather I am afraid, that the deified national

State and the State regarded as a utopia are just such nominalistic structures; and the recognition of them, let us say the recognition of Germany, has something not binding about it because it has nothing to do with personal substance and qualitative content. Nothing is asked about that, and when one says "Germany" and declares that to be his connecting link, he does not need to validate it at all. He will be asked by nobody, not even by himself, how much Germanism he in fact and in a personal – that is, in a qualitative sense – represents and realizes; or how far he is in a position to serve the assertion of a German form of life in the world. It is that which I call nominalism, or rather the fetish of names, which in my opinion is the ideological worship of idols.'

'Good, Hubmeyer,' said Deutschlin. 'All you say is quite right, and in any case I admit that your criticism has brought us closer to the problem. I disagreed with Matthaeus Arzt because the domination of the utilitarian principle in the economic field does not suit me; but I entirely agree with him that the theonomic sanction in itself, that is to say the religious in general, has something formalistic and unobjective about it. It needs some kind of down-to-earth, empirical content or application or confirmation, some practice in obedience to God. And so now Arzt has chosen socialism and Carl Teutleben nationalism. These are the two between which we have today to choose. I deny that there is an outbidding of ideologies, since today nobody is beguiled by the empty word "freedom". There are in fact just these two possibilities, of religious submission and religious realization: the social and the national. But as ill luck will have it, both of them have their drawbacks and dangers, and very serious ones. Hubmeyer has expressed himself very tellingly on a certain nominalistic hollowness and personal lack of substance so frequently evident in the acceptance of the national; and, generally speaking, one should add that it is futile to fling oneself into the arms of a reinvigorating objectivism if it means nothing for the actual shaping of one's personal life but is only valid for solemn occasions, among which indeed I count the intoxication of sacrificial death. To a genuine sacrifice two valuations and qualitative ingredients belong: that of the thing and that of the sacrifice. . . . But we have cases where the personal substance, let us say, was very rich in Germanness and quite involuntarily objectivated itself also as sacrifice; yet where acknowledgement of the folk-bond not only utterly failed, but there was even a permanent and violent negation of it, so that the tragic sacrifice consisted precisely in the conflict between being and confession. . . . So much for tonight about the national sanction. As for the social, the hitch is that when everything in the economic field is regulated in the best possible manner, the problem of the meaning and fulfilment of existence and a worthy conduct of life is left open, just as open as it is today. Some day we shall have universal economic administration of the world, the complete victory of collectivism. Good; the relative insecurity of man due to the catastrophic social character of the capitalistic system will have disappeared; that is, there will have vanished from human life the last memory of risk and loss – and with it the intellectual problem. One asks oneself why then continue to live . . .'

'Would you like to retain the capitalist system, Deutschlin,' asked Arzt – 'because it keeps alive the memory of the insecurity of human life?'

'No, I would not, my dear Arzt,' answered Deutschlin with some heat. 'Still, I may be allowed to indicate the tragic antinomies of which life is full.'

'One doesn't need to have them pointed out,' sighed Dungersheim. 'It is certainly a desperate situation, and the religious man asks himself whether the world really is the single work of a benevolent God and not rather a combined effort, I will not say with whom.'

'What I should like to know,' remarked von Teutleben, 'is whether the young of other nations lie about like us, plaguing themselves with problems and antinomies.'

'Hardly,' answered Deutschlin contemptuously. 'They have a much easier and more comfortable time intellectually.'

'The Russian revolutionary youth,' Arzt asserted, 'should be excepted. There, if I am not mistaken, there is a tireless discursive argumentation and a cursed lot of dialectic tension.'

'The Russians,' said Deutschlin sententiously, 'have profundity but no form. And in the west they have form but no profundity. Only we Germans have both.'

'Well, if that is not a nationalistic sanction!' laughed Hubmeyer.

'It is merely the sanction of an idea,' Deutschlin asserted. 'It is the demand of which I speak. Our obligation is exceptional, certainly not the average, for that we have already attained. What is and what ought to be – there is a bigger gulf between them with us than with others, simply because the "ought to be", the standard, is so high.'

'In all that,' Dungersheim warned us, 'we probably ought not to consider the national, but rather to regard the complex of problems as bound up with the existence of modern man. But it is the case, that since the direct faith in being has been lost, which in earlier times was the result of being fixed in a pre-existent universal order of things, I mean the ritually permeated regulations which had a certain definite bearing on the revealed truth . . . that since the decline of faith and the rise of modern society our relations which men and things have become endlessly complicated and refracted, there is nothing left but problems and uncertainties, so that the design for truth threatens to end in resignation and despair. The search rising from disintegration, for the beginnings of new forces of order, is general; though one may also agree that it is particularly serious and urgent among us Germans, and that the others do not suffer so from historical destiny, either because they are stronger or because they are duller –'

'Duller,' pronounced von Teutleben.

'That is what you say, Teutleben. But if we count to our honour as a nation our sharp awareness of the historical and psychological complex of problems, and identify with the German character the endeavour after new universal regulation, we are already on the point of prescribing for ourselves a myth of doubtful genuineness and not doubtful arrogance: namely, the national, with its structural romanticism of the warrior type, which is nothing but natural paganism with Christian trimmings and identifies Christus as "Lord of the heavenly hosts". But that is a position decisively threatened from the side of the demons . . .'

'Well, and?' asked Deutschlin. 'Daemonic powers stand beside the order-making qualities in any vital movement.'

'Let us call things by their names,' demanded Schappeler – or it might have been Hubmeyer. 'The daemonic, the German word for that is the instincts. And that is just it: today even, along with the instincts, propaganda is made for claims to all sorts of sanctions, and that one, too, I mean, it takes them in and trims up the old idealism with the psychology of instinct, so that there arises the dazzling impression of a thicker density of reality. But just on that account the bid can be pure swindle.'

At this point one can only say 'and so on'; for it is time to put an end to the

reproduction of that conversation – or of such conversations. In reality it had
no end, it went on deep into the night, on and on, with 'bipolar position' and
'historically conscious analysis', with 'extratemporal qualities', 'ontological
naturalism', 'logical dialectic', and 'practical dialectic': painstaking, shore-
less, learned, tailing off into nothing – that is, into slumber, to which our
leader Baworinski recommended us, for in the morning – as it already almost
was – we should be due for an early start. That kind nature held sleep ready,
to take up the conversation and rock it in forgetfulness, was a grateful
circumstance, and Adrian, who had not spoken for a long time, gave it
expression in a few words as we settled down.

'Yes, good night, lucky we can say it. Discussions should always be held
just before going to bed, your rear protected by sleep. How painful, after an
intellectual conversation, to have to go about with your mind so stirred up.'

'That is just an escapist psychology,' somebody grumbled – and then the
first sounds of heavy breathing filled our loft with its announcement of
relaxation and surrender to the vegetative state; of that a few hours sufficed
to restore youth's elasticity. For next day along with physical activity and
the enjoyment of natural beauty, they would continue the usual theological
and philosophical debates with almost interminable mutual instruction,
opposition, challenge, and reply. It was the month of June, and the air was
filled with the heavy scent of jasmine and elder-blossom from the gorges of
the wooded heights that cross the Thuringian basin. Priceless it was to
wander for days through the countryside, here almost free from industry,
the well-favoured, fruitful land, with its friendly villages, in clusters of
latticed buildings. Then coming out of the farming region into that of mostly
grazing land, to follow the storied, beech- and pine-covered ridge road, the
'Rennsteig', which, with its view deep down into the Werra valley, stretches
from the Frankenwald to Eisenach on the Hörsel. It grew ever more
beautiful, significant, romantic; and neither what Adrian had said about the
reserve of youth in the face of nature, nor that about the desirability of being
able to retire to slumber after intellectual discussion seemed to have any
cogency. Even to him it scarcely applied; for, except when his headaches
made him silent, he contributed with animation to the daily talks; and if
nature lured from him no very enthusiastic cries and he looked at it with a
certain musing aloofness, I do not doubt that its pictures, rhythms, the
melodies of its upper airs, penetrated deeper into his soul than into those of
his companions. It has even happened that some passage of pure, free beauty
standing out from the tense intellectuality of his work has later brought to
my mind those days and the experiences we shared.

Yes, they were stirring hours, days, and weeks. The refreshment of the
out-of-doors life, and the oxygen in the air, the landscape, and the historical
impressions, thrilled these young folk and raised their spirits to a plane
where thought moved lavishly in free experimental flight as it will at that time
of life. In later, more arid hours of an after-university professional career,
even an intellectual one, there would be scarcely any such occasion. Often I
looked at them during their theological and philosophical debates and
pictured to myself that to some among them their Winfried period might in
later years seem the finest time of their lives. I watched them and I watched
Adrian, with the clear perception that it would not be so with him. I, as a
non-theologian, was a guest among them; he, though a theologian, was even
more of one. Why? I felt, not without a pang, the foreordained gulf between
his existence and that of these striving and high-purposed youths. It was the
difference of the life-curve between good, yes, excellent average, which was

destined to return from that roving, seeking student life to its bourgeois courses, and the other, invisibly singled out, who would never forsake the hard route of the mind, would tread it, who knew whither, and whose gaze, whose attitude, never quite resolved in the fraternal, whose inhibitions in his personal relations made me and probably others aware that he himself divined this difference.

By the beginning of his fourth semester I had indications that my friend was thinking of dropping his theological course, even before the first exams.

Chapter Fifteen

Adrian's relations with Wendell Kretschmar had never been broken off or weakened. The young 'studiosus' of the divine science saw the musical mentor of his schooldays in every vacation, when he came to Kaisersaschern; visited him and consulted him in the organist's quarters in the Cathedral; met him at Uncle Leverkühn's house, and persuaded the parents to invite him once or twice to Buchel for the weekend, where they took extended walks and also got Jonathan Leverkühn to show the guest Chladni's sound-patterns and the devouring drop. Kretschmar stood very well with the host of Buchel, now getting on in years. His relations with Frau Elsbeth were more formal if by no means actually strained. Perhaps she was distressed by his stutter, which just for that reason got worse in her presence and in direct conversation with her. It was odd, after all. In Germany music enjoys that respect among the people which in France is given to literature; among us nobody is put off or embarrassed, uncomfortably impressed, or moved to disrespect or mockery by the fact that a man is a musician; so I am convinced that Elsbeth Leverkühn felt entire respect for Adrian's elder friend, who, moreover, practised his activity as a salaried man in the service of the Church. Yet during the two and a half days which I once spent with him and Adrian at Buchel, I observed in her bearing towards the organist a certain reserve and restraint, held in check but not quite done away by her native friendliness. And he, as I said, responded with a worsening of his impediment amounting a few times almost to a calamity. It is hard to say whether it was that he felt her unease and mistrust or whatever it was, or because on his own side, spontaneously, he had definite inhibitions amounting to shyness and embarrassment in her presence.

As for me, I felt sure that the peculiar tension between Kretschmar and Adrian's mother had reference to Adrian; I divined this because in the silent struggle that went on I stood in my own feeling between the two parties, inclining now to the one and now to the other. What Kretschmar wanted, what he talked about on those walks with Adrian, was clear to me, and privately my own wishes supported him. I thought he was right when, also in talk with me, he pleaded for the musical calling of his pupil, that he should become a composer, with determination, even with urgency. 'He has,' he said, 'the composer's eye; he bends on music the look of the initiate, not of the vaguely enjoying outsider. His way of discovering thematic connexions that the other kind of man does not see; of perceiving the articulations of a short extract in the form of question and answer; altogether of seeing from the inside how it is made, confirms me in my judgement. That he shows no productive impulse, does not yet write or naïvely embark upon youthful productions, is only to his credit; it is a question of his pride, which prevents him from producing epigonal music.'

I could only agree with all that. But I could thoroughly understand as well the protective concern of the mother and often felt my solidarity with her, to the point of hostility to the other side. Never shall I forget a scene in the living-room at Buchel when we chanced to sit there together, the four of us: mother and son, Kretschmar and I. Elsbeth was in talk with the musician, who was puffing and blowing with his impediment; it was a mere chat, of which Adrian was certainly not the subject. She drew her son's head to her as he sat beside her, in the strangest way, putting her arm about him, not round his shoulders but round his head, her hand on his brow, and thus, with the gaze of her black eyes directed upon Kretschmar and her sweet voice speaking to him, she leaned Adrian's head upon her breast.

But to return: it was not alone these meetings that sustained the relation between master and pupil. There was also frequent correspondence, an exchange, I believe every two weeks, between Halle and Kaisersaschern, about which Adrian from time to time informed me and of which I even got to see some part. It seemed that Kretschmar was considering taking a piano and organ class in the Hase private conservatoire in Leipzig, which next to the famous State Music School in that city was rejoicing in a growing reputation, constantly increased during the next ten years, up to the death of the capital musician Clemens Hase (it no longer plays any role, even if it still exists). I learned this fact in Michaelmas 1904. At the beginning of the next year Wendell accordingly left Kaisersaschern to take over his new position, and from then on the correspondence went forward between Halle and Leipzig, to and fro: Kretschmar's sheets covered on one side with large, scratching, spluttering letters; Adrian's replies on rough yellow paper, in his regular, slightly old-fashioned, rather florid script, written, as one could see, with a round-hand pen. I saw a draft of one of them, very compactly written, like figures, full of fine additions and corrections – I had early become familiar with his way of writing and read it quite easily – and he also showed me Kretschmar's reply to it. He did this, obviously, in order that I need not be too much surprised by the step he proposed to take when he should have actually settled on it. For that he had not as yet, was hesitating very much, doubting and examining himself, the letter makes clear; he obviously wanted to be advised by me – God knows whether in a sense to encourage or to warn.

There could not be and would not have been on my side any possibility of surprise, even if I had been faced with the fact without preparation. I knew what was on the way: whether it would actually come to pass was another question; but so much was clear to me too, that since Kretschmar's move to Leipzig, his chances of getting his way were considerably improved.

Adrian's letter showed a more than average capacity to look at himself critically, and as a confession its ironic humility touched me very much. To his one-time mentor, now aspiring to be that again and much more, he set forth the scruples that held him back from a decision to change his profession and fling himself into the arms of music. He halfway admitted that theology, as an empiric study, had disappointed him: the reasons of course being to seek not in that revered science, nor with his academic teachers, but in himself. That was already plain from the fact that he certainly could not say what other, better choice he could then have made. Sometimes, when he took counsel with himself on the possibilities of a shift, he had, during these years, considered choosing mathematics, in which, when he was at school, he had always found 'good entertainment' (his very words). But with a sort of horror at himself he saw it coming, that if he made this discipline his own, bound himself over, identified himself with it, he would very soon be disillusioned, bored; get as sick and tired of it as though he 'had ladled it in with a cooking-spoon' (this grotesque simile also I recall literally). 'I cannot conceal from your respected self,' he wrote (for he sometimes fell into old-fashioned phrases and spellings), 'neither you nor myself, that with your *apprendista* it is a god-forsaken case. It is not just an everyday thing with me, I would not lain it thus; it addresses itself to your verye bowells of compassion more than makes your heart leap up for joy.' He had, he said, received from God the gift of a 'toward wit'; from childhood up and with less than common pain had grasped everything offered in his education – too easily, 'belike', for any of it to win his proper respect. Too easily for blood and brains ever to have got properly warmed up for the sake of a subject and by effort over it. 'I fear,' he wrote, 'dear and beloved friend and master, I am a lost soul, a black sheep; I have no warmth. As the Gode Boke hath it, they shall be cursed and spewed out of the mouth who are neither cold nor warm but lukewarm. Lukewarm I should not call myself. I am cold out of all question; but in my judgement of myself I would pray to dissent from the taste of that Power whose it is to apportion blessing and cursing.'

He went on:

'Oddly enough, it was best at the grammar school, there I was still pretty much in the right place, because in the upper forms they deal out the greatest variety of thinges, one after the other, changing the subject from one five-and-forty minutes to the next – in other words there was still no profession. But even those five-and-forty minutes were too long, they bored me – and boredom is the coldest thing in the world. After fifteen minutes at most I had all that the good man chammed over with the other boys for thirty more. Reading the authors, I read on further; I had done so at home, and if I mought not always give answer, 'twas but because I was already in the next lesson. Three quarters of an hour of Anabasis was too much of one thing for my patience, in sign thereof my mygryms came on' (he meant his headaches) 'and never did they procede from fatigue due to effort, but from satiety, from cold boredom, and, dear master and friend, sith I no longer am a young bachelor springing from branch to branch but have married me with one plot and one profession, it has truly gone hevyli indeed with me.

'In feith, ye will not believe that I hold myself too good for any profession. On the contrary, I am pitiful of that I make mine own, and ye may see in that an homage, a declaration of love for music, a special position towards her, that in her case I should feel quite too deeply pitiful.

'You will ask if it was not so with theology? But I submitted thereunto; not so much, though there was somewhat of that too therein, that I saw in it the highest of the sciences; but for that I would fain humble myself, bow the knee, and be chastened, to castigate my cold contumacy, in short out of *contritio*. I wanted the sack of heyre, the spiked girdle beneath. I did what those did in earlier times who knocked at the gate of the cloister of strict observance. It has its absurd and comic sides, this professionally cloistered life, but assaye to understand that a secret terror warned me not to forsake it, to put the Scriptures under the bench and scape into the art to which you introduced me, and about which I feel that for me to practise it were shrewidness and shame.

'Ye think me called to this art, and give me to understand that the "step aside" to her were no long one. My Lutheranism agrees, for it sees in theology and music neighbouring spheres and close of kin; and besides, music has always seemed to me personally a magic marriage between theology and the so diverting mathematic. Item, she has much of the laboratory and the insistent activity of the alchemists and nigromancers of yore, which also stood in the sign of theology, but at the same time in that of emancipation and apostasy; it was apostasy, not from the feith, that was never possible, but *in* the feith; for apostasy is an act of feith and everything is and happens in God, most of all the falling from Him.'

My quotations are very nearly literal, even where they are not quite so. I can rely very well on my memory, and besides I committed much of it to paper at once after reading the draft, and in particular this about apostasy.

He then excused himself for the digression, which scarcely was one, and went on to the practical question of what branch of musical activity he should envisage in case he yielded to Kretschmar's pressure. He pointed out that he was useless, from the start and admittedly, for solo virtuosity. 'It pricketh betimes that will be a sharp thorn', he wrote, quoting Kumpf, and that he had come too late into contact with the instrument, or even with the idea, from which followed of course, the clear conclusion that he lacked any instinctive urge in that direction. He had gone to the keyboard not out of desire to master it, but out of private curiosity about music itself; he was entirely lacking in the gypsy blood of the concert artist, who produced himself before the public through music, music being the occasion he took. To that went mental premises which he did not satisfy: desire for love-affairs with the crowd, for laurel wreaths and bowing and kowtowing to applause. He avoided the adjectives which would actually have made clear what he meant: he did not say that even if he had not come to it too late, he was too self-conscious, too proud, too difficult, too solitary, to be a virtuoso.

These same objections, he went on, stood in the way of a career as a conductor. As little as a keyboard juggler could he see himself as a baton-waving, frock-coated prima donna of the orchestra, an interpreting ambassador and gala-representative of music on earth. But now there did escape him a word that belonged in the same class with those which I just said would have fitted the case: he spoke of being unsocial; he called himself that, and meant no compliment. This quality he judged, was the expression of a want of warmth, sympathy, love, and it was very much in question whether one could, lacking them, be a good artist, which after all and always means being a lover and beloved of the world. Now putting these two aside, the solo artist and the conductor, what was left? Forsooth, music herself, the promise and vow to her, the hermetic laboratory, the gold-kitchen: composition. 'Wonderful! Ye will initiate me, friend Albertus Magnus, into the mysteries of theory and certes I feel, I know aforehand, as already I know a little from experience, I shalbe no backward adeptus. I shall grasp all the shifts and controls, and that easily, in truth because my mind goeth to meet them, the ground is prepared, it already nourishes some seed therein. I will refine on the *prima materia*, in that I add to it the *magisterium* and with spirit and fire drive the matter through many limbecs and retorts for the refining thereof. What a glorious mystery! I know none higher, deeper, better; none more thrilling, or occult; none whereto less persuasion were necessary to persuade.

'And yet, why does an inward voice warn me: "*O homo fuge*"? I cannot give answer unto the question very articulately. Only this much I can say: I fear to make promises to art, because I doubt whether my nature – quite aside from the question of a gift – is calculated to satisfy her; because I must disclaim the robust naïveté which, so far as I can see – among other things, and not least among them – pertaineth to the nature of the artist. In its place my lot is a quickly satisfied intelligence, whereof, I suppose, I may speak, because I call heaven and hell to witness that I am not in vain of it; it is that, together with the accompanying proneness to fatigue and disgust (with headake), which is the ground of my fear and concern. It will, it ought to, decide me to refrain. Mark me, good master, young as I am I am wel enow seen therein to know, and should not be your pupil did I not, that it passeth far beyond the pattern, the canon, the tradition, beyond what one learns from others, the trick, the technique. Yet it is undeniable that there is a lot of all that in it, and I see it coming (for it lieth also in my nature, for good or ill, to look beyond) that I am embarrassed at the insipidness which is the supporting structure, the conditioning solid substance of even the work of genius, at the elements thereof which are training and common property, at use and wont in achieving the beautiful; I blush at all that, weary thereof, get head-ake therefrom and that right early.

'How stupid, how pretentious it would be to ask: "Do you understand that?" For how should you not? It goes like this, when it is beautiful: the cellos intone by themselves, a pensive, melancholy theme, which questions the folly of the world, the wherefore of all the struggle and striving, pursuing and plaguing – all highly expressive and decorously philosophical. The cellos enlarge upon this riddle awhile, head-shaking, deploring, and at a certain point in their remarks, a well-chosen point, the chorus of wind instruments enters with a deep full breath that makes your shoulders rise and fall, in a choral hymn, movingly solemn, richly harmonized, and produced with all the muted dignity and mildly restrained power of the brass. Thus the sonorous melody presses on up to nearly the height of a climax, which, in accordance with the law of economy it avoids at first, gives way, leaves open, sinks away, postpones, most beautifully lingers, then withdraws and gives place to another theme, a songlike, simple one, now jesting, now grave, now popular, apparently brisk and robust by nature but sly as you make them, and for someone with some subtle cleverness in the art of thematic analysis and transformation it proves itself amazingly pregnant and capable of utter refinement. For a while this little song is managed and deployed, cleverly and charmingly, it is taken apart, looked at in detail, varied, out of it a delightful figure in the middle register is led up into the most enchanting heights of fiddles and flutes, lulls itself there a little, and when it is at its most artful, then the mild brass has again the word with the previous choral hymn and comes into the foreground. The brass does not start from the beginning as it did the first time, but as though its melody had already been there for a while; and it continues, solemnly, to that climax from which it wisely refrained the first time, in order that the surging feeling, the Ah-h-effect, might be the greater: now it gloriously bestrides its theme, mounting unchecked, with weighty support from the passing notes on the tuba, and then, looking back, as it were, with dignified satisfaction on the finished achievement, sings itself decorously to the end.

'Dear friend, why do I have to laugh? Can a man employ the traditional or sanctify the trick with greater genius? Can one with shrewder sense achieve the beautiful? And I, abandoned wretch, I have to laugh, particularly at the grunting supporting notes of the bombardone. Bum, bum, bum, bang! I may have tears in my eyes at the same time, but the desire to laugh is

irresistible – I have always had to laugh, most damnably, at the most
mysterious and impressive phenomena. I fled from this exaggerated sense of
the comic into theology, in the hope that it would give relief to the tickling –
only to find there too a perfect legion of ludicrous absurdities. Why does
almost everything seem to me like its own parody? Why must I think that
almost all, no, all the methods and conventions of art today *are good for
parody only?* – These are of course rhetorical questions, it was not that I still
expected an answer to them. But such a despairing heart, such a damp squib
as I am, you consider as "gifted" for music and summon me to you and to its
service, instead of rather leaving me humbly to tarry with God and
theology?'

Thus Adrian's confession in avoidance. And Kretschmar's reply: that
document I have not by me. It was not found among the papers Leverkühn
left. He must have preserved it for a while and then in some moving to
Munich, to Italy, to Pfeiffering, it must have got lost. But I retain it in my
memory almost as precisely as Adrian's own, even though I made no notes
on it. The stutterer stuck by his summons, his monitions and allurements.
Not a word in Adrian's letter, he wrote, could have made him for a moment
falter in his conviction that it was music for which fate destined the writer,
after which he hankered as music after him, and against which, half
cowardly, half capricious, he had hidden himself behind these half-true
analyses of his character and constitution, as previously behind theology, his
first and absurd choice. 'Affectation, Adri – and the increase in your
headaches is the punishment for it.' His sense of the ludicrous of which he
boasted, or complained, would suit with art far better than with his present
unnatural occupation, for art, on the contrary, could use it; could in general,
much better use the repellent characteristics he attributed to himself than he
believed or made pretence that he believed it could. He, Kretschmar, would
leave the question open, how far Adrian was accusing himself in order to
excuse his corresponding accusations against art; for this painting art as a
marriage with the mob, as kiss-throwing, gala-posturing, as a bellows to blow
up the emotions, was facile misconstruction and a wilful one too. What he
was trying to do was to excuse himself on account of certain characteristics,
while there, on the other hand, were the very ones art demanded. Art needed
just his sort today – and the joke, the hypocritical, hide-and-seek joke, was
that Adrian knew it perfectly well. The coolness, the 'quickly satisfied
intelligence', the eye for the stale and absurd, the early fatigue, the capacity
for disgust – all that was perfectly calculated to make a profession of the
talent bound up with it. Why? Because it belonged only in part to the private
personality; for the rest it was of an extra-individual nature, the expression
of a collective feeling for the historical exhaustion and vitiation of the means
and appliances of art, the boredom with them and the search for new ways.
'Art strides on,' Kretschmar wrote, 'and does so through the medium of the
personality, which is the product of the tool of the time, and in which
objective and subjective motives combine indistinguishably, each taking on
the shape of the others. The vital need of art for revolutionary progress and
the coming of the new addresses itself to whatever vehicle has the strongest
subjective sense of the staleness, fatuity, and emptiness of the means still
current. It avails itself of the apparently unvital, of that personal satiety and
intellectual boredom, that disgust at seeing "how it works"; that accursed
itch to look at things in the light of their own parody; that sense of the
ridiculous – I tell you that the will to life and to living, growing art puts on
the mask of these faint-hearted personal qualities, to manifest itself therein,

to objectivate, to fulfill itself. Is that too much metaphysics for you? But it is just precisely enough of it, precisely the truth, the truth which at bottom you know yourself. Make haste, Adrian, and decide. I am waiting. You are already twenty, and you have still a good many tricks of the trade to get used to, quite hard enough to stimulate you. It is better to get a headache from exercises in canons, fugues, and counterpoint than from confuting the Kantian confutation of the evidence for the existence of God. Enough of your theological spinsterhood!

> Virginity is well, yet must to motherhood;
> Unear'd she is a soil unfructified for good.'

With this quotation from the *Cherubinic Wandersmann* the letter ended, and when I looked up from it I met Adrian's subtle smile.

'Not badly parried, don't you think?' he asked.

'By no means,' said I.

'He knows what he wants,' he went on, 'and it is rather humiliating that I do not.'

'I think you do too,' I said. For indeed in his own letter I had not seen an actual refusal, nor indeed had I believed he wrote it out of affectation. That is certainly not the right word for the will to make harder for oneself a hard decision, by deepening it with self-distrust. I already saw with emotion that the decision would be made; and it had become the basis for the ensuing conversation about our immediate futures. In any case, our ways were parting. Despite serious short-sightedness I was declared fit for military service, and intended to put in my year at once; I was to do it in Naumburg with the regiment of the 3rd Field Artillery. Adrian, on whatever grounds – narrow-chestedness, or his habitual headaches – was indefinitely excused; and he planned to spend some weeks at Buchel, in order, as he said, to discuss with his parents his change of profession. It came out that he would put it to them as though it involved merely a change of university. In a way, that was how he put it to himself too. He would, so he would tell them, bring his music more into the foreground, and accordingly he was going to the city where the musical mentor of his schooldays was working. What did not come out was that he was giving up theology. In fact, his actual intention was to enrol himself again at the university and attend lectures in philosophy in order to make his doctorate in that school.

At the beginning of the winter semester, in 1905, Leverkühn went to Leipzig.

Chapter Sixteen

It scarcely needs saying that our good-bye was outwardly cool and reserved. There was hardly even a pressure of the hand, an exchange of looks. Too often in our young days we had parted and met again for us to have kept the habit of shaking hands. He left Halle a day earlier than I; we had spent the previous evening together at the theatre, without any of the Winfried group. He was leaving next moring, and we said good-bye on the street, as we had hundreds of times before. I could not help marking my farewell by calling

him by name – his first name, as was natural to me, but he did not follow suit.
'So long!' he said, that was all; he had the phrase from Kretschmar, and used
it half-mockingly, as a quotation, having in general a definite liking to quote,
to make word-plays on something or someone. He added some jest about the
solider's life I was now to pursue, and we went our different ways.

He was right not to take the separation seriously. After at most a year,
when my military service should be finished, we would come together, one
place or another. Still, it was in a way a break, the end of one chapter, the
beginning of another, and if he seemed not to be conscious of the fact, I was,
with a certain pang, well aware of it. By going to him in Halle I had, so to
speak, prolonged our schooldays; we had lived there much as in
Kaisersaschern. Even the time when I was a student and he still at school I
cannot compare with the change now impending. Then I had left him
behind in the familiar frame of the gymnasium and the paternal city and had
continued to return thither. Only now, it seemed to me, did our lives become
detached, only now were both of us beginning on our own two feet. Now
there would be an end to what seemed to me so necessary, though so futile
withal; I can but describe it in the words I used above: I should no longer
know what he did or experienced, no more be able to be near him, to keep
watch over him, I must leave his side just at the very moment when
observation of his life, although it could certainly change nothing in it,
seemed most highly desirable. I mean when he abandoned the scholarly
career, 'put the Bible under the bench', to use his own words, and flung
himself into the arms of music.

It was a significant decision, one pregnant with fate. In a way it cancelled
the more immediate past and linked up with moments of our common life
lying far, far back, the memory of which I bore in my heart: the hour when I
had found the lad experimenting with his uncle's harmonium, and still
further back, our canon-singing with Hanne the stable-girl, under the
linden tree. It made my heart lift up for joy, this decision of his – and at the
same time contract with fear. I can only compare the feeling with the catch in
the breath that a child feels in a swing as it flies aloft, the mingled exultation
and terror. The rightness of the change, its inevitability, the correction of
the false step, the misrepresentation theology had been: all that was clear to
me, and I was proud that my friend no longer hesitated to acknowledge the
truth. Persuasion, indeed, had been necessary to bring him to it; and
extraordinary as were the results I expected from the change, and despite all
my joyful agitation, I took comfort from being able to tell myself that I had
no part in the persuasions – or at most had supported them by a certain
fatalistic attitude, and a few words such as 'I think you know, yourself.'

Here I will follow on with a letter I had from him two months after I
entered the service at Naumburg. I read it with feelings such as might move
a mother at a communication of that kind from her son – only that of course
one withholds that sort of thing from one's mother, out of propriety. I had
written to him three weeks before, ignorant of his address, in care of Herr
Wendell Kretschmar at the Hase conservatoire; had described my new, raw
state and begged him, if ever so briefly, to tell me how he lived and fared in
the great city, and about the programme of his studies. I preface his reply
only by saying that its antiquated style was of course intended as a parody of
grotesque Halle experiences and the language idiosyncrasies of Ehrenfried
Kumpf. At the same time in both hides and reveals his own personality and
stylistic leanings and his employment of the parodic, in a highly characteristic and indicative way.

He wrote:

Leipzig, Friday after
Purificationis 1905
In the Peterstrasse, house the 27th

Most honourable, most illustrious, learned, and well-beloved Magister and Ballisticus!

We thank you kindly for the courtesy of your communication and the highly diverting tidings touching your present arrangements, so full of discipline, dullness, and hardship as they be. Your tales of the whip-cracking and springing to order, the curry-combing and spit-and-polish, have made us heartily to laugh: above all that one of the under-officer which even as he planes and polishes and breketh to harness, yet holdeth so much in estimation your high education and grete leaning that in the canteen you must needs mark off for him all the metres according to feet and *morae* because this kind of learning seemeth to him the high prick of intellectual aristocracy. In requital thereof we will an we hold out counter thee with some right folish facecies and horseplay which we fell into here that you too mayst have to wonder and to laugh thereat. Albeit first our friendly hert and good will, trusting and playing that thou maist almost joyfully bear the rod and in tract of time be so holpen thereby, till at the last in braid and buttons thou goest forth as a reserve sergeant major.

Here the word is: Trust God, honour the King, do no man any nuisance. On the Pleisse, the Parthe, and the Elster existence and pulse are manifestly other than on the Saale; for here many people be gathered togyder, more than seven hundred thousand; which from the outset bespeaketh a certain sympathy and tolerance; as the Lord hath already for Nineveh's sin a knowing and humorous eye when He says excusingly: 'Such a great city, therein more than a hundred thousand men.' Thus maist thou think how among seven hundred thousand forbearance is counselled when in the autumn fair-times whereof I as novice had even now a taste, more stream from all parts of Europe, and from Persia, Armenia, and other the Asiatic lands.

Not as though this Nineveh, particularly doth like me, 'tis not the fairest city of my fatherland. Kaisersaschern is fairer; yet may easier be both fair and stately, sithence it needs but be olde and quiet and have no pulse. Is gorgeously builded, my Leipzig, of clear stone as out of a costly box of toy bricks. The common people's tongue is a devilishly lewd speech so that one shrinks before every booth before one bargains. It is even as though our mildly slumbering Thuringian were woke up to a seven-hundred-thousand-man impudence and smattered abhominably, jaw stuck out – horrible, dreadful, but, God keep us, certes meaning no harm, and mixed with self-mockery which they can graunt unto themselves on the ground of their world-pulse. *Centrum musicae, centrum* of the printing trade and the book rag-fair, illustrious universitie, albeit scattered in respect to buildings, for the chief building is in Augustusplatz, the library hard by the Cloth hall, and to the divers faculties long severall college buildings, as the Red House on the Promenade to the philosophic, to the juristic the *Collegium Beatae Viginis*, in my Peterstrasse, where I found forthwith fresh from the station, on the next way into the town, fitting lodging and accommodation. Came early in the afternoon, left my fardels at the station, got hither as directed, read the notice on the rain-pipe, range, and was straightway agreed with the fat landlady with the fiendish brogue on the two rooms on the ground floor.

Still so early that I had on that same day looked over almost the whole town in the first flush of arrival – this time really with a guide, to wit the porter who fetched my portmanteo from the station; hence at the last the farce and foolery of which I spake and may still reherse.

The fat frau made no bones about the clavicymbal, they are used to that here. Sha'n't be assaulting her ears to much for I am chiefly working on theory, with books and pen and paper, the harmonium and the *punctum contra punctum*, quite off my own bat, I mean under the supervision and general direction of *amicus* Kretschmar, to whom every few days I take that I have practised and wrought, for his criticism, good or bad. Good soul was uncommon glad that I came, and embraced me for that I was not minded to betray his hope. And he will hear not of my going to the conservatoire, either the big one or the Hase, where he teaches; it were, he says, no atmosphere for me, I must rather do as Father Hadyn did, who had no preceptor at all, but got himself the *Gradus ad Parnassum* of Fux and some music of the time, in special the Hamburg Bach, and therewith sturdily practised his trade. Just between ourselves, the study of harmony makes me for to yawn, but with counterpoint I wax quick and lusty, cannot concoct enough merry frolics in this enchanted field, with joyous passion soyle the never-ending problems and have already put together on paper a whole stook of droll studies in canon and fugue, even gotten some praise from the Master therefore. That is creative work, requirith phantasy and invention; playing dominoes with chords, without a theme is meseemeth neither flesh nor fowl. Should not one learn all that about suspensions, passing-notes, modulation, preparations and resolution, much better *in praxi* from hearing, experiencing, and inventing oneself, then out of a boke? But altogether, now, and *par aversionem* it is foolishness, this unthinking division of counterpoint and harmony, sith they interact so intimately that one cannot teach them sunderlye but only in the whole, as music – in so far as it can be taught.

Wherefore I am industrious, *zelo virtutis*, yea almost over-burdened and overwhelmed with matters, for I go to lectures at the academie in hist. phil. by Lautensack and Encyclopedia of the philosophical sciences as well as logic from the famous Bermeter. *Vale. Jam satis est.* Herewith I commit you to the Lord, may He preserve you and all clear souls. Your most obedient servant, as they say in Halle. – I have made you much too curious about the jocus and jape, and what is afoot betwixt me and Satan; not much to it after all, except that porter led me astray on the evening of the first day – a base churl like that, with a strap round his waist, a red cap and a brass badge and a rain-cape, same vile lingo as everybody else here. Bristly jaw; looked to me like unto our Schleppfuss by reason of his little beard, more than slightly, even, when I bethink, or is he waxen more like in my recollection? Heavier and fatter, that were from the beer. Introduces himself to me as a guide and proved it by his brass badge and his two or three scrapes of French and English, diabolical pronunciation; 'peautiful puilding, antiquidé extrèment indéressant'.

Item: we struck a bargain, and the churl shewed me everything, two whole hours, took me everywhere, to the Pauluskirche with wondrously chamfered cloisters, the Thomaskirche on account of Johann Sebastian, and his grave in St John's, where is also the Reformation monument, and the new Cloth Hall. Lively it was in the streets, for as I said whilere the autumn fair still happened to be, and all sorts of banners and hangings advertising furs and other wares hung out at windows down the house-fronts, there was great bustle and prease in all the narrow streets, particularly in the heart of the town, nigh the old Town Hall, where the chap shewed me the palace, and Auerbach's inn and the still standing tower of the Pleissenburg – where Luther held his disputacyon with Eck. Great shoving and shouldering in the narrow streets behind the market, very old, with steep gabled roofs; connected by a criss-crosse labyrinth of covered courts and passages, and adjoining warehouses and cellars. All this close packed with wares and the hosts of people look at you with outlandish eyen and speak in tongues you've never heard a syllable of afore. Right exciting, and you felt the pulse of the world beating in your own body.

By little and little it gat dark, lights came on, the streets emptied, I was aweary and ahungered. I bade my guide draw to an ende by shewing me an inn where I could eat. 'A good one?' he asks, and winks. 'A good one,' quoth I, 'so it be not too dear.' Takes me to a house in a little back lane behind the main street – brass railing to the steps up to the door – polished as bright as the fellow's badge, and a lantern over the door, red as the fellow's cap. I pay him, he wishes me 'Good appetite!' and shogs off. I ring, the door opens of itself, and in the hall is a dressed-up madame coming towards me, with carmine cheeks, a string of wax-coloured beads on her blubber, and greets me with most seemely gest, fluting and flirting, ecstatic as though she had been longing for me to come, ushers me through portières into a glistering room, with panelled tapestries, crystal chandelier, candelabra with mirrors behind them; satin couches, and on them sitting your nymphs and daughters of the wilderness, ribaudes, laced muttons all, six or seven, morphos, clear-wings, esmeraldas, et cetera, clad or unclad, in tulle, gauze, spangs, hair long and floating, hair short with heart-breakers; paps bare, thick poudered, arms with bangles, they look at you with expectant eyes, glistering in the light of the chandelier.

Look at me, mark wel, not thee. A hothouse the fellow, the small-beer-Schleppfuss, had brought me into. I stood, not showing what I was feeling, and there opposite me I see an open piano, a friend, I rush up to it across the carpet and strike a chord or twain, standing up, I wot still what it was, because the harmonic problem was just in my mind, modulation from B major to C major, the brightening semitone step, as in the hermit's prayer in the finale of the *Freischütz*, at the entry of timpani, trumpets, and oboes on the six-four chord on G. I wot it now, afterwards, but then I wist not, I but fell upon it. A brown wench puts herself nigh me, in a little Spanish jacket, with a big gam, snub nose, almond eyes, an Esmeralda, she brushed my cheek with her arm. I turn around, push the wench away with my knee, and fling myself back through the lust-hell, across the carpets, past the mincing madam, through the entry and down the steps without touching the brass railing.

There you have the trifle, so it befell me, told at its length, in payment for the roaring corporal to whom you teach the *artem metrificandi*. Herewith amen – and pray for me. Only a Gewandhaus concert heard up till now with Schumann's Third as *pièce de résistance*. A critic of that time belauded the comprehensive world-view of this music, which sounds like very un-objective gabble – the classicists made themselves thoroughly merry over it. But it did have some sense, for it defines the improvement in their status which music and musicians owe to romanticism. It emancipated her from the sphere of a small-town specialism and piping and brought her into contact with the great world of the mind, the general artistic and intellectual movement of the time – we should not forget that. All that proceeds from the Beethoven of the last period and his polyphony; and I find it extraordinarily significant that the opponents of the romantic movement, that is of an art which progresses from the solely musical into the universally intellectual sphere, were the same people who also opposed and deplored Beethoven's later development. Have you ever thought how differently, how much more suffering and significant the individualization of the voice appears in his greatest works than in the older music where it is treated with greater skill? There are judgements which make one laugh by the crass truthfulness of them, which are at the same time a judgement on the judge. Handel said of Gluck: 'My cook understands more about counterpoint than he does' – I love this pronouncement of a fellow-musician!

Playing much Chopin, and reading about him. I love the angelic in his figure, which reminds me of Shelley: the peculiarly and very mysteriously veiled, unapproachable, withdrawing, unadventurous flavour of his being, that not wanting to know, that rejection of material experience, the sublime incest of his fantastically delicate and seductive art. How much speaks for the man the deep, intent friendship of Delacroix, who writes to him: '*J'espère vous voir ce soir, mais ce moment est capable de me faire devenir fou.*' Everything possible for the Wagner of painting! But there are quite a few things in Chopin which, not only harmonically but also in a general, psychological sense more than anticipate Wagner, indeed surpass him. Take the C-sharp minor Nocturne op. 27, No. 2, and the duet that begins after the enharmonic change from C-sharp minor to D-flat major. That surpasses in despairing beauty of sound all the *Tristan* orgies – even in the intimate medium of the piano, though not as a grand battle of voluptuosity; without the bull-fight character of a theatrical mysticism robust in its corruption. Take above all his ironic relation to tonality, his teasing way with it, obscuring, ignoring, keeping it fluctuating, and mocking at accidentals. It goes far, divertingly and thrillingly far....

With the exclamation: '*Ecce epistola!*' the letter ends. Added is: 'Goes without saying you destroy this at once.' The signature is an initial, that of the family name: the *L*, not the *A*.

Chapter Seventeen

The explicit order to destroy this letter I did not obey – and who on that ground will condemn a friendship which can claim for itself the description 'deeply intent' used therein of Delacroix's friendship for Chopin? I did not obey it, in the first instance because I felt the need to read again and again a piece of writing at first run through so quickly; to study it, not so much read as study, stylistically and psychologically. Then, with the passage of time, the moment to destroy it had passed too; I learned to regard it as a document of which the order to destroy was a part, so that by its documentary nature it cancelled itself out.

So much I was certain of from the start: it was not the letter as a whole that had given occasion to the direction at the end; but only a part of it, the so-called *facetie* and farce, the experience with the fatal porter. But again, that part was the whole letter, on account of that part it was written; not for my amusement – doubtless the writer had known that the 'jape' would have nothing comic about it for me – but rather to shake off a painful impression, for which I, the friend of his childhood, was of course the only repository. All the rest was only trimmings, wrappings, pretext, putting off, and afterwards a covering-up again with talk, music-critical *aperçus*, as though nothing had happened. Upon the *anecdote* – to use a very objective word – everything focuses; it stands in the background from the beginning on, announces itself in the first lines and is postponed. Still untold, it plays into the jests about the great city Nineveh and the tolerant sceptical quotation from the Bible. It comes near being told at the place where for the first time there is mention of the porter; then it is dropped again. The letter is ostensibly finished before it is told – '*Jam satis est*' – and then, as though it had almost gone out of the writer's head, as though only Schleppfuss's quoted greeting brought it back, it is told 'to finish off with', including the extraordinary reference back to his father's lectures on butterflies. Yet it is not allowed to form the end of the letter, rather some remarks about Schumann, the romantic movement, Chopin, are appended to it, obviously with the intention of detracting from its weight, and so causing it to be forgotten – or more correctly, probably, to make it, out of pride, look as though that were the idea; for I do not believe the intention existed that I, the reader, should overlook the core of the letter.

Very remarkable to me, even on the second reading, was the fact that the style, the travesty or personal adaptation of Kumpf's old-German, prevailed only until the adventure was recounted and then was dropped regardless, so that the closing pages are entirely uncoloured by it and show a perfectly modern style. Is it not as though the archaizing tone had served its purpose as soon as the tale of the false guide is on paper? As though it is given up afterwards, not so much because it is unsuitable for the final observations put in to divert the attention as because from the date onwards it was only introduced in order to be able to *tell the story* in it, which by that means gets its proper atmosphere? And what atmosphere, then? I will characterize it, however little the designation I have in mind will seem applicable to a jest. It is the religious atmosphere. So much was clear to me: on account of its historical affinity with the religious, the language of the Reformation – or the flavour of it – had been chosen for a letter which was to bring me this story. Without it, how could the word have been written down that pressed to be written down: 'Pray for me!' There could be no better example of the quotation as disguise, the parody as pretext. And just before it was another, which even at the first reading went through and through me, and which has just as little to do with humour, bearing as it does an undeniably mystical, thus religious stamp: the word 'lust-hell'.

Despite the coolness of the analysis to which I there and then subjected Adrian's letter, few readers will have been deceived about the real feelings with which I read and reread it. Analysis has necessarily the appearance of coolness, even when practised in a state of profound agitation. Agitated I was, I was even beside myself. My fury at the obscene prank of that small-beer Schleppfuss knew no bounds – yet it was an impersonal fury, no evidence at all of prudishness in myself. I was never prudish, and if that Leipzig procurer had played his trick on me I should have known how to put a good face on it. No, my present feelings had entirely to do with Adrian's nature and being; and for that, indeed, the word 'prudish' would be perfectly silly and unsuitable. Vulgarity itself might here have been inspired with a sense of the need to spare and protect.

In my feelings the fact played no small part that he should have told me the adventure at all, told it weeks after it had happened, breaking through a reserve otherwise absolute and always respected by me. However strange it may seem, considering our long intimacy, we had never touched in any personal or intimate way on the subject of love, of sex, of the flesh. We had never come on it otherwise than through the medium of art and literature, with reference to the manifestations of passion in the intellectual sphere. At such times he spoke in an objectively knowledgeable way divorced from any personal element. Yet how could it have been absent in a being like him? That it was not there was evidence enough in his repetition of certain doctrines taken over from Kretschmar on the not contemptible role of the sensual in art, and not only in art; in some of his comments on Wagner, and in such spontaneous utterances as that about the nudity of the human voice and the intellectual compensation provided for it through highly complicated art-forms in the old vocal music. That sort of thing had nothing old-maidish about it; it showed a free, unforced contemplation of the world of fleshly desire. But agin, it was not indicative of my nature but of his that every time at such turns in the conversation I felt something like a shock, a catch, a slight shrinking within me. It was, to express myself strongly, as though one heard an angel holding forth on sin. One could expect no flippancy or vulgarity, no banal bad jokes. And yet one would feel put off; acknowledging his intellectual right to speak, one would be tempted to beg: 'Hush, my friend! Your lips are too pure, too stern for such matters.'

In fact, Adrian's distaste for the coarse or lascivious was forbidding and forthright. I knew exactly the wry mouth, the contemptuous expression with which he recoiled when that sort of thing was even remotely approached. At Halle, in the Winfried circle, he was fairly safe: religious propriety, at least in word, spared him attacks upon his fine feeling. Women, wives, 'the girls', affairs, were never the subject of conversation among the members. I do not know how these young theologians did in fact, each for himself, behave, whether or not they preserved themselves in chastity for Christian marriage. As for myself, I will confess that I had tasted of the apple, and at that time had relations for seven or eight months with a girl of the people, a cooper's daughter, a connexion which was hard enough to keep from Adrian – though truly I scarcely believe that he noticed it – and which I severed without ill feeling at the end of that time as the creature's lack of education bored me and I had never anything to say for myself with her except just the one thing. I had gone into it not so much out of hot blood as impelled by curiosity, vanity, and the desire to translate into practice that frankness of the ancients about sexual matters which was part of my theoretic convictions.

But precisely this element of intellectual complacence to which I, it may be a little pedantically, pretended, was entirely lacking in Adrian's attitude. I will not speak of Christian inhibitions nor yet apply the shibboleth 'Kaisersaschern', with its various implications, partly middle-class and conventional, yet coloured as well with a medievally lively horror of sin. That would do the truth scant justice and not suffice either to call out the loving consideration with which his attitude inspired me, the anger I felt at any injury he might receive. One simply could not and would not picture Adrian in any situation of gallantry; that was due to the armour of purity, chastity, intellectual pride, cool irony, which he wore; it was sacred to me, sacred in a certain painful and secretly mortifying way. For painful and mortifying – except perhaps to the malicious soul – is the thought that purity is not given to this life in the flesh; that instinct does not spare the loftiest intellectual pride, nor can arrogance itself refuse its toll to nature. One may only hope that this derogation into the human, and thereby also into the beast, may by God's will fulfil itself in some form of beauty, forbearance, and spiritual elevation, in feelings veiled and purified by devotion.

Must I add that precisely in cases like my friend's there is the least hope of this? The beautifying, veiling, ennobling, I mean, is a work of the soul, in a court of appeal interceding, mediating, itself instinct with poetry; where spirit and desire interpenetrate and appease each other in a way not quite free from illusion; it is a stratum of life peculiarly informed with sentiment, in which, I confess, my own humanity feels at ease, but which is not for stronger tastes. Natures like Adrian's have not much 'soul'. It is a fact, in which a profoundly observant friendship has instructed me, that the proudest intellectuality stands in the most immediate relation of all to the animal, to naked instinct, is given over most shamelessly to it; hence the anxiety that a person like me must suffer through a nature like Adrian's – hence too my conviction that the accursed adventure of which he had written was in its essence frightfully symbolic.

I saw him standing at the door of that room in the house of joy; slowly comprehending, eyeing the waiting daughters of the wilderness. Once – I had the picture clearly before me – I had seen him pass through the alien atmosphere of Mütze's tavern in Halle. So now I saw him move blindly to the piano and strike chords – what chords he only afterwards knew himself. I saw the snub-nosed girl beside him, Hetaera esmeralda: her powdered bosoms in Spanish bodice – saw her brush his cheek with her arm. Violently, across space and back in time, I yearned thither. I felt the impulse to push the witch away from him with my knee as he had pushed the music stool aside to gain his freedom. For days I felt the touch of her flesh on my own cheek and knew with abhorrence and sheer terror that it had burned upon his ever since. Again I beg that it be considered indicative not of me but of him that I was quite unable to take the event on its lighter side. There was no light side there. If I have even remotely succeeded in giving the reader a picture of my friend's character, he must feel with me the indescribably profaning, the mockingly debasing and dangerous nature of this contact.

That up to then he had 'touched' no woman was and is to me an unassailable fact. Now the woman had touched him – and he had fled. Nor is there in this flight any trace of the comic, let me assure the reader, in case he incline to seek such in it. Comic, at most, this avoidance was, in the bitter-tragic sense of futility. In my eyes Adrian had not escaped, and only very briefly, certainly, did he feel that he had. His intellectual pride had suffered the trauma of contact with soulless instinct. Adrian was to return to the place whither the betrayer had led him.

Chapter Eighteen

May not my readers ask whence comes the detail in my narrative, so precisely known to me, even though I could not have been always present, not always at the side of the departed hero of this biography? It is true that repeatedly, for extended periods, I lived apart from Adrian: during my year of military service, at the end of which I resumed my studies at the

University of Leipzig and became familiar with his life and circle there. So also for the duration of my educational travels to the classic lands in the years 1908 and 1909. Our reunion on my return was brief, as he already cherished the purpose of leaving Leipzig and going to southern Germany. The longest period of separation followed thereupon: the years when after a short stay in Munich he was in Italy with his friend the Silesian Schildknapp. Meanwhile I first spent my probation time at the Boniface gymnasium in Kaisersaschern and then entered upon my teaching office there. Only in 1913, when Adrian had settled in Pfeiffering in Upper Bavaria and I had transferred to Freising, were we near each other; but then it was to have before my eyes, for seventeen years, with no – or as good as no – interruption, that life already long since marked by fate, that increasingly vehement activity, until the catastrophe of 1930.

He had long since ceased to be a beginner in music, that curiously cabbalistic craft, at once playful and profound, artful and austere, when he placed himself again under the guidance, direction, supervision of Wendell Kretschmar in Leipzig. His rapid progress was winged by an intelligence grasping everything as it flew and distracted at most by anticipatory impatience in the field of what could be taught, in the technique of composition, form, and orchestration. It seemed that the two-year theological episode in Halle had not weakened his bond with music or been any actual interruption to his preoccupation with it. His letter had told me something about his eager and accumulating exercises in counterpoint. Kretschmar laid even greater stress on the technique of orchestration; even in Kaisersaschern he had made him orchestrate movements from sonatas, string quartets; which then, in long conversations, would be discussed, criticized, and corrected. He went so far as to ask him to orchestrate the piano reductions of single acts from operas unknown to Adrian, and the comparison of that which the pupil tried, who had heard and read Berlioz, Debussy, and the German and Austrian late romantics, with that which Grétry or Cherubini had actually done made master and pupil laugh. Kreschmar was at that time at work on his own composition, *The Statue*, and gave his pupil one or the other scene in *particell* for instrumentation and then showed him what he himself had done or intended. Here was occasion for abundant debates, in which of course the superior experience of the master held the field, but once at least, nevertheless, the intuition of the apprentice won a victory. For a chord combination that Kretschmar rejected at first sight as being doubtful and awkward finally seemed to him more characteristic than what he himself had in mind, and at the next meeting he declared that he would like to take over Adrian's idea.

The latter felt less proud than one would expect. Teacher and pupil were in their musical instincts and intuitions at bottom very far apart, since in art almost of necessity the aspiring student finds himself addressed to the technical guidance of a craftsmanship already become somewhat remote, owing to the difference of a generation. Then it is well at least if the master guesses and understands the hidden leanings of the youth; he may even be ironic on the score of them if he takes care not to stand in the way of their development. Thus Kretschmar lived in the natural, taken-for-granted conviction that music had found its definitely highest manifestation and effect in orchestral composition; and this Adrian no longer believed. To the boy of twenty, more than to his elders, the close link of the most highly developed instrumental technique with a harmonic conception was more than a historical view. With him it had grown to be something like a state of mind, in which past and future merged together; the cool gaze he directed upon the hypertrophy of the post-romantic monster orchestra, the need he felt for its reduction and return to the ancillary role that it had played at the time of the preharmonic, the polyphonic vocal music; his tendency in this direction and thus to oratorio, a species in which the creator of *The Revelation of St John* and the *Lamentation of Dr Faustus* would later achieve his highest and boldest flights – all this came out very early in word and deed.

His studies in orchestration under Kretschmar's guidance were not the less zealous on that account. For he agreed with his teacher that one must have command over what has been achieved even though one no longer finds it essential. He once said to me that a composer who is sick of orchestral impressionism and therefore no longer learns instrumentation seemed to him like a dentist who no longer learns how to treat the roots of teeth and goes back to the barber technique because it has lately been discovered that dead teeth give people rheumatism of the joints. This comparison, extraordinarily far-fetched yet so characteristic of the intellectual atmosphere of the time, continued to be an oft-quoted allusion between us, and the 'dead tooth' preserved by skilful embalming of the root became a symbol for certain very modern refinements of the orchestral palette, including his own symphonic fantasy *Ocean Lights*. This piece he wrote in Leipzig, still under Kretschmar's eye, after a holiday trip to the North Sea with Rüdiger Schildknapp. Kretschmar later arranged a semi-public performance of it. It is a piece of exquisite tone-painting, which gives evidence of an astonishing feeling for entrancing combinations of sound, at first hearing almost impossible for the ear to unravel. The cultured public saw in the young composer a highly gifted successor to the Debussy-Ravel line. That he was not, and he scarcely included this demonstration of colouristic and orchestral ability in the list of his actual productions; almost as little, indeed, as the wrist-loosening and calligraphic practice with which he had once occupied himself under Kretschmar's direction: the six- to eight-part choruses, the fugue with the three themes for string quintet with piano accompaniment, the symphony, whose *particell* he brought him by bits and whose instrumentation he discussed with him; the Cello Sonata in A minor with the very lovely slow movement, whose theme he would later use in one of his Brentano songs. That sound-sparkling *Ocean Lights* was in my eyes a very remarkable instance of how an artist can give his best to a thing in which he privately no longer believes, insisting on excelling in artistic devices which for his consciousness are already at the point of being worn out. 'It is acquired root-treatment,' he said to me. 'I don't rise to streptococcus disinfection.' Every one of his remarks showed that he considered the genre of 'tone-painting', of 'nature moods', to be fundamentally out of date.

But to be frank, this disillusioned masterpiece of orchestral brilliance already bore within itself the traits of parody and intellectual mockery of art, which in Leverkühn's later work so often emerged in a creative and uncanny way. Many found it chilling, even repellent and revolting, and these were the better, if not the best sort, who thus judged. All the superficial lot simply called it witty and amusing. In truth parody was here the proud expedient of a great gift threatened with sterility by a combination of scepticism, intellectual reserve, and a sense of the deadly extension of the kingdom of the banal. I trust I have put that aright. My uncertainty and my feeling of responsibility are alike great, when I seek to clothe in words thoughts that are not primarily my own, but have come to me only through my friendship with Adrian. Of a lack of *naïveté* I would not speak, for in the end *naïveté* lies at the bottom of being, all being, even the most conscious and complicated. The conflict – almost impossible to simplify – between the inhibitions and the productive urge of inborn genius, between chastity and passion, just that is the *naïveté* out of which such an artist nature lives, the soil for the difficult, characteristic growth of his work; and the unconscious effort to get for the 'gift' the productive impulse, the necessary little ascendancy over the impediments of unbelief, arrogance, intellectual self-consciousness: this instinctive effort stirs and becomes decisive at the moment when the mechanical studies preliminary to the practice of an art begin to be combined with the first personal, while as yet entirely ephemeral and preparatory plastic efforts.

Chapter Nineteen

I speak of this because, not without tremors, not without a contraction of my heart, I have now come to the fateful even which happened about a year after I received in Naumburg the letter I quoted from Adrian; somewhat more than a year, that is, after his arrival in Leipzig and that first night of the city of which the letter tells. In other words, it was not long before – being released from the service – I went to him again and found him, while outwardly unchanged, yet in fact a marked man, pierced by the arrow of fate. In narrating this episode, I feel I should call Apollo and the Muses to my aid, to inspire me with the purest, most indulgent words: indulgent to the sensitive reader, indulgent to the memory of my departed friend, indulgent lastly to myself, to whom the telling is like a serious personal confession. But such an invocation betrays to me at once the contradiction between my own intellectual conditioning and the coloration of the story I have to tell, a coloration that comes from quite other strata of tradition, altogether foreign to the blitheness of classical culture. I began this record by expressing doubt whether I was the right man for the task. The arguments I had to adduce against such doubts I will not repeat. It must suffice that, supported on them, strengthened by them, I propose to remain true to my undertaking.

I said that Adrian returned to the place whither the impudent messenger had brought him. One sees now that it did not happen so soon. A whole year long the pride of the spirit asserted itself against the injury it had received, and it was always a sort of consolation to me to feel that his surrender to the naked instinct that had laid its spiteful finger on him had not lacked all and every human nobility or psychological veiling. For as such I regard every fixation of desire, however crude, on a definite and individual goal. I see it in the moment of choice, even though the will thereto be not 'free' but impudently provoked by its object. A trace of purifying love can be attested so soon as the instinct wears the face of a human being, be it the most anonymous, the most contemptible. And there is this to say, that Adrian went back to that place on account of one particular person, of her whose touch burned on his cheek, the 'brown wench' with the big mouth, in the little jacket, who had come up to him at the piano and whom he called Esmeralda. It was she whom he sought there – and did not find her.

The fixation, calamitous as it was, resulted in his leaving the brothel after his second and voluntary visit the same man as after the first, involuntary one; not, however, without having assured himself of the place where she was now. It had the further result that under a musical pretext he made rather a long journey to reach her whom he desired. It happened that the first Austrian performance of *Salome*, conducted by the composer himself, was to take place in Graz, the capital of Styria, in May 1906. Some months earlier Adrian and Kretschmar had gone to Dresden to see its actual première; and he told his teacher and the friends whom he had meantime made in Leipzig that he wanted to be present at this gala performance and hear again that successful revolutionary work, whose aesthetic sphere did not at all attract him, but which of course interested him in a musical and technical sense, particularly as the setting to music of a prose dialogue. He travelled alone, and one cannot be sure whether he carried out his ostensible purpose and went from Graz to Pressburg, possibly from Pressburg to Graz; or whether he simply pretended to stay in Graz and confined himself to the visit to Pressburg (in Hungarian, Pozsony). She whose mark he bore had been hidden in a house there, having to leave her former place for hospital treatment. The hunted hunter found her out.

My hand trembles as I write; but in quiet, collected words I will say what I know, always consoled to a certain extent by the thought to which I gave utterance above, the idea of choice, the thought that something obtained here like a bond of love, which lent to the coming together of the precious youth and that unhappy creature a gleam of soul. Though of course this consolation is inseparable from the other thought, so much more dreadful, that love and poison here once and for ever became a frightful unity of experience; the mythological unity embodied in the arrow.

It does look as though in the poor thing's mind something answered the feeling which the youth brought to her. No doubt she remembered that fleeting visit. Her approach, that caressing of his cheek with her bare arm, might have been the humble and tender expression of her receptivity for all that distinguished him from the usual clientèle. And she learned from his own lips that he made the journey thither on her account. She thanked him, even while she warned him against her body. I know it from Adrian: she warned him – is not this something like a beneficent distinction between the higher humanity of the creature and her physical part, fallen to the gutter, sunk to a wretched object of use? The unhappy one warned him who asked of her, warned him away from 'herself'; that means an act of free elevation of soul above her pitiable physical existence, an act of human disassociation from it, an act of sympathy, an act – if the word be permitted me – of love. And, gracious heaven, was it not also love, or what was it, what madness, what deliberate, reckless tempting of God, what compulsion to comprise the punishment of the sin, finally what deep, deeply mysterious longing for daemonic conception, for a deathly unchaining of chemical change in his nature was at work, that having been warned he despised the warning and insisted upon possession of this flesh?

Never without a religious shudder have I been able to think of this embrace, in which the one staked his salvation, the other found it. Purifying, justifying, sublimating, it must have blessed the wretched one, that the other travelled from afar and refused whatever the risk to give her up. It seems that she gave him all the sweetness of her womanhood, to repay him for what he risked. She might thus know that he never forgot her; but it is no less true that it was for her own sake he who never saw her again, remembered; and her name – that which he gave her from the beginning – whispers magically, unheard by anyone but me, throughout his work. I may be taxed with vanity, but I cannot refrain from speaking here of the discovery which he one day silently confirmed. Leverkühn was not the first composer, and he will not have been the last, who loved to put mysteries, magic formulas, and charms into his works. The fact displays the inborn tendency of music to superstitious rites and observances, the symbolism of numbers and letters. Thus in my friend's musical fabric a five- to six-note series, beginning with B and ending on E flat, with a shifting E and A between, is found strikingly often, a basic figure of peculiarly nostalgic character, which in differing harmonic and rhythmic garb, is given now to this part now to that, often in its inversion, as it were turned on its axis, so that while the intervals remain the same, the sequence of the notes is altered. It occurs at first in the probably most beautiful of the thirteen Brentano songs composed in Leipzig, the heart-piercing lied: '*O lieb Mädel, wie schlecht bist du*', which is permeated with it; but most particularly in the late work, where audacity and despair mingle in so unique a way, the *Weheklag of Dr Faustus*, written in Pfeiffering, where the inclination shows even more strongly to use those intervals also in a simultaneous-harmonic combination.

The letters composing this note-cipher are: h, e, a, e, e-flat: hetaera esmeralda.*

Adrian returned to Leipzig and expressed himself as entertained and full of admiration for the powerful and striking opera he was supposed to have heard a second time and possibly really had. I can still hear him say about the author of it: 'What a gifted good fellow! The revolutionary as a Sabbath-day child, pert and *conciliant*. How after great expense of affronts and dissonances everything turns into good nature, beer good nature, gets all buttered up, so to speak, appeasing the philistine and telling him no harm was meant.... But a hit, a palpable hit!' Five weeks after he had resumed his musical and philosophical studies a local affection decided him to consult a physician. The specialist, by name Dr Erasmi – Adrian had chosen him from the street directory – was a powerful man, with a red face and a pointed black beard. It obviously made him puff to stoop and even in a upright posture he breathed in pants with his lips open. The habit indicated oppression, but it also looked like contemptuous indifference, as though the man would dismiss or intended to dismiss something by saying 'Pooh, pooh!' He puffed like that during the whole examination, and then, in contradiction of his pooh-poohing, declared the necessity for a thorough and rather lengthy treatment, on which he at once embarked. On three successive days Adrian went to him. Then Erasmi arranged a break of three days. Adrian was to come back on the fourth. When the patient – who was not ailing, his general state of health being entirely unaffected – returned at four o'clock on the appointed day, something utterly unexpected and startling confronted him.

He had always had to ring at the door of the apartment, which was up three steep flights of stairs in a gloomy building in the old city, and wait for a maid to open. But this time he found both outer and inner doors open, that to the waiting-room, the consulting-room, and facing him a door into the living-room, the so-called 'best room' with two windows. Yes, there the windows were wide open too, and all four curtains blew in and out in the draught. In the middle of the room lay Dr Erasmi, with his beard sticking up, his eyes fast shut, in a white shirt with cuffs, lying on a tufted cushion in an open coffin on two trestles.

*The English *B* is represented in German by *H*.

What was going on, why the dead man lay there so alone and open to the wind, where the maid and Frau Dr Erasmi were, whether perhaps the people from the undertaking establishment were waiting to screw on the lid, or were coming back at once – at what singular moment the visitor had been brought to the spot, was never made clear. When I came to Leipzig, Adrian could only describe to me the bewilderment in which he, after staring for a moment, had gone down the stairs again. He seems not to have inquired further into the doctor's sudden death, seems not to have been interested. He merely thought that the man's constant puffing and blowing had always been a bad sign.

With secret repugnance, struggling against unreasoning horror, I must now relate that Adrian's second choice also stood under an unlucky star. He took two days to recover from the shock. Then he again had recourse to the Leipzig directory, chose another name, and put himself in the care of a certain Dr Zimbalist, in one of the business streets off the Markplatz. On the ground floor was a restaurant, then a piano warehouse; the doctor's house occupied part of the upper story, a porcelain shield with his name on it being downstairs in the lobby. The dermatologist's two waiting-rooms, one reserved for female patients, were adorned with growing plants, palms and house trees in pots. Medical books and magazines lay about, for instance an illustrated history of morals, in the room where Adrian for the first and second time awaited his treatment.

Dr Zimbalist was a small man with horn spectacles, an oval bald spot running from the brow to the back of the head between two growths of reddish hair, and a moustache left growing only immediately under the nostrils, as was then the fashion in the upper classes and would later become the attribute of a world-famous face. His speech was slovenly and he inclined to bad masculine jokes. But one had not the impression that he felt very jolly. One side of his cheek was drawn up in a sort of tic, the corner of the mouth as well, and the eye winked in sympathy; the whole expression was crabbed and craven to a degree; he looked no-good, he looked odious. Thus Adrian described him to me and thus I see him.

Now this is what happened: Adrian had gone twice for treatment; he went a third time. As he mounted the stairs he met, between the first and second storeys, the physician coming down between two sturdy men wearing stiff hats on the backs of their heads. Dr Zimbalist's eyes were cast down like those of a man taking heed to his steps on the stairs. One of his wrists were linked with the wrist of one of his companions by a bracelet and little chain. Looking up and recognizing his patient, he twitched his cheek sourly, nodded at him and said: 'Another time!' Adrian, his back to the wall, disconcerted, faced the three and let them pass; looked after them awhile as they descended and then followed them down. He saw them mount a waiting car and drive off at a fast pace. Thus ended the continuation of Adrian's cure by Dr Zimbalist, after its earlier interruption. I must add that he troubled himself as little about the circumstances of his second bad shot as about the extraordinary atmosphere of his first one. Why Zimbalist had been taken away, and at the very hour for which an appointment had been made – he let that rest. But as though frightened off, he never took up the cure again after that and went to no other doctor. He did so the less in that the local affection healed itself without further treatment and disappeared, and as I can confirm and would sustain against any professional doubts, there were no manifest secondary symptoms. Adrian suffered once, in Wendell Kretschmar's lodgings, where he had just presented some studies in

composition, a violent attack of giddiness, which made him stagger and
forced him to lie down. It passed into a two days' migraine, which except for
its severity was not different from other earlier attacks of the same kind.
When I came back to Leipzig, once more a civilian, I found my friend
unchanged in his walks and ways.

Chapter Twenty

Or was he? If during our year of separation he had not become a different
person, at least he was now more definitely that which he was, and this was
enough to impress me, especially since I had probably a little forgotten what
he had been. I have described the coolness of our parting in Halle. Our
reunion, at the thought of which I had so rejoiced, was not lacking in the
same quality, so that I, put off, both amused and dismayed, had to swallow
my feelings and suppress whatever surged upwards into my consciousness.
That he would fetch me from the station I had not expected. I had even not
let him know the hour. I simply sought him out in his lodgings, before I had
looked out for any myself. His landlady announced me, and I entered the
room, calling him in a loud and joyful shout.

He sat at his desk, an old-fashioned one with a roll top and cabinet, writing
down notes. 'Hallo!' said he, not looking up. 'Just a minute, we can talk.'
And went on for some minutes with his work, leaving it to me to remain
standing or to make myself comfortable. The reader must not misinterpret
this, any more than I did. It was evidence of old-established intimacy, a life
in common which could not be in the least affected by a year's separation. It
was simply as though we had parted the day before. Even so I was a little
dashed, if at the same time amused, as the characteristic does amuse me. I
had long since let myself down in one of the armless upholstered chairs
flanking the book-table, when he screwed the top on his fountain-pen and
approached me, without particularly looking me in the face.

'You've come just at the right time,' he said, and sat down on the other
side of the table. 'The Schaff-Gosch quartet is playing op. 132 tonight.
You'll come along?'

I understood that he meant Beethoven's late work, the A-minor String
Quartet.

'Since I'm here,' I replied, 'I'll come with you. It will be good to hear the
Lydian movement, the "Thanksgiving for Recovery"; I've not heard it for a
long time.'

'That beaker,' he said, 'I drain at every feast. My eyes run over.' And he
began to talk about the Church modes and the Ptolemaic or 'natural' system,
whose six different modes were reduced by the tempered, i.e. the false
system to two, major and minor; and about superiority in modulation of the
'pure' scale over the tempered one. This he called a compromise for home
use, as also the tempered piano was a thing precisely for domestic consumption, a transient peace-pact, not a hundred and fifty years old, which
had brought to pass all sorts of considerable things, oh, very considerable,
but about which we should not imagine that everything was settled for
eternity. He expressed great pleasure over the fact that it was an astronomer

and mathematician named Ptolemy, a man from Upper Egypt, living in Alexandria, who had established the best of all known scales, the natural or right one. That proved again, he said, the relation between music and astronomy, as it had been shown already by Pythagoras' cosmic theory of harmony. Now and then he came back to the quartet and its third movement, referring to its strange character, its suggestion of a moon-landscape, and the enormous difficulty of performing it.

'At bottom,' said he, 'every one of the four players has to be a Paganini and would have to know not only his own part but the three others' as well, else it's no use. Thank God, one can depend on the Schaff-Gosch. Today it can be done, but it is only just playable, and in his time it was simply not. The ruthless indifference of one who has risen above it towards the sheer earthly difficulties of technique is to me the most colossally entertaining thing in life. "What do I care about your damned fiddle?" he said to somebody who complained.'

We laughed – and the odd thing was, simply that we had never even said how do you do.

'Besides,' he said, 'there is the fourth movement, the incomparable finale, with the short, marchlike introduction and that noble recitative of the first violin, with which as suitably as possible the theme is prepared. Only it is vexatious, if you don't want to call it gratifying, that in music, at least in this music, there are things for which one cannot scare up, out of the whole rich realm of language, do what you like, any properly characterizing epithet or combination of epithets. I have been tormenting myself over that these days: you cannot find any adequate term for the spirit, the attitude, the behaviour of this theme. For there is a lot of behaviour there. Tragic? Bold? Defiant, emphatic, full of élan, the height of nobility? None of them good. And "glorious" is of course only throwing in your hand. You finally land at the objective direction, the name: *Allegro appassionato*. That is the best after all.'

I agreed. 'Perhaps,' I thought, 'this evening we might think of something else.'

'You must see Kretschmar soon,' it occurred to him to say. 'Where do you live?'

I told him I would go to a hotel for the night and look out something suitable in the morning.

'I understand,' he said, 'your not asking me to find something. One cannot leave it to anyone else. I have,' he added, 'told the people in Café Central about you and your arrival. I must take you there soon.'

By the people he meant the group of young intellectuals whose acquaintance he had made through Kretschmar. I was convinced that his attitude towards them was very like what it had been towards the Winfried brethren in Halle, and when I said it was good to hear that he had quickly found suitable contacts in Leipzig he answered:

'Well, contacts ...'

Schildknapp, the poet and translator, he added, was the most satisfactory. But even he had a way, out of a sort of not precisely superior self-confidence, of always refusing, as soon as he saw anyone wanted anything of him or needed or tried to claim him. A man with a very strong – or perhaps on the other hand not so strong – feeling of independence, he said. But sympathetic, entertaining, and besides so short of money that he himself had to help out.

What he had wanted of Schildknapp, who as a translator lived intimately with the English language and was altogether a warm admirer of everything English, emerged as we continued to talk. I learned that Adrian was looking for a theme for an opera and years before he seriously approached the task, had had *Love's Labour's Lost* in mind. What he wanted of Schildknapp, who was musically equipped as well, was the preparation of the libretto. But the other, partly on account his own work, and partly, I surmise, because Adrian would hardly have been able to pay him in advance, would not hear of it. Well, later I myself did my friend this service. I like to think back to our first groping talk about it, on this very evening. And I found my idea confirmed: the tendency to marriage with the word, to vocal articulation, more and more possessed him. He was practising almost exclusively the composition of lieder, short and long songs, even epic fragments, taking his material from a Mediterranean anthology, which in a fairly happy German version included Provençal and Catalan lyrics of the twelfth and thirteenth centuries, Italian poetry, the loftiest visions of the *Divina Commedia*, and some Spanish and Portuguese things. It was, at that musical time of day and at the young adept's age, almost inevitable that here and there the influence of Gustav Mahler should be perceptible. But then would come a tone, a mood, a glimpse, a something lone-wandering and unique: it stood strange and firm on its own feet; and in such things we recognize today the master of the grotesque *Vision of the Apocalypse*.

This was clearest in the songs of the series taken from the *Purgatorio* and the *Paradiso*, chosen with a shrewd sense of their affinity with music. Thus in the piece which especially took me, and Kretschmar too had called very good, where the poet in the light of the planet Venus sees the smaller lights – they are the spirits of the blessed – some more quickly, the others more slowly, 'according to the kind of their regard of God' drawing their circles, and compares this to the sparks that one distinguishes in the song 'when the one twines round the other'. I was surprised and enchanted at the reproduction of the sparks in the fire, of the entwining voices. And still I did not know whether I should give the preference to these fantasies on the light in light or to the introspective, more-thought-than-seen-pieces – those where all is rejected questioning, wrestling with the unfathomable, where 'doubt springs at the foot of truth' and even the cherub who looks into God's depths measures not the gulf of the everlasting resolve. Adrian had here chosen the frightfully stern sequence of verses which speak of the condemnation of innocence and ignorance, and incomprehensible justice is questioned which delivers over to hell the good and pure but not baptized, not reached by faith. He had persuaded himself to put the thundering response in tones which announce the powerlessness of the creaturely good before Good in itself: the latter, being itself the source of justice, cannot give way before anything that our human understanding is tempted to call unjust. This rejection of the human in favour of an unattainable absolute foreordination angered me. And altogether, though I acknowledge Dante's greatness as a poet, I always feel put off by his tendency to cruelty and scenes of martyrdom. I recall that I scolded Adrian for choosing this almost intolerable passage as his theme. It was then that I met a look from his eye which I had not seen before; it had made me question whether I was quite right in asserting that I found him unchanged after our year's separation. This look was something new, and it remained peculiar to him, even though one encountered it only from time to time and indeed without especial occasion. Mute, veiled, musing, aloof to the point of offensiveness, full of a chilling melancholy, it ended in a smile with closed lips, not unfriendly, yet mocking, and with that gesture of turning away, so habitual, so long familiar to me.

The impression was painful and, intentional or not, it wounded. But I quickly forgave him as he went on, and I heard the moving musical diction given to the parable in the *Purgatorio* of the man who carries a light on his back at night, which does not light him but lights up the path of those coming after. The tears came in my eyes. I was still happier over the altogether successful shaping of the address, only nine lines long, of the poet to his allegorical song, which speaks so darkly and difficultly, with no prospect of its hidden sense being understood of the world. Thus, its creator lays upon it, may it implore perception if not of its depth at least of its beauty. 'So look at least, how beautiful I am!' The way the music strives upward out of the difficulties, the artful confusion, the mingled distresses of its first part to the tender light of the final cry and there is touchingly resolved – all that I straightway found admirable and did not hide my delighted approbation.

'So much the better if it is good for something already,' said he. In later talks it became clear what he meant by 'already'. The word had not to do with his youth; he meant that he regarded the composition of the songs, however much devotion he gave to the single task, on the whole only as practice for a complete work in words and music which hovered before his mind's eye, the text of which was to be the Shakespeare comedy. He went about theoretically to glorify this bond with the word, which he would put in practice. Music and speech, he insisted, belonged together, they were at bottom one, language was music, music a language; separate, one always appealed to the other, imitated the other, used the other's tools, always the one gave itself to be understood as substitute of the other. How music could be first of all word, be thought and planned as word, he would demonstrate to me by the fact that Beethoven had been seen composing in words. 'What is he writing there in his notebooks?' it had been asked. 'He is composing.' 'But he is writing words, not notes.' Yes, that was a way he had. He usually sketched in words the course of ideas in a composition, at most putting in a few notes here and there. – Adrian dwelt upon this, it visibly charmed him. The creative thought, he said, probably formed its own and unique intellectual category, but the first draft hardly ever amounted to a picture, a statue in words – which spoke for the fact that music and speech belonged together. It was very natural that music should take fire at the word, that the word should burst forth out of music, as it did towards the end of the Ninth Symphony. Finally it was a fact that the whole development of music in Germany strove towards the word-tone drama of Wagner and therein found its goal.

'One goal,' said I, referring to Brahms and to the absolute music in the 'light on his back'. He agreed to the qualification, the more easily because what he had vaguely in mind was as un-Wagnerian as possible, and most remote from nature-daemony and the theatrical quality of the myth: a revival of opéra bouffe in a spirit of the most artificial mockery and parody of the artificial: something highly playful and highly precious; its aim the ridicule of affected asceticism and that euphuism which was the social fruit of classical studies. He spoke with enthusiasm of the theme, which gave opportunity to set the lout and 'natural' alongside the comic sublime and make both ridiculous in each other. Archaic heroics, rodomontade, bombastic etiquette tower out of forgotten epochs in the person of Don Armado, whom Adrian rightly pronounced a consummate figure of opera. And he

quoted verses to me in English, which obviously he had taken to his heart:
the despair of the witty Biron at his perjured love of her who had two pitch-
balls stuck in her face for eyes; his having to sigh and watch for 'by heaven
one that will do the deed, though Argus were her eunuch and her guard'.
Then the judgement upon this very Biron: 'You shall this twelvemonth term
from day to day Visit the speechless sick, and still converse With groaning
wretches'; and his cry: 'It cannot be: mirth cannot move a soul in agony!' He
repeated the passage and declared that some day he would certainly compose
it, also the incomparable talk in the fifth act about the folly of the wise, the
helpless, blinded, humiliating misuse of wit to adorn the fool's cap of
passion. Such utterance, he said, as that of the two lines:

> The blood of youth burns not with such excess
> As gravity's revolt to wantonness

flourishes only on the heights of poetic genius.

I rejoiced at this admiration, this love, even though the choice of matter
was not quite to my taste. I have always been rather unhappy at any mockery
of humanistic extravagances; it ends by making humanism itself a subject for
mirth. Which did not prevent me from preparing the libretto for him when
he was ready. What I at once tried my best to dissuade him from was his
strange and utterly impractical idea of composing the comedy in English,
because he found that the only right, dignified, authentic thing; also because
it seemed indicated, on account of the plays on words and the old English
verse with doggerel rhyme. The very important objection, that a text in
a foreign language would destroy every prospect of its appearance on a
German stage, he did not consider, because he altogether declined to
imagine a contemporary public for his exclusive, eccentric, fantastic dreams.
It was a baroque idea, but rooted deep in his nature, combined as that
was of haughty shyness, the old-German provincialism of Kaisersaschern,
and an out-and-out cosmopolitanism. Not for nothing was he a son of the
town where Otto III lay buried. His dislike of his own very Germanness
(it was that, indeed, which drew him to the Anglicist and Anglomaniac
Schildknapp) took the two disparate forms of a cocoonlike withdrawal from
the world and an inward need of world-wideness. These it was made him
insist on expecting a German concert audience to listen to songs in a foreign
language – or, more realistically put, on preventing their hearing them.
In fact, he produced during my Leipzig year compositions on poems by
Verlaine and the beloved William Blake, which were not sung for decades.
The Verlaine ones I heard later in Switzerland. One of them is the
wonderful poem with the closing line: *'C'est l'heure exquise';* another the
equally enchanting *'Chanson d'Automne';* a third the fantastically melancholy, preposterously melodious three-stanza poem that begins with the
lines: *'Un grand sommeil noir Tombe sur ma vie'.* Then a couple of mad
and dissolute pieces from the *'Fêtes galantes': Hê! Bonsoir, la Lune!'* and
above all the macabre proposal, answered with giggles: *'Mourons ensemble,
voulezvous?'* – As for Blake's extraordinary poesy, he set to music the stanzas
about the rose, whose life was destroyed by the dark secret love of the
worm which found its way into her crimson bed. Then the uncanny sixteen
lines of 'A Poison Tree', where the poet waters his wrath with his tears,
suns it with smiles and soft deceitful wiles, so that an alluring apple ripens,
with which the thievish friend poisons himself: to the hater's joy he lies
dead in the morning beneath the tree. The evil simplicity of the verse was
completely reproduced in the music. But I was even more profoundly

impressed at the first hearing by a song to words by Blake, a dream of a chapel all of gold before which stand people weeping, mourning, worshipping, not daring to enter in. There rises the figure of a serpent who knows how by force to make an entry into the shrine; the slimy length of its body it drags along the costly floor and gains the altar, where it vomits its poison out on the bread and on the wine. 'So,' ends the poet, with desperate logic, therefore and thereupon, 'I turned into a sty and laid me down among the swine.' The dream anguish of the vision, the growing terror, the horror of pollution, finally the wild renunciation of a humanity dishonoured by the sight – all this was reproduced with astonishing power in Adrian's setting.

But these are later things, though all of them belong to Leverkühn's Leipzig years. On that evening, then, after my arrival we heard the Schaff-Gosch concert together and next day visited Wendell Kretschmar, who spoke to me privately about Adrian's progress in a way that made me proud and glad. Nothing, he said, did he fear less, than ever to have to regret his summons to a musical career. A man so self-assured, so fastidious in matters of taste and 'pleasing the public', would of course have difficulties, outwardly as well as inwardly; but that was quite right, in such a case, since only art could give body to a life which otherwise would bore itself to death with its own facility. – I enrolled myself with Lautensack and the famous Bermeter, glad that I need not hear any more theology for Adrian's sake; and allowed myself to be introduced to the circle at Café Central, a sort of bohemian club, which had pre-empted a smoky den in the tavern, where the members read the papers afternoons, played chess, and discussed cultural events. They were students from the conservatoires, painters, writers, young publishers, also beginning lawyers with an interest in the arts, a few actors, members of the Leipzig Kammerspiele, under strong literary influence – and so on. Rüdiger Schildknapp, the translator, considerably older than we were, at the beginning of the thirties, belonged, as I have said, to this group. As he was the only one with whom Adrian stood on terms of any intimacy, I too approached him, and spent many hours with them both together. That I had a critical eye on the man whom Adrian dignified with his friendship will, I fear, be evident in the present sketch of his personality, though I will endeavour, as I always have endeavoured, to do him justice.

Schildknapp was born in a middle-sized town in Silesia, the son of a post-office official whose position elevated him above the lower ranks without leading to the higher administrative posts reserved for men with university degrees. Such a position requires no certificate or juristic training; it is arrived at after a term of years of preliminary service by passing the examinations for secretary in chief. Such had been the career of the elder Schildknapp. He was a man of proper upbringing and good form, also socially ambitious; but the Prussian hierarchy either shut him out of the upper circles of the town or, if they did by exception admit him, gave him to taste humiliation there. Thus he quarrelled with his lot and was an aggrieved man, a grumbler, visiting his unsuccessful career on his own family's head. Rüdiger, his son, portrayed to us very vividly, filial respect giving way before a sense of the ridiculous, how the father's social embitterment had poisoned his own, his mother's and his brothers' and sisters' lives; the more because it expressed itself, in accordance with the man's refinement, not in gross unpleasantness but as a finer capacity for suffering, and an exaggerated self-pity. He might come to the table and bite violently on a cherrystone in the fruit soup, breaking a crown on one of his teeth. 'Yes, you see,' he would say, his voice trembling, stretching out his hands, 'that is how it is, that's what happens to me, that is the way I am, it is in myself, it has to be like this! I had looked forward to this meal, and felt some appetite; it is a warm day and the cold fruit dish had promised me some refreshment. Then this has to happen. Good, you can see that joy is not my portion. I give it up. I will go back to my room. I hope you will enjoy it,' he would finish in a dying voice, and quit the table, well knowing that joy would certainly not be their portion either.

The reader can picture Adrian's mirth at the drolly dejected reproduction of scenes experienced with youthful intensity. Of course we had always to check our merriment and remember that this was the narrator's father we were dealing with. Rüdiger assured us that the elder's feeling of social inferiority had communicated itself to them all in greater or less degree: he himself had taken it with him, a sort of spiritual wound, from his parents' house. Apparently his irritation over it was one of the reasons why he would not give his father the satisfaction of wiping out the stain in the person of his son, for he had frustrated the elder's hope of seeing the younger a member of government. Rüdiger had finished at the gymnasium and gone to the university. But he had not even got so far as an assessorship, devoting himself to literature instead, and preferring to forfeit any assistance from home rather than to satisfy the father's obnoxious wishes. He wrote poems in free verse, critical essays and short stories in a neat prose style. But partly under economic pressure, partly also because his own production was not exactly copious, he devoted most of his time to translation, chiefly from his favourite language, English. He not only supplied several publishers with German versions of English and American literary provender, but also got himself commissioned by a Munich publisher of de luxe editions and literary curiosities to translate English classics, Skelton's dramatic moralities, some pieces of Fletcher and Webster, certain didactic poems of Pope; and he was responsible for excellent German editions of Swift and Richardson. He supplied this sort of produce with well-found prefaces, and contributed to his translations a great deal of conscientiousness, taste, and feeling for style, likewise a preoccupation with the exactness of the reproduction, matching phrase for phrase and falling more and more victim to the charms and penalties of translation. But his work was accompanied by a mental state which on another plane resembled his father's. He felt himself to be a born writer, and spoke bitterly of being driven by necessity to till another's field, wearing himself out on work which only distinguished him in a way he found insulting. He wanted to be a poet, in his own estimation he was one; that on account of his tiresome daily bread he had to sink to a middleman's position in literature put him in a critical and derogatory frame towards the contributions of others and was the subject of his daily plaint. 'If only I had time,' he used to say; 'if I could work instead of drudging, I would show them!' Adrian was inclined to believe it, but I, perhaps judging too harshly, suspected that what he considered an obstacle was really a welcome pretext with which he deceived himself over his lack of a genuine and telling creative impulse.

With all this, one must not imagine him as morose or sullen; on the contrary he was very jolly, even rather feather-headed, gifted with a definitely Anglo-Saxon sense of humour and in character just that which the English call boyish. He was always immediately acquainted with all the sons of Albion who came to Leipzig as tourists, idlers, music-students; talked with them with complete elective adaptation of his speech to theirs, chattering nonsense thirteen to the dozen and imitating irresistibly their struggles in German, their accents, their all too correct mistakes in ordinary everyday exchange, their foreign weakness for the written language: as for instance *Besichtigen Sie jenes!* when all they meant was: *Sehen Sie das!* And he looked just like them. I have not yet mentioned his appearance: it was very good, and – apart from the clothes, shabby and always the same, to which his poverty condemned him – elegant and gentlemanly, and rather sporting. His features were striking, their aristocratic character marred only by a soft, loose-lipped mouth such as I have often noticed among Silesians. Tall, broad-shouldered, long-legged, narrow-hipped, he wore day in, day out the same checked breeches, the worse for wear, long woollen stockings, stout yellow shoes, a coarse linen shirt open at the throat, and over it a jacket of a colour already vague, with sleeves that were a little short. But his hands were very aristocratic, with long fingers and beautifully shaped, oval, rounded nails. The whole was so undeniably 'portrait of a gentleman' that in his everyday clothes, in themselves an offence to society, he could frequent circles where evening dress was the rule. The women preferred him just as he was to his rivals in correct black and white, and at such receptions he might be seen surrounded by unaffectedly admiring femininity.

And yet! And again! His needy exterior, excused by the tiresome want of money, could not affect adversely his rank as cavalier and gentleman or prevent the native truth from showing through and counteracting it. But this very 'truth' was itself in part a deception, and in this complicated sense Schildknapp was a fraud. He looked like an athlete, but his looks were misleading, for he practised no sport, except a little ski-ing with his English friends in winter in the Saxon Alps; and he was subject to a catarrh of the bladder, which in my opinion was not quite negligible. Despite his tanned face and broad shoulders his health was not always sound and as a younger man he had spit blood; in other words, tended to be tubercular. The women were not quite so lucky with him as he was with them, so far as I saw; at least not individually, for collectively they enjoyed his entire devotion. It was a roving, all-embracing devotion, it referred to the sex as such, and the possibilities for happiness presented to him by the entire world; for the single instance found him inactive, frugal, reserved. That he could have as many love-affairs as he chose seemed to satisfy him, it was as though he shrank from every connexion with the actual because he saw therein a theft from the possible. The potential was his kingdom, its endless spaces his domain – therein and thus far he was really a poet. He had concluded from his name that his forebears had been giant attendants on knights and princes, and although he had never sat a horse, nor ever tried to do so, he felt himself a born horseman. He ascribed it to atavistic memory, a blood heritage, that he very often dreamed of riding; he was uncommonly convincing when he showed us how natural it was for him to hold the reins in the left hand and pat the horse's neck with the right. – The most common phrase in his mouth was 'One ought to'. It was the formula for a wistful reflection upon possibilities for the fulfilment of which the resolve was lacking. One ought to do – this and that, have this or that. One ought to write a novel about Leipzig society: one ought, if even as a dish-washer, to take a trip round the world; one ought to study physics, astronomy; one ought to acquire a little land and cultivate the soil in the sweat of one's brow. If we went into a grocery to have some coffee ground, he was capable of saying when we came out, with a contemplative head-shake: 'One ought to keep a grocery.'

I have referred to his feeling of independence. It had expressed itself early, in his rejection of government service and a choice of free-lance life. Yet he was on the other hand the servant of many gentlemen and had something of the parasite about him. And why should he not, with his narrow means, make use of his good exterior and social popularity! He got himself invited out a good deal, ate luncheon here and there in Leipzig houses, even in rich Jewish ones, though one might hear him drop anti-Semitic remarks. People who feel slighted, not treated according to their deserts, yet rejoice in an aristocratic physique, often seek satisfaction in racial self-assertion. The special thing in his case was that he did not like the Germans either, was saturated with their social and national sense of inferiority and expressed it by saying that he would just as soon or sooner stick with the Jews. On their side, the Jewish publishers' wives and bankers' ladies looked up to him with the profound admiration of their race for German master-blood and long legs and greatly enjoyed making him presents: the knitted stockings, belts, sweaters, and scarves which he wore were mostly gifts, and not always quite unprompted. When he went shopping with a lady he might point to something and say: 'Well, I would not spend money on that. At most I would take it for a gift.' And took it for a gift, with the bearing of one who had certainly said he would not give money for it. For the rest, he asserted his independence to himself and others by the fundamental refusal to be obliging: when one needed him, he was definitely not to be had. If a place was vacant at dinner and he was asked to fill in, he unfailingly declined. If somebody wished to assure himself of an agreeable companion for a prescribed sojourn at a cure, Schildknapp's refusal was the more certain the clearer it was that the other set store by his company. It was thus he had rejected Adrian's proposal that he make the libretto for *Love's Labour's Lost*. Yet he was fond of Adrian, he was really attached to him, and Adrian did not take it ill that he refused. He was altogether very tolerant of Schildknapp's weaknesses, over which the man himself laughed; and much too grateful for his sympathetic talk, his stories about his father, his English whimsies, to have wished to bear him a grudge. I have never seen Adrian laugh so much, laugh even to tears, as when he and Rüdiger Schildknapp were together. A true humorist, the latter knew how to draw a momentarily overwhelming funniness from the most unlikely things. It is a fact that the chewing of a dry ruck fills the ears of the chewer with a deafening crunch, shutting him away from the outer world; and Schildknapp demonstrated at tea that a rusk-chewing company could not possibly understand each other and would have to confine themselves to 'What did you say?' 'Did you speak?' 'Just a moment, please!' How Adrian would laugh when Schildknapp fell out with his own reflection in the mirror! He was vain, that is, not in a common way, but in poetic reference to the endless potential of happiness in the world, far outbidding his own power of resolution, for which he wished to keep himself young and handsome; he was aggrieved at the tendency of his face to be prematurely wrinkled and weather-beaten. And his mouth did have something old-man about it, together with the nose drooping straight down over it, which otherwise one was willing to call classic. One could readily see how Rüdiger would look when he was old, adding a wrinkled brow, lines from nose to mouth, and various crow's-feet. He would approach his features mistrustfully to the glass, pull a wry face, hold his chin with thumb and forefinger, stroke his cheek in disgust and then wave his face away with the other hand so expressively that we, Adrian and I, burst out in loud laughter.

What I have not yet mentioned is that his eyes were exactly the same colour as Adrian's. There was really a remarkable similarity: they showed just the same mixture of blue, grey, and green, and both had the same rust-coloured ring round the pupil. However strange it may sound, it always seemed to me, seemed so with a certain soothing conviction, that Adrian's laughter-loving friendship for Schildknapp had to do with this likeness in the colour of their eyes – which is equivalent to saying that it rested upon an indifference as profound as it was light-hearted. I scarcely need to add that they always addressed each other with their last names and *Sie*. If I did not know how to entertain Adrian as Schildknapp did, I did have our childhood tie, our *du*, to my advantage over the Silesian.

Chapter Twenty-one

This morning, while my good Helene was preparing our morning drink and a brisk Upper Bavarian autumn day began to clear away the usual early mists, I read in my paper of the successful revival of our submarine warfare, to which inside twenty-four hours not less than twelve ships, among them two large passenger steamers, an English and a Brazilian, with five hundred passengers, have fallen victim. We owe this success to a new torpedo of fabulous properties which German technicians have succeeded in constructing, and I cannot repress a certain satisfaction over our ever alert spirit of invention, our national gift of not being swerved aside by however many set-backs. It stands wholly and entirely at the service of the regime which brought us into this war, laid the Continent literally at our feet and replaced the intellectual's dream of a European Germany with the upsetting, rather brittle reality, intolerable, so it seems to the rest of the world, of a German Europe. But my involuntary satisfaction gives way to the thought that such incidental triumphs as the new sinkings or the splendid commando feat of snatching the fallen dictator of Italy from his prison can only serve to arouse false hopes and lengthen out a war which in the view of any reasonable and sensible man can no longer be won. Such is also the opinion of the head of our Freising theological seminary Monsignor Hinterpförtner; he has confessed it to me in so many words, in private conversation as we sat over our evening glasses – a man who has nothing in common with the passionate scholar about whom in the summer the Munich student uprising centred, so horribly quenched in blood. Monsignor Hinterpförtner's knowledge of the world permits him no illusion, not even that which clings to the distinction between losing the war and not winning it. For that only veils the truth that we have played *va banque* and that the failure of our hopes of world conquest amounts to a first-class national catastrophe.

I say all this to remind the reader of the historical conditions under which I am setting down Leverkühn's biography, and to point out how the excited state bound up with my subject constantly assimilates itself to that produced by the shattering events of the time. I do not speak of distraction; for – at least so it seems to me – events have not actually the power of distracting me from my task. Even so, and despite my personal security, I may say that the times are not precisely favourable to the steady pursuance of such a work as this. And, moreover, just during the Munich disorders and executions, I got an influenza with fever and chills, which for ten days confined me to my bed and necessarily affected for some time the physical and mental powers of a man now sixty years old. It is no wonder that spring and summer have passed into autumn, and autumn is now well advanced, since I committed to paper the first lines of this narrative. Meanwhile we have experienced the destruction of our noble cities from the air, a destruction that would cry to heaven if we who suffer were not ourselves laden with guilt. As it is, the cry is smothered in our throats; like King Claudius's prayer, it can 'never to heaven go'. There is outcry over these crimes against culture, crimes that we ourselves invoked; how strange it sounds in the mouths of those who trod the boards of history as the heralds and bringers of a world-rejuvenating barbarism, revelling in atrocity. Several times the shattering, headlong destruction has come breath-takingly near my retreat. The frightful bombardment of the city of Dürer and Willibald Pirkheimer was no remote event; and when the last judgement fell on Munich too, I sat pallid, shaking like the walls, the doors, and the windowpanes in my study – and with trembling hand wrote on at this story of a life. For my hand trembles in any case, on account of my subject; it cannot much matter to me that it trembles a little more due to terror from without.

We have lived through, with the sort of hope and pride which the unfolding of German might must rouse in us, the new offensive of our Wehrmacht against the Russian hordes defending their inhospitable but obviously dearly loved land. It was an offensive which after a few weeks passed over into a Russian one and since then has led to endless, unavoidable abandonment of territory – to speak only of territory. With profound consternation we read of the landing of American and Canadian troops on the south-east coast of Sicily, the fall of Syracuse, Catania, Messina, Taormina. We learned, with a mixture of terror and envy – pierced by the knowledge that we ourselves were not capable of it, in either a good or a bad sense – how a country whose mental state still permitted it to draw the foregone conclusion from a succession of scandalous defeats and losses relieved itself of its great man, in order somewhat later to submit to unconditional surrender. That is what the world demands of us too, but to consent to it our most desperate situation would still be much too holy and dear. Yes, we are an utterly indifferent people; we deny and reject the foregone conclusion; we are a people of mightily tragic soul, and our love belongs to fate – to any fate, if only it be one, even destruction kindling heaven with the crimson flames of the death of the gods!

The advance of the Muscovites into our destined granary, the Ukraine, and the elastic retreat of our troops to the Dnieper line accompanied my work, or rather my work accompanied those events. Some days since, the untenability of this defence line too seems proved, although our Führer, hurrying up, ordered a mighty halt to the retreat, uttered his trenchant rebuke, the words 'Stalingrad psychosis', and commanded that the line of the Dneiper be held at all costs. The price, any price, was paid, in vain; whither, how far, the red flood the papers speak of will still pour on its left to our powers of imagination – and these are already inclined to reckless excess. For it belongs in the realm of the fantastic, it offends against all order and expectation that Germany itself should become the theatre of one of Germany's wars. Twenty-five years ago at the very last moment we escaped that fate. But now our increasingly tragic and heroic psychology seems to prevent us from quitting a lost cause before the unthinkable becomes fact. Thank God, wide stretches still lie between our home soil and destruction rushing on from the east. We may be prepared to take some painful losses now on this front in order to defend in greater strength our European territory against the deadly enemies of the German order advancing from the west. The invasion of our beautiful Sicily by no means proved that it was possible for the foe to gain a footing on the Italian mainland. But unhappily it did turn out to be possible, while in Naples last week a communistic revolt broke out in support of the Allies which made that city appear no longer a place worthy of German troops. After conscientious destruction of the library, and leaving a time bomb behind in the post office, we made our exit with our heads high. And now there is talk of invasion tests in the Channel, supposed to be covered with ships, and the civilian takes unlawful leave to ask himself whether what happened in Italy and farther up the peninsula can happen, all the prescribed beliefs in the inviolability of Fortress Europa to the contrary, also in France or some other place.

Yes, Monsignor Hinterpförtner is right: we are lost. In other words, the war is lost; but that means more than a lost campaign, it means in very truth that *we* are lost: our character, our cause, our hope, our history. It is all up with Germany, it will be all up with her. She is marked down for collapse, economic, political, moral, spiritual, in short all-embracing, unparalleled, final collapse. I suppose I have not wished for it, this that threatens, for it is madness and despair. I suppose I have not wished for it, because my pity is too deep, my grief and sympathy are with this unhappy nation, when I think of the exultation and blind ardour of its uprising, the breaking out, the breaking-up, the breaking-down; the purifying and fresh start, the national new birth of ten years ago, that seemingly religious intoxication – which then betrayed itself to any intelligent person for what it was by its curdity, vulgarity, gangsterism, sadism, degradation, filthiness – ah, how unmistakably it bore within itself the seeds of this whole war! My heart contracts painfully at the thought of that enormous investment of faith, zeal, lofty historic emotion; all this we made, all this is now puffed away in a bankruptcy without compare. No, surely I did not want it, and yet – I have been driven to want it, I wish for it today and will welcome it, out of hatred for the outrageous contempt of reason, the vicious violation of the truth, the cheap, filthy backstairs mythology, the criminal degradation and confusion of standards; the abuse, corruption, and blackmail of all that was good, genuine, trusting, and trustworthy in our old Germany. For liars and lickspittles mixed us a poison draught and took away our senses. We drank – for we Germans perenially yearn for intoxication – and under its spell, through years of deluded high living, we committed a superfluity of shameful deeds, which must now be paid for. With what? I have already used the word, together with the word 'despair' I write it. I will not repeat it: not twice could I control my horror or my trembling fingers to set it down again.

Asterisks too are a refreshment for the eye and mind of the reader. One does not always need the greater articulation of a Roman numeral, and I could scarcely give the character of a main section to the above excursus into a present outside of Adrina Leverkühn's life and work. No, asterisks will serve capitally to give proportion to my page; and below them I will round out this section with some further information about Adrian's Leipzig years, though I realize that as a chapter it makes an impression of heterogeneous elements – as though it were not enough that I did not succeed better with what came before. I have re-read it all: Adrian's dramatic wishes and plans, his earliest songs, the painful gaze that he had acquired during our separation; the intellectual fascinations of Shakespearian comedy, Leverkühn's emphasis on foreign songs and his own shy cosmopolitanism; then the bohemian Café Central club, winding up with the portrait of Rüdiger Schildknapp, given in perhaps unjustifiable detail. And I quite properly ask myself whether such uneven material can actually make up a single chapter. But let me remember that from the first I had to reproach myself for the absence of a controlled and regular structure in my work. My excuse is always the same: my subject is too close to me. What is lacking is distance, contrast, mere differentiation between the material and the hand that shapes it. Have I not said more than once that the life I am treating of was nearer to me, dearer, more moving than my own? And being so near, so moving, and so intimate, it is not mere 'material' but a *person*, and that does not lend itself to artistic treatment. Far be it from me to deny the seriousness of art, but when it becomes serious, then one rejects art and is not capable of it. I can only repeat that paragraphs and asterisks are in this book merely a concession to the eyes of the reader, and that I, if I had my way, would write down the whole in one burst and one breath, without any division, yes, without paragraphing or intermissions. I simply have not the courage to submit such an insensate text to the eyes of the reading public.

Having spent a year with Adrian in Leipzig, I know how he lived during the other three of his stay there; his manner of life being so regular and conservative that I found it rigid and sometimes even depressing. Not for nothing, in that first letter, had he expressed his sympathy for Chopin's lack of adventurous spirit, his 'not wanting to know'. He too wanted to know nothing, see nothing, actually experience nothing, at least not in any obvious, exterior sense of the word. He was not out for change, new sense impressions, distraction, recreation. As for the last, he liked to make fun of people who are constantly having a 'little change', constantly getting brown and strong – and nobody knew for what. 'Relaxation,' he said, 'is for those to whom it does no good.' He was not interested in travel for the sake of sightseeing or 'culture'. He scorned the delight of the eye, and sensitive as his hearing was, just so little had he ever felt urged to train his sight in the forms of plastic art. The distinction between eye-men and ear-men he considered indefeasibly valid and correct and counted himself definitely among the latter. As for me, I have never thought such a distinction could be followed through thick and thin, and in his case I never quite believed in the unwillingness and reluctance of the eye. To be sure, Goethe too says that music is something inborn and native, requiring no great nourishment from outside and no experience drawn from life. But after all there is the inner vision, the perception, which is something different and comprehends more than mere seeing. And more than that, it is profoundly contradictory that a man should have, as Leverkühn did, some feeling for the human eye, which after all speaks only to the eye, and yet refuse to perceive the outer world through that organ. I need only mention the names of Marie Godeau, Rudi Schwerdtfeger, and Nepomuk Schneidewein to bring home to myself Adrian's receptivity, yes, weakness, for the magic of the blue, the black and the blue. Of course I am quite clear that I am doing wrong to bombard the reader with unfamiliar names when the actual appearance of their owners in these pages is still far off; it is a barefaced blunder which may well make one question the freedom of the will. What, indeed, is free will? I am quite aware that I have put down under a compulsion these too empty, too early names.

Adrian's journey to Graz, which did not occur for the journey's sake, was one interruption in the even flow of his life. Another was the excursion with Schildknapp to the sea, the fruit of which one can claim to be that one-movement symphonic tone-poem. The third exception, related to the second, was a journey to Basel, which he made in company with his teacher Kretschmar to attend the performances of sacred music of the baroque period, which the Basel Chamber Choir gave in St Martin's Church, Kretschmar was to play the organ. They gave Monteverdi's Magnificat, some organ studies by Frescobaldi, an oratorio by Carissimi, and a cantata by Buxtehude. This '*musica riservata*' made a strong impression on Adrian, as a music of emotion, which in a rebound from the constructivism of the Netherlanders treated the Bible world with astonishing human freedom, with a declamatory expressiveness, and clothed it in a boldly descriptive instrumental garb. The impression it made was very strong and lasting. He wrote and spoke much to me about this outburst of modernity in Monteverdi's musical devices: he spent much time in the Leipzig library, and practised Carissimi's *Jephtha* and the *Psalms of David* by Schütz. Who could fail to recognize in the quasi-ecclesiastical music of his later years, the *Apocalypse* and the *Faustus*, the stylistic influence of this madrigalism? Always dominant in him was a will to go to extremes of expression; together with the intellectual passion for austere order, the *linear* style of the Netherlands composers. In other words, heat and cold prevail alongside each other in his work; sometimes in movements of the greatest genius they play into each other, the *espressivo* takes hold of the strict counterpoint, the objective blushes with feeling. One gets the impression of a glowing mould; this, like nothing else, has brought home to me the idea of the daemonic.

As for the connexion between Adrian's first journey to Switzerland and the earlier one to Sylt, it had come about thus: that little mountain land, culturally so active and unhampered, had and has a Society of Musicians, a *Tonkünstler Verein*, which holds regular orchestral practices, the so-called *lectures d'orchestre*. A jury of authorities, that is, permits young aspirants to present their compositions, which are then given a try-out by one of the symphony orchestras of the country and its conductor, the public being excluded and only professionals admitted. Thus the young composer has an opportunity to hear his creation, to get experience and have his imagination instructed by the reality of sound. Such a try-out was held in Geneva at almost the same time with the Basel concert, by the Orchestre de la Suisse Romande, and Wendell Kretschmar had succeeded through his connexions in having Adrian's *Meerleuchten* – by exception the work of a young German – put on the programme. For Adrian it was a complete surprise: Kretschmar had amused himself by keeping him in the dark. He still knew nothing when he went with his teacher from Basel to Geneva for the trial performance, and there sounded under Herr Ansermet's baton his 'root treatment', that piece of darkly sparkling impressionism which he himself did not take seriously, had not taken seriously even when he wrote it. Of course while it was being performed he sat on pins and needles. To know himself being identified by the audience with an achievement which he himself had got beyond and which for him means only a trifling with something not taken in earnest: that must be for the artist a grotesque torment. Thank God, signs of applause or displeasure were forbidden at these performances. Privately he received words of praise or blame, exception was taken, shortcomings pointed out in French and German; he said nothing, either way, and anyhow he agreed with no one. A week or ten days he remained with Kretschmar in Geneva, Basel and Zürich and came into brief contact with musical circles there.

They will not have had much joy of him, nor even known how to take him, at least in so far as they set store by inoffensiveness, expansiveness, friendly responsiveness. Individuals here and there might have been touched by his shyness and understood the solitude that wrapped him, the difficulties of his life – indeed, I know that such was the case and I find it illuminating. In my experience there is in Switzerland much feeling for suffering, much understanding of it, which, more than in other places of advanced culture, for instance intellectual Paris, is bound up with the old civic life of the towns. Here was a hidden point of contact. On the other hand, the introverted Swiss mistrust of the Reich-German met here a special case of German mistrust of the 'world' – strange as it may seem to apply the word 'world' to the tight little neighbouring country by way of contrasting it with the broad and mighty German Reich with its immense cities. But the comparison has indisputable justice on its side. Switzerland, neutral, many-tongued, affected by French influence, open to western airs, is actually, despite its small size, far more 'world', far more European territory than the political colossus of the north, where the word 'international' has long been a reproach, and a smug provincialism has made the air spoilt and stuffy. I have already spoken of Adrian's inner cosmopolitanism. But German citizenship of the world was always something different from worldliness; and my friend was just the soul to be made uneasy by the 'world', and feel himself outside of it. A few days earlier than Kretschmar he returned to Leipzig, certainly a world-minded city, yet one where the world is present more as a guest than at home; that city where people talk so outlandishly – and where first desire had touched his pride. That experience was profound, it was shattering; he had not expected it from the world, and I think it did much to estrange him from it. It is indeed quite false, and nothing but German provincial conceitedness, to deny depth to the world. But the depth is a world-depth; and it is a destiny, like another, which one must accept as such, to be born to the provincial – and thus so much the more uncanny – depth of Germany.

Adrian kept without changing during the whole four and a half years he spent in Leipzig his two-room quarters in Peterstrasse, near the Collegium Beatae Virginis, where he had again pinned the magic square above his cottage piano. He attended lectures in philosophy and the history of music; read and excerpted in the library and brought Kretschmar his exercises to be criticized: piano pieces, a 'concerto' for string orchestra, and a quartet for flute, clarinet, basset horn, and bassoon. I mention the pieces which were known to me and are still extant, though never published. What Kretschmar did was to point out weak places, recommend corrections of tempo, the enlivening of a stiffish rhythm, the better articulation of a theme. He pointed out to him a middle part that came to nothing, a bass that did not move. He put his finger on a transition that was only makeshift, not organic, and compromising the natural flow of the composition. Actually, he only told him what the artistic sense of the pupil might have said itself, or what it had already told him. A teacher is the personified conscience of the pupil, confirming him in his doubt, explaining his dissatisfactions, stimulating his urge to improve. But a pupil like Adrian at bottom needed no mentor or corrector at all. He deliberately brought to Kretschmar unfinished things in order to be told what he knew already, then to laugh at the artistic sense, the connoisseurship, of his teacher, which entirely coincided with his own: the understanding which is the actual agent of the work-idea – not the idea of a particular work but the idea of the opus itself, the objective and harmonic creation complete, the manager of its unified organic nature; which sticks the cracks together, stops up the holes, brings out that 'natural flow' – which was not there in the first place and so is not natural at all, but a product of art – in short, only in retrospect and indirectly does this manager produce the impression of the spontaneous and organic. In a work there is much seeming and sham, one could go further and say that as 'a work' it is seeming in and for itself. Its ambition is to make one believe that it is not made, but born, like Pallas Athene in full fig and embossed armour from Jupiter's head. But that is a delusion. Never did a work come like that. It is work: art-work for appearance's sake – and now the question is whether at the present stage of our consciousness, our knowledge, our sense of truth, this little game is still permissible, still intellectually possible, still to be taken seriously; whether the work as such, the construction, self-sufficing, harmonically complete in itself, still stands in any legitimate relation to the complete insecurity, problematic conditions, and lack of harmony of our social situation; whether all seeming, even the most beautiful, even precisely the beautiful, has not today become a lie.

One asks, I say, or rather I learned to ask myself, through my intercourse with Adrian, whose sharp-sightedness, or if I may invent a word, sharp-feelingness, in these matters was of extreme incorruptibility. Insights fundamentally remote from my own native easygoingness he expressed in talk as casual *aperçus*; and they pained me, not because of wounded feeling but on his account; they hurt, depressed, distressed me, because I saw in them dangerous aggravations of his nature, inhibitions hampering the development of his gifts. I have heard him say:

'The work of art? It is a fraud. It is something the burgher wishes there still were. It is contrary to truth, contrary to serious art. Genuine and serious is only the very short, the highly consistent musical moment ...'

How should that not have troubled me, when after all I knew that he himself aspired to a 'work', and was planning an opera!

Again, I have heard him say: 'Pretence and play have the conscience of art against them today. Art would like to stop being pretence and play, it would like to become knowledge.'

But what ceases to conform to his definition, does that not cease to exist altogether? And how will art live as knowledge? I recalled what he had written from Halle to Kretschmar about the extension of the kingdom of the banal. Kretschmar had not allowed it to upset his belief in the calling of his pupil. But these later criticisms, levelled against pretence and play, in other words against form itself, seemed to indicate such an extension of the kingdom of the banal, of the no longer permissible, that it threatened to swallow up art itself. With deep concern I asked myself what strain and effort, intellectual tricks, by-ways, and ironies would be necessary to save it, to reconquer it, and to arrive at a work which as a travesty of innocence confessed to the state of knowledge from which it was to be won.

My poor friend had been instructed one day, or rather one night, from frightful lips, by an awful ally, in more detail on the subject I here touch upon. The document is extant, I will report on it in its proper place. It first illuminated and clarified the instinctive fears which Adrian's remarks aroused in me. But what I called above the 'travesty of innocence': how often, from early on, did it strangely stand out in his work. That work contains, on a developed musical plane, against a background of the most extreme tensions, 'banalities' – of course not in a sentimental sense nor in that of a buoyant complacency, but banalities rather in the sense of a technical primitivism, specimens of naïveté or sham naïveté which Meister Kretschmar, in so gifted a pupil, let pass with a smile. He did so, certainly because he understood them not as first-degree naïvetés, if I may so express myself, but as something the other side of the new and cheap: as audacities dressed in the garment of the primitive. The thirteen Brentano songs are also to be regarded in this light. To them, before I leave the subject, I must certainly devote a few words; they often affect one like at once a mockery and a glorification of the fundamental, a painfully reminiscent ironic treatment of tonality, of the tempered system, of traditional music itself.

That Adrian in these Leipzig years so zealously devoted himself to the composition of lieder doubtless came about because he regarded this lyric marrying of music with words as a preparation for the dramatic composition he had in mind. Probably it was also connected with the scruples he felt on the score of the destiny, the historic situation of art itself, of the automonous work. He misdoubted form, calling it pretence and play. Thus the small and lyric form of the lied might stand to him as the most acceptable, most serious, and truest; it might seem to him soonest to fulfil his theoretic demand for brevity and condensation. But it is not only that several of these productions, as for instance the '*O lieb Mädel*' with the letter symbol, further the Hymns, the '*Lustigen Musikanten*', the 'Huntsman to the Shepherds', and others, are quite long. Yet Leverkühn wanted them all regarded and treated together, as a whole, proceeding from one definite, fundamental stylistic conception, the congenial contact with a particular, amazingly lofty, and deeply dream-sunken poet soul. He would never permit the performance of single pieces, but always only the full cycle, a stern reservation, which in his lifetime stood very much in the way of their performance in public, especially since one of them, the 'Jolly Musicians', is written for a quintet of voices, mother, daughter, the two brothers, and the boy who 'early broke his leg'; that is, for alto, soprano, baritone, tenor, and a child's voice; these, partly in ensemble, partly solo, partly in duet (the two brothers) must perform No. 4 of the cycle. It was the first one that Adrian orchestrated, or more correctly, he set it at once for a small orchestra of strings, woodwind, and percussion; for in the strange poem much is said of the pipes and tambourine, the bells and cymbals, the jolly violin trills, with which the fantastic, frightened little troupe, by night 'when us no human eye does see' draws into the magic spell of its airs the lovers in their chamber, the drunken guests, the lonely maiden. In mood and spirit and piece, like a spectral serenade, the music at once lovely and tortured, is unique. And still I hesitate to award it the palm among the thirteen, several of which challenge music in a more inward sense and fulfil themselves more deeply in it than this one which treats of music in words.

'*Grossmutter Schlangenköchin*' is another one of the songs, this '*Maria, wo bist du zur Stube gewesen?*' This seven times repeated 'Oh woe, Frau Mother, what woe!' that was incredibly intuitive art actually calls up the unearthly thrills and shudders so familiar to us in the field of the German folk-song. For it is really the case that this music, wise and true and over-shrewd, here continually and painfully woos the folk-air. The wooing remains unrealized, it is there and not there, sounds fleetingly, echoes, fades into a style musically foreign to it, from which after all it constantly seeks to escape. The artistic effect is striking: it appears like a cultural paradox, which by inversion of the natural course of development, where the refined and intellectual grow out of the elementary, the former here plays the role of the original, out of which the simple continually strives the wrest itself free.

Wafteth the meaning pure of the stars
Soft through the distance unto my ears –

that is the sound, almost lost in space, the cosmic ozone of another poem, wherein spirits in golden barks traverse the heavenly sea and the ringing course of gleaming songs wreathes itself down and wells up again:

All is so gently and friendly combining,
Hand seeketh hand in sympathy kind,
Lights through the night wind trusting, consoling,
All is in union for ever entwined.

Very rarely in all literature have word and music met and married as here. Here music turns its eye upon itself and looks at its own being. These notes, that consoling and trusting offer each other the hand; that weaving and winding of all things in likeness and change – of such it is, and Adrian Leverkühn is its youthful master.

Kretschmar, before he left Leipzig to become first Kapellmeister in the Lübeck State Opera House, saw to the publication of the Brentano songs. Schott in Mainz took them on commission; that is, Adrian, with Kretschmar's and my help (we both shared in it) guaranteed the cost of printing and remained the owner, in that he assured the publishers of a share in the profits amounting to twenty per cent of the net receipts. He strictly supervised the piano reduction, demanded a rough, mat paper, quarto format, wide margins and notes printed not too close together. And he insisted upon a note at the beginning to the effect that performances in clubs and concerts were only by the author's permission and only permitted for all thirteen pieces as a whole. This was taken offence at as pretentious and, together with the boldness of the music itself, put difficulties in the way of their becoming known. In 1922, not in Adrian's presence, but in mine, they were sung in the Tonhalle in Zürich, under the direction of the excellent Dr Volkmar Andreae. This part in *'Die lustigen Musikanten'* of the boy who 'early broke his leg' was sung by a boy unfortunately really crippled, using a crutch, little Jacob Nägli. He had a voice pure as a bell, that went straight to the heart.

In passing, the pretty original edition of Clemens Brentano's poems which Adrian used in his work had been a present from me; I brought the little volume for him from Naumburg to Leipzig. Of course the thirteen songs were quite his own choice. I had no smallest influence upon that. But I may say that almost song for song they followed my own wish and expectations. – I do not mean they were my personal choice, nor will the reader find them so. For what had I, really, what had my culture and ethics to do with these words and visions of the romantic poet, these dreams of a child-world and folk-world which yet are for ever floating off, not to say degenerating, into the supernatural and spectral? I can only answer that it was the music of the words themselves which led me to make the gift – music which lies in these verses, so lightly slumbering that the slightest touch of the gifted hand was enough to awake it.

Chapter Twenty-two

When Leverkühn left Leipzig, in September 1910, at a time when I had already begun to teach in the gymnasium at Kaisersaschern, he first went home to Buchel to attend his sister's wedding, which took place at that time and to which I and my parents were invited. Ursula, now twenty-years-old, was marrying the optician Johannes Schneidewein of Langensalza, an excellent man whose acquaintance she had made while visiting a friend in the charming little Salza town near Erfurt. Schneidewein, ten or twelve years older than his bride, was a Swiss by birth, of Bernese peasant stock. His trade, lens-grinding, he had learned at home, but he had somehow drifted into Germany and there opened a shop with eye-glasses and optical goods of all sorts, which he conducted with success. He had very good looks and had kept his Swiss manner of speech, pleasant to the ear, deliberate, formal, interspersed with survivals of old-German expressions oddly solemn to hear. Ursel Leverkühn had already begun to take them on. She too, though no beauty, was an attractive creature, resembling her father in looks, in manner more like her mother, brown-eyed, slim, and naturally friendly. The two made a pair on whom the eye rested with approval. In the years between 1911 and 1923 they had four children born to them: Rosa, Ezekiel, Raimund, and Nepomuk, pretty creatures all of them, and Nepomuk, the youngest, was an angel. But of that later, only quite at the end of my story.

The wedding party was not large: the Oberweiler clergyman, the schoolmaster, the justice of the peace, with their wives; from Kaisersaschern besides us Zeitbloms only Uncle Nikolaus; relatives of Frau Leverkühn from Apolda; a married pair, friends of the Leverkühns, with their daughter, from Weissenfels; brother George, the farmer, and the dairy manageress Frau Luder – that was all. Wendell Kretschmar sent a telegram with good wishes from Lübeck, which arrived during the midday meal at the house in Buchel. It was not an evening party. It had assembled betimes in the morning; after the ceremony in the village church we gathered round a capital meal in the dining-room of the bride's home, bright with copper cooking-vessels. Soon afterwards the newly wedded pair drove off with old Thomas to the station at Weissenfels, to begin the journey to Dresden; the wedding guests still sat awhile over Frau Luder's good fruit liqueurs.

Adrian and I took a walk that afternoon to the Cow Trough and up Mount Zion. We needed to talk over the text of *Love's Labour's Lost*, which I had undertaken and about which we had already had much discussion and correspondence. I had been able to send him from Athens and Syracuse the scenario and parts of the German versification, in which I based myself on Tieck and Hertzberg and occasionally, when condensation was necessary, added something of my own in as adequate a style as possible. I was determined at least to put before him a German version of the libretto, although he still stuck to his project of composing the opera in English.

He was visibly glad to get away from the wedding party and out of doors. The cloud over his eyes showed that he was suffering from headache. It had been odd, in church and at the table, to see the same sign in his father too. That this nervous complaint set in precisely on festal occasions, under the influence of emotion and excitement, is understandable. It was so with the elder man. In the son's case the psychical ground was rather that he had taken part only of necessity and with reluctance in this sacrificial feast of a maidenhead, in which, moreover, his own sister was concerned. At least he clothed his discomfort in words which recognized the simplicity, good taste, and informality of our affair, the absence of 'customs and curtsyings' as he put it. He applauded the fact that it had all taken place in broad daylight, the wedding sermon had been short and simple, and at table there had been no offensive speeches – or rather, to avoid offence, no speeches at all. If the veil, the white shroud of virginity, the satin grave-shoes had been left out as well, it would have been still better. He spoke particularly of the favourable impression that Ursel's betrothed, now her husband, had made upon him.

'Good eyes,' he said. 'Good stock, a sound, clean, honest man. He could court her, look at her to desire her, covet her as a Christian wife, as we theologians say, with justified pride at swindling the Devil out of the carnal concomitant and making a sacrament of it, the sacrament of Christian marriage. Very droll, really, this turning the natural and sinful into the sacrosanct just by putting in the word Christian – by which it is not fundamentally altered. But one has to admit that the domestication of sex, which is evil by nature, into Christian marriage was a clever makeshift.'

'I do not like,' I replied, 'to have you make over the natural to evil. Humanism, old and new, considers that an aspersion on the sources of life.'

'My dear chap, there is not much there to asperse.'

'One ends,' I said undeterred, 'by denying the works of God; one becomes the advocate of nothing. Who believes in the Devil, already belongs to him.'

He gave his short laugh.

'You never understand a joke. I spoke as a theologian and so necessarily like a theologian.'

'Never mind,' I said, laughing as well. 'You usually take your jokes more seriously than your seriousness.' We carried on this conversation on the community bench under the maple trees on Mount Zion, in the sunshine of the autumn afternoon. The fact was that at that time I myself was going courting, though the wedding and even the public engagement had to wait on my being confirmed in my position. I wanted to tell him about Helene and of my proposed step, but his remarks did not precisely encourage me.

'And they twain shall be one flesh,' he began again: 'Is it not a curious blessing? Pastor Schröder, thank God, spared himself the quotation. In the presence of the bridal pair it is rather painful to hear. But it is only too well meant, and precisely what I mean by domestication. Obviously the element of sin, of sensuality, of evil lust together, is conjured away out of marriage – for lust is certainly only in flesh of two different kinds, not in one, and that they are to be one flesh is accordingly soothing but nonsensical. On the other hand, one cannot wonder enough that one flesh has lust for another; it is a phenomenon – well, yes, the entirely exceptional phenomenon of love. Of course, love and sensuality are not to be separated. One best absolves love from the reproach of sensuality by identifying the love element in sensuality itself. The lust after strange flesh means a conquest of previously existing resistances, based on the strangeness of I and You, your own and the other person's. The flesh – to keep the Christian terminology – is normally inoffensive to itself only. With another's it will have nothing to do. Now, if all at once the strange flesh become the object of desire and lust, then the relation of the I and the You is altered in a way for which sensuality is only an empty word. No, one cannot get along without the concept of love, even when ostensibly there is nothing spiritual in play. Every sensual act means tenderness, it is a give and take of desire, happiness through making happy, a manifestation of love. "One flesh" have lovers never been; and the prescription would drive love along with lust out of marriage.'

I was peculiarly upset and bewildered by his words and took care not to look at him, though I was tempted. I wrote down above how I always felt when he spoke of the things of the flesh. But he had never come out of himself like this, and it seemed to me that there was something explicit and unlike him about the way he spoke, a kind of tactlessness too, against himself and also against his auditor. It disturbed me, together with the idea that he said it when his eyes were heavy with headache. Yet with the sense of it I was entirely in sympathy.

'Well roared, lion!' I said, as lightly as possible. 'That is what I call standing up to it! No, you have nothing to do with the Devil. You do know that you have spoken much more as a humanist than as a theologian?'

'Let us say a psychologist,' he responded. 'A neutral position. But they are, I think, the most truth-loving people.'

'And how would it be,' I proposed, 'if we just once spoke quite simply, personally and like ordinary citizens? I wanted to tell you that I am about to –'

I told him what I was about to do, told him about Helene, how I had met her and we had got to know each other. If, I said, it would make his congratulations any warmer, he might be assured that I had dispensed him beforehand from any 'customs and curtsyings' at my wedding feast.

He was greatly enlivened.

'Wonderful!' he cried. 'My dearest fellow – wilt marry thyself! What a goodly idea! Such things always take one by surprise, though there is nothing surprising about them. Accept my blessing! "But, if thou marry, hang me by the neck, if horns that year miscarry!"'

'"Come, come, you talk greasily,"' I quoted out of the same scene. 'If you knew the girl and the spirit of our bond, then you would know that there is no need to fear for my peace of mind, but that on the contrary everything is directed towards the foundation of love and tranquillity, a fixed and undisturbed happiness.'

'I do not doubt it,' said he, 'and doubt not of its success.'

A moment he seemed tempted to press my hand, but desisted. There came a pause in the talk, then as we walked home it turned to our all-important topic, the opera, and the scene in the fourth act, with the text of which we had been joking, and which was among those I definitely wanted to leave out. Its verbal skirmish was really offensive, and dramatically it was not indispensable. In any case there had to be cuts. A comedy should not last four hours – that was and remains the principal objection to the *Meistersinger*. But Adrian seemed to have planned to use precisely the 'old sayings' of Rosaline and Boyet, the 'Thou canst not hit it, hit it, hit it', and so on for the contrapuntal passages of his overture, and altogether haggled over every episode, although he had to laugh when I said that he reminded me of Kretschmar's Beissel and his naïve zeal to set half the world to music. Anyhow he denied being embarrassed by the comparison. He still retained some of the half-humorous respect he had felt when he first heard about the wonderful novice and lawgiver of music. Absurdly enough, he had never quite ceased to think of him, and lately had thought of him oftener than ever.

'Remember,' he said, 'how I once defended his childish tyranny with the "master" and "servant" notes against your reproach of silly rationalism. What instinctively pleased me was itself something instinctive, in naïve agreement with the spirit of music: the wish, which showed itself in a comic way, to write something to the nature of the "strict style". On another, less childish plane we would need people like him, just as his flock had need of him then: we need a system-master, a teacher of the objective and organization, with enough genius to unite the old-established, the archaic, with the revolutionary. One ought to –'

He had to laugh.

'I'm talking like Schildknapp. One ought to. What all ought one not to?'

'What you say,' I threw in, 'about the archaic-revolutionary schoolmaster has something very German about it.'

'I take it,' he responded, 'that you use the word not as a compliment, but in a descriptive and critical way, as you should. However, it could mean something necessary to the time, something promising a remedy in an age of destroyed conventions and the relaxing of all objective obligations – in short, of a freedom that begins to lie like a mildew upon talent and to betray traces of sterility.'

I started at the word. Hard to say why, but in his mouth, altogether in connexion with him, there was something dismaying about it, something wherein anxiety mixed in an odd way with reverence. It came from the fact that in his neighbourhood sterility, threatened paralysis, arrest of productivity could be thought of only as something positive and proud, only in connexion with pure and lofty intellectuality.

'It would be tragic,' I said, 'if unfruitfulness should ever be the result of freedom. But there is always the hope of the release of the productive powers, for the sake of which freedom is achieved.'

'True,' he responded. 'And she does for a while achieve what she promised. But freedom is of course another word for subjectivity, and some fine day she does not hold out any longer, some time or other she despairs of the possibility of being creative out of herself and seeks shelter and security in the objective. Freedom always inclines to dialectic reversals. She realizes herself very soon in constraint, fulfils herself in the subordination to law, rule, coercion, system – but to fulfil herself therein does not mean she therefore ceases to be freedom.'

'In your opinion,' I laughed: 'So far as she knows. But actually she is no longer freedom, as little as dictatorship born out of revolution is still freedom.'

'Are you sure of it?' he asked. 'But anyhow that is talking politics. In art, at least, the subjective and the objective intertwine to the point of being indistinguishable, one proceeds from the other and takes the character of the other, the subjective precipitates as objective and by genius is again awaked to spontaneity, 'dynamized', as we say; it speaks all at once the language of the subjective. The musical conventions today destroyed were not always so objective, so objectively imposed. They were crystallizations of living experiences and as such long performed an office of vital importance: the task of organization. Organization is everything. Without it there is nothing, least of all art. And it was aesthetic subjectivity that took on the task, it undertook to organize the work out of itself, in freedom.'

'You are thinking of Beethoven.'

'Of him and of the technical principle through which a dominating subjectivity got hold of the musical organization; I mean the development, or working out. The development itself had been a small part of the sonata, a modest republic of subjective illumination and dynamic. With Beethoven it becomes universal, becomes the centre of the whole form, which, even where it is supposed to remain conventional, is absorbed by the subjective and is newly created in freedom. The form of variations, something archaic, a residuum, becomes a means by which to infuse new life into form. The principle of development plus variation technique extends over the whole sonata. It does that in Brahms, as thematic working-out, even more radically. Take him as an example of how subjectivity turns into objectivity. In him music abstains from all conventional flourishes, formulas, and residua and so to speak creates the unity of the work anew at every moment, out of freedom. But precisely on that account freedom becomes the principle of an all-round economy that leaves in music nothing casual, and develops the utmost diversity while adhering to the identical material. Where there is nothing unthematic left, nothing which could not show itself to derive from the same basic material, there one can no longer speak of a "free style".'

'And not of the "strict style" in the old sense, either!'

'Old or new, I will tell you what I understand by "strict style". I mean the complete integration of all musical dimensions, their neutrality towards each other due to complete organization.'

'Do you see a way to do that?'

'Do you know,' he countered, 'when I came nearest to the "strict style"?'

I waited. He spoke so low as to be hard to hear, and between his teeth, as he used to when he had headache.

'Once in the Brentano cycle,' he said, 'in *"O lieb Mädel"*. That song is entirely derived from a fundamental figure, a series of interchangeable intervals, the five notes B, E, A, E, E-flat, and the horizontal melody and the vertical harmony are determined and controlled by it, in so far as that is possible with a basic motif of so few notes. It is like a work, a key word, stamped on everything in the song, which it would like to determine entirely. But it is too short a word and in itself not flexible enough. The tonal space it affords is too limited. One would have to go on from here and take larger words out of the twelve letters, as it were, of the tempered semitone alphabet. Words of twelve letters, certain combinations and interrelations of the twelve semitones, series of notes from which a piece and all the movements of a work must strictly derive. Every note of the whole composition, both melody and harmony, would have to show its relation to this fixed fundamental series. Not one might recur until the other notes have sounded. Not one might appear which did not fulfil its function in the whole structure. There would no longer be a free note. That is what I would call "strict composition".'

'A striking thought,' said I. 'Rational organization through and through, one might indeed call it. You would gain an extraordinary unity and congruity, a sort of astronomical regularity and legality would be obtained thereby. But when I picture it to myself, it seems to me that the unchanged recurrence of such a succession of intervals, even when used in different parts of the texture, and in rhythmic variations, would result in a probably unavoidable serious musical impoverishment and stagnation.'

'Probably,' he answered, with a smile which showed that he had been prepared for this reservation. It was the smile that brought out strongly his likeness to his mother, but with the familiar look of strain which it would show under pressure of the migraine.

'And it is not so simple either. One must incorporate into the system all possible techniques of variation, including those decried as artificial; that is, the means which once helped the "development" to win its hold over the sonata. I ask myself why I practised so long under Kretschmar the devices of the old counterpoint and covered so much paper with inversion fugues, crabs, and inversions of crabs. Well now, all that should come in handy for the ingenious modification of the twelve-note word. In addition to being a fundamental series it could find application in this way, that every one of its intervals is replaced by its inversion. Again, one could begin the figure with its last note and finish it on its first, and then invert this figure as well. So then you have four modes, each of which can be transposed to all the twelve notes of the chromatic scale, so that forty-eight different versions of the basic series may be used in a composition and whatever other variational diversions may present themselves. A composition can also use two or more series as basic material, as in the double and triple fugue. The decisive factor is that every note, without exception, has significance and function according to its place in the basic series or its derivatives. That would guarantee what I call the indifference to harmony and melody.'

'A magic square,' I said. 'But do you hope to have people hear all that?'

'Hear?' he countered. 'Do you remember a certain lecture given for the Society for the Common Weal from which it followed that in music one certainly need not hear everything? If by "hearing" you understand the precise realization in detail of the means by which the highest and strictest order is achieved, like the order of the planets, a cosmic order and legality – no, that way one would not hear it. But this order one will or would hear, and the perception of it would afford an unknown aesthetic satisfaction.'

'Very remarkable,' said I. 'The way you describe the thing, it comes to a sort of composing before composition. The whole disposition and organization of the material would have to be ready when the actual work should begin, and all one asks is: which is the actual work? For this preparation of the material is done by variation, and the creative element in variation, which one might call the actual composition, would be transferred back to the material itself – together with the freedom of the composer. When he went to work, he would no longer be free.'

'Bound by a self-imposed compulsion to order, hence free.'

'Well, of course the dialectic of freedom is unfathomable. But he could scarcely be called a free inventor of his harmony. Would not the making of chords be left to chance and accident?'

'Say, rather, to the context. The polyphonic dignity of every chord-forming note would be guaranteed by the constellation. The historical events – the emancipation of dissonance from its resolution, its becoming "absolute" as it appears already in some passages of the later Wagner – would warrant any combination of notes which can justify itself before the system.'

'And if the constellation produced the banal: consonance, common-chord harmonics, the worn-out, the diminished seventh?'

'That would be a rejuvenation of the worn-out by the constellation.'

'I see there a restorative element in your Utopia. It is very radical, but it relaxes the prohibition which after all already hung over consonance. The return to the ancient forms of variation is a similar sign.'

'More interesting phenomena,' he responded, 'probably always have this double face of past and future, probably are always progressive and regressive in one. They display the equivocalness of life itself.'

'Is that not a generalization?'

'Of what?'

'Of our domestic experiences as a nation?'

'Oh, let us not be indiscreet! Or flatter ourselves either. All I want to say is that our objections – if they are meant as objections – would not count against the fulfilment of the old, the ever repeated demand to take hold and make order, and to resolve the magic essence of music into human reason.'

'You want to put me on my honour as a humanist,' said I. 'Human reason! And besides, excuse me; "constellation" is your every other word. But surely it belongs more to astrology. The rationalism you call for has a good deal of superstition about it – of belief in the incomprehensibly and vaguely daemonic, the kind of thing we have in games of chance, fortune-telling with cards, and shaking dice. Contrary to what you say, your system seems to me more calculated to dissolve human reason in magic.'

He carried his closed hand to his brow.

'Reason and magic,' said he, 'may meet and become one in that which one calls wisdom, initiation; in belief in the stars, in numbers ...'

I did not go on, as I saw that he was in pain. And all that he had said seemed to me to bear the mark of suffering, to stand in its sign, however intellectually remarkable it may have been. He himself seemed not to care for more conversation; his idle humming and sighing betrayed the fact as we sauntered on. I felt, of course, vexed and inwardly shook my head, silently reflecting as I walked that a man's thoughts might be characterized by saying that he had a headache; but that did not make them less significant.

We spoke little on the rest of the way home. I recall that we paused by the Cow Trough, took a few steps away from the path and looked into it, with the reflection of the setting sun in our faces. The water was clear: one could see that the bottom was flat only near the edge; it fell off rapidly into darkness. The pond was known to be very deep in the middle.

'Cold,' said Adrian, motioning with his head; 'much too cold to bathe. – Cold,' he repeated a moment later, this time with a definite shiver, and turned away.

My duties obliged me to go back that evening to Kaisersaschern. He himself delayed a few days longer his departure for Munich, where he had decided to settle. I see him pressing his father's hand in farewell – for the last time; he knew it not. I see his mother kiss him and, perhaps in the same way as she had done that time with Kretschmar in the living-room, lean his head on her shoulder. He was not to return to her, he never did. She came to him.

Chapter Twenty-three

'He that would eat the kernel must crack the nut,' he wrote to me, copying Kumpf, from the Bavarian capital a few weeks later. He meant that he had begun the composition of *Love's Labour's Lost*, and he urged me to send the rest of the text. He needed, he said, to be able to see it as a whole, and he wanted, for the sake of providing musical links and connexions, to anticipate the setting of some later parts of the libretto.

He lived in the Rambergstrasse, near the Academy, as a lodger with the widow of a Senator from Bremen, named Rodde, who with her two daughters occupied a ground-floor flat in a still new house. The room they gave him, fronting the quiet street, to the right of the entrance door, appealed to him on account of its cleanliness and impersonally comfortable furnishings. He had soon fully made it his own with more intimate belongings, books and notes. There was indeed one rather pointless decoration, relic of some past enthusiasm, framed in nutwood, on the left-hand wall: Giacomo Meyerbeer at the piano, with inspired gaze attacking the keys, surrounded by the hovering forms of characters from his operas. However, the apotheosis did not too much displease the young maestro, and when he sat in the basket-chair at his work-table, a simple green-covered extension-table, he had his back to it. So he let it stay.

A little harmonium, which might remind him of early days, stood in his room and was of use to him. But as the Frau Senator kept mostly to the garden side of the house, in the rear, and the daughters were invisible in the mornings, the grand piano in the salon, a rather old but soft-toned Bechstein, was also at his service. This salon was furnished with upholstered fauteuils, bronze candelabra, little gilt 'occasional chairs', a sofa-table with a brocade cover, and a richly framed, very much darkened oil painting of 1850, representing the Golden Horn with a view of Galata. All these things were easily recognized as the remnant of a once well-to-do bourgeois household. The salon was not seldom the scene of small social affairs, into which Adrian let himself be drawn, at first resisting, then as a habit, and finally, as circumstances brought it about, rather like a son of the house. It was the artist or half-artist world that gathered there, a house-broke Bohemia, so to speak: well-bred yet free-and-easy, and amusing enough to fulfil the expectations that had caused the Frau Senator to move from Bremen to the southern capital. Frau Senator Rodde's background was easy to imagine. Her bearing and looks were ladylike: she had dark eyes, neatly waved hair only a little grey, an ivory complexion, and pleasant, rather well-preserved features. Her long life had been spent as an honoured member of a patrician society, presiding over a household full of servants and responsibilities. After the death of her husband (whose solemn likeness, in the garb of office, also adorned the salon) her circumstances were greatly reduced, so that she was probably not able to maintain her position in her accustomed milieu. At the same time there were now released in her certain still keen desires of an unexhaustible and probably never satisfied love of life, in some humanly warmer sphere. She entertained, she explained, in the interest of her daughters, but yet largely, as was pretty clear, to enjoy herself and hold court. One amused her best with mild little salacities, not going too far, jokes about barmaids, models, artists, to which she responded with a high, affected, suggestive laugh from between her closed lips.

Obviously her daughters, Inez and Clarissa, did not not care for this laugh; they exchanged cold and disapproving looks, which showed all the irritation of grown children at the unsatisfied humanity in their mother's nature. In the case of the younger, Clarissa, the uprooting out of her hereditary middle class had been conscious, deliberate, and pronounced. She was a tall blonde, with large features whitened by cosmetics, a full lower lip and underdeveloped chin; she was preparing for a dramatic career and studied with an elderly actor who played father parts at the Hoftheater. She wore her golden-yellow hair in bold and striking style, under hats like cart-wheels, and she loved eccentric feather boas. Her imposing figure could stand these things very well and absorb their extravagance into her personality. Her tendency to the macabre and bizarre made her interesting to the masculine world which paid her homage. She had a sulphur-coloured tomcat named Isaac, whom she put in mourning for the deceased Pope by trying a black satin bow on his tail. The death's head motif appeared repeatedly in her room; there was actually a prepared skeleton, in all his toothiness; and a bronze paperweight that bore the hollow-eyed symbol of mortality and 'healing' lying on a folio bearing the name of Hippocrates. The book was hollow, the smooth bottom of it being screwed in with four tiny screws, which could be unscrewed with a fine instrument. Later, after Clarissa had taken her life with the poison from this box, Frau Senator Rodde gave me the object as a memento and I have it still.

A tragic deed was also the elder sister, Inez. She represented – or shall I say: yet she represented? – the conservative element in the little family; being a living protest against its transplantation, against everything South German, the art-metropolis, Bohemia, her mother's evening parties. She turned her face obstinately back to the old, paternal, middle-class strictness and dignity. Still one got the impression that this conservastism was a defence mechanism against certain tensions and dangers in her own nature; though intellectually she ascribed some importance to these as well. She was more delicate in figure than Clarissa, with whom she got on very well, whereas she distinctly though unobtrusively turned away from her mother. Heavy ash-blonde hair weighed down her head, so that she held it thrust out sidewise, with extended neck. Her mouth wore a pinched smile, her nose was rather beaked; the expression of her blue eyes, blurred by the drooping lids, was weakly, dull, suspicious; it was a look of knowledge and suffering, if not without some effort at roguishness. Her upbringing had been no more than highly correct: she had spent two years in an aristocratic girls' boarding-school in Karlsruhe, patronized by the court. She occupied herself with no art or science, but laid stress on acting as daughter of the house. She read much, wrote extraordinarily literary letters 'back home' – to the past, her boarding-house mistress and earlier friends. Secretly she wrote verse. Her sister showed me one day a poem by her, called 'The Miner'. I still remember the first stanza:

> *A miner I who in the dark shaft mines*
> *Of the soul, descending fearless from the light*
> *To where the golden ore of anguish shines*
> *With fugitive priceless glimmer through the night.*

I have forgotten the rest, except the last line:

> *And never more upwards to joy I yearn.*

So much for the present about the daughters, with whom Adrian came into relations as housemates. They both looked up to him and influenced their mother to follow suit, although she found him not very 'artistic'. As for the guests of the house, some of them, including Adrian or, as the hostess said, 'our lodger, Herr Dr Leverkühn', a larger or smaller group, might be invited to supper in the Rodde dining-room, which was furnished with an oak sideboard much too monumental and richly carved for the room. Others came in at nine o'clock or later, for music, tea and talk. There were Clarissa's male and female colleagues, one or the other ardent young man who rolled his *r*'s and girls with voices placed well forwards; a couple named Knöterich – the man, Konrad Knöterich, a native of Munich, looked like a primitive

German, Sugambian or Ubian, he only lacked the bushy tuft on top. He had some vaguely artistic occupation, had probably been a painter, but now dabbled at making instruments, and played the cello wildly and inaccurately, snorting violently as he played. His wife, Natalia, also had something to do with painting; she was an exotic brunette with a trace of Spanish blood, wearing earrings and black ringlets dangling on her cheeks. Then there was a scholar, Dr Kranich, a numismatic expert, and Keeper of the Cabinet of Coins: clear, decided, cheerful and sensible in conversation, though with a hoarse asthmatic voice. There were two friends, both painters belonging to the Secession group, Leo Zink and Baptist Spengler; one an Austrian from near Bozen, a jester by social technique, an insinuating clown, who in a gentle drawl ceaselessly made fun of himself and his exaggeratedly long nose. He was a faunish type, making the women laugh with the really very droll expression of his close-set eyes – always a good opening. The other, Spengler, from central Germany, with a flourishing blond moustache, was a sceptical man of the world, with some means, no great worker, hypochondriac, well-read, always smiling and blinking rapidly as he talked. Inez Rodde mistrusted him very much – why, she did not say, but to Adrian she called him disingenuous, a sneak. Adrian said that he found Spengler intelligent and agreeable to talk to. He responded much less to the advances of another guest, who really took pains to woo Adrian's reserve and shyness. This was Rudolf Schwerdtfeger, a gifted young violinist, member of the Zapfenstösser Orchestra, which next to the Hoftheater orchestra played a prominent role in the musical life of the town and in which he was one of the first violins. Born in Dresden, but in origin low-German, of medium height and neat build, and with a shock of flaxen hair, he had the polish, the pleasing versatility of the Saxon, and was in equal measure good-natured and desirous to please. He loved society and spent all his free time in at least one but oftener two or three evening parties, blissfully absorbed in flirtation with the other sex, young girls as well as more mature women. Leo Zink and he were on a cool, sometimes even ticklish footing; I have often noticed that charmers do not appreciate each other, a fact equally applicable to masculine and to feminine conquistadores. For my part I had nothing against Schwerdtfeger, I even liked him sincerely, and his early, tragic death, which had for me its own private and peculiar horror, shook me to my depths. How clearly I still see the figure of this young man: his boyish way of shrugging up one shoulder inside his coat and drawing down one corner of his mouth in a grimace. It was further his naïve habit to watch someone talking, very tense, as it were in a fury of concentration, his lips curled, his steel-blue eyes burrowing into the speaker's face, seeming to fix now on one eye and now on the other. What good qualities too did he not have quite aside from his talent, which one might almost reckon as one of his charms! Frankness, decency, open-mindedness, an artistic integrity, indifference to money and possessions – in short, a certain cleanness; all these looked out of his – I repeat it – beautiful steel-blue eyes and shone in a face full of youthful attractiveness if just slightly like a pug dog's. He often played with the Frau Senator, who was no indifferent pianist – and this somewhat encroached upon Knöterich, who wanted to sweep his cello, whereas the company were looking forward to hearing Rudolf. His playing was neat and cultivated, his tone not large, but of beautiful sweetness and technically not a little brilliant. Seldom has one heard certain things of Vivaldi, Vieuxtemps and Spohr, the C-minor Sonata of Grieg, even the Kreutzer Sonata, and compositions by César Franck,

262 *Doctor Faustus*

more faultlessly played. With all this he was simple, untouched by letters, but concerned for the good opinion of prominent men of intellect – not only out of vanity but because he seriously set store by intercourse with them and wanted to elevate and round himself out by its means. He at once had his eye on Adrian, paid court to him, practically neglecting the ladies; consulted his judgement, asked to be accompanied – Adrian at that time always refused – showed himself eager for musical and extra-musical conversation, and was put off by nor reserve or rebuff. That may have been a sign of uncommon ingenuousness; but it displayed unselfconscious understanding and native culture as well. Once when Adrian, on account of a headache and utter distaste for society, had excused himself to the Frau Senator and remained in his room, Schwerdtfeger suddenly appeared, in his cut-away and black tie, to persuade him, ostensibly on behalf of several or all of the guests, to join them. They were so dull without him ... It was even embarrassing, on the whole, for Adrian was by no means a lively social asset. I do not know if he let himself be persuaded. Probably it was in order to win him over that Schwerdtfeger said he was voicing the wish of the company; yet my friend must have felt a certain pleasant surprise at such invincible attentiveness.

I have now rather fully introduced the personae of the Rodde salon, mere figures at present, whose acquaintance, together with other members of Munich society I later made as a professor from Freising. Rüdiger Schildknapp joined the group quite soon; Adrian's example having instructed him that one should live in Munich instead of Leipzig, he pulled himself together to act upon the conviction. The publisher of his translations from English classics had his offices in Munich, a fact of practical importance for Rüdiger; besides that he had probably missed Adrian, whom he at once began to delight with his stories about his father and his '*Besichtigen Sie jenes!*' He had taken a room in the third storey of a house in Amalienstrasse, not far from his friend; and there he now sat at his table, by nature quite exceptionally in need of fresh air, the whole winter through with wide-open windows, wrapped in mantle and plaid, vaporizing cigarettes and wrestling, half full of hatred, half passionately absorbed in his problems, and striving after the exact German value for English words, phrases, and rhythms. At midday he ate with Adrian, in the Hoftheater restaurant or in one of the *Keller* in the centre of the city; but very soon, through Leipzig connexions, he had entrée to private houses, and managed aside from evening invitations to have here and there a cover laid for him at the midday meal, perhaps after he had gone shopping with the housewife and intrigued her by a display of his lordly poverty. Such invitations came from his publisher, proprietor of the firm of Radbruch & Co. in the Fürstenstrasse; and from the Schlaginhaufens, an elderly well-to-do and childless pair, the husband of Swabian origin and a private scholar, the wife from a Munich family. They had a somewhat gloomy but splendid house in the Briennerstrasse, where their pillared salon was the meeting-place of a society of mingled aristocratic and artistic elements. Nothing better pleased the housewife, a von Plausig by birth, than to have both elements represented in the same person, as in the General-Intendant of the Royal Theatres, His Excellency von Riedesel, who was often a guest. Schildknapp also dined with the industrialist Bullinger, a rich paper-manufacturer, who occupied the *bel étage* in the block of flats built by himself in Wiedemayerstrasse on the river; with the family of a director of the Pschorrbräu joint-stock company; and in other houses.

At the Schlaginhaufens' Rüdiger had also introduced Adrian, who then, a monosyllabic stranger, met the titled stars of the artist world, the Wagner heroine Tanya Orlanda, Felix Mottl, ladies from the Bavarian court, the 'descendant of Schiller', Herr von Gleichen-Russwurm, who wrote books on cultural history; also other writers who wrote nothing at all but made themselves socially interesting as specialists in the art of conversation, superficially and without tangible results. However, it was here that Adrian made the acquaintance of Jeanette Scheurl, a woman of peculiar charm and sincerity, a good ten years older than he, daughter of a deceased Bavarian government official. Her mother was a Parisian, a paralysed old lady, confined to her chair but full of mental energy, who had never given herself the trouble of learning German. She had no need to, since French was by good fortune generally the mode and hers so to speak ran on wheels, gaining her both living and position. Mme Scheurl lived near the Botanical Gardens with her three daughters, of whom Jeanette was the eldest; their quarters were small, the atmosphere entirely Parisian. In her little salon she gave extraordinarily popular musical teas, where the exemplary organs of the court singers male and female filled the little rooms to bursting, and the blue coaches from the court often stood in front of the house.

Jeanette was a writer of novels. Grown up between two languages, she wrote ladylike and original studies of society in a charmingly incorrect idiom peculiar to herself alone. They did not lack psychological or melodic charm and were definitely a literary achievement. She noticed Adrian at once, and took to him; he, in his turn, felt at home in her presence and conversation. She was aristocratically ugly and good form, with a face like a sheep, where the high-born and the low-born met, just as in her speech her French was mingled with Bavarian dialect. She was extraordinarily intelligent and at the same time enveloped in the naïvely inquiring innocence of the spinster no longer young. Her mind had something fluttering and quaintly confused about it, at which she herself laughed more heartily than anyone else – though by no means in the fashion of Leo Zink, who laughed at himself as a parlour trick, whereas she did the same out of sheer lightness of heart and sense of fun. She was very musical, a pianist, a Chopin enthusiast, a writer on Schubert; on friendly terms with more than one bearer of a great name in the contemporary world of music. Her first conversation with Adrian had been a gratifying exchange upon the subject of Mozart's polyphony and his relations to Bach. He was and remained her attached friend for many years.

But no one will suppose that the city he had chosen to live in really took him to her bosom or ever made him her own. The beauty of the grandiose village under the melting blue of the Alpine sky, with the mountain stream rushing and rippling through it: that might please his eye; the self-indulgent comfort of its ways, the suggestion it had of all-the-year-round carnival freedom, might make even his life easier. But its spirit – *sit venia verboo!* – its atmosphere, a little mad and quite harmless; the decorative appeal to the senses, the holiday and artistic mood of this self-satisfied Capua: all that was of course foreign to the soul of a deep, stern nature like his. It was indeed the fitting and proper target for that look of his I had so long observed: veiled and cold and musingly remote, followed by the smile and averted face.

The Munich I speak of is the Munich of the late Regency, with only four years between it and the war, whose issue was to turn its pleasantness to morbidness and produce in it one sad and grotesque manifestation after another; this capital city of beautiful vistas, where political problems confined themselves to a capricious opposition between a half-separatist folk-Catholicism and the lively liberalism professed by the supporters of the Reich; Munich, with its palaces of decorative crafts, its recurring exhibitions, its *Bauern*-balls in carnival time, its seasonal '*Märzbräu*' carouses and week-long monster fair on the 'Oktoberwiese', where a stout and lusty folkishness, now long since corrupted by modern mass methods, celebrated its saturnalia; Munich, with its residuary Wagnerism, its esoteric coteries performing their aesthetic devotions behind the Siegestor; its Bohemia, well bedded down in public approval and fundamentally easy going. Adrian looked on at all that, moved in it, tasted of it, during the nine months that he spent at this time in Oberbayern – an autumn, a winter, and a spring. At the artist festivals that he attended with Schildknapp in the illusory twilight of artistically decorated ballrooms he met members of the Rodde circle, the young actors, the Knöterichs, Dr Kranich, Zink and Spengler, the daughters of the house. He sat on a table with Inez and Clarissa, Rüdiger, Spengler and Kranich, perhaps Jeanette Scheurl. And Schwerdtfeger, in peasant dress or in the Florentine *Quattrocento* which set off his handsome legs and made him look like Botticelli's youth in the red cap, would come up, dissolved in festival mirth, all intellectual elevation quite forgot, and in order to be 'nice' invite the Rodde girls to dance. 'Nice' was his favourite word: he insisted on having everything happen 'nicely' and on leaving out all that was not 'nice'. He had many obligations and pending flirtation in the room, but it would not have seemed 'nice' to him to neglect entirely the ladies of the Rambergstrasse, with whom he was on a brotherly footing. This compulsion to be 'nice' was so visible in his business-like approach that Clarissa said pertly:

'Good heavens, Rudolf, if you didn't put on the air of a knight rescuing a damsel in distress! I assure you we have danced enough, we do not need you at all.'

'Need!' he replied, with pretended anger, in his rather guttural voice. 'And the needs of my heart are not to count at all?'

'Not a brass farthing,' said she. 'Anyhow, I am too big for you.'

But she would go off with him even so, proudly tilting her insufficient chin, with no hollow under the full lip. Or it was Inez he had asked, who with pinched lips and drooping head followed him to the dance. But he was 'nice' not alone to the sisters. He kept a guard over his forgetfulness. Suddenly, especially if someone had declined to dance, he might become serious and sit down at the table with Adrian and Baptist Spengler. The latter was always in a domino, and drinking red wine. Blinking, a dimple in his cheek above the thick moustaches he would be citing the Goncourt diaries or the letters of Abbé Galiani, and Schwerdtfeger, positively furious with attention, would sit and bore his gaze into the speaker's face. Or he would talk with Adrian about the programme of the next Zapfenstösser concert; or demand, as though there were no more pressing interest or obligations anywhere, that Adrian explain and enlarge upon something that he had lately said at the Roddes' about music, about the state of the opera, or the like. He would devote himself to Adrian, take his arm and stroll with him at the edge of the crowd, round the hall, addressing him with the carnival *du*, heedless that the other did not respond. Jeanette Scheurl told me later that when Adrian once returned to the table after such a stroll, Inez Rodde said to him:

'You shouldn't give him the pleasure. He wants everything.'

'Perhaps Herr Leverkühn wants everything too,' remarked Clarissa, supporting her chin on her hand.

Adrian shrugged his shoulders.

'What he wants,' he responded, 'is that I should write a violin concerto for him with which he can be heard in the provinces.'

'Don't do it,' Clarissa said again. 'You wouldn't think of anything but prettinesses if you considered him while you were doing it.'

'You have too high an opinion of my flexibility,' he retorted, and had Baptist Spengler's bleating laugh on his side.

But enough of Adrian's participation in the Munich joy of life. Trips into the environs, justly celebrated if somewhat spoiled by mass resort, he made with Schildknapp, mostly on the latter's initiative. Even in the glittering winter they spent days in Ettal, Oberammergau, Mittenwald; and when spring came, these excursions increased, to the famous lakes and the theatrical castles built by the nation's madman. Often they went on bicycles (for Adrian loved them as a means of independent travel) at random into the greening country, lodging at night humbly or pretentiously, just as it fell out. I am reminded of the fact because it was thus that Adrian made acquaintance with the place that he later chose as the permanent setting of his life: Pfeiffering near Waldshut and the Schweigestill farm.

The little town of Waldshut, devoid of interest or charm, lies on the Garmisch-Partenkirchen line, an hour from Munich. The next station, only ten minutes farther on, is Pfeiffering or Pfeffering, where the through trains do not stop. They leave to one side the onion-shaped dome of Pfeiffering church, rising out of a landscape which at this point is in no way remarkable. Adrian and Rüdiger visited the place by mere chance. They did not even spend the night at the Schweigestills', for both had to work next morning and must take the train back from Waldshut to Munich. The had eaten their midday meal in the little square at Waldshut, and as the time-table left them some hours to spare, they rode along the tree-lined highway to Pfeiffering, pushed their bicycles through the village, inquired of a child the name of the near-by pond, and heard that it was called the Klammer; cast a glance at the tree-crowned height, the Rohmbühel, and asked for a glass of lemonade from a barefoot girl under the gate of the manor-house, which was adorned with ecclesiastical arms. They asked less from thirst than because the massive and characteristic peasant baroque structure attracted their attention. The yard dog on his chain bayed loudly, and the girl shouted at him: 'Kaschperl, hush your noise!'

I do not know how far Adrian took notice at that time; or whether it was only afterwards, gradually and from memory, that he recognized certain correspondences, transposed, as it were, into another but not far removed key. I incline to the belief that the discovery at first remained unconscious and only later, perhaps as in a dream, came to him as a surprise. At least he did not utter a syllable to Schildknapp, nor did he ever mention to me the singular correspondence. Of course I may be mistaken. Pond and hill, the gigantic old tree in the courtyard – an elm, as a matter of fact – with its round green bench, and still other details might have attracted him at his first glance; it may be no dream was needed to open his eyes. That he said nothing is of course no proof at all.

It was Frau Else Schweigestill who advanced towards the travellers with dignified tread, met them at the gate, gave a friendly ear to their wants, and made lemonade in tall glasses with long spoons. She served it in the best room, left of the entry, a sort of peasant hall, with a vaulted ceiling, a huge table, window embrasures which showed the thickness of the walls, and the Winged Victory of Samothrace in plaster above the tall, gaily painted press. There was a dark brown piano as well. The room was not used by the family,

Frau Schweigestill explained as she sat down with her guests. They sat of evenings in a smaller room diagonally opposite, near the house door. The building had much extra space; farther along on this side was another sightly room, the so-called Abbot's chamber, probably thus named because it had served as study to the head of the Augustine Order of monks, who had once presided over the place. So it had formerly been a cloister; but for three generations Schweigestills had been settled here.

Adrian mentioned that he himself was country-bred, though he had lived now for some time in towns. He inquired how much land there was and learned that there was about forty acres of ploughed land and meadow, with a wood-lot as well. The low building with the chestnut trees on the vacant space opposite the courtyard also belonged to the property. Once it had been occupied by lay brothers, now it was nearly always empty and scarcely furnished enough to live in. Summer before last a Munich painter and his wife had rented it; he wanted to make landscapes of the neighbourhood, the Waldshut moors and so on, and had done some pretty views, though rather gloomy, being painted in a dull light. Three of them had been hung in the Glaspalast, she had seen them there herself, and Herr Director Stiglmayer of the Bavarian Exchange Bank had bought one. The gentlemen were painters themselves?

She very likely mentioned the tenants in order to raise the subject and find out with whom she had to deal. When she heard that no, they were a writer and a musician, she lifted her brows respectfully and said that was more unusual and interesting. Painters were thick as blackberries. The gentlemen had seemed serious people to her, whereas painters were mostly a loose lot, without much feeling for the serious things of life – she did not mean the practical side, earning money and that, no, when she said serious she meant the dark side of life, its hardships and troubles, but she did not mean to be unfair to artists: her lodger, for instance, had been an exception to that kind of lightheaded gentry, he begin a quiet, reserved sort of man, rather lowspirited if anything – and his pictures had looked like that too, the atmosphere of the moors, and the lonely woods and meadows, yes, it was perhaps surprising that Director Stiglmayer should have bought one, the gloomiest of all, of course he was a financial man, but maybe he had a streak of melancholy himself.

She sat with them, bolt upright, her brown hair, only touched with grey, drawn smoothly away from the parting, so that you saw the white skin; in her checked apron, an oval brooch at the opening of her frock, her well-shaped, capable little hands with the plain wedding ring folded together on the table.

She liked artists, she said. Her language, seasoned with dialect, with *halt* and *fei* and *gellen's ja*, was yet not coarse. Artists were people of understanding, she thought, and understanding was the best and most important thing in life, the way artists were so lively depended on that, she would say, at bottom, there was a lively and a serious kind of understanding, and it had never come out yet which one was better, maybe the best of all was still another one, a quiet kind of understandingness, anyhow artists, of course, had to live in the towns, because that was where the culture was, that they spent their time on, but actually they belonged more with peasant folk, who lived in the middle of nature and so nearer to understanding, much more than with townspeople, because these had had their understanding stunted, or else they had smothered it up for the sake of being regular and that came to the same thing, but she did not want to be unfair to the townsfolk either, there were always exceptions, maybe one didn't always know, and Director

Stiglmayer, just to mention him again, when he bought the gloomy painting had shown he was a man of understanding, and not only artistic either.

Hereupon she offered her guests coffee and pound-cake; but Schildknapp and Adrian preferred to spend what time they had left looking at the house and grounds, if she would be so good as to show them.

'Willingly,' said she; 'only too bad my Maxl' (that was Herr Schweigestill) 'is out on the farm with Gereon, that's our son, they wanted to try a new manure-spreader Gereon bought, so the gentlemen will have to make do with me.'

They would not call that making-do, they answered, and went with her through the massively built old house. They looked at the houseplace in front, where the prevailing odour of pipe tobacco was strongest; farther back was the Abbot's room, very pleasing, not very large, and rather earlier in style than the exterior architecture of the house, nearer 1600 than 1700; wainscoted, with carpetless wooden floor and stamped leather hangings below the beamed ceiling. There were pictures of saints on the walls of the flat-arched window embrasures, and leaded windowpanes that had squares of painted glass let into them. There was a niche in the wall, with a copper water-kettle and basin, and a cupboard with wrought-iron bolts and locks. There was a corner bench with leather cushions, and a heavy oak table not far from the window, built like a chest, with deep drawers under the polished top and a sunken middle part where a carved reading-desk stood. Above it there hung down from the beamed ceiling a huge chandelier with the remains of wax candles still sticking in it, a piece of Renaissance decoration with horns, shovel-antlers, and other fantastic shapes sticking out irregularly on all sides.

The visitors praised the Abbot's room warmly. Schildknapp, with a reflective head-shake, even thought that one ought to settle down an live here; but Frau Schweigestill had her doubts whether it would not be too lonely for a writer, too far from life and culture. And she led her guests up the stairs to the upper storey, to show them a few of the numerous bedrooms, in a row on a whitewashed, musty corridor. They were furnished with bedsteads and chests in the style of the painted one below, and only a few were supplied with the towering feather beds in peasant syle. 'What a lot of rooms!' they exclaimed. Yes, they were mostly empty, replied the hostess. One or two might be occupied temporarily. For two years, until last autumn, a Baroness von Handschuchsheim had lived there and wandered about through the house: a lady of rank, whose ideas, as Frau Schweigestill expressed it, had not been able to fit in with those of the rest of the world so that she had sought refuge here from the conflict. She, Frau Else Schweigestill, had got on very well with her and liked to talk with her; had sometimes even succeeded in making her laugh at her own outlandish notions. But unfortunately it had been impossible either to do away with these or to prevent them from gaining ground; in the end the dear Baroness had had to be placed in professional care.

Frau Schweigestill came to the end of this tale as they went back down the stair again and out into the courtyard to have a glimpse of the stables. Another time, she said, before that, one of the many sleeping rooms had been occupied by a Fräulein from the best social circles who had here brought her child into the world – taking with artists she could call things, though not people, by their right names – the girl's father as a judge of the high court, up in Bayreuth, and had got himself an electric automobile and that had been the beginning of all the trouble, for he had hired a chauffeur too, to drive him to his office, and this young man, not a bit out of the common run, only very smart in his braided livery, had made the girl lose her head altogether, she had got with child by him, and when that was plain to see there had been outbreaks of rage and despair, hand-wringing and hair-tearing, cursing, wailing, berating on the part of the parents, such as one would not have dreamt possible, of understanding there had been none, either of an artistic or a natural kind, nothing but a crazy fear for their social reputation, like people in towns have, and the girl had regularly writhed on the floor before her parents, beseeching and sobbing while they shook their fists, and in the end mother and daughter fainted at the very same minute, but the high judge found his way here one day and talked with her, Frau Schweigestill, a little man with a pointed grey beard and gold eye-glasses, quite bowed with affliction and they had made up that the girl be brought to bed here secretly, and afterwards, under the pretext of anaemia, should stop on for a while. And when the high official had turned to go, he had turned round again and with tears behind his gold glasses had pressed her hand again with the words: 'Thank you, thank you, for your understanding and goodness,' but he meant understanding for the bowed-down parents, not for the girl.

She came, then, a poor thing, with her mouth always open and her eyebrows up, and while she awaited her hour she confided a good deal in Frau Schweigestill. She was entirely reasonable about her own guilt and did not pretend that she had been seduced – on the contrary, Carl, the chauffeur, had even said: 'It's no good, Fräulein, better not,' but it had been stronger than she was, and she had always been ready to pay with death, and would do, and being ready for death, so it seemed to her, made up for the whole thing, and she had been very brave when her time came, and her child, a girl, was brought into the world with the help of good Dr Kürbis, the district physician, to whom it was all one how a child came, if everything was otherwise in order an no transverse positions, but the girl had remained very weak, despite good nursing and the country air, she had never stopped holding her mouth open and her eyebrows up, and her cheeks seemed hollower than ever and after a while her little high-up father came to fetch her away and at the sight of her, tears came in his eyes behind the gold eye-glasses. The infant was sent to the Grey Sisters in Bamberg, but the mother was from then on only a very grey sister herself, with a canary-bird and a tortoise which her parents gave her out of pity, and she had just withered away in her room in a consumption, the seeds of which had probably always been in her. Finally they sent her to Davos, but that seemed to have been the finishing touch, for she died there almost at once, just as she had wished and wanted it, and if she had been right in her idea that everything had been evened up by the readiness for death, then she was quits and had got what she was after.

They visited the stables, looked at the horses and the pigsties while their hostess was talking about the girl she had sheltered. They went to look at the chickens and the bees behind the house, and then the guests asked what they owed her and were told nothing at all. They thanked her for everything and rode back to Waldshut to take their train. That the day had not been wasted and that Pfeiffering was a remarkable spot, to that they both heartily agreed.

Adrian kept the picture in his mind; but for a long time it did not determine his decisions. He wanted to go away, but farther away than an hour's journey towards the mountains. Of the music of *Love's Labour's Lost* he had written the piano sketch of the expository scenes; but then he had got stuck, the parodistic artificiality of the style was hard to keep up, needing as it did a supply of whimsicality constantly fresh and sustained. He felt a desire for more distant air, for surroundings of greater unfamiliarity. Unrest possessed him. He was tired of the family pension in Rambergstrasse; its privacy had been an uncertain quantity, people could always intrude on it. 'I am looking,' he wrote to me, 'I keep asking round about and hankering for news of a place buried from and untroubled by the world, where I could hold speech alone, with my life, my destiny ...' Strange, ominous words! Must not my hand tremble, must I not feel cold in the pit of my stomach, at thought of the meeting, the holding speech, the compact for which he, consciously or unconsciously, sought a theatre?

It was Italy on which he decided; whither he, at an unusual time for a tourist, the beginning of June and the summer, set off. He had persuaded Rüdiger Schildknapp to go with him.

Chapter Twenty-four

In the long vacation of 1912 and still from Kaisersaschern, I, with my young bride, visited Adrian and Schildknapp in the nest they had found in the Sabine Hills. It was the second summer the friends had spent there. They had wintered in Rome, and in May, as the heat strengthened, they had again sought the mountains and the same hospitable house where, in a sojourn lasting three months, they had learned to feel at home the year before.

The place was Palestrina, birthplace of the composer; ancient Praeneste, and as Penestrino citadel of the Colonna princes, mentioned by Dante in the twenty-seventh canto of the *Inferno*: a picturesque hillside settlement, reached from the church below by a lane of shallow steps, overhung by houses and not even of the cleanest. A sort of little black pig ran about on the steps, and one of the pack mules that passed up and down with its projecting load might push the unwary pedestrian to the wall. The street continued on above the village as a mountain road, past a Capuchin friary, up to the top of the hill and the acropolis, only surviving in a few ruins and the remnant of an ancient theatre. Helene and I climbed up several times to these dignified relics during our visit, whereas Adrian, who 'did not want to see anything', had never in all those months got further than the shady garden of the Capuchin friary, his favourite spot.

The Manardi house, where Adrian and Rüdiger lodged, was probably the most imposing in the place, and although the family were six in number, they easily took us in as well. It was on the lane, a sober, solid edifice, almost like a palazzo or castello, which I judged to be from about the second third of the seventeenth century, with spare decorative mouldings under the flat, slightly profiled tiled roof; it had small windows and a door decorated in early baroque style, but boarded up, with the actual door-opening cut into the boarding and furnished with a tinkling little bell. Extensive quarters had been vacated for our friends on the ground floor, consisting chiefly of a two-windowed living-room as large as a salon, with stone floors like all the rest of the house. It was shaded, cool, a little dark, and very simply furnished, with wicker chairs and horsehair sofas, and in fact so large that two people could carry on their work there separated by considerable space, neither disturbing the other. Adjoining were the roomy bedchambers, also very sparsely furnished, a third one being opened for us.

The family dining-room and the much larger kitchen, in which friends from the village were entertained, lay in the upper storey. The kitchen had a vast and gloomy chimney, hung with fabulous ladles and carving-knives and -forks which might have belonged to an ogre; while the shelves were full of copper utensils, skillets, bowls, platters, tureens, and mortars. Here Signora Manardi reigned, called Nella by her family – I believe her name was Peronella. She was a stately Roman matron, with arched upper lip, not very dark, the good eyes and hair were only chestnut brown, with at most a faint silver network on the smooth head. Her figure was full and well-proportioned, the impression she made both capable and rustically simple, as one saw her small work-hardened hands, the double widow's ring on the right one, poised on the firm strong hips, bound by their stiff apron-strings.

She had but one daughter from her marriage, Amelia, a girl of thirteen or fourteen years, inclined to weak-headedness. Amelia had a habit, at table, of moving spoons or forks to and fro in front of her eyes and repeating with a questioning intonation some word that had stuck in her mind. A little time previously an aristocratic Russian family had lodged with the Manardis, whose head, a count or prince, had been a seer of ghosts and from time to time had given the family unquiet nights, by shooting at wandering spirits who visited him in his chamber. All this naturally enough made an impression on Amelia; it was the reason why she often and insistently questioned her spoons: '*Spiriti, spiriti?*' But she could remember lesser matters as well; for instance it had happened that a German tourist had once made the mistake of saying: '*La* melona', the word being feminine in German though masculine in Italian; and now the child would sit wagging her head, following with her forlorn look the movement of her spoons and murmuring '*La melona, la melona?*' Signora Peronella and her brothers paid no heed or did not hear; such things were an everyday matter to them and only if the guest seemed put off would they smile at him, less in excuse than almost tenderly, as though the child had done something winning.

Helene and I soon got used to Amelia's uncanny murmurs; as for Adrian and Schildknapp, they were no longer conscious of them.

The housewife's brothers, of whom I spoke, were two, on older and one younger than herself: Ercolano Manardi, lawyer, mostly called *l'avvocato* for short, yet with some satisfaction too, he being the pride of the otherwise unlettered and rustic family, a man of sixty with bristling grey moustaches and a hoarse, complaining voice, which began with an effort like a donkey's bray; and Sor Alfonso, the younger, perhaps in the middle of his forties, intimately addressed by his family as Alfo, a farmer. Often, returning from our afternoon walk in the *campagna*, we saw him coming home from his fields on his little long-ears, his feet almost on the ground, under a sunshade, with blue glasses on his nose. The lawyer apparently no longer practised his profession, he only read the newspaper, read it indeed all the time; on hot days he permitted himself to do it sitting in his room in his drawers, with the door open. He drew down upon himself the disapproval of Sor Alfo, who found that the man of law – '*quest'uomo*' he called him in this connexion – took too much upon himself. Loudly, behind his brother's back he censured this provocative licence and would not be talked round by his sister's soothing words, to the effect that the advocate was a full-blooded man, in danger of a heat stroke, which made light clothing a necessity to him. Then '*quest'uomo*' should at least keep the door shut, retorted Alfo, instead of exposing himself in so *négligé* a state to the eyes of his family and the *distinti forestieri*. A higher education did not justify such offensive slackness. It was clear that a certain animosity was being expressed by the *contadino* against the educated member of the family, under a well-chosen pretext indeed – although, or even because, Sor Alfo in the depths of his heart shared the family admiration for the lawyer, whom they considered the next thing to a statesman. But the politics of the brothers were in many matters far asunder, for the advocate was of a conservative and devout cast. Alfonso on the other hand a free-thinker, *libero pensatore*, and a critical mind, hostile to Church, monarchy, and government, which he painted as permeated with scandalous corruption. '*A capito, che sacco di birbaccioni*' (did you understand what a pack of rascals they are?), he would close his indictment, much more articulately than the advocate, who after a few gasping protests would retire behind his newspaper.

A connexion of the three, brother of Signora Nella's deceased husband, Dario Manardi, a mild, grey-bearded rustic, walking with a stick, lived with his simple, ailing wife in the family house. They did their own housekeeping while Signora Peronella provided for us seven from her romantic kitchen – the brothers, Amelia, the two permanent guests, and the visiting pair – with an amplitude that bore no relation to the modest pension price. She was inexhaustible. For when we had already enjoyed a powerful minestra, larks and polenta, scallopini in Marsala, a joint of mutton or boar with compote, thereto much salad, cheese and fruit, and our friends had lighted their government-monopoly cigarettes to smoke with the black coffee, she might say as one suggesting a captivating idea: 'Signori, a little fish perhaps?' A purple country wine which the advocate drank like water, in great gulps, croaking the while – a growth too fiery really to be recommended as a table beverage twice daily, yet on the other hand a pity to water it – served to quench our thirst. The *padrona* encouraged us with the words: 'Drink, drink! *Fa sangue il vino.*' But Alfonso upbraided her, saying it was a superstition.

The afternoons were spent in beautiful walks, during which there were many hearty laughs at Rüdiger Schildknapp's Anglo-Saxon jokes; down to the valley by roads lined with mulberry bushes and out a stretch into the well-cultivated country with its olive trees and vine garlands, its tilled fields divided into small holdings separated by stone walls with almost monumental entrance gates. Shall I express how much – aside from the being with Adrian again – I enjoyed the classic sky, where during the weeks of our stay not one single cloud appeared; the antique mood that lay over the land and now and then expressed itself visibly, as for instance in the rim of a well, a picturesque shepherd, a goat's head suggestive of Pan? A smiling, slightly ironic nod was Adrian's only response to the raptures of my humanistic soul. Artists pay little heed to their surroundings so long as these bear no direct relation to their own field of work; they see in them no more than an indifferent frame, either more or less favourable to production. We looked towards the sunset as we returned to the little town, and another such splendour of the evening sky I have not seen. A golden layer, thick and rich like oil, bordered with crimson, was on the western horizon; the sight was utterly extraordinary and so beautiful that it might well exhilarate and expand the soul. So I confess I felt slightly put off when Schildknapp, gesturing towards the marvellous spectacle, shouted his '*Besichtigen Sie jenes!*' and Adrian burst out into the grateful laughter which Rüdiger humour always drew from him. For it seemed to me he seized the occasion to

laugh at Helene's and my emotion and even at the glory of nature's
magnificence as well.

I have already mentioned the garden of the cloister above the town, to
which our friends climbed every morning with their portfolios to work
apart. They had asked permission of the monks to sit there and it had been
benignly granted. We often accompanied them into the spice-scented shade
of the not-too-well-tended plot surrounded by crumbling walls, where we
would leave them to their devices and invisible to them both, who were
themselves invisible to each other, isolated by bushes of oleander, laurel,
and broom, spend the increasingly hot afternoon, Helene with her crochet-
work, I with a book, but dwelling in my thoughts on the pleasurable
excitement of the knowledge that Adrian was working on his opera close by.

On the badly out-of-tune square piano in the friends' living-room he
played to us once during our stay – unfortunately only once – from the
completed sections, mostly already scored for a specially chosen orchestra,
of the 'pleasant well-conceited comedy *Love's Labour's Lost*', as the piece was
called in 1598. He played characteristic passages and a few complete scene
sequences: the first act, including the scene outside Armado's house, and
several later numbers which he had partly anticipated: in particular Biron's
monologues, which he had had especially in mind for the first, the one in
verse at the end of the third act, as well as the prose one in the fourth: 'They
have pitched a toil, I am toiling in a pitch – pitch that defiles'; which, while
always preserving the atmosphere of the comic and grotesque, expresses
musically still better than the first the deep and genuine despair of the young
man over his surrender to the suspect black beauty, his raging abandonment
of self-mockery: 'By the Lord, this love is as mad as Ajax; it kills sheep; it
kills me, I a sheep': this partly because the swift-moving, unjointed,
ejaculatory prose, with its many plays on words, inspired the composer to
invent musical accents of quite peculiar fantasticality; partly, also, because
in music the repetition of the significant and already familiar, the suggestive
or subtle invention, always makes the strongest and most speaking impression. And in the second monologue elements of the first are thus
delightfully recalled to the mind. This was true above all for the embittered
self-castigation of the heart because of its infatuation with the 'whitely
wanton with a velvet brow, with two pitch-balls stuck in her face for eyes',
and again quite particularly for the musical picture of these beloved
accursed eyes: a melisma darkly flashing out of the sound of combined cellos
and flutes, half lyrically passionate and half burlesque, which in the prose, at
the place 'O, but her eye – by this light, but for her eye, I would not love her',
recurs in a wildly caricatured way, where the darkness of the eyes is
intensified by the pitch, but the lightning flash of them is this time given to
the piccolo.

There can be no doubt that the strangely insistent and even unnecessary,
dramatically little justified characterization of Rosaline as a faithless,
wanton, dangerous piece of female flesh – a description given to her only in
Biron's speeches, whereas in the actual setting of the comedy she is no more
than pert and witty – there can be no doubt that this characterization springs
from a compulsion, heedless of artistic indiscrepancies, on the poet's part, an
urge to bring in his own experiences and, whether it fits or not, to take poetic
revenge for them. Rosaline, as the lover never tires of portraying her, is the
dark lady of the second sonnet sequence, Elizabeth's maid of honour,
Shakespeare's love, who betrayed him with the lovely youth. And the 'part
of my rhyme and here my melancholy' with which Biron appears on the

stage for the prose monologue ('Well, she hath one o' my sonnets already') is one of those which Shakespeare addressed to this black and whitely beauty. And how does Rosaline come to apply to the sharp-tongued, merry Biron of the play such wisdom as:

> *The blood of youth burns not with such excess*
> *As gravity's revolt to wantonness?*

For he is young and not at all grave, and by no means the person who could give occasion to such a comment as that it is lamentable when wise men turn fools and apply all their wit to give folly the appearance of worth. In the mouth of Rosaline and her friends Biron falls quite out of his role; he is no longer Biron, but Shakespeare in his unhappy affair with the dark lady; and Adrian, who had the sonnets, that profoundly extraordinary trio of poet, friend, and beloved, always by him in an English pocket edition, had been from the beginning at pains to assimilate the character of his Biron to this particular and favourite dialogue and to give him a music which, in suitable proportion to the burlesquing style of the whole, makes him 'grave' and intellectually considerable, a genuine sacrifice to a shameful passion.

That was beautiful, and I praised it highly. And how much reason there was besides for praise and joyful amaze in what he played to us! One could say in earnest what the learned hair-splitter Holofernes says of himself: 'This is a gift that I have, simple, simple: a foolish extravagant spirit, full of forms, figures, shapes, objects, ideas, apprehensions, motions, revolutions: these are begot in the ventricle of memory, nourished in the womb of pia mater, and delivered upon the mellowing of occasion.' Wonderful! In a quite incidental, a ludicrous setting the poet there gives an incomparably full description of the artist essence, and involuntarily one referred it to the mind that was here at work to transfer Shakespeare's satirical youthful work into the sphere of music.

Shall I completely pass over the little hurt feeling, the sense of being slighted, which I felt on the score of the subject itself, the mockery of classical studies, which in the play appear as ascetic preciosity! Of the caricature of humanism not Adrian but Shakespeare was guilty, and from Shakespeare too come the ideas wrenched out of their order in which the conceptions 'culture' and 'barbarism' play such a singular role. That is intellectual monkishness, a learned over-refinement deeply contemptuous of life and nature both, which sees the barbaric precisely in life and nature, in directness, inhumanity, feeling. Biron himself, who puts in some good words for nature to the sworn *précieux* of the groves of academe, admits that he has 'for barbarism spoke more than for that angel knowledge you can say.' The angel knowledge is indeed made ridiculous, but again only through the ridiculous; for the 'barbarism' into which the group falls back, the sonnet-drunk infatuation that is laid upon them as a punishment for their disastrous alliance, is caricature too, in brilliant style, love-persiflage; and only too well did Adrian's music see to it that in the end feeling came no better off than the arrogant forswearing of it. Music, so I felt, was by its very nature called to lead men out of the sphere of absurd artificiality into fresh air, into the world of nature and humanity. But it refrained. That which the noble Biron calls barbarism, that is to say the spontaneous and natural, celebrates here no triumph.

As art this music of my friend was admirable indeed. Contemptuous of a mass display, he had originally wanted to score for the classical Beethoven orchestra; and only for the sake of the bombastic and absurd figure of the

Spaniard Armado had he introduced a second pair of horns, three trombones, and a bass tuba. But everything was in strict chamber-music style, a delicate airy filigree, a clever parody in notes, ingenious and humoristic, rich in subtle, high-spirited ideas. A music-lover who had tired of romantic democracy and popular moral harangues and demanded an art for art's sake, an ambitionless – or in the most exclusive sense ambitious – art for artists and connoisseurs, must have been ravished by this self-centred and completely cool esoteric; but which now, as esoteric, in the spirit of the piece in every way mocked and parodistically exaggerated itself, thus mixing into its ravishment a grain of hopelessness, a drop of melancholy.

Yes, admiration and sadness mingled strangely as I contemplated this music. 'How beautiful!' the heart said to itself – mine at least said so – 'and how sad!' The admiration was due to a witty and melancholy work of art, an intellectual achievement which deserved the name of heroic, something just barely possible, behaving like arrogant travesty. I know not how otherwise to characterize it than by calling it a tense, sustained, neck-breaking game played by art at the edge of impossibility. It was just this that made one sad. But admiration and sadness, admiration and doubt, is that not almost the definition of love? It was with a strained and painful love for him and what was his that I listened to Adrian's performance. I could not say much; Schildknapp, who always made a very good, receptive audience, expressed the right things much more glibly and intelligently than I. Even afterwards, at dinner, I sat benumbed and absent at the Manardi table, moved by feelings with which the music we had heard so fully corresponded. '*Bevi, bevi!*' said the padrona. '*Fa sangue il vino!*' And Amelia moved her spoons to and fro before her face and murmured: '*Spiriti? Spiriti?*'

This evening was one of the last which we, my good wife and I, spent with the two friends in their novel quarters. A few days later, after a stay of three weeks, we had to leave and begin the return journey to Germany. The others for months still, on into the autumn, remained true to the idyllic uniformity of their existence between cloister garden, family table, *campagna* framed in rich gold, and stone-floored study, where they spent the evenings by lamplight. So it had the whole of the summer before, and their winter way of life in the town had not been essentially different. They lived in via Torre Argentina, near the Teatro Costanzi and the Pantheon, three flights up, with a landlady who gave them breakfast and luncheon. In a near-by *trattoria* they took their dinner at charge of a monthly sum. The role of the cloister garden of Palestrina was played in Rome by the Villa Doria Pamfili, where on warm spring and autumn days they pursued their labours beside a classically lovely fountain where from time to time a roving and pasturing cow or horse came to drink. Adrian seldom failed the afternoon municipal concerts in Piazza Colonna. On occasion there was an evening of opera; as a rule they spent it quietly playing dominoes over a glass of hot orange punch, in a quiet corner of some café.

More extended society than this they had none – or as good as none. Their isolation was almost as complete in Rome as in the country. The German element they avoided entirely – Schildknapp invariably took to flight so soon as a sound of his mother tongue struck on his ear. He was quite capable of getting out of an omnibus or train when there were 'Germans' in it. But their solitary way of life – solitary *à deux*, it is true – gave little opportunity to make even Italian friends. Twice during the winter they were invited by a lady of indefinite origins who patronized art and artists, Mme de Coniar, to whom Rüdiger Schildknapp had a Munich letter of introduction. In her home on the Corso, decorated with personally signed photographs in plush and silver frames, they met hordes of international artists, theatre people, painters, musicians, Polish, Hungarians, French, also Italians; but individual persons they soon lost sight of. Sometimes Schildknapp separated from Adrian to drink malmsey with young Britishers into whose arms his English predilection had driven him; to make excursions to Tivoli or the Trappist monastery at Quattro Fontane, to consume eucalyptus brandy and talk nonsense with them as a relief from the consuming difficulties of the art of translation.

In short, in town as in the isolation of the country village, the two led a life remote from the world and mankind, entirely taken up by the cares of their work. At least one can so express it. And shall I say that the departure from the Manardi house, however unwillingly I now as always left Adrian's side, was accompanied with a certain private feeling of relief? To utter it is equivalent to the obligation of justifying the feeling, and that is hard to do without putting myself and others in a somewhat laughable light. The truth is: in a certain point, *in puncto puncti* as young people like to say, I formed in the company a somewhat comic exception and fell so to speak out of the frame; namely, in my quality and way of life as a benedict, which paid tribute to what we half excusingly, half glorifyingly called 'nature'. Nobody else in the castello-house on the terraced lane did so. Our excellent hostess, Signora Peronella, had been a widow for years, her daughter Amelia was a half-idiot child. The brothers Manardi, lawyer and peasant, seemed to be hardened bachelors, yes, one could imagine that neither of them had ever laid a finger on a woman. There was Cousin Dario, grey and mild, with a tiny, ailing little wife, a pair whose love could certainly be interpreted only in the *caritas* sense of the word. And finally there were Adrian and Rüdiger Schildknapp, who spent month after month in this austere and peaceful circle that we had learned to know, living not otherwise than did the cloistered monks above. Would not that, for me, the ordinary man, have something mortifying and depressing about it?

Of Schildknapp's particular relation to the wide world of possibilities for happiness, and of his tendency to be sparing with them, as he was sparing with himself, I have spoken before. I saw in it the key to his way of life, it served me as explanation for the fact, otherwise hard for me to understand, that he succeeded in it. It was otherwise with Adrian, although I felt certain that this community of chastity was the basis of their friendship, or if the word is too strong, their life together. I suspect that I have not succeeded in hiding from the reader a certain jealousy of the Silesian's relations with Adrian; if so, he may also understand that it was this life in common, this bond of continence, with which after all my jealousy had to do.

If Schildknapp, let us say, lived as a roué of the potentialities, Adrian – I could not doubt it – since that journey to Graz or otherwise Pressburg, lived the life of a saint – as indeed he had done up to then. But now I trembled at the thought that his chastity since then, since that embrace, since his passing contagion and the loss of his physicians, sprang no longer from the ethos of purity but from the pathos of impurity.

There had always been in his nature something of *noli me tangere*. I knew that; his distaste for the too great physical nearness of people, his dislike of 'getting in each other's steam', his avoidance of physical contact, were familiar to me. He was in the real sense of the word a man of disinclination, avoidance, reserve, aloofness. Physical cordialities seemed quite impossible to associate with his nature, even his handshake was infrequent and hastily performed. More plainly than ever this characteristic came out during my visit and to me, I cannot say why, it was as though the 'Touch me not!' the 'three paces off', had to some extent altered its meaning, as though it were not so much that an advance was discouraged as that an advance from the other side was shrunk from and avoided – and this, undoubtedly, was connected with his abstention from women.

Only a friendship as keen-eyed and penetrating as mine could feel or divine such a change of significance; and may God keep me from letting my pleasure in Adrian's company be affected thereby! What was going on in him could shatter me but never sever me from him. There are people with whom it is not easy to live; but to leave impossible.

Chapter Twenty-five

The document to which repeated reference has been made in these pages, Adrian's secret record, since his demise in my possession and guarded like a frightful and precious tresure, here it is, I offer it herewith. The biographical moment has come. And accordingly I myself must cease to speak, since in spirit I have turned my back on his deliberately chosen refuge, shared with the Silesian, where I had sought him out. In this twenty-fifth chapter the reader hears Adrian's voice direct.

But is it only his? This is a dialogue which lies before us. Another, quite other, quite frightfully other, is the principal speaker, and the writer, in his stone-floored living-room, only writes down what he heard from that other. A dialogue? Is it really a dialogue? I should be mad to believe it. And therefore I cannot believe that in the depths of his soul Adrian himself considered to be actual that which he saw and heard – either while he heard and saw it or afterwards, when he put it on paper; notwithstanding the cynicisms with which his interlocutor sought to convince him of his objective presence. But if he was not there, that visitor – and I shudder at the admission which lies in the very words, seeming even conditionally and as a possibility to entertain his actuality – then it is horrible to think that those cynicisms too, those jeerings and jugglings, came out of the afflicted one's own soul . . .

It goes without saying that I have no idea of turning over Adrian's manuscript to the printer. With my own hand I will transcribe it word for word in my text from the music-paper covered with his script, which I characterized earlier in these memoirs: his small, old-fashioned, florid, very black round-hand, the writing of a scribe, a monk, one might say. He used his music notepaper obviously because no other was at hand at the moment, or because the little shop down in the Piazza St Agapitus had no proper writing-paper. There are always two lines on the upper five-line system and two on the bass; the white spaces in between are covered throughout with two lines each.

Not with entire definiteness can the time of writing be made out, for the document bears no date. If my conviction is worth anything, it was certainly not written after our visit to the mountain village or during our stay there. Either it comes from earlier in the summer, of which we spent three weeks with the friends, or it dates from the summer before, the first they spent as guests of the Manardis. That at the time we were there the experience which is the basis of the manuscript lay already in the past; that Adrian at that time had already had the conversation which follows, amounts with me to a certainty; so does it that he wrote it down at once after the event, presumably the very next day.

So now I copy it down – and I fear that no distant explosions jarring my retreat will be needed to make my hand shake as I write and my letters to be ill-formed.

Whist, mum's the word. And certes I schal be mum, will hold my tunge, were it sheerly out of shame, to spare folkes feelings, for social considerations forsooth! Am firmly minded to keep fast hold on reason and decency, not giving way even up till the end. But seen Him I have, at last, at last. He was with me, here in this hall, He sought me out; unexpected, yet long expected. I held plenteous parley with Him, and now thereafter I am vexed but sith I am not certain whereat I did shake all the whole time: an 'twere at the cold, or at Him. Did I beguile myself, or He me, that it was cold, so I might quake and thereby certify myself that He was there, Himself in person? For verily no man but knows he is a fool which quaketh at his proper brain-maggot; for sooner is such welcome to him and he yieldeth without or shaking or quaking thereunto. Mayhap He did but delude me, making out by the brutish cold I was no fool and He no figment, since I a fool did quake before Him? He is a wily-pie.

Natheles I will be mum, will hold my tonge and mumchance hide all down here on my music-paper, whiles my old jester-fere *in eremo*, far away in the hall, travails and toils to turn the loved outlandish into the loathed mother tongue. He weens that I compose, and were he to see that I write words, would but deem Beethoven did so too.

All the whole day, poor wretch, I had lien in the dark with irksome mygrym, retching and spewing, as happeth with the severer seizures. But at eventide quite suddenly came unexpected betterment. I could keep down the soup the Mother brought me (*'Poveretto!'*); with good cheer drank a glass of *rosso* (*'Bevi! bevi!'*) and on a sudden felt so staunch as to allow myself a cigarette. I could even have gone out, as had been arranged the day before. Dario M. wanted to take us down to his club and introduce us to the better sort of Praenestensians, show us reading-room, billiard-room, and about the place. We had no heart to offend the good soul, but it came down to Sch. going alone, I being forgiven due to my attack. From *pranzo* he stalked off with a sour countenance, down the street at Dario's side to the farmers and philistines, and I stopped by myself.

I sate alone here, by my lamp, nigh to the windows with shutters closed, before me the length of the hall, and read Kirkegaard on Mozart's *Don Juan*.

Then in a clap I am stricken by a cutting cold, even as though I sat in a winter-warm room and a window had blown open towards the frost. It came not from behind me, where the windows lie; it falls on me from in front. I start up from my boke and look abroad into the hall, belike Sch. is come back for I am no more alone. There is some bodye there in the mirk, sitting on the horse-hair sofa that stands almost in the myddes of the room, nigher the door, with the table and chairs, where we eat our breakfasts. Sitting in the sofa-corner with legs crossed; not Sch., but another, smaller than he, in no wise so imposing and not in truth a gentilman at all. But the cold keeps percing me.

'Chi e costà?' is what I shout with some catch in my throat, propping my

hands on the chair-arms, in such wise that the book falls from my knees to the floore. Answers the quiet, slow voice of the other, a voice that sounds trained, with pleasing nasal resonance:
'Speak only German! Only good German without feignedness or dissimulation. I understand it. It happens to be just precisely my favoured language. Whiles I understand only German. But fet thee a cloak, a hat and rug. Thou art cold. And quiver and shake thou wilt, even though not taking a cold.'
'Who says *thou* to me?' I ask, chafing.
'I,' he says. 'I, by your leave. Oh, thou meanest because thou sayst to nobody thou, not even to thy jester gentilman, but only to the trusty playfere, he who clepes thee by the first name but not thou him. No, matter. There is already enough between us for us to say thou. Well then: wilt fet thyself some warm garment?'
I stare into the half-light, fix him angrily in mine eye. A man: rather spindling, not nearly so tall as Sch., smaller even then I. A sports cap over one ear, on the other side reddish hair standing up from the temple; reddish lashes and pink eyes, a cheesy face, a drooping nose with wry tip. Over diagonal-striped tricot shirt a chequer jacket; sleeves too short, with sausage-fingers coming too far out; breeches indecently tight, worn-down yellow shoes. An ugly customer, a bully, a *strizzi*, a rough. And with an actor's voice and eloquence.
'Well?' he says again.
'First and foremost I fain would know,' say I in quaking calm, 'who is bold enough to force himself in to sit down here with me.'
'First and foremost,' he repeats. 'First and foremost is not bad at all. But you are oversensitive to any visit you hold to be unexpected and undesired. I am no flattering claw-back come to fetch you into company, to woo you that you may join the musical circle; but to talk over our affairs. Wilt fetch thy things? It is ill talking with teeth chattering.'
I sat a few seconds longer, not taking my eyes off him. And the cutting cold, coming from him, rushes at me, so that I feel bare and bald before it in my light suit. So I go. Verily I stand up and pass through the next door to the left, where my bedchamber is (the other's being further down on the same side), take my winter cloke out of the presse that I wear in Rome on *tramontana* days and it had to come along as I wist not where I might leave it else; put my hat on too, take my rug and so furnished go back to my place.
There he still sits in his, just as I left him.
'Ye're still there,' say I, turning up my coat-collar and wrapping my plaid about my knees – 'even after I've gone and come back? I marvel at it. For I've a strong suspicion y'are not there at all.'
'No?' he asks in his trained voice, with nasal resonance. 'For why?'   I:
'Because it is nothing likely that a man should seat himself here with me of an evening, speaking German and giving out cold, with pretence to discuss with me gear whereof I wot nor would wot naught. Miche more like is it I am waxing sicke and transferring to your form the chills and fever against the which I am wrapped, sneaped by frost, and in the beholding of you see but the source of it.'
He (quietly and convincingly laughing, like an actor): 'Tillyvally, what learned gibberidge you talk! In good playne old German, tis fond and frantick. And so artificial! A clever artifice, an 'twere stolen from thine own opera! But we make no music here, at the moment. Moreover it is pure hypochondria. Don't imagine any infirmities! Have a little pride and don't lose grip of yourself! There's no sickness breaking out, after the slight attack

you are in the best of youthful health. But I cry you mercy, I would not be tactless, for what is health? Thuswise, my goodly fere, your sickness does not break out. You have not a trace of fever and no occasion wherefore you should ever have any.'

I: 'Further, because with every third word ye utter you uncover your nothingness. You say nothing save things that are in me and come out of me but not out of you. You jape old Kumpf with turns of phrase yet look not as though you ever had been in academie or higher school or ever sat next to me on the scorner's bench. You talk of the needy gentilman and of him to whom I speak in the singular number, and even of such as have done so and reaped but little thank. And of my opera you speak too. Whence could you know all that?'

He (laughs again his practised laugh, shaking his head as at some priceless childishness): 'Yea, whence? But see, I do know it. And you will conclude therefrom to your own discredit that you do not see aright? That were truly to set all logick upsodown, as one learns at the schools. 'Twere better to conclude, not that I am not here in the flesh, but that I, here in my person, am also he for whom you have taken me all the whole time.'

I: 'And for whom do I take you?'

He (politely reproachful): 'Tut, tut! Do not lain it thus, as though you had not been long since expecting me! You wit aswel as I that our relation demands a dispicion. If I am – and that I ween you do now admit – then I can be but One. Or do you mean, what I hyght? But you can still recall all the scurrile nicknames from the schoole, from your first studies, when you had not put the Good Boke out of the door and under the bench. You have them all at your fingers' ends, you may elect one – I have scant others, they are well-nigh all nicknames, with the which people, so to speke, chuck me under the chin: that comes from my good sound German popularity. A man is gratified by popularity, I trow, even when he has not sought it out and at bottom is convinced that it rests on false understanding. It is always flattering, always does a bodye good. Choose one yourself, if you would call me by name, although you commonly do not call people by name at all; for lack of interest you do not know what they hight. But choose any one you list among the pet names the peasants give me. Only one I cannot and will not abide because it is distinctly a malicious slander and fits me not a whit. Whosoever calls me *Dicis et non facis* is in the wrong box. It too may even be a finger chucking my chin, but it is a calumny. I do ywisse that I say, keep my promise to a tittle; that is precisely my business principle, more or less as the Jews are the most reliable dealers, and when it comes to deceit, well, it is a common saying that it was always I, who believe in good faith and rightwiseness, who am beguiled.'

I: '*Dicis et non es.* Ye would forsoothe sit there against me on the sofa and speak outwardly to me in good Kumpfish, in old-German snatches? Ye would visit me deliberately here in Italy of all places, where you are entirely out of your sphere and not on the peasant tongue at all? What an absurd want of style! In Kaisersaschern I could have suffered it. At Wittenberg or on the Wartburg, even in Leipzig you would have been credible to me. But not here under this pagan and Catholic sky!'

He (shaking his head and pained clucking with his tongue): 'Tch, tch, tch! always this same distrust, this same lack of self-confidence! If you had the courage to say unto yourself: "Where I am, there is Kaisersaschern" – well and good, the thing would be in frame, the Herr aestheticus would needs moan no more over lack of style. Cocksblood! You would have the right to speak like that, yet you just haven't the courage or you act as though you lacked it. Self-belittlement, my friend – and you underestimate me too, if you limit me thuswise and try to make a German provincial of me. I am in fact German. German to the core, yet even so in an older, better way, to wit cosmopolitan from my heart. Wouldst deny me away, wouldst refuse to consider the old German romantic wander-urge and yearning after the fair land of Italy! German I am, but that I should once in good Düreresque style freeze and shiver after the sun, that Your Excellency will not grant me – not even when quite aside from the sun, I have delicate and urgent business here, with a fine, well-created human being ...'

Here an unspeakable disgust came over me, so that I shuddered violently. But there was no real difference between the grounds of my shudder; it might be at one and the same time for cold, too; the draught from him had got abruptly stronger, so that it went through my overcoat and pierced me to my marrow. Angrily I ask:

'Cannot you away with this nuisance, this icy draught?'

He: 'Alas no, I regret not to be able to gratify you. But the fact is, I *am* cold. How otherwise could I hold out and find it possible to dwell where I dwell?'

I (involuntary): 'You mean in the brenning pit of fier?'

He (laughs as though tickled): 'Capital! Said in the good robust and merry German way. It has indeed many other pretty names, scholarly, pathetical, the Herr Doctor ex-Theologus knows them all, as *carcer, exitium, confutatio, pernicies, condemnatio,* and so on. But there is no remedy, the familiar German, the comic ones are still my favourites. However, let us for the nonce leave that place and the nature of it. I see by your face, you are at the point of asking about it; but that is far off, not in the least a brenning question – you will forgive me the bourd, that it is not brenning! There is time for it, plenteous, boundless time – time is the actual thing, the best we give, and our gift the houre-glass – it is so fine, the little neck, through which the red sand runs, a threadlike trickle, does not minish at all to the eye in the upper cavitie, save at the very end; then it does seem to speed and to have gone fast. But that is so far away, the narrow part, it is not worth talking or thinking about. Albeit inasmuch as the glass is set and the sand has begun to run; for this reason, my good man, I would fain come to an understanding with you.'

I (full scornfully): 'Extraordinarily Dürerish. You love it. First "how will I shiver after the sun"; and then the houre-glasse of the *Melancolia.* Is the magic square coming too? I am prepared for everything, can get used to everything. Get used to your shamelessness, your thee-ing and thou-ing and trusty fere-ing, which soothly always go particularly against the wood. After all I say "thou" only to myself, which of likelihood explains why you do. According to you I am speaking with black Kaspar, which is one of the names, and so Kaspar and Samiel are one and the same.'

He: 'Off you go again!'

I: 'Samiel, It giveth a man to laugh. Where then is your C-minor fortissimo of stringed tremoli, wood and trombones, ingenious bug to fright children, the romantic public, coming out of the F-sharp minor of the Glen as you out of your abyss – I wonder I hear it not!'

He: 'Let that be. We have many a lovelier instrument and you shall hear them. We shall play for you, when you be ripe to hear. Everything is a matter of ripeness and of dear time. Just that I would speak of with you. But Samiel – that's a folish form. I am all for that is of the folk; but Samiel, too foolish,

Johann Ballhorn from Lübeck corrected it. Sammael it is. And what signifies Sammael?'

I (defiant, do not answer).

He: 'What, ne'er a word but mum? I like the discreet way in which you leave me to put it in German. It means angel of death.'

I (between my teeth, which will not stay properly closed): 'Yes, distinctly, that is what you look like! Just like unto an angel, exactly. Do you know how you look? Common is not the word for it. Like some shameless scum, a lewd losel, a make-bate, that is how you look, how you have found good to visit me – and no angel!'

He (looking down at himself, with his arms stretched out): 'How then, how then? How do I look? No, it is really good that you ask me if I wot how I look, for by my troth I wot not. Or wist not, you called it to my attention. Be sure, I reck nothing at all to my outward appearance. I leave it so to say to itself. It is sheer chance how I look, or rather, it comes out like that, it happeth like that according to the circumstances, without my taking heed. Adaptation, mimicry, you know it, of course. Mummery and jugglery of mother Nature, who always has her tongue in her cheek. But you won't, my good fere, refer the adaptation, about which I know just as much and as little as the leaf butterfly, to yourself, and take it ill of me. You must admit that from the other side it has something suitable about it – on that side where you got it from, and indeed forewarned, from the side of your pretty song with the letter symbol – oh, really ingeniously done, and almost as though by inspiration:

> *When once thou gavest to me*
> *At night the cooling draught,*
> *With poison didst undo me*
>
> *Then on the wound the serpent*
> *Fastened and firmly sucked –*

Really gifted. That is what we recognized betimes and why from early on we had an eye on you – we saw that your case was quite definitely worth the trouble, that it was a case of the most favourable situation, whereof with only a little of our fire lighted under it, only a little heating, elation, intoxication, something brilliant could be brought out. Did not Bismarck say something about the Germans needing half a bottle of champagne to arrive at their normal height? Meseems he said something of the sort. And that of right. Gifted but halt is the German – gifted enough to be angry with his paralysis, and to overcome it by hand-over-head illumination. You, my good man, well knew what you needed, and took the right road when you made your journey and *salva venia* summoned your French beloved to you.'

'Hold thy tongue!'

'Hold thy tongue? We are coming on. We wax warm. At last you drop the polite plural number and say "thou", as it should be between people who are in league and contract for time and eternity.'

'Will ye hold your tongue still?'

'Still? But we have been still for nigh five years and must after all sometime hold parley and advise over the whole and over the interesting situation wherein you find yourself. This is naturally a thing to keep wry about, but after all not at the length – when the houre-glasse is set, the red sand has begun to run through the fine-fine neck – ah, but only just begun! It is still almost nothing, what lies underneath, by comparison with all there is on top; we give time, plenteous time, abundant time by the eye, the end whereof we do not need to consider, not for a long time yet, nor need to trouble yet awhile even of the point of time where you could begin to take heed to the ending, where it might come to '*Respice finem*'. Sithence it is a variable point, left to caprice and temper, and nobody knows where it should begin, and how nigh to the end one should lay it out. This is a good bourd and capital arrangement: the uncertainty and the free choice of the moment when the time is come to heed the eynde, overcasts in mist and jest the view of the appointed limit.'

'Fables, fantasies!'

'Get along, one cannot please you, even against my psychology you are harsh – albeit you yourself on your Mount Zion at home called psychology a nice, neutral middle point and psychologists the most truth-loving people. I fable not a whit when I speak of the given time and the appointed end; I speak entirely to the point. Wheresoever the houre-glasse is set up and time fixed, unthinkable yet measured time and a fixed end, there we are in the field, there we are in clover. Time we sell – let us say twenty-four years – can we see to the end of that? Is it a good solid amount? Therewith a man can live at rack and manger like a lord and astonish the world as a great nigromancer with much divel's work; the lenger it goes on, the more forget all paralysis and in highly illuminated state rise out of himselfe, yet never transcend but remain the same, though raised to his proper stature by the half-bottle of champagne. In drunken bliss he savours all the rapture of an almost unbearable draught, til he may with more or less of right be convinced that a like infusion has not been in a thousand years and in certain abandoned moments may simply hold himself a god. How will such an one come to think about the point of time when it is become time to give heed to the end! Only, the end is ours, at the end he is ours, that has to be agreed on, and not merely silently, how silent so ever it be else, but from man to man and expressly.'

I: 'So you would sell me time?'

He: 'Time? Simple time? No, my dear fere, that is not devyll's ware. For that we should not earn the reward, namely that the end belongs to us. What manner of time, that is the heart of the matter! Great time, mad time, quite bedivelled time, in which the fun waxes fast and furious, with heaven-high leaping and springing – and again, of course, a bit miserable, very miserable indeed, I not only admit that, I even emphasize it, with pride, for it is sitting and fit, such is artist-way and artist-nature. That, as is well known, is given at all times to excess on both sides and is in quite normal way a bit excessive. Alway the pendulum swings very wide to and fro between high spirits and melancholia, that is usual, is so to speak still according to moderate bourgeois Nueremberg way, in comparison with that which we purvey. For we purvey the uttermost in this direction; we purvey towering flights and illuminations, experiences of upliftings and unfetterings, of freedom, certainty, facility, feeling of power and triumph, that our man does not trust his wits – counting in besides the colossal admiration for the made thing, which could soon bring him to renounce every outside, foreign admiration – the thrills of self-veneration, yes, of exquisite horror of himself, in which he appears to himself like an inspired mouthpiece, as a godlike monster. And correspondingly deep, honourably deep, doth he sink in between-time, not only into void and desolation and unfruitful melancholy but also into pains and sicknesse – familiar incidentally, which had alway been there, which belong to his character, yet which are only most honorably enhanced by the

illumination and the well-knowen "sack of heyre". Those are pains which a
man gladly pays, with pleasure and pride, for what he has so much enjoyed,
pains which he knows from the fairy-tale, the pains which the little sea-
maid, as from sharp knives, had in her beautiful human legs she got herself
instead of her tail. You know Andersen's Little Sea-maid? She would be a
sweetheart for you! Just say the word and I will bring her to your couch.'

I: 'If you could just keep quiet, prating jackanapes that you are!'

He: 'How now! Need you always make a rude answer? Always you expect
me to be still. But silence is not my motto, I do not belong to the
Schweigestill family. And Mother Else, anyhow, has prattled in all proper
discretion no end to you about her odd occasional guests. Neither am I come
hither for the sake of silence to a pagan foreign land; but rather for express
confirmation between us two and a firm contract upon payment against
completion. I tell you, we have been silent more than four years – and now
everything is taking the finest, most exquisite, most promising course, and
the bell is now half cast. Shall I tell you how it stands and what is afoot?'

I: 'It well appeareth I must listen.'

He: 'Wouldst like to besides, and art well content that thou canst hear. I
trow forsooth you are on edge to hear and would grumble and growl an I
kept it back, and that of right too. It is such a snug, familiar world wherein
we are together, thou and I – we are right at home therein, pure
Kaisersaschern, good old German air, from anno MD or thereabouts,
shortly before Dr Martinus came, who stood on such stout and sturdy
footing with me and threw the roll, no, I mean the ink-pot at me, long before
the thirty years' frolic. Bethink thee what lively movement of the people was
with you in Germany's midst, on the Rhine and all over, how full of agitation
and unrest, anxiety, presentiments; what press of pilgrims to the Sacred
Blood at Niklashausen in the Tauberthal, what children's crusades,
bleeding of the Host, famine, Peasants' League, war, the pest at Cologne,
meteors, comets, and great omens, nuns with the stigmata, miraculous
crosses on men's garments, and that amazing standard of the maiden's shift
with the Cross, whereunder to march against the Turk! Good time,
divellishly German time! Don't you feel all warm and snug at the memory?
There the right planets come together in the sign of the Scorpion, as Master
Dürer has eruditely drawn in the medical broadsheet, there came the tender
little ones, the swarms of animated corkscrews, the loving guests from the
West Indies into the German lands, the flagellants – ah, now you listen! As
though I spake of the marching guild of penitents, the Flagellants, who
flailed for their own and all other sins. But I mean those flagellates, the
invisible tiny ones, the kind that have scourges, like our pale Venus, the
spirochaeta pallida, that is the true sort. But th'art right, it sounds so
comfortingly like the depths of Middle Ages and the *flagellum haereticorum
fascinariorum*. Yea, verily, as *fascinarii* they may well shew themselves, our
devotees, in the better cases, as in yours. They are moreover quite civilized
and domesticated long since, and in old countries where they have been so
many hundred years at home, they do not play such merry pranks and coarse
preposterous jokes as erstwhile, with running sore and plague and worm-
eaten nose. Baptist Spengler the painter does not look as though he, his body
wrapped up in hair, would have to shake the warning rattle withersoever he
went.'

I: 'Is he like that – Spengler?'

He: 'Why not? I suppose you think you are the only one in like case? I
know thou haddest thine liefer quite by thyself and art vexed at any

comparison. My dear fellow, a man always has a great many companions. Spengler, of course is an Esmeraldus. It is not without reason that he blinks, so sly and shamefast, and not for nothing does Inez Rodde call him a sneak. So it is: Leo Zink, the *Faunus ficarius*, has always heretofore escaped; but it got the clean, clever Spengler early on. Yet be calm, withhold your jealousy. It is a banal, tedious case, productive of nothing at all. He is no python, in whom we bring sensational deeds to pass. A little brighter, more given to the intellectual he may be become since the reception and would peradventure list not so much on reading the Goncourt journals or Abbé Galiani if he had not the relation with the higher world, nor had the privy memorandum. Psychology, my dear friend. Disease, indeed I mean repulsive, individual, private disease, makes a certain critical contrast to the world, to life's mean, puts a man in a mood rebellious and ironic against the bourgeois order, makes its man take refuge with the free spirit, with books, in cogitation. But more it is not with Spengler. The space that is still allotted him for reading, quoting, drinking red wine, and idling about, it isn't we who have sold it to him, it is anything rather than genialized time. A man of the world, just singed by our flame, weary, mildly interesting, no more. He rots away, liver, kidneys, stomach, heart, bowels; some day his voice will be a croak, or he will be deaf, after a few years he will ingloriously shuffle off this coyle, with a cynical quip on his lips – what then? It forceth but little, there was never any illumination, enhancing or enthusiasm, for it was not of the brain, not cerebral, you understand – our little ones in that case made no force of the upper and noble, it had obviously no fascination for them, it did not come to a metastasis into the metaphysical, metavenereal, meta-infectivus ...'

I (with venom): 'How long must I needs sit and freeze and listen to your intolerable gibberish?'

He: 'Gibberish? Have to listen? That's a funny chord to strike. In mine opinion you listen very attentively and are but impatient to know more, yea and all. You have just asked eagerly after your friend Spengler in Munich, and if I had not cut you off, you would avidly have asked me all this whole time about hell's fiery pit. Don't, I beg of you, pretend you're put on. I also have my self-respect, and know that I am no unbidden guest. To be short, the meta-spirochaetose, that is the meningeal process, and I assure you, it is just as though certain of the little ones had a passion for the upper storey, a special preference for the head region, the meninges, the dura mater, the tentorium, and the pia, which protect the tender parenchyma inside and from the moment of the first general contagion swarmed passionately hither.'

I: 'It is with you as you say. The rampallion seems to have studied *medicinam*.'

He: 'No more than you theology, that is in bits and as a specialist. Will you gainsay that you studied the best of the arts and sciences also only as specialist and amateur? Your interest had to do with – me. I am obliged to you. But wherefore should I, Esmeralda's friend and co-habitant, in which quality you behold me before you, not have a special interest in the medical field concerned, which borders on it, and be at home in it as a specialist? Indeed, I constantly and with the greatest attention follow the latest results of research in this field. Item, some doctores assert and swear by Peter and Paul there must be brain specialists among the little ones, amateurs in the cerebral sphere, in short a *virus nerveux*. But these experts are in the aforementioned box. It is arsie-versie in the matter, for 'tis the brain which gapes at their visitation and looks forward expectantly, as you to mine, that it invites them to itself, draws them unto it, as though it could not bear at all to wait for them. Do you still remember? The philosopher, *De anima*: "the acts of the person acting are performed on him the previously disposed to suffer it." There you have it: on the disposition, the readiness, the invitation, all depends. That some men be more qualified to the practising of witchcraft, than others, and we know well how to discern them, of that already are aware the worthy authors of the *Malleus*.'

I: 'Slanderer, I have no connexion with you. I did not invite you.'

He: 'La, la, sweet innocence! The far-travelled client of my little ones was I suppose not forewarned? And your doctors too you chose with sure instinct.'

I: 'I looked them out in the directory. Whom should I have asked? And who could have told me that they would leave me in the lash? What did you do with my two physicians?'

He: 'Put them away, put them away. Oh, of course we put the blunderers away in your interest. And at the right moment iwis, not too soon and not too late, when they had got the thing in train with their quackery and quicksilvery, and if we had left them they might have botched the beautiful case. We allowed them the provocation, then *basta* and away with them! So soon as they with their specific treatment had properly limited the first, cutaneously emphasized general infiltration, and thus given a powerful impetus to the metastasis upwards, their business was accomplished, they had to be removed. The fools, to wit, do not know, and if they know they cannot change it, that by the general treatment the upper, the meta-venereal processes are powerfully accelerated. Indeed, by not treating the fresh stages it is often enough forwarded; in short, the way they do it is wrong. In no case could we let the provocation by quackery and quickery go on. The regression of the general penetration was to be left to itself, that the progression up there should go on pretty slowly, in order that years, decades, of nigromantic time should be saved for you, a whole houre-glasseful of divel-time, genius-time. Narrow and small and finely circum-scribed it is today, four years after you got it, the place up there in you; but it is there, the hearth, the workroom of the little ones, who on the liquor way, the water way as it were, got there, the place of incipient illumination.'

I: 'Do I trap you, blockhead? Do you betray yourself and name to me yourself the place in my brain, the fever hearth, that makes me imagine you, and without which you were not? Betrayest to me that in excited state I see and hear you, yet you are but a bauling before my eyes!'

He: 'The Great God Logick! Little fool, it is topside the other waie: I am not the product of your pia hearth up there, rather the hearth enables you to perceive me, understand, and without it, indeed, you would not see me. Is therefore my existence dependent on your incipient drunkenness? Do I belong in your subjective? I ask you! Only patience, what goes on and progresses there will give you the capacity for a great deal more, will conquer quite other impediments and make you to soar over lameness and halting. Wait till Good Friday, and 'twill soon be Easter! Wait one, ten, twelve years, until the illumination, the dazzling radiance as all lame scruples and doubts fall away and you will know for what you pay, why you make over body and soul to us. Then shall osmotic growths *sine pudore* sprout out of the apothecary's sowing. . . .'

I (start up): 'Hold thy foul mouth! I forbid thee to speak of my father!'

He: 'Oh, thy father is not so ill placed in my mouth. He was a shrewd one, always wanting to speculate the elements. The mygrim, the point of attack for the knife-pains of the little sea-maid – after all, you have them from him ... Moreover, I have spoken quite correctly: osmosis, fluid diffusion, the proliferation process – the whole magic intreats of these. You have there the spinal sac with the pulsating column of fluid therein, reaching to the cerebrum, to the meninges, in whose tissues the furtive venereal meningitis is at its soundless stealthy work. But our little ones could not reach into the inside, into the parenchyma, however much they are drawn, however much they longingly draw thither – without fluid diffusion, osmosis, with the cell-fluid of the pia watering it, dissolving the tissue, and paving a way inside for the scourges. Everything comes from osmosis, my friend, in whose teasing manifestations you so early diverted yourself.'

I: 'Your baseness makes me to laugh. I wish Schildknapp would come back that I might laugh with him. I would tell him father-stories, I too. Of the tears in my father's eyes, when he said: "And yet they are dead!"'

He: 'Cock's body! You were right to laugh at his ruthful tears – aside from the fact that whoever has, by nature, dealings with the tempter is always at variance with the feelings of people, always tempted to laugh when they weep, and weep when they laugh. What then does "dead" mean, when the flora grows so rankly, in such diverse colours and shapes? And when they are even heliotropic? What does "dead" mean when the drop displays such a healthy appetite? What is sick, what well, my friend, about that we must not let the philistine have the last word. Whether he does understand life so well remains a question. What has come about by the way of death, of sickness, at that life has many a time clutched with joy and let itself be led by it higher and further. Have you forgotten what you learned in the schools, that God can bring good out of evil and that the occasion to it shall not be marred? Item, a man must have been always ill and mad in order that others no longer need be so. And where madness begins to be malady, there is nobody knows at all. If a man taken up in a rapture write in a margent note: "Am blissful! Am beside myself! That I call new and great! Seething bliss of inspiration! My cheeks glow like molten iron! I am raging, you will all be raging, when this comes to you! Then God succour your poor sely souls!" Is that still mad healthiness, normal madness, or has he got it in the *meninges*? The bourgeois is the last to diagnose; for long in any case nothing further about it strikes him as strange, because forsooth artists are queer birds anyhow. If next day on a rebound he cry: "Oh, flat and stale! Oh, a dog's life, when a man can do nothing! Were there but a war, so that somewhat would happen! If I could croak in good style! May hell pity me, for I am a son of hell!" Does he really mean that? Is it the literal truth that he says there of hell, or is it only metaphor for a little normal Dürer melancolia? In summa, we simply give you that for which the classic poet, the lofty and stately genius, so beautifully thanked his gods:

> All do the gods give, the Eternal,
> To their favourites, wholly:
> All the joys, the eternal,
> All the pangs, the eternal,
> Wholly.'

I: 'Mocker and liar! *Si diabolus non esset mendax et homicida!* If I must listen, at least speak to me not of sane and sound greatness and native gold! I know that gold made with fire instead of the sun is not genuine.'

He: 'Who says so? Has the sun better fire then the kitchen? And the sane and sound greatness! Whenever I hear of such, I laugh! Do you believe in anything like an *ingenium* that has nothing to do with hell? *Non datur!* The artist is the brother of the criminal and the madman. Do you ween that any important work was ever wrought except its maker learned to understand the way of the criminal and madman? Morbid and healthy! Without the morbid would life all its whole life never have survived. Genuine and false! Are we land-loping knaves? Do we draw the good things out of the nose of nothing? Where nothing is there the Devil too has lost his right and no pallid Venus produces anything worth while! We make naught new – that is other people's matter. We only release, only set free. We let the lameness and selfconsciousness, the chaste scruples and doubts go to the Devil. We physic away fatigue merely by a little charm-hyperaemia, the great and the small, of the person and of the time. That is it, you do not think of the passage of time, you do not think historically, when you complain that such and such a one could have it "wholly", joys and pains endlessly, without the hour-glass being set for him, the reckoning finally made. What he in his classical decades could have without us, certainly, that, nowadaies, we alone have to offer. And we offer better, we offer only the right and true – that is no lenger the classical, my friend, what we give to experience, it is the archaic, the primeval, that which long since has not been tried. Who knows today, who even knew in classical times, what inspiration is, what genuine, old, primeval enthusiasm, insicklied critique, unparalysed by thought or by the mortal domination of reason – who knows the divine raptus? I believe, indeed, the Devil passes for a man of destructive criticism? Slander and again slander, my friend! Gog's sacrament! If there is anything he cannot abide, if there's one thing in the whole world he cannot stomach, it is destructive criticism. What he wants and gives is triumph over it, is shining sparkling, vainglorious unreflectiveness!'

I: 'Charlatan!'

He: 'Yea, of a truth. When you set right the grossest false understandings about yourself, more out of love of truth than of self, then you are a cheap jack. I will not let my mouth be stopped by your shamefast ungraciousness; I know that you are but suppressing your emotions, you are listening to me with as much pleasure as the maid to the whisperer in church . . . Let us just for an instance take the "idea" – what you call that, what for a hundred years or so you have been calling it, sithence earlier there was no such category, as little as musical copyright and all that. The idea, then, a matter of three, four bars, no more, isn't it? All the residue is elaboration, sticking at it. Or isn't it? Good. But now we are all experts, all critics: we note that the idea is nothing new, that it all too much reminds us of something in Rimsky-Korsakov or Brahms. What is to be done? You just change it. But a changed idea, is that still an idea? Take Beethoven's notebooks. There is no thematic conception there as God gave it. He remoulds it and adds "Meilleur". Scant confidence in God's prompting, scant respect for it is expressed in that "Meilleur" – itself not so very enthusiastic either. A genuine inspiration, immediate, absolute, unquestioned, ravishing, where there is no choice, no tinkering, no possible improvement; where all is as a sacred mandate, a visitation received by the possessed one with faltering and stumbling step, with shudders of awe from head to foot, with tears of joy blinding his eyes: no, that is not possible with God, who leaves the understanding too much to do. It comes but from the divel, the true master and giver of such rapture.'

Even as he spake, and easily, a change came over the fellow: as I looked straight at him meseemed he was different, sat there no longer a rowdy losel, but changed for the better, I give my word. He now had on a white collar and a bow tie, horn-rimmed spectacles on his hooked nose. Behind them the dark, rather reddened eyes gleamed moistly. A mixture of sharpness and softness was on the visage; nose sharp, lips sharp, yet soft the chin with a dimple, a dimple in the cheek too – pale and vaulted the brow, out of which the hair retreats towards the top, yet from there to the sides thick, standing up black and woolly: a member of the intelligentsia, writer on art, on music for the ordinary press, a theoretician and critic, who himself composes, so far as thinking allows him. Soft, thin hands as well, which accompany his talk with gestures of refined awkwardness, sometimes delicately stroking his thick hair at temples and back. This was now the picture of the visitor in the sofa-corner. Taller he had not grown, and above all the voice, nasal, distinct, cultivated, pleasing, had remained the same; it kept the identity in all the fluidity of appearance. Then I hear him speak and see his wide lips, pinched in at the corners under the badly shaved upper one, protrude as he articulates.

'What is art today? A pilgrimage on peas. There's more to dancing in these times than a pair of red shoon, and you are not the only one the devil depresses. Look at them, your colleagues – I know, of course, that you do not look at them, you don't look in their direction, you cherish the illusion that you are alone and want everything for yourself, all the whole curse of the time. But do look at them for your consolation, your fellow-inaugurators of the new music, I mean the honest, serious ones, who see the consequences of the situation, I speak not of the folklorists and neo-classic asylists whose modernness consists in their forbidding themselves a musical outbreak and in wearing with more or less dignity the style-garment of a pre-individualistic period. Persuade themselves and others that the tedious has become interesting, because the interesting has begun to grow tedious.'

I had to laugh, for although the cold continued to pursue me, I must confess that since his alteration I felt more comfortable in his presence. He smiled as well: that is, the corners of his mouth tensed a little and he slightly narrowed his eyes.

'They are powerless too,' he went on, 'but I believe we, thou and I, lever prefer the decent impotence of those who scorn to cloak the general sickness under colour of a dignified mummery. But the sickness is general, and the straightforward ones shew the symptoms just as well as the producers of back-formations. Does not production threaten to come to an end? And whatever of serious stuff gets on to paper betrays effort and distaste. Extraneous, social grounds? Lack of demand? And as in the pre-liberal period the possibility of production depends largely on the chance of a Maecenas? Right, but as explanation doesn't go far enough. Composing itself has got too hard, devilishly hard. Where work does not go any longer with sincerity how is one to work? But so it stands, my friend, the masterpiece, the self-sufficient form, belongs to traditional art, emancipated art rejects it. The thing begins with this: that the right of command over all the tone-combinations ever applied by no means belongs to you. Impossible the diminished seventh, impossible certain chromatic passing notes. Every composer of the better sort carries within himself a canon of the forbidden, the self-forbidding, which by degrees includes all the possibilities of tonality, in other words all traditional music. What has become false, worn-out cliché, the canon decides. Tonal sounds, chords in a composition with the technical horizon of today, outbid every dissonance. As such they are to be used, but cautiously and only *in extremis*, for the shock is worse than the harshest discord of old. Everything depends on the technical horizon. The

diminished seventh is right and full of expression at the beginning of op.
111. It corresponds to Beethoven's whole technical niveau, doesn't it? – the
tension between consonance and the harshest dissonance known to him.
The principle of tonality and its dynamics lend to the chord its specific
weight. It has lost it – by a historical process which nobody reverses. Listen
to the obsolete chord; even by itself alone it stands for a technical general
position which contradicts the actual. Every sound carries the whole, carries
the whole story in itself. But therefore the judgement of the ear, what is right
and what wrong, is indisputably and directly related to it, to this one chord,
in itself not false, entirely without abstract reference to the general technical
niveau: we have there a claim on rightness which the sound image makes
upon the artist – a little severe, don't you think? Then does not his activity
exhaust itself in the execution of the thing contained within the objective
conditions of production? In every bar that one dares to think, the situation
as regards technique presents itself to him as a problem. Technique in all
aspects demands of him every moment that he do justice to it, and give the
only right answer which it at any moment permits. It comes down to this,
that his compositions are nothing more than solutions of that kind; nothing
but solving of technical puzzles. Art becomes critique. That is something
quite honourable, who denies it? Much rebellion in strict obedience is
needed, much independence, much courage. But the danger of being
uncreative – what do you think? Is it perhaps still only a danger, or is it
already a fixed and settled fact?'

He paused. He looked at me through his glasses with his humid reddened
eyes, raised his hand in a fastidious gesture, and stroked his hair with his two
middle fingers. I said:

'What are you waiting for? Should I admire your mockery? I have never
doubted ye would know how to say to me what I know. Your way of
producing it is very purposeful. What you mean by it all is to shew me that I
could avail myself of, nor have, no one otherwise then the divel to kindle me
to my work. And ye could at the same time not exclude the theoretic
possibility of spontaneous harmony between a man's own needs and the
moment, the possibility of "rightness", of a natural harmony, out of which
one might create without a thought or any compulsion.'

He (laughing): 'A very theoretic possibility, in fact. My dear fellow, the
situation is too critical to be dealt with without critique. Moreover I reject
the reproach of a tendentious illumination of things. We do not need to
involve ourselves further in dialectic extravagances on your account. What I
do not deny is a certain general satisfaction which the state of the "work"
generally vouchsafes me. I am against "works", by and large. Why should I
not find some pleasure in the sickness which has attacked the idea of the
musical work? Don't blame it on social conditions. I am aware you tend to do
so, and are in the habit of saying that these conditions produce nothing fixed
and stable enough to guarantee the harmony of the self-sufficient work.
True, but unimportant. The prohibitive difficulties of the work lie deep in
the work itself. The historical movement of the musical material has turned
against the self-contained work. It shrinks in time, it scorns extension in
time, which is the dimensions of a musical work, and lets it stand empty. Not
out of impotence, not out of incapacity to give form. Rather from a ruthless
demand for compression, which taboos the superfluous, negates the phrase,
shatters the ornament, stands opposed to any extension of time, which is the
life-form of the work. Work, time, and pretence, they are one, and together
they fall victim to critique. It no longer tolerates pretence and play, the

fiction, the self-glorification of form, which censors the passions and human suffering, divides out the parts, translates into pictures. Only the non-fictional is still permissible, the unplayed, the undisguised and untransfigured expression of suffering in its actual moment. Its impotence and extremity are so ingrained that no seeming play with them is any longer allowed.'

I (very ironically): 'Touching, touching! The devil waxes pathetic. The poor devil moralizes. Human suffering goes to his heart. How high-mindedly he shits on art! You would have done better not to mention your antipathy to the work if you did not want me to realize that you animadversions are naught but divel-farting.'

He (unperturbed): 'So far, so good. But at bottom you do agree that to face the facts of the time is neither sentimental nor malicious. Certain things are no longer possible. The pretence of feeling as a compositional work of art, the self-satisfied pretence of music itself, has become impossible and no longer to be preserved – I mean the perennial notion that prescribed and formalized elements shall be introduced as though they were the inviolable necessity of the single case. Or put it the other way round: the special case behaving as though it were identical with the prescribed and familiar formula. For four hundred years all great music has found its satisfaction in pretending that this unity has been accomplished without a break – it has pleased itself with confusing the conventional universal law to which it is subject with its own peculiar concern. My friend, it cannot go on. The criticism of ornament, convention, and the abstract generality are all the same one. What it demolishes is the pretence in the bourgeois work of art; music, although she makes no picture, is also subject to it. Certainly, this "not making a picture" gives her an advantage over the other arts. But music too by untiringly conforming her specific concerns to the ruling conventions has as far as she could played a role in the highbrow swindle. The inclusion of expression in the general appeasement is the innermost principle of musical pretence. It is all up with it. The claim to consider the general harmonically contained in the particular contradicts itself. It is all up with the once blindingly valid conventions, which guaranteed the freedom of play.'

I: 'A man could know that and recognize freedom above and beyond all critique. He could heighten the play, by playing with forms out of which, as he well knew, life has disappeared.'

He: 'I know, I know. Parody. It might be fun, if it were not so melancholy in its aristocratic nihilism. Would you promise yourself much pleasure and profit from such tricks?'

I (retort angrily): 'No.'

He: 'Terse and testy. But why so testy? Because I put to you friendly questions of conscience, just between ourselves? Because I shewed you your despairing heart and set before your eyes with the expert's insight the difficulties absolutely inseparable from composition today? You might even so value me as an expert. The Devil ought to know something about music. If I mistake not, you were reading just now in a book by the Christian in love with aesthetics. He knew and understood my particular relation to this beautiful art – the most Christian of all arts, he finds – but Christian in reverse, as it were: introduced and developed by Christianity indeed, but then rejected and banned as the Divel's Kingdom – so there you are. A highly theological business, music – the way sin is, the way I am. The passion of that Christian for music is true passion, and as such knowledge and corruption in one. For there is true passion only in the ambiguous and ironic. The highest passion concerns the absolutely questionable ... No, musical I am indeed, don't worry about that. I have sung you the role of poor Judas because of the difficulties into which music like everything else has got today. Should I not have done so? But I did it only to point out to you that you should break through them, that you should lift yourselves above them to giddy heights of self-admiration, and do such things that you will behold them only with shudders of awe.'

I: 'An annunciation, in fact. I am to grow osmotic growths.'

He: 'It comes to the same thing. Ice crystals, or the same made of starch, sugar and cellulose, both are Nature; we ask, for which shall we praise Nature more. Your tendency, my friend, to inquire after the objective, the so-called truth, to question as worthless the subjective, pure experience: that is truly petty bourgeois, you ought to overcome it. As you see me, so I exist to you. What serves it to ask whether I really am? Is not "really" what works, is not truth experience and feeling? What uplifts you, what increases your feeling of power and might and domination, damn it, that is the truth – and whether ten times a lie when looked at from the moral angle. This is what I think: that an untruth of a kind that enhances power holds its own against any ineffectively virtuous truth. And I mean too that creative, genius-giving disease, disease that rides on high horse over all hindrances, and springs with drunken daring from peak to peak, is a thousand times dearer to life than plodding healthiness. I have never heard anything stupider than that from disease only disease can come. Life is not scrupulous – by morals it sets not a fart. It takes the reckless product of disease, feeds on and digests it, and as soon as it takes it to itself it is health. Before the fact of fitness for life, my good man, all distinction of disease and health falls away. A whole host and generation of youth, receptive, sound to the core, flings itself on the work of the morbid genius, made genius by disease; admires it, praises it, exalts it, carries it away, assimilates it unto itself and makes it over to culture, which lives not on home-made bread alone, but as well on provender and poison from the apothecary's shop at the sign of the Blessed Messengers. Thus saith to you the unbowdlerized Sammael. He guarantees not only that towards the end of your houre-glasse years your sense of your power and splendour will more and more outweigh the pangs of the little seamaid and finally mount to most triumphant well-being, to a sense of bursting health, to the walk and way of a god. That is only the subjective side of the thing, I know; it would not suffice, it would seem to you unsubstantial. Know, then, we pledge you the success of that which with your help you will accomplish. You will lead the way, you will strike up the march of the future, the lads will swear by your name who thanks to your madness will no longer need to be mad. On your madness they will feed in health, and in them you will become healthy. Do you understand? Not only will you break through the paralysing difficulties of the time – you will break through time itself, by which I mean the cultural epoch and its cult, and dare to be barbaric, twice barbaric indeed, because of coming after the humane, after all possible root-treatment and bourgeois *raffinement*. Believe me, barbarism even has more grasp of theology than has a culture fallen away from cult, which even in the religious has seen only culture, only the humane, never excess, paradox, the mystic passion, the utterly unbourgeois ordeal. But I hope you do not marvel that "the Great Adversary" speaks to you of religion. Gog's nails! Who else, I should like to know, is to speak of it today? Surely not the liberal theologian! After all I am by now its sole custodian! In whom will you recognize theological existence if not in me? And who can lead a theological existence without me? The religious is certainly my line: as certainly as it is not the line of bourgeois culture. Since culture fell away from the cult and made a cult of itself, it has become nothing else then a falling away; and all the world after a mere five hundred years is as sick and tired of it as though, *salva venia*, they had ladled it in with cooking-spoons.'

It was now, it was even a little before this, when he was uttering his taunts and mockage about the theological existence of the Devil and being the guardian of the religious life, speaking in flowing language like a lectour, that I noticed the merchaunte before me on the sofa had changed again; he seemed no longer to be the spectacled intellectual and amateur of music who had awhile been speaking. And he was no lenger just sitting in his corner, he was riding *légèrement*, half-sitting, on the curved arm of the sofa, his fingertips crossed in his lap and both thumbs spread out. A little parted beard on his chin wagged up and down as he talked, and above his open lips with the sharp teeth behind them was the little moustache with stiff twisted points. I had to laugh, in all my frozenness, at his metamorphosis into the old familiar.

'Obedient servant,' I say. 'I ought to know you; and I find it most civil of you to give me a *privatissimum* here in our hall. As ye now are, my Protean friend, I look to find you ready to quench my thirst for knowledge and conclusively demonstrate your independent presence by telling me not only things I know but also of some I would like to know. You have lectured me a good deal about the houre-glasse time you purvey; also about the payment in pains to be made now and again for the higher life; but not about the end, about what comes afterwards, the eternal obliteration. That is what excites curiosity, and you have not, long as you have been squatting there, given space to the question in all your talk. Shall I not know the price in cross and kreuzer? Answer me: what is life like in the Dragon's Den? What have they to expect, who have listened to you, in the *spelunca*?

He (laughs a falsetto laugh): 'Of the *pernicies*, the *confutatio* you want to have knowledge? Call that prying, I do, the exuberance of the youthful scholar. There is a time enough, so much that you can't see to the end of it, and so much excitement coming first – you will have a plenty to do besides taking heed to the end, or even noticing the moment when it might be time to take heed to the ending. But I'll not deny you the information and do not need to palliate, for what speak thereof – that is, one can really not speak of it at all, because the actual is beyond what by word can be declared; many words may be used and fashioned, but all together they are but tokens, standing for names which do not and cannot make claim to describe what is never to be described and denounced in words. That is the secret delight and security of hell, that it is not to be informed on, that it is protected from speech, that it just is, but cannot be public in the newspaper, be brought by any word to critical knowledge, wherefor precisely the words "subterranean", "cellar", "thick walls", "soundlessness", "forgottenness", "hopelessness", are the poor, weak symbols. One must just be satisfied with symbolism, my good man, when one is speaking of hell, for there everything ends – not only the word that describes, but everything altogether. This is indeed the chiefest characteristic and what in most general terms is to be uttered about it: both that which the newcomer thither first experiences, and what at first with his as it were sound senses he cannot grasp, and will not understand, because his reason or what limitation soever of his understanding prevents him, in short because it is quite unbelievable enough to make him turn white as a sheet, although it is opened to him at once on greeting, in the most emphatic and concise words, that *"here everything leaves off"*. Every compassion, every grace, every sparing, every last trace of consideration for the incredulous, imploring objection "that you verily cannot do so unto a soul": it is done, it happens, and indeed without being called to any reckoning in words; in soundless cellar, far down beneath God's hearing, and happens to all eternity. No, it is bad to speak of it, lies aside from and outside of speech, language has naught to do with and no connexion with it, wherefore she knows not rightly what timeform to apply to it and helps herself perforce with the future tense, even as it is written: "There shall be wailing and gnashing of teeth." Good; these are a few word-sounds, chosen out of a rather extreme sphere of language, yet but weak symbols and without proper reference to what "shall be" there, unrecorded, unreckoned, between thick walls. True it is that inside these echoless walls it gets right loud, measureless loud, and by much overfilling the ear with screeching and beseeching, gurgling and groaning, with yauling and bauling and caterwauling, with horrid winding and grinding and racking ectasies of anguish no man can hear his own tune, for that it smothers in the general, in the thick-clotted diapason of trills and chirps lured from this everlasting dispensation of the unbelievable combined with the irresponsible. Nothing forgetting the dismal groans of lust mixted therewith; since endless torment, with no possible collapse, no swoon to put a period thereto, degenerates into shameful pleasure, wherefore such as have some intuitive knowledge speak indeed of the "lusts of hell". And therewith mockage and the extreme of ignominy such as belongs with martydom; for this bliss of hell is like a deep-voiced pitiful jeering and scorn of all the immeasureable anguish; it is accompanied by whinnying laughter and the pointing finger; whence the doctrine that the damned have not only torment but also mockery and shame to bear; yea, that hell is to be defined as a monstrous combination of suffering and derision, unendurable yet to be endured world without end. There will they devour their proper tongues for greatness of the agony, yet make no common cause on that account, for rather they are full of hatred and scorn against each other, and in the midst of their trills and quavers hurl at one another the foulest oaths. Yea, the finest and proudest, who never let a lewd word pass their lips, are forced to sue the filthiest of all. A part of their torment and lust of shame standeth therein that they must cogitate the extremity of filthiness.'

I: 'Allow me, this is the first word you have said to me about what manner of suffering the damned have to bear. Pray note that you have only lectured to me on the affects of hell but not about what objectively and in fact must await the damned.'

He: 'Your curiosity is childish and indiscreet. I put that in the foreground; but I am very well aware indeed, my good soul, what hides behind it. You assaye to question me in order to be feared, to be afraid of the pangs of hell. For the thought of backward turning and rescue, of your so-called soul-heal, of withdrawing from the promise lurks in the back of your mind and you are acting to summon up the *attritio cordis*, the heartfelt anguish and dread of what is to come, of which you may well have heard, that by it man can arrive at the so-called blessedness. Let me tell you, that it is an entirely exploded theology. The attrition-theory has been scientifically superseded. It is shown that *contritio* is necessary, the real and true protestant remorse for sin, which means not merely fear repentance by churchly regulation but inner, religious conversion; ask yourself whether you are capable of that; ask yourself, your pride will not fail of an answer. The longer the less will you be able and willing to let yourself in for *contritio*, sithence the extravagant life you will lead is a great indulgence, out of the which a man does not so simply find the way back into the good safe average. Therefore, to your reassurance be it said, even hell will not afford you aught essentially new, only the more or less accustomed, and proudly so. It is at bottom only a continuation of the extravagant existence. To knit up in two words its quintessence, or if you like its chief matter, is that it leaves its denizens only the choice between extreme cold and an extreme heat which can melt granite. Between these two states they flee roaring to and fro, for in the one the other always seems heavenly refreshment but is at once and in the most hellish meaning of the word intolerable. The extreme in this must please you.'

I: 'It liketh me. Meanwhile I would warn you lest you feel all too certain of me. A certain shallowness in your theology might tempt you thereto. You rely on my pride preventing me from the *contritio* necessary to salvacion, and do not bethink yourself that there is a prideful *contritio*. The remorse of Cain, for instance, who was of the firm persuasion that his sin was greater than could ever be forgiven him. The *contritio* without hope, as complete disbelief in the possibility of mercy and forgiveness, the rocklike firm conviction of the sinner that he has done too grossly for even the Everlasting Goodness to be able to forgive his sin – only that is the true *contritio*. I call your attention to the fact that it is the nighest to redemption, for Goodness the most irresistible of all. You will admit that the everyday sinner can be but very moderately interesting to Mercy. In his case the act of grace has but little impetus, it is but a feeble motion. Mediocrity, in fact, has no theological status. A capacity for sin so healless that it makes its man despair from his heart of redemption – that is the true theological way to salvation.'

He: 'You are a sly dog! And where will the likes of you get the single-mindedness, the naïve recklessness of despair, which would be the premise for this singfull waye to salvacion? Is it not playne to you that the conscious speculation on the charm which great guilt exercises on Goodness makes the act of mercy to the uttermost unpossible to it?'

I: 'And yet only through this *non plus ultra* can the high prick of the dramatic-theological existence be arrived at; I mean the most abandoned guilt and the last and most irresistible challenge to the Everlasting Goodness.'

He: 'Not bad. Of a truth ingenious. And now I will tell you that precisely heads of your sort comprise the population of hell. It is not so easy to get into hell, we should long have been suffering for lack of space if we let Philip and Cheyney in. But your theologian in grain, your arrant wily-pie who speculates on speculation because he has speculation in his blood already from the father's side – there must be foul work an he did not belong to the divel.'

As he said that, or even somewhat afore, the fellow changed again, the way clouds do, without knowing it, apparently; is no longer sitting on the arm of the couch before me in the room; there back in the sofa-corner is the unspeakable losel, the cheesy rapscallion in the cap, with the red eyes. And says to me in his slow, nasal, actor's voice:

'To make an end and a conclusion will be agreeable to you. I have devoted much time and tarried long to entreat of this matter with you – I hope and trust you realize. But also you are an attractive case, that I freely admit. From early on we had an eye on you, on your quick, arrogant head, your mighty *ingenium* and *memoriam*. They have made you study theology, as your conceit devised it, but you would soon name yourself no longer of theologians, but put the Good Boke under the bench and from then on stuck to the figures, characters, and incantations of music, which pleased us not a little. For your vaine glory aspired to the elemental, and you thought to gain it in the form most mete for you, where algebraic magic is married with corresponding cleverness and calculation and yet at the same time it always boldly warres against reason and sobriety. But did we then not know that you were too clever and cold and chaste for the element; and did we not know that you were sore vexed thereat and piteously bored with your shamefast cleverness? Thus it was our busily prepensed plan that you should run into our arms, that is of my little one, Esmeralda, and that you got it, the illumination, the aphrodisiacum of the brain, after which with body and soul and mind you so desperately longed. To be short, between us there needs no crosse way in the Spesser's Wood and no cercles. We are in league and business – with your blood you have affirmed it and promised yourself to us, and are baptized ours. This my visit concerns only the confirmation thereof. Time you have taken from us, a genius's time, high-flying time, full twenty-four years *ab dato recessi*, which we set to you as the limit. When they are finished and fully expired, which is not to be foreseen, and such a time is also an eternity – then you shall be fetched. Against this meanwhile shall we be in all things subject and obedient, and hell shall profit you, if you renay all living creature, all the Heavenly Host and all men, for that must be.'

I (in an exceeding cold draught): 'What? That is new. What signifies the *clausula*?'

He: 'Renounce, it means. What otherwise? Do you think that jealousy dwells in the height and not also in the depths? To us you are, fine, well-create creature, promised and espoused. Thou maist not love.'

I (really have to laugh): 'Not love! Poor divel! Will you substantiate the report of your stupidity and wear a bell even as a cat, that you will base business and promise on so elastic, so ensnaring a concept as love? Will the Devil prohibit lust? If it be not so, then he must endure sympathy, yea, even *caritas*, else he is betrayed just as it is written in the books. What I have invited, and wherefore you allege that I have promised you – what is then the source of it, prithee, but love, even if that poisoned by you with God's sanction? The bond in which you assert we stand has itself to do with love, you doating fool. You allege that I wanted it and repaired to the wood, the crosse-waye, for the sake of the work. But they say that work itself has to do with love.'

He (laughing through his nose): 'Do, re, mi! Be assured that thy psychological feints do not trap me, any better than do the theological. Psychology – God warrant us, do you still hold with it? That is bad, bourgeois nineteenth century. The epoch is heartily sick of it, it will soon be a red rag to her, and he will simply get a crack on the pate, who disturbs life by psychology. We are entering into times, my friend, which will not be hood-winked by psychology . . . This *en passant*. My condition was clear and direct, determined by the legitimate jealousy of hell. Love is forbidden you, in so far as it warms. Thy life shall be cold, therefore thou shalt love no human being. What are you thinking then? The illumination leaves your mental powers to the last unimpaired, yes, heightens them to an ecstatie of delirium – what shall it then go short of save the dear soul and the priceless life of feeling? A general chilling of your life and your relations to men lies in the nature of things – rather it lies already in your nature; in feith we lay upon you nothing new, the little ones make nothing new and strange out of you, they only ingeniously strengthen and exaggerate all that you already are. The coldness in you is perhaps not prefigured, as well as the paternal head paynes out of which the pangs of the little sea-maid are to come? Cold we want you to be, that the fires of creation shall be hot enough to warm yourself in. Into them you will flee out of the cold of your life...'

I: 'And from the burning back to the ice. It seems to be hell in advance, which is already offered me on earth.'

He: 'It is that extravagant living, the only one that suffices a proud soul. Your arrogance will probably never want to exchange with a lukewarm one. Do you strike with me? A work-filled eternity of human life shall you enjoy. When the houre-glasse runs out, then I shall have good power to deal and dole with, to move and manage the fine-created Creature after my way and my pleasure, be it in life, soul, flesh, blood or goods – to all eternity!'

There it was again, the uncontrollable disgust that had already seized me once before and shaken me, together with the glacial wave of cold which came over me again from the tight-trousered *strizzi* there. I forgot myself in a fury of disgust, it was like a fainting-fit. And then I heard Schildknapp's easy, everyday voice, he sat there in the sofa-corner, saying to me:

'Of course you didn't miss anything. Newspapers and two games of billiards, a round of Marsala and the good souls calling the *governo* over the coals.'

I was sitting in my summer suit, by my lamp, the Christian's book on my knee. Can't be anything else: in my excitement I must have chased the losel out and carried my coat and rug back before Schildknapp returned.

Chapter Twenty-six

It consoles me to be able to tell myself that the reader cannot lay to my charge the extraordinary size of the last chapter, which considerably exceeds the disquieting number of pages in the one of Kretschmar's lectures. The unreasonable demand made upon the reader does not lie at my door and need not trouble me. To mitigate Adrian's account by subjecting it to any kind of editing; to dismiss the 'dialogue' in a few numbered paragraphs (will the reader please note the protesting quotation-marks I have given the word, without concealing from myself that they can remove from it only part of its indwelling horror); to do this no regard for the possible failure of the reader's capacity could possibly move me. With rueful loyalty I had to reproduce a given thing; to transfer it from Adrian's music paper to my manuscript; and that I have done, not only word for word, but also, I may say, letter for letter – often laying down the pen to recover myself, to measure my study floor with heavy, pensive tread or to throw myself on my sofa with my hands clasped upon my brow. So that, however strange it may seem, this chapter, which I had only to copy down, actually did not leave my sometimes trembling hand any faster than the earlier ones which I composed myself.

To copy, understandingly and critically, is in fact – at least for me, and Monsignor Hinterpförtner agrees with me – an occupation as intensive and time-consuming as putting down one's own thoughts. It is likely that the reader may before now have underestimated the number of days and weeks that I had spent upon the life-story of my departed friend. It is even more probable that his imagination will have fallen behind the point of time at which I am composing the present lines. He may laugh at my pedantry, but I consider it right to let him know that since I began writing almost a year has passed; and that whilst I have been composing the last chapters, April 1944 has arrived.

That date, of course, is the point where I now stand in my actual writing and not the one up to which my narrative has progressed. That has only reached the autumn of 1912, twenty months before the outbreak of the last war, when Adrian and Rüdiger Schildknapp came back from Palestrina to Munich and he lodged at first in Pension Gisela in Schwabing. I do not know why this double time-reckoning arrests my attention or why I am at pains to point out both the personal and the objective, the time in which the narrator moves and that in which the narrative does so. This is a quite extraordinary interweaving of time-units, destined, moreover, to include even a third: namely, the time which one day the courteous reader will take for the reading of what has been written; at which point he will be dealing with a three-fold ordering of time: his own, that of the chronicler, and historic time.

I will not lose myself further in these speculations, to my mind as idle as they are agitating. I will only add that the word 'historic' fits with a far more sinister emphasis the time in which, than about which, I write. In these last days the battle for Odessa has been raging, with heavy losses ending in the recapture by the Russians of the famous city on the Black Sea – though the enemy was not able to disorganize our retreat. The case will be the same with Sebastopol, another of our pledges unto death, which the obviously superior antagonist appears to mean to wrest from us. Meanwhile the terrors of almost daily air raids upon our beleagured Fortress Europa grows into incredible dimensions. What does it avail that many of these monsters, raining down ever more powerful, more horrible explosives, fall victim to our heroic defence? Thousands darken the skies of our fiercely united continent, and ever more of our cities fall in ruins. Leipzig, which played so significant a part in Leverkühn's development and tragedy, has lately been struck with might and main; its famous publishing quarter is, I hear, a heap of rubble, with immeasurable destruction of educational and literary property: a very heavy loss not only for us Germans but altogether for the world which makes culture its concern, but which in blindness or in even-handedness, I will not venture to say which, appears to pocket up the loss.

Yes, I fear it will prove our destruction that a fatally inspired policy has brought us into conflict with two powers at once: one of them richest in man-power and revolutionary *élan*; the other mightiest in productive capacity. It seems, indeed, that this American production-machine did not even need to run to capacity to throw out an absolutely crushing abundance of war material. That the flabby democracies did know after all how to use these frightful tools is a staggering revelation, weaning us daily from the mistaken idea that war is a German prerogative, and that all other peoples must prove to be bunglers and amateurs in the art. We have begun – Monsignor Hinterpförtner and I are no longer exceptions – to expect anything and everything from the war technique of the Anglo-Saxons. The fear of invasion grows: we await the attack, from all sides, with preponderance of material and millions of soldiers, on our European fortress – or shall I say our prison, our madhouse? It is expected, and only the most impressive

accounts of our measures against enemy landings, measures that really do
seem tremendous, and are, indeed, designed to protect us and our hemi-
sphere from the loss of our present leaders, only these accounts can preserve
our mental balance and prevent our yielding to the general horror of the
future.

Certainly the time in which I write has vastly greater historical momen-
tum than the time of which I write, Adrian's time, which brought him only
to the threshold of our incredible epoch. I feel as though one should call out to
him, as to all those who are no longer with us and were not with us when it
began: 'Lucky you!' and a fervent 'Rest in peace!' Adrian is safe from the
days we dwell in. The thought is dear to me, I prize it, and in exchange for
that certainty I accept the terrors of the time in which I myself continue to
live on. It is to me as though I stood here and lived for him, lived instead of
him; as though I bore the burden his shoulders were spared, as though I
showed my love by taking upon me living for him, living in his stead. The
fancy, however illusory, however foolish, does me good, it flatters the always
cherished desire to serve, to help, to protect him – this desire which during
the lifetime of my friend found so very little satisfaction.

It is worthy of remark that Adrian's stay in the Schwabing pension lasted
only a few days and that he made no effort to find a suitable permanent
dwelling in the city. Schildknapp had already written from Italy to his
former abode in the Amalienstrasse and arranged to be received there. But
Adrian was not thinking either of returning to his old place at Frau Senator
Rodde's or even of remaining in Munich. His resolve seemed to have been
taken long since and silently; he did not even go out to Pfeiffering near
Waldshut to look over the ground again and close the bargain, but did it all
by one telephone conversation and that a brief one. He called up the
Schweigestills from Pension Gisela – it was Mother Else herself who
answered the call – introduced himself as one of the two bicyclists who had
been privileged to inspect the house and farm, and asked whether and at
what price they could let him have a sleeping-chamber in the upper storey
and in the daytime the Abbot's room on the ground floor. Frau Schweigestill
let the price rest for the moment – it proved to be very modest – but was
concerned to find out which of the two earlier visitors it was, the writer or the
musician. She obviously laboured to bring back her impressions of the visit
and realize which was the musician; then she expressed some misgiving,
though only in his own interest and from his own point of view. Even this she
put only in the form that she thought he must know best what suited him.
They, the Schweigestills, she said, did not set up to be pension-keepers as a
business, they only took in occasionally, so to speak from case to case,
lodgers and mealers; that the gentlemen had been able to gather the other
time from what she said, and whether he, the speaker, represented such an
occasion and such a case, that she must leave him to judge, he would have it
pretty quiet and dull with them, and primitive as far as conveniences went,
no bathroom, no W.C., just a peasant make-shift outside the house, and she
did wonder that a gentleman of – if she had heard aright – not yet thirty,
given to one of the fine arts, wanted to take quarters in the country, so far
away from the centres of culture, but wonder was maybe not the right word,
it was not hers and her husband's way to wonder, and if maybe it was just
that he was looking for, because really most folks did wonder too much, then
he might come, but it better be thought about, especially since Maxl, her
husband, and she set store by an arrangement not made just out of some

quirk and giving notice after they tried it a bit, but meaning from the first to bide, you understand, *net wahr, gellen's ja?* and so on.

He was coming for good, answered Adrian, and he had considered a long time. The kind of life that awaited him he had tried within himself, found it good and espoused it. On the price, a hundred and twenty marks a month, he was agreed. The choice of bedroom he left to her, and was looking forward with pleasure to the Abbot's room. In three days he would move in.

And so it was. Adrian employed his brief stay in the city in making arrangements with a copyist recommended to him (I think by Kretschmar), first bassoon in the Zapfenstösser orchestra, a man named Griepenkerl, who earned a bit of money in this way. He left in his hands a part of the partitur of *Love's Labour's Lost.* He had not quite finished with the work in Palestrina, was still orchestrating the last two acts, and was not yet quite clear in his mind about the sonata-form overture, the original conception of which had changed very much by the introduction of that striking second theme, itself quite foreign to the opera, playing so spirited a part in the recapitulation and closing allegro. He had besides much trouble with the time-markings and so on, which for extended stretches he had during composition neglected to put in. Moreover it was clear to me that not by chance had the end of his Italian sojourn and the end of the work failed to coincide. Even if he had consciously striven for such a coincidence, an unconscious intuition had prevented it. He was far too much the man of the *semper idem,* of self-assertion against circumstances, to regard it as desirable to come to the end of a task pursued in a former scene at the actual moment when he changed it for a new one. For the sake of the inner continuity it would be better, so he said to himself, to bring with him into the new situation a remnant of the old occupation, and only to fix the inward eye on something new when the outward new should have become routine.

With his never heavy luggage, to which belonged a brief-case with his scores and the rubber tub which in Italy too had furnished his bath, he travelled to his goal from the Starnberger station on one of the local trains, which stopped not only in Waldshut but ten minutes later in Pfeiffering. Two boxes of books and some oddments had been left to follow by freight train. It was near the end of October, the weather, still dry, was already raw and gloomy. The leaves were falling. The son of the house of Schweigestill, Gereon, the same who had introduced the new manure-spreader, a young farmer rather disobliging and curt but obviously knowing his business, awaited the guest at the little station, on the box of a trap with a high frame and stiff springs. While the luggage was put in, he let the thong of his whip play across the backs of the team of sturdy brown horses. Not many words were exchanged on the drive. Adrian had seen from the train the Rohmbühel with its crown of trees, the grey mirror of the Klammer; now his eyes rested on these sights from close at hand. Soon the cloisterbaroque of the Schweigestill house came in sight; in the open square of the courtyard the vehicle rounded the old elm in the middle, whose leaves were now mostly lying on the bench beneath.

Frau Schweigestill stood under the gateway with the ecclesiastical coat of arms; beside her was her daughter Clementine, a brown-eyed country girl in modest peasant dress. Their words of greeting were drowned in the yapping of the yard dog, who in great excitement stepped into his food basin and almost dragged his straw-strewn kennel from its moorings. It was no use for mother and daughter, and even the stable-girl, Waltpurgis, helping to hand down the luggage, her bare feet caked with dung, to should at him:

'Kaschperl, hush your noise, be quiet!' The dog raved on and Adrian, after
he had watched awhile smiling, went up to him. 'Suso, Suso?' said he, not
raising his voice, in a certain surprised and admonishing tone, and behold,
probably from the influence of the soothing monotone, the animal became
almost immediately quiet and allowed the magician to put out a hand and
stroke his head, scarred with old bites, while the creature looked up at him
with deeply serious yellow eyes.

'Courage you've got! My respects,' said Frau Else when Adrian came back
to the gate. 'Most folks are feart of the beast and when he takes on, like now,
one don't blame them, the young schoolmaster from the village who used to
come to the children, oh, my, he was a poor body, he said everytime: "That
dog, Frau Schweigestill, I'm just feart of him." '

'Yes, yes,' laughed Adrian, nodding, and they went into the house, into
the pipe-tobacco air, and up to the upper storey, along the white damp-
smelling walls, where the goodwife showed him his bedroom with the gay
clothes-press and the high-piled white bed. They had added something
extra, a green reclining-chair with a knitted rug for the feet on the pine floor.
Gereon and Waltpurgis brought up the bags.

Here and on the way downstairs they talked about arrangements for the
guest's comfort, continuing in the Abbot's room, that characteristically
patriarchal chamber, of which Adrian had long since mentally taken
possession: about the large jug of hot water in the morning, the strong early-
morning coffee, the times for meals; Adrian was not to take them with the
family, they had not expected that, their hours being too early for him. At
half past one and at eight he was to be served preferably in the big front room
(the peasant salon with the Nike and the square piano), Frau Schweigestill
thought. It was always at his disposal. And she promised him light diet,
milk, eggs, toast, vegetable soup, a good red beefsteak with spinach at
midday, and afterwards a medium-sized omelet, with apple-sauce – in short.
things that were nourishing and agreeable to a delicate stomach like his.

'The stummick, my lord, it ain't mostly the stummick at all, eh, it's the
head, the pernickety, overstrained head, it works on the stummick, even
when 't ain't nothing wrong with it, like the way it is with seasickness and
sick headache aha, he sometimes has it pretty bad?' She thought so already,
from his looking so hard at the blinds and curtains in the bedroom; darkness,
lying in the dark, night, black, especially no light in the eyes, that was the
right thing, as long as the misery went on, and very strong tea, real sour with
lemon. Frau Schweigestill was not unacquainted with migraine – that is, she
had never had it herself but her Maxl had suffered from it periodically when
he was younger, in time it had gone away. She would hear no apologies from
the guest on the score of his infirmity, or his having smuggled a chronic
patient into the house, so to speak; she said only: 'Oh, get along with you!'
Something of the sort, she thought, one would have guessed, for when
anyone like him from over there where culture is going on came out to
Pfeiffering like that, he would have his reasons for it, and obviously it was a
case that had a claim on the understanding. Herr Leverkühn! But he'd come
to the right address for understanding, if not for culture, eh? – and so on and
so on, good woman that she was.

Between her and Adrian, as they stood or walked about, arrangements
were made, which, surprisingly perhaps to both of them, were to regulate his
outward existence for nineteen years. The village carpenter was called in to
measure the space beside the doors in the Abbot's room for shelves to hold
Adrian's books, not higher than the old panelling under the leather

hangings; also the chandelier with the stumps of wax candles was wired for electricity. Various other changes came about through time, in the room that was destined to see the birth of so many masterpieces to this day largely withheld from public knowledge and admiration. A carpet almost covering the floor, only too necessary in winter, soon hid the worn boards; and to the corner bench, the only seat in the room besides the Savonarola chair in front of the work-table, there was added after a few days without any fastidious regard for style, which was not in Adrian's line, a very deep reading- and easy-chair covered with grey velvet, from Bernheimer's in Munich, a commendable piece, which together with its separate stool, a tabouret with a cushion, deserved the name of chaise-longue; it took the place of a divan, and did its owner almost two decades of service.

The purchases – the carpet and chair from the furnishing shop in the Maximiliansplatz – I mention partly with the aim of making it clear that there was convenient opportunity for communication with the city by numerous trains, some of them fast ones which took less than an hour. So that Adrian did not, as Frau Schweigestill's way of talking would lead one to think, bury himself in solitude by setting in Pfeiffering, cut off from 'culture'. Even when he visited an evening entertainment, an academy concert or the Zapfenstösser orchestra, and opera performance or an evening company – and that too did happen – there was an eleven-o'clock train for him to travel home in. Of course he could not then count on being fetched from the station with the Schweigestill cart; in such cases he arranged beforehand with a Waldshut livery, or even, to his great satisfaction, returned on foot, on clear winter nights, by the road along the pond to the sleeping courtyard of the Schweigestill house. On these occasions he gave a sign to Kaschperl-Suso, at this hour free of his chain, that he might not rouse the house. He did this with a little metal pipe tuned by means of a screw whose higher notes were of such an extreme vibration that the human ear could scarcely hear them from close by. On the other hand they had a very strong effect and at a surprising distance on the quite differently constituted ear-drum of the dog, and Kaschperl kept mum as a mouse when the mysterious sound, heard by no one else, came to him through the night.

It was curiosity, but it was also a power exerted by my friend, whose cool, reserved person, shy despite his haughtiness, was far from unattractive, that brought people out to visit him in his retreat. I will give Schildknapp the precedence which he did actually possess: of course he was the first to come, to see how Adrian did in the place they had found out together. After that, especially in the summer-time, he often spent the week-end in Pfeiffering. Zink and Spengler came on their bicycles, for Adrian, on his shopping tours in town, has paid his respects to the Roddes in Rambergstrasse and the two painters had heard from the daughters of Adrian's return and his present address. Probably Spengler's was the initiative in the visit, for Zink, more gifted and active as a painter than the other, but much less fine as a human being, had no instinctive sympathy for Adrian and was certainly only present as Spengler's inseparable: flattering, in the Austrian manner, with kiss-the-hand and disingenuous 'Marvellous, marvellous!' at everything he saw, while at bottom unfriendly. His clownishness, the farcical effects he could produce with his long nose and the close-lying eyes which had such an absurdly hypnotic effect on women, made no play with Adrian, however grateful the latter always was for being amused. Vanity detracts from wit; the knavish Zink had a tiresome mania of attending to every word, to see whether he could not get a *double entendre* out of it, and this, as he probably saw, did not precisely enchant Adrian.

Spengler, blinking, a dimple in his cheek, laughed, or bleated, heartily at such little contretemps. The sexual interested him in a literary sense, sex and esprit lying with him very close together – which in itself is not so far wrong. His culture – we know indeed, his feeling for what was subtle, witty, discriminating – was founded on his accidental and unhappy relation to the sphere of sex, the physical fixation on it, which was sheer bad luck, and not further characteristic of his temperament or his sexuality. He smiled and prattled, in the language of that now vanished cultural and aesthetic epoch, about events in the world of artists and bibliophiles; retailed Munich gossip and dwelt very drolly on a story of how the Grand Duke of Weimar and the dramatic poet Richard Voss, travelling together in the Abruzzi, were set upon by genuine bandits – of course engaged by Voss. To Adrian, Spengler made clever politenesses about the Brentano song cycle, which he had bought and studied at the piano. He delivered himself at that time of the remark that occupation with these songs ended by spoiling one, quite definitely and almost dangerously. Afterwards one could hardly find pleasure in anything in that field. Said other quite good things about being spoiled, of which the needy artist himself was in the greatest danger, it seemed: it might be disastrous for him. For with every finished work he made life harder for himself, and in the end impossible. Spoilt by the extraordinary, his taste ruined for anything else, he must at last deteriorate through despair of executing the impossible. The problem for the highly gifted artist was how, despite his always increasing fastidiousness, his spreading disgust, he could still keep within the limits of the possible.

Thus the witty Spengler – solely on the basis of his specific fixation, as his blinking and bleating showed. The next guests were Jeanette Scheurl and Rudi Schwerdtfeger, who came to tea to see how Adrian did.

Jeanette and Schwerdtfeger sometimes played together, for the guests of old Mme Scheurl as well as privately, and they had planned the trip to Pfeiffering, and Rudi had done the telephoning. Whether he proposed it or whether it was Jeanette I do not know. They argued over it in Adrian's presence and each put on the other the merit of the attention they paid him. Jeanette's droll impulsiveness speaks for her initiative; on the other hand, it was very consistent with Rudi's amazing familiarity. He seemed to be of opinion that two years ago he had been *per du* with Adrian, whereas after all that had only been in carnival time, and even then entirely on Rudi's side. Now he blithely took it up again and desisted, with entire unconcern, only when Adrian for the second or third time refused to respond. The unconcealed merriment of Fräulein Scheurl at this repulse of his devotion moved him not at all. No trace of confusion showed in his blue eyes, which could burrow with such penetrating naïveté into the eyes of anyone who was making clever, learned, or cultured remarks. Even today I think of Schwerdtfeger and ask myself whether he actually understood how solitary Adrian was, thus how needy and exposed to temptation; whether he wanted to try his charms – to put it crudely, to get round him. Beyond a doubt he was born for conquest; but I should be afraid of doing him wrong were I to see him from this side alone. He was also a good fellow and an artist, and the fact that Adrian and he were later actually *per du* and called each other by their first names I should like not to regard as a cheap triumph of Schwerdtfeger's mania for pleasing people, but rather to refer it to his honestly recognizing the value of this extraordinary human being. I should like to think he was truly drawn to Adrian, and that his own feeling was the source of the unerring and staggering self-confidence which finally made conquest of coldness and melancholy. A fatal triumph! But I have fallen into my old, bad habit and got ahead of my story.

In her broad-brimmed hat, with a thin veil stretched across her nose, Jeanette Scheurl played Mozart on the square piano in the Schweigestills' pleasant 'big room', and Rudi Schwerdtfeger whistled with such artistry that one laughed for sheer pleasure. I heard him later at the Roddes' and Schlaginhaufens', and got him to tell me how, as quite a little lad, before he had violin lessons, he had begun to develop this technique and never stopped whistling the music he heard, or practising what he learned. His performance was brilliant, professional, fit for any cabaret, almost more impressive than his violin-playing; he must have been organically just right for it. The cantilena was wonderfully pleasing, more like a violin than a flute, the phrasing masterly, the little notes, staccato or legato, coming out with delicious precision, never or almost never faltering. In short, it was really capital, and not the least diverting thing about it was the combination of whistling 'prentice and serious artist which it presented. One involuntarily smiled as one applauded; Schwerdtfeger himself laughed like a boy, wriggling his shoulders in his jacket and making his little grimace with the corner of his mouth.

These, then, were Adrian's first guests in Pfeiffering. And soon I came myself and on fine Sundays strolled at his side round the pond and up the Rohmbühel. Only that one winter, after his return from Italy, did I live at any distance from him, for at Easter 1913 I had got my position at the Freising academy, our family's Catholic connexion being useful in this respect. I left Kaisersaschern and settled with wife and child at the edge of the Isar, in this dignified city, seat of a bishopric for hundreds of years, where with the exception of some months during the war I have passed my own life in convenient touch with the capital and also with my friend, and shared, in love and solicitude, the stresses and the tragedy of his.

Chapter Twenty-seven

Bassoonist Griepenkerl had done a good and grateful piece of work on the score of *Love's Labour's Lost*. Just about the first words Adrian said to me when we met concerned the all but flawless copy and his joy over it. He also showed me a letter that the man had written to him in the midst of his exacting labours, wherein he expressed with intelligence a sort of anxious enthusiasm for the object of his pains. He could not, so he told its author, express how it took his breath away with its boldness, the novelty of its ideas. Not enough could he admire the fine subtlety of the workmanship, the versatile rhythms, the technique of instrumentation, but which an often considerable complication of parts was made perfectly clear; above all, the rich fantasy of the composition, showing itself in the manifold variations of a given theme. He instanced the beautiful and withal half-humorous music that belongs to the figure of Rosaline, or rather expresses Biron's desperate feeling for her, in the middle part of the tripartite bourrée in the last act, this witty revival of the old French dance; it must, he said, be characterized as brilliant and deft in the highest sense of the words. He added that this bourrée was not a little characteristic of the démodé archaic element of social conventionality which so charmingly but also so challengingly contrasted with the 'modern', the free and more than free, the rebel parts, disdaining tonal connexion of the work. He feared indeed that these parts of the score, in all their unfamiliarity and rebellious heresy, would be better received than the strict and traditional. Here it often amounted to a rigidity, a more academic than artistic speculation in notes, a mosaic scarcely any longer effective musically, seeming rather more to be read than to be heard – and so on.

We laughed.

'When I hear of hearing!' said Adrian. 'In my view it is quite enough if something has been heard *once*; I mean when the artist thought it out.'

After a while he added: 'As though people ever heard what had been heard then! Composing means to commission the Zapfenstösser orchestra to execute an angelic chorus. And anyhow I consider angelic choruses to be highly speculative.'

For my part I thought Griepenkerl was wrong in his sharp distinction between archaic and modern elements in the work. 'They blend into and interpenetrate,' I said, and he accepted the statement but showed little inclination to go into what was fixed and finished; preferring apparently to put it behind him as not further interesting. Speculations about what to do with it, where to send it, to whom to show it, he left to me. That Wendell Kretschmar should have it to read was the important thing to him. He sent it to Lübeck, where the stutterer still was, and the latter actually produced it there, in a German version, a year later, after war had broken out – I was not present – with the result that during the performance two thirds of the audience left the theatre. Just as it is supposed to have happened six years before at the Munich première of Debussy's *Pelléas et Mélisande*. There were only two more performances of Adrian's opera, and it was not, for the time, to penetrate beyond the Hansa city on the Trave. The local critics agreed to a man with the judgement of the lay audience and jeered at the 'decimating' music which Herr Kretschmar had taken up with. Only in the *Lübeck Börsenkurier* an old music-professor named Immerthal – doubtless dead long since – spoke of an error of justice which time would put right, and declared in crabbed, old-fashioned language that the opera was a work of the future, full of profound music, that the writer was of course a mocker but a 'god-witted man'. This striking expression, which I had never before heard or read, nor ever since, made a peculiar impression on me. And as I have never forgotten it or the knowledgeable old codger who coined it, I think it must be counted to his honour by the posterity he invoked as witness against his spineless and torpid fellow-critics.

At the time when I moved to Freising, Adrian was busy with the composition of some songs and lieder, German and foreign, or rather, English. In the first place he had gone back to William Blake and set to music a very strange poem of this favourite author of his. 'Silent, Silent Night', in four stanzas of three lines each, the last stanza of which dismayingly enough runs:

> *But an honest joy*
> *Does itself destroy*
> *For a harlot coy.*

These darkly shocking verses the composer had set to very simple harmonies, which in relation to the tone-language of the whole had a 'falser', more heart-rent, uncanny effect than the most daring harmonic tensions, and made one actually experience the common chord growing monstrous. 'Silent, Silent Night' is arranged for a piano and voice. He set two poems by Keats, *Ode to a Nightingale* and the shorter *Ode to Melancholy* with a string-quartet accompaniment, which indeed left far behind and below it the traditional conception of an accompaniment. For in fact it was an extremely artificial form of variation in which no note of the singing voice and the four instruments was unthematic. There reigns here without interruption the closest relation between the parts so that the relation is not that of melody and accompaniment, but in all strictness that of constantly alternating primary and secondary parts.

They are glorious pieces – and almost unsung up till today, owing to the language they are in. Odd enough to make me smile was the expressiveness with which the composer enlarges in the 'Nightingale' on the demand for southern sweetness of life which the song of the 'immortal Bird' arouses in the soul of the poet. For, after all, Adrian in Italy had never displayed much gratitude or enthusiasm about the consolations of a sunny world, which make one forget the 'weariness, the fever, and the fret Here, where men sit and hear each other groan'. Musically the most priceless, the most perfect, beyond doubt, is the resolution and dissipation of the vision at the end, the

> *Adieu! the fancy cannot cheat so well*
> *As she is famed to do, deceiving elf.*
> *Adieu! adieu! thy plaintive anthem fades*
>
> *Fled is that music – do I wake or sleep?*

I can well understand how the beauty of the poems, like that of an antique vase, challenged the music to crown them; not to make them completer, for they are complete, but to articulate more strongly and to throw into relief their proud and melancholy charm; to lend more lastingness to the priceless moment of their every detail than is granted to the breathed-out words; to such moments of condensed imagery as in the third stanza of the *Ode on Melancholy*, the image of the 'sovran shrine' which veiled Melancholy has in the temple of delight, though seen of none save him whose strenuous tongue can burst Joy's grape against his palate fine – all that is so brilliant that it scarcely leaves the music anything to say. It may be that it can only injure it, unless by simply speaking with it, and so lingering it out. I have often heard say that a poem must not be too good to furnish a good lied. Music is at home in the task of gilding the mediocre. Just as real virtuosity in an actor shows up more brilliantly in a poor piece. But Adrian's relation to art was too proud and critical for him to wish to let his light shine in darkness. He had to look very high, intellectually, where he was to feel himself called a musician, and so the German poem to which he gave himself productively is also of the highest rank if without the intellectual distinction of the Keats lyrics. In place of literary exquisiteness we have something more monumental, the high-pitched, sounding pathos of the religious hymn, which with its invocations and depictions of majesty and mildness yields even more to the music, is more faithfully compliant with it than are those British images with their Greek nobility.

It was Klopstock's *Spring Festival*, the famous song of the 'Drop to the

Bucket', which Leverkühn, with but few textual abbreviations, had composed for baritone, organ, and string orchestra – a thrilling piece of work, which was performed, through the efforts of some courageous conductors friendly to the new music, during the first World War and some years after it in several German music-centres and also in Switzerland. It received the enthusiastic approval of a minority and of course some spiteful and stupid opposition too. These performances contributed very much to the fact that at latest in the twenties an aura of esoteric fame began to unfold about the name of my friend. But this much I will say: deeply as I was moved – not yet really surprised – by this outburst of religious feeling, which was the purer and more pious for the restraint and absence of cheap effects, no harp-twanging (though the text is actually a challenge to it), no drum to give back the thunder of the Lord; however much went to my heart certain beauties not at all achieved by the hackneyed tone-painting: the magnificent truths of the paean; the oppressively slow movement of the black cloud; the twice-repeated thundering 'Jehovah!' when 'the shattered wood steams' (a powerful passage); the so new and enlightened concord of the high register of the organ with the strings at the end, when the Deity comes, no longer in storm, but in hushed murmurings and beneath it 'arches the bow of peace'; yet despite all these I have never understood the work in its real spiritual sense, its inward necessity, its purpose, informed by fear, of seeking grace in praise. Did I at that time know the document, which my readers now know too, the record of the 'dialogue' in the stone-floored sala? Only conditionally could I have named myself before that 'a partner in your sorrow's mysteries', as it says in the 'Ode on Melancholy'; only with the right of a general concern since our boyhood days for his soul's health; but not through actual knowledge, as it then stood. Only later did I learn to understand the composition of the *Spring Festival* as what it was: a plea to God, an atonement for sin, a work of *attritio cordis*, composed, as I realized with shudders, under the threat of that visitor insisting that he was really visible.

But in still another sense did I fail to understand the personal and intellectual background of this production based on Klopstock's poems. For I did not, as I should have done, connect it with conversations I had with him at this time, or rather he had with me, when he gave me, quite circumstantially, with great animation, accounts of studies and researches in fields very remote from my curiosity or my scientific comprehension; thrilling enrichments, that is, of his knowledge of nature and the cosmos. And now he strongly reminded me of the older Leverkühn's musing mania for 'speculating the elements'.

Indeed, the composer of this setting for the *Spring Festival* did not conform to the poet's words that he 'would not fling himself in the ocean of the worlds'; that only about the drop in the bucket, about the earth, would he hover and adore. For Adrian did fling himself into the immense, which astro-physical science seeks to measure, only to arrive at measures, figures, orders of greatness with which the human spirit has no longer any relation, and which lose themselves in the theoretic and abstract, in the entirely non-sensory, not to say non-sensical. Moreover I will not forget that it all began with a dwelling on the 'drop', which does not ill deserve this name, as it consists mainly of water, the water of the oceans, which on the occasion of the creation 'also ran out from the hand of the Almighty'. On it, at first, we dwelt, and its dark secrets; for the wonders of the depths of the sea, the extravagant living things down there where no sun's ray penetrates, were the first matters of which Adrian told me, and indeed in such a strange and startling way that I was both entertained and bewildered, for he spoke as though he had personally seen and experienced it all.

Of course he had only read of these things, had got books about them and fed his fancy. But whether he had so concentrated on them, had so mastered these pictures mentally, or out of whatever whim it was, he pretended that in the region of the Bermudas, some nautical miles east of St George, he had himself gone down into the sea and been shown by his companion the natural phenomena of the deeps. He spoke of this companion as an American scholar named Akercocke, in company with whom he was supposed to have set up a new deep-sea record.

I remember this conversation most vividly. It occurred at a week-end I was spending in Pfeiffering, after the simple meal served us in the big piano-room, when the primly clad young Clementine had kindly brought us each our half-litre mug of beer, and we sat smoking Zechbauer cigars, light and good. It was about the hour when Suso, the yard dog, in other words Kaschperl, was loosed from his chain and allowed to range the court-yard.

Then Adrian embarked with gusto on his jest, which he related to me in the most circumstantial manner: how he and Professor Akercocke climbed into a bullet-shaped diving-bell of only one point two metres inside diameter, equipped somewhat like a stratosphere balloon, and were dropped by a crane from the companion ship into the sea, at this point very deep. It had been more than exciting – at least for him, if not for his mentor or cicerone, from whom he had procured this experience and who took the thing more coolly as it was not his first descent. Their situation inside the two-ton hollow ball was anything but comfortable, but was compensated for by the knowledge of their perfect safety, absolutely watertight as it was, capable of withstanding immense pressure. It was provided with a supply of oxygen, a telephone, high-voltage searchlights, and quartz windows all round. Somewhat longer than three hours in all they spent beneath the surface of the ocean; it had passed like a dream, thanks to the sights they were vouchsafed, the glimpses into a world whose soundless, frantic foreignness was explained and even justified by its utter lack of contact with our own.

Even so it had been a strange moment, and his heart had missed a beat, when one morning at nine o'clock the four-hundred pound armoured door had closed behind them and they swayed away from the ship and plunged into the water, crystal clear at first, lighted by the sun. But this illumination of the inside of our 'drop in the bucket' reached down only some fifty-seven metres. For at that depth light has come to an end; or rather, a new, unknown, irrelevant world here begins, into which Adrian with his guide went down to nearly fourteen times that depth, some thirty-six hundred feet, and there remained for half an hour, almost every moment painfully aware that a pressure of five hundred thousand tons rested upon their shelter.

Gradually, on the way down, the water had taken on a grey colour, that of a darkness mixed with some still undaunted rays of light. Not easily did these become discouraged; it was the will and way of them to make light and they did so to their uttermost, so that the next stage of light's exhaustion and retreat actually had more colour than the previous one. Through the quartz windows the travellers looked into a blue-blackness hard to describe; perhaps best compared to the dull colour of the horizon on a clear thawing day. After that, indeed long before the hand of the indicator stood at seven hundred and fifty to seven hundred and sixty-five metres, came solid blackness all round, the blackness of interstellar space whither for eternities no weakest sun-ray had penetrated, the eternally still and virgin night, which now had to put up with a powerful artificial light from the upper world, not of cosmic origin, in order to be looked at and looked through.

Adrian spoke of the itch one felt to expose the unexposed, to look at the unlooked-at, the not-to-be and not-expecting-to-be looked-at. There was a feeling of indiscretion, even of guilt, bound up with it, not quite allayed by the feeling that science must be allowed to press just as far forwards as it is given the intelligence of scientists to go. The incredible eccentricities, some grisly, some comic, which nature here achieved, forms and features which seemed to have scarcely any connexion with the upper world but rather to belong to another planet: these were the product of seclusion, sequestration, or reliance on being wrapped in eternal darkness. The arrival upon Mars of a human conveyance travelling through space – or rather, let us say, upon that half of Mercury which is eternally turned away from the sun – could excite no greater sensation in the inhabitants – if any – of that 'near' planet, than the appearance of the Akercocke diving-bell down here. The mass curiosity with which these inconceivable creatures of the depths had crowded round the cabin had been indescribable – and quite indescribable too was everything that went whisking past the windows in a blur of motion: frantic caricatures of organic life; predatory mouths opening and shutting; obscene jaws, telescopic eyes; the paper nautilus; silver- and gold-fish with goggling eyes on top of their heads; heteropods and pteropods, up to two or three yards long. Even those that floated passively in the flood, monsters compact of slime, yet with arms to catch their prey, polyps, acalephs, skyphomedusas – they all seemed to have been seized by spasms of twitching excitement.

It might well be that all these natives of the deep regarded this light-radiating guest as an outsize variation of themselves, for most of them could do what it could; that is to say, give out light by their own power. The visitors, Adrian said, had only to put out their own searchlight, when an extraordinary spectacle unfolded outside. Far and wide the darkness of the sea was illuminated by shooting and circling will-o'-the-wisps, caused by the light with which many of the creatures were equipped, so that in some cases the entire body was phosphorescent, while others had a searchlight, an electric lantern, with which presumably they not only lighted the darkness of their path, but also attracted their prey. They also probably used it in courtship. The ray from some of the larger ones cast such an intense white light that the observers' eyes were blinded. Others had eyeballs projecting on stalks; probably in order to perceive at the greatest possible distance the faintest gleam of light meant to lure or warn.

The narrator regretted that it was not possible to catch any of these monsters of the deep, at least some of the utterly unknown ones, and bring them to the surface. In order to do so, however, one would have to preserve for them while ascending the same tremendous atmospheric pressure they were used to and adapted to in their environment – the same that rested on our diving-bell – a disturbing thought. In their habitat the creatures counteracted it by an equal pressure of their tissues and cavities; so that if the outside pressure were decreased, they would inevitably burst. Some of them, alas, burst now, on coming into contact with the diving-bell: the watchers saw an unusually, large flesh-coloured wight, rather finely formed, just touch the vessel and fly into a thousand pieces.

Thus Adrian told his tale, as we smoked our cigars; quite as though he had himself been present and had all these things shown to him. He carried out the jest so well, with only half a smile, that I could but stare amazed even while I laughed and marvelled at his tale. His smile also probably expressed a teasing amusement at a certain resistance on my side, which must have been obvious to him, for he well knew my lack of interest, even amounting to distaste, for the tricks and mysteries of the natural, for 'nature' altogether, and my allegiance to the sphere of the human and articulate. Obviously this knowledge of his was in large part what led him to go on with his reports or, as he put it, his experiences of the monstrously extra-human; plunging, carrying me along with him, *'in den Ozean der Welten alle'*.

The transition was made easy for him by his previous descriptions. The alien, fantastic nature of the deep-sea life, which seemed no longer to belong to the same planet with us, was a point of departure. Another was the Klopstock phrase 'The Drop to the Bucket': how well its admiring humility described our own quite secondary position in the cosmos! This on account of our utter insignificance to any larger view; the almost undiscoverable situation not only of the earth but of our whole planetary system, the sun with its seven satellites, within the vortex of the Milky Way, to which it belongs – *'our'* Milky Way, to say nothing of the millions of other ones. The word 'our' lends a certain intimacy to the vastness to which it refers; it takes the feeling of 'home' and almost comically magnifies it into breath-takingly extended space, wherein then we are to consider ourselves as established if humble citizens. And here the tendency of nature to the spherical seems to be carried through: this was a third point to which Adrian linked his discourse on the cosmos; arriving at it partly through the strange experience of the sojourn in the hollow ball, the Akercocke diving-bell in which he purported to have spent some hours. In a hollow ball, so he was instructed, we all and sundry passed our days; for in the galactic system wherein we occupied an infinitesimal point somewhere at one side, the situation was as follows:

It was shaped more or less like a flat watch; round, and much less thick than its circumference: an aggregation not literally immeasurable but still truly vast, a whirling disk of concentrated hosts of stars and star systems, star clusters, double stars, which described elliptical orbits about each other; of gas clouds, nebulae, planetary nebulae, stellar nebulae, and so on. But this disk was only comparable to the flat round surface which results when one cuts an orange in half: for it was enclosed all round by a vapour of other stars, which again could not strictly speaking be called immeasurable, but as raised to a very high power of vastness and in whose spaces, mostly empty spaces, the given objects were so distributed that the whole structure formed a ball. Somewhere deep within this absurdly sparsely settled ball, belonging, in a very minor category, scarcely worth mention and not even easy to find, to the disk or condensed swarm of worlds, was the fixed star about which, along with its greater and smaller companions, sported the earth and its little moon. 'The sun' – a body little deserving of the definite article – a gas ball registering six thousand degrees of heat on its surface, and a mere million and a half kilometres in diameter, was as far distant from the centre of the galactic inner plane as that was thick through – in other words, thirty thousand light-years.

My general information permitted me to associate a concept, however imprecise, with the words 'light-year'. It was, of course, a spatial concept and the word meant the span that light puts behind it in the course of a whole earth-year, at a speed peculiar to it, of which I had a vague idea but Adrian had in his head the exact figure of 186,000 miles per second. So a light-year amounted to a round and net figure of six trillion miles, and the eccentricity of our solar system amounted to thirty thousand times as much, while the whole diameter of the galactic hollow ball came to two hundred thousand light-years.

No, it was not immeasurable, but it was in this way that it was to be measured. What is one to say to such an assault upon the human understanding? I confess to being so made that nothing but a resigned if also somewhat contemptuous shoulder-shrug remains to me in face of such ungraspable, such stunning statistics. Enthusiasm for size, being overwhelmed by size – that is no doubt a mental pleasure; but it is only possible in connexions which a human being can grasp. The Pyramids are large, Mont Blanc and the inside of the dome of St Peter's are large, unless one prefer to reserve this attribute of largeness to the mental and moral world, the nobility of the heart and of thought. The data of the cosmic creation are nothing but a deafening bombardment of our intelligence with figures furnished with a comet's tail of a couple of dozen ciphers, and comporting themselves as though they still had something, anything, to do with measurement and understanding. There is in all, this monstrousness nothing that could appeal to the likes of me as goodness, beauty, greatness; and I shall never understand the glory-to-God mental attitude which certain temperaments assume when they contemplate the 'works of God', meaning by the phrase the physics of the universe. And is a construction to be hailed as 'the works of God' when one may just as reasonably say: 'Well, what then?' instead of 'Glory to the Lord'? The first rather than the second seems to me the right answer to two dozen ciphers after a one or even after a seven, which really adds nothing to it; and I can see no sort of reason to fall in the dust and adore the fifth power of a million.

It was also a telling fact that Klopstock in his soaring poesy expressing and arousing a fervid reverence confines himself to the earth – the drop in the bucket – and leaves the quintillions alone. My friend Adrian, the composer of Klopstock's hymns, does, as I say, dwell on this aspect; but I should do wrong to arouse the impression that he does so with any sort of emotion or emphasis. Adrian's way of dealing with these insanities was cold, in-different, coloured by amusement at my unconcealed distaste. But also it displayed a certain initiated familiarity, a persistence, I mean, in the fiction that he had derived his knowledge not simply through reading, but rather by personal transmission, instruction, demonstration, experience, perhaps from his above-mentioned mentor, Professor Akercocke, who it appeared had been with him not only down in the darkness of the ocean deeps, but also up among the stars . . . He behaved in a way as though he had got it from his mentor, and indeed more or less through observation, that the physical universe – this word in its widest and furthest connotation – should be called neither finite nor infinite, because both words describe something some-how static, whereas the true situation was through and through dynamic in its nature, and the cosmos, at least for a long time, more precisely for nineteen hundred million years, has been in a state of furious expansion – that is, of explosion. Of this we were left in no doubt, due to the redshift of the light which reaches us from numerous milky-way systems at a known distance from us; the stronger alteration of colour of this light towards the red end of the spectrum is in proportion to the greater distance from us of these nebulae. Obviously they were moving away from us; and with the farthest ones, complexes one hundred and fifty million light-years away, particles of radioactive substance developed, amounting to twenty-five thousand kilometres a second, a rate of speed compared with which the splintering of a bursting shell was at a snail's pace. If then all the galaxies were to rush away from each other in the most exaggerated space of time, then the word 'explosion' would just be – or rather had not for a long time been – adequate to describe the state of the world-pattern and its way of expansion. It might once have been static, earlier, and been simply a milliard light-years in diameter. As things were now, one could speak indeed of expansion, but not of any constant expansion, 'finite' or 'infinite'. It seemed that his guide had been able to assure the questioner only of the fact that the sum of the collective existing galaxies was in the order of size of a hundred milliards, of which only a modest million were accessible to our telescopes.

Thus Adrian, smoking and smiling. I appealed to his conscience and demanded from him an admission that this spooking about with statistics forever escaping into the void could not possibly stir one to a feeling of the majesty of God or give rise to any moral elevation. It all looked very much more like devil's juggling.

'Admit,' said I to him, 'that the horrendous physical creation is in no way religiously productive. What reverence and what civilizing process born of reverence can come from the picture of a vast impropriety like this of the exploding universe? Absolutely none. Piety, reverence, intellectual decency, religious feeling, are only possible about men and through men, and by limitation to the earthly and human. Their fruit should, can and will be a religiously tinged humanism, conditioned by feeling for the transcendental mystery of man, by the proud consciousness that he is no mere biological being, but with a decisive part of him belongs to an intellectual and spiritual world, that to him the Absolute is given, the ideas of truth, of freedom, of justice; that upon him the duty is laid to approach the consummate. In this pathos, this obligation, this reverence of man for himself, is God; in a hundred milliards of Milky Ways I cannot find him.'

'So you are against the works,' he answered, 'and against physical nature, from which man comes and with him his incorporeal part, which in the end does occur in other places in the cosmos. Physical creation, this monstrosity of a world set-up, so annoying to you, is contestably the premise for the moral, without which it would have no soil, and perhaps one must call the good the flower of evil – *une fleur du mal*. But your *homo Dei* is after all – or not after all, I beg pardon, I mean before all – a part of this abominable nature – with not a very generous quantum of potential spirituality. Moreover it is amusing to see how much your humanism, and probably all humanism, inclines to the medieval geocentric – as it obviously must. In the popular belief, humanism is friendly to science; but it cannot be, for one cannot consider the subjects of science to be devil's work without seeing the same in science itself. That is Middle Ages. The Middle Ages were geocentric and anthropocentric. The Church, in which they survived, has set itself to oppose astronomical knowledge in the humanistic spirit; bedevilled and forbidden it to the honour of the human being; out of humanity has insisted on ignorance. You see, your humanism is pure Middle Ages. Its concern is a cosmology proper to Kaisersaschern and its towers: it leads to astrology, to observation of the position of the planets, the constellation and its favourable or unfavourable indications – quite naturally and rightly, for nothing is clearer than the intimate interdependence of the bodies of a cosmic little group so closely bound together as our solar system, and their near neighbourly mutual reference.'

'We have already talked about astrological conjuncture,' I broke in. 'It was long ago, we were talking round the Cow Pond, and it was a musical conversation. At that time you defended the constellation.'

'I still defend it today,' he answered. 'Astrological times knew a lot. They knew, or divined, things which science in its broadest scope is coming back to. That diseases, plagues, epidemics have to do with the position of the stars was to those times an intuitive certainty. Today we have got so far as to debate whether germs, bacteria, organisms which, we say, can produce an influenza epidemic on earth come from other planets – Mars, Jupiter, or Venus.'

Contagious diseases, plague, black death, were probably not of this planet; as, almost certainly indeed, life itself has not its origin on our globe, but came hither from outside. He, Adrian, had it on the best authority that it came from neighbouring stars which are enveloped in an atmosphere more favourable to it, containing much methane and ammonia, like Jupiter, Mars and Venus. From them, or from one of them – he left me the choice – life had once, borne by cosmic projectiles or simply by radiation pressure, arrived upon our formerly sterile and innocent planet. My humanistic *homo Dei*, that crowning achievement of life, was together with his obligations to the spiritual in all probability the produce of the marsh-gas fertility of a neighbouring star.

'The flower of evil,' I repeated, nodding.

'And blooming mostly in mischief,' he added.

Thus he taunted me, not only with my kindly view of the world, but also by persisting in the whimsical pretence of a personal, direct, and special knowledge about the affairs of heaven and earth. I did not know, but I might have been able to tell myself, that all this meant something, meant a new work: namely, the cosmic music which he had in his mind, after the episode of the new songs. It was the amazing symphony in one movement, the orchestral fantasy that he was working out during the last months of 1913 and the first of 1914, and which very much against my expressed wish bore the title *Marvels of the Universe*. I was mistrustful of the flippancy of the name and suggested the title *Symphonia cosmologica*. But Adrian insisted, laughing, on the other, mock-pathetic, ironic name, which certainly better prepared the knowing for the out-and-out bizarre and unpleasant character of the work, even though often these images of the monstrous and uncanny were grotesque in a solemn, formal, mathematical way. This music has simply nothing in common with the spirit of the *Spring Celebration*, which after all was in a certain way the preparation for it: I mean with the spirit of humble glorification. If certain musical features of the writing peculiar to Adrian had not indicated the author, one could scarcely believe that the same mind brought forth both. Nature and essence of that nearly thirty-minutes-long orchestral world-portrait is mockery, a mockery which all too well confirms my opinion expressed in conversation, that preoccupation with the immeasurable extra-human affords nothing for piety to feed on: a luciferian sardonic mood, a sneering travesty of praise which seems to apply not only to the frightful clockwork of the world-structure but also the medium used to describe it: yes, repeatedly with music itself, the cosmos of sound. The piece has contributed not a little to the reproach levelled at the art of my friend, as a virtuosity antipathetic to the artist mind, a blasphemy, a nihilistic sacrilege.

But enough on this theme. The next two chapters I mean to devote to some social experiences which I shared with Adrian Leverkühn at the turn of the year 1913–14, during the last Munich carnival before the outbreak of the war.

Chapter Twenty-eight

I have already said that the lodger at the Schweigestills' did not quite bury himself in his cloistral solitude, guarded by Kaschperl-Suso. Though sporadically and with reserve, he cultivated a certain social life. Even so, he seemed to cling to the soothing necessity of an early leave-taking and fixed departure by the eleven-o'clock train. We met at the Roddes' in Rambergstrasse, with whose circle – Schwerdtfeger the fiddler and whistler, the Knöterichs, Dr Kranich, Zink and Spengler – I had got on a friendly footing; further at the Schalginhaufens', also at the home of Radbruch, Schildknapp's publisher, in Fürstenstrasse, and in the elegant *bel étage* of the Rhineland paper-manufacturer Bullinger, where also Rüdiger introduced us.

At the Roddes', as well as in the pillared Schlaginhaufen salon, they enjoyed my viola d'amore, and in any case it was the only contribution that I, a scholar and schoolmaster, never very lively in conversation, could make to this society. In the Rambergstrasse it was particularly the asthmatic Dr Kranich and Baptist Spengler who kept me to it: the one of his antiquarian interests (he liked to talk with me, in his clearly articulated, well-arranged sentences about numismatics and about the historical development of the viola family), the other out of a general taste for the out-of-the-way and even the decadent. Still I had in that house to have regard for Konrad Knöterich's craving to make himself heard playing cello and snorting the while. And the little audience had a justified preference for Schwerdtfeger's captivating violin-playing. So much the more did it flatter my vanity (I deny it not) that there was a lively demand from the much larger and more elevated public which the ambition of Frau Dr Schlaginhaufen, née von Plausig, knew how to gather round her and her hard-of-hearing, Swabian-speaking husband. I had always cultivated my music merely as an amateur; but I was almost always obliged to bring my instrument with me to the Briennerstrasse, to regale the company with a chaconne or sarabande from the seventeenth century, a *'plaisir d'amour'* from the eighteenth, or to perform a sonata by Ariosti, the friend of Handel, or one of Haydn's written for the viola di bordone but quite possible for the viola d'amore as well.

Not only from Jeanette Scheurl did suggestions like the last proceed, but also from the General-Intendant, Excellency von Riedesel, whose patronage of the old instrument and old music did not indeed, as with Kranich, stem from scholarly or antiquarian interest, but was purely conservative in its origin, a great difference of course. This courtier, a former cavalry colonel, who had been appointed to his present post simply and solely because it had been well known that he played piano a little (how many centuries ago it seems, that one could become a General-Intendant solely because one was 'noble' and played the piano a little!), Baron Riedesel, then, saw in everything old and historic a bulwark against the new and subversive, a sort of feudal argument against it, and supported it in this sense, without in fact understanding anything about it. For just as little as one understands the new and the young, without being at home in the traditional, just so must love for the old remain ungenuine and sterile if one shut oneself away from the new, which with historical inevitability grows out of it. Thus Riedesel esteemed and protected the ballet, and forsooth because it was 'graceful'. The word meant to him a shibboleth, a conservative arguing-point against the modern and insurrectionary. Of the traditional world of the Russian and French ballets, represented by a Tchaikovsky, a Ravel, a Stravinsky, he had no notion; ideas about the classical ballet such as those which the last-named Russian master later enunciated were remote from his mind; ballet as a triumph of plan and measure over unstable feeling, of order over chance, as a pattern of conscious, appolline activity, a paradigm for art. What hovered before his mind's eye were simply gauze petticoats, toe-pointing, tripping, and arms bent 'gracefully' over heads, under the eyes of a court society asserting the 'ideal', reprobating the hateful problematical, these sitting in their loges, while a well-trained bourgeoisie filled the parterre.

Well, there was much Wagner played at the Schlaginhaufens', since the dramatic soprano Tania Orlanda, tremendous woman, and the heroic Harald Kioeielund, a man already stout, with a pince-nez and brazen voice, were frequent guests. But without Wagner's work, loud and violent as it was, Herr Riedesel and his Hoftheater could not have existed, so it was received, more or less, into the kingdom of the feudal and 'graceful' and respect was paid it, the more readily because there were already newer works which went still further, so that one could reject them, and play off Wagner against them as a conservative. Thus His Excellence himself could flatter the singers by playing their accompaniments on the piano, although his pianistic virtuosity was scarcely equal to the task and more than once compromised the effect. I did not care for it when Kammersänger Kioeielund brayed out Siegfried's pretty dull and long-winded smith's songs so that all the vases and glass-ware in the salon rattled and rang in sympathy. But I confess that I am not proof against such a heroic female voice as the Orlanda's was at that time. The weight of her personality, the power of her organ, her practised technique produced the convincing illusion of a regal female soul possessed by lofty emotion. When she sang Isolde's *'Frau Minne kenntest du nicht'*, and marked by an energetic downward thrust of her arms the ecstatic *'Die Fackel, wär's meines Lebens Licht lachend sie zu löschen zagt' ich nicht'*, it did not lack much for me, with tears in my eyes, to have knelt before the singer as she stood triumphantly smiling, overwhelmed with applause. Moreover it was Adrian who had accompanied her, and he too smiled when he rose from the piano-stool and his eyes dwelt on my face, moved as it was almost to weeping.

It does one good, among such impressive performances, to contribute something oneself to the artistic entertainment, and I was gratified when Excellence von Riedesel, seconded at once by our long-legged hostess, urged me in his south-German pronunciation, and voice made more strident by his officer's training, to repeat the andante and minuet of Mildandre (1770) which I had once before played on my seven strings. How weak is man! I was grateful to him, I utterly forgot my dislike of his smooth and empty aristocrat's face, which out of sheer imperturbable insolence positively shone; with the twisted blond moustaches, the smooth-shaven cheeks, and the gleaming monocle in the eye under the bleached brows. To Adrian, as well I knew, this titled gentleman was a figure beyond judgement or sentence, beyond hatred or scorn, yes, beyond laughter; he was not worth a shoulder-shrug – and just so, actually, I felt myself. But at such a moment, when he challenged me to contribute something 'graceful', that the company might recover from the attack of the revolutionary arriviste, I could not help acceding to his request.

It was very strange, partly painful and partly comic, to observe Riedesel's conservatism in contact with another brand of the same thing. Here it was a matter not so much of 'still' as 'again'; for this was an after- and anti-revolutionary conservatism, a revolt against bourgeois liberal standards from the other end, not from the rear but from the front; not from the old but from the new. Such a contact was encouraging as well as bewildering to the simple old conservatism; and occasion for it was afforded in our day, even in the Schlaginhaufen salon, where the social ambitions of the hostess brought people of every stripe together. For example, one of the guests was the private scholar Dr Chaim Breisacher, a racial and intellectual type in high, one might almost say reckless development and of a fascinating ugliness. Here, obviously with a certain malicious pleasure, he played the role of ferment and foreigner. The hostess approved his dialectic readiness, produced with a decided Palatinate accent; also his turn for paradox, which made the ladies clap their hands over their heads in demure jubilation. As for himself, it was probably snobbishness that made him take pleasure in this society, as well as the need of astonishing elegant simplicity with ideas which, in a literary circle, would have made less of a sensation. I did not like him in the least, always saw in him an intellectual intrigant, and was convinced that he was repugnant to Adrian as well, although, on grounds to me unclear, we never came to any detailed conversation about Breisacher. But the man's scent for the intellectual weather of the time, his nose for the newest views, I have never denied, and some of all that I met for the first time in his person and his conversation in society.

He was a polyhistor, who knew how to talk about anything and every-thing; he was concerned with the philosophy of culture, but his views were anti-cultural, in so far as he gave out to see in the whole history of culture nothing but a process of decline. The most contemptuous word on his lips was the word 'progress'; he had an annihilating way of pronouncing it; and one felt that the conservative scorn which he devoted to the idea was regarded by himself as the true legitimation of his presence in this society, the mark of his fitness for it. He had wit, but of no very sympathetic kind; as when he poured scorn on the development of painting from the primitive flat to the presentation of perspective. To condemn as incapacity or ignorance, even as clumsy primitivism, the rejection of perspective eye-deception by preperspective art; even pityingly to shrug the shoulder over it: this he declared to be the peak of silly modern arrogance. Rejection, renunciation, disdain were not incapacity, nor uninstructedness, nor evidence of poverty. As though illusion were not the cheapest principle in art, the most suited to the mob, as though it were not simply a sign of elevated taste to wish to know nothing of it! The gift of wanting to know nothing of certain things was very close to wisdom, was even part of it; but it had unfortunately been lost, and ordinary, impudent know-nothings called themselves progressive.

The guests of Frau Schlaginhaufen née von Plausig somehow found themselves very much at home listening to these remarks. They may have felt that Breisacher was not quite the right person to make them, but scarcely that they might not be the right people to applaud them.

It was the same thing, he said, with the change-over of music from monody to part-music, to harmony, which people liked to think of as cultural progress, when actually it had been just an acquisition of barbarism.

'That is ... pardon, barbarism?' croaked Herr von Riedesel, who was of course accustomed to see in the barbaric a form, if a slightly compromising one, of the conservative.

'Yes indeed, Excellence. The origins of polyphonic music – that is, of singing simultaneously in fifths and fourths – lie remote from the centre of musical civilization, far from Rome, where the beautiful voice and the cult of it were at home. They lie in the raw-throated north and seem to have been a sort of compensation for the rawness. They lie in England and France, particularly in savage Britain, which was the first to accept the third into harmony. The so-called higher development, the complication, the progress are thus sometimes the achievement of barbarism. I leave it to you whether this is to be praised or not ...'

It was clear and plain that he was making fun of His Excellence and the whole company, at the same time as he was ingratiating himself with them as a conservative. Obviously he did not feel comfortable so long as any of his audience knew what they were to think. Of course polyphonic vocal music, this invention of progressivist barbarism, became the object of his conservative protection so soon as the historical transition from it to the harmonic-chordal principle and therewith to instrumental music of the last two centuries was complete. This, then, was the decline, namely the deterioration of the great and only true art of counterpoint, the cool and sacred play of numbers, which, thank God, had had nothing to do with prostitution of feeling or blasphemous dynamic; and in this decline, right in the middle of it, belonged the great Bach from Eisenach, whom Goethe quite rightly called a harmonist. A man was not the inventor of the well-tempered clavichord, accordingly of the possibility of understanding every note ambiguously and exchanging them enharmonically, and thus of the newer harmonic romanticism of modulation, without deserving the hard name which the wise one of Weimar gave him. Harmonic counterpoint? There was not such a thing. It was neither fish nor flesh. The softening, the effeminizing and falsification, the new interpretation put on the old and genuine polyphony understood as a combined sounding of various voices into the harmonic-chordal, had already begun in the sixteenth century, and people like Palestrina, the two Gabrielis, and our good Orlando di Lasso here on the spot had already played their shameful part in it. These gentlemen brought us the conception of the vocal polyphonic art, 'humanly' at first, oh yes, and seemed to us therefore the greatest masters of this style. But that was simply because for the most part they delighted in a purely chordal texture of phrase, and their way of treating the polyphonic style had been miserably weakened by their regard for the harmonic factor, for the relation of consonance and dissonance.

While everybody marvelled and laughed and clapped his knees at these irritating remarks, I sought Adrian's eye, but he would not look at me. As for von Riedesel, he was a prey to sheer confusion.

'Pardon me,' he said, 'permit me ... Back, Palestrina ...'

These names wore for him the nimbus of conservative authority, and here they were being assigned to the realm of modernistic disintegration. He sympathized – and at the same time found it all so unnatural that he even took his monocle out of his eye, thus robbing his face of every gleam of intelligence. He fared no better when Breisacher's cultural harangue shifted its theme to the field of Old Testament criticism, thus turning to his own personal sphere of origin, the Jewish race or people and its intellectual history. Even here he adhered to a double-faced, a crass and malicious conservatism. According to him, decline, besottedness, loss of every contact with the old and genuine, had set in earlier and in a more respectable place than anyone could have dreamed. I can only say that it was on the whole frantically funny. Biblical personages – revered by every Christian child – King David, King Solomon, and the prophets drivelling about dear God in heaven, these were the already debased representatives of an exploded late theology, which no longer had any idea of the old and genuine Hebraic actuality of Jahve, the Elohim of the people; and in the rites with which at the time of genuine folkishness they served this national god or rather forced him to physical presence, saw only 'riddles of primeval time'. He was particularly cutting about Solomon 'the wise', and treated him with so little ceremony that the gentlemen whistled through their teeth and the ladies cheered as well as they could for amazement.

'Pardon,' said von Riedesel. 'I am, to put it mildly . . . King Solomon in all his glory . . . Should you not –'

'No, Excellence, I should not,' answered Breisacher. 'The man was an aesthete unnerved by erotic excesses and in a religious sense a progressivist blockhead, typical of the back-formation of the cult of the effectively present national god, the general concept of the metaphysical power of the folk, into the preaching of an abstract and generally human god in heaven; in other words, from the religion of the people to the religion of the world. To prove it we only need to read the scandalous speech which he made after the first temple was finished, where he asks: "But will God indeed dwell on the earth?" as though Israel's whole and unique task had not consisted therein, that it should build God a dwelling, a tent, and provide all means for His constant presence. But Solomon was so bold as to declaim: "Behold, the heaven and heaven of heavens cannot contain Thee; how much less this house that I have builded!" That is just twaddle and the beginning of the end, that is the degenerate conception of the poets of the Psalms; with whom God is already entirely exiled into the sky, and who constantly sing of God in heaven, whereas the Pentateuch does not even know it as the seat of the Godhead. There the Elohim goes on ahead of the people in a pillar of fire, there He will dwell among the people, go about among the people and have His shambles – to avoid the thin word "altar" substituted by a later humanity. Is it conceivable for a psalmist to make God ask: "Do I then eat the flesh of bulls and drink the blood of goats?" To put such words in God's mouth is already simply unheard of, a slap of impertinent enlightenment in the face of the Pentateuch, which expressly described the sacrifice as "the bread" – that is, as the actual nourishment of Jahve. It is only a step from this question, as also from the phrases of Solomon the "wise", to Maimonides, supposedly the greatest rabbinical scholar of the Middle Ages, actually an assimilator of Aristotle, who manages to "explain" the sacrifice as a concession by God to the heathen instincts of the people – ha, ha! Good, the sacrifice of blood and fat, which once, salted and seasoned with savoury smells, fed God, made Him a body, held Him to the present, is for the psalmist only a "symbol"' (I can still hear the accents of ineffable contempt in which Dr Breisacher uttered the word); 'one no longer slaughters the beast, but, incredibly enough, gratitude and humility. "Whoso offereth praise", is the word now, "glorifieth me"! And another time: "The sacrifices of God are a broken spirit." In short, all that ceased long ago, to be folk and blood and religious reality; it is nothing any more but weak water-gruel.'

So much as a taste of Breisacher's highly conservative exegesis. It was as
amusing as it was repulsive. He could not say enough to display the genuine
cult of the real and by no means abstractly universal, hence also not 'almighty'
and 'all-present' God of the people as a magic technique, a manipulation of
dynamic forces physically not without its risks, in which mishaps might
easily occur, catastrophic short circuits due to mistakes and failures. The
sons of Aaron had died because they had brought on 'strange fire'. That was
an instance of a technical mischance, the consequence of an error.
Somebody named Uzza had laid hands on the chest, the so-called ark of the
covenant, as it threatened to slip when it was being transported by wagon,
and he fell dead on the spot. That too was a transcendental dynamic
discharge, occurring through negligence – the negligence, indeed, of King
David, who was too fond of playing the harp, and had no real understanding
of things any more; for he had the ark conveyed as the Philistines did, by
wagon instead of on bearing-poles according to the well-founded prescript
of the Pentateuch. David indeed, was quite as ignorant of origins and quite
as besotted, not to say brutalized, as Solomon his son. He was too ignorant,
for instance, to realize the dynamic dangers of a general census of the
population; and by instituting one had brought about a serious biological
misfortune, an epidemic with high mortality; a reaction of the metaphysical
powers of the people, which might have been foreseen. For a genuine folk
simply could not stand such a mechanizing registration, the dissolution by
enumeration of the dynamic whole into similar individuals ...

It merely gratified Breisacher when a lady interposed and said she had not
known that a census was such a sin.

'Sin?' he responded, in an exaggeratedly questioning tone. No, in the
genuine religion of a genuine folk such colourless theological conceptions as
sin and punishment never occurred, in their merely ethical causal connexion. What we had here was the causality of error, a working accident.
Religion and ethics represented the decline of a religion. All morality was 'a
purely intellectual' misunderstanding of the ritual. Was there anything
more god-forsaken than the 'purely intellectual'? It had remained for the
characterless world-religion, out of 'prayer' – *sit venia verbo* – to make a
begging appeal for mercy, an 'O Lord', 'God have mercy', a 'Help' and
'Give' and 'Be so good'. Our so-called prayer ... 'Pardon!' said von
Riedesel, this time with real emphasis. 'Quite right, of course, but "Head
bare at prayer" was always my –'

'Prayer,' finished Dr Breisacher relentlessly, 'is the vulgarized and
rationalistically watered-down late form of something very vital, active and
strong: the magic invocation, the coercion of God.'

I really felt sorry for the Baron. Here was his aristocratic conservatism
outbid by the frightfully clever playing of atavistic cards; by a radical
conservatism that no longer had anything aristocratic about it, but rather
something revolutionary; something more disrupting than any liberalism,
and yet, as though in mockery, possessing a laudable conservative appeal.
All that must bewilder the very depths of his soul. I imagined it giving him a
sleepless night, but my sympathy may have been exaggerated. Certainly not
everything that Breisacher said was correct. One could easily have disputed
him and pointed out that the spirited condemnation of the sacrifice is not
found first of all in the prophets but in the Pentateuch itself; for it is Moses
who bluntly declares that the sacrifice is secondary and lays all the emphasis
on obedience to God and the keeping of His commandments. But a sensitive
man does not like to disturb another; it is unpleasant to break in on a train of

thought with logical or historical objections; even in the anti-intellectual such a man respects and spares the intellectual. Today we see, of course, that it was the mistake of our civilization to have practised all too magnanimously this respect and forbearance. For we found after all that the opposite side met us with sheer impudence and the most determined intolerance.

I was already thinking of all these things when at the beginning of this work I made an exception to my general profession of friendliness towards the Jewish people, confessing that I had run across some pretty annoying specimens, and the name of the scholar Breisacher slipped prematurely from my pen. Yet can one quarrel with the Jewish spirit when its quick hearing and receptivity for the coming thing, the new, persists also in the most extraordinary situations, where the avant-garde coincides with the re-actionary? In any case, it was at the Schlaginhaufens', and through this very Breisacher, that I first came in touch with the new world of anti-humanity, of which my easy-going soul till then had known nothing at all.

Chapter Twenty-nine

The Munich carnival season, that period between Epiphany and Ash Wednesday, was celebrated by common consent with dance and mirth, with flaming cheeks and flashing eyes, and with all sorts of public and private entertainments. The carnival of 1914, in which I, the still youthful academy professor from Freising, alone or in company with Adrian, took part, has remained in my memory, a vivid or rather a portentous image. It was indeed the last carnival before the beginning of the four-year war which has now telescoped with the horrors of today into one historical epoch; the last one before the so-called 'first World War', which put an end for ever to the idyll of aesthetic guilelessness in the city on the Isar and its dionysiac easy-goingness – if I may put it like that. And it was also the time in which certain individual destinies in our circle of acquaintance unfolded before my eyes, and, almost unheeded outside our circle, led up to naked catastrophe. I go into it in these pages because what happened did to some extent touch the life and destiny of my hero, Adrian Leverkühn; yes, in one of them, to my actual knowledge, he was involved and active in an obscure and fatal way.

I am not referring to the case of Clarissa Rodde, the proud and flippant blonde who toyed with the macabre. She still lived among us, in her mother's house, and shared in the carnival gaieties. Soon afterwards, however, she prepared to leave town and fill an engagement as *jeune première* in the provinces, which her teacher, who played father parts at the Hoftheater, had got for her. The engagement proved a failure; and her teacher, a man of experience named Seiler, must be absolved from all responsibility for it. He had written a letter one day to the Frau Senator saying that his pupil was extraordinarily intelligent and full of enthusiasm, but that she had not enough natural gift for a successful career on the stage. She lacked, he said, the first requisite of all dramatic art, the instinct of the play-actor – what one calls theatre blood; and in all conscience he felt constrained to advise against her continuing. This had led to a *crise de nerves*, an outburst of despair on Clarissa's part, which went to the mother's heart, and Seiler had been asked to terminate the training and use his connexions to get her a start as a beginner.

It is now twenty-four years since Clarissa's lamentable destiny fulfilled itself, as I shall relate in its proper place in my story. Here I have in mind what happened to her delicate and suffering sister Inez, who cultivated the past and its regrets – and to poor Rudi Schwerdtfeger, of whom I thought with horror when I mentioned just now, almost involuntarily, the share of the recluse Adrian Leverkühn in these events. The reader is already used to my anticipations and will not interpret them as muddle-headedness and disregard of literary conventions. The truth is simply that I fix my eye in advance with fear and dread, yes, with horror on certain things which I shall sooner or later have to tell; they stand before me and weigh me down, and I try to distribute their weight by referring to them beforehand, of course not comprehensibly to anybody but myself. I let them a little way out of the bag and hope by this means to make the telling more tolerable to myself, to take out the sting and mitigate the distress. So much in excuse of a 'faulty' technique of narration and in explanation of my difficulties. I scarcely need to say that Adrian was remote from the beginnings of the events I shall speak of here, being aware of them only to a certain extent and that only through me, who had much more social curiosity or shall I say human sympathy.

As I mentioned earlier, neither of the two Rodde sisters, Clarissa and Inez, got on particularly well with their mother, the Frau Senator, and they not seldom betrayed that the informal, slightly lax and bohemian air of her salon, the uprooted existence, upholstered though it was with the remnants of upper-middle-class elegance, got on their nerves. They strained away from the hybrid milieu, but in different directions. The proud Clarissa reached outwards towards a definite career as an actress for which, as her master had finally been forced to say, she lacked a real calling. While, on the other hand, the refined and pensive Inez, who was at bottom afraid of life, yearned back to the refuge, the psychological security of an assured bourgeois position, the route to which was marriage, for love if possible, but in God's name even without love. Inez walked this road, of course with the cordial approval of her mother, and came to grief, as her sister did on hers. It turned out tragically enough that this solution was not the right one: that neither for Inez personally, nor for her circumstances in view of the times she lived in, this upsetting and undermining social epoch, did it hold out any hope of satisfaction.

At this time there approached her a certain Dr Helmut Institoris, instructor in aesthetics and the history of art at the Technical Institute in Munich, where he lectured on aesthetic theory and the history of Renaissance architecture and handed round photographs in class. He had good prospects of being called one day to the university, of becoming professor, member of the Academy and so on; especially when he, a bachelor from a solid Würzburg family, in expectancy of a good inheritance, should have enhanced his dignity by setting up a household of his own where he could gather society about him. He went courting, and he did not worry about the financial situation of the girl he courted. On the contrary, he belonged to those men who prefer in marriage to have all the economic power in their hands and to have their wives dependent on them.

Such an attitude does not speak for conscious strength. And Institoris was in fact not a strong man; one realized it in the aesthetic admiration he showed for everything bursting with exuberant vitality. He was blond and dolichocephalic, rather small and very good form, with smooth hair, parted and slightly oiled. A blond moustache drooped over his mouth, and behind the gold-rimmed glasses the blue eyes wore a gentle, high-minded expression, which made it hard to understand – or perhaps precisely did make one understand – that he respected and revered brute force, but of course only when it was beautiful. He belonged to a type bred in those decades – the kind of man who, as a Baptist Spengler once aptly put it, 'when consumption glows in his cheeks, keeps on shrieking: "How stark and beautiful is life!" '

Well, Institoris did not shriek, on the contrary he spoke rather softly, with a lisp, even when he celebrated the Italian Renaissance as a time that 'reeked of blood and beauty'. He was not consumptive, had at most, like nearly everybody, been slightly tubercular in his youth. But he was delicate and nervous, suffered from his sympathetic nerve, in his solar plexus, from which so many anxieties and early fears of death proceed, and was an habitué of a sanatorium for the wealthy in Meran. Surely he promised himself – and his doctors promised him – an improvement in his health resulting from the regularity of a comfortable married life.

In the winter of 1913–14 he approached our Inez Rodde in a way that made one guess it would end in an engagement. However, the affair dragged on for some time, into the early years of the war: doubt and conscience-searching on both sides probably induced a long and careful testing, to see whether they were truly born for each other. But when one saw the 'pair' together in the Frau Senator's salon, to which Institoris had correctly sought an introduction, or in public places, often sitting apart and talking, it was just this question which seemed to be at issue between them, whether directly or not, and the friendly observer, seeing something like a trial engagement in the offing involuntarily discussed the subject too within himself.

That it was Inez upon whom Helmut had cast his eye might surprise one at first, but one understood it better in the end. She was no Renaissance female – anything but that, in her temperamental sensitiveness, with her veiled glance, full of melancholy and distinction; her head drooping on the slender, extended stalk and the little pursed-up mouth that seemed to indicate a feeble and fluctuating love of mischief. But on the other hand, the wooer would not have known how to cope with his own ideal either; his masculine superiority would have been found sorely wanting – one only needed to imagine him paired with a full and rounded nature like the Orlanda's to smile and be convinced. And Inez was by no means without feminine charm; it was understandable that man on the look-out might have fallen in love with her heavy hair, her little dimpling hands, her aristocratic air of setting store by herself. She might be what he needed. Her circumstances attracted him: namely, her patrician origin, on which she laid stress, though it was slightly breathed upon by her present transplanted state; the faint suggestion that she had come down in the world, and thus threatened no superiority. Indeed, he might cherish the thought that in making her his he would be raising and rehabilitating her. A widowed mother, half-impoverished, a little pleasure-seeking; a sister who was going on the stage; a circle more or less bohemian: these were connexions which did not, in combination with his own dignity, displease him, especially since socially he lost nothing by them, did not endanger his career, and might be sure that Inez, correctly and amply supplied by the Frau Senator with a dowry of linen, perhaps even silver, would make a model housewife and hostess.

Thus things looked to me, as seen from Dr Institoris's side. If I tried to look at him with the girl's eyes, the thing ceased to be plausible. I could not, even using all my imagination, ascribe to the man, unimpressive as he was, absorbed in himself, refined indeed, with an excellent education, but physically anything but commanding (he even had a tripping gait), any appeal for the other sex; whereas I felt that Inez, with all her maiden reserve and austerity, needed such an appeal. Added to this was the contrast between the philosophical views, the theoretic posture towards life, assumed by the two – which might be considered diametrical and exemplary. It was, to put it briefly, the antithesis between aesthetics and ethics, which in fact largely dominated the cultural dialectics of the time and was to some extent embodied in these two young people: the conflict between a doctrinaire glorification of 'life' in its splendid unthinkingness, and the pessimistic reverence for suffering, with its depth and wisdom. One may say that at its source this contrast had formed a personal unity and only through time fell out and strove against itself. Dr Institoris was in the very marrow of his bones a man of the Renaissance – one feels like commenting 'Good God!' – and Inez Rodde quite explicitly a child of pessimistic moralism. For a world that 'reeked of blood and beauty' she had no use at all, and as for 'life' she was seeking shelter from it in a strictly orthodox, modish, economically well-upholstered marriage, which should protect her from all possible blows of fate. It was ironic that the man – the manikin – who seemed desirous to offer her this shelter raved about beautiful ruthlessness and Italian poisoners.

I doubt that they, when they were alone, discussed any controversies of world-wide bearing. They talked of things nearer at hand and simply tried to see how it would be to be engaged. Philosophical discussion as a social diversion belonged more to the larger group; and I do remember several occasions when we were all sitting together, perhaps round an alcove table in a ballroom, and the view of the two clashed in conversation. Institoris might assert that only human beings with strong and brutal instincts could create great works; and Inez would protest, contending that it had often been highly Christian characters, bowed down by conscience, refined by suffering, their view of life marked by melancholy, from whom had come great things in art. Such antitheses I found idle and ephemeral; they seemed to do no justice to actual fact, the seldom happy and certainly always precarious balance of vitality and infirmity which genius obviously is. But in this discussion one side represented that which it was, namely sickliness, the other that which it worshipped, namely strength; and both must be allowed to have their voice.

Once, I recall, as we sat together (the Knöterichs, Zink and Spengler, Schildknapp and his publisher Radbruch were also of the party) the friendly difference arose not between the lovers, as one tended to call them, but amusingly enough between Institoris and Rudi Schwerdtfeger, who was sitting with us, very charming in his huntsman's costume. I no longer clearly remember the discussion; anyhow the disagreement arose from a quite innocent remark of Schwerdtfeger's about which he had surely thought little or nothing. It was about 'merit', so much I know; something fought for, achieved, accomplished by will-power and self-conquest, and Rudolf, who praised the occurrence warmly, and called it deserving, could not in the least understand what Institoris meant by denying any value to it and refusing to recognize any virtue that had to sweat for it to that extent. From the point of view of beauty, he said, it was not the will but the gift that was to be praised; it alone could be called meritorious. Effort was plebeian; aristocratic and therefore alone meritorious was solely what happened out of instinct, involuntary and with ease. Now, the good Rudi was no hero or conqueror, and had never in his life done anything that did not come easy to him, as for instance his capital violin playing. But what the other said did go against the grain with him, and although he dimly felt that the subject had something 'higher' about it, out of his own reach, he would not let himself be talked down. He looked Institoris in the face, his lip curled angrily, and his blue eyes bored into the other's, first the right and then the left, by turns.

'After all, that is just nonsense,' he said, but in a contained, rather subdued voice, betraying that he did not feel so sure of his argument. 'Merit is merit, and a gift isn't a merit. You are always talking about beauty, doctor, but after all it is beautiful when somebody triumphs over himself and does something better than nature gave him to do. What do you say, Inez?' he turned appealingly to her with his question, in perfect innocence, for he had no idea of the fundamentally opposed nature of her views and Helmut's.

'You are right,' she answered, a faint glow rising in her cheeks. 'At least I think so. A gift is pleasing; but the word "merit" implies admiration of a different kind, not applicable to a gift nor to the instinctive at all.'

'There you have it!' cried Schwerdtfeger triumphantly, and Institoris laughed back:

'By all means. You went to the right shop.'

There was something strange here; nobody could help feeling it, at least for the moment; nor did the flush in Inez's cheek immediately subside. It was just in her line to disagree with her lover in all such questions. But it was not in her line to agree with the boy Rudolf. He was utterly unaware that there was such a thing as immoralism, and one cannot well agree with a thesis while not understanding its opposite – at least not before it has been explained to him. In Inez's verdict, although it was logically quite natural and justified, there was after all something that put one off, and that something was underlined for me by the burst of laughter with which her sister Clarissa greeted Schwerdtfeger's undeserved triumph. It surely did not escape this haughty person with the too short chin when superiority, on grounds which have nothing to do with superiority, gave something away and was just as certainly of the opinion that it gave nothing away.

'There!' she cried. 'Jump up, Rudolf, say thank you, hop up, laddy, and bow! Fetch your rescuer an ice and engage her for the next waltz!'

That was always her way. She always stood up for her sister and said 'Up with you!' whenever it was a matter of Inez's dignity. She said it to Institoris, too, the suitor, when he behaved with something less than alacrity in his gallantries, or was slow in the uptake. Altogether out of pride she held with superiority, looked out for it, and showed herself highly surprised when she thought it did not get its due. If *he* wants something of *you*, she seemed to say, you have to hop up. I well remember how she once said: 'Hop up!' to Schwerdtfeger on Adrian's behalf, he having expressed a wish – I think it was a ticket for Jeannette Scheurl to the Zapfenstösser orchestra and Schwerdtfeger made some objection. 'Yes, Rudolf, you just hop along and get it,' she said. 'For heaven's sake, have you lost your legs?'

'No, no,' said he, 'I only, certainly, of course I – but –'

'But me no buts,' she cut him short, condescendingly, half farcically but also half reproachfully. And Adrian as well as Schwerdtfeger laughed; the latter, making his usual boyish grimace with the corner of his mouth and shrugging his shoulder inside his jacket, promised that he should be served.

It was as though Clarissa saw in Rudolf the sort of suitor who had to 'hop'; and in fact he constantly, in the most naïve way, confidingly and unabashedly sued for Adrian's favour. About the real suitor who was courting her sister she often tried to worm an opinion out of me – and Inez herself did the same, in a shyer, more refined way, drawing back almost at once, as though she wanted to hear, and yet wanted to hear and know nothing. Both sisters had confidence in me; that is, they seemed to consider me capable of just evaluation of others, a capacity, of course, which, if it is to inspire full confidence, must stand outside any situation and view it with unclouded eye. The role of confidant is always at once gratifying and painful, for one always plays it with the premise that one does not come into consideration oneself. But how much better it is, I have often told myself, to inspire the world with confidence than to rouse its passion! How much better to seem to it 'good' than 'beautiful'!

A 'good' man, that was in Inez Rodde's eyes probably one to whom the world stands in a purely ethical relation, not an aesthetically stimulated one; hence her confidence in me. But I must say that I served the sisters somewhat unequally and expressed my opinions about Institoris in a form proper to the person who asked for them. In conversation with Clarissa I spoke far more as I really felt; expressed myself as a psychologist about the motives of his choice and his hesitations (anyhow the hesitation was not all on one side), and did not scruple to poke a little fun at his 'Miss Nancy' ways and worship of 'brute instinct'. She seemed to concur. When Inez herself talked to me, it was not the same. I deferred to feelings which *pro forma* I assumed in her, without actually believing in them; deferred to the reasonable grounds on which in all probability she would marry the man, and spoke with sober regard of his solid qualities, his knowledge, his human decency, his capital prospects. To give my words adequate warmth and yet not too much was a delicate task; for it seemed to me equally a responsibility whether I strengthened the girl in her doubts and depreciated the security for which she yearned, or on the other hand encouraged her to give herself while cherishing such doubts. I even had some ground for feeling, now and then, that I ran more of a risk by encouraging than by dissuading.

The truth was that she soon had enough of my opinions about Helmut Institoris and went on with her confidences in a general way, asking my opinion about certain other persons in the circle, for instance Zink and Spengler, or, for another example, Schwerdtfeger. What did I think about his violin-playing, she asked; about his character, whether and how much I respected him, what shade of seriousness or humour my regard showed. I answered as best I could, with all possible justice, quite as I have spoken of Rudolf in these pages, and she listened attentively, enlarging on my friendly commendation with some remarks of her own, to which again I could only agree, though I was rather struck by her insistence. Considering the girl's character, her confirmed and mistrustful view of life, her ideas were not surprising, but applied to this particular subject I must say they rather put me off.

Yet after all it was no wonder that she, knowing the attractive young man so much longer than I, and like Clarissa in a brother-and-sister relation with him, had observed him more closely and had more matter for a confidential conversation. He was a man without vice, she said (she used a milder word, yet it was clear that was what she meant); a clean man, hence his confidingness, for cleanness was confiding (a touching word in her mouth, since she herself was not confiding at all, save by exception to me). He did not drink, taking nothing but slightly sugared tea, without cream, three times a day; he did not smoke, or at most only occasionally, he did not make a habit of it. For all such masculine pacifiers (I think I remember the word) – in short, for narcotics – flirtation was his substitute; he was utterly given to flirtation, he was a born flirt. She did not mean love or friendship; both of these by his very nature and, so to speak, under his hands became flirtation. A poseur? Yes and no. Certainly not in the ordinary vulgar sense. One need only see him with Bullinger, the manufacturer, who plumed himself so enormously on his money, and liked to sing:

'*A happy heart and healthy blood*
Are better than much gold and goods'

just to make people envious of his money. Rudolf was not like that at all. But he made it hard for one to feel sure of him all the time. His coquetry, his nice manners, his social coxcombry, his love of society altogether were really something frightful. Did I not find, she asked, that this whole free-and-easy, aesthetic life here in this place, for instance the smart Biedermeier celebration which we had lately attended in the Cococello Club, was in torturing contrast to the sadness and disillusionments of life? Did I not know, like her, that shudder at the spiritual vacuity which reigned in the average gathering, in glaring contrast to the feverish excitement induced by the wine, the music, and the under-currents of human relations? Sometimes one could see how somebody talked with somebody else, preserving all the social forms, while his mind was entirely absent, fixed on another person at whom he was looking . . . And then the disorder of the scene afterwards, the rubbish strewn about, the desolation of an empty salon at the end of an entertainment! She confessed that sometimes after she got home she wept for an hour before falling asleep . . .

So she went on, expressing a general criticism and disapproval, and seeming to have forgotten Rudolf. But when she came back to him one had little doubt that he had been in her mind all the time. When she called him a coxcomb, she said, she meant something very harmless, almost laughable; yet if often made one feel sad. For instance, he was always the last comer at a party, he had to feel himself waited for, other people must always wait for him. Then he set store by rivalry and social jealousy: would tell how he had been at such and such houses, yesterday at the Langewiesches', or whoever his friends were; or at the Rollwagens', who had the two thoroughbred daughters ('it always upsets me just to hear that word'). But he always spoke apologetically as though he really meant: 'I have to appear there now and again, after all.' Though one could be sure that he said the same thing in the other place and tried to create the illusion that he liked them best – just as though everybody set great store by that. Yet he was so sure he was bringing joy to everybody that there was something contagious about it. He came to tea at five o'clock and said he had promised to be somewhere else between half past five and six, at the Langewiesches' or Rollwagens' – probably it was not true at all. Then he stopped on until half past six, to show that he would rather be here, that he was so entertained where he was that the others would just have to wait. And was so certain that one would be pleased that one actually was pleased.

We laughed, but I did so with reserve, for I saw distress written on her face. She spoke as though she thought it necessary – did she really think it necessary? – to warn me not to put too much confidence in Schwerdtfeger's amiable attentions. There was nothing to them. She had once happened to hear, from a little distance, word for word, how he implored somebody, to whom she knew him to be profoundly indifferent, to remain at a gathering, not to go away; spoke in a low voice, with charming, intimate inflections: 'Ah, do, come on, be sweet, stay with me.' So now, when he spoke to her in the same way, or to me, it might be, the words would mean nothing at all.

In short, she confessed to a painful distrust of his seriousness, or any display he made of attention and sympathy – for instance, if one was not well and he came to see one. All that happened, as I myself would learn, only to be 'nice' and because it was proper and socially the done thing, not from any inner feeling, one must not imagine it. One might even expect actual bad taste. Somebody once warned him in jest not to make some girl – or it might perhaps have been a married woman – unhappy, and he had actually answered, arrogantly: 'Oh, there are so many unhappy!' She had heard it with her own ears. One could only think: 'God save me from the humiliation of belonging to a man like that!'

But she did not want to be hard – perhaps the word 'humiliation' was too strong. I must not misunderstand her, she did not doubt that there was a certain fund of nobility in Rudolf's character. Sometimes even in company one could alter his loud and common mood to a gentler, more serious one, simply by a quiet word or surprised glance. It had really happened like that more than once, for Rudolf was extraordinarily susceptible; and then the Langewiesches and Rollwagens and whatever their names were became for the time mere shadows and phantoms for him. Yet it was enough for him to breathe other air, be exposed to other influences, to bring about a complete estrangement, a hopeless aloofness in the place of confidence and mutual understanding. Then he would feel it, for he really had fine feelings, and would try remorsefully to put things right. It was funny, and touching, but to restore good relations he might repeat some more or less apt phrase you had used, or a quotation you had once made from a book, to show that he had not forgotten, that he was at home among the higher things. Really it was enough to make one weep. And when he took leave for the evening, he showed his readiness to be sorry and do better: he came and said good-bye and made little jokes in dialect, at which one rather winced, for perhaps one was suffering from fatigue. But then when he had shaken hands all round he came back and said good-bye again, quite simply, so that one was able to respond. And that meant a good exit for him, which he simply had to have. At the two other houses he was going to he probably did the same thing . . .

Have I said enough? This is no novel, in whose composition the author reveals the hearts of his characters indirectly, by the action he portrays. In a biography, of course, I must introduce things directly, by name, and simply state such psychological factors as have a bearing on the life I am describing. But after the singular expressions which my memory leads me to write down, expressions of what I might call a specific intensity, there can be no doubt as to the fact to be communicated. Inez Rodde was in love with young Schwerdtfeger. There were only two questions to be asked: first, did she know it, and second, when, at what point had her original brother-sister relation with him assumed this ardent and distressful colour?

The first question I answer with a yes. So well-read a girl, one might say psychologically trained, keeping watch with a poet's eye upon her own experiences must certainly have had an insight into the growth of her own feeling – however surprising, yes, unbelievable the development might have seemed to her at first. The apparent *naïveté* with which she bared her heart to me was no evidence of ignorance; for what looked like simplicity was partly a compulsive desire to communicate and partly a motion of confidence in me, a strangely disguised confidence, for to some extent she was pretending that she thought me simple enough not to understand; and that was in itself a sort of confidence. But actually she knew and was glad to know that the truth was not escaping me since, to my honour be it spoken, she trusted her secret with me. She might do so, of course, might be certain of my discretion and my human sympathy, however hard it naturally is for a man to enter into the feelings of a woman on fire with love for somebody of his own sex. It is much easier for us to follow the feelings of a man for a woman – even though he be entirely indifferent to her himself – than to put himself in the place of a woman in love with another man. One does not at bottom 'understand' that, one just accepts it as a well-bred man should, in objective respect for a law of nature – and indeed the attitude of a man is usually more tolerant and benevolent that that of a woman, who mostly casts a jealous eye on a friend who tells her a man is in love with her, even though she cares nothing at all for the man.

I did not fail, then, in friendly good will, even though I was prevented by nature from understanding in the sense of fellow-feeling. My God, little Schwerdtfeger! His facial structure had something of the pug about it, his voice was guttural, he was more like a boy than a man, the lovely blue of his eyes, his good straight growth and captivating violin-playing and whistling, his general niceness admitted and agreed. Well, then, Inez Rodde loved him. Not blindly, but for that reason suffering the more; and my inward attitude was that of her mocking sister Clarissa, who looked down her nose at the other sex: I should have liked to say to him: 'Hop man! Hop up and do your duty – what do you think of yourself?'

But hopping was not so simple, even if Rudolf had acknowledged the obligation. For there was Helmut Institoris, the bridegroom, or bridegroom *in spe*, Institoris the suitor. And here I come back to the question: since when had Inez's sisterly relations with Rudolf turned into passionate love? My human powers of intuition told me: it had happened when Dr Helmut approached her, as man to woman, and began to woo her. I was and remain convinced that Inez would never have fallen in love with Schwerdtfeger without the entry of Institoris into her life. He wooed her, but in a sense for another. A man not passionate himself could by his courtship and the trains of thought connected with it arouse the woman in her; it might go that far. But he could not arouse it for himself, though on grounds of good sense she was ready to accept him – that far it did not go. Instead her awakened femininity turned straightway to another man, towards whom thus far she had consciously felt only tranquil sisterly feelings – and now others had been released in her. It was not that she found him 'the right one' or worthy of her love. No, it was her melancholy nature, seeking unhappiness, which fixed upon him as its object; upon him from whom she had heard with disgust the words: 'There are so many unhappy ones!'

And stranger still: her inadequate suitor's predilection for soullessness and the beauty of instinct, so repugnant to her own views – had she not fallen victim to it herself, in her love for Rudolf? She was, in a way, betraying Institoris with his own convictions; for did not Rudolf represent to her wise and disillusioned gaze something like sweet unthinking life itself?

Compared with Institoris, who was a mere instructor in the beautiful, Rudolf had on his side the advantage of art at first hand: art, nourisher of the passions, transcender of the human. For by his art the person of the beloved is elevated, from art the emotions ever draw fresh food, when the artist's own individuality is associated with the joys his art purveys. Inez at bottom despised the aesthetic traffic of the sense-loving city into which she had been transplanted by her mother's craving for a less strait-laced life. But for the sake of her bourgeois security she took part in the festivities of a community which was just one great art-society, and this it was emperilled the security she sought. My memory preserves pregnant and disquieting images of this time; I see us, the Roddes, the Knöterichs perhaps, and myself, after a particularly brilliant performance of a Tchaikovsky symphony in the Zapfenstösser concert hall, standing in the crowd in one of the front rows and applauding. The conductor had motioned the orchestra to stand up to receive the thanks of the audience for its beautiful work. Schwerdtfeger, a little to the left of the first violin, whose place he was soon to take, stood with his instrument under his arm, warm and beaming, face towards the hall and nodding to us with not quite permissible familiarity, while Inez, at whom I could not resist stealing a glance, with her head thrust out, her mouth mischievously pursed, kept her eyes obstinately directed at some other point on the stage, perhaps on the leader, or no, farther alone, on the harps. Or another time I see Rudolf himself, all on fire over a classic performance by a guest colleague, standing in the front of an almost emptied hall, applauding up at the stage where the soloist stood bowing for the tenth time. Two steps away, among the disarray of chairs, stands Inez, who sees him and waits for him to stop clapping, turn round and speak to her. He does not turn, he continues to applaud. But out of the corner of his eye he looks – or perhaps not quite looks, perhaps his blue eyes are only the slightest shade turned from a direct gaze up at the platform and towards the corner where she stands and waits. He does not pause in his enthusiastic activity. Another few seconds and she turns away, pale with anger, lines between her brows, and moves towards the door. At once he stops clapping and follows her. At the door he overtakes her; she puts on an air of chilling surprise to find him here, to find that he exists at all. Refuses to speak, refuses her hand, her eyes, and hastens out.

I see that it was ill-judged of me to try to set down all the trifling minutiae which were the harvest of my observant eye. They are not worth printing, the reader may easily find them puerile or be annoyed by what seems like idle and boring speculation. But he must consider that I am suppressing a hundred others that got caught as it were in the net of my perceptions, the perceptions of a sympathetic and benevolent friend; thanks to the calamity they added up to, I cannot so easily dismiss them from my mind. For years I watched the oncoming of a catastrophe, insignificant, it is true, in the light of world events; and I held my peace about what I saw and feared. Only to Adrian did I once speak, at the beginning, in Pfeiffering, although I had on the whole small inclination, always feeling a certain reluctance to discuss the love-affairs of our circle with him, who lived in monkish detachment from everything of the sort. Yet I did so: I told him in confidence that Inez Rodde, although about to engage herself to Institoris, was, so far as my observations went, hopelessly and fatally in love with Rudi Schwerdtfeger. We were sitting in the Abbot's room, playing chess.

'That's news!' he said. 'You probably want me to miss my move and lose my castle.'

He smiled, shook his head, and added: 'Poor soul!'

Then, as he considered his next play, with a pause between the sentences: 'But that's no joke for him. – He must see to it that he gets out of it whole.'

Chapter Thirty

The first glowing August days of 1914 found me changing from one crowded train to another, waiting in stations swarming with people, their platforms piled with left-behind luggage, on a head-long journey from Freising to Naumburg in Thuringia, where as reserve vice-sergeant-major I was joining my regiment.

War had broken out. The fate that so long had brooded over Europe was upon us, it raged. In the guise of a disciplined execution of all the plans previously made and rehearsed, it raged through our cities and towns, as terror and exaltation, as the inevitable, as 'destiny'; as awareness of power and readiness for sacrifice, in the heads and hearts of men. It may well be, I like to think so, that elsewhere, in both enemy and allied countries, this short cut of fate was felt more as a catastrophe and '*grand malheur*'. We in the field heard these words so often from the lips of Frenchwomen, who did have the war on their soil, in their homes and on their hearths: '*Ah, monsieur, la guerre, quel grand malheur!*' But in our Germany its effect was undeniably and preeminently enthusiasm, and from a world-stagnation that could go on no longer; as hope for the future, an appeal to duty and manhood, in short as a holiday for heroes. My Freising top-formers had hot heads and glowing eyes. Youthful thirst for adventure, impatience to be off, were naïvely mingled with satisfaction at an early release from school. They stormed the recruiting stations, and I was glad that they need not look down on me for a stay-at-home.

I would by no means deny that I fully shared in the popular exultation which I just sought to characterize, though its more extravagant ebullitions were foreign to my nature. My conscience, speaking generally, was not perfectly clear. Such a 'mobilization' for war, however stern and grim a face it wears, must always have something about it like an unlicensed holiday; however unreservedly one's duty, it seems a little like playing truant, like running away, like yielding to unbridled instinct. A settled man like me scarcely felt at ease in it all; and aside from personal and temperamental discomfort, I dimly felt a moral doubt: had we as a nation been so well-behaved up to now that this abandon, these transports, were legitimate? But now the moment had come for readiness to sacrifice and die; that carries one along over everything, it is so to speak the last word, after it there is no more to be said. If the war is felt more or less clearly as a general visitation, in which the individual, as well as the individual people, is ready to stand his man and atone with his blood for the weaknesses and sins of the time, including his own; if he thinks of himself as a sacrifice by which the old Adam is put away and from which in unity a new and higher life will be wrested, then our everyday morals are outbid by the abnormal and must be silent. Neither would I forget that then we went with relatively pure hearts and clean hands to war and did not think we had so behaved at home that a general and catastrophic blood-letting must needs be regarded as the inevitable logical consequence of our domestic doings. Thus it was five years ago. God help us, but not thirty! Justice and law, the habeas corpus, freedom and human dignity had been tolerably honoured in the land. Of course the sword-waving of that fundamentally unsoldierly play-actor, made for anything but war, who sat on the imperial throne was painful to the man of culture; moreover his attitude to the things of the mind was that of a retarded mentality. But his influence on them had exhausted itself in empty gestures of regulation. Culture had been free, she had stood at a respectable height; and though she had long been used to a complete absence of relations with the governing power, her younger representatives might see in a great national war, such as now broke out, a means of achieving a form of life in which state and culture might become one. In this we displayed the preoccupation with self which is peculiar to us: our naïve egoism finds it unimportant, yes, takes it entirely for granted, that for the sake of our development (and we are always developing) the rest of the world, further on than ourselves and not at all possessed by the dynamic of catastrophe, must shed its blood. They take that ill of us, not quite unfairly; for ethically speaking, the only way a people can achieve a higher form of communal life is not by a foreign war, but by a civil one – even with bloodshed. The idea is repugnant to us; yet we thought at all, on the contrary we found it glorious, that our national unification – and even so a partial, a compromise unification – cost three serious wars. We were already long since a great power, we were quite used to it, and it did not make us as happy as we had expected. The feeling that it had not made us more winning, that our relation to the world had rather worsened than improved, lay, unconfessed, deep in our hearts. A new break-through seemed due: we would become a dominating world power – but such a position was not to be achieved by means of mere moral 'home-work'. War, then, and if needs must, war against everybody, to convince everybody and to win; that was our lot, our 'sending' (the very word we use is Germanic, the idea pre-Christian, the whole concept a tragically mythological, musical-dramatic motif); that was what fate had willed, and we – only we! – enthusiastically responded and set forth. We were bursting with the consciousness that this was Germany's century, that history was holding her hand out over us; that after Spain, France, England, it was our turn to put our stamp on the world and be its leader; that the twentieth century was ours; that now, at the end of the bourgeois epoch begun some hundred and twenty years before, the world was to renew itself in our sign, in the sign of a never up to the end quite defined military socialism.

This picture, not to call it an idea, possessed all our heads, companionably side by side with another: the belief that we were forced into war, that sacred necessity called us to take our weapons – those well-polished weapons whose readiness and excellence always induced a secret temptation to test them. Then there was the fear of being overrun from all sides, from which fate only our enormous strength protected us, our power of carrying the war straightway into other lands. Attack and defence were the same, in our case: together they made up the feeling of a providence, a calling, a great hour, a sacred necessity. The peoples beyond our borders might consider us disturbers of the peace if they chose, enemies of life and not to be borne with; but we had the means to knock the world on the head until it changed its mind and came not only to admire but to love us.

Let nobody think I am being jocose. There is no occasion for that, first of all because I can by no means pretend to have excluded myself from the general emotion. I genuinely shared it, even though my normal staid professorial attitude would have held me aloof from any loud manifestation, or even have caused in me some slight protest, a subconscious misgiving at thinking and feeling what everybody else thought and felt. People of my sort have doubts whether every man's thoughts are the right ones. And still, it is a great pleasure to the superior individual, just once – and where should one find this once, if not here and now? – to lose himself altogether in the general.

I stopped two days in Munich to make my farewells in various quarters and supply some details of my equipment. The city was seething. There was a religious solemnity in the air, as well as cases of panic, rage, and dread; as for instance when the wild rumour sprang up that the water supply was poisoned, or a Serbian spy was supposed to have been discovered in the crowd. In order not to be taken for one and cut down by mistake, Dr Breisacher, whom I met on the Ludwigstrasse, had decorated his coat with numerous little red, white, and black rosettes and flags. The state of war, the passing of the supreme authority from the civil to the military, and to a General Staff issuing proclamations, was accepted with mingled confidence and apprehension. It was soothing to know that the members of the royal family, who as commanders had left for headquarters, would have competent chiefs of staff at their side and could commit no royal ineptnesses. Under those circumstances they were loudly cheered on their way. I saw regiments, with nosegays tied to their rifle-barrels, marching out of barrack gates, accompanied by women with handkerchiefs to their faces, while civilian crowds quickly gathered and shouted godspeed, and the peasant lads promoted to heroship smiled back, proud, stupid, and shy. I saw a very young officer, in marching kit, standing on the back platform of a tram, faced to the rear, staring before him and into himself, obviously busy with thoughts of his own young life; then he pulled himself together and with a hasty smile looked round to see if anyone had noticed.

Again I was glad to feel that my situation was the same as his and that I need not remain behind those who were marching to protect their land. At least in the beginning I was the only one of our circle to go. The country was strong enough in man-power to afford to be particular, to consider cultural interests, to admit to much unfitness and to hurl to the front only the perfectly sound of our youth and manhood. In nearly all the men of our group there turned out to be some kind of weakness, something we had scarcely known, but it now procured their exemption. Knöterich, the Sugambian, was slightly tubercular. Zink, the artist, suffered from asthmatic attacks like whooping-cough and used to withdraw from society to get rid of them; his friend Baptist Spengler was ailing, as we know, everywhere by turns. Bullinger the business man was still young, but it appeared that as an industrialist he was indispensable. The Zapfenstösser orchestra was too important a feature of the city's artistic life for its members, among them Rudi Schwerdtfeger, not to be exempted from the service. Anyhow the occasion served to inform us, to our momentary surprise, that Rudi, in his earlier life, had had an operation that cost him one of his kidneys. He lived, we suddenly heard, with only one. That was quite enough, it appeared, and the ladies soon forgot all about it.

I could go on to mention many a case of reluctance, protection, favouritism, in the circles that frequented the Schlaginhaufens and the ladies Scheurl near the Botanical Gardens: circles where there was a fundamental objection to this war, as there had been to the last one: memories of the

Rhenish alliance, Francophile sentiments, Catholic dislike of Prussia, and so on. Jeanette Scheurl was unhappy to tears. She was in despair over the savage flaring-up of the antagonism between the two countries to which she belonged, and which in her opinion ought to complement each other, instead of fighting. '*J'en ai assez jusqu'à la fin de mes jours*,' she said with angry sobs. Despite my dissimilar feelings I could but grant her a cultural sympathy.

To say good-bye to Adrian, whose personal detachment from the whole scene was the most understandable thing in the world to me, I went out to Pfeiffering, whence the son of the house, Gereon, had already departed with several horses for his base. I found Rüdiger Schildknapp there, for the present still free, spending a weekend with our friend. He had served in the marines and would be taken later, but after some months he was again released. It was not very different in my own case: let me say at once that I remained in the field a bare year, till the Argonne battles of 1915, and was shipped home, with the Cross I had earned only by putting up with discomforts and by catching a typhus infection.

So much by way of preface. Rüdiger's judgement of the war was conditioned by his admiration for the English, as was Jeanette Scheurl's by her French blood. The British declaration of war had gone home to him, his mood was unusually sombre. We should never in his opinion have challenged England by the treaty-breaking march into Belgium. France and Russia – well and good, one might take them on. But England? It was frightful folly. So then, inclined to an irritated realism, he saw in the war only filth, stench, horrible amputations, sexual licence, and lice and jeered his fill at the ideological journalism that turned an utter nuisance into a glorious event. Adrian did not gainsay him, and I, despite my deeper feelings, yet willingly conceded that there was some truth in what he said.

The three of us ate in the great Nike room that evening, and as Clementina Schweigestill moved to and fro quietly serving us, I asked news of how Adrian's sister Ursula fared in Langensalza. Her marriage was of the happiest, it seemed; she had recovered very well from a weakness of the lung, a slight apical catarrh, which she had got after three childbeds in quick succession, in 1911, 1912, and 1913. It was the Schneidewein offspring Rosa, Ezekiel, and Raimund who saw then the light. The period between these three and the next was a full decade; it would be ten years before the enchanting Nepomuk made his appearance.

During the meal and afterwards in the Abbot's room there was much talk on political and moral subjects. We spoke of the legendary manifestation of the German national character, which was supposed to reveal itself at moments of historical crisis like this – I referred to it with a certain emotion, in order to offset a little the drastically empirical interpretation that Schildknapp considered the only possible one: Germany's traditional role, the trespass against Belgium, which was so reminiscent of Frederick the Great's attack upon formally neutral Saxony; the yell of outrage that went up from the world, and the speech of our philosophical Chancellor, with its ingeniously presented admission of guilt, its folk-proverb: 'Necessity knows no law', its plea to God in contempt of an old legal paper, in face of living necessity. It was due to Rüdiger that we ended by laughing; for he accepted my somewhat emotional representations and then turned into irresistible absurdity all this dignified regret, noble brutality, and respectable mischief-making by parodying the tall philosopher who had dressed up in poetic moralizations a strategic plan long since determined on. We might laugh, but there was no amusement in the virtuous roar that went up from a stunned world at this execution of a cut-and-dried plan of campaign, knowledge of which had long been public property. However, I saw that our host liked this line much better and was glad of the chance to laugh; so I willingly joined in, not without recalling what Plato had said of comedy and tragedy: how they grow on the same tree and a change of lighting suffices to make one into the other.

All together I did not allow my sympathy for Germany's necessity, her moral isolation and public proscription, which, so it seemed to me, was only the expression of the general fear of her strength and advantage in preparedness (I did admit that we reckoned the strength and the advantage as a harsh consolation in our outlawed state) – all together, I say, I did not allow my patriotic emotion, which was so much harder to explain than that of the others, to be dampened by the cold water thrown on our national traits. Indeed, I gave it words, walking up and down the room, while Schildknapp in the deep easy-chair smoked his shag pipe, and Adrian stood, the most of the time, in front of his old-German work-table with the sunken centre and the reading- and writing-desk set on it. For oddly enough he wrote on a slanting surface, like Erasmus in Holbein's portrait. A few books lay on the table: a little volume of Kleist, with the book-mark at the essay on marionettes; the indispensable volume of Shakespeare sonnets and another book with some of the plays – *Twelfth Night* I think, *Much Ado about Nothing*, and I believe *Two Gentlemen of Verona*. His work in hand lay there too: sheets, drafts, beginnings, notes, sketches in various stages of incompletion; often only the top line of the violin part or the wood-wind was filled out and quite below the progression of the bass, but between them simply white space, elsewhere the harmonic connexion and the instrumental grouping were already made clear by the jotting down of the other orchestral parts. With his cigarette between his lips he would step up to the desk to look at his work, just as a chess-player measures on the chequered field the progress of a game, to which musical composition bears so suggestive a resemblance. We were all so comfortable together that he might even take a pencil and enter a clarinet or horn figure somewhere if he thought well of it.

We knew nothing precise about what was occupying him, now that that music of the cosmos had appeared in print from Schott's Sons in Mainz, under the same arrangements as the Brentano songs. Actually it was the suite of dramatic grotesques, whose themes, so we heard, he had taken from the old history and anecdote book, the *Gesta Romanorum*. He was trying these, without yet knowing whether anything would come of it or if he would continue. In any case, the characters were not to be men but puppets (hence the Kleist). As for the *Marvels of the Universe*, there was to have been a foreign performance of that solemn and arrogant work had not the war brought the plan to nothing. We had spoken of it at table. The Lübeck performances of *Love's Labour's Lost*, even unsuccessful as they had proved, together with the mere existence of the Brentano cycle, had made some impression, and Adrian's name had begun in the inner circles of the art to have a certain esoteric and tentative fame – even this hardly at all in Germany and decidedly not in Munich. But there were other, more perceptive regions. A few weeks earlier he had had a letter from a Monsieur Monteux, director of the Russian ballet in Paris, former member of the Colonne orchestra, wherein this experimentally-minded director had announced his intention of producing the *Marvels of the Universe*, together with some orchestral parts of *Love's Labour's Lost* as a concert pure and simple. He had in mind

the Théâtre des Champs Élysées for the performance, and invited Adrian to
come to Paris, probably in order to rehearse and conduct his own works. We
had not asked our friend whether he would, under favourable conditions,
accept. In any case, the circumstances were now such that there could be no
further talk of it.

I still see myself walking up and down the carpet and boards of the old
wainscoted room, with its overpowering chandelier, its wall cupboards with
their wrought-iron hinges, the flat leather cushions on the corner bench, and
the deep embrasures of the windows; walking up and down and holding
forth at large about Germany; more for myself and certainly more for
Schildknapp than for Adrian, from whom I expected no interest. Used to
teaching and to talking, and, when I got warmed up, no bad talker, I do not
dislike listening to myself and take a certain pleasure in my command over
words. Not without lively gesture I challenged Rüdiger to set down what I
said to the wartime journalism which so annoyed him. Surely one might be
permitted a little psychological participation in the national and even
touching traits which our otherwise multiform German character was
evincing in this historic hour. In the last analysis, what we were dealing with
was the psychology of the break-through.

'In a nation like ours,' I set forth, 'the psychological is always the primary
and actually motivating; the political action is of the second order of
importance: reflex, expression, instrument. What the break-through to
world power, to which fate summons us, means at bottom, is the break-
through to the world – out of an isolation of which we are painfully
conscious, and which no vigorous reticulation into world economy has been
able to break down since the founding of the Reich. The bitter thing is that
the practical manifestation is an outbreak of war, though its true interpretation is longing, a thirst for unification.'

'God bless your studies,' I heard Adrian say here in a low voice, with a
half-laugh. He had not even glanced up from his notes as he quoted the old
student tag.

I remained standing and looked at him; he paid no heed. 'You mean,' I
retorted, 'that I am talking nonsense?'

'Pardon,' he hastily returned. 'I lapsed into student lingo, because your
oratio reminded me so much of our straw-threshing disputes of anno so-
and-so – what were the fellows' names? I notice I begin to forget them' (he
was twenty-nine at the time). 'Deutschmeyer? Dungersleben?'

'You mean the redoubtable Deutschlin,' I said; 'and there was one called
Dungersheim. A Hubmeyer and Teutleben there were too. You have never
had a memory for names. They were good, serious chaps.'

'Certainly, of course. And look here, there was a Schappeler, and a
socialist named Arzt. What do you say now? You did not even belong to their
faculty. But today I seem to hear them when I hear you. Straw-threshing –
by which I only mean once a student, always a student. Academic life keeps
one young and critical.'

'You did belong to their faculty,' said I, 'and yet you were at bottom more
a guest than I. Of course, Adri. I was only a student, and you may well be
right, I am one still. But so much the better if the academic keeps one young,
if it preserves loyalty to the spirit, to free thought, to the higher interpretation of the crude event –'

'Are we talking about loyalty?' he asked. 'I understood that Kaisersaschern
would like to become a world capital. That is not very loyal.'

'Get along with you,' I cried, 'you understood nothing of the sort and you understand very well what I meant about the German break-through to the world.'

'It would not help much if I did understand, for at present, anyhow, the crude event will just make our shut-inness and shut-offness more complete, however far your military swarm into Europe. You see: I cannot go to Paris, you go there instead of me. Good too! Between ourselves, I would not have gone anyhow. You help me out of an embarrassment –'

'The war will be short,' I said in a suppressed voice, for his words affected me painfully. 'It cannot last long. We pay for the swift break-through with a wrong, an acknowledged one, which we declare ourselves ready to make good. We must take it on ourselves ...'

'And will know how to carry it with dignity,' he broke in. 'Germany has broad shoulders. And who denies that a real break-through is worth what the tame world calls a crime? I hope you don't suppose that I think small of the idea which it pleases you to chew over, in your straw. There is at bottom only one problem in the world, and this is its name. How does one break through? How does one get into the open? How does one burst the cocoon and become a butterfly? The whole situation is dominated by the question. Here too,' said he, and twitched the little red marker in the volume of Kleist on the table – 'here too it treats of the break-through, in the capital essay on marionettes, and it is called straight out "the last chapter of the history of the world". But it is talking only about the aesthetic, charm, free grace, which actually is reserved to the automaton and the god; that is, to the unconscious or an endless consciousness, whereas every reflection lying between nothing and infinity kills grace. The consciousness must, this writer thinks, have gone through an infinity in order that grace find itself again therein; and Adam must eat a second time from the tree of knowledge in order to fall back into the state of innocence.'

'How glad I am,' I put in, 'that you have just read that! It is gloriously thought, and you are quite right to bring it into connexion with the break-through. But do not say that it is speaking only of aesthetics, do not say *only*! One does wrong to see in aesthetics a separate and narrow field of the humane. It is much more that that, it is at bottom everything, it attracts or repels, the poet attaches to the word "grace" the very widest possible meaning. Aesthetic release or the lack of it is a matter of one's fate, dealing out happiness or unhappiness, companionship or hopeless if proud isolation on earth. And one does not need to be a philologian to know that what is odious is also what is hated. Craving to break through from bondage, to cease being sealed up in the odious – tell me that I am straw-threshing again; but I feel, I have always felt and will assert against strongly held opposition, that this German is *kat exochen*, profoundly German, the very definition of Germanism, of a psychology threatened with envelopment, the poison of isolation, provincial boorishness, neurosis, implicit Satanism ...'

I broke off. He eyed me, and I believe the colour left his cheeks. The look he cast on me was the look, the familiar one that made me almost equally unhappy, no matter whether myself or another was its object: wordless, veiled, coldly remote to the point of offensiveness, followed by the smile with closed lips and sneeringly dilating nostrils – and then the turning away. He moved away from the table, not towards Schildknapp, but to the window niche, where he had hung a saint's picture on the panelling. Rüdiger talked away. In his opinion, he said, I was to be congratulated on going straight into the field, and actually on horse-back. One should ride into the field or else not go at all. And he patted the neck of an imaginary nag. We laughed, and our parting when I left for the train was easy and cheerful. Good that it was not sentimental, it would have seemed tasteless. But Adrian's look I carried with me to war – perhaps it was that, and not the typhus infection from lice, which brought me home so soon, back to his side.

Chapter Thirty-one

'You go there instead of me,' Adrian had said. And we did not get to Paris. Shall I confess that, privately and apart from the historical point of view, I felt a deep, intimately personal shame? Weeks long we had sent home terse, affectedly laconic dispatches, dressing our triumphs in cold matter-of-fact. Liége had long since fallen, we had won the battle for Lorraine. In accordance with the fixed master-plan we had swung with five armies across the Meuse, had taken Brussels, Namur, carried the day at Charleroi and Longwy, won a second series of battles at Sedan, Rethel, Saint-Quentin, and occupied Reims. We advanced as though on wings. It was just as we had dreamed: by the favour of the god of war, at destiny's nod, we were borne as on pinions. To gaze without flinching at the flames we kindled, could not help kindling, was incumbent upon our manhood, it was the supreme challenge to our heroic courage. I can still see vividly the picture of a gaunt Gaulish wife, standing on a height round which our battery was moving; at its foot a village lay shattered and smoking. 'I am the last!' she cried, with a gesture of tragic power, such as is given to no German woman to make. '*Je suis la dernière!*' Raising her fists, she hurled her curses down on our heads, repeating three times: '*Méchants! Méchants! Méchants!*'

We looked the other way. We had to win, and ours was the hard trade of triumph. That I felt wretched enough myself sitting my horse, plagued with coughing and the racking pain in my limbs due to wet nights under canvas, actually afforded me a certain consolation.

Yet many more villages we shot up, still borne on victory's pinions. Then came the incomprehensible, the apparently senseless thing: the order to retreat. How should we have understood it? We belonged to the army group Hausen, south of Châlons-sur-Marne, streaming on to Paris, as the von Kluck group were doing at other points. We were ignorant that somewhere, after a five-day battle, the French had crushed von Bülow's right wing – reason enough for the anxious cautiousness of a supreme commander who had been elevated to his rank on account of his uncle, to order a general withdrawal. We passed some of the villages that we had left smoking in our rear, and the hill where the tragic woman had stood. She was not there.

The wings were trustless. It should not have been. It had not been a war to be won in one swift onslaught. But as little as those at home did we understand what that meant. We did not understand the frantic jubilation of the world over the result of the battle of the Marne; over the fact that the short war on which our salvation hung had turned into a long one, which we could not stand. Our defeat was now only a matter of time, and of cost to the foe. We could have laid our weapons down and forced our leaders to an immediate peace, if only we had understood. But even among them probably only one here and there dared to think of it. After all, they had scarcely realized that the age of localized war had gone by and that every campaign to which we felt ourselves driven must end in a world conflagration. In such a one the advantage of the inner line, the fanatical devotion of the troops, the high state of preparedness, and a firmly based strong authoritarian state had held out the chance of a lightning triumph. If this failed – and it stood written that it must fail – then, whatever we might still for years accomplish, we were lost in principle and before we began: this time, next time, always.

We did not know. Slowly the truth tortured its way into us; while the war, a rotting, decaying, misery-creating war, though from time to time flaring up in flattering, deceiving successes, this war, of which I too had said it *must* not last long, lasted four years. Shall I here and now go into details of that long-drawn-out giving way and giving up, the wearing out of our powers and our equipment, the shabbiness and shortages of life, the under-nourishment, the loss of morale from the deprivations, the lapses into dishonesty and the gross luxury of the profiteer? I might well be censured for recklessly overstepping the limits of my purpose, which is personal and biographical. I lived through it all from the beginning to the bitter end in the hinterland, as a man on furlough and at length mustered out, given back to his teaching profession at Freising. For before Arras, during the second period of struggle for that fortified place, which lasted from the beginning of May until far on in July of 1915, the delousing measures were obviously inadequate; an infection took me for weeks to the isolation barracks, then for another month to a convalescent home for the sick and wounded in Taunus. At last I no longer resisted the idea that I had fulfilled my duty to my fatherland and would do better to serve in my old place the cause of education.

That I did, and might once more be husband and father in the frugal home, whose walls and their too familiar contents, spared perhaps for destruction by future bombing, today still form the frame of my retired and impoverished life. It should be said once more, certainly not in any boastful sense, but as a mere statement, that I led my own life, without precisely neglecting it, only as it were as an aside, with half my attention, with my left hand; that my real concern and anxiety were centred upon the existence of my childhood friend, to be back in whose nearness made me so rejoice – if the word I use can describe the slight chill, the shiver of dread, the painful lack of response which were my portion from him in the increasingly productive isolation of his life. 'To have an eye on him', to watch over his extraordinary and puzzling course, always seemed to mine its real and pressing task. It made up its true content, and thus it is I speak of the emptiness of my present days.

The place he had elected as his home – 'home' in that sense I have spoken of, assimilative, and not altogether acceptable – was a relatively fortunate choice. During the years of approaching defeat and ever more gnawing stringency, he was, thank God, on the Schweigestill farm as tolerably cared for as one could wish, without knowledge or appreciation of the state of things, almost unaffected by the slowly corroding changes under which our blockaded and invested country suffered, even while militarily still on the offensive. He took everything as a matter of course, without any words, as something that proceeded from him and lay in his nature, whose power of inertia and fixation on the *semper idem* persisted in the face of outward circumstance. His simple dietary needs the Schweigestill household could always satisfy. More than that, and soon after my return from the field, he came under the care of two females who had approached him quite independently of each other and appointed themselves his devotees. These were the damsels Meta Nackedey and Kunigunde Rosenstiel: one a piano-teacher, the other an active partner in a factory for the production of sausage cases. It is certainly remarkable: a budding reputation such as had begun to attach itself to Leverkühn's name is unknown to the general, having its seat in the initiate sphere, on the heights of connoisseurship; from those heights the invitation to Paris had come. But at the same time it may also be reflected in humbler, lowlier regions, in the needy souls of poor creatures who stand out from the masses through some sensibility of loneliness and suffering dressed up as 'higher aspirations'; and these may find their happiness in a worship still fittingly paid to the rarest values. That it is women, and unmarried ones, need not surprise us; for human resignation is certainly the source of a prophetic intuition, which is not the less estimable because its origins are humble. There was not the least question that the immediately personal here played a considerable role; indeed, it predominated over the intellectual values; which even so, in both cases, could only be grasped and estimated in vague outline, as a matter of feeling and intuition. I myself, speaking as one who early submitted his own head and heart to the phenomenon of Adrian's cool and bafflingly self-contained existence, have I the smallest right to mock at the fascination which his aloneness, the nonconformity of his life, exerted upon these women? The Nackedey was a scurrying, deprecating creature, some thirty years old, forever dissolving in blushes and modesty, who speaking or listening blinked spasmodically and appealingly behind the pince-nez she wore, nodding her head and wrinkling up her nose. She, one day, when Adrian was in the city, had found herself beside him on the front platform of a tram, and when she discovered it, had rushed in headless flight through the crowd to the rear platform. Then, having collected herself for a few minutes, she had gone back, to speak to him by name, to tell him, blushing and paling by turns, her own, to add something of her circumstances and to say that she held his music sacred – to all which he had listened and then thanked her. Upon this followed their acquaintance, which Meta had certainly not brought about in order to let it drop. She paid a visit of homage to Pfeiffering, with a bouquet; and cultivated it from then on, in free competition with the Rosenstiel, both sides spurred on by jealousy. The Rosenstiel had begun it differently.

She was a raw-boned Jewess, of about the same age as Nackedey, with thick, unmanageable woolly hair and brown eyes where timeless grief stood written for the daughter of Zion despoiled and her people as a forsaken hearth. A capable business woman in not a very refined line (for the manufacture of sausage cases has something gross about it, certainly), she had the elegiac habit of beginning all her sentences with 'ah'. Ah, yes! Ah, no! Ah, believe me! Ah, why not? Ah, I will go to Nuremburg tomorrow: she would say these things in a deep harsh, desolate, complaining voice, and even when asked How are you? she would reply: 'Ah, very well.' But it was not the same when she wrote, which she uncommonly liked to do. For not only was Kunigunde, as almost all Jews are, very musical, but also she had, though without any extensive reading, much purer and more fastidious relations with the German language than the national average, yes, than most of the learned. She had set in train the acquaintance with Adrian, which of her own motion she always called a friendship (indeed, in time it did become something like that), with an excellent letter, a long, well-turned protestation of devotion, in content not really extraordinary, but stylistically formed on the best models of an older, humanistic Germany. The recipient read it with a certain surprise, and on account of its literary quality it could not possibly be passed over in silence. She kept on writing to him at

Pfeiffering, quite aside from her frequent visits: explicitly, not very objectively, in matter not further exciting, but in language very meticulous, clear and readable; not hand-written, moreover, but done on her business typewriter, with an ampersand for 'and', expressing a reverence which more nearly to define or justify she was either too shy or else incapable. It was just reverence, an instinctive reverence and devotion preserved loyally through-out many years; you simply had to respect such a capital person, quite aside from any other capacities she might have. I at least did so, and took pains to pay the same silent respect to the elusive Nackedey; whereas Adrian simply accepted the tributes and devotion of these followers of his with the utter heedlessness of his nature. And was my lot then so different from theirs? I can count it to my credit that I took pains to be benevolent towards them, while they, quite primitively, could not endure each other and when they met measured each other with narrowed eyes. In a certain sense I was of their guild and might have been justified in feeling irritation over this reduced and spinsterish reproduction of my own relation to Adrian.

These two, then, coming always with full hands during the hunger-years, when he was already well taken care of so far as the essentials were concerned, brought him everything imaginable that could be got hold of in underhand ways: sugar, tea, coffee, chocolate, cakes, preserves, tobacco for cigarettes. He could make presents to me, to Schildknapp, and to Rudi Schwerdtfeger, whose assumption of intimacy never wavered; and the names of those devoted women were often called blessed among us! As for the cigarettes, Adrian never gave up smoking except when forced to on the days when the migraine, with its violent attacks like seasickness fell on him, and he kept his bed in a darkened room, as happened two or three times in the month. Otherwise he could not do without the stimulant and diversion; it had become a habit rather late, during his Leipzig time, and now, at least during his work, he must, so he said, have the interlude of rolling and inhaling else he could not hold out so long. At the time when I returned to civil life he was greatly given to the habit; and my impression was that he practised it not so much for the sake of the *Gesta*, though this was ostensibly the cure, as it was because he was trying to put the *Gesta* behind him and be ready for new demands upon his genius. On his horizon, I am sure of it, there was already rising – probably since the outbreak of war, for a power of divination like his must have recognized therein a deep cleft and discontinuity, the opening of a new period of history, crowded with tumult and disruptions, agonies and wild vicissitudes – on the horizon of his creative life, I say, there was already rising the '*Apocalypsis cum figuris*', the work which was to give this life such a dizzying upward surge. Until then, so at least I see the process, he was employing the waiting-time with the brilliant marionette fantasies.

Adrian had learned through Schildknapp of the old book that passes for the source of most of the romantic myths of the Middle Ages. It is a translation from the Latin of the oldest Christian collection of fairytales and legends. I am quite willing to give Adrian's favourite with the like-coloured eyes due credit for the suggestion. They had read it together in the evenings and it appealed to Adrian's sense of the ridiculous, his craving to laugh, yes, to laugh until he cried. That was a craving which my less suggestible nature never knew how to feed, being hampered as well by an anxious feeling that all this dissolving in mirth had about it something unsuited to a nature I loved even while I feared it. Rüdiger, the like-eyed, shared my apprehensions not a whit. Indeed, I concealed them; they never hindered me from joining sincerely in such moods of abandon when they came about. But in the Silesian one marked a distinct satisfaction, as though he had performed a task, a mission, when he had managed to reduce Adrian to tears of laughter; and certainly he succeeded in a most fruitful and acceptable way with the old book of fables and jests.

I am of opinion that the *Gesta* – in their historical uninstructedness, pious Christian didacticism, and moral *naïveté*, with their eccentric casuistry of parricide, adultery, and complicated incest; their undocumented Roman emperors, with daughters whom they fantastically guarded and then offered for sale under the most hair-splitting conditions – it is not to be denied, I say, that all these fables, presented in a solemn Latinizing and indescribably naïve style of translation, concerning knights in pilgrimage to the Promised Land, wanton wives, artful procuresses, clerics given to the black arts, do have an extraordinarily diverting effect. They were in the highest degree calculated to stimulate Adrian's penchant for parody, and the thought of dramatizing them musically in condensed form for the puppet theatre occupied him from the day he made their acquaintance. There is for instance the fundamentally unmoral fable, anticipating the *Decameron*, 'of the godless guile of old women', wherein an accomplice of guilty passion, under a mask of sanctity succeeds in persuading a noble and even exceptionally decent and honourable wife, while her confiding husband is gone on a journey, that she is sinfully minded to a youth who is consumed with desire for her. The witch makes her little bitch fast for two days, and then gives it bread with mustard to eat, which causes the little animal to shed copious tears. Then she takes it to the virtuous lady, who receives her respectfully, since everybody supposes she is a saint. But when the lady looks at the weeping little bitch and asks in surprise what causes its tears, the old woman behaves as though she would rather not answer. When pressed to speak, she confesses that this little dog is actually her own all-too-chaste daughter, who by reason of the unbending denial of her favour to a young man on fire for her had driven him to his death; and now, in punishment therefor, she has been turned into this shape and of course constantly weeps tears of despair over her doggish estate. Telling these deliberate lies, the procuress weeps too, but the lady is horrified at the thought of the similarity of her own case with that of the little dog and tells the old woman of the youth who suffers for her. Thereupon the woman puts it seriously before her what an irretrievable pity it would be if she too were to be turned into a little dog; and is then commissioned to fetch the groaning suitor that in God's name he may cool his lust, so that the two at the instance of a godless trick celebrate the sweetest adultery.

I still envy Rüdiger for having been the first to read aloud this tale to our friend, in the Abbot's room; although I confess that if it had been myself the effect might not have been the same. Moreover his contribution to the future work was limited to this first stimulation. When the point was reached of preparing the fables for the puppet stage, the casting of them in dialogue form, he refused his offices, for lack of time, or out of his well-known refractory sense of freedom. Adrian did not take it ill of him, but did what he could by himself for as long as I was away, sketching in the scenarios freely and more or less the dialogue, after which it was I who in my spare time quickly gave them their final form in mixed prose and rhymed lines.

The singers who according to Adrian's plan lend their voices to the acting puppets had to be given their places among the instruments in the orchestra, a very small one, composed of violin and double-bass, clarinet, bassoon, trumpet, and trombone, with percussion for one man, and a set of bells. With them is a speaker who, like the *testis* in the oratorio, condenses the plot in narration and recitative.

This loose treatment is most successful in the fifth, the real kernel of the suite, the tale 'Of the Birth of the Holy Pope Gregory', a birth whose sinful singularity is by no means the end of the story; and all the shocking circumstances accompanying the hero's life not only are no hindrance to his final elevation to be the Vice-Regent of Christ on earth, but make him, by God's peculiar favour, called and destined to·that seat. The chain of complications is long, and I may as well relate in this place the history of the royal and orphaned brother–sister pair: the brother who loved the sister more than he should, so that he loses his head and puts her into a more than interesting condition, for he makes her the mother of a boy of extraordinary beauty. It is this boy, a brother–sister child in all the ill meaning of the word, about whom everything turns. The father seeks to do penance by a crusade to the Holy Land, and there finds his death; the child presses on towards uncertain destinies. For the Queen, resolved not to have the infant so monstrously begot baptized on her own responsibility, puts him and his princely cradle into a cask and entrusts him, not without a tablet of instructions and gold and silver for his upbringing, to the waves of the sea, which bring him 'on the sixth feast-day' to the neighbourhood of a cloister presided over by a pious Abbot. The Abbot finds him, baptizes him with his own name, Gregory, and gives him an education perfectly suited to the lad's unusual physical and mental endowments. Meanwhile the sinful mother, to the regret of her whole realm, makes a vow not to marry, quite obviously not only because she regards herself as unconsecrate and unworthy of a Christian marriage but because she still cherishes a shameful loyalty to the departed brother. A powerful Duke of a foreign land seeks her hand, which she refuses: he is so wroth that he lays siege to her kingdom, overruns and conquers it, all but a single fortified city into which she retires. Now the youth Gregory, having learned of his origins, thinks to make a pilgrimage to the Holy Sepulchre; but instead arrives by chance in his mother's city, where he learns of the misfortune of the head of the kingdom, has himself brought before her, and offers her, who as the story says 'looks at him sharply' but does not know him, his services. He conquers the cruel Duke, frees the country, and is proposed by her retainers to the liberated Queen as her husband. She is indeed somewhat coy and asks for a day – only one – to think it over; and then against her oath she consents, so that, with the greatest approval and jubilation of the whole country, the marriage takes place and frightful is unsuspectingly heaped upon frightful, when the son of sin mounts the marriage bed with his own mother. I will not go further into all that; all I want is to describe the heavily emotional climax of the plot, which in the puppet theatre comes into its own in so surprising and admirable a way. At the very beginning the brother asks the sister why she looks so pale and 'why the upper part of thine eyelids darken'; and she answers him: 'It is no wonder, for I am with child and indeed full of remorse.' When the news comes that her sinful brother–husband is dead she breaks out in the remarkable lament: 'Gone is my hope, gone is my strength, my only brother, my second I!' and then covers the corpse with kisses from the soles of his feet to the crown of his head, so that her knights, unpleasantly impressed with such exaggerated grief, see themselves constrained to tear their sovereign lady away from the dead. Or when she becomes aware with whom she lives in tender wedded love, and says to him; 'O my sweet son, thou art my only child, thou art my spouse and lord, thou art mine and my brother's son, O my sweet child, and O thou my God, why hast thou let me be born!' For so it is: by means of the tablet she had once written with her own hand, which she finds in the private chamber of her husband, she learns with whom she shares her couch, thank God without having borne him another brother and grandson of her brother. And now it is his turn to think of a penitential pilgrimage, which he straightway barefoot undertakes. He comes to a fisherman who, 'by the fineness of his limbs', recognizes that he has no ordinary traveller before him, and the two agree that the utmost isolation is the only fitting thing. He rows him out sixteen miles into the ocean, to a rock where great seas surge, and there, chains being laid to his feet and the key thereof flung into the waves, Gregory spends seventeen years doing penance. At the end of this period there comes overwhelming, but to himself, it seems, scarce surprising favour and exaltation. For the Pope dies in Rome, and hardly is he dead when there comes down a voice from heaven: 'Seek out Gregory the man of God and set him up as My vicar on earth!' Then messengers haste in all directions and arrive at the place of that fisherman, who bethinks himself. Then he catches a fish, in whose belly he finds the key once sunk in the depths of the sea. He rows the messengers to the stone of penance and they cry up to it: 'O Gregory, thou man of God, come down to us from the stone, for God wills for thee to be set up for His vicar upon earth!' And what does he answer them? 'If that please God,' he says calmly, 'may His will be done!' But as he comes to Rome and when the bells are to be rung, they do not wait but ring of themselves, all the bells ring of their own accord, in witness to the fact that so pious and edifying a pope had never been before. And the holy man's fame reaches his mother, and she rightly decides that her life can be better entrusted to no one else than to this chosen one; so she departs for Rome to confess to the Holy father, who, as he receives her confession, recognizes her and says: 'O my sweet mother, sister, and wife, O my friend! The Devil thought to lead us to hell, but the greater power of God has prevented him.' And he builds her a cloister where she rules as Abbess, but only for a short time. For it is soon vouchsafed to them both to render up their souls to God.

Upon this extravagantly sinful, simple, and appealing tale then, did Adrian concentrate all the possible wit and terror, all the childlike fervour, fantasy, and solemnity of musical presentation, and probably one may apply to the whole production, but above all to this particular tale, the singular invention of the old Lübeck professor, the word 'God-witted'. The memory comes back to me, because the *Gesta* actually show something like a return to the musical style of *Love's Labour's Lost*, while the tone language of the *Marvels of the Universe* leans more to that of the *Apocalypse* or even the *Faust*. Such anticipations and overlappings often occur in creative life; but I can explain to myself the artistic attraction which this material had for my friend: it was an intellectual charm, not without a trace of malice and solvent travesty, springing as it did from a critical rebound after the swollen pomposity of an art epoch nearing its end. The musical drama had taken its materials from the romantic sagas, the myth-world of the Middle Ages, and thus suggested that only such objects were worthy of music, or suited to its nature. Here the conclusion seemed to be drawn; in a right destructive way, indeed, in that the bizarre, and particularly the farcically erotic, takes the place of the moralizing and priestly, all inflated pomp of production is rejected and the action transferred to the puppet theatre, in itself already burlesque. Adrian was at pains when he was at work on the *Gesta* to study the specific possibilities of the puppet play; and the Catholic-baroque popular fondness for the theatre, which was rife in the region where he led his hermit life, afforded him opportunity. Close by, in Waldshut, lived a druggist who carved and dressed marionettes, and Adrian repeatedly visited the man. He also travelled to Mittenwald, the fiddle village in the valley of the upper Isar, where the apothecary was an amateur of the same art and with the help of his wife and his clever sons produced puppet plays after Pocci and Christian Winter in the town, attracting large audiences of townsfolk and strangers. Leverkühn saw and studied these too; also, as I noticed, the very ingenious hand puppets and shadow-plays of the Javanese.

Those were enjoyable and stimulating evenings when he played for us – that is, to me, Schildknapp, and very likely Rudi Schwerdtfeger, who persisted in being present now and then – on the old square piano in the deep windowed room with the Nike, the latest-written parts of his amazing scores, in which the harmonically most dominating, the rhythmically labyrinthine was applied to the simplest material, and again a sort of musical children's trumpet style to the most extraordinary. The meeting of the Queen with the holy man whom she had borne to her brother, and whom she had embraced as spouse, charmed tears from us such as had never filled our eyes, uniquely mingled of laughter and fantastic sensibility. Schwerdtfeger, in abandoned familiarity, availed himself of the licence of the moment: with a 'You've done it magnificently!' embraced Adrian and pressed him to his heart. I saw Rüdiger's mouth, always a bitter one, give a wry twist and could not myself resist murmuring: 'Enough!' and putting out my hand to quench the unquenchable and restrain the unrestrained.

Rudolf may have had some trouble in following the conversation that ensued after the private performance in the Abbot's room. We spoke of the union of the advanced with the popular, the closing of the gulf between art and accessibility, high and low, as once in a certain sense it had been brought about by the romantic movement, literary and musical. But after that had followed a new and deeper cleavage and alienation between the good and the easy, the worth-while and the entertaining, the advanced and the generally enjoyable, which has become the destiny of art. Was it sentimentality to say that music – and she stood for them all – demanded with growing consciousness to step out of her dignified isolation, to find common ground without becoming common, and to speak a language which even the musically untaught could understand, as it understood the Wolf's Glen and the Jungfernkranz and Wagner? Anyhow, sentimentality was not the means to this end, but instead and much sooner irony, mockery; which, clearing the air, made an opposing party against the romantic, against pathos and prophecy, sound-intoxication and literature and a bond with the objective and elemental – that is, with the rediscovery of music itself as an organization of time. A most precarious start. For how near did not lie the false primitive, and thus the romantic again! To remain on the height of intellect; to resolve into the matter-of-course the most exclusive productions of European musical development, so that everybody could grasp the new; to make themselves its master, applying it unconcernedly as free building material and making tradition felt, recoiled into the opposite of the epigonal; to make technique, however high it had climbed, entirely unimportant, and all the arts of counterpoint and instrumentation to disappear and melt together to an effect of simplicity very far from simplicity, an intellectually winged simplicity – that seemed to be the object and the craving of art.

It was mostly Adrian who talked, only slightly seconded by us. Excited by the playing, he spoke with flushed cheeks and hot eyes, slightly feverish; not in a steady stream but more as just throwing out remarks, yet with so much animation that I felt I had never seen him, either in mine or in Rüdiger's presence, so eloquently taken out of himself. Schildknapp had given expression to his disbelief in the deromanticizing of music. Music was after all too deeply and essentially bound up with the romantic ever to reject it without serious natural damage to itself. To which Adrian:

'I will gladly agree with you, if you mean by the romantic a warmth of feeling which music in the service of technical intellectuality today rejects. It is probably self-denial. But what we called the purification of the complicated into the simple is at bottom the same as the winning back of the vital and the power of feeling. If it were possible – whoever succeeded in – how would you say it?' he turned to me and then answered himself: '– the breakthrough, you would say; whoever succeeded in the break-through from intellectual coldness into a touch-and-go world of new feeling, him one should call the saviour of art. Redemption,' he want on, with a nervous shoulder-shrug, 'a romantic word, and a harmonic writer's word, shop talk for the cadence-blissfulness of harmonic music. Isn't it amusing that music for a long time considered herself a means of release, whereas she herself, like all the arts, needed to be redeemed from a pompous isolation, which was the fruit of the culture-emancipation, the elevation of culture as a substitute for religion – from being alone with an élite of culture, called the public, which soon will no longer be, which even now no longer is, so that soon art will be entirely alone, alone to die, unless she were to find her way to the folk, that is, to say it unromantically, to human beings?'

He said and asked that all in one breath in a lowered, conversational tone, but with a concealed tremor which one understood only when he finished:

'The whole temper of art, believe me, will change, and withal into the blither and more modest; it is inevitable, and it is a good thing. Much melancholy ambition will fall away from her, and a new innocence, yes, harmlessness will be hers. The future will see in her, she herself will once more see in herself, the servant of a community which will comprise far more than "education" and will not have culture but will perhaps be a culture. We can only with difficulty imagine such a thing; and yet it will be, and be the natural thing: an art without anguish, psychologically healthy, not solemn, unsadly confiding, an art *per du* with humanity . . .'

He broke off, and we all three sat silent and shaken. It is painful and heart-stirring at once to hear talk of isolation from the community, remoteness from trust. With all my emotion I was yet in my deepest soul unsatisfied with his utterance, directly dissatisfied with him. What he had said did not fit with him, his pride, his arrogance if you like, which I loved, and to which art has a right. Art is mind, and mind does not at all need to feel itself obligated to the community, to society – it may not, in my view, for the sake of its freedom, its nobility. An art that 'goes in unto' the folk, which makes her own the needs of the crowd, of the little man, of small minds, arrives at wretchedness, and to make it her duty *is* the worst small-mindedness, and the murder of mind and spirit. And it is my conviction that mind, in its most audacious, unrestrained advance and researches, can, however unsuited to the masses, be certain in some indirect way to serve man – in the long run men.

Doubtless that was also the natural opinion of Adrian. But it pleased him to deny it, and I was very much mistaken if I looked at that as a contradiction of his arrogance. More likely it was an effort to condescend, springing from the same arrogance. If only there had not been that trembling in his voice when he spoke of the need of art to be redeemed, of art being *per du* with humanity! That was feeling: despite everything it tempted me to give his hand a stolen pressure. But I did not do so; instead I kept an eye on Rudi Schwerdtfeger lest he again be moved to embrace him.

Chapter Thirty-two

Inez Rodde's marriage to Professor Dr Helmut Institoris took place at the beginning of the war, when the country was still in good condition and strong in hope, and I myself still in the field, in the spring of 1915. It went off with all the proper bourgeois flourishes: ceremonies civil and religious and a wedding dinner in the Hôtel Vier Jahreszeiten, after which the young pair left for Dresden and the Saxon Switzerland. Such was the outcome of a long probation on both sides, which had evidently led to the conclusion that they were suited to each other. The reader will note the irony which I, truly without malice, express in the word 'evidently', for such a condition either did not exist or else had existed from the beginning, and no development had occurred in the relations between the two since Helmut had first approached the daughter of the deceased Senator. What on both sides spoke for the union did so at the moment of betrothal and marriage no more and no less than it had in the beginning, and nothing new had been added. But the classic adage: 'Look before you leap' had been formally complied with, and the very length of the test, added to the pressure due to the war, seemed finally to demand a positive solution. Indeed, it had ripened in haste several other unsettled affairs. Inez's consent, however, which she – on psychological or shall I say material grounds, that is to say for commonsense reasons – had always been more or less ready to give, had been the readier because Clarissa, towards the end of the previous year, had left Munich and entered on her first engagement in Celle on the Aller, so that her sister was left alone with a mother of whose bohemian leanings, tame as they were, she disapproved.

The Frau Senator, of course, felt a joyous satisfaction with the good bourgeois settlement her child was making, to which she had materially contributed by the entertaining she did and the social activities of her home. At her own expense she had thereby served the easy-going 'south-German' love of life, which was her way of making up for what she had lost, and had her fading charms paid court to by the men she invited, Knöterich, Kranich, Zink and Spengler, the young dramatic students, and so on. Yes, I do not go too far, perhaps in the end only just far enough, when I say that even with Rudi Schwerdtfeger she was on a jesting, teasing travesty of a mother-and-son footing. Uncommonly often when she talked with him her familiar affected cooing laugh could be heard. But after all I have intimated or rather expressed about Inez's inner life, I can leave it to the reader to imagine the mingled distaste and embarrassment that she felt at the sight of her mother's philandering. It has happened in my presence that during such a scene she left the drawing-room with flushed cheeks and shut herself in her room, at whose door after a quarter of an hour, as she had probably hoped and expected, Rudolf knocked to ask why she had gone away. Surely he knew the answer to his question; as surely it could not be put in words. He would tell her how much her presence was missed and coax her in all the tender notes in his voice, including of course the brotherly ones, to come back. He would not rest until she promised – perhaps not with him, she would not quite do that, but a little while after him – to return to the company.

I may be pardoned for adding this supplement, which impressed itself on my memory, though it had been comfortably dropped out of Frau Senator Rodde's now that Inez's betrothal and marriage were accomplished fact. She had provided the wedding with due pomp and circumstance, and in the absence of any considerable dowry had not failed to supply a proper equipment of linen and silver. She even parted with various pieces of furniture from former days, such as carved chests and this or that gilt 'occasional chair', to contribute to the furnishings of the imposing new house which the young pair had rented in Prinzregentenstrasse, two flights up, looking out on the English Garden. Yes, as though to prove to herself and others that her social undertakings and all the lively evenings in her drawing-room had really only served to further her daughters' prospects of happiness and settlement in life, she now expressed a distinct wish to retire, an inclination to withdraw from the world. She no longer entertained, and a year after Inez's marriage she gave up her apartment in the Rambergstrasse and put her widowed existence upon an altered footing. She moved out to Pfeiffering, where almost without Adrian being aware of it she took up her residence in the low building on the square opposite the Schweigestill courtyard, with the chestnuts in front of it, where formerly the painter of the melancholy landscapes of the Waldshut moors had had his quarters.

It is remarkable what charm this modest yet picturesque corner of the earth possessed for every sort of distinguished resignation or bruised humanity. Perhaps the explanation lay in the character of the proprietors and especially in that of the stout-hearted landlady Frau Else Schweigestill and her power of 'understanding'. She was amazingly clear-sighted, and she displayed her gift in occasional talk with Adrian, as when she told him that the Frau Senator was moving in across the road. 'It's pretty plain to see,' she said in her peasant singsong, 'easy as an'thing, I see it with half an eye, Herr Leverkühn, eh! – she got out of conceit with city folk's doings and lady and gentleman manners and ways, because she feels her age and she's singin' small, it takes different people different ways, I mean, eh, some don't care a hoot, they brazen it out and they look good too, they just get more restless and roguish, eh, and put on false fronts and make ringlets of their white hairs maybe and so on and so forth, real peart, and don't do any more like they used to, and act audacious and it often takes the men more than you'd think, eh, but with some that don't go, and don't do, so when their cheeks fall in and their necks get scrawny like a hen and nothin' to do for the teeth when you laugh, so they can't hold out, and grieve at their looks in the glass and act like a sick cat and hide away, and when 'taint the neck and the teeth, then it's the hair, eh, and with this one it's the hair's the worst, I could tell right off, otherways it's not so bad, none of it, but the hair, it's goin' on top, eh, so the part's gone to rack and ruin and she can't do anythin' any more with the tongs, and so she's struck all of a heap, for it's a great pain, believe me, and so she just gives up the ghost eh, and moves out in the country, to Schweigestills', and that's all 'tis.'

Thus the mother, with her smoothly drawn hair, just lightly silvered, with the parting in the middle showing the white skin. Adrian, as I said, was little affected by the advent of the lodger over the way, who when she first visited the house, was brought by their landlady to greet him. Then out of respect for his work she matched his reserve with her own and only once just at first had him for tea with her, in the two simple whitewashed low-ceilinged rooms on the ground floor, behind the chestnut trees, furnished quaintly enough with the elegant bourgeois relics of her former household, the candelabra, the stuffed easy-chairs, the Golden Horn in its heavy frame, the grand piano with the brocaded scarf. From then on, meeting in the village or on their walks, they simply exchanged friendly greetings or stopped a few minutes to chat about the sad state of the country and the growing food shortages in the cities. Out here one suffered much less, so that the retirement of the Frau Senator had a practical justification and even became a genuine interest, for it enabled her to provide her daughters and also former friends of the house, like the Knöterichs, with supplies from Pfeiffering: eggs, butter, flour, sausages, and so on. During the worst years she made quite a business out of packing and posting provisions. The Knöterichs had taken over Inez Rodde, now rich and settled and well wadded against life, into their own social circle from the little group who had attended her mother's evenings. They also invited the numismatist Dr Kranich, Schildknapp, Rudi Schwerdtfeger, and myself; but not Zink and Spengler, nor the little theatre people who had been Clarissa's colleagues. Instead their other guests were from university circles, or older and younger teachers of the two academies and their wives. With the Spanish-exotic Frau Knöterich, Natalie, Inez was on friendly or even intimate terms, this although the really attractive woman had the reputation, pretty well confirmed, of being a morphine addict; a rumour that was justified by my observation of the speaking brilliance of her eyes at the beginning of an evening and her occasional disappearance in order to refresh her gradually waning spirits. I saw that Inez, who set such store by patrician dignity and conservative propriety, who indeed had only married to gratify those tastes, chose to go about with Natalie rather than with the staid spouses of her husband's colleagues, the typical German professors' wives. She even visited and received Natalie alone. And thus was revealed to me anew the split in her nature; the fact that despite her nostalgia for it, the bourgeois life had no real viability for her.

That she did not love her husband, that rather limited teacher of aesthetics, wrapped in his dreams of beauty and brutality, I could not doubt. It was a conscious love of respectability that she devoted to him, and so much is true, that she upheld with consummate distinction, refined yet more by her expression of delicate and fastidious roguishness, her husband's station in life. Her meticulous conduct of his household and his social activities might even be called pedantic; and she achieved it under economic conditions which year by year made it harder and harder to sustain the standards of bourgeois correctness. To aid her in the care of the handsome and expensive apartment with its Persian rugs and shining parquetry floors she had two well-trained maidservants, dressed very *comme il faut* in little caps and starched apron-strings. One of them served as lady's maid. To ring for this Sophie was her passion. She did it all the time, to enjoy the aristocratic service and assure herself of the protection and care she had bought with her marriage. It was Sophie who had to pack the numberless trunks and boxes she took with her when she went to the country with Institoris, to Tegernsee or Berchtesgaden, if only for a few days. These mountains of luggage with which she weighed herself down at every smallest excursion out of her nest were to me likewise symbolic of her need of protection and her fear of life.

I must describe a little more particularly the immaculate eight-roomed apartment in the Prinzregentenstrasse. It had two drawing-rooms, one of which, more intimately furnished, served as family living-room; a spacious dining-room in carved oak, and a gentlemen's den and smoking-room supplied with leather-upholstered comfort. The sleeping-room of the married pair had twin beds with a semblance of a tester in polished yellow pear-wood above them. On the toilette-table the glittering bottles, the silver tools were ranged in rows according to size. All this was a pattern, one which still survived for some years into the period of disintegration: a pattern establishment of German bourgeois culture, not least by virtue of the 'good books' you found everywhere in living- and reception-rooms. The collection, on grounds partly representative, partly psychological, avoided the exciting and disturbing. It was dignified and cultured, with the histories of Leopold von Ranke, the works of Gregorovius, art histories, German and French classics – in short, the solid and conservative – as its foundation. With the years the apartment grew more beautiful, or at least fuller and more elaborate; for Dr Institoris knew this or that Munich artist of the more conservative Glaspalast school. His taste in art, despite all his theoretic espousal of the gorgeous and barbaric, was decidedly tame. In particular there was a certain Nottebohm, a native of Hamburg, married, hollow-cheeked, with a pointed beard; a droll man, clever at frightfully funny imitations of actors, animals, musical instruments, and professors, a patron of the now declining carnival festival, as a portraitist clever at the social technique of catching subjects and as an artist, I may say, possessing a glossy and inferior painting style. Institoris, accustomed to professional familiarity with masterpieces, either did not distinguish between them and deft mediocrity, or else he thought his commissions were a due of friendship, or else he asked nothing better than the refined and inoffensive for the adornment of his walls. Therein doubtless he was supported by his wife, if not on grounds of taste, then as a matter of feeling. So they both had themselves done for good money by Nottebohm, very like and not at all speaking portraits, each alone and both together; and later, when children came, the funny man made a life-size family group of all the Institorises, a collection of wooden dolls, on the respectable canvas of which a great deal of highly varnished oil paint had been expended. All these adorned the reception-rooms, in rich frames, provided with their own individual electric lighting above and below.

When children came, I said. For children did come; and with what address, what persistent, one might almost say heroic ignoring of circumstances less and less favourable to the patrician and bourgeois were they cared for and brought up – for a world, one might say, as it had been and not as it was to become. At the end of 1915 Inez presented her husband with a small daughter, named Lucrezia, begot in the polished yellow bedstead with the tester, next to the symmetrically ranged silver implements on her toilette-table. Inez declared at once that she intended to make of her a perfectly brought-up young girl, *une jeune fille accomplie*, she said in her Karlsruhe French. Two years later came twins, also female; they were christened Aennchen and Riekchen, with the same correct pomp and cèremony, at home, with chocolate, port wine, and dragées. The christening basin was silver, with a garland of flowers. All three were fair, charmingly pampered, lisping little beings, concerned about their frocks and sashes, obviously under pressure from the mother's perfection-compulsion. They were sensitive-plants grown in the shade, pathetically taken up with themselves. They spent their early days in costly bassinets with silk curtains, and were taken out to drive in little go-carts of the most elegant construction, with rubber wheels, under the lime trees of the Prinzregentenstrasse. They had a wet-nurse from 'the people', decked out in the traditional costume and ribbons like a lamb for the sacrifice. Inez did not nurse her children herself, the family doctor having advised against it. Later a Fräulein, a trained kindergarten teacher, took charge of them. The light, bright room where they grew up, where their little beds stood, where Inez visited them whenever the claims of the household and her own person permitted, had a frieze of fairy-stories round the walls, fabulous dwarf furniture, a gay linoleum-covered floor, and a world of well-ordered toys, teddy-bears, lambs on wheels, jumping-jacks, Käthe Kruse dolls, railway trains, on shelves along the walls – in short, it was the very pattern of a children's paradise, correct in every detail.

Must I say now, or repeat, that with all this correctness things were by no means correct, that they rested on self-will, not to say on a lie, and were not only more and more challenged from without, but for the sharper eye, the eye sharpened by sympathy, were crumbling within, they gave no happiness, neither were they truly believed in or willed. All this good fortune and good taste always seemed to me a conscious denial and whitewashing of the problem. It was in strange contradiction to Inez's cult of suffering, and in my opinion the woman was too shrewd not to see that the ideal little bourgeois brood which she had wilfully made of her children was the expression and over-all correction of the fact that she did not love them, but saw in them the fruits of a connexion she had entered into with a bad conscience as a woman and in which she lived with physical repulsion.

Good God, it was certainly no intoxicating bliss for a woman to go to bed with Helmut Institoris! So much I understand of feminine dreams and demands; and I always had to imagine that Inez had merely tolerated receiving her children from him, out of a sense of duty and so to speak with her head turned away. For they were his, the looks of all three left no doubt of that, the likeness with him being much stronger than that with the mother, possibly because her psychological participation when she conceived them had been so slight. And I would in no way impugn the masculine honour of the little man. He was certainly a whole man, even in a manikin edition, and through him Inez learned desire – a hapless desire, a shallow soil whereon her passion was to spring up and grow rank.

I have said that Institoris, when he began to woo the maiden Inez, had actually done so for another. And so it was now too: as a husband he was only the awakener of errant longings, of a half-experience of joy at bottom only frustrating, which demanded fulfilment, confirmation, satisfaction, and made the pain she suffered on Rudi Schwerdtfeger's account, which she had so strangely revealed to me, flare up into passion. It is quite clear: when she was the object of courtship she began distressfully to think of him; as disillusioned wife she fell in love with him, in full consciousness and with utter abandonment to feeling and desire. And there can be no doubt that the young man could not avoid responding to this feeling towards him, coming as it did from a suffering and spiritually superior being. I had almost said it would have been 'still finer' if he had *not* listened to it – and I could hear her sister's 'Hop, man, hop, what's the matter with you – jump up!' Again, I am not writing a novel, and I do not claim the writer's omniscient eye, penetrating into the dramatic development of an affair hidden from all the rest of the world. But so much is certain: that Rudolf, driven into a corner, quite involuntarily and with a 'What shall I do?' obeyed that haughty command, and I can very well imagine how his passion for flirtation, in the beginning a harmless amusement, betrayed him into situations more and more exciting and enflaming, ending in a liaison, which without this tendency of his to play with fire, he could have avoided.

In other words, under cover of the bourgeois propriety she had so nostalgically longed for as a refuge, Inez Institoris lived in adultery with a man in years, a youth in mental constitution and behaviour, a ladies' pet who made her suffer and doubt, just as a frivolous woman will cause anguish to a serious and loving man. In his arms then, her senses, aroused by an unloving marriage, found satisfaction. She lived thus for years, from a time which if I am right was not long after marriage up to the end of the decade; and when she no longer so lived, it was because he whom she sought with all her strength to hold escaped her. It was she who, while playing the part of exemplary housewife and mother, managed the affair, manipulated and concealed the daily artifices and the double life, which naturally gnawed at her nerves and terrified her by threatening the precarious loveliness of her looks: for instance, it deepened the two furrows between her blonde brows until she looked almost maniacal. And then, despite all the caution, cunning, and self-control used to hide such devious ways from society's eyes, the will to do so is never, on either side, quite clear or consistent. As for the man, of course it must flatter him if his good fortune is at least suspected; while for the woman it is a point of secret sexual pride to have it guessed that she need not content herself with the caresses, by nobody very highly rated, of her husband. So I scarcely deceive myself when I assume that knowledge of Inez Institoris's side-slip was fairly widespread in her Munich circle, although I have never, except with Adrian Leverkühn, exchanged a word with anybody on the subject. Yes, I would go so far as to reckon with the possibility that Helmut himself knew the truth: a certain admixture of cultured decency, deprecating and regretful toleration, and – love of peace, speaks for the supposition, and it does happen far from seldom that society takes the spouse for the only blind one, while he thinks that except for himself no one knows anything. This is the comment of an elderly man who has observed life.

I had not the impression that Inez troubled herself overmuch about what people knew. She did her best to prevent their knowing, but that was more to preserve the convenances; whoever actually must know, let them, so long as they left her alone. Passion is too much taken up with itself to be able to conceive that anyone would be seriously against it. At least, it is so in matters of love, where feeling claims for itself every right in the world and, however forbidden and scandalous, quite involuntarily reckons on understanding. How could Inez, if she considered herself otherwise quite unperceived, have taken my own knowledge so completely for granted? But she did so, as good as regardless, except that no name was mentioned, in an evening conversation which we had – it would be in the autumn of 1916 – and which obviously was of moment to her. At that time, unlike Adrian, who when he had spent the evening in Munich used to stick to his eleven o'clock train back to Pfeiffering, I had rented a room in Schwabing, Hohenzollernstrasse, not far behind the Siegesthor, in order to be independent and on occasion to have a roof over my head in the city. So when as a near friend I was asked to the Institorises' for the evening meal, I could readily accept the invitation given by Inez at table and seconded by her husband to keep her company after supper, when Helmut, who was to play cards at the Allotria Club, should have left the house. He went out shortly after nine, wishing us a pleasant evening. Then the mistress of the house and her guest sat alone in the family living-room. It was furnished with cushioned wicker chairs, and a bust of Inez, in alabaster, made by an artist friend, stood on a pedestal: very like, very piquant, considerably under life-size, but an uncommonly speaking likeness, with the heavy hair, the veiled glance, the delicate, outstretched neck, the mouth pursued in a disdainful sort of mischief.

And again I was the confidant, the 'good' man, rousing no emotion, in contrast to the world of the irresistible, which was incorporated for Inez in the youth about whom she longed to talk to me. She said it herself: the things happening and having happened, the joy, the love and suffering, did not come into their own if they remained wordless, were only enjoyed and suffered. They were not satisfied in night and silence. The more secret they were, the more they required a third party, the intimate friend, the good man, to whom and with whom one could talk about them – and that was I. I saw it and took my role upon myself.

For a while after Helmut left, as it were while he was within hearing, we spoke of indifferent things. Then suddenly, almost abruptly, she said:

'Serenus, do you blame, do you despise and condemn me?'

It would have been silly to pretend I did not understand.

'By no means, Inez,' I replied. 'God forbid! I have always been told: "Vengeance is mine, I will repay." I know He includes the punishment in the sin and saturates it therewith so that one cannot be distinguished from the other and happiness and punishment are the same. You must suffer very much. Would I sit here if I were constituted a moral judge over you? That I fear for you I do not deny. But I would have kept that to myself if not for your question whether I blame you.'

'What is suffering, what fear and humiliating danger,' said she, 'in comparison with the one sweet, indispensable triumph, without which one would not live; to hold to its better self that frivolous, evasive, worldly, torturing, irresponsible charmingness, which yet has true human value; to drive its flippancy to serious feeling, to possess the elusive, and at last, at last, not only once but for confirmation and reassurance never often enough, to see it in the state that suits its worth, the state of devotion of deep suspiring passion!'

I do not say the woman used exactly these words, but she expressed herself in like ones. She was well read, accustomed to articulate her inner life in speech; as a girl she had even attempted verse. What she said had a cultured precision and something of the boldness that always arises when language tries seriously to achieve feeling and life, to make them first truly live, to exhaust them in it. This is no everyday effort, but a product of emotion, and in so far feeling and mind are related, but also in so far mind gets its thrilling effect. As she went on speaking, seldom listening, with half an ear, to what I threw in, her words, I must frankly say, were soaked in a sensual bliss that makes me scruple to report them directly. Sympathy, discretion, human reverence prevent me, and also, maybe, a philistine reluctance to impose anything so painful upon the reader. She repeated herself often in a compulsive effort to express in better terms what she had already said without in her opinion doing it justice. And always there was this curious equation of worthiness with sensual passion, this fixed and strangely drunken idea that inward worthiness could only fulfil itself, realize itself, in fleshly desire, which obviously was something of like value with 'worth'; that it was at once the highest and the most indispensable happiness to keep them together. I cannot describe the glowing albeit melancholy and insecure, unsatisfied notes in her voice as she spoke of this mixture of the two conceptions *worth* and *desire*; how much desire appeared as the profoundly serious element, sternly opposed to the hated 'society' one, 'society' where true worth in play and coquetry betrayed itself; which was the inhuman, treacherous element of its exterior surface amiability; and which one must take from it, tear from it, to have it alone, utterly alone, alone in the most final sense of the word. The disciplining of lovableness till it became love: that was what it amounted to; but at the same time there was more abstruse matter, about something wherein thought and sense mystically melted into one; the idea that the contradiction between the frivolity of society and the melancholy untrustworthiness of life in general was resolved in his embrace, the suffering it caused most sweetly avenged.

Of what I said myself I scarcely know by now any details, except one question intended of course to point out her erotic over-estimation of the object of her love and to inquire how it was possible: I remember I delicately hinted that the being to whom she devoted it was not after all actually so vital, glorious, or consummately desirable; that the military examination had showed a physiological functional defect and the removal of an organ. The answer was in the sense that this defect only brought the lovable closer to the suffering soul; that without it there would have been no hope at all, it was just that which had made the fickle one accessible to the cry of pain; more still, and revealing enough: that the shortening of life which might result from it was more of a consolation and assurance to her who demanded possession than it was a moderation of her love. For the rest, all the strangely embarrassing details from that first talk were repeated now, only resolved in almost spiteful satisfaction: he might now make the same deprecating remark that he would have to show himself at the Langewiesches' or the Rollwagens' (people whom one did not know oneself) and thus betray that he said the same thing to them; but now there was triumph in the thought. The 'raciness' of the Rollwagen girls was no longer worrying or distressing: mouth to mouth with him, the sting was drawn from those too ingratiating requests to indifferent people that they really must stop on longer with him. As for that frightful 'There are so many unhappy ones already'; there was a kind of sigh on which the ignominy of the words was blown away. This woman was plainly filled with the thought that while she did indeed belong to the world of enlightenment and suffering, yet at the same time she was a woman and in her femininity possessed a means of snatching life and happiness for herself, of bringing arrogance to her feet and her heart. Earlier, indeed, by a look, a serious word, one could put light-headedness a moment in a thoughtful mood, temporarily win it; one could oblige it, after a flippant farewell, to turn back and correct it by a silent and serious one. But now these temporary gains had been confirmed in possession, in union; in so far as possession and union were possible in duality, in so far as a brooding femininity could secure them. It was this which Inez mistrusted, betraying her lack of faith in the loyalty of the beloved. 'Serenus,' said she, 'it is inevitable. I know it, he will leave me.' And I saw the folds between her brows deepen and her face take on a half-mad expression. 'But then woe to him! And woe to me!' she added tonelessly, and I could not help recalling Adrian's words when I first told him about the affair: 'He must see that he gets out of it whole.'

For me the talk was a real sacrifice. It lasted two hours, and much self-denial, human sympathy, friendly goodwill were needed to hold out. Inez seemed conscious of that too, but I must say that her gratitude for the patience, time, and nervous strain one devoted to her was, oddly enough, unmistakably mixed with a sort of malicious satisfaction, a dog-in-the-manger attitude expressing itself in an occasional enigmatic smile. I cannot think of it today without wondering how I bore it so long. In fact we sat on until Institoris got back from the Allotria, where he had been playing tarok with some gentlemen. An expression of embarrassed conjecture crossed his face when he saw us still there. He thanked me for so kindly taking his place and I did not sit down again after greeting him. I kissed the hand of the mistress of the house and left, really unnerved, half angry, half sorry, and went through the silent empty streets to my quarters.

Chapter Thirty-three

The time of which I write was for us Germans an era of national collapse, of capitulation, of uprisings due to exhaustion, of helpless surrender into the hands of strangers. The time *in* which I write, which must serve me to set down these recollections here in my silence and solitude, this time has a horribly swollen belly, it carries in its womb a national catastrophe compared with which the defeat of those earlier days seems a moderate misfortune, the sensible liquidation of an unsuccessful enterprise. Even an ignominious issue remains something other and more normal than the judgement that now hangs over us, such as once fell on Sodom and Gomorrah; such as the first time we had not after all invoked.

That it approaches, that it long since became inevitable: of that I cannot believe anybody still cherishes the smallest doubt. Monsignor Hinterpförtner and I are certainly no longer alone in the trembling – and at the same time, God help us, secretly sustaining – realization. That it remains shrouded in silence is uncanny enough. It is already uncanny when among a great host of the blind some few who have the use of their eyes must live with scaled lips. But it becomes sheer horror, so it seems to me, when everybody knows and everybody is bound to silence, while we read the truth from each other in eyes that stare or else shun a meeting.

I have sought faithfully, from day to day, to be justified of my biographical task. In a permanent state of excitement I have tried to give worthy shape to the personal and intimate; and I have let go by what has gone by in the outer world during the time in which I write. The invasion of France, long recognized as a possibility, has come, a technical and military feat of the first, or rather of an altogether unique order, prepared with the fullest deliberation, in which we could the less prevent the enemy since we did not dare concentrate our defence at the single point of landing, being uncertain whether or not to regard it as one among many further attacks at points we could not guess. Vain and fatal both were our hesitations. This was the one. And soon troops, tanks, weapons, and every sort of equipment were brought on shore, more than we could throw back into the sea. The port of Cherbourg, we could confidently trust, had been put out of commission by the skill of German engineers; but it surrendered after a heroic radiogram to the Führer from the Commandant as well as the Admiral. And for days now a battle had been raging for the Norman city of Caen – a struggle which probably, if our fears see truly, is already the opening of the way to the French capital, that Paris to which in the New Order the role of European Luna Park and house of mirth was assigned, and where now, scarcely held in check by the combined strength of the German and French police, resistance is boldly raising its head.

Yes, how much has happened that had its effect on my own solitary activities, while yet I refused to look without-doors! It was not many days after the amazing landing in Normandy that our new reprisal weapon, already many times mentioned with heartfelt joy by our Führer, appeared on the scene of the western theatre of war: the robot bomb, a most admirable means of offence, which only sacred necessity could inspire in the mind of inventive genius; these flying messengers of destruction, sent off in numbers without a crew from the French coast, which explode over southern England, and unless all signs fail, have become a real calamity to the foe. Are they capable of averting actual catastrophe from us? Fate did not will the installations should be ready in time to prevent or disturb the invasion. Meantime we read that Perugia is taken. It lies, though we do not say so, between Rome and Florence. We already hear whispers of a strategic plan to abandon the whole peninsula, perhaps to free more troops for the faltering defence in the east, whither our soldiers want at no price at all to be sent. A Russian wave is rolling up; it has taken Vitebsk and now threatens Minsk, the capital of White Russia, after whose fall, so our whispering news service tells us, there will be no longer any stopping them in the east either.

No stopping them! My soul, think not on it! Do not venture to measure what it would mean if in this our uniquely frightful extremity the dam should break, as it is on the point of doing, and there were no more hold against the boundless hatred that we have fanned to flame among the peoples round us! True, by the destruction of our cities from the air, Germany has long since become a theatre of war; but it still remains for it to become so in the most actual sense, a sense that we cannot and may not conceive. Our propaganda even has a strange way of warning the foe against the wounding of our soil, the sacred German soil, as against a horrible crime ... The sacred German soil! As though there were anything still sacred about it, as though it were not long since deconsecrate over and over again, through uncounted crimes against law and justice and both morally and *de facto* laid open to judgement and enforcement! Let it come! Nothing more remains to hope, to wish, to will. The cry for peace with the Anglo-Saxon, the offer to continue alone the war against the Sarmatic flood, the demand that some part of the condition of unconditional surrender be remitted, in other words that they treat with us – but with whom? All that is nothing but eye-wash: the demand of a regime which will not understand, even today seems not to understand, that its staff is broken, that it must disappear, laden with the curse of having made itself, us, Germany, the Reich, I go further and say all that is German, intolerable to the world.

Such at the moment is the background of my biographical activity. It seemed to me I owed a sketch of it to the reader. As for the background of my actual narrative, up to the point whither I have brought it, I have characterized it at the beginning of this chapter in the phrase 'into the hands of strangers'. 'It is frightful to fall into the hands of strangers': this sentence and the bitter truth of it I thought through and suffered through, often, in those days of collapse and surrender. For as a German, despite a univer-salistic shading which my relation to the world takes on through my

Catholic tradition, I cherish a lively feeling for the national type, the characteristic life-idiom of my country, so to speak, its idea, the way it asserts itself as a facet of the human, against other no doubt equally justifiable variations of the same, and can so assert itself only by a certain outward manifestation, sustained by a nation standing erect on its feet. The unexampled horror of a decisive military defeat overwhelms this idea, physically refutes it, by imposing an ideology foreign to it – and in the first instance bound up with words, with the way we express ourselves. Handed over utterly into the power of this foreign ideology, one feels with all one's being that just because it is foreign it bodes no good. The beaten French tasted this awful experience in 1870, when their negotiators, seeking to soften the conditions of the victors, priced very high the renown, '*la gloire*', ensuing from the entry of our troops into Paris. But the German statesmen answered them that the word *gloire* or any equivalent of it did not occur in our vocabulary. They talked about it in hushed voices, in the French Chamber. Anxiously they tried to comprehend what it meant to surrender at discretion to a foe whose conceptions did not embrace the idea of *gloire*.

Often and often I thought of it, when the Jacobin-Puritan virtue jargon, which four years long had disputed the war propaganda of the 'agreed peace', became the current language of victory. I saw it confirmed that it is only a step from capitulation to pure abdication and the suggestion to the conqueror that he would please take over the conduct of the defeated country according to his own ideas, since for its own part it did not know what to do. Such impulses France knew, forty-seven years before, and they were not strange to us now. Still they are rejected. The defeated must continue somehow to be reponsible for themselves; outside leading-strings are there only for the purpose of preventing the Revolution which fills the vacuum after the departure of the old authority from going to extremes and endangering the bourgeois order of things for the victors. Thus in 1918 the continuation of the blockade after we laid down our arms in the west served to control the German Revolution, to keep it on bourgeois-democratic rails and prevent it from degenerating into the Russian proletarian. Thus bourgeois imperialism crowned with the laurels of vitory, could not do enough to warn against 'anarchy'; not firmly enough reject all dealing with workmen's and soldiers' councils and bodies of that kind, not clearly enough protest that only with a settled Germany could peace be signed and only such would get enough to eat. What we had for a government followed this paternal lead, held with the National Assembly against the dictatorship of the proletariat and meekly waved away the advances of the Soviets, even when they concerned grain-deliveries. Not to my entire satisfaction, I may add. As a moderate man and son of culture I have indeed a natural horror of radical revolution and the dictatorship of the lower classes, which I find it hard, owing to my tradition, to evisage otherwise than in the image of anarchy and mob rule – in short, of the destruction of culture. But when I recall the grotesque anecdote about the two saviours of European civilization, the German and the Italian, both of them in the pay of finance capital, walking together through the Uffizi Gallery in Florence, where they certainly did not belong, and one of them saying to the other that all these 'glorious art treasures' would have been destroyed by Bolshevism if heaven had not prevented it by raising them up – when I recall all this, then my notions about classes and masses take on another colour, and the dictatorship of the proletariat begins to seem to me, a German burgher, an ideal situation compared with the now possible one of the dictatorship of the scum of the earth. Bolshevism to my knowledge has never destroyed any works of art. That was far more within the sphere of activity of those who assert that they are protecting us from it. There did not lack much for their zeal in destroying the things of the spirit – a zeal that is entirely foreign to the masses – to have made sacrifice of the works of the hero of these pages, Adrian Leverkühn. For there is no doubt that their truimph and the historical sanction to regulate this world according to their beastly will would have destroyed his life-work and his immortality.

Twenty-six years ago it was revulsion against the self-righteous blandishments of the rhetorical burgher and 'son of the revolution', which proved stronger in my heart than the fear of disorder, and made me want just what he did not: that my conquered country should turn towards its brother in tribulation, towards Russia. I was ready to put up with the social revolution – yes, to agee to it – which would arise from such comradery. The Russian Revolution shook me. There was no doubt in my mind of the historical superiority of its principles over those of the powers which set their foot on our necks.

Since then history has taught me to regard with other eyes our conquerors of that day, who will shortly conquer us again in alliance with the revolution of the East. It is true that certain strata of bourgeois democracy seemed and seem today ripe for what I termed the dictatorship of the scum: willing to make common cause with it to linger out their privileges. Still, leaders have arisen, who like myself, who am a son of humanism, saw in this dictatorship the ultimate that can or may be laid upon humanity and moved their world to a life-and-death struggle against it. Not enough can these men be thanked, and it shows that the democracy of the western lands, in all the anachronistic state of their institutions through the passage of time, all the rigidity of their conceptions of freedom in resisting the new and inevitable, is after all essentially in the line of human progress, of goodwill to the improvement of society and its renewal, alteration, rejuvenation; it shows that western democracy is after all capable by its own nature, of a transition into conditions more justified of life.

All this by the way. What I want to recall here in this biography is the loss of authority of the monarchic military state, so long the form and habit of our life; it was far advanced as defeat approached and now with defeat it is complete. Its collapse and abdication result in a situation of permanent hunger and want, progressive depreciation of the currency, progressive laxity and loose speculation, a certain regrettable and unearned dispensing of civilian freedom from all restraint, the degeneration of a national structure so long held together by discipline into debating groups of masterless citizens. Such a very gratifying sight that is not, and no deduction can be made from the word 'painful' when I use it here to characterize the impressions I got as a purely passive observer from the gatherings of certain 'Councils of Intellectual Workers' then springing up in Munich hotels. If I were a novel-writer, I could make out of tortured recollections a most lively picture of such a futile and flagitious assemblage. There was a writer of belles-lettres, who spoke, not without charm, even with sybaritic and dimpling relish, on the theme of 'Revolution and Love of Humanity', and unloosed a free discussion – all too free, diffuse, and confused – by such misbegotten types as only see the light at moments like this: lunatics, dreamers, clowns, flibbertigibbets and fly-by-nights, plotters and small-time philosophers. There were speeches for and against love of human kind, for and against the authorities, for and against the people. A little girl spoke a piece, a common soldier was with difficulty prevented from reading to the end a manuscript that began 'Dear citizens and citizenesses!' and would doubtless have gone on the whole night; an angry student launched an embittered invective against all the previous speakers, without vouchsafing to the assemblage a single positive expression of opinion – and so on. The audience revelled in rude interruptions; it was turbulent, childish, and uncivilized, the leadership was incapable, the air frightful, and the result less than nothing. I kept looking round and asking myself whether I was the only sufferer; and I was grateful at last to be out of doors, where the tram service had stopped hours before and the sound of some probably entirely aimless shots echoed through the winter night.

Leverkühn, to whom I conveyed these impression of mine, was unusually ailing at this time, in a way that had something humiliating in its torments. It was as though he were pinched and plagued with hot pincers, without being in immediate danger of his life. That, however, seemed to have arrived at its nadir, so that he was just prolonging it by dragging on from one day to the next. He had been attacked by a stomach ailment, not yielding to any dietary measures, beginning with violent headache, lasting several days and recurring in a few more; with hours, yes, whole days of retching from an empty stomach, sheer misery, undignified, niggling, humiliating, ending in utter exhaustion and persistent sensitivity to light after the attack had passed. There was no thought that the condition might be due to psychological causes, the tribulations of the time, the national defeat with its desolating consequences. In his rustic, not to say cloistered retreat, far from the city, these things scarcely touched him, though he was kept posted on them, not through the newspapers, which he never read, but by his so sympathetic and yet so unruffled housekeeper, Frau Else Schweigestill. The events, which certainly for a man of insight were not a sudden shock but the coming to pass of the long expected, could produce in him scarcely a shoulder-shrug, and he found my efforts to see in the evil the good which it might conceal, to be in the same vein as the comment which I had made at the war's beginning – and that makes me think of that cold, incredulous 'God bless your studies!' with which he then answered me.

And still! Little as it was possible to connect his worsening health in any temperamental way with the national misfortune, yet my tendency to see the one in the light of the other and find symbolic parallels in them, this inclination, which after all might be due simply to the fact that they were happening at the same time, was not diminished by his remoteness from outward things, however much I might conceal the thought and refrain from bringing it up even indirectly.

Adrian had not asked for a physician, because he wanted to interpret his sufferings as familiar and hereditary, as merely an acute intensification of his father's migraine. It was Frau Schweigestill who at last insisted on calling in Dr Kürbis, the Waldshut district physician, the same who had once delivered the Fräulein from Bayreuth. The good man would not hear of migraine, since the often excessive pains were not one-sided as is the case with migraine but consisted in a raging torment in and above both eyes, and moreover were considered by the physician to be a secondary symptom. His diagnosis, stated with all reserve, was of something like a stomach ulcer, and while he prepared the patient for a possible haemorrhage, which did not occur, he prescribed a solution of nitrate of silver to be taken internally. When this did not answer he went over to strong doses of quinine, twice daily, and that did in fact give temporary relief. But at intervals of two weeks, and then for two whole days, the attacks, very like violent seasickness, came back; and Kürbis's diagnosis began to waver or rather he settled on a different one: he decided that my friend's sufferings were definitely to be ascribed to a chronic catarrh of the stomach with considerable dilation on the right side, together with circulatory stoppages which decreased the flow of blood to the brain. He now prescribed Karlsbad effervescent salts and a diet of the smallest possible volume, so that the fare consisted of almost nothing but tender meat. He prohibited liquids, soup and vegetables, flour and bread. This treatment was directed towards the desperately violent acidity from which the patient suffered, and which Kürbis was inclined to ascribe at least in part to nervous causes – that is, to a central influence, the brain, which here for the first time began to play a role in his diagnostic speculations. More and more, after the dilation of the stomach had been cured without diminishing the headaches and nausea, he shifted his explanation of the symptoms to the brain, confirmed therein by the emphatic demand of the patient to be spared the light. Even when he was out of bed he spent entire half-days in a densely dark room. One sunny morning had been enough to fatigue his nerves so much that he thirsted after darkness and enjoyed it like a beneficient element. I myself have spent many hours of the day talking with in the Abbot's room where it was so dark that only after the eyes got used to it could one see the outlines of the furniture and a pallid gleam upon the walls.

About this time ice-caps and morning cold showers for the head were prescribed, and they did better than the other means, though only as palliatives, whose ameliorating effects did not justify one in speaking of a cure. The unnatural condition was not removed, the attacks recurred intermittently, and the afflicted one declared he could stand them if it were not for the permanent and constant pain in the head, above the eyes, and that indescribable, paralysis-like feeling all over from the top of the head to the tips of the toes, which seemed to affect the organs of speech as well. The sufferer's words dragged, perhaps unconsciously, and he moved his lips so idly that what he said was badly articulated. I think it was rather that he did not care, for it did not prevent him from talking; and I sometimes even got the impression that he exploited the impediment and took pleasure in saying things in a not quite articulate way, only half meant to be understood, speaking as though out of a dream, for which he found this kind of communication suitable. He talked to me about the little sea-maid in Andersen's fairy-tale, which he uncommonly loved and admired; not least the really capital picture of the horrid kingdom of the sea-witch, behind the raging whirlpools, in the wood of polyps, whither the yearning child ventured in order to gain human legs instead of her fish's tail, and through the love of the dark-eyed prince (while she herself had eyes 'blue as the depths of sea') perhaps to win, like human beings, an immortal soul. He played with the comparison between the knife-sharp pains which the beautiful dumb one found herself ready to bear every step she took on her lovely new white pins and what he himself had ceaselessly to endure. He called her his sister in affliction and made intimate, humorous, and objective comments on her behaviour, her wilfulness, and her sentimental infatuation for the two-legged world of men.

'It begins,' he said, 'with the cult of the marble statue that had got down to the bottom of the sea, the boy, who is obviously by Thorwaldsen, and her illegitimate taste for it. Her grandmother should have taken the thing away from her instead of letting her plant a rose-red mourning wreath in the blue sand. They had let her go through too much, too early, after that the yearning and the hysterical over-estimation of the upper world and the immortal soul cannot be controlled. An immortal soul – but why? A perfectly absurd wish; it is much more soothing to know that after death one will be the foam on the sea, as Nature wills. A proper nixie would have taken this empty-headed prince, who did not know how to value her and who married someone else before her face and eyes, led him to the marble steps of his palace, drawn him into the water, and tenderly drowned him instead of making her fate depend as she did on his stupidity. Probably he would have loved her much more passionately with the fish-tail she was born with than with those extremely painful legs . . .'

And with an objectivity that could only be in jest, but with drawn brows and reluctantly moving, half-articulating lips, he spoke of the aesthetic advantages of the nixie's shape over that of the forked human kind, of the charm of the lines with which the feminine form flowed from the hips into the smooth-scaled, strong, and supple fish-tail, so well adapted for steering and darting. He rejected all idea of a monstrosity, whatever attaches in the popular mind to mythological combinations of the human and the animal; and declared that he did not find admissible mythological fictions of that kind. The sea-wife had a perfectly complete and charming organic reality, beauty and inevitability; you saw that at once, when she became so pathetically déclassée after she had bought herself legs, which nobody thanked her for. Here we unquestionably had a perfectly natural pheno-menon, nature herself was guilty of it, *if* she was guilty of it, which he did not believe, in fact he knew better – and so on.

I still hear him speaking, or murmuring, with a sinister humour which I answered as lightly; with some misgiving as usual in my heart, along with silent admiration for the whimsical relish he knew how to extract from the pressure obviously resting on him. It was this that made me agree to his rejecting the proposal which Dr Kürbis at that time in duty bound put before him: he recommended or asked consideration for a consultation with a higher medical authority; but Adrian avoided it, would have none of it. He had, he said, in the first place full confidence in Kürbis; but also he was convinced that he, more or less alone, out of his own nature and powers, would have to get rid of the evil. This corresponded with my own feelings. I should have been more inclined to a change of air, a sojourn at a cure, which the doctor also suggested, without, as we might have expected, being able to persuade the patient. Much too much was he dependent on his elected and habitual frame of house and courtyard, church-tower, pond, and hill; too much on his ancient study, his velvet chair, to let himself in for exchanging all this, even for four weeks, for the abomination of a resort existence, with table d'hôte, promenade, and band. Above all, he pleaded for consideration for Frau Schweigestill, whom he would not wish to offend by preferring some outside, public care and service to hers. He felt, he said, far and away better provided for here, in her understanding, humanly wise and motherly care. Really one might ask where else he could have what he had here, with her who brought him according to the new regimen every four hours something to eat: at eight o'clock an egg, cocoa, and rusk, at twelve a little steak or cutlet, at four soup, meat, and vegetable, at eight o'clock cold joint and tea. This diet was beneficial. It guarded against the fever attending the digestion of hearty meals.

The Nackedey and Kunigunde Rosenstiel came by turns to Pfeiffering. They brought flowers, preserves, peppermint lozenges, and whatever else the market shortages allowed. Not always, in fact only seldom were they admitted, which put neither of them off. Kunigunde consoled herself with particularly well-turned letters in the purest, most stately German. This consolation, true, the Nackedey lacked.

I was always glad to see Rüdiger Schildknapp, with his Adrian-eyes, at my friend's retreat. His presence had a soothing and cheering effect; would it had oftener been vouchsafed! But Adrian's illness was just one of those serious cases which always seemed to paralyse Rüdiger's obligingness; we know how the feeling of being urgently desired made him jib and refuse. He did not lack excuses, I mean rationalizations of this odd psychological trait: wrapped up in his literary bread-winning, this confounded translation, he could really scarcely get away, and besides, his own health was suffering under the bad food conditions. He often had intestinal catarrh and when he appeared in Pfeiffering – for he did come now and again – he wore a flannel bodybelt, also a damp bandage in a gutta-percha sheath, a source of bitter wit and Anglo-Saxon jokes for him and thus a diversion for Adrian, who could raise himself with no one so well as with Rüdiger above the torments of the body into the free air of jest and laughter.

Frau Senator Rodde came too, of course, from time to time, crossing the road from her over-furnished retreat to inquire of Frau Schweigestill about Adrian's health if she could not see him herself. If he could receive her, or if they met out of doors, she told him about her daughters, and when she smiled kept her lips closed over a gap in her front teeth, for here too, in addition to the hair, there were losses which made her shun society. Clarissa, she said, loved her profession and did not falter in pursuit of it, despite a certain coldness on the part of the public, carping critics, and the impertinent cruelty of this or that producer who tried to distract her by calling 'Tempo, tempo!' from the wings when she was about to enjoy a solo scene. The first engagement in Celle had come to an end and the next one had not carried her much further: she was playing the juvenile lead in remote East Prussian Elbing. But she had prospects of an engagement in the west, in Pforzheim, whence it was but a step to the stage of Karlsruhe or Stuttgart. The main thing, in this profession, was not to get stuck in the provinces, but to be attached betimes to an important state theatre or a private one in a metropolis. Clarissa hoped to succeed. But from her letters, at least those to her sister, it appeared that her success was of a more personal, that is erotic, kind rather than an artistic one. Many were the snares to which she saw herself exposed; repulsing them took much of her energy and mocking coolness. To Inez, though not to her mother directly, she announced that a rich warehouse-owner, a well-preserved man with a white beard, wanted to make her his mistress and set her up extravagantly with an apartment, a car, and clothes – when she could silence the regisseur's impudent 'Tempo!' and make the critics fall in line. But she was much too proud to establish her life on such foundations. It was her personality, not her person, that was important to her. The rich man was turned down and Clarissa went on fighting her way in Elbing.

About her daughter Institoris in Munich Frau Rodde talked in less detail; her life was not so lively or eventful, more normal and secure – regarded superficially, and Frau Rodde obviously wanted to regard it thus. I mean she represented Inez's marriage as happy, which was certainly a large order of sentimental superficiality. The twins had just been born, and the Frau Senator spoke with simple feeling of the event, of the three spoilt little darlings, whom she visited from time to time in their ideal nursery.

Expressly and with pride she praised her older daughter for the unbending will-power with which she kept her housekeeping up to the mark despite all contrary circumstances. You could not tell whether the Frau Senator really did not know what the birds on the house-tops talked about, the Schwerdtfeger affair, or whether she only pretended. Adrian, as the reader knows, knew of it from me. But one day he received Rudolf's confession – a singular business indeed.

The violinist was most sympathetic during the acute illness of our friend, loyal and attached; yes, it seemed as though he wanted to use the occasion to show how much store he set by Adrian's favour and good will. It was often my impression that he believed he could use the sufferer's reduced and as he probably thought more or less helpless state to exert his quite imperturbable ingratiatingness, enforced by all his personal charm, to conquer a coolness, dryness, and ironic withdrawal which annoyed him, on grounds more or less serious, or hurt him, or wounded his vanity, or possibly some genuine feeling on his part – God knows what it was. In speaking of Rudolf's inconstant nature – as one has to speak of it – one runs a risk of saying too much. But also one should not say too little, and for my part this nature and its manifestations appeared to me always in the light of an absolutely naïve, childish, yes, puckish possession, whose reflection I sometimes saw laughing out of his so very pretty blue eyes.

Suffice it to say that Schwerdtfeger zealously concerned himself with Adrian's condition. He often rang up to inquire of Frau Schweigestill and offered to come out whenever a visit might be tolerable or welcome. Soon afterwards, on a day when there was an improvement, he would appear; he displayed the most winning delight at the reunion, and twice at the beginning addressed Adrian with *du*, only the third time, as Adrian did not respond, to correct himself and be satisfied with the first name and *Sie*. As a sort of consolation and by way of experiment Adrian sometimes called him Rudolf, though never Rudi, as everybody else did, and he dropped this too after a while. However, he congratulated the violinist on the great success he had recently had in a Nuremberg concert, and particularly with his playing of Back's Partita in E major for violin alone, which had received the liveliest commendation from public and press. The result was his appearance as soloist at one of the Munich Academy concerts in the Odeon, where his clean, sweet, technically perfect interpretation of Tartini pleased everybody extraordinarily. They put up with his 'small tone'. He had musical and also personal compensations to make up for it. His rise to the position of leader in the Zapfenstösser orchestra – the former holder having retired to devote himself to teaching – was by this time a settled thing, despite his youth, and he looked considerably younger than he was, yes, remarkably enough, younger than when I first met him.

But with all this, Rudi appeared depressed by certain circumstances of his private life; in short by his liaison with Inez Institoris, about which he relieved himself in private to Adrian. 'In private' is even an understatement, for the conversation took place in a darkened room, each being aware of the other's presence only as a shadowy outline; and that was, no doubt, an encouragement and easement to Schwerdtfeger in his confidences. The day was an uncommonly brilliant one in January 1919, with sunshine, blue sky, and glittering snow, and Adrian, soon after Rudolf appeared and the first greetings took place, out of doors, was seized with such severe head pains that he asked his guest to share with him at least for a while the well-tried remedy of darkness. They had exchanged the Nike salon, where they had sat at first, for the Abbot's room, shutting out the light with blinds and hangings, so that it was as I had known it: at first complete night to the eyes, then they learned to distinguish more or less the position of the furniture and perceived the weakly trickling shimmer of the outer light, a pallid gleam on the walls. Adrian, in his velvet chair, excused himself many times into the darkness on account of the inconvenience, but Schwerdtfeger, who had taken the Savonarola chair at the writing table, was entirely satisfied. If it did the other good – and he could well understand how it would do so – then he preferred it that way too. They talked with lowered voices, partly on account of Adrian's condition, partly because one tends to lower one's voice in the dark. It even produces a certain inclination to silence, to the extinction of speech; but Schwerdtfeger's Dresden upbringing did not tolerate any pauses. He chatted away over the bad patches, in defiance of the uncertainty one is in under such conditions about the other party's reactions. They skimmed over the desperate political situation, the fights in the capital, came to speak of the latest in the musical world, and Rudolf, in the purest tone, whistled something from Falla's *Nights in the Gardens of Spain* and Debussy's Sonata for flute, viola, and harp. He whistled the bourrée from *Love's Labour's Lost* too, precisely in the right pitch, and then the comic theme of the weeping little dog from the puppet play *Of the Godless Guile*, without being able to judge whether Adrian cared for it or not. At length he sighed and said he did not feel like whistling, but on the contrary was heavy-hearted, or perhaps not that so much as angry, vexed, impatient, also worried and not knowing what to do, and so, after all, heavy-hearted. Why? To answer that was not so easy and not even permissible, or at most among friends, where you were not obliged to be so careful about this man-of-honour attitude that you must keep your affairs with women to yourself. He was accustomed to observe it, he was no chatterbox. But he was not merely a man of honour either, people mistook him when they thought so, a shallow amoroso and man of pleasure: that was loathsome. He was a man and an artist; he had no use for this man-of-honour attitude; and certainly Adrian knew, for everybody did, what he meant. In short, it was about Inez Rodde, or rather Institoris, and his relations with her, which he could not help. 'I can't help it, Adrian, believe me! I never seduced her, but she me, and the horns of little Institoris, to use that silly expression, are altogether her work, not mine. What do you do when a woman clings to you like a drowning person and simply will have you for her lover? Do you leave your garment in her hands and flee? No, people do not do that now, there are other man-of-honour rules, you are not to say so, especially if the woman is pretty, though in rather a fatal and suffering way.' But he was fatal and suffering too, a nervous and often afflicted artist, he wasn't a young light-head or sonny-boy, whatever people thought. Inez imagined all sorts of things about him, quite falsely, and that resulted in a crooked sort of relationship, as though such a relation in and for itself were not crooked enough, with the silly situations it was always bringing about and the need of caution every minute. Inez got round all that better than he did, for the simple reason that she was so passionately in love; he could say that because she was so on the basis of her false imaginings. He was at a disadvantage because he was not in love: 'I never have loved her, I admit it openly, I always just had friendly and brotherly feelings for her, and that I let myself in with her like this and the stupid thing drags on because she clings to it, that is just a matter of duty and decency on my side.' But he must in confidence say this: that it was awkward, yes, degrading, when the passion, a really desperate passion, was on the woman's side while the man was just doing his knightly duty. It reversed the possessive relation somehow and led to an uncomfortable preponderance on the part of the woman so that he must say that Inez behaved with his person and his body as actually and rightly a man behaves with a woman, added to which her morbid and feverish jealousy, quite unjustified anyhow, had to do with the undivided possession of his person; unjustified, as he said, for he had enough with her, in fact enough *of* her and her clinging, and his invisible auditor could scarcely conceive what a refreshment for him, under these circumstances, was the society of a man so highly placed and by him very highly esteemed, the sphere of such a one and conversation with him. People mostly judged him falsely; he much preferred having a serious, elevating, and worth-while talk with such a man to going to bed with women; yes, if he were to characterize himself, he thought, after detailed self-examination, it would be as a platonic nature.

And suddenly, as it were in illustration of what he had just said, Rudi came to speak of the violin concerto which he so greatly wished to have Adrian write for him, if possible with all rights of performance reserved. That was his dream. 'I need you, Adrian, for my advancement, my development, my purification, in a way, from all those other affairs. On my word, that is the way I feel, I've never been more in earnest about anything, about what I need. And the concerto I want from you, that is just the most concrete, I mean the most symbolic expression for this need. And you would do it wonderfully, much better than Delius or Prokofiev – with an unheard-of simple and singable first theme in the main movement that comes in again after the cadenza. That is always the best moment in the classic violin concerto, when after the solo acrobatics the first theme comes in again. But you don't need to do it like that, you don't need to have a cadenza at all, that is just a convention. You can throw them all overboard, even the arrangement of the movements, it doesn't need to have any movements, for my part you can have the *allegro molto* in the middle, a real "Devil's trill", and you can juggle with the rhythm, as only you can do, and the *adagio* can come at the end, as transfiguration – it couldn't be too unconventional, and anyhow I want to put that down, that it will make people cry. I want to get it into myself so I could play it in my sleep, and brood over it and love every note like a mother, and you would be the father – it would be between us like a child, a platonic child – yes, *our* concerto, that would be so exactly the fulfilment of everything that I understand by platonic.'

Thus Schwerdtfeger. I have in these pages spoken many times in his favour, and today too, when I go over it all again I feel mildly towards him, to a considerable extent touched by his tragic end. But the reader will now understand better certain expressions which I applied to him, that 'impish *naïveté*' or childish devilry in his nature. In Adrian's place – but there is really no sense in putting myself in his place; I would not have tolerated some of the things Rudi said. It was distinctly an abuse of the darkness. Not only that he repeatedly went too far in his frankness about his relations with Inez – but also he went too far in another direction, culpably and impishly too far, betrayed by the darkness, I might say, if the notion of any betrayal is in place and one ought not to speak instead of an impudent intrusion of familiarity upon solitude.

That is in fact the right description of Rudi Schwerdtfeger's relation to Adrian Leverkühn. The plan took years to carry out, and a certain sad success cannot be denied to it. In the long run the defencelessness of solitude against such a wooing was proved, certainly to the destruction of the wooer.

Chapter Thirty-four

Not only with the little sea-maid's knifelike pains did Leverkühn at the time of his worst state of health compare his own torments. In conversation he had another parallel, which he visualized with remarkable clarity. I called it to mind when some months later, in the spring of 1919, the illness lifted like a miracle from off him, and his spirit, phoenixlike, rose to its fullest freedom and most amazing power, in an unchecked, not to say unbridled, anyhow an unintermitted flow of almost breathless productivity. But just that very thing betrayed to me that the two states, the depressive and exalted, were not inwardly sharply distinguished from each other. They were not separate and without all connexion, for the present state had been preparing in the former one and to some extent had already been contained in it – just as indeed, on the other hand, the outbreak of the healthy and creative epoch was by no means a time of enjoyment, but rather in its own way one of affliction, of painful urgency and compulsion ... Ah, I write badly! My eagerness to say everything at once makes my sentences run over, hurries them away from the thought they began by intending to express, and makes them seem to rush on and lose it from sight. I shall do well to take the reproof from the reader's mouth. The way my ideas tumble over themselves and get lost is a result of the excitement generated by my memory of this time, the time after the collapse of the authoritarian German state, with its far-reaching accompanying laxity, which affected me as well, laying siege to my settled view of the world with new conceptions hard for it to digest. I felt that an epoch was ending, which had not only included the nineteenth century, but gone far back to the end of the Middle Ages, to the loosening of scholastic ties, the emancipation of the individual, the birth of freedom. This was the epoch which I had in very truth regarded as that of my more extended spiritual home, in short the epoch of bourgeois humanism. And I felt as I say that its hour had come; that a mutation of life would be consummated; the world would enter into a new, still nameless constellation. And moreover this feeling of mine, riveting my attention, was a product not only of the end of the war but already the product of its beginning, fourteen years after the turn of the century. It had laid at the bottom of the panic, the awful sense of destiny which people like me felt at that time. No wonder the disintegration of defeat increased this feeling to its highest pitch, no wonder either that in a defeated country like Germany it occupied the mind far more than among the victorious nations, whose average mental state, precisely on account of victory, was much more conservative. They by no means felt the war as the massive and decisive historical break which it seemed to us. They saw in it a disturbance, now happily past, after which life could return to the path out of which it had been thrust. I envied them. I envied in particular France, for the sanction which, at least apparently, had been vouchsafed by the victory to its conservative bourgeois intellectual constitution; for the sense of security in the classic and rational, which it might draw from its triumph. Certainly, I should at that time have felt better and more at home the other side of the Rhine that here, where, as I said, much that was new, alarming, and destructive, which none the less my conscience obliged me to take stock of, urged itself upon my world-picture. And here I think of the distracting discussion evenings in the Schwabing apartment of a certain Sixtus Kridwiss, whose acquaintance I made at the Schlaginhaufens'. I will come back to those evenings presently, only saying for the moment that the gatherings and intellectual conferences, in which I often out of pure conscientiousness took part, set about me shrewdly. And at this same time with my whole deeply stirred and often dismayed soul I was sharing intimately in the birth of a work which did not fail of certain bold and prophetic associations with those same conferences; which confirmed and realized them on a higher, more creative plane ... When I add that besides all this I had my teaching work to perform and might not neglect my duties as head of a family, it will be understood that I was subject to a strain which together with a diet low in calories reduced me physically not a little.

This too I say only to characterize the fleeting, insecure times we lived in; certainly not to direct the reader's attention upon my inconsiderable person, to which only a place in the background of these memoirs is fitting. I have already given expression to my regret that my zeal to communicate must here and there give an impression of flightiness. It is however a wrong impression, for I stick very well by my trains of thought, and have not forgotten that I intended to introduce a second striking and pregnant comparison, in addition to that with the little sea-maid, which Adrian made at the time of his utmost and torturing sufferings.

'How do I feel?' he said to me. 'Quite a lot like Johannes Martyr in the cauldron of oil. You must imagine it pretty much like that. I squat there, a pious sufferer, in the tub, with a lively wood fire crackling underneath, faithfully fanned up by a bravo with a hand-bellows, and in the presence of Imperial Majesty who looks on from close by. It is the Emperor Nero, you must know, a magnificent big Turk with Italian brocade on his back. The hangman's helper in a flowing jacket and a codpiece pours the boiling oil over the back of my neck from a long-handled ladle, as I duly and devoutly squat. I am basted properly, like a roast, a hell-roast; it is worth seeing, and you are invited to mingle with the deeply interested persons behind the barrier, the magistrates, the invited public, partly in turbans and partly in good old-German caps with hats on top of them. Respectable townsfolk – and their pensive mood rejoices in the protection of halberdiers. One points out to the other what happens to a hell-roast. They have two fingers on the cheek and two under the nose. A fat man is raising his hand, as though to say: "God save us all!" On the women's faces, simple edification. Do you see it? We are all close together, the scene is faithfully filled with figures. Nero's little dog has come too, so there shan't be even a tiny empty space. He has a cross little fox-terrier face. In the background you see the towers and gables and pointed oriels of Kaisersaschern ...'

Of course he should have said Nuremberg. For what he described – described with the same intimate confidence as he had the tapering of the nixie's body into the fish-tail, so that I recognized it long before he got to the end – was the first sheet of Dürer's series of woodcuts of the Apocalypse. How could I not have recalled the comparison, when later Adrian's purpose slowly revealed itself, though at the time it seemed far-fetched to me, while immediately suggesting certain vague divinations. This was the work which he was mastering, the while it mastered him; for which his powers were slowly gathering head while they lay stretched in torments. Was I not right to say that the depressive and the exalted states of the artist, illness and health, are by no means sharply divided from each other? That rather in illness, as it were under the lee of it, elements of health are at work, and elements of illness, working geniuslike, are carried over into health? It is not otherwise, I thank the insight given me by a friendship which caused me much distress and alarm, but always filled me too with pride: genius is a form of vital power deeply experienced in illness, creating out of illness, through illness creative.

The conception of the apocalyptic oratorio, the secret preoccupation with it, then, went far back into a time of apparently complete exhaustion, and the vehemence and rapidity with which afterward, in a few months, it was put on paper always gave me the idea that that period of prostration had been a sort of refuge and retreat, into which his nature withdrew, in order that, unspied on, unsuspected, in some hidden sanctuary, shut away by suffering from our healthy life, he might preserve and develop conceptions for which ordinary wellbeing would never summon the reckless courage. Indeed, they seemed to be as it were robbed from the depths, fetched up from there and brought to the light of day. That his purpose only revealed itself to me by degrees from visit to visit, I have already said. He wrote, sketched, collected, studied, combined; that could not be hidden from me, with inward satisfaction I realized it. Anticipatory announcements came out, from week to week, in a half-joking half-silence; in a repulse that out of fear or annoyance protected a not quite canny secret; in a laugh, with drawn brows; in phrases like 'Stop prying, keep your little soul pure!' or 'You always hear about it soon enough!' or, more frankly, somewhat readier to confess: 'Yes, there are holy horrors brewing; the theological virus, it seems, does not get out of one's blood so easily. Without your knowing it, it leaves a strong precipitate.'

The hint confirmed suspicions that had arisen in my mind on seeing what he read. On his work-table I discovered an extraordinary old volume: a thirteenth-century French metrical translation of the *Vision of St Paul*, the Greek text of which dates back to the fourth century. To my question about where it came from he answered:

'The Rosenstiel got it. Not the first curiosity she had dug up for me. An enterprising female that. It has not escaped her that I have a weakness for people who have been "down below". By below I mean in hell. That makes a bond between people as far apart as Paul and Virgil's Aeneas. Remembering how Dante refers to them as brothers, as two who have been down below?'

I remembered. 'Unfortunately,' I said, 'your *filia hospitalis* can't read that to you.'

'No,' he laughed, 'for the old French I have to use my own eyes.'

At the time, that is, when he could not have used them, as the pain above and in their depths made reading impossible, Clementine Schweigestill often had to read aloud to him: matter indeed that came oddly enough but after all not so unsuitably from the lips of the kindly peasant girl. I myself had seen the good child with Adrian in the Abbot's room: he reclined in the Bernheim chaise-longue while she sat very stiff-backed in the Savonarola chair at the table and in touchingly plaintive, painfully high-German schoolgirl accents read aloud out of the discoloured old cardboard volume. It too had probably come into the house through the offices of the keen-nosed Rosenstiel: it was the ecstatic narrative of Mechthild of Magdeburg. I sat down noiselessly in a corner and for some time listened with astonishment to this quaint, devout, and blundering performance.

So then I learned that it was often thus. The brown-eyed maiden sat by the sufferer, in her modest Bavarian peasant costume, which betrayed the influence of the parish priest: a frock of olive-green wool, high-necked, with a thick row of tiny metal buttons, the bodice that flattened the youthful bosom ending in a point over the wide gathered skirt that fell to her feet. As sole adornment she wore below the neck ruche a chain made of old silver coins. So she sat and read or intoned, in her naïve accents, from writings to which surely the parish priest could have had no objection: the early Christian and medieval accounts of visions and speculations about the other world. Now and then Mother Schweigestill would put her head round the door to look for her daughter, whom she might have needed in the house; but she nodded approvingly at the pair and withdrew. Or perhaps she too sat down to listen for ten minutes on a chair near the door, then noiselessly disappeared. If it was not the transports of Mechthild that Clementine rehearsed, then it was those of Hildegarde of Bingen; if neither of these, then a German version of the *Historia ecclesiastica gentis anglorum* by the learned monk known as the Venerable Bede: a work in which is transmitted a good part of the Celtic fantasies about the beyond, the visionary experiences of early Irish and Anglo-Saxon times. This whole ecstatic literature from the pre-Christian and early Christian eschatologies forms a rich fabric of tradition, full of recurrent motifs. Into it Adrian spun himself round like a cocoon, to stimulate himself for a work which should gather up all their elements into one single focus, assemble them in one pregnant, portentous synthesis and in relentless transmission hold up to humanity the mirror of the revelation, that it might see wherein what is oncoming and near at hand.

'And end is come, the end is come, it watcheth for thee, behold, it is come. The morning is come unto thee, O thou that dwellest in the land.' These words Leverkühn makes his *testis*, the witness, the narrator, announce in a spectral melody, built up of perfect fourths and diminished fifths and set above pedal harmonies alien to the key; they then form the text of the boldly archaic *responsorium*, which they unforgettably repeat by two four-part choruses in contrary motion. These words, indeed, do not belong to the Revelation of St John, they originate in another layer, the prophecy of the Babylonian exile, the visions and lamentations of Ezekiel, to which, moreover, the mysterious epistle from Patmos, from the time of Nero, stands in a relation of the most singular dependence. Thus the 'eating of the little book', which Albrecht Dürer also boldly made the subject of one of his woodcuts, is taken almost word for word from Ezekiel, down to the detail that it (or the 'roll', therein 'lamentations and mourning and woe') in the mouth of the obediently eating one was as honey for sweetness. So also the great whore, the woman on the beast, is quite extensively prefigured, with similar turns of phrase. In depicting her the Nuremberger amused himself by using the portrait study he had brought with him of a Venetian courtesan. In fact there is an apocalyptic tradition which hands down to these ecstatics visions and experiences to a certain extent already framed, however odd it may seem, psychologically, that a raving man should rave in the same pattern as another who came before him; that one is ecstatic not independently, so to speak, but by rote. Still it seems to be the case, and I point out it in connexion with the statement that Leverkühn in the text for his incommensurable choral work by no means confined himself to the

Revelation of St John, but took in this whole prophetic tradition, so that his work amounts to the creation of a new and independent Apocalypse, a sort of résumé of the whole literature. The title, *Apocalypsis cum figuris*, is in homage to Dürer and is intended to emphasize the visual and actualizing, the graphic character, the minuteness, the saturation, in short, of space with fantastically exact detail; the feature is common to both works. But it is far from being the case that Adrian's mammoth fresco follows the Nuremberger's fifteen illustrations in any programmatic sense. True, many words of the same mysterious document which also inspired Dürer underlie this frightful and consummate work of tonal art. But Adrian broadened the scope both of choral recitative and of ariosa by including also much from the Lamentations in the Psalter, for instance that piercing 'For my soul is full of troubles and my life draweth nigh unto the grave', as also the expressive denunciations and images of terror from the Apocrypha; then certain fragments from the Lamentations of Jeremiah, today unspeakably offensive in their effect; and even remoter matter still, all of which must contribute to produce the general impression of a view opening into the other world and the final reckoning breaking in, of a journey into hell, wherein are worked through the visional representations of the hereafter, in the earlier, shamanistic stages, as well as those developed from antiquity and Christianity, down to Dante. Leverkühn's tone-picture draws much from Dante's poem; and still more from that crowded wall, swarming with bodies, where here angels perform staccato on trumpets of destruction, there Charon's bark unloads its freight, the dead rise, saints pray, daemonic masks await the nod of the serpent-wreathed Minos, the damned man, voluptuous in flesh, clung round, carried and drawn by grinning sons of the pit, makes horrid descent, covering one eye with his hand and with the other staring transfixed with horror into the bottomless perdition; while not far off Grace draws up two sinning souls from the snare into redemption – in short, from the groups and the scenic structure of the Last Judgment.

A man of culture, such as I am, when he essays to talk about a work with which he is in such painfully close touch may be pardoned for comparing it with existing and familiar cultural monuments. To do this gives me the needed reassurance, still needed even as it was at the time when I was present with horror, amaze, consternation, and pride, at its birth – an experience that I suppose was due to my loving devotion to its author but actually went beyond my mental capacities, so that I trembled and was carried away. For after that first period when he repulsed me and hugged his secret, he then began to give the friend of his childhood access to his doing and striving; so that at every visit to Pfeiffering – and of course I went as often as I could, and almost always over Saturday and Sunday – I was allowed to see new parts as they developed, also accretions and drafts, of a scope at times fairly incredible. Here were vastly complex problems, technical and intellectual, subjecting themselves to the strictest law. Contemplating the mere manufacture of the work a steady-going man used to a moderate bourgeois rate of accomplishment might well go pale with terror. Yes, I confess that in my simple human fear the largest factor was, I should say, the perfectly uncanny rapidity with which the work came to be: the chief part of it in four and a half months, a period which one would have allowed for the mere mechanical task of putting it down.

Obviously and admittedly this man lived at the time in a state of tension so high as to be anything but agreeable. It was more like a constant tyranny: the flashing up and stating of a problem, the task of composition (over which he had heretofore always lingered), was one with its lightning-like solution. Scarcely did it leave him time to follow with the pen the haunting and hunting inspirations which gave him no rest, which made him their slave. Still in the most fragile health, he worked ten hours a day and more, broken only by a short pause at midday and now and then a walk round the pond or up the hill, brief excursions more like flight than recreation. One could see by his step, first hasty and then halting, that they were merely another form of unrest. Many a Sunday evening I spent with him and always remarked how little he was his own master, how little he could stick to the everyday, indifferent subjects which he deliberately chose, by way of relaxation, to talk about with me. I see him suddenly stiffen from a relaxed posture; see his gaze go staring and listening, his lips part and – unwelcome sight to me – the flickering red rise in his cheeks. What was that? Was it one of those melodic illuminations to which he was, I might almost say, exposed and with which powers whereof I refuse to know aught kept their pact with him? Was it one of those so mightily plastic themes in which the apocalyptic work abounds, rising to his mind, there at once to be checked and chilled, to be bridled and bitted and made to take its proper place in the whole structure? I see him with a murmured 'Go on, go on!' move to his table, open the folder of orchestral drafts with such violence as sometimes to tear one, and with a grimace whose mingled meaning I will not try to convey but which in my eyes distorted the lofty, intelligent beauty his features wore by right, read to himself, where perhaps was sketched that frightful chorus of humanity fleeing before the four horsemen, stumbling, fallen, overridden; or there was noted down the awful scream given to the mocking, bleating bassoon, the 'Wail of the Bird' or perhaps that song and answer, like an antiphony, which on first hearing so gripped my heart – the harsh choral fugue to the words of Jeremiah:

> *Wherefore doth a living man complain,*
> *A man for the punishment of his sins?*
> *Let us search and try our ways,*
> *And turn again to the Lord . . .*
>
> *We have transgressed and have rebelled:*
> *Thou hast not pardoned.*
> *Thou has covered with anger*
> *And persecuted us:*
> *Thou hast slain, thou hast not pitied . . .*
>
> *Thou hast made us as the offscouring*
> *And refuse in the midst of the people.*

I call the piece a fugue, and it gives that impression, yet the theme is not faithfully repeated, but rather develops with the development of the whole, so that a style is loosened and in a way reduced *ad absurdum*, to which the artist seems to submit himself – which cannot occur without reference back to the archaic fugal forms of certain canzoni and ricercari of the pre-Bach time, in which the fugue theme is not always clearly defined and adhered to.

Here or there he might look, seize his pen, throw it down again, murmur: 'Good, till tomorrow,' and turn back to me, the flush still on his brow. But I knew or feared that the 'till tomorrow' would not be adhered to: that after I left he would sit down and work out what had so unsummoned flashed into his mind as we talked. Then he would take two luminol tablets to give sleep the soundness which must compensate for its briefness. For next day he would begin again at daybreak. He quoted:

> '*Up, psalter and harp* –
> *I will be early up.*'

He lived in fear that the state of illumination with which he was blest – or with which he was afflicted – might be untimely withdrawn. And in fact he did suffer a relapse. It was shortly before he got to the end, that frightful finis, which demanded all his courage and which, so far from being a romantic music of redemption, relentlessly confirms the theologically negative and pitiless character of the whole. It was, I say, just before he made port with those roaring brass passages, heavily scored and widely spaced out, which make one think of an open abyss wherein one must hopelessly sink. The relapse lasted for three weeks with pain and nausea, a condition in which, in his own words, he lost the memory of what it meant to compose, or even how it was done. It passed. At the beginning of August 1919 he was working again; and before this month, with its many hot, sunny days, was over, his task was finished. The four and a half months which I gave as the period of production are reckoned up to the beginning of the relapse. Including the final working period, the sketch of the *Apocalypse* had taken him, in all, amazingly enough, six months to put on paper.

Chapter Thirty-four

(*Continued*)

And now: is that all I have to say in his biography about this work of my departed friend: this work a thousandfold hated, thought of with shuddering and yet a hundredfold beloved and exalted? No, I still have much on my heart about it and about certain of its characteristics, which – of course, with undeviating admiration – disturbed and depressed me, or better put, absorbed my attention even while they disturbed my mind. But at the same time I had it in mind to connect those very qualities and characteristics with the abstract speculations to which I was exposed in the house of Herr Sextus Kridwiss and to which I referred on an earlier page. I am free to confess that the novel experiences of those Kridwiss evenings, combined with my participation in Adrian's solitary work, were responsible for the mental strain of my life at that time and in the end for the loss of a good twelve pounds' weight.

Kridwiss was an expert in the graphic arts and fine editions, collector of east-Asiatic coloured wood-carvings and ceramics, a field in which, invited by this or that cultural organization, he gave interesting and well-informed lectures in various cities of the Reich and even abroad. He was an ageless, rather dainty little gentleman, with a strong Rhenish-Hessian accent and uncommon intellectual liveliness. He seemed not to have connexions of any opinion-forming kind so far as one could tell, but out of pure curiosity 'listened in' at all the events of the day; and when this or that came to his ears he would describe it as '*scho' enorm wischtich*'. The reception-room of his house in Martiusstrasse, Schwabing, was decorated with charming Chinese paintings in India ink and colour (from the Sung period!) and he made it a meeting-place for the leading or rather the initiate members of the intellectual life of Munich, as many of them as the good city harboured in her walls. Kridwiss arranged informal discussion evenings for gentlemen, intimate round-table sittings of not more than eight or ten personalities; one put in an appearance at about nine o'clock and with no great entertainment on the part of the host proceeded to free association and the exchange of ideas. Of course intellectual high tension was not unintermittedly sustained; the talk often slipped into comfortable everyday channels, since thanks to Kridwiss's social tastes and obligations the level was rather uneven. For instance there took part in the sessions two members of the grand-ducal house of Hesse-Nassau, then studying in Munich, friendly young folk whom the host with a certain *empressement* called the beautiful princes. In their presence, if only because they were so much younger than the rest of us, we practised a certain reserve. I cannot say however that they disturbed us much. Often a more highbrow conversation went painlessly over their heads, while they smiled in modest silence or made suitably serious faces. More annoying for me personally was the presence of Dr Chaim Breisacher, the lover of paradox, already known to the reader. I long ago admitted that I could not endure the man; but his penetration and keen scent appeared to be indispensable on these occasions. I was also irritated by the presence of Bullinger, the manufacturer; he was legitimated only by his high income tax, but he talked dogmatically on the loftiest cultural themes.

I must confess further that really I could feel no proper liking to any of the table-round, nor extend to any of them a feeling of genuine confidence. Helmut Institoris was also a guest, and him I except, since I had friendly relations with him through his wife; yet even here the associations evoked were painful ones, though on other grounds. But one might ask what I could have against Dr Unruhe, Egon Unruhe, a philosophic palaeozoologist who in his writings brilliantly combined a profound knowledge of geological periods and fossilization with the interpretation and scientific verification of our store of primitive sagas. In this theory, a sublimated Darwinism if you like, everything there became true and real, though a sophisticated humanity had long since ceased to believe it. Yes, whence my distrust of this learned and conscientiously intellectual man? Whence the same distrust of Professor Georg Vogler, the literary historian, who had written a much esteemed history of German literature from the point of view of racial origins, wherein an author is discussed and evaluated not as a writer and comprehensively trained mind, but as the genuine blood-and-soil product of his real, concrete, specific corner of the Reich, engendering him and by him engendered. All that was very worthy, strong-minded, fit and proper, and critically worth thinking about. The art-critic and Dürer scholar Professor Gilgen Holzschuher, another guest, was not acceptable to me either, on grounds similarly hard to justify; and the same was true without reservation of the poet Daniel zur Höhe who was often present. He was a lean man of thirty in a black cleric-like habit closed to the throat, with a profile like a bird of prey and a hammering delivery, as for instance: 'Yes, yes, yes, yes, not so bad, oh certainly, one may say so!' nervously and continuously tapping the floor the while with the balls of his feet. He loved to cross his arms on his chest or thrust one hand Napoleon-like in his coat, and his poet dreams dealt with a world subjected by sanguinary campaigns to the pure spirit, by it held in terror and high discipline, as he had described it in his work, I believe his only one, the *Proclamations*. It had appeared before the war, printed on hand-made paper, a lyrical and rhetorical outburst of riotous terrorism, to which one had to concede considerable verbal power. The signatory to these proclamations was an entity named *Christus Imperator Maximus*, a commanding energumen who levied troops prepared to die for the subjection of the globe. He promulgated messages like Orders of the Day, stipulated abandonedly ruthless conditions, proclaimed poverty and chastity, and could not do enough in the hammering, first-pounding line to exact unquestioned and unlimited obedience. 'Soldiers!' the poem ended, 'I deliver to you to plunder – *the World!*'

All this was 'beautiful' and mightily acclaimed as such; 'beautiful' in a cruelly and absolutely beauty-ous way, in the impudently detached, flippant, and irresponsible style poets permit themselves: it was, in fact, the tallest aesthetic misdemeanour I have ever come across. Helmut Institoris, of course, was sympathetic; but indeed both author and work had enjoyed a measure of serious respect from the public, and my antipathy was not quite so sure of itself, because I was conscious of my general irritation with the whole Kridwiss circle and the pretensions of its cultural position, of which my intellectual conscience forced me to take account.

I will try, in as small space as possible, to sketch the essential of these experiences, which our host rightly found 'enormously important' and which Daniel zur Höhe accompanied with his stereotyped 'Oh yes, yes, yes, not so bad, yes, certainly, one may say so', even when it did not exactly go so far as the plundering of the world by the touch and dedicated soldiery of *Christus Imperator Maximus*. That was, of course, only symbolic poesy, whereas the interest of the conferences lay in surveys of sociological actualities, analyses of the present and the future, which even so had something in common with the ascetic and 'beautiful' nightmares of Daniel's fantasy. I have called attention above, quite apart from these evenings, to the disturbance and destruction of apparently fixed values of life brought about by the war, especially in the conquered countries, which were thus in a psychological sense further on than the others. Very strongly felt and objectively confirmed was the enormous loss of value which the individual had sustained, the ruthlessness which made life today stride away over the single person and precipitate itself as a general indifference to the sufferings and destruction of human beings. This carelessness, this indifference to the individual fate, might appear to be the result of the four years' carnival of blood just behind us; but appearances were deceptive. As in many another respect here too the war only completed, defined, and drastically put in practice a process that had been on the way long before and had made itself the basis of a new feeling about life. This was not a matter for praise or blame, rather of objective perception and statement. However, the least passionate recognition of the actual, just out of sheer pleasure in recognition, always contain some shade of approbation; so why should one not accompany such objective perceptions of the time with a many-sided, yes, all-embracing critique of the bourgeois tradition? By the bourgeois tradition I mean the values of culture, enlightenment, humanity, in short of such dreams as the uplifting of the people through scientific civilization. They who practised this critique were men of education, culture, science. They did it, indeed, smiling; with a blithness and intellectual complacency which lent the thing a special, pungent, disquieting, or even slightly perverse charm. It is probably superfluous to state that not for a moment did they recognize the form of government which we got as a result of defeat, the freedom that fell in our laps, in a word the democratic republic, as anything to be taken seriously as the legitimized frame of the new situation. With one accord they treated it as emphemeral, as meaningless from the start, yes, as a bad joke to be dismissed with a shrug.

They cited de Tocqueville, who had said that out of revolution as out of a common source two streams issued, the one leading men to free arrangements, the other to absolute power. In the free arrangements none of the gentlemen conversationalists at Kridwiss's any longer believed, since the very concept was self-contradictory: freedom by the act of assertion being driven to limit the freedom of its antagonist and thus to stultify itself and its own principles. Such was in fact its ultimate fate, though oftener the prepossession about 'human rights' was thrown overboard at the start. And this was far more likely than that we would let ourselves in today for the dialectic process which turned freedom into the dictatorship of its party. In the end it all came down to dictatorship, to force, for with the demolition of the traditional national and social forms through the French Revolution an epoch had dawned which, consciously or not, confessedly or not, steered its course towards despotic tyranny over the masses; and they, reduced to one uniform level, atomized, out of touch, were as powerless as the single individual.

'Quite right, quite right. Oh, indeed, yes, one may say so!' zur Höhe assured us, and pounded with his feet. Of course one may say so; only one might, for my taste, dealing with this description of a mounting barbarism, have said so with rather more fear and trembling and rather less blithe satisfaction. One was left with the hope that the complacency of these gentlemen had to do with their recognition of the state of things and not with the state of things in itself. Let me set down as clearly as I can a picture of this distressing good humour of theirs. No one will be surprised that, in the conversations of this avant-garde of culture and critique, a book which had appeared seven years before the war, *Réflexions sur la violence* by Sorel, played an important part. The author's relentless prognostication of war and anarchy, his characterization of Europe as the war-breeding soil, his theory that the peoples of our continent can unite only in the one idea, that of making war – all justified its public in calling it the book of the day. But even more trenchant and telling was its perception and statement of the fact that in this age of the masses parliamentary discussion must prove entirely inadequate for the shaping of political decisions; that in its stead the masses would have in the future to be provided with mythical fictions, devised like primitive battle-cries, to release and activate political energies. This was in fact the crass and inflaming prophecy of the book; that popular myths or rather those proper for the masses would become the vehicle of political action; fables, insane visions, chimeras, which needed to have nothing to do with truth or reason or science in order to be creative, to determine the course of life and history, and to prove themselves dynamic realities. Not for nothing, of course, did the book bear its alarming title; for it dealt with violence as the triumphant antithesis of truth. It made plain that the fate of truth was bound up with the fate of the individual, yes, identical with it: being for both truth and the individual a cheapening, a devaluation. It opened a mocking abyss between truth and power, truth and life, truth and the community. It showed by implication that precedence belonged far more to the community; that truth had the community as its goal, and that whoever would share in the community must be prepared to scrap considerable elements of truth and science and line up for the *sacrificium intellectus*.

And now imagine (here is the 'clear picture' I promised to give) how these gentlemen, scientists themselves, scholars and teachers – Vogler, Unruhe, Holzschuher, Institoris and Breisacher as well – revelled in a situation which for me had about it so much that was terrifying, and which they regarded as either already in full swing or inevitably on the way. They amused themselves by imagining a legal process in which one of these mass myths was up for discussion in the service of the political drive for the undermining of the bourgeois social order. Its protagonists had to defend themselves against the charge of lying and falsification; but plaintiff and defendant did not so much attack each other as in the most laughable way miss each other's points. The fantastic thing was the mighty apparatus of scientific witness which was invoked – quite futilely – to prove that humbug was humbug and a scandalous affront to truth. For the dynamic, historically creative fiction, the so-called lie and falsification, in other words the community-forming belief, was simply inaccessible to this line of attack. Science strove, on the plane of decent, objective truth, to confute the dynamic lie, but arguments on that plane could only seem irrelevant to the champions of the dynamic, who merely smiled a superior smile. Science, truth – good God! The dramatic expositions of the group were possessed by the spirit and the accent of ejaculation. They could scarcely contain their mirth at the desperate campaign waged by reason and criticism against wholly untouchable, wholly invulnerable belief. And with their united powers they knew how to set science in a light of such comic impotence that even the 'beautiful princes', in their childlike way, were brilliantly entertained. The happy board did not hesitate to prescribe to justice, which had to say the last word and pronounce the judgement, the same self-abnegation which they themselves practised. A jurisprudence that wished to rest on popular feeling and not to isolate itself from the community could not venture to espouse the point of view of theoretic, anti-communal, so-called truth; it had to prove itself modern as well as patriotic, patriotic in the most modern sense, by respecting the fruitful *falsum*, acquitting its apostles, and dismissing science with a flea in its ear.

'Oh yes, yes, yes, certainly, one may say so' – thump, thump.

Although I felt sick at my stomach, I would not play the spoilsport; I showed no repugnance, but rather joined as well as I could in the general mirth; particularly since this did not necessarily mean agreement but only, at least provisionally, a smiling, gratified intellectual recognition of what was or was to be. I did once suggest that 'if we wanted to be serious for a moment', we might consider whether a thinking man, to whom the extremity of our situation lay very much at heart, would not perhaps do better to make truth and not the community his goal, since the latter would indirectly and in the long run be better served by truth, even the bitter truth, than by a train of thought which proposed to serve it at the expense of truth, but actually, by such denial, destroyed from within in the most unnatural way the basis of genuine community. Never in my life have I made a remark that fell more utterly and completely flat than this one. I admit that it was a tactless remark, unsuited to the prevailing intellectual climate, and permeated with an idealism of course well known, only too well known, well known to the point of being bad taste, and merely embarrassing to the new ideas. Much better was it for me to chime in with the others; to look at the new, to explore it, and instead of offering it futile and certainly boring opposition, to adapt my conceptions to the course of the discussion and in the frame of them to make myself a picture of the future and of a world even now, if unawares, in the throes of birth – and this no matter how I might be feeling in the pit of my stomach.

It was an old-new world of revolutionary reaction, in which the values bound up with the idea of the individual – shall we say truth, freedom, law, reason – were entirely rejected and shorn of power, or else had taken on a meaning quite different from that given them for centuries. Wrenched away from the washed-out theoretic, based on the relative and pumped full of fresh blood, they were referred to the far higher court of violence, authority, the dictatorship of belief – not, let me say, in a reactionary, anachronistic way as of yesterday or the day before, but so that it was like the most novel setting back of humanity into medievally theocratic conditions and situations. That was as little reactionary as though one were to describe as regression the track round a sphere, which of course leads back to where it started. There it was: progress and reaction, the old and the new, the past and the future became one; the political Right more and more coincided with the Left. That thought was free, that research worked without assumptions: these were conceptions which, far from representing progress, belonged to a superseded and uninteresting world. Freedom was given to thought that it might justify force; just as seven hundred years ago reason had been free to discuss faith and demonstrate dogma; for that she was there, and for that today thinking was there, or would be there tomorrow. Research *certainly* had assumptions – of course it had! They were force, the authority of the community; and indeed they were so taken for granted as such that science never came upon the thought that perhaps it was not free. Subjectively, indeed, it was free, entirely so, within an objective restraint so native and incorporate that it was in no way felt as a fetter. To make oneself clear as to what was coming and to get rid of the silly fear of it one need only remind oneself that the absoluteness of definite premises and sacrosanct conditions had never been a hindrance to fancy and individual boldness of thought. On the contrary: precisely because from the very first medieval man had received a closed intellectual frame from the Church as something absolute and taken for granted, he had been far more imaginative than the burgher of the individualist age; he had been able to surrender himself far more freely and sure-footedly to his personal fantasy.

Oh, yes, force created a firm ground under the feet: it was anti-abstract, and I did very well to conceive to myself, working together with Kridwiss's friends, how the old-new would in this and that field systematically transform life. The pedagogue, for instance, knew that in elementary instruction even today the tendency was to depart from the primary learning of letters and sounds and to adopt the method of word-learning; to link writing with concrete looking at things. This meant in a way a departure from the abstract universal letter-script, not bound up with speech; in a way a return to the word-writing of earlier peoples. I thought privately: why words anyhow, why writing, why speech? Radical objectivity must stick to things and to them only. And I recalled a satire of Swift's in which some learned scholars with reform gone to their heads decided, in order to save their lungs and avoid empty phrases, to do away altogether with words and speech and to converse by pointing to the things themselves, which in the interest of understanding were to be carried about on the back in as large numbers as possible. It is a very witty piece of writing: for the women, the masses, and the analphabetic, they it is who rebel against the innovation and insist on talking in words. Well, my interlocutors did not go so far with their proposals as Swift's scholars. They wore the air of disinterested observers, and as 'enorm wischtisch' they fixed their eyes on the general readiness, already far advanced, to drop out of hand our so-called cultural conquests for the sake of simplification regarded as inevitable and timely. One might, if one chose, describe it as deliberate rebarbarization. Was I to trust my ears? But now I had to laugh, yet at the same time was amazed when the gentlemen at this point came upon the subject of dental medicine and quite objectively began to talk about Adrian's and my symbolic musical critique of the dead tooth. I am sure I went the colour of a turkey-cock for laughing, while listening to a discussion, pursued with the same intellectual satisfaction as before, about the growing tendency of dentists to pull out forthwith all teeth with dead nerves; since it had been concluded – after a long, painstaking, and refined development in the nineteenth-century technique of root treatment – that they were to be regarded as infectious foreign bodies. Observe – it was Dr Breisacher who acutely pointed this out, and met with general agreement – that the hygienic point of view therein represented must be considered, in a way, as a rationalization of the fundamental tendency to let things drop, to give up, to get away, to simplify. For in a matter of hygiene it was quite in place to suspect an ideological basis. There was no doubt that in the future, after we had begun to practise a large-scale elimination of the unfit, the diseased and weak-minded, we would justify the policy by similar hygienic arguments for the purification of society and the race. Whereas in reality – none of those present denied, but on the contrary rather emphasized the fact – that the real reason lay far deeper down, in the renunciation of all the humane softness of the bourgeois epoch; in an instinctive self-preparation of humanity for harsh and sinister times which mocked our human ideals; for an age of over-all wars and revolutions which would probably take us back far behind the Christian civilization of the Middle Ages; in a return to the dark era before it arose after the collapse of the classic culture ...

Chapter Thirty-four

(Conclusion)

It will perhaps be granted that man labouring to digest such novelties as these might lose twelve pounds' weight. Certainly I should not have lost them if I had not taken seriously my experiences at the Kridwiss sessions, but had stood firm in the conviction that these gentlemen were talking nonsense. However, that was not in the least the way I felt. I did not for a moment conceal from myself that with an acuity worthy of note they had laid their fingers on the pulse of the time and were prognosticating accordingly. But I must repeat that I should have been so endlessly grateful, and perhaps should have lost only six pounds instead of twelve, if they themselves had been more alarmed over their findings or had opposed to them a little ethical criticism. They might have said: Unhappily it looks as though things would follow this and this course. Consequently one must take steps to warn people of what is coming and do one's best to prevent it. But what in a way they were saying was: It is coming, it is coming, and when it is here it will find us on the crest of the moment. It is interesting, it is even good, simply by virtue of being what is inevitably going to be, and to recognize it is sufficient of an achievement and satisfaction. It is not our affair to go on to do anything against it. – Thus these learned gentlemen, in private. But that about the satisfaction of recognizing it was a fraud. They sympathized with what they recognized; without this sympathy they could not have recognized it. That was the whole point, and because of it, in my irritation and nervous excitement, I lost weight.

No, all that is not quite right. Merely through my conscientious visits to the Kridwiss group and the ideas to which I deliberately exposed myself, I should not have got thinner by twelve pounds or even half as much. I should never have taken all that speechifying to heart if it had not constituted a cold-blooded intellectual commentary upon a fervid experience of art and friendship: I mean the birth of a work of art very near to me, near through its creator, not through itself, that I may not say, for too much belonged to it that was alien and frightful to my mind. In that all too homelike rural retreat there was being built up with feverish speed a work which had a peculiar kinship with, was in spirit a parallel to, the things I had heard at Kridwiss's table-round.

At that table had been set up as the order of the day a critique of tradition which was the result of the destruction of living values long regarded as inviolable. The comment had been explicitly made – I do not recall by whom, Breisacher, Unruhe, Holzschuher? – that such criticism must of necessity turn against traditional art-forms and species, for instance against the aesthetic theatre, which had lain within the bourgeois circle of life and was a concern of culture. Yes. And right there before my very eyes was taking place the passing of the dramatic form into the epic, the music drama was changing to oratorio, the operatic drama to operatic cantata – and indeed in a spirit, a fundamental state of mind, which agreed very precisely with the derogatory judgements of my fellow-talkers in the Martiusstrasse about the position of the individual and all individualism in the world. It was, I will say, a state of mind, which, no longer interested in the psychological, pressed for the objective, for a language that expressed the absolute, the binding and compulsory, and in consequence by choice laid on itself the pious fetters of pre-classically strict form. How often in my strained observation of Adrian's activity I was forced to remember the early impressions we boys had got from that voluble stutterer, his teacher, with his antithesis of 'harmonic subjectivity' and 'polyphonic objectivity'! The track round the sphere, of which there had been talk in those torturingly clever conversations at Kridwiss's, this track, on which regress and progress, the old and the new, past and future, became one – I saw it all realized here, in a regression full of modern novelty, going back beyond Bach's and Handel's harmonic art to the remoter past of true polyphony.

I have preserved a letter which Adrian sent to me at that time to Freising from Pfeiffering, where he was at work on the hymn of 'a great multitude, which no man could number, of all nations, and kindreds, and people, and tongues, standing before the throne and before the Lamb' (see Dürer's seventh sheet). The letter asked me to visit him, and it was signed Perotinus Magnus; a suggestive joke and playful identification full of self-mockery, for this Perotinus was in charge of church music at Notre Dame in the twelfth century, a composer whose directions contributed to the development of the young art of polyphony. The jesting signature vividly reminded me of a similar one of Richard Wagner, who at the time of *Parsifal* added to his name signed to a letter the title 'Member of the High Consistory'. For a man who

is not an artist the question is intriguing: how serious is the artist in what
ought to be, and seems, his most pressing and earnest concern; how seriously
does he take himself in it, and how much tired disillusionment, affectation,
flippant sense of the ridiculous is at work? If the query were unjustified, how
then could that great master of the musical theatre, at work on this his most
consecrated task, have mocked himself with such a title? I felt much the same
at sight of Adrian's signature. Yes, my questioning, my concern and anxiety
went further and in the silence of my heart dealt with the legitimacy of his
activity, his claim in time to the sphere into which he had plunged, the recreation of which he pursued at all costs and with the most developed means.
In short, I was consumed with loving and anxious suspicion of an
anaestheticism which my friend's saying: 'the antithesis of bourgeois culture
is not barbarism, but collectivism', abandoned to the most tormenting
doubts.

Here no one can follow me who has not as I have experienced in his very
soul how near aestheticism and barbarism are to each other: aestheticism as
the herald of barbarism. I experienced this distress certainly not for myself
but in the light of my friendship for a beloved and emperilled artist soul. The
revival of ritual music from a profane epoch has its dangers. It served indeed
the ends of the Church, did it not? But before that it had served less civilized
ones, the ends of the medicine-man, magic ends. That was in times when all
celestial affairs were in the hands of the priest-medicine-man, the priest-
wizard. Can it be denied that this was a pre-cultural, a barbaric condition of
cult-art; and is it comprehensible or not that the late and cultural revival of
the cult in art, which aims by atomization to arrive at collectivism, seizes
upon means that belong to a stage of civilization not only priestly but
primitive? The enormous difficulties which every rehearsal and performance of Leverkühn's *Apocalypse* presents, have directly to do with all that.
You have there ensembles which begin as 'speaking' choruses and only by
stages, by the way of the most extraordinary transitions, turn into the richest
vocal music; then choruses which pass through all the stages from graded
whisperings, antiphonal speech, and humming up to the most polyphonic
song – accompanied by sounds which begin as mere noise, like tom-toms
and thundering gongs, savage, fanatical, ritual, and end by arriving at the
purest music. How often has this intimidating work, in its urge to reveal in
the language of music the most hidden things, the beast in man as well as his
sublimest stirrings, incurred the reproach both of blood-boltered barbarism
and of bloodless intellectuality! I say incurred; for its idea, in a way, is to take
in the life-history of music, from its pre-musical magic, rhythmical,
elementary stage to its most complex consummation; and thus it does
perhaps expose itself to such reproaches not only in part but as a whole.

Let me give an illustration that has always been the target of scorn and
hatred, and hence the special object of my painful human feeling. But first I
must go back a little. We all know that it was the earliest concern, the first
conquest of the musician to rid sound of its raw and primitive features, to fix
to one single note the singing which in primeval times must have been a
howling glissando over several notes, and to win from chaos a musical
system. Certainly and of course: ordering and normalizing the notes was the
condition and first self-manifestation of what we understand by music. Stuck
there, so to speak, a naturalistic atavism, a barbaric rudiment from pre-
musical days, is the gliding voice, the glissando, a device to be used with the
greatest restraint on profoundly cultural grounds; I have always been
inclined to sense in it an anti-cultural, anti-human appeal. What I have in

mind is Leverkühn's preference for the glissando. Of course 'preference' is not the right word; I only mean that at least in this work, the *Apocalypse*, he makes exceptionally frequent use of it, and certainly these images of terror offer a most tempting and at the same time most legitimate occasion for the employment of that savage device. In the place where the four voices of the altar order the letting loose of the four avenging angels, who mow down rider and steed, Emperor and Pope, and a third of mankind, how terrifying is the effect of the trombone glissandos which here represent the theme! This destructive sliding through the seven positions of the instrument! The theme represented by howling – what horror! And what acoustic panic results from the repeated drum-glissandos, an effect made possible on the chromatic or machine drum by changing the tuning to various pitches during the drum-roll. The effect is extremely uncanny. But most shattering of all is the application of the glissando to the human voice, which after all was the first target in organizing the tonic material and ridding song of its primitive howling over several notes: the return, in short, to this primitive stage, as the chorus of the *Apocalypse* does it in the form of frightfully shrieking human voices at the opening of the seventh seal, when the sun became black and the moon became as blood and the ships are overturned.

I may be allowed here to say a word on the treatment of the chorus in my friend's work: this never before attempted breaking-up of the choral voices into groups both interweaving with and singing against each other; into a sort of dramatic dialogue and into single cries which, to be sure, have their distant classic model in the crashing answer 'Barrabam!' of the *St Matthew Passion*. The *Apocalypse* has no orchestral interludes; but instead the chorus more than once achieves a marked and astonishing orchestral effect: this in the choral variations which represent the paean of the hundred and forty-four thousand redeemed, filling the heavens with their voices, here the four choral parts simply sing in the same rhythm, while the orchestra adds to and sets against them the richest, most varied and contrasting ones. The extremely harsh clashes produced by the part-writing in this piece (and not here alone) have offered much occasion for spiteful jeers. But so it is: so must one accept it; and I at least do so, consenting if amazed. The whole work is dominated by the paradox (if it is a paradox) that in it dissonance stands for the expression of everything lofty, solemn, pious, everything of the spirit; while consonance and firm tonality are reserved for the world of hell, in this context a world of banality and commonplace.

But I wanted to say something else: I wanted to point out the singular interchange which often takes place between the voices and the orchestra. Chorus and orchestra are here not clearly separated from each other as symbols of the human and the material world; they merge into each other, the chorus is 'instrumentalized', the orchestra as it were 'vocalized', to that degree and to that end that the boundary between man and thing seems shifted: an advantage, surely, to artistic unity, yet – at least for my feeling – there is about it something oppressive, dangerous, malignant. A few details: the part of the 'Whore of Babylon, the Woman on the Beast, with whom the kings of the earth have committed fornication', is, surprisingly enough, a most graceful coloratura of great virtuosity; its brilliant runs blend at times with the orchestra exactly like a flute. On the other hand, the muted trumpet suggests a grotesque *vox humana*, as does also the saxophone, which plays a conspicuous part in several of the small chamber orchestras which accompany the singing of the devils, the shameful round of song by the sons of the

Pit. Adrian's capacity for mocking imitation, which was rooted deep in the melancholy of his being, became creative here in the parody of the different musical styles in which the insipid wantonness of hell indulges: French impressionism is burlesqued, along with bourgeois drawing-room music. Tchaikovsky, music-hall, the syncopations and rhythmic somersaults of jazz – like a tilting-ring it goes round and round, gaily glittering, above the fundamental utterance of the main orchestra, which, grave, sombre, and complex, asserts with radical severity the intellectual level of the work as a whole.

Forward! I have still so much on my heart about this scarcely opened testament of my friend; it seems to me I shall do best to go on, stating my opinions in the light of that reproach whose plausibility I admit though I would bite my tongue out sooner than recognize its justice: the reproach of barbarism. It has been levelled at the characteristic feature of the work, its combination of very new and very old; but surely this is by no means an arbitrary combination; rather it lies in the nature of things: it rests, I might say, on the curvature of the world, which makes the last return unto the first. Thus the elder art did not know rhythm as music later understood it. Song was set according to the metrical laws of speech, it did not run articulated by bars and musical periods; rather it obeyed the spirit of free recitation. And how is it with the rhythm of our, the latest, music? Has it too not moved nearer to a verbal accent? Has it not been relaxed by an excessive flexibility? In Beethoven there are already movements of a rhythmic freedom foreshadowing things to come – a freedom which in Leverkühn is complete but for his bar-lines, which, as an ironically conservative conventional feature, he still retained. But without regard to symmetry, and fitted exclusively to the verbal accent, the rhythm actually changes from bar to bar. I spoke of impressions which, unimportant as they seem to the reason, work on in the subconscious mind and there exercise a decisive influence. So it was now: the figure of that queer fish across the ocean of his arbitrary, ingenuous musical activity, of whom another queer fish, Adrian's teacher, had told us in our youth, and about whom my companion expressed himself with such spirited approval as we walked home that night: the figure and the history of Johann Conrad Beissel was such an impression. Why should I behave as though I had not already, long ago and repeatedly thought of that strict schoolmaster and beginner in the art of song, at Ephrata across the sea? A whole world lies between his naïve unabashed theory and the work of Leverkühn, pushed to the very limits of musical erudition, technique, intellectuality. And yet for me, the understanding friend, the spirit of the inventor of the 'master' and 'servant' notes and of musical hymn-recitation moves ghostlike in it.

Do I, with these personal interpolations, contribute anything which will explain that reproach which hurts me so, which I seek to interpret without making the smallest concession to it: the reproach of barbarism? It has probably more to do with a certain touch, like an icy finger, of mass-modernity in this work of religious vision, which knows the theological almost exclusively as judgement and terror: a touch of 'streamline', to venture the insulting word. Take the *testis*, the witness and narrator of the horrid happenings: the 'I, Johannes', the describer of the beasts of the abyss, with the heads of lions, calves, men, and eagles – this part, by tradition assigned to a tenor, is here given to a tenor indeed but one of almost castrato-like high register, whose chilly crow, objective, reporterlike, stands in terrifying contrast to the content of his catastrophic announcements. When in 1926 at the festival of the International Society for New Music at Frankfurt the *Apocalypse* had its first and so far its last performance (under Klemperer) this extremely difficult part was taken and sung in masterly fashion by a tenor with the voice of a eunuch, named Erbe, whose piercing communications did actually sound like 'Latest News of World Destruction'. That was altogether in the spirit of the work, the singer had with the greatest intelligence grapsed the idea. – Or take as another example of easy technical facility in horror, the effect of being at home in it: I mean the loud-speaker effects (in an oratorio!) which the composer has indicated in various places and which achieve an otherwise never realized gradation in the volume and distance of the musical sound: of such a kind that by means of the loud-speaker some parts are brought into prominence, while others recede as distant choruses and orchestras. Again think of the jazz – certainly very incidental – used to suggest the purely infernal element: one will bear with me for making bitter application of the expression 'streamlined' for a work which, judged by its intellectual and psychological basic mood, has more to do with Kaisersaschern than with modern slickness and which I am fain to characterize as a dynamic archaism.

Soullessness! I well know this is at bottom what they mean who apply the word 'barbaric' to Adrian's creation. Have they ever, even if only with the reading eye, heard certain lyrical parts – or may I only say moments? – of the *Apocalypse*: song passages accompanied by a chamber orchestra, which could bring tears to the eyes of a man more callous than I am, since they are like a fervid prayer for a soul. I shall be forgiven for an argument more or less into the blue; but to call soullessness the yearning for a soul – the yearning of the little sea-maid – that is what I would characterize as barbarism, as inhumanity!

I write it down in a mood of self-defence; and another emotion seizes me: the memory of that pandemonium of laughter, of hellish merriment which, brief but horrible, forms the end of the first part of the *Apocalypse*. I hate, love, and fear it; for – may I be pardoned for this all too personal excuse? I have always feared Adrian's proneness to laughter, never been able, like Rüdiger Schildknapp, to play a good second to it; and the same fear, the same shrinking and misgiving awkwardness I feel at this gehennan gaudium, sweeping through fifty bars, beginning with the chuckle of a single voice and rapidly gaining ground, embracing choir and orchestra, frightfully swelling in rhythmic upheavals and contrary motions to a *fortissimo tutti*, an overwhelming, sardonically yelling, screeching, bawling, bleating, howling, piping, whinnying salvo, the mocking, exulting laughter of the Pit. So much do I shudder at this episode in and for itself, and the way it stands out by reason of its position in the whole, this hurricane of hellish merriment, that I could hardly have brought myself to speak of it if it were not that here, precisely here, is revealed to me, in a way to make my heart stop beating, the profoundest mystery of this music, which is a mystery of identity.

For this hellish laughter at the end of the first part has its pendant in the truly extraordinary chorus of children which, accompanied by a chamber orchestra, opens the second part: a piece of cosmic music of the spheres, icily clear, glassily transparent, of brittle dissonances indeed, but withal of an – I would like to say – inaccessibly unearthly and alien beauty of sound, filling the heart with longing without hope. And this piece, which has won, touched, and ravished even the reluctant, is in its musical essence, for him who has ears to hear and eyes to see, the devil's laughter all over again. Everywhere is Adrian Leverkühn great in making unlike the like. One knows his way of modifying rhythmically a fugal subject already in its first answer, in such a way that despite a strict preservation of its thematic essence it is as repetition no longer recognizable. So here – but nowhere else as here is the effect so profound, mysterious and great. Every word that turns into sound the idea of Beyond, of transformation in the mystical sense, and thus of change, transformation, transfiguration, is here exactly reproduced. The passages of horror just before heard are given, indeed, to the indescribable children's chorus at quite a different pitch, and in changed orchestration and rhythms; but in the searing, susurrant tones of spheres and angels there is not one note which does not occur, with rigid correspondence, in the hellish laughter.

That is Adrian Leverkühn. Utterly. That is the music he represents; and that correspondence is its profound significance, calculation raised to mystery. Thus love with painful discrimination has taught me to see this music, though in accordance with my own simple nature I would perhaps have been glad to see it otherwise.

Chapter Thirty-five

The new numeral stands at the head of a chapter that will report a death, a human catastrophe in the circle round my friend. And yet, my God, what chapter, what sentence, what word that I have written has not been pervaded by the catastrophic, when that has become the air we breathe! What word did not shake, as only too often the hand that wrote it, with the vibrations not alone of the catastrophe towards which my story strives but simultaneously of that cataclysm in whose sign the world – at least the bourgeois, the human world – stands today?

Here we shall be dealing with a private, human disaster, scarcely noted by the public. To it many factors contributed: masculine rascality, feminine frailty, feminine pride and professional unsuccess. It is twenty-two years since, almost before my eyes, Clarissa Rodde the actress, sister of the just as obviously doomed Inez, went to her death: at the end of the winter season of 1921–2, in the month of May, at Pfeiffering in her mother's house and with scant consideration for that mother's feelings, with rash and resolute hand she took her life, using the poison that she had long kept in readiness for the moment when her pride could not longer endure to live.

I will relate in a few words the events which led to the frightful deed, so shattering to us all though at bottom we could hardly condemn it, together with the circumstances under which it was committed. I have already mentioned that her Munich teacher's warnings had proved all too well founded: Clarissa's artistic career had not in the course of years risen from lowly provincial beginnings to more respectable and dignified heights. From Elbing in East Prussia she went to Pforzheim in Baden – in other words she advanced not at all or very little, the larger theatres of the Reich gave her not a thought. She was a failure or at least lacking any genuine success, for the simple reason, so hard for the person concerned to grasp, that her natural talent was not equal to her ambition. No genuine theatre blood gave body to her knowledge or her hopes or won for her the minds and hearts of the contrarious public. She lacked the primitive basis, that which in all art is the decisive thing but most of all in the art of the actor – whether that be to the honour or the dishonour of art and in particular the art of the stage.

There was another factor which added to Clarissa's emotional confusion. As I had long before observed with regret, she did not make a clear distinction between her stage life and her real one. Possibly just because she was no true actress, she played actress even outside the theatre. The personal and physical nature of stage art led her to make up in private life with rouge and cosmetics, exaggerated hairdressing and extravagant hats: an entirely unnecessary and mistaken self-dramatization which affected her friends painfully, invited criticism from the conventional, and encouraged the licentious. All this without wish or intention on her part, for Clarissa was the most mockingly aloof, chaste, and high-minded creature imaginable, though her armour of arrogance may well have been a defence mechanism against the demands of her own femininity. If so, she was the blood sister of Inez Institoris, the beloved – or *ci-devant* beloved – of Rudi Schwerdtfeger.

In any case, to that well-preserved sixty-year-old man who wanted to make her his mistress, there succeeded this or that unchronicled trifler with less solid prospects, or one or another favourable critic who might have been useful to her but being repulsed revenged himself by pouring public scorn on her performance. And finally fate overtook her and put to shame her contemptuous way of looking down her nose. It was a defeat the more lamentable in that the conqueror of her maidenhood was not at all worthy of his triumph and was not even so deemed by Clarissa herself. He was a pseudo-Mephistopheles, a Pforzheim petticoat-chaser, back-stage hanger-on and provincial roué, by profession a criminal lawyer. He was equipped for conquest with nothing but a cheap and cynical eloquence, fine linen, and much black hair on his hands. One evening after the play, probably a little the worse for wine, the prickly but at bottom shy, inexperienced, and defenceless creature yielded to his practised technique of seduction and afterwards was prey to the most scathing self-contempt. For the betrayer had indeed been able to capture her senses for the moment but she actually felt for him only the hatred his triumph aroused, together with a certain astonishment that she, Clarissa Rodde, could have been thus betrayed. She scornfully rejected his further addresses; but she was frightened lest he might betray their relation – in fact he was already threatening to do so as a means of bringing pressure.

Meanwhile decent human prospects had opened to the girl in her disillusioned and nervous state. Among her social connexions she had made the acquaintance of a young Alsatian businessman who sometimes came over from Strasbourg to Pforzheim and had fallen desperately in love with the proud and stately blonde. Clarissa was not at this time entirely without an engagement; having remained for another season at the Pforzheim theatre, though only in secondary and unrewarding parts. Even so, the re-engagement was due to the sympathy and mediation of an elderly dramatist, who while sceptical as to her acting abilities esteemed her general intellectual and human worth, which was so greatly, even disadvantageously superior to the average among the little stage folk. Perhaps, who knows, this man even loved her, but was too much resigned to the disappointments and disillusionments of life to summon up courage to declare his inclination.

At the beginning of the new season, then, Clarissa met the young man who promised to rescue her from her unsuccessful career and to offer her as his wife a peaceful and secure, yes, well-furnished existence in a sphere strange to her, indeed, but socially not alien with her own origins. With unmistakable joy and hope, with gratitude, yes, with a tenderness rooted in her gratitude, she wrote to her sister and even to her mother of Henri's wooing and also about the disapproval of his family. He was about the same age as Clarissa, his mother's darling, his father's business partner, and altogether the light of his family's eyes. He put his case to them with ardour and strength of purpose; but it would have taken more than that to overcome all at once the prejudice of his bourgeois clan against an itinerant actress and a *boche* into the bargain. Henri understood his family's concern for refinement and good taste, their fear that he might be getting entangled. It was not so easy to convince them that he would by no means be doing so in bringing Clarissa home; the best way would be for him to present her personally to his loving parents, jealous brothers and sisters, and prejudiced aunts, and towards this goal he had been working for weeks, that they might consent and arrange an interview. In regular letters and repeated trips to Pforzheim he reported progress to his betrothed.

Clarissa was confident of success. Her social equality, only clouded by the profession she was ready to renounce, must become plain to Henri's anxious clan at a personal meeting. In her letters and during a visit she made to Munich she took for granted her coming official betrothal and the future she anticipated. The future, to be sure, looked quite different from the earlier dreams of this uprooted child of patrician stock, striving towards intellectual and artistic goals. But now it was her haven, her happiness: a bourgeois happiness, which obviously looked more acceptable because it possessed the charm of novelty; the foreign nationality was a new frame into which she would be transplanted. In fancy she heard her future children prattling in French.

Then the spectre of her past rose up to blast her hopes. It was a stupid, cynical, ignoble spectre but bold and ruthless; and it put her to shame, it drove the poor soul into a corner and brought her to her death. That villain learned in the law, to whom in a weak moment she had surrendered, used his single conquest to enforce her. Henri's family, Henri himself should learn of their relation if she did not yield to him again. From all that we later learned, there must have been desperate scenes between the murderer and his victim. In vain the girl implored him – on her knees at last – to spare her, to release her, not to make her pay for her peace with the betrayal of the man who loved her, whose love she returned. Precisely this confession roused the wretch to cruelty. He made no bones of saying that in giving herself to him now, she was buying peace only for the moment, buying the trip to Strasbourg, the betrothal. He would never release her: to pay himself for his present silence he would compel her to his will whenever he chose. He would speak out as soon as she denied her debt. She would be forced to live in adultery: a just punishment for her philistinism, for what the wretch called her cowardly retreat into bourgeois society. If all that went wrong, if even without his treachery her little bridegroom learned the truth, then there still remained the last resort, the outcrowing drug which for so long she had kept in that object d'art, the book with the death's-head on the lid. Not for nothing had she felt superior to life and made macabre mock of it by her possession of the Hippocratic drug – a mock that was more in character than the bourgeois peace treaty with life for which she had been preparing.

In my opinion the wretch, aside from satisfying his lust, had aimed at her death. His abnormal vanity demanded a female corpse on his path, he itched to have a human being die and perish, if not precisely for him, yet on his account. Alas, that Clarissa had to gratify him! She saw the situation clearly, just as I see it, as we all had to see it. Once again she yeilded, to gain a present peace, and was thereby more than ever in his power. She probably thought that once accepted by the family, once married to Henri and safe in another country, she would find ways and means to defy her oppressor. It was not to be. Obviously her tormentor had made up his mind not to let matters go as far as marriage. An anonymous letter referring in the third person to Clarissa's lover did its work with Henri and his Strasbourg family. He sent it to her that she might, if possible, deny it. His accompanying letter did not precisely display an unshakeable faith and love.

Clarissa received the registered letter in Pfeiffering, where after the close of the Pforzheim theatre season she was spending a few weeks with her mother in the cottage under the chestnut trees. It was early afternoon. The Frau Senator saw her daughter hurrying back from a walk she had taken alone, after the midday meal. They met on the little open place in front of the house and Clarissa brushed past her mother with a blank, dazed look and fugitive smile, into her own room, where with a swift and violent movement she turned the key in the door. Next door the old lady presently heard her daughter at the wash-hand-stand, gargling her throat – we know now that it was to cool the fearful corrosive action of the acid. Then there was silence – long and uncanny. After twenty minutes the Frau Senator knocked and called Clarissa's name. Repeatedly and urgently she called but no answer came. The frightened woman, with her scanty hair awry over her brow, her partly toothless gums, ran across to the main building and in half-choked words told Frau Schweigestill; that experienced soul followed her with a manservant. After repeated knocking and calling they forced the door. Clarissa lay with open eyes on the sofa at the foot of the bed, a piece from the seventies or eighties of the last century, with a back and side arm; I knew it from the Rambergstrasse. She had retreated there when death came upon her while she gargled her throat.

'Not anythin' to do, dear Frau Senator,' said Frau Schweigestill, one finger on her cheek, shaking her head, at sight of the half-sitting, half-lying figure. The same only too convincing sight met my eyes when I hurried over from Freising, having been informed by our landlady on the telephone. I took the wailing mother in my arms, a distressed and consolatory family friend; we stood beside the body together with Frau Schweigestill and Adrian. Dark blue spots of congested blood on Clarissa's lovely hands and on her face indicated death by quick suffocation, the abrupt paralysis of the organs of breathing by a dose of cyanide large enough to kill a regiment. On the table, empty, the screws taken out of the bottom, was that bronze container, the book with the name Hippocrates in Greek letters, and the skull upon it. There was a hasty pencilled note to her betrothed, with the words: '*Je t'aime. Une fois je t'ai trompé, mais je t'aime.*'

The young man came to the funeral, the arrangements for which fell to my lot. He was heart-broken – or rather he was *désolé*, which of course quite wrongly does not sound quite so serious, somehow a little more like a phrase. I would not cast doubt on the pain with which he cried out: 'Ah, monsieur, I loved her enough to pardon her. Everything might have been well – and now – *comme ça!*'

Yes, '*comme ça!*' It really might all have been otherwise if he had not been such a son of his family and if Clarissa had had in him a more responsible support.

That night we wrote, Adrian, Frau Schweigestill, and I, while the Frau Senator in the deepest grief sat by the rigid husk of her child, the public announcement of the death. It had to be signed by Clarissa's nearest relatives, and we were to give it an unmistakably palliating tone. We agreed on a formula which said that the deceased had died after grave and incurable affliction. This was read by the Munich dean on whom I called to get consent for the church service so intensely desired by the Frau Senator. I did not begin too diplomatically, for I naïvely admitted in confidence that Clarissa had preferred death to a life of dishonour. The man of God, a sturdy cleric of true Lutheran type, would not listen to me. Frankly, it took me some time to understand that on the one hand, indeed, the Church did not wish to see herself put on one side; but on the other she was not ready to give her parting blessing to a declared suicide, however honourable a one. In short, the sturdy cleric wanted nothing else than that I should tell him a lie. So then I came round with almost ridiculous promptness, described the event as incomprehensible; allowed that a mistake, a wrong bottle was quite possible, yes, probable. Whereupon the fat-head showed himself flattered by the weight we attached to the services of his firm and declared himself ready to conduct the funeral.

It took place in the Munich Waldfried cemetery, attended by the whole circle of friends of the Rodde family. Rudi Schwerdtfeger, Zink and Spengler, even Schildknapp, they were all there. The mourning was sincere, for everybody had been fond of poor, proud, pert Clarissa. Inez Institoris, in deepest black, represented her mother, who did not appear. The daughter received the condolences with dignity, her delicate neck stretched out. In this tragic outcome of her sister's struggle I could not help seeing an ill omen for her own fate. And in speaking with her I got the impression that she rather envied than mourned for her sister. Her husband's income was more and more reduced by the fall of the exchange, in some circles so desired and promoted. The bulwark of luxury, her protection against life, threatened to fail the frightened woman; it was already doubtful whether they could keep the expensive home on the English Garden. As for Rudi Schwerdtfeger, he had indeed paid Clarissa the last honours; but he left the cemetery as soon as he could after his condolences to the relatives. Adrian commented on their briefness and formality.

This was probably the first time Inez had seen her lover since he broke off their affair – I fear rather brutally, for to do it 'nicely' was hardly possible in view of the desperation with which she clung to him. As she stood there beside her slender husband, at her sister's grave, she was a forsaken woman, and in all likelihood desperately unhappy. But she had gathered round her a little group of women as a consolation and substitute, and they now stood with her, more for her sake than in Clarissa's honour. To this close little circle, partnership, corporation, club, or what you will, belonged Natalie Knöterich as Inez's nearest friend; also a divorced woman writer, a Rumanian-Siebenbügerin, author of various farces and mistress of a bohemian salon in Schwabing; the actress Rosa Zwitscher, a performer who frequently displayed great nervous intensity; and one or two other females whom it is unnecessary to describe, especially since I am not certain of their active membership in the group.

The cement that bound them together was – as the reader is already prepared to hear – morphine. It was an extremely strong bond; for the confraternity not only helped each other out with their unhealthy partnership in the drug that was their bliss and bane; but also on the moral side there exists a sad yet tender mutual respect and solidarity among the slaves of the craving. In this case the sinners were also held together by definite

philosophy or motto originating with Inez Institoris and subscribed to by all
the five or six friends. Inez, that is, espoused the view – I have on occasion
heard it from her lips – that pain is an indignity, that it is shameful to suffer.
But quite aside from that concrete and particular humiliation from physical
or emotional suffering, life in and for itself, mere existence, animal
existence, was an ignoble fetter and unworthy burden, and it was nothing
less than noble and high-minded, it was an exercise of a human right, it was
intellectually justifiable to slough off the burden, so to speak, to win
freedom, ease, and as it were bodiless well-being by providing the physical
with the blessed stuff which purveyed such emancipation from suffering.

That such a philosophy took in its stride the physically ruinous consequences of the self-indulgent habit, belonged obviously to its nobility, and
probably it was the consciousness of their common early ruin that stimulated
the companions to such tenderness, yes, to being tenderly in love with each
other. Not without repulsion did I observe their raptures, the lighting up
of their glances, their gushing embraces and kisses when they met in society.
Yet I confess my private impatience with this dispensation – confess it
with a certain surprise, since I do not at all care for myself in the role
of carping pharisee. It may be the sentimental disingenuousness to which
the vice leads, or is always immanent in it, that causes my unconquerable
distaste. Moreover I took amiss the reckless indifference to her children
which Inez displayed as this evil habit grew on her; it stamped as false
all her pretended devotion to her coddled little white-skinned darlings. In
short, the woman had become deeply offensive to me after I knew and
saw what she let herself in for. She perfectly saw that I had given her up,
and repaid the perception with a smile which in its hysterical malice
reminded me of that other smile on her face when for two hours on end
she had assumed my human sympathy with her love and her lust.

Indeed, she had small ground to be cheerful; for the way she debased
herself was a sorry sight. Probably she took over-doses which did not
increase her animation but reduced her to a state in which she could not
appear in public. Mme Zwitscher acted more brilliantly by the help of the
drug, and it actually heightened Natalie Knöterich's charm. But it happened
repeatedly to poor Inez that she came half-dazed to the table and sat with
glazed eyes and nodding head with her eldest daughter and her worried
and petty little husband, at the still well-kept-up board sparkling with silver
and glass. But one admission I will make: Inez, as we know, committed
a few years later a capital crime, which aroused general horror and put
an end to her bourgeois existence. I shuddered at the awful deed; at the
same time, in memory of my old friendship, I felt almost, nay, I felt
definitely proud that in all her sunken state she found the strength, the
furious energy to commit it.

Chapter Thirty-six

O Germany, thou art undone! And I am mindful of thy hopes. Those hopes, I mean, which you aroused (it may even be that you did not share them) after your former relatively mild collapse and the abdication of the Empire. The world then placed on you certain hopes; and you seemed – aside from that reckless, utterly crazy, desperate, and hysterical 'inflation' of your own misery, the giddy heavenward climb of the exchange – that aside, you seemed for some years to be about to justify, to some extent, those hopes.

True, the fantastic improprieties of that period, a deliberate attempt to make faces at the rest of the world, were really not unlike what we have seen since 1933 and of course since 1939. On a smaller scale they too were monstrously incredible and exaggerated; the scene displayed the same vicious sans-culottism. But the debauch on 'change, the bombast of despair did one day come to an end; the face of our economic life lost its distorted, insane grimace and assumed a look of returning sanity. An epoch of psychological convalescence seemed to be dawning. There was some hope for Germany of social progress in peace and freedom; of adult and forward-looking effort; of a voluntary adaptation of our thoughts and feelings to those of the normal world. Despite all her inherent weakness and self-hatred, this was beyond a doubt the meaning and the hope of the German republic – again, the hope I mean is the one she awakened in the world outside. It was an attempt, a not utterly and entirely hopeless attempt (the second since the failure of Bismarck and his unification performance) to normalize Germany in the sense of Europeanizing or 'democratizing' it, of making it part of the social life of peoples. Who will deny that much honest belief in the possibility of this process was alive in the other countries? Who will dispute the existence of a hopeful movement, plain to see on every hand among us Germans, save in this or that unregenerate spot – for instance typically in our good city of Munich?

I am speaking of the twenties of the twentieth century, in particular of course of their second half, which quite seriously witnessed nothing less than a shift of the cultural centre from France to Germany. It is a telling fact that, as I mentioned earlier, the first performance of Adrian Leverkühn's apocalpytic oratorio took place in Germany – or more precisely its first complete performance. The scene was Frankfurt, always one of the most friendly and free-minded cities of the Reich. Even so, it did not come about without angry opposition, bitter reproaches and outcries against the piece as a mockery of art, an expression of nihilism, a crime against music, in short, to use the current and fashionable condemnation, as a specimen of cultural Bolshevism. But the work, and the audacity which presented it, found intelligent and eloquent defenders: about the year 1927 courageous friendliness to the outer world and the cause of freedom was at its height, as an offset

to the nationalistic-Wagnerian-romantic forces of reaction, at home particularly in Munich. It was certainly an element of our public life in the first
half of the decade. I am thinking cultural events like the Music Festival in
Weimer in 1920 and the first one at Donaueschingen in the following year.
On both occasions, unfortunately in the absence of the composer, some
works of Leverkühn were given, together with those of other artists
representative of the new intellectual and musical attitude. The audience
was by no means unreceptive; I might say that they were, in the field of art,
republican-minded. In Weimar the Cosmic Symphony was conducted by
Bruno Walter with a particularly sure rhythmical sense. At the festival in
Baden, in cooperation with Hans Platner's famous marionette theatre, they
gave all five pieces of the *Gesta Romanorum* an experience ravishing the
feelings to and fro between pious emotion and laughter as never before.

But I would also recall the share which German artists and friends of art
had in the founding of the International Society for Contemporary Music,
in 1922, and the performances by the society two years later in Prague, when
choral and instrumental portions of Adrian's *Apocalypsis cum figuris* were
given before a public including famous guests from all the lands of music.
The composition had already appeared in print, not, like Leverkühn's
earlier work, published by Schott in Mainz but by the 'Universal Editions'
in Vienna, whose youthful editor Dr Edelmann was scarcely thirty years old
but already played an influential part in the musical life of central Europe.
One day Edelmann bobbed up unexpectedly in Pfeiffering, in fact even
before the *Apocalypse* was finished (it was in the weeks of interruption
through the attack of illness) to offer the guest of the Schweigestills his
service as editor and publisher. The visit was supposed to be in connexion
with an article on Adrian's work, which had recently appeared in the
advanced radical Vienna musical magazine *Anbruch*, from the pen of the
Hungarian musicologist and culture-philosopher Desiderius Fehér. Fehér
has expressed himself with great warmth about the high intellectual level
and religious content of the music; its pride and despair, its diabolic
cleverness, amounting to afflatus; he invoked the attention of the world of
culture, with ardour increased by the writer's confessed chagrin at not
having himself discovered this most interesting and thrilling phenomenon.
He had, as he put it, needed to be guided from outside, from above, from a
sphere higher than all learning, the sphere of love and faith, in a word the
eternal feminine. In short the article, which mingled the analytical with the
lyrical in a way congenial to its theme, gave one a glimpse, even though in a
very vague outline, of a female figure who was its real inspirer: a sensitive
woman, wise and well-informed, actively at work for her faith. But as Dr
Edelmann's visit had turned out to be prompted by the Vienna publication,
one might say that indirectly it too was an effect of that fine and scrupulous
love and energy in the background.

Only indirectly? I am not quite sure. I think it possible that the young
musician and man of business may have received direct stimulation,
suggestion, and instruction from that sphere, and I am strengthened in my
guess by the fact that he knew more than the rather mystery-making article
had allowed itself to tell. He knew the name and mentioned it – not at once,
not as accepted fact, but in the course of the conversation, towards the end.
In the beginning he had almost been refused admission; then, when he had
managed to get himself received, he had asked Leverkühn to tell him about
his present work and he heard about the oratorio. Was that for the first time?
I doubt it. Adrian was suffering almost to the point of collapse; but in the

end was prevailed upon to play, in the Nike room, considerable portions
from the manuscript, whereupon Dr Edelmann secured it on the spot for the
'Editions'. The contract came from the Bayerischer Hof in Munich next
day. But before he left he had asked Adrian, using the Viennese mode of
address modelled on the French: 'Meister, do you know' (I think he even
said 'Does Meister know') 'Frau von Tolna?'

I am about to do something that would, in a novel, break all the canons:
I mean to introduce into the narrative an invisible character. This invisible
figure is Frau Von Tolna and I cannot set her before the reader's eye or
give the smallest idea of her outward appearance, for I have not seen her and
never had a description of her, since no one I know ever saw her either. I
leave it an open question whether Dr Edelmann himself, or only that
associate editor of the *Anbruch* who was a countryman of hers, could boast of
her acquaintance. As for Adrian, he answered in the negative the question
put by the Viennese. He did not know the lady, he said; but he did not, in his
turn, ask who she was, nor did Edelmann give any explanation of his
question, other than merely by saying: 'At all events, you have' (or 'Meister
has') 'no warmer admirer than she.'

Obviously he regarded the negative reply as the conditioned and guarded
truth that it was. Adrian could answer as he did because his relation to the
Hungarian noblewoman lacked any personal contact; I may add that by
mutual consent it was always to lack it, to the end. It is another matter that
for a long time they had carried on a correspondence, in which she showed
herself the shrewdest and most initiate connoisseur of his work, the most
devoted friend, confidante, and counsellor, unconditionally and unfailingly
at his service; while on his side he went to the furthest limits of communicativeness and confidingness of which a solitary soul like his is capable.
We know of those other needy, yearning female beings who by selfless
devotion won a modest niche in the life-history of this certainly immortal
genius. Here now is a third, of quite different mould, not only equalling in
disinterestedness those other simpler souls, but even excelling them in the
ascetic renunciation of any direct approach, the inviolable observance of his
privacy, the aloofness, the restraint, the persistent invisibility. None of this,
of course, was due to shyness or awkwardness, for this was a woman of the
world, who to the hermit of Pfeiffering, did really represent the world: the
world as he loved it, needed it, and so far as he could stand it; the world at a
distance, keeping itself removed out of tact and good sense.

I set down here what I know of this extraordinary being. Mme de Tolna
was the wealthy widow of a dissipated nobleman, who however had not died
of his excesses but in a racing accident. She was left childless, the owner of a
palace in Budapest, a vast estate a few hours south of the capital, near
Stuhlweissenburg, between the Plattensee and the Danube, and besides
these a castellated villa on the same lake, Balaton. The estate, with its
splendid, comfortably modernized eighteenth-century manor-house,
comprised enormous wheat-growing tracts and extensive sugar-beet plan-
tations, the harvests being manufactured in refining works on the property
itself. None of these residences – palatial town house, manorial estate, or
summer villa – did the owner occupy for long at a time. Mostly, one may say
almost always, she was travelling, leaving her homes, to which she obviously
did not cling, from which restlessness or painful memories drove her
away, to the care of managers and major-domos. She lived in Paris, Naples,
Egypt, and Engadine, attended from place to place by a lady's maid, a
male official something like a courier and quartermaster, and a body-

physician for her sole service, which made one suspect that she was in delicate health.

Her mobility however seemed not to suffer; and combined with an enthusiasm resting on instinct, intuition, knowledge, sensibility – God knows what! – mysterious perception, soul-affinity, she commanded most unusual resources. It turned out that this woman had been present, mingling unobtrusively in the audience wherever people had been bold enough to perform any of Adrian's music: in Lübeck, at the much-ridiculed première of his opera; in Zürich, in Weimar, in Prague. How often she had been near him in Munich and so near to his lodging, without revealing herself, I would not know. But she also – it came out by accident – knew Pfeiffering; had secretly made acquaintance with the setting of Adrian's activity, his immediate surroundings; and, if I am not mistaken, stood under the window of the Abbot's Chamber and gone away unseen. All that is thrilling enough; but even stranger, summoning up the image of the devout pilgrim is a fact which I learned long afterwards and also more or less by chance: she had actually gone to Kaisersaschern, was acquainted with Oberweiler and the Buchel farm itself, and thus was aware of the parallel – to me always faintly depressing – between Adrian's childhood setting and the frame of his later life.

I forgot to say that she had not omitted Palestrina, the village in the Sabine Hills. She spent some weeks in the Manardi house and, it appeared, made quick and close friends with Signora Manardi. When in her half-German, half-French letters she mentioned the Signora, she called her Mère Manardi. She gave the same title to Frau Schweigestill, whom, according to her own evidence, she had seen without being seen or noticed. And herself? Was it her idea to attach herself to all these maternal figures and call them sisters? What name fitted her in relation to Adrian Leverkühn? What did she want or claim? A protecting deity, an Egeria, a soul-mate? The first letter she wrote, from Brussels, was accompanied by a gift sent to him in homage: a ring the like of which I have never seen – though in all conscience that does not mean much, since the present writer is little versed in the precious material things of this world. It was a jewel of great beauty and – to me – incalculable value. The engraved hoop itself was old Renaissance work; the stone a splendid specimen of clear pale-green emerald from the Urals, cut with large facets, a glorious sight. One could imagine that it had once adorned the hand of a prince of the Church – the pagan inscription it bore was scarcely evidence to the contrary. On the hard upper facet of the precious beryl two lines were graven in the tiniest Greek characters. Translated they ran somewhat like this:

> *What a trembling seized on the laurel-bush of Appollo!*
> *Trembles the entire frame! Flee, profane one! Depart!*

It was not hard for me to place the lines as the beginning of a hymn to Apollo, by Callimachus. They describe with unearthly terror the sign of an epiphany of the god at his shrine. The writing, with all its tininess, was clear and sharp. Rather more blurred was the sign carved beneath, like a vignette. Under a glass it revealed itself as a winged snakelike monster whose tongue was clearly arrow-shaped. The mythological fantasy made me think of the sting or shot-wound of the Chrysaen Philoctetes and the spithet Aeschylus has for the arrow: 'hissing winged snake'; I recalled too the connexion between the arrow of Phoebus and the ray of the sun.

I can testify that Adrian was childishly delighted with this considerable gift, speaking of a sympathetic someone in the background. He accepted it without a thought, though he never, in fact, showed himself to others wearing it, but instead made a practice – or shall I say a ritual? – of putting it on for his working hours. I know that during the writing of the whole of the *Apocalypse* he wore the jewel on his left hand.

Did he think that a ring is the symbol of a bond, a fetter, yes, of possession? Obviously he thought no such thing; seeing in that precious link of an invisible chain, which he stuck on his finger while he composed, nothing more than a sort of bridge between his hermit state and the outside world; as a mere cloudy symbol of a personality, about whose features or individual traits he evidently inquired far less than I did. Was there, I asked myself, something in the woman's outward appearance that might explain the fundamental condition of her relations with Adrian, the invisibility, the avoidance, the rule that they should never set eyes on each other? She might be ugly, lame, crippled, disfigured by a skin ailment. I do not so interpret it: but rather think that if some blemish existed it lay in the realm of the spirit and taught her to understand every sort of need for consideration and scrupulous tact. Adrian never once sought to break that law; he silently acquiesced in the bounds set to the relationship within the realms of intellect and spirit.

I use unwillingly this banal phrase. There is something colourless and weak about it, not consistent with the practical energy characteristic of this care, a concern, and devotion, remote and shrouded though it was. During the composition of the *Apocalypse* the two carried on an exchange of letters altogether objective in their content, hers evincing a serious and solid European culture, both musically and generally speaking. My friend's correspondent knew how to give him suggestions for the textual structure of the work, from material not easily accessible. It turned out, for instance, that that old-French metrical version of the vision of St Paul had come to him from the 'outer world'. The same outer world was constantly, if by roundabout ways and through intermediaries, active on his behalf. It was 'the world' which instigated that stimulating article in the *Anbruch*, certainly the only publication where enthusiasm for Leverkühn's music could get a hearing. It was 'the world' which saw to it that the 'Universal Editions' had secured the oratorio while it was still being written. In 1921 it put at the disposal of the Platner marionette theatre, privately, so that the source of the gift was left vague, considerable sums for the expensive and musically adequate production of the *Gesta* in Domaueschingen.

I must dwell a little on this point, and the sweeping gesture accompanying it, this 'putting at the disposal of'. Adrian could have no shadow of doubt that he might command any and every resource of this woman of the world who had become the recluse's devotee. Her wealth was obviously a burden on her conscience, although she had never known life without it and probably would not have known how to live. To lay on the altar of genius as much of it as possible, as much as she ever dared to offer, was her confessed desire; and if Adrian had wished, his whole manner of life might have changed from one day to the next on the costly scale of that gem, adorned with which only the four walls of the Abbot's chamber ever saw him. He knew it as well as I did. I need not say that he never for a moment seriously considered it. Differently constituted from me, for whom some intoxication had always lain in the thought of vast wealth lying at his feet, which he need only grasp to secure himself a princely existence, he had certainly never actually come to grips with such an idea. But once, when by exception he had left his Pfeiffering nest on a journey, he had had a fleeting glimpse, tasted an experimental sip, of the almost regal form of life which privately I could not help wishing might be permanently his.

That is twenty years since, and came about when he accepted the standing invitation of Mme de Tolna to live for as long as he chose in one of her residences – that is, of course, when she was not there. He was then, in the spring of 1924, in Vienna, where in the Ehrbar Hall and in the setting of one of the so-called *Anbruch* evenings Rudi Schwerdtfeger at last and finally played the violin concerto written for him. It was a great success, not least for Rudi himself. I say not least, and mean above all; for a certain concentration of interest on the art of the interpreter is inherent in the intention of the work, which, though the hand of the musician is unmistakable, is not one of Leverkühn's highest and proudest effects, but at least in part has something complimentary and condescending, I might better say affable about it which reminded me of an early prophecy from lips now forever mute. – Adrian declined to appear before the applauding audience at the end of the piece and left the house while we were looking for him. We found him later, the producer, the beaming Rudi, and I, in the restaurant of the little hotel in the Herrengasse where he stopped alone, Schwerdtfeger having thought it due to himself to go to a hotel in the Ring.

The celebration was brief – Adrian had headache. But it seems the temporary relaxation of his plan of life led him to decide next day not to return at once to the Schweigestill's but to please his friend of the outer world by visiting her Hungarian estate. The condition that she should be absent was complied with, for she was at the time in Vienna, though invisibly. He sent a wire to the estate making announcement of his visit, and hasty arrangements were made by messages to and fro. He set off, not accompanied by me, for much to my regret I could scarcely spare time even for the concert. This time it was not Rüdiger Schildknapp either. The like-eyed one did not exert himself to go to Vienna – probably he did not have the money. No, quite naturally it was Rudi Schwerdtfeger, who was already on the spot and free. Moreover, he had just collaborated successfully with Adrian in their common enterprise, and his indefatigable self-confidence had been crowned with success – a success heavy with fate.

In this company, then, Adrian was received on the estate as though he were the lord of the manor come home from abroad. The two spent twelve days in stately domesticity in the dix-huitième salons and apartments of Castle Tolna, in drives through the princely estate and along the gay shores of the Plattensee, attended by an obsequious retinue, some of whom were Turks. They might use and enjoy a library in five languages; two glorious grand pianos stood on the platform of the music-room; there was a house organ and every conceivable luxury. Adrian said that in the village belonging to the property the deepest poverty prevailed and an entirely archaic, pre-revolutionary stage of development. Their guide, the manager of the estate, himself told them, with compassionate head-shakings, as a fact worth mention, that the villagers only had meat one day in the year, at Christmas, and had not even tallow candles, but literally went to bed with the chickens. To alter these shocking conditions, to which habit and ignorance had rendered those who saw them callous – for instance the indescribable filth of the village street, the utter lack of sanitation in the dwelling-hovels – would have amounted to a revolutionary deed, to which no single individual, certainly not a woman, could bring herself. But one may suspect that the sight of the village was among the things which prevented

Adrian's invisible friend from spending much time upon her own property.

But I am not the man to give more than a bare sketch of this slightly fantastic episode in my friend's austere life. I was not at his side and could not have been, even had he asked me. It was Schwerdtfeger, he could describe it. But he is dead.

Chapter Thirty-seven

I should do better to deal with this section as I did with some earlier ones: not giving it a number of its own, but treating it simply as a continuation. To go on without any marked caesura would be correct for the subject of the narrative is the same: 'the outer world', and the history of my departed friend's connexion or lack of connexion with it. At this point however, all mystery, all delicacy, all discretion are abandoned. No longer is 'the world' embodied in the figure of a shrouded tutelary goddess showering priceless symbolic gifts. In her place we have the international business man and concert agent, naïvely persistent, profuse of promises, rebuffed by no reserve, certainly superficial, yet for all that to me even an engaging type. We met him in the person of Herr Saul Fitelberg, who appeared in Pfeiffering one lovely day in late summer when I happened to be there. It was a Saturday afternoon, and Sunday morning early I was returning home as it was my wife's birthday. For at least an hour he amused Adrian and me and made us laugh; and then, with his business unaccomplished – in so far as there had been anything so concrete as business about it – he departed with complete equanimity.

It was the year 1923; one cannot say that the man had waked up very early. However, he had not waited for the Prague and Frankfurt concerts; they belonged to a future by then not very distant. But there had been Weimar, and Donaueschingen, aside from the Swiss performances of Leverkühn's youthful works: it took no extraordinary intuition to guess that here was something to prize and to promote. And the *Apocalypse* had appeared in print, and I think it quite possible that Monsieur Saul was in a position to study that work. In short, the man had picked up the scent, he wanted to make a kill, to build up a reputation, discover a genius and as his manager introduce him to a social world always and above all avid for new things. Such were the motives that led him to force his way so blandly into the retreat where genius created and suffered.

Here is how it happened: I had reached Pfeiffering early in the afternoon; Adrian and I returned soon after four from a walk in the meadows after tea and saw to our surprise an automobile standing in the courtyard by the elm tree. It was not an ordinary taxi, but more like a private car, the kind one sees, with chauffeur, out in front of an automobile business, for hire by the hour or the day. The driver, whose uniform was designed to carry the same idea, stood beside the car smoking, and as we passed him he lifted his peak cap with a broad grin, probably thinking of the jokes his amazing passenger had made on the way. Frau Schweigestill came towards us from the house, a visiting-card in her hand, and spoke in a subdued and startled voice. A man was there, she told us, a 'man of the world' – the phrase, as she whispered it, and as a rapid summing-up of a guest she had that moment clapped eyes on, had something uncannily perceptive about it, almost sibylline. Perhaps the euphemism is more understandable coupled with the other which Frau Else supplied on top of it: she called the man a crazy loon. '*Scher Madame*', was what he had called her, and after that '*petite maman*', and he had pinched Clementine's cheek. Frau Else had shut the girl into her room until the 'man of the world' should be gone. But she couldn't send him off with a flea in his ear, eh, him coming like that from Munich in a car? So there he was, waiting in the big room. With misgiving we examined the card, which gave us all the information we needed; it read: 'Saul Fitelberg. *Arrangements musicaux. Représentant de nombreux artistes prominents.*' I rejoiced that I was on the spot to protect Adrian; I should not have liked him to be delivered over alone to this '*représentant*'. We betook ourselves to the Nike room.

Fitelberg was already standing at the door, and although Adrian let me go in first, the man's whole attention was at once addressed to him. After one cursory glance at me through his horn-rimmed glasses he swung his whole plump body round to look beyond me at the man on whose account he had let himself in for the expense of a two hours' auto journey. Of course it is no great feat to distinguish between a simple high-school teacher and a man set apart by genius. But the visitor's swift orientation, his glib recognition of my unimportance despite my walking in ahead, his pounce on his proper prey – all in all, it was an impressive performance.

'Cher maître,' he began, with a smile, rattling off his speech with a harsh accent but uncommon fluency: 'Comme je suis heureux, comme je suis ému de vous trouver! Même pour un homme gâté, endurci comme moi, c'est toujours une expérience touchante de recontrer un grand homme. – Enchante, monsieur le professeur,' he added in passing as Adrian presented me, and put out his hand carelessly, turning again at once to the right address.

'Vous maudirez l'intrus, cher Monsieur Leverkühn,' said he, accenting the name on the last syllable as though it were spelt Le Vercune. 'Mais pour moi, étant une fois à Munich, c'était tout à fait impossible de manquer – oh, yes, I speak German,' he interrupted himself, with the same not unpleasant hard quality in his voice: 'Not well, not perfectly, but I can make myself understood. Du reste, je suis convaincu that you know French perhaps. Your settings to the Verlaine poems are the best evidence in the world. Mais après tout, we are on German soil – how German, how homely, how full of character! I am enchanted with the idyllic setting in which you, Maître, have been so wise as to settle down ... Mais oui, certainement, let us sit down, many thanks, a thousand thanks!'

He was a man of perhaps forty, fat, not pot-bellied but fleshy and soft in his limbs and his thick white hands; smooth-shaven, full-faced, with a double chin, strongly marked arched brows, and lively almond-shaped eyes full of southern meltingness behind the horn-rimmed glasses. His hair was thinning, but he had sound white teeth which were always visible, for he smiled all the time. He was dressed in elegant summer clothes, a waisted striped blue flannel suit and canvas shoes with yellow leather bands. Mother Schweigestill's description of him was amusingly justified by his easy manner and refreshing lightness of touch. Like his rapid-fire, slightly indistinct, always rather high-pitched voice, sometimes breaking into a treble, his airiness was peculiar to his whole bearing, counteracting the plumpness of his person, while actually, in a way, in harmony with it. I found this lightness of touch refreshing; it had become part of him, and it did actually inspire the absurdly soothing conviction that we all take life unconscionable hard. It seemed always to be saying: 'Why not? So what? Means nothing. Let's be happy!' And involuntarily one strove to chime in.

That he was anything but stupid will be evident when I repeat his conversation, which is still fresh in my mind. I shall do well to leave the word entirely to him, since whatever Adrian or I interpolated or replied played scarcely any role. We sat down at one end of the massive long table which was the chief furnishing of the peasant room: Adrian and I next to each other, our guest opposite. He did not beat about the bush very long; his hopes and intents came out quite soon.

'Maître,' said he, 'I quite understood how you must cling to the distinguished retirement of the abode you have chosen – oh, yes, I have seen it all, the hill, the pond, the village, and church, et puis cette maison pleine de dignité avec son hôtesse maternelle et vigoureuse. Madame Schweige-still! Ça veut dire: "Je sais me taire. Silence, silence!" Comme c'est charmant! How long have you lived here? Ten years? Without a break – or nearly so? C'est étonnant! But oh, how easy to understand! And still, figurez-vous, I have come to tempt you away, to betray you to a temporary unfaithfulness, to bear you on my mantle through the air and show you the kingdoms of the earth and the glory of them – or even more, to lay them at your feet ... Forgive my pompous way of talking. It is really ridiculously exagéré, especially as far as the "glories" go. It is not so grand as that, nothing so very thrilling about those glories; I am saying that who after all am the son of little people, living in very humble circumstances, really *miese*, you know, from Lublin in the middle of Poland; of really quite little Jewish parents – I am a Jew, you must know, and Fitelberg is a very ordinary, low-class, Polish-German-Jewish name; only I have made it the name of a respected protagonist of avant-garde culture, whom great artists call their friend. C'est la verité pure, simple et irréfutable. The reason is that from my youth up I have aspired to higher things, more intellectual and interesting – above all to whatever is a novelty and sensation – the scandalous today which tomorrow will be the fashion, the dernier cri, the best-seller – in short, art. A qui le dis-je? Au commencement était le scandale.

'Thank God, that lousy Lublin lies far behind me. More than twenty years I have been living in Paris – will you believe it, for a whole year I attended philosophy lectures at the Sorbonne! But à la longue they bored me. Not that philosophy couldn't be a best-seller too. It could, but for me it is too abstract. And I have a vague feeling that it is in Germany one should study metaphysics – perhaps the Herr Professor, my honoured vis-à-vis, will agree with me ... After that I had a little boulevard theatre, small, exclusive, un creux, une petite caverne for a hundred people, nommée "Théâtre des fouberies gracieuses". Isn't that a peach of a name? But what would you, the thing wasn't financially possible. So few seats, they had to be so high-priced, we had to make presents of them. We were lewd enough, I do assure you; but too high-brow too, as they say in English. James Joyce, Picasso, Ezra Pound, the Duchesse de Clermont-Tonnère – it wasn't enough of an audience. En un mot, the fourberies gracieuses had to fold up after a short season. But the experiment was not entirely without fruit, for it had put me in touch with the leaders of the artistic life of Paris, painters, musicians, writers. In Paris today – even here I may say it – beats the pulse of the living world; and in my position as director, it opened to me the doors of several aristocratic salons where all these artists gathered ...

'Perhaps that surprises you? Perhaps you will say "How did he do it? How did the little Jewish boy from Polish provinces manage to move in on these

fastidious circles, all among the *crème de la crème?*" Ah, gentlemen, nothing
easier. How quickly one learns to tie a white tie, to enter a salon with
complete nonchalance, even if it goes a few steps down and to forget the
sensation that you don't know what to do with your hands! After that you
just keep on saying "madame": "Ah, madame, O madame, que pensez-
vous, madame; on me dit, madame, que vous êtes fanatique de musique?"
That is as good as all there is to it. Believe me, from the outside these things
are exagéré.

'Enfin, I cashed in on the connexions I owed to the Fourberies, and they
multiplied when I opened my agency for the presentation of contemporary
music. Best of all, I had found myself, for as I stand here, I am a born
impresario; I can't help it, it is my joy and pride, I find my satisfaction et mes
délices in discovering talent, genius, interesting personalities, beating the
drum, making society mad with enthusiasm or at least with excitement, for
that is all they ask, et nous nous recontrons dans ce désir. Society demands to
be excited, challenged, torn in sunder for and against; it is grateful for that as
for nothing else, for the diversion and the turmoil qui fournit le sujet for
caricatures in the papers and endless, endless chatter. The way to fame, in
Paris, leads through notoriety – at a proper première people jump up several
times during the evening and yell "Insulte! Impudence! Bouffonerie
ignominieuse!" while six or seven initiates, Erik Satie, a few surréalistes,
Virgil Thomson, shout from the loges: "Quelle précision! Quel esprit! C'est
divin! C'est suprême! Bravo! Bravo!"

'I fear I shock you, messieurs – if not Monsieur Le Vercune, then perhaps
the Herr Professor. But in the first place I hasten to add that a concert
evening never yet broke down in the middle; that is not what even the most
outraged want at bottom; on the contrary they want to go on being outraged,
that is what makes them enjoy the evening, and besides, remarkable as it is,
the informed minority always command the heavier guns. Of course I do not
mean that every performance of outstanding character must go as I have
described it. With proper publicity, adequate intimidation beforehand, one
can guarantee an entirely dignified result; and in particular if one were to
present today a citizen of a former enemy nation, a German, one could count
on an entirely courteous reception from the public.

'That is indeed the sound speculation upon which my proposition, my
invitation is based. A German, un boche qui par son génie appartient au
monde et qui marche á la tête du progrès musical! That is today a most
piquant challenge to the curiosity, the broad-mindedness, the snobisme, the
good breeding of the public – the more piquant, the less this artist disguises
his national traits, his Germanisme, the more he gives occasion for the cry:
"Ah, ça c'est bien allemand, par exemple!" For that you do, cher Maître,
why not say so? You give this occasion everywhere – not so much in your
beginnings, the time of the *Phosphorescence de la mer* and your comic opera,
but later and more and more from work to work. Naturellement, you think I
have in mind your ferocious discipline, and que vous enchaînez votre art
dans un système de règles inexorables et néo-classiques, forcing it to move in
these iron bands – if not with grace, yet with boldness and esprit. But if it is
that that I mean, I mean at the same time more than that when I speak of
your qualité d'allemand; I mean – how shall I put it? – a certain four-
squareness, rhythmical heaviness, immobility, grossièreté, which are old-
German – en effet, entre nous, one finds them in Bach too. Will you take
offence at my criticism? Non, j'en suis sûr – you are too great. Your themes –
they consist almost throughout of even note values, minims, crotchets,

quavers; true enough, they are syncopated and tied but for all that they remain clumsy and unweildy, often with a hammering, machinelike effect. C'est "boche" dans un degré fascinant. Don't think I am finding fault, it is simply énormément charactéristique and in the series of concerts of international music which I am arranging, this note is quite indispensable ...

'You see, I am spreading out my magic cloak. I will take you to Paris, to Brussels, Antwerp, Venice, Copenhagen. You will be received with the intensest interest. I will put the best orchestras and soloists at your service. You shall direct the *Phosphorescence*, portions of *Love's Labour's Lost*, your Cosmologic Symphony. You will accompany on the piano your songs by French and English poets and the whole world will be enchanted that a German, yesterday's foe, displays this broad-mindedness in the choice of his texts – ce cosmopolitisme généreux et versatile! My friend Madame Maia de Strozzi-Pečič, a Croatian, today perhaps the most beautiful soprano voice in the two hemispheres, will consider it an honour to sing your songs. For the instrumental part of Keats's hymns I will engage the Flonzaley Quartet from Geneva or the Pro Arte from Brussels. The very best of the best – are you satisfied?

'What do I hear – you do not conduct? You don't? And you would not play piano? You decline to accompany your own songs? I understand. Cher Maître, je vous comprends à demi-mot! It is not your way to linger with the finished work. For you the doing of a work is its performance, it is done when it is written down. You do not play it, you do not conduct it, for you would straightway change it, resolve it in variations and variants, develop it further and perhaps spoil it. How well I understand! Mais c'est dommage, pourtant. The concerts will suffer a decided loss of personal appeal. Ah, bah, we must see what we can do. We must look about among the world-famous conductors to interpret – we shall not need to look long. The permanent accompanist of Madame de Strozzi-Pečič will take over for the songs, and if only you, Maître, are simply present and show yourself to the public, nothing will be lost, everything will be gained.

'But that is the condition – ah, non! You cannot inflict upon me the performance of your works *in absentia*. Your personal appearance is indispensable, particulièrement à Paris, where musical renown is made in three or four salons. What does it cost you to say a few times: "Tout le monde sait, madame, que votre jugement musical est infaillible?" It costs you nothing and you will have a lot of satisfaction from it. As social events my productions rank next after the premières of Diaghilev's Ballet Russe – if they do rank after them. You would be invited out every evening. Nothing harder, generally speaking, than getting into real Paris society. But for an artist nothing is easier, even if he is only standing in the vestibule to fame, I mean the sensational appeal. Curiosity levels every barrier, it knocks the exclusive right out of the field ...

'But why do I talk so much about elegant society and its itches? I can see that I am not succeeding in kindling your curiosity, cher Maître. How could I? I have not seriously been trying to. What do you care about elegant society? Entre nous, what do I care about it? For business reasons – this and that. But personally? Not that much. This milieu, this Pfeiffering and your presence, Maître, do not a little to make me realize my indifference, my contempt, for that world of frivolity and superficiality. Dites-moi donc: don't you come from Kaisersaschern on the Saale? What a serious, dignified place of origin! Well, for me, I call Lublin my birthplace – likewise a dignified spot and grey with age, from which one carries into life a fund of sévérité, un état d'âme solennel et un peu gauche . . . Ah, I am the last person to want to glorify elegant society to you. But Paris will give you the chance to make the most interesting and stimulating contacts among your brothers in Apollo, among the sons of the Muses, your aspiring colleagues and peers, painters, writers, stars of the ballet, above all musicians. The summits of European tradition and experiment, they are all my friends, and they are ready to be yours. Jean Cocteau the poet, Massine the ballet-master, Manuel de Falla the composer, Les Six, the six great ones of the new music – this whole elevated, audacious amusing, aggressive sphere, it waits only for you, you belong to it, as soon as ever you will . . .

'Is it possible that I read in your manner a certain resistance even to that? But here, cher Maître, every shyness, every embarras is really quite out of place – whatever may be the ground for such habits of seclusion. I am far from searching for grounds; that they exist is quite enough for my cultivated and I may say respectful perceptions. This Pfeiffering, ce refuge étrange et érémitique – there must be some peculiar and interesting psychological association: I do not ask, I consider all possibilities, I frankly bring them all up, even the most fantastic. Eh bien, what then? Is that a reason for embarras in a sphere where there reigns unlimited freedom from prejudice? A freedom from prejudice which for its part has its own good reasons too? Oh, la la! Such a circle of arbiters elegantiarum and society cheer-leaders is usually an assortment of demi-fous excentriques, expended souls and elderly crapules – un impresario, c'est un espèce d'infirmier, voilà!

'And now you see how badly I conduct my affair, in what utterly maladroit fashion! That I point it out is all that speaks in my favour. With the idea of encouraging you I anger your pride and work with my eyes open against my interests. For I tell myself, of course, that people like you – though I should speak not of people like you, but only of yourself – you regard your existence, your *destin* as something unique and consider it too sacred to lump it in with anyone else's. You do not want to hear about other *destinées*, only about your own, as something quite unique – I know, I understand. You abhor all generalizing, classifying, subsuming, as a derogation of your dignity. You insist on the incomparableness of the personal case. You pay tribute to an arrogant personal uniqueness – maybe you have to do that. "Does one live when others live?" I have read that question somewhere, I am not sure precisely where, but in some very prominent place. Privately or publicly you will ask it; only out of good manners and for appearance's sake do you take notice of each other if you do take notice of each other. Wolf, Brahms, and Bruckner lived for years in the same town – Vienna, that is – but avoided each other the whole time and none of them, so far as I know, ever met the others. It would have been penible too, considering their opinions of each other. They did not judge or criticize like colleagues; their comments were meant to annihilate, to leave their author alone in the field. Brahms thought as little as possible of Bruckner's symphonies, he called them huge shapeless serpents. And Bruckner's opinion of Brahms was very low. He found the first theme of the D-minor Concerto very good, but asserted that Brahms never came near inventing anything so good a second time. You don't want to know anything of each other. For Wolf Brahms meant le dernier ennui. And have you ever read his critique of Bruckner's Seventh in the Vienna *Salonblatt*? There you have his opinion of the man's importance. He charged him with "lack of intelligence" – avec quelque raison, for Bruckner was of course what one calls a simple, childlike soul, wholly given to his majestic figured-bass music

and a complete idiot in all matters of European culture. But if one happens
on certain utterances of Wolf about Dostoyevsky, in his letters, qui sont
simplement stupéfiant, one is driven to ask what kind of mind he had
himself. The text of his unfinished opera *Manuel Venegas*, which a certain
Dr Hörnes has restored, he called a wonder, Shakespearian, the height of
poetic creation, and became offensive when friends expressed their doubts.
Moreover, not satisfied with composing a hymn for male voices, *To the
Fatherland*, he wanted to dedicate it to the German Kaiser. What do you say
to that? The memorial was rejected. Tout cela est un peu embarrassant, n'est
ce pas? Une confusion tragique.

'Tragique, messieurs. I call it that, because in my opinion the unhappiness of the world rests on the disunity of the intellect, the stupidity, the lack
of comprehension, which separates its spheres from each other. Wagner
poured scorn on the picturesque impressionism of his time, calling it all
"daubs" – he was sternly conservative in that field. But his own harmonic
productions have a lot to do with impressionism, they lead up to it and as
dissonances often go beyond the impressionistic. Against the Paris daubers
he set up Titian as the true and the good. A la bonne heure! But actually his
taste in art was more likely somewhere between Piloty and Makart, the
inventor of the decorative bouquet; while Titian was more in Lenbach's
line, and Lenbach had an understanding of Wagner that made him call
Parsifal music-hall stuff – to the Master's very face. Ah, ah, comme c'est
mélancholique, tout ça!

'Gentlemen, I have been rambling frightfully. I mean I have wandered
from my subject and my purpose. Take my garrulity as an expression of the
fact that I have given up the idea that brought me here. I have convinced
myself that it is not possible. You will not set foot on my magic cloak. I am
not to introduce you to the world as your entrepreneur. You decline, and
that ought to be a bigger disappointment to me than it actually is.
Sincèrement, I ask myself whether it really is one at all. One may come to
Pfeiffering with a practical purpose in mind – but that must always take
second place. One comes, even if one is an impresario, first of all to salute a
great man. No failure on the practical side can decrease this pleasure,
especially when a good part of it consists in the disappointment. So it is, cher
Maître: your inaccessibility gives me among other things satisfaction as well;
that is due to the understanding, the sympathy which I involuntarily feel
towards it. I do so against my own interests, but I do it – as a human being, I
might say, if that were not too large a category; perhaps I ought to express
myself more specifically.

'You probably do not realize, cher Maître, how German is your ré-
pugnance, which, if you will permit me to speak en psychologue, I find
characteristically made up of arrogance and a sense of inferiority, of scorn
and fear. I might call it the ressentiment of the serious-minded against the
salon world. Well, I am a Jew, you know, Fitelberg is undeniably a Jewish
name, I have the Old Testament in my bones, a thing no less serious-minded
than being German is, and not conducive to a taste for the sphere of the
valse brillante. In Germany the superstition prevails that there is nothing
but a valse brillante outside its borders and nothing but serious-mindedness
inside them. And still, as a Jew one feels sceptical towards the world, and
leans to German serious-mindedness – at the risk, of course of getting kicked
in the pants for one's pains. To be German, that means above all to be
national – and who expects a Jew to be nationalistic? Not only that nobody
would believe him, but everybody would bash his head in for having the

impudence to try it on. We Jews have everything to fear from the German character, qui est essentiellement antisémitique; and that is reason enough, of course, for us to plump for the worldly side and arrange sensational entertainments. It does not follow that we are windbags, or that we have fallen on our heads. We perfectly well know the difference between Gounod's *Faust* and Goethe's, even when we speak French, then too ...

'Gentlemen, I say all that only out of pure resignation. On the business side, we have said everything. I am as good as gone; I have the door-handle in my hand, we have got up, I am still running on just pour prendre congé. Gounod's *Faust*, gentlemen – who turns up his nose at it? Not I, and not you, I am glad to know. A pearl – a marguerite full of the most ravishing musical inventions. Laisse-moi, laisse-moi contempler – enchanting! Massenet is enchanting, he too. He must have been particularly charming as a teacher – as professor at the Conservatoire, there are little stories about it. From the beginning his pupils in composition were urged to produce, no matter whether or not they were technically able to write a movement free from flaws. Humane, n'est-ce pas? Not German, it isn't, but humane. A lad came to him with a song just composed – fresh, showing some talent. "Tiens," says Massenet, "that is really quite nice. Listen, of course you must have a little friend; play it to her, she will certainly love it and the rest will happen of itself." It is certain what he meant by "the rest", probably various things, both love and art. Have you pupils, Master? They wouldn't be so fortunate. But you have none. Bruckner had some. He had from the first wrestled with music and its sacred difficulties, like Jacob with the angel, and he demanded the same from his pupils. Years on end they had to practise the sacred craft, the fundamentals of harmony and the strict style before they were allowed to make a song, and this music-teaching had not the faintest connexion with any little friend. A man may have a simple, childlike temperament; but music is the mysterious revelation of the highest wisdom, a divine service, and the profession of music-teacher a priestly office ...

'Comme c'est respectable! Pas précisément humain mais extrêmement respectable. Why should we Jews, who are a priestly people, even when we are minaudering about in Parisian salons, not feel drawn to the Germans and let outselves lean to the German side and an ironic view, as against the world, against art for the little friend? In us nationalism would be impertinent enough to provoke a pogrom. We are international – but we are pro-German, like nobody else in the world, simply because we can't help perceiving the role of Germany and Judaism on earth. Une analogie frappante! In just the same way they are both hated, despised, feared, envied, in the same measure they alienate and are alienated. People talk about the age of nationalism. But actually there are only two nationalisms, the German and the Jewish, and all the rest is child's play. – Is not the downright Frenchness of an Anatole France and purest cosmopolitanism alongside German isolation in the subjective and the Jewish conceit of the chosen race ... France – a nationalistic pseudonym. A German writer could not well call himself Germany, such a name one gives to a battleship. He has to content himself with German – and that is a Jewish name, oh la, la.

'Gentlemen, this is now really the door-knob. I am already outside. I must just say one more thing. The Germans should leave it to the Jews to be pro-German. With their nationalism, their pride, their foible of "differentness", their hatred of being put in order and equalized, their refusal to let themselves be introduced into the world and adopted socially, they will get into trouble, real Jewish trouble, je vous le jure. The Germans should let the

Jew be the médiateur between them and society, be the manager, the
impresario. He is altogether the right man for it, one should not turn him
out, he is international, and he is pro-German. Mais c'est en vain. Et c'est
très dommage! Am I still talking? No, I left long ago. Cher Maître, j'étais
enchanté. J'ai manqué ma mission but I am delighted. Mes respects,
monsieur le professeur. Vous m'avez assisté trop peu, mais je ne vous en
veux pas. Mille choses à Madame Schwei-ge-still. Adieu, adieu . . .'

Chapter Thirty-eight

My readers are aware that Adrian in the end complied with Rudi
Schwerdtfeger's long-cherished and expressed desire, and wrote for him a
violin concerto of his own. He dedicated to Rudi personally the brilliant
composition, so extraordinarily suited to a violin technique, and even
accompanied him to Vienna for the first performance. In its place I shall
speak about the circumstance that some months later, towards the end of
1924, he was present at the later performances in Berne and Zürich. But first
I should like to discuss with its very serious implications, my earlier,
perhaps premature – perhaps, coming from me, unfitting – critique of the
concerto. I said that it falls somewhat out of the frame of Leverkühn's
ruthlessly radical and uncompromising work as a whole. And I suggested
that this was due to a kind of concession to concert virtuosity as shown in the
musical attitude of the piece. I cannot help thinking that posterity will agree
with my 'judgement' – my God, how I hate the word! – and what I am doing
here is simply giving the psychological explanation of a phenomenon to
which the key would otherwise be lacking.

There is one strange thing about the piece: cast in three movements, it has
no key-signature, but, if I may so express myself, three *tonalities* are built
into it: B-flat major, C major, and D major, of which, as a musician can see,
the D major forms a sort of secondary dominant, the B-flat major a sub-
dominant, while the C major keeps the strict middle. Now between these
keys the work plays most ingeniously, so that for most of the time none
of them clearly comes into force but is only indicated by its proportional
share in the general sound-complex. Throughout long and complicated
sections all three are superimposed one above the other, until at last, in a way
electrifying to any concert audience, C major openly and triumphantly
declares itself. There, in the first movement, inscribed '*andante amoroso*', of
a dulcet tenderness bordering on mockery, there is a leading chord which to
my ear has something French about it: C, G, E, B-flat, D, F-sharp, A, a
harmony which, with the high of the violin above it, contains, as one sees,
the tonic chords of those three main keys. Here one has, so to speak, the soul
of the work, also one has in it the soul of the main theme of this movement,
which is taken up again in the third, a gay series of variations. In its way it is a
wonderful stroke of melodic invention, a rich, intoxicating cantilena of great
breadth, which decidedly has something showy about it, and also a
melancholy that does not lack in grace if the performer so interpret it. The
characteristically delightful thing about the invention is the unexpected and
subtly accentuated rise of the melodic line after reaching a certain high

climax, by a further step, from which then, treated in the most perfect, perhaps all too perfect taste, it flutes and sings itself away. It is one of those physically effective manifestations capturing head and shoulders, bordering on the 'heavenly', of which only music and no other art is capable. And the tutti-glorification of just this theme in the last part of the variation movement brings the bursting out into the open C major. But just before it comes a bold flourish – a plain reminiscence of the first violin part leading to the finale of Beethoven's A-minor Quartet; only that here the magnificent phrase is followed by something different, a feast of melody in which the parody of being carried away becomes a passion which is seriously meant and therefore creates a somewhat embarrassing effect.

I know that Leverkühn, before composing the piece, studied very carefully the management of the violin in Bériot, Vieux-temps, and Wieniawski and then applied his knowledge in a way half-respectful, half caricature and moreover with such a challenge to the technique of the player – especially in the extremely abandoned and virtuoso middle movement, a scherzo, wherein there is a quotation from Tartini's Devil's Trill Sonata – that the good Rudi had his work cut out to be equal to the demands upon him. Beads of sweat stood out beneath his blond locks every time he performed it, and the whites of his pretty azure eyes were bloodshot. But how much he got out of it, how much opportunity for 'flirtation' in a heightened sense of the word, lay in a work which I to the Master's very face called 'the apotheosis of salon music'! I was, of course, certain beforehand that he would not take the description amiss, but accept it with a smile.

I cannot think of that hybrid production without recalling a conversation which took place one evening at the home of the Bullinger, the Munich manufacturer. Bullinger, as we know, occupied the *bel étage* of an elegant apartment-house he had built in Wiedemayerstrasse; beneath its windows, the Isar, that uncorrupted glacial stream, purled past in its well-regulated bed. The Croesus entertained some fifteen guests at seven o'clock dinner; he kept open house, with a trained staff, and a lady housekeeper who presided with affectedly elegant manners and obviously would have liked to marry. The guests were mostly people in the financial and business world. But it was known that Bullinger loved to air his views at large in intellectual circles; and on occasion he would gather a selection of artistic and academic elements for an evening in his agreeable quarters. No one, myself included, I confess, saw any reason to despise his cuisine or the spacious amenities of his drawing-rooms as a setting for stimulating discussion.

This time the group consisted of Jeanette Scheurl, Herr and Frau Knöterich, Schildknapp, Rudi Schwerdtfeger, Zink and Spengler, Kranich the numismatist, Radbruch the publisher and his wife, the actress Zwitscher, the farce-writer from Bukovina, whose name was Binder-Majoresku, myself and my dear wife. Adrian, urged by me and also by Schildknapp and Schwerdtfeger, was there too. I do not inquire whose plea had been decisive, nor do I flatter myself in the least that it was mine. At table he sat next to Jeanette, whose society was always a comfort to him, and he saw other familiar faces about him as well; so he seemed not to regret having yielded but rather to have enjoyed the three hours of his stay. I remarked again with unspoken amusement the involuntary attention and more or less timid reverence paid to him. After all, he was only thirty-nine years old, and besides, but few of the guests present possessed enough musical knowledge for such an attitude on any rational grounds. It amused me, I say; yet gave me a pang at my heart as well. For the behaviour of these people was really due to the indescribable atmosphere of aloofness which he carried about wherever he went. In increasing degree, more and more perceptible and baffling as the years went by, it wrapped him round and gave one the feeling that he came from a country where nobody else lived.

This evening, as I said, he seemed quite comfortable; he was even conversational, which I ascribed in some degree to the effects of Bullinger's champagne-and-bitters cocktail and his wonderful Pfalz wine. Adrian talked with Spengler, who was already in wretched health, his disease having attacked his heart, and laughed with the rest of us at the clowneries of Leo Zink, who leaned back at table and covered himself with his huge damask serviette like a sheet up to his fantastic nose and folded his hands peacefully atop. Adrian was even more amused by the jester's adroitness when we were called on to look at a well-intentioned still-life by Bullinger, who dabbled in oils. To save the company the embarrassment of criticizing it, Zink examined the painting with a thousand acclamations and Good-graciouses which might mean anything and nothing; looked at it from every point of view and even turned it over and looked at the back. This gush of ecstatic yet wholly meaningless verbiage was Zink's social technique; at bottom he was not a pleasant man, and this was his way of taking part in conversations that went over his head as dilettante painter and enthusiast of carnival balls. He even practised it in the conversation I have in mind, touching the fields of aesthetics and ethics.

It developed as a sequel to some gramophone music with which the host regaled us after the coffee, as we smoked and drank liqueurs. Very good gramophone records had begun to be produced, and Bullinger played several enjoyable ones for us from his valuable cabinet; the well-recorded waltzes from the Gounod's *Faust* came first, I remember. Baptis Spengler could only criticize them on the ground that they were drawing-room music, much too elegant for folk-dances on the meadow. It was agreed that their style was more suitable in the case of the charming ball-music in Berlioz's *Symphonie fantastique* and we asked to hear a record of the latter. It was not there; but Rudi Schwerdtfeger whistled the air faultlessly, in violin timbre, pure and perfect, and laughed at the applause, shrugging his shoulder inside his coat, in the way he had, and drawing down one corner of his mouth in a grimace. By way of comparision with the French somebody now demanded something Viennese: Lanner, Johann Strauss the younger. Our host gave us willingly from his store, until a lady – it was Frau Radbruch, the publisher's wife – suggested that with all this frivolous stuff we might be boring the great composer who was present. Everybody, in concern, agreed with her; Adrian, who had not understood, asked what she had said. When it was repeated he made lively protest. In God's name no, that was all a mistake. No one could take more pleasure than he in these things – in their way they were masterly.

'You underestimate my musical education,' said he. 'In my early days I had a teacher' (he looked across at me with his deep, subtle, lovely smile) 'crammed full of the whole world of sound; a bubbling enthusiast, too much in love with every, I really mean every, organized noise, for me to have learned any contempt from him. There was no such thing as being "too good" for any sort of music. A man who knew the best, the highest and austerest; but for him music was music – if it just was music. He objected to Goethe's saying that art is concerned with the good and difficult; he held that "light" music is difficult too, if it is good, which it can be, just as well as "heavy" music. Some of that stuck by me, I got it from him. Of course I have always grasped the idea that one must be very well anchored in the good and "heavy" to take up with the "light".'

There was silence in the room. What he had said, at bottom, was that he alone had the right to enjoy the pleasant things we had been regaled with. They tried not to understand it thus, but they suspected that was what he meant. Schildknapp and I exchanged looks. Dr Kranich went 'H'm, h'm.' Jeanette Scheurl whispered '*Magnifique!*' Leo Zink's fatuous 'Jesus, Jesus!' rose above the rest, in pretended acclamation, but really out of spite. 'Genuine Adrian Leverkühn!' cried Schwerdtfeger, red in the face from one Vieille Cure after another, but also, I felt sure, out of private chagrin.

'You haven't by chance,' Adrian went on, 'Delilah's D-sharp major aria from *Sansom* by Saint-Saëns?' The question was addressed to Bullinger, who found great satisfaction in replying:

'Not have it? My dear sir, what do you think of me? Here it is – not at all "by chance", I assure you!'

Adrian answered: 'Oh, good! It came into my head, because Kretschmar, my teacher, he was an organist, a fugue-man, you must know, had a peculiarly passionate feeling for the piece, a real *faible*. He could laugh at it too, but that did not lessen his admiration, which may have concerned only the consummateness of the thing in its own genre. Listen.'

The needle touched the plate, Bullinger put down the heavy lid. Through the loud-speaker poured a proud mezzo-soprano voice, which did not much trouble about clear enunciation: you understood: '*Mon coeur s'ouvre à ta voix*' and not a great deal else. But the singing, unfortunately accompanied by a rather whining orchestra, was wonderful in its warmth, tenderness, sombre lament for happiness, like the melody, which indeed in both of the structurally similar strophes of the aria reaches its full beauty only in the middle and finishes in a way to overpower the senses, especially the second time, when the violin, now quite sonorous, emphasizes with pleasing effect the voluptuous vocal line and repeats the closing figure in delicate and melancholy postlude.

They were moved. One lady wiped an eye with her embroidered party handkerchief. 'Crazy beautiful!' said Bullinger, using a phrase now in favour among stricter connoisseurs, who rejected the sentimental 'lovely'. It might be said to be used here exactly in its right and proper place, and perhaps that was what amused Adrian.

'Well, there!' he said, laughing. 'You understand now how a serious man can be capable of adoring the thing. Intellectual beauty it has not, of course, it is typically sensual. But after all one must not blush for the sensual, nor be afraid of it.'

'And yet, perhaps,' Dr Kranich was heard to say. He spoke as always, very clearly, with distinct articulation, though wheezing with asthma. 'Perhaps, after all, in art. In this realm in fact one may, or one should, be afraid of the nothing-but-sensual; one should be ashamed of it, for, as the poet said, it is the common, the vulgar: "Vulgar is everything that does not speak to the mind and spirit and arouses nothing but a sensual interest."'

'A noble saying,' Adrian responded. 'We shall do well to let it echo for a bit in our minds before we think of anything to dispute it.'

'And what would you think of then?' the scholar wanted to know.

Adrian had made a grimace, shrugged a shoulder, as much as to say: 'I can't help the facts.' Then he replied:

'Idealism leaves out of count that the mind and spirit are by no means addressed by the spiritual alone; they can be most deeply moved by the animal sadness of sensual beauty. They have even paid homage to frivolity. Philine, after all, is nothing but a little strumpet, but Wilhelm Meister, who is not so very different from his creator, pays her a respect in which the vulgarity of innocent sensuality is openly denied.'

'His complaisance, his toleration of the questionable,' returned the numismatist, 'have never been looked on as the most exemplary traits of our Olympian's character. And one may see a danger to culture when the spirit closes its eyes to the vulgar and sensual, or even winks at them.'

'Obviously we have different opinions as to the danger.'

'You might as well say I am a coward, at once!'

'God forbid! A knightly defender of fear and censure is no coward, he is simply knightly. For myself, I would only like to break a lance for a certain breadth of view in matters of artistic morality. One grants it, or allows it, it seems to me, more readily in other arts than in music. That may be very honourable but it does seriously narrow its field. What becomes of the whole jingle-jangle if you apply the most rigorously intellectual standards? A few "pure spectra" of Bach. Perhaps nothing else audible would survive at all.'

A servant came round with whisky, beer, and soda-water on a huge tray.

'Who would want to be a spoil-sport?' said Kranich, and got a 'Bravo!' and a clap on the shoulder from Bullinger. To me, and very likely to some of the other guests, the exchange was a duel suddenly struck up between uncompromising mediocrity and painful depth of experience. But I have interpolated this scene, not only because I feel the close connexion between it and the concerto upon which Adrian was then at work, but also because even then both concerto and conversation directed my attention to the person of the young man upon whose obstinate insistence the piece had been written and for whom it represented a conquest in more than one sense of the word. Probably it is my fate to be able to speak only stiffly, dryly, and analytically about the phenomenon of love: of that which Adrian had one day characterized to me as an amazing and always somewhat unnatural alteration in the relation between the I and the not-I. Reverence for the mystery in general, and personal reverence as well, combine to close my lips or make me chary of words when I come to speak of the transformation, always in the sign of the daemonic, the phenomenon in and for itself half miraculous which negatives the singleness of the individual soul. Even so, I will show that it was a specific sharpening of my wits through my classical scholarship, an acquirement which otherwise tends rather to take the edge off one's reactions towards life, which puts me in a position to see or understand as much as I did.

There remains no doubt – I say it in all calmness – that tireless, self-confident perseverance, put off by nothing, had won the day over aloofness and reserve. Such a conquest, considering the polarity – I emphasize the word – the polarity of the partners, the intellectual antithesis between them could have only one definite character, and that, in a freakish sort of way, was what had always been sought and striven after. It is perfectly clear to me that a man of Schwerdtfeger's make-up had always, whether consciously or not, given this particular meaning and coloration to his wooing of Adrian – though of course I do not mean that it lacked nobler motives. On the contrary, the suitor was perfectly serious when he said how necessary Adrian's friendship was the fulfilment of his nature, how it would develop, elevate, improve it. But he was illogical enough to use his native gift of coquetry – and then to feel put off when the melancholy preference he aroused did not lack the signs of ironic eroticism.

To me the most remarkable and thrilling thing about all this was to see how the victim did not see that he had been bewitched. He gave himself credit for an initiative that belonged entirely to the other party, and was full of fantastic astonishment at frankly reckless and regardless advances that might better be called seduction. Yes, Adrian talked about the *miracle* of that undaunted single-mindedness, undistracted by melancholy or emotion; I have little doubt that his astonishment went back to that distant evening when Schwerdtfeger appeared in his room to beg him to come back because the party was so dull without him. And yet in these so-called miracles you could always see poor Rudi's 'higher', his free and decent characteristics as an artist, which I have repeatedly celebrated. There is a letter which Adrian at about the time of the Bullinger dinner wrote to Schwerdtfeger, who could of course have destroyed it but which, partly out of sentiment, partly as a trophy he did in fact preserve. I refrain from quoting it, merely characterizing it as a human document which affects the reader like the baring of a wound and whose painful lack of reserve the writer probably considered an uttermost hazard. It was not. And the way it proved not to be was really beautiful. At once, with all expedition, with no torturing delay, Rudi's visit to Pfeiffering followed. There were explanations, there was assurance of the profoundest gratitude; the revelation of a simple, bold, and utterly sincere bearing, zealously concerned to obviate all humiliation ... That I must commend, I cannot help it. And I suspect – and in a way approve – that on this occasion the composition and dedication of the violin concerto were decided on.

It took Adrian to Vienna. It took him, with Rudi Schwerdtfeger, to the estate in Hungary. When they returned, Rudolf rejoiced in the prerogative that up to then, from our childhood on, had been mine alone: he and Adrian were *per du*.

Chapter Thirty-nine

Poor Rudi! Brief was the triumph of your childish daemony. It had entered into a field of power far more charged with fate, far more daemonic than its own, which speedily shattered, consumed and extinguished it. Unhappy '*Du*'! It was inappropriate to the blue-eyed mediocrity that had achieved it: nor could he who so far condescended refrain from avenging the humiliation inseparable from the condescension, pleasurable though that may have been. The revenge was automatic, cold-eyed, secret. But let me tell my tale.

In the last days of 1924 the successful violin concerto was repeated in Berne and Zurich, as part of two performances of the Swiss Chamber Orchestra, whose director, Herr Paul Sacher, had invited Schwerdtfeger, on very flattering terms and with the express wish that the composer might honour the occasion with his presence. Adrian demurred, but Rudolf knew how to plead and the recent '*Du*' was strong enough to open the way for what was to come.

The concerto occupied a place in the middle of a programme including German classics and contemporary Russian music. It was performed twice: in the Hall of the Conservatorium at Berne and also in Zürich, in the

Tonhalle. Thanks to the exertions of the soloist, who gave all he had to its
execution, the piece fully asserted both its fascination and its intellectual
appeal. True, the critics remarked a certain lack of unity in the style, even in
the level of the composition, and the public too was slightly more reserved
than in Vienna. However, it not only gave the performers a lively ovation but
on both evenings insisted on the appearance of the composer, who gratified
his interpreter by appearing repeatedly hand in hand with him to acknowledge the applause. I was not present at this twice repeated unique event, the
exposure of the recluse in person to the gaze of the crowd. I was out of it. I
heard about it, however, from Jeanette Scheurl, who was in Zürich for the
second performance and also met Adrian in the private house where he and
Schwerdtfeger lodged.

It was in the Mythenstrasse, near the lake, the home of Herr and Frau,
Reiff, an elderly, wealthy, childless pair. They were friends of art, who had
always enjoyed extending hospitality to prominent artists on tour and
entertaining them socially. The husband was a retired silk-manufacturer, a
Swiss of the old democratic mould. He had a glass eye, which imparted a
rather stony expression to his bearded face and belied his character, for he
was of a lively and liberal frame and loved nothing better than playing the
gallant with prima donnas and soubrettes in his drawing-room. Sometimes
he entertained the company, not too badly, with his cello, accompanied by
his wife, who came from Germany and had once been a singer. She lacked
his sense of humour, but was the energetic, hospitable housewife personified, warmly seconding her husband's pleasure at entertaining celebrities and giving their drawing-rooms an atmosphere of unforced virtuosity.
She had in her boudoir a whole tableful of photographs of European
celebrities, gratefully dedicated to the Reiff hospitality.

Even before Schwerdtfeger's name had appeared in the papers the couple
had invited him, for as an open-handed Maecenas the old industrialist heard
sooner than ordinary people about coming musical events. They had
promptly extended the invitation to Adrian so soon as they knew he was
coming too. Their apartment was spacious, there was plenty of room for
guests; in fact on their arrival from Berne the two musicians found Jeanette
Scheurl already installed, for she came every year for a few weeks on a visit.
But it was not Jeanette Scheurl next to whom Adrian was placed at the
supper the Reiffs gave for a small circle of friends after the concert.

The master of the house sat at the head of the table, drinking orange-juice
out of wonderfully engraved crystal, and despite his staring gaze exchanging
free and easy repartee with the dramatic soprano of the municipal theatre, a
powerful female who in the course of the evening thumped herself repeatedly on the breast with her fist. There was another opera singer there, the
heroic baritone, a Balt by birth, a tall man with a booming voice, who, however, talked with intelligence. Then of course Kapellmeister Sacher, who
had arranged the concert, Dr Andreae, the regular conductor of the Tonhalle, and Dr Schuh, the excellent music-critic of the *Neue Züricher Zeitung*
– all these were present with their wives. At the other end of the table Frau
Reiff energetically presided between Adrian and Schwerdtfeger, next to
whom sat, respectively, a young, or still young professional woman, Mlle
Godeau, a French Swiss, and her aunt, a thoroughly good-natured, almost
Russian-looking old dame with a little moustache. Marie (in other words
Mlle Godeau) addressed her as '*ma tante*' or Tante Isabeau; she apparently
lived with her niece as companion and housekeeper.

It is undoubtedly incumbent on me to give a picture of the niece, since a little later, for excellent reasons, my eyes dwelt long upon her in anxious scrutiny. If ever the word 'sympathetic' was indispensable to the description of a person, it is so in the present case, when I seek to convey the picture of this woman: from head to foot, in every feature, with every word, every smile, every expression of her being, she corresponded to the tranquil, temperate, aesthetic, and moral climate purveyed by this word. She had the loveliest black eyes in the world. I will begin with them; black as jet they were, as tar, as ripe blackberries; eyes not large indeed, but with a clear and open shine from their dark depths, under brows whose fine, even line had as little to do with cosmetics as had the temperate native red of the gentle lips. There was nothing artificial, no make-up about her, no accentuation by borrowed colour. Her native genuine sweetness – the way, for instance, in which the dark-brown hair was drawn back from her brow and sensitive temples, leaving the ears free and lying heavy at the back of her neck – set its stamp on the hands as well. They were sensible and beautiful, by no means small, but slender and small-boned, the wrists encircled by the cuffs of a white silk blouse. And just so too the throat rose out of a flat white collar, slender and round like a column, crowned by the piquantly pointed oval of the ivory-tinted face. The shapely little nose was remarkable for the animation of the open nostrils. Her not precisely frequent smile, her still less frequent laugh, which always caused a certain appealing look of strain round the almost translucent region of the temples, revealed the enamel of her even, close-set teeth.

It will be seen that I seek to summon up in a spirit of painstaking love the figure of this woman whom Adrian for a short time thought to marry. It was in that white silk evening blouse which so enhanced – perhaps with intention – her brunette type that I too saw Marie for the first time. Afterwards I saw her chiefly in one of her still more becoming simple everyday and travelling costumes of dark tartan with patent-leather belt and mother-of-pearl buttons; or else in the knee-length smock which she put on over it when she worked with lead-pencils and coloured crayons at her drawing-board. She was a designer, so Adrian had been told by Frau Reiff; an artist who sketched and worked out for the smaller Paris opera and vaudeville stages, the Gaieté Lyrique, the old Théâtre du Trianon, the figurines, costumes and settings which then served as models for costumiers and decorators. The artist, a native of Nyon on Lake Geneva, lived and worked in the tiny rooms of a flat on the Ile de Paris, companioned by Tante Isabeau. Her reputation for inventiveness and industry was on the increase, as were her professional grasp of costume history and her fastidious taste. Her present visit in Zürich was a business one; and she told her neighbour on the right that in a few weeks she would be coming to Munich, where she was to create the settings for a modern comedy of manners at the Schauspielhaus.

Adrian divided his attention between her and the hostess, while opposite him the tired but happy Rudi joked with '*ma tante*'. She laughed till the tears ran down; often she leaned over with her face and shaking voice to repeat something her neighbour had just said and her niece absolutely must hear. Marie would nod and smile, obviously pleased to see her aunt so well amused; her eyes rested gratefully on the source of the old lady's enjoyment, while he in his turn did his utmost to provoke her to yet another repetition of what he had said. Mlle Godeau talked with Adrian, answering his questions about her work in Paris, about recent productions of the French ballet and opera which were only partly known to him, works by Poulenc, Auric, Rieti. They exchanged animated views on Ravel's *Daphnis et Chloé* and the *Jeux* of

Debussy, Scarlatti's music to the *Donne di buon umore* by Goldini, Cimarosa's *Il Matriminio segreto*, and *L'Education manquée* by Chabrier. For some of these Marie had designed new settings, and she made sketches on her place card to illustrate solutions for various scenic problems. Saul Fitelberg she knew – oh, of course! It was then she showed the gleaming enamel of her teeth, her voice rang out in a hearty laugh, and her temples got that lovely look of strain. Her German was effortless, with a slight, delightful foreign accent; her voice had a warm, appealing quality, it was a singing voice, a 'material' beyond a doubt. To be specific, not only was it like Elsbeth Leverkühn's in colour and register but sometimes one really might think, as one listened, that one heard the voice of Adrian's mother.

But a company of fifteen people, like this one, usually breaks up on rising from table into groups and makes fresh contacts. Adrian scarcely exchanged a word after supper with Marie Godeau. Sacher, Andreae, and Schuh, with Jeanette Scheurl, engaged him in a long conversation about Zürich and Munich musical events, while the Paris ladies, with the opera singers, the host and hostess, and Schwerdtfeger, sat at the table with the priceless Sèvres service and with amazement watched the elderly Herr Reiff empty one cup of strong coffee after another. He declared in his impressive Swiss German that he did it by his doctor's advice, to strengthen his heart and make him fall asleep more easily. The three house guests retired soon after the departure of the rest of the company. Mlle Godeau was staying for several days with her aunt at Hotel Eden au Lac. When Schwerdtfeger, who was to accompany Adrian the next morning to Munich, bade them good-bye, he expressed a lively hope of seeing them there later. Marie waited a moment, until Adrian echoed the wish, and then pleasantly reciprocated.

The first weeks of June 1925 had gone by when I read in the paper that my friend's attractive Zürich table partner had arrived in our capital and with her aunt was staying in Pension Gisela in Schwabing; not by chance, for Adrian told me he had recommended it to her. He had stopped there for a few days on his return from Italy. The Schauspielhaus, in order to arouse interest in the coming première, had given publicity to the news of her arrival; it was at once confirmed to us by an invitation from the Schlaginhaufens to spend the next Saturday evening with them to meet the well-known stage designer.

I cannot describe the suspense with which I looked forward to this meeting. Curiosity, pleasurable expectation, apprehension, mingled in my mind and resulted in profound excitement. Why? Not – or not only – because Adrian on his return from Switzerland had told me among other things of his meeting with Marie and had given me a description of her which, as a simple statement, included the likeness of her voice to his mother's and in other ways besides had made me prick up my ears. Certainly it was no enthusiastic portrayal, on the contrary his words were quiet and casual, his manner unembarrassed, he talked looking off into the room. But that the meeting had made an impression on him was clear, if only because he knew Marie's first and her last name. And we know that in society he seldom knew the name of the person he spoke with. Of course he did much more than merely mention her, besides.

But that was not all that caused my heart to beat so strangely in joy and fear. On my next visit to Pfeiffering, Adrian let fall remarks to the effect that he had now lived here a very long time. He might possibly make changes in his outward life; at least he might soon put an end to his hermit state: he was considering matters, and so on. In short you could interpret his remarks only as an intention to marry. I had the courage to ask whether his hints were connected with a certain social event in Zürich; to that he replied:

'Who can prevent you from making guesses? Anyhow this cabined, cribbed, confined space is not at all the right theatre. If I mistake not, it was on Mount Zion, back home, that you once made me similar revelations. We ought to climb up to the Rohmbühel for this conversation.'

Imagine my astonishment!

'My dear friend,' said I, 'this is a sensation, it is thrilling.'

He advised me to moderate my transports. He would soon be forty; that he thought was warning enough not to put off the step. I was not to ask any more questions. I would see in good time. I did not conceal from myself my joy that this new idea meant the severance of the impish and anomalous bond with Schwerdtfeger; I rejoiced to interpret it as a conscious means to that end. How the fiddler and whistler would take it was a minor matter, which did not unduly upset me since Schwerdtfeger had already, with the concert, arrived at the goal of his childish ambition. After that triumph, I thought, he would be ready to take a more reasonable place in Adrian Leverkühn's life. But what I was revolving in my mind was my friend's singular way of speaking of his intention as though its realization depended on himself alone; as though he did not need to give a thought to the girl's consent. I was more than ready to approve a self-confidence so strong as to assume that it needed only to choose, only to make known its choice. And yet I did feel some trepidation at this *naïveté*, it seemed to me like another manifestation of that remoteness and other-worldness he carried about like an aura. Against my will, I doubted whether this man was made to win the love of women. If I were quite candid with myself, I even doubted that he believed it himself. I thought perhaps he struggled against the feeling and purposely so put it as though his success were a matter of course. Whether the woman of his choice had so far any inkling of his feelings and plans remained obscure.

It remained obscure so far as I was concerned even after the evening party in the Briennerstrasse where I first met Marie Godeau. How much I liked her will be clear from the description I gave above. Not only the mild dark depth of her eyes – and I knew what an appeal that must make to Adrian's sensibilities – her delightful smile, her musical voice; not only these won me to her, but also the friendly and intelligent seriousness of her character, the directness so far above all cooing femininity, the decision, even the bluntness of the independent, capable woman. It rejoiced me to think of her as Adrian Leverkühn's life-partner; I could well understand the feeling she gave him. Did not 'the world' come near to him in her, the world from which he shrank – and, in an artistic and musical sense, that part of the world which was outside Germany? And it came in the most serious, friendly guise, awakening confidence, promising fulfilment, encouraging him to abandon his recluse state. Did he not love her out of his own world of musical theology, oratorio, mathematical number-magic? It gave me hope, it excited me, to see these two human beings together in one room, although in fact they were not together for long at a time. Once a shift in the grouping brought Marie, Adrian, myself and another person together, when I removed myself almost at once in the hope that the other person would take the hint and move off too.

The affair at the Schlaginhaufens' was not a dinner but a nine-o'clock evening company with a buffet in the dining-room next the salon. The picture had changed considerably since the war. There was no Baron Riedesel to represent the claims of the 'graceful' in art: that piano-playing cavalry officer had disappeared through history's trapdoor. Herr von Gleichen-Russwurm, the descendant of the poet Schiller, was not there either. He had been convicted of attempted conspiracy to defraud and been retired from the world to a sort of voluntary arrest on his Bavarian estate. His scheme had been consummately ingenious, as well as sheerly crazy and incredible besides. The Baron had insured a piece of jewellery for a sum higher than its value, and had then ostensibly sent it, carefully packed, to be reset by a jeweller in another city. When the packet arrived, there was nothing found in it but a dead mouse. This mouse had most incompetently failed to perform the task expected of it by the sender. Obviously the idea had been to have it gnaw through the wrappings and get away, leaving the conclusion to be drawn that the parcel had somehow got a hole in it through which the valuable piece had fallen out and got lost. The insurance would then have been due. But the wretched little animal had died without making the hole that was to have explained the absence of the jewel. And the inventor of this ingenious knavery was most comically exposed. Possibly he had got the idea from some book on the history of culture and fallen victim to his own erudition. Or again, the confusion in moral standards prevailing at the time may have been responsible for his freakish inspiration.

Our hostess, née von Plausig, had had by now to resign herself to the loss of many things, among them the idea of bringing art and aristocracy together in her salon. The presence of some former ladies of the court, talking French with Jeanette Scheurl, reminded one of old times. Otherwise, mingling among the stars of the theatre one saw this or that deputy of the Catholic People's party and a few higher and not so high functionaries of the new state. Some of them were people of family, such as a certain Herr von Stengel, indefatigably jolly and ready for anything. But there were other elements, anathema in word and deed to the 'liberalistic' republic, whose intention to avenge the German 'shame', their conviction that they represented a coming world, was written large on their brows.

Well, it is always like that: an observer might have found that I spent more time with Marie Godeau and her good Tantchen than Adrian did, who doubtless was there on her account. He had greeted her at once with obvious pleasure, but after that spent most of his time with his dear Jeanette and the Social-Democratic member, a serious and knowledgeable admirer of Bach. My own conduct was natural after all that Adrian had confided to me, quite aside from the attractiveness of the object. Rudi Schwerdtfeger was there too; Tante Isabeau was enchanted to see him again. He made her laugh – and Marie smile – as he had in Zürich, but did not interrupt a sedate conversation we had about Paris and Munich events in the world of art, also political and European ones, relations between France and Germany; just at the end for a few minutes Adrian joined our group, standing. He always had to catch the eleven-o'clock train to Waldshut, and his stay that evening had lasted scarcely an hour and a half. The rest of us remained a little longer.

This was, as I said, on Saturday evening. Some days later, on a Thursday, I heard from him by telephone.

Chapter Forty

He called me up in Freising and said he wanted to ask a favour of me. His voice was level and subdued, indicating headache. He had the feeling, he said, that one should do the honours of Munich a bit for the ladies in Pension Gisela. The idea was to offer them an excursion into the country, just now at its best in this beautiful winter weather. He made no claim to have originated the plan, it had come from Rudi Schwerdtfeger. But he had taken it up and thought it over. They had been considering Füssen and Neu-Schwanstein. But perhaps Oberammergau would be even better, with a sledge from there to Ettal; he personally was fond of the cloister, and they might drive by way of Linderhof, also a curiosity worth seeing. What did I think?

I said I thought the idea and also the choice of Ettal were excellent.

'Of course you must both come with us,' he said, 'you and your wife. We'll make it a Saturday – so far as I know you have no classes on Saturday this semester. Let us say a week from the day after tomorrow unless there is too big a thaw. I have told Schildknapp already; he is mad about that sort of thing and wants to go on skis and be drawn by the sledge.'

I said I thought all that was capital.

He wanted to make this much clear, he went on. The plan, as he had said, was originally Schwerdtfeger's, but I would probably understand his, Adrian's, wish that they should not get that impression in Pension Gisela. He would not like to have Rudolf invite them, but rather laid stress on doing it himself, though even so not too directly. Would I be so good as to wangle the thing for him in such a way that before my next visit to Pfeiffering, in other words the next day but one, I called upon the ladies in their pension and in a sense as his messenger, if only by inference, brought them the invitation?

'You would be obliging me very much by this friendly service,' he ended with a curious formality.

I began to put some questions in my turn, but then suppressed them and simply promised him to carry out his wish, assuring him that I was very much pleased with the enterprise, for him and for all of us. So I was. I had already seriously asked myself how the intentions he had confided to me were to be furthered and things set going. It did not seem advisable just to leave to chance further occasions for meeting with the woman of his choice. The situation did not afford a very wide margin, it had to be helped out, there was need of initiative – and here it was. Was the idea really Schwerdtfeger's, or had Adrian merely put it off on him out of shyness at assuming quite contrary to his nature the role of a lover, and suddenly taking thought for social affairs and sleighing-parties? All this seemed to me so much beneath his dignity that I wished he had told the truth rather than make the fiddler responsible for the idea; yet I could not quite suppress the question whether our pixy platonist might not have had a hand in the enterprise.

But as for questions, after all I had but one: why did Adrian – if he wanted to let Marie know that he was making plans in order to see her – not address himself to her direct, ring her up, even go to Munich, call on the ladies and put his plans before them? I did not know then that what was involved was a tendency, an idea, in a way a sort of rehearsal for something to come later; a pattern, I mean, of sending to the beloved – for that is what I must call her – and leaving it to someone else to speak to her.

The first time it was I to whom he entrusted the message, and I readily performed my office. Then it was that I saw Marie in the white smock she wore over the collarless plaid blouse, and very well it became her. I found her at her drawing-board, a flat, heavy piece of wood set up at a slant, with an electric light fastened to it. She rose to greet me. We sat perhaps twenty minutes in the little sitting-room. Both ladies proved receptive to the attention shown to them, and welcomed with enthusiasm the plan for an excursion, of which I only said that I had not originated it – and after dropping the remark that I was on the way to my friend Leverkühn. They said that without such gallant escorts they might probably have never seen anything of the famous environment of Munich or the Bavarian Alps. The day was fixed on, the time of meeting. I was able to bring Adrian a gratifying report; I made it quite circumstantial, weaving into it praises of Marie's appearance in her working smock. He thanked me in the words, spoken so far as I could hear without humour:

'Well, you see, it is a good thing after all to have reliable friends.'

The railway line to the village of the Passion Play is for most of the distance the same as the Garmisch-Partenkirchen line, only branching off at the end. It goes through Waldshut and Pfeiffering. Adrian lived halfway to our goal, so it was only the rest of us, Schwerdtfeger, Schildknapp, the guests from Paris, and my wife and myself who forgathered at about ten in the morning at the station in Munich. Without Adrian we covered the first hour through the flat and frozen countryside, beguiling the time with sandwiches and red wine brought by my wife. Schildknapp made us all laugh by his exaggerated eagerness to get as much as the rest: 'Don't make the long fellow come short,' he clamoured in English, using a nickname he went by among us. His natural, unconcealed, and amusingly parodied fear of not getting enough to eat was irresistibly comic; with goggling eyes he chewed a tongue sandwich in imitation of a starving man. All these jests were unmistakably for Mlle Godeau's benefit; he liked her, of course, as much as the rest of us did. She was wearing a most becoming olive-green winter costume, trimmed with bands of brown fur. A sort of suggestibility in my nature, simply because I knew what was toward, tempted me to revel again and again in the sight of her eyes, the pitch-black, coal-black, merry gleam between the darkness of her lashes.

When Adrian joined us, greeted with shouts by our high-spirited group, I got a sudden start – if that is the right word for my feelings, and truly there was something startling about them. We were sitting at close quarters, not in a compartment but in an open section of a second-class coach of a through train. Thus Adrian had under his own eyes the whole range of blue and black and like-coloured ones: attraction and indifference, stimulation and equability, there they all were and would remain for the whole day, which thus stood in a way in the sign of this constellation, perhaps ought to stand in it, that the initiated might recognize therein the real idea of the excursion.

There was a natural fitness in the fact that after Adrian joined us the landscape began to rise and the mountain scenery under snow, though still at some distance, to come into view. Schildknapp distinguished himself by knowing the names of this or that ridge or wall. The Bavarian Alps boast no august or awe-inspiring giants. Yet in their pure white dress they afforded a scene of glorious winter splendour, mounting bold and austere between wooded gorge and wide expanse as we wound among them. The day, however, was cloudy, inclined to frost and snow, and was to clear only towards evening. Our attention even in the midst of conversation was mostly given to the view. Marie led the talk to their common experience in Zürich, the evening in the Tonhalle and the violin concerto. I looked at Adrian talking with her. He had sat down on the opposite bench; she was between Schildknapp and Schwerdtfeger, while Tantchen chattered good-naturedly with Helene and me. I could see that he had to guard himself as he gazed at her face, her black eyes. With his blue ones Rudolf looked on, watched Adrian's absorption, and then saw how he checked himself and turned away. Did he feel recompensed by the praises that Adrian was singing in his behalf? Marie had modestly refrained from any expression of opinion about the music; so they spoke only of the performance, and Adrian emphatically declared that even with the soloist himself sitting opposite, he could not refrain from calling his playing masterly, consummate, simply incomparable. He added a few cordial, even glowing words about Rudi's artistic development in general and his undoubtedly great future.

The man thus spoken of seemed to disclaim the praise; he said: 'Now, now!' and '*Tu' di fei halten,*' and protested that the Master was exaggerating frightfully; but he was red with pleasure. Not a doubt but he was overjoyed to have himself praised to the skies in Marie's hearing; but his delight in the fact that it was Adrian who extolled him was just as manifest, and his gratitude expressed itself in admiration of Adrian's way of speaking. Marie had heard and read about the part performance of the *Apocalypse* in Prague, and she asked about the work. Adrian put her off.

'Let us,' he said, 'not speak of these pious peccadilloes!' Rudi was enchanted.

'Pious peccadilloes!' he repeated, in ecstasy. 'Did you hear that? The way he talks! How he knows how to use words! He is masterly, our Master!'

And he pressed Adrian's knee. He was one of those people who always have to touch and feel – the arm, the shoulder, the elbow. He did it even to me, and also to women, most of whom did not dislike it.

In Oberammergau our little party walked about through the spick and span village, admiring the quaint peasant houses with their rich ornament of carven balconies and ridge-poles; distinguishing those of the Apostles, the Saviour, and the Mother of God. While they climbed the near-by Calvarienberg I left them for a little while to find a livery stable I knew and engage a sledge. I joined them for dinner at an inn that had a glass dance-floor lighted from beneath and surrounded by little tables. During the theatre season it was doubtless crowded with foreigners; now, to our satisfaction, it was almost empty. There were only two groups of other guests: at one table an invalidish gentleman with a nursing sister in attendance, at the other a party of young folk come out for the winter sports. From a platform an orchestra of five instruments dispensed light music; they displeased no one by the long intervals they made between the pieces. What they played was trivial and they played even that badly and haltingly. After our roast fowl Rudi Schwerdtfeger could stand it no longer and made up his mind to let his light shine, as it says in the Good Book. He took the violinist's fiddle away from him, and after turning it round in his hands and seeing where it came from, he improvised magnificently on it, weaving in, to the amusement of our party, some snatches from the cadenza of 'his' concerto. The orchestra stood open-mouthed. Then he asked the pianist, a weary-eyed youth who had certainly dreamed of something higher than his present occupation, if he could accompany Dvořàk's *Humoresque*, and on the mediocre fiddle played the popular piece, with its many grace notes, charming glides, and pretty double stopping; so pertly and brilliantly that he won loud applause from everybody in the place, ourselves and the neigh-bouring tables, the amazed musicians, and the two waiters as well.

It was after all a stereotyped pleasantry, as Schildknapp jealously muttered in my ear; but charming and dramatic too, in short 'nice', in perfect Rudi Schwerdtfeger style. We stayed longer than we meant, the other guests having left, over our coffee and gentian brandy. We even had a little dance ourselves, on the glass floor: Schildknapp and Schwerdtfeger dancing by turns with Mlle Godeau and my good Helene, God knows what sort of dance, under the benevolent eye of the three who refrained. The sledge was waiting outside, a roomy one with a pair of horses and well provided with fur rugs. I took the place next the coachman and Schildknapp made good his threat of being dragged on skis behind us – the driver had brought a pair. The other five found comfortable quarters in the body of the vehicle. It was the most happily planned part of the programme, aside from the fact that Rüdiger's virile enterprise miscarried. Standing in the icy wind, dragged over all the bumps in the road, showered with snow, he caught cold in his most sensitive place and fell victim to one of his intestinal catarrhs, which kept him in bed for days. Of course this misfortune was only revealed afterwards. I, for my part, love to be borne along, snugly wrapped and warm, to the subdued chiming of the bells, through the pure, sharp, frosty air; so it seemed to me that everybody else felt the same. To know that behind me Adrian and Marie were sitting looking into each other's eyes made my heart beat with a mixture of curiosity, joy, concern, and fervent hope.

Linderhof, the small rococo castle of Ludwig II, lies among woods and mountains in a remote solitude of splendid beauty. Never was there a more fairy-tale retreat for a misanthropic monarch. But despite all the enthusiasm induced by the magic of the locality, we felt put off by the taste which that prince displayed in his ceaseless itch to build, in reality an expression of the compulsion to glorify his regal estate. We stopped at Linderhof and guided by the castellan went through the sumptuous overladen little rooms which formed the 'living-apartments' of the fantastic abode. There the mad monarch spent his days, consumed with the idea of his own majesty; von Bülow played to him, and he listened to the beguiling voice of Kainz. In the castles of princes the largest room is usually the throne-room. Here there is none. Instead there is the bedchamber, of a size very striking compared with the smallness of the living-rooms. The state bed, raised solemnly on a dais and looking rather short on account of its exaggerated width, is flanked like a bier with gold candelabra.

With due and proper interest, if with some private head-shaking, we took it all in and then under a brightening sky continued on our way to Kloster Ettal, which has a solid architectural reputation on account of its Benedictine Abbey and baroque church. I recall that as we drove and later while we took our evening meal in the cleanly hotel opposite the cloister we talked at length about the 'unhappy' King (why, really, unhappy?) into whose eccentric sphere we had penetrated. The discussion was intermitted only by a visit to the church; it was in the main a controversy between Rudi

Schwerdtfeger and me over the so-called madness, the incapacity for reigning, the dethronement and legal restraint of Ludwig. To Rudi's great astonishment I pronounced all that unjustifiable, a brutal piece of philistinism, and in addition a political move in the interest of the succession.

Rudi took his stand on the interpretation, not so much popular as bourgeois and official, that the King was 'completely crackers' as he put it. It had been absolutely necessary for the sake of the country to turn him over to psychiatrists and keepers and set up a mentally sound regency. He, Rudolf, did not understand why there should be any question about it. In the way he had when some point of view was completely new to him, he bored his blue eyes into my right and my left in turn as I spoke and his lips curled angrily. I must say that I surprised even myself by the eloquence which the subject aroused in me, although before that day I had scarcely given it a thought. I found that unconsciously I had formed quite decided opinions. Insanity, I explained, was an ambiguous conception, used quite arbitrarily by the average man, on the basis of criteria very much open to question. Very early, and in close correspondence with his own averageness, the philistine established his personal standards of 'reasonable' behaviour. What went beyond those norms was insanity. But a sovereign King, surrounded by devotion, dispensed from criticism and responsibility, licensed, in support of his dignity, to live in a style forbidden to the wealthiest private man, could give way to such fantastic tastes and tendencies; to the gratification of such baffling passions and desires, such nervous attractions and repulsions, that a haughty and consummate exploitation of them might very easily look like madness. To what mortal below this regal elevation would it be given to create for himself, as Ludwig had done, gilded solitudes in chosen sites of glorious natural beauty! These castles, certainly, were monuments of royal misanthropy. But if we are hardly justified in considering it a symptom of mental aberration when a man of average equipment avoids his fellows, why then should it be allowable to do so when the same taste is able to gratify itself on a regal scale?

But six learned professional alienists had established the insanity of the King and declared the necessity for his internment.

Those compliant alienists had done what they did because they were called on to do it. Without ever seeing Ludwig, without having examined him even according to their own methods, without ever having spoken a word to him. A conversation with him about music and poetry would just as well have convinced those idiots of his madness. On the basis of their verdict this man was deprived of the right to dispose of his own person, which doubtless departed from the normal, though it by no means followed that he was mad. They degraded him to the status of a patient, shut him up in his castle by the lake, unscrewed the door-knobs and barred the windows. He had not put up with it, he had sought freedom or death and in death had taken his doctor-jailer with him: that was evidence of his sense of dignity, but no convincing proof of the diagnosis of madness. Nor did the bearing of his entourage speak for it, they having been ready to fight on his behalf; nor the fanatical love of the peasants, eager to die for their 'Kini'. When they had seen him driving through his mountains, at night, alone, wrapped in furs, in a golden sledge with outriders, in the gleam of torches, they had seen no madman, but a King after their own rude romantic hearts. And if he had succeeded in swimming across the lake, as he had obviously meant to do, they would have come to his rescue on the other side with pitchforks and flails against all the medicos and politicians in the world.

But his frantic extravagance was a definite sign of an unbalanced mind; it had become intolerable; and his powerlessness to govern had followed upon his unwillingness to govern: he had merely dreamed his kingship, refusing to exercise it in any normal form. In such a way no state can survive.

'Oh, nonsense, Rudolf. A normally contructed minister-president can govern a modern federated state even if the king is too sensitive to stand the sight of his and his colleagues' faces. Bavaria would not have been ruined even if they had gone on letting Ludwig indulge in his solitary hobbies, and the extravagance of a king meant nothing, it was just words, a pretext and swindle. The money stayed in the country and stonemasons and gold-beaters got rich on his fairy palaces. More than that, the estates had paid for themselves over and over, with the entrance fees drawn from the romantic curiosity of two hemispheres. We ourselves had today contributed to turn the madness into good business ... Why, I don't understand you, Rudolf,' I cried. 'You open your mouth in astonishment at my apologia, but I am the one who has the right to be surprised at you and not to understand how you, precisely you – I mean as an artist, and anyhow, just you ...'

I sought for words to explain why I was surprised, and found none. My eloquence faltered; and all the time I had the feeling that it was an impropriety for me to hold forth like that in Adrian's presence. He should have spoken. And yet perhaps it was better that I did it; for my mind misgave me lest he be capable of agreeing with Schwerdtfeger. I had to prevent that by speaking myself, in his proper spirit. I thought Marie Godeau was also taking my action in that sense, regarding me, whom he had sent to her about the day's excursion, as his mouthpiece. For she looked at him while I was working myself up, as though she were listening to him and not to me. For his part, indeed, he had an enigmatic smile on his lips, a smile that was far from confirming me as his representative.

'What is truth?' he said at last. And Rüdiger Schildknapp chimed in at once, asserting that truth had various aspects, of which in the present case the medical and practical were perhaps not the highest ones, yet even so could not quite be brushed aside. In the naturalistic view of truth, he added, the dull and the melancholy were remarkably enough united. That was not to be taken as an attack on 'our Rudolf', who certainly was not melancholic; but it might pass as a characterization of a whole epoch, the nineteenth century, which had exhibited a distinct tendency to both dullness and gloom. Adrian laughed – not of course, out of surprise. In his presence one had always the feeling that all the ideas and points of view made vocal round about him were present in himself; that he, ironically listening, left it to the individual human constitutions to express and represent them. The hope was expressed that the young twentieth century might develop a more elevated and intellectually a more cheerful temper. Then the conversation split up and exhausted itself in disjointed speculation on the signs, if any, that this might come to pass. Fatigue began to set in, following on all our activity in the wintry mountain air. The time-table too put in its word, we summoned our driver, and under a brilliantly starry sky drove to the little station and waited on the platform for the Munich train.

The homeward journey was a quiet one, if only out of respect for the slumbering Tantchen. Schildknapp now and then made a low-voiced remark to Mlle Godeau. I reassured myself, in conversation with Schwerdtfeger, that he had taken nothing amiss. Adrian talked commonplaces with Helene. Against all expectation and to my unspoken gratification and amusement, he did not leave us in Waldshut but insisted on accompanying our Paris guests back to Munich and their pension. The rest of us said good-bye at the station and went our ways, while he escorted aunt and niece in a taxi to their pension – a chivalrous act which in my eyes had the meaning that he spent the last moments of the declining day only in the company of the black eyes.

The usual eleven-o'clock train bore him back to his modest retreat, where from afar off he announced his coming by the high notes of his pipe to the watchful and prowling Kaschperl-Suso.

Chapter Forty-one

My sympathetic readers and friends: let me go on with my tale. Over Germany destruction thickens. Rats grow fat on corpses housed in the rubble of our cities; the thunder of the Russian cannon rolls on towards Berlin; the crossing of the Rhine was child's play to the Anglo-Saxons; our own will seems to have united with the enemy's to make it that. 'An end is come, the end is come, it watcheth for thee, behold it is come. The morning is come unto thee, O thou that dwellest in the land.' But let me go on. What happened between Adrian and Rudi Schwerdtfeger only two days after that so memorable excursion, what happened and how it happened – I know, let the objection be ten times raised that I could not know it because I was not there. No, I was not there. But today it is psychological fact that I was there, for whoever has lived a story like this, lived it through, as I have lived this one, that frightful intimacy makes him an eye- and ear-witness even to its hidden phases.

Adrian phoned and asked the companion of his Hungarian journey to come to him at Pfeiffering. He must come as soon as possible, for the matter was pressing. Rudolf was always compliant. He received the summons at ten in the morning – during Adrian's working hours, in itself an unusual event – and by four in the afternoon the violinist was on the spot. He was to play that evening at a subscription concert by the Zapfenstösser orchestra – Adrian had never once thought of it.

'You ordered me,' Rudolf said, 'what's up?'

'I'll tell you at once,' answered Adrian. 'But the great thing is that you are here. I am glad to see you, even more than usual. Remember that!'

'A golden frame for whatever you have to say,' responded Rudi, with a wonderfully flowery turn of phrase.

Adrian suggested that they should take a walk, one talked better walking. Schwerdtfeger agreed with pleasure, only regretting that he had not much time, he had to be at the station for the six-o'clock train, so as not to be late for his concert. Adrian struck his forehead and begged pardon for his forgetfulness. Perhaps Rudi would find it more understandable when he heard what he had to say.

It was thawing. The snow where it had been shovelled was melting and settling; the paths were beginning to be slushy; the friends wore their overshoes, Rudolf had not even taken off his short fur jacket, and Adrian had put on his camel's-hair ulster. They walked towards the Klammerweiher and round its banks. Adrian asked what the evening programme was to be. 'Again Brahms's First as *pièce de résistance* – again the "Tenth Symphony"?

Well, you should be pleased: you have some good things in the adagio.'
Then he related that as a lad beginning piano, long before he knew anything
about Brahms, he had invented a motif almost identical with the highly
romantic horn theme in the last movement, though without the rhythmical trick of the dotted quaver following the semiquaver, but melodi-
cally in the same spirit.

'Interesting,' said Schwerdtfeger.

'Well, and our Saturday excursion?' Had he enjoyed himself? Did he
think the others had?

'Could not have gone off better,' declared Rudolf. He was sure that
everybody remembered the day with pleasure, except probably
Schildknapp, who had overdone himself and was now ill in bed. 'He is
always too ambitious when ladies are present.' Anyhow, he, Rudolf, had no
reason to be sympathetic, for Rüdiger had been rather rude to him.

'He knows you can take a joke.'

'So I can. But he did not need to rub it in like that after Serenus had borne
down so hard with his loyalist propaganda.'

'He is a schoolmaster. We have to let him instruct and correct.'

'With red ink, yes. At the moment I feel quite indifferent to both of them –
now I am here and you have something to tell me.'

'Quite right. And when we talk about the excursion we are actually on the
subject – a subject about which you could oblige me very much.'

'Oblige you?'

'Tell me, what do you think of Marie Godeau?'

'The Godeau? Everybody must like her – surely you do too?'

'Like is not quite the right word. I will confess to you that ever since
Zürich she has been very much in my mind, quite seriously, so that it is hard
to bear the thought of the meeting as a mere episode, after which she will go
away and I may never see her again. I feel as though I should like – as though
I must – always see her and have her about me.'

Schwerdtfeger stood still and looked at the speaker, first in the one eye and
then in the other.

'Really?' said he, going on again, with bent head.

'It is true,' Adrian assured him. 'I am sure you won't take it ill of me for
confiding in you. It is precisely because I feel I can rely on you.'

'You may rely on me,' Rudolf murmured.

Adrian went on:

'Look at it humanly speaking. I am getting on in years – I am by now forty.
Would you, as my friend, want me to spend the rest of my life in this cloister?
Consider me, I say, as a human being who suddenly realizes, with a sort of
pang at the lateness of the hour, that he would like a real home, a companion
congenial in the fullest sense of the word; in short, a warmer and more
human atmosphere round him. Not only for the sake of comfort, to be better
bedded down; but most of all because he hopes to get from it good and fine
things for his working energy and enthusiasm, for the human content of his
future work.'

Schwerdtfeger was silent for a few paces. Then he said in a depressed
tone:

'You've said human and human being four times. I've counted. Frankness
for frankness: something shrinks together inside me, it makes me squirm
when you use the word as you do use it in reference to yourself. It sounds so
incredibly unsuitable – yes, humiliating, in your mouth. Excuse me saying
so. Has your music been inhuman up till now? Then it owes its greatness to

its inhumanity. Forgive the simplicity of the remark, but I would not want to hear any humanly inspired work from you.'

'No? You really mean that? And yet you have already three times played one before the public? And had it dedicated to you? I know you are not saying cruel things to me on purpose. But don't you think it's cruel to let me know that only out of inhumanity I am what I am and that humanity is not becoming to me? Cruel, and thoughtless – anyhow cruelty always comes of thoughtlessness. That I have nothing to do with humanity, may have nothing to do with it, that is said to me by the very person who had the amazing patience to win me over for the human and persuaded me to say *du*; the person in whom for the first time in my life I found human warmth.'

'It seems to have been a temporary makeshift.'

'And suppose it were? Suppose it were a matter of getting into practice, a preliminary stage, and none the less worth while for all that? A man came into my life; by his heartfelt holding out he overcame death – you might really put it like that. He released the human in me, taught me happiness. It may never be known or be put in any biography. But will that diminish its importance, or dim the glory which in private belongs to it?'

'You know how to turn things very flatteringly for me.'

'I don't turn them, I just state them as they are.'

'Anyhow, we are not speaking of me but of Marie Godeau. In order always to see her and have her about you, as you say, you must take her for your wife.'

'That is my wish and hope.'

'Oh! Does she know?'

'I am afraid not. I am afraid I do not command the means of expression to bring my feelings and desires home to her. It embarrasses me to play the languishing swain in the company of others.'

'Why don't you go to see her?'

'Because I shrink from the idea of coming down on her with confessions and offers when on account of my awkwardness she has probably not the faintest idea of my feelings. In her eyes I am still the interesting recluse. I dread her failure to understand and the hasty repulse that might be the result.'

'Why don't you write to her?'

'Because it might embarrass her even more. She would have to answer, and I don't know if she is good at writing. What pains she would have to take to spare me if she had to say no! And how it would hurt me! I dread the abstractness of an exchange like that – it strikes me it could be a danger to my happiness. I don't like to think of Marie, alone, by herself, uninfluenced by any personal contact – I might almost say personal pressure – having to write an answer to a written proposal. You see, I am afraid of both ways: the direct attack and the approach by letter.'

'Then what way do you see?'

'I told you that in this difficult situation you could be a great help to me. I would send you to her.'

'Me?'

'You, Rudi. Would it seem so absurd to you if you were to consummate your service to me – I am tempted to say to my salvation – by being my mediator, my agent, my interpreter between me and life, my advocate for happiness? Posterity might not hear of it – again, perhaps it might. It is an idea of mine, an inspiration, the way something comes when you compose. You must always assume beforehand that the inspiration is not altogether new. What is there in notes themselves, that is altogether new? But the way it looks just here, in this light, in this connexion, something that has always been there may be new, new-alive, one might say; original and unique.'

'The newness is my least concern. What you are saying is new enough to stagger me. If I understand you, I am to pay your addresses to Marie for you, ask for her hand for you?'

'You do understand me – you could scarcely mistake. The ease with which you do so speaks for the naturalness of the thing.'

'Do you think so? Why don't you send your Serenus?'

'You are probably making fun of my Serenus. Obviously it amuses you to picture my Serenus as love's messenger. We just spoke of personal impressions which the girl should not be quite without in making her decision. Don't be surprised that I imagine she would incline her ear to your words more than to anything such a sober-sides as my Serenus could say.'

'I do not feel in the least like joking, Adri – because in the first place it goes to my heart and makes me feel solemn, the role you assign to me in your life, and even before posterity. I asked about Zeitblom because he has been your friend so much longer –'

'Yes, longer.'

'Good, then only longer. But don't you think this only would make his task easier and himself better at it?'

'Listen, how would it be if we just dropped him out of our minds? In my eyes he has nothing to do with love-affairs and that sort of thing. It is you, not he, in whom I have confided, you know the whole story, I have opened to you the most secret pages in the book of my heart, as they used to say. If you now open them to her and let her read; if you talk to her of me, speak well of me, by degrees betray my feelings, and the life-wishes bound up with them! Try her, gently, appealingly – "nicely", the way you have – try if she, well, yes, if she could love me! Will you? You don't have to bring me her final consent – God forbid! A little encouragement is quite enough as a conclusion to your mission. If you bring me that much back, that the thought of sharing my life with me is not utterly repugnant to her, not exactly monstrous – then my turn will come and I will speak with her and her aunt myself.'

They had left the Rohmbühel on their left and walked through the little pine wood behind it, where the water was dripping from the boughs. Now they struck into the path at the end of the village, which brought them back home. Here and there a cottager or peasant saluted by name the long-standing lodger of the Schweigestills. Rudolf, after a little while, began again:

'You may be sure that it will be easy for me to speak well of you. So much the more, Adri, because you praised me so to her. But I will be quite open with you – as open as you have been with me. When you asked me what I thought of Marie Godeau, I had the answer ready that everybody must like her. I will confess that there was more in that answer than there seemed. I should never have admitted it to you if you had not, as you put it with such old-world poetry, let me read the book of your heart.'

'You see me truly inpatient for your confession.'

'You've really heard it already. The girl – you don't like the word – the woman then, Marie, – I am not indifferent to her either; and when I say not indifferent, even that is not quite the right way to put it. She is the nicest loveliest feminine creature, I think, that has come my way. Even in Zürich – after I had played, I had played *you* and was feeling warm and susceptible, she already charmed me. And here – you know it was I suggested the excursion, and in the interval, as you do not know, I had seen her: I had tea in Pension Gisela, with her and Tante Isabeau, we had such a nice time ... I repeat, Adri, that I only come to speak of it on account of our present talk and our mutual frankness.'

Leverkühn was silent a little. Then he said, in an oddly faltering and neutral voice:

'No, I did not know that – about your feelings nor about the tea. I seem to have been so ridiculous as to forget that you are flesh and blood too and not wrapped up in asbestos against the transaction of the lovely and precious. So you love her, or let us say, you are in love with her. But now let me ask you one thing; does it stand so that our intentions cut across each other, so that you want to ask her to be your wife?'

Schwerdtfeger seemed to consider. He said:

'No, I hadn't thought of that yet.'

'How you talk, Adrian! Don't say such things! No, I hadn't thought of that either.'

'Well, then, let me tell you that your confession, your open and gratifying confession, is much more likely to make me stick to my request than to put me off it.'

'What do you mean?'

'I mean it in more than one sense. I thought of you for this service of love because you would be much more in your element than, let us say, Serenus Zeitblom. You give out something he has not got to give, which seems to be favourable to my wishes and hopes. But aside from this: it seems now that you even to a certain extent share my feelings, though not, as you assure me, my hopes. You will speak out of your own feelings for me and my hopes. I cannot possibly think of a more ordained or desirable wooer.'

'If you look at it like that –'

'Do not think I see it only in that light. I see it also in the light of a sacrifice, and you can certainly demand that I should look at it like that. Demand it then, with all the emphasis you can summon! For that means that you, the sacrifice recognized as sacrifice, still want to make it. You make it in the spirit of the role that you play in my life, as a final contribution to the merit you have acquired for the sake of my humanity; the service which perhaps may remain hidden, or perhaps be revealed. Do you consent?'

Rudolf answered:

'Yes, I will go and do your errand to the best of my powers.'

'We will shake hands on it,' said Adrian, 'when you leave.'

They had got back to the house, and Schwerdtfeger had still time to have a bite with his friend in the Nike-saal. Gereon Schweigestill had put the horse in for him: despite Rudolf's plea not to make trouble himself, Adrian accompanied him to the station, bouncing on the seat of the little cart.

'No, it is the right thing to do, this time quite particularly,' he declared.

The accommodating local train drew up at the little Pfeiffering halt. The two clasped hands through the open window.

'Not another word,' said Adrian: 'Only "nicely"!'

He raised his arm as he turned to go. He never again saw the traveller whom the train bore away. He only received a letter from him – a letter to which he denied all answer.

Chapter Forty-two

The next time I was with him, ten or eleven days later, the letter was already in his hands and he announced to me his definite decision not to answer it. He looked pale and made the impression of a man who has had a heavy blow. A tendency, which indeed I had noticed in him some time back, to walk with his head and torso slightly bent to one side was now more marked. Still he was, or purported to be, perfectly calm, even cool, and seemed almost to need to excuse himself for his shoulder-shrugging composure over the treachery he had been the victim of.

'I hardly think,' he said, 'you expected any outburst of moral indignation. A disloyal friend. Well, what of it? I cannot feel greatly outraged at the way of the world. It is bitter, of course; you ask yourself whom you can trust, when your own right hand strikes you in the breast. But what will you have? Friends are like that today. What remains with me is chagrin – and the knowledge that I deserve to be whipped.'

I asked what he had to be ashamed of.

'Of behaviour,' he answered, 'so silly that it reminds me of a schoolboy who finds a bird's nest and out of sheer joy shows it to another boy who then goes and steals it.'

What could I say except:

'It is no sin or shame to be trusting, surely; they are the portion of the thief.'

If only I could have met his self-reproaches with a little more conviction! But the truth was that I agreed with him. His whole attitude, the whole set-up with the second-hand wooing, and Rudolf of all people as go-between: I found it forced, devious, unseemly. I needed only to imagine that instead of speaking myself to my Helene, instead of using my own tongue, I had sent some attractive friend of mine to tell her my love, to see the whole equivocal absurdity of what he had done. But why then object to his remorse – if remorse it was that spoke in his words and manner? He had lost friend and beloved at one blow. And by his own fault, one must admit. If only one could have been quite certain – if only I myself had been certain – that we were dealing with a fault, an unconscious false step, a fatal lack of judgement! If only the suspicion had not stolen into my brooding mind that he had to some extent foreseen what would happen and that it had come about as he wanted it to! Could he have seriously conceived the idea that what Rudolf 'gave out' – in other words the young man's undeniable sexual appeal – could be made to work and woo for him, Adrian? Was it credible that he had counted on it? Sometimes the speculation arose in my mind that while putting it as though urging the other to a sacrifice, he had elected himself as the actual victim; that he deliberately brought together what really did belong together, in an affinity of 'niceness' and charm in order to abdicate and retreat again into his fastness. But such an idea was more like me than it was like him. Such a motive, so soft and sacrificial, such abnegation might have sprung from my reverence for him and lain at the bottom of an apparent gaucherie, a so-called stupidity that he was supposed to have committed. But events were to bring me face to face with a reality harsher, colder, crueller than my good nature would have been capable of without stiffening in icy horror. That was a reality without witness or proof; I recognized it only by its staring gaze; and for all of me it shall remain dumb, for I am not the man to give it words.

I am certain that Schwerdtfeger, so far as he knew himself, went to Marie Godeau with the best and most correct intentions. But it is no less certain that these intentions had never from the first been very firm on their feet. They were endangered from within, prone to relax, to melt, to change their character. His vanity had been flattered by what Adrian had been at pains to impress upon him about his personal significance for the life and humanity of his great friend; he had accepted the interpretation, so skilfully instilled, that his present mission arose out of this significance. But jealousy worked against those first feelings. He resented the fact that Adrian, after the conquest he had made of him, had changed his mind; that he, Rudolf, now counted for nothing except as a tool and instrument. I believe that in his secret heart he now felt free, in other words not bound to repay with good faith the other's disloyalty and egotism. This is fairly clear to me. And it is clear, too, that to go wooing for another man is an intriguing enterprise, particularly for a fanatical male coquette, whose morale must have been prone to relax in the anticipation of a flirtation even if only a vicarious one.

Does anyone doubt that I could tell what happened between Rudolf and Marie Godeau, just as I knew the whole course of the dialogue between him and Adrian in Pfeiffering? Does anyone doubt that I was 'there'? I think not. But I also think, that a precise account is no longer useful or desirable. Its issue, heavy with fate, however delightful it looked at first to others if not to me, was not, we must assume, the fruit of only one interview. A second was necessary and inevitable after the way in which Marie dismissed him the first time. It was Tante Isabeau whom Rudolf met when he entered the little vestibule of the pension. He inquired after the niece and asked if he might have a few words of private conversation with her, in the interest of a third party. The old lady directed him to the living- and working-room with a mischievous smile which betrayed her disbelief in the existence of the third party. He entered and was greeted by Marie with surprise and pleasure; she was about to inform her aunt when he told her, to her increasing if obviously not unpleasant astonishment, that her aunt knew he was here and would come in after he had spoken with herself on a weighty and wonderful theme. What did she reply? Something jesting and commonplace, of course. 'I am certainly most curious,' or the like. And asked the gentleman to sit down comfortably for his recital.

He seated himself in an easy-chair beside her drawing-board. Nobody could say he broke his word. He kept it, honourably. He spoke to her of Adrian, of his importance and greatness, of which the public would only slowly become aware; of his, Rudolf's admiration, his devotion to the extraordinary man. He talked of Zürich, and of the meeting at the Schlaginhaufens', of the day in the mountains. He revealed to her that his friend loved her — but how does one reveal to a woman that another man loves her? Do you bend over her, gaze into her eyes, take in an appealing grasp the hand that you profess to hope you may lay in another's? I do not know. I had to convey only an invitation to an excursion, not an offer of marriage. All I know is that she hastily drew back her hand, either from his or only from her lap, where it had been lying; that a blush overspread the southern paleness of her face and the laughter disappeared from her eyes. She did not understand, she was really not sure she understood. She inquired if she had understood aright: was Rudolf proposing to her for Dr Leverkühn? Yes, he said, he was; actuated by friendship and a sense of duty. Adrian, in his scrupulous delicacy, had asked him to represent him and he felt he could not refuse. Her distinctly cool, distinctly mocking comment, that it was certainly very kind of him, was not calculated to relieve his embarrassment. The extraordinary nature of his situation and role only now struck him, mingled with the thought that something not very complimentary to her was involved in it. Her manner expressed sheer surprise and umbrage – and that both startled and secretly pleased him. He struggled for a while, stammering, to justify himself. She did not know, he said, how hard it was to refuse a man like that. And he had felt to some extent responsible for the turn Adrian's life had taken, because it had been he who had moved him to the Swiss journey and thus brought about the meeting with Marie. Yes, it was strange: the violin concerto was dedicated to him, but in the end it had been the medium of the composer's meeting with her. He begged her to understand that his sense of responsibility had largely contributed to his readiness to perform this service for Adrian.

Here there was another quick withdrawal of the hand which he had tried to take as he pleaded with her. She answered that he need not trouble himself further, it was not important that she should understand the role he had assumed. She regretted to be obliged to shatter his friendly hopes, but though she was of course not unimpressed by the personality of his principal, the reverence she felt for the great man had nothing to do with any feelings that could form the basis of a union for which he had argued with so much eloquence. The acquaintance with Dr Leverkühn had been a source of pleasure and an honour as well; but unfortunately the answer that she must now give would probably make further meetings too painful. She sincerely regretted being obliged to take the view that Dr Leverkühn's messenger and representative was also necessarily affected by this change in the situation. Certainly after what had happened it would be better and less embarrassing if they did not meet again. And now she must bid him a friendly farewell: 'Adieu, monsieur!'

He implored her: 'Marie!' But she merely expressed her amazement at his use of her first name and repeated her farewell – the sound of her voice rings clearly in my ears: 'Adieu, monsieur!'

He went, his tail between his legs – to all appearance, that is. Inwardly he was blissful. Adrian's plan of marrying had turned out to be the nonsensical idea it had been from the first, and she had taken it very ill indeed that he had been willing to espouse it. She had been enchantingly angry. He did not hasten to let Adrian know the result of his visit, overjoyed as he was to have saved his own face by the honest admission that he was not himself indifferent to her. What he did now was to sit down and compose a letter to Mlle Godeau. He said that he could not submit to her 'Adieu monsieur'; for the sake of his life and reason he must see her again, and put to her in person the question which he here wrote down with his whole heart and soul: did she not understand that a man, out of veneration for another man, could sacrifice his own feelings and act regardless of them, making himself a selfless advocate of the other's desire? And could she not further understand that the suppressed, the loyally controlled feelings must burst forth, freely, exultantly, so soon as the other man proved to have no prospects of success? He begged her pardon for the treason, which he had committed against nobody but himself. He could not regret it, but he was overjoyed that there was no longer any disloyalty involved if he told her that – he loved her.

In that style. Not unclever. Winged by his genius for flirtation, and, as I fully believe, all unconscious that in substituting his own wooing for Adrian's, his declaration of love remained bound up with an offer of marriage which of his own motion, considering his nature, would never have entered his flirtatious head. Tante Isabeau read the letter aloud to Marie, who had been unwilling to accept it. Rudolf received no reply. But two days later he had himself announced to Tante by the housemaid at Pension Gisela and was not refused entrance. Marie was out. After his first visit, as the old lady with sly reproof betrayed to him, she had wept a few tears on her Tante's breast. Which in my view was an invention of Tante. She emphasized her niece's pride. Marie's was a proud nature but full of deep feeling, she said. Definite hope of another meeting she could not give him. But she would say this much, that she herself would spare no pains to represent to her niece the uprightness of his conduct.

In another two days he was there again. Mme Ferblantier – this was Tante's name, she was a widow – went in to her niece. She remained some time; at last she came out and with an encouraging twinkle ushered him in. Of course he had brought flowers.

What else is there to say? I am too old and sad to relish describing a scene whose details can be of moment to no one. Rudolf repeated his wooing, only this time not for Adrian but himself. Of course the feather-headed youth was as suited to the married state as I am to the role of Don Juan. But it is idle to speculate on the chances for future happiness of a union doomed to no future at all, destined to be brought to naught by a violent blow from the hand of fate. Marie had dared to love the breaker of hearts, the fiddler with the 'little tone', whose artistic gifts and certain success had been vouched for to her by so weighty an authority. She confided in herself to hold and bind him, in her power to domesticate the wild-fowl she had caught. She gave him her hands, received his kiss, and it was not four-and-twenty hours before the glad news had gone the rounds of our circle that Rudi was caught, that Konzertmeister Schwerdtfeger and Marie Godeau were an engaged pair. We also heard that he would not renew his contract with the Zapfenstösser orchestra but marry in Paris and there devote his services to a new musical group just being organized, called the Orchestre Symphonique.

No doubt he was very welcome there, and just as certainly the arrangements to release him went forward slowly in Munich, where there was reluctance to let him go. However, his presence at the next concert – it was the first after that one to which he had come back at the last minute from Pfeiffering – was interpreted as a sort of farewell performance. The conductor, Dr Edschmidt, had chosen for the evening an especially house-filling programme, Berlioz and Wagner, and, as they say, all Munich was there. Familiar faces looked from the rows of seats, and when I stood up I had to bow repeatedly: there were the Schlaginhaufens and their social circle, the Radbruchs with Schildknapp, Jeanette Scheurl, Mmes Zwitscher and Binder-Majoresku, and the rest, all of whom had certainly come with the thought uppermost in their minds of seeing Benedict the married man, in other words Rudi Schwerdtfeger, up there, left front, at his music-stand. His betrothed was not present; we heard that she had returned to Paris. I bowed to Inez Institoris. She was alone, or rather with the Knöterichs and without her husband, who was unmusical and would be spending the evening at the Allotria. She sat rather far back, in a frock so simple as to look almost poverty-stricken; her head thrust forward on its slanting stalk, her eyebrows raised, the mouth pursed in that look of not quite innocent mischief. As she returned my greeting I could not help the irritating impression that she was forever smiling in malicious triumph over that evening in her living-room and her exploitation of my long-suffering sympathy.

As for Schwerdtfeger, well knowing how many curious eyes he would meet, he scarcely during the whole evening looked down into the parterre. At the times when he might have done so, he listened to his instrument or turned over the score.

The last number was the overture to the *Meistersinger*, played with breadth and élan. The crashing applause, loud enough anyhow, rose still higher as Ferdinand Edschmidt motioned to the orchestra to stand up, and put out his hand gratefully to his Konzertmeister. By then I was already in the aisle, intent on my overcoat, which was handed out before there was a crowd round the garde-robe. I intended to walk for at least a part of my way home; that is, to my stop in Schwabing. But in front of the building I met a gentleman of the Kridwiss group, the Dürer expert. Professor Gilgen Holzschuher, who had also been at the concert. He involved me in a conversation which began with a criticism of the evening's programme: this combination of Berlioz and Wagner, of foreign virtuosity and German mastery, was tasteless, and also it only ill concealed a political tendency. All too much it looked like pacifism and German-French rapprochement; this Edschmidt was known to be a republican and nationally unreliable. The thought had spoilt his whole evening. Unfortunately, everything today was politics, there was no longer any intellectual clarity. To restore it we must above all have at the head of our great orchestras men of unquestionably German views.

I did not tell him that it was he himself who was making politics of everything, and that the word 'German' is today by no means synonymous with intellectual clarity, being, as it is, a party cry. I only suggested that a great deal of virtuosity, foreign or not, was after all a component of Wagner's internationally so well-tolerated art – and then charitably distracted his mind by speaking of an article on problems of proportion in Gothic architecture, which he had recently written for the periodical *Art and Artists*. The politeness I expressed about it rendered him quite happy, pliable and unpolitical; I utilized this bettered mood to bid him good-bye and turn right as he turned left in front of the hall.

I went by way of the upper Türkenstrasse, reached the Ludwigstrasse, and walked along the silent Monumental-Chaussée (asphalted now, years ago), on the left side, in the direction of the Siegestor. The evening was cloudy and very mild, and my overcoat began to feel oppressive, so I stopped at the Theresienstrasse halt to pick up a tram to Schwabing. I don't know why it took so long for one to come, but there are always many blocks in the traffic. At last number ten appeared, quite conveniently for me; I can still see and hear it approaching from the Feldherrnhalle. These Munich trams, painted in the Bavarian light-blue, are heavily built and either for that reason or some characteristic of the subsoil make considerable noise. Electric sparks flashed under the wheels of the vehicle and even more on top of the contact with the pole, where they sent out hissing showers of cold flame.

The car stopped, I got on in front and went inside. Close to the sliding door was an empty seat, obviously just vacated. The tram was full, two gentlemen stood clinging to straps at the rear door. Most of the passengers were home-goers from the concert. Among them, in the middle of the opposite bench, sat Schwerdtfeger, with his violin-case between his knees. Under his overcoat he wore a white cache-nez over his dress tie, but as usual was bareheaded. Of course he had seen me come in, but he avoided my eye. He looked young and charming, with his unruly waving blond locks, his colour heightened by his recent honourable exertions; by contrast the blue eyes seemed a little swollen. But even that became him, as did the curling lips that could whistle in so masterly a fashion. I am not a quick observer, only by degrees was I aware of other people I knew. I exchanged a greeting with Dr Kranich, who sat on Schwerdtfeger's side of the tram, at some distance from him, near the rear door. Bending forward by chance, I was aware to my surprise of Inez Institoris, on the same bench with myself, several seats away, towards the middle of the tram, diagonally opposite to Rudi Schwerdtfeger. I say to my surprise, for certainly this was not her way home. But a few seats farther on I saw her friend Frau Binder-Majoresku, who lived far out in Schwabing, beyond the 'Grossen Wirt', so I assumed the Inez was going to drink tea with her.

But now I could see why Schwerdtfeger kept his head mostly turned to the right so that I saw only his rather too blunt profile. I was not the only person he wanted to ignore: the man whom he must regard as Adrian's alter ego. I reproached him mentally: why did he have to take just this particular tram? It was probably an unjust reproach, for he had not necessarily got in at the same time with Inez. She might have got in later, as I had, or if it had been the other way he could hardly have rushed out again at sight of her.

We were passing the university, and the conductor, in his felt boots, was standing in front of me to take my ten pfennige and give me my ticket, when the incredible thing happened – at first, like everything entirely unexpected, quite incomprehensible. There was a burst of shooting: sharp, abrupt, shattering detonations, one after the other, three, four, five, with furious, deafening rapidity. Over there Schwerdtfeger, his violin-case still in his hands, sank first against the shoulder and then into the lap of the lady next to him on the right, who for her part, the one on his left as well, leaned away from him in horror, while a general commotion ensued in the vehicle, more like flight and shrieking panic than any activity showing presence of mind. Out in front the driver, God knows why, kept up a ceaseless clamour like mad on the bell, perhaps to summon the police. Of course there were none within hearing. There was an almost dangerous surging to and fro inside the tram, which had come to a stop. Many passengers were pushing to get out, while others, curious or anxious to do something, squeezed in from the platforms. The two gentlemen who had been standing in the gangway had like me flung themselves on Inez – of course far too late. We did not need to 'wrest' the revolver from her, she had let it fall, or rather cast it from her in the direction of her victim. Her face was white as paper, with sharply defined, bright-red spots on the cheekbones. She had her eyes shut and an insane smile was on her pursed-up mouth.

They held her by the arms, and I rushed over to Rudolf, who had been stretched out on the now empty bench. On the other side, bleeding, in a fainting-fit, lay the lady upon whom he had fallen. She had received a glancing wound in the arm, which turned out not to be serious.

Several people were standing by Rudolf, among them Dr Kranich,
holding his hand.

'What a horrible, senseless, irrational deed!' said he, pale in the face, but
in his clear, scholarly, well-articulated, short-winded way of speaking. He
said 'hor-r-r-ible', as actors often pronounce it. He added that he had never
more regretted not being a doctor instead of only a numismatist; and actually
at that moment the knowledge of coins did seem to me the most futile of the
branches of science, more futile even than philology, a position by no means
easy to sustain. In fact there was no doctor present, not among all those
concert-goers, though doctors are usually music-lovers, so many of them
being Jews. I bent over Rudolf. He gave signs of life, but was frightfully
injured. There was a bleeding wound under one eye. Other bullets had, it
turned out, gone into the throat, the lungs, and the coronary arteries. He
lifted his head and tried to say something; but bubbles of blood welled out
between his lips, whose gentle fullness seemed all at once so touching to me;
his eyes rolled and his head fell back with a thud on the bench.

I cannot express the mournful pity which almost overcame me. I felt that
in a way I had always loved him and I must confess that my sympathy for
him was far stronger than for her, the unhappy creature who by suffering
and by pain-deadening, demoralizing vice had been worked up to the
revolting deed. I made myself known as a close friend of both parties and
advised that the wounded man be carried over into the university, where the
janitor could telephone for the police and an ambulance, and where, to my
knowledge, there was a small first-aid station. I arranged that they should
bring the author of the crime thither as well.

All this was done. A studious, spectacled young man had with my help
lifted poor Rudolf from the tram, behind which, by now, two of three more
had come to a stop. Out of one of these hurried up a doctor with an
instrument-case and directed, rather superfluously, the work of carrying
Rudolf in. A reporter came too, asking questions. The memory still tortures
me of the trouble we had to rouse the janitor from his basement quarters.
The doctor, a youngish man, who introduced himself to everybody, tried to
administer first aid to the now unconscious victim after we had laid him on a
sofa. The ambulance came with surprising quickness. Rudolf died, as the
doctor after examination indicated to me was unfortunately probable, on the
way to the hospital.

As for me I attached myself to the later arriving police and their now
convulsively sobbing charge, to make known her connexions and bespeak
her admission into the psychiatric clinic. But this, for the present night, was
not permitted.

It struck midnight from the church when I left the office and, looking
about for an auto, set out to perform the painful duty that still remained to
me. I felt bound to go to Prinzregentenstrasse, to inform the little husband,
as gently as might be, of what had happened. I got a chance of a car when it
was no longer worth while. I found the house-door barred, but the light went
on when I rang and Institoris himself came down – to find me instead of his
wife at the door. He had a way of snapping his mouth open for air and
drawing his lower lip across his teeth.

'Oh, what is it?' he said. 'It is you? How is she coming? ... Has
something –?'

I said almost nothing on the stairs. Above in the living-room, where I had
heard Inez's distressing confessions, I told him, after a few words of
preparation, what had happened and what I had been witness to. He had

been standing, and after I had done he sat down suddenly in one of the basket chairs. But after that he displayed the self-control of a man who has lived a long time in an oppressive and threatening atmosphere.

'So then,' said he, 'it came like that.' And it was clear that his dread had concerned chiefly the manner in which the inevitable tragedy would be consummated.

'I will go to her,' he declared, and stood up again. 'I hope they will let me speak to her there' (he meant in the police cells).

I could not give him much hope for tonight. But he said in a shaken voice that he thought it was his duty to try; flung on his coat and hastened off.

Alone in the room, with Inez's bust, distinguished and sinister, looking down from its pedestal, my thoughts went thither where it will be believed they had in the last hour often and constantly gone. One more painful announcement it seemed to me had to be made. But a strange rigidity that seized on my limbs and even the muscles of my face prevented me from lifting the receiver and asking to be connected with Pfeiffering. No, that is not quite true, I did lift it, I held it dangling in my hand and heard the muffled voice, as from the depths of the sea, of the Fräulein at the other end. But a realization born of my already morbid exhaustion that I was about to disturb quite uselessly the nocturnal peace of the Schweigestill household, that it was not necessary to tell Adrian now, that I should only in a way be making myself ridiculous, checked my intention and I put the receiver down.

Chapter Forty-three

My tale is hastening to its end – like all else today. Everything rushes and presses on, the world stands in the sign of the end – at least it does for us Germans. Our 'thousand-year' history, refuted, reduced *ad absurdum*, weighed in the balance and found unblest, turns out to be a road leading nowhere, or rather into despair, an unexampled bankruptcy, a *descensus Averno* lighted by the dance of roaring flames. If it be true, as we say in Germany, that every way to the right goal must also be right in each of its parts, then it will be agreed that the way that led to this sinful issue – I use the word in its strictest, most religious sense – was everywhere wrong and fatal, at every single one of its turns, however bitter it may be for love to consent to such logic. To recognize because we must our infamy is not the same thing as to deny our love. I, a simple German man and scholar, have loved much that is German. My life, insignificant but capable of fascination and devotion, has been dedicated to my love for a great German man and artist. It was always a love full of fear and dread, yet eternally faithful to this German whose inscrutable guiltiness and awful end had no power to affect my feeling for him – such love it may be as is only a reflection of the everlasting mercy.

Awaiting the final collapse, beyond which the mind refuses its office, I have withdrawn within my Freising hermitage and shun the sight of our horribly punished Munich: the fallen statues, the gaping eyeholes in the façades, which both disguise the yawning void behind them and advertise it by the growing piles of rubble on the pavements. My heart contracts in pity for the reckless folly of my own sons, who, like the masses of the people, trusted, exulted, struggled, and sacrificed and now long since are reduced, with millions of their like, to staring at the bitter fruit of disillusion as it mellows into decay and final utter despair. To me, who could not believe in their belief or share their hopes, they will be brought no nearer by the present agony of their souls. They will still lay it to my charge – as though things would have turned out differently had I dreamed with them their insane dream. God help them! I am alone with my old Helene, who cares for my physical part, and to whom sometimes I read aloud from my pages such portions as suit her simplicity. In the midst of ruin all my thoughts are addressed to the completion of this work.

The *Apocalypsis cum figuris*, that great and piercing prophecy of the end, was performed at Frankfurt on the Main in February 1926, about a year after the frightful events that I chronicled in my last chapter. It may have been due in part to the disheartenment they left in their wake that Adrian could not bring himself to break through his usual retirement and be present at the performance, a highly sensational event, also one accompanied by much malicious abuse and shallow ridicule. He never heard the work, one of the two chief monuments of his proud and austere life; but after all he used to say about 'hearing' I do not feel entitled to lament the fact. Besides myself, who took care to be free for the occasion, from our circle of acquaintances there was present only our dear Jeanette Scheurl, who despite her narrow means made the journey to Frankfurt and reported on the performance to her friend at Pfeiffering, in her very individual mixed French and Bavarian dialect. Adrian especially prized this peasant-aristocrat, her presence had a beneficial and soothing effect on him, like a sort of guardian spirit. Actually I have seen him sitting hand in hand with her in a corner of the Abbot's room silent and as it were in safe-keeping. This hand-in-hand was not like him, it was a change which I saw with emotion, even with pleasure, but yet not quite without anxiety.

More than ever too, at that time, he liked to have Rüdiger Schildknapp with him. True, the like-eyed one was chary as ever of his presence, but when our shabby gentleman did appear he was ready for one of those long walks across country which Adrian loved, especially when he was unable to work; for Rüdiger seasoned his idleness with bitter and grotesque humour. Poor as a church-mouse, he had at that time much trouble with his neglected and decayed teeth and talked about nothing but dishonest dentists who pretended to treat him out of friendship but then suddenly presented impossible bills. He railed about conditions of payment, which he had neglected to observe, and then had been compelled to find another man, well knowing that he never could or would satisfy him – and more of the same. They had tortured him by pressing a considerable bridge on roots which had been left in and shortly began to loosen under the weight, so that the grisly prospect, the removal of the artificial structure, was imminent, and the consequence would be more bills which he could not pay. 'It is all going to pieces,' he announced in hollow tones; but had no objection when Adrian laughed till he cried at all this misery. Indeed it seemed Rüdiger could look down on it himself and bend double with schoolboy laughter.

This gallows humour of his made his company just the right thing for our recluse. I am unfortunately without talent in that line, but I did what I could to encourage the mostly recalcitrant Rüdiger to visit Pfeiffering. Adrian's life during this whole year was idle and void. He fell victim to a dearth of ideas, his mental stagnation tormented, depressed, and alarmed him, as his letters showed; indeed he put forward his condition as the chief ground for his refusal to go to Frankfurt. It was impossible for him to think about things he had already done while in a state of incapacity to do better. The past was only tolerable if one felt above it, instead of having to stare stupidly at it aware of one's present impotence. Fallow and hollow, he called his state: a dog's life, a *vie végétale*, without past or future, root or fruit, an idyll too idle for words. The one saving grace was that he could rail at it. Actually he could pray for a war, a revolution, any external convulsion just to shock him out of his torpor. Of composition he had literally not the smallest conception, not the faintest memory of how it was done; he confidently believed that he would never write another note. 'May hell have pity on me!' 'Pray for my poor soul!' such expressions repeated themselves in the letters. They filled me with gloom, yet on the other hand could even raise my spirits, as I reflected that after all only the youthful playmate and nobody else in the world could be the recipient of such confidences.

In my replies I tried to console him by pointing out how hard it is for human beings to think beyond their immediate situation. It is a matter of feeling and not of reason: prone to consider the present their abiding lot, they are incapable, so to speak, of seeing round the corner – and that probably applies more to bad situations than to good ones. Adrian's low morale was easily explainable by the cruel disappointments he had lately suffered. And I was weak and 'poetical' enough to compare the fallow ground of his mind with the 'winter-resting earth', in whose womb life, preparing new shoots, worked secretly on. I felt myself that the image was inapplicable to the extremes of Adrian's nature, his swing between penitential paralysis and compensating creative release. The stagnation of his impulse to create was accompanied though not caused by a new low-water mark in his physical state: severe attacks of migraine confined him to darkness; catarrh of the stomach, bronchial tubes, and throat attacked him by turns, particularly during the winter of 1926, and would of itself have been enough to prevent the trip to Frankfurt. It did in fact prevent another journey which humanly speaking was still more immediate and urgent, but categorically forbidden by his doctor.

At the end of the year, at the same age, seventy-five years and strange to say almost on the same day, Max Schweigestill and Jonathan Leverkühn departed this life: the father and proprieter of Adrian's Bavarian asylum and home, and his own father up in Buchel. The mother's telegram announcing the peaceful passing of Jonathan Leverkühn, the speculator of the elements, found his son standing at the bier of that equally quiet and thoughtful smoker with the other dialect. 'Maxl' had gradually handed over the business to Gereon, his heir, just as Jonathan had done to George; now he had stepped aside for ever. Adrian might be certain that Elsbeth Leverkühn bore this loss with the same quiet resignation, the same understanding acceptance of the human lot, as Mother Schweigestill showed. A journey to Saxon Thuringia to the burial was out of the question in Adrian's present condition. But despite fever and weakness he insisted, against his doctor's advice, on taking part the following Sunday in the funeral of his old friend, in the village church at Pfeiffering. It was attended by hosts of people from the region round about. I too paid last honours to the departed, with the feeling that I was doing honour to Jonathan as well. We went back on foot to the Schweigestill house, oddly and rather irrationally moved as we noted that the odour of the old man's pipe tobacco, though he himself was gone, still hung on the air of living-room and passage just as it always had.

'That lasts,' Adrian said, 'a long time, maybe as long as the house. In Buchel too. The time we last, a little shorter, a little longer, we call immortality.'

That was after Christmas; the two fathers, their faces already half-turned away, half-estranged from earthly things, had still been present at the Christmas feast. Now, as the light waxed, in the beginning of the new year, Adrian's health markedly improved, the succession of harassing attacks came to an end. He seemed psychologically to have overcome the shipwreck of his life-plans and all the damage bound up with it, his mind rose up, a giant refreshed – indeed, his trouble might now be to keep his poise in the storm of ideas rushing upon him. This (1927) was the year of the high and miraculous harvest of chamber music: first the ensemble for three strings, three wood-wind instruments, and piano, a discursive piece, I might say, with very long themes, in the character of an improvisation, worked out in many ways without ever recurring undisguised. How I love the yearning, the urgent longing, which characterized it; the romantic note – since after all it is treated with the strictest of modern devices – thematic, indeed, but with such considerable variation that actually there are no 'reprises'. The first movement is expressly called 'fantasia', the second is an adagio surging up in a powerful crescendo, the third the finale, which begins lightly enough, almost playfully, becomes increasingly contrapuntal and at the same time takes on more and more a character of tragic gravity, until it ends in a sombre epilogue like a funeral march. The piano is never used for harmonic fillings, its part is soloistic as in a piano concerto – probably a survival from the violin concerto. What I perhaps most profoundly admire is the mastery with which the problem of sound-combination is solved. Nowhere do the wind instruments cover up the strings, but always allow them to have their own say and alternate with them; only in a very few places are strings and wind instruments combined in a tutti. If I am to sum up the whole impression: it is as though one were lured from a firm and familiar setting-out into ever remoter regions – everything comes contrary to expectation. 'I have,' Adrian said to me, 'not wanted to write a sonata but a novel.'

This tendency to musical prose comes to its height in the string quartet, Leverkühn's most esoteric work, perhaps, which followed on the heels of the ensemble piece. Where, otherwise, chamber music forms the playground for thematic work, here it is almost provocatively avoided. There are altogether no thematic connexions, developments, variations, and no repetitions; unbroken, in an apparently entirely free way, the new follows, held together by similarity of tone or colour, or, almost more, by contrast. Of traditional forms not a trace. It is as though the Master, in this apparently anarchic piece, was taking a deep breath for the *Faust* cantata, the most coherent of his works. In the quartet he only followed his ear, the inner logic of the idea. At the same time polyphony predominates in the extreme, and every part is quite independent at every moment. The whole is articulated by very clearly contrasted tempi, although the parts are to be played without interruption. The first part, inscribed *moderato*, is like a profoundly reflective, tensely intellectual conversation, like four instruments taking counsel among themselves, an exchange serious and quiet in its course, almost without dynamic variety. There follows a presto part as though whispered in delirium, played muted by all four instruments, then a slow movement, kept shorter, in which the viola leads throughout, accompanied by interjections from the other instruments, so that one is reminded of a song-scene. In the '*Allegro con fuoco*' the polyphony is given free rein in long lines. I know nothing more stirring than the end, where it is as though there were tongues of flame from all four sides, a combination of runs and trills which gives the impression of a whole orchestra. Really, by resetting the widely spaced chords and using the best registers of every instrument, a sonority is achieved which goes beyond the usual boundaries of chamber music; and I do not doubt that the critics will hold it against the quartet altogether that it is an orchestral piece in disguise. They will be wrong. Study of the score shows that the most subtle knowledge of the string-quartet medium is involved. Indeed, Adrian had repeatedly expressed to me the view that the old distinctions between chamber music and orchestral music are not tenable, and that since the emancipation of colour they merge into one another. The tendency to the hybrid, to mixing and exchanging, as it showed itself already in the treatment of the vocal and instrumental elements in the *Apocalypse,* was growing on him. 'I have learned in my philosophy courses, that to set limits already means to have passed them. I have always stuck by that.' What he meant was the Hegel-Kant critique, and the saying shows how profoundly his creative power sprang from the intellect – and from early impressions.

This is entirely true of the *Trio* for violin, viola, and cello: scarcely playable, in fact to be mastered technically only by three virtuosos and astonishing as much by its fanatical emphasis on construction, the intellectual achievement it exhibits, as by the unsuspected combination of sound, by which an ear coveting the unknown has won from the three instruments a combinational fantasy unparalleled. 'Impossible, but refreshing,' so Adrian in a good mood characterized the work, which he had begun to write down even during the composition of the ensemble piece, carried in his mind and developed, burdened as it was with the work on the quartet, of which one would have thought that it alone must have consumed a man's organizing powers for long and to the utmost. It was an exuberant interweaving of inspirations, challenges, realizations, and resummonings to the mastery of new tasks, a tumult of problems which broke in together with their solutions – 'a night,' Adrian said, 'where it doesn't get dark for the lightnings.'

'A rather sharp and spasmodic sort of illumination,' he would add. 'What then – I am spasmodic myself, it gets me by the hair like the devil and goes along me so that my whole carcass quivers. Ideas, my friend, are a bad lot, they have hot cheeks, they make your own burn too, in none too lovesome a way. When one has a humanist for a bosom friend, one ought to be able to make a clear distinction between bliss and martyrdom ...' He added that sometimes he did not know whether the peaceful incapacity of his former state were not preferable in comparison with his present sufferings.

I reproached him with ingratitude. With amazement, with tears of joy in my eyes, yet secret and loving concern, I read and heard, from week to week, what he put on paper: in the neatest, most precise, yes, even elegant notation, betraying not a trace of 'spasms'. This was what, as he fancifully put it, his familiar friend Mr Akercocke told him to do and demanded of him. In one breath, or rather in one breathlessness, he wrote down the three pieces, any one of which would have been enough to make memorable the year of its production; actually he began with the draft of the trio on the very day on which he finished the 'lento' of the quartet, which he composed last. 'It goes,' he once wrote to me, when I had been unable to visit him for two weeks, 'as though I had studied in Cracow.' I did not understand the allusion until I recalled that at Cracow, in the sixteenth century, courses were publicly given in magic.

I can assure my readers that I paid great attention to his archaic style and allusions, which he had always been given to but now even more frequently, or should I say 'oftimes', came into his letters and even his speech. The reason was soon to be made clear. The first hint came when I saw among his papers a note that he had written with a broad pen-nib: 'This sadnesse moved Dr Faustum that he made note of his lamentacyon.'

He saw what I was looking at and took away the slip of paper with 'Fie on a gentleman and brother! What concerns you not, meddle not with!' What he was planning and thought to carry out, no man aiding, he still kept from me. But from that moment on I knew what I knew. It is beyond all doubt that the year of the chamber music, 1927, was also the year when the *Lamentation of Dr Faustus* was conceived. Incredible as it sounds, while his mind was wrestling with problems so highly complicated that one can imagine their being mastered only by dint of the shortest, most exclusive concentrations, he was already looking ahead, reaching out, casting forward, with the second oratorio in view: the crushing *Lamentation*. From his serious preoccupation with that work he was at first distracted by another interest, both priceless and heart-piercing.

Chapter Forty-four

Ursula Schneidewein, Adrian's sister in Langensalza, gave birth to her first three children, one after the other, in 1911, 1912, and 1913. After that she had lung trouble and spent some months in a sanatorium in the Harz Mountains. The trouble, a catarrh of the apex of the lung, then seemed to have been cured, and throughout the ten years that passed before the birth of her youngest, little Nepomuk, Ursula had been a capable wife and mother to her family, although the years of privation during and after the war took the bloom off her health. She was subject to colds, beginning in the head and going to the bronchial cords; her looks, belied by her sweet-tempered and active ways, were if not precisely ailing, yet delicate and pale.

The pregnancy of 1923 seemed rather to increase than to lower her vitality. True, she got round from it rather slowly, and the feverish affection, which ten years before had brought her to the sanatorium flickered up afresh. There had been some talk of interrupting her housewifely duties a second time for special treatment. But the symptoms died away – under the influence as I strongly suspect of psychological well-being, maternal happiness, and joy in her little son, who was the most placid, friendly, affectionate, easy-to-tend baby in the world. For some years the brave woman kept sturdy and strong; until May of 1928, when the five-year-old Nepomuk got a severe attack of measles, and the anxious day-and-night nursing of the exceptionally beloved child became a heavy drain upon the mother's strength. She herself had an attack of illness, after which the cough and the fluctuations of temperature did not subside; and now the doctor insisted on a sojourn at a cure, which, without undue optimism, he reckoned at half a year.

This was what brought Nepomuk Schneidewein to Pfeiffering. His sister Rosa, seventeen years old, and her brother Ezekiel, a year younger, were employed in the shop; while the fifteen-year-old Raimund was still at school. Rosa had of course the natural duty of keeping house for her father in her mother's absence and was likely to be too busy to take over the care of her little brother. Ursula had thought of Adrian. She wrote that the doctor would consider it a happy solution if the little convalescent could spend some time in the country air of Upper Bavaria. She asked her brother to sound his landlady, whether or not Frau Else would be willing to play the part of mother or grandmother to the little one for a time. Else Schweigestill, and even more enthusiastically Clemetine, readily consented; and in the middle of June of that year Johannes Schneidewein took his wife to the same sanatorium, near Suderode in the Harz, where she had been benefited before; while Rosa and her little brother travelled south, bringing him to the bosom of her uncle's second home.

I was not present when the brother and sister arrived in the courtyard, Adrian described the scene to me: the whole house, mother, daughter, Gereon, maidservants and menservants, in sheer delight laughing for pure pleasure, stood about the little man and could not gaze enough at so much loveliness. Especially the womenfolk of course were quite besides themselves, and of the women in particular the servants. They bent over the little one in a circle, convulsed with rapture; squatted down beside him and called on Jesus, Mary, and Joseph at sight of the beautiful little lad. His sister stood looking on indulgently: clearly she had expected nothing different, being used to see everyone fall in love with the youngest of the family.

Nepomuk – Nepo as his family called him, or 'Echo' as ever since he began to prattle he had called himself, quaintly missing out the first consonant – was dressed with warm-weather rustic simplicity in a sleeveless white cotton shirt, linen shorts, and worn leather shoes on his stockingless feet. But it always seemed as though one were looking at a fairy princeling. The graceful perfection of the small figure with the slender, shapely legs, the indescribable comeliness of the little head, long in shape, covered with an innocent tumble of light hair; the features despite their childishness with something There was his smile, of course not quite free from coquetry and conscious-lashed clear blue eyes, ineffably pure and sweet, at once full of depth and sparkling with mischief – no, it was not even all these together that gave such an impression of faerie, of a guest from some finer, tinier sphere. For there was besides the stance and bearing of the child as he stood in the centre of the circle of 'big people' all exclaiming, laughing, even sighing with emotion. There was his smile, of course not quite free from conquetry and conscious-ness of the charm he wielded; hid words and gestures, sweetly instructive, benignly condescending, as though he were a friendly ambassador from that other, better clime. There was the silvery small voice and what it uttered, still with baby blunders, in the father's slightly drawling, weighty Swiss speech, which the mother had early taken over. The little man rounded his *r*'s on his tongue; he paused between syllables; he accompanied his words, in a way I have never seen before in a child, with vague but expressive explanatory gestures of arms and hands, often quite unconnected with what he said, and rather puzzling while at the same time wholly delicious.

So much for the moment as a description of Nepo Schneidewein, or Echo as everybody, following his example, straightway called him. It is written by one not present when he came, and only as clumsy words can approximate the scene. How many writers before me have bemoaned the inadequacy of language to arrive at visualization or to produce an exact portrait of an individual! The word is made for praise and homage; to the word it is given to astonish, to admire, and to bless; it may characterize a phenomenon through the emotion it arouses; but it cannot conjure up or reproduce. Instead of attempting the impossible I shall probably do more for my adorable little subject by confessing that today, after fully seventeen years, tears come to my eyes when I think of him, while at the same time the thought of him fills me with an odd, ethereal, not quite sublunary lifting of the heart.

The replies he made, with that bewitching play of gesture, to questions about his mother, his journey, his stay in the great city of Munich, has as I said a pronounced Swiss accent and much dialect, rendered in the silvery timbre of his voice: '*huesli*' for house, '*a bitzli*' for a little bit. He liked to say 'well': 'Well, it was lovely.' Fragments of grown-up language came too: if he had not remembered something, he said it had 'slipped his mind'. And finally he said: 'Well, nothing more of news' – obviously because he wanted to break up the group, for the words fell from his honey-sweet lips: 'Echo thinks best to not be outdoors any more. Better go in the huesli and see the uncle.' And he put out his hand to his sister to take him in. But just then Adrian, who had been resting and putting himself to rights, came out to welcome his niece.

'And so this,' said he, after he had greeted the young girl and exclaimed over her likeness to her mother, 'is the new member of the family?'

He held Nepomuk's hand, gazed into the starry eyes, and soon was lost in the sweet depths of that azure upturned smile.

'Well, well!' was all he said, nodding slowly at the girl and then turning back to gaze again. His emotions could escape nobody, certainly not the child. So when Echo addressed his uncle for the first time, his words, instead of sounding forward, seemed to be placating and making light of something, loyally reducing it to simple and friendly terms: 'Well, you are glad I did come, yes?' Everyone laughed, Adrian too.

'I should say so,' he answered. 'And I hope you are glad too, to make our acquaintance.'

'It is most pleasant meeting all,' the child said quaintly.

The others would have burst out laughing again, but Adrian shook his head at them with his finger on his lips.

'The child,' he said softly, 'must not be bewildered by our laughter. And there is no ground for laughter, do you think, Mother Schweigestill?' turning to her.

'Not a speck,' said she in an exaggeratedly firm voice, and put the corner of her apron to her eye.

'So let us go in,' he decided, and took Nepomuk's hand again to lead him. 'Of course you have a little refreshment for our guests.'

Accordingly, in the Nike salon, Rosa Schneidewein was served with coffee and the little one with milk and cake. His uncle sat with him at the table and watched him as he ate, daintily. Adrian talked with his niece the while, but did not hear much that she said, so taken up he was with looking at the elf and just as much with controlling his feelings, not to betray them and make them a burden. His concern was unnecessary, for Echo seemed no longer to mark mere silent admiration for enraptured looks; while it would have been a sin to miss that sweet lifting of the eyes in thanks for handing the jam or a piece of cake.

At length the little man uttered the single word: ''Nuff.' It was, his sister explained, what he had always said from a tiny child, when he had done; it meant 'Echo has had enough.' When Mother Schweigestill would have pressed him to take something more, he said with a certain superior reasonableness:

'Echo would be best without it.'

He rubbed his eyes with his little fists, a sign that he was sleepy. They put him to bed, and while he slept Adrian talked with Sister Rosa in his workroom. She was to stay only till the third day, her duties in Langensalza summoned her home. When she left, Nepomuk wept a little, but then promised to be 'good' until she came to fetch him. My God how he kept his word! How incapable he was of not keeping it! He brought something like a state of bliss, a constant heart-warming gaiety and tenderness not only to the farm but to the village as well, and even as far as Waldshut. For the Schweigestills, mother and daughter, eager to be seen with him, confident of the same rapturous reception everywhere, took him with them to the apothecary, the shoemaker, the general store, in order that everybody might hear him 'speak his piece', with bewitching play of gesture and impressive, deliberate enunciation: about Pauline, who was bur-r-nt up, out of *Struwwelpeter*, or Jochen, who did come home from play so dir-rty that Mrs Duck and Mr Drake were amazed and even Mr Pig was per-rfectly dazed. The Pfeiffering pastor heard him recite his prayer, with folded hands held out before his face – a strange old prayer it was, beginning 'Naught availeth for timely Death.' And the pastor, in his emotion, could only say: 'Ah, thou dear child of God, thou little blessed one!' stroking his hair with a white priestly hand and presenting him with a coloured picture of the Lamb of God. The schoolmaster felt 'a new man' after talking with him. At market and in the street every third person asked Fräul'n Clementine or Mother Schweigestill what was this had dropped down from heaven. People stared and nudged each other: 'Just look, just look!' or else, not very differently from the pastor: 'Ah, dear little one, little blessed one!' Women, in most cases, showed a tendency to kneel down in front of Nepomuk.

When I was next at the farm, two weeks had already passed since he came; he had settled in and was well known to the neighbourhood. I saw him first at a distance: Adrian showed him to me round the corner of the house, sitting on the ground in the kitchen garden at the back, between a strawberry and a vegetable bed, one little leg stretched out, the other half drawn up, his hair falling in strands on his forehead. He was looking, it seemed with somewhat detached approval, at a picturebook his uncle had given him, holding it on his knee, with the right hand at the margin. But the little left hand and arm, with which he turned the page, unconsciously continuing the turning motion remained in the air in an incredibly graceful posture beside the book, the small hand open. To me it seemed I had never seen a child so ravishingly posed. I could not even in fancy conceive my own affording such a sight; to myself I thought that thus must the little angels up above turn the pages of their heavenly choirbooks.

We went up to him, that I might make the acquaintance of the wonder-child, I did so with pedagogic restraint, with a view to reducing the situation to the everyday, and determined not to be sentimental. I put on a strict face, frowned, pitched my voice low, and spoke to him in the proper brisk and patronizing way: 'Well, my son? Being a good lad, eh? And what are we up to here?' But even as I spoke I seemed to myself unspeakably fatuous; and even worse, he saw it too, apparently shared my view, and felt ashamed on my account. He hung his head, drawing down his mouth as one does to keep from laughing; it so upset me that I said nothing more for some time. He was not yet of an age when a lad is expected to stand up and be respectful to his

elders; he deserved, if any creature ever did, the tender consideration and
indulgence we grant to those not long on this earth, unpractised and strange
to its ways. He said we should 'sitty down' and so we did, with the manikin
between us in the grass, and looked at his picturebook with him. It was
probably among the most acceptable of the children's books in the shop,
with pictures in English taste, a sort of Kate Greenaway style and not at all
bad rhymes. Nepomuk (I called him that, not Echo; the latter I was idiot
enough to find 'sentimental') knew almost all of them by heart, and 'read'
them to us, following the lines with his finger, of course always in the wrong
place.

The strange thing is that today I know those verses by heart myself, only
because I had heard them once – or it may have been more than once –
recited in that little voice of his, with its enchanting intonation. How well I
still know the one about the organ-grinders who met at a street corner, one of
whom had a grudge against the other so that neither would budge from the
spot. I could recite to any child – though not nearly so well as Echo did –
what the neighbours had to bear from the hullabaloo those hurdy-gurdies
kept up. The mice did keep a fasting feast, the rats they ran away. It ends:

> *And only one, a puppy-dog,*
> *Listened till silence fell;*
> *And when he got back to his home*
> *That dog felt far from well.*

You would have to see the little lad's troubled head-shake and hear his
voice fall as he recounted the indisposition of the little dog. You would have
to see the minuscule grandezza of his bearing as he imitated the two quaint
little gentlemen meeting each other on the beach:

> *Good morning, m'sieur!*
> *No bathing, I fear!*

This for several reasons: first because the water is so wet and only forty-
three degrees, but also 'three guests from Sweden' are there:

> *A swordfish, a sawfish and shark*
> *Swimming close in you can mark.*

He uttered so drolly this confidential warning, had such a large-eyed way
of enumerating the three undesirable guests, and fell into a key so mingled of
horror and satisfaction at the news that they were swimming close in, that we
both burst out laughing. He looked into our faces, observing our merriment
with roguish curiosity, mine in particular, I thought – probably he wanted to
see whether my uncalled-for schoolmaster solemnity was being thawed out.

Good heavens, it certainly was! After my first foolish attempts I did not
return to it, except that I always addressed this little ambassador from
childhood and fairyland as Nepomuk, speaking in a firm voice and only
calling him Echo when I mentioned him to his uncle, who like the women
had taken up the name. The reader will understand that the pedagogue in me
felt somewhat disturbed or even embarrassed at this incontestably adorable
loveliness, which yet was a prey to time, destined to mature and partake of
the earthly lot. In no long space the smiling azure of these eyes would lose
their other-world purity. This face, this angelic air, as it were an explicit
aura of childlikeness; the lightly cleft chin, the charming mouth, which
when he smiled showed the gleaming milk teeth; the lips that then became
somewhat fuller than in repose, and at their corners showed two softly

curving lines coming from the fine little nose and setting off his mouth and chin from his cheeks: this face, I say, would become the face of a more or less ordinary boy, whom one would have to treat practically and prosaically and who would have no reason to greet a pedagogic approach with any of the ironic understanding betrayed by Nepomuk. And yet there was something here – that elfin mockery seemed to express a consciousness of it – which put it out of one's power to believe in time and time's common work, or its action upon this pure and precious being. Such was the impression it gave of its extraordinary completeness in itself; the conviction it inspired that this was a manifestation of 'the child' on earth; the feeling that it had 'come down to us' as, I say it again, an envoy of message-bearer; all this lulled the reason in dreams beyond the claims of logic and tinged with the hues of our Christian theology. It could not deny inevitable growth; but it took refuge in the sphere of the mythical and timeless, the simultaneous and abiding, wherein the Saviour's form as a grown man is no contradiction to the Babe in the Mother's arms which He also is; which He always is, always before His worshipping saints lifting His little hand in the sign of the Cross.

What extravagance, what fanaticism, it will be said! But I can do no more than give account of my own experience, and I must confess that the slightly other-worldly existence of this child always produced in me a sense of my own clumsiness. But I should have patterned myself – and tried to do so – on Adrian, who was no schoolman but an artist and took things as they came, apparently without thought of their proneness to change. In other words, he gave to impermanent becoming the character of being; he believed in the image: a tranquillizing belief, so at least it seemed to me, which, adjusted to the image, would not let its composure be disturbed no matter how unearthly that image might be. Echo, the fairy princeling, had come; very well, one must treat him according to his kind, and that was all. Such seemed to be Adrian's position. Of course he was far removed from the frowning brow or any avuncular 'That's a good lad'. But on the other hand, he left 'little angel' ecstasies to simpler folk. He behaved to the little one with a delicacy and warmth, smiling or serious as occasion called it out; without flattery or fawning, even without tenderness. It is a fact that I never saw him caress the child, scarcely even smooth his hair. Only he liked to walk with him in the fields, hand in hand.

But however he behaved, he could not deceive me: I saw that his little nephew's appearance had made a bright spot in his life, that he loved him from the first day on. No mistaking the fact that the sweet, light, elfin charm, working as it were without a trace despite the child's serious, old-fashioned language, occupied and filled his days, although he had the boy with him only at certain times. The child's care of course fell on the women; and as mother and daughter had much else to do, he often played by himself in some safe spot. Owing to the measles he still needed as much sleep as quite small children do, and slept during the day in addition to the usual afternoon nap, dropping off wherever he happened to be. 'Night!' he would say, just as when he went to bed. In fact 'Night!' was his good-bye on all occasions, when he or anyone else went away. It was the companion-piece to the ' 'Nuff' he always said when he had had enough. He would offer his little hand, too, when he said 'Night' before he fell asleep in the grass or as he sat in his chair. I once found Adrian in the back garden sitting on a very narrow bench made of three boards nailed together, watching Echo asleep at his feet. 'He gave me his hand first,' he announced when he looked up and saw me. He had not heard me approach.

Else and Clementine Schweigestill told me that Nepomuk was the best, most biddable, untroublesome child they had ever seen – which agreed with the stories of his earliest days. Actually I have known him to weep when he hurt himself, but never howl or roar or blubber as unruly children do. It would have been unthinkable. If he were forbidden, as for instance at an inconvenient time, to go with the stable-boy to the horses, or with Waltpurgis into the cow-stalls, he would assent to the verdict quite readily and even say: 'In a little while, maybe tomorrow or next day,' in a tone meant to console the grown-ups who, certainly against their will, had denied the request. Yes, he would even pat the disappointed one as though to say: 'Don't take it to heart! Next time you won't have to refuse, maybe you can let me.'

It was the same when he could not go to Adrian in the Abbot's room. He was much drawn to his uncle, even in the first two weeks; by the time I got there it was plain that he clung especially to Adrian and wanted to be with him. Of course this was partly because it was the unusual, a treat, while the society of the women was a commonplace. Yet how could it have escaped him that this man, his mother's brother, occupied among the rustics of Pfeiffering a unique, honoured, even rather intimidating place? And their respectful bearing must also make the boy eager to be with his uncle. But one cannot say that Adrian met the little boy half-way. Whole days might go by and he would not see him, would deny himself the undoubtedly beloved sight. Then again they would spend long hours together; taking walks hand in hand as far as the little one could go, strolling in friendly silence or chatting in Echo's little language, through the countryside lush with the season in which he had come and sweet with scents of lilac, alder-bush, and jasmine. The light-footed lad would be before him in the narrow lanes between walls of corn already ripening yellow for the harvest, their blades, with nodding ears as high as himself, mounting out of the mould.

Out of the earth, I might better say, for the little one said it, expressing his joy that heaven gave the 'firsty earff' a drink last night.

'A drink, Echo?' asked his uncle, letting pass the rest of the child's metaphorical language. 'You mean the rain?'

'Yes, the rain,' his little companion agreed more explicitly; but he would not go further into the matter.

'Imagine, he talks about the earth being thirsty, and uses a figure of speech like that,' Adrian related to me next time, in wonder. 'Isn't that a bit strange? Yes,' he nodded, with a certain amazed recognition, 'he is pretty far along.'

When he was obliged to go in to the city, Adrian brought the boy all sorts of presents: various animals, a jack-in-the-box, a toy railway with lights that switched on and off as it roared round the curves; a magic casket in which the greatest treasure was a glass filled with red wine which did not run out when the glass was turned upside down. Echo liked these things, of course, but when he had played with them he soon said: ''Nuff,' and much preferred to have his uncle show and explain some object of grown-up use – always the same and always new, for a child's persistence and appetite are great in matters of entertainment. The carved ivory paper-knife, the globe turning on its axis, with broken land-masses, deep bays, strange-shaped inland seas, and vast blue-dyed oceans; the clock on the chimney-piece that struck the hours, whose weights one could wind up with a crank out of the well into which they had sunk; those were some of the wonders which the little boy coveted to examine, when the slender figure stood at the door, and the little voice inquired:

'Are you look cross because I do come?'

'No, Echo, not very cross. But the weights are only half-way down.'

In this case it might be the music-box he asked for. It was my contribution, I had brought it to him: a small brown box to be wound up underneath. The roller, provided with metal tongues, turned along the tuned teeth of a comb and played, at first briskly and daintily, then slowly running down, three well-harmonized, demure little tinkling melodies, to which Echo listened always with the same rapt attention, the same unforgettable mixture of delight, surprise, and dreamy musing.

His uncle's manuscripts too, those runes strewn over the staves, adorned with little stems and tails, connected by slurs and strokes, some blank, some filled in with black; he liked to look at them too and have it explained what all those marks were about – just between ourselves, they were about him, and I should like to know whether he divined that, whether it could be read in his eyes that he gathered it from the master's explanations. This child, sooner than any of us, was privileged to get an 'insight' into the drafts of the score of Ariel's songs, on which Adrian was privately at work. He had combined the first, full of ghostly 'dispersèd' voices of nature, the 'Come unto these yellow sands', with the second, pure loveliness. 'Where the bee sucks, there suck I', into a single song for soprano, celeste, muted violin, an oboe, a bass clarinet, and the flageolet notes of the harp. And truly he who hears these 'gently spiriting' sounds or even hears them by reading alone, with his spirit's ear, may well ask for Ferdinand: 'Where should this music be? I' th' air or th' earth?' For he who made it has caught in its gossamer, whispering web not only the hovering childlike-pure, bewildering light swiftness of 'my dainty Ariel', but the whole elfin world from the hills, brooks, and groves which in Prospero's description as weak masters and demi-puppets by moonshine for their pastime midnight mushrooms make and the green sour ringlets whereof the ewe not bites. Echo always asked to see once more the place in the notes where the dog says 'Bow-wow' and the chanticleer cries 'Cock-a-diddle-dow'. And Adrian told him about the wicked witch Sycorax and her little slave, whom she, because he was a spirit too delicate to obey her earthy and abhorred commands, confined in a cloven pine, in which plight he spent a dozen painful years, until the good master of spells came and freed him. Nepomuk wanted to know how old the little spirit was when he was imprisoned and then how old when he was freed, after twelve years. But his uncle said that the spirit had no age, that he was the same after as before imprisonment, the same child of air – with which Echo seemed content.

The Master of the Abbot's room told him other stories, as well as he could remember them. Rumpelstiltskin, Falada and Rapunzel and the Singing, Soaring Lark; for the stories the little one had to sit on his uncle's knee, sidewise, sometimes putting one arm round his neck. 'Well, that does sound most nice,' he would say when the tale was done; but often he went to sleep with his head on the story-teller's breast. Then his uncle sat without moving, his chin resting lightly on the hair of the sleeping child, until one of the women came and fetched him away.

As I said, for days they might keep the child from him, because he was busy, or perhaps a headache shut him away in silence and darkness.

But after such a day, when he had not seen Echo, he liked to go when the child was put to bed, softly, hardly seen, to his room to hear the evening prayer. The child said his prayers lying on his back, his hands folded on his chest, one or both of the women being present. They were very singular things he recited, the heavenly blue of his eyes cast up to the ceiling, and he

had a whole range of them so that he hardly ever said the same ones two
evenings running.

> *Whoso hedeth Goddes stevene*
> *In hym is God and he in hevene.*
> *The same commaunde myselfe would keepe,*
> *And me insure my seemely slepe.*
>
> *Amen.*

Or:

> *A mannes misdeede, however grete,*
> *On Goddes merci he may wait,*
> *My sinne to Him a lytyl thynge is,*
> *God doth but smile and pardon bringes.*
>
> *Amen.*

Or:

> *Whoso for this brief cesoun*
> *Barters hevens blysse*
> *Hath betrayed his resoun*
> *His house the rainbow is:*
> *Give me to build on the firme grounde*
> *And Thy eternal joys to sound.*
>
> *Amen.*

Or, remarkable for its unmistakable coloration by the Protestant doctrine of
predestination:

> *Through sin no let has been,*
> *Save when some goode be seen.*
> *Mannes good deede shall serve him wel,*
> *Save that he were born for hell.*
> *O that I may and mine I love*
> *Be borne for blessedness above!*
>
> *Amen.*

Or sometimes:

> *The sun up-hon the divell shines*
> *And parts as pure away*
> *Keep me safe in the vale of earthe,*
> *Till that I pay the debt of deathe.*
>
> *Amen.*

And lastly:

> *Mark, whoso for other pray*
> *Himself he saves that waye.*
> *Echo prayes for all gainst harms,*
> *May God hold him too in His armes.*
>
> *Amen.*

This verse I myself heard him say, and was greatly touched; I think he did
not know I was there.

Outside the door Adrian asked: 'What do you say to this theological
speculation? He prays for all creation, expressly in order that he himself may
be included. Should a pious child know that he serves himself in that he

prays for others? Surely the unselfishness is gone so soon as one sees that it is of use.'

'You are right that far,' I replied. 'But he turns the thing into unselfishness so soon as he may not pray only for himself but does so for us all.'

'Yes, for us all,' Adrian said softly.

'Anyhow we are talking as though he had thought these things up himself. Have you ever asked him where he learned them, from his father or from whom?'

The answer was: 'Oh, no, I would rather let the question rest and assume that he would not know.'

It seemed that the Schweigestills felt the same. So far as I know they never asked the child the source of his little evening prayers. From them I heard the ones which I had not listened to from outside. I had them recited to me at a time when Nepomuk Schneidewein was no longer with us.

Chapter Forty-five

He was taken from us, that strangely seraphic little being was taken from this earth – oh, my God, why should I seek soft words for the harshest, most incomprehensible cruelty I have ever witnessed? Even yet it tempts my heart to bitter murmur, yes, to rebellion. He was set on with frightful, savage fury and in a few days snatched away by an illness of which there had been for a long time no case in the vicinity. Our good Dr Kürbis was greatly surprised by the violence of its recurrence; but he told us that children convalescing from measles or whooping-cough were susceptible to it.

The whole thing lasted scarcely two weeks, including the earliest signs that all was not quite well with the child; from those beginnings no one – I believe no one at all – even dreamed of the horror to come. It was the middle of August; the harvest was in full swing, with a considerable increase in the number of hands. For two months Nepomuk had been the joy of the house. Now a slight cold glazed the sweet clarity of his eyes; it was surely only this annoying affection that took away his appetite, made him fretful, and increased the drowsiness to which he had been subject ever since we knew him. He said ''Nuff' to all that was offered him: food, play, picture-books, fairy-tales. ''Nuff,' he said, his little face painfully drawn, and turned away. Soon there appeared an intolerance of light and sound, more disquieting still. He seemed to feel that the wagons driving into the yard made more noise than usual, that voices were louder. 'Speak more low,' he begged, whispering to show them how. Not even the delicate tinkling of the music-box would he hear; at once uttered his tortured ''Nuff, 'nuff!' stopped the works himself, and then wept bitterly. He fled from the high-summer sunshine of yard and garden, went indoors and crouched there, rubbing his eyes. It was hard to watch him seeking comfort, going from one to another of his loving ones, putting his arms about their necks, only after a little to turn disconsolate away. Thus he clung to Mother Schweigestill, to Clementine, to Waltpurgis. The same impulse brought him to his uncle, to press himself against his breast, to look up at him, even to smile faintly and listen to his

gentle words. But then the little head would droop lower and lower; he
would murmur: 'Night!' slip to his feet, and go away with unsteady
tread.

The doctor came. He gave him some drops for his nose and prescribed a
tonic, but did not conceal his fear that a more serious illness was setting in.
In the Abbot's room he expressed this concern to his patient of many years.

'You think so?' asked Adrian, going pale.

'The thing doesn't look quite right to me,' the doctor said.

'Right?'

The words had been repeated in such a startled, almost startling tone that
Kürbis asked himself if he had not gone too far.

'Well, in the sense I mentioned,' he answered. 'You yourself might look
better too, sir. Your heart is set on the little lad?'

'Oh, yes,' was the reply. 'It is a responsibility, doctor. The child was given
in our charge here in the country to strengthen his health ...'

'The clinical picture, in so far as one can speak of such a thing,' responded
the doctor, 'gives no warrant for a discouraging diagnosis. I will come again
tomorrow.'

He did so, and now he could diagnose the case with all too much certainty.
Nepomuk had had an abrupt vomiting spell, like the outbreak of an illness;
head pains set in accompanied by moderate fever and within a few hours had
obviously become all but intolerable. When the doctor came the child had
already been put to bed and was holding his head with both hands, uttering
shrieks which went on as long as his breath held out, a martyrdom to all who
heard them, and they could be heard throughout the house. At intervals he
put out his little hands to those about him, crying: 'Echo's head, Echo's
head!' Then another violent spell of vomiting would fetch him upright, to
sink back again in convulsions.

Kürbis tested the child's eyes, the pupils of which were tiny and showed a
tendency to squint. The pulse raced. Muscular contractions developed, and
an incipient rigidity of the neck. It was cerebro-spinal meningitis, inflammation of the meninges. The good man pronounced the name with a
deprecating movement of the head shoulderwards, probably in the hope that
they might not know the almost complete powerlessness of medical science
in the face of this fatal onslaught. A hint lay in his suggestion that they might
telegraph and let the parents know. The presence of the mother, at least,
would probably have a soothing effect on the little patient. He also asked for
a consultation with a physician from the capital, as he wanted to share the
responsibility of a case which was unfortunately not at all light. 'I am a
simple man,' he said. 'This is a case for higher authority.' A gloomy irony
lay, I believe, in his words. In any case, he was quite competent to undertake
the spinal puncture necessary to confirm the diagnosis as well as to afford the
only possible relief from the pains. Frau Schweigestill, pale but capable, as
ever loyal to the 'human', held the moaning child in bed, chin and knees
almost touching, and between the separated vertebrae Kürbis drove his
needle into the spinal canal and drew out the fluid drop by drop. Almost at
once the frantic headache yielded. If it returned, the doctor said – he knew
that after a couple of hours it must return, for the relief from pressure given
by drawing off the fluid from the brain cavity lasted only that long – then
they must use, besides the indispensable ice-bag, the chloral which he
prescribed and ordered from the county town.

After the puncture Nepomuk fell into a sleep of exhaustion. But then he
was roused by fresh vomiting, skull-splitting headache, and convulsions

that shook his small frame. The heart-rending moans and yelling screams began again: the typical 'hydrocephalic shriek', against which only the physician, precisely because he knows it is typical, is tolerably armed. The typical leaves one calm, only what we think of as individual puts us beside ourselves. Science is calm. Science did not, however, prevent our good country doctor from going over quite soon from the bromide and chloral preparations to morphine, which was more efficacious. He may have decided as much for the sake of the family – I have in mind particularly one of its members – as out of pity for the martyred child. Only once in twenty-four hours might the fluid be drawn off, and for only two of these did the relief last. Twenty-two hours of shrieking, writhing torture, of a child, of this child, who folded his twitching little hands and stammered: 'Echo will be good, Echo will be good!' Let me add that for those who saw him a minor symptom was perhaps the most dreadful of all: the squinting of the heaven's blue eyes, caused by the paralysis of the eye-muscles accompanying the rigidity of the neck. It changed the sweet face almost beyond recognition, horribly; and in combination with the gnashing of the teeth, which presently began, gave it a look as though he were possessed.

Next afternoon, fetched from Waldshut by Gereon Schweigestill, the consulting authority arrived from Munich. He was a Professor von Rothenbuch; Kürbis had suggested him among others and Adrian had chosen him on account of his great reputation. He was a tall man, with one eye half-closed as though from constant examination. He had a social presence and had been ennobled personally by the late King; was much sought after and high-priced. He vetoed the morphine, as its effect might obscure the appearance of a coma, 'which has not yet supervened'. He permitted only codeine. Obviously he was primarily concerned with the typical progress of the case and a clear clinical picture in all its stages. After the examination he confirmed the dispositions of his obsequious rural colleague: avoidance of light, head kept cook and bedded high, very gentle handling, alcohol rubs, concentrated nourishment; it would probably become necessary to give it by a tube through the nose. Very likely because he was not in the home of the child's parents his sympathy was candid and unequivocal. A clouding of the consciousness, legitimate and not prematurely induced by morphine would not be long in appearing, and would grow progressively worse. The child would suffer less, and finally not at all. Even more unsightly symptoms, therefore, must not be taken too seriously. After he had had the goodness to carry out the second puncture with his own hands, he took a dignified leave and did not return.

For my part, I was kept posted daily on the dreadful situation by Mother Schweigestill on the telephone. Only on Saturday, the fourth day after the onslaught of the disease, could I get to Pfeiffering. By then, after furious spasms which seemed to stretch the little body on the rack and made his eyeballs roll up in his head, the coma had set in. The shrieking stopped; there remained only the gnashing of the teeth. Frau Schweigestill, worn with lack of sleep, her eyes swollen with weeping, met me at the door and urged me to go at once to Adrian. There was time enough to see the poor baby, whose parents had been with him since the night before. I would see soon enough. But the Herr Doctor, he needed me to talk to him, just between ourselves things weren't right with him, sometimes it seemed to her he was talking crazy like.

In distress of mind I went to him. He sat at his desk and as I entered glanced up, almost with contempt. Shockingly pale, he had the same red

eyes as the rest of the household; with his mouth firmly shut, he kept
mechanically moving his tongue to and fro inside his lower lips.

'Is that you, good soul?' he said as I went to him and laid my hand on his
shoulder. 'What are you doing here? This is no place for you. Cross yourself,
like this, forehead to shoulders, the way you learned as a child. That will
keep you safe.'

And when I spoke a few words of consolation and hope:

'Spare yourself,' he roughly interrupted; 'spare yourself the humanistic
quibbles. He is taking him. Just let him make it short. Perhaps he can't make
it any shorter, with his miserable means.'

And he sprang up, stood against the wall, and leaned the back of his head
against the panelling.

'Take him, monster!' he cried, in a voice that pierced me to the marrow.
'Take him, hell-hound, but make all the haste you can, if you won't tolerate
any of this either, cur, swine, viper! I thought,' he said in a low confidential
voice, and turned to me suddenly, taking a step forwards and looking at me
with a lost, forlorn gaze I shall never forget, 'I thought he would concede this
much after all, maybe just this; but no, where should he learn mercy, who is
without any bowels of compassion? Probably it was just exactly this he had
to crush in his beastly fury. Take him, scum, filth, excrement!' he shrieked,
and stepped away from me again as though back to the Cross. 'Take his
body, you have power over that. But you'll have to put up with leaving me
his soul, his sweet and precious soul, that is where you lose out and make
yourself a laughing-stock – and for that I will laugh you to scorn, aeons on
end. Let there be eternities rolled between my place and his, yet I shall know
that he is there whence you were thrown out, orts and draff that you are! The
thought will be moisture on my tongue and a hosannah to mock you in my
foulest cursings!'

He covered his face with his hands, turned round and leaned his forehead
against the wall.

What could I say? Or do? How could I meet such words? 'But my dear
fellow, for heaven's sake be calm! You are beside yourself, your sufferings
make you imagine preposterous things.' That is the sort of thing one says,
and out of reverence for the psyche, especially in the case of such a man,
one does not think of the physical remedies, sedatives, bromide, and so on,
even though we had them in the house.

To my imploring efforts at consolation he only responded:

'Save yourself the trouble, just cross yourself, that's what's going on up
there. Do it not only for yourself, but at the same time for me and my guilty
soul. What a sin, what a crime' – he was sitting now at his desk, his temples
between his fists – 'that we let him come, that I let him be near me, that I
feasted my eyes on him! You must know that children are tender stuff, they
are receptive for poisonous influences –'

Now it was I, in very truth, who cried out and indignantly repudiated his
words.

'Adrian, no!' I cried. 'What are you doing, torturing yourself with absurd
accusations, blaming yourself for a blind dispensation that could snatch
away the dear child, perhaps too dear for this earth, wherever he chanced to
be! It may rend our hearts but must not rob us of our reason. You have done
nothing but loving-kindness to him ...'

He only waved me aside. I sat perhaps an hour with him, speaking softly
now and then, and he muttered answers that I scarcely understood. Then I
said I would visit the patient.

'Yes, do that,' he retorted and added, hardly:

'But don't talk the way you did at first: "Well my lad, that's a good boy," and so on. In the first place he won't hear you, and then it would most likely offend your humanistic taste.'

I was leaving when he stopped me, calling my name, my last name, Zeitblom, which sounded hard too. And when I turned round:

'I find,' he said, 'that it is not to be.'

'What, Adrian, is not to be?'

'The good and noble,' he answered me; 'what we call the human, although it is good, and noble. What human beings have fought for and stormed citadels, what the ecstatics exultantly announced – that is not to be. It will be taken back. I will take it back.'

'I don't quite understand, dear man. What will you take back?'

'The Ninth Symphony,' he replied. And then no more came, though I waited for it.

Dazed and grievously afflicted I went up into the fatal room. The atmosphere of the sick-chamber reigned there, clean and bare, heavy with the odours of drugs, though the windows were wide open. But the blinds were almost shut, only a crack showed. Several people were standing round Nepomuk's bed. I put out my hand to them, my eyes already on the dying child. He lay on his side, his legs drawn up, elbows and knees together. The cheeks were very flushed; he drew a breath, then one waited long for the next. His eyes were not quite closed, but between the lashes no iris showed, only blackness, for the pupils had grown unevenly larger, they had almost swallowed up the colour. Yet it was good when one saw the mirroring black. For sometimes it was white in the crack, and then the little arms pressed closer to the sides, the grinding spasm, cruel to see but perhaps no longer felt, twisted the little limbs.

The mother was sobbing. I had squeezed her hand, I did so again. Yes, she was there, Ursel, the brown-eyed daughter of the Buchel farm, Adrian's sister; and the woebegone face of the now thirty-nine-year-old woman moved me as I saw, stronger than ever, the paternal, the old-German features of Jonathan Leverkühn. With her was her husband, to whom the wire had been sent and he had fetched her from Suderode: Johannes Schneidewein, a tall, fine-looking, simple man with a blond beard, with Nepomuk's blue eyes, with the honest and sober speech that Ursula had early caught from him, whose rhythm we had known in the timbre of Echo, our sprite.

With the others in the room, aside from Frau Schweigestill, who was moving to and fro, was the woolly-haried Kunigunde Rosenstiel. On a visit she had been allowed to make she had learned to know the little lad and treasured him passionately in her melancholy heart. She had at that time, on her typewriter with the ampersand and on the letter-paper of her inelegant firm, written a long letter to Adrian in model German describing her feelings. Now, driving Meta Nackedey from the field, she had succeeded in relieving the Schweigestills and then Ursel Schneidewein in the care of the child; changed his ice-bag, rubbed him with spirit, tried to give him food and medicine, and at night unwillingly and seldom yielded to another her place by his bed.

The Schweigestills, Adrian, his family, Kunigunde, and I ate an almost silent meal in the Nike-saal together, one of the women rising very often to look to the patient. On Sunday morning I should have, hard as it was, to leave Pfeiffering. I still had a whole stack of Latin unseens to correct for

Monday. I parted from Adrian with soothing hopes on my lips, and the way
he left me was better than the way he had received me the day before. With a
sort of smile he spoke, in English, the words:
'"Then to the elements. Be free, and fare thou well!"'
He turned quickly away.

Nepomuk Schneidewein, Echo, the child, Adrian's last love, fell on sleep
twelve hours later. His parents took the little coffin with them, back to their
home.

Chapter Forty-six

For nearly four weeks now I have entered nothing in these records; deterred
in the first place by a sort of mental exhaustion caused by reliving the scenes
described in the last chapter, and secondly by the events of today, now
rushing headlong on each other's heels. Foreseen as a logical sequence, and
in a way longed for, they now after all excite an incredulous horror. Our
unhappy nation, undermined by fear and dread, incapable of understanding, in dazed fatalism lets them pass over its head, and my spirit too, worn
with old sorrow, weary with old wrong, is helplessly exposed to them as well.

Since the end of March – it is now the 25th of April in this year of destiny
1945 – our resistance in the west has been visibly disintegrating. The papers,
already half-unmuzzled, register the truth. Rumour, fed by enemy announcements on the radio and stories told by fugitives, knows no censor-
ship, but carries the individual details of swiftly spreading catastrophe about
the land, into regions not yet swallowed, not yet liberated by it, and even
hither into my retreat. No hold any more: everybody surrenders, everybody
runs away. Our shattered, battered cities fall like ripe plums. Darmstadt,
Würzburg, Frankfurt are gone; Mannheim and Cassell, even Münster and
Leipzig are in foreign hands. One day the English reached Bremen, the
Americans were at the gates of Upper Franconia; Nuremberg, city of the
national celebrations so uplifting to unenlightened hearts, Nuremberg
surrendered, The great ones of the regime, who wallowed in power, riches,
and wrong, now rage and kill themselves: justice is done.

Russian corps after taking Königsberg and Vienna were free to force the
Oder; they moved a million strong against the capital, lying in its rubble,
already abandoned by all the government officials. Russian troops carried
out with their heavy artillery the sentence long since inflicted from the air.
They are now approaching the centre of Berlin. Last year the horrible man
escaped with his life – by now surely only an insanely flaring and flickering
existence – from the plot of desperate patriots trying to salvage the future of
Germany and the last remnant of her material goods. Now he has commanded his soldiery to drown in a sea of blood the attack on Berlin and to
shoot every officer who speaks of surrender. And the order has been in
considerable measure obeyed. At the same time strange radio messages in
German, no longer quite sane, rove the upper air; some of them commend
the population to the benevolence of the conquerors, even including the
secret police, who they say have been much slandered. Others are
transmitted by a 'freedom movement' christened Werwolf: a band of raving-

mad lads who hide in the woods and break out nightly; they have already deserved well of the Fatherland by many a gallant murder of the invaders. The fantastic mingles with the horrible: up to the very end the crudely legendary, the grim deposit of saga in the soul of the nation is invoked, with all its familiar echoes and reverberations.

A transatlantic general has forced the population of Weimar to file past the crematories of the neighbouring concentration-camp. He declared that these citizens – who had gone in apparent righteousness about their daily concerns and sought to know nothing, although the wind brought to their noses the stench of burning human flesh – he declared that they too were guilty of the abominations on which he forced them now to turn their eyes. Was that unjust? Let them look, I look with them. In spirit I let myself be shouldered in their dazed or shuddering ranks. Germany had become a thick-walled underground torture-chamber, converted into one by a profligate dictatorship vowed to nihilism from its beginnings on. Now the torture-chamber has been broken open, open lies our shame before the eyes of the world. Foreign commissions inspect those incredible photographs everywhere displayed, and tell their countrymen that what they have seen surpasses in horribleness anything the human imagination can conceive. I say our shame. For is it mere hypochondria to say to oneself that everything German, even the German mind and spirit, German thought, the German Word, is involved in this scandalous exposure and made subject to the same distrust? Is the sense of guilt quite morbid which makes one ask oneself the question how Germany, whatever her future manifestations, can ever presume to open her mouth in human affairs?

Let us call them the sinister possibilities of human nature in general that here come to light. German human beings, tens of thousands, hundreds of thousands of them it is, who have perpetrated what humanity shudders at; and all that is German now stands forth as an abomination and a warning. How will it be to belong to a land whose history witnesses this hideous default; a land self-maddened, psychologically burnt-out, which quite understandably despairs of governing itself and thinks it for the best that it become a colony of foreign powers; a nation that will have to live shut in like the ghetto Jews, because a frightfully swollen hatred round all its borders will not permit it to emerge; a nation that cannot show its face outside?

Curses, curses on the corrupters of an originally decent species of human being, law-abiding, only too docile, only all too willingly living on theory, who thus went to school to Evil! How good it is to curse – or rather how good it would be, if only the cursing came from a free and unobstructed heart! We are present at the last gasp of a blood state which, as Luther put it, 'took on its shoulders' immeasurable crimes; which roared and bellowed to the ravished and reeling masses proclamations cancelling all human rights; which set up its gaudy banners for youth to march under, and they marched, with proud tread and flashing eyes, in pure and ardent faith. But a patriotism which would assert that a blood state like that was so forced, so foreign to our national character that it could not take root among us: such a patriotism would seem to me more high-minded than realistic. For was this government, in word and deed, anything but the distorted, vulgarized, besmirched symbol of a state of mind, a notion of world affairs which we must recognize as both genuine and characteristic? Indeed, must not the Christian and humane man shrink as he sees it stamped upon the features of our greatest, the mightiest embodiments of our essential Germanness? I ask – and should I not? Ah, it is no longer in question that his beaten people now standing wild-eyed in face of the void stand there just because they have failed, failed horribly in their last and uttermost attempt to find the political form suited to their particular needs.

Yet how strangely the times, these very times in which I write, are linked with the period that forms the frame of this biography! For the last two years of my hero's rational existence, the two years 1929 and 1930, after the shipwreck of his marriage plans, the loss of his friend, the snatching away of the marvellous child – those years were part and parcel of the mounting and spreading harms which then overwhelmed the country and now are being blotted out in blood and flames.

And for Adrian Leverkühn they were years of immense and highly stimulated, one is tempted to say monstrous creative activity, which made even the sympathetic onlooker giddy. One could not help feeling that it was by way of being a compensation and atonement for the loss of human happiness and mutual love which had befallen him. I spoke of two years, but that is incorrect, since only a part of each, the second half of one and some months of the other, sufficed to produce the whole composition, his last and in a somewhat historical sense his utmost work; the symphonic cantata *The Lamentation of Dr Faustus*, the plan of which, as I have already explained, goes back to before the advent of little Nepomuk Schneidewein in Pfeiffering. To it I will now devote my poor powers.

But first I must not fail to shed some light upon the personal condition of its creator, a man now forty-four years old; to speak of his appearance and way of life as they then seemed to my always anxious and observant eye. What I should first set down is the fact – I have mentioned it earlier in these pages – that his looks, which, so long as he was smooth-shaven, had shown such a likeness to his mother, had of late considerably altered. The change was due to a dark growth of beard, mixed with grey, a sort of chin-beard, with the addition of a drooping little strip of moustache. Though much heavier on the chin, it did not leave the cheeks free; but even on the chin it was heavier at the sides than in the middle, and thus was not like an imperial. One bore with the unfamiliarity resulting from the partial covering of the features, because it was this beard – and perhaps a growing tendency he had to carry his head on one side – that gave his countenance something spiritualized and suffering, even Christlike. I could not help loving this expression, and felt that my sympathy with it was justified in that obviously it did not indicate weakness but went with an almost excessive energy and an unexceptionable state of health, which my friend could not enough celebrate. He dwelt on it in the somewhat retarded, sometimes hesitant, sometimes slightly monotonous manner of speech which I had lately noted in him and which I liked to explain as a sign of productive absorption, of self-control and poise in the midst of a distracting whirl of ideas. The irksome physical conditions that had victimized him so long, the catarrh of the stomach, the throat trouble, the tormenting attacks of headache were all gone, his day was his own, and freedom to work in it. He himself declared his health to be perfect, magnificent; and one could read in his eyes the creative energy with which he daily arose to his task. It filled me with pride, yet again it made me fearful of relapses. His eyes, in his former state half overhung by the drooping lids, were now almost exaggeratedly wide open, and above the iris one saw a strip of white. That might perhaps alarm me, the more because there was about the widened gaze a fixity – or shall I say it was a stare? – the nature of which I puzzled over until it occurred to me that it depended on the unvarying size of the not quite round, rather irregularly lengthened pupils, as though they remained unaffected by any alteration in the lighting.

I am talking about a rigidness to some extent internal, one needed to be a very much concerned observer to perceive it. There was another, more obvious and striking manifestation of an opposite kind, noticed by our dear Jeanette Scheurl, who mentioned it to me after a visit. She need not have, of course. This was the recent habit, for instance when he was thinking, of moving his eyeballs rapidly to and fro rather far, from one side to the other, rolling them as we say. Some people might be startled by it. If I myself found it easy – and it seems to me I did find it so – to lay such habits, eccentric enough if you like, to the enormous strain he was under; yet privately I was relieved to think that except for myself scarcely anyone saw him, and that precisely because I feared outsiders might be alarmed. In practice, any sort of social intercourse with the city was now excluded. Invitations were declined by the faithful landlady on the telephone, or even remained unanswered. Short trips on errands were given up, the last one having been made to buy toys for the dead child. Clothes that had been worn to evening parties and on public occasions hung unused in his wardrobe, his dress was the simplest everyday. Not a dressing-gown, for he never used one, even in the mornings, only when he got up in the night and sat an hour or two in his chair. But a loose coat like a pea-jacket, closed to the throat so that he needed no tie, worn with some odd pair of checked trousers, loose and unpressed; such was at this time his habitual garb. He wore it out of doors too, for the regular indispensable long walks he took to get the air into his lungs. One might have spoken of an unkemptness in his appearance if his natural distinction had not, on intellectual grounds, belied the statement.

For whom, indeed, should he have taken pains? He saw Jeanette Scheurl, with whom he went through certain seventeenth-century music she had brought with her (I remember a chaconne of Jacopo Melani which literally anticipates a passage in *Tristan*). From time to time he saw Rüdiger Schildknapp, the like-eyed, with whom he laughed. I could not refrain from thinking desolately that only the like eyes were left, the black and the blue ones having disappeared ... He saw, lastly, me, when I went to spend the week-end. And that was all. Moreover, there were few hours in which he could wish for society, for not excepting Sunday (which he had never 'kept holy') he worked eight hours a day, with an intermission for an afternoon rest in a darkened room. So that on my visits to Pfeiffering I was left very much to myself. As though I regretted it! I was near him, near the source of the beloved work, beloved through all my sufferings and shudderings. For a decade and a half now it has been a buried, forbidden treasure, whose resurrection may come about through the destructive liberation we now endure. There were years in which we children of the dungeon dreamed of a hymn of exultation, a *Fidelio*, a Ninth Symphony, to celebrate the dawn of a freed Germany – freed by herself. Now only this can avail us, only this will be sung from our very souls: the *Lamentation* of the son of hell, the lament of men and God, issuing from the subjective, but always broadening out as it were laying hold on the Cosmos; the most frightful lament ever set up on this earth.

Woe, woe! A *De Profundis*, which in my zeal and love I am bound to call matchless. Yet has it not – from the point of view of creative art and musical history as well as that of individual fulfilment – a jubilant, a highly triumphant bearing upon this awe-inspiring faculty of compensation and redress? Does it not mean the 'break-through' of which we so often talked when we were considering the destiny of art, its state and hour? We spoke of it as a problem, a paradoxical possibility: the recovery, I would not say the reconstitution – and yet for the sake of exactness I will say it – of expressivism, of the highest and profoundest claim of feeling to a stage of intellectuality and formal strictness, which must be arrived at in order that we may experience a reversal of this calculated coldness and its conversion into a voice expressive of the soul and a warmth and sincerity of creature confidence. Is that not the 'break-through'?

I put in the form of a question what is nothing more than the description of a condition that has its explanation in the thing itself as well as in its artistic and formal aspect. The *Lamentation*, that is – and what we have here is an abiding, inexhaustibly accentuated lament of the most painfully Ecce-homo kind – the *Lamentation* is expression itself; one may state boldly that all expressivism is really lament; just as music, so soon as it is conscious of itself as expression at the beginning of its modern history, becomes lament and '*lasciatemi morire*', the lament of Ariadne, to the softly echoing plaintive song of nymphs. It does not lack significance that the *Faust* cantata is stylistically so strongly and unmistakably linked with the seventeenth century and Monteverdi, whose music – again not without significance – favoured the echo-effect, sometimes to the point of being a mannerism. The echo, the giving back of the human voice as nature-sound, and the revelation of it *as* nature-sound, is essentially a lament: Nature's melancholy 'Alas!' in view of man, her effort to utter his solitary state. Conversely, the lament of the nymphs on its side is related to the echo. In Leverkühn's last and loftiest creation, echo, favourite device of the baroque, is employed with unspeakably mournful effect.

A lament of such gigantic dimensions is, I say, of necessity an expressive work, a work of expression, and therewith it is a work of liberation; just as the earlier music, to which it links itself across the centuries, sought to be a liberation of expression. Only that the dialectic process – by which, at the stage of development that this work occupies, is consummated by the change from the strictest constraint to the free langauge of feeling, the birth of freedom from bondage – the dialectic process appears as endlessly more complicated in its logic, endlessly more miraculous and amazing than at the time of the madrigalists. Here I will remind the reader of a conversation I had with Adrian on a long-ago day, the day of his sister's wedding at Buchel, as we walked round the Cow Trough. He developed for me – under pressure of a headache – his idea of the 'strict style', derived from the way in which, as in the lied '*O lieb Mädel, wie schlecht bist du*', melody and harmony are determined by the permutation of a fundamental five-note motif, the symbolic letters h, e, a, e, e-flat. He showed me the 'magic square' of a style of technique which yet developed the extreme of variety out of identical material and in which there is no longer anything unthematic, anything that could not prove itself to be a variation of an ever constant element. This style, this technique, he said, admitted no note, not one, which did not fulfil its thematic function in the whole structure – there was no longer any free note.

Now, have I not, when I attempted to give some idea of Leverkühn's apocalyptic oratorio, referred to the substantial identity of the most blest with the most accurst, the inner unity of the chorus of child angels and the hellish laughter of the damned? There, to the mystic honour of one sensitive to it, is realized a Utopia in form, of terrifying ingenuity, which in the *Faust* cantata becomes universal, seizes upon the whole work and, if I may so put it, causes it to be completely swallowed up by thematic thinking. This giant 'lamento' (it lasts an hour and a quarter) is very certainly non-dynamic, lacking in development, without drama, in the same way that concentric rings made by a stone thrown into water spread even farther, without drama and always the same. A mammoth variation-piece of lamentation – as such negatively related to the finale of the Ninth Symphony with its variation of exultation – broadens out in circles, each of which draws the other resistlessly after it: movements, large-scale variations, which correspond to the textual units of chapters of a book and in themselves are nothing else than series of variations. But all of them go back for the theme to a highly plastic fundamental figure of notes, which is inspired by a certain passage of the text.

We recall that in the old chap-book which tells the story of the arch-magician's life and death, sections of which Leverkühn with a few bold adaptations put together as the basis of his movements, Dr Faustus, as his hour-glass is running out, invites his friends and familiars 'magistros, Baccalaureos and other students', to the village of Rimlich near Wittenberg, entertains them there hospitably all day long, at night takes one more drink of 'Johann's wine' with them, and then in an address both dignified and penitential announces and gives them to know his fate and that its fulfilment is now at hand. In this '*Oratio Fausti ad Studiosos*' he asks them, when they find him strangled and dead, charitably to convey his body into the earth; for he dies, he says, as a bad and as a good Christian; a good one by the power of his repentence, and because in his heart he always hopes for mercy on his soul; a bad one in so far as he knows that he is now facing a horrible end and the Devil will and must have his body. These words: 'For I die as a good and as a bad Christian', form the general theme of the variations. If you count the syllables, there are twelve, and all twelve notes of the chromatic scale are set to it, with all the thinkable intervals therein. It already occurs and makes itself felt long before it is reintroduced with the text, in its place as a choral group – there is no true solo in the *Faustus* – rising up until the middle, then descending, in the spirit and inflexion of the Monteverdi *Lamento*. It is the basis of all the music – or rather, it lies almost as key behind everything and is responsible for the identity of the most varied forms – that identity which exists between the crystalline angelic choir and the hellish yelling in the *Apocalypse* and which has now become all-embracing: a formal treatment strict to the last degree, which no longer knows anything unthematic, in which the order of the basic material becomes total, and within which the idea of a fugue rather declines into an absurdity, just because there is no longer any free note. But it serves now a higher purpose; for – oh, marvel, oh, deep diabolic jest! – just by virtue of the absoluteness of the form the music is, as language, freed. In a more concrete and physical sense the work is done, indeed, before the composition even begins, and this can now go on wholly unrestrained; that is, it can give itself over to expression, which, thus lifted beyond the structural element, or within its uttermost severity, is won back again. The creator of '*Fausti Weheklage*' can, in the previously organized material, unhampered, untroubled by the already given structure, yield himself to subjectivity; and so this, his technically most rigid work, a work of extreme calculation, is at the same time purely expressive. The return to Monteverdi and the style of his time is what I meant by 'the reconstruction of expressiveness', of expressiveness in its first and original manifestation, expressiveness as lament.

Here marshalled and employed are all the means of expression of that

emancipatory epoch of which I have already mentioned the echo-effect –
especially suitable for a work based wholly on the variation-principle, and
thus to some extent static, in which every transformation is itself already the
echo of the previous one. It does not lack echo-like continuations, the
further repetition of the closing phrase of a theme in higher pitch. There are
faint reminiscences of Orphic lamentation, which make Orpheus and Faust
brothers as invokers of the world of shades: as in that episode where Faust
summons Helen, who is to bear him a son. There are a hundred references to
the tone and spirit of the madrigal, and a whole movement, the exhortation
to his friends at the meal on the last night, is written in strict madrigal form.

But precisely in the sense of résumé there are offered musical moments of
the greatest conceivable possibility of expression: not as mechanical
imitation or regression, of course; no, it is like a perfectly conscious control
over all the 'characters' of expressiveness which have ever been precipitated
in the history of music, and which here, in a sort of alchemical process of
distillation, have been refined to fundamental types of emotional significance, and crystallized. Here is the deep-drawn sigh at such words as: 'Ah,
Faustus, thou senceles, wilfull, desperate herte! Ah, ah, reason, mischief,
presumption, and free will . . .' the recurrent suspensions, even though only
as a rhythmical device, the chromatic melody, the awful collective silence
before the beginning of a phrase, repetitions such as in that '*Lasciatemi*', the
lingering-out of syllables, falling intervals, dying-away declamations –
against immense contrast like the entry of the tragic chorus, *a capella* and in
full force, after Faust's descent into hell, an orchestral piece in the form of
grand ballet-music and galop of fantastic rhythmic variety – an overwhelming outburst of lamentation after an orgy of infernal jollity.

This wild conception of the carrying-off of Faust as a dance-furioso
recalls most of all the spirit of the *Apocalypsis cum figuris*; next to it, perhaps,
the horrible – I do not hesitate to say cynical – choral scherzo, werein 'the
evil spirit sets to at the gloomy Faustus with strange mocking jests and
sayings' – that frightful 'then silence, suffer, keepe faith, abstain; of thy ill lot
to none complayne; it is too late, of Gode dispair, thy ill luck runneth
everywhere.' But for the rest, Leverkühn's late work has little in common
with that of his thirties. It is stylistically purer, darker in tone as a whole and
without parody, not more conservative in its facing towards the past, but
mellower, more melodious; more counterpoint than polyphony – by which I
mean the lesser parts for all their independence pay more heed to the main
part, which often dies away in long melodic curves, and the kernel of which,
out of which everything develops, is just that twelve-note idea: 'For I die as a
bad and as a good Christian.' Long ago I said in these pages that in *Faustus*
too that letter symbol, the Hetaera-Esmeralda figure, first perceived by me,
very often governs melody and harmony: that is to say, everywhere where
there is reference to the bond and the vow, the promise and the blood pact.

Above all the *Faust* cantata is distinguished from the *Apocalypse* by its
great orchestral interludes, which sometimes only express in general the
attitude of the work to its subject, a statement, a 'Thus it is'. But sometimes,
like the awful ballet-music of the descent to hell, they also stand for parts of
the plot. The orchestration of his horror-dance consists of nothing but wind
instruments and a continuous accompaniment, which, composed of two
harps, harpsichord, piano, celeste, glockenspiel, and percussion, pervades
the work throughout as a sort of 'continuo', appearing again and again. Some
choral pieces are accompanied only by it. To others, wind instruments, to
still others strings are added; others again have a full orchestral accompani-

ment. Purely orchestral is the end: a symphonic adagio, into which the chorus of lament, opening powerfully after the inferno-galop, gradually passes over – it is, as it were, the reverse of the 'Ode to Joy', the negative, equally a work of genius, of that transition of the symphony into vocal jubilation. It is the revocation.

My poor, great friend! How often, reading in this achievement of his decline, his posthumous work, which prophetically anticipates so much destruction, have I recalled the distressful words he uttered at the death of the child. It is not to be, goodness, joy, hope, that was not to be, it would be taken back, it must be taken back! 'Alas, it is not to be!' How the words stand, almost like a musical direction, above the choral and orchestral movements of '*Dr Fausti Wehe-klag*'; how they speak in every note and accent of this 'Ode to Sorrow'! He wrote it, no doubt, with his eye on Beethoven's Ninth, as its counterpart in a most melancholy sense of the word. But it is not only that it more than once formally negates the symphony, reverses it into the negative; no, for even in the religious it is negative – by which I do not at all mean it denies the religious. A work that deals with the Tempter, with apostasy, with damnation, what else could it be but a religious work? What I mean is a conversion, a proud and bitter change of heart, as I, at least, read it in the 'friendly plea' of Dr Faustus to the companions of his last hour, that they should betake themselves to bed, *sleep in peace*, and let naught trouble them. In the frame of the cantata one can scarcely help recognizing this instruction as the conscious and deliberate reversal of the 'Watch with me' of Gethsemane. And again the Johann's wine, the draught drunk by the parting soul with his friends, has an altogether ritual stamp, it is conceived as another Last Supper. But linked with it is an inversion of the temptation idea, in such a way that Faust rejects as temptation the thought of being saved: not only out of formal loyalty to the pact and because it is 'too late', but because with his whole soul he despises the posivitism of the world for which one would save him, the lie of its godliness. This becomes clearer still and is worked out even more powerfully in the scene with the good old doctor and neighbour who invites Faust to come to see him, in order to make a pious effort to convert him. In the cantata he is clearly drawn in the character of a tempter; and the tempting of Jesus by Satan is unmistakably suggested; as unmistakably also is the '*Apage!*' by the proudly despairing 'No!' uttered to false and flabby middle-class piety.

But another and last, truly the last change of mind must be thought on, and that profoundly. At the end of this work of endless lamentation, softly, above the reason and with the speaking unspokenness given to music alone, it touches the feelings. I mean the closing movement of the piece, where the choir loses itself and which sounds like the lament of God over the lost state of His world, like the Creator's rueful 'I have not willed it.' Here, towards the end, I find that the uttermost accents of mourning are reached, the final despair achieves a voice, and – I will not say it, it would mean to disparage the uncompromising character of the work, its irremediable anguish to say that it affords, down to its very last note, any other consolation than what lies in voicing it, in simply giving sorrow words; in the fact, that is, that a voice is given the creature for its woe. No, this dark tone-poem permits up to the very end no consolation, appeasement, transfiguration. But take our artist paradox: grant that expressiveness – expression as lament – is the issue of the whole construction: then may we not parallel with it another, a religious one, and say too (though only in the lowest whisper) that out of the sheerly irremediable hope might germinate? It would be but a hope beyond hopelessness, the transcendence of despair – not betrayal to her, but the miracle that passes belief. For listen to the end, listen with me: one group of instruments after another retires, and what remains, as the work fades on the air, is the high G of a cello, the last word, the last fainting sound, slowly dying in a pianissimo-fermata. Then nothing more: silence, and night. But that tone which vibrates in the silence, which is no longer there, to which only the spirit hearkens, and which was the voice of mourning, is so no more. It changes its meaning; it abides as light in the night.

Chapter Forty-seven

'Watch with me!' In his cantata Adrian might if he chose transform that cry of human and divine agony into the masculine pride and self-confidence of his Faust's 'Sleep quietly and fear nothing!' But the human remains, after all: the instinctive longing, if not for aid, then certainly for the presence of human sympathy, the plea: 'Forsake me not! Be about me at my hour!'

And so, when the year 1930 was almost half gone, in the month of May, Leverkühn, by various means, invited a company to Pfeiffering, all his friends and acquaintances, even some whom he knew but little or not at all, a good many people, as many as thirty: partly by written cards, partly through me, and again by some of those invited passing on the invitation to others. Some again, out of sheer curiosity invited themselves, in other words begged an invitation from me or some other member of the more intimate circle. On his cards Adrian had let it be known that he wished to give a favourably disposed group of friends some idea of his just finished choral symphonic work, by playing some of its characteristic parts on the piano. He thus aroused the interest of certain people whom he had not thought of inviting, as for instance the dramatic soprano Tanya Orlanda and Herr Kioeielund, who had themselves bidden through the Schlaginhaufens; and the publisher Radbruch and his wife, who attached themselves to Schildknapp. Adrian had also sent a written card to Baptist Spengler, though he certainly must have known that Spengler had not been for a month and more among the living. That intellectual and wit, only in the middle of his forties, had most regrettably succumbed to his heart trouble.

As for me, I admit I was not at ease about the whole affair. Why it is hard to say. This summons to a large number of people most of whom were both inwardly and outwardly very remote from him to come to his most intimate retreat, to the end that they should be initiated into his most intimate work: it was not like Adrian; it made me uneasy, not so much in itself as because it seemed a strange thing for him to do. Though in and for itself it went against me too. On whatever grounds – and I do think I have indicated the grounds – in my heart I liked better to feel he was alone in his refugium, seen only by his humanly minded, respectful, and devoted hosts and by us few, Schildknapp, our dear Jeanette, the adoring Rosenstiel and Nackedey and myself, than to have the eyes of a mixed gathering, not used to him, focused on him who in his turn was not used to the world. But what was there for me to do but put my hand to the enterprise which he himself had already gone so far in, to carry out his instructions and do my telephoning? There were no regrets; on the contrary, as I said, only additional requests for an invitation.

Not only did I look with disfavour on the whole affair, I will go further in my confession and set down that I was tempted to remain away myself. Yet against that course was my anxious sense of duty, the feeling that I must, willy-nilly, be present and watch over everything. And so on that Saturday afternoon I betook myself with Helene to Munich, where we caught the local train for Waldshut-Garmisch. We shared the compartment with Schildknapp, Jeanette Scheurl, and Kunigunde Rosenstiel. The rest of the guests were scattered in different coaches, with exception of the Schlaginhaufen pair, the Swabian-speaking old rentier and the former von Plausig, who together with their friends from the opera made the trip by car. They arrived before we did, and the car did good service in Pfeiffering, going to and fro several times between the little station and Hof Schweigestill and conveying the guests by groups, such of them, that is, as did not prefer to walk. The weather held, though a storm rumbled faintly on the horizon. No arrangements had been made to fetch the guests; and Frau Schweigestill, whom Helene and I sought out in the kitchen explained to us in no small consternation that Adrian had not said a word to prepare her for the invasion. Now in all haste, with Clementine's help, she was making sandwiches for these people, to be served with coffee and sweet cider.

Meanwhile the baying of old Suso or Kaschperl, jumping about and rattling his chain in front of his kennel, seemed never to stop; he became quiet only when no more guests came and the company had gathered in the Nike salon, whither the servants hastily fetched chairs from the family quarters and even from the sleeping-chambers above. In addition to the guests already named, I mention a few more of those present, at random and from memory: the wealthy Bullinger, Leo Zink, the painter, whom neither Adrian nor I really liked and whom he had presumably invited along with the departed Spengler; Helmut Institoris, now a sort of widower; the clearly articulating Dr Kranich, Frau Binder-Majorescu, the Knöterichs, the hollow-cheeked jester and academy portrait-painter Nottebohm and his wife, brought by Institoris. Also there were Sixtus Kridwiss and the members of his discussion group: Dr Unruhe, the researcher into the strata of the earth, Professors Vogler and Holzschuher, Daniel zur Höhe, the poet, in a black buttoned-up frock coat, and to my great annoyance even that quibbling sophist Chaim Breisacher. The professional musical element was represented, in addition to the opera singers, by Dr Edschmid, the director of the Zapfenstösser orchestra. To my utter astonishment – and probably not only to mine – who should have found his way hither but Baron Gleichen-Russwurm, who, so far as I know, was making his first social appearance since that affair with the mouse, and had brought his wife with him, a full-bosomed, elegant Austrian dame. It appeared that Adrian, eight days beforehand, had sent an invitation to his estate, and most likely the so fantastically compromised descendant of the poet Schiller had joyfully seized upon the unique opportunity to reinstate himself in society.

Well, so all these people, some thirty, as I said, at first stood about expectantly in the salon, greeted each other, exchanged their feelings of anticipation. Rüdiger Schildknapp, in his everlasting shabby sports clothes, was surrounded by females. Women, in fact, formed the majority of the guests. I heard the voices of the dramatic singers rising euphoniously above all the rest; the clear, asthmatic articulation of Dr Kranich; Bullinger's swaggering tones, the assurances of Kridwiss that this gathering and what it promised was '*sho'enorm wichtich*', and zur Höhe's concurrence: '*Ja wohl, man kann es sagen*', as he pounded with the balls of his feet. The Baroness

Gliechen moved about, seeking sympathy for the obscure fatality that had befallen her and her husband: 'You know about this *ennui* we have had,' she was saying to all and sundry. From the beginning I had observed that many of the guests did not notice Adrian's presence and spoke as though we were still waiting for him, simply because they did not recognize him. He was sitting at the heavy oval table in the centre of the room, where we had once talked with Saul Fitelberg; he had his back to the light, and was dressed in his everyday clothes. But several guests asked me who the gentleman was, and when, at first in some surprise, I set them right they hastened with an 'Oh, really!' of sudden enlightenment to greet their host. How he must have changed, under my very eyes, for that to be possible! Of course, the beard made a great difference, and I said so to those who could not feel convinced that it was he. Near his chair the woolly-headed Rosenstiel stood erect for a long time, like a sentinel; this was why Meta Nackedey kept as far off as possible, in a remote corner of the room. However, Kunigunde had the decency to leave her post after a while, whereon the other adoring soul occupied it straightway. Open on the rack of the square piano against the wall stood the score of *The Lamentation of Dr Faustus.*

I kept my eyes on my friend, and while talking with one and another of the guests did not miss the sign which he gave me with his head and eyebrows, to the effect that I should have people take their seats. I did so at once, inviting those nearest me, making signs to those farther off, and even bringing myself to clap hands for silence, that the announcement might be made that Dr Leverkühn would now begin his lecture. A man knows by a certain numbness of the features that he has gone pale; the drops of perspiration which may come out on his brow are deathly cold as well. My hands, when I very feebly clapped them, shook as they shake now when I set myself to write down the horrible memory.

The audience obeyed with fair alacrity. Silence and order were quickly established. It happened that at the table with Adrian sat the old Schlaginhaufens, Jeanette Sheurl, Schildknapp, my wife and myself. The other guests were irregularly bestowed at both sides of the room, on various kinds of seats, the sofa, painted wooden chairs, horsehair arm-chairs; some of the men leaned against the walls. Adrian showed no sign of gratifying the general expectation, mine included, by going to the piano. He sat with his hands folded, his head drooped to one side, looking straight in front of him, yet hardly with an outward gaze. He began in the now complete hush to address the assembly, in the slightly monotonous, rather faltering voice I was familiar with; in the sense of a greeting, it seemed to me at first, and at first it really was that. I must bring myself to add that he often mis-spoke – and in my agony I dug my nails into my palms – and in correcting one mistake made another, so that after a while he paid no further attention, but simply passed them over. Anyhow, I need not have been so agonized over his various irregularities of pronunciation, for he used in part, as he had always enjoyed doing in writing, a sort of elder German, with its defects and open sentence-structure, always with something doubtful and unregulated about it; how long ago is it, indeed, that out tongue outgrew the barbaric and got tolerably regulated as to grammar and spelling!

He began in a low murmur, so that very few understood his opening sentence or made anything out of it. Perhaps they took it as a whim, rhetorical flourish; it went something like this:

'Esteemed, in especial and beloved brethren and sisters.'

After that he was silent for a little, as though considering, his cheek resting against one hand that was supported by the elbow on the table. What followed was also taken as a whimsical introductory, intended to be humorous; and although the immobility of his features, the weariness of his looks, his pallor contradicted the idea, yet a responsive laugh ran through the room, a slight sniff, a titter from the ladies.

'Firstly,' said he, 'I will exhibit to you my thankfulness for the courtesy and the friendship, both undeserved by me, ye have vouchsafed in that ye are come hither into this place, afoot and by wagon, since out of the desolation of this retreat I have written to and called you, likewise had you written to and called by my leal famulus and special friend, which yet knoweth how to put me in remembrance of our school-days from youth up, since we did study together at Halla; but thereof, and of how high-mindedness and abominacyon did in that study already begin, more hereafter in my Sermoni.'

Some of them looked over at me and smirked, who out of emotion was unable to smile, feeling that our dear man did not look as though he thought of me with any such particular tenderness. But just the fact that they saw tears in my eyes diverted most of them; and I remember with disgust that at this point Leo Zink loudly blew his big nose, the butt of most of his own jokes, to caricature my perceptible emotion. His performance elicited more titters. Adrian seemed not to notice.

'Before aught else,' he went on, 'must I pray' (he said 'play', corrected it, and then went back again to his mistake) 'and beg you not to take it amiss or crosswise that our hound Praestigiar, he is called Suso but of a truth is named Praestigiar, did demean himself so ill and make so hellish a yauling and bauling that you have for my sake undergone stress and strain. It were better we handed each of you a whistle we have pitched so high that only the hound can hear it and understand from afar off that good and bidden friends are coming, coveting to hear in what manner of life under his guard I have lived these many years.'

There was another polite laugh at his words about the whistle, but it sounded strained. He continued, and said:

'Now have I a friendly Christian request to you, that ye may not take and receive in evil part my homily, but that ye would rather construe it all to the best, inasmuch as I verily crave to make unto you, good and sely ones, which if not without sin are yet but ordinarily and tolerably sinful, wherefore I cordially despise yet fervidly envy you, a full confession from one human being to another, for now the houre-glasse standeth before my eyes, the finishing whereof I must carefully expect: when the last grain runs through the narrow neck and he will fetch me, to whom I have given myselfe so dearly with my proper blood that I shall both body and soul everlastingly be his and fall in his hands and his power when the glass is run and the time, which is his ware, be full expired.'

Again here and there somebody tittered or sniffed; but others shook their heads and made disapproving noises as though the words had been in bad taste. Some of the guests put on a look of dark foreboding.

'Know, then,' said he, at the table, 'ye good and godly folk' (he said 'god and goodly'), 'with your modest sins and resting in Goodes godness, for I have suppressed it so long in me but will no longer hide it, that already since my twenty-first year I am wedded to Satan and with due knowing of peril, out of well-considered courage, pride, and presumption because I would win glory in this world, I made with him a bond and vow, so that all which during the term of four-and-twenty years I brought forth, and which mankind justly regarded with mistrust, is only with his help come to pass and is divel's work, infused by the angel of death. For I well thought that he that will eat the kernel must crack the nut, and one must today take the divel to favour, because to great enterprise and devises one can use and have none other save him.'

A strained and painful stillness now reigned in the room. Only a few listened unperturbed; there were many raised eyebrows, and faces wherein one read: 'What is all this and what is it leading up to?' If he had but once smiled or put on a face to explain his words as a mystification got up by the artist, matters would have been halfway made good. But he did not, he sat there in dead earnest. Some of the guests looked inquiringly at me, as if to ask what it all meant and how I would account for it. Perhaps I ought to have intervened and broken up the meeting. But on what pretext? The only explanations were humiliating and extreme; I felt that I must let things take their course, in the hope that he would soon begin to play and give us notes instead of words. Never had I felt more strongly the advantage that music, which says nothing and everything, has over the unequivocal word; yes the saving responsibility of all art, compared with the bareness and baldness of unmediated revelation. But to interrupt not only went against my sense of reverence, but also my very soul cried out to hear, even though among those who listened with me only very few were worthy. Only hold out and listen, I said in my heart to the others, since after all he did invite you as his fellow human beings!

After a reflective pause my friend went on.

'Believe not, dear brothers and sisters, that for the promission and conclusion of the pact a crosse way in the wood, many circles and impure conjuration were needed, since already St Thomas teacheth that for falling away there needs not words with which invocation takes place, rather any act be enough, even without express allegiance. For it was but a butterfly, a bright cream-licker, Hetaera Esmeralda, she charmed me with her touch, the milk-witch, and I followed after her into the twilit shadowy foliage that her transparent nakedness loveth, and where I caught her, who in flight is like a wind-blown petal, caught her and caressed with her, defying her warning, so did it befall. For as she charmed me, so she bewitched me and forgave me in love – so I was initiate, and the promise confirmed.'

I started for now came a voice from the audience: it came from Daniel zur Höhe the poet, in his priestly garment, pounding with his feet and hammering out his words:

'It is beautiful. It has beauty. Very good, oh, very good, one may say so!'

Some people hissed. I too turned disapprovingly towards the speaker, though privately I was grateful for what he said. His words were silly enough; but they classified what we were hearing, put it under a soothing and recognized rubric, namely the aesthetic, which, inapplicable as that was and however much it angered me, did make me feel easier. For it seemed to me that a sort of relieved 'Ah-h!' went through the audience, and one lady, Radbruch the publisher's wife, was encouraged by zur Höhe's words to say:

'One thinks one is hearing poetry.'

Alas, one did not think so for long! This aesthetic interpretation, however conveniently offered, was not tenable. What we heard had nothing at all in common with zur Höhe the poet's tall tomfooleries about obedience, violence, blood, and world-plunder. This was dead sober earnest, a confession, the truth, to listen to which a man in extreme agony of soul had called together his fellow-men – an act of fantastic good faith, moreover, for one's fellow-men are not meant or made to face such truth otherwise than with cold shivers and with the conclusion that, when it was no longer possible to regard it as poetry, they very soon unanimously and audibly came to about it.

It did not look as though those interpolations had reached our host at all. His thoughts, whenever he paused in his address, obviously made him inaccessible to them.

'But only mark,' he resumed, 'heartily respected loving friends, that you have to do with a god-forsaken and despairing man, whose carcass belongeth not in consecrate earth, among Christians dead in the faith, but on the horse-dung with the cadavers of dead animals. On the bier, I say to you beforehand, you will always find it lying on its face, and though you turn it fives times you will ever find it on its face. For long before I dallied with the poison butterfly, my forward soul in high mind and arrogance was on the way to Satan though my goal stood in doubt; and from youth up I worked towards him, as you must know, indeed, that man is made for hell or blessedness, made and foredestined, and I was born for hell. So did I feed my arrogance with sugar, studying divinity at Halla Academie, yet not for the service of God but the other, and my study of divinity was secretly already the beginning of the bond and the disguised move not Biblewards, but to him the great religiosus. For who can hold that will away, and 'twas but a short step from the divinity school over to Leipzig and to music, that I solely and entirely then busied myself with figuris, characteribus, formis conjurationum, and what other so ever are the names of invocations and magic.

'So my desperate heart hath trifled all away. I had I suppose a good toward wit and gifts gratiously given me from above which I could have used in all honour and modesty, but felt all-too well: it is the time when uprightly and in pious sober wise, naught of work is to be wrought and art grown unpossible without the divel's help and fires of hell under the cauldron . . . Yea verily, dear mates, that art is stuck and grown too heavy and scorneth itselfe and God's poor man knoweth no longer where to turn in his sore plight, that is belike the fault in the times. But an one invite the divel as guest, to pass beyond all this and get to the break-through, he chargeth his soul and taketh the guilt of the time upon his own shoulders, so that he is damned. For it hath been said "Be sober, and watch!" But that is not the affair of some; rather, instead of shrewdly concerning themselves with what is needful upon earth that it may be better there, and discreetly doing it, that among men such order shall be stablished that again for the beautiful work living soil and true harmony be prepared, man playeth the truant and breaketh out in hellish drunkenness; so giveth he his soul thereto and cometh among the carrion.

'So, courteous and beloved brothers and sisters have I borne me, and let nigromantia, carmina, incantatio, veneficium, and what names so ever be all my aim and striving. And I soon came to the speech of that one, the make-bate, the losel, in the Italian room, have held much parley with him, and he had much to tell me of the quality, fundament, and substance of hell. Sold me time too, four-and-twenty years, boundless to the eye, and promised too great things and much fire under the cauldron, to the end that not withstanding I should be capable of the work although it were too hard and my head too shrewd and mocking thereto. Only certes I should suffer the knives of pain therefor, even in the time, as the little sea-maid suffered them in her legs, which was my sister and sweet bride, and named Hyphialta. For he brought her me to my bed as my bed-sister that I gan woo her and loved her ever more, whether she came to me with the fishes tail or with legs. Oftentimes indeed she came with the tail, for the pains she suffered as with knives in the legs outweighed her lust, and I had much feeling for the wise wherein her tender body went over so sweetly into the scaly tail. But higher was my delight even so in the pure human form and so for my part I had greater lust when she came to me in legs.'

There was a stir in the room. Somebody was leaving, the old Schlaginhaufen pair it was: they got up from our table and looking neither right nor left, on tiptoe, the husband guiding his spouse by the elbow passed through the seated groups and out at the door. Not two minutes went by before the noise and the throbbing of their engine were heard, starting up in the yard. They were driving away.

Many of the audience were upset by this, for now they had lost their means of conveyance to the station. But there was no perceptible inclination among the guests to follow the Schlaginhaufens' example. They all sat spellbound, and when quiet was restored outside, zur Höhe raised his voice again in his dogmatic 'Beautiful! Ah, indeed yes, it is beautiful.'

I too was just on the point of opening my mouth, to beg our friend to make an end of the introduction and play to us from the work itself, when he, unaffected by the incident, continued his address:

'Thereupon did Hyphialta get with child and accounted me a little son, to whom with my whole soul I clung, a hallowed little lad, lovelier than is ever born, and as though come hither from afar and of old stamp. But since the child was flesh and blood and it was ordained that I might love no human being, he slew it, merciless, and used thereto mine own proper eyes. For you must know that when a soul is drawn violently to evil, its gaze is venomous and like to a basilisk, and chiefly for children. So this little son full of sweet sayings went from me hence, in August-month, though I had thought anon such tenderness might be let. I had well thought before that I, as devil's disciple, might love in flesh and blood what was not female, but he wooed me for my thou in boundless confidence, until I graunted it. Hence I must slay him too, and sent him to his death by force and order. For the magisterulus had marked that I was minded to marry me and was exceeding wroth, sith in the wedded state he saw apostasy from him, and a trick for atonement. So he forced me to use precisely this intent, that I coldly murdered the trusting one and will have confessed it today and here before you all, that I sit before you also as murtherer.'

Another group of guests left the room at this point: little Helmut Institoris got up in silent protest, white, his underlip drawn across his teeth. So did his friends the academy portraitist Nottebohm, and his markedly bourgeois high-chested wife, whom we used to call 'the maternal bosom'. They all went out in silence. But outside they had probably not held their tongues, for shortly afterwards Frau Schweigestill came quietly in, in her apron, with her smooth grey head, and stood near the door, with folded hands. She listened as Adrian said:

'But whatever sinner was I, ye friends, a murtherer, enemy to man, given to divelish concubinge, yet aside from all that I have ever busied myself as a worker and did never arrest' (again he seemed to bethink and correct himself, but went back to 'arrest' again), 'arrest not rist, but toiled and moiled and produced hard things, according to the word of the apostle: "Who seeks hard things, to him it is hard." For as God doth nothing great through us, without our unction, so neither the other. Only the shame and the intellectual mockery and what in the time was against the work, that he kept aside, the residue I had to do myself, even also after strange infusions. For there was oftentimes heard by me all manner of instrument: an organ or positive, more delectable then harpes, lutes, fiddles, trombones, clarigolds, citerns, waigths, anomes, cornets, and hornpipes, four of each, that I had thought myself in heaven had I not known differently. Much of it I wrote down. Often too, certain children were with me in the room, boys and girls who sang to me a motet from sheets of notes, smiled a funny little knowing smile and exchanged their glances. They were most pretty children. Sometimes their hair was lifted as though from hot air and they smoothed it again with their pretty hands, that were dimpled and had little rubies on them. Out of their nostrils curled sometimes little yellow worms, crawled down to their breasts and disappeared –'

These words were the signal for another group of listeners to leave the room: the scholars Unruhe, Vogler, and Holzschuher, one of whom I saw press the base of his palms to his temples as he went out. But Sixtus Kridwiss, at whose house they held their discussions, kept his place, looking much excited. Even after these had gone, there remained some twenty persons, though many of them had risen and seemed ready to flee. Leo Zink had his eyebrows raised in malicious anticipation, saying 'Jessas, na!' just as he did when he was pronouncing on somebody's painting. A little troop of women had gathered round Leverkühn as though to protect him: Kunigunde Rosenstiel, Meta Nackedey, Jeanette Scheurl – these three. Else Schweigestill held aloof.

And we heard:

'So the Evil One hath strengthened his words in good faith through four-and-twenty years and all is finished up till the last, with murther and lechery have I brought it to fullness and perhaps through Grace good can come of what was create in evil, I know not. Mayhap to God it seemeth I sought the hard and laboured might and main, perhaps, perhaps it will be to my credit that I applied myself and obstinately finished all – but I cannot say and have not courage to hope for it. My sin is greater than that it can be forgiven me, and I have raised it to its height, for my head speculated that the contrite unbelief in the possibility of Grace and pardon might be the most intriguing of all for the Everlasting Goodness, where yet I see that such impudent calculation makes compassion unpossible. Yet basing upon that I went further in speculation and reckoned that this last depravity must be the uttermost spur for Goodness to display its everlastingness. And so then, that I carried on an atrocious competition with the Goodness above, which were more inexhaustible, it or my speculation – so ye see that I am damned, and there is no pity for me that I destroy all and every beforehand by speculation.

'But since my time is at an end, which aforetime I bought with my soul, I have summoned you to me before my end, courteous and loving brethren and sisters, to the end that my ghostly departure may not be hidden from you. I beseech you hereupon, ye would hold me in kindly remembrance, also others whom perchance to invite I forgat, with friendly commendations to salute and not to misdeam anything done by me. All this bespoke and beknown, will I now to take leave to play you a little out of the construction which I heard from the lovely instrument of Satan and which in part the knowing children sang to me.'

He stood up, pale as death.

'This man,' in the stillness one heard the voice of Dr Kranich, wheezing yet clearly articulate: 'This man is mad. There has been for a long time no doubt of it, and it is most regrettable that in our circle the profession of alienist is not represented. I, as a numismatist, feel myself entirely incompetent in this situation.'

With that he too went away.

Leverkühn, surrounded by the women, Schildknapp, Helene, and myself, had sat down at the brown square piano and flattened the pages of the score with his right hand. We saw tears run down his cheeks and fall on the keyboard, wetting it, as he attacked the keys in a strongly dissonant chord. At the same time he opened his mouth as though to sing, but only a wail which will ring for ever in my ears broke from his lips. He spread out his arms, bending over the instrument and seeming about to embrace it, when suddenly, as though smitten by a blow, he fell sideways from his seat and to the floor.

Frau Schweigestill, though she had stood farther off, was by him sooner than the rest of us, who, I know not why, wavered a second before we moved. She lifted the head of the unconscious man and holding him in her motherly arms she cried to those still in the room, standing anigh and gaping: 'Let me see the backs of ye, all and sundry! City folk all, with not a smitch of understanding, and there's need of that here! Talked about th'everlasting mercy, poor soul, I don't know if it goes's far's that, but human understanding, believe me, that does!'

Epilogue

It is finished. An old man, bent, well-nigh broken by the horrors of the times in which he wrote and those which were the burden of his writing, looks with dubious satisfaction on the high stack of teeming paper which is the work of his industry, the product of these years filled to running over with past memories and present events. A task has been mastered, for which by nature I was not the man, to which I was not born, but rather called by love and loyalty – and by my status as eyewitness. What these can accomplish, what devotion can do, that has been done – I must needs be content.

When I began writing down these memories, the biography of Adrian Leverkühn, there existed with reference to its author as much as to the art of its subject not the faintest prospect of its publication. But now that the monstrous national perversion which then held the Continent, and more than the Continent, in its grip, has celebrated its orgies down to the bitter end; now that its prime movers have had themselves poisoned by their physicians, drenched with petrol and set on fire, that nothing of them might remain – now, I say, it might be possible to think of the publication of my labour of love. But those evil men willed that Germany be destroyed down to the ground; and one dares not hope it could very soon be capable of any sort of cultural activity, even the printing of a book. In actual fact I have sometimes pondered ways and means of sending these pages to America, in order that they might first be laid before the public in an English translation. To me it seems as though this might not run quite counter to the wishes of my departed friend. True, there comes the thought of the essentially foreign impression my book must make in that cultural climate and coupled with it the dismaying prospect that its translation into English must turn out, at least in some all too radically German parts, to be an impossibility.

What I further foresee is the feeling of emptiness which will be my lot when after a brief report on the closing scenes of the great composer's life I shall have rendered my account and drawn it to a close. The work on it, harrowing and consuming as it has been, I shall miss. As the regular performance of a task it kept me busy and filled the years which would have been still harder to bear in idleness. I now look about me for an activity which could in future replace it. And at first I look in vain. It is true, the barriers that eleven years ago kept me from practising my profession have now fallen to the guns of history. Germany is free, in so far as one may apply the word to a land prostrate and proscribed. It may be that soon nothing will stand in the way of my return to teaching. Monsignor Hinterpförtner has already taken occasion to refer to the possibility. Shall I once more impress upon the hearts of my top-form pupils in the humanities the cultural ideas in which reverence for the deities of the depths blends with the civilized cult of Olympic reason and clarity, to make for a unity in uprightness? But ah, I fear that in this savage decade a generation of youth has grown up which understands my language as little as I theirs. I fear the youth of my land has become too strange for me to be their teacher still. And more: Germany herself, the unhappy nation, is strange to me, utterly strange and that because, convinced of her awful end, I drew back from her sins and hid from them in my seclusion. Must I not ask myself whether or not I did right? And again: did I actually do it? I have clung to one man, one suffering, significant human being, clung unto death; and I have depicted his life, which never ceased to fill me with love and grief. To me it seems as though this loyalty might atone for my having fled in horror from my country's guilt.

Reverence forbids me to describe Adrian's condition when he came to himself after the twelve hours' unconsciousness into which the paralytic stroke at the piano had plunged him. No, not to himself did he come; rather he found himself as a stranger, who was only the burnt-out husk of his personality, having at bottom nothing to do with him who had been called Adrian Leverkühn. After all, the word 'dementia' originally meant nothing else than this aberration from self, self-alienation.

I will say this much: that he did not remain in Pfeiffering. Rüdiger Schildknapp and I assumed the hard duty of conveying the patient, treated by Dr Kürbis with sedatives for the journey, to Munich and a private hospital for nervous diseases, in Nymphenburg, directed by Dr von Hösslin. There Adrian remained for three months. The prognosis of the specialist stated without reservation that this was a disease of the brain which could only run its course. But in the measure that it did so, it would pass through the present crass manifestations and with a suitable treatment arrive at quieter, though unfortunately not more hopeful phases. This information it was which after some consultation determined Schildknapp and myself to delay our announcement of the catastrophe to Adrian's mother, Elsbeth Leverkühn at Buchel. It was certain that on the receipt of such news she would hasten to him; and if more calmness might be hoped for, it seemed no more than human to spare her the intolerable, shattering spectacle of her child before that was in any measure improved by institutional treatment.

Her child! For that and nothing more was Adrian Leverkühn again. She came one day, the old mother, when the year was passing into autumn. She came to Pfeiffering, to take him back to his Thuringian home, the scene of his childhood, to which his outward frame of life had so long stood in such singular correspondence. She came to a helpless infant, who had no longer any memory of his manhood's proud flight, or at most some very dark and obscure vision buried in his depths; who clung to her skirts of yore, and whom as in early days she must – or might – tend and coax and reprove for being 'naughty'. Anything more fearfully touching or lamentable cannot be imagined that to see a free spirit, once bold and defiant, once soaring in a giddy arc above an astonished world, now creeping broken back to his mother's arms. But my conviction, resting on unequivocal evidence, is that the maternal experiences from so tragic and wretched a return, in all its grief, some appeasement as well. The Icarus-flight of the hero son, the steep ascent of the male escaped from her outgrown care, is to a mother an error both sinful and incomprehensible: in her heart, with secret anger she hears the austere, estranging words: 'Woman, what have I to do with thee?' And when he falls and is shattered she takes him back, the 'poor, dear child', to her bosom, thinking nothing else than that he would have done better never to have gone away.

I have reason to believe that within the blackness of his spirit's night Adrian felt a horror of this soft humiliation; that an instinctive repulsion, a remnant of his pride was still alive, before he surrendered with gloomy relish to the comfort which an exhausted spirit must after all find in complete mental abdication. Evidence of this compulsive rebellion and of urge to flight from the maternal is supplied, at least in part, by the attempt at suicide which he made when we had succeeded in making him understand that Elsbeth Leverkühn had been told of his illness and was on her way to him. What happened was this:

After three months' treatment in the von Hösslin establishment, where I was allowed to see my friend only seldom and always only for a few minutes, he achieved a degree of composure – I do not say improvement – which enabled the physician to consent to private care in quiet Pfeiffering. Financial reasons too spoke for this course. And so once more the patient's familiar surroundings received him. At first he continued under the supervision of the attendant who had brought him back. But his behaviour seemed to warrant the removal of this precaution, and for the time being he was attended by the family, particularly by Frau Schweigestill. Gereon had brought a capable daughter-in-law into the house (Clementine had become the wife of the Waldshut station-master) and the mother was now retired, with leisure to devote her human feeling to her lodger, who after all these years had become, though so much above her, something like her son. He trusted her as he did no one else. To sit hand in hand with her in the Abbot's room or in the garden behind the house was obviously most soothing to him. I found him thus when I went for the first time to Pfeiffering. The look he directed upon me as I approached had something violent and unbalanced about it, quickly resolved, to my great grief, in gloomy repugnance. Perhaps he recognized in me the companion of his sane existence, all memory of which he rejected. On a cautious hint from Frau Else that he should speak 'nicely' to me, his face only darkened still more, its expression was even menacing. There was nothing for me to do save in sadness to withdraw.

The moment had now come to compose the letter which should as gently as possible inform his mother of the facts. To delay longer would have been unfair to her, and the answering telegram announcing her arrival followed without a day's delay. As I said, Adrian had been told; but it was hard to know if he had grasped the news. An hour later, however, when he was supposed to be asleep, he escaped unnoticed from the house. Gereon and a farmhand came up with him by the Klammerweiher; he had removed his outer clothing and was standing up to his neck where the water deepened so abruptly from the bank. He was just disappearing when the men plunged after him and brought him out. As they were bringing him back to the house he spoke repeatedly of the coldness of the water and added that it was very hard to drown oneself in a pond one had bathed and swum in often as a boy. But that he had never done in the Klammer pool, only in its counterpart at Buchel, the Cow Trough.

My guess, which amounts almost to certainty, is that a mystic idea of salvation was behind his frustrated attempt to escape. The idea is familiar to the older theology and in particular to early Protestantism: namely, that those who had invoked the Devil could save their souls by 'yielding their bodies'. Very likely Adrian acted in this sense, among others, and God alone knows whether we did right in not letting him so act up to the end. Not all that happens in madness is therefore simply to be prevented, and the obligation to preserve life was in this case obeyed in scarcely anyone's interest save the mother's – for undoubtedly the maternal would prefer an irresponsible son to a dead one.

She came, Jonathan Leverkühn's brown-eyed widow with the smooth white head, bent on taking her lost and erring son back into childhood. When they met, Adrian trembled for a long time, resting his head on the breast of the woman he called *Mutter* and *Du*. Frau Schweigestill, who kept out of the way, he called *Mutter* and *Sie*. Elsbeth spoke to her son, in the still melodious voice which all her life long she had refrained from song. But during the journey north into central Germany, accompanied fortunately by the attendant familiar to Adrian, there came without warning or occasion an outburst of rage against his mother, an unexpected seizure, which obliged Frau Leverkühn to retire to another compartment for the remainder, almost half of the journey, leaving the patient alone with his attendant.

It was an isolated occurrence. Nothing of the sort happened again. When she approached him as they arrived in Weissenfels he joined her with demonstrations of love and pleasure, followed her at her heels to Buchel, and was the most docile of children to her who expended herself on his care with a fullness of devotion which only a mother can give. At Buchel, where likewise for years a daughter-in-law had presided and two grandchildren were growing up, he occupied the upstairs room he had once shared with his elder brother, and once more it was the old linden, instead of the elm, whose boughs stirred in the breeze beneath his window and whose marvellous scent he seemed to enjoy. They could confidently leave him free to sit and dream the hours away on the round bench where once the loud-voiced stable-girl had taught us children how to sing canons. His mother took care that he got exercise: arm in arm they often walked through the quiet countryside. When they met someone he would put out his hand; she did not restrain him, and they would all exchange greetings in turn while standing.

As for me, I saw our dear man again in 1935, being by then *emeritus*. I found myself at Buchel, a sorrowful gratulant on the occasion of his fiftieth birthday. The linden was in bloom, he sat beneath it, his mother beside him. I confess my knees trembled as I approached him with flowers in my hand. He seemed grown smaller, which might be due to the bent and drooping posture, from which he lifted to me a narrow face, an Ecce-homo countenance, despite the healthy country colour, with woeful open mouth and vacant eyes. In Pfeiffering he had wished not to recognize me. Now there was no doubt at all that, despite reminders from his mother, he connected with my appearance no memories whatever. Of what I said to him about his birthday, the meaning of my visit, he obviously understood nothing. Only the flowers seemed to arouse his interest for a moment, then they lay forgotten.

I saw him once more in 1939, after the conquest of Poland, a year before his death, which his mother, at eighty, still survived. She led me up the stair to his room, entering it with the encouraging words: 'Just come in, he will not notice you!' while I stood profoundly moved at the door. At the back of the room, on a sofa, the foot end of which was towards me, so that I could look into his face, there lay under a light woollen coverlet he that was once Adrian Leverkühn, whose immortal part is now so called. The colourless hands, whose sensitive shape I had always loved, lay crossed on his breast, like a saint's on a medieval tomb. The beard, grown greyer, still lengthened more the hollow face, so that it was now strikingly like an El Greco nobleman's. What a mocking game Nature here played, one might say: presenting a picture of the utmost spirituality, just there whence the spirit had fled! The eyes lay deep in their sockets, the brows were bushier; from under them the apparition directed upon me an unspeakably earnest look, so searching as to be almost threatening. It made me quail; but even in a second it had as it were collapsed, the eyeballs rolled upwards, half disappearing under the lids and ceaselessly moving from side to side. I refused the mother's repeated invitation to come closer, and turned weeping away.

On the 25th August 1940 the news reached me in Freising that that remnant of a life had been quenched: a life which had given to my own, in love and effort, pride and pain, its essential content. At the open grave in the little Oberweiler churchyard stood with me, besides the relatives, Jeanette Scheurl, Rüdiger Schildknapp, Kunigunde Rosenstiel, and Meta Nackedey; also a stranger, a veiled unknown, who disappeared as the first clods fell on the coffin.

Germany, the hectic on her cheek, was reeling then at the height of her dissolute triumphs, about to gain the whole world by virtue of the one pact she was minded to keep, which she had signed with her blood. Today, clung round by demons, a hand over one eye, with the other staring into horrors, down she flings from despair to despair. When will she reach the bottom of the abyss? When, out of uttermost hopelessness – a miracle beyond the power of belief – will the light of hope dawn? A lonely man folds his hands and speaks: 'God be merciful to thy poor soul, my friend, my Fatherland!'

Author's Note

It does not seem supererogatory to inform the reader that the form of musical composition delineated in Chapter Twenty-two, known as the twelve-tone or row system, is in truth the intellectual property of a contemporary composer and theoretician, Arnold Schönberg. I have transferred this technique in a certain ideational context to the fictitious figure of a musician, the tragic hero of my novel. In fact the passages of this book that deal with musical theory are indebted in numerous details to Schönberg's *Harmonielehre*.

Mario
and the
Magician

TRANSLATED FROM THE GERMAN BY

H.T. Lowe-Porter

The atmosphere of Torre di Venere remains unpleasant in the memory. From the first moment the air of the place made us uneasy, we felt irritable, on edge; then at the end came the shocking business of Cipolla, that dreadful being who seemed to incorporate, in so fateful and so humanly impressive a way, all the peculiar evilness of the situation as a whole. Looking back, we had the feeling that the horrible end of the affair had been preordained and lay in the nature of things; that the children had to be present at it was an added impropriety, due to the false colours in which the weird creature presented himself. Luckily for them, they did not know where the comedy left off and the tragedy began; and we let them remain in their happy belief that the whole thing had been a play up till the end.

Torre di Venere lies some fifteen kilometres from Portoclemente, one of the most popular summer resorts on the Tyrrhenian Sea. Portoclemente is urban and elegant and full to overflowing for months on end. Its gay and busy main street of shops and hotels runs down to a wide sandy beach covered with tents and pennanted sandcastles and sunburnt humanity, where at all times a lively social bustle reigns, and much noise. But this same spacious and inviting fine-sanded beach, this same border of pine grove and near, presiding mountains, continues all the way along the coast. No wonder then that the same competition of a quiet kind should have sprung up farther on. Torre di Venere – the tower that gave the town its name is gone long since, one looks for it in vain – is an offshoot of the larger resort, and for some years remained an idyll for the few, a refuge for more unworldly spirits. But the usual history of such places repeated itself: peace has had to retire farther along the coast, to Marina Petriera and dear knows where else. We all know how the world at once seeks peace and puts her to flight – rushing upon her in the fond idea that they two will wed, and where she is, there it can be at home. It will even set up its Vanity Fair in a spot and be capable of thinking that peace is still by its side. Thus Torre – though its atmosphere so far is more modest and contemplative than that of Portoclemente – has been quite taken up, by both Italians and foreigners. It is no longer the thing to go to Portoclemente – though still so much the thing that it is as noisy and crowded as ever. One goes next door, so to speak: to Torre. So much more refined, even, and cheaper to boot. And the attractiveness of these qualities persists, though the qualities themselves long ago ceased to be evident. Torre has got a Grand Hotel. Numerous pensions have sprung up, some modest, some pretentious. The people who own or rent the villas and pinetas overlooking the sea no longer have it all their own way on the beach. In July and August it looks just like the beach at Portoclemente: it swarms with a screaming, squabbling, merrymaking crowd, and the sun, blazing down like mad, peels the skin off their necks. Garish little flat-bottomed boats rock on the glittering blue, manned by children, whose mothers hover afar and fill the air with anxious cries of Nino! and Sandro! and Bice! and Maria! Pedlars step across the legs of recumbent sunbathers, selling flowers and corals, oysters, lemonade, and *cornetti al burro*, and crying their wares in the breathy, full-throated southern voice.

Such was the scene that greeted our arrival in Torre: pleasant enough, but after all, we thought, we had come too soon. It was the middle of August, the Italian season was still at its height, scarcely the moment for strangers to learn to love the special charms of the place. What an afternoon crowd in the cafés on the front! For instance, in the Esquisito, where we sometimes sat and were served by Mario, that very Mario of whom I shall have presently to tell. It is well-nigh impossible to find a table; and the various orchestras contend together in the midst of one's conversation with bewildering effect. Of course, it is in the afternoon that people come over from Portoclemente. The excursion is a favourite one for the restless denizens of that pleasure resort, and a Fiat motor-bus plies to and fro, coating inch-thick with dust the oleander and laurel hedges along the highroad – a notable if repulsive sight.

Yes, decidedly one should go to Torre in September, when the great public has left. Or else in May, before the water is warm enough to tempt the Southerner to bathe. Even in the before and after seasons Torre is not empty, but life is less national and more subdued. English, French, and German prevail under the tent-awnings and in the pension dining-rooms; whereas in August – in the Grand Hotel, at least, where, in default of private addresses, we had engaged rooms – the stranger finds the field so occupied by Florentine and Roman society that he feels quite isolated and even temporarily *déclassé*.

We had, rather to our annoyance, this experience on the evening we arrived, when we went in to dinner and were shown to our table by the waiter in charge. As a table, it had nothing against it, save that we had already fixed our eyes upon those on the veranda beyond, built out over the water, where little red-shaded lamps glowed – and there were still some tables empty, though it was as full as the dining-room within. The children went into raptures at the festive sight, and without more ado we announced our intention to take our meals by preference on the veranda. Our words, it appeared, were prompted by ignorance; for we were informed, with somewhat embarrassed politeness, that the cosy nook outside was reserved for the clients of the hotel: *di nostri clienti*. Their clients? But we were their clients. We were not tourists or trippers, but boarders for a stay of some three or four weeks. However, we forbore to press for an explanation of the difference between the likes of us and that clientèle to whom it was vouchsafed to eat out there in the glow of the red lamps, and took our dinner by the prosaic common light of the dining-room chandelier – a thoroughly ordinary and monotonous hotel bill of fare, be it said. In Pensione Eleonora, a few steps landward, the table, as we were to discover, was much better.

And thither it was that we moved, three or four days later, before we had had time to settle in properly at the Grand Hotel. Not on account of the veranda and the lamps. The children, straightway on the best of terms with waiters and pages, absorbed in the joys of life on the beach, promptly forgot those colourful seductions. But now there arose, between ourselves and the veranda clientèle – or perhaps more correctly with the compliant management – one of those little unpleasantnesses which can quite spoil the pleasure of a holiday. Among the guests were some high Roman aristocracy, a Principe X and his family. These grand folk occupied rooms close to our own, and the Principessa, a great and a passionately maternal lady, was thrown into a panic by the vestiges of a whooping-cough which our little ones had lately got over, but which now and then still faintly troubled the unshatterable slumbers of our youngest-born. The nature of this illness is not clear, leaving some play for the imagination. So we took no offence at our elegant neighbour for clinging to the widely held view that whooping-cough is acoustically contagious and quite simply fearing lest her children yield to the bad example set by ours. In the fullness of her feminine self-confidence she protested to the management, which then, in the person of the proverbial frock-coated manager, hastened to represent to us, with many expressions of regret, that under the circumstances they were obliged to transfer us to the annexe. We did our best to assure him that the disease was in its very last stages, that it was actually over, and presented no danger of infection to anybody. All that we gained was permission to bring the case before the hotel physician – not one chosen by us – by whose verdict we must then abide. We agreed, convinced that thus we should at once pacify the Princess and escape the trouble of moving. The doctor appeared, and behaved like a faithful and honest servant of science. He examined the child and gave his opinion: the disease was quite over, no danger of contagion was present. We drew a long breath and considered the incident closed – until the manager announced that despite the doctor's verdict it would still be necessary for us to give up our rooms and retire to the *dépendance*. Byzantinism like this outraged us. It is not likely that the Principessa was responsible for the wilful breach of faith. Very likely the fawning management had not even dared to tell her what the physician said. Anyhow, we made it clear to his understanding that we preferred to leave the hotel altogether and at once – and packed our trunks. We could do so with a light heart, having already set up casual friendly relations with Casa Eleonora. We had noticed its pleasant exterior and formed the acquaintance of its proprietor, Signora Angiolieri, and her husband: she slender and black-haired, Tuscan in type, probably at the beginning of the thirties, with the dead ivory complexion of the southern woman, he quiet and bald and carefully dressed. They owned a larger establishment in Florence and presided only in summer and early autumn over the branch in Torre di Venere. But earlier, before her marriage, our new landlady had been companion, fellow traveller, wardrobe mistress, yes, friend, of Eleonora Duse and manifestly regarded that period as the crown of her career. Even at our first visit she spoke of it with animation. Numerous photographs of the great actress, with affectionate inscriptions, were displayed about the drawing-room, and other souvenirs of their life together adorned the little tables and *étagères*. This cult of a so interesting past was calculated, of course, to heighten the advantages of the signora's present business. Nevertheless our pleasure and interest were quite genuine as we were conducted through the house by its owner and listened to her sonorous and staccato Tuscan voice relating anecdotes of that immortal mistress, depicting her suffering saintliness, her genius, her profound delicacy of feeling.

Thither, then, we moved our effects, to the dismay of the staff of the Grand Hotel, who, like all Italians, were very good to children. Our new quarters were retired and pleasant, we were within easy reach of the sea through the avenue of young plane trees that ran down to the esplanade. In the clean, cool dining-room Signora Angiolieri daily served the soup with her own hands, the service was attentive and good, the table capital. We even discovered some Viennese acquaintances, and enjoyed chatting with them after luncheon, in front of the house. They, in their turn, were the means of our finding others – in short, all seemed for the best, and we were heartily glad of the change we had made. Nothing was now wanting to a holiday of the most gratifying kind.

And yet no proper gratification ensued. Perhaps the stupid occasion of our change of quarters pursued us to the new ones we had found. Personally, I admit that I do not easily forget these collisions with ordinary humanity, the naïve misuse of power, the injustice, the sycophantic corruption. I dwelt upon the incident too much, it irritated me in retrospect – quite futilely, of course, since such phenomena are only all too natural and all too much the rule. And we had not broken off relations with the Grand Hotel. The children were as friendly as ever there, the porter mended their toys, and we sometimes took tea in the garden. We even saw the Principessa. She would come out, with her firm and delicate tread, her lips emphatically corallined, to look after her children, playing under the supervision of their English governess. She did not dream that we were anywhere near, for so soon as she appeared in the offing we sternly forbade our little one even to clear his throat.

The heat – if I may bring it in evidence – was extreme. It was African. The power of the sun, directly one left the border of the indigo-blue wave, was so frightful, so relentless, that the mere thought of the few steps between the beach and luncheon was a burden, clad though one might be only in pyjamas. Do you care for that sort of thing? Weeks on end? Yes, of course, it is proper to the south, it is classic weather, the sun of Homer, the climate wherein human culture came to flower – and all the rest of it. But after a while it is too much for me, I reach a point where I begin to find it dull. The burning void of the sky, day after day, weighs one down; the high coloration, the enormous *naïveté* of the unrefracted light – they do, I dare say, induce light-heartedness, a carefree mood born of immunity from downpours and other meteorological caprices. But slowly, slowly, there makes itself felt a lack: the deeper, more complex needs of the northern soul remain unsatisfied. You are left barren – even, it may be, in time, a little contemptuous. True, without that stupid business of the whooping-cough I might not have been feeling these things. I was annoyed, very likely I wanted to feel them and so half-unconsciously seized upon an idea lying ready to hand to induce, or if not to induce, at least to justify and strengthen my attitude. Up to this point, then, if you like, let us grant some ill will on our part. But the sea; and the mornings spent extended upon the fine sand in face of its eternal splendours – no, the sea could not conceivably induce such feelings. Yet it was none the less true that, despite all previous experience, we were not at home on the beach, we were not happy.

It was too soon, too soon. The beach, as I have said, was still in the hands of the middle-class native. It is a pleasing breed to look at, and among the young we saw much shapeliness and charm. Still, we were necessarily surrounded by a great deal of very average humanity – a middle-class mob, which, you will admit, is not more charming under this sun than under one's own native sky. The voices these women have! It was sometimes hard to believe that we were in the land which is the western cradle of the art of song. '*Fuggièro!*' I can still hear that cry, as for twenty mornings long I heard it close behind me, breathy, full-throated, hideously stressed, with a harsh open *e*, uttered in accents of mechanical despair. '*Fuggièro! Rispondi almeno!*' Answer when I call you! The *sp* in *rispondi* was pronounced like *shp*, as Germans pronounce it; and this, on top of what I felt already, vexed my sensitive soul. The cry was addressed to a repulsive youngster whose sunburn had made disgusting raw sores on his shoulders. He outdid anything I have ever seen for ill-breeding, refractoriness, and temper and was a great coward to boot, putting the whole beach in an uproar, one day, because of his outrageous sensitiveness to the slightest pain. A sand-crab had pinched his toe in the water, and the minute injury made him set up a cry of heroic proportions – the shout of an antique hero in his agony – that pierced one to the marrow and called up visions of some frightful tragedy. Evidently he considered himself not only wounded, but poisoned as well; he crawled out on the sand and lay in apparently intolerable anguish, groaning '*Ohi!*' and '*Ohimè!*' and threshing about with arms and legs to ward off his mother's tragic appeals and the questions of the bystanders. An audience gathered round. A doctor was fetched – the same who had pronounced objective judgement on our whooping-cough – and here again acquitted himself like a man of science. Good-naturedly he reassured the boy, telling him that he was not hurt at all, he should simply go into the water again to relieve the smart. Instead of which, Fuggièro was borne off the beach, followed by a concourse of people. But he did not fail to appear next morning, nor did he leave off spoiling our children's sandcastles. Of course, always by accident. In short, a perfect terror.

And this twelve-year-old lad was prominent among the influences that, imperceptibly at first, combined to spoil our holiday and render it unwholesome. Somehow or other, there was a stiffness, a lack of innocent enjoyment. These people stood on their dignity – just why, and in what spirit, it was not easy at first to tell. They displayed much self-respectingness; towards each other and towards the foreigner their bearing was that of a person newly conscious of a sense of honour. And wherefore? Gradually we realized the political implications and understood that we were in the presence of a national ideal. The beach, in fact, was alive with patriotic children – a phenomenon as unnatural as it was depressing. Children are a human species and a society apart, a nation of their own, so to speak. On the basis of their common form of life, they find each other out with the greatest ease, no matter how different their small vocabularies. Ours soon played with natives and foreigners alike. Yet they were plainly both puzzled and disappointed at times. There were wounded sensibilities, displays of assertiveness – or rather hardly assertiveness, for it was too self-conscious and too didactic to deserve the name. There were quarrels over flags, disputes about authority and precedence. Grown-ups joined in, not so much to pacify as to render judgement and enunciate principles. Phrases were dropped about the greatness and dignity of Italy, solemn phrases that spoilt the fun. We saw our two little ones retreat, puzzled and hurt, and were put to it to explain the situation. These people, we told them, were just passing through a certain stage, something rather like an illness, perhaps; not very pleasant, but probably unavoidable.

We had only our own carelessness to thank that we came to blows in the end with this 'stage' – which, after all, we had seen and sized up long before now. Yes, it came to another 'cross-purposes', so evidently the earlier ones had not been sheer accident. In a word, we became an offence to the public morals. Our small daughter – eight years old, but in physical development a good year younger and thin as a chicken – had had a good long bathe and gone playing in the warm sun in her wet costume. We told her that she might take off her bathing-suit, which was stiff with sand, rinse it in the sea, and put it on again, after which she must take care to keep it cleaner. Off goes the costume and she runs down naked to the sea, rinses her little jersey, and comes back. Ought we to have foreseen the outburst of anger and resentment which her conduct, and thus our conduct, called forth? Without delivering a homily on the subject, I may say that in the last decade our attitude towards the nude body and our feelings regarding it have undergone, all over the world, a fundamental change. There are things we 'never think about' any more, and among them is the freedom we had permitted to this by no means provocative little childish body. But in these parts it was taken as a challenge. The patriotic children hooted. Fuggièro whistled on his fingers. The sudden buzz of conversation among the grown people in our neighbourhood boded no good. A gentleman in city togs, with a not very apropos bowler hat on the back of his head, was assuring his outraged womenfolk that he proposed to take punitive measures; he stepped up to us, and a philippic descended on our unworthy heads, in which all the emotionalism of the sense-loving south spoke in the service of morality and discipline. The offence against decency of which we had been guilty was, he said, the more to be condemned because it was also a gross ingratitude and an insulting breach of his country's hospitality. We had criminally injured not only the letter and spirit of the public bathing regulations, but also the honour of Italy; he, the gentleman in the city togs, knew how to defend that honour and proposed to see to it that our offence against the national dignity should not go unpunished.

We did our best, bowing respectfully, to give ear to this eloquence. To contradict the man, overheated as he was, would probably be to fall from one error into another. On the tips of our tongues we had various answers: as, that the word 'hospitality', in its strictest sense, was not quite the right one, taking all the circumstances into consideration. We were not literally the guests of Italy, but of Signora Angiolieri, who had assumed the role of dispenser of hospitality some years ago on laying down that of familiar friend to Eleonora Duse. We longed to say that surely this beautiful country had not sunk so low as to be reduced to a state of hypersensitive prudishness. But we confined ourselves to assuring the gentleman that any lack of respect, any provocation on our parts, had been the farthest from our thoughts. And as a mitigating circumstance we pointed out the tender age and physical slightness of the little culprit. In vain. Our protests were waved away, he did not believe in them; our defence would not hold water. We must be made an example of. The authorities were notified, by telephone, I believe, and their representative appeared on the beach. He said the case was '*molto grave*'. We had to go with him to the Municipio up in the Piazza, where a higher official confirmed the previous verdict of '*molto grave*', launched into a stream of the usual didactic phrases – the selfsame tune and words as the man in the bowler hat – and levied a fine and ransom of fifty lire. We felt that the adventure must willy-nilly be worth to us this much of a contribution to the economy of the Italian government; paid, and left. Ought we not at this point to have left Torre as well?

If we only had! We should thus have escaped that fatal Cipolla. But circumstances combined to prevent us from making up our minds to a change. A certain poet says that it is indolence that makes us endure uncomfortable situations. The *aperçu* may serve as an explanation for our inaction. Anyhow, one dislikes voiding the field immediately upon such an event. Especially if sympathy from other quarters encourages one to defy it. And in the Villa Eleonora they pronounced as with one voice upon the injustice of our punishment. Some Italian after-dinner acquaintances found that the episode put their country in a very bad light, and proposed taking the man in the bowler hat to task, as one fellow citizen to another. But the next day he and his party had vanished from the beach. Not on our account, of course. Though it might be that the consciousness of his impending departure had added energy to his rebuke; in any case his going was a relief. And, furthermore, we stayed because our stay had by now become remarkable in our own eyes, which is worth something in itself, quite apart from the comfort or discomfort involved. Shall we strike sail, avoid a certain experience so soon as it seems not expressly calculated to increase our enjoyment or our self-esteem? Shall we go away whenever life looks like turning in the slightest uncanny, or not quite normal, or even rather painful and mortifying? No, surely not. Rather stay and look matters in the face, brave them out; perhaps precisely in so doing lies a lesson for us to learn. We stayed on and reaped as the awful reward of our constancy the unholy and staggering experience with Cipolla.

I have not mentioned that the after season had begun, almost on the very day we were disciplined by the city authorities. The worshipful gentleman in the bowler hat, our denouncer, was not the only person to leave the resort. There was a regular exodus, on every hand you saw luggage-carts on their way to the station. The beach denationalized itself. Life in Torre, in the cafés and the pinetas, become more homelike and more European. Very likely we might even have eaten at a table on the glass veranda, but we refrained, being content at Signora Angiolieri's – as content, that is, as our evil star would let us be. But at the same time with this turn for the better came a change in the weather: almost to an hour it showed itself in harmony with the holiday calendar of the general public. The sky was overcast; not that it grew any cooler, but the unclouded heat of the entire eighteen days since our arrival, and probably long before that, gave place to a stifling sirocco air, while from time to time a little ineffectual rain sprinkled the velvety surface of the beach. Add to which, that two thirds of our intended stay at Torre had passed. The colourless, lazy sea, with sluggish jellyfish floating in its shallows, was at least a change. And it would have been silly to feel retrospective longings after a sun that had caused us so many sighs when it burned down in all its arrogant power.

At this juncture, then, it was that Cipolla announced himself. Cavaliere Cipolla he was called on the posters that appeared one day stuck up everywhere, even in the dining-room of Pensione Eleonora. A travelling virtuoso, an entertainer, *'forzatore, illusionista, prestidigatore'*, he called himself, who proposed to wait upon the highly respectable population of Torre di Venere with a display of extraordinary phenomena of a mysterious and staggering kind. A conjuror! The bare announcement was enough to turn our children's heads. They had never seen anything of the sort, and now our present holiday was to afford them this new excitement. From that moment on they besieged us with prayers to take tickets for the performance. We had doubts, from the first, on the score of the lateness of the hour, nine o'clock; but gave way, in the idea that we might see a little of what Cipolla had to offer, probably no great matter, and then go home. Besides, of course, the children could sleep late next day. We bought four tickets off Signora Angiolieri herself, she having taken a number of the stalls on commission to sell them to her guests. She could not vouch for the man's performance, and we had no great expectations. But we were conscious of a need for diversion, and the children's violent curiosity proved catching.

The Cavaliere's performance was to take place in a hall where during the season there had been a cinema with a weekly programme. We had never been there. You reached it by following the main street under the wall of the '*palazzo*', a ruin with a 'For sale' sign, that suggested a castle and had obviously been built in lordlier days. In the same street were the chemist, the hairdresser, and all the better shops; it led, so to speak, from the feudal past the bourgeois into the proletarian, for it ended off between two rows of poor fishing-huts, where old women sat mending nets before the doors. And here, among the proletariat, was the hall, not much more, actually, than a wooden shed, though a large one, with a turreted entrance, plastered on either side with layers of gay placards. Some while after dinner, then, on the appointed evening, we wended our way thither in the dark, the children dressed in their best and blissful with the sense of so much irregularity. It was sultry, as it had been for days; there was heat lightning now and then, and a little rain; we proceeded under umbrellas. It took us a quarter of an hour.

Our tickets were collected at the entrance, our places we had to find ourselves. They were in the third row left, and as we sat down we saw that, late though the hour was for the performance, it was to be interpreted with even more laxity. Only very slowly did an audience – who seemed to be relied upon to come late – begin to fill the stalls. These comprised the whole auditorium; there were no boxes. This tardiness gave us some concern. The children's cheeks were already flushed as much with fatigue as with excitement. But even when we entered, the standing-room at the back and in the side aisles was already well occupied. There stood the manhood of Torre di Venere, all and sundry, fisherfolk, rough-and-ready youths with bare forearms crossed over their striped jerseys. We were well pleased with the presence of this native assemblage, which always adds colour and animation to occasions like the present; and the children were frankly delighted. For they had friends among these people – acquaintances picked up on afternoon strolls to the farther ends of the beach. We would be turning homeward, at the hour when the sun dropped into the sea, spent with the huge effort it had made and gilding with reddish gold the oncoming surf; and we would come upon bare-legged fisherfolk standing in rows, bracing and hauling with long-drawn cries as they drew in the nets and harvested in dripping baskets their catch, often so scanty, of *frutta di mare*. The children looked on, helped to pull, brought out their little stock of Italian words, made friends. So now they exchanged nods with the 'standing-room' clientèle; there was Guiscardo, there Antonio, they knew them by name and waved and called across in half-whispers, getting answering nods and smiles that displayed rows of healthy white teeth. Look, there is even Mario, Mario from the Esquisito, who brings us the chocolate. He wants to see the conjuror, too, and he must have come early, for he is almost in front; but he does not see us, he is not paying attention; that is a way he has, even though he is a waiter. So we wave instead to the man who lets out the little boats on the beach; he is there too, standing at the back.

It had got to a quarter past nine, it got to almost half past. It was natural that we should be nervous. When would the children get to bed? It had been a mistake to bring them, for now it would be very hard to suggest breaking off their enjoyment before it had got well under way. The stalls had filled in time; all Torre, apparently, was there: the guests of the Grand Hotel, the guests of Villa Eleonora, familiar faces from the beach. We heard English and German and the sort of French that Rumanians speak with Italians. Madame Angiolieri herself sat two rows behind us, with her quiet, bald-headed spouse, who kept stroking his moustache with the two middle fingers of his right hand. Everybody had come late, but nobody too late. Cipolla made us wait for him.

He made us wait. That is probably the way to put it. He heightened the suspense by his delay in appearing. And we could see the point of this, too – only not when it was carried to extremes. Towards half past nine the audience began to clap – an amiable way of expressing justifiable impatience, evincing as it does an eagerness to applaud. For the little ones, this was a joy in itself – all children love to clap. From the popular sphere came loud cries of '*Pronti!*' '*Cominciamo!*' And lo, it seemed now as easy to begin as before it had been hard. A gong sounded, greeted by the standing rows with a many-voiced 'Ah-h!' and the curtains parted. They revealed a platform furnished more like a schoolroom than like the theatre of a conjuring performance – largely because of the blackboard in the left foreground. There were a common yellow hatstand, a few ordinary straw-bottomed chairs, and farther back a little round table holding a water carafe and glass, also a tray with a liqueur glass and a flask of pale yellow liquid. We had still a few seconds of time to let these things sink in. Then, with no darkening of the house, Cavaliere Cipolla made his entry.

He came forward with a rapid step that expressed his eagerness to appear before his public and gave rise to the illusion that he had already come a long way to put himself at their service – whereas, of course, he had only been standing in the wings. His costume supported the fiction. A man of an age hard to determine, but by no means young; with a sharp, ravaged face, piercing eyes, compressed lips, small black waxed moustache, and a so-called imperial in the curve between mouth and chin. He was dressed for the street with a sort of complicated evening elegance, in a wide black pelerine with velvet collar and satin lining; which, in the hampered state of his arms, he held together in front with his white-gloved hands. He had a white scarf round his neck; a top hat with a curving brim sat far back on his head. Perhaps more than anywhere else the eighteenth century is still alive in Italy, and with it the charlatan and mountebank type so characteristic of the period. Only there, at any rate, does one still encounter really well-preserved specimens. Cipolla had in his whole appearance much of the historic type; his very clothes helped to conjure up the traditional figure with its blatantly, fantastically foppish air. His pretentious costume sat upon him, or rather hung upon him, most curiously, being in one place drawn too tight, in another a mass of awkward folds. There was something not quite in order about his figure, both front and back – that was plain later on. But I must emphasize the fact that there was not a trace of personal jocularity or clownishness in his pose, manner, or behaviour. On the contrary, there was complete seriousness, an absence of any humorous appeal; occasionally even a cross-grained pride, along with that curious, self-satisfied air so character-istic of the deformed. None of all this, however, prevented his appearance from being greeted with laughter from more than one quarter of the hall.

All the eagerness had left his manner. The swift entry had been merely an expression of energy, not of zeal. Standing at the footlights he negligently drew off his gloves, to display long yellow hands, one of them adorned with a seal ring with a lapis-lazuli in a high setting. As he stood there, his small hard eyes, with flabby pouches beneath them, roved appraisingly about the hall, not quickly, rather in a considered examination, pausing here and there upon a face with his lips clipped together, not speaking a word. Then with a display of skill as surprising as it was casual, he rolled his gloves into a ball and tossed them across a considerable distance into the glass on the table. Next from an inner pocket he drew forth a packet of cigarettes; you could see by the wrapper that they were the cheapest sort the government sells. With

his fingertips he pulled out a cigarette and lighted it, without looking, from a
quick-firing benzine lighter. He drew the smoke deep into his lungs and let it
out again, tapping his foot, with both lips drawn in an arrogant grimace and
the grey smoke streaming out between broken and saw-edged teeth.

With a keenness equal to his own his audience eyed him. The youths at the
rear scowled as they peered at this cocksure creature to search out his secret
weaknesses. He betrayed none. In fetching out and putting back the
cigarettes his clothes got in his way. He had to turn back his pelerine, and in
so doing revealed a riding-whip with a silver claw-handle that hung by a
leather thong from his left forearm and looked decidedly out of place. You
could see that he had on not evening clothes but a frock-coat, and under this,
as he lifted it to get at his pocket, could be seen a striped sash worn about the
body. Somebody behind me whispered that this sash went with his title of
Cavaliere. I give the information for what it may be worth – personally, I
never heard that the title carried such insignia with it. Perhaps the sash was
sheer pose, like the way he stood there, without a word, casually and
arrogantly puffing smoke into his audience's face.

People laughed, as I said. The merriment had become almost general
when somebody in the 'standing seats', in a loud, dry voice, remarked:
'*Buona sera.*'

Cipolla cocked his head. 'Who was that?' asked he, as though he had been
dared. 'Who was that just spoke? Well? First so bold and now so modest?
Paura, eh?' He spoke with a rather high, asthmatic voice, which yet had a
metallic quality. He waited.

'That was me,' a youth at the rear broke into the stillness, seeing himself
thus challenged. He was not far from us, a handsome fellow in a woollen
shirt, with his coat hanging over one shoulder. He wore his curly, wiry hair
in a high, dishevelled mop, the style affected by the youth of the awakened
Fatherland; it gave him an African appearance that rather spoiled his looks.
'*Bè!* That was me. It was your business to say it first, but I was trying to be
friendly.'

More laughter. The chap had a tongue in his head. '*Ha sciolto la
scilinguàgnolo,*' I heard near me. After all, the retort was deserved.

'Ah, bravo!' answered Cipolla. 'I like you, *giovanotto*. Trust me, I've had
my eye on you for some time. People like you are just in my line. I can use
them. And you are the pick of the lot, that's plain to see. You do what you
like. Or is it possible you have ever not done what you liked – or even, maybe,
what you didn't like? What somebody else liked, in short? Hark ye, my
friend, that might be a pleasant change for you, to divide up the willing and
the doing and stop tackling both jobs at once. Division of labour, *sistema
americano, sa*'*!* For instance, suppose you were to show your tongue to this
select and honourable audience here – your whole tongue, right down to the
roots?'

'No, I won't,' said the youth, hostilely. 'Sticking out your tongue shows a
bad bringing-up.'

'Nothing of the sort,' retorted Cipolla. 'You would only be *doing* it. With
all due respect to your bringing-up, I suggest that before I count ten, you
will perform a right turn and stick out your tongue at the company here
farther than you knew yourself that you could stick it out.'

He gazed at the youth, and his piercing eyes seemed to sink deeper into
their sockets. '*Uno!*' said he. He had let his riding-whip slide down his arm
and made it whistle once through the air. The boy faced about and put out
his tongue, so long, so extendedly, that you could see it was the very

uttermost in tongue which he had to offer. Then turned back, stony-faced, to his former position.

'That was me,' mocked Cipolla, with a jerk of his head towards the youth. '*Bè!* That was me.' Leaving the audience to enjoy its sensations, he turned towards the little round table, lifted the bottle, poured out a small glass of what was obviously cognac, and tipped it up with a practised hand.

The children laughed with all their hearts. They had understood practically nothing of what had been said, but it pleased them hugely that something so funny should happen, straightaway, between that queer man up there and somebody out of the audience. They had no preconception of what an 'evening' would be like and were quite ready to find this a priceless beginning. As for us, we exchanged a glance and I remember that involuntarily I made with my lips the sound that Cipolla's whip had made when it cut the air. For the rest, it was plain that people did not know what to make of a preposterous beginning like this to a sleight-of-hand performance. They could not see why the *giovanotto*, who after all in a way had been their spokesman, should suddenly have turned on them to vent his incivility. They felt that he had behaved like a silly ass and withdrew their countenances from him in favour of the artist, who now came back from his refreshment table and addressed them as follows:

'Ladies and gentlemen,' said he, in his wheezing, metallic voice, 'you saw just now that I was rather sensitive on the score of the rebuke this hopeful young linguist saw fit to give me' – '*questo linguista di belle speranze*' was what he said, and we all laughed at the pun. 'I am a man who sets some store by himself, you may take it from me. And I see no point in being wished a good evening unless it is done courteously and in all seriousness. For anything else there is no occasion. When a man wishes me a good evening he wishes himself one, for the audience will have one only if I do. So this lady-killer of Torre di Venere' (another thrust) 'did well to testify that I have one tonight and that I can dispense with any wishes of his in the matter. I can boast of having good evenings almost without exception. One not so good does come my way now and again, but very seldom. My calling is hard and my health not of the best. I have a little physical defect which prevented me from doing my bit in the war for the greater glory of the Fatherland. It is perforce with my mental and spiritual parts that I conquer life – which after all only means conquering oneself. And I flatter myself that my achievements have aroused interest and respect among the educated public. The leading newspapers have lauded me, the *Corriere della Sera* did me the courtesy of calling me a phenomenon, and in Rome the brother of the *Duce* honoured me by his presence at one of my evenings. I should not have thought that in a relatively less important place' (laughter here, at the expense of poor little Torre) 'I should have to give up the small personal habits which brilliant and elevated audiences had been ready to overlook. Nor did I think I had to stand being heckled by a person who seems to have been rather spoilt by the favours of the fair sex.' All this of course at the expense of the youth whom Cipolla never tired of presenting in the guise of *donnaiuolo* and rustic Don Juan. His persistent thin-skinnedness and animosity were in striking contrast to the self-confidence and the wordly success he boasted of. One might have assumed that the *giovanotto* was merely the chosen butt of Cipolla's customary professional sallies, had not the very pointed witticisms betrayed a genuine antagonism. No one looking at the physical parts of the two men need have been at a loss for the explanation, even if the deformed man had not constantly played on the other's supposed success with the fair sex.

'Well,' Cipolla went on, 'before beginning our entertainment this evening, perhaps you will permit me to make myself comfortable.'

And he went towards the hatstand to take off his things.

'*Parla benissimo,*' asserted somebody in our neighbourhood. So far, the man had done nothing; but what he had said was accepted as an achievement, by means of that he had made an impression. Among southern peoples speech is a constituent part of the pleasure of living, it enjoys far livelier social esteem than in the north. That national cement, the mother tongue, is paid symbolic honours down here, and there is something blithely symbolical in the pleasure people take in their respect for its form and phonetics. They enjoy speaking, they enjoy listening; and they listen with discrimination. For the way a man speaks serves as a measure of his personal rank; carelessness and clumsiness are greeted with scorn, elegance and mastery are rewarded with social *éclat*. Wherefore the small man too, where it is a question of getting his effect, chooses his phrase nicely and turns it with care. On this count, then, at least, Cipolla had won his audience; though he by no means belonged to the class of men which the Italian, in a singular mixture of moral and aesthetic judgements, labels '*simpatico*'.

After removing his hat, scarf, and mantle he came to the front of the stage, settling his coat, pulling down his cuffs with their large cuff-buttons, adjusting his absurd sash. He had very ugly hair; the top of his head, that is, was almost bald, while a narrow, black-varnished frizz of curls ran from front to back as though stuck on; the side hair, likewise blackened, was brushed forward to the corners of the eyes – it was, in short, the hairdressing of an old-fashioned circus-director, fantastic, but entirely suited to his outmoded personal type and worn with so much assurance as to take the edge off the public's sense of humour. The little physical defect of which he had warned us was now all too visible, though the nature of it was even now not very clear: the chest was too high, as is usual in such cases; but the corresponding malformation of the back did not sit between the shoulders, it took the form of a sort of hips or buttocks hump, which did not indeed hinder his movements but gave him a grotesque and dipping stride at every step he took. However, by mentioning his deformity beforehand he had broken the shock of it, and a delicate propriety of feeling appeared to reign throughout the hall.

'At your service,' said Cipolla. 'With your kind permission, we will begin the evening with some arithmetical tests.'

Arithmetic? That did not sound much like sleight-of-hand. We began to have our suspicion that the man was sailing under a false flag, only we did not yet know which was the right one. I felt sorry on the children's account; but for the moment they were content simply to be there.

The numerical test which Cipolla now introduced was as simple as it was baffling. He began by fastening a piece of paper to the upper right-hand corner of the blackboard; then lifting it up, he wrote something underneath. He talked all the while, relieving the dryness of his offering by a constant flow of words, and showed himself a practised speaker, never at a loss for conversational turns of phrase. It was in keeping with the nature of his performance, and at the same time vastly entertained the children, that he went on to eliminate the gap between stage and audience, which had already been bridged over by the curious skirmish with the fisher lad: he had representatives from the audience mount the stage, and himself descended the wooden steps to seek personal contact with his public. And again, with individuals, he fell into his former taunting tone. I do not know how far that was a deliberate feature of his system; he preserved a serious, even a peevish air, but his audience, at least the more popular section, seemed convinced that that was all part of the game. So then, after he had written something and covered the writing by the paper, he desired that two persons should come up on the platform and help to perform the calculations. They would not be difficult, even for people not clever at figures. As usual, nobody volunteered, and Cipolla took care not to molest the more select portion of his audience. He kept to the populace. Turning to two sturdy young louts standing behind us, he beckoned them to the front, encouraging and scolding by turns. They should not stand there gaping, he said, unwilling to oblige the company. Actually, he got them in motion; with clumsy tread they came down the middle aisle, climbed the steps, and stood in front of the blackboard, grinning sheepishly at their comrades' shouts and applause. Cipolla joked with them for a few minutes, praised their heroic firmness of limb and the size of their hands, so well calculated to do this service for the public. Then he handed one of them the chalk and told him to write down the numbers as they were called out. But now the creature declared that he could not write! '*Non so scrivere*,' said he in his gruff voice, and his companion added that neither did he.

God knows whether they told the truth or whether they wanted to make game of Cipolla. Anyhow, the latter was far from sharing the general merriment which their confession aroused. He was insulted and disgusted. He sat there on a straw-bottomed chair in the centre of the stage with his legs crossed, smoking a fresh cigarette out of his cheap packet; obviously it tasted the better for the cognac he had indulged in while the yokels were stumping up the steps. Again he inhaled the smoke and let it stream out between curling lips. Swinging his leg, with his gaze sternly averted from the two shamelessly chuckling creatures and from the audience as well, he stared into space as one who withdraws himself and his dignity from the contemplation of an utterly despicable phenomenon.

'Scandalous,' said he, in a sort of icy snarl. 'Go back to your places! In Italy everybody can write – in all her greatness there is no room for ignorance and unenlightenment. To accuse her of them, in the hearing of this international company, is a cheap joke, in which you yourselves cut a very poor figure and humiliate the government and the whole country as well. If it is true that Torre di Venere is indeed the last refuge of such ignorance, then I must blush to have visited the place – being, as I already was, aware of its inferiority to Rome in more than one respect –'

Here Cipolla was interrupted by the youth with the Nubian coiffure and his jacket across his shoulder. His fighting spirit, as we now saw, had only abdicated temporarily, and he now flung himself into the breach in defence of his native heath. 'That will do,' said he loudly. 'That's enough jokes about Torre. We all come from the place and we won't stand strangers making fun of it. These two chaps are our friends. Maybe they are no scholars, but even so they may be straighter than some folks in the room who are so free with their boasts about Rome, though they did not build it either.'

That was capital. The young man had certainly cut his eyeteeth. And this sort of spectacle was good fun, even though it still further delayed the regular performance. It is always fascinating to listen to an altercation. Some people it simply amuses, they take a sort of kill-joy pleasure in not being principals. Others feel upset and uneasy, and my sympathies are with these latter, although on the present occasion I was under the impression that all this was part of the show – the analphabetic yokels no less than the *giovanotto* with the jacket. The children listened well pleased. They understood not at all, but the sound of the voices made them hold their breath. So this was a 'magic evening' – at least it was the kind they have in Italy. They expressly found it 'lovely'.

Cipolla had stood up and with two of his scooping strides was at the footlights.

'Well, well, see who's here!' said he with grim cordiality. 'An old acquaintance! A young man with his heart at the end of his tongue' (he used the word *linguaccia*, which means a coated tongue, and gave rise to much hilarity). 'That will do, my friends,' he turned to the yokels. 'I do not need you now, I have business with this deserving young man here, *con questo torregiano de Venere*, this tower of Venus, who no doubt expects the gratitude of the fair as a reward for his prowess –'

'*Ah, non scherziamo!* We're talking earnest,' cried out the youth. His eyes flashed, and he actually made as though to pull off his jacket and proceed to direct methods of settlement.

Cipolla did not take him too seriously. We had exchanged apprehensive glances; but he was dealing with a fellow countryman and had his native soil beneath his feet. He kept quite cool and showed complete mastery of the situation. He looked at his audience, smiled, and made a sideways motion of the head towards the young cockerel as though calling the public to witness how the man's bumptiousness only served to betray the simplicity of his mind. And then, for the second time, something strange happened, which set Cipolla's calm superiority in an uncanny light, and in some mysterious and irritating way turned all the explosiveness latent in the air into matter for laughter.

Cipolla drew still nearer to the fellow, looking him in the eye with a peculiar gaze. He even came halfway down the steps that led into the auditorium on our left, so that he stood directly in front of the troublemaker, on slightly higher ground. The riding-whip hung from his arm.

'My son, you do not feel much like joking,' he said. 'It is only too natural, for anyone can see that you are not feeling too well. Even your tongue, which leaves something to be desired on the score of cleanliness, indicates acute disorder of the gastric system. An evening entertainment is no place for people in your state; you yourself, I can tell, were of several minds whether you would not do better to put on a flannel bandage and go to bed. It was not good judgement to drink so much of that very sour white wine this afternoon. Now you have such a colic you would like to double up with the pain. Go ahead, don't be embarrassed. There is a distinct relief that comes from bending over, in cases of intestinal cramp.'

He spoke thus, word for word, with quiet impressiveness and a kind of stern sympathy, and his eyes, plunged the while deep in the young man's, seemed to grow very tired and at the same time burning above their enlarged tear-ducts – they were the strangest eyes, you could tell that not manly pride alone was preventing the young adversary from withdrawing his gaze. And presently, indeed, all trace of its former arrogance was gone from the bronzed young face. He looked open-mouthed at the Cavaliere and the open mouth was drawn in a rueful smile.

'Double over,' repeated Cipolla. 'What else can you do? With a colic like that you *must* bend. Surely you will not struggle against the performance of a perfectly natural action just because somebody suggests it to you?'

Slowly the youth lifted his forearms, folded and squeezed them across his body; it turned a little sideways, then bent, lower and lower, the feet shifted, the knees turned inward, until he had become a picture of writhing pain, until he all but grovelled upon the ground. Cipolla let him stand for some seconds thus, then made a short cut through the air with his whip and went with his scooping stride back to the little table, where he poured himself out a cognac.

'*Il boit beaucoup,*' asserted a lady behind us. Was that the only thing that struck her? We could not tell how far the audience grasped the situation. The fellow was standing upright again, with a sheepish grin – he looked as though he scarcely knew how it had all happened. The scene had been followed with tense interest and applauded at the end; there were shouts of '*Bravo, Cipolla!*' and '*Bravo, giovanotto!*' Apparently the issue of the duel was not looked upon as a personal defeat for the young man. Rather the audience encouraged him as one does an actor who succeeds in an unsympathetic role. Certainly his way of screwing himself up with cramp had been highly picturesque, its appeal was directly calculated to impress the gallery – in short, a fine dramatic performance. But I am not sure how far the audience were moved by that natural tactfulness in which the south excels, or how far it penetrated into the nature of what was going on.

The Cavaliere, refreshed, had lighted another cigarette. The numerical tests might now proceed. A young man was easily found in the back row who was willing to write down on the blackboard the numbers as they were dictated to him. Him too we knew; the whole entertainment had taken on an intimate character through our acquaintance with so many of the actors. This was the man who worked at the greengrocer's in the main street; he had served us several times, with neatness and dispatch. He wielded the chalk with clerkly confidence, while Cipolla descended to our level and walked with his deformed gait through the audience, collecting numbers as they were given, in two, three, and four places, and calling them out to the grocer's assistant, who wrote them down in a column. In all this, everything on both sides was calculated to amuse, with its jokes and its oratorical asides. The artist could not fail to hit on foreigners, who were not ready with their figures, and with them he was elaborately patient and chivalrous, to the great amusement of the natives, whom he reduced to confusion in their turn, by making them translate numbers that were given in English or French. Some people gave dates concerned with great events in Italian history. Cipolla took them up at once and made patriotic comments. Somebody shouted 'Number one!' The Cavaliere, incensed at this as at every attempt to make game of him, retorted over his shoulder that he could not take less than two-place figures. Whereupon another joker cried out 'Number two!' and was greeted with the applause and laughter which every reference to natural functions is sure to win among southerners.

When fifteen numbers stood in a long straggling row on the board, Cipolla called for a general adding-match. Ready reckoners might add in their heads, but pencil and paper were not forbidden. Cipolla, while the work went on, sat on his chair near the blackboard, smoked and grimaced, with the complacent, pompous air cripples so often have. The five-place addition was soon done. Somebody announced the answer, somebody else confirmed it, a third had arrived at a slightly different result, but the fourth agreed with the first and second. Cipolla got up, tapped some ash from his coat, and lifted the paper at the upper right-hand corner of the board to display the writing. The correct answer, a sum close on a million, stood there; he had written it down beforehand.

Astonishment, and loud applause. The children were overwhelmed. How had he done that, they wanted to know. We told them it was a trick, not easily explainable offhand. In short, the man was a conjuror. This was what a sleight-of-hand evening was like, so now they knew. First the fisherman had cramp, and then the right answer was written down beforehand – it was all simply glorious, and we saw with dismay that despite the hot eyes and the hand of the clock at almost half past ten, it would be very hard to get them away. There would be tears. And yet it was plain that this magician did not 'magick' – at least not in the accepted sense, of manual dexterity – and that the entertainment was not at all suitable for children. Again, I do not know, either, what the audience really thought. Obviously there was grave doubt where its answers had been given of 'free choice'; here and there an individual might have answered of his own motion, but on the whole. Cipolla certainly selected his people and thus kept the whole procedure in his own hands and directed it towards the given result. Even so, one had to admire the quickness of his calculations, however much one felt disinclined to admire anything else about the performance. Then his patriotism, his irritable sense of dignity – the Cavaliere's own countrymen might feel in their element with all that and continue in a laughing mood; but the combination certainly gave us outsiders food for thought.

Cipolla himself saw to it – though without giving them a name – that the nature of his powers should be clear beyond a doubt to even the least-instructed person. He alluded to them, of course, in his talk – and he talked without stopping – but only in vague, boastful, self-advertising phrases. He went on awhile with experiments on the same lines as the first, merely making them more complicated by introducing operations in multiplying, subtracting, and dividing; then he simplified them to the last degree in order to bring out the method. He simply had numbers 'guessed' which were previously written under the paper; and the guess was nearly always right. One guesser admitted that he had had in mind to give a certain number, when Cipolla's whip went whistling through the air, and a quite different one slipped out, which proved to be the 'right' one. Cipolla's shoulders shook. He pretended admiration for the powers of the people he questioned. But in all his compliments there was something fleering and derogatory; the victims could scarcely have relished them much, although they smiled, and although they might easily have set down some part of the applause to their own credit. Moreover, I had not the impression that the artist was popular with his public. A certain ill will and reluctance were in the air, but courtesy kept such feelings in check, as did Cipolla's competency and his stern self-confidence. Even the riding-whip, I think, did much to keep rebellion from becoming overt.

From tricks with numbers he passed to tricks with cards. There were two packs, which he drew out of his pockets, and so much I still remember, that the basis of the tricks he played with them was as follows: from the first pack he drew three cards and thrust them without looking at them inside his coat. Another person then drew three out of the second pack, and these turned out to be the same as the first three – not invariably all the three, for it did happen that only two were the same. But in the majority of cases Cipolla triumphed, showing his three cards with a little bow in acknowledgment of the applause with which his audience conceded his possession of strange powers – strange whether for good or evil. A young man in the front row, to our right, an Italian, with proud, finely chiselled features, rose up and said that he intended to assert his own will in his choice and consciously to resist any influence, of whatever sort. Under these circumstances, what did Cipolla think would be the result? 'You will,' answered the Cavaliere, 'make my task somewhat more difficult thereby. As for the result, your resistance will not alter it in the least. Freedom exists, and also the will exists; but freedom of the will does not exist, for a will that aims at its own freedom aims at the unknown. You are free to draw or not to draw. But if you draw, you will draw the right cards – the more certainly, the more wilfully obstinate your behaviour.'

One must admit that he could not have chosen his words better, to trouble the waters and confuse the mind. The refractory youth hesitated before drawing. Then he pulled out a card and at once demanded to see if it was among the chosen three. 'But why?' queried Cipolla. 'Why do things by halves?' Then, as the other defiantly insisted, '*E servito*,' said the juggler, with a gesture of exaggerated servility; and held out the three cards fanwise, without looking at them himself. The left-hand card was the one drawn.

Amid general applause, the apostle of freedom sat down. How far Cipolla employed small tricks and manual dexterity to help out his natural talents, the deuce only knew. But even without them the result would have been the same: the curiosity of the entire audience was unbounded and universal, everybody both enjoyed the amazing character of the entertainment and unanimously conceded the professional skill of the performer. '*Lavora bene*,' we heard, here and there in our neighbourhood; it signified the triumph of objective judgement over antipathy and repressed resentment.

After his last, incomplete, yet so much the more telling success, Cipolla had at once fortified himself with another cognac. Truly he did 'drink a lot', and the fact made a bad impression. But obviously he needed the liquor and the cigarettes for the replenishment of his energy, upon which, as he himself said, heavy demands were made in all directions. Certainly in the intervals he looked very ill, exhausted and hollow-eyed. Then the little glassful would redress the balance, and the flow of lively, self-confident chatter run on, while the smoke he inhaled gushed out grey from his lungs. I clearly recall that he passed from the card-tricks to parlour games – the kind based on certain powers which in human nature are higher or else lower than human reason: on intuition and 'magnetic' transmission; in short, upon a low type of manifestation. What I do not remember is the precise order things came in. And I will not bore you with a description of these experiments; everybody knows them, everybody has at one time or another taken part in this finding of hidden articles, this blind carrying out of a series of acts, directed by a force that proceeds from organism to organism by unexplored paths. Everybody has had his little glimpse into the equivocal, impure, inexplicable nature of the occult, has been conscious of both curiosity and contempt, has shaken his head over the human tendency of those who deal in it to help themselves out with humbuggery, though, after all, the humbuggery is no disproof whatever of the genuineness of the other elements in the dubious amalgam. I can only say here that each single circumstance gains in weight and the whole greatly in impressiveness when it is a man like Cipolla who is the chief actor and guiding spirit in the sinister business. He sat smoking at the rear of the stage, his back to the audience while they conferred. The object passed from hand to hand which it was his task to find, with which he was to perform some action agreed upon beforehand. Then he would start to move zigzag through the hall, with his head thrown back and one hand outstretched, the other clasped in that of a guide who was in the secret but enjoined to keep himself perfectly passive, with his thoughts directed upon the agreed goal. Cipolla moved with the bearing typical in

these experiments: now groping upon a false start, now with a quick forward
thrust, now pausing as though to listen and by sudden inspiration correcting
his course. The roles seemed reversed, as the artist himself pointed out, in his
ceaseless flow of discourse. The suffering, receptive, performing part was
now his, the will he had before imposed on others was shut out, he acted in
obedience to a voiceless common will which was in the air. But he made it
perfectly clear that it all came to the same thing. The capacity for self-
surrender, he said, for becoming a tool, for the most unconditional and utter
self-abnegation, was but the reverse side of that other power to will and to
command. Commanding and obeying formed together one single principle,
one indissoluble unity; he who knew how to obey knew also how to
command, and conversely; the one idea was comprehended in the other, as
people and leader were comprehended in one another. But that which was
done, the highly exacting and exhausting performance, was in every case his,
the leader's and mover's, in whom the will became obedience, the obedience
will, whose person was the cradle and womb of both, and who thus suffered
enormous hardship. Repeatedly he emphasized the fact that his lot was a
hard one – presumably to account for his need of stimulant and his frequent
recourse to the little glass.

Thus he groped his way forward, like a blind seer, led and sustained by the
mysterious common will. He drew a pin set with a stone out of its hiding-
place in an Englishwoman's shoe, carried it, halting and pressing on by
turns, to another lady – Signora Angiolieri – and handed it to her on bended
knee, with the words it had been agreed he was to utter. 'I present you with
this in token of my respect,' was the sentence. Their sense was obvious but
the words themselves not easy to hit upon, for the reason that they had been
agreed on in French; the language complication seemed to us a little
malicious, implying as it did a conflict between the audience's natural
interest in the success of the miracle, and their desire to witness the
humiliation of this presumptuous man. It was a strange sight: Cipolla on his
knees before the signora, wrestling, amid efforts at speech, after knowledge
of the preordained words. I must say something,' he said, 'and I feel clearly
what it is I must say. But I also feel that if it passed my lips it would be
wrong. Be careful not to help me unintentionally!' he cried out, though very
likely that was precisely what he was hoping for. '*Pensez très fort*,' he cried all
at once, in bad French, and then burst out with the required words – in
Italian, indeed, but with the final substantive pronounced in the sister
tongue, in which he was probably far from fluent: he said *vénération* instead
of *venerazione*, with an impossible nasal. And this partial success, after the
complete success before it, the finding of the pin, the presentation of it on his
knees to the right person – was almost more impressive than if he had got the
sentence exactly right, and evoked bursts of admiring applause.

Cipolla got up from his knees and wiped the perspiration from his brow.
You understand that this experiment with the pin was a single case, which I
describe because it sticks in my memory. But he changed his method several
times and improvised a number of variations suggested by his contact with
his audience; a good deal of time thus went by. He seemed to get particular
inspiration from the person of our landlady; she drew him on to the most
extraordinary displays of clairvoyance. 'It does not escape me, madame,' he
said to her, 'that there is something unusual about you, some special and
honourable distinction. He who has eyes to see descries about your lovely
brow an aureola – if I mistake not, it once was stronger than now – a slowly
paling radiance ... hush, not a word! Don't help me. Beside you sits your

husband – yes?' He turned towards the silent Signor Angiolieri. 'You are the husband of this lady, and your happiness is complete. But in the midst of this happiness memories rise . . . the past, signora, so it seems to me, plays an important part in your present. You knew a king . . . has not a king crossed your path in bygone days?'

'No,' breathed the dispenser of our midday soup, her golden-brown eyes gleaming in the noble pallor of her face.

'No? No, not a king; I meant that generally, I did not mean literally a king. Not a king, not a prince, and a prince after all, a king of a loftier realm; it was a great artist, at whose side you once – you would contradict me, and yet I am not wholly wrong. Well, then! It was a woman, a great, a world-renowned woman artist, whose friendship you enjoyed in your tender years, whose sacred memory overshadows and transfigures your whole existence. Her name? Need I utter it, whose fame has long been bound up with the Fatherland's, immortal as its own? Eleonora Duse,' he finished, softly and with much solemnity.

The little woman bowed her head, overcome. The applause was like a patriotic demonstration. Nearly everyone there knew about Signora Angiolieri's wonderful past; they were all able to confirm the Cavaliere's intuition – not least the present guests of Casa Eleonora. But we wondered how much of the truth he had learned as the result of professional inquiries made on his arrival. Yet I see no reason at all to cast doubt, on rational grounds, upon powers which, before our very eyes, became fatal to their possessor.

At this point there was an intermission. Our lord and master withdrew. Now I confess that almost ever since the beginning of my tale I have looked forward with dread to this moment in it. The thoughts of men are mostly not hard to read; in this case they are very easy. You are sure to ask why we did not choose this moment to go away – and I must continue to owe you an answer. I do not know why. I cannot defend myself. By this time it was certainly eleven, probably later. The children were asleep. The last series of tests had been too long, nature had had her way. They were sleeping in our laps, the little one on mine, the boy on his mother's. That was, in a way, a consolation; but at the same time it was also ground for compassion and a clear leading to take them home to bed. And I give you my word that we wanted to obey this touching admonition, we seriously wanted to. We roused the poor things and told them it was now high time to go. But they were no sooner conscious than they began to resist and implore – you know how horrified children are at the thought of leaving before the end of a thing. No cajoling has any effect, you have to use force. It was so lovely, they wailed. How did we know what was coming next? Surely we could not leave until after the intermission; they liked a little nap now and again – only not go home, only not go to bed, while the beautiful evening was still going on!

We yielded, but only for the moment, of course – so far as we knew – only for a little while, just a few minutes longer. I cannot excuse our staying, scarcely can I even understand it. Did we think, having once said A, we had to say B – having once brought the children hither we had to let them stay? No, it is not good enough. Were we ourselves so highly entertained? Yes, and no. Our feelings for Cavaliere Cipolla were of a very mixed kind, but so were the feelings of the whole audience, if I mistake not, and nobody left. Were we under the sway of a fascination which emanated from this man who took so strange a way to earn his bread; a fascination which he gave out independently of the programme and even between the tricks and which paralysed our resolve? Again, sheer curiosity may account for something. One was curious to know how such an evening turned out; Cipolla in his remarks having all along hinted that he had tricks in his bag stranger than any he had yet produced.

But all that is not it – or at least it is not all of it. More correct it would be to answer the first question with another. Why had we not left Torre di Venere itself before now? To me the two questions are one and the same, and in order to get out of the impasse I might simply say that I had answered it already. For, as things had been in Torre in general: queer, uncomfortable, troublesome, tense, oppressive, so precisely they were here in this hall tonight. Yes, more than precisely. For it seemed to be the fountain-head of all the uncanniness and all the strained feelings which had oppressed the atmosphere of our holiday. This man whose return to the stage we were awaiting was the personification of all that; and, as we had not gone away in general, so to speak, it would have been inconsistent to do it in the particular case. You may call this an explanation, you may call it inertia, as you see fit. Any argument more to the purpose I simply do not know how to adduce.

Well, there was an interval of ten minutes, which grew into nearly twenty. The children remained awake. They were enchanted by our compliance, and filled the break to their own satisfaction by renewing relations with the popular sphere, with Antonio, Guiscardo, and the canoe man. They put their hands to their mouths and called messages across, appealing to us for the Italian words. 'Hope you have a good catch tomorrow, a whole netful!' They called to Mario, Esquisito Mario: '*Mario, una cioccolata e biscotti!*' And this time he heeded and answered with a smile: '*Subito, signorini!*' Later we had reason to recall this kindly, if rather absent and pensive smile.

Thus the interval passed, the gong sounded. The audience, which had scattered in conversation, took their places again, the children sat up straight in their chairs with their hands in their laps. The curtain had not been dropped. Cipolla came forward again, with his dipping stride, and began to introduce the second half of the programme with a lecture.

Let me state once for all that this self-confident cripple was the most powerful hypnotist I have ever seen in my life. It was pretty plain now that he threw dust in the public eye and advertised himself as a prestidigitator on account of police regulations which would have prevented him from making his living by the exercise of his powers. Perhaps this eyewash is the usual thing in Italy; it may be permitted or even connived at by the authorities. Certainly the man had from the beginning made little concealment of the actual nature of his operations; and this second half of the programme was quite frankly and exclusively devoted to one sort of experiment. While he still practised some rhetorical circumlocutions, the tests themselves were one long series of attacks upon the will-power, the loss or compulsion of volition. Comic, exciting, amazing by turns, by midnight they were still in full swing; we ran the gamut of all the phenomena this natural–unnatural field has to show, from the unimpressive at one end of the scale to the monstrous at the other. The audience laughed and applauded as they followed the grotesque details; shook their heads, clapped their knees, fell very frankly under the spell of this stern, self-assured personality. At the same time I saw signs that they were not quite complacent, not quite unconscious of the peculiar ignominy which lay, for the individual and for the general, in Cipolla's triumphs.

Two main features were constant in all the experiments: the liquor glass and the claw-handled riding-whip. The first was always invoked to add fuel to his demoniac fires; without it, apparently, they might have burned out. On this score we might even have felt pity for the man; but the whistle of his scourge, the insulting symbol of his domination, before which we all cowered, drowned out every sensation save a dazed and outbraved submission to his power. Did he then lay claim to our sympathy to boot? I was struck by a remark he made – it suggested no less. At the climax of his experiments, by stroking and breathing upon a certain young man who had offered himself as a subject and already proved himself a particularly susceptible one, he had not only put him into the condition known as deep trance and extended his insensible body by neck and feet across the backs of two chairs, but had actually sat down on the rigid form as on a bench, without making it yield. The sight of this unholy figure in a frock-coat squatted on the stiff body was horrible and incredible; the audience, convinced that the victim of this scientific diversion must be suffering, expressed its sympathy: '*Ah, poveretto!*' Poor soul, poor soul! '*Poor soul!*' Cipolla mocked them, with some bitterness. 'Ladies and gentlemen, you are barking up the wrong tree. *Sono io il poveretto.* I am the person who is suffering. I am the one to be pitied.' We pocketed the information. Very good. Maybe the experiment was at his expense, maybe it was he who had suffered the cramp when the *giovanotto* over there had made the faces. But appearances were all against it; and one does not feel like saying *poveretto* to a man who is suffering to bring about the humiliation of others.

I have got ahead of my story and lost sight of the sequence of events. To this day my mind is full of the Cavaliere's feats of endurance; only I do not recall them in their order – which does not matter. So much I do know: that the longer and more circumstantial tests, which got the most applause, impressed me less than some of the small ones which passed quickly over. I remember the young man whose body Cipolla converted into a board, only because of the accompanying remarks which I have quoted. An elderly lady in a cane-seated chair was lulled by Cipolla into the delusion that she was on a voyage to India and gave a voluble account of her adventures by land and sea. But I found this phenomenon less impressive than one which followed immediately after the intermission. A tall, well-built, soldierly man was unable to lift his arm, after the hunchback had told him that he could not and given a cut through the air with his whip. I can still see the face of that stately, mustachioed colonel smiling and clenching his teeth as he struggled to regain his lost freedom of action. A staggering performance! He seemed to be exerting his will, and in vain; the trouble, however, was probably simply that he could not will. There was involved here that recoil of the will upon itself which paralyses choice – as our tyrant had previously explained to the Roman gentleman.

Still less can I forget the touching scene, at once comic and horrible, with Signora Angiolieri. The Cavaliere, probably in his first bold survey of the room, had spied out her ethereal lack of resistance to his power. For actually he bewitched her, literally drew her out of her seat, out of her row, and away with him whither he willed. And in order to enhance his effect, he bade Signor Angiolieri call upon his wife by her name, to throw, as it were, all the weight of his existence and his rights in her into the scale, to rouse by the voice of her husband everything in his spouse's soul which could shield her virtue against the evil assaults of magic. And how vain it all was! Cipolla was standing at some distance from the couple, when he made a single cut with his whip through the air. It caused our landlady to shudder violently and

turn her face towards him. 'Sofronia!' cried Signor Angiolieri – we had not
known that Signora Angiolieri's name was Sofronia. And he did well to call,
everybody saw that there was no time to lose. His wife kept her face turned in
the direction of the diabolical Cavaliere, who with his ten long yellow fingers
was making passes at his victim, moving backwards as he did so, step by step.
Then Signora Angiolieri, her pale face gleaming, rose up from her seat,
turned right round, and began to glide after him. Fatal and forbidding sight!
Her face as though moonstruck, stiff-armed, her lovely hands lifted a little at
the wrists, the feet as it were together, she seemed to float slowly out of her
row and after the tempter. 'Call her, sir, keep on calling,' prompted the
redoubtable man. And Signor Angiolieri, in a weak voice, called: 'Sofronia!'
Ah, again and again he called; as his wife went farther off he even curved one
hand round his lips and beckoned with the other as he called. But the poor
voice of love and duty echoed unheard, in vain, behind the lost one's back;
the signora swayed along, moonstruck, deaf, enslaved; she glided into the
middle aisle and down it towards the fingering hunchback, towards the door.
We were convinced, we were driven to the conviction, that she would have
followed her master, had he so willed it, to the ends of the earth.

'*Accidente!*' cried out Signor Angiolieri, in genuine affright, springing up
as the exit was reached. But at the same moment the Cavaliere put aside, as it
were, the triumphal crown and broke off. 'Enough, signora, I thank you,' he
said, and offered his arm to lead her back to her husband. 'Signor,' he
greeted the latter, 'here is your wife. Unharmed, with my compliments, I
give her into your hands. Cherish with all the strength of your manhood a
treasure which is so wholly yours, and let your zeal be quickened by knowing
that there are powers stronger than reason or virtue, and not always so
magnanimously ready to relinquish their prey!'

Poor Signor Angiolieri, so quiet, so bald! He did not look as though he
would know how to defend his happiness, even against powers much less
demoniac than these which were now adding mockery to frightfulness.
Solemnly and pompously the Cavaliere retired to the stage, amid applause to
which his eloquence gave double strength. It was this particular episode, I
feel sure, that set the seal upon his ascendancy. For now he made them
dance, yes, literally; and the dancing lent a dissolute, abandoned, topsy-
turvy air to the scene, a drunken abdication of the critical spirit which had so
long resisted the spell of this man. Yes, he had had to fight to get the upper
hand – for instance against the animosity of the young Roman gentleman,
whose rebellious spirit threatened to serve others as a rallying-point. But it
was precisely upon the importance of example that the Cavaliere was so
strong. He had the wit to make his attack at the weakest point and to choose
as his first victim that feeble, ecstatic youth whom he had previously made
into a board. The master had but to look at him, when this young man would
fling himself back as though struck by lightning, place his hands rigidly at
his sides, and fall into a state of military somnambulism, in which it was
plain to any eye that he was open to the most absurd suggestion that might be
made to him. He seemed quite content in his abject state, quite pleased to be
relieved of the burden of voluntary choice. Again and again he offered
himself as a subject and gloried in the model facility he had in losing
consciousness. So now he mounted the platform, and a single cut of the whip
was enough to make him dance to the Cavaliere's orders, in a kind of
complacent ecstasy, eyes closed, head nodding, lank limbs flying in all
directions.

It looked unmistakably like enjoyment, and other recruits were not long in coming forward: two other young men, one humbly and one well dressed, were soon jigging alongside the first. But now the gentleman from Rome bobbed up again, asking defiantly if the Cavaliere would engage to make him dance too, even against his will.

'Even against your will,' answered Cipolla, in unforgettable accents. That frightful *'anche se non vuole'* still rings in my ears. The struggle began. After Cipolla had taken another little glass and lighted a fresh cigarette he stationed the Roman at a point in the middle aisle and himself took up a position some distance behind him, making his whip whistle through the air as he gave the order: *'Balla!'* His opponent did not stir. *'Balla!'* repeated the Cavaliere incisively, and snapped his whip. You saw the young man move his neck round in his collar; at the same time one hand lifted slightly at the wrist, one ankle turned outward. But that was all, for the time at least; merely a tendency to twitch, now sternly repressed, now seeming about to get the upper hand. It escaped nobody that here a heroic obstinacy, a fixed resolve to resist, must needs be conquered; we were beholding a gallant effort to strike out and save the honour of the human race. He twitched but danced not; and the struggle was so prolonged that the Cavaliere had to divide his attention between it and the stage, turning now and then to make his riding-whip whistle in the direction of the dancers, as it were to keep them in leash. At the same time he advised the audience that no fatigue was involved in such activities, however long they went on, since it was not the automatons up there who danced, but himself. Then once more his eye would bore itself into the back of the Roman's neck and lay siege to the strength of purpose which defied him.

One saw it waver, that strength of purpose, beneath the repeated summons and whip-crackings. Saw with an objective interest which yet was not quite free from traces of sympathetic emotion – from pity, even from a cruel kind of pleasure. If I understand what was going on, it was the negative character of the young man's fighting position which was his undoing. It is likely that *not* willing is not a practicable state of mind; *not* to want to do something may be in the long run a mental content impossible to subsist on. Between not willing a certain thing and not willing at all – in other words, yielding to another person's will – there may lie too small a space for the idea of freedom to squeeze into. Again, there were the Cavaliere's persuasive words, woven in among the whip-crackings and commands, as he mingled effects that were his own secret with others of a bewilderingly psychological kind. *'Balla!'* said he. 'Who wants to torture himself like that? Is forcing yourself your idea of freedom? *Una ballatina!* Why, your arms and legs are aching for it. What a relief to give way to them – there, you are dancing already! That is no struggle any more, it is a pleasure!' And so it was. The jerking and twitching of the refractory youth's limbs had at last got the upper hand; he lifted his arms, then his knees, his joints quite suddenly relaxed, he flung his legs and danced, and amid bursts of applause the Cavaliere led him to join the row of puppets on the stage. Up there we could see his face as he 'enjoyed' himself; it was clothed in a broad grin and the eyes were half-shut. In a way, it was consoling to see that he was having a better time than he had had in the hour of his pride.

His 'fall' was, I may say, an epoch. The ice was completely broken, Cipolla's triumph had reached its height. The Circe's wand, that whistling leather whip with the claw handle, held absolute sway. At one time – it must have been well after midnight – not only were there eight or ten persons dancing on the little stage, but in the hall below a varied animation reigned, and a long-toothed Anglo-Saxoness in a pince-nez left her seat of her own motion to perform a tarantella in the centre aisle. Cipolla was lounging in a cane-seated chair at the left of the stage, gulping down the smoke of a cigarette and breathing it impudently out through his bad teeth. He tapped his foot and shrugged his shoulders, looking down upon the abandoned scene in the hall; now and then he snapped his whip backwards at a laggard upon the stage. The children were awake at the moment. With shame I speak of them. For it was not good to be here, least of all for them; that we had not taken them away can only be explained by saying that we had caught the general devil-may-careness of the hour. By that time it was all one. Anyhow, thank goodness, they lacked understanding for the disreputable side of the entertainment, and in their innocence were perpetually charmed by the unheard-of indulgence which permitted them to be present at such a thing as a magician's 'evening'. Whole quarter-hours at a time they drowsed on our laps, waking refreshed and rosy-cheeked, with sleep-drunken eyes, to laugh to bursting at the leaps and jumps the magician made those people up there make. They had not thought it would be so jolly; they joined with their clumsy little hands in every round of applause. And jumped for joy upon their chairs, as was their wont, when Cipolla beckoned to their friend Mario from the Esquisito, beckoned to him just like a picture in a book, holding his hand in front of his nose and bending and straightening the forefinger by turns.

Mario obeyed. I can see him now going up the stairs to Cipolla, who continued to beckon him, in that droll, picture-book sort of way. He hesitated for a moment at first; that, too, I recall quite clearly. During the whole evening he had lounged against a wooden pillar at the side entrance, with his arms folded, or else with his hands thrust into his jacket pockets. He was on our left, near the youth with the militant hair, and had followed the performance attentively, so far as we had seen, if with no particular animation and God knows how much comprehension. He could not much relish being summoned thus, at the end of the evening. But it was only too easy to see why he obeyed. After all, obedience was his calling in life; and then, how should a simple lad like him find it within his human capacity to refuse compliance to a man so throned and crowned as Cipolla at that hour? Willy-nilly he left his column and with a word of thanks to those making way for him he mounted the steps with a doubtful smile on his full lips.

Picture a thickset youth of twenty years, with clipped hair, a low forehead, and heavy-lidded eyes of an indefinite grey, shot with green and yellow. These things I knew from having spoken with him, as we often had. There was a saddle of freckles on the flat nose, the whole upper half of the face retreated behind the lower, and that again was dominated by thick lips that parted to show the salivated teeth. These thick lips and the veiled look of the eyes lent the whole face a primitive melancholy – it was that which had drawn us to him from the first. In it was not the faintest trace of brutality – indeed, his hands would have given the lie to such an idea, being unusually slender and delicate for a southerner. They were hands by which one liked being served.

We knew him humanly without knowing him personally, if I may make that distinction. We saw him nearly every day, and felt a certain kindness for his dreamy ways, which might at times be actual inattentiveness, suddenly transformed into a redeeming zeal to serve. His mien was serious, only the children could bring a smile to his face. It was not sulky, but uningratiating, without intentional effort to please – or rather, it seemed to give up being pleasant in the conviction that it could not succeed. We should have remembered Mario in any case, as one of those homely recollections of travel which often stick in the mind better than more important ones. But of his circumstances we knew no more than that his father was a petty clerk in the Municipio and his mother took in washing.

His white waiter's-coat became him better than the faded striped suit he wore, with a gay coloured scarf instead of a collar, the ends tucked into his jacket. He neared Cipolla, who however did not leave off that motion of his finger before his nose, so that Mario had to come still closer, right up to the chair-seat and the master's legs. Whereupon the latter spread out his elbows and seized the lad, turning him so that we had a view of his face. Then gazed him briskly up and down, with a careless, commanding eye.

'Well, *ragazzo mio*, how comes it we make acquaintance so late in the day? But believe me, I made yours long ago. Yes, yes, I've had you in my eye this long while and known what good stuff you were made of. How could I go and forget you again? Well, I've had a good deal to think about ... Now tell me, what is your name? The first name, that's all I want.'

'My name is Mario,' the young man answered, in a low voice.

'Ah, Mario. Very good. Yes, yes, there is such a name, quite a common name, a classic name too, one of those which preserve the heroic traditions of the Fatherland. *Bravo! Salve!*' And he flung up his arm slantingly above his crooked shoulder, palm outward, in the Roman salute. He may have been slightly tipsy by now, and no wonder; but he spoke as before, clearly, fluently, and with emphasis. Though about this time there had crept into his voice a gross, autocratic note, and a kind of arrogance was in his sprawl.

'Well, now, Mario *mio*,' he went on, 'it's a good thing you came this evening, and that's a pretty scarf you've got on; it is becoming to your style of beauty. It must stand you in good stead with the girls, the pretty pretty girls of Torre –'

From the row of youths, close by the place where Mario had been standing, sounded a laugh. It came from the youth with the militant hair. He stood there, his jacket over his shoulder, and laughed outright, rudely and scornfully.

Mario gave a start. I think it was a shrug, but he may have started and then hastened to cover the movement by shrugging his shoulders, as much as to say that the neckerchief and the fair sex were matters of equal indifference to him.

The Cavaliere gave a downward glance.

'We needn't trouble about him,' he said. 'He is jealous, because your scarf is so popular with the girls, maybe partly because you and I are so friendly up here. Perhaps he'd like me to put him in mind of his colic – I could do it free of charge. Tell me, Mario. You've come here this evening for a bit of fun – and in the daytime you work in an ironmonger's shop?'

'In a café,' corrected the youth.

'Oh, in a café. That's where Cipolla nearly came a cropper! What you are is a cup-bearer, a Ganymede – I like that, it is another classical allusion – *Salvietta!*' Again the Cavaliere saluted, to the huge gratification of his audience.

Mario smiled too. 'But before that,' he interpolated, in the interest of accuracy, 'I worked for a while in a shop in Portoclemente.' He seemed visited by a natural desire to assist the prophecy by dredging out its essential features.

'There, didn't I say so? In an ironmonger's shop?'

'They kept combs and brushes,' Mario got round it.

'Didn't I say that you were not always a Ganymede? Not always at the sign of the serviette? Even when Cipolla makes a mistake, it is a kind that makes you believe in him. Now tell me: Do you believe in me?'

An indefinite gesture.

'A halfway answer,' commented the Cavaliere. 'Probably it is not easy to win your confidence. Even for me, I can see, it is not so easy. I see in your features a reserve, a sadness, *un tratto di malinconia* . . . tell me' (he seized Mario's hand persuasively) 'Have you troubles?'

'*Nossignore,*' answered Mario, promptly and decidedly.

'You *have* troubles,' insisted the Cavaliere, bearing down the denial by the weight of his authority. 'Can't I see? Trying to pull the wool over Cipolla's eyes, are you? Of course, about the girls – it is a girl, isn't it? You have love troubles?'

Mario gave a vigorous head-shake. And again the *giovanotto*'s brutal laugh rang out. The Cavaliere gave heed. His eyes were roving about somewhere in the air; but he cocked an ear to the sound, then swung his whip backwards, as he had once or twice before in his conversation with Mario, that none of his puppets might flag in their zeal. The gesture had nearly cost him his new prey: Mario gave a sudden start in the direction of the steps. But Cipolla had him in his clutch.

'Not so fast,' said he. 'That would be fine, wouldn't it? So you want to skip, do you, Ganymede, right in the middle of the fun, or rather, when it is just beginning? Stay with me, I'll show you something nice. I'll convince you. You have no reason to worry, I promise you. This girl – you know her and others know her too – what's her name? Wait! I read the name in your eyes, it is on the tip of my tongue and yours too –'

'Silvestra!' shouted the *giovanotto* from below.

The Cavaliere's face did not change.

'Aren't there the forward people?' he asked, not looking down, more as in undisturbed converse with Mario. 'Aren't there the young fighting-cocks that crow in season and out? Takes the word out of your mouth, the conceited fool, and seems to think he has some special right to it. Let him be. But Silvestra, your Silvestra – ah, what a girl that is! What a prize! Brings your heart into your mouth to see her walk or laugh or breathe, she is so lovely. And her round arms when she washes, and tosses her head back to get the hair out of her eyes! An angel from paradise!'

Mario stared at him, his head thrust forward. He seemed to have forgotten the audience, forgotten where he was. The red rings round his eyes had got larger, they looked as though they were painted on. His thick lips parted.

'And she makes you suffer, this angel,' went on Cipolla, 'or, rather, you make yourself suffer for her – there is a difference, my lad, a most important difference, let me tell you. There are misunderstandings in love, maybe nowhere else in the world are there so many. I know what you are thinking: what does this Cipolla, with his little physical defect, know about love? Wrong, all wrong, he knows a lot. He has a wide and powerful understanding of its workings, and it pays to listen to his advice. But let's leave Cipolla out, cut him out altogether and think only of Silvestra, your peerless Silvestra! What ! Is she to give any young gamecock the preference, so that he can laugh while you cry? To prefer him to a chap like you, so full of feeling and so sympathetic? Not very likely, is it? It is impossible – we know better,

Cipolla and she. If I were to put myself in her place and choose between the two of you, a tarry lout like that – a codfish, a sea-urchin – and a Mario, a knight of the serviette, who moves among gentlefolk and hands round refreshments with an air – my word, but my heart would speak in no uncertain tones – it knows to whom I gave it long ago. It is time that he should see and understand, my chosen one! It is time that you see me and recognize me, Mario, my beloved! Tell me, whom am I?'

It was grisly, the way the betrayer made himself irresistible, wreathed and coquetted with his crooked shoulder, languished with the puffy eyes, and showed his splintered teeth in a sickly smile. And alas, at his beguiling words, what was come of our Mario? It is hard for me to tell, hard as it was for me to see; for here was nothing less than an utter abandonment of the inmost soul, a public exposure of timid and deluded passion and rapture. He put his hands across his mouth, his shoulders rose and fell with his pantings. He could not, it was plain, trust his eyes and ears for joy, and the one thing he forgot was precisely that he could not trust them. 'Silvestra!' he breathed, from the very depths of his vanquished heart.

'Kiss me!' said the hunchback. 'Trust me, I love thee. Kiss me here.' And with the tip of his index finger, hand, arm, and little finger outspread, he pointed to his cheek, near the mouth. And Mario bent and kissed him.

It had grown very still in the room. That was a monstrous moment, grotesque and thrilling, the moment of Mario's bliss. In that evil span of time, crowded with a sense of the illusiveness of all joy, one sound became audible, and that not quite at once, but on the instant of the melancholy and ribald meeting between Mario's lips and the repulsive flesh which thrust itself forward for his caress. It was the sound of a laugh, from the *giovanotto* on our left. It broke into the dramatic suspense of the moment, coarse, mocking, and yet – or I must have been grossly mistaken – with an undertone of compassion for the poor bewildered, victimized creature. It had a faint ring of that '*Poveretto*' which Cipolla had declared was wasted on the wrong person, when he claimed the pity for his own.

The laugh still rang in the air when the recipient of the caress gave his whip a little swish, low down, close to his chair-leg, and Mario started up and flung himself back. He stood in that posture staring, his hands one over the other on those desecrated lips. Then he beat his temples with his clenched fists, over and over; turned and staggered down the steps, while the audience applauded, and Cipolla sat there with his hands in his lap, his shoulders shaking. Once below, and even while in full retreat, Mario hurled himself round with legs flung wide apart; one arm flew up, and two flat shattering detonations crashed through applause and laughter.

There was instant silence. Even the dancers came to a full stop and stared about, struck dumb. Cipolla bounded from his seat. He stood with his arms spread out, slanting as though to ward everybody off, as though next moment he would cry out: 'Stop! Keep back! Silence! What was that?' Then, in that instant, he sank back in his seat, his head rolling on his chest; in the next he had fallen sideways to the floor, where he lay motionless, a huddled heap of clothing, with limbs awry.

The commotion was indescribable. Ladies hid their faces, shuddering, on the breasts of their escorts. There were shouts for a doctor, for the police. People flung themselves on Mario in a mob, to disarm him, to take away the weapon that hung from his fingers – that small, dull-metal, scarcely pistol-shaped tool with hardly any barrel – in how strange and unexpected a direction had fate levelled it!

And now – now finally, at last – we took the children and led them towards the exit, past the pair of *carabinieri* just entering. Was that the end, they wanted to know, that they might go in peace? Yes, we assured them, that was the end. An end of horror, a fatal end. And yet a liberation – for I could not, and I cannot, but find it so!

A Man
and
His Dog

TRANSLATED FROM THE GERMAN BY

H.T. Lowe-Porter

He Comes Round the Corner

When spring, the fairest season of the year, does honour to its name, and when the trilling of the birds rouses me early because I have ended the day before at a seemly hour, I love to rise betimes and go for a half-hour's walk before breakfast. Strolling hatless in the broad avenue in front of my house, or through the parks beyond, I like to enjoy a few draughts of the young morning air and taste its blithe purity before I am claimed by the labours of the day. Standing on the front steps of my house, I give a whistle in two notes, tonic and lower fourth, like the beginning of the second phrase of Schubert's Unfinished Symphony; it might be considered the musical setting of a two-syllabled name. Next moment, and while I walk towards the garden gate, the faintest tinkle sounds from afar, at first scarcely audible, but growing rapidly louder and more distinct; such a sound as might be made by a metal licence-tag clicking against the trimming of a leather collar. I face about, to see Bashan rounding the corner of the house at top speed and charging towards me as though he meant to knock me down. In the effort he is making he has dropped his lower lip, baring two white teeth that glitter in the morning sun.

He comes straight from his kennel, which stands at the back of the house, between the props of the veranda floor. Probably, until my two-toned call set him in this violent motion, he had been lying there snatching a nap after the adventures of the night. The kennel has curtains of sacking and is lined with straw; indeed, a straw or so may be clinging to Bashan's sleep-rumpled coat or even sticking between his toes – a comic sight, which reminds me of a painstakingly imagined production of Schiller's *Die Räuber* that I once saw, in which old Count Moor came out of the Hunger Tower tricot-clad, with a straw sticking pathetically between his toes. Involuntarily I assume a defensive position to meet the charge, receiving it on my flank, for Bashan shows every sign of meaning to run between my legs and trip me up. However at the last minute, when a collision is imminent, he always puts on the brakes, executing a half-wheel which speaks for both his mental and his physical self-control. And then, without a sound – for he makes sparing use of his sonorous and expressive voice – he dances wildly round me by way of greeting, with immoderate plungings and waggings which are not confined to the appendage provided by nature for the purpose but bring his whole hind quarters as far as his ribs into play. He contracts his whole body into a curve, he hurtles into the air in a flying leap, he turns round and round on his own axis – and curiously enough, whichever way I turn, he always contrives to execute these manoeuvres behind my back. But the moment I stoop down and put out my hand he jumps to my side and stands like a statue, with his shoulder against my shin, in a slantwise posture, his strong paws braced against the ground, his face turned upwards so that he looks at me upside-down. And his utter immobility, as I pat his shoulder and murmur encouragement, is as concentrated and fiercely passionate as the frenzy before it had been.

Bashan is a short-haired German pointer – speaking by and large, that is, and not too literally. For he is probably not quite orthodox, as a pure matter of points. In the first place, he is a little too small. He is, I repeat, definitely undersized for a proper pointer. And then his forelegs are not absolutely straight, they have just the suggestion of an outward curve – which also detracts from his qualifications as a blood-dog. And he has a tendency to a dewlap, those folds of hanging skin under the muzzle, which in Bashan's case are admirably becoming but again would be frowned on by your fanatic for pure breeding, as I understand that a pointer should have taut skin round the neck. Bashan's colouring is very fine. His coat is a rusty brown with black stripes and a good deal of white on chest, paws, and under side. The whole of his snub nose seems to have been dipped in black paint. Over the broad top of his head and on his cool hanging ears the black and brown combine in a lovely velvety pattern. Quite the prettiest thing about him, however, is the whorl or stud or little tuft at the centre of the convolution of white hairs on his chest, which stands out like the boss on an ancient breastplate. Very likely even his splendid coloration is a little too marked and would be objected to by those who put the laws of breeding above the value of personality, for it would appear that the classic pointer type should have a coat of one colour or at most with spots of a different one, but never stripes. Worst of all from the point of view of classification, is a hairy growth hanging from his muzzle and the corners of his mouth; it might with some justice be called a moustache and goatee, and when you concentrate on it, close at hand or even at a distance, you cannot help thinking of an airedale or a schnauzer.

But classification aside, what a good and good-looking animal Bashan is, as he stands there straining against my knee, gazing up at me with all his devotion in his eyes! They are particularly fine eyes, too, both gentle and wise, if just a little too prominent and glassy. The iris is the same colour as his coat, a rusty brown; it is only a narrow rim, for the pupils are dilated into pools of blackness and the outer edge merges into the white of the eye wherein it swims. His whole head is expressive of honesty and intelligence, of manly qualities corresponding to his physical structure: his arched and swelling chest where the ribs stand out under the smooth and supple skin; the narrow haunches, the veined, sinewy legs, the strong, well-shaped paws. All these bespeak virility and a stout heart; they suggest hunting blood and peasant stock – yes, certainly the hunter and game dog do after all predominate in Bashan, he is genuine pointer, no matter if he does not owe his existence to a snobbish system of inbreeding. All this, probably, is what I am really telling him as I pat his shoulder-blade and address him with a few disjointed words of encouragement.

So he stands and looks and listens, gathering from what I say and the tone of it that I distinctly approve of his existence – the very thing which I am at pains to imply. And suddenly he thrusts out his head, opening and shutting his lips very fast, and makes a snap at my face as though he meant to bite off my nose. It is a gesture of response to my remarks, and it always makes me recoil with a laugh, as Bashan knows beforehand that it will. It is a kiss in the hair, half caress, half teasing, a trick he has had since puppyhood, which I have never seen in any of his predecessors. And he immediately begs pardon for the liberty, crouching, wagging his tail, and behaving funnily embarrassed. So we go out through the garden gate and into the open.

We are encompassed with a roaring like that of the sea; for we live almost directly on the swift-flowing river that foams over shallow ledges at no great distance from the poplar avenue. In between lie a fenced-in grass plot planted with maples, and a raised pathway skirted with huge aspen trees, bizarre and willowlike of aspect. At the beginning of June their seed-pods strew the ground far and wide with woolly snow. Upstream, in the direction of the city, construction troops are building a pontoon bridge. Shouts of command and the thump of heavy boots on the planks sound across the river; also, from the farther bank, the noise of industrial activity, for there is a locomotive foundry a little way downstream. Its premises have been lately enlarged to meet increased demands, and light streams all night long from its lofty windows. Beautiful glittering new engines roll to and fro on trial runs; a steam whistle emits wailing head-tones from time to time; muffled thunderings of unspecified origin shatter the air, smoke pours out of the many chimneys to be caught up by the wind and borne away over the wooded country beyond the river, for it seldom or never blows over to our side. Thus in our half-suburban, half-rural seclusion the voice of nature mingles with that of man, and over all lies the bright-eyed freshness of the new day.

It might be about half past seven by official time when I set out; by suntime, half past six. With my hands behind my back I stroll in the tender sunshine down the avenue, cross-hatched by the long shadows of the poplar trees. From where I am I cannot see the river, but I hear its broad and even flow. The trees whisper gently, song-birds fill the air with their penetrating chirps and warbles, twitters and trills; from the direction of the sunrise a plane is flying under the humid blue sky, a rigid, mechanical bird with a droning hum that rises and falls as it steers a free course above river and fields. And Bashan is delighting my eyes with the beautiful long leaps he is making across the low rail of the grass-plot on my left. Backwards and forwards he leaps – as a matter of fact he is doing it because he knows I like it; for I have often urged him on by shouting and striking the railing, praising him when he fell in with my whim. So now he comes up to me after nearly every jump to hear how intrepidly and elegantly he jumps. He even springs up into my face and slavers all over the arm I put out to protect it. But the jumping is also to be conceived as a sort of morning exercise, and morning toilet as well, for it smooths his ruffled coat and rids it of old Moor's straws.

It is good to walk like this in the early morning, with senses rejuvenated and spirit cleansed by the night's long healing draught of Lethe. You look confidently forward to the day, yet pleasantly hesitate to begin it, being master as you are of this little untroubled span of time between, which is your good reward for good behaviour. You indulge in the illusion that your life is habitually steady, simple, concentrated, and contemplative, that you belong entirely to yourself – and this illusion makes you quite happy. For a human being tends to believe that the mood of the moment, be it troubled or blithe, peaceful or stormy, is the true, native, and permanent tenor of his existence; and in particular he likes to exalt every happy chance into an inviolable rule and to regard it as the benign order of his life – whereas the truth is that he is condemned to improvisation and morally lives from hand to mouth all the time. So now, breathing the morning air, you stoutly believe that you are virtuous and free; while you ought to know – and at bottom do know – that the world is spreading its snares round your feet, and that most likely tomorrow you will be lying in your bed until nine, because you sought it at two in the morning hot and befogged with impassioned discussion. Never mind. Today you, a sober character, an early riser, you are the right master for that stout hunter who has just cleared the railings again out of sheer joy in the fact that today you apparently belong to him alone and not to the world.

We follow the avenue for about five minutes, to the point where it ceases to be an avenue and becomes a gravelly waste along the river-bank. From this we turn away to our right and strike into another covered with finer gravel, which has been laid out like the avenue and like it provided with a cycle-path, but is not yet built up. It runs between low-lying, wooded lots of land, towards the slope which is the eastern limit of our river neighbourhood and Bashan's theatre of action. On our way we cross another road, equally embryonic, running along between fields and meadows. Farther up, however, where the tram stops, it is quite built up with flats. We descend by a gravel path into a well-laid-out, park-like valley, quite deserted, as indeed the whole region is at this hour. Paths are laid out in curves and rondels, there are benches to rest on, tidy playgrounds, and wide plots of lawn with fine old trees whose boughs nearly sweep the grass, covering all but a glimpse of trunk. They are elms, beeches, limes, and silvery willows, in well-disposed groups. I enjoy to the full the well-landscaped quality of the scene, where I may walk no more disturbed than if it belonged to me alone. Nothing has been forgotten – there are even cement gutters in the gravel paths that lead down the grassy slopes. And the abundant greenery discloses here and there a charming distant vista of one of the villas that bound the spot on two sides.

Here for a while I stroll along the paths, and Bashan revels in the freedom of unlimited level space, galloping across and across the lawns like mad with his body inclined in a centrifugal plane; sometimes, barking with mingled pleasure and exasperation, he pursues a bird which flutters as though spellbound, but perhaps on purpose to tease him, along the ground just in front of his nose. But if I sit down on a bench he is at my side at once and takes up a position on one of my feet. For it is a law of his being that he only runs about when I am in motion too; that when I settle down he follows suit. There seems no obvious reason for this practice; but Bashan never fails to conform to it.

I get an odd, intimate, and amusing sensation from having him sit on my foot and warm it with the blood-heat of his body. A pervasive feeling of sympathy and good cheer fills me, as almost invariably when in his company and looking at things from his angle. He has a rather rustic slouch when he sits down; his shoulderblades stick out and his paws turn negligently in. He looks smaller and squatter than he really is, and the little white boss on his chest is advanced with comic effect. But all these faults are atoned for by the lofty and dignified carriage of the head, so full of concentration. All is quiet, and we two sit there absolutely still in our turn. The rushing of the water comes to us faint and subdued. And the senses become alert for all the tiny, mysterious little sounds that nature makes: the lizard's quick dart, the note of a bird, the burrowing of a mole in the earth. Bashan pricks up his ears – in so far as the muscles of naturally drooping ears will allow them to be pricked. He cocks his head to hear the better; and the nostrils of his moist black nose keep twitching sensitively as he sniffs.

Then he lies down, but always in contact with my foot. I see him in profile, in that age-old, conventionalized pose of the beast-god, the sphinx: head and chest held high, forelegs close to the body, paws extended in parallel lines. He has got overheated, so he opens his mouth, and at once all the intelligence of his face gives way to the merely animal, his eyes narrow and blink and his rosy tongue lolls out between his strong white pointed teeth.

How We Got Bashan

In the neighbourhood of Tölz there is a mountain inn, kept by a pleasingly buxom, black-eyed damsel, with the assistance of a growing daughter, equally buxom and black-eyed. This damsel it was who acted as go-between in our introduction to Bashan and our subsequent acquisition of him. Two years ago now that was; he was six months old at the time. Anastasia – for so the damsel was called – knew that we had had to have our last dog shot; Percy by name, a Scotch collie by breeding and a harmless, feeble-minded aristocrat who in his old age fell victim to a painful and disfiguring skin disease which obliged us to put him away. Since that time we had been without a guardian. She telephoned from her mountain height to say that she had taken to board a dog that was exactly what we wanted and that it might be inspected at any time. The children clamoured to see it, and our own curiosity was scarcely behind theirs; so the very next afternoon we climbed up to Anastasia's inn, and found her in her roomy kitchen full of warm and succulent steam, preparing her lodgers' supper. Her face was brick-red, her brow was wet, the sleeves were rolled back on her plump arms, and her frock was open at the throat. Her young daughter went to and fro, an industrious kitchen-maid. They were glad to see us and thoroughly approved of our having lost no time in coming. We looked about; whereupon Resi, the daughter, led us up to the kitchen table, and squatting with her hands on her knees, addressed a few encouraging words beneath it. Until then, in the flickering half-light, we had seen nothing; but now we perceived something standing there, tied by a bit of rope to the table-leg: an object that must have made any soul alive burst into half-pitying laughter.

Gaunt and knock-kneed he stood there with his tail between his hind legs, his four paws planted together, his back arched, shaking. He may have been frightened, but one had the feeling that he had not enough on his bones to keep him warm; for indeed the poor little animal was a skeleton, a mere rack of bones with a spinal column, covered with a rough fell and stuck up on four sticks. He had laid back his ears – which muscular contraction never fails to extinguish every sign of intelligence and cheer in the face of any dog. In him, who was still entirely puppy, the effect was so consummate that he stood there expressive of nothing but wretchedness, stupidity, and a mute appeal for our forbearance. And his hirsute appendages, which he has to this day, were then out of all proportion to his size and added a final touch of sour hypochondria to his appearance.

We all stooped down and began to coax and encourage this picture of misery. The children were delighted and sympathetic at once, and their shouts mingled with the voice of Anastasia as, standing by her cooking-stove, she began to furnish us with the particulars of her charge's origins and history. He was named, provisionally, Lux, she said, in her pleasant, level voice; and was the offspring of irreproachable parents. She had herself known the mother and of the father had heard nothing but good. Lux had seen the light on a farm in Hugelfing; and it was only due to a combination of circumstances that his owners were willing to part with him cheaply. They had brought him to her inn because there he might be seen by a good many people. They had come in a cart, Lux bravely running the whole twenty kilometres behind the wheels. She, Anastasia, had thought of us at once, knowing that we were on the look-out for a good dog and feeling certain that we should want him. If we so decided, it would be a good thing all round. She was sure we should have great joy of him, he in his turn would have found a good home and be no longer lonely in the world, and she, Anastasia, would know that he was well taken care of. We must not be prejudiced by the figure he cut at the moment; he was upset by his strange surroundings and uncertain of himself, but his good breeding would come out strong before long. His father and mother were of the best.

Ye-es – but perhaps not quite well matched?

On the contrary; that is, they were both of them good stock. He had excellent points – she, Anastasia, would vouch for that. He was not spoilt, either, his needs were modest – and that meant a great deal, nowadays. In fact, up to now he had had nothing to eat but potato-parings. She suggested that we take him home on trial; if we found that we did not take to him she would receive him back and refund the modest sum that was asked for him. She made free to say this, not minding at all if we took her up. Because, knowing the dog and knowing us, both parties, as it were, she was convinced that we should grow to love him, and never dream of giving him up.

All this she said and a great deal more in the same strain in her easy, comfortable, voluble way, working the while over her stove, where the flames shot up suddenly now and then as though we were in a witches' kitchen. She even came and opened Lux's jaws with both hands to show us his beautiful teeth and – for some reason or other – the pink grooves in the roof of his mouth. We asked knowingly if he had had distemper; she replied with a little impatience that she really could not say. Our next question – how large would he get – she answered more glibly: he would be about the size of our departed Percy, she said. There were more questions and answers; a good deal of warm-hearted urging from Anastasia, prayers and pleas from the children, and on our side a feeble lack of resolution. At last we begged for a little time to think things over; she agreed, and we went thoughtfully valley-wards, changing impressions as we went.

But of course the children had lost their hearts to the wretched little quadruped under the table; in vain we affected to jeer at their lack of judgement and taste, feeling the pull at our own heartstrings. We saw that we should not be able to get him out of our heads; we asked ourselves what would become of him if we scorned him. Into what hands would he fall? The question called up a horrid memory, we saw again the knacker from whom we had rescued Percy with a few timely and merciful bullets and an honourable grave by the garden fence. If we wanted to abandon Lux to an uncertain and perhaps gruesome fate, then we should never have seen him at all, never cast eyes upon his infant whiskered face. We knew him now, we felt a responsibility which we could disclaim only by an arbitrary exercise of authority.

So it was that the third day found us climbing up those same gentle foothills of the Alps. Not that we had decided to buy – no, we only saw that, as things stood, the matter could hardly have any other outcome.

This time we found Frau Anastasia and her daughter drinking coffee, one at each end of the long kitchen table, while between them he sat who bore provisionally the name of Lux, in his very attitude as he sits today, slouching over with his shoulder-blades stuck out and his paws turned in. A bunch of wild flowers in his worn leather collar gave him a festive look, like a rustic bridegroom or a village lad in his Sunday best. The daughter, looking very trim herself in the tight bodice of her peasant costume, said that she had adorned him thus to celebrate his entry into his new home. Mother and daughter both told us they had never been more certain of anything in their lives than that we would come back to fetch him – they knew that we would come this very day.

So there was nothing more to say. Anastasia thanked us in her pleasant way for the purchase price – ten marks – which we handed over. It was clear that she had asked it in our interest rather than in hers or that of the dog's owners; it was by way of giving Lux a positive value, in terms of money, in our eyes. We quite understood, and paid it gladly. Lux was untied from his table-leg and the end of the rope laid in my hand; we crossed Anastasia's door-step followed by the warmest, most cordial assurances and good wishes.

But the homeward way, which it took us an hour to cover, was scarcely a triumphal procession. The bridegroom soon lost his bouquet, while everybody we met either laughed or else jeered at his appearance – and we met a good many people, for our route lay through the length of the market town at the foot of the hill. The last straw was that Lux proved to be suffering from an apparently chronic diarrhoea, which obliged us to make frequent pauses under the villagers' eyes. At such times we formed a circle round him to shield his weakness from unfriendly eyes – asking ourselves whether this was not distemper already making its appearance. Our anxiety was uncalled-for: the future was to prove that we were dealing with a sound and cleanly constitution, which has been proof against distemper and all such ailments up to this day.

Directly we got home we summoned the maids to make acquaintance with the new member of the family and express their modest judgement of his worth. They had evidently been prepared to praise; but, reading our own insecurity in our eyes, they laughed loudly, turning their backs upon the appealing object and waving him off with their hands. We doubted whether they could understand the nature of our financial transaction with the benevolent Anastasia and in our weakness declared that we had had him as a present. Then we led Lux into the veranda and regaled him with a hearty meal of scraps.

He was too frightened to eat. He sniffed at the food we urged upon him, but was evidently, in his modesty, unable to believe that these cheese-parings and chicken-bones were meant for him. But he did not reject the sack stuffed with seaweed which we had prepared for him on the floor. He lay there with his paws drawn up under him, while within we took counsel and eventually came to a conclusion about the name he was to bear in the future.

On the following day he still refused to eat; then came a period when he gulped down everything that came within reach of his muzzle; but gradually he settled down to a regular and more fastidious regimen, this result roughly corresponding with his adjustment to his new life in general, so that I will not dwell further upon it. The process of adaptation suffered an interruption one day – Bashan disappeared. The children had taken him into the garden and let him off the lead for better freedom of action. In a momentary lapse of vigilance he had escaped through the hole under the garden gate and gained the outer world. We were grieved and upset at his loss – at least the masters of the house were, for the maids seemed inclined to take light-heartedly the loss of a dog which we had received as a gift; perhaps they did not even consider it a loss. We telephoned wildly to Anastasia's inn, hoping he might find his way thither. In vain, nobody had seen him; two days passed before we heard that Anastasia had word from Hugelfing that Lux had put in an appearance at his first home some hour and a half before. Yes, he was there, his native idealism had drawn him back to the world of his early potato-parings; through wind and weather he had trotted alone the twelve or fourteen miles which he had first covered between the hind wheels of the farmer's cart. His former owners had to use it again to deliver him into Anastasia's hands once more. On the second day after that we went up to reclaim the wanderer, whom we found as before, tied to the table-leg, jaded and dishevelled, bemired from the mud of the roads. He did show signs of being glad to see us again – but then, why had he gone away?

The time came when it was plain that he had forgotten the farm – yet without having quite struck root with us; so that he was a masterless soul and like a leaf carried by the wind. When we took him walking we had to keep close watch, for he tended to snap the frail bond of sympathy which was all that as yet united us and to lose himself unobtrusively in the woods, where, being quite on his own, he would certainly have reverted to the condition of his wild forebears. Our care preserved him from this dark fate, we held him fast upon his civilized height and to his position as the comrade of man, which his race in the course of millennia has achieved. And then a decisive event, our removal to the city – or a suburb of it – made him wholly dependent upon us and definitely a member of the family.

Notes on Bashan's Character and Manner of Life

A man in the Isar valley had told me that this kind of dog can become a nuisance, by always wanting to be with his master. Thus I was forewarned against taking too personally Bashan's persistent faithfulness to myself, and it was easier for me to discourage it a little and protect myself at need. It is a deep-lying patriarchal instinct in the dog which leads him – at least in the more manly, outdoor breeds – to recognize and honour in the man of the house and head of the family his absolute master and overlord, protector of the hearth; and to find in the relation of vassalage to him the basis and value of his own existence, whereas his attitude towards the rest of the family is much more independent. Almost from the very first day Bashan behaved in this spirit towards me, following me with his trustful eyes that seemed to be begging me to order him about – which I was chary of doing, for time soon showed that obedience was not one of his strong points – and dogging my footsteps in the obvious conviction that sticking to me was the natural order of things. In the family circle he always sat at my feet, never by any chance at anyone else's. And when we were walking, if I struck off on a path by myself, he invariably followed me and not the others. He insisted on being with me when I worked; if the garden door was closed he would disconcert me by jumping suddenly in at the window, bringing much gravel in his train and flinging himself down panting beneath my desk.

But the presence of any living thing – even a dog – is something of which we are very conscious; we attend to it in a way that is disturbing when we want to be alone. Thus Bashan could become a quite tangible nuisance. He would come up to me wagging his tail, look at me with devouring gaze, and prance provocatively. On the smallest encouragement he would put his fore-paws on the arm of my chair, lean against me, and make me laugh with his kisses in the air. Then he would examine the things on my desk, obviously under the impression that they must be good to eat since he so often found me stooped above them; and so doing would smudge my freshly written page with his broad, hairy hunter's paws. I would sharply call him to order and he would lie down on the floor and go to sleep. But when he slept he dreamed, making running motions with all four paws and barking in a subterranean but perfectly audible sort of way. I quite comprehensibly found this distracting; in the first place the sound was uncannily ventrilo-quistic, in the second it gave me a guilty feeling. For this dream life was obviously an artificial substitute for real running, hunting, and open-air activity; it was supplied to him by his own nature because his life with me did not give him as much of it as his blood and his senses required. I felt touched; but since there was nothing for it, I was constrained in the name of my higher interests to throw off the incubus, telling myself that Bashan brought altogether too much mud into the room and also that he damaged the carpet with his claws.

So then the fiat went forth that he might not be with me or in the house when I was there – though of course there might be exceptions to the rule. He was quick to understand and submit to the unnatural prohibition, as being the inscrutable will of his lord and master. The separation from me – which in winter often lasted the greater part of the day – was in his mind only a separation, not a divorce or severance of connexions. He may not be with me, because I have so ordained. But the not being with me is a kind of negative being with me, just in that it is carrying out my command. Hence we can hardly speak of an independent existence carried on by Bashan during the hours when he is not by my side. Through the glass door of my study I can see him on the grass-plot in front of the house, playing with the children and putting on an absurd avuncular air. He repeatedly comes to the door and sniffs at the crack – he cannot see me through the muslin curtains – to assure himself of my presence within; then he sits down and mounts guard with his back to the door. Sometimes I see him from my window prosing along on the elevated path between the aspen trees; but this is only to pass the time, the excursion is void of all pride or joy in life; in fact it is unthinkable that Bashan should devote himself to the pleasures of the chase on his own account, though there is nothing to prevent him from doing so and my presence, as will be seen, is not always an unmixed advantage.

Life for him begins when I issue from the house – though, alas, it does not always begin even then! For the question is, when I do go out, which way am I going to turn: to the right, down the avenue, the road towards the open and our hunting-ground, or towards the left and the place where the trams stop, to ride into town? Only in the first case is there any sense in accompanying me. At first he used to follow me even when I turned left; when the tram thundered up he would look at it with amazement and then, suppressing his fears, land with one blind and devoted leap among the crowd on the platform. Thence being dislodged by the popular indignation, he would gallop along on the ground behind the roaring vehicle which so little resembled the cart he once knew. He would keep up with it as long as he could, his breath getting shorter and shorter. But the city traffic bewildered his rustic brains; he got between people's legs, strange dogs fell on his flank, he was confused by a volume and variety of smells, the like of which he had never imagined, irresistibly distracted by house-corners impregnated with lingering ancient scents of old adventures. He would fall behind; sometimes he would overtake the tram again, sometimes not; sometimes he overtook the wrong one, which looked just the same, ran blindly in the wrong direction, farther and farther into a mad, strange world. Once he only came home after two days' absence, limping and starved to death, and seeking the peace of the last house on the river-bank, found that his lord and master had been sensible enough to get there before him.

This happened two or three times. Then he gave it up and definitely declined to go with me when I turned to the left. He always knows instantly whether I have chosen the wild or the world, directly I get outside the door. He springs up from the mat in the entrance where he has been waiting for me and in that moment divines my intentions; my clothes betray me, the cane I carry, probably even my bearing: my cold and negligent glance or on the other hand the challenging eye I turn upon him. He understands. In the one case he tumbles over himself down the steps, he whirls round and round like a stone in a sling as in dumb rejoicing he runs before me to the gate. In the other he crouches, lays back his ears, the light goes out of his eyes, the fire I have kindled by my appearance dies down to ashes, and he puts on the guilty look which men and animals alike wear when they are unhappy.

Sometimes he cannot believe his eyes, even though they plainly tell him that there is no hope for the chase today. His yearning has been too strong. He refuses to see the signs, the urban walking-stick, the careful city clothes. He presses beside me through the gate, turns round like lightning, and tries to make me turn right, by running off at a gallop in that direction, twisting his head round and ignoring that fatal negative which I oppose to his efforts. When I actually turn to the left he comes back and walks with me along the hedge, with little snorts and head-tones which seem to emerge from the high tension of his interior. He takes to jumping to and fro over the park railings, although they are rather high for comfort, and he gives little moans as he leaps, being evidently afraid of hurting himself. He jumps with a sort of desperate gaiety which is bent on ignoring reality; also in the hope of beguiling me by his performance. For there is still a little – a very little – hope that I may still leave the highroad at the end of the park and turn left after all by the roundabout way past the pillarbox, as I do when I have letters to post. But I do that very seldom; so when that last hope has fled, then Bashan sits down and lets me go my way.

There he sits, in that clumsy rustic posture of his, in the middle of the road and looks after me as far as he can see me. If I turn my head he pricks up his ears, but he does not follow; even if I whistled he would not, for he knows it would be useless. When I turn out of the avenue I can still see him sitting there, a small, dark, clumsy figure in the road, and it goes to my heart, I have pangs of conscience as I mount the tram. He has waited so long – and we all know what torture waiting can be! His whole life is a waiting – waiting for the next walk in the open, a waiting that begins as soon as he is rested from the last one. Even his night consists of waiting; for his sleep is distributed throughout the whole twenty-four hours of the day, with many a little nap on the grass in the garden, the sun shining down warm on his coat, or behind the curtains of his kennel, to break up and shorten the empty spaces of the day. Thus his night sleep is broken too, not continuous, and manifold instincts urge him abroad in the darkness; he dashes to and fro all over the garden – and he waits. He waits for the night watchman to come on his rounds with his lantern and when he hears the recurrent heavy tread heralds it, against his own better knowledge, with a terrific outburst of barking. He waits for the sky to grow pale, for the cocks to crow at the nursery-gardener's close by; for the morning breeze to rise among the tree-tops – and for the kitchen door to be opened, so that he may slip in and warm himself at the stove.

Still, the night-time martyrdom must be mild compared with what Bashan has to endure in the day. And particularly when the weather is fine, either winter or summer, when the sunshine lures one abroad and all the muscles twitch with the craving for violent motion – and the master, without whom it is impossible to conceive doing anything, simply will not leave his post behind the glass door. All that agile little body, feverishly alive with pulsating life, is rested through and through, is worn out with resting; sleep is not to be thought of. He comes up on the terrace outside my door, lets himself down with a sigh that seems to come from his very heart, and rests his head on his paws, rolling his eyes up patiently to heaven. That lasts but a few seconds, he cannot stand the position any more, he sickens of it. One other thing there is to do. He can go down again and lift his leg against one of the little formal arbor-vitae trees that flank the rose-bed – it is the one to the right that suffers from his attentions, wasting away so that it has to be replanted every year. He does go down, then, and performs this action, not because he needs to, but just to pass the time. He stands there a long time, with very little to show for it, however – so long that the hind leg in the air begins to tremble and he has to give a little hop to regain his balance. On four legs once more he is no better off than he was. He stares stupidly up into the boughs of the ash trees, where two birds are flitting and chirping; watches them dart off like arrows and turns away as though in contempt of such light-headedness. He stretches and stretches, fit to tear himself apart. The stretching is very thorough; it is done in two sections, thus: first the forelegs, lifting the hind ones into the air; second the rear quarters, by sprawling them out on the ground; both actions being accompanied by tremendous yawning. Then that is over too, cannot be spun out any longer, and if you have just finished an exhaustive stretching you cannot do it over again just at once. He stands still and looks gloomily at the ground. Then he begins to turn round on himself, slowly and consideringly, as though he wanted to lie down, yet was not quite certain of the best way to do it. Finally he decides not to; he moves off sluggishly to the middle of the grass-plot, and once there flings himself violently on his back and scrubs to and fro as though to cool off on the shaven turf. Quite a blissful sensation, this, it seems, for his paws jerk and he snaps in all directions in a delirium of release and satisfaction. He drains this joy down to its vapid dregs, aware that it is fleeting, that you cannot roll and tumble more than ten seconds at most, and that no sound and soul-contenting weariness will result from it, but only a flatness and returning boredom, such as always follows when one tries to drug oneself. He lies there on his side with his eyes rolled up, as though he were dead. Then he gets up and shakes himself, shakes as only his like can shake without fearing concussion of the brain; shakes until everything rattles, until his ears flop together under his chin and foam flies from his dazzling white teeth. And then? He stands perfectly still in his tracks, rigid, dead to the world, without the least idea what to do next. And then, driven to extremes, he climbs the steps once more, comes up to the glass door, lifts his paw and scratches – hesitantly, with his ears laid back, the complete beggar. He scratches only once, quite faintly; but this timidly lifted paw, this single, faint-hearted scratch, to which he has come because he simply cannot think of anything else, are too moving. I get up and open the door, though I know it can lead to no good. And he begins to dance and jump, challenging me to be a man and come abroad with him. He rumples the rugs, upsets the whole room and makes an end of all my peace and quiet. But now judge for yourself if, after I have seen Bashan wait like this, I can find it easy to go off in the tram and leave him, a pathetic little dot at the end of the poplar avenue!

In the long twilights of summer, things are not quite so bad: there is a good chance that I will take an evening walk in the open and thus even after long waiting he will come into his own and with good luck be able to start a hare. But in winter if I go off in the afternoon it is all over for the day, all hope must be buried for another four-and-twenty hours. For night will have fallen; if I go out again our hunting-grounds will lie in inaccessible darkness and I must bend my steps towards the traffic, the lighted streets, and city parks up the river – and this does not suit Bashan's simple soul. He came with me at first, but soon gave it up and stopped at home. Not only that space and freedom were lacking; he was afraid of the bright lights in the darkness, he shied at every bush, at every human form. A policeman's flapping cloak could make him swerve aside with a yelp or even lead him to attack the officer with a courage born of desperation; when the latter, frightened in his turn, would let loose a stream of abuse to our address. Unfortunate episodes mounted up when Bashan and I went out together in the dark and the damp. And speaking of policemen reminds me that there are three classes of human beings whom Bashan does especially abhor: policemen, monks, and chimney-sweeps. He cannot stand them, he assails them with a fury of barking wherever he sees them or when they chance to pass the house.

And winter is of course the time of year when freedom and sobriety are with most difficulty preserved against snares; when it is hardest to lead a regular, retired, and concentrated existence; when I may even seek the city a second time in the day. For the evening has its social claims, pursuing which I may come back at midnight, with the last tram, or losing that am driven to return on foot, my head in a whirl with ideas and wine and smoke, full of roseate views of the world and of course long past the point of normal fatigue. And then the embodiment of that other, truer, soberer life of mine, my own hearthstone, in person, as it were, may come to meet me; not wounded, not reproachful, but on the contrary giving me joyous welcome and bringing me back to my own. I mean, of course, Bashan. In pitchy darkness, the river roaring in my ears, I turn into the poplar avenue, and after the first few steps I am enveloped in a soundless storm of prancings and swishings; on the first occasion I did not know what was happening. 'Bashan?' I inquire into the blackness. The prancings and swishings redouble – is this a dancing dervish or a berserk warrior here on my path? But not a sound; and directly I stand still, I feel those honest, wet, and muddy paws on the lapels of my raincoat, and a snapping and flapping in my face, which I draw back even as I stoop down to pat the lean shoulder, equally wet with snow or rain. Yes, the good soul has come to meet the tram. Well informed as always upon my comings and goings, he has got up at what he judged to be the right time, to fetch me from the station. He may have been waiting a long while, in snow or rain, yet his joy at my final appearance knows no resentment at my faithlessness, though I have neglected him all day and brought his hopes to naught. I pat and praise him, and as we go home together I tell him what a fine fellow he is and promise him (that is to say, not so much him as myself) that tomorrow, no matter what the weather, we two will follow the chase together. And resolving thus, I feel my worldly preoccupations melt away; sobriety returns; for the image I have conjured up of our hunting-ground and the charms of its solitude is linked in my mind with the call to higher, stranger, more obscure concerns of mine.

There are still other traits of Bashan's character which I should like to set down here, so that the gentle reader may get as lively and speaking an image of him as is anyway possible. Perhaps the best way would be for me to compare him with our deceased Percy; for a better-defined contrast than that between these two never existed within the same species. First and foremost we must remember that Bashan was entirely sound in mind, whereas Percy, as I have said, and as often happens among aristocratic canines, had always been mad, through and through, a perfectly typical specimen of frantic over-breeding. I have referred to this subject before, in a somewhat wider connexion; here I only want, for purposes of comparison, to speak of Bashan's infinitely simpler, more ordinary mentality, expressed for instance in the way he would greet you, or in his behaviour on our walks. His manifestations were always within the bounds of a hearty and healthy common sense; and never even bordered on the hysterical, whereas Percy's on all such occasions overstepped them in a way that was at times quite shocking.

And even that does not quite cover the contrast between these two creatures; the truth is more complex and involved still. Bashan is coarser-fibred, true, like the lower classes; but like them also he is not above complaining. His noble predecessor, on the other hand, united more delicacy and a greater capacity for suffering, with an infinitely firmer and prouder spirit; despite all his foolishness he far excelled in self-discipline the powers of Bashan's peasant soul. In saying this I am not defending any aristocratic system of values. It is simply to do honour to truth and actuality that I want to bring out the mixture of softness and hardiness, delicacy and firmness in the two natures. Bashan, for instance, is quite able to spend the coldest winter night out of doors, behind the sacking curtains of his kennel. He has a weakness of the bladder which makes it impossible for him to remain seven hours shut up in a room; we have to fasten him out, even in the most inhospitable weather, and trust to his robust constitution. Sometimes after a particularly bitter and foggy winter night he comes into the house with his moustache and whiskers like delicately frosted wires; with a little cold, even, and coughing, in the odd, one-syllabled way that dogs have. But in a few hours he has got all over it and takes no harm at all. Whereas we should never have dared to expose our silken-haired Percy to such rigours. Yet Bashan is afraid of the slightest pain, behaving so abjectly that one would feel disgusted if the plebeian simplicity of his behaviour did not make one laugh instead. When he goes stalking in the underbrush. I constantly hear him yelping because he has been scratched by a thorn or a branch has struck him in the face. If he hurts his foot or skins his belly a little, jumping over a fence, he sets up a cry like an antique hero in his death-agony; comes to me hobbling on three legs, howling and lamenting in an abandonment of self-pity – the more piercingly, the more sympathy he gets – and this although in fifteen minutes he will be running and jumping again as though nothing had happened.

With Percival it was otherwise; he clenched his jaws and was still. He was afraid of the dog-whip, as Bashan is too; and tasted it, alas, more often than the latter, for in his day I was younger and quick-tempered and his witlessness often assumed a vicious aspect which cried out for chastisement and drove me on to administer it. When I was quite beside myself and took down the lash from the nail where it hung, Percy might crawl under a table or a bench. But not a sound would escape him under punishment; even at a second flailing he would give vent only to a fervent moan if it stung worse than usual – whereas the base-born Bashan will howl abjectly if I so much as raise my arm. In short, no sense of honour, no strictness with himself. And anyhow, it seldom comes to corporal punishment, for I long ago ceased to make demands upon him contrary to his nature, of a kind which would lead to conflict between us.

For example, I never asked him to learn tricks; it would be of no use. He is not talented, no circus dog, no trained clown. He is a sound, vigorous young hunter, not a professor. I believe I remarked that he is a capital jumper. No obstacle too great, if the incentive be present: if he cannot jump it he will scrabble up somehow and let himself fall on the other side – at least, he conquers it one way or another. But it must be a genuine obstacle, not to be jumped through or crawled under; overwise he would think it folly to jump. A wall, a ditch, a fence, a thickset hedge, are genuine obstacles; a crosswise bar, a stick held out, are not, and you cannot jump over them without going contrary to reason and looking silly. Which Bashan refuses to do. He refuses. Try to make him jump over some such unreal obstacle; in the end you will be reduced to taking him by the scruff of the neck, in your anger, and flinging him over, while he whimpers and yaps. Once on the other side he acts as though he had done just what you wanted and celebrates the event in a frenzy of barking and capering. You may coax or you may punish; you cannot break down his reasonable resistance to performing a mere trick. He is not unaccommodating, he sets store by his master's approval, he will jump over a hedge at my will or my command, and not only when he feels like it himself, and enjoys very much the praise I bestow. But over a bar or a stick he will not jump, he will crawl underneath – if he were to die for it. A hundred times he will beg for forgiveness, forbearance, consideration; he fears pain, fears it to the point of being abject. But no fear and no pain can make him capable of a performance which in itself would be child's-play for him, but for which he obviously lacks all mental equipment. When you confront him with it, the question is not whether he will jump or not; that is already settled, and the command means nothing to him but a beating. To demand of him what reason forbids him to understand and hence to do is simply in his eyes to seek a pretext for blows, strife, and disturbance of friendly relations – it is merely the first step towards all these things. Thus Bashan looks at it, so far as I can see, and I doubt whether one may properly charge him with obstinacy. Obstinacy may be broken down, in the last analysis it cries out to be broken down; but Bashan's resistance to performing a trick he would seal with his death.

Extraordinary creature! So close a friend and yet so remote; so different from us, in certain ways, that our language has not power to do justice to his canine logic. For instance, what is the meaning of that frightful circumstan- tiality – unnerving alike to the spectator and to the parties themselves – attendant on the meeting of dog and dog; or on their first acquaintance or even on their first sight of each other? My excursions with Bashan have made me witness to hundreds of such encounters, or, I might better say, forced me to be an embarrassed spectator at them. And every time, for the duration of the episode, my old familiar Bashan was a stranger to me, I found it impossible to enter into his feelings or behaviour or understand the tribal laws which governed them. Certainly the meeting in the open of two dogs, strangers to each other, is one of the most painful, thrilling, and pregnant of all conceivable encounters; it is surrounded by an atmosphere of the last uncanniness, presided over by a constraint for which I have no preciser name; they simply cannot pass each other, their mutual embarrassment is frightful to behold.

I am not speaking of the case where one of the parties is shut up behind a hedge or a fence. Even then it is not easy to interpret their feelings – but at least the situation is less acute. They sniff each other from far off, and Bashan suddenly seeks shelter in my neighbourhood, whining a little to give vent to a distress and oppression which simply no words can describe. At the same time the imprisoned stranger sets up a violent barking, ostensibly in his character as a good watch-dog, but passing over unconsciously into a whimpering much like Bashan's own, an unsatisfied, envious, distressful whine. We draw near. The strange dog is waiting for us, close to the hedge, grousing and bemoaning his impotence; jumping at the barrier and giving every sign – how seriously one cannot tell – of intending to tear Bashan to pieces if only he could get at him. Bashan might easily stick close to me and pass him by; but he goes up to the hedge. He has to, he would even if I forbade him; to remain away would be to transgress a code older and more inviolable than any probibition of mine. He advances, then, and with a modest and inscrutable bearing performs that rite which he knows will soothe and appease the other – even if temporarily – so long as the stranger performs it too, though whining and complaining in the act. Then they both chase wildly along the hedge, each on his own side, as close as possible, neither making a sound. At the end of the hedge they both face about and dash back again. But in full career both suddenly halt and stand as though rooted to the spot; they stand still, facing the hedge, and put their noses together through it. For some space of time they stand thus, then resume their curious, futile race shoulder to shoulder on either side of the barrier. But in the end my dog avails himself of his freedom and moves off – a frightful moment for the prisoner! He cannot stand it, he finds it namelessly humiliating that the other should dream of simply going off like that. He raves and slavers and contorts himself in his rage; runs like one mad up and down his enclosure; threatens to jump the hedge and have the faithless Bashan by the throat; he yells insults behind the retreating back. Bashan hears it all, it distresses him, as his manner shows. But he does not turn round, he jogs along beside me, while the cursings in our rear die down into whinings and are still.

Such the procedure when one of the parties is shut up. Embarrassments multiply when both of them are free. I do not relish describing the scene: it is one of the most painful and equivocal imaginable. Bashan has been bounding light-heartedly beside me; he comes up close, he fairly forces himself upon me, with a sniffling and whimpering that seem to come from his very depths. I still do not know what moves his utterance, but I recognize it at once and gather that there is a strange dog in the offing. I look about – yes, there he comes, and even at this distance his strained and hesitating mien betrays that he has already seen Bashan. I am scarcely less upset than they; I find the meeting most undesirable. 'Go away,' I say to Bashan. 'Why do you glue yourself to my leg? Can't you go off and do your business by yourselves?' I try to frighten him off with my cane. For if they start biting –

which may easily happen, with reason or without – I shall find it most unpleasant to have them between my feet. 'Go away!' I repeat, in a lower voice. But Bashan does not go away, he sticks in his distress the closer to me, making as brief a pause as he can at a tree-trunk to perform the accustomed rite; I can see the other dog doing the same. We are now within twenty paces, the suspense is frightful. The strange dog is crawling on his belly, like a cat, his head thrust out. In this posture he awaits Bashan's approach, poised to spring at the right moment for his throat. But he does not do it, nor does Bashan seem to expect that he will. Or at least he goes up to the crouching stranger, though plainly trembling and heavy-hearted; he would do this, he is obliged to do it, even though I were to act myself and leave him to face the situation alone by striking into a side path. However painful the encounter, he has no choice, avoidance is not to be thought of. He is under a spell, he is bound to the other dog, they are bound to each other with some obscure and equivocal bond which may not be denied. We are now within two paces.

Then the other gets up, without a sound, as though he had never been behaving like a tiger, and stands there just as Bashan is standing profoundly embarrassed, wretched, at a loss. They cannot pass each other. They probably want to, they turn away their heads, rolling their eyes sideways; evidently the same sense of guilt weighs on them both. They edge cautiously up to each other with a hang-dog air; they stop flank to flank and sniff under each other's tails. At this point the growling begins, and I speak to Bashan low-voiced and warn him, for now is the decisive moment, now we shall know whether it will come to biting or whether I shall be spared that rude shock. It does come to biting, I do not know how, still less why: quite suddenly they are nothing but a raging tumult and whirling coil out of which issue the frightful guttural noises that animals make when they engage. I may have to engage too, with my cane, to forestall a worse calamity; I may try to get Bashan by the neck or the collar and hold him up at arm's length in the air, the stranger dog hanging on by his teeth. Other horrors there are, too, which I may have to face – and feel them afterwards in all my limbs during the rest of our walk. But it may be, too, that after all the preliminaries the affair will pass tamely off and no harm done. At best it is hard to part the two; even if they are not clenched by the teeth, they are held by that inward bond. They may seem to have passed each other, they are no longer flank to flank, but in a straight line with their heads in opposite directions; they may not even turn their heads, but only be rolling their eyes backwards. There may even be a space between them – and yet the painful bond still holds. Neither knows if the right moment for release has come, they would both like to go, yet each seems to have conscientious scruples. Slowly, slowly, the bond loosens, snaps; Bashan bounds lightly away, with, as it were, a new lease of life.

I speak of these things only to show how under stress of circumstance the character of a near friend may reveal itself as strange and foreign. It is dark to me, it is mysterious; I observe it with head-shakings and can only dimly guess what it may mean. And in all other respects I understand Bashan so well. I feel such lively sympathy for all his manifestations! For example, how well I know that whining yawn of his when our walk has been disappointing, too short, or devoid of sporting interest; when I have begun the day late and only gone out for a quarter of an hour before dinner. At such times he walks beside me and yawns – an open, impudent yawn to the whole extent of his jaws, an animal, audible yawn insultingly expressive of his utter boredom. 'A fine master I have!' it seems to say. 'Far in the night last night I met him at the bridge and now he sits behind his glass door and I wait for him dying of boredom. And when he does go out he only does it to come back again before there is time to start any game. A fine master! Not a proper master at all – really a rotten master, if you ask me!'

Such was the meaning of his yawn, vulgarly plain beyond all misunderstanding. And I admit that he is right, that he has a just grievance, and I put out a hand to pat his shoulder consolingly or to stroke his head. But he is not, under such circumstances, grateful for caresses; he yawns again, if possible more rudely than before, and moves away from my hand, although by nature, in contrast to Percy and in harmony with his own plebian sentimentality, he sets great store by caresses. He particularly likes having his throat scratched and has a funny way of guiding one's hand to the right place by energetic little jerks of his head. That he has no room just now for endearments is partly due to his disappointment, but also to the fact that when he is in motion – and that means that I also am – he does not care for them. His mood is too manly; but it changes directly I sit down. Then he is all for friendliness again and responds to it with clumsy enthusiasm.

When I sit reading in a corner of the garden wall, or on the lawn with my back to a favourite tree, I enjoy interrupting my intellectual preoccupations to talk and play with Bashan. And what do I say to him? Mostly his own name, the two syllables which are of the utmost personal interest because they refer to himself and have an electric effect upon his whole being. I rouse and stimulate his sense of his own ego by impressing upon him – varying my tone and emphasis – that he *is* Bashan and that Bashan is his name. By continuing this for a while I can actually produce in him a state of ecstasy, a sort of intoxication with his own identity, so that he begins to whirl round on himself and send up loud exultant barks to heaven out of the weight of dignity that lies on his chest. Or we amuse ourselves, I by tapping him on the nose, he by snapping at my hand as though it were a fly. It makes us both laugh, yes, Bashan has to laugh too; and as I laugh I marvel at the sight, to me the oddest and most touching thing in the world. It is moving to see how under my teasing his thin animal cheeks and the corners of his mouth will twitch, and over his dark animal mask will pass an expression like a human smile, or at least some ungainly, pathetic semblance of one. It gives way to a look of startled embarrassment, then transforms the face by appearing again...

But I will go no further nor involve myself in more detail of the kind. Even so I am dismayed at the space I have been led on to give to this little description; for what I had in mind to do was merely to display, as briefly as I might, my hero in his element, on the scene where he is most at home, most himself, and where his gifts show to best advantage; I mean, of course, the chase. But first I must give account to my reader of the theatre of these delights, my landscape by the river and Bashan's hunting-ground. It is a strip of land intimately bound up with his personality, familiar, loved, and significant to me like himself; which fact, accordingly, without further literary justification or embellishment, must serve as the occasion for my description.

The Hunting-Ground

The spacious gardens of the suburb where we live contain many large old trees that rise above the villa roofs and form a striking contrast to the saplings set out at a later period. Unquestionably they are the earliest inhabitants, the pride and adornment of a settlement which is still not very old. They have been carefully protected and preserved, so far as was possible; when any one of them came into conflict with the boundaries of the parcels of land, some venerable silvery moss-grown trunk standing exactly on a border-line, the hedge makes a little curve round it, or an accommodating gap is left in a wall, and the ancient towers up half on public, half on private ground, with bare snow-covered boughs or adorned with its tiny, late-coming leaves.

They are a variety of ash, a tree that loves moisture more than most – and their presence here shows what kind of soil we have. It is not so long since human brains reclaimed it for human habitation; not more than a decade or so. Before that it was a marshy wilderness, a breeding-place for mosquitoes, where willows, dwarf poplars, and other stunted growths mirrored themselves in stagnant pools. The region is subject to floods. There is a stratum of impermeable soil a few yards under the surface; it has always been boggy, with standing water in the hollows. They drained it by lowering the level of the river – engineering is not my strong point, but anyhow it was some such device, by means of which the water which cannot sink into the earth now flows off laterally into the river by several subterranean channels, and the ground is left comparatively dry – but only comparatively, for Bashan and I, knowing it as we do, are acquainted with certain low, retired, and rushy spots, relics of the primeval condition of the region, whose damp coolness defies the summer heat and makes them a grateful place wherein to draw a few long breaths.

The whole district has its peculiarities, indeed, which distinguish it at a glance from the pine forests and moss-grown meadows which are the usual setting of a mountain stream. It has preserved its original characteristics even since it was acquired by the real-estate company; even outside the gardens the original vegetation preponderates over the newly planted. In the avenues and parks, of course, horse-chestnuts and quick-growing maple trees, beeches, and all sorts of ornamental shrubs have been set out; also rows of French poplars standing erect in their sterile masculinity. But the ash trees, as I said, are the aborigines; they are everywhere, and of all ages, century-old giants and tender young seedlings pushing their way by hundreds, like weeds, through the gravel. It is the ash, together with the silver poplar, the aspen, the birch, and the willow, that gives the scene its distinctive look. All these trees have small leaves, and all this small-leaved foliage is very striking by contrast with the huge trunks. But there are elms too, spreading their large, varnished, saw-edged leaves to the sun. And everywhere too are masses of creeper, winding round the young trees in the underbrush and inextricably mingling its leaves with theirs. Little thickets of slim alder trees stand in the hollows. There are few lime trees, no oaks or firs at all, in our domain, though there are some on the slope which bounds it to the east, where the soil changes and with it the character of the vegetation. There they stand out black against the sky, like sentinels guarding our little valley.

It is not more than five hundred yards from slope to river – I have paced it out. Perhaps the strip of river-bank widens a little, farther down, but not to any extent; so it is remarkable what landscape variety there is in this small area, even when one makes such moderate use of the playground it affords along the river as do Bashan and I, who rarely spend more than two hours there, counting our going and coming. There is such diversity that we need hardly take the same path twice or ever tire of the view or be conscious of any limitations of space; and this is due to the circumstance that our domain divides itself into three quite different regions or zones. We may confine ourselves to one of these or we may combine all three: they are the neighbourhood of the river and its banks, the neighbourhood of the opposite slope, and the wooded section in the middle.

The wooded zone, the parks, the osier brakes, and the riverside shrubbery take up most of the breadth. I search in vain for a word better than 'wood' to describe this strange tract of land. For it is no wood in the usual sense of the word: not a pillared hall of even-sized trunks, carpeted with moss and fallen leaves. The trees in our hunting-ground are of uneven growth and size, hoary giants of willows and poplars, especially along the river, though also deeper in; others ten or fifteen years old, which are probably as large as they will grow; and lastly a legion of slender trees, young ashes, birches, and alders in a nursery garden planted by nature herself. These look larger than they are; and all, as I said, are wound round with creepers which give a look of tropical luxuriance to the scene. But I suspect them of choking the growth of their hosts, for I cannot see that the trunks have grown any thicker in all the years I have known them.

The trees are of few and closely related species. The alder belongs to the birch family, the poplar is after all not very different from a willow. And one might say that they all approach the willow type; foresters tell us that trees tend to adapt themselves to their local conditions, showing a certain conformity, as it were, to the prevailing mode. It is the distorted, fantastic, witchlike silhouette of the willow tree, dweller by still and by flowing waters, that sets the fashion here, with her branches like broom-splints and her crooked-fingered tips; and all the others visibly try to be like her. The silver poplar apes her best; but often it is hard to tell poplar from birch, so much is the latter beguiled by the spirit of the place to take on misshapen forms. Not that there are not also plenty of very shapely and well-grown single specimens of this lovable tree, and enchanting they look in the favouring glow of the late afternoon sun. In this region the birch appears as a slender silver bole with a crown of little, separate leaves atop; as a lovely, lithe, and well-grown maiden; it has the prettiest of chalk-white trunks, and its foliage droops like delicate languishing locks of hair. But there are also birches colossal in size, that no man could span with his arms, the bark of which is only white high up, but near the ground has turned black and coarse and is seamed with fissures.

The soil is not like what one expects in a wood. It is loamy, gravelly, even sandy. It seems anything but fertile, and yet, within its nature, is almost luxuriantly so; for it is overgrown with tall, rank grass, often the dry, sharp-cornered kind that grows on dunes. In winter it covers the ground like trampled hay; not seldom it cannot be distinguished from reeds, but in other places it is soft and fat and juicy, and among it grow hemlock, coltsfoot, nettles, all sorts of low-growing things, mixed with tall thistles and tender young tree shoots. Pheasants and other wildfowl hide in this vegetation, which rolls up to and over the gnarled roots of the trees. And everywhere the wild grape and the hop-vine clamber out of the thicket to twine round the trunks in garlands of flapping leaves, or in winter with bare stems like the toughest sort of wire.

Now, all this is not a wood, it is not a park, it is simply an enchanted garden, no more and no less. I will stand for the word – though of course nature here is stingy and sparse and tends to the deformed; a few botanical names exhausting the catalogue of her performance. The ground is rolling, it constantly rises and falls away, so that the view is enclosed on every hand, with a lovely effect of remoteness and privacy. Indeed, if the wood stretched for miles to right and left, as far as it reaches lengthwise, instead of only a hundred and some paces on each side from the middle, one could not feel more secluded. Only by the sense of sound is one made aware of the friendly nearness of the river; you cannot see it, but it whispers gently from the west. There are gorges choked with shrubbery – elder, privet, jasmine, and wild cherry – on close June days the scent is almost overpowering. And again there are low-lying spots, regular gravel-pits, where nothing but a few willow-shoots and a little sage can grow, at the bottom or on the sides.

And all this scene never ceases to exert a strange influence upon me, though it has been my almost daily walk for some years. The fine massed foliage of the ash puts me in mind of a giant fern; these creepers and climbers, this barrenness and this damp, this combination of lush and dry, have a fantastic effect; to convey my whole meaning, it is a little as though I were transported to another geological period, or even to the bottom of the sea – and the fantasy has this much of fact about it, that water did stand here once, for instance in the square low-lying meadow basins thick with shoots of self-sown ash, which now serve as pasture for sheep. One such lies directly behind my house.

The wilderness is crossed in all directions by paths, some of them only lines of trodden grass or gravelly trails, obviously born of use and not laid out – though it would be hard to say who trod them, for only by way of unpleasant exception do Bashan and I meet anyone here. When that happens he stands stock-still and gives a little growl which very well expresses my own feelings too. Even on the fine summer Sunday afternoons which bring crowds of people to walk in these parts – for it is always a few degrees cooler here – we remain undisturbed in our fastness. They know it not; the water is the great attraction, as a rule, the river in its course; the human stream gets as close as it can, down to the very edge if there is no flood, rolls along beside it, and then back home again. At most we may come on a pair of lovers in the shrubbery; they look at us wide-eyed and startled out of their nest, or else defiantly as though to ask what objection we have to their presence or their behaviour. All which we disclaim by beating swift retreat, Bashan with the indifference he feels for everything that does not smell like game; I with a face utterly devoid of all expression, either approving or the reverse.

But these woodland paths are not the only way we have of reaching my park. There are streets as well – or rather there are traces, which once were streets, or which once were to have been streets, or which, by God's will, may yet become streets. In other words: there are signs that the pickaxe has been at work, signs of a hopeful real-estate enterprise for some distance beyond the built-up section and the villas. There has been some far-sighted planning on the part of the company which some years ago acquired the land; but their plans went beyond their capacity for carrying them out, for the villas were only a part of what they had in mind. Building-lots were laid out; an area extending for nearly a mile down the river was prepared, and doubtless still remains prepared, to receive possible purchasers and home-loving settlers. The building society conceived things on a rather large scale. They enclosed the river between dykes, they built quays and planted gardens, and, not content with that, they had embarked on clearing the woods, dumped piles of gravel, cut roads through the wilderness, one or two lengthwise and several across the width: fine, well-planned roads, or at least the first steps towards them, made of coarse gravel, with a wide footpath and indications of a kerb-stone. But no one walks there save Bashan and myself, he on the good stout leather of his four paws, I in hobnailed boots on account of the gravel. For the stately villas projected by the company are still non-existent, despite the good example I set when I built my own house. They have been, I say, non-existent for ten, no, fifteen years; it is no wonder that a kind of blight has settled upon the enterprise and discouragement reigns in the bosom of the building society, a disinclination to go on with their project.

However, things had got so far forward that these streets, though not built up, have all been given names, just as though they were in the centre of the town or in a suburb. I should very much like to know what sort of speculator he was who named them; he seems to have been a literary chap with a fondness for the past: there is an Opitzstrasse, a Flemmingstrasse, a Bürgerstrasse, even an Adalbert-Stifterstrasse – I walk on the last-named with especial reverence in my hobnailed boots. At all the corners stakes have been driven in the ground with street signs affixed to them, as is usual in suburbs where there are no house-corners to receive them; they are the usual little blue enamel plates with white lettering. But alas, they are rather the worse for wear. They have stood here far too long, pointing out the names of vacant sites where nobody wants to live; they are monuments to the failure, the discouragement, and the arrested development of the whole enterprise. They have not been kept up or renewed, the climate has done its worst by them. The enamel has scaled off, the lettering is rusty, there are ugly broken-edged gaps which make the names sometimes almost illegible. One of them, indeed, puzzled me a good deal when I first came here and was spying about the neighbourhood. It was a long name, and the word 'street' was perfectly clear, but most of the rest was eaten by rust; there remained only an *S* at the beginning, an *E* somewhere about the middle, and another *E* at the end. I could not reckon with so many unknown quantities. I studied the sign a long time with my hands behind my back, then continued along the footpath with Bashan. I thought I was thinking about something else, but all the time my brains were privately cudgelling themselves, and suddenly it came over me. I stopped with a start, stood still, and then hastened back, took up my former position, and tested my guess. Yes, it fitted. The name of the street where I was walking was Shakespeare Street.

The streets suit the signboards and the signboards suit the streets – it is a strange and dreamlike harmony in decay. The streets run through the wood they have broken into; but the wood does not remain passive. It does not let the streets stop as they were made, through decade after decade, until at last people come and settle on them. It takes every step to close them again; for what grows here does not mind gravel, it flourishes in it. Purple thistles, blue sage, silvery shoots of willow, and green ash seedlings spring up all over the road and even on the pavement; the streets with the poetic names are going back to the wilderness, whether one likes it or not; in another ten years Opitzstrasse, Flemmingstrasse, and the rest will be closed, they will probably as good as disappear. There is at present no ground for complaint; for from the romantic and picturesque point of view there are no more beautiful streets in the world than they are now. Nothing could be more delightful than strolling through them in their unfinished, abandoned state, if one has on stout boots and does not mind the gravel. Nothing more agreeable to the eye than looking from the wild garden beneath one's feet to the humid massing of fine-leafed foliage that shuts in the view – foliage such as Claude Lorrain used to paint, three centuries ago. Such as he used to paint, did I say? But surely he painted *this*. He was here, he knew this scene, he studied it. If my building-society man had not confined himself to the literary field, one of these rusty street signs might have borne the name of Claude.

Well, that is our middle or wooded region. But the eastern slope has its own charms not to be despised, either by me or by Bashan, who has his own reasons, which will appear hereafter. I might call this region the zone of the brook; for it takes its idyllic character as landscape from the stream that flows through it, and the peaceful loveliness of its beds of forget-me-not makes it a fit companion-piece to the zone on the other side with its rushing river, whose flowing, when the west wind blows, can be faintly heard even all the way across our hunting-ground. The first of the made crossroads through the wood runs like a causeway from the poplar avenue to the foot of the hillside, between low-lying pasture-ground on one side and wooded lots of land on the other. And from there a path descends to the left, used by the children to coast on in winter. The brook rises in the level ground at the bottom of this descent. We love to stroll beside it, Bashan and I, on the right or the left bank at will, through the varied territory of our eastern zone. On our left is an extent of wooded meadow, and a nursery-gardening establishment; we can see the backs of the buildings, and sheep cropping the clover, presided over by a rather stupid little girl in a red frock. She keeps propping her hands on her knees and screaming at her charges at the top of her lungs in a harsh, angry, and imperious voice. But she seems to be afraid of the majestic old ram, who looks enormously fat in his thick fleece and who does as he likes regardless of her bullying ways. The child's screams rise to their height when the sheep are thrown into a panic by the appearance of Bashan; and this almost always happens quite against his will or intent, for he is profoundly indifferent to their existence, behaves as though they were not there, or even deliberately and contemptuously ignores them in an effort to forestall an attack of panic folly on their part. Their scent is strong enough to me, though not unpleasant; but it is not a scent of game, so Bashan takes no interest in harrying them. But let him make a single move, or merely appear on the scene, and the whole flock, but now grazing peacefully over the meadow and bleating in their curiously human voices, some bass, some treble, suddenly collect in a huddled mass of backs and go dashing off, while the imbecile child stoops over and screams at them until her voice cracks and her eyes pop out of her head. Bashan looks up at me as though to say: Am I to blame, did I do anything at all?

But once something quite the opposite happened, that was even more extraordinary and distressing than any panic. A sheep, a quite ordinary specimen, of medium size and the usual sheepish face, save for a narrow-lipped little mouth turned up at the corners into a smile which gave the creature an uncommonly sly and fatuous look – this sheep appeared to be smitten with Bashan's charms. It followed him; it left the flock and the pasture-ground and followed at his heels, wherever he went, smiling with extravagant stupidity. He left the path, and it followed. He ran, it galloped after. He stopped, it did the same, close behind him and smiling its inscrutable smile. Embarrassment and dismay were painted on Bashan's face, and certainly his position was highly distasteful. For good or for ill it lacked any kind of sense or reason. Nothing so consummately silly had ever happened to either of us. The sheep got farther and farther away from its base, but it seemed not to care for that; it followed the exasperated Bashan apparently resolved to part from him nevermore, but to be at his side whithersoever he went. He stuck close at my side; not so much alarmed – for the which there was no cause – as ashamed of the disgraceful situation. At last, as though he had had enough of it, he stood still, turned round, and gave a menacing growl. The sheep bleated – it was like a man's laugh, a spiteful laugh – and put poor Bashan so beside himself that he ran away with his tail between his legs, the sheep bounding absurdly behind him.

Meanwhile we had got a good way from the flock; the addlepated little girl was screaming fit to burst, and not only bending her knees but jerking them up and down as she screamed till they touched her face, and she looked from a distance like a demented dwarf. A dairymaid in an apron came running, her attention being drawn by the shrieks or in some other way. She had a pitchfork in one hand; with the other she held her breasts, that shook up and down as she ran. She tried to drive back the sheep with the pitchfork – it had started after Bashan again – but unsuccessfully. The sheep did indeed spring away from the fork in the right direction, but then swung round again to follow Bashan's trail. It seemed no power on earth would divert it. But at last I saw what had to be done and turned round. We all marched back, Bashan beside me, behind him the sheep, behind the sheep the maid with the pitchfork, the child in the red frock bouncing and stamping at us all the while. It was not enough to go back to the flock, we had to do the job thoroughly. We went into the farmyard and to the sheep-pen, where the farm girl rolled back the big door with her strong right arm. We all went inside, all of us; and then the rest of us had to slip out again and shut the door in the face of the poor deluded sheep, so that it was taken prisoner. And then, after receiving the farm girl's thanks, Bashan and I might resume our interrupted walk, to the end of which Bashan preserved a sulky and humiliated air.

So much for the sheep. Beyond the farm buildings is an extensive colony of allotments, that looks rather like a cemetery, with its arbours and little summer-houses like chapels and each tiny garden neatly enclosed. The whole colony has a fence round it, with a latticed gate, through which only the owners of the plots have admission. Sometimes I have seen a man with his sleeves rolled up digging his few yards of vegetable-plot – he looked as though he were digging his own grave. Beyond this come open meadows full of mole-hills, reaching to the edge of the middle wooded region; besides the moles, the place abounds in field-mice – I mention them on account of Bashan and his multifarious joy of the chase.

But on the other, the right side, the brook and the hillside continue, the latter, as I said, with great variety in its contours. The first part is shadowed

and gloomy and set with pines. Then comes a sand-pit which reflects the
warm rays of the sun; then a gravel-pit, then a cataract of bricks, as though a
house had been demolished up above and the rubble simply flung down the
hill, damming the brook at the bottom. But the brook rises until its waters
flow over the obstacle and go on, reddened with brick-dust and dyeing the
grass along its edge, to flow all the more blithely and pellucidly farther on,
with the sun making diamonds spark on its surface.

I am very fond of brooks, as indeed of all water, from the ocean to the
smallest reedy pool. If in the mountains in the summertime my ear but catch
the sound of plashing and prattling from afar, I always go to seek out the
source of the liquid sounds, a long way if I must; to make the acquaintance
and to look in the face of that conversable child of the hills, where he hides.
Beautiful are the torrents that come tumbling with mild thunderings down
between evergreens and over stony terraces; that form rocky bathing-pools
and then dissolve in white foam to fall perpendicularly to the next level. But
I have pleasure in the brooks of the flatland too, whether they be so shallow
as hardly to cover the slippery, silver-gleaming pebbles in their bed, or as
deep as small rivers between overhanging, guardian willow trees, their
current flowing swift and strong in the centre, still and gently at the edge.
Who would not choose to follow the sound of running waters? Its attraction
for the normal man is of a natural, sympathetic sort. For man is water's
child, nine-tenths of our body consists of it, and at a certain stage the foetus
possesses gills. For my part I freely admit that the sight of water in whatever
form or shape is my most lively and immediate kind of natural enjoyment;
yes, I would even say that only in contemplation of it do I achieve true self-
forgetfulness and feel my own limited individuality merge into the universal. The sea, still-brooding or coming on in crashing billows, can put me
in a state of such profound organic dreaminess, such remoteness from
myself, that I am lost to time. Boredom is unknown, hours pass like minutes,
in the unity of that companionship. But then, I can lean on the rail of a little
bridge over a brook and contemplate its currents, its whirlpools, and its
steady flow for as long as you like; with no sense or fear of that other flowing
within and about me, that swift gliding away of time. Such love of water and
understanding of it make me value the circumstance that the narrow strip of
ground where I dwell is enclosed on both sides by water.

But my little brook here is the simplest of its kind, it has no particular or
unusual characteristics, it is quite the average brook. Clear as glass, without
any guile, it does not dream of seeming deep by being turbid. It is shallow
and candid and makes no bones of betraying that there are old tins and the
mouldering remains of a laced shoe in its bed. But it is deep enough to serve
as a home for pretty, lively, silver-grey little fish, which dart away in zigzags
at our approach. In some places it broadens into a pool, and it has willows on
its margin, one of which I love to look at as I pass. It stands on the hillside, a
little removed from the water; but one of the boughs has bent down and
reached across and actually succeeded in plunging its silvery tip into the
flowing water. Thus it stands revelling in the pleasure of this contact.

It is pleasant to walk here in the warm breeze of summer. If the weather is
very warm Bashan goes into the stream to cool his belly; not more than that,
for he never of his own free will wets the upper parts. He stands there with
his ears laid back and a look of virtue on his face and lets the water stream
round and over him. Then he comes back to me to shake himself, being
convinced that this can only be accomplished in my vicinity – although he
does it so thoroughly that I receive a perfect shower-bath in the process. It is

no good waving him off with my stick or with shoutings. Whatever seems to him natural and right and necessary, that he will do.

The brook flows on westward to a little hamlet that faces north between the wood and the hillside. At the beginning of this hamlet is an inn, and at this point the brook widens into another pool where women kneel to wash their clothes. Crossing the little footbridge, you strike into a road going back towards the city between wood and meadow. But on the right of the road is another through the wood, by which in a few minutes you can get back to the river.

And so here we are at the river zone, and the river itself is in front of us, green and roaring and white with foam. It is really nothing more than a mountain torrent; but its ceaseless roaring pervades the whole region round, in the distance subdued, but here a veritable tumult which – if one cannot have the ocean itself – is quite a fair substitute for its awe-inspiring swell. Numberless gulls fill the air with their cries; autumn, winter, and spring they circle screaming round the mouths of the drainpipes which issue here, seeking their food. In summer they depart once more for the lakes higher up. Wild and half-wild duck also take refuge here in the neighbourhood of the town for the winter months. They rock on the waves, are whirled round and carried off by the current, rise into the air to escape being engulfed, and then settle again on quieter water.

And this river tract also is divided into areas of varying character. At the edge of the wood is the gravelly expanse into which the poplar avenue issues; it extends for nearly a mile downstream, as far as the ferry-house, of which I will speak presently. At this point the underbrush comes nearly down to the river-bed. And all the gravel, as I am aware, constitutes the beginnings of the first and most important of the lengthwise streets, magnificently conceived by the real-estate company as an esplanade, a carriage-road bordered by trees and flowers – where elegantly turned-out riders were to hold sweet converse with ladies leaning back in shiny landaus. Beside the ferry-house, indeed, is a sign, already rickety and rotting, from which one can gather that the site was intended for the erection of a café. Yes, there is the sign – and there it remains, but there is no trace of the little tables, the hurrying waiters and coffee-sipping guests; nobody has bought the site, and the esplanade is nothing but a desert of gravel, where sage and willow-shoots are almost as thick as in Opitz- and Flemmingstrasse.

Down close to the river is another, narrower gravel waste, as full of weeds as the bigger one. Along it are grassy mounds supporting telegraph poles. I like to use this as a path, by way of variety – also because it is cleaner, though more difficult, to walk on it than on the actual footpath, which in bad weather is often very muddy, though it is actually the proper path, extending for miles along the river, finally going off into trails along the bank. It is planted on the river side with young maple and birch trees; on the other side the original inhabitants stand in a row – willows, aspens, and silver poplars of enormous size. The river-bank is steep and high and is ingeniously shored up with withes and concrete to prevent the flooding which threatens two or three times in the year, after heavy rains or when the snows melt in the hills. At several points there are ladder-like wooden steps leading down to the river-bed – an extent of mostly dry gravel, six or eight yards wide. For this mountain torrent behaves precisely as its like do, whether large or small: it may be, according to the conditions up above, either the merest green trickle, hardly covering the stones, where long-legged birds seem to be standing on the water; or it may be a torrent alarming in its power and

extent, filling the wide bed with raging fury, whirling round tree-branches
and old baskets and dead cats and threatening to commit much damage.
Here, too, there is protection against floods in the shape of woven hurdles
put in slanting to the stream. When dry, the bed is grown up with wiry grass
and wild oats, as well as that omnipresent shrub the blue sage; there is fairly
good walking, on the strip of flat stones at the extreme outer edge, and it
affords me a pleasant variety, for though the stone is not of the most
agreeable to walk on, the close proximity of the river atones for much, and
there is even sometimes sand between the gravel and the grass; true, it is
mixed with clay, it has not the exquisite cleanness of sea-sand, but after all it
is sand. I am taking a walk on the beach that stretches into the distance at the
edge of the wave, and there is the sound of the surge and the cry of the gulls,
there is that monotony that swallows time and space and shuts one up as in a
dream. The river roars eddying over the stones, and halfway to the ferry-
house the sound is augmented by a waterfall that comes down by a diagonal
canal and tumbles into the larger stream, arching as it falls, shining glassily
like a leaping fish, and seething perpetually at its base.

Lovely to walk here when the sky is blue and the ferry-boat flies a flag,
perhaps in honour of the fine weather or because it is a feast-day of some
sort. There are other boats here too, but the ferry-boat is fast to a wire cable
attached to another, thicker cable that is spanned across the stream and runs
along it on a little pulley. The current supplies the motive power, the
steering is done by hand. The ferryman lives with his wife and child in the
ferry-house, which is a little higher up than the upper footpath; the house
has a kitchen-garden and a chicken-house and the man undoubtedly gets it
rent-free in his office as ferryman. It is a sort of dwarf villa, rather flimsy,
with funny little outcroppings of balconies and bay-windows, and seems to
have two rooms below and two above. I like to sit on the little bench on the
upper footpath close to the tiny garden – with Bashan squatting on my foot
and the ferryman's chickens stalking round about me, jerking their heads
forward with each step. The cock usually comes and perches on the back of
the bench with his green bersaglieri tail-feathers hanging down behind; he
sits thus beside me and measures me with a fierce side-glance of his red eye. I
watch the traffic; it is not crowded, hardly even lively; indeed, the ferry-boat
runs only at considerable intervals. The more do I enjoy it when on one side
or the other a man appears, or a woman with a basket, and wants to be put
across; the 'Boat ahoy!' is an age-old, picturesque cry, with a poetry not
impaired by the fact that the business is done somewhat differently
nowadays. Double flights of steps for those coming and going lead down to
the river-bed and to the landings, and there is an electric push-button at the
side of each. So when a man appears on the opposite bank and stands looking
across the water, he does not put his hands round his mouth and call. He
goes up to the push-button, puts out his hand, and pushes. The bell rings
shrilly in the ferryman's villa; that is the 'Boat ahoy!' even so, and it is poetic
still. Then the man waits and looks about. And almost at the moment when
the bell rings, the ferryman comes out of his little official dwelling, as though
he had been standing behind the door or sitting on a chair waiting for the
signal. He comes out, and the way he walks suggests that he has been
mechanically put in motion by the ringing of the bell. It is like a shooting-
booth when you shoot at the door of a little house and if you hit it a figure
comes out, a sentry or a cow-girl. The ferryman crosses his garden at a
measured pace, his arms swinging regularly at his sides; over the path and
down the steps to the river, where he pushes off the ferry-boat and holds the

steering-gear while the little pulley runs along the wire above the stream and the boat is driven across. The man springs in, and once safely on this side hands over his penny and runs briskly up the steps, going off right or left. Sometimes, when the ferryman is not well or is very busy in the house, his wife or even his little child comes out to ferry the stranger across. They can do it as well as he, and so could I, for it is an easy office, requiring no special gift or training. He can reckon himself lucky to have the job and live in the dwarf villa. Anyone, however stupid, could do what he does, and he knows this, of course, and behaves with becoming modesty. On the way back to his house he very politely says: '*Grüss Gott*' to me as I sit there on the bench between Bashan and the cock; you can see that he likes to be on good terms with everybody.

There is a tarry smell, a breeze off the water, a slapping sound against the ferry-boat. What more can one want? Sometimes these things call up a familiar memory: the water is deep, it has a smell of decay – that is the Lagoon, that is Venice. But sometimes there is a heavy storm, a deluge of rain; in my macintosh, my face streaming with wet, I take the upper path, leaning against the strong west wind, which in the poplar avenue has torn the saplings away from their supports. Now one can see why all the trees are bent in one direction and have somewhat lop-sided tops. Bashan has to stop often to shake himself, the water flies off him in every direction. The river is quite changed: swollen and dark yellow it rolls threateningly along, rushing and dashing in a furious hurry this way and that; its muddy tide takes up the whole extra bed up to the edge of the undergrowth, pounding against the cement and the willow hurdles – until one is glad of the forethought that put them there. The strange thing about it is that the water is *quiet*; it makes almost no noise at all. And there are no rapids in its course now, the stream is too high for that. You can only see where they were by the fact that its waves are higher and deeper there than elsewhere, and that their crests break backwards instead of forwards like the surf on a beach. The waterfall is insignificant now, its volume is shrunken, no longer vaulted, and the boiling water at its base is almost obliterated by the height of the flood. Bashan's reaction to all this is simple unmitigated astonishment that things can be so changed. He cannot get over it, cannot understand how it is that the dry territory where he is wont to run about has disappeared, is covered by water. He flees up into the undergrowth to get away from the lashing of the flood; looks at me and wags his tail, then back at the water, and has a funny, puzzled way of opening his jaws crookedly, shutting them again and running his tongue round the corner of his mouth. It is not a very refined gesture, in fact rather common, but very speaking, and as human as it is animal – in fact it is just what an ordinary simple-minded man might do in face of a surprising situation, very likely scratching his neck at the same time.

Having gone into some detail in describing the river zone, I believe I have covered the whole region and done all I can to bring it before my reader's eye. I like my description pretty well, but I like the reality of nature even better. It is more vivid and various; just as Bashan himself is warmer, more living and hearty than his imaginary presentment. I am attached to this landscape, I owe it something, and am grateful; therefore, I have described it. It is my park and my solitude; my thoughts and dreams are mingled and interwoven with images from it, as the tendrils of climbing plants are with the boughs of its trees. I have seen it at all times of day and all seasons of the year: in autumn, when the chemical odour of decaying vegetation fills the air, when all the thistles have shed their down, when the great beeches in my park have spread a rust-coloured carpet of leaves on the meadow and the liquid golden afternoons merge into romantic, theatrical early evenings, with the moon's sickle swimming in the sky, when a milk-brewed mist floats above the lowlands and a crimson sunset burns through the black silhouettes of the tree-branches. In autumn, but in winter too, when the gravel is covered with snow and softly levelled off so that one can walk on it in overshoes; when the river looks black as it flows between sallow frost-bound banks, and the cries of hundreds of gulls fill the air from morning to night. But my freest and most familiar intercourse with it is in the milder months, when no extra clothing is required, to dash out quickly, between two showers, for a quarter of an hour; to bend aside in passing a bough of black alder and get a glimpse of the river as it flows. We may have had guests, and I am left somewhat worn down by conversation, between my four walls, where it seems the breath of the strangers still hovers on the air. Then it is good not to linger but to go out at once and stroll in Gellertstrasse or Stifterstrasse, to draw a long breath and get the air into one's lungs. I look up into the sky, I gaze into the tender depths of the masses of green foliage, and peace returns once more and dwells within my spirit.

And Bashan is always with me. He had not been able to prevent the influx of strange persons into our dwelling though he had lifted up his voice and objected. But it did no good, so he had withdrawn. Now he rejoices to be with me again in our hunting-ground. He runs before me on the gravel path, one ear negligently cocked, with that sidewise gait dogs have, the hind legs not just exactly behind the forelegs. And suddenly I see him gripped, as it were, body and soul, his stump of tail switching furiously, erect in the air. His head goes forward and down, his body lengthens out, he makes short dashes in several directions, and then shoots off in one of them with his nose to the ground. He has struck a scent. He is off after a hare.

The Chase

The region round is full of game, and we hunt it; that is, Bashan does and I look on. Thus we go hunting: hares, partridges, fieldmice, moles, ducks, and gulls. Neither do we shrink from larger game, we stalk pheasant, even deer, if one of them, in winter, happens to stray into our preserve. It is quite a thrilling sight to see the slender long-legged creature, yellow against the snow, running away, with its white buttocks bobbing up and down, in flight from my little Bashan. He strains every nerve, I look on with the greatest sympathy and suspense. Not that anything would ever come of it, nothing ever has or will. But the lack of concrete results does not affect Bashan's passionate eagerness or mar my own interest at all. We pursue the chase for its own sake, not for the prey nor for any other material advantage. Bashan is, as I have said, the active partner. He does not expect from me anything more than my moral support, having no experience, immediate and personal, that is, of more direct cooperation. I say immediate and personal for it is more than likely that his forebears, at least on the pointer side, know what the chase should really be like. I have sometimes asked myself whether some memory might still linger in him, ready to be awakened by a chance sight or sound. At his level the life of the individual is certainly less sharply distinguished from the race than is the case with human beings, birth and death must be a less far-reaching shock; perhaps the traditions of the stock are preserved unimpaired, so that it would only be an apparent contradiction to speak of inborn experiences, unconscious memories which, when summoned up, would have the power to confuse the creature as to what were its own individual experiences or give rise to dissatisfaction with them. I indulge in this thought, but finally put it from me, as Bashan obviously put from him the rather brutal episode which gave rise to my speculations.

When we get out to follow the chase it is usually midday, half past eleven or twelve; sometimes, on particularly warm summer days, we go late in the afternoon, six o'clock or so – or perhaps we go then for the second time. But on the afternoon walk things are very different with me – not at all as they were on my careless morning stroll. My freshness and serenity have departed long since, I have been struggling and taking thought, I have overcome difficulties, have had to grit my teeth and tussle with a single detail while at the same time holding a more extended and complex context firmly in mind, concentrating my mental powers upon it down to its furthermost ramifications. And my head is tired. It is the chase with Bashan that relieves and distracts me, gives me new life, and puts me back into condition for the rest of the day, in which there is still something to be done.

Of course we do not select each day a certain kind of game to hunt – only hares, for instance, or only ducks. Actually we hunt everything that comes – I was going to say, within reach of our guns. So that we do not need to go far before starting something, actually the hunt can begin just outside the garden gate; for there are quantities of moles and field-mice in the meadow bottom behind the house. Of course these fur-bearing little creatures are not properly game at all. But their mysterious, burrowing little ways, and especially the slyness and dexterity of the field-mice, which are not blind by day like their brethren the moles, but scamper discreetly about on the ground, whisking into their holes at the approach of danger, so that one cannot even see their legs moving – all this works powerfully upon Bashan's instincts. Besides, they are the only wild creatures he ever catches. A field-mouse, a mole, makes a morsel not to be despised, in these lean days, when he often finds nothing more appetizing than porridge in the dish beside his kennel.

So then I and my walking-stick will scarcely have taken two or three steps up the poplar avenue, and Bashan will have scarcely opened the ball with his usual riotous plunges, when I see him capering off to my right – already he is in the grip of his passion, sees and hears nothing but the maddening invisible activities of the creatures all round him. He slinks through the grass, his whole body tense, wagging his tail and lifting his legs with great caution; stops, with one foreleg and one hind leg in the air, eyes the ground with his head on one side, muzzle pointed, ear muscles stiffly erected – so that his ear-laps fall down in front, each side of his eyes. Then with both forepaws raised he makes a sudden forward plunge, and another; looking with a puzzled air at the place where something just now was but is not any more. Then he begins to dig. I feel a strong desire to follow him and see what he gets. But if I did we should never get farther, his whole zeal for the chase would be expended here on the spot. So I go on. I need not worry about his losing me. Even if he stops behind a long time and has not seen which way I turned, my trail will be as clear to him as though I were the game he seeks, and he will follow it, head between his paws, even if I am out of sight; already I can hear his licence-tag clinking and his stout paws thudding in my rear. He shoots past me, turns round, and wags his tail to announce that he is on the spot.

But in the woods, or out on the meadows by the brook, I do stop often and watch him digging for a mouse, even though the time allotted for my walk is nearly over. It is so fascinating to see his passionate concentration, I feel the contagion myself and cannot help a fervent wish that he may catch something and I be there to see. The spot where he has chosen to dig looks like any other – perhaps a mossy little mound and among the roots at the foot of a birch tree. But he has heard and scented something at that spot, perhaps even viewed it as it whisked away; he is convinced that it is there in its burrow underground, he has only to get at it – and he digs away for dear life, oblivious of all else, not angry, but with the professional passion of the sportsman – it is a magnificent sight. His little striped body, the ribs showing and muscles playing under the smooth skin, is drawn in at the middle, his hind quarters stand up in the air, the stump of a tail vibrating in quick time; his head with his forepaws is down in the slanting hole he has dug and he turns his face aside as he plies his iron-shod paws. Faster and faster, till earth and little stones and tufts of grass and fragments of tree-roots fly up almost into my face. Sometimes he snorts in the silence, when he has burrowed his nose well into the earth, trying to smell out the motionless, clever, frightened little beast that is besieged down there. It is a muffled snorting; he draws in the air hastily and empties his lungs again the better to scent the fine, keen, faraway, and buried effluvium. How does the creature feel when he hears the snorting? Ah, that is its own affair, or God's, who has made Bashan the enemy of field-mice. Even the emotion of fear is an enhancement of life; and who knows, if there were no Bashan the mouse might find time hang heavy on its hands. Besides, what would be the use of all its beady-eyed cleverness and mining skill, which more than balance what Bashan can do, so that the attacker's success is always more than problematical? In short, I do not feel much pity for the mouse, privately I am on Bashan's side and cannot always stick to my role of onlooker. I take my walking-stick and dig out some pebble or gnarled piece of root that is too firmly lodged for him to move. And he sends up a swift, warm glance of understanding to me as he works. With his mouth full of dirt, he chews away at the stubborn earth and the roots running through it, tears out whole chunks and throws them aside, snorts again into his hole and is encouraged by the freshened scent to renewed attack on it with his claws.

In nearly every case all this labour is vain. Bashan will give one last cursory look at the scene and then with soil sticking to his nose, and his legs black to the shoulder, he will give it up and trot off indifferently beside me. 'No go, Bashan,' I say when he looks up at me. 'Nothing there,' I repeat, shaking my head and shrugging my shoulders to make my meaning clear. But he needs no consolation, he is not in the least depressed by his failure. The chase is the thing, the quarry a minor matter. It was a good effort, he thinks, in so far as he casts his mind back at all to his recent strenuous performance – for already he is bent on a new one, and all three of our zones will furnish him plenty of opportunity.

But sometimes he actually catches the mouse. I have my emotions when that happens, for he gobbles it alive, without compunction, with the fur and the bones. Perhaps the poor little thing was not well enough advised by its instincts, and chose for its hole a place where the earth was too soft and loose and easy to dig. Perhaps its gallery was not long enough and it was too terrified to go on digging, but simply crouched there with its beady eyes popping out of its head for fright, while the horrible snorting came nearer and nearer. And so at last the iron-shod paw laid it bare and scooped it up –

out into the light of day, a lost little mouse! It was justified of its fears; luckily these most likely reduced it to a semi-conscious state, so that it will hardly have noticed being converted into porridge.

Bashan holds it by the tail and dashes it against the ground, once, twice, thrice; there is the faintest squeak, the very last sound which the godforsaken little mouse is destined to make on this earth, and now Bashan snaps it up in his jaws, between his strong white teeth. He stands with his forelegs braced apart, his neck bent, and his head stuck out while he chews, shifting the morsel in his mouth and then beginning to munch once more. He crunches the tiny bones, a shred of fur hangs from the corner of his mouth, it disappears and all is over. Bashan begins to execute a dance of joy and triumph round me as I stand leaning on my stick as I have been standing to watch the whole procedure. 'You are a fine one!' I say, nodding in grim tribute to his prowess. 'You are a murderer, you know, a cannibal!' He only redoubles his activity – he does everything but laugh aloud. So I walk on, feeling rather chilled by what I have seen, yet inwardly amused by the crude humours of life. The event was in the natural order of things, and a mouse lacking in the instinct of self-preservation is on the way to be turned into pulp. But I feel better if I happen not to have assisted the natural order with my stick but to have preserved throughout my attitude of onlooker.

It is startling to have a pheasant burst out of the undergrowth where it was perched asleep or else hoping to be undiscovered, until Bashan's unerring nose ferreted it out. The big, rust-coloured, long-tailed bird rises with a great clapping and flapping and a frightened, angry, cackling cry. It drops its excrement into the brush and takes flight with the absurd headlessness of a chicken to the nearest tree, where it goes on shrieking murder, while Bashan claws at the trunk and barks furiously up at it. 'Get up, get up!' he is saying. 'Fly away, you silly object of my sporting instincts, that I may chase you!' And the bird cannot resist his loud voice, it rises rustling from the bough and flies on heavy wing through the tree-tops, squawking and complaining, Bashan following below, with ardour, but preserving a stately silence.

This is his joy. He wants and knows no other. For what would happen if he actually caught the pheasant? Nothing at all: I have seen him with one in his claws – he may have stolen upon it while it slept so that the awkward bird could not rise – and he stood over it embarrassed by his triumph, without an idea what to do. The pheasant lay in the grass with its neck and one wing sprawled out and shrieked without stopping – it sounded as though an old woman were being murdered in the bushes, and I hastened up to prevent, if I could, something frightful happening. But I quickly convinced myself that there was no danger. Bashan's obvious helplessness, the half curious, half disgusted look he bent on his capture, with his head on one side, quite reassured me. The old-womanish screaming at his feet got on his nerves, the whole affair made him feel more bothered than triumphant. Perhaps, for his honour as a sportsman, he plucked at the bird – I think I saw him pulling out a couple of feathers with his lips, not using his teeth, and tossing them to one side with an angry shake of the head. But then he moved away and let it go. Not out of magnanimity, but because the affair seemed not to have anything to do with the joyous hunt and so was merely stupid. Never have I seen a more nonplussed bird. It had given itself up for lost, and appeared not to be able to convince itself to the contrary: awhile it lay in the grass as though it were dead. Then it staggered along the ground a little way, fluttered up on a tree, looked like falling off it, but pulled itself together and flew away heavily, with dishevelled plumes. It did not squawk, it kept its bill shut.

Without a sound it flew across the park, the river, the woods on the other side, as far away as possible and certainly it never came back.

But there are plenty of its kind in our hunting-ground and Bashan hunts them in all honour and according to the rules of the game. Eating mice is the only blood-guilt he has on his head and even that is incidental and superfluous. The tracking out, the driving up, the chasing – these are ends in themselves to the sporting spirit, and are plainly so to him, as anybody would see who watched him at his brilliant performance. How beautiful he becomes, how consummate, how ideal! Like a clumsy peasant lad, who will look perfect and statuesque as a huntsman among his native rocks. All that is best in Bashan, all that is genuine and fine, comes out and reaches its flower at these times. Hence his yearning for them, his repining when they fruitlessly slip away. He is no terrier, he is true hunter and pointer, and joy in himself as such speaks in every virile, valiant, native pose he assumes. Not many other things rejoice my eye as does the sight of him going through the brush at a swinging trot, then standing stock-still, with one paw daintily raised and turned in, sagacious, serious, alert, with all his faculties beautifully concentrated. Then suddenly he whimpers. He has trod on a thorn and cries out. Ah, yes, that too is natural, it is amusing to see that he has the courage of his simplicity. It could only passingly mar his dignity, next moment his posture is as fine as ever.

I look at him and recall a time when he lost all his nobility and distinction and reverted to the low physical and moral state in which we found him in the kitchen of that mountain inn and from which he climbed painfully enough to some sort of belief in himself and the world. I do not know what ailed him; he had bleeding from the mouth or nose or throat, I do not know which to this day. Wherever he went he left traces of blood behind: on the grass in our hunting-ground, the straw in his kennel, on the floor in the house – though we could not discover any wound. Sometimes his nose looked as though it had been dipped in red paint. When he sneezed he showered blood all over, and then trod in it and left the marks of his paws about. He was carefully examined without result, and we felt more and more disturbed. Was he tubercular? Or had he some other complaint to which his species was prone? When the mysterious affliction did not pass off after some days, we decided to take him to a veterinary clinic.

Next day at about noon I kindly but firmly adjusted his muzzle, the leather mask which Bashan detests as he does few other things, always trying to get rid of it by shaking his head or rubbing it with his paws. I put him on the plaited leather lead and led him thus harnessed up the poplar avenue, through the English Gardens, and along a city street to the Academy, where we went under the arch and crossed the courtyard. We were received into a waiting-room where several people sat, each holding like me a dog on a lead. They were dogs of all sizes and kinds, gazing dejectedly at each other over their muzzles. There was a matron with her apoplectic pug, a liveried manservant with a tall, snow-white Russian greyhound, which from time to time gave a hoarse, aristocratic cough; a countryman with a dachshund which seemed to need orthopaedic assistance, its legs being entirely crooked and put on all wrong. And many more. The attendant let them in one by one into the consulting-room, and after a while it became the turn of Bashan and me.

The Professor was a man in advanced years, wearing a white surgeon's coat and a gold eye-glass. His hair was curly, and he seemed so mild, expert, and kindly that I would have unhesitatingly entrusted myself and all my family to him in any emergency. During my recital he smiled benevolently at his patient, who sat there looking up at him with equal trustfulness. 'He has fine eyes,' said he, passing over Bashan's moustaches in silence. He said he would make an examination at once, and poor Bashan, too astounded to offer any resistance, was with the attendant's help stretched out on the table forthwith. And then it was touching to see the physician apply his black stethoscope and auscultate my little man just as I have more than once had it done to me. He listened to his quick-breathing doggish heart, listened to all his organs, in various places. Then with his stethoscope under his arm he examined Bashan's eyes and nose and the cavity of his mouth, and gave a temporary opinion. The dog was a little nervous and anaemic, he said, but otherwise in good condition. The origin of the bleeding was unclear. It might be an epistaxis or a haematemesis. But equally well it might be tracheal or pharyngeal haemorrhage. Perhaps for the present one might characterize it as a case of haemoptysis. It would be best to keep the animal under careful observation. I might leave it with them and look in at the end of a week.

Thus instructed, I expressed my thanks and took my leave, patting Bashan on the shoulder by way of good-bye. I saw the attendant take the new patient across the courtyard to some back buildings opposite the entrance, Bashan looking back at me with a frightened and bewildered face. And yet he might have felt flattered, as I could not help feeling myself, at having the Professor call him nervous and anaemic. No one could have foretold of him in his cradle that he would one day be called those things or discussed with such gravity and expert knowledge.

But after that my walks abroad were as unseasoned food to the palate; I had little relish of them. No dumb paean of joy accompanied my going out, no glorious excitement of the chase surrounded my footsteps. The park was a desert, time hung on my hands. During the period of waiting I telephoned several times for news. Answer came through a subordinate that the patient was doing as well as possible under the circumstances – but the circumstances – for better or worse – were never described in more detail. So when the week came round again, I betook myself to the clinic.

Guided by numerous signs and arrows I arrived without difficulty before the entrance of the department where Bashan was lodged, and, warned by another sign on the door, forbore to knock and went straight in. The medium-sized room I found myself in reminded me of a carnivora-house – a similar atmosphere prevailed. Only here the menagerie odour seemed to be kept down by various sweetish-smelling medicinal fumes – a disturbing and oppressive combination. Wire cages ran round the room, most of them occupied. Loud baying greeted me from one of these, at the open door of which a man, who seemed to be the keeper, was busy with rake and shovel. He contented himself with returning my greeting while going on with his work, and left me to my own devices.

I had seen Bashan directly I entered the door, and went up to him. He was lying behind his bars on a pile of tan-bark or some such stuff, which contributed its own special odour to the animal and chemical smells in the room. He lay there like a leopard – but a very weary, sluggish, and disgusted leopard. I was startled by the sullen indifference with which he met me. His tail thumped the floor once or twice, weakly; only when I spoke to him did he lift his head from his paws, and even then he let it fall again at once and blinked gloomily to one side. There was an earthenware dish of water at the back of his pen. A framed chart, partly printed and partly written, was

fastened to the bars, giving his name, species, sex, and age and showing his
temperature curve. 'Bastard pointer,' it said, 'named Bashan. Male. Two-
years-old. Admitted on such and such a day of the month and the year, for
observation of occult blood.' Underneath followed the fever curve, drawn
with a pen and showing small variations; also daily entries of his pulse. Yes,
his temperature was taken, and his pulse felt, by a doctor; in his direction
everything was being done. But I was distressed about his state of mind.

'Is that one yours?' asked the keeper, who had now come up, his tools in
his hands. He had on a sort of gardening apron and was a squat red-faced
man with a round beard and rather bloodshot brown eyes that were quite
strikingly like a dog's in their humid gaze and faithful expression.

I answered in the affirmative, referred to my telephone conversations and
the instructions I had had to come back today, and said I should like to hear
how things stood. The man looked at the chart. Yes, the dog was suffering
from occult blood, that was always a long business, especially when one did
not know where it came from. But was not that always the case? No, they did
not really know yet. But the dog was there to be observed, and he would be.
And did he still bleed? Yes, now and then he did. And had he fever? I asked,
trying to read the chart. No, no fever. His temperature and pulse were quite
normal, about ninety beats a minute, he ought to have that much, and if he
had not, then they would have to observe him even more carefully. Except
for the bleeding, the dog was really doing all right. He had howled at first, of
course; he had howled for twenty-four hours, but after that he was used to it.
He didn't eat much, for a fact, but then he hadn't much exercise, and
perhaps he wasn't a big eater. What did they give him? Soup, said the man.
But as he had said, the dog didn't eat much at all. 'He seems depressed,' I
remarked with an assumption of objectivity. Yes, that was true, but it didn't
mean much. After all it wasn't very much fun for a dog to lie cooped up like
that under observation. They were all depressed, more or less. That is, the
good-natured ones, some dogs got mean and treacherous. He could not say
that of Bashan. He was a good dog, he would not get mean if he stayed there
all his days. I agreed with the man, but I did so with pain and rebellion in my
heart. How long then, I asked, did they reckon to keep him here? The man
looked at the chart again. Another week, he said, would be needed for the
observation, the Herr Professor had said. I'd better come and ask again in
another week; that would be two weeks in all, then they would be able to say
more about the possibility of getting rid of the haemorrhages.

I went away, after trying once more to rouse up Bashan by renewed calls
and encouragement. In vain. He cared as little for my going as for my
coming. He seemed weighed down by bitter loathing and despair. He had
the air of saying: 'Since you were capable of having me put in this cage, I
expect nothing more from you.' And, actually, had he not enough ground to
despair of reason and justice? What had he done that this should happen to
him and that I not only let it happen but took steps to bring it about? And yet
my intentions had been of the best. He had bled, and though it seemed to
make no difference to him, I thought it sensible that we should call in
medical advice, he being a dog in good circumstances. And then we had
learned that he was anaemic and nervous – as though he were the daughter of
some upper-class family. And then it had to come out like this! How could I
explain to him we were treating him with great distinction, in shutting him
up like a jaguar, without sun, air, or exercise, and plaguing him every day
with a thermometer?

On the way home I asked myself these things; and if before then I had missed Bashan, now worry about him was added to my distress: worry over his state and reproaches to my own address. Perhaps after all I had taken him to the clinic only out of vanity and arrogance. And added to that may I not have secretly wished to get rid of him for a while? Perhaps I had a craving to see what it would be like to be free of his incessant watching of me; to be able to turn calmly to right or left as I pleased, without having to realize that I had been to another living creature the source of joy or of bitter disappointment. Certainly while Bashan was interned I felt a certain inner independence which had long been strange to me. No one exasperated me by looking through the glass door with the air of a martyr. No one put up a hesitating paw to move me to laughter and relenting and persuade me to go out sooner than I wished. Whether I sought the part or kept my room concerned no one at all. It was quiet, pleasant, and had the charm of novelty. But lacking the accustomed spur I hardly went out at all. My health suffered, gradually I approached the condition of Bashan in his cage; and the moral reflection occurred to me that the bonds of sympathy were probably more conducive to my own well-being than the selfish independence for which I had longed.

The second week went by, and on the appointed day I stood with the round-bearded keeper before Bashan's cage. Its inmate lay on his side on the tan-bark, there were bits of it on his coat. He had his head flung back as he lay and was staring with dull, glazed eyes at the bare whitewashed wall. He did not stir. I could scarcely see him breathe; but now and then his chest rose in a long sigh that made the ribs stand out, and fell again with a faint, heart-rending resonance from the vocal cords. His legs seemed to have grown too long, and his paws large out of all proportion, as a result of his extraordinary emaciation. His coat was rough and dishevelled and had, as I said, tan-bark sticking in it. He did not look at me, he seemed not to want to look at anything ever any more.

The bleeding, so the keeper said, had not altogether and entirely disappeared, it came back now and again. Where it came from was still not quite clear; in any case it was harmless. If I liked I could leave the dog here for further observation, to be quite certain, or I could take him home, because the bleeding might disappear just as well there as here. I drew the plaited lead out of my pocket – I had brought it with me – and said that I would take him with me. The keeper thought that was a sensible thing to do. He opened the grating and we summoned Bashan by name, both together and in turn, but he did not come, he kept on staring at the whitewashed wall. But he did not struggle when I put my arm into the cage and pulled him out by the collar. He gave a spring and landed with his four feet on the floor, where he stood with his tail between his legs and his ears laid back, the picture of wretchedness. I picked him up, tipped the keeper, and went to the front office to pay my debt; at the rate of seventy-five pfennigs a day plus the medical examination it came to twelve marks fifty. I led Bashan home, breathing the animal-chemical odours which still clung to his coat.

He was broken, in body and in spirit. Animals are more primitive and less inhibited in giving expression to their mental state – there is a sense in which one might say they are more human: descriptive phrases which to us have become mere metaphor still fit them literally, we get a fresh and diverting sense of their meaning when we see it embodied before our eyes. Bashan, as we say, 'hung his head'; that is, he did it literally and visibly, till he looked like a worn-out cab-horse, with sores on its legs, standing at the cab-rank, its skin twitching and its poor fly-infested nose weighed down towards the pavement. It was as I have said: those two weeks at the clinic had reduced him to the state he had been in at the beginning. He was the shadow of his former self – if that does not insult the proud and joyous shadow our Bashan once cast. The hospital smell he had brought with him wore off after repeated soapy baths till you got only an occasional whiff; but it was not with him as with human beings: he got no symbolic refreshment from the physical cleansing. The very first day, I took him out to our hunting-ground, but he followed at my heel with his tongue lolling out; even the pheasants perceived that it was the close season. For days he lay as he had lain in his cage at the clinic, staring with glazed eyes, flabby without and within. He showed no healthy impatience for the chase, did not urge me to go out – indeed it was rather I who had to go and fetch him from his kennel. Even the reckless and indiscriminate way he wolfed his food recalled those early unworthy days. But what a joy to see him slowly finding himself again! Little by little he began to greet me in the morning in his old naïve, impetuous way, storming upon me at my first whistle instead of limping morosely up; putting his forepaws on my chest and snapping playfully at my face. Gradually there returned to him his old out-of-doors pride and joy in his own physical prowess; once more he delighted my eyes with the bold and beautiful poses he took, the sudden bounds with his feet drawn up, after some creature stirring in the long grass ... He forgot. The ugly and to Bashan senseless episode sank into the past, unresolved indeed, unclarified by comprehension, that being of course impossible; it was covered by the lapse of time, as must happen sometimes to human beings. We went on living and what had not been expressed became by degrees forgotten ... For several weeks, at lengthening intervals, Bashan's nose showed red. Then the phenomenon disappeared, it was no more, it only had been, and so it was no matter whether it had been an epistaxis or a haematemesis.

Well, there! Contrary to my own intentions, I have told the story of the clinic. Perhaps my reader will forgive the lengthy digression and come back to the park and the pleasures of the chase, where we were before the interruption. Do you know that long-drawn wailing howl to which a dog gives vent when he summons up his utmost powers to give chase to a flying hare? In it rage and rapture mingle, desire and the ecstasy of despair. How often have I heard it from Bashan! It is passion itself, deliberate, fostered passion, drunkenly revelled in, shrilling through our woodland scene, and every time I hear it near or far a fearful thrill of pleasure shoots through my limbs. Rejoiced that Bashan will come into his own today, I hasten to his side, to see the chase if I can; when it roars past me I stand spellbound – though the futility of it is clear from the first – and look on with an agitated smile on my face.

And the hare, the common, frightened little hare? The air whistles through its ears, it lays back its ears, it lays back its head and runs for its life, it scrabbles and bounds with Bashan behind it yelling all he can; its yellow-white scut flies up in the air. And yet at the bottom of its soul, timid as that is and acquainted with fear, it must know that its peril cannot be grave, that it will get away, as its brothers and sisters have done before it, and itself too under like circumstances. Never in his life has Bashan caught one of them, nor will he ever; the thing is as good as impossible. Many dogs, they say, are the death of a hare, a single dog cannot achieve it, even one much speedier and more enduring than Bashan. The hare can 'double' and Bashan cannot – and that is all there is to it. For the double is the unfailing natural weapon of those born to seek safety in flight; they always have it by them, to use at the decisive moment; when Bashan's hopes are highest – then they are dashed to the ground, and he is betrayed.

There they come, dashing diagonally through the brush, across the path in front of me, and on towards the river: the hare silently hugging his little trick in his heart, Bashan giving tongue in high head-tones. 'Be quiet!' I think. 'You are wasting your wind and your lung-power and you ought to save them if you want to catch him up.' Thus I think because in my heart I am on Bashan's side, some of his fire has kindled me, I fervently hope he may catch the hare – even at the risk of seeing it torn to shreds before my eyes. How he runs! It is beautiful to see a creature expending the utmost of its powers. He runs better than the hare does, he has stronger muscles, the distance between them visibly diminishes before I lose sight of them. And I make haste too, leaving the path and cutting across the park towards the river-bank, reaching the gravelled street in time to see the chase come raging on – the hopeful, thrilling chase, with Bashan on the hare's very heels; he is still, he runs with his jaw set, scent just in front of his nose urges him to a final effort. – 'One more push, Bashan!' I think, and feel like shouting: 'Well run, old chap, remember the double!' But there it is; Bashan does make one more push, and the misfortune is upon us: at that moment the hare gives a quick, easy, almost malicious twitch at right angles to the course, and Bashan shoots past from his rear, howling helplessly and braking his very best so that dirt and pebbles fly into the air. Before he can stop, turn round, and get going in the other direction, yelling all the time as in great mental torment, the hare has gained so much ground that it is out of sight; for while he was braking so desperately Bashan could not watch where it went.

It is no use, I think; it is beautiful but futile; this while the chase fades away through the park. It takes a lot of dogs, five or six, a whole pack. Some of them to take it on the flank, some to cut off its way in front, some to corner it, some to catch it by the neck. And in my excited fancy I see a whole pack of bloodhounds with their tongues out rushing on the hare in their midst.

It is my passion for the chase makes me have these fancies, for what has the hare done to me that I should wish him such a horrible death? Bashan is nearer to me, of course, it is natural that I should feel with him and wish for his success. But the hare is after all a living creature too, and he did not play his trick on my huntsman out of malice, but only from the compelling desire to live yet awhile, nibble young tree-shoots, and beget his kind. It would be different, I go on in my mind, if this cane of mine – I lift it and look at it – were not a harmless stick, but a more serious weapon, effective like lightning and at a distance, with which I could come to Bashan's assistance and hold up the hare in mid career, so that it would turn a somersault and lie dead on the ground. Then we should not need another dog, and it would be Bashan's only task to rouse the game. Whereas as things stand it is Bashan who sometimes rolls over and over in his effort to brake. The hare sometimes does too, but it is nothing to it, it is used to such things, they do not make it feel miserable, whereas it is a shattering experience for Bashan, and might even quite possibly break his neck.

Often such a chase is all over in a few minutes; that is, when the hare succeeds after a short length in ducking into the bushes and hiding, or else by doubling and feinting in throwing off its pursuer, who stands still, hesitating, or makes short springs in this and that direction, while I in my bloodthirstiness shout encouragement and try to show him with my stick the direction the hare took. But often the hunt sways far and wide across the landscape and Bashan's furious baying sounds like a distant bugle-horn, now near, now remote; I go my own way, knowing that he will return. But in what a state he does return, at last! Foam drips from his lips, his ribs flutter, and his loins are lank and expended, his tongue lolls out of his jaws, which yawn so wide as to distort his features and give his drunken, swimming eyes a weird Mongolian slant. His breath goes like a trip-hammer. 'Lie down and rest, Bashan,' say I, 'or your lungs will burst!' and I want to give him time to recover. I am alarmed for him when it is cold, when he pumps the air by gasps into his overheated insides and it gushes out again in a white stream; when he swallows whole mouthfuls of snow to quench his furious thirst. He lies there looking helplessly up at me, now and then licking up the slaver from his lips, and I cannot help teasing him a bit about the invariable futility of all his exertions. 'Where is the hare, Bashan?' I ask. 'Why don't you bring it to me?' He thumps with his tail on the ground when I speak; his sides pump in and out less feverishly, and he gives a rather embarrassed snap – for how can he know that I am mocking him because I feel guilty myself and want to conceal it? For I did not play my part in his enterprise, I was not man enough to hold the hare, as a proper master should have done. He does not know this, and so I can make fun of him and behave as though it were all his fault.

Strange things sometimes happen on these occasions. Never shall I forget the day when the hare ran into my arms. It was on the narrow clayey path above the river. Bashan was in full cry; I came from the wood into the river zone, struck across through the thistles of the gravelly waste, and jumped down the grassy slope to the path just in time to see the hare, with Bashan fifteen paces behind it, come bounding from the direction of the ferry-house towards which I was facing. It leaped right into the path and came towards me. My first impulse was that of the hunter towards his prey: to take advantage of the situation and cut off its escape, driving it back if possible into the jaws of the pursuer joyously yelping behind. I stood fixed on the spot, quite abandoned to the fury of the chase, weighting my cane in my hand as the hare came towards me. A hare's sight is poor, that I knew; hearing and smell are the senses that guide and preserve it. It might have taken me for a tree as I stood there; I hoped and foresaw it would do so and thus fall victim to a frightful error, the possible consequences of which were not very clear to me, though I meant to turn them to our advantage. Whether it did at any time make this mistake is unclear. I think it did not see me at all until the last minute, and what it did was so unexpected as to upset all my plans in a trice and cause a complete and sudden revulsion in my feelings. Was it beside itself with fright? Anyhow, it jumped straight at me, like a dog, ran up my overcoat with its forepaws and snuggled its head into me, me whom it should most fear, the master of the chase! I stood bent back with my arms raised; I looked down at the hare and it looked up at me. It was only a second, perhaps only part of a second, that this lasted. I saw the hare with such extraordinary distinctness, its long ears, one of which stood up, the other hung down; its large, bright, short-sighted, prominent eyes, its cleft lip and the long hairs of its moustache, the white on its breast and little paws; I felt or thought I felt the throbbing of its hunted heart. And it was strange to see it so clearly and have it so close to me, the little genius of the place, the inmost beating heart of our whole region, this ever-fleeing little being which I had never seen but for brief moments in our meadows and bottoms, frantically and drolly getting out of the way – and now, in its hour of need, not knowing where to turn, it came to me, it clasped as it were my knees, a human being's knees: not the knees, so it seemed to me, of Bashan's master, but the knees of a man who felt himself master of hares and this hare's master as well as Bashan's. It was, I say, only for the smallest second. Then the hare had dropped off, taken again to its uneven legs, and bounded up the slope on my left; while in its place there was Bashan, Bashan giving tongue in all the horrid head-tones of his hue and cry. When he got within reach he was abruptly checked by a deliberate and well-aimed blow from the stick of the hare's master, which sent him yelping down the slope with a temporarily disabled hind quarter. He had to limp painfully back again before he could take up the trail of his by this time vanished prey.

Finally, there are the waterfowl, to our pursuit of which I must devote a few lines. We can only go after them in winter and early spring, before they leave their town quarters – where they stay for their food's sake, and return to their lakes in the mountains. They furnish, of course, much less exciting sport than can be got out of the hares; still, it has its attractions for hunter and hound – or, rather, for the hunter and his master. For me the charm lies in the scenery, the intimate bond with living water; also it is amusing and diverting to watch the creatures swimming and flying and try provisionally to exchange one's personality for theirs and enter into their mode of life.

The ducks lead a quieter, more comfortable, more bourgeois life than do the gulls. They seem to have enough to eat, on the whole, and not to be tormented by the pangs of hunger – their kind of food is regularly to be had, the table, so to speak, always laid. For everything is fish that comes to their net: worms, snails, insects – even the ooze of the river-bed. So they have plenty of time to sit on the stones in the sun, doze with their bills tucked under one wing, and preen their well-oiled plumes, off which the water rolls in drops. Sometimes they take a pleasure-ride on the waves, with their pointed rumps in the air; paddling this way and that and giving little self-satisfied shrugs.

But the nature of gulls is wilder and more strident; there is a dreary monotony about what they do, they are the eternally hungry bird of prey, swooping all day long in hordes across the waterfall, croaking about the drainpipes that disgorge their brown streams into the river. Single gulls hover and pounce down upon a fish now and then, but this does not go far to satisfy their inordinate mass hunger; they have to fill in with most unappetizing-looking morsels from the drains, snatching them from the water in flight and carrying them off in their crooked beaks. They do not like the river-bank. But when the river is low, they huddle together on the rocks that stick out of the water – the scene is white with them, as the cliffs and islets of northern oceans are white with hosts of nesting eider-duck. I like to watch them rise all together with a great cawing and take to the air, when Bashan barks at them from the bank, across the intervening stream. They need not be frightened, certainly they are in no danger. He has a native aversion to water; but aside from that he would never trust himself to the current, and he is quite right, it is much stronger than he and would soon sweep him away and carry him God knows where. Perhaps into the Danube – but he would only arrive there after having suffered a river-change of a very drastic kind, as we know from seeing the bloated corpses of cats on their way to some distant bourne. Bashan never goes farther into the water than the point where it begins to break over the stones. Even when he seems most tense with the pleasure of the chase and looks exactly as though he meant to jump in the very next minute, one knows that under all the excitement his sense of caution is alert and that the dashings and rushings are pure theatre –

empty threats, not so much dictated by passion as cold-bloodedly undertaken in order to terrify the web-footed tribe.

But the gulls are too witless and poor-spirited to make light of his
performance. He cannot get to them himself, but he sends his voice
thundering across the water; it reaches them, and it, too, has actuality; it is an
attack which they cannot long resist. They try to at first, they sit still, but a
wave of uneasiness goes through the host, they turn their heads, a few lift
their wings, and suddenly they all rush up into the air, like a white cloud,
whence issue the bitterest, most fatalistic screams, Bashan springing hither
and thither on the rocks, to scatter their flight and keep them in motion, for
it is motion that he wants, they are not to sit quiet, they must fly, fly up and
down the river so that he may chase them.

He scampers along the shore far and wide, for everywhere there are ducks,
sitting with their bills tucked in homely comfort under their wings; and
wherever he comes they fly up before him. He is like a jolly little hurricane
making a clean sweep of the beach. Then they plump down on the water
again, where they rock and ride in comfort and safety, or else they fly away
over his head with their necks stretched out, while below on the shore he
measures the strength of his leg-muscles quite creditably against those of
their wings.

He is enchanted, and really grateful to them if they will only fly and give
him occasion for this glorious race up and down the beach. It may be that
they know what he wants and turn the fact to their own advantage. I saw a
mother duck with her brood – this was in spring, all the birds had forsaken
the river and only this one was left with her fledglings, not yet able to fly. She
had them in a stagnant puddle left by the last flood in the low-lying bed of the
shrunken river, and there Bashan found them, while I watched the event
from the upper path. He jumped into the puddle and lashed about, furiously
barking, driving the family of ducklings into wild disorder. He did them no
harm, of course, but he frightened them beyond measure; the ducklings
flapped their stumps of wings and scattered in all directions, and the duck
was overtaken by an attack of the maternal heroism which will hurl itself
blind with valour upon the fiercest foe to protect her brood; more, will even
by a frenzied and unnatural display of intrepidity bully the attacker into
surrender. She opened her beak to a horrific extent, she ruffled up her
feathers, she flew repeatedly into Bashan's face, she made onslaught after
onslaught, hissing all the while. The grim seriousness of her behaviour was
so convincing that Bashan actually gave ground in confusion, though
without definitely retiring from the field, for each time after retreating he
would bark and advance anew. Then the mother duck changed her tactics:
heroics having failed, she took refuge in strategy. Probably she knew Bashan
already and was aware of his foibles and the childish nature of his desires.
She left her children in the lurch – or she pretended to; she took to flight, she
flew up above the river, 'pursued' by Bashan. At least, he thought he was
pursuing her, in reality it was she who was leading him on, playing on his
childish passion, leading him by the nose. She flew downstream, then
upstream, she flew farther and farther away, Bashan racing equal with her
along the bank; they left the pool with the ducklings far behind, and at length
both dog and duck disappeared from my sight. Bashan came back to me after
a while; the simpleton was quite winded and panting for dear life. But when
we passed the pool again on our homeward way, it was empty of its brood.

So much for the mother duck. As for Bashan, he was quite grateful for the
sport she had given him. For he hates the ducks who selfishly prefer their

bourgeois comfort and refuse to play his game with him, simply gliding off into the water when he comes rushing along, and rocking there in base security before his face and eyes, heedless of his mighty barking, heedless too – unlike the nervous gulls – of all his feints and plungings. We stand there, Bashan and I, on the stones at the water's edge, and two paces away a duck floats on the wave, floats impudently up and down, her beak pressed coyly against her breast; safe and untouched and sweetly reasonable she bobs up and down out there, let Bashan rave as he will. Paddling against the current, she keeps abreast of us fairly well; yet she is being slowly carried down, closer and closer to one of those beautiful foaming eddies in the stream. In her folly she rides with her tail turned towards it – and now it is only a yard away. Bashan loudly gives tongue, standing with his forelegs braced against the stones; and in my heart I am barking with him, I am on his side and against that impudent, self-satisfied floating thing out there. I wish her ill. Pay attention to our barking, I address her mentally; do not hear the whirlpool roar – and then presently you will find yourself in an unpleasant and undignified situation and I shall be glad! But my malicious hopes are not fulfilled. For at the rapid's very edge she flutters up into the air, flies a few yards upstream, and then, oh, shameless hussy, settles down again.

I recall the feelings of baffled anger with which we looked at that duck – and I am reminded of another occasion, another and final episode in this tale of our hunting-ground. It was attended by a certain satisfaction for my companion and me, but had its painful and disturbing side as well; yes, it even gave rise to some coolness between us, and if I could have foreseen it I would have avoided the spot where it took place.

It was a long way out, beyond the ferry-house, downstream, where the wilds that border the river approach the upper road along the shore. We were going along this, I at an easy pace, Bashan in front with his easy, lopsided lope. He had roused a hare – or, if you like, it had roused him – had stirred up four pheasants, and now was minded to give his master a little attention. A small bevy of ducks were flying above the river, in v-formation, their necks stretched out. They flew rather high and closer to the other shore, so that they were out of our reach as game, but moving in the same direction as ourselves. They paid no attention to us and we only cast casual glances at them now and then.

Then it happened that opposite to us on the other bank, which like ours was steep here, a man struck out of the bushes, and directly he appeared upon the scene he took up a position which fixed our attention, Bashan's no less than mine, upon him at once. We stopped in our tracks and faced him. He was a fine figure of a man, though rather rough-looking; with drooping moustaches, wearing puttees, a frieze hat cocked down over his forehead, wide velveteen trousers and jerkin to match, over which hung numerous leather straps, for he had a rucksack slung on his back and a gun over his shoulder. Or rather he had had it over his shoulder; for he no sooner appeared than he took it in his hand, laid his cheek along the butt, and aimed it diagonally upwards at the sky. He took a step forwards with one putteed leg, the gun-barrel rested in the hollow of his left hand, with the arm stretched out and the elbow against his side. The other elbow, with the hand on the trigger, stuck out at his side, and we could see his bold, foreshortened face quite clearly as he sighted upwards. It looked somehow very theatrical, this figure standing out above the boulders on the bank, against a background of shrubbery, river, and open sky. But we could have gazed for only a moment when the dull sound of the explosion made me start, I had waited for it with such inward tension. There was a tiny flash at the same time; it looked pale in the broad daylight; a puff of smoke followed. The man took one slumping pace forwards, like an operatic star, with his face and chest lifted towards the sky, his gun hanging from the strap in his right fist. Something was going on up there where he was looking and where we now looked too. There was a great confusion and scattering, the ducks flew in all directions wildly flapping their wings with a noise like wind in the sails, they tried to volplane down – then suddenly a body fell like a stone onto the water near the other shore.

This was only the first half of the action. But I must interrupt my narrative here to turn the vivid light of my memory upon the figure of Bashan. I can think of large words with which to describe it, phrases we use for great occasions: I could say that he was thunderstruck. But I do not like them, I do not want to use them. The large words are worn out, when the great occasion comes they do not describe it. Better use the small ones and put into them every ounce of their weight. I will simply say that when Bashan heard the explosion, saw its meaning and consequence, he started; and it was the same start which I have seen him give a thousand times when something surprises him, only raised to the *n*th degree. It was a start which flung his whole body backwards with a right-and-left motion, so sudden that it jerked his head against his chest and almost bounced it off his shoulders with the shock; a start which made his whole body seem to be crying out: What! What! What was that? Wait a minute, in the devil's name! *What was that?* He looked and listened with that sort of rage in which extreme astonishment expresses itself; listened within himself and heard things that had always been there, however novel and unheard-of the present form they took. Yes, from this start, which flung him to right and left and halfway round on his axis, I got the impression that he was trying to look at himself, trying to ask: What am I? Who am I? Is this me? At the moment when the duck's body plopped on the water he bounded forwards to the edge of the bank, as though he were going to jump down to the river-bed and plunge in. But he bethought himself of the current and checked his impulse; then, rather shamefaced, devoted himself to staring, as before.

I looked at him, somewhat disturbed. After the duck had fallen I felt that we had had enough and suggested that we go on our way. But he had sat down on his haunches, facing the other shore, his ears erected as high as they would go. When I said: 'Well, Bashan, shall we go on?' he turned his head only the briefest second as though saying, with some annoyance: Please don't disturb me! And kept on looking. So I resigned myself, crossed my legs, leaned on my cane, and watched to see what would happen.

The duck – no doubt one of those that had rocked in such pert security on the water in front of our noses – went driving like a wreck on the water, you could not tell which was head and which tail. The river is quieter at this point, its rapids are not so swift as they are farther up. But even so, the body was seized by the current, whirled round, and swept away. If the man was not concerned only with sport but had a practical goal in view, then he would better act quickly. And so he did, not losing a moment – it all went very fast. Even as the duck fell he had rushed forward stumbling and almost falling down the slope, with his gun held out at arm's length. Again I was struck with the picturesqueness of the sight, as he came down the slope like a robber or smuggler in a melodrama, in the highly effective scenery of boulder and bush. He held somewhat leftwards, allowing for the current, for the duck was drifting away and he had to head it off. This he did successfully, stretching out the butt end of the gun and bending forward with his feet in the water. Carefully and painstakingly he piloted the duck towards the stones and drew it to shore.

The job was done, the man drew a long breath. He put down his weapon against the bank, took his knapsack from his shoulders, and stuffed the duck inside; buckled it on again, and thus satisfactorily laden and using his gun as a stick, he clambered over the boulders and up the slope.

'Well, he got his Sunday joint,' thought I, half enviously, half approvingly. 'Come, Bashan, let's go now, it's all over.' Bashan got up and turned round on himself, but then he sat down again and looked after the man, even after he had left the scene and disappeared among the bushes. It did not occur to me to ask him twice. He knew were we lived, and he might sit here goggling, after it was all over, as long as he thought well. It was quite a long walk home and I meant to be stirring. So then he came.

He kept beside me on our whole painful homeward way, and did not hunt. Nor did he run diagonally a little ahead, as he does as a rule when not in a hunting mood; he kept behind me, at a jog-trot, and put on a sour face, as I could see when I happened to turn round. I could have borne with that and should not have dreamed of being drawn; I was rather inclined to laugh and shrug my shoulders. But every thirty or forty paces he *yawned* – and that I could not stand. It was that impudent gape of his, expressing the extreme of boredom, accompanied by a throaty little whine which seems to say: Fine master I've got! No master at all! Rotten master, if you ask me! – I am always sensitive to the insulting sound, and this time it was almost enough to shake our friendship to its foundations.

'Go away!' said I. 'Get out with you! Go to your new friend with the blunderbuss and attach yourself to him! He does not seem to have a dog, perhaps he could use you in his business. He is only a man in velveteens, to be sure, not a gentleman, but in your eyes he may be one; perhaps he is the right master for you, and I honestly recommend you to suck up to him – now that he has put a flea in your ear to go with your others.' (Yes, I actually said that!) 'We'll not ask if he has a hunting-licence, or if you won't both get into fine trouble some day at your dirty game – that is your affair, and, as I tell you, my advice is perfectly sincere. You think so much of yourself as a hunter! Did you ever bring me a hare of all those I let you chase? Is it my fault that you do not know how to double, but must come down with your nose in the gravel at the moment when agility is required? Or a pheasant, which in these lean times would be equally welcome? And now you yawn! Get along, I tell you. Go to your master with the puttees and see if he knows how to scratch your neck and make you laugh. I'll wager he does not know how to laugh a decent laugh himself. Do you think he is likely to have you put under scientific observation when you decide to suffer from occult blood, or that when you are his dog you will be pronounced nervous and anaemic? If you do, then you'd better get along. But you may be over-estimating the respect which that kind of master would have for you. There are certain distinctions – that kind of man with a gun is very keen on them: native advantages or disadvantages, to make my meaning clearer, trouble-some questions of pedigree and breeding, if I must be plain. Not everybody passes these over on grounds of humanity and fine feeling; and if your wonderful master reproaches you with your moustaches the first time you and he have a difference of opinion, then you may remember me and what I am telling you now.'

With such biting words did I address Bashan as he slunk behind me on our way home. And though I did not utter but only thought them, for I did not care to look as though I were mad, yet I am convinced that he got my meaning perfectly, at least in its main lines. In short, it was a serious quarrel, and when we got home I deliberately let the gate latch behind me so that he could not slip through and had to climb over the fence. I went into the house without even looking round, and shrugged my shoulders when I heard him yelp because he scratched his belly on the rail.

But all that is long ago, more than six months. Now, like our little clinical episode, it has dropped into the past. Time and forgetfulness have buried it, and on their alluvial deposit where all life lives, we too live on. For a few days Bashan appeared to mope. But long ago he recovered all his joy in the chase, in mice and moles and pheasant, hares and waterfowl. When we return home, at once begins his period of waiting for the next time. I stand at the house door and turn towards him; upon that signal he bounds in two great leaps up the steps and braces his forepaws against the door, reaching as far up as he can that I may pat him on the shoulder. 'Tomorrow, Bashan,' say I; 'that is, if I am not obliged to pay a visit to the outer world.' Then I hasten inside, to take off my hobnailed boots, for the soup stands waiting on the table.

The
Black Swan

TRANSLATED FROM THE GERMAN BY
Willard R. Trask

In the twenties of our century a certain Frau Rosalie von Tümmler, a widow for over a decade, was living in Düsseldorf on the Rhine, with her daughter Anna and her son Eduard, in comfortable if not luxurious circumstances. Her husband, Lieutenant-Colonel von Tümmler, had lost his life at the very beginning of the war, not in battle, but in a perfectly senseless automobile accident, yet still, one could say, 'on the field of honour' – a hard blow, borne with patriotic resignation by his wife, who, then just turned forty, was deprived not only of a father for her children, but, for herself, of a cheerful husband, whose rather frequent strayings from the strict code of conjugal fidelity had been only the symptom of a superabundant vitality.

A Rhinelander by ancestry and in dialect, Rosalie had spent the twenty years of her marriage in the busy industrial city of Duisburg, where von Tümmler was stationed; but after the loss of her husband she had moved, with her eighteen-year-old daughter and her little son, who was some twelve years younger than his sister, to Düsseldorf, partly for the sake of the beautiful parks that are such a feature of the city (for Frau von Tümmler was a great lover of Nature), partly because Anna, a serious girl, had a bent for painting and wanted to attend the celebrated Academy of Art. For the past ten years, then, the little family had lived in a quiet linden-bordered street of villas, named after Peter von Cornelius, where they occupied the modest house which, surrounded by a garden and equipped with rather outmoded but comfortable furniture dating from the time of Rosalie's marriage, was often hospitably opened to a small circle of relatives and friends – among them professors from the Academies of Art and Medicine, together with a married couple or two from the world of industry – for evening gatherings which, though always decorous in their merriment, tended, as the Rhineland custom is, to be a little bibulous.

Frau von Tümmler was sociable by nature. She loved to go out and, within the limits possible to her, to keep open house. Her simplicity and cheerfulness, her warm heart, of which her love for Nature was an expression, made her generally liked. Small in stature, but with a well-preserved figure, with hair which, though now decidedly grey, was abundant and wavy, with delicate if somewhat ageing hands, the backs of which the passage of years had discoloured with freckle-like spots that were far too many and far too large (a symptom to counteract which no medication has yet been discovered), she produced an impression of youth by virtue of a pair of fine, animated brown eyes, precisely the colour of husked chestnuts, which shone out of a womanly and winning face composed of the most pleasant features. Her nose had a slight tendency to redden, especially in company, when she grew animated; but this she tried to correct by a touch of powder – unnecessarily, for the general opinion held that it became her charmingly.

Born in the spring, a child of May, Rosalie had celebrated her fiftieth birthday, with her children and ten or twelve friends of the house, both ladies and gentlemen, at a flower-strewn table in an inn garden, under the parti-coloured light of Chinese lanterns and to the chime of glasses raised in fervent or playful toasts, and had been gay with the general gaiety – not quite without effort: for some time now, and notably on that evening, her health had been affected by certain critical organic phenomena of her time of life, the extinction of her physical womanhood, to whose spasmodic progress she responded with repeated psychological resistance. It induced states of anxiety, emotional unrest, headaches, days of depression, and an irritability which, even on that festive evening, had made some of the humorous discourses that the gentlemen had delivered in her honour seem insufferably stupid. She had exchanged glances tinged with desperation with her daughter, who, as she knew, required no predisposition beyond her habitual intolerance to find this sort of punch-inspired humour imbecilic.

She was on extremely affectionate and confidential terms with this daughter, who, so much older than her son, had become a friend with whom she maintained no taciturn reserve even in regard to the symptoms of her state of transition. Anna, now twenty-nine and soon to be thirty, had remained unmarried, a situation which was not unwelcome to Rosalie, for, on purely selfish grounds, she preferred keeping her daughter as her household companion and the partner of her life to resigning her to a husband. Taller than her mother, Fräulein von Tümmler had the same chestnut-coloured eyes – and yet not the same, for they lacked the naïve animation of her mother's, their expression being more thoughtful and cool. Anna had been born with a club-foot, which, after an operation in her childhood that produced no permanent improvement, had always excluded her from dancing and sports and indeed from all participation in the activities and life of the young. An unusual intelligence, a native endowment fortified by her deformity, had to compensate for what she was obliged to forgo. With only two or three hours of private tutoring a day, she had easily got through school and passed her final examinations, but had then ceased to pursue any branch of academic learning, turning instead to the fine arts, first to sculpture, then to painting, in which, even as a student, she had struck out on a course of the most extreme intellectualism, which, disdaining mere imitation of nature, transfigured sensory content into the strictly cerebral, the abstractly symbolical, often into the cubistically mathematical. It was with dismayed respect that Frau von Tümmler looked at her daughter's paintings, in which the highly civilized joined with the primitive, the decorative with profound intellection, an extremely subtle feeling for colour combinations with a sparse asceticism of style.

'Significant, undoubtedly significant, my dear child,' she said. 'Professor Zumsteg will think highly of it. He has confirmed you in this style of painting and he has the eye and the understanding for it. One has to have the eye and the understanding for it. What do you call it?'

'Trees in Evening Wind.'

'Ah, that gives a hint of what you were intending. Are those cones and circles against the greyish-yellow background meant to represent trees – and that peculiar spiralling line the wind? Interesting, Anna, interesting. But, heavens above, child, adorable Nature – what you do to her! If only you would let your art offer something to the emotions just once – paint something for the heart, a beautiful floral still life, a fresh spray of lilac, so true to life that one would think one smelt its ravishing perfume, and a pair of delicate Meissen porcelain figures beside the vase, a gentleman blowing kisses to a lady, and with everything reflected in the gleaming, polished table-top . . .'

'Stop, stop, Mama! You certainly have an extravagant imagination. But no one can paint like that any more!'

'Anna, you don't mean to tell me that, with your talent, you can't paint something like that, something to refresh the heart!'

'You misunderstand me, Mama! It's not a question of whether I can. Nobody can. The state of the times and of art no longer permits it.'

'So much the more regrettable for the times and art! No, forgive me, child, I did not mean to say quite that. If it is life and progress that make it impossible, there is no room for regret. On the contrary, it would be regrettable to fall behind. I understand that perfectly. And I understand too that it takes genius to conceive such an expressive line as this one of yours. It doesn't express anything to me, but I can see beyond doubt that it is extremely expressive.'

Anna kissed her mother, holding her palette and wet brush well away from her. And Rosalie kissed her too, glad in her heart that her daughter found in her work – which, if abstract and, as it seemed to her, deadening, was still an active handicraft – found in her artist's smock comfort and compensation for much that she was forced to renounce.

How greatly a limping gait curtails any sensual appreciation, on the part of the opposite sex, for a girl as such, Fräulein von Tümmler had learned early, and had armed herself against the fact with a pride which (in turn, as these things go), in cases where a young man was prepared despite her deformity to harbour an inclination towards her, discouraged it through coldly aloof disbelief and nipped it in the bud. Once, just after their change of residence, she had loved – and had been grievously ashamed of her passion, for its object had been the physical beauty of the young man, a chemist by training, who, considering it wise to turn science into money as rapidly as possible, had, soon after attaining his doctorate, manoeuvred himself into an important and lucrative position in a Düsseldorf chemical factory. His swarthy, masculine handsomeness, together with an openness of nature which appealed to men too, and the proficiency and application which he had demonstrated, aroused the enthusiasm of all the girls and matrons in Düsseldorf society, the young and the old being equally in raptures over him; and it had been Anna's contemptible fate to languish where all languished, to find herself condemned by her senses to a universal feeling, confronted with whose depth she struggled in vain to keep her self-respect.

Dr Brünner (such was the paragon's name), precisely because he knew himself to be practical and ambitious, entertained a certain corrective inclination towards higher and more recondite things, and for a time openly sought out Fräulein von Tümmler, talked with her, when they met in society, of literature and art, tuned his insinuating voice to a whisper to make mockingly derogatory remarks to her concerning one or another of his adorers, and seemed to want to conclude an alliance with her against the mediocrities, who, refined by no deformity, importuned him with improper advances. What her own state was, and what an agonizing happiness he aroused in her by his mockery of other women – of that he seemed to have no inkling, but only to be seeking and finding protection, in her intelligent companionship, from the hardships of the amorous persecution whose victim he was, and to be courting her esteem just because he valued it. The temptation to accord it to him had been strong and profound for Anna, though she knew that, if she did, it would only be in attempt to extenuate her weakness for his masculine attraction. To her sweet terror, his assiduity had begun to resemble a real wooing, a choice, and a proposal; and even now Anna could not but admit that she would helplessly have married him if he had ever come to the point of speaking out. But the decisive word was never uttered. His ambition for higher things had not sufficed to make him disregard her physical defect nor yet her modest dowry. He had soon detached himself from her and married the wealthy daughter of a manufacturer, to whose native city of Bocum, and to a position in her father's chemical enterprise there, he had then betaken himself, to the sorrow of the female society of Düsseldorf and to Anna's relief.

Rosalie knew of her daughter's painful experience, and would have known of it even if the latter, at the time, in a moment of uncontrollable effusion, had not wept bitter tears on her mother's bosom over what she called her shame. Frau von Tümmler, though not particularly clever in other respects, had an unusually acute perception, not malicious but purely a matter of sympathy, in respect to everything that makes up the existence of a woman, psychologically and physiologically, to all that Nature has inflicted upon woman; so that in her circle hardly an event or circumstance in this category escaped her. From a supposedly unnoticed and private smile, a blush, or a brightening of the eyes, she knew what girl was captivated by what young man, and she confided her discoveries to her daughter, who was quite unaware of such things and had very little wish to be made aware of them. Instinctively, now to her pleasure, now to her regret, Rosalie knew whether a woman found satisfaction in her marriage or failed to find it. She infallibly diagnosed a pregnancy in its very earliest stage, and on these occasions, doubtless because she was concerned with something so joyously natural, she would drop into dialect – '*Da is wat am kommen*,' she would say, meaning 'something's on the way.' It pleased her to see that Anna ungrudgingly helped her younger brother, who was well along in secondary school, with his homework; for, by virtue of a psychological shrewdness as naïve as it was keen, she divined the satisfaction that the superiority implied by this service to the male sex brought to the jilted girl.

It cannot be said that Rosalie took any particular interest in her son, a tall, lanky redheaded boy, who looked like his dead father and who, furthermore, seemed to have little talent for humanistic studies, but instead dreamed of building bridges and highways and wanted to be an engineer. A cool friendliness, expressed only perfunctorily, and principally for form's sake, was all that she offered him. But she clung to her daughter, her only real friend. In view of Anna's reserve, the relation of confidence between them might have been described as one-sided, were it not that the mother simply knew everything about her repressed child's emotional life, had known the proud and bitter resignation her soul harboured, and from that knowledge had derived the right and the duty to communicate herself with equal openness.

In so doing, she accepted, with imperturbable good humour, many a fondly indulgent or sadly ironical or even somewhat pained smile from her daughter and confidante, and, herself kindly, was glad when she was kindly treated, ready to laugh at her own simple-heartedness, convinced that it was happy and right – so that, if she laughed at herself, she laughed too at Anna's wry expression. It happened quite often – especially when she gave full rein to her fervour for Nature, to which she was for ever trying to win over the intellectual girl. Words cannot express how she loved the spring, *her* season, in which she had been born, and which, she insisted, had always brought her, in a quite personal way, mysterious currents of health, of joy in life. When birds called in the new mild air, her face became radiant. In the garden, the first crocus and daffodil, the hyacinths and tulips sprouting and flaunting in the beds around the house, rejoiced the good soul to tears. The darling violets along country roads, the gold of flowering broom and forsythia, the red and the white may trees – above all, the lilac, and the way the chestnuts lighted their candles, white and red – her daughter had to admire it all with her and share her ecstasy. Rosalie fetched her from the north room that had been made into a studio for her, dragged her from her abstract handicraft; and with a willing smile Anna took off her smock and accompanied her mother for hours together; for she was a surprisingly good walker and if in company she concealed her limp by the utmost possible economy of movement, when she was free and could stump along as she pleased, her endurance was remarkable.

The season of flowering trees, when the roads became poetic, when the dear familiar landscape of their walks clothed itself in charming, white and rosy promise of fruit – what a bewitching time! From the flower catkins of the tall white poplars bordering the watercourse along which they often strolled, pollen sifted down on them like snow, drove with the breeze, covered the ground; and Rosalie, in raptures again, knew enough botany to tell her daughter that poplars are 'dioecious', each plant bearing only flowers of one sex, some male, others female. She discoursed happily on wind pollination – or, rather, on Zephyrus' loving service to the children of Flora, his obliging conveyance of pollen to the chastely awaiting female stigma – a method of fertilization which she considered particularly charming.

The rose season was utter bliss to her. She raised the Queen of Flowers on standards in her garden, solicitously protected it, by the indicated means, from devouring insects; and always, as long as the glory endured, bunches of duly refreshed roses stood on the whatnots and little tables in her boudoir – budding, half-blown, full-blown – especially red roses (she did not favour the white), of her own raising or attentive gifts from visitors of her own sex who were aware of her passion. She could bury her face, eyes closed, in such a bunch of roses and, when after a long time she raised it again, she would swear that it was the perfume of the gods; when Psyche bent, lamp in hand, over sleeping Cupid, surely his breath, his curls and cheeks, had filled her sweet little nose with this scent; it was the aroma of heaven, and she had no doubt that, as blessed spirits there above, we should breathe the odour of roses for all eternity. Then we shall very soon, was Anna's sceptical comment, grow so used to it that we simply shan't smell it any more. But Frau von Tümmler reprimanded her for assuming a wisdom beyond her years: if one was bent on scoffing, such an argument could apply to the whole state of beatitude, but joy was none the less joy for being unconscious. This was one of the occasions on which Anna gave her mother a kiss of tender indulgence and reconciliation, and then they laughed together.

Rosalie never used manufactured scents or perfumes, with the single exception of a touch of Eau de Cologne from C. M. Farina in the Jülichsplatz. But whatever Nature offers to gratify our sense of smell – sweetness, aromatic bitterness, even heady and oppressive scents – she loved beyond measure, and absorbed it deeply, thankfully, with the most sensual fervour. On one of their walks there was a declivity, a long depression in the ground, a shallow gorge, the bottom of which was thickly overgrown with jasmine and alder bushes, from which, on warm, humid days in June with a threat of thunder showers, fuming clouds of heated odour welled up almost stupefyingly. Anna, though it was likely to give her a headache, had to accompany her mother there time and again. Rosalie breathed in the heavy, surging vapour with delighted relish, stopped, walked on, lingered again, bent over the slope, and sighed: 'Child, child, how wonderful! It is the breath of nature – it is! – her sweet, living breath, sun-warmed and drenched with moisture, deliciously wafted to us from her breast. Let us enjoy it with reverence, for we too are her children.'

'At least you are, Mama,' said Anna, taking the enthusiast's arm and drawing her along at her limping pace. 'She's not so fond of me and she gives me this pressure in my temples with her concoction of odours.'

'Yes, because you are against her,' answered Rosalie, 'and pay no homage to her with your talent, but want to set yourself above her through it, turn her into a mere theme for the intellect, as you pride yourself on doing, and transpose your sense perceptions into heaven knows what – into frigidity. I respect it, Anna; but if I were in Mother Nature's place, I should be as offended with all of you young painters for it as she is.' And she seriously proposed to her that if she was set upon transposition and absolutely must be abstract, she should try, at least once, to express odours in colour.

This idea came to her late in June, when the lindens were in flower – again for her the one lovely time of year, when for a week or two the avenues of trees outside filled the whole house, through the open windows, with the indescribably pure and mild, enchanting odour of their late bloom, and the smile of rapture never faded from Rosalie's lips. It was then that she said: 'That is what you painters should paint, try your artistry on that! You don't want to banish Nature from art entirely; actually, you always start from her in your abstractions, and you need something sensory in order to in-tellectualize it. Now, odour, if I may say so, is sensory and abstract at the same time, we don't see it, it speaks to us ethereally. And it ought to fascinate you to convey an invisible felicity to the sense of sight, on which, after all, the art of painting rests. Try it! What do you painters have palettes for? Mix bliss on them and put it on canvas as chromatic joy, and then label it "Odour of Lindens", so that people who look at it will know what you were trying to do.'

'Dearest Mama, you are astonishing!' Fräulein von Tümmler answered. 'You think up problems that no painting teacher would ever dream of! But don't you realize that you are an incorrigible romanticist with your synaesthetic mixture of the senses and your mystical transformation of odours into colours?'

'I know – I deserve your erudite mockery.'

'No, you don't – not any kind of mockery,' said Anna fervently.

Yet on a walk they took one afternoon in mid-August, on a very hot day, something strange befell them, something that had a suggestion of mockery. Strolling along between fields and the edge of a wood, they suddenly noticed an odour of musk, at first almost imperceptibly faint, then stronger, It was Rosalie who first sniffed it and expressed her awareness by an 'Oh! Where does that come from?' but her daughter soon had to concur: Yes, there was some sort of odour, and, yes, it did seem to be definable as musky – there was not doubt about it. Two steps sufficed to bring them within sight of its source, which was repellent. It was there by the roadside, seething in the sun, with blowflies covering it and flying all around it – a little mound of excrement, which they preferred not to investigate more closely. The small area represented a meeting-ground of animal, or perhaps human faeces with some sort of putrid vegetation, and the greatly decomposed body of some small woodland creature seemed to be present too. In short, nothing could be nastier than the teeming little mound; but its evil effluvium, which drew the blowflies by hundreds, was, in its ambivalence, no longer to be called a stench but must undoubtedly be pronounced the odour of musk.

'Let us go,' the ladies said simultaneously, and Anna, dragging her foot along all the more vigorously as they started off, clung to her mother's arm. For a time they were silent, as if each had to digest the strange impression for herself. Then Rosalie said:

'That explains it – I never did like musk, and I don't understand how anyone can use it as a perfume. Civet, I think, is in the same category. Flowers never smell like that, but in natural-history class we were taught that many animals secrete it from certain glands – rats, cats, the civet-cat, the musk-deer. In Schiller's *Kabale und Liebe* – I'm sure you must remember it – there's a little fellow, some sort of a toady, an absolute fool, and the stage direction says that he comes on screeching and spreads an odour of musk through the whole parterre. How that passage always made me laugh!'

And they brightened up. Rosalie was still capable of the old warm laughter that came bubbling from her heart – even at this period when the difficult organic adjustments of her time of life, the spasmodic withering and disintegration of her womanhood, were troubling her physically and psychologically. Nature had given her a friend in those days, quite close to home, in a corner of the Palace Garden ('Paintbox' Street was the way there). It was an old, solitary oak tree, gnarled and stunted, with its roots partly exposed, and a squat trunk, divided at a moderate height into thick knotty branches, which themselves ramified into knotty offshoots. The trunk was hollow here and there and had been filled with cement – the Park Department did something for the gallant centenarian; but many of the branches had died and, no longer producing leaves, clawed, crooked and bare, into the sky; others, only a scattered few but on up to the crown, still broke into verdure each spring with the jaggedly lobed leaves, which have always been considered sacred and from which the victor's crown is twined. Rosalie was only too pleased to see it – about the time of her birthday she followed the budding, sprouting, and unfolding of the oak's foliage on those of its branches and twigs to which life still forced its way, her sympathetic interest continuing from day to day. Quite close to the tree, on the edge of the lawn in which it stood, there was a bench; Rosalie sat down on it with Anna, and said:

'Good old fellow! Can you look at him without being touched, Anna – the way he stands there and keeps it up? Look at those roots, woody, and thick as your arm, how broadly they clasp the earth and anchor themselves in the nourishing soil. He has weathered many a storm and will survive many more. No danger of his falling down! Hollow, cemented, no longer able to produce a full crown of leaves – but when his time comes, the sap still rises in him – not everywhere, but he manages to display a little green, and people respect it and indulge him for his courage. Do you see that thin little shoot up there with its leaf-buds nodding in the wind? All around it things haven't gone as they should, but the little twig saves the day.'

'Indeed, Mamma, it gives cause for respect, as you say,' answered Anna. 'But if you don't mind, I'd rather go home now. I am having pains.'

'Pains? Is it your – but of course, dear child, how could I have forgotten! I reproach myself for having brought you with me. Here I am staring at the old tree and not worrying about your sitting there bent over. Forgive me. Take my arm and we will go.'

From the first, Fräulein von Tümmler had suffered severe abdominal pains in advance of her periods – it was nothing in itself, it was merely, as even the doctors had put it, a constitutional infliction that had to be accepted. Hence, on the short walk home, her mother could talk about it to the suffering girl soothingly and comfortingly, with well-intentioned cheerfulness, and indeed – and particularly – with envy.

'Do you remember,' she said, 'it was like this the very first time, when you were still just a young thing and it happened to you and you were so frightened but I explained to you that it was only natural and necessary and something to be glad over and that it was really a sort of day of glory because it showed that you had finally ripened into a woman? You have pains beforehand – it's a trial, I know, and not strictly necessary, I never had any; but it happens; aside from you, I know of two or three cases where there are pains, and I think to myself: Pains, *à la bonne heure!* – for us women, pains are something different from what they are elsewhere in Nature and for men; they don't have any, except when they're sick, and then they carry on terribly; even Tümmler did that, your father, as soon as he had a pain anywhere, even though he was an officer and died the death of a hero. Our sex behaves differently about it; it takes pain more patiently, we are the long-suffering, born for pain, so to speak. Because, above all, we know the natural and healthy pain, the God-ordained and sacred pain of childbirth, which is something absolutely peculiar to woman, something men are spared, or denied. Men – the fools! – are horrified, to be sure, by our half-unconscious screaming, and reproach themselves and clasp their heads in their hands; and, for all that we scream, we are really laughing at them. When I brought you into the world, Anna, it was very bad. From the first pain it lasted thirty-six hours, and Tümmler ran around the apartment the whole time with his head in his hands, but despite everything it was a great festival of life, and I wasn't screaming myself, *it* was screaming, it was a sacred ecstasy of pain. With Eduard, later, it wasn't half so bad, but it would still have been more than enough for a man – our lords and masters would certainly want no part in it. Pains, you see, are usually the danger-signals by which Nature, always benignant, warns that a disease is developing in the body – look sharp there, it means, something's wrong, do something about it quick, not so much against the pain as against what the pain indicates. With us it can be like that too, and have that meaning, of course. But, as you know yourself, your abdominal pain before your periods doesn't have that meaning, it doesn't warn you of anything. It's a sport among the species of women's pains and as such it is honourable, that is how you must take it, as a vital function in the life of a woman. Always, so long as we are that – a woman, no longer a child and not yet an incapacitated old crone – always, over and over, there is an intensified welling up of the blood of life in our organ of motherhood, by which precious Nature prepares it to receive the fertilized egg, and if one is present, as, after all, even in my long life, was the case only twice and with a long interval between, then our monthly doesn't come, and we are pregnant. Heavens, what a joyous surprise when it stopped the first time for me, thirty years ago! It was you, my dear child, with whom I was blessed, and I still remember how I confided it to Tümmler and, blushing, laid my face against his and said, very softly: "Robert, it's happened, all the signs point that way, and it's my turn now, *da is wat am kommen...*"'

'Dearest Mama, please just do me the favour of not using dialect, it irritates me at the moment.'

'Oh, forgive me, darling – to irritate you now is the last thing I meant to do. It's only that, in my blissful confusion, I really did say that to Tümmler. And then – we are talking about natural things, aren't we? – and, to my mind, Nature and dialect go together somehow, as Nature and the people go together – if I'm talking nonsense, correct me, you are so much cleverer than I am. Yes, you are clever, and, as an artist, you are not on the best of terms with Nature but insist on transposing her into concepts, into cubes and spirals, and, since we're speaking of things going together, I rather wonder if they don't go together too, your proud, intellectual attitude towards Nature, and the way she singles you out and sends you pains at your periods.'

'But, Mama,' said Anna, and could not help laughing, 'you scold me for being intellectual, and then propound absolutely unwarrantable intellectual theories yourself!'

'If I can divert you a little with it, child, the most naïve theory is good enough for me. But what I was saying about women's natural pains I mean perfectly seriously, it should comfort you. Simply be happy and proud that, at thirty, you are in the full power of your blood. Believe me, I would gladly put up with any kind of abdominal pains if it were still with me as it is with you. But unfortunately that is over for me, it has been growing more and more scanty and irregular, and for the last two months it hasn't happened at all. Ah, it has ceased to be with me after the manner of women, as the Bible says, in reference to Sarah, I think – yes, it was Sarah, and then a miracle of fruitfulness was worked in her, but that's only one of those edifying stories, I suppose – that sort of thing doesn't happen any more today. When it has ceased to be with us after the manner of women, we are no longer women at all, but only the dried-up husk of a woman, worn out, useless, cast out of nature. My dear child, it is very bitter. With men, I believe, it usually doesn't stop as long as they are alive. I know some who at eighty still can't let a woman alone, and Tümmler, your father, was like that too – how I had to pretend not to see things even when he was a lieutenant-colonel! What is fifty for a man? Provided he has a little temperament, fifty comes nowhere near stopping him from playing the lover, and many a man with greying temples still makes conquests even among young girls. But we, take it all in all, are given just thirty-five years to be women in our life and our blood, to be complete human beings, and when we are fifty, we are superannuated, our capacity to breed expires, and, in Nature's eyes, we are nothing but old rubbish!'

To these bitter words of acquiescence in the ways of Nature, Anna did not answer as many women would doubtless, and justifiably, have answered. She said:

'How you talk, Mama, and how you revile and seem to want to reject the dignity that falls to the elderly woman when she has fulfilled her life, and Nature, which you love after all, translates her to a new, mellow condition, an honourable and more lovable condition, in which she still can give and be so much, both to her family and to those less close to her. You say you envy men because their sex life is less strictly limited than a woman's. But I doubt if that is really anything to be respected, if it is a reason for envying them; and in any case all civilized peoples have always rendered the most exquisite honours to the matron, have even regarded her as sacred – and we mean to regard you as sacred in the dignity of your dear and charming old age.'

'Darling' – and Rosalie drew her daughter close as they walked along –

'you speak so beautifully and intelligently and well, despite your pains, for which I was trying to comfort you, and now you are comforting your foolish mother in her unworthy tribulations. But the dignity, and the resignation, are very hard, my dear child, it is very hard even for the body to find itself in its new situation, that alone is torment enough. And when there are heart and mind besides, which would still rather not hear too much of dignity and the honourable estate of a matron, and rebel against the drying up of the body – that is when it really begins to be hard. The soul's adjustment to the new constitution of the body is the hardest thing of all.'

'Of course, Mama, I understand that very well. But consider: body and soul are one; the psychological is no less a part of Nature than the physical; Nature takes in the psychological too, and you needn't be afraid that your psyche can long remain out of harmony with the natural change in your body. You must regard the psychological as only an emanation of the physical; and if the poor soul thinks that she is saddled with the all too difficult task of adjusting herself to the body's changed life, she will soon see that she really has nothing to do but let the body have its way and do its work on herself too. For it is the body that moulds the soul, in accordance with its own conditions.'

Fräulein von Tümmler had her reasons for saying this, because, about the time that her mother made the above confidence to her, a new face, an additional face, was very often to be seen at home, and the potentially embarrassing developments which were under way had not escaped Anna's silent, apprehensive observation.

The new face – which Anna found distressingly commonplace, anything but distinguished by intelligence – belonged to a young man named Ken Keaton, an American of about twenty-four whom the war had brought over and who had been staying in the city for some time, giving English lessons in one household or another or simply commandeered for English conversation (in exchange for a suitable fee) by the wives of rich industrialists. Eduard had heard of these activities towards Easter of his last year in school and had earnestly begged his mother to have Mr Keaton teach him the rudiments of English a few afternoons a week. For though his school offered him a quantity of Greek and Latin, and fortunately a sufficiency of mathematics as well, it offered no English, which, after all, seemed highly important for his future goal. As soon as, one way or another, he had got through all those boring humanities, he wanted to attend the Polytechnic Institute and after that, so he planned, go to England for further study or perhaps straight to the El Dorado of technology, the United States. So he was happy and grateful when, respecting his clarity and firmness of purpose, his mother readily acceded to his wish; and his work with Keaton, Mondays, Wednesdays, and Saturdays, gave him great satisfaction – because it served his purpose, of course, but then too because it was fun to learn a new language right from the rudiments, like an abecedarian, beginning with a little primer: words, their often outlandish orthography, their most extraordinary pronunciation, which Ken, forming his l's even deeper down in his throat than the Rhinelanders and letting his r's sound from his gums unrolled, would illustrate with such drawn-out exaggeration that he seemed to be trying to make fun of his own mother tongue. 'Scrr-ew the top on!' he said. 'I sllept like a top.' 'Alfred is a tennis play-err. His shoulders are thirty inches brr-oaoadd.' Eduard could laugh, through the whole hour and a half of the lesson, at Alfred, the broad-shouldered tennis player, in whose praise so much was said with the greatest possible use of 'though' and 'thought' and 'taught' and 'tough', but he made very good progress, just because Ken, not being a learned pedagogue, used a free and easy method – in other words, improvised on whatever the moment brought and hammering away regardless, through patter, slang, and nonsense, initiated his willing pupil into his easy-going, humorous, efficient vernacular.

Frau von Tümmler, attracted by the jollity that pervaded Eduard's room, sometimes looked in on the young people and took some part in their profitable fun, laughed heartily with them over 'Alfred, the tennish play-err', and found a certain resemblance between him and her son's young tutor, particularly in the matter of his shoulders, for Ken's too were splendidly broad. He had, moreover, thick blond hair, a not particularly handsome though not unpleasant, guilelessly friendly boyish face, to which in these surroundings, however, a slight Anglo-Saxon cast of features lent a touch of the unusual; that he was remarkably well built was apparent despite his loose, rather full clothes; with his long legs and narrow hips, he produced an impression of youthful strength. He had very nice hands, too, with a not too elaborate ring on the left. His simple, perfectly unconstrained yet not rude manner, his comical German, which became as undeniably English-sounding in his mouth as the scraps of French and Italian that he knew (for he had visited several European countries) – all this Rosalie found very pleasant; his great naturalness in particular prepossessed her in his favour; and now and again, and finally almost regularly, she invited him to stay for dinner after Eduard's lesson, whether she had been present at it or not. In part her interest in him was due to her having heard that he was very successful with women. With this in mind, she studied him and found the rumour not incomprehensible, though it was not quite to her taste when, having to eructate a little at table, he would put his hand over his mouth and say 'Pardon me!' – which was meant for good manners, but which, after all, drew attention to the occurrence quite unnecessarily.

Ken, as he told them over dinner, had been born in a small town in one of the Eastern states, where his father had followed various occupations – broker, manager of a gas station – from time to time too he had made some money in the real-estate business. Ken had attended high school, where, if he was to be believed, one learned nothing at all – 'by European standards', as he respectfully added – after which, without giving the matter much thought, but merely with the idea of learning something more, he had entered a college in Detroit, Michigan, where he had earned his tuition by the work of his hands, as dishwasher, cook, waiter, campus gardener. Frau von Tümmler asked him how, through all that, he had managed to keep such white, one might say aristocratic hands, and he answered that, when doing rough work, he had always worn gloves – only a short-sleeved polo shirt, or nothing at all from the waist up, but always gloves. Most workmen, or at least many of them – construction workers, for example – did that back home, to avoid getting horny proletarian hands, and they had hands like a lawyer's clerk, with a ring.

Rosalie praised the custom, but Keaton differed. Custom? The word was too good for it, you couldn't call it a 'custom', in the sense of the old European folk customs (he habitually said 'Continental' for 'European'). Such an old German folk custom, for example, as the 'rod of life' – village lads gathering fresh birch and willow rods at Christmas or Easter and striking ('peppering' or 'slashing', they called it) the girls, and sometimes cattle and trees, with them to bring health and fertility – that was a 'custom', an age-old one, and it delighted him. When the peppering or slashing took place in spring, it was called 'Smack Easter'.

The Tümmlers had never heard of Smack Easter and were surprised at Ken's knowledge of folklore. Eduard laughed at the 'rod of life', Anna made a face, and only Rosalie, in perfect agreement with their guest, showed herself delighted. Anyhow, he said, it was something very different from wearing gloves at work, and you could look a long time before you found anything of the sort in America, if only because there were no villages there and the farmers were not farmers at all but entrepreneurs like everyone else and had no 'customs'. In general, despite being so unmistakably American in his entire manner and attitude, he displayed very little attachment to his great country. He 'didn't care for America'; indeed, with its pursuit of the dollar and insensate church-going, its worship of success and its colossal mediocrity, but, above all, its lack of historical atmosphere, he found it really appalling. Of course, it had a history, but that wasn't 'history', it was simply a short, boring 'success story'. Certainly, aside from its enormous deserts, it had beautiful and magnificent landscapes, but there was 'nothing behind them', while in Europe there was so much behind everything, particularly behind the cities, with their deep historical perspectives. American cities – he 'didn't care for them'. They were put up yesterday and might just as well be taken away tomorrow. The small ones were stupid holes, one looking exactly like another, and the big ones were horrible, inflated monstrosities, with museums full of bought-up European cultural treasures. Bought, of course, was better than stolen, but not *much* better, for, in certain places things dating from AD 1400 and 1200 were as good as stolen.

Ken's irreverent chatter aroused laughter; they took him to task for it too, but he answered that what made him speak as he did was precisely reverence, specifically a respect for perspective and atmosphere. Very early dates, AD 1100, 700, were his passion and his hobby, and at college he had always been best at history – at history and at athletics. He had long been drawn to Europe, where early dates were at home, and certainly, even without the war, he would have worked his way across, as a sailor or dishwasher, simply to breathe historical air. But the war had come at just the right moment for him; in 1917 he had immediately enlisted in the army, and all through his training he had been afraid that the war might end before it brought him across to Europe. But he had made it – almost at the last minute he had sailed to France, jammed into a troop transport, and had even got into some real fighting, near Compiègne, from which he had carried away a wound, and not a light one, so that he had had to lie in hospital for weeks. It had been a kidney wound, and only one of his kidneys really worked now, but that was quite enough. However, he said, smiling, he was, in a manner of speaking, disabled, and he drew a small disability pension, which was worth more to him than the lost kidney.

There was certainly nothing of the disabled veteran about him, Frau von Tümmler observed, and he answered: 'No, thank heaven, only a little cash!'

On his release from the hospital, he had left the service, had been 'honourably discharged' with a medal for bravery, and had stayed on for an indefinite time in Europe, which he found 'wonderful' and where he revelled in early dates. The French cathedrals, the Italian campaniles, *palazzi*, and galleries, the Swiss villages, a place like Stein am Rhein – all that was 'most delightful indeed'. And the wine everywhere, the *bistros* in France, the *trattorie* in Italy, the cosy *Wirtshäuser* in Switzerland and Germany, 'at the sign of the Ox', 'of the Moor', 'of the Star' – where was there anything like that in America? There was no wine there – just 'drinks', whisky and rum, and no cool pints of Elässer or Tiroler or Johannisberger at an oak table in a historical taproom or a honeysuckle arbour. Good heavens! People in America simply didn't know how to live.

Germany! That was the country he loved, though he really had explored it very little and in fact knew only the places on the Bodensee, and of course – but that he knew really well – the Rhineland. The Rhineland, with its charming, gay people, so amiable, especially when they were a bit 'high'; with its venerable cities, full of atmosphere. Trier, Aachen, Coblenz, 'Holy' Cologne – just try calling an American city 'holy' – 'Holy Kansas City', ha-ha! The golden treasure, guarded by the nixies of the Amissouri River – ha-ha-ha – 'Pardon me!' Of Düsseldorf and its long history from Merovingian days, he knew more than Rosalie and her children put together, and he spoke of Pepin the Short, of Barbarossa, who built the Imperial Palace at Rindhusen, and of the Salian Church at Kaiserswerth, where Henry IV was crowned King as a child, of Albert of Berg and John William of the Palatinate, and of many other things and people, like a professor.

Rosalie said that he could teach history too, just as well as English. There was too little demand, he replied. Oh, not at all, she protested. She herself, for instance, whom he had made keenly aware of how little she knew, would begin taking lessons from him at once. He would be 'a little shy' about it, he confessed; in answer she expressed something that she had feelingly observed: It was strange and to a certain degree painful that in life shyness was the rule between youth and age. Youth was reserved in the presence of age because it expected no understanding of its green time of life from age's dignity, and age feared youth because, though admiring it whole-heartedly, simply as youth, age considered it due to its dignity to conceal its admiration under mockery and assumed condescension.

Ken laughed, pleased and approving. Eduard remarked that Mama really talked like a book, and Anna looked searchingly at her mother. She was decidedly vivacious in Mr Keaton's presence, unfortunately even a little affected at times; she invited him frequently, and looked at him, even when he said 'Pardon me' behind his hand, with an expression of motherly compassion which to Anna – who, despite the young man's enthusiasm for Europe, his passion for dates like 700, and his knowledge of all the time-honoured pothouses in Düsseldorf, found him totally uninteresting – appeared somewhat questionable in point of motherliness and made her not a little uncomfortable. Too often, when Mr Keaton was to be present, her mother asked, with nervous apprehension, if her nose was flushed. It was, though Anna soothingly denied it. And if it wasn't before he arrived, it flushed with unwonted violence when she was in the young man's company. But then her mother seemed to have forgotten all about it.

Anna saw rightly: Rosalie had begun to lose her heart to her son's young tutor, without offering any resistance to the rapid budding of her feeling, perhaps without being really aware of it, and in any case without making any particular effort to keep it a secret. Symptoms that in another woman could not have escaped her feminine observation (a cooing and exaggeratedly delighted laughter at Ken's chatter, a soulful look followed by a curtaining of the brightened eyes), she seemed to consider imperceptible in herself – if she was not boasting of her feeling, was not too proud of it to conceal it.

The situation became perfectly clear to the suffering Anna one very summery, warm September evening, when Ken had stayed for dinner and

Eduard, after the soup, had asked permission, on account of the heat, to take off his jacket. The young men, was the answer, must feel no constraint; and so Ken followed his pupil's example. He was not in the least concerned that, whereas Eduard was wearing a coloured shirt with long sleeves, he had merely put on his jacket over his sleeveless white jersey and hence now displayed his bare arms – very handsome, round, strong, white young arms, which made it perfectly comprehensible that he had been as good at athletics in college as at history. The agitation which the sight of them caused in the lady of the house, he was certainly far from noticing, nor did Eduard have any eyes for it. But Anna observed it with pain and pity. Rosalie, talking and laughing feverishly, looked alternately as if she had been drenched with blood and frighteningly pale, and after every escape her fleeing eyes returned, under an irresistible attraction, to the young man's arms and then, for rapt seconds, lingered on them with an expression of deep and sensual sadness.

Anna, bitterly resentful of Ken's primitive guilelessness, which, however, she did not entirely trust, drew attention, as soon as she found even a shred of an excuse, to the evening coolness, which was just beginning to penetrate through the open French window, and suggested, with a warning against catching cold, that the jackets be put on again. But Frau von Tümmler terminated her evening almost immediately after dinner. Pretending a headache, she took a hurried leave of her guest and retired to her bedroom. There she lay stretched on her couch, with her face hidden in her hands and buried in the pillow, and, overwhelmed with shame, terror, and bliss, confessed her passion to herself.

'Good God, I love him, yes, love him, as I have never loved, is it possible? Here I am, retired from active service, translated by Nature to the calm, dignified estate of matronhood. Is it not grotesque that I should still give myself up to lust, as I do in my frightened, blissful thoughts at the sight of him, at the sight of his godlike arms, by which I insanely long to be embraced, at the sight of his magnificent chest, which, in wretchedness and rapture, I saw outlined under his jersey? Am I a shameless old woman? No, not shameless, for I am ashamed in his presence, in the presence of his youth, and I do not know how I ought to meet him and look him in the eyes, the ingenuous, friendly boy's eyes, which expect no burning emotion from me. But it is I who have been struck by the rod of life, he himself, all unknowing, has slashed me and peppered me with it, he has given me my Smack Easter! Why did he have to tell us of it, in his youthful enthusiasm for old folk customs? Now the thought of the awakening stroke of his rod leaves my inmost being drenched, inundated with shameful sweetness. I desire him – have I ever desired before? Tümmler desired me, when I was young, and I consented, acquiesced in his wooing, took him in marriage in his commanding manhood, and we gave ourselves up to lust when he desired. This time it is I who desire, of my own will and motion, and I have cast my eyes on him as a man casts his eyes on the young woman of his choice – this is what the years do, it is my age that does it and his youth. Youth is feminine, and age's relationship to it is masculine, but age is not happy and confident in its desire, it is full of shame and fear before youth and before all Nature, because of its unfitness. Oh, there is much sorrow in prospect for me, for how can I hope that he will be pleased by my desire, and, if pleased, that he will consent to my wooing, as I did to Tümmler's. He is no girl, with his firm arms, not he – far from it, he is a young man, who wants to desire for himself and who, they say, is very successful in that way with women. He has as

many women as he wants, right here in town. My soul writhes and screams
with jealousy at the thought. He gives lessons in English conversation to
Louise Pfingsten in Pempelforter Strasse and to Amélie Lützenkirchen,
whose husband, the pottery-manufacturer, is fat, short-winded, and lazy.
Louise is too tall and has a bad hairline, but she is only just thirty-eight and
knows how to give melting looks. Amélie is only a little older, and pretty,
unfortunately she is pretty, and that fat husband of hers gives her every
liberty. Is it possible that they lie in his arms, or at least one of them does,
probably Amélie, but it might be that stick of a Louise at the same time –in
those arms for whose embrace I long with fervour that their stupid souls
could never muster? That they enjoy his hot breath, his lips, his hands that
caress their bodies? My teeth, still so good, and which have needed so little
attention – my teeth gnash, I gnash them, when I think of it. My figure too is
better than theirs, worthier than theirs to be caressed by his hands, and what
tenderness I should offer him, what inexpressible devotion! But they are
flowing springs, and I am dried up, not worth being jealous of any more.
Jealousy, torturing, tearing, crushing jealousy! That garden party at the
Rollwagens' – the machine-factory Rollwagen and his wife – where he was
invited too – wasn't it there that with my own eyes, which see everything, I
saw him and Amélie exchange a look and a smile that almost certainly
pointed to some secret between them? Even then my heart contracted with
choking pain, but I did not understand it, I did not think it was jealousy
because I no longer supposed myself capable of jealousy. But I am, I
understand that now, and I do not try to deny it, no, I rejoice in my torments
– there they are, in marvellous disaccord with the physical change in me.
The psychological only an emanation of the physical, says Anna, and the
body moulds the soul after its own condition? Anna knows a lot, Anna knows
nothing. No, I will not say that she knows nothing. She has suffered, loved
senselessly and suffered shamefully, and so she knows a great deal. But that
soul and body are translated together to the mild, honourable estate of
matronhood – there she is all wrong, for she does not believe in miracles,
does not know that Nature can make the soul flower miraculously, when it is
late, even too late – flower in love, desire, and jealousy, as I am experiencing
in blissful torment. Sarah, the old grey crone, heard from behind the tent
door what was still appointed for her, and she laughed. And God was angry
with her and said: Wherefore did Sarah laugh? I – I will not have laughed. I
will believe in the miracle of my soul and my senses, I will revere the miracle
Nature has wrought in me, this agonizing shy spring in my soul, and I will be
shamefaced only before the blessing of this late visitation...'
Thus Rosalie, communing with herself, on that evening. After a night of
violent restlessness and a few hours of deep morning sleep, her first thought
on waking was of the passion that had smitten her, blessed her, and to deny
which, to reject it on moral grounds, simply did not enter her head. The poor
woman was enraptured with the survival in her soul of the ability to bloom in
sweet pain. She was not particularly pious, and she left the Lord God out of
the picture. Her piety was for Nature, and it made her admire and prize what
Nature, as it were against herself, had worked in her. Yes, it was contrary to
natural seemliness, this flowering of her soul and senses; though it made her
happy, it did not encourage her, it was something to be concealed, kept
secret from all the world, even from her trusted daughter, but especially
from him, her beloved, who suspected nothing and must suspect nothing –
for how dared she boldly raise her eyes to his youth?
Thus into her relationship to Keaton there entered a certain submissive-

ness and humility which were completely absurd socially, yet which Rosalie, despite her pride in her feeling, was unable to banish from it, and which, on any clear-sighted observer – and so on Anna – produced a more painful effect than all the vivacity and excessive gaiety of her behaviour in the beginning. Finally even Eduard noticed it, and there were moments when brother and sister, bowed over their plates, bit their lips, while Ken, uncomprehendingly aware of the embarrassed silence, looked questioningly from one to another. Seeking counsel and enlightenment, Eduard took an opportunity to question his sister.

'What's happening to Mama?' he asked. 'Doesn't she like Keaton any more?' And as Anna said nothing, the young man, making a wry face, added: 'Or does she like him too much?'

'What are you thinking of?' was the reproving answer. 'Such things are no concern of yours, at your age. Mind your manners, and do not permit yourself to make unsuitable observations!' But she went on: he might reverently remind himself that his mother, as all women eventually must, was having to go through a period of difficulties prejudicial to her health and well-being.

'Very new and instructive for me!' said the senior in school ironically; but the explanation was too general to suit him. Their mother was suffering from something more specific, and even she, his highly respected sister, was visibly suffering – to say nothing of his young and stupid self. But perhaps, young and stupid as he was, he could make himself useful by proposing the dismissal of his too attractive tutor. He had, he could tell his mother, got enough out of Keaton; it was time for him to be 'honourably discharged' again.

'Do so, dear Eduard,' said Anna, and he did.

'Mama,' he said, 'I think we might stop my English lessons, and the constant expense I have put you to for them. Thanks to your generosity, I have laid a good foundation, with Mr Keaton's help; and by doing some reading by myself I can see to it that it will not be lost. Anyway, no one ever really learns a foreign language at home, outside of the country where everybody speaks it and where one is entirely dependent on it. Once I am in England or America, after the start you have generously given me, the rest will come easily. As you know, my final examinations are approaching, and there is none in English. Instead I must see to it that I don't flunk the classical languages, and that requires concentration. So the time has come – don't you think? – to thank Keaton cordially for his trouble and in the most friendly way possible to dispense with his services.'

'But Eduard,' Frau von Tümmler answered at once, and indeed at first with a certain haste, 'what you say surprises me, and I cannot say that I approve of it. Certainly, it shows great delicacy of feeling in you to wish to spare me further expenditure for this purpose. But the purpose is a good one, it is important for your future, as you now see it, and our situation is not such that we cannot meet the expenses of language lessons for you, quite as well as we were able to meet those of Anna's studies at the Academy. I do not understand why you want to stop halfway in your project to gain a mastery of the English language. It could be said, dear boy – please don't take it in bad part – that you would be making me an ill return for the willingness with which I met your proposal. Your final examinations – to be sure, they are a serious matter, and I understand that you will have to buckle down to your classical languages, which come hard to you. But your English lessons, a few times a week – you don't mean to tell me that they wouldn't be more of a recreation, a healthy distraction for you, than an additional strain. Besides – and now let me pass to the personal and human side of the matter – the relationship between Ken, as he is called, or rather Mr Keaton, and our family has long since ceased to be such that we could say to him: "You're no longer needed", and simply give him his marching orders. Simply announce: "Sirrah, you may withdraw." He has become a friend, almost a member of the family, and he would quite rightly be offended at such a dismissal. We should all feel his absence – Anna especially, I think, would be upset if he no longer came and enlivened our table with his intimate knowledge of the history of Düsseldorf, stopped telling us all about the quarrel over right of succession between the duchies of Jülich and Cleves, and about Elector John William on his pedestal in the market place. You would miss him too, and so, in fact, should I. In short, Eduard, your proposal is well meant, but it is neither necessary nor, indeed, really possible. We had better leave things as they are.'

'Whatever you think best, Mama,' said Eduard, and reported his ill success to his sister, who answered:

'I expected as much, my boy. After all, Mama has described the situation quite correctly, and I saw much the same objections to your plan when you announced it to me. In any case, she is perfectly right in saying that Keaton is pleasant company and that we should all regret his absence. So just go on with him.'

As she spoke, Eduard looked her in the face, which remained impassive; he shrugged his shoulders and left. Ken was waiting for him in his room, read a few pages of Emerson or Macaulay with him, then an American mystery story, which gave them something to talk about for the last half hour, and stayed for dinner, to which he had long since ceased to be expressly invited. His staying on after lessons had become a standing arrangement; and Rosalie, on the recurring days of her untoward and timorous, shame-clouded joy, consulted with Babette, the housekeeper, over the menu, ordered a choice repast, provided a full-bodied Pfälzer or Rüdesheimer, over which they would linger in the living-room for an hour after dinner, and to which she applied herself beyond her wont, so that she could look with better courage at the object of her unreasonable love. But often too the wine made her tired and desperate; and then whether she should stay and suffer in his sight or retire and weep over him in solitude became a battle which she fought with varying results.

October having brought the beginning of the social season, she also saw Keaton elsewhere than in her own house – at the Pfingstens' in Pempelforter Strasse, at the Lützenkirchens', at big receptions at Chief Engineer Rollwagen's. On these occasions she sought and shunned him, fled the group he had joined, waited in another, talking mechanically, for him to come and bestow some notice on her, knew at any moment where he was, listened for his voice amid the buzz of voices, and suffered horribly when she thought she saw signs of a secret understanding between him and Louise Pfingsten or Amélie Lützenkirchen. Although the young man had nothing in particular to offer except his fine physique, his complete naturalness and friendly simplicity, he was liked and sought out in this circle, contentedly profited by the German weakness for everything foreign, and knew very well that his pronunciation of German, the childish turns of phrase he used in speaking it, made a great hit. Then, too, people were glad to speak English with him. He could dress as he pleased. He had no evening clothes; social usages, however, had for many years been less strict, a dinner jacket was no longer absolutely obligatory in a box at the theatre or at an evening party, and even on occasions where the majority of the gentlemen present wore evening dress, Keaton was welcome in ordinary street clothes, his loose, comfortable apparel, the belted brown trousers, brown shoes, and grey woollen jacket.

Thus unceremoniously he moved through drawing-rooms, made himself agreeable to the ladies to whom he gave English lessons, as well as to those by whom he would gladly have been prevailed upon to do the same – at table first cut a piece of his meat, then laid his knife diagonally across the rim of his plate, let his left arm hang, and, managing his fork with the right, ate what he had made ready. He adhered to this custom because he saw that the ladies on either side of him and the gentleman opposite observed it with such great interest.

He was always glad to chat with Rosalie, whether in company or *tête-à-tête* – not only because she was one of his sources of income but from a genuine attraction. For whereas her daughter's cool intelligence and intellectual pretensions inspired fear in him, the mother's true-hearted womanliness impressed him sympathetically, and, without correctly reading her feelings (it did not occur to him to do that), he allowed himself to bask in the warmth that radiated from her to him, took pleasure in it, and felt little concern over certain concomitant signs of tension, oppression, and confusion, which he interpreted as expressions of European nervousness and therefore held in high regard. In addition, for all her suffering, her appearance at this time acquired a conspicuous new bloom, a rejuvenescence, upon which she received many compliments. Her figure had always preserved its youthfulness, but what was so striking now was the light in her beautiful brown eyes – a light which, if there was something feverish about it, nevertheless added to her charm – was her heightened colouring, quick to return after occasional moments of pallor, the mobility of feature that characterized her face (it had become a little fuller) in conversations that inclined to gaiety and hence always enabled her to correct any involuntary expression by a laugh. A good deal of loud laughter was the rule at these convivial gatherings, for all partook liberally of the wine and punch, and what might have seemed eccentric in Rosalie's manner was submerged in the general atmosphere of relaxation, in which nothing caused much surprise. But how happy she was when it happened that one of the women said to her, in Ken's presence: 'Darling, you are astonishing! How ravishing you look this evening! You eclipse the girls of twenty. Do tell me, what fountain of youth have you discovered?' And even more when her beloved corroborated: 'Right you are! Frau von Tümmler is perfectly delightful tonight.' She laughed, and her deep blush could be attributed to her pleasure in the flattery. She looked away from him, but she thought of his arms, and again she felt the same prodigious sweetness drenching, inundating her inmost being – it had been a frequent sensation these days, and other women, she thought, when they found her young, when they found her charming, must surely be aware of it.

It was on one of these evenings, after the gathering had broken up, that she failed in her resolve to keep the secret of her heart, the illicit and painful but fascinating psychological miracle that had befallen her, wholly to herself and not to reveal it even to Anna's friendship. An irresistible need for communication forced her to break the promise she had made to herself and to confide in her brilliant daughter, not only because she yearned for understanding sympathy but also from a wish that what Nature was bringing to pass in her should be understood and honoured as the remarkable human phenomenon that it was.

A wet snow was falling; the two ladies had driven home through it in a taxicab about midnight. Rosalie was shivering. 'Allow me, dear child,' she said, 'to sit up another half-hour with you in your cosy bedroom. I am freezing, but my head is on fire, and sleep, I fear, is out of the question for some time. If you would make tea for us, to end the evening, it wouldn't be a bad idea. That punch of the Rollwagens' is hard on one. Rollwagen mixes it himself, but he hasn't the happiest knack of it, pours a questionable orange cordial into the Moselle and then adds domestic champagne. Tomorrow we shall have terrible headaches again, a bad "hangover". Not you, that is. You are sensible and don't drink much. But I forget myself, chattering away, and don't notice that they keep filling my glass and think it is still the first. Yes, make tea for us, it's just the thing. Tea stimulates, but it soothes at the same time, and a cup of hot tea, taken at the right moment, wards off a cold. The rooms were far too hot at the Rollwagens' – at least, I thought so – and then the foul weather outdoors. Does it mean spring already? At noon today in the park I thought I really sniffed spring. But your silly mother always does that as soon as the shortest day has passed and the light increases again. A good idea, turning on the electric heater; there's not much heat left here at this hour. My dear child, you know how to make us comfortable and create just the right intimate atmosphere for a little *tête-à-tête* before we go to bed. You see, Anna, I have long wanted to have a talk with you, and – you are quite right –you have never denied me the opportunity. But there are things, child, to express which, to discuss which, requires a particularly intimate atmosphere, a favourable hour, which loosens one's tongue...'

'What sort of things, Mama? I haven't any cream to offer you. Will you take a little lemon?'

'Things of the heart, child, things of Nature, wonderful, mysterious, omnipotent Nature, who sometimes does such strange, contradictory, indeed incomprehensible things to us. You know it too. Recently, my dear Anna, I have found myself thinking a great deal about your old – forgive me for referring to it – your *affaire de cœur* with Brünner, about what you went through then, the suffering of which you complained to me in an hour not unlike this, and which, in bitter self-reproach, you even called a shame, because, that is, of the shameful conflict in which your reason, your judgement, was engaged with your heart, or, if you prefer, with your senses.'

'You are quite right to change the word, Mama. "Heart" is sentimental nonsense. It is inadmissible to say "heart" for something that is entirely different. Our heart speaks truly only with the consent of our judgement and reason.'

'You may well say so. For you have always been on the side of unity and insisted that Nature, simply of herself, creates harmony between soul and body. But that you were in a state of disharmony then – that is, between your wishes and your judgement – you cannot deny. You were very young at the time, and your desire had no reason to be ashamed in Nature's eyes, only in the eyes of your judgement, which called it debasing. It did not pass the test of your judgement, and that was your shame and your suffering. For you are proud, Anna, very proud; and that there might be a pride in feeling alone, a pride of feeling which denies that it has to pass the test of anything and be responsible to anything – judgement and reason and even Nature herself – that you will not admit, and in that we differ. For to me the heart is supreme, and if Nature inspires feelings in it which no longer become it, and seems to create a contradiction between the heart and herself – certainly it is painful and shameful, but the shame is only for one's unworthiness and, at bottom, is sweet amazement, is reverence, before Nature and before the life that it pleases her to create in one whose life is done.'

'My dear Mama,' replied Anna, 'let me first of all decline the honour that you accord to my pride and my reason. At the time, they would have miserably succumbed to what you poetically call my heart if a merciful fate had not intervened; and when I think where my heart would have led me, I cannot but thank God that I did not follow its desires. I am the last who would dare to cast a stone. However, we are not talking of me, but of you, and I will not decline the honour you accord me in wishing to confide in me. For that is what you wish to do, is it not? What you say indicates it, only you have spoken in such generalities that everything remains dark, show me, please, how I am to refer them to you and how I am to understand them!'

'What should you say, Anna, if your mother, in her old age, were seized by an ardent feeling such as rightfully belongs only to potent youth, to maturity, and not to a withered womanhood?'

'Why the conditional, Mama? It is quite obvious that you are in the state you describe. You're in love?'

'The way you say that, my sweet child! How freely and bravely and openly you speak the words which would not easily come to my lips, and which I have locked up in me so long, together with all the shameful joy and grief that they imply – have kept secret from everyone, even from you, so closely that you really used to be startled out of your dream, the dream of your belief in your mother's matronly dignity! Yes, I'm in love, I love with ardour and desire and bliss and torment, as you once loved in your youth. My feeling can as little stand the test of reason as yours could, and if I am even proud of the spring with which Nature has made my soul flower, which she has miraculously bestowed upon me, I yet suffer, as you once suffered, and I have been irresistibly driven to tell you all.'

'My dear, darling, Mama! Then do tell me! When it is so hard to speak, questions help. Who is it?'

'It cannot but be a shattering surprise to you, my child. The young friend of the house. Your brother's tutor.'

'Ken Keaton?'

'Yes.'

'Ken Keaton. So that is it. You needn't fear, Mother, that I shall begin exclaiming "Incomprehensible!" – though most people would. It is so easy and so stupid to call a feeling incomprehensible if one cannot imagine oneself having it. And yet – much as I want to avoid hurting you – forgive my anxious sympathy for asking a question. You speak of an emotion inappropriate to your years, complain of entertaining feelings of which you are no longer worthy. Have you ever asked yourself if he, this young man, is worthy of your feelings?'

'He – worthy? I hardly understand what you mean. I love, Anna. Of all the young men I have ever seen, Ken is the most magnificent.'

'And that is why you love him. Shall we try reversing the positions of cause and effect and perhaps get them in their proper places by doing so? May it not be that he only seems so magnificent to you because you are ... because you love him?'

'Oh, my child, you separate what is inseparable. Here in my heart my love and his magnificence are one.'

'But you are suffering, dearest, best Mama, and I should be so infinitely glad if I could help you. Could you not try, for a moment – just a moment of trying it might do you good – not to see him in the transfiguring light of your love, but by plain daylight, in his reality, as the nice, attractive – that I will grant you! – attractive lad he is, but who, such as he is, in and for himself, has so little to inspire passion and suffering on his account?'

'You mean well, Anna, I know. You would like to help me, I am sure of it. But it cannot be accomplished at his expense, by your doing him an injustice. And you do him injustice with your "daylight", which is such a false, misleading light. You say that he is nice, even attractive, and you mean by it that he is an average human being with nothing unusual about him. But I tell you he is an absolutely exceptional human being, with a life that touches one's heart. Think of his simple background – how, with iron strength of will, he worked his way through college, and excelled all his fellow students in history and athletics, and how he then hastened to his country's call and behaved so well as a soldier that he was finally "honourably discharged" . . .'

'Excuse me, Mama, but that is the routine procedure for everyone who doesn't actually do something dishonourable.'

'Everyone. You keep harping on his averageness, and, in doing so, by calling him, if not directly, then by implication, a simple-minded ingenuous youngster, you mean to talk me out of him. But you forget that ingenuousness can be something noble and victorious, and that the background of his ingenuousness is the great democratic spirit of his immense country . . .'

'He doesn't like his country in the least.'

'And for that very reason he is a true son of it; and if he loves Europe for its historical perspectives and its old folk customs, that does him honour too, and sets him apart from the majority. And he gave his blood for his country. Every soldier, you say, is "honourably discharged". But is every soldier given a medal for bravery, a Purple Heart, to show that the heroism with which he flung himself on the enemy cost him a wound, perhaps a serious one?'

'My dear Mama, in war, I think, one man catches it and another doesn't, one falls and another escapes, without its having much to do with whether he is brave or not. If somebody has a leg blown off or a kidney shot to pieces, a medal is a sop, a small compensation for his misfortune, but in general it is no indication of any particular bravery.'

'In any case, he sacrificed one of his kidneys on the altar of his fatherland!'

'Yes, he had that misfortune. And, thank heaven, one can at a pinch make do with only one kidney. But only at a pinch, and it *is* a lack, a defect, the thought of it does rather detract from the magnificence of his youth, and in the common light of day, by which he ought to be seen, does show him up, despite his good – or let us say normal – appearance, as not really complete, as disabled, as a man no longer perfectly whole.'

'Good God – Ken no longer complete, Ken not a whole man! My poor child, he is complete to the point of magnificence and can laugh at the lack of a kidney – not only in his own opinion, but in everyone's – that is, in the opinion of all the women who are after him, and in whose company he seems to find his pleasure! My dear, good, clever Anna, don't you know why, above all other reasons, I have confided in you, why I began this conversation? Because I wished to ask you – and I want your honest opinion – if, from your observation, you believe that he is having an affair with Louise Pfingsten, or with Amélie Lützenkirchen, or perhaps with both of them – for which, I assure you, he is quite complete enough! That is what keeps me suspended in the most agonizing doubt, and I hope very much that I shall get the truth from you, for you can look at things more calmly, by daylight, so to speak ...'

'Poor, darling Mama, how you torture yourself, how you suffer! It makes me so unhappy. But, to answer you: I don't think so – of course, I know very little about his life and have not felt called upon to investigate it – but I don't think so, and I have never heard anyone say that he has the sort of relationship you suspect, either with Frau Pfingsten or Frau Lützenkirchen. So please be reassured, I beg of you!'

'God grant, dear child, that you are not simply saying it to comfort me and pour balm on my wound, out of pity! But pity, don't you see, even though perhaps I am seeking it from you, is not in place at all, for I am happy in my torment and shame and filled with pride in the flowering spring of pain in my soul – remember that, child, even if I seem to be begging for pity!'.

'I don't feel that you are begging. But in such a case the happiness and pride are so closely allied with the suffering that, indeed, they are identical with it, and even if you looked for no pity, it would be your due from those who love you and who wish for you that you would take pity on yourself and try to free yourself from this absurd enchantment ... Forgive my words; they are the wrong ones, of course, but I cannot be concerned over words. It is you, darling, for whom I am concerned and not only since today, not only since your confession, for which I am grateful to you. You have kept your secret locked within you with great self-control; but that there has been some secret, that, for months now, you have been in some peculiar and crucial situation, could not escape those who love you, and they have seen it with mixed feelings.'

'To whom do you refer by your "they"?'

'I am speaking of myself. You have changed strikingly in these last weeks, Mama – I mean, not changed, I'm not putting it right, you are still the same, and if I say "changed", I mean that a sort of rejuvenescence has come over you – but that too isn't the right word, for naturally it can't be a matter of any actual, demonstrable rejuvenescence in your charming person. But to my eyes, at moments, and in a certain phantasmagoric fashion, it has been as if suddenly, out of your dear matronly self, stepped the Mama of twenty years ago, as I knew her when I was a girl – and even that was not all, I suddenly thought I saw you as I had never seen you, as you must have looked, that is, when you were a girl yourself. And this hallucination – if it was a mere hallucination, but there was something real about it too – should have delighted me, should have made my heart leap with pleasure, should it not? But it didn't, it only made my heart heavy, and at those very moments when you grew young before my eyes, I pitied you terribly. For at the same time I saw that you were suffering, and that the phantasmagoria to which I refer not only had to do with your suffering but was actually the expression of it, its manifestation, a "flowering spring of pain", as you just expressed it. Dear Mama, how did you happen to use such an expression? It is not natural to you. You are a simple being, worthy of all love; you have sound, clear eyes, you let them look into Nature and the world, not into books – you have never read much. Never before have you used expressions such as poets create, such lugubrious, sickly expressions, and if you do it now, it has a tinge of –'

'Of what, Anna? If poets use such expressions it is because they *need* them, because emotion and experience force them out of them, and so it is surely, with me, though you think them unbecoming in me. You are wrong. They are becoming to whoever needs them, and he has no fear of them, because

they are forced out of him. But your hallucination, or phantasmagoria –
whatever it was that you thought you saw in me – I can and will explain to
you. It was the work of *his* youth. It was my soul's struggle to match his
youth, so that it need not perish before him in shame and disgrace.'

Anna wept. They put their arms round each other, and their tears
mingled.

'That too,' said the lame girl with an effort, 'what you have just said, dear
heart, that too is of a piece with the strange expression you used, and, like
that, coming from your lips, it has a ring of destruction. This accursed
seizure is destroying you, I see it with my eyes, I hear it in your speech. We
must check it, put a stop to it, save you from it, at any cost. One forgets,
Mama, what is out of one's sight. All that is needed is a decision, a saving
decision. The young man must not come here any longer, we must dismiss
him. That is not enough. You see him elsewhere when you go out. Very well,
we must prevail upon him to leave the city. I will take it upon myself to
persuade him. I will talk to him in a friendly way, point out to him that he is
wasting his time and himself here, that he has long since exhausted
Düsseldorf and should not hang around here for ever, that Düsseldorf is not
Germany, of which he must see more, get to know it better, that Munich,
Hamburg, Berlin are there for him to sample, that he must not let himself be
tied down, must live in one place for a time, then in another, until, as is his
natural duty, he returns to his own country and takes up a regular
profession, instead of playing the invalid language-teacher here in Europe.
I'll soon impress it upon him. And if he declines and insists on sticking to
Düsseldorf, where, after all, he has connexions, we will go away ourselves.
We will give up our house here and move to Cologne or Frankfurt or to some
lovely place in the Taunus, and you will leave here behind you what has been
torturing you and trying to destroy you, and with the help of "out of sight",
you will forget. Out of sight – it is all that is needed, it is an infallible remedy,
for there is no such thing as not being able to forget. You may say it is a
disgrace to forget, but people do forget, depend upon it. And in the Taunus
you will enjoy your beloved Nature and you will be our old darling Mama
again.'

Thus Anna, with great earnestness, but how unavailingly!

'Stop, stop, Anna, no more of this, I cannot listen to what you are saying!
You weep with me, and your concern is affectionate indeed, but what you
say, your proposals, are impossible and shocking to me. Drive him away?
Leave here ourselves? How far your solicitude has led you astray! You speak
of Nature, but you strike her in the face with your demands, you want me to
strike her in the face, by stifling the spring of pain with which she has
miraculously blest my soul! What a sin that would be, what ingratitude,
what disloyalty to her, to Nature, and what a denial of my faith in her
beneficent omnipotence! You remember how Sarah sinned? She laughed to
herself behind the door and said: "After I am waxed old shall I have
pleasure, my lord being old also?" But the Lord God was angry and said:
"Wherefore did Sarah laugh?" In my opinion, she laughed less on account
of her own withered old age than because her lord, Abraham, was likewise so
old and stricken in years, already ninety-nine. And what woman could not
but laugh at the thought of indulging in lust with a ninety-nine-year-old
man, for all that a man's love life is less strictly limited than a woman's. But
my lord is young, is youth itself, and how much more easily and temptingly
must the thought come to me – Oh, Anna, my loyal child, I indulge in lust,
shameful and grievous lust, in my blood, in my wishes, and I cannot give it

up, cannot flee to the Taunus, and if you persuade Ken to go – I believe I should hate you to my dying day!'

Great was the sorrow with which Anna listened to these unrestrained, frenzied words.

'Dearest Mama,' said she in a strained voice, 'you are greatly excited. What you need now is rest and sleep. Take twenty drops of valerian in water, or even twenty-five. It is a harmless remedy and often very helpful. And rest assured that, for my part, I will undertake nothing that is opposed to your feeling. May this assurance help to bring you the peace of mind which, above all things, I desire for you! If I spoke slightingly of Keaton, whom I respect as the object of your affection, though I cannot but curse him as the cause of your suffering, you will understand that I was only trying to see if it would not restore your peace of mind. I am infinitely grateful for your confidence, and I hope, indeed I am sure, that by talking to me you have somewhat lightened your heart. Perhaps this conversation was the prerequisite for your recovery – I mean, for your restored peace of mind. Your sweet, happy heart, so dear to us all, will find itself again. It loves in pain. Do you not think that – let us say, in time – it could learn to love without pain and in accordance with reason? Love, don't you see? –' (Anna said this as she solicitously led her mother to her bedroom, so that she could herself drop the valerian into her glass) 'love – how many things it is, what a variety of feelings are included in the word, and yet how strangely it is always love! A mother's love for her son, for instance – I know that Eduard is not particularly close to you – but that love can be very heartfelt, very passionate, it can be subtly yet clearly distinguished from her love for a child of her own sex, and yet not for an instant pass the bounds of mother love. How would it be if you were to take advantage of the fact that Ken could be your son, to make the tenderness you feel for him maternal, let it find a permanent place, to your own benefit as mother love?'

Rosalie smiled through her tears.

'And thus establish the proper understanding between body and soul, I take it?' she jested sadly. 'My dear child, the demands that I make on your intelligence! How I exhaust it and misuse it! It is wrong of me, for I trouble you to no purpose. Mother love – it is something like the Taunus all over again ... Perhaps I'm not expressing myself quite clearly now? I *am* dead tired, you are right about that. Thank you, darling, for your patience, your sympathy! Thank you too for respecting Ken for the sake of what you call my affection. And don't hate him at the same time, as I should have to hate you if you drove him away! He is Nature's means of working her miracle in my soul.'

Anna left her. A week passed, during which Ken Keaton twice dined at the Tümmlers'. The first time, an elderly couple from Duisburg were present, relatives of Rosalie's; the woman was a cousin of hers. Anna, who well knew that certain relationships and emotional tensions inevitably emanate an aura that is obvious, particularly to those who are in no way involved, observed the guests keenly. Once or twice she saw Rosalie's cousin look wonderingly first at Keaton, then at the hostess; once she even detected a smile under the husband's moustache. That evening she also observed a difference in Ken's behaviour towards her mother, a quizzical change and readjustment in his reactions, observed too that he would not let it pass when, laboriously enough, she pretended not to be taking any particular notice of him, but forced her to direct her attention to him. On the second occasion no one else was present. Frau von Tümmler indulged in a scurrilous performance, directed at her daughter and inspired by her recent conversation with her, in which she mocked at certain of Anna's counsels and at the same time turned the travesty to her own advantage. It had come out that Ken had been very much on the town the previous night – with a few of his cronies, an art-school student and two sons of manufacturers, he had gone on a pub-crawl that had lasted until morning, and, as might have been expected, had arrived at the Tümmlers' with a 'first-class hangover' as Eduard, who was the one to let out the story, expressed it. And the end of the evening, when the good nights were being said, Rosalie gave her daughter a look that was at once excited and crafty – indeed, kept her eyes fixed on her for a moment as she held the young man by the lobe of his ear and said:

'And you, son, take a serious word of reproof from Mama Rosalie and understand hereafter that her house is open only to people of decent behaviour and not to night-owls and disabled beer-swillers who are hardly up to speaking German or even to keeping their eyes open! Did you hear me, you good-for-nothing? Mend your ways! If bad boys tempt you, don't listen to them, and from now on stop playing so fast and loose with your health! Will you mend your ways, will you?' As she spoke, she kept tugging at his ear, and Ken yielded to the slight pull in an exaggerated way, pretended that the punishment was extraordinarily painful, and writhed under her hand with a most pitiable grimace, which showed his fine white teeth. His face was near to hers, and speaking directly into it, in all its nearness, she went on:

'Because if you do it again and don't mend your ways, you naughty boy, I'll banish you from the city – do you know that? I'll send you to some quiet place in the Taunus where, though Nature is very beautiful, there are no temptations and you can teach the farmers' children English. This time, go and sleep it off, you scamp!' And she let go of his ear, took leave of the nearness of his face, gave Anna one more pale, crafty look, and left.

A week later something extraordinary happened, which astonished, touched, and perplexed Anna von Tümmler in the highest degree – perplexed her because, though she rejoiced in it for her mother's sake, she did not know whether to regard it as fortunate or unfortunate. About ten o'clock in the morning the chambermaid brought a message asking her to see the mistress in her bedroom. Since the little family breakfasted separately – Eduard first, then Anna, the lady of the house last – she had not yet seen her mother that day. Rosalie was lying on the chaise-longue in her bedroom, covered with a light cashmere shawl, a little pale, but with her nose flushed. With a smile of rather studied languor, she nodded to her daughter as she came stumping in, but said nothing, so that Anna was forced to ask:

'What is it, Mama? you aren't ill, are you?'

'Oh no, my child, don't be alarmed, I'm not ill at all. I was very much tempted, instead of sending for you, to go to you myself and greet you. But I am a little in need of coddling, rest seems to be indicated, as it sometimes is for us women.'

'Mama! What do you mean?'

Then Rosalie sat up, flung her arms round her daughter's neck, drew her down beside her on to the edge of the chaise-longue, and, cheek to cheek with her, whispered in her ear, quickly, blissfully, all in a breath:

'Victory, Anna, victory, it has come back to me, come back to me after such a long interruption, absolutely naturally and just as it should be for a mature, vigorous woman! Dear child, what a miracle! What a miracle great, beneficent nature has wrought in me, how she has blessed my faith! For I believed, Anna, and did not laugh, and so now kind Nature rewards me and takes back what she seemed to have done to my body, she proves that it was a mistake and re-establishes harmony between soul and body, but not in the way that you wished it to happen. Not with the soul obediently letting the body act upon it and translate it to the dignified estate of matronhood, but the other way round, the other way round, dear child, with the soul proving herself mistress over the body. Congratulate me, darling, there is reason for it! I am a woman again, a whole human being again, a functioning female, I can feel worthy of the youthful manhood that has bewitched me, and no longer need lower my eyes before it with a feeling of impotence. The rod of life with which it struck me has reached not my soul alone but my body too and has made it a flowing fountain again. Kiss me, my darling child, call me blessed, as blessed I am, and, with me, praise the miraculous power of great, beneficent Nature!'

She sank back, closed her eyes, and smiled contentedly, her nose very red.

'Dear, sweet Mama,' said Anna, willing enough to rejoice with her, yet sick at heart, 'this is truly a great, a moving event, it testifies to the richness of your nature, which was already evident in the freshness of your feeling and now gives that feeling such power over your bodily functions. As you see, I am entirely of your opinion – that what has happened to you physically is psychological in origin, is the product of your youthfully strong feeling. Whatever I may at times have said about such things, you must not think me such a Philistine that I deny the psychological any power over the physical and hold that the latter has the last word in the relationship between them. Each is dependent upon the other – that much even I know about Nature and its unity. However much the soul may be subject to the body's circumstances – what the soul, for its part, can do to the body often verges on the miraculous, and your case is one of the most splendid examples of it. Yet, permit me to say that this beautiful, animating event, of which you are so proud – and rightly, you may certainly be proud of it – on me, constituted as I am, it does not make the same sort of impression that it makes on you. In my opinion, it does not change things much, my best of mothers, and it does not appreciably increase my admiration for your nature – or for Nature in general. Club-footed, ageing spinster that I am, I have every reason not to attach much importance to the physical. Your freshness of feeling, precisely in contrast to your physical age, seemed to me splendid enough, enough of a triumph – it almost seemed to me a purer victory of the soul than what has happened now, than this transformation of the indestructible youth of your heart into an organic phenomenon.'

'Say no more, my poor child! What you call my freshness of feeling, and now insist that you enjoyed, you represented to me, more or less bluntly, as sheer folly, through which I was making myself ridiculous, and you advised me to retreat into a motherly dowagerhood, to make my feeling maternal. Well, it would have been a little too early for that, don't you think so now, my pet? Nature has made her voice heard against it. She has made my feeling her concern and has unmistakably shown me that it need not be ashamed before her nor before the blooming young manhood which is its object. And do you really mean to say that does not change things much?'

'What I mean, my dear, wonderful Mama, is certainly not that I did not respect Nature's voice. Nor, above all things, do I wish to spoil your joy in her decree. You cannot think that of me. When I said that what had happened did not change things much, I was referring to outward realities, to the practical aspects of the situation, so to speak. When I advised you –

when I fondly wished that you might conquer yourself, that it might not even be hard for you to confine your feeling for the young man – forgive me for speaking of him so coolly – for our friend Keaton, rather, to maternal love, my hope was based on the fact that he could be your son. That fact, you will agree, has not changed, and it cannot but determine the relationship between you on either side, on your side and on his too.'

'And on his too. You speak of two sides, but you mean only his. You do not believe that he could love me except, at best, as a son?'

'I will not say that, dearest and best Mama.'

'And how could you say it, Anna, my true-hearted child! Remember, you have no right to, you have not the necessary authority to judge in matters of love. You have little perception in that realm, because you gave up early, dear heart, and turned your eyes away from such things. Intellect offered you a substitute for Nature – good for you, that is all very fine! But how can you undertake to judge and to condemn me to hopelessness? You have no power of observation and do not see what I see, do not perceive the signs which indicate to me that his feeling is ready to respond to mine. Do you mean to say that at such moments he is only trifling with me? Would you rather consider him insolent and heartless than to grant me the hope that his feeling may correspond to mine? What would be so extraordinary in that? For all your aloofness from love, you cannot be unaware that a young man very often prefers a mature woman to an inexperienced girl, to a silly little goose. Naturally, a nostalgia for his mother may enter in – as, on the other hand, maternal feelings may play a part in an elder woman's passion for a young man. But why say this to you? I have a distinct impression that you recently said something very like it to me.'

'Really? In any case, you are right, Mama, I agree with you completely in what you say.'

'Then you must not call me past hope, especially today, when Nature has recognized my feeling. You must not, despite my grey hair, at which, so it seems to me, you are looking. Yes, unfortunately I am quite grey. It was a mistake that I didn't begin dyeing my hair long ago. I can't suddenly start now, though Nature has to a certain extent authorized me to. But I can do something for my face, not only by massage, but also by using a little rouge. I don't suppose you children would be shocked?'

'Of course not, Mama! Eduard will never notice, if you go about it a little discreetly. And I . . . though I think that artificiality will not go too well with your deep feeling for Nature, why, it is certainly no sign against Nature to help her out a little in such an accepted fashion.'

'So you agree with me? After all, the thing is to prevent a fondness for being mothered from playing too large a part, from predominating, in Ken's feeling. That would be contrary to my hopes. Yes, dear, loyal child, this heart – I know that you do not like talking and hearing about the "heart" – but my heart is swollen with pride and joy, with the thought of how very differently I shall meet his youth, with what a different self-confidence. Your mother's heart is swollen with happiness and life!'

'How beautiful, dearest Mama! And how charming of you to let me share in your great happiness! I share it, share it from my heart, you cannot doubt it, even if I say that a certain concern intrudes even as I rejoice with you – that is very like me, isn't it? – certain scruples – *practical* scruples, to use the word which, for want of a better, I used before. You speak of your hope, and of all that justifies you in entertaining it – in my opinion, what justifies it above all is simply your own lovable self. But you fail to define your hope more precisely, to tell me what its goal is, what expression it expects to find in the reality of life. Is it your intention to marry again? To make Ken Keaton our stepfather? To stand before the altar with him? It may be cowardly of me, but as the difference in your ages is equivalent to that between a mother and her son, I am a little afraid of the astonishment which such a step would arouse.'

Frau von Tümmler stared at her daughter.

'No,' she answered, 'the idea is new to me, and if it will calm your apprehensions, I can assure you that I do not entertain it. No. Anna, you silly thing, I have no intention of giving you and Eduard a twenty-four-year-old stepfather. How odd of you to speak so stiffly and piously of "standing before the altar"!'

Anna remained silent; her eyelids lowered a little, she gazed past her mother into space.

'Hope –' said her mother, 'who can define it, as you want me to? Hope is hope – how can you expect that it will inquire into practical goals, as you put it? What Nature has granted me is so beautiful that I can only expect something beautiful from it, but I cannot tell you how I think that it will come, how it will be realized, and where it will lead. That is what hope is like. It simply doesn't think – least of all about "standing before the alatar".'

Anna's lips were slightly twisted. Between them she spoke softly, as if involuntarily and despite herself:

'That would be a comparatively reasonable idea.'

Frau von Tümmler stared in bewilderment at her crippled daughter – who did not look at her – and tried to read her expression.

'Anna!' she cried softly. 'What are you thinking, what does this behaviour mean? Allow me to say that I simply don't recognize you! Which of us, I ask you, is the artist – I or you? I should never have thought that you could be so far behind your mother in broad-mindedness – and not only behind her, but behind the times in its freer manners! In your art you are so advanced and profess the very latest thing, so that a simple person like myself can scarcely follow you. But morally you seem to be living God knows when, in the old days, before the war. After all, we have the republic now, we have freedom, and ideas have changed very much, towards informality, towards laxity, it is apparent everywhere, even in the smallest things. For example, nowadays young men consider it good form to let their handkerchiefs, of which you used to see only a little corner protruding from the breast pocket, hang far out – why, they let them hang out like flags, half the handkerchief; it is clearly a sign, even a conscious declaration, of a republican relaxation of manners. Eduard lets his handkerchief hang out too, in the way that is the fashion, and I see it with a certain satisfaction.'

'Your observation is very fine, Mama. But I think that, in Eduard's case, your handkerchief symbol is not to be taken too personally. You yourself often say that the young man – for such by this time he has really become – is a good deal like our father, the lieutenant-colonel. Perhaps it is not quite tactful of me to bring Papa into our conversation and our thoughts at the moment. And yet –'

'Anna, your father was an excellent officer and he fell on the field of honour, but he was a rake and a Don Juan to the very end, the most striking example of the elastic limits of a man's sexual life, and I constantly had to shut both eyes on his account. So I cannot consider it particularly tactless that you should refer to him.'

'All the better, Mama – if I may say so. But Papa was a gentleman and an officer, and he lived, despite all that you call his rakishness, according to certain concepts of honour, which mean very little to me, but many of which Eduard, I believe, has inherited. He not only resembles his father outwardly, in figure and features. In certain circumstances, he will involuntarily react in his father's fashion.'

'Which means – in what circumstances?'

'Dear Mama, let me be perfectly frank, as we have always been with each other! It is certainly conceivable that a relationship such as you vaguely anticipate between Ken Keaton and yourself could remain completely concealed and unknown to society. However, what with your delightful impulsiveness and your charming inability to dissimulate and bury the secrets of your heart, I have my doubts as to how well it could be carried off. Let some young whipper-snapper make mocking allusions to our Eduard, give him to understand that it is known that his mother is – how do people put it? – leading a loose life, and he would strike him, he would box the fellow's ears, and who knows what dangerous kind of official nonsense might result from his chivalry?'

'For heaven's sake, Anna! What things you imagine! You are excruciating. I know you are doing it out of solicitude, but it is cruel, your solicitude, as cruel as small children condemning their mother . . .'

Rosalie cried a little. Anna helped her to dry her tears, affectionately guiding the hand in which she held her handkerchief.

'Dearest, best Mama, forgive me! How reluctant I am to hurt you! But you – don't talk of children condemning! Do you think I would not look – no, not tolerantly, that sounds too supercilious – but reverently, and with the tenderest concern, on what you are determined to consider your happiness? And Eduard – I hardly know how I happened to speak of him – it was just because of his republican handkerchief. It is not a question of us, nor only of people in general. It is a question of you, Mama. Now, you said that you were broad-minded. But are you, really? We were speaking of Papa and of certain traditional concepts by which he lived, and which, as he saw them, were not infringed by the infidelities to upset you with. That you forgave him for them again and again was because, fundamentally, as you must realize, you were of the same opinion – you were, in other words, conscious that they had nothing to do with real dèbauchery. He was not born for that, he was no libertine at heart. No more are you. I, at most, as an artist, have deviated from type in that respect, but then again, in another way, I am unfitted to make any use of my emancipation, of my being morally *déclassée*.'

'My poor child,' Frau von Tümmler interrupted her, 'don't speak of yourself so gloomily!'

'As if I were speaking of myself at all!' answered Anna. 'I am speaking of you, of you, it is for you that I am so deeply concerned. Because, for you, it would really be debauchery to do what, for Papa, the man about town, was simply dissipation, doing violence neither to himself nor to the judgement of society. Harmony between body and soul is certainly a good and necessary thing, and you are proud and happy because Nature, your beloved Nature, has granted it to you in a way that is almost miraculous. But harmony between one's life and one's innate moral convictions is, in the end, even more necessary, and where it is disrupted the only result can be emotional disruption, and that means unhappiness. Don't you feel that this is true? That you would be living in opposition to yourself if you made a reality out of what you now dream? Fundamentally, you are just as much bound as Papa was to certain concepts, and the destruction of that allegiance would be no less than the destruction of your own self . . . I say it as I feel it – with anxiety. Why does that word come to my lips again – "destruction"? I know that I have used it once before, in anguish, and I have had the sensation more than once. Why must I keep feeling as if this whole visitation, whose happy victim you are, had something to do with destruction? I will confess something to you. Recently, just a few weeks ago, after our talk when we drank tea late that night in my room and you were so excited, I was tempted to go to Dr Oberloskamp, who took care of Eduard when he had jaundice, and of me once, when I had laryngitis and couldn't swallow – you never need a doctor; I was tempted, I say, to talk to him about you and about what you had confided to me, simply for the sake of setting my mind at rest on your account. But I rejected the idea, I rejected it almost at once, out of pride, Mama, out of pride in you and for you, and because it seemed to me degrading to turn your experience over to a medical man who, with the help of God, is competent for jaundice and laryngitis, but not for deep human ills. In my opinion, there are sicknesses that are too good for the doctor.'

'I am grateful to you for both, my dear child,' said Rosalie, 'for the concern which impelled you to talk with Oberloskamp about me, and for your having repressed the impulse. But then what can induce you to make the slightest connexion between what you call my visitation – this Easter of my womanhood, what the soul has done to my body – and the concept of sickness? Is happiness – sickness? Certainly, it is not lightmindedness either, it is living, living in joy and sorrow, and to live is to hope – the hope for which I can give no explanation to your reason.'

'I do not ask for any explanation from you, dearest Mama.'

'Then go now, child. Let me rest. As you know, a little quiet seclusion is indicated for us women on such crowning days.'

Anna kissed her mother and stumped out of the bedroom. Once separated, the two women reflected on the conversation they had just held. Anna had neither said, nor been able to say, all that was on her mind. How long, she wondered, would what her mother called 'the Easter of her womanhood', this touching revivification, endure in her? And Ken, if, as was perfectly plausible, he succumbed to her – how long would *that* last? How constantly her mother, in her late love, would be cast into trepidation by every younger woman, would have to tremble from the very first day, for his faithfulness, even his respect! At least it was to the good that she did not conceive of happiness simply as pleasure and joy but as life with its suffering. For Anna uneasily foresaw much suffering in what her mother dreamed.

For her part, Frau Rosalie was more deeply impressed by her daughter's remonstrances than she had allowed to appear. It was not so much the thought that, under certain circumstances, Eduard might have to risk his young life for her honour – the romantic idea, though she had wept over it, really made her heart beat with pride. But Anna's doubts of her 'broad-mindedness', what she had said about debauchery and the necessary harmony between one's life and one's moral convictions, preoccupied the good soul all through her day of rest and she could not but admit that her daughter's doubts were justified, that her views contained a good part of truth. Neither, to be sure, could she suppress her most heartfelt joy at the thought of meeting her young beloved again under such new circumstances. But what her shrewd daughter had said about 'living in contradiction to herself', she remembered and pondered over, and she strove in her soul to associate the idea of renunciation with the idea of happiness. Yes, could not renunciation itself be happiness, if it were not a miserable necessity but were practised in freedom and in conscious equality? Rosalie reached the conclusion that it could be.

Ken presented himself at the Tümmlers' three days after Rosalie's great physiological reassurance, read and spoke English with Eduard, and stayed for dinner. Her happiness at the sight of his pleasant, boyish face, his fine teeth, his broad shoulders and narrow hips, shone from her sweet eyes, and their sparkling animation justified, one might say, the touch of artificial red which heightened her cheeks and without which, indeed, the pallor of her face would have been in contradiction to that joyous fire. This time, and thereafter every time Ken came, she had a way, each week, of taking his hand when she greeted him and drawing his body close to hers, at the same time looking earnestly, luminously, and significantly into his eyes, so that Anna had the impression that she very much wished, and indeed was going, to tell the young man of the experience her nature had undergone. Absurd apprehension! Of course nothing of that sort occurred, and all through the rest of the evening the attitude of the lady of the house towards her young guest was a serene and settled kindliness from which both the affected motherliness with which she had once teased her daughter, as well as any bashfulness and nervousness, any painful humility, were gratifyingly absent.

Keaton, who to his satisfaction had long been aware that, even such as he was, he had made a conquest of this grey-haired but charming European woman, hardly knew what to make of the change in her behaviour. His respect for her had, quite understandably, diminished when he became aware of her weakness; the latter, on the other hand, had in turn attracted and excited his masculinity; his simple nature felt sympathetically drawn to hers, and he considered that such beautiful eyes, with their youthful penetrating gaze, quite made up for fifty years and ageing hands. The idea of entering into an affair with her, such as he had been carrying on for some time – not, as it happened, with Amélie Lützenkirchen or Louise Pfingsten, but with another woman of the same set, whom Rosalie had never thought of – was by no means new to him, and, as Anna observed, he had begun, at least now and again, to change his manner towards his pupil's mother, to speak to her in a tone that was provocatively flirtatious.

This, the good fellow soon found, no longer seemed quite to come off. Despite the handclasp by which, at the beginning of each meeting, she drew him close to her, so that their bodies almost touched, and despite her intimate, searching gaze into his eyes, his experiments in this direction encountered a friendly but firm dignity which put him in his place, forbade any establishment of what he wished to establish, and, instantly dispelling his pretensions, reduced his attitude to one of submission. The meaning of the repeated experience escaped him. 'Is she in love with me or not?' he asked himself, and blamed her repulses and her reprobation on the presence of her children, the lame girl and the schoolboy. But his experience was no different when it happened that he was alone with her for a time in a drawing-room corner – and no different when he changed the character of his little advances, abandoning all quizzicalness and giving them a seriously tender, a pressing, almost passionate tone. Once, using the unrolled palatal 'r' which so delighted everyone, he tried calling her 'Rosalie' in a warm voice – which, simply as a form of address, was, in his American view, not even a particular liberty. But, though for an instant she had blushed hotly, she had almost immediately risen and left him, and had given him neither a word nor a look during the rest of that evening.

The winter, which had proved to be mild, bringing hardly any cold weather and snow, but all the more rain instead, also ended early that year. Even in February there were warm, sunny days redolent of spring. Tiny leaf buds ventured out on branches here and there. Rosalie, who had lovingly greeted the snowdrops in her garden, could rejoice far earlier than usual, almost prematurely, in the daffodils – and, very soon after, in the short-stemmed crocuses too, which sprouted everywhere in the front garden of villas and in the Palace Garden, and before which passers-by halted to point them out to one another and to feast on their particoloured profusion.

'Isn't it remarkable,' said Frau von Tümmler to her daughter, 'how much they resemble the autumn colchicum? It's practically the same flower! End and beginning – one could mistake them for each other, they are so alike – one could think one was back in autumn in the presence of a crocus, and believe in spring when one saw the last flower of the year.'

'Yes, a slight confusion,' answered Anna. 'Your old friend Mother Nature has a charming propensity for the equivocal and for mystification in general.'

'You are always quick to speak against her, you naughty child, and where I succumb to wonder, you mock. Let well enough alone; you cannot laugh me out of my tender feeling for her, for my beloved Nature, least of all now, when she is just bringing in my season – I call it mine because the season in which we were born is peculiarly akin to us, and we to it. You are an Advent child, and you can truly say that you arrived under a good sign – almost under the dear sign of Christmas. You must feel a pleasant affinity between yourself and that season, which, even though cold, makes us think of joy and warmth. For really, in my experience, there is a sympathetic relation between ourselves and the season that produced us. Its return brings something that confirms and strengthens, that renews our lives, just as spring has always done for me – not because it is spring, or the prime of the year, as the poets call it, a season everyone loves, but because I personally belong to it, and I feel that it smiles at me quite personally.'

'It does indeed, dearest Mama,' answered the child of winter. 'And rest assured that I shan't speak a single word against it!'

But it must be said that the buoyancy of life which Rosalie was accustomed – or believed she was accustomed – to receive from the approach and unfolding of 'her' season was not, even as she spoke of it, manifesting itself quite as usual. It was almost as if the moral resolutions which her conversation with her daughter had inspired in her, and to which she so steadfastly adhered, went against her nature, as if, despite them, or indeed because of them, she were 'living in contradiction to herself'. This was precisely the impression that Anna received, and the limping girl reproached herself for having persuaded her mother to a continence which her own liberal view of life in no sense demanded but which had seemed requisite to her only for the dear woman's peace of mind. What was more, she suspected herself of unacknowledged evil motives. She asked herself if she, who had once grievously longed for sensual pleasure, but had never experienced it, had not secretly begrudged it to her mother and hence had exhorted her to chastity by all sorts of trumped-up arguments. No, she could not believe it of herself, and yet what she saw troubled and burdened her conscience.

She saw that Rosalie, setting out on one of the walks she so loved, quickly grew tired, and that it was she who, inventing some household task that must be done, insisted on turning home after only half an hour or even sooner. She rested a great deal, yet despite this limitation of her physical activity, she lost weight, and Anna noticed with concern the thinness of her forearms when she happened to see them exposed. People no longer asked her at what fountain of youth she had been drinking. There was an ominous, tired-looking blueness under her eyes, and the rouge which, in honour of the young man and of her recovery of full womanhood, she put on her cheeks created no very effective illusion against the yellowish pallor of her complexion. But as she dismissed any inquiries as to how she felt with a cheerful, 'I feel quite well – why should you think otherwise?' Fräulein von Tümmler gave up the idea of asking Dr Oberloskamp to investigate her mother's failing health. It was not only a feeling of guilt which led her to this decision; piety too played a part – the same piety that she had expressed when she said that there were sicknesses which were too good to be taken to a doctor.

So Anna was all the more delighted by the enterprise and confidence in her strength which Rosalie exhibited in connexion with a little plan that was agreed on between herself, her children, and Ken Keaton, who happened to be present one evening as they lingered over their wine. A month had not yet passed since the morning Anna had been called to her mother's bedroom to hear the wonderful news. Rosalie was as charming and gay as in the old days that evening, and she could have been considered the prime mover of the excursion on which they had agreed – unless Ken Keaton was to be given the credit, for it was his historical chatter that had led to the idea. He had talked about various castles and strongholds he had visited in the Duchy of Berg – of the Castle on the Wupper, of Bensberg, Ehreshoven, Gimhorn, Homburg, and Krottorf; and from these he went on to the Elector Carl Theodore, who, in the eighteenth century, had moved his court from Düsseldorf, first to Schwetzingen and then to Munich – but that had not prevented his Statthalter, a certain Count Grottstein, from embarking on all sorts of important architectural and horticultural projects here: it was under him that the Electoral Academy of Art was conceived, the Palace Garden was first laid out, and Jägerhof Castle was built – and, Eduard added, in the same year, so far as he knew, Holterhof Castle too, a little to the south of the city, near the village of the same name. Of course, Holterhof too, Keaton confirmed, and then, to his own amazement, was obliged to admit that he had never laid eyes on that creation of the late Rococo nor even visited its park, celebrated as it was, which extended all the way to the Rhine. Frau von Tümmler and Anna had, of course, taken the air there once or twice, but they had never succeeded in viewing the interior of the charmingly situated castle, nor had Eduard.

'*War et nit all jibt!*' said the lady of the house, using, in jocular disapproval, the local equivalent of 'Will wonders never cease!' It was always an indication of good spirits when she dropped into dialect. 'Fine Düsseldorfers you are,' she added, 'the lot of you!' One had never been there at all, and the others had not seen the interior of the jewel of a castle which every tourist made it a point to be shown through! 'Children,' she cried, 'this has gone on too long, we must not allow it. An excursion to Holterhof – for the four of us! And we will make it within the next few days! It is so beautiful now, the season is so enchanting and the barometer is steady. The buds will be opening in the park, it may well be pleasanter in its spring array than in the heat of summer, when Anna and I went walking there. Suddenly I feel a positive nostalgia for the black swans which – you remember, Anna – glided over the moats in such melancholy pride with their red bills and oar-feet. How they disguised their appetite in condescension when we fed them! We must take along some bread for them ... Let's see, today is Friday – we will go Sunday, is that settled? Only Sunday would do for Eduard, and for Mr Keaton too, I imagine. Of course there will be a crowd out on Sunday, but that means nothing to me, I like mixing with people in their Sunday best, I share in their enjoyment, I like being where there's "something doing" – at the outdoor carnivals at Oberkassel, when it smells of fried food and the children are licking away at red sugar-sticks and, in front of the circus tent, such fantastically vulgar people are tinkling and tootling and shouting. I find it marvellous. Anna thinks otherwise. She finds it sad. Yes you do, Anna – and you prefer the aristocratic sadness of the pair of black swans in the moat ... I have an inspiration, children – we'll go by water! The trip by land on the street railway is simply boring. Not a scrap of woods and hardly an open field. It's much more amusing by water, Father Rhine shall convey us. Eduard, will you see to getting the steamer timetable? Or, just a moment, if we want to be really luxurious, we'll indulge ourselves and hire a private motor-boat for the trip up the Rhine. Then we'll be quite by ourselves, like the black swans ... All that remains to be settled is whether we want to set sail in the morning or the afternoon.'

The consensus was in favour of the morning. Eduard thought that, in any case, he had heard that the castle was open to visitors only into the early hours of the afternoon. It should be Sunday morning, then. Under Rosalie's energetic urging, the arrangements were soon made and agreed on. It was Keaton who was designated to charter the motor-boat. They would meet again at the point of departure, the Rathaus quay, by the Water-gauge Clock, the day after tomorrow at nine.

And so they did. It was a sunny and rather windy morning. The quay was jammed with a crowd of pushing people who, with their children and their bicycles, were waiting to go aboard one of the white steamers of the Cologne-Düsseldorf Navigation Company. The chartered motor-boat lay ready for the Tümmlers and their companion. Its master, a man with rings in his ear-lobes, clean-shaven upper lip, and a reddish mariner's beard under his chin, helped the ladies aboard. The party had hardly seated themselves on the curved bench under the awning, which was supported by stanchions, before he got under way. The boat made good time against the current of the broad river, whose banks, incidentally, were utterly prosaic. The old castle tower, the crooked tower of the Lambertuskirche, the harbour installations, were left behind. More of the same sort of thing appeared beyond the next bend in the river – warehouses, factory buildings. Little by little, behind the stone jetties which extended from the shore into the river, the country became more rural. Hamlets, old fishing villages – whose names Eduard, and Keaton too, knew – lay, protected by dykes, before a flat landscape of meadows, fields, willow-bushes, and pools. So it would be, however many windings the river made, for a good hour and a half, until they reached their destination. But how right they had been, Rosalie exclaimed, to decide on the boat instead of covering the distance in a fraction of the time by the horrible route through the suburbs! She seemed to be heartily enjoying the elemental charm of the journey by water. Her eyes closed, she sang a snatch of some happy tune into the wind, which at moments was almost stormy: 'O water-wind, I love thee; lovest thou me, O water-wind?' Her face, which had grown thinner, looked very appealing under the little felt hat with the feather, and the grey-and-red-checked coat she had on – of light woollen material with a turn-down collar – was very becoming to her. Anna and Eduard had also worn coats for the voyage, and only Keaton, who sat between mother and daughter, contented himself with a grey sweater under his tweed jacket. His handkerchief hung out, and, suddenly opening her eyes and turning, Rosalie stuffed it deep into his breast pocket.

'Propriety, propriety, young man!' she said, shaking her head in decorous reproof.

He smiled: 'Thank you,' and then wanted to know what song it was she had just been singing.

'Song?' she asked. 'Was I singing? That was only singsong, not a song.' And she closed her eyes again and hummed, her lips scarcely moving: 'How I love thee, O water-wind!'

Then she began chattering through the noise of the motor, and – often having to hold on to her hat, which the wind was trying to tear from her still abundant, wavy grey hair – expatiated on how it would be possible to extend the Rhine trip beyond Holterhof, to Leverkusen and Cologne, and from there on past Bonn to Godesberg and Bad Honnef at the foot of the Siebengebirge. It was beautiful there, the trim watering-place on the Rhine, amid vineyards and orchards, and it had an alkaline mineral spring that was very good for rheumatism. Anna looked at her; she knew that her mother now suffered intermittently from lumbago, and had once or twice considered going to Godesberg or Honnef with her in the early summer, to take the waters. There was something almost involuntary in the way she chattered on about the beneficial spring, catching her breath as she spoke into the wind; it made Anna think that her mother was even now not free from the shooting pains that characterize the disease.

After an hour they breakfasted on a few ham sandwiches and washed them down with port from little travelling-cups. It was half past eleven when the boat made fast to a flimsy landing-stage, inadequate for larger vessels, which was built out into the river near the castle and the park. Rosalie paid off the boatman, as they had decided that it would after all be easier to make the return journey by land, on the street railway. The park did not extend quite to the river. They had to follow a rather damp footpath across a meadow, before a venerable, seigniorial landscape, well cared for and well clipped, received them. From an elevated circular terrace, with benches in yew arbours, avenues of magnificent trees, most of them already in bud, though many shoots were still hidden under their shiny brown covers, led in various directions – finely gravelled promenades, often arched over by meeting branches, between rows, and sometimes double rows, of beeches, yews, lindens, horse-chestnuts, tall elms. Rare and curious trees, brought from distant countries, were also to be seen, planted singly on stretches of lawn – strange conifers, fern-leafed beeches, and Keaton recognized the Californian sequoia and the swamp cypress with its supplementary breathing-roots.

Rosalie took no interest in these curiosities. Nature, she considered, must be familiar, or it did not speak to the heart. But the beauty of the park did not seem to hold much charm for her. Scarcely glancing up now and again at the proud tree-trunks, she walked silently on, with Eduard at her side, behind his young tutor and the hobbling Anna – who, however, soon hit on a manoeuvre to change the arrangement. She stopped and summoned her brother to tell her the names of the avenue they were following and of the winding footpath that crossed it just there. For all these paths and avenues had old, traditional names, such as 'Fan Avenue', 'Trumpet Avenue', and so on. Then, as they moved on, Anna kept Eduard beside her and left Ken behind with Rosalie. He carried her coat, which she had taken off, for not a breath of wind stirred in the park and it was much warmer than it had been on the water. The spring sun shone gently through the high branches, dappled the roads, and played on the faces of the four, making them blink. In her finely tailored brown suit, which closely sheathed her slight, youthful figure, Frau von Tümmler walked at Ken's side, now and again casting a veiled, smiling look at her coat as it hung over his arm. 'There they are!' she cried, and pointed to the pair of black swans; for they were now walking along the poplar-bordered moat, and the birds, aware of the approaching visitors, were gliding nearer, at a stately pace, across the slightly scummy water. 'How beautiful they are! Anna, do you recognize them? How majestically they carry their necks! Where is the bread for them?' Keaton pulled it out of his pocket, wrapped in newspaper, and handed it to her. It was warm from his body, and she took some of the bread and began to eat it.

'But it's stale and hard,' he cried, with a gesture that came too late to stop her.

'I have good teeth,' she answered.

One of the swans, however, pushing close against the bank, spread its dark wings and beat the air with them, stretching out its neck and hissing angrily up at her. They laughed at its jealousy, but at the same time felt a little afraid. Then the birds received their rightful due. Rosalie threw them the stale bread, piece after piece, and, swimming slowly back and forth, they accepted it with imperturbable dignity.

'Yet I fear,' said Anna as they walked on, 'that the old devil won't soon forget your robbing him of his food. He displayed a well-bred pique the whole time.'

'Not at all,' answered Rosalie. 'He was only afraid for a moment that I would eat it all and leave none for him. After that, he must have relished it all the more, since I relished it.'

They came to the castle, to the smooth circular pond which mirrored it and in which, to one side, lay a miniature island bearing a solitary poplar. On the expanse of gravel before the flight of steps leading to the gracefully winged structure, whose considerable dimensions its extreme daintiness seemed to efface, and whose pink façade was crumbling a little, stood a number of people who, as they waited for the eleven o'clock conducted tour, were passing the time by examining the armorial pediment with its figures, the clock, heedless of time and supported by an angel, which surmounted it, the stone wreaths above the tall white portals, and comparing them with the descriptions in their guidebooks. Our friends joined them, and, like them, looked at the charmingly decorated feudal architecture, up to the *œils-de-bœuf* in the slate-coloured garret storey. Figures clad with mythological scantiness, Pan and his nymphs, stood on pedestals beside the long windows, flaking away like the four sandstone lions which, with sullen expressions, their paws crossed, flanked the steps and the ramp.

Keaton was enthusiastic over so much history. He found everything 'splendid' and 'excitingly continental'. Oh dear, to think of his own prosaic country across the Atlantic! There was none of this sort of crumbling aristocratic grace over there, for there had been no Electors and Landgraves, able, in absolute sovereignty, to indulge their passion for magnificence, to their own honour and to the honour of culture. However, his attitude towards the culture which, in its dignity, had not moved on with time, was not so reverent but that, to the amusement of the waiting crowd, he impudently seated himself astride the back of one of the sentinel lions, though it was equipped with a sharp spike, like certain toy horses whose rider can be removed. He clasped the spike in front of him with both hands, pretended, with cries of 'Hi!' and 'Giddap!', that he was giving the beast the spurs, and really could not have presented a more attractive picture of youthful high spirits. Anna and Eduard avoided looking at their mother.

Then bolts creaked, and Keaton hastened to dismount from his steed, for the caretaker, a man wearing military breeches and with his left sleeve empty and rolled up – to all appearances a retired non-commissioned officer whose service injury had been compensated by this quiet post – swung open the central portal and admitted the visitors. He stationed himself in the lofty doorway and, letting them file past him, not only distributed entrance tickets from a small pad, but managed too, with his one hand, to tear them half across. Meanwhile, he had already begun to talk; speaking out of his crooked mouth in a hoarse, gravelly voice, he rattled off the information which he had learned by rote and repeated a thousand times: that the sculptured decoration on the façade was by an artist whom the Elector had summoned for the purpose from Rome; that the castle and the park were the work of a French architect; and that the structure was the most important example of Rococo on the Rhine, though it exhibited traces of the transition to the Louis Seize style; that the castle contained fifty-five rooms and had cost eight hundred thousand taler – and so on.

The vestibule exhaled a musty chill. Here, standing ready in rows, were large boat-shaped felt slippers, into which, amid much snickering from the ladies, the party were obliged to step for the protection of the precious parquets, which were, indeed, almost the chief objects of interest in the apartments dedicated to pleasure, through which, awkwardly shuffling and sliding, the party followed their droning one-armed guide. Of different patterns in the various rooms, the central intarsias represented all sorts of star shapes and floral fantasies. Their gleaming surfaces received the reflections of the visitors, of the cambered state furniture, while tall mirrors, set between gilded pillars wreathed in garlands and tapestry fields of flowered silk framed in gilded listels, repeatedly interchanged the images of the crystal chandeliers, the amorous ceiling paintings, the medallions and emblems of the hunt and music over the doors, and, despite a great many blind-spots, still succeeded in evoking the illusion of rooms opening into one another as far as the eye could see. Unbridled luxuriousness, unqualified insistence on gratification, were to be read in the cascades of elegant ornamentation, of gilded scrollwork, restricted only by the inviolable style and taste of the period that had produced them. In the round banquet room, around which, in niches, stood Apollo and the Muses, the inlaid woodwork of the floor gave place to marble, like that which sheathed the walls. Rosy *putti* drew back a painted drapery from the pierced cupola, through which the daylight fell, and from the galleries, as the caretaker said, music had once floated down to the banqueters below.

Ken Keaton was walking beside Frau von Tümmler, with his hand under her elbow. Every American takes his lady across the street in this fashion. Separated from Anna and Eduard, among strangers, they followed close behind the caretaker, who hoarsely, in stilted textbook phrases, unreeled his text and told the party what they were seeing. They were not, he informed them, seeing everything that was to be seen. Of the castle's fifty-five rooms, he went on – and, following his routine, dropped for a moment into vapid insinuation, though his face, with its crooked mouth, remained wholly aloof from the playfulness of his words – not all were simply open without further ado. The gentry of those days had a great taste for jokes and secrets and mysteries, for hiding-places, in the background, retreats that, offering opportunities, were accessible through mechanical tricks – such as this one here, for example. And he stopped beside a pier glass, which, in response to his pressing upon a spring, slid aside, surprising the sightseers by a view of a narrow circular staircase with delicately latticed banisters. Immediately to the left, on a pedestral at its foot, stood an armless three-quarters torso of a man with a wreath of berries in his hair and kirtled with a spurious festoon of leaves; leaning back a little, he smiled down into space over his goat's beard, priapic and welcoming. There were ah's and oh's. 'And so on,' said the guide, as he said each time, and returned the trick mirror to its place. 'And so too,' he said, walking on; and made a tapestry panel, which had nothing to distinguish it from the others, open as a secret door and disclose a passageway leading into darkness and exhaling an odour of mould. 'That's the sort of thing they liked,' said the one-armed caretaker. 'Other times, other manners,' he added, with sententious stupidity, and continued the tour.

The felt boats were not easy to keep on one's feet. Frau von Tümmler lost one of hers; it slid some distance away over the smooth floor, and while Keaton laughingly retrieved it and, kneeling, put it on her foot again, they were overtaken by the party of sightsers. Again he put his hand under her elbow, but, with a dreamy smile, she remained standing where she was, looking after the party as it disappeared into further rooms; then, still supported by his hand, she turned and hurriedly ran her fingers over the tapestry, where it had opened.

'You aren't doing it right,' he whispered. 'Let me. It was here.' He found the spring, the door responded, and the mouldy air of the secret passageway enveloped them as they advanced a few steps. It was dark around them. With a sigh drawn from the uttermost depths of her being Rosalie flung her arms round the young man's neck; and he too happily embraced her trembling form. 'Ken, Ken,' she stammered, her face against his throat, 'I love you, I love you, and you know it, I haven't been able to hide it from you completely, and you, and you, do you love me too, a little, only a little, tell me, can you love me with your youth, as Nature has bestowed it on me to love you in my grey age? Yes? yes? Your mouth then, oh, at last, your young mouth, for which I have hungered, your dear lips, like this, like this – Can I kiss? Tell me, can I, my sweet awakener? I can do everything, as you can. Ken, love is strong, a miracle, so it comes and works great miracles. Kiss me, darling! I have hungered for your lips, oh how much, for I must tell you that my poor head slipped into all sorts of sophistries, like thinking that broad-mindedness and libertinism were not for me, and that the con-tradiction between my way of life and my innate convictions threatened to destroy me. Oh, Ken, it was the sophistries that almost destroyed me, and my hunger for you ... It is you, it is you at last, this is your hair, this is your mouth, this breath comes from your nostrils, the arms that I know are round me, this is your body's warmth, that I relished and the swan was angry...'

A little more, and she would have sunk to the ground before him. But he held her, and drew her along the passage, which grew a little lighter. Steps descended to the open round arch of a door, behind which murky light fell from above on an alcove whose tapestries were worked with billing pairs of doves. In the alcove stood a sort of causeuse beside which a carved Cupid with blindfolded eyes held a thing like a torch. There, in the musty dampness, they sat down.

'Ugh, it smells of death,' Rosalie shuddered against his shoulder. 'How sad, Ken my darling, that we have to be here amid this decay. It was in kind Nature's lap, fanned by her airs, in the sweet breath of jasmines and alders, that I dreamed it should be, it was there that I should have kissed you for the first time, and not in this grave! Go away, stop it, you devil, I will be yours, but not in this mould. I will come to you tomorrow, in your room, tomorrow morning, perhaps even tonight. I'll arrange it, I'll play a trick on my would-be-wise Anna . . .' He made her promise. And indeed they felt too that they must rejoin the others, either by going on or by retracing their steps. Keaton decided in favour of going on. They left the dead pleasure chamber by another door, again there was a dark passageway, it turned, mounted, and they came to a rusty gate, which, in response to Ken's strenuous pushing and tugging, shakily gave way and which was so overgrown outside with leathery vines and creepers that they could hardly force their way through. The open air received them. There was a plash of waters; cascades flowed down behind broad beds set with flowers of the early year, yellow narcissi. It was the back garden of the castle. The group of visitors was just approaching from the right; the caretaker had left them; Anna and her brother were bringing up the rear. The pair mingled with the foremost, who were beginning to scatter towards the fountains and in the direction of the wooded park. It was natural to stand there, look around, and go to meet the brother and sister. 'Where in the world have you been?' And: 'That's just what we want to ask *you*!' And: 'How could we possibly lose sight of one another so?' Anna and Eduard had even, they said, turned back to look for the lost couple, but in vain. 'After all, you couldn't have vanished from the face of the earth,' said Anna. 'No more than you,' Rosalie answered. None of them looked at the others.

Walking between rhododendrons, they circled the wing of the castle and arrived at the pond in front of it, which was quite close to the street-railway stop. If the boat trip upstream, following the windings of the Rhine, had been long, the return journey on the tram, speeding noisily through industrial districts and past colonies of workmen's houses, was correspondingly swift. The brother and sister now and again exchanged a word with each other or with their mother, whose hand Anna held for a while because she had seen her trembling. The party broke up in the city, near the Königsallee.

Frau von Tümmler did not go to Ken Keaton. That night, towards morning, a severe indisposition attacked her and alarmed the household. What, on its first return, had made her so proud, so happy, what she had extolled as a miracle of Nature and the sublime work of feeling, reappeared calamitously. She had had the strength to ring, but when her daughter and the maid came hurrying in, they found her lying in a faint in her blood.

The physician, Dr Oberloskamp, was soon on the spot. Reviving under his ministrations, she appeared astonished at his presence.

'What, Doctor, you here?' she said. 'I suppose Anna must have troubled you to come? But it is only "after the manner of women" with me.'

'At times, my dear Frau von Tümmler, these functions require a certain supervision,' the grey-haired doctor answered. To her daughter he declared categorically that the patient must be brought, preferably by ambulance, to the gynaecological hospital. The case demanded the most thorough examination – which, he added, might show that it was not dangerous.

Certainly, the metrorrhagias – the first one, of which he had only now heard, and this alarming recurrence – might well be caused by a myoma, which could easily be removed by an operation. In the hands of the director and chief surgeon of the hospital, Professor Muthesius, her dear mother would receive the most trustworthy care.

His recommendations were followed – without resistance on Frau von Tümmler's part, to Anna's silent amazement. Through it all, her mother only stared into the distance with her eyes very wide open.

The bimanual examination, performed by Muthesius, revealed a uterus far too large for the patient's age, abnormally thickened tissue in the tube, and, instead of an ovary already greatly reduced in size, a huge tumour. The curettage showed carcinoma cells, some of them characteristically ovarian; but others left no doubt that cancer cells were entering into full development in the uterus itself. All the malignancy showed signs of rapid growth.

The professor, a man with a double chin, a very red complexion, and water-blue eyes into which tears came easily – their presence having nothing whatever to do with the state of his emotions – raised his head from the microscope.

'Condition extensive, if you ask me,' he said to his assistant, whose name was Dr Knepperges. 'However, we will operate, Knepperges. Total extirpation, down to the last connective tissue in the true pelvis and to all lymphatic tissue, can in any case prolong life.'

But the picture that the opening of the abdominal cavity revealed, in the white light of the arc-lamps, to the doctors and nurses, was too terrible to permit any hope even of a temporary improvement. The time for that was long since past. Not only were all the pelvic organs already involved; the peritoneum too showed, to the naked eye alone, the murderous cell groups, all the glands of the lymphatic system were carcinomatously thickened, and there was no doubt that there were also foci of cancer cells in the liver.

'Just take a look at this mess, Knepperges,' said Muthesius. 'Presumably it exceeds your expectations.' That it also exceeded his own, he gave no sign. 'Ours is a noble art,' he added, his eyes filling with tears that meant nothing, 'but this is expecting a little too much of it. We can't cut all that away. If you think that you observe metastasis in both ureters, you observe correctly. Uremia cannot but soon set in. Mind you, I don't deny that the uterus itself is producing the voracious brood. Yet I advise you to adopt my opinion, which is that the whole story started from the ovary – that is, from immature ovarian cells which often remain there from birth and which, after the menopause, through heaven knows what process of stimulation, begin to develop malignantly. And then the organism, *post festum*, if you like, is shot through, drenched, inundated, with estrogen hormones, which leads to hormonal hyperplasia of the uteral mucous membrane, with concomitant haemorrhages.'

Knepperges, a thin, ambitiously conceited man, made a brief, covertly ironical bow of thanks for the lecture.

'Well, let's get on with it, *ut aliquid fieri videatur*,' said the professor. 'We must leave her what is essential for life, however steeped in melancholy the word is in this instance.'

Anna was waiting upstairs in the hospital room when her mother, who had been brought up by the elevator, returned on her stretcher and was put to bed by the nurses. During the process she awoke from her post-narcotic sleep and said indistinctly:

'Anna, my child, he hissed at me.'

'Who, dearest Mama?'

'The black swan.'

She was already asleep again. But she often remembered the swan during the next few weeks, his blood-red bill, the black beating of his wings. Her suffering was brief. Uremic coma soon plunged her into profound unconsciousness, and, double pneumonia developing, her exhausted heart could only hold out for a matter of days.

Just before the end, when it was but a few hours away, her mind cleared again. She raised her eyes to her daughter, who sat at her bedside, holding her hand.

'Anna,' she said, and was able to push the upper part of her body a little towards the edge of the bed, closer to her confidante, 'do you hear me?'

'Certainly I hear you, dear, dear Mama.'

'Anna, never say that Nature deceived me, that she is sardonic and cruel. Do not rail at her, as I do not. I am loth to go away – from you all, from life with its spring. But how should there be spring without death? Indeed, death is a great instrument of life, and if for me it borrowed the guise of resurrection, of the joy of love, that was not a lie, but goodness and mercy.'

Another little push, closer to her daughter, and a failing whisper:

'Nature – I have always loved her, and she – has been loving to her child.'

Rosalie died a gentle death, regretted by all who knew her.

Confessions
of
Felix Krull,
Confidence Man

TRANSLATED FROM THE GERMAN BY

Denver Lindley

Chapter One

As I take up my pen at leisure and in complete retirement – furthermore, in good health, though tired, so tired that I shall only be able to proceed by short stages and with frequent pauses for rest – as I take up my pen, then, to commit my confessions to this patient paper in my own neat and attractive handwriting, I am assailed by a brief misgiving about the educational background I bring to an intellectual enterprise of this kind. But since everything I have to record derives from my own immediate experience, errors, and passions, and since I am therefore in complete command of my material, the doubt can apply only to my tact and propriety of expression, and in my view these are less the product of study than of natural talent and a good home environment. This last has not been wanting, for I come of an upper-class though somewhat dissolute family; for several months my sister Olympia and I were looked after by a Fräulein from Vevey, though it is true she presently had to decamp because female contention arose between her and my mother, with my father as its object; my godfather Schimmelpreester, with whom I was on the most intimate terms, was a greatly admired artist whom everyone in our little town called 'Herr Professor' though it is doubtful whether he was officially entitled to this distinction; and my father, though corpulent, possessed much personal charm and always laid great stress on the choice and lucid use of words. He had French blood on his grandmother's side, had himself spent his student years in France, and, as he assured us, knew Paris like the palm of his hand. He was fond of sprinkling his conversation with French phrases such as '*c'est ça*', '*épatant*', '*parfaitement*', and the like. To the end of his days he remained a great favourite with the ladies. This only by way of preface and out of its proper sequence. As to my natural instinct for good form, that is something I have always been able to count on all too well, as my whole career of fraud will prove, and in the present literary undertaking I believe I can rely on it implicitly. Moreover I am resolved to employ the utmost frankness in my writing, without fear of being reproached for vanity or impudence. For what moral value or significance can attach to confessions written from any point of view except that of truthfulness?

The Rhine Valley brought me forth – that highly favoured and benign region, harsh neither in its climate nor in the quality of its soil, rich in cities and villages, peopled by a merry folk – it must be among the sweetest regions of the habitable globe. Here, sheltered from rough winds by the mountains of the Rhine district and happily exposed to the southern sun, flourish those famous communities whose very names make the winebibber's heart rejoice – Rauenthal, Johannisberg, Rüdesheim – and here, too, is that favoured town in which, only a few years after the glorious founding of the German Empire, I first saw the light of day. It lies slightly to the west of the bend the river makes at Mainz. With a population of some four thousand souls, it is renowned for its sparkling wines and is one of the principal ports of call for the steamers plying up and down the Rhine. Thus the gay city of Mainz was very near, as were the Taunus Baths, patronized by high society – Homburg, Langenschwalbach, and Schlangenbad. The last could be reached in a half-hour trip by narrow-gauge railway. How many summertime excursions we made, my parents, my sister Olympia, and I, by boat, by carriage, or on the train! Enticements lay in every direction, for nature and human ingenuity had everywhere provided charms and delights for our enjoyment. I can still see my father in his comfortable checked summer suit as we sat in the garden of some inn – a little way back from the table because his paunch prevented him from drawing up close – immersed in his enjoyment of a dish of prawns washed down by golden wine. My godfather Schimmelpreester was often with us, keenly studying people and landscape through his big artist's glasses and absorbing both great and small into his artist's soul.

My poor father owned the firm of Engelbert Krull, makers of the now discontinued brand of champagne *Loreley extra cuvée*. Their cellars lay on the bank of the Rhine not far from the landing, and often as a boy I used to linger in the cool vaults, wandering pensively along the stone-paved passages that led back and forth between the high shelves, examining the array of bottles which lay on their sides in slanting rows. 'There you lie,' I thought to myself (though of course at that time I could not give such apt expression to my thoughts), 'there you lie in the subterranean twilight, and within you the bubbling golden sap is clearing and maturing, the sap that will enliven so many hearts and awaken a brighter gleam in so many eyes! Now you look plain and unpromising, but one day you will rise to the upper world magnificently adorned, to take your place at feasts, at weddings, to send your corks popping to the ceilings of private dining-rooms and evoke intoxication, irresponsibility, and desire in the hearts of men.' So, or approximately so, spoke the boy; and this much at least was true, the firm of Engelbert Krull paid unusual attention to the outside of their bottles, those final adornments that are technically known as the coiffure. The compressed corks were secured with silver wire and gilt cords fastened with purplish-red wax; there was, moreover, an impressive round seal – such as one sees on ecclesiastical bulls and old state documents – suspended from a gold cord; the necks of the bottles were liberally wrapped in gleaming silver foil, and their swelling bellies bore a flaring red label with gold flourishes round the edges. This label had been designed for the firm by my godfather Schimmelpreester and bore a number of coats of arms and stars, my father's monogram, the brand name, *Loreley extra cuvée*, all in gold letters, and a female figure, arrayed only in bangles and necklaces, sitting with legs crossed on top of a rock, her arm raised in the act of combing her flowing hair. Unfortunately it appears that the quality of the wine was not entirely commensurate with the splendour of its coiffure. 'Krull,' I have heard my godfather Schimmelpreester say to my father, 'with all due respect to you, your champagne ought to be forbidden by law. Last week I let myself be talked into drinking half a bottle, and my system hasn't recovered from the shock yet. What sort of vinegar goes into that brew? And do you use petroleum or fusel oil to doctor it with? The stuff's simply poison. Look out for the police!' At this my poor father would be embarrassed, for he was a gentle man and unable to hold his own against harsh criticism.

'It's easy enough for you to laugh, Schimmelpreester,' he would reply, gently stroking his belly with his fingertips in his usual fashion, 'but I have to keep the price down because there is so much prejudice against the domestic product – in short, I give the public something to increase its confidence. Besides, competition is so fierce, my friend, I'm hardly able to go on.' Thus my father.

Our villa was a charming little estate on a gentle slope that commanded a view of the Rhine. The terraced garden was liberally adorned with earthenware gnomes, mushrooms, and all kind of lifelike animals; on a pedestal stood a mirrored glass sphere, which distorted faces most comically; there were also an aeolian harp, several grottoes, and a fountain whose streams made an ingenious figure in the air, while silvery goldfish swam in its basin. As for the interior decoration of our house, it was, in accordance with my father's taste, both cosy and cheerful. Pleasant nooks offered repose, and in one corner stood a real spinning-wheel; there were innumerable knick-knacks and decorations – conch shells, glass boxes, and bottles of smelling-salts – which stood about on *étagères* and velvet-covered tables; countless downy cushions covered in embroidered silk were strewn everywhere on sofas and daybeds, for my father loved to have a soft place to lie down; the curtain rods were halberds, and between the rooms were those airy portières made of bamboo tied with strings of glass beads. They look almost as solid as a door, but one can walk through them without raising a hand, and they part and fall back with a whispering click. Over the outside door was an ingenious mechanism, activated by air pressure as the door closed, which played with a pleasing tinkle the opening bars of Strauss's '*Freut euch des Lebens*'.

Chapter Two

Such was the home in which I was born one mild, rainy day in the merry month of May – a Sunday, to be exact. From now on I mean to follow the order of events conscientiously and to stop anticipating. If reports are true, the birth was slow and difficult and required the assistance of our family doctor, whose name was Mecum. It appears that I – if I may so refer to that far-away and foreign little being – was extremely inactive and made no attempt to aid my mother's efforts, showing no eagerness whatever to enter the world which later I was to love so dearly. Nevertheless, I was a healthy, well-formed child and thrived most promisingly at the breast of my excellent wet-nurse. Frequent reflection on this subject, moreover, inclines me to the belief that this reluctance to exchange the darkness of the womb for the light of day is connected with my extraordinary gift and passion for sleep, a characteristic of mine from infancy. I am told that I was a quiet child, not given to crying or troublemaking, but inclined to sleep and doze to an extent most convenient for my nurse. And despite the fact that later on I had such a longing for the world and its people that I mingled with them under a variety of names and did all I could to win them to myself, yet I feel that in night and slumber I have always been most at home. Even without being physically fatigued I have always been able to fall asleep with the greatest ease and pleasure, to lose myself in far and dreamless forgetfulness, and to awake after ten or twelve or even fourteen hours of oblivion even more refreshed and enlivened than by the successes and accomplishments of my waking hours. There might seem to be a contradiction between this love of sleep and my great impulse towards life and love, about which I intend to speak in due course. As I have already mentioned, however, I have devoted much thought to this matter and I have clearly perceived more than once that there is no contradiction but rather a hidden connexion and correspondence. In fact, it is only now, when I have turned forty and have become old and weary, when I no longer feel the old irrepressible urge towards the society of men but live in complete retirement, it is only now that my capacity for sleep is impaired so that I am in a sense a stranger to it, my slumbers being short and light and fleeting; whereas even in prison – where there was plenty of opportunity – I slept better than in the soft beds of the Palace Hotel. But I am falling again into my old fault of anticipating.

Often enough I heard from my parents' lips that I was a Sunday child, and, although I was brought up to reject every form of superstition, I have always thought there was a secret significance in that fact taken in connexion with my Christian name of Felix (for so I was called, after my godfather Schimmelpreester), and my physical fitness and attractiveness. Yes, I have always believed myself favoured of fortune and of Heaven, and I may say that, on the whole, experience has borne me out. Indeed, it has been peculiarly characteristic of my career that whatever misfortunes and sufferings it may have contained have always seemed an exception to the natural order, a cloud, as it were, through which the sun of my native luck continued to shine. After this digression into generalities, I shall continue to sketch in broad strokes the picture of my youth.

An imaginative child, my games of make-believe gave my family much entertainment. I have often been told, and seem still to remember, that when I was still in dresses I liked to pretend I was the Kaiser and would persist in this game for hours at a time with the greatest determination. Sitting in my little go-cart, which my nurse would push around the garden or the entrance hall of the house, I would draw down my mouth as far as I could so that my upper lip was unnaturally lengthened and would blink my eyes slowly until the strain and strength of my emotion made them redden and fill with tears. Overwhelmed by a sense of my age and dignity, I would sit silent in my little wagon, while my nurse was instructed to inform all we met who I was, since I should have taken any disregard of my fancy much amiss. 'I am taking the Kaiser for a drive,' she would announce, bringing the flat of her hand to the side of her head in an awkward salute, and everyone would pay me homage. In particular, my godfather Schimmelpreester, a great joker, would encourage my pretence for all he was worth whenever we met. 'Look, there he goes, the old hero!' he would say with an exaggeratedly deep bow. Then he would pretend to be the populace and, standing beside my path, would shout: 'Hurray, hurray!' throwing his hat, his cane, even his eye-glasses into the air, and he would split his sides laughing when, from excess of emotion, tears would roll down my long-drawn face.

I used to play the same sort of game when I was older and could no longer demand the cooperation of grown-ups – which, however, I did not miss, glorying as I did in the independent and self-sufficient exercise of my imagination. One morning, for example, I awoke resolved to be an eighteen-year-old prince named Karl, and I clung to this fantasy all day long; indeed, for several days, for the inestimable advantage of this kind of game is that it never needs to be interrupted, not even during the almost insupportable hours spent in school. Clothed in a sort of amiable majesty, I moved about, holding lively imaginary conversations with the governor or adjutant I had in fantasy assigned to myself; and the pride and happiness I felt at my secret superiority are indescribable. What a glorious gift is imagination, and what satisfaction it affords! The other boys of the town seemed to me dull and limited indeed, since they obviously did not share my ability and were consequently ignorant of the secret joys I could derive from it by a simple act of will, effortlessly and without any outward preparation. They were common fellows, to be sure, with coarse hair and red hands, and they would have had trouble persuading themselves that they were princes – and very foolish they would have looked, too. Whereas my hair was silken soft, as it seldom is in the male sex, and it was fair; like my blue-grey eyes, it provided a fascinating contrast to the golden brown of my skin, so that I hovered on the borderline between blond and dark and might have been considered either. My hands, which I began to take care of early, were distinguished without being too narrow, never clammy, but dry and agreeably warm, with well-shaped nails that it was a pleasure to see. My voice, even before it changed, had an ingratiating tone and could fall so flatteringly upon the ear that I liked more than anything to listen to it myself, especially when I was alone and could blissfully engage in long, plausible, but quite meaningless conversations with my imaginary adjutant, accompanying them with extravagant gestures. Such personal advantages are mostly intangible and are recognizable only in their effect; they are, moreover, difficult to put into words, even for someone unusually talented. In any case, I could not conceal from myself that I was made of superior stuff, or, as people say, of finer clay, and I do not shrink from the charge of self-complacency in saying so. If someone accuses me of self-complacency, it is a matter of complete indifference to me for I should have to be a fool or a hypocrite to pretend that I am of common stuff, and it is therefore in obedience to truth that I repeat that I am of the finest clay.

I grew up solitary, for my sister Olympia was several years older than I; I indulged in strange, introspective practices, of which I shall give two examples. First, I took it into my head to study the human will and to practise on myself its mysterious, sometimes supernatural effects. It is a well-known fact that the muscles controlling the pupils of our eyes react involuntarily to the intensity of the light falling upon them. I decided to bring this reaction under voluntary control. I would stand in front of my mirror, concentrating all my powers in a command to my pupils to contract or expand, banishing every other thought from my mind. My persistent efforts, let me assure you, were, in fact, crowned with success. At first as I stood bathed in sweat, my colour coming and going, my pupils would flicker erratically; but later I actually succeeded in contracting them to the merest points and then expanding them to great, round, mirror-like pools. The joy I felt at this success was almost terrifying and was accompanied by a shudder at the mystery of man.

There was another interior activity that often occupied me at that time and that even today has not lost its charm for me. I would ask myself: which is better, to see the world small or to see it big? The significance of the question was this: great men, I thought, field-marshals, statesmen, empire-builders, and other leaders who rise through violence above the masses of mankind must be so constituted as to see the world small, like a chessboard, or they would never possess the ruthless coldness to deal so boldly and cavalierly with the weal and woe of the individual. Yet it was quite possible, on the other hand, that such a diminishing point of view, so to speak, might lead to one's doing nothing at all. For if you saw the world and the human beings in it as small and insignificant and were early persuaded that nothing was worth while, you could easily sink into indifference and indolence and contemptuously prefer your own peace of mind to any influence you might exert on the spirits of men. Added to that, your coldness and detachment would certainly give offence and cut you off from any possible success you might have achieved involuntarily. Is it preferable, then, I would ask myself, to regard the world and mankind as something great, glorious, and significant, justifying every effort to obtain some modicum of esteem and fame? Against this one might argue that with so magnifying and respectful a view one can easily fall a victim to self-depreciation and loss of confidence, so that the world passes you by as an uncertain, silly boy and gives itself to a more manly lover. On the other hand, such genuine credulity and artlessness has its advantages too, since men cannot but be flattered by the way you look up to them; and if you devote yourself to making this impression, it will give weight and seriousness to your life, lending it meaning in your own eyes and leading to your advancement. In this way I pondered, weighing the pros and cons. It has always been a part of my nature, however, to hold instinctively to the second position, considering the world a great and infinitely enticing phenomenon, offering priceless satisfactions and worthy in the highest degree of all my efforts and solicitude.

Chapter Three

Visionary experiments and speculations of this kind served to isolate me inwardly from my contemporaries and schoolmates in the town, who spent their time in more conventional ways. But it is also true, as I was soon to learn, that these boys, the sons of winegrowers and government employees, had been warned by their parents to stay away from me. Indeed, when I experimentally invited one of them to our house, he told me to my face that he couldn't come because our family was not respectable. This pained me and made me covet an association that otherwise I should not have cared for. It must be admitted, however, that the town's opinion of our household had a certain justification.

I referred above to the disturbance in our family life caused by the presence of the Fräulein from Vevey. My poor father, in point of fact, was infatuated with the girl and pursued her until he gained his ends, or so it appeared, for quarrels arose between him and my mother and he left for Mainz, where he remained for several weeks enjoying a bachelor's life, as he had occasionally done before. My mother was entirely wrong in treating my poor father with such lack of respect. She was an unprepossessing woman and no less a prey to human weaknesses than he. My sister Olympia, a fat and inordinately sensual creature, who later had some success in comic opera, resembled her in this respect – the difference between them and my poor father being that theirs was a coarse-grained greed for pleasure, whereas his foibles were never without a certain grace. Mother and daughter lived on terms of unusual intimacy: I recall once seeing my mother measure Olympia's thigh with a tape measure, which gave me food for thought for several hours. Another time, when I was old enough to have some intuitive understanding of such matters though no words to express them, I was an unseen witness when my mother and sister together began to flirt with a young painter who was at work in the house. He was dark-eyed youth in a white smock, and they painted a green moustache on his face with his own paint. In the end they roused him to such a pitch that he pursued them giggling up the attic stairs.

Since my parents bored each other to distraction they often invited guests from Mainz and Wiesbaden, and then our house was the scene of merriment and uproar. It was a gaudy crowd who attended these gatherings: actors and actresses, young businessmen, a sickly young infantry lieutenant who was later engaged to my sister; a Jewish banker with a wife who awesomely overflowed her jet-embroidered dress in every direction; a journalist in velvet waistcoat with a lock of hair over his brow, who brought a new helpmeet along every time. They would usually arrive for seven-o'clock dinner, and the feasting, dancing, piano-playing, rough-housing, and shrieks of laughter went on all night. The tide of pleasure rose especially high at carnival time and at the vintage season. My father, who was very expert in such matters, would set off the most splendid fireworks in the garden; the whole company would wear masks and unearthly light would play upon the earthenware dwarfs. All restraint was abandoned. It was my misfortune at that time to have to attend the local high school, and many mornings when I came down to the dining-room for breakfast, face freshly washed, at seven o'clock or half-past, I would find the guests still sitting over coffee and liqueurs, sallow, rumpled, and blinking in the early light. They would give me an uproarious welcome.

When I was no more than half grown I was allowed, along with my sister Olympia, to take part in these festivities. Even when we were alone we always kept a good table, and my father drank champagne mixed with soda water. But at these parties there were endless courses prepared by a chef from Wiesbaden assisted by our own cook: the most tempting succession of sweets, savouries, and ices; *Loreley extra cuvée* flowed in streams, but many good wines were served as well. There was, for instance, Berncasteler Doctor, whose bouquet especially appealed to me. In later life I became acquainted with still other notable brands and could, for instance, casually order *Grand Vin* Château Margaux or *Grand Cru* Château Mouton-Rothschild – two noble wines.

I love to recall the picture of my father presiding at the head of the table, with his white pointed beard, and his paunch spanned by a white silk waistcoat. His voice was weak and sometimes he would let his eyes drop in a self-conscious way and yet enjoyment was written large on his flushed and shining face. '*C'est, ça*', he would say, '*épatant*', '*parfaitement*' – and with his fingers, which curved backwards at the tips, he would give delicate touches to the glasses, the napkins, and the silver. My mother and sister would surrender themselves to mindless gluttony interrupted only by giggling flirtations behind their fans with their tablemates.

After dinner, when cigar smoke began to eddy around the gas chandeliers, there were dancing and games of forfeit. As the evening advanced I used to be sent to bed; but since sleep was impossible in that din, I would wrap myself in my red woollen bedspread and in this becoming costume return to the feast, where I was received by all the ladies with cries of joy. Snacks and refreshments, punch, lemonade, herring salad, and wine jellies were served in relays until the morning coffee. Dancing was unconstrained and the games of forfeit became a pretext for kissing and fondling. The ladies, *décolleté*, bent low over the backs of chairs to give the gentlemen exciting glimpses of their bosoms, and the high point of the evening would come when some joker turned out the gaslight amid general uproar and confusion.

It was mostly these social affairs that provoked the town gossip that called our household disreputable, but I learned early that it was the economic aspect of the situation that was principally in question. For it was rumoured (and with only too much justification) that my poor father's business was in desperate straits, and that the expensive fireworks and dinners would inevitably furnish the *coup de grâce*. My sensitivity early made me aware of this general distrust, and it combined, as I have said, with certain peculiarities of my character to cause me first and last a good deal of pain. It was therefore all the more delightful to have the experience that I now set down with special pleasure.

The summer that I was eight years old my family and I went to spend several weeks at the famous near-by resort of Langenschwalbach. My father was taking mud-baths for his gout, and my mother and sister made themselves conspicious on the promenade by the exaggerated size of their hats. There as elsewhere our opportunities for social advancement were meagre. The natives, as usual, avoided us. Guests of the better class kept themselves very much to themselves as they usually do; and such society as we met did not have much to recommend it. Yet I liked Langenschwalbach and later on often made such resorts the scene of my activities. The tranquil, well-regulated existence and the sight of aristocratic, well-groomed people in the gardens or at sport satisfied an inner craving. But the strongest attraction of all was the daily concert given by a well-trained orchestra for the guests of the cure. Though I have never taken occasion to acquire any skill in that dreamlike art, I am a fanatical lover of music; even as a child I could not tear myself away from the pretty pavilion where a becomingly uniformed band played selections and potpourris under the direction of a leader who looked like a gipsy. For hours on end I would crouch on the steps of this little temple of art, enchanted to the marrow of my bones by the ordered succession of sweet sounds and watching with rapture every motion of the musicians as they manipulated their instruments. In particular I was thrilled by the gestures of the violinists, and when I went home I delighted my parents with an imitation performed with two sticks, one long and one short. The swinging movement of the left arm when producing a soulful tone, the soft gliding motion from one position to the next, the dexterity of the fingering in virtuoso passages and cadenzas, the fine and supple bowing of the right wrist, the cheek nestling in utter abandonment on the violin – all this I succeeded in reproducing so faithfully that the family, and especially my father, burst into enthusiastic applause. Being in high spirits because of the beneficial effects of the baths, he conceived the following little joke with the connivance of the long-haired, almost inarticulate little conductor. They bought a small, cheap violin and plentifully greased the bow with Vaseline. As a rule little attention was paid to my appearance, but now I was dressed in a pretty sailor suit complete with gold buttons and lanyard, silk stockings, and shiny patent-leather shoes. And one Sunday afternoon at the hour of the promenade I took my place beside the little conductor and joined in the performance of a Hungarian dance, doing with my fiddle and Vaselined bow what I had done before with my two sticks. I make bold to say my success was complete.

The public, both distinguished and undistinguished, streamed up from all sides and crowded in front of the pavilion to look at the infant prodigy. My pale face, my complete absorption in my task, the lock of hair falling over my brow, my childish hands and wrists in the full, tapering sleeves of the becoming blue sailor suit – in short, my whole touching and astonishing little figure captivated all hearts. When I finished with the full sweep of the bow across all the fiddle strings, the garden resounded with applause and delighted cries from male and female throats. After the band-master had safely got my fiddle and bow out of the way, I was picked up and set down on the ground, where I was overwhelmed with praises and caresses. The most aristocratic ladies and gentlemen stroked my hair, patted my cheeks and hands, called me an angel child and an amazing little devil. An aged Russian princess, wearing enormous white side curls and dressed from head to toe in violet silk, took my head between her beringed hands and kissed my brow, beaded as it was with perspiration. Then in a burst of enthusiasm she snatched a lyre-shaped diamond brooch from her throat and pinned it on my blouse, amid a perfect torrent of ecstatic French. My family approached and my father made excuses for the defects of my playing on the score of my tender years. I was taken to the confectioner's, where at three different tables I was treated to chocolate and cream puffs. The children of the noble family of Siebenklingen, whom I had admired from a distance while they regarded me with haughty aloofness, came up and asked me to play croquet, and while our parents drank coffee together I went off with them in the seventh heaven of delight, my diamond brooch still on my blouse. That was one of the happiest days of my life, perhaps the happiest. A cry was raised that I should play again, and the management of the casino actually approached my father, and asked for a repeat performance, but he refused, saying that he had only permitted me to play by way of exception and that repeated public appearances would not be consistent with my social position. Besides, our stay in Bad Langenschwalbach was drawing to a close . . .

Chapter Four

I will now speak of my godfather Schimmelpreester, who was by no means an ordinary man. In build he was short and thick-set. He had thin, prematurely grey hair, which he wore parted over one ear so that almost all of it was brushed across the crown. He was clean-shaven, with a hook nose and thin, compressed lips, and he wore large round glasses in celluloid frames. His face was further remarkable for the fact that it was bare above the eyes; that is, there were no eyebrows; his whole appearance gave the impression of a sharp and bitter turn of mind; there was proof of this in the splenetic interpretation he used to give to his own name. 'Nature,' he would say, 'is nothing but mould and corruption, and I am her high priest. The high priest of mould, that's the real meaning of Schimmelpreester. But why I am called Felix, God only knows.' He came from Cologne, where he had once moved in the best circles and had served as carnival steward. But for reasons that remained obscure he had been obliged to leave the place; he had gone into retirement in our little town, where very soon – a number of years before I was born – he became a family friend of my parents. At all our evening gatherings he was a regular and indispensable guest, in high favour with young and old. When he tightened his lips and fixed the ladies with appraising eyes, through his round eye-glasses, they would scream and raise their arms for protection. 'Ooh, the painter!' they would cry. 'What eyes he has! Now he is looking straight through us, right into our hearts. Mercy, Professor, please take your eyes away.' But however much he was admired, he himself had no very high regard for his calling and often made highly ambiguous remarks about the nature of artists. 'Phidias,' he used to say, 'also called Pheidias, was a man of more than ordinary gifts, as may be gathered from the fact that he was convicted and put in jail for embezzling the gold and ivory entrusted to him for his statue of Athena. Pericles, who found him out, allowed him to escape from prison, thereby proving himself not only expert in art but, what is more important, an expert in understanding the nature of the artist, and Phidias or Pheidias went to Olympia, where he was commissioned to make the great gold-and-ivory Zeus. And what did he do? He stole again. And imprisoned in Olympia he died. A striking combination. But that is the way people are. They want talent, which is in itself something out of the ordinary. But when it comes to the other oddities that are always associated with it, and perhaps essential to it, they will have none of them and refuse them all understanding.' Thus my godfather. I have been able to recall his comments verbatim, because he repeated them so often and always with the same turns of phrase.

As I have said, we lived on terms of mutual affection; indeed, I believe that I enjoyed his special favour, and often as I grew older it was my particular delight to act as his model, dressing up in all sorts of costumes, of which he had a large and varied collection. His studio was a sort of storeroom with a large window, under the roof of a little house that stood by itself on the bank of the Rhine. He rented this house and lived in it with an old serving-woman, and there on a rude, home-made dais, I would sit to him, as he called it, for hours on end while he brushed and scraped and painted away. Several times I posed in the nude for a large picture out of Greek mythology that was to adorn the dining-room of a wine-dealer in Mainz. When I did this my godfather was lavish in his praises; and indeed I was a little like a young god, slender, graceful, yet powerful in build, with a golden skin and flawless proportions. These sittings still constitute a unique memory. Yet I enjoyed even more, I think, the 'dressing up' itself; and that took place not only in the studio but at our house as well. Often when my godfather was to dine with us he would send up a large bundle of costumes, wigs, and accessories and try them all on me after the meal, sketching any particularly good effect on the lid of a cardboard box. 'He's a natural costume boy,' he would say, meaning that everything became me, and that in each disguise I assumed I looked better and more natural than in the last. I might appear as a Roman flute-player in a short tunic, a wreath of roses twined in my curly locks; as an English page in snug-fitting satin with lace collar and plumed hat; as a Spanish bull-fighter in spangled jacket and broad-brimmed hat; as a youthful abbé at the time of powdered white wigs, with cap and bands, mantle and buckled shoes; as an Austrian officer in white military tunic with sash and dagger; or as a German mountaineer in leather breeches and hobnailed boots, with a tuft of goat's hair in my green felt hat – whatever the costume, the mirror assured me that I was born to wear it, and my audience declared that I looked to the life exactly the person whom I aimed to represent. My godfather even asserted that with the aid of costume and wig I seemed not only able to put on whatever social rank or personal characteristics I chose, but could actually adapt myself to any given period or century. For each age, my godfather would say, imparts to its children its own facial stamp; whereas I, in the costume of a Florentine dandy of the late Middle

Ages, would look as though I had stepped out of a contemporary portrait, and yet be no less convincing in the full-bottomed wig that was the fashionable ideal of a later century. Ah, those were glorious hours! But when they were over and I resumed my ordinary dull dress, how indescribably boring seemed all the world by contrast, in what depths of dejection did I spend the rest of the evening!

Of Schimmelpreester I shall say no more in this place. Later on, at the end of my exacting career, he was to intervene in my destiny decisively and providentially ...

Chapter Five

As I search my mind for further impressions of my youth, I am at once reminded of the day when I first attended the theatre, in Wiesbaden with my parents. I should mention here that in my description of my youth I am not adhering to strict chronological order, but am treating my younger days as a whole and moving freely from incident to incident. When I posed for my godfather as a Greek god I was between sixteen and eighteen years of age and thus no longer a child, though very backward at school. But my first visit to the theatre fell in my fourteenth year – though even so my physical and mental development, as will presently be seen, was well advanced and my receptivity to impressions of certain kinds much greater than ordinary. What I saw that evening made the strongest impression on me and gave me endless food for thought.

We first visited a Viennese café, where I drank a cup of punch and my father imbibed absinthe through a straw – this in itself was calculated to stir me to the depths. But how can one describe the fever that possessed me when we drove in a cab to the theatre and entered the lighted auditorium with its tiers of boxes? The women fanning their bosoms in the balconies, the men leaning over their chairs to chat; the hum and buzz of conversation in the orchestra, where we presently took our seats; the odours which streamed from hair and clothing to mingle with that of the illuminating gas; the confusion of sounds as the orchestra tuned up; the voluptuous frescoes that depicted whole cascades of rosy, foreshortened nymphs – certainly all this could not but rouse my youthful senses and prepare my mind for all the extraordinary scenes to come. Never before except in church had I seen so many people gathered together in a large and stately auditorium; and this theatre with its impressive seating arrangements and its elevated stage where privileged personages, brilliantly costumed and accompanied by music, went through their dialogues and dances, their songs and routines – certainly all this was in my eyes a temple of pleasure, where men in need of edification gathered in darkness and gazed upward open-mouthed into a realm of brightness and perfection where they beheld their hearts' desire.

The play that was being given was unpretentious, a work of the loose-zoned muse, as people say. It was an operetta whose name I have, to my sorrow, forgotten. Its scene was Paris, which delighted my poor father's heart, and its central figure was an idle attaché, a fascinating rogue and lady-killer, played by that star of the theatre, the well-loved singer Müller-Rosé. I heard his real name from my father, who enjoyed his personal acquaintance, and the picture of this man will remain for ever in my memory. He is probably old and worn-out now, like me, but at that time his power dazzled all the world, myself included; it made so strong an impression upon me that it belongs to the decisive experiences of my life. I say dazzled, and it will be seen hereafter how much meaning I wish to convey by that word. But first I must try to set down my still vivid recollections of Müller-Rosé's effect on me.

On his first entrance he was dressed in black, and yet he radiated sheer brilliance. In the play he was supposed to be coming from some meeting-place of the gay world and to be slightly intoxicated, a state he was able to counterfeit in agreeable and sublimated fashion. He wore a black cloak with a satin lining, patent-leather shoes, evening dress, white kid gloves, and a top hat; his hair was parted all the way to the back of his head in accordance with the military fashion of the day. Every article of his attire was so well pressed, and fitted with such flawless perfection, that it could not have lasted more than a quarter-hour in real life. He seemed indeed, not to belong to this world. In particular his top hat, which he wore nonchalantly tipped forward over his brow, was the ideal and model of what a top hat should be, without a particle of dust or roughness and with the most beautiful reflections, just as in a picture. And this higher being had a face to match, rosy, fine as wax, with almond-shaped, black-rimmed eyes, a small, short, straight nose, a perfectly clear-cut, coral-red mouth, and a little black moustache as even as if it had been drawn with a paintbrush, following the outline of his arched upper lip. Staggering with a fluid grace such as drunken men do not possess in everyday life, he handed his hat and stick to an attendant, slipped out of his cloak, and stood there in full evening dress, with diamond studs in his thickly pleated shirt-front. As he drew off his gloves, laughing and chatting in a silvery voice, you could see that the backs of his hands were white as milk and adorned with diamond rings, but that the palms were as pink as his face. He stood before the footlights on one side of the stage and sang the first stanza of a song about what a wonderful life it was to be an attaché and a ladies' man. Then he spread out his arms, snapped his fingers, and drifted delightedly to the other side of the stage, where he sang the second stanza and made his exit, only to be recalled by loud applause. The third stanza he sang in mid-stage in front of the prompter's box. Then with careless grace he plunged into the action of the play. He was supposed to be very rich, which in itself lent his figure a magical charm. He appeared in a succession of costumes: snow-white sports clothes with a red belt; a full-dress, fancy uniform – yes, at one ticklish and sidesplitting moment in sky-blue silk drawers. The complications of the plot were audacious, adventurous, and *risqué* by turns. One saw him at the feet of a countess, at a champagne supper with two ambitious daughters of joy, and standing with raised pistol confronting a dull-witted rival in a duel. And not one of these elegant but strenuous exercises was able to disarrange a single fold of his shirt-front, extinguish any of the reflections in his top hat, or overheat his rosy countenance. He moved so easily within the frame of the musical and dramatic conventions that they seemed, far from restricting him, to release him from the limitations of everyday life. His body seemed informed to the fingertips with a magic for which we have only the vague and inadequate word 'talent', and which obviously gave him as much pleasure as it did us. To watch him take hold of the silver head of his cane or plunge both hands in his trouser pockets was a spontaneous delight; the way he rose from a chair, bowed, made his exits and entrances, possessed such delightful self-assurance that it filled one's heart with the joy of life. Yes, that was it: Müller-Rosé dispensed the joy of life – if that phrase can be used to describe the precious and painful feeling, compounded of envy, yearning, hope, and love, that the sight of beauty and lighthearted perfection kindles in the souls of men.

The audience in the orchestra was made up of middle-class citizens and their wives, clerks, one-year servicemen, and girls in blouses; and despite the rapture of my own sensations I had presence of mind and curiosity enough to look about me and interpret their feelings. The expression on their faces was both silly and blissful. They were wrapped in self-forgetful absorption, a smile played about their lips, sweeter and more lively in the little shop-girls, more brooding and thoughtful in the grown-up women, while the faces of the men expressed that benevolent admiration which plain fathers feel in the presence of sons who have exceeded them and realized the dreams of their youth. As for the clerks and the young soldiers, everything stood wide open in their upturned faces – eyes, mouths, nostrils, everything. And at the same time they were smiling. Suppose we were up there in our underdrawers, how should we be making out? And look how boldly he behaves with those ambitious tarts, as though he had been dealing with them all his life! When Müller-Rosé left the stage, shoulders slumped and virtue seemed to go out of the audience. When he strode triumphantly from back-stage to footlights, on a sustained note, his arms outspread, bosoms rose as though to meet him, and satin bodices strained at the seams. Yes, this whole shadowy assembly was like an enormous swarm of nocturnal insects, silently, blindly, and blissfully rushing into a blazing fire.

My father enjoyed himself royally. He had followed the French custom and brought his hat and stick into the theatre with him. When the curtain fell he put on the one and with the other pounded long and loud on the floor. '*C'est épatant,*' he repeated several times, quite weak from enthusiasm. But when it was all over and we were outside in the lobby among a crowd of exalted clerks, who were quite obviously trying to imitate their hero in the way they walked, held their canes, and regarded their reddened hands, my father said to me: 'Come along, let's shake hands with him. By God, weren't we on intimate terms, Müller and I? He will be *enchanté* to see me again.' And after instructing the ladies to wait for us in the vestibule, we actually went off to hunt up Müller-Rosé.

Our way lay through the darkened director's box beside the stage and then through a narrow iron door into the wings. The half-darkened stage was animated by the eerie activity of scene-shifting. A girl in red livery, who had played the role of a lift-boy, was leaning against the wall sunk in thought. My poor father pinched her playfully where her figure was at its broadest and asked her the way to the dressing-rooms, which she irritably pointed out. We went through a whitewashed corridor, where naked gas-jets flared in the confined air. From behind several doors came loud laughter and angry voices, and my father gestured with his thumb to call my attention to these manifestations. At the end of the narrow passage he knocked on the last door, pressing his ear to it as he did so. From within came a gruff shout: 'Who's there?' or 'What the devil?' I no longer remember the words spoken in that clear, rude voice. 'May I come in?' asked my father, whereupon he was instructed to do something quite different, which I must not mention in these pages. My father smiled his deprecatory smile and called through the door: Müller, it's Krull, Engelbert Krull. I suppose I may shake your hand after all these years?' There was a laugh from inside and the voice said: 'Oh, so it's you, you old rooster! Always out for a good time, eh?' And as he opened the door he went on: 'I don't imagine my nakedness will do you any harm!' We went in. I shall never forget the disgusting sight that met my boyish eyes.

Müller-Rosé was seated at a grubby dressing-table in front of a dusty, speckled mirror. He had nothing on but a pair of grey cotton drawers, and a man in shirt-sleeves was massaging his back, the sweat running down his own face. Meanwhile the actor was busy wiping face and neck with a towel already stiff with rouge and grease-paint. Half of his countenance still had the rosy coating that had made him radiant on the stage but now looked merely pink and silly in contrast to the cheese-like pallor of his natural complexion. He had taken off the chestnut wig and I saw that this own hair was red. One of his eyes still had deep black shadows beneath it and metallic dust clung to the lashes; the other was inflamed and watery and squinted at us impudently. All this I might have borne. But not the pustules with which Müller-Rosé's back, chest, shoulders, and upper arms were thickly covered. They were horrible pustules, red-rimmed, suppurating, some of them even bleeding; even today I cannot repress a shudder at the thought of them. Our capacity for disgust, let me observe, is in proportion to our desires; that is, in proportion to the intensity of our attachment to the things of this world. A cool indifferent nature would never have been shaken by disgust to the extent that I was then. As a final touch, the air in the room, which was overheated by an iron stove, was compounded of the smell of sweat and the exhalations from the pots and jars and sticks of grease-paint that littered the table so that at first I thought I could not stand it for more than a minute without being sick.

However, I did stand it and looked about – but I can add nothing to this description of Müller-Rosé's dressing-room. Indeed, I should perhaps be ashamed at reporting so little and at such length about my first visit to a theatre, if I were not writing primarily for my own amusement and only secondarily for the public. It is not my intention to maintain dramatic suspense; I leave such effects to the writers of imaginative fictions, who are intent on giving their stories the beautiful and symmetrical proportions of works of art – whereas my material comes from my own experience alone and I feel I may make use of it as I think best. Thus I shall dwell on those experiences and encounters that brought me particular understanding and illumination about the world and myself, passing by more quickly what is less precious to me.

I have almost forgotten what Müller-Rosé and my poor father chatted about – no doubt because I had not time to pay attention. For it is undoubtedly true that we receive stronger impressions through the senses than through words. I recall that the singer – though surely the applause that had greeted him that evening must have reassured him about his triumph – kept asking my father whether he had made a hit and how much of a hit he had made. How well I understood his uneasiness! I even have a vague memory of some rather vulgar witticisms he injected into the conversation. To some gloating comment of my father's, for example, he replied: 'Shut your trap –' adding at once: 'or you'll fall through it.' But I lent only half an ear, as I have said, to this and other examples of his mental accomplishments, being completely absorbed in my own sense impressions.

This then – such was the tenor of my thoughts – this grease-smeared and pimply individual is the charmer at whom the twilight crowd was just now gazing so soulfully! This repulsive worm is the reality of the glorious butterfly in whom those deluded spectators believed they were beholding the realization of all their own secret dreams of beauty, grace, and perfection! Is he not like one of those repellent little creatures that have the power of glowing phosphorescently at night? But the grown-up people in the audience, who on the whole must know about life, and who yet were so frightfully eager to be deceived, must they not have been aware of the deception? Or did they privately not consider it one? And that is quite possible. For when you come to think of it, which is the real shape of the glow-worm: the insignificant little creature crawling about on the palm of your hand, or the poetic spark that swims through the summer night? Who would presume to say? Rather recall the picture you saw before: the giant swarms of poor moths and gnats, rushing silently and madly into the enticing flame! What unanimity in agreeing to let oneself be deceived! Here quite clearly there is in operation a general human need, implanted by God Himself in human nature, which Müller-Rosé's abilities are created to satisfy. This beyond doubt is an indispensable device in life's economy, which this man is kept and paid to serve. What admiration he deserves for his success tonight and obviously every night! Restrain your disgust and consider that, in full knowledge and realization of his frightful pustules, he was yet able – with the help of grease-paint, lighting, music, and distance – to move before his audience with such assurance as to make them see in him their heart's ideal and thereby enliven and edify them infinitely.

Consider further and ask yourself what it was that impelled this miserable mountebank to learn the art of transfiguring himself every night. What are the secret sources of the charm that possessed him and informed him to the fingertips? To learn the answer, you have but to recall (for you know it well!) the ineffable power, which there are no words monstrously sweet enough to describe, that teaches the firefly to glow. Remind yourself how this man could not hear often enough or emphatically enough the assurance that he had truly given pleasure, pleasure altogether out of the ordinary. It was the devotion and drive of his heart towards that yearning crowd that made him skilful in his art; and if he bestows on them joy of life and they satiate him with their applause for doing so, is not that a mutual fulfilment, a meeting and marriage of his yearning and theirs?

Chapter Six

The above lines indicate the general tenor of my hot and excited thoughts as I sat in Müller-Rosé's dressing-room, and again and again in the following days and weeks they returned to this subject with trance-like persistence. It was a subject that always aroused emotions so profound and shattering, such a drunkenness of yearning, hope, and joy, that even today, despite my weariness, the mere memory makes my heart beat faster. In those days my feelings were of such violence that they threatened to burst my frame; indeed, they often actually made me ill and thus served as an excuse for my staying away from school.

I consider it superfluous to dwell on the reasons for my increasing detestation of that malignant institution. I am only able to live in conditions that leave my spirit and imagination completely free; and so it is that the memory of my years in prison is actually less hateful to me than the recollection of the slavery and fear to which my sensitive boyish soul was subjected through the ostensibly honourable discipline in the small square white school-house down there in the town. Add to this the feeling of isolation, the sources of which I have indicated, and it is not surprising that I soon hit on the idea of escaping from school more often than on Sundays and holidays.

In carrying out this idea I was helped a good deal by a playful diversion I had long indulged in – the imitation of my father's handwriting. A father is the natural and nearest model for the growing boy who is striving to adapt himself to the adult world. Similarity of physique and the mystery of their relationship incline the boy to admire in his parent's conduct all that he himself is still incapable of and to strive to imitate it – or rather it is, perhaps, his very admiration that unconsciously leads him to develop along the lines heredity has laid down. Even when I was still making great hens' tracks on my lined slate, I already dreamed of guiding a steel pen with my father's swiftness and sureness; and many were the pages I covered later with efforts to copy his hand from memory, my fingers grasping the pen in the same delicate fashion as his. His writing was not, in fact, hard to imitate, for my poor father wrote a childish, copy-book hand, quite undeveloped, its only peculiarity being that the letters were very tiny and separated by long hairlines to an extent I have never seen anywhere else. This mannerism I quickly mastered to perfection. As for the signature 'E. Krull', in contrast to the angular Gothic letters of the text, it had a Latin cast. It was surrounded by a perfect cloud of flourishes, which at first sight looked difficult to copy, but were in reality so simple in conception that with them I succeeded best of all. The lower half of the *E* made a wide sweep to the right, in whose ample lap, so to speak, the short syllable of the last name was neatly enclosed. A second flourish arose from the *u*, embracing everything before it, cutting the curve of the *E* in two places and ending in an s-shaped downstroke flanked like the curve of the *E* with ornamental rows of dots. The whole signature was higher than it was long, it was naïve and baroque; thus it lent itself so well to my purpose that in the end its inventor would have certified my product as his own. But what was more obvious, once I had acquired this skill for my own entertainment, than to put it to work in the interests of my intellectual freedom? 'On the 7th instant,' I wrote, 'my son Felix was afflicted by severe stomach cramps which compelled him to stay away from school, to the regret of yours –E. Krull.' And again: 'An infected gumboil, together with a sprained right arm, compelled Felix to keep his room from the 10th to the 14th of this month. Therefore, much to our regret, he was unable to attend school. Respectfully yours – E. Krull.' When this succeeded, nothing prevented me from spending the school hours of one day or even of several wandering freely outside the town or lying stretched out in a green field, in the whispering shade of the leaves, dreaming the dreams of youth. Sometimes I hid in the ruins of the old episcopal palace on the Rhine; sometimes, even, in stormy winter weather, in the hospitable studio of my godfather Schimmelpreester, who rebuked me for my conduct in tones that showed he was not without a certain sympathy for my motives.

Now and again, however, I stayed at home in bed on school days – and not always, as I have explained, without justification. It is a favourite theory of mine that every deception which fails to have a higher truth as its roots and is simply a barefaced lie is by that very fact so grossly palpable that nobody can fail to see through it. Only one kind of lie has a chance of being effective: that which in no way deserves to be called deceit, but is the product of a lively imagination which has not yet entered wholly into the realm of the actual and acquired those tangible signs by which alone it can be appraised at its proper worth. Although it is true that I was a sturdy boy, who, except for the usual childish ailments, never had anything serious the matter with him, it was nevertheless not a gross deception when I decided one morning to avoid the painful oppressions of school by becoming an invalid. For why should I subject myself to such treatment when I had at hand the means of neutralizing the cruel power of my intellectual lords and masters? No, the painfully intense excitement and exaltation which, as I have explained, accompanied certain states of mind used often to overwhelm me to such an extent as to produce in combination with my abhorrence of the misunder-standings and drudgery of a day in school, a condition that created a solid basis of truth for my behaviour. I was effortlessly provided with the means of gaining the sympathy and concern of the doctor and of my family.

I did not at first produce my symptoms for an audience, but for myself alone. On a certain day when my need for freedom and the possession of my own soul had become overpowering, my decision was made and became irrevocable through the simple passage of time. The latest possible hour for rising had been passed in brooding; downstairs breakfast had been put on the table by the maid and was growing cold; all the dull fellows in town were trudging off to school; daily life had begun, and I was irretrievably committed to a course of rebellion against my taskmasters. The audacity of my conduct made my heart flutter and my stomach turn over. I noted that my fingernails had taken on a bluish tint. The morning was cold and all I needed to do was to throw off the covers for a few moments and lie relaxed in order to bring on the most convincing attack of chills and chattering teeth. All that I am saying is, of course, highly indicative of my character. I have always been very sensitive, susceptible, and in need of care; and everything I have accomplished in my active life has been the result of self-conquest – indeed, must be regarded as a moral achievement of a high order. If it were otherwise I should never, either then or later, have succeeded, merely by willing my mind and body to relax, in producing the appearance of physical illness and thus inclining those about me to tenderness and concern. To counterfeit illness effectively could never be within the powers of a coarse-grained man. But anyone of finer stuff, if I may repeat the phrase, is always, though he may never be ill in the crude sense of the word, on familiar terms with suffering and able to control its symptoms by intuition. I closed my eyes and then opened them to their widest extent, making them look appealing and plaintive. I knew without a mirror that my hair was rumpled from sleep and fell in damp strands across my brow, and that my face was pale. I made it look sunken by a device of my own, drawing in my cheeks and unobtrusively holding them in with my teeth. This made my chin appear longer, too, and gave me the appearance of having grown thin overnight. A dilation of the nostrils and an almost painful twitching of the muscles at the corners of the eyes contributed to this effect. I put my basin on a chair beside my bed, folded my blue-nailed fingers across my breast, made my teeth chatter from time to time, and thus awaited the moment when somebody would come to look for me.

That happened rather late, for my parents loved to lie abed, and so two or three school hours had passed before it was noticed that I was still in the house. Then my mother came upstairs and into the room to ask if I was ill. I looked at her wide-eyed, as though in my dazed condition it was hard for me to tell who she was. Then I said yes, I thought I must be ill. What was the trouble then, she asked. 'My head . . . pains in my bones . . . And why am I so cold?' I answered in a monotonous voice, speaking with an effort and tossing myself from side to side in the bed. My mother was sympathetic. I do not believe she took my sufferings very seriously, but her sensibilities were far in excess of her reason and she could not bring herself to spoil the game. Instead, she joined in and began to support me in my performance. 'Poor child,' she said, laying her forefinger on my cheek and shaking her head in pity, 'don't you want something to eat.' I declined with a shudder, pressing my chin on my chest. This strict consistency in my behaviour sobered her, made her seriously concerned, and, so to speak, startled her out of her enjoyment in our joint game; that anyone should refuse food and drink for frivolous reasons went quite beyond her powers of imagination. She looked at me with a growing sense of reality. When she had got this far I helped her to a decision by a display of art as arduous as it was effective. Starting up in bed with a fitful, shuddering motion, I drew my basin towards me and bent over it with spasmodic twitchings and contortions of my whole body, such as no one could witness without profound emotion unless he had a heart of stone. 'Nothing in me . . .' I gasped between my writhings, lifting my wry and wasted face from the basin. 'Threw it all up in the night . . .' And then I launched upon my main effort, a prolonged attack of cramps and retching which made it seem that I would never breathe again. My mother held my head, repeatedly calling me by name in an effort to bring me to myself. By the time my limbs finally began to relax she was quite overcome and, exclaiming: 'I'll send for Düsing!' she rushed out of the room. I sank back among the pillows exhausted but full of indescribable joy and satisfaction.

How often I had imagined such a scene, how often I had practised it in my mind before I caused it to become a reality! I don't know whether people will understand if I say that I seemed to be in a happy dream when I first gave it concrete expression and achieved complete success. Not everyone can do such a thing. One may dream of it, but not do it. Suppose, a man thinks, something awful were to happen to me: suppose I were to faint or blood were to gush out of my nose, or I were to have some kind of seizure – then how quickly the world's harsh unconcern would turn into attention, sympathy, and belated remorse! But the flesh is obtusely strong and enduring, it holds out long after the mind has felt the necessity of sympathy and care; it will not manifest the alarming tangible symptoms that would make an onlooker see himself in a similar plight and would speak with stern voice to the conscience of the world. But I – I had produced these symptoms as effectively as though I had nothing to do with their appearance. I had improved upon nature, realized a dream; and only he who has succeeded in creating a compelling and effective reality out of nothing, out of sheer inward knowledge and contemplation – in short, out of nothing more than imagination and the daring exploitation of his own body – he alone understands the strange and dream-like satisfaction with which I rested from my creative task.

An hour later Health Councillor Düsing arrived. He had been our family physician ever since the death of old Dr Mecum, who had ushered me into the world. Dr Düsing was tall and stooped, with bad carriage and bristling grey hair; he was either rubbing his long nose between thumb and forefinger all the time or rubbing his big bony hands. This man might have been dangerous to my enterprise. Not through his professional ability, probably, which was, I believe, of the slightest (though a true doctor devoted to science and to the pursuit of medicine for its own sake is easiest of all to deceive), but through a certain native human shrewdness, which is often the whole stock in trade of inferior characters. This unworthy disciple of Aesculapius was both stupid and ambitious and had achieved his title through personal influence, exploitation of wine-house acquaintances, and the receipt of patronage; he was always going to Wiesbaden to advance his interests with the authorities. Most indicative to me was the fact that he did not receive the patients who came to his waiting-room in the order in which they arrived, but took the more influential first, letting the humbler sit and wait. His manner towards the former class was obsequious, towards the latter harsh and cynical, indicating often that he did not believe in their complaints. I am convinced he would not have stopped at any lie, corruption, or bribery that might ingratiate him with his superiors or recommend him as a zealous party man to those in power; such behaviour was consistent with the shrewd common sense he relied on to see him through in default of higher qualifications. Although my poor father's position was already doubtful, as a businessman and a taxpayer, he still belonged to the influential classes of the town, and Dr Düsing naturally wished to stand well with him. It may even be that the wretched man willingly seized every opportunity to school himself in corruption, and may have believed for this reason that he ought to make common cause with me.

Whenever he came and sat by my bed with the usual avuncular phrases like: 'Well, well, what have we here?' or: 'What seems to be wrong today?' the moment would come when a wink, a smile, or a significant little pause would encourage me to admit that we were partners in the deceptive little game of playing sick – 'school sick' as he would probably have called it. Never did I make the smallest response to his advances. Not out of caution, for he would probably not have betrayed me, but out of pride and contempt. At each of his attempts I only looked all the more ailing and helpless, my cheeks grew hollower, my breathing shorter and more irregular, my mouth more lax. I was quite prepared to go through another attack of vomiting if needs must; and so persistently did I fail to understand his worldly wisdom that in the end he had to abandon this approach in favour of a more scientific one.

That was not very easy for him. First because of his stupidity; and secondly because the clinical picture I presented was very general and indefinite in character. He thumped my chest and listened to me all over, peered down my throat with the aid of a spoon handle, annoyed me by taking my temperature, and finally, for better or worse, was forced to express his opinion. 'Migraine,' he said. 'No cause for alarm. We know our young friend's tendency in this direction. Unfortunately his stomach is involved in no small degree. I prescribe rest, no visits, little conversation, and preferably a darkened room. Besides, citric acid and caffeine have proved valuable in these cases. I'll write a prescription ...' If, however, there had been a few cases of grippe in the town, he would say: 'Grippe, dear Frau Krull, with gastric complications. Yes, that's what our friend has caught! The inflammation of the respiratory tract is as yet insignificant, but it's detectable. You do cough, don't you, dear boy? I also observe an elevation of temperature, which will no doubt increase in the course of the day. Moreover, the pulse is rapid and irregular.' And, with his hopeless lack of imagination, he could think of nothing but to prescribe a certain bitter-sweet tonic wine from the druggist's, which, moreover, I liked very much. I found it induced a state of warm and quiet satisfaction after my victory in battle.

Indeed, the medical profession is not different from any other: its members are, for the most part, ordinary empty-headed dolts, ready to see what is not there and to deny the obvious. Any untrained person, if he is a connoisseur and lover of the body, exceeds them in his knowledge of its subtler mysteries and can easily lead them around by the nose. The inflammation of the respiratory tract was something I had not thought of, and so had not included in my performance. But once I had forced the doctor to drop his theory of 'school sickness', he had to fall back on grippe, and to that end had to assume that my throat was inflamed and my tonsils swollen, which was just as little the case. He was quite right about the fever – though the fact entirely disproved his first diagnosis by presenting a genuine clinical phenomenon. Medical science maintains that fever can be caused only by an infection of the blood through some agent or other, and that fever on other than physical grounds does not exist. That is absurd. My readers will be as convinced as I that I was not really ill when Health Councillor Düsing examined me. But I was highly excited; I had concentrated my whole being upon an act of will; I was drunk with the intensity of my own performance in my role of parodying nature – a performance that had to be masterly if it was not to be ridiculous; I was delirious with the alternate tension and relaxation necessary to give reality, in my own eyes and others', to a condition that did not exist; and all this so heightened and enhanced my organic processes that the doctor was actually able to read the result on the thermometer. The same explanation applies to the pulse. When the Councillor's head was pressed against my chest and I inhaled the animal odour of his dry, grey hair, I had it in my power to feel a violent reaction that made my heart beat fast and irregularly. And as for my stomach, Dr Düsing said that it too was affected, whatever other diagnosis he produced; and it was true enough that it was an uncommonly sensitive organ, pulsing and contracting with every stir of emotion, so that I could properly speak of a throbbing stomach where others under stress of circumstances speak of a throbbing heart. Of this phenomenon the doctor was aware and he was not a little impressed by it.

And so he prescribed his acid tablets or his bitter-sweet tonic wine and stayed for a while sitting on my bed chatting and gossiping with my mother; while I lay breathing irregularly through my flaccid lips and staring vacantly at the ceiling. My father used to come in, too, and look at me self-consciously, avoiding my glance. He would take advantage of the occasion to consult the doctor about his gout. Then I was left to spend the day alone – perhaps two or three days – on short rations, to be sure, which tasted all the better for their sparseness, given over to dreams of my brilliant career in the world. When my healthy young appetite rebelled at the diet of gruel and Zwieback, I would get cautiously out of bed, noiselessly open the top of my little desk, and partake of the chocolates that almost always lay there in abundant store.

Chapter Seven

Where had I procured them? They had come into my possession in a strange, almost fantastic fashion. Down in the town on a corner of what was, comparatively speaking, our busiest street, there was a neat and attractively stocked delicatessen shop, a branch, if I am not mistaken, of a Wiesbaden firm. It was patronized by the best society. My way to school led me past this shop daily and I had dropped in many times, coin in hand, to buy cheap sweets, fruit drops, or barley sugar. But on going in one day I found it empty not only of customers but of assistants as well. There was a little bell on a spring over the door, and this had rung as I entered; but either the inner room was empty or its occupants had not heard the bell – I was and remained alone. The glass door at the rear was covered by some pleated material. At first the emptiness surprised and startled me, it even gave me an uncanny feeling; but presently I began to look about me, for never before had I been able to contemplate undisturbed the delights of such a spot. It was a narrow room, with a rather high ceiling, and crowded from floor to ceiling with eatables. There were rows and rows of hams and sausages of all shapes and colours – white, yellow, red, and black; fat and lean and round and long – rows of tinned preserves, cocoa and tea, bright translucent glass bottles of honey, marmalade, and jam; round bottles and slender bottles, filled with liqueurs and punch – all these things crowded every inch of the shelves from top to bottom. Then there were glass showcases where smoked mackerel, lampreys, flounders, and eels were displayed on platters to tempt the appetite. There were dishes of Italian salad, crayfish spreading their claws on blocks of ice, sprats pressed flat and gleaming goldenly from open boxes; choice fruits – garden strawberries and grapes as beautiful as though they had come from the Promised Land; rows of sardine tins and those fascinating little white earthenware jars of caviar and *foie gras*. Plump chickens dangled their necks from the top shelf, and there were trays of cooked meats, ham, tongue, beef, and veal, smoked salmon, and breast of goose, with the slender slicing knife lying ready to hand. There were all sorts of cheeses under glass bells, brick-red, milk-white, and marbled, also the creamy ones that overflow their silver foil in golden waves. Artichokes, bundles of asparagus, truffles, little liver sausages in silver paper – all these things lay heaped in rich profusion; while on other tables stood open tin boxes full of fine biscuits, spice cakes piled in criss-cross layers, and glass urns full of dessert chocolates and candied fruits.

I stood enchanted, straining my ears and breathing in the delightful atmosphere and the mixed fragrance of chocolate and smoked fish and earthy truffles. My mind was filled with memories of fairy-tale kingdoms, of underground treasure chambers where Sunday children might fill their pockets and boots with precious stones. It was indeed either a fairy-tale or a dream! Everyday laws and prosaic regulations were all suspended. One might give free rein to one's desires and let imagination roam in blissful unrestraint. So great was the joy of beholding this bountiful spot completely at my disposal that I felt my limbs begin to jerk and twitch. It took great self-control not to burst into a cry of joy at so much newness and freedom. I spoke into the silence, saying: 'Good day' in quite a loud voice; I can still remember how my strained, unnatural tones died away in the stillness. No one answered. And my mouth literally began to water like a spring. One quick, noiseless step and I was beside one of the laden tables. I made one rapturous grab into the nearest glass urn, filled as it chanced with pralines, slipped a fistful into my coat pocket, then reached the door, and in the next second was safely round the corner.

No doubt I shall be accused of common theft. I will not deny the accusation, I will simply withdraw and refuse to contradict anyone who chooses to mouth this paltry word. But the word – the poor, cheap, shopworn word, which does violence to all the finer meanings of life – is one thing, and the primeval absolute deed for ever shining with newness and originality is quite another. It is only out of habit and sheer mental indolence that we come to regard them as the same. And the truth is that the word, as used to describe or characterize a deed, is no better than one of those wire fly-swatters that always miss the fly. Moreover, whenever an act is in question, it is not the what nor the why that matters (though the second is the more important), but simply and solely the who. Whatever I have done or committed, it has always been first of all *my* deed, not Tom's or Dick's or Harry's; and though I have had to accept being labelled, especially by the law, with the same name as ten thousand others, I have always rebelled against such an unnatural identification in the unshakeable belief that I am a favourite of the powers that be and actually composed of finer flesh and blood. The reader, if I ever have one, will pardon this digression into the abstract, which perhaps ill suits me since I am not trained in abstract thought. But I regard it as my duty to reconcile him as far as I can to the eccentricities of my way of life or, if this should prove impossible, to prevent him betimes from reading further.

When I got home I went up to my room, still wearing my overcoat, spread my treasures out on the table, and examined them. I had hardly believed that they were real and would still be there; for how often do priceless things come into our possession in dreams, yet when we wake, our hands are empty. No one can share my lively joy unless he can imagine that the treasures vouchsafed him in a delightful dream are ready and waiting for him on the coverlet of his bed in the light of morning, as though left over from the dream. They were of the best quality, those candies wrapped in silver paper, filled with sweet liqueurs and flavoured creams; but it was not alone their quality that enchanted me; even more it was the carrying over of my dream treasure into my waking life that made up the sum of my delight – a delight too great for me not to think of repeating it when occasion offered. For whatever reason – I did not consider it my duty to speculate – the delicatessen shop occasionally proved to be unattended at noon. This did not happen often or regularly, but after a longer or shorter interval it would occur, and I could tell by strolling slowly past the glass door with my schoolbag on my shoulder. I would return and go in, having learned to open the door so gently that the little bell did not ring, the clapper simply quivering on its wire. I would say 'Good morning', just in case, quickly seize whatever was available, never shamelessly, but rather choosing moderately – a handful of sweets, a slice of honey cake, a bar of chocolate – so that very likely nothing was ever missed. But in the incomparable expansion of my whole being which accompanied these free and dream-like forays upon the sweets of life, I thought I could clearly recognize anew the nameless sensation that had been so long familiar to me as the result of certain trains of thought and introspection.

Chapter Eight

Unknown reader! I have put aside my fluent pen for purposes of reflection and self-examination before treating a theme on which I have had earlier occasion to touch lightly in the course of my confessions. It is now my conscientious duty to dwell on it at somewhat greater length. Let me say immediately that whoever expects from me a lewd tone or scabrous anecdote will be disappointed. It is rather my intention to see that the dictates of morality and good form should be combined with the frankness which I promised at the outset of this enterprise. Pleasure in the salacious for its own sake, though an almost universal fault, has always been incomprehensible to me, and verbal excesses of this kind I have always found the most repulsive of all, since they are the cheapest and have not the excuse of passion. People laugh and joke about these matters precisely as though they were dealing with the simplest and most amusing subject in the world, whereas the exact opposite is the truth; and to talk of them in a loose and careless way is to surrender to the mouthings of the mob the most important and mysterious concern of nature and of life. But to return to my confession.

First of all I must make clear that the above-mentioned concern began very early to play a role in my life, to occupy my thoughts, to shape my fancies and form the content of my childish enterprises – long, that is, before I had any words for it or could possibly form any general ideas of its nature or significance. For a considerable time, that is, I regarded my tendency to such thoughts and the lively pleasure I had in them to be private and personal to myself. Nobody else, I thought, would understand them, and it was in fact advisable not to talk of them at all. Lacking any other means of description, I grouped all my emotions and fancies together under the heading of 'The Best of All' or 'The Great Joy' and guarded them as a priceless secret. And thanks to this jealous reserve, thanks also to my isolation, and a third motive to which I shall presently return, I long remained in a state of intellectual ignorance which corresponded little to the liveliness of my senses. As far back as I can remember, this 'Great Joy' took up a commanding position in my inner life – indeed, it probably began further back than my conscious memory extends. For small children are ignorant and in that sense innocent; but to maintain that theirs is an angelic purity is certainly a sentimental superstition that would not stand the test of objective examination. For myself at least, I have it from an excellent authority (whom I shall shortly identify) that even at my nurse's breast I displayed the most unambiguous evidence of sensual pleasure – and this tradition has always seemed highly credible to me, as indicative of the eagerness of my nature.

In actual fact my gifts for the pleasures of love bordered on the miraculous; even today it is my conviction that they far exceeded the ordinary. I had early grounds to suspect that this was so, but my suspicions were converted to certainty by the evidence of that person who told me of my precocious behaviour at my nurse's breast. For several years I carried on a secret relationship with this person. I refer to our housemaid Genovefa, who had been with us from a tender age and was in her early thirties when I reached sixteen. She was the daughter of a sergeant-major and for a long time had been engaged to the station master at a little station on the Frankfurt–Niederlahnstein line. She had a good deal of feeling for the refinements of life, and although she did all the hard work in the house, her position was halfway between a servant and a member of the family. Her marriage was – for lack of money – only a distant prospect; and the long waiting must have been a genuine hardship for the poor girl. In person she was a voluptuous blonde with exciting green eyes and a graceful way of moving. But despite the prospect of spending her best years in renunciation she never lowered herself to heeding the advances of soldiers, labourers, or such people, for she did not consider herself one of the common folk, and felt only disgust for the way they spoke and the way they smelt. It was different with the son of the house, who may well have won her favour as he developed, and she may have had the feeling that in satisfying him she was not only performing a domestic duty but advancing her social position. Thus it happened that my desires encountered no serious resistance.

I am far from inclined to go into details about an episode that is too common to be of interest to a cultivated public. In brief, my godfather Schimmelpreester had dined with us one evening and later we had spent the time trying on costumes. When I went up to bed it happened – not without her connivance – that I met Genovefa in the dark corridor outside the door of my attic room. We stopped to talk, by degrees drifted into the room itself, and ended by occupying it together for the night. I well remember my mood. It was one of gloom, disillusion, and boredom such as often seized me after an evening of trying on costumes – only this time it was even more severe than usual. I had resumed my ordinary dress with loathing, I had an impulse to tear it off, but no desire to forget my misery in slumber. It seemed to me that my only possible consolation lay in Genovefa's arms – yes, to tell the truth, I felt that in complete intimacy with her I should find the continuation and logical conclusion of my brilliant evening and the proper goal of my adventuring among the costumes from my godfather's wardrobe. However that may be, the soul-satisfying unimaginable delights I experienced on Genovefa's white, well-nourished breast defy description. I cried aloud for bliss, I felt myself borne heavenwards. And my desire was not of a selfish nature, for characteristically I was truly inflamed only by the joy Genovefa evinced. Of course, every possibility of comparison is out of the question; I can neither demonstrate nor disprove, but I was then and am now convinced that with me the satisfaction of love is twice as sweet and twice as penetrating as with the average man.

But it would be unjust to conclude that because of my extraordinary endowment I became a libertine and ladykiller. My difficult and dangerous life made great demands on my powers of concentration – I had to be careful not to exhaust myself. I have observed that with some the act of love is a trifling matter, which they discharge perfunctorily, going their way as though nothing had happened. As for me, the tribute I bought was so great as to leave me for a time quite empty and deprived of the power to act. True, I have often indulged in excesses, for the flesh is weak and I found the world all too ready to satisfy my amorous requirements. But in the end and on the whole I was of too manly and serious a temper not to return from sensual relaxation to a necessary and healthful austerity. Moreover, is not purely animal satisfaction the grosser part of what as a child I had instinctively called 'The Great Joy'? It enervates us by satisfying us too completely; it makes us bad lovers of the world because on the one hand it robs life of its bloom and enchantment while on the other hand it impoverishes our own capacity to charm, since only he who desires is amiable and not he who is satiated. For my part, I know many kinds of satisfaction finer and more subtle than this crude act which is after all but a limited and illusory satisfaction of appetite; and I am convinced that he has but a coarse notion of enjoyment whose activities are directed point-blank to that goal alone. Mine have always been on a broader, larger, and more general scale; they found the most piquant viands where others would not look at all; they were never precisely defined or specialized – and it was for this reason among others that despite my special aptitude I remained so long innocent and unconscious, a child and dreamer indeed, my whole life long.

Chapter Nine

Herewith I leave a subject in the treatment of which I believe I have not for a moment transgressed the canons of propriety and good taste, and hasten forward to the tragic moment which was the turning-point in my career and which terminated my sojourn under my parents' roof. But first I must mention the betrothal of my sister Olympia to Second Lieutenant Übel of the Second Nassau Regiment, stationed in Mainz. The betrothal was celebrated on a grand scale but led to no practical consequences. It was broken off under the stress of circumstances and my sister, after the break-up of our family, went on the stage in comic opera. Übel was a sickly young man, inexperienced in life. He was a constant guest at our parties, and it was there, excited by dancing, games of forfeit, and Berncasteler Doctor, and fired by the calculated glimpses that the ladies of our household granted so freely, that he fell passionately in love with Olympia. Longing for her with the desirousness of weak-chested people and probably overestimating our position and importance, he actually went down on his knees one evening and, almost weeping with impatience, spoke the fatal words. To this day I am amazed that Olympia had the face to accept him, for she certainly did not love him and had doubtless been informed by my mother of the true state of our affairs. But she probably thought it was high time to make sure of some refuge, however insubstantial, from the oncoming storm; and it may even have been indicated to her that her engagement to an army officer, however poor his prospects, might delay the catastrophe. My poor father was appealed to for his consent and gave it with an embarrassed air and little comment; thereupon the family event was communicated to the assembled guests, who received the news with loud huzzahs and christened it, so to speak, with rivers of *Loreley extra cuvée*. After that, Lieutenant Übel came almost daily from Mainz to visit us, and did no little damage to his health by constant attendance upon the object of his sickly desire. When I chanced to enter the room where the betrothed pair had been left alone for a little while, I found him looking so distracted and cadaverous that I am convinced the turn affairs presently took was a piece of unmixed good fortune for him.

As for me, my mind was chiefly occupied in these weeks with the fascinating subject of the change of name my sister's marriage would bring with it. I remember that I envied her almost to the point of dislike. She who for so long had been called Olympia Krull would sign herself in future Olympia Übel – and that fact alone possessed all the charm of novelty. How tiresome to sign the same name to letters and papers all one's life long! The hand grows paralysed with irritation and disgust – what a pleasant refreshment and stimulation of the whole being comes, then, from being able to give oneself a new name and to hear oneself called by it! It seemed to me that the female sex enjoys a great advantage over the male through being afforded at least once in life the opportunity of enjoying this restorative tonic – whereas for a man any change is practically forbidden by law. As I personally, however, was not born to lead the easy and sheltered existence of the majority, I have often disregarded a prohibition that ran counter to both my safety and my dislike of the humdrum and everyday. In doing so I have displayed a very considerable gift of invention and I mention now, by way of anticipation, the peculiar charm of that place in my notes where I first speak of the occasion on which I laid aside like a soiled and worn-out garment the name to which I was born, to assume another which for elegance and euphony far surpassed that of Lieutenant Übel.

But events had taken their course in the midst of the betrothal, and ruin – to express myself metaphorically – knocked with a bony knuckle on our door. Those malicious rumours about my poor father's business, the avoidance we suffered from all and sundry, the gossip about our domestic affairs, all these were most cruelly confirmed by the event – to the miserable satisfaction of the prophets of doom. The wine-drinking public had more and more eschewed our brand. Lowering the price (which could not, of course, improve the product) did nothing to allure the gay world, nor did the enticing design produced to oblige the firm and against his better judgement by my good-natured godfather Schimmelpreester. Presently sales dropped to zero, and ruin fell upon my poor father in the spring of the year I became eighteen.

At that time I was, of course, entirely lacking in business experience – nor am I any better off in that respect now, since my own career, based on imagination and self-discipline, gave me little business training. Accordingly I refrain from exercising my pen on a subject of which I have no detailed knowledge and from burdening the reader with an account of the misfortunes of the Loreley Sparkling Wine Company. But I do wish to give expression to the warm sympathy I felt for my father in these last months. He sank more and more into speechless melancholy and would sit about the house with head bent, the fingers of his right hand gently caressing his rounded belly, ceaselessly and rapidly blinking his eyes. He made frequent trips to Mainz, sad expeditions no doubt designed to raise cash or to find some new source of credit; he would return from these excursions greatly depressed, wiping his forehead and eyes with his batiste handkerchief. It was only at the evening parties we still held in our villa, when he sat at table with his napkin tied around his neck, his guests about him, and his glass in his hand, presiding over the feast, that anything like comfort revisited him. Yet in the course of one such evening there occurred a most unpleasant exchange between my poor father and the Jewish banker, husband of the jet-laden female. He, as I later learned, was one of the most hard-hearted cut-throats who ever lured a harried and unwary businessman into his net. Very soon thereafter came that solemn and ominous day – yet for me refreshing in its novelty and excitement – when my father's factory and business premises failed to open, and a group of cold-eyed, tight-lipped gentlemen appeared at our villa to attack our possessions. My poor father had filed a petition in bankruptcy, expressed in graceful phrases and signed with that naïve, ornamental signature of his which I knew so well how to imitate, and the proceedings had solemnly begun.

On that day, because of our disgrace, I had an excuse for staying away from school – and I may say here that I was never permitted to finish my course. This was due, first, to my having never been at any pains to hide my aversion to the despotism and dullness which characterized that institution, and secondly because our domestic circumstances and ultimate downfall filled the masters with venom and contempt. At the Easter holidays after my poor father's failure, they refused to give me my graduation certificate, thus presenting me with the alternative of staying on in a class below my age or of leaving school and losing the social advantages of a certificate. In the happy consciousness that my personal abilities were adequate to make up for the loss of so trifling an asset, I chose the latter course.

Our financial collapse was complete; it became clear why my poor father had put it off so long and involved himself so deeply in the toils of the usurers, for he was aware that when the crash came, it would reduce him to total beggary. Everything went under the hammer: the warehouses (but who wanted to buy so notoriously bad a product as my father's wine?), the real estate – that is, the cellars and our villa, encumbered as they were with mortgages to two-thirds of their value, mortgages on which the interest had not been paid for years – the dwarfs, the toadstools and earthenware animals in the garden – yes, even the mirrored ball and the Aeolian harp went the same sad way. The inside of the house was stripped of every pleasant luxury: the spinning-wheel, the down cushions, the glass boxes and smelling-salts all went at public auction; not even the halberds over the windows or the portières were spared; and if the little device over the entrance door that played the Strauss melody as the door closed still jingled unmindful of the desolation, it was only because it had not been noticed by its legal owners.

One could hardly say at first that my father gave the impression of a broken man. His features even expressed a certain satisfaction that his affairs, having passed beyond his own competence, now found themselves in such good hands; and since the bank that had purchased our property let us for very pity remain for the time being within its bare walls, we still had a roof over our heads. Temperamentally easy-going and good-natured, he could not believe his fellow human beings would be so pedantically cruel as to reject him utterly; he was actually naïve enough to offer himself as director to a local company that manufactured sparkling wine. Contemptuously rejected, he made other efforts to re-establish himself in life – and if he had succeeded would no doubt have resumed his old practice of feasting and fireworks. But when everything failed he at last gave up; and as he probably considered that he was only in our way and that we might get along better without him, he decided to make an end of it all.

It was five months after the opening of the bankruptcy proceedings, and autumn had begun. Since Easter I had not gone back to school and was enjoying my temporary freedom and absence of definite prospects. We had gathered in our bare dining-room, my mother, my sister Olympia, and I, to eat our meagre meal, and were waiting for the head of the house. But when we had finished our soup and he had not yet appeared, we sent Olympia, who had always been his favourite, to summon him. She had scarcely been gone three minutes when we heard her give a prolonged scream and run still screaming upstairs and down and then distractedly up again. Chilled to the marrow of my bones and prepared for the worst, I hurried to my father's room. There he lay on the floor, his clothes loosened, his hand resting on his protuberant belly, beside him the fatal shining thing with which he had shot himself through his gentle heart. Our maid Genovefa and I lifted him to the sofa, and while she ran for the doctor, and my sister Olympia still rushed screaming through the house, and my mother for very fear would not stir out of the dining-room, I stood beside the body of my sire, now growing cold, with my hand over my eyes and paid him the tribute of my flowing tears.

Chapter One

These papers have lain for a long time under lock and key; for at least a year now indifference towards the enterprise and doubt of my success have kept me from continuing my confessions, piling page on page in faithful sequence. For although I have often maintained that I am setting down these reminiscences principally for my own occupation and amusement, I will now honour truth in this respect, too, and admit freely that I have in secret and as it were out of the corner of my eye given some heed to the reading public as well; indeed, without the encouraging hope of their interest and approval I should hardly have had the perseverance to continue my work even this far. At this point, however, I have had to decide whether these true recollections, conforming modestly to the facts of my life, could compete with the inventions of writers, especially for the favour of a public whose satiety and insensitivity – the result of just such crass productions – cannot be exaggerated. Heaven knows, I said to myself, what excitement, what sensationalism, people will expect in a book whose title seems to place it side by side with murder mysteries and detective stories – whereas my life story, though it does indeed appear strange and often dreamlike, is totally devoid of stage effects and rousing dénouements. And so I thought I must abandon hope.

Today, however, my eyes chanced to fall on the composition in question; once more and not without emotion I ran through the chronicle of my childhood and early youth; aroused, I continued to spin out my reminiscences in imagination; and as certain striking moments in my career appeared vividly before me, I was quite unable to believe that incidents which exercise so enlivening an effect on me could fail to entertain the reading public as well. If I recall, for example, one of the great houses of Germany where, masquerading as a Belgian aristocrat, I sat in the midst of a distinguished company, chatting over coffee and cigars with the director of police, an unusually humane man with a deep understanding of the human heart, discussing the characteristics of confidence men and their appropriate punishment; or if I recollect, just to choose a case in point, the fateful hour of my first arrest, when a young novice among the police officers who came to fetch me was so impressed by the gravity of the occasion and so confused by the magnificence of my bedchamber that he knocked at the open door, carefully wiped his shoes, and humbly murmured: 'Permit me', thereby earning a glower of rage from the officer in charge: then I cannot deny myself the cheery hope that although my disclosures, in respect of vulgar excitement and satisfaction of common curiosity, may be put in the shade by the fables of the novelists, yet to compensate, they will be all the more certain to triumph in the end through a certain refined impressiveness and fidelity to truth. Accordingly my desire has been rekindled to continue and complete these reminiscences; and it is my intention while doing so to exercise, in the matter of purity of style and propriety of expression, even greater care, if possible, than hitherto, so that my offerings may pass muster even in the best houses.

Chapter Two

I take up the thread of my story exactly where I dropped it – that is, at the moment when my poor father, driven into a corner by the hardheartedness of his contemporaries, took his own life. To provide a proper funeral presented difficulties, for the Church averts her face from an act such as his, and even a morality independent of canonical dogma must disapprove it too. Life is by no means the highest good, so precious it must be clung to in all circumstances. Instead it seems to me we should regard it as a heavy and exacting task that has been assigned us, one which we have in some sense chosen and which we are absolutely obliged to carry through with loyal perseverance. To abandon it before our time is unquestionably an act of dereliction. In this particular case, however, my judgement was suspended and converted into wholehearted sympathy – especially since we survivors held it of great moment that the departed should not go to his grave unblessed – my mother and sister, because of what people would say and out of a tendency to bigotry (for they were zealous Catholics); I, however, because I am conservative by nature and have always had an unforced affection for traditional procedures in preference to the vulgarities of progress. Accordingly, since the women's courage failed them, I undertook to persuade the official town minister, Spiritual Counsellor Chateau, to take charge of the obsequies.

I encountered that cheerful and worldly cleric, who had only recently assumed office in our town, at his lunch, which consisted of an omelet *fines herbes* and a bottle of Liebfraumilch, and he received me kindly. For Spiritual Counsellor Chateau was an elegant priest who most convincingly personified the nobility and distinction of his Church. Although he was small and stout he possessed much grace of manner, swayed his hips expertly and attractively when he walked, and was master of the most charmingly accomplished gestures. His manner of speech was studied and impeccable, and below his silky black cassock peeped black silk socks and patent-leather shoes. Freemasons and antipapists maintained that he wore them simply because he suffered from sweaty, evil-smelling feet; but even today I consider that malicious gossip. Although I was as yet personally unknown to him, with a wave of his plump, white hand he invited me to sit down, shared his meal with me, and, in the manner of a man of the world, gave every indication of believing my report, which was to the effect that my poor father, in the process of examining a long unused gun, had been struck down by a shell that went off unexpectedly. This, then, is what he gave the appearance of believing, as a matter of policy, no doubt (for very likely in times like these the Church must rejoice when people sue for her gifts even deceitfully). He bestowed words of human comfort on me and declared himself ready to conduct the priestly rites of burial, the cost of which my godfather Schimmelpreester had nobly engaged to pay. His Reverence thereupon made some notes concerning the manner of life of the departed, which I was at pains to portray as both honourable and happy, and finally he directed to me certain questions about my own circumstances and prospects, which I answered in general and approximate terms. 'My dear son,' was the general tenor of his reply, 'you seem hitherto to have conducted yourself somewhat carelessly. As yet, however, nothing is lost, for your personality makes a pleasing impression and I should like to praise you in particular for the agreeable quality of your voice. I should be much surprised if Fortuna did not prove gracious to you. I make it my business at all times to recognize those with bright prospects, such as have found favour in the eyes of God, for a man's destiny is written on his brow in characters that are not indecipherable to the expert.' And therewith he dismissed me.

Cheered by the words of this clever man, I hastened back to my mother and sister to tell them the happy outcome of my mission. The funeral, I must, alas, admit, turned out to be less impressive than one might have hoped, for the participation of our fellow citizens was meagre in the extreme, a not surprising fact so far as our townspeople were concerned. But where were our other friends, who in his prosperous days had watched my poor father's fireworks and had done so well by his Berncasteler Doctor? They stayed away, less from ingratitude perhaps than simply because they were people who had no taste for those solemn occasions on which one's attention is directed towards the external, and avoided them as something upsetting, a course of action that certainly bespeaks an indifferent character. Among them all only Lieutenant Übel, of the Second Nassau Regiment in Mainz, put in an appearance, though in civilian clothes, and it was thanks to him that my godfather Schimmelpreester and I were not the only ones to follow the swaying coffin to the grave.

Nevertheless, the reverend gentleman's prophecy continued to ring in my ears, for it not only accorded completely with my own presentiments and impressions, but came from a source to which I could attribute particular authority in these arcane matters. To say why would be beyond most people's competence; I believe, however, that I can at least outline the reasons. In the first place, belonging to a venerable hierarchy like the Catholic clergy develops one's perception of the gradations of human worth to a far subtler degree than life in ordinary society can do. Now that this simple thought has been safely stated, I shall go a step further and in doing so I shall try to be consistent and logical. We are here talking about a perception and therefore about a function of our material nature. Now, the Catholic form of worship, in order to lead us to what lies beyond the world of the senses, takes special account of that world and works with it, takes it into consideration in every possible way, and more than any other explores its secrets. An ear accustomed to lofty music, to harmonies designed to arouse a presentiment of heavenly choruses – should not such an ear be sensitive enough to detect inherent nobility in a human voice? An eye familiar with the most gorgeous pomp of colour and form, prefiguring the majesty of the heavenly mansions – should not such an eye be especially quick to detect the signs of mysterious favour in charm and natural endowment? An organ of smell familiar with and taking pleasure in clouds of incense in houses of worship, an organ of smell that in former times would have perceived the lovely odour of sanctity – should it not be able to detect the immaterial yet nevertheless corporeal exhalation of a child of fortune, a Sunday child? And one who has been ordained to preside over the loftiest secret of the Church, the mystery of Flesh and Blood – should he not be able to differentiate, thanks to his higher sensibility, between the more distinguished and the meaner forms of human clay? With these carefully chosen words I flatter myself that I have given my thoughts the completest possible expression.

In any case, the prophecy I had received told me nothing that my insight and opinion of myself did not confirm in the happiest fashion. At times, to be sure, depression weighed my spirit down, for my body, which once an artist's hand had fixed on canvas in a legendary role, was clothed in ugly and shabby garments, and my position in the small town could only be called disgraceful – indeed, suspect. Of disreputable family, son of a bankrupt and suicide, an unsuccessful student without any real prospect in life, I was the object of dark and contemptuous glances; and though my fellow townsmen from whom they came were, in my opinion, superficial and unattractive, they could not but wound painfully a nature such as mine. For as long as I was compelled to stay there, they made it distressing for me to appear in the public streets. This period reinforced the tendency to misanthropy and withdrawal from the world which had always been a part of my character, a tendency that can go so amiably hand in hand with an eager delight in the world and its people. And yet something mingled in those glances – nor was this the case simply among my townswomen – that one might have described as unwilling admiration and that in more auspicious circumstances would have promised the finest recompense for my inner distress. Today, when my face is haggard and my limbs show the marks of age, I can say without conceit that my nineteen years had fulfilled all that my tender youth had promised, and that even in my own estimation I had bloomed into a most attractive young man. Blond and brown at once, with melting blue eyes, a modest smile on my lips, a charmingly husky voice, a silken gleam in my hair, which was parted on the left and brushed back from my forehead in a decorous wave, I would have seemed as appealing to my simple fellow countrymen as later I seemed to the citizens of other parts of the world, if their sight had not been confused and clouded by their awareness of my misfortunes. My physique, which in earlier days had pleased the artistic eye of my godfather, Schimmelpreester, was by no means robust, and yet every limb and muscle was developed with a symmetry usually found only in devotees of sport and muscle-building exercises – whereas I, in dreamer's fashion, had always shunned bodily exercise and had done nothing of an outdoor kind to promote my physical development. It must further be observed that texture of my skin was of an extraordinary delicacy, and so very sensitive that, even when I had no money, I was obliged to provide myself with soft, fine soaps, for if I used the common, cheap varieties, even for a short time, they chafed it raw.

Natural gifts and innate superiorities customarily move their possessors to a lively and respectful interest in their heredity. And so at this time one of my absorbing occupations was to search about among the likenesses of my ancestors – photographs and daguerreotypes, medallions and silhouettes, in so far as these could be helpful – trying to discover in their physiognomies some anticipation or hint of my own person in order that I might know to whom among them I might perhaps owe special thanks. My reward, however, was meagre. I found, to be sure, among my relations and forebears on my father's side much by way of feature and bearing that provided a glimpse of preparatory experiments on the part of nature (just as I made a point of saying earlier, for example, that my poor father, despite his corpulence, was on the friendliest footing with the Graces). On the whole, however, I had to conclude that I did not owe much to heredity; and unless I was to assume that at some indefinite point in history there had been an irregularity in my family tree whereby some cavalier, some great nobleman must be reckoned among my natural forebears, I was obliged, in order to explain the source of my superiorities, to look within myself.

What was it really about the words of the divine that had made such an extraordinary impression on me? Today I can answer precisely, just as at the time I was instantly certain about it in my own mind. He had praised me – and for what? For the agreeable tone of my voice. But that is an attribute or gift that in the common view has nothing at all to do with one's deserts and is no more considered a subject for praise than a cock eye, a goitre, or a club foot is thought blameworthy. For praise or blame, according to the opinion of our middle-class world, is applicable to the moral order only, not to the natural; to praise the latter seems in such a view unjust and frivolous. That Town Minister Chateau happened to think otherwise struck me as wholly new and daring, as the expression of a conscious and defiant independence that had a heathenish simplicity about it and at the same time stimulated me to happy reverie. Was it not difficult, I asked myself, to make a sharp distinction between natural deserts and moral? These portraits of uncles, aunts, and grandparents had taught me how few, indeed, of my assets had come to me by way of natural inheritance. Was it true that I had had so little to do, in an inner sense, with the development of those assets? Had I not instead the assurance that they were my own work, to a significant degree, and that my voice might quite easily have turned out common, my eyes dull, my legs crooked, had my soul been less watchful? He who really loves the world shapes himself to please it. If, furthermore, the natural is a consequence of the moral, it was less unjust and capricious than might have appeared for the reverend gentleman to praise me for the pleasing quality of my voice.

Chapter Three

A few days after we had consigned my father's mortal remains to the earth, we survivors, together with my godfather, Schimmelpreester, assembled for a deliberation or family council, for which our good friend arranged to come out to our villa. We had been officially informed that we should have to vacate the premises by New Year's Day, and so it had become urgently necessary for us to make serious plans about our future residence.

In this connexion I cannot praise highly enough the counsel and assistance of my godfather. Nor can I express sufficient gratitude for the plans and suggestions that extraordinary man had worked out for each of us. These proved in the sequel to be altogether happy and fruitful inspirations, especially for me.

Our former salon, once furnished with refinement and elegance and filled so often with an atmosphere of joy and festivity, now barren, pillaged, and hardly furnished at all, was the sorry scene of our conference. We sat in one corner on cane-bottomed walnut chairs, which had been part of the dining-room furniture, around a small green table that was really a nest of four or five fragile tea or serving tables.

'Krull!' my godfather began (in his comfortable, friendly way he used to call my mother simply by her last name). 'Krull!' he said, turning towards her his hooked nose and those sharp eyes without brows or lashes, which were so strangely emphasized by the celluloid frames of his glasses, 'you hang your head, you look limp, and you're entirely wrong to act like that. The bright and cheery possibilities of life only reveal themselves after that truly cleansing catastrophe which is correctly called social ruin, and the most hopeful situation in life is when things are going so badly for us that they can't possibly go worse. Believe me, dear friends, I am thoroughly familiar with this situation, through inner experience if not in a material sense! Furthermore, you are not really in it yet and that's bound to be what's weighing down the wings of your soul. Courage, my dear! Arouse your spirit of initiative! Here the game is up, but what of it? The wide world lies before you. Your small personal account in the Bank of Commerce is not yet entirely exhausted. With that remaining nest egg you shall set yourself up to keep lodgers in some big city, Wiesbaden, Mainz, Cologne, or even Berlin. You are at home in the kitchen – forgive my inept expression – you know how to make a pudding out of crumbs and a tangy hash out of day-before-yesterday's leftovers. Furthermore, you are used to having people around you, used to feeding them and entertaining them. And so you will rent a few rooms, you will let it be known that you are ready to take in boarders and lodgers at reasonable rates, you will go on living as you have hitherto, only now you will let the consumers pay and thereby get your profit. It will simply be a matter of your patience and good humour producing an atmosphere of cheerfulness and comfort among your clients, and I should be much surprised if your institution does not prosper and expand.'

Here my godfather paused, and we had an opportunity to give heartfelt expression to our approval and thanks. Presently he took up his discourse again.

'As far as Lympchen is concerned,' he continued (that was my sister's pet name), 'the obvious idea would be for her to remain with her mother and follow her natural vocation of making their guests' stay agreeable, and it is undeniable that she would prove herself an admirable and attractive *filia hospitalis*. Indeed, the chance of making herself useful in this capacity will always remain open. But for a start, I have something better in mind for her. In the days of your prosperity she learned to sing a little. Not to amount to much, her voice is weak, but it has a pleasant, tender quality, and her other advantages, which spring to the eye, add to its effectiveness. Solly Meerschaum in Cologne is a friend of mine from the old days and his principal business interest is a theatrical agency. He will have no trouble finding a place for Olympia either in a light-opera troupe, at first of the simpler sort, or in a music-hall company – and her first outfit will be paid for out of what remains of my ill-gotten gains. At the start her career will be dark and difficult. She may have to wrestle with life. But if she shows signs of character (which is more important than talent) and knows how to profit by her single talent, which consists of so many pounds, her path will swiftly lead upward from her lowly beginning – possibly to glittering heights. Of course, I, for my part, can only indicate general directions and sketch in possibilities; the rest is your affair.'

Shrieking with joy, my sister flew to our counsellor and threw her arms around his neck. During his next words she kept her head hidden on his breast.

'Now,' he said, and it was easy to see that what was coming lay especially close to his heart, 'in the third place I come to our fancy-dress boy.' (The reader will understand the reference contained in this epithet.) 'I have given thought to the problem of his future and, despite considerable difficulties in the way of finding a solution, I think I have hit upon one, though it may be only of a temporary kind. I have even begun a foreign correspondence on the subject; with Paris, to be specific – I'll explain in a moment. In my opinion, the most important thing is to introduce him to that way of life to which, through a misunderstanding, the school authorities thought they ought not to grant him honourable admittance. Once we have him in the clear the flood tide will bear him along and bring him, as I confidently hope, to happy shores. Now it seems to me that in his case a career as a hotel waiter offers the most hopeful prospects: both as a career in itself (which can lead to very lucrative positions in life) and thanks to those bypaths which open up here and there to left and right of the main thoroughfare and have provided a livelihood for many a Sunday's child before now. The correspondence I mentioned has been with the director of the Hotel Saint James and Albany in Paris, on the rue Saint-Honoré not far from the Place Vendôme (a central location, that is; I'll show it to you on my map) – with Isaak Stürzli, an intimate friend since the days when I lived in Paris. I have put Felix's family background and personal qualities in the most favourable light and I have vouched for his polish and his adroitness. He has a smattering of French and English; he will do well in the immediate future to extend his knowledge of these languages as much as possible. In any case, as a favour to me, Stürzli is prepared to accept him on probation – at first, to be sure, without a salary. Felix will have free board and lodging and he will also be given some help in acquiring his livery, which will certainly be very becoming to him. In short, here is a way, here are space and a favourable environment for the development of his gifts, and I count on our fancy-dress boy to wait upon the distinguished guests of the Saint James and Albany to their complete satisfaction.'

It is easy to imagine that I showed myself no less grateful to this splendid man than the women. I laughed for joy and embraced him in complete ecstasy. My cramped and odious native place disappeared at once, and the great world opened before me; Paris, that city whose very memory had made my poor father weak with joy throughout his life, arose in brightest majesty before my inner eye. However, the matter was not so simple, there was indeed a difficulty, or, as people say, a hitch; for I could not and might not go in search of the wide world until the matter of my military service was attended to; until my papers were in order, the borders of the Empire were insuperable barriers, and the question presented all the more disquieting an aspect since, as the reader knows, I had not succeeded in gaining the prerogatives of the educated class and would have to enter the barracks as a common recruit if I was found fit for service. This circumstance, this difficulty which I had hitherto put out of mind so lightly, weighed heavily on my heart at the moment when I was so elated by hope; and when I hesitantly mentioned the matter, it transpired that neither my mother and sister nor even Schimmelpreester had been aware of it: the former out of womanly ignorance and the latter because, as an artist, he was accustomed to pay scant attention to political and official affairs. Furthermore, he confessed to complete helplessness in this case; for, as he irritably explained, he did not have any sort of connexion with army doctors and there was therefore no chance of exerting personal influence on the authorities; I could just see about getting my head out of this noose myself.

Thus I turned out to be entirely dependent on my own resources in this very ticklish matter, and the reader will judge whether I rose to the occasion.

In the meanwhile, however, my youthful and volatile spirits were diverted and distracted in a variety of ways by the prospect of leaving, the imminent change of scene, and our preparations. My mother hoped to be taking in lodgers and boarders by New Year, and so the move was to be made before the Christmas holiday. We had finally fixed on Frankfurt am Main as our goal because of the greater opportunities afforded by so large a city.

How lightly, how impatiently does youth, bent on taking the wide world by storm, turn its back, contemptuous and unfeeling, on its little homeland, without once looking round at the towers and vineyard-covered hills! And yet, however much a man may have outgrown it and may continue to outgrow it, its ridiculous, too familiar image still remains in the background of his consciousness, or emerges from it strangely after years of complete forgetfulness: what was absurd becomes estimable; among the actions, impressions, successes of one's life abroad, at every juncture, one takes secret thought for that small world, at every increase in one's fortunes one asks inwardly what it may be saying or what it might say, and this is true especially when one's homeland has behaved unkindly, unjustly, and obtusely towards one. While he is dependent on it, the youth defies it; but when it has released him and may long since have forgotten him, of his own free will he gives it the authority to pass judgement on his life. Yes, some day, after many years rich in excitement and in change, he will probably be drawn back to his birthplace, he will yield to the temptation, conscious or unconscious, to show himself to its narrow view in all the glitter he has gained abroad, and with mixed anxiety and derision in his heart, he will feast upon its astonishment – just as, in due course, I shall report of myself.

I wrote a polite letter to the aformentioned Stürzli in Paris, asking him to be patient on my account since I was not free to cross the border right away but must wait until the question of my fitness for military service had been decided – a decision, I ventured to add, that would probably prove favourable for reasons in no way affecting my future calling. Our remaining possessions were quickly transferred to packing cases and hand luggage. Among them were six magnificent starched shirts that my godfather had given me as a parting gift and that were to stand me in good stead in Paris. And one gloomy winter day we three, leaning out to wave from the window of the departing train, saw the fluttering red handkerchief of our good friend disappear in the fog. I only saw that splendid man once again.

Chapter Four

I shall pass quickly over the first confused days following our arrival in Frankfurt, for it pains me to recall the distressing role we were obliged to play in that rich and resplendent centre of commerce, and I should be afraid of earning the reader's displeasure by a circumstantial account of our situation. I say nothing of the dingy hostelry or boarding-house, unworthy of the name of hotel which it arrogated to itself, where, for reasons of economy, my mother and I spent several nights, my sister Olympia having parted company with us at the junction of Wiesbaden in order to seek her fortune in Cologne with Meerschaum, the agent. For my own part, I spent those nights on a sofa teeming with vermin that both stung and bit. I say nothing of our painful wanderings through that great, cold-hearted city, so unfriendly to poverty, in search of an abode we could afford, until, in a mean section, we finally came on one that had just been vacated and that corresponded fairly well to my mother's idea of a starting-place. It consisted of four small, sunless rooms and an even smaller kitchen, and was situated on the ground floor of a rear building, with a view of ugly courtyards. As, however, it cost only forty marks a month, and as it ill became us to be fastidious, we rented it on the spot and moved in the same day.

Whatever is new holds infinite charm for the young, and although this gloomy domicile could not be compared even faintly with our cheerful villa at home, I nevertheless felt cheered by the unfamiliar surroundings and satisfied to the point of boisterousness. With rough and ready helpfulness I joined my mother in the necessary preliminaries, moving furniture, unpacking cups and plates from protective wood-shavings, stocking shelves and cupboards with pots and pans; I also undertook to negotiate with our landlord, a repulsively fat man with vulgar manners, about the necessary alterations in our quarters. 'Fat-belly', however, obstinately refused to pay for them, and in the end my mother had to dip into her own pocket-book so that the rooms we hoped to rent would not look completely dilapidated. This came hard, for the costs of moving and settling in had been high, and if our paying guests did not put in an appearance, our establishment would be threatened with bankruptcy before it was properly started.

On the very first evening, as we were standing in the kitchen eating our supper of fried eggs, we decided, for reasons of pious and happy memory, to call our establishment 'Pension Loreley', and we immediately communicated this decision to my godfather Schimmelpreester, on a postcard we jointly composed; next day I hurried to the office of Frankfurt's leading newspaper with an advertisement couched in modest yet enticing terms and designed, by the use of boldface type, to impress that poetic name on the public consciousness. Because of the expense, we were unable for several days to put up a sign on the house facing the street that would attract the attention of passers-by to our establishment. How describe our jubilation when, on the sixth or seventh day after our arrival, the mail from home brought a package of mysterious shape with my godfather Schimmelpreester's name on it? It contained a metal sign one end of which was bent at a right angle and pierced by four holes. It bore, painted by the artist's own hand, that female figure clothed only in jewellery which had adorned our bottle labels, with the inscription: 'Pension Loreley' emblazoned in gold letters beneath it. When this had been fastened to the corner of the house facing the street in such a way that the fairy of the rock pointed with outstretched, ring-bedecked hand across the courtyard to our establishment, it produced the most beautiful effect.

As it turned out, we did get customers: first of all in the person of a young technician or mechanical engineer, a solemn, quiet, even morose man, clearly discontented with his lot, who, nevertheless, paid punctually and led a discreet and orderly life. He had been with us barely a week when two other guests arrived together: members of the theatrical profession – a comic bass, unemployed because of having lost his voice completely, heavy and jolly in appearance but in a furious temper as a result of his misfortune and determined to restore his organ through persistent and futile exercises which sounded as though someone were drowning inside a hogshead and shouting for help; and with him his female supplement, a red-haired chorus girl with long, rose-coloured fingernails, who wore a dirty dressing-gown – a pathetic, frail creature who seemed to have chest trouble, but whom the singer, either on account of her shortcomings or simply to give vent to his general bitterness, beat frequently and severely with his braces, without, however, making her at all dubious about him or his affection for her.

These two, then, occupied a room together, the machinist another; the third served as a dining-room, where we all consumed the meals my mother skilfully concocted out of very little. As I did not wish to share a room with my mother, for obvious reasons of propriety, I slept on a kitchen bench with bedding spread over it, and washed myself at the kitchen sink, mindful that this state of affairs could not last and that, in one way or another, my road would soon have a turning.

The Pension Loreley began to flourish; the guests, as I have indicated, drove us into a corner, and my mother could properly look forward to an enlargement of the enterprise and the acquisition of a maid. In any case, the business was on its feet, my assistance was no longer required, and, left to myself, I saw that until I departed for Paris or was compelled to put on a uniform, there would be a prolonged period of leisurely waiting of the sort that is so welcome to a high-minded youth – indeed, so necessary for his inner development. Education is not won in dull toil and labour; rather it is the fruit of freedom and apparent idleness; one does not achieve it by exertion, one breathes it in; some secret machinery is at work to that end, a hidden industry of the senses and the spirit, consonant with an appearance of complete vagabondage, is hourly active to promote it, and you could go so far as to say that one who is chosen learns even in his sleep. For one must after all be of educable stuff in order to be educated. No one grasps what he has not possessed from birth, and you can never yearn for what is alien. He who is made of common clay will never acquire education; he who does acquire it was never crude. And here once again it is very hard to draw a just and clear distinction between personal desert and what are called favourable circumstances; if, on the one hand, beneficent fortune had placed me in a big city at the right moment and granted me time in abundance, on the other hand it must be said that I was entirely deprived of the means which alone throw open the many places of entertainment and education such a city contains. And in my studies I had, as it were, to be content with pressing my face against the magnificent gates of a pleasure garden.

At this time I devoted myself to sleep almost to excess, usually sleeping until lunchtime, often until much later, eating a warmed-up meal in the kitchen or even a cold one, and afterwards lighting a cigarette, a gift from our machinist (who knew how greedy I was for this pleasure and how unable I was to provide it for myself out of my own funds). I did not leave the Pension Loreley until late in the afternoon, four or five o'clock. At that hour the fashionable life of the city reached its height, rich ladies rode out in their carriages to pay calls or go shopping, the coffee houses were filling, and the shop windows began to come magnificently alight. Then it was that I betook myself to the centre of town, embarking on a journey of pleasure and entertainment through the populous streets of the famous city, from which I would not return to my mother's house until the grey of dawn, though usually with much profit.

Now observe this youth in ragged clothes, alone, friendless, and lost in the crowd, wandering through this bright and alien world. He has no money with which to take any real part in the joys of civilization. He sees them proclaimed and touted on the placards stuck on advertising pillars, so excitingly that they would arouse curiosity and desire in even the dullest (whereas he is especially impressionable) – and he must content himself with reading their names and being aware of their existence. He sees the portals of the theatres festively open and dares not join the crowd that goes streaming in; he stands dazzled in the unearthly light that spills across the pavement from music halls and vaudeville houses, in front of which, perhaps, some gigantic Negro, his countenance and purple costume blanched by the white brilliance, towers fabulously in tricorn hat, waving his staff – and he cannot accept the flashing-toothed invitation and the enticements of the spiel. But his senses are lively, his mind attentive and alert; he sees, he enjoys, he assimilates; and if at first the rush of noise and faces confuses this son of a sleepy country town, bewilders him, frightens him indeed, nevertheless he possesses mother wit and strength of mind enough slowly to become master of his inner turmoil and turn it to good purpose for his education, his enthusiastic researches.

And what a happy institution the shop window is! How lucky that stores, bazaars, salons, that market places and emporia of luxury do not stingily hide their treasures indoors, but shower them forth in glittering profusion, in inexhaustible variety, spreading them out like a splendid offering behind shining plate glass. Brighter than day on a winter's afternoon is the illumination of these displays: rows of little gas flames at the bottoms of the windows keep the panes from frosting over. And there stood I, protected from the cold only by a woollen scarf wrapped around my neck (for my overcoat, inherited from my poor father, had long since gone to the pawnshop for a paltry sum), devouring with my eyes these wares, these precious and splendid wares, and paying no attention to the cold and damp that worked their way up from my feet to my thighs.

Whole suites were arranged in the windows of the furniture shops: drawing-rooms of stately luxury, bed-chambers that acquainted one with every intimate refinement of cultivated life; inviting little dining-rooms, where the damask-covered, flower-bedecked tables, surrounded by comfortable chairs, shimmered enchantingly with silver, fine porcelain, and fragile glassware; princely salons in formal style with candelabra, fireplaces, and brocaded armchairs; and I never tired of observing how firmly and splendidly the legs of this noble furniture rested on the colourful, softly glowing Persian carpets. Farther on, the windows of the haberdasher and a fashion shop drew my attention. Here I saw the wardrobes of the rich and great, from satin dressing-gowns and silk-lined smoking-jackets to the evening severity of the tail-coat, from the alabaster collar in the latest, most favoured style to the delicate spat and the mirror-bright patent-leather shoe, from the pin-striped or dotted shirt with French cuffs to the costly fur jacket; here their hand luggage was displayed before me, those knapsacks of luxury, of pliant calfskin or expensive alligator, which looks as though it were made out of little squares; and I learned to know the appurtenances of a high and discriminating way of life, the bottles, the hair-brushes, the dressing-cases, the boxes with plates and cutlery and collapsible spirit stoves of finest nickel; fancy waistcoats, magnificent ties, sybaritic underclothes, morocco slippers, silk-lined hats, deerskin gloves, and socks of gauzy silk were strewn in seductive display; the youth could fix in his memory the wardrobe requirements of a man of fashion down to the last, sturdy, convenient button. But perhaps I needed only to slip across the street, carefully and adroitly dodging between carriages and honking buses, to arrive at the windows of an art gallery. There I saw the treasures of the decorative industry, such objects of a high and cultivated visual lust as oil paintings by the hands of masters, gleaming porcelain figures of animals of various sorts, beautifully shaped eathenware vessels, small bronze statues, and dearly would I have liked to pick up and fondle those poised and noble bodies.

But what sort of splendour was it a few steps farther on that held me rooted to the spot in amazement? It was the window display of a big jeweller and goldsmith – and here nothing but a fragile pane of glass divided the covetousness of a freezing boy from all the treasures of fairyland. Here, more than anywhere else, my first dazzled enchantment was combined with the eagerest desire to learn. Pearl necklaces, palely shimmering on lace runners, arranged one above another, big as cherries in the middle and decreasing symmetrically towards the sides, ending in diamond clasps, and worth whole fortunes; diamond jewellery bedded on satin, sharply glittering with all the colours of the rainbow and worthy to adorn the neck, the bosom, the head of queens; smooth golden cigarette cases and cane heads, seductively displayed on glass shelves; and everywhere, carelessly strewn, polished precious stones of magnificent colour: blood-red rubies; grass-green, glossy emeralds; transparent blue sapphires that held a star-shaped light; amethysts whose precious violet shade is said to be due to organic content; mother-of-pearl opals whose colour changed as I shifted my position; single topazes; fanciful arrangements of gems in all the shadings of the spectrum – all this was not only a joy to the senses, I studied it, I immersed myself completely in it, I tried to decipher the few price tags that were visible, I compared, I weighed by eye, for the first time I became aware of my love for the precious stones of the earth, those essentially quite worthless crystals whose elements through a playful whim of nature have combined to form these precious structures. It was at this time that I laid the groundwork for my later reliable connoisseurship in this magical domain.

Shall I speak too of the flower ships out of whose doors, when they were opened, gushed the moist, warm perfumes of paradise, and behind whose windows I saw those sumptuous flower baskets, adorned with gigantic silk bows, that one sends to women as evidence of one's attention? Or of the stationery stores whose display taught me what sort of notepaper a cavalier uses for his correspondence, and how the initials of one's name are engraved on it with crest and coat of arms? Or the windows of the perfumers and hairdressers, where in glittering elegant rows shone the many different scents and essences that come from France, and the delicate instruments used for the manicure and the care of the face were displayed in richly lined cases? The gift of seeing had been granted me and it was my be-all and end-all at this time – an instructive gift, to be sure, when material things, the enticing, educational aspects of the world, are its object. But how much more profoundly does the gift of perception engage one's feelings! Perception, that visual feasting on the human spectacle as it unfolds in the fashionable districts of a great city – whither I went by preference – how very different from the attraction of inanimate objects must be the pull it exerts on the longings and curiosity of a passionately ambitious youth!

O scenes of the beautiful world! Never have you presented yourselves to more appreciative eyes. Heavens knows why one in particular among the nostalgic pictures I stored up at that time has sunk so deeply into me and clings so persistently in my memory that despite its unimportance, its insignificance indeed, it fills me with delight even today. I shall not resist the temptation to record it here, though I know very well that a story-teller – and it is as a story-teller that I present myself in these pages – ought not to encumber the reader with incidents of which 'nothing comes', to put the matter bluntly, since they in no way advance what is called 'the action'. But perhaps it is in some measure permissible, in the description of one's own life, to follow not the laws of art but the dictates of one's heart.

Once more, it was nothing, it was only charming. The stage was above my head – an open balcony of the *bel étage* of the great Hotel Zum Frankfurter Hof. Onto it stepped one afternoon – it was so simple that I apologize – two young people, as young as myself, obviously a brother and sister, possibly twins – they looked very much alike – a young man and a young woman moving out together into the wintry weather. They did so out of pure high spirits, hatless, without protection of any kind. Slightly foreign in appearance, dark-haired, they might have been Spanish, Portuguese, South American, Argentinian, Brazilian – I am simply guessing – but perhaps, on the other hand, they were Jews – I could not swear they were not and I would not on that account be shaken in my enthusiasm, for gently reared children of that race can be most attractive. Both were pretty as pictures – the youth not a whit less than the girl. In evening dress, both of them, the youth with a pearl in his shirt-front, the girl wearing one diamond clip in her rich, dark, attractively dressed hair and another at her breast, where the flesh-coloured silk of her princess gown met the transparent lace of the yoke and sleeves.

I trembled for the safety of their attire, for a few damp snowflakes were falling and some of them came to rest on their wavy black hair. But they carried on their childish family prank for only two minutes at most, only long enough to point out to each other, as they leaned laughing over the railing, some incident in the street. Then they pretended to shiver with cold, knocked one or two snowflakes from their clothes, and withdrew into their room, where the light was at once turned on. They were gone, the enchanting phantasmagoria of an instant, vanished never to be seen again. But for a long time I continued to lean against the lamp-post, staring up at their balcony, while I tried in imagination to force my way into their existence; and not on that night only but on many following nights, when I lay down on my kitchen bench exhausted from wandering and watching, my dreams were of them.

Dreams of love, dreams of delight, and a longing for union – I cannot name them otherwise, though they concerned not a single image but a double creature, a pair fleetingly but profoundly glimpsed, a brother and sister – a representative of my own sex and of the other, the fair one. But the beauty lay here in the duality, in the charming doubleness, and if it seems more than doubtful that the appearance of the youth alone on the balcony would have inflamed me in the slightest, apart perhaps from the pearl in his shirt, I am almost equally sure that the image of the girl alone, without her fraternal complement, would never have lapped my spirit in such sweet dreams. Dreams of love, dreams that I loved precisely because – I firmly believe – they were of primal indivisibility and indeterminateness, double; and that really means only then a significant whole blessedly embracing what is beguilingly human in both sexes.

Dreamer and idler! I hear the reader addressing me. Where are your adventures? Do you propose to entertain me throughout your whole book with such fine-spun quiddities, the so-called experiences of your covetous idleness? No doubt, until the policeman drove you away, you pressed your forehead and nose against the big glass panes and peered into the interior of elegant restaurants through the openings in the cream-coloured curtains – stood in the mixed, spicy odours that drifted up from the kitchen through cellar gratings and saw Frankfurt's high society, served by attentive waiters, dining at little tables on which stood shaded candles and candelabra and crystal vases with rare flowers? So I did – and I am astounded at how accurately the reader is able to report the visual joys I purloined from the beau monde, just exactly as though he had had his own nose pressed against that pane. So far as 'idleness' is concerned, he will very soon see the inaccuracy of any such description and will, like a gentleman, withdraw it and apologize. Let it be said now, however, that, divorcing myself from the spectator's role, I sought and found a personal relationship with that world to which I was drawn by nature. I would, to wit, linger around the entrances of the theatres at closing-time and, like an active and obliging lad, make myself useful to the exalted public that streamed chattering out of the lobbies, stimulated by the delights of art. I would do this by hailing droshkies and summoning waiting carriages. I would rush out in front of a droshky to stop it in front of the marquee for my patron, or I would run some distance up the street to catch one and then drive back, sitting beside the coachman. Swinging down like a lackey, I would open the door for the people who were waiting, with a bow so perfect as to startle them. To summon the private coupés and coaches, I would inquire in flattering fashion the names of their fortunate owners and I took no small delight in shouting those names and titles down the street in a clear, strong voice – Privy Councillor Streisand! Consul General Ackerbloom! Lieutenant-Colonel von Stralenheim or Adelsleben! And then the horses would drive up. Many names were quite difficult and their owners hesitated to tell them to me, doubtful of my ability to pronounce them. A dignified married couple, for example, with an obviously unmarried daughter, was named Crequis de Mont-en-fleur, and what pleased surprise all three showed at the correctness and elegance with which that name rang out when they finally entrusted it to me, that name compounded, as it were, of sneezes and giggles terminating in a nasal but flowery poesy! It came to the ears of their fairly far-off and aged family coachman like the clarion morning call of chanticleer, so that there was no delay in bringing up the old-fashioned but well-washed carriage and the plump, dun-coloured pair.

Many a welcome coin, often enough a silver one, was slipped into my hand for these services tendered to Society. But more precious to my heart, a dearer, more reassuring reward was mine as well – an intercepted look of astonishment, of attentive kindliness on the part of the world, a glance that measured me with pleased surprise; a smile that dwelt on my person with amazement and curiosity; and so carefully did I treasure up these secret triumphs that I could today report them more easily than almost anything else, however significant and profound.

What a wonderful phenomenon it is, carefully considered, when the human eye, that jewel of organic structures, concentrates its moist brilliance on another human creature! This precious jelly, made up of just as ordinary elements as the rest of creation, affirming, like a precious stone, that the elements count for nothing, but their imaginative and happy combination counts for everything – this bit of slime embedded in a bony hole, destined some day to moulder lifeless in the grave, to dissolve back into watery refuse, is able, so long as the spark of life remains alert there, to throw such beautiful, airy bridges across all the chasms of strangeness that lie between man and man!

Of delicate and subtle matters one should speak delicately and subtly, and so a supplementary observation will be cautiously inserted here. Only at the two opposite poles of human contact, where there are no words or at least no more words, in the glance and in the embrace, is happiness really to be found, for there alone are unconditional freedom, secrecy, and profound ruthlessness. Everything by way of human contact and exchange that lies between is lukewarm and insipid; it is determined, conditioned, and limited by manners and social convention. Here the word is master – that cool, prosaic device, that first begetter of tame, mediocre morality, so essentially alien to the hot, inarticulate realm of nature that one might say every word exists in and for itself and is therefore no better than claptrap. I say this, I, who am engaged in the labour of describing my life and am exerting every conceivable effort to give it a belletristic form. And yet verbal communication is not my element; my truest interest does not lie there. It lies rather in the extreme, silent regions of human intercourse – that one, first of all, where strangeness and social rootlessness still create a free, primordial condition and glances meet and marry irresponsibly in dreamlike wantonness; but then, too, the other in which the greatest possible closeness, intimacy, and commingling re-establish completely that wordless primordial condition.

Chapter Five

But I am conscious of a look of concern on the reader's face lest as a result of all these tokens of kindliness I may have forgotten, frivolously and completely, the matter of my military obligations, and so I hasten to assure him that this was by no means the case; I had instead kept my eye fixed constantly and uneasily on that fatal question. It is true that after I had reached a decision about handling this unpleasant problem, my uneasiness turned, to a certain extent, into the kind of happy nervousness we feel when we are about to test our abilities in a great, indeed excessive, enterprise and – here I must curb my pen and, out of calculation, resist in some measure the temptation to blurt out everything in advance. For since my intention has steadily strengthened to give this little composition to the press, if I ever get to the end of it, and thus present it to the public, I should be much in the wrong if I did not obey those general rules and maxims professional writers use to maintain interest and tension, against which I should be sinning grossly if I yielded to my inclination to blurt out the best at once and, so to speak, burn up all my powder in advance.

Let just this much be said: I went to work with great thoroughness, with scientific precision in fact, and took good care not to underestimate the difficulties in my path, for plunging ahead was never my way of undertaking a serious enterprise; instead I have always felt that precisely those actions of extreme daring which are almost incredible to the common crowd require the coolest consideration and the most delicate foresight, if their result is not to be defeat, shame, and ridicule – and I have not fared badly. Not content with informing myself exactly as to the methods and practices of the recruiting office and the nature of the regulations on which it acted (which I accomplished partly through conversations with our machinist boarder who had seen military service, and partly with the help of a general reference work in several volumes which another boarder, hopeful of improving himself, had installed in his room), once my plan was sketched in general outline, I saved up one and a half marks from my tips for fetching carriages to buy a publication I had discovered in a bookshop window, a publication of clinical character in the reading of which I immersed myself with both enthusiasm and profit.

Just as a ship requires ballast, so talent requires knowledge, but it is equally certain that we can really assimilate, indeed have a real right to, only just so much knowledge as our talent demands and hungrily draws to itself in each urgent, individual instance, in order to acquire the requisite substance and solidity. I devoured with the greatest joy the instructive content of that little book, and translated what I had aquired into certain practical exercises carried out by candlelight in front of a mirror in the nightly privacy of my kitchen, exercises that would have looked foolish to a secret observer but with which I was pursuing a clear and reasoned goal. Not a word more about it here! The reader will be compensated shortly for this momentary deprivation.

Before the end of January, in compliance with official regulations, I had reported in writing to the military authorities, enclosing my birth certificate, which was in perfect order, as well as the necessary certificate of good behaviour from the Police Bureau, the reticent and negative form of which (to wit, that concerning my way of life nothing reprehensible was known to the authorities) made me childishly angry and uncomfortable. At the beginning of March, just as twittering birds and sweet breezes were charmingly heralding the advent of spring, I was obliged by statute to present myself at the recruiting centre for an initial interview and, summoned to Wiesbaden, I travelled thither by train, fourth class, in a fairly relaxed state of mind, for I knew that the die could hardly be cast that day and that almost everyone comes up before the final authority, which is known as the Superior Recruiting Commission on the Fitness and Enrolment of Youth. My expectations proved correct. The episode was brief, hurried, unimportant, and my memories of it have faded. I was measured up and down, tapped, and questioned, and received no information in return. Dismissed and, for the time being, free, as though on the end of a long tether, I went for a walk in the splendid parks that adorn the spa, amused myself by training my eye in the fine stores in the casino colonnade, and returned to Frankfurt the same day.

But when two more months had passed (half of May was over and a premature midsummer heat hung over the district), the day arrived when my respite ended, the long tether I spoke of figuratively was hauled in, and I had to present myself for recruitment. My heart beat hard when I found myself seated once more on the narrow bench of a fourth-class compartment in the Wiesbaden train, surrounded by characters of the lower sort, and borne on wings of steam towards the moment of decision. The prevailing closeness lulled my travelling-companions into a nodding doze, but could not be allowed to enervate me; awake and alert I sat there, automatically on guard against leaning back, while I tried to picture the circumstances in which I should have to prove myself, and which, to judge by experience, would turn out to be quite different from any I could prefigure. If my feelings were apprehensive as well as happy, it was not because I had any serious doubts about the outcome. That was quite definite in my mind. I was completely determined to go all the way, yes, even if it proved necessary to put all the latent powers of body and soul into the game (in my opinion, it is silly to undertake any great enterprise without being prepared to do this), and I did not for an instant doubt that I was bound to succeed. What made me apprehensive was simply my being uncertain how much of myself I should have to give, what sort of sacrifice in enthusiasm and energy I should have to make to gain my ends – in other words, a sort of tenderness towards myself which had been part of my character of old and could quite easily have turned into softness and cowardice had not more manly qualities evened the balance and held it steady.

I can still see before my eyes, the low, large room, with wooden beams, into which I was roughly herded by the guard and which I found, on entering, filled with a great crowd of young men. Located on the second floor of a dilapidated and abandoned barracks on the outer edge of the city, this cheerless room offered through four bare windows a view of suburban fields disfigured by all sorts of refuse, tin cans, rubbish, and waste. Seated behind an ordinary kitchen table, papers and writing-materials spread out before him, a harsh-voiced sergeant called out names. Those summoned had to pass through a doorless entry into a passage where they stripped to a state of nature and then entered an adjoining room, the real scene of the examination. The behaviour of the man in charge was brutal and deliberately frightening. Frequently he thrust out his fists and legs, yawning like an animal, or made merry, as he ran through the roster, over the impressive degrees of those who appeared before him, headed for that decisive corridor. 'Doctor of philosophy!' he shouted, laughing derisively as though he meant to say: 'We'll beat it out of you, my young friend!' All this aroused fear and revulsion in my heart.

The business of conscription was in full swing but it advanced slowly, and as it proceeded in alphabetical order, those whose names began with letters well along in the alphabet had to resign themselves to a long wait. An oppressive silence hung over the assembly, which consisted of young men from the most varied walks of life. You saw helpless country bumpkins and unruly young representatives of the urban proletariat; semi-refined shop employees and simple sons of toil; there was even a member of the theatrical profession, who aroused much covert merriment by his plump, dark appearance; hollow-eyed youths of uncertain profession, without collars and with cracked patent-leather shoes; mothers' darlings just out of Latin school, and gentlemen of more advanced years with pointed beards, pallid faces, and the delicate deportment of scholars, pacing through the room, restless and painfully intent, conscious of their undignified position. Three or four of the potential recruits whose names would soon be called stood barefooted near the door, stripped to their undershirts, their clothes over their arms, hat and shoes in their hands. Others were sitting on the narrow benches that ran around the room or, perched on one thigh on the window-sills, were making friends and exchanging subdued comments on each other's physical peculiarities and the vicissitudes of conscription. Once in a while, no one knew how, rumours circulated from the room where the board was sitting that the number of those already accepted for service was very large and so the chances of escaping, for those who had not yet been examined, were improving, rumours no one was in a position to verify. Here and there in the crowd jokes and coarse comments broke out about the men already called up, who had to stand about almost entirely naked, and they were laughed at with increasing openness until the biting voice of the uniformed man at the table restored a respectful silence.

I for my part remained aloof as always, took no part in the idle chatter or the coarse jokes, and replied in chilly and evasive fashion when I was spoken to. Standing at an open window (for the human smell in the room had become distressing), I glanced from the desolate landscape outside to the mixed gathering in the room, and let the hours run by. I should have liked to get a glimpse of the neighbouring room where the commission sat, so as to form an impression of the examining doctor; but this was impossible and I kept emphasizing to myself that nothing depended on that particular individual and that my fate rested not in his hands but in mine alone. Boredom weighed heavily on the spirits of those around me. I, however, did not suffer from it, first because I have always been patient by nature, can endure long periods unoccupied, and love the free time those addicted to mindless activity either squander or obliterate; moreover, I was in no hurry to engage in the daring and difficult feat that awaited me, but was instead grateful for the prolonged leisure in which to collect, accustom, and prepare myself.

Noon was already approaching when names beginning with the letter *K* came to my ears. But, as though fate were bent on teasing me, there were a great many, and the list of Kammachers, Kellermanns, and Kilians, as well as Knolls and Krolls, seemed to have no end, so that when my name was finally pronounced by the man at the table, I set about the prescribed toilet rather unnerved and weary. I can declare, however, that my weariness not only failed to detract from my resolution but actually strengthened it.

For that particular day I had put on one of those starched white shirts my godfather had given me at parting, which until now I had conscientiously saved; I had realized in advance that here one's linen would be of special importance and so I now stood at the entrance to the passage, between two fellows in checked, faded cotton shirts, conscious that I could afford to be seen. To the best of my knowledge, no word of ridicule was directed at me from the room, and even the sergeant at the table looked at me with the sort of respect that underlings, used to being subordinate, never deny to elegance of manner and attire. I was quick to notice how curiously he compared the information on his list with my appearance; indeed, he was so engrossed in this study that for a moment he neglected to call my name again at the appropriate time, and I had to ask him whether I was to step inside. He said yes. I crossed the threshold on bare soles and, alone in the passage, placed my clothes on the bench beside those of my predecessor, put my shoes underneath, and took off my starched shirt as well; I folded it neatly and added it to the rest of my outfit. Then I waited alertly for further instructions.

My feeling of tension was painful, my heart hammered irregularly, and I incline to believe that the blood left my face. But with this agitation there was mixed another, happier feeling, to describe which there are no words readily available. Somewhere or other – perhaps in an aphorism or *aperçu* that I came on while reading in prison or glancing through the daily paper – this notion has come to my attention; that nakedness, the condition in which nature brought us forth, is levelling and that no sort of injustice or order of precedence can obtain between naked creatures. This statement, which immediately aroused my anger and resistance, may seem flatteringly self-evident to the crowd, but it is not true in the least, and one might almost say by way of correction that the true and actual order of precedence is established only in that original state, and that nakedness can only be called just in so far as it proclaims the naturally unjust constitution of the human race, unjust in that it is aristocratic. I had perceived this long ago, when my godfather Schimmelpreester's artistry had conjured up my likeness on canvas in its higher significance, and on all those other occasions, as in public baths, where men are freed of their accidental trappings, and step forth in and for themselves. So, too, from that moment on, I was filled with joy and lively pride that I was to present myself before a high commission not in the misleading garb of a beggar but in my own free form.

The end of the passage adjoining the committee room was open, and although a wooden partition blocked my view of the examination scene, I was able to follow its course very accurately by ear. I heard the words of command with which the staff doctor directed the recruit to bend this way and that, to show himself from all sides, heard the short questions and the answers, rambling accounts of an inflammation of the lung, which obviously failed of their transparent purpose, for they were presently cut short by a declaration of unconditional fitness for service. This verdict was repeated by other voices, further instructions followed, the order to withdraw was given, pattering steps approached, and presently the conscript joined me: a poor specimen, I saw, with a brown streak around his neck, plump shoulders, yellow spots on his upper arms, coarse knees, and big, red feet. In the narrow space I was careful to avoid contact with him. At that moment my name was called in a sharp and nasal voice and simultaneously the assisting NCO appeared in front of the cabinet and motioned to me; I stepped out from behind the partition, turned to the left, and strode with dignified but modest bearing to the place where the doctor and the commission awaited me.

At such moments one is blind, and it was only in blurred outline that the scene penetrated to my at once excited and bemused consciousness: obliquely to my right a longish table cut off one corner of the room, and at this the gentlemen sat in a row, some bending forward, some leaning back, some in uniform, some in civilian clothes. To the left of the table stood the doctor, he, too, very shadowy in my eyes, especially since he had the window at his back. I, however, inwardly repelled by so many importunate glances turned on me, bemused by the dream-like sensation of being in a highly vulnerable and defenceless position, seemed to myself to be alone, cut off from every relationship, nameless, ageless, floating free and pure in empty space, a sensation I have preserved in memory as not only not disagreeable but actually precious. The fibres of my body might continue to quiver, my pulse go on beating wildly and irregularly; nevertheless, from then on, my spirit, if not sober, was yet completely calm, and what I said and did in the sequel happened as though without my co-operation and in the most natural fashion – indeed, to my own momentary amazement. Here exactly lies the value of long advance preparation and conscientious immersion in what is to come: at the critical moment something somnambulistic occurs, half-way between action and accident, doing and being dealt with, which scarcely requires our attention, all the less so because the demands actuality makes on us are usually lighter than we expected, and we find ourselves, so to speak, in the situation of a man who goes into battle armed to the teeth only to discover that the adroit use of a single weapon is all he needs for victory. To protect himself the more readily in minor contingencies the prudent man practises what is most difficult, and he is happy if he needs only the most delicate and subtle weapons in order to triumph, as he is naturally averse to anything gross and crude and accommodates himself to their use only in cases of necessity.

'That's a one-year man,' I heard a deep benevolent voice say from the commission table, as though in explanation, but immediately thereafter I was disgusted to hear another, that sharp and nasal voice, declare by way of correction that I was only a recruit.

'Step up,' said the staff doctor. His voice was a rather weak tremolo. I obeyed with alacrity and, standing close in front of him, I made this statement with an absurd but not unpleasant positiveness:

'I am entirely fit for service.'

'That's not for you to judge,' he broke in angrily, thrusting his head forward and shaking it violently. 'Answer what I ask you and refrain from such remarks!'

'Certainly, Surgeon General,' I said softly, although I knew very well that he was nothing but a senior staff doctor, and I looked at him with startled eyes. I could now make him out a little better, He was lean of build, and his uniform blouse hung on him in loose folds. His sleeves, their facings reaching almost to the elbows, were so long that half of each hand was covered and only the thin fingers stuck out. A full beard, sparse and narrow, of a neutral dark shade like the wiry hair on his head, lengthened his face, and this effect was the more pronounced because of his hollow cheeks and his habit of letting his lower jaw sag with his mouth half open. A pince-nez in a silver frame that was bent out of shape sat in front of his narrowed, reddened eyelids in such a way that one lens rested awkwardly against the lid while the other stood far out.

This was the external appearance of my partner. He smiled woodenly at my manner of address and glanced out of the corner of his eye at the table where the commission sat.

'Lift your arms. State your position in civil life,' he said, and at the same time, like a tailor, put a green tape measure with the white figures on it around my chest.

'It is my intention,' I replied, 'to devote myself to hotel service.'

'Hotel service? So, it is your intention. When do you intend to do this?'

'I and mine have reached an understanding that I am to begin this career after I have finished my military service.'

'Hm. I did not ask you about your people. Who are your people?'

'Professor Schimmelpreester, my godfather, and my mother, the widow of a champagne-manufacturer.'

'So, so the widow of a champagne-manufacturer. And what are you doing at present? Are you nervous? Why are your shoulders jerking and twitching that way?'

I had in fact begun, since I had been standing there, half unconsciously and entirely spontaneously, an oddly contrived twisting of the shoulders, an action by no means obtrusive but recurring frequently, which had somehow seemed appropriate. I replied thoughtfully:

'No. It has never for an instant crossed my mind that I might be nervous.'

'Then stop that jerking!'

'Yes, Surgeon General,' I said shamefacedly, and yet at the same instant I jerked again, a fact he appeared to overlook.

'I am not the Surgeon General,' he bleated at me sharply, and shook his outstretched head so violently that the pince-nez threatened to drop off and he was forced to push it back in place with all five fingers of his right hand, an action that could do nothing to remedy the root of the trouble, the fact that it was bent.

'Then I beg your pardon,' I replied very softly and penitently.

'Just answer my question!'

Confused, without comprehension, I looked around me, glanced, too, as though in entreaty at the row of commissioners, in whose deportment I thought I had detected a certain sympathy and interest. Finally I sighed without speaking.

'I have asked about your present occupation.'

'I assist my mother,' I replied with restrained enthusiasm, 'in the operation of a quite large boarding-house or rooming-house in Frankfurt am Main.'

'My compliments,' he said ironically. 'Cough!' he then commanded immediately, for he had placed a black stethoscope against my chest and was bending over to listen to my heart.

I had to cough again and again while he poked about on my body with his instrument. Thereupon he exchanged the stethoscope for a little hammer that he picked up from a near-by table, and he began to tap.

'Have you had any serious illness?' he asked meanwhile.

I replied: 'No, colonel! Never serious ones! To the best of my knowledge I am entirely healthy and have always been so, if I may pass over certain insignificant fluctuations in my health, and I feel myself qualified in the highest degree for any form of military service.'

'Silence!' he said, suddenly interrupting his auscultation and glancing angrily up into my face from his stooping position. 'Leave the question of your military fitness to me and don't make so many irrelevant observations! You continually talk irrelevancies!' he repeated as though distracted, and, interrupting his examination, he straightened up and stepped back from me a little. 'Your manner of speech is lacking in restraint. That struck me some time ago. What is your position anyway? What schools have you attended?'

'I went through six grades at high school,' I replied softly, feigning distress at having alienated and offended him.

'And why not the seventh?'

I let my head hang and threw him an upward glance that may well have spoken for me and struck the recipient to the heart. 'Why do you torment me?' I asked with this look. 'Why do you force me to speak? Don't you hear, don't you feel, don't you see that I am a refined and remarkable youth who, beneath an agreeable and conventional exterior, hides deep wounds that life has cruelly inflicted on him? Is it delicate of you to force me to reveal my shame before so many respectable gentlemen?' Thus my glance; and, discriminating reader, it was by no means a lie, even though its piteous plaint at this particular instant was the product of calculation and design. For lies and hypocrisy refer properly to a sensation that is illegitimately produced because its outward expression corresponds to no true and deep experience, a state of affairs that can only result in pathetic, bungling apishness. Should we not, however, be able to command the timely and useful manifestation of our own precious experiences? Briefly, sadly, and reproachfully my glance spoke of early acquaintance with the injustices and misfortunes of life. Then I sighed deeply.

'Answer,' said the senior staff doctor in a milder tone.

Struggling with myself, I replied hesitantly: 'I was passed over at school and did not complete the course because of a recurrent indisposition that on several occasions confined me to my bed and frequently prevented me from attending class. Also, the teachers thought in their duty to reproach me with lack of attention and diligence, which depressed me very much and disheartened me, since I was not aware of any failure or carelessness in this respect. And yet it so happened that at times a good deal escaped me, I did not hear it or absorb it, whether a classroom exercise was in question or the prescribed homework, whose completion I neglected because I knew nothing about it, not because I entertained other and unsuitable thoughts but because it was exactly as though I had not been present, had not been there in the classroom when the assignments were given out, and this led to reprimands and severe disciplinary measures on the part of the authorities, and on my own part to great –'

Here I could no longer find words, grew confused, fell silent, with my shoulders twitching strangely.

'Stop!' he said. 'Do you have trouble hearing? Step farther back there! Repeat what I say.' And now with laughable distortions of his thin lips and sparse beard, he began to whisper cautiously: 'Nineteen, twenty-seven,' and other figures which I took pains to say after him promptly and exactly; for like all my faculties my hearing was not simply normal but of a special acuity and fineness, and I saw no reason to hide this fact. And so I understood and repeated compound numbers that he only breathed out, and my unusual talent seemed to fascinate him, for he pressed on with the experiment further and further, sending me into the remotest corner of the room in order to hide rather than communicate numbers of four figures at a distance of six or seven yards, and then with pursed mouth he directed significant glances at the commissioner's table when I, half-guessing, understood and repeated what he believed he had barely let slip across his lips.

'Well,' he said finally with pretended indifference, 'you hear very well. Step up here again and tell us precisely how this indisposition that occasionally kept you from school manifested itself.'

Obediently I approached.

'Our family doctor,' I replied, 'Health Councillor Düsing, used to explain it as a kind of migraine.'

'So, you had a family doctor. Health Councillor, was he? And he explained it as migraine! Well, how did it show itself, this migraine? Describe an attack for us. Did you have headaches?'

'Headaches, too!' I replied in surprise, looking at him with respect. 'A kind of roaring in both ears and especially a great feeling of distress and fear or rather a timorousness of the whole body, which finally turns into a spasm of choking so violent that it almost hurls me out of bed.'

'Spasms of choking?' he said. 'Any other spasms?'

'No, certainly no others,' I assured him with great earnestness.

'But the roaring in the ears?'

'A roaring in the ears did certainly often accompany it.'

'And when did the attacks occur? Possibly when there had been preceding excitement of some sort? Some specific cause?'

'If I am right,' I replied hesitantly and with a questioning glance, 'during my school days they often ensued just after an incident – that is, a difficulty of the sort I told –'

'When you failed to hear certain things just as though you had not been there?'

'Yes, Surgeon-in-Chief.'

'Hm,' he said. 'And now just think back and tell us carefully whether you noticed any signs that regularly preceded and heralded this condition when it seemed to you that you weren't present. Don't be hesitant. Overcome your natural embarrassment and tell us frankly whether you noticed anything of the sort at such times.'

I looked at him, looked him resolutely in the eye for a considerable time, while I nodded my head, heavily, slowly, and as it were in bitter reflection.

'Yes, I often feel strange; strange, alas, was and is very often my state of mind,' I finally said softly and reflectively. 'Often it seems as though I have suddenly come close to an oven or a fire, so hot do my limbs feel, first my legs, then the upper parts, and this is accompanied by a kind of tickling or prickling that astonishes me, all the more so because at the same time I have before my eyes a play of colour that is really beautiful but that nevertheless terrifies me; and if I may come back to the prickling for a moment, one might describe it as ants running over one.'

'Hm. And after this you fail to hear certain things?'

'Yes, that is so, superintendent, sir! There is a great deal I don't understand about my nature, and even at home it has caused me embarrassment, for at times I know I have involuntarily dropped my spoon at the table and stained the tablecloth with soup, and afterwards my mother scolds me because I, a full-grown man, behave so boorishly in the presence of our guests – theatrical artists and scholars they are, for the most part.'

'So, you drop your spoon? And only notice it a bit later? Tell me, did you ever tell your family doctor, this Health Councillor or whatever that civilian title is, about these little irregularities?'

Softly and dejectedly I replied that I had not.

'And why not?' the other persisted.

'Because I was ashamed,' I replied falteringly, 'and did not want to tell anyone; it seemed to me that I must keep it secret. And then, too, I hoped secretly that in time it would go away. And I would never have thought I could have enough confidence in anyone to confess to him what very strange experiences I sometimes have.'

'Hm,' he said, twitching his sparse beard derisively, 'because you probably thought they would simply explain it all as migraine. Didn't you say,' he went on, 'that your father was a distiller?'

'Yes – that is, he owned a sparkling-wine establishment on the Rhine,' I said, politely confirming his words and at the same time correcting them.

'Right, a sparkling-wine establishment! And so your father was probably a distinguished connoisseur of wine, wasn't he?'

'He was indeed, superintendent, sir!' I said happily, while a wave of amusement visibly swept the commission table. 'Yes, he was indeed.'

'And no hypocrite about himself either, rather a man who loved a good drop, was he not, and, as the saying goes, a mighty drinker before the Lord?'

'My father,' I replied evasively, as though withdrawing my levity, 'was love of live itself. That much I can agree to.'

'So, so, love of life. And what did he die of?'

I was silent. I glanced at him, then bowed my head. And in an altered voice I replied:

'May I most humbly request the battalion surgeon to be so kind as not to insist on his question?'

'You are not permitted to refuse any information whatsoever!' he replied in a shrill bleat. 'What I ask you is asked with deliberation and your answers are important. In your own interest I warn you to tell us truthfully the manner of your father's death.'

'He received a church funeral,' I said with heaving breast, and my excitement was too great for me to report things in their proper order. 'I can bring you papers to prove that he was buried from a church, and inquiries will show that a number of officers and Professor Schimmelpreester walked behind the coffin. Spiritual Counsellor Chateau himself said in his funeral oration,' I went on with increasing vehemence, 'that the gun went off accidentally as my father was examining it, and if his hand shook and he was not completely master of himself, that was because we had been visited by a great calamity.'

I said 'great calamity' and made use of other extravagant and figurative expressions. 'Ruin had knocked at our door with her bony knuckles,' I said, beside myself, knocking in the air with my own bent index finger by way of illustration, 'for my father had fallen into the toils of evil men, bloodsuckers, who cut his throat and everything was sold and squandered – the glass – harp,' I stammered foolishly, and felt myself change colour, for now something altogether astounding was about to happen to me, 'the Aeolian – wheel –' and at that instant this is what occurred.

My face became contorted – but that tells very little. In my opinion, it was contorted in an entirely new and terrifying fashion, such as no human passion could produce, but only a satanic influence and impulse. My features were literally thrust apart in all directions, upward and downward, right and left, only to be violently contracted towards the centre immediately thereafter; a horrible, one-sided grin tore at my left, then at my right cheek, compressing each eye in turn with frightful force while the other became so enormously enlarged that I had the distinct and frightful feeling that the eyeball must pop out – and it could have done so for all of me – let it happen! Whether or not it popped out was hardly the important question, and in any case this was not the moment for tender solicitude about my eye. If, however, so unnatural a play of expression might well have aroused in those present that extreme distaste which we call horror, it was nevertheless only the introduction and prelude to a real witch's Sabbath of face-making, a whole battle of grimaces, fought out during the following seconds on my youthful countenance. To recount in detail the distortions of my features, to describe completely the horrible positions in which mouth, nose, brows, and cheeks – in short, all the muscles of my face – were involved, changing constantly, moreover, so that not a single one of these facial deformities repeated itself – such a description would be far too great an undertaking. Let just this much be said, that the emotional experiences which might correspond to these physiognomical phenomena, the sensations of mindless cheerfulness, blank astonishment, wild lust, inhuman torment, and tooth-grinding rage, simply could not be of this world, but must rather belong to an infernal region where our earthly passions, magnified to monstrous proportions, would find themselves horribly reproduced. But is it not true that those emotions whose expressions we assume really do reproduce themselves in premonitory and shadowy fashion in our souls? Meanwhile the rest of my body was not still, though I remained standing in one spot. My head lolled and several times it twisted almost entirely around just as if Old Nick were in the act of breaking my neck; my shoulders and arms seemed on the point of being wrenched out of their sockets, my hips were bowed, my knees turned inward, my belly was hollowed, while my ribs seemed to burst the skin over them; my teeth were clamped together, not a single finger but was fantastically bent into a claw. And so, as though stretched on a hellish engine of torture, I remained for perhaps two-thirds of a minute.

I was not conscious during this most difficult and consequently lengthy period, at least I was not aware of my surroundings and audience, for to keep them in mind was rendered wholly impossible by the rigours of my condition. Rough shouts reached my ears as though from a great distance without my being able to understand them. Coming to myself on a chair,

which the army doctor had hurriedly pushed under me, I choked violently
on some stale, warmish tap water which this scholar in uniform had been at
pains to pour down my throat. Several of the gentlemen of the commission
had sprung up and were bending forward over the green table with
expressions of consternation, indignation, and even disgust. Others revealed
more sympathetically their amazement at the impressions they had received.
I saw one who was holding both fists against his ears; probably through some
kind of contagion, he had twisted his own face into a grimace; another had
two fingers of his right hand pressed against his lips and was blinking his
eyelids with extraordinary rapidity. As far as I myself was concerned, I had
no sooner looked about me with a restored but naturally shocked expression
than I hastened to put an end to a scene that could only appear unseemly to
me. I rose from my chair quickly and bewilderedly and took up a military
posture beside it, which, to be sure, ill-suited my naked human state.

The doctor had stepped back, with the glass still in his hand.

'Have you come to your senses?' he asked with a mixture of anger and
sympathy.

'At your service, sir,' I replied in a zealous tone.

'And do you retain any recollection of what you have just gone through?'

'I humbly beg your pardon,' I replied. 'For a moment I was a little
distraught.'

Short, rather harsh laughter answered me from the commission table.
There was repeated murmuring of the word 'distraught'.

'You certainly didn't seem to be paying very close attention,' the doctor
said dryly. 'Did you come here in a state of excitement? Were you specially
anxious about the decision on your fitness for service?'

'I must admit,' I replied, 'that it would have been a great disappointment
to be turned down, and I hardly know how I could have broken such news to
my mother. In earlier days she was used to having many members of the
officers' corps in her home, and she regards the Army with the greatest
admiration. For this reason it is especially important to her for me to be taken
into the service, and she not only looks forward to conspicuous advantages in
respect of my education but also, and in particular, to a desirable strengthening of my health, which occasionally leaves something to be desired.'

He seemed to regard my words with contempt and as worthy of no further
consideration.

'Rejected,' he said, putting down the glass on the little table where lay the
instruments of his profession, the measuring-tape, stethoscope, and little
hammer. 'The barracks is no health resort,' he snapped at me over his
shoulder, turning to the gentlemen at the commission table.

'This person summoned for duty,' he explained in a thin bleat, 'suffers
from epileptoid attacks, the so-called equivalents, which are sufficient to
negate absolutely his fitness for service. My examination shows that there is
obviously a hereditary taint from his alcoholic father, who, after his business
failure, ended his life by suicide. The appearance of the so-called aura was
unmistakable in the patient's obviously embarrassed descriptions.
Furthermore the feeling of severe distress which, as we have heard, at times
confined him to bed and which my colleague in civil life,' (here a wooden
derision appeared once more on his thin lips) 'attempted to diagnose as so-
called migraine, is to be scientifically designated as a depressed condition
following a precedent attack. Especially significant for the nature of the
illness is the secrecy the patient observed in regard to his symptoms; for
though he is obviously of a communicative character, he kept them secret

from everyone, as we heard. It is worth noting that even today there persists in the consciousness of many epileptics something of that mystical, religious attitude which the ancient world adopted towards this nervous disorder. This individual came here in a tense and excited emotional state. Indeed, his exalted way of speaking made me suspicious. Furthermore there were indications of a nervous disorder in the extremely irregular though organically sound beat of his heart and the habitual twitching of the shoulders, which he appeared unable to control. As an especially fascinating symptom I should like to draw your attention to the really astounding hyperacuity of hearing which the patient manifested upon further examination. I have no hesitation in connecting this super-normal sensory sharpness with the rather severe attack we have witnessed, which had perhaps been latent for hours and was instantly precipitated by the excitement I induced in the patient through my unwelcome questions. I recommend to you' – he concluded his clear and learned survey and turned condescendingly to me – 'that you put yourself in the hands of a competent doctor. You are rejected.'

'Rejected,' repeated the sharp, nasal voice that I knew.

Aghast I stood there, not moving from the spot.

'You are exempt from service and may go.' These words were spoken, not without some traces of sympathy and kindliness, by that bass voice whose possessor had discriminatingly taken me for a one-year serviceman.

Then I rose on tiptoe and said with beseechingly raised brows: 'Would it not be possible to try? Is it not conceivable that a soldier's life would improve my health?'

Some of the gentlemen at the commission table laughed so that their shoulders shook, but the doctor remained harsh and truculent.

'I repeat,' he said, rudely throwing the words at my feet, 'that the barracks are not a health resort. Dismissed!' he bleated.

'Dismissed!' repeated the sharp, nasal voice, and a new name was called. 'Latte' it was, if I remember correctly, for it was now the turn of the letter *L*, and a tramp with shaggy chest appeared on the scene. I, however, bowed and withdrew to the passage. While I put on my clothes the assisting NCO kept me company.

Happy of course and yet serious in mood, and wearied by experiences so extreme as hardly to lie within the human range, to which I had surrendered myself, acting and being acted upon; still preoccupied in particular by the significant comments the army doctor had made about the esteem formerly attached to the mysterious sickness from which he believed I was suffering, I paid hardly any attention to the intimate chatter of the underling, with his inadequate stripes, watered hair, and waxed moustaches; it was only later that I remembered his simple words.

'Too bad,' he said, looking at me, 'too bad about you, Krull, or whatever your name is! You're a promising fellow, you might have amounted to something in the Army. One can see right away whether a man is going to get anywhere with us. Too bad about you; you have what it takes, that's certain, you would certainly have made a first-rate soldier. Who knows if you mightn't have been made sergeant-major if you'd surrendered!'

It was only afterwards, as I have said, that this confidential speech reached my consciousness. While hurrying wheels bore me homeward, I thought to myself that the fellow might well have been right; yes, when I pictured how admirably, how naturally and convincingly a uniform would have become me, what a satisfying effect my figure would have made in it, I almost regretted that I had had to dismiss on principle this way of attaining a form of existence that would so well become me and a world where a sense for the natural hierarchy is obviously so highly developed.

More mature consideration, however, compelled me to realize that my entering that world would have been a gross mistake and error. I had not, after all, been born under the sign of Mars – at least not in the specific and actual sense! For although martial severity, self-discipline, and danger had been the conspicuous characteristics of my strange life, its primary prerequisite and basis had been freedom, a necessity completely irreconcilable with any kind of commitment to a grossly factual situation. Accordingly, if I lived *like* a soldier it would have been a silly misapprehension to believe that I should therefore live *as* a soldier; yes, if it is permissible to describe and define intellectually an emotional treasure as noble as freedom, then it may be said that to live like a soldier but not as a soldier, figuratively but not literally, to be allowed in short to live symbolically, spells true freedom.

Chapter Six

After this victory (a real victory of David over Goliath, if I may say so), the moment not having yet arrived for my induction into the Paris hotel, I returned for the nonce to that existence on the streets of Frankfurt which I have already sketched in broad outline – an existence of sensitive loneliness amid the tumult of the world. As I drifted footloose through the bustle of the great city, I could have found, had I desired it, abundant opportunity for conversation and companionship with a variety of individuals who might outwardly have seemed to be living lives very like my own. This, however, was by no means my intention; I either avoided such contacts entirely or took care that they never became intimate; for in early youth an inner voice had warned me that close association, friendship, and companionship were not to be my lot, but that I should instead be inescapably compelled to follow my strange path alone, dependent entirely upon myself, rigorously self-sufficient. Furthermore, it seemed to me that if I made myself common in the least, fraternized with acquaintances or, as my poor father would have said, put myself on a *frère-et-cochon* footing – if, in short, I spent myself in a loose sociability – I should literally do violence to some secret part of my nature, should, so to speak, thin the vital sap and disastrously weaken and reduce the tension of my being.

When, therefore, I had to deal with inquisitiveness and importunity – as would happen, for instance, in the café where I would sit late beside a stickly little marble-topped table – I would behave with that courtesy which better befits my taste and character than rudeness and is, moreover, incomparably better protection. For rudeness makes one common; it is courtesy that creates distinctions. And so I summoned courtesy to my aid on those occasions when unwelcome proposals (I assume that the reader schooled in the multifarious world of the emotions will not be astounded) were made to me from time to time in more or less veiled and diplomatic language by men of a certain sort. It is small wonder, considering the appealing face nature granted me ánd the altogether winning appearance that my miserable clothing could not conceal – the scarf around my neck, my mended coat, and broken shoes. For the petitioners of whom I speak and who, of course, belonged to the higher levels of society this mean exterior served as an incitement to desire and an encouragement as well; it was, on the other hand, a barrier between me and the world of fashionable women. I do not mean that there was any lack of attention from that quarter, or of involuntary interest in my naturally favoured person, indications I joyfully noted and remembered. How often have I seen the egotistical, absent-minded smile fade at sight of me from some pure white face scented with eau-de-lis and the face assume an expression of almost suffering tenderness! Your black eyes, precious creature in the brocade evening wrap, grew attentive, wide, almost afraid, they penetrated my rags till I felt their searching touch, on my bare body, they returned inquiringly to my clothes, your glance met mine, absorbed it deep within, while your little head tilted a trifle backward as though you were drinking, you returned my glance, plunged deep into my eyes with a sweet, uneasy, importunate attempt to understand. Then, of course, you had to turn away 'indifferently', had to enter your wheeled home, and yet when you were already half-way into your silken cage and your servant, with an air of fatherly benevolence, was handing me a coin, the charms of your person seen from behind, tightly spanned by figured cloth of gold, illuminated by the moonlight of the great lamps in the lobby of the opera house, still seemed to hesitate irresolutely in the narrow frame of the carriage door.

No, indeed, there was no lack of silent encounters, one of which I have just summoned up – with emotion. On the whole, however, what good was I to women in gold evening gowns? A penniless youth, I could hardly expect more from them than a shrug of the shoulders. The beggarliness of my appearance, the absence of everything that constitutes the cavalier, wholly devalued me in their eyes and altogether banished me from the radius of their attention. Women only notice 'gentlemen' – and I was not one. Matters stood quite otherwise with certain vagrant gentlemen, eccentrics who were seeking neither a woman nor a man, but some extraordinary being in between. And I was that extraordinary being. That is why I needed so much evasive courtesy to calm their importunate enthusiasm; at times, indeed, I found myself compelled to reason with and soothe some beseeching and inconsolable individual.

I refrain from pronouncing moral judgement on a craving which, when I was the object of it, seemed not incomprehensible. Rather I may say with the Roman that I regard nothing human as alien to me. In the story of my personal education in love, however, the following incident must be recorded.

Of all the varieties of humankind which the great city presented to view, one was especially strange – whose very existence in our workaday world afforded no little food for the imagination – one that must needs attract the particular attention of a youth bent on self-education. It was that variety of female known as public persons, daughters of joy, or simply creatures or, more genteelly, priestesses of Venus, nymphs, and Phrynes. They either lay together in licensed houses or at night wandered the streets in certain sections, holding themselves, with official sanction or toleration, at the disposal of a world of men at once needy and able to pay. It always seemed to me that this arrangement, seen, if I am right, as one should see everything – that is, with a fresh eye undimmed by habit – that this phenomenon, I say, intrudes on our dull-mannered age like a colourful and romantic survival from a gaudier epoch. Its very existence always produced an enlivening and pleasurable effect on me. To visit those particular houses was beyond my means. On the streets and in the cafés, however, I had plenty of opportunity to study these enticing creatures. Nor did this interest remain one-sided; indeed, if I could congratulate myself on sympathetic attention from any quarter, it was from these flitting nightbirds, and before long, despite my habitual attitude of aloofness, I had established personal relations with some of them.

Birds of death is the popular name for the small owls and hawks which, it is said, fly at night against the windows of those who are sick unto death and lure their fearful souls into the open with the cry: 'Come with me!' Is it not strange that this same formula is used by the disreputable sisterhood when its members, strolling beneath the street lamps, boldly yet covertly summon men to debauchery? Some are corpulent as sultanas, tightly encased in black satin, against which the powdered whiteness of their faces glares in ghostly contrast; others in turn are of a sickly emaciation. Their makeup is crass, designed for effectiveness in the blaze and shadow of nocturnal streets. Raspberry lips glow in chalk-white faces; others have put rosy powder on their cheeks. Their brows are sharply and clearly arched, their eyes, lengthened at the corners by the use of eyebrow pencil and darkened at the edge of the lower lid, often show an unnatural brilliance induced by drugs. Imitation diamonds blaze in their ears; large feather hats nod on their heads; and in their hands all carry little bags, known as reticules or pompadours, in which are hidden toilet articles, lipstick, powder, and certain preventive devices. Thus they stroll past you on the sidewalk, touching your arm with theirs; their eyes, agleam in the street light, are directed sideways at you, their lips are twisted in a hot, provocative smile, and hastily, furtively whispering the enticing cry of the bird of death, they gesture with a short, sidewise motion of the head towards some undefined promise, as though for a man of courage who followed their invitation and summons there awaited somewhere a wonderful, never tasted, illimitable joy.

As I repeatedly observed this secret scene from a distance and with rapt attention, I saw too how the well-dressed gentlemen either remained unmoved or entered into negotiations and, if these proved satisfactory, went off with buoyant step in company with their lascivious guides. The creatures did not approach me for this purpose, for my poor attire promised no pecuniary gain from my patronage. Soon, however, I was to rejoice in their private and unprofessional favour. If, mindful of my economic impotence, I did not dare approach them, it not infrequently happened that after a curious and approving examination of my person they would begin a conversation with me in the most cordial manner, inquiring in a comradely way about my occupation and interests – to which I would lightly reply that I was staying in Frankfurt for purposes of amusement. In the conversations that took place in entries and archways between me and members of this gaudy sisterhood they expressed their interest in me in the most various ways in their coarse, outspoken vocabulary. Such persons, let me say parenthetically, ought not to talk. Silently smiling, glancing, gesturing, they are significant; but once they open their mouths they run the risk of sobering us and losing their own halo. For speech is the foe of mystery and the pitiless betrayer of the commonplace.

My friendly association with them was not devoid of a certain attractive tinge of danger, for the following reason. Whoever makes a career of catering to desire and earns a living by so doing is not in consequence by any means exempt from that particular human weakness; he would not otherwise devote himself so completely to its cultivation, stimulation, and satisfaction. He would understand it less thoroughly if it were not especially alive in him, yes, if he were not in his own person a true child of desire. So it happens, as we well know, that these girls usually have a bosom friend, a private lover, besides the many lovers to whom they give themselves professionally. Coming from the same lowly world, he calculatingly bases his way of life on their dream of bliss just as they do theirs on the dreams of others. These fellows are rash and violent characters for the most part, and though they lavish on their girls the joys of non-professional tenderness, supervise and regulate their work, and provide them with a certain knightly protection, they make themselves absolute lords and masters, confiscate most of the earnings, and if the returns are unsatisfactory, beat the girls unmercifully, a chastisement they bear willingly and happily. The authorities are hostile to this profession and persecute it constantly. Therefore in these flirtations I was exposing myself to a double danger; first, that I might be mistaken by the police for one of these rude cavaliers and picked up, and, on the other hand, that I might arouse the jealousy of these tyrants and have a taste of the knives with which they make so free. Thus caution was enjoined from both directions, and if more than one of the sisterhood let me see clearly that she would not be averse for once to neglecting her tedious profession in favour of my company, for a long time this double consideration stood firmly in the way – until in one particular case it was, in its graver aspect at least, happily suspended.

One evening, then – I had been applying myself with particular pleasure and persistence to my study of city life, and the night was far advanced – I was resting in a medium-grade café, at once weary and excited from my wanderings, a glass of punch in front of me. A wicked wind was sweeping the streets, and the rain mixed with snow that fell unremittingly made me reluctant to go in search of my distant lodgings; but my present refuge, too, was in an inhospitable state; some of the chairs had already been piled on the tables, charwomen were at work with wet rags on the dirty floor, the waiters were lolling about, disgruntled and half asleep, and if despite all this I still lingered, it was principally because I was finding it harder than usual to abandon the sights of the world for sleep.

Desolation reigned in the room. Next to one wall a man who looked like a cattle-dealer slept, leaning forward with his cheek on his leather money-belt. Opposite him two aged men with pince-nez, no doubt incapable of sleep, played dominoes in complete silence. But not far from me, only two tables away, with a little glass of green liqueur in front of her, sat a stranger, a girl easily recognizable as one of Them, but someone I had never seen before. We examined each other with mutual approval.

She was marvellously foreign in appearance; from underneath a red wool cap perched on one side of her head, straight glossy black hair fell in a page-boy bob, half covering cheeks that looked slightly concave beneath the prominent cheekbones. Her nose was blunt, her mouth wide and painted red, and her eyes, which slanted up at the outer corners, shimmered with an indeterminate colour, indeterminate too in the direction of their gaze in a way altogether her own and unlike other people's. With her red cap she wore a canary-yellow jacket under which the delicate contours of her body revealed themselves as spare but rounded. Nor did I fail to notice that she was long-legged after the fashion of a filly, something that always appealed strongly to my taste. When she lifted the green liqueur to her lips, the fingers of her hand were spread outward and upward, and for some reason, I do not know why, that hand looked hot – perhaps because the veins on the back stood out so prominently. She had, too, the strange habit of pushing her underlip forward and up, rubbing it against the other.

And so I exchanged glances with her, though her slanting, shimmering eyes never clearly betrayed in what direction she was looking, and finally, after we had thus taken each other's′ measure for a while, I noticed not without youthful confusion that she had favoured me with the signal, that sideways nod towards the wanton and unknown, with which her guild accompany the enticing call of the bird of death. In pantomime I turned one of my pockets inside out; but, replying with a shake of her head to indicate I need not worry about money, she repeated the signal and, counting out the coins for her green liqueur on the marble table-top, got up and moved smoothly to the door.

I followed her without delay. Dirty slush lay on the pavement, rain drove down at an angle, and the big, misshapen flakes that accompanied it settled on our shoulders, face, and arms like soft, wet animals. I was therefore well content when my unknown bride signalled a cab that was wobbling by. In broken German she gave the driver her address, which was in a street unknown to me, slipped in, and I, drawing the rattling door shut behind me, sank on the shabby cushions beside her.

Only after the nocturnal vehicle had again set itself into jogging motion did our conversation begin. I scruple to set it down, for I am sensible enough to see that its freedom lies beyond the compass of my voluble and chatty pen. It was without introduction, this conversation, it was without polite conventions of any sort; from the very beginning it had the free, exalted irresponsibility that is usually a characteristic only of dreams, where our 'I' associates with shadows that have no independent life, with creations of its own, in a way that is after all impossible in waking life where one flesh-and-blood being exists in actual separation from another. Here it happened, and I happily admit that I was moved to the depths of my soul by the intoxicating strangeness of the experience. We were not alone and even less were we as two; for duality ordinarily creates an inhibiting social situation – and there could be no talk of that here. My darling had a way of putting her leg over mine as though she were simply crossing her own; everything she said and did was marvellously unconstrained, bold and free as lonely thoughts are, and I was joyously ready to follow her lead.

In brief, this exchange consisted in the expression of the lively attraction we had immediately felt for each other, in the exploration, explanation, analysis of this attraction, as well as in an agreement to cultivate it in every way, augment it, and turn it to account. My companion for her part lavished on me many words of praise that reminded me distantly of certain expressions of that wise cleric, the Spiritual Counsellor at home, except that hers were at once more inclusive and more emphatic. For at first glance, so she assured me, anyone who knew anything about such matters could see that I had been created and predestined for the service of love, that I would indeed provide the world and myself with much pleasure and much joy if I hearkened to this special calling and arranged my life entirely to that end. Moreover, she wished to be my instructress and to put me through a thorough schooling, for it was obvious that my gifts still required the direction of an expert hand ... This I understood from what she said, but only approximately, for just as her appearance was foreign, her speech was broken and ungrammatical; indeed, she really did not know German at all, so that her words and expressions were often completely absurd and verged strangely upon the irrational – a fact that increased the dream-like quality of her company. It must be especially and specifically noted, however, that her behaviour was devoid of any frivolity or light-mindedness; instead she maintained in all circumstance – and how strange the circumstances sometimes were! – a severe, almost fierce seriousness, both then and during the whole time of our association.

After prolonged jolting and rattling the carriage finally stopped, we got out, and my friend paid the driver. Then we went upward through a dark, cold stairwell which smelled of dead lamp-wicks, and my guide opened the door to her room, just opposite the stairs. Here it was suddenly very warm; the smell of a greatly over-heated iron stove mingled with the heavy, flowery scent of cosmetics, and when the hanging lamp was lighted, a deep-red glow suffused the room. Comparative luxury surrounded me; on little velvet-topped tables stood colourful vases with dried sheaves of palm leaves, paper flowers, and peacocks' feathers; soft, furry hides lay about; a canopy bed with hangings of red wool adorned with gold braid dominated the room, and there was a great abundance of mirrors, even in places where one does not ordinarily expect them – as, for instance, in the canopy of the bed and in the wall at its side. But since we were filled with longing to know each other completely, we set to work at once, and I stayed with her until the following morning.

Rozsa, this was my antagonist's name, had been born in Hungary, but of the most doubtful antecedents; her mother had been employed in a travelling circus to leap through tissue-paper-covered hoops, and who her father had been remained wholly obscure. She had early shown a very marked inclination to unlimited *galanterie*, and while she was still young she had been placed, by no means against her will, in a house of ill-fame in Budapest, where she had spent a number of years as the establishment's chief attraction. But a businessman from Vienna, who believed he could not live without her, had extracted her from this den of iniquity by dint of great cunning plus the active co-operation of a society for the suppression of the white-slave trade and had installed her in his home. No longer young, and prone to apoplexy, he had been excessive in expressing his joy at possessing her and had unexpectedly passed away in her arms. Thus Rozsa had found herself left to her own devices. Living by her arts, she had moved from city to city and had only recently settled in Frankfurt. Unsatiated and unsatisfied by her purely professional activities, she had entered into a permanent relationship with a man who had originally been a butcher's assistant. His fierce energy and wild virility, however, had led him to choose pimping, extortion, and other kinds of blackmail as his calling. This fellow had made himself Rozsa's master and had derived the best part of his income from her amorous activities. But on account of some bloody deed he had been picked up by the police and had been forced to leave her unattended for a protracted period. As she was by no means inclined to give up her private pleasure, she had turned her eyes towards me and had chosen the quiet, still-untrained youth as her bosom companion.

She told me this simple tale in a relaxed hour, and I reciprocated with a condensed version of my own earlier life. For the rest, however, both then and in the future, conversation played a very minor role in our association, for Rozsa restricted herself to simple, practical directions and commands, accompanied by short, excited cries, which were survivals from her earliest youth – that is, from the circus ring. But on those occasions when our conversation took a broader turn, it was devoted to mutual admiration and praise, for the promise that we had held for each other at our first encounter was richly confirmed, and my mistress, for her part, gave me repeated and unsolicited assurance that my adroitness and prowess in love exceeded her fondest expectations.

Here, earnest reader, I am in the same position as once before in these pages when I was relating certain early and happy experiences with the sweets of life and I added a warning not to confuse an act with the name it goes by, or to make the elementary mistake of dismissing something living and specific with a general term. For if I now set down the fact that for a number of months, until my departure from Frankfurt, I was on intimate terms with Rozsa, often stayed with her, secretly superintended the conquests she made on the street with those slanted, shimmering eyes and gliding play of her underlip, sometimes, even, was there in hiding when she received her paying customers (occasions that gave me small grounds for jealousy) and did not disdain to accept a reasonable share of the proceeds, one might well be tempted to apply a short, ugly word to my way of life at that time and to lump me summarily with those dark gallants about whom I was talking above. Whoever thinks that actions make people equal may go ahead and take refuge in this simple procedure. For my own part, I am in agreement with folk wisdom which holds that when two persons do the same thing it is no longer the same; yes, I go further and maintain that labels such as 'drunkard', 'gambler', or even 'wastrel' not only do not embrace and define the actual living case, but in some instances do not even touch it. This is my point of view; others may judge differently about this confession – in respect to which it should be remembered that I am making it of my own free will and could quite easily have passed over it in silence.

If, however, I have treated the present interlude in as much detail as good taste will permit, it is because in my view it was of the most crucial importance for my education; not in the sense that it especially advanced my knowledge of the world or in itself refined my social manners – for that purpose my wild Eastern blossom was by no means the right person. And yet the word 'refine' can claim a place here, which I withhold only in order to clarify my meaning. For our vocabulary offers no other term for the profit I derived, in person and character, from my association with this exacting and beloved mistress, whose demands coincided so precisely with my gifts. Moreover, here one must think not only of a refinement *in* love but also *through* love. These italics must be understood aright, for they point to a distinction between, and at the same time an amalgamation of, means and ends, in which the former take on a narrower and more specific meaning and the latter a far more general one. Somewhere in these pages I have already remarked that because of the extraordinary demands life imposed on my energies it was not permissible for me to squander myself in enervating passion. Now, however, during the six-month period that is signalized by the name of the inarticulate but audacious Rozsa I did just that – except that the censorious word 'enervating' comes from the vocabulary of hygiene, and its appropriateness to certain important instances is very doubtful. For it is the enervating that benerves us – if certain vital prerequisites are met – and makes us capable of performances and enjoyments in the world that are beyond the compass of the un-benerved. I take no little pride in my invention of this word 'benerved' with which I have quite spontaneously enriched our vocabulary; it is intended to serve as the scientific antonym to the virtuously deprecatory 'enervate'. For I know from the very bottom of my being that I could never have borne myself with so much subtlety and elegance in the many vicissitudes of my life if I had not passed through Rozsa's naughty school of love.

Chapter Seven

With the coming of Michaelmas the leaves began to fall from the trees that bordered our streets, and the moment arrived for me to take up the position my godfather Schimmelpreester had secured for me through his international connexions. One cheery morning, after a tender farewell from my mother – the pension had acquired a maid and was enjoying a modest success – with my few possessions packed in one small suitcase, hurrying wheels bore me towards my new goal in life – no less than the capital city of France.

They hurried, rattled, and jolted, those wheels, beneath the communicating compartments of a third-class carriage. On the yellow wooden benches a mixed lot of depressingly insignificant travellers of the poorer sort went on with their miserable existence throughout the day, snoring, smacking their lips, gossiping, and playing cards. My own interest was mainly attracted by some children between two and four years of age. Although they were blubbering and roaring intermittently, I gave them some chocolate creams out of a bag my mother had included among my supplies; for I have always liked to share. Later I did a great deal of good with the treasures that passed from the hands of the rich into mine. The little ones came tripping up to me, repeatedly touching me with their sticky hands and speaking to me in lisps and gurgles. They were delighted when I replied in exactly the same fashion. Now and again this intercourse earned me a benevolent glance from the grown-ups, despite their schooling in reserve – not that I had any such purpose in view. On the contrary, this day's journey taught me afresh that the more receptive one's mind and soul to human charm, the more abysmally depressing one finds the sight of human rag-tag and bob-tail. I know very well these people can do nothing about their ugliness; they have their little joys and no doubt their heavy sorrows; in short, like other creatures they love, suffer, and endure life. From a moral point of view, every one of them very likely has a claim to our sympathy. But the alert and sensitive aesthetic perception that Nature has endowed me with compels me to avert my eyes. Only at the tenderest age are they tolerable, like these waifs to whom I gave chocolates and whom I set roaring with laughter by using their own language, thus paying sociability its due.

Moreover, I shall now take occasion to say for the reader's reassurance that this was the last time I ever travelled third class, companioned by misery. What is called fate, and is actually ourselves, working through unknown but infallible laws, soon found ways and means of keeping this from ever happening again.

My ticket, of course, was in perfect order, and in my own fashion I relished the fact that it was so irreproachable – that consequently I myself was irreproachable and when, in the course of the day, the honest conductors in their smart uniforms visited me in my wooden carriage to examine and punch my ticket, they returned it each time with silent official approval. Silent of course and expressionless: that is, with an expression of indifference that was barely animated and bordered on affectation. This prompted me to reflect on the aloofness, the stand-offishness, amounting almost to lack of interest, which one human being, especially an official, feels compelled to manifest towards his fellows. This honest man who punched my valid ticket earned his livelihood thereby; somewhere a home awaited him – there was a wedding ring on his finger – he had a wife and children. But I had to behave as though the thought of his human associations could never occur to me, and any question about them, revealing that I did not regard him simply as a convenient marionette, would have been completely out of order. On the other hand I had my own particular human background about which he might have inquired. But this, for one thing, was not his privilege and, for another, was beneath his dignity. He was concerned only with the validity of the ticket held by a passenger who was no less a marionette than he. What became of me once the ticket had been used was something he must coldly disregard.

There is something strangely unnatural and downright artificial in this behaviour, though one must admit that to abandon it would be going too far for various reasons – indeed, even slight departures usually result in embarrassment. This time, in fact, towards evening, when the conductor, lantern at waist, returned my ticket, he accompanied it with a prolonged glance and a smile that was obviously inspired by my youth.

'You going to Paris?' he asked, though my destination was clear to see.

'Yes, inspector,' I replied, nodding cordially. 'That's where I'm bound.'

'What are you planning to do there?' he took the further liberty of asking.

'Just imagine!' I replied. 'Thanks to a recommendation I am going into the hotel business.'

'Think of that!' he said. 'Well, lots of luck!'

'Good luck to you, too, chief inspector,' I replied. 'Please give my regards to your wife and children.'

'Yes, thanks – well, what do you know!' He laughed in embarrassment, mixing his words up oddly, and hastened to leave. But on his way out he tripped over a non-existent obstacle, so completely had this human touch upset him.

I felt very cheerful at the border station, too, where we all had to get out with our luggage for the customs inspection. My heart was light and pure, for my small bag actually did not contain anything I had to hide from the eyes of the inspectors. Even the necessity of a very long wait (since the officials understandably gave distinguished travellers precedence over those of the meaner sort, whose possessions they then all the more thoroughly mussed and mauled) was not able to cloud my sunny mood. When the man before whom I was finally permitted to spread out my meagre belongings at first seemed bent on shaking every shirt and sock to see whether some contraband might not fall out, I immediately engaged him in a conversation I had composed in advance and thus quickly won him over and kept him from mauling everything out. Frenchmen naturally love and honour conversation – and quite rightly! That, after all, is what distinguishes human beings from animals, and it is certainly not unreasonable to assume that a human being distinguishes himself the more from animals, the better he speaks – especially in French. For France regards its language as the language of mankind, exactly, I imagine, as those happy tribes of ancient Greeks took their idiom for the only human mode of expression, holding everything else for barbaric barking and quacking – an opinion the rest of mankind involuntarily subscribed to, more or less, inasmuch as it regarded Greek, as we today do French, as the finest.

'*Bonsoir, monsieur le commissaire!*' I greeted the inspector, dwelling with a kind of muted hum on the third syllable of the word '*commissaire*'. '*Je suis tout à fait à votre disposition avec tout ce que je possède. Voyez en moi un jeune homme très honnête, profondément dévoué à la loi et qui n'a absolument rien à déclarer. Je vous assure que vous n'avez jamais examiné une pièce de baggage plus innocente.*'

'*Tiens!*' he said, looking at me more closely. '*Vous semblez être un drôle de petit bonhomme. Mais vous parlez assez bien. Êtes-vous Français?*'

'*Oui et non,*' I replied. '*A peu près. À moitié – à demi, vous savez. En tout cas, moi, je suis un admirateur passioné de la France et un adversaire irréconciliable de l'annexion de l'Alsace-Lorraine!*'

His face took on an expression that I might describe as deeply moved. '*Monsieur,*' he said decisively, '*je ne vous gêne plus longtemps. Fermez votre malle et continuez votre voyage à la capitale du monde avec les bons vœux d'un patriote français!*'

And while I was stuffing back my odds and ends of linen, still expressing my thanks, he was already putting his chalk mark on the top of my open bag. In the course of my hasty repacking, however, chance decreed that this piece of luggage should lose some of the innocence I had quite honestly ascribed to it, for an additional small item slipped into it that had not been there before. To be specific: beside me at the tin-roofed luggage counter, behind which the inspectors carried on their activities, a middle-aged lady, wearing a mink coat and a velvet cloche adorned with heron feathers, was engaged in a heated altercation with the official in charge, who obviously held a different view from hers about the value of some of her possessions, certain pieces of lace which he held in his hand. Her handsome luggage, from which he had plucked forth the lace in question, was strewn about, several pieces of it so close to my own possessions as to be mixed up with them; nearest of all was a very costly small morocco case, almost square in shape, and it was this that had unexpectedly slipped into my little bag along with the other things while my friend was inscribing his chalk mark on top. This was an occurrence rather than an action, and it happened quite secretly; the case simply smuggled itself in, so to speak, as a by-product of the good humour that my friendly relations with the authorities of this country had produced in me. Actually during the rest of my trip I hardly thought about my accidental acquisition and I only fleetingly considered the possibility that the lady might have missed her jewel-case while repacking. Eventually I was to find out more about that.

And so at the end of a trip that, with interruptions, had lasted twelve hours, the train rolled slowly into the Gare du Nord. While porters busily and loquaciously helped the wealthy travellers with their numerous pieces of baggage, while some of the latter were exchanging embraces and kisses with friends who had come to meet them, while even the conductors condescended to receive handbags and blanket rolls handed to them out of doors and windows, the lonely youth descended into this tumult from his refuge for third-class members of society. Observed by no one, his small suitcase in his hand, he departed from the noisy, rather unattractive hall. Outside on the dirty street (a shower was falling) the driver of a fiacre saw I was carrying a suitcase, and lifted his whip invitingly in my direction, calling to me: 'Eh! Shall we drive, *mon petit?*' or '*mon vieux*' or something of the sort. And yet how was I to pay for the ride? I had almost no money, and if that little case foreshadowed an improvement in my financial position, its contents could certainly not be put to immediate use. Besides, it would hardly have been proper to arrive at my future place of employment in a fiacre. It was my intention to make my way there on foot, even though it might be a considerable distance, and I politely inquired from passers-by the direction I must take to reach the Place Vendôme – for reasons of discretion I mentioned neither the hotel nor even the rue Saint-Honoré. I did this several times, but no one I asked so much as slowed his step to give ear to my inquiry. And yet I did not look like a beggar, for my mother had in the end disgorged a few talers to spruce me up a bit for my journey. My shoes had been newly soled and mended, and I wore a warm, short jacket with patch pockets, and a becoming sports cap to match, below which my blond hair showed attractively. But a young fellow who does not hire a porter and carries his possessions through the street without engaging a fiacre is a stepson of our civilization, not worthy of a single glance. To be more precise, a feeling of anxiety warns others against having anything whatever to do with him. He is suspected of a disquieting attribute: to wit, poverty; and he is therefore suspected of even worse things as well. It thus seems wisest to society simply to avert her eyes from this damaged product of her order. 'Poverty,' it is said, 'is no sin,' but that is just talk. To its possessor it is highly sinister – half defect, half undefined, reproach; it is in every way extremely repulsive, and any association with it may lead to unpleasant consequences.

This attitude towards poverty has often been painfully brought home to me, and it was so on this occasion. Finally, I stopped a little old woman, who, for what reason I do not know, was pushing ahead of her a child's cart filled with all sorts of pots and pans; and it was she who not only pointed out the direction in which I must go, but also described the place where I could get a bus that would take me to the famous square. I could at least spare the few sous this form of transportation would cost and so I was happy to have this information. Moreover, the longer the good old woman looked at me in giving these directions, the wider her toothless mouth stretched in the friendliest of smiles. Finally, she patted me on the cheek with her hard hand, saying: '*Dieu vous bénisse, mon enfant!*' This caress made me happier than many another that I was to receive in the future from fairer hands.

For the traveller who enters the streets of Paris from that particular station, the first impression of the city is not by any means enchanting; but splendour and magnificence increase apace as he nears the glittering centre. If in manly fashion I repressed the timidity I felt, it was yet with astonishment and delighted reverence that, from my narrow seat in the omnibus, my little suitcase on my knee, I looked out upon the flaming magnificence of those avenues and squares, at the confusion of carriages, crowds of pedestrians, the sparkling stores that proffered everything, the inviting cafés and restaurants, and the blinding theatre façades with their white arc lights or hanging gaslights. Meanwhile, the conductor pronounced names I had often heard lovingly uttered by my poor father: 'Place de la Bourse', 'rue du Quatre Septembre', 'Boulevard des Capucines', 'Place de l'Opéra', and many others.

The uproar, pierced by the shrill cries of newsboys, was deafening, and the lights made one's head swim. In front of the cafés, sheltered by the marquees, men in hats and coats sat at little tables, their canes between their knees, and looked out as though from a loge at the crowds hurrying by. Meanwhile, dark figures stooped to snatch cigarette butts from between their feet. To them the gentlemen paid no heed nor did they seem distressed by this creeping occupation. They obviously considered it a persistent and accepted feature of that civilization whose happy tumult they were in a secure position to enjoy.

It is the proud rue de la Paix that connects the Place de l'Opéra with the Place Vendôme. Here, then, beside the pillar surmounted by the statue of the might Emperor, I left the bus and went afoot in search of my real goal, the rue Saint-Honoré, which as travellers know, runs parallel to the rue de Rivoli. It proved easy to find, and from a distance, in letters of impressive size and brilliance, the name of the Hotel Saint James and Albany sprang to my eyes.

There people were arriving and departing. Gentlemen about to get into carriages already loaded with their luggage, were handing tips to the servants who had looked after them; porters were carrying into the building the bags of new arrivals. I know the reader will smile when I admit that I was almost overcome by timidity at the thought of boldly entering this imposing, expensive, fashionably located edifice. But did not right and duty combine to encourage me? Had I not been directed and engaged to come here, and was not my godfather Schimmelpreester on intimate terms with the general manager of the establishment? Nevertheless, modesy bade me choose, not one of the two revolving glass doors through which the guests were entering, but rather the side entrance through which the porters passed. The latter, however, whatever they may have taken me for, motioned me back; I was not one of them. Nothing remained for me but to go in through one of those magnificent revolving doors, my little bag in my hand. In the process of negotiating it, I had, to my shame, to be helped by a page-boy in a diminutive red tail-coat who was posted there. '*Dieu vous bénisse, mon enfant!*' I said to him, automatically using the words of that good old woman – at which he burst into as hearty a roar of laughter as the children with whom I had been playing on the train.

I found myself in a stately lobby with porphyry columns and a gallery circling it at the height of the entresol. Crowds surged back and forth, and people dressed for travel sat in the deep armchairs arranged on the carpeted floor beneath the columns. Among them were several ladies who held tiny, shivering dogs in their laps. A boy in livery officiously tried to take my bag out of my hand, but I resisted and turned to the right towards the easily identifiable concierge's desk. There a gentleman with cold unfriendly eyes, dressed in a gold-braided frock-coat and obviously accustomed to large tips, was dispensing information in three or four languages to the crowd clustered around his desk. From time to time, smiling benignly, he would hand room keys to such of the hotel's guests as asked for them. I had to stand there a long time before I had an opportunity to ask him whether he thought the general manager, Monsieur Stürzli, was in, and where I might perhaps have the opportunity of presenting myself to him.

'You wish to speak to Monsieur Stürzli?' he asked with insolent surprise. 'And who are you?'

'A new employee of the *éstablissement*,' I replied. 'With the highest personal recommendations to *monsieur le directeur.*'

'*Etonnant!*' replied this benighted man, and added with a disdain that cut me to the quick: 'No doubt Monsieur Stürzli has been awaiting your visit with painful impatience for hours. Perhaps you would be so good as to take yourself a few steps farther on to the reception desk.'

'A thousand thanks, *monsieur le concierge*,' I replied. 'And may large tips come your way from every side, so that you will soon be able to retire to private life!'

'Idiot!' I heard him call after me. But that neither concerned nor disturbed me. I carried my suitcase over to the reception desk, which was indeed only a few steps away, on the same side of the lobby. It was even more densely beleaguered. Numerous travellers vied for the attention of the two gentlemen in severe morning coats who were in charge, inquiring for their reservations, learning the numbers of the rooms assigned to them, signing the register. To work my way forward to the desk cost me much patience; finally I stood face to face with one of the gentlemen, a still young man with a small waxed moustache, a pince-nez, and a sallow, indoor complexion.

'You wish a room?' he asked, since I had deferentially waited to be spoken to.

'Oh, no indeed – not that, *monsieur le directeur*,' I answered smiling. 'I am a member of the staff, if I may already say so. My name is Krull, first name Felix, and I am reporting here by arrangement between Monsieur Stürzli and his friend, my godfather Professor Schimmelpreester. I am to be employed as an assistant in this hotel. That is –'

'Step back!' he commanded hastily in a low voice. 'Wait! Step all the way back!' And at this a faint flush tinged his sallow cheeks. He glanced about uneasily, as though the fact of a new employee, not yet in uniform, appearing before the hotel guests as if he were a human being, had caused him the most acute embarrassment. Some of those busy at the desk were, indeed, glancing at me curiously. They interrupted their filling up of forms to look round at me.

'*Certainement, monsieur le directeur!*' I answered in subdued tones, and withdrew well behind those who had come after me. There were not many of them, however, and after a few minutes the reception desk was entirely clear, though it would not be for long.

'Well, now what about you?' The gentleman of the indoor complexion was finally forced to turn to where I was standing some way off.

'*L'employé-volontaire Félix Kroull*,' I replied without moving from the spot, for I wanted to force him to invite me to approach.

'Well, come here!' he said nervously. 'Do you think I want to keep shouting at you at this distance?'

'I withdrew on your orders, *monsieur le directeur*,' I replied, approaching eagerly, 'and I was just waiting for you to countermand them.'

'My orders,' he interposed, 'were only too necessary. What are you doing here? What possessed you to march into the lobby like one of our guests and mix willy-nilly with the clientele?'

'I beg a thousand pardons,' I said contritely, 'if that was a mistake. I knew of no other way to reach you except by frontal attack through the revolving door and the lobby. But I assure you I would not have hesitated to take the dirtiest, darkest, most secret way if that had been necessary to gain your presence.'

'What kind of talk is this?' he replied, and once more a faint flush tinged his sallow cheeks. This tendency in him to blush pleased me.

'You seem,' he added, 'either a fool or possibly a little too intelligent.'

'I hope,' I replied, 'to prove quickly enough to my superiors that my intelligence functions within precisely the right limits.'

'It seems to me very doubtful,' he said, 'whether you will have the chance. I don't know at the moment of any vacancy in our staff.'

'Nevertheless, I take the liberty of pointing out,' I reminded him, 'that we are dealing with a firm agreement between *monsieur le directeur général* and a boyhood friend of his, who held me at the baptismal font. I have intentionally refrained from asking for Monsieur Stürzli, for I know very well that he is not dying of impatience to see me and I am under no illusions that I will see that gentleman soon or perhaps ever. But that is of minor importance. Instead, all my desires and efforts have been directed towards paying my respects to you, *monsieur le directeur*, and learning from you, and from you alone, where, how, and in what manner of service I can prove myself useful to the *établissement*.'

'*Mon Dieu, mon Dieu!*' I heard him murmur. Nevertheless, he took down a bulky volume from a shelf on the wall and searched angrily through it, repeatedly licking the two middle fingers of his right hand. Presently he stopped at an entry and said to me:

'At least get away from here as fast as you can and go wherever you belong! Your employment has been provided for, that much is correct –'

'But that's the important point,' I remarked.

'*Mais oui, mais oui!* Bob' – he turned to one of the half-grown bellboys sitting on a bench at the back of the office, hands on knees, waiting for errands – 'show this individual to the *dortoir des employés* number four on the top floor. Use the service elevator! You will hear from us early tomorrow,' he added sharply to me. 'Go!'

The freckled boy, obviously English, went with me.

'Why don't you carry my bag a little way?' I said to him. 'I can tell you both my arms are lame from lugging it.'

'What will you give me?' he asked in broadly accented French.

'I have nothing.'

'Well, I'll do it anyway. Don't feel pleased about *dortoir* number four! It is very bad. We are all very badly housed. Also the food is bad and the pay too. But a strike is out of the question. Too many are ready to take our places. That whole crowd of pirates ought to be exterminated. I am an anarchist, you must know, *voilà ce que je suis*.'

He was a very nice, childish youngster. We rode up together in the service lift to the fifth floor, the garret, and there he let me pick up my bag again, pointed to a door in the ill-lit carpetless corridor and said: '*Bonne chance*.'

The plate on the door showed it was the right one. As a precaution I knocked, but there was no answer. Although it was already after ten o'clock, the dormitory was still completely dark and empty. Its appearance, when I turned on the electric light bulb that hung unshielded from the ceiling, was indeed far from attractive. Eight beds, with grey flannel blankets and flat, obviously long-unwashed pillows, were arranged like bunks, two and two, one above the other, along the side walls. Between them open shelves were set against the walls to the height of the upper bunk, and on these the occupants had placed their bags. The room, whose single window seemed to open on an air shaft, offered no further conveniences, nor was there any space for them, since its width was considerably less than its length, leaving very little room in the middle. At night, obviously, one would have to put one's clothes at the bottom of one's bed or in a bag on the shelf.

Well, I thought, you need not have gone to so much trouble to escape the barracks, for it could not have been more Spartan there than in this room – probably somewhat cosier. A bed of roses, however, was something I had not been accustomed to for a long time – not since the break-up of my happy home. Moreover, I knew that a man and his circumstances usually come to a tolerable adjustment; indeed, that the latter, however difficult they may appear at the start, show, if not for everyone, then at least for the more fortunate, a certain flexibility that is not altogether a question of habit. The same situations are not the same for everyone, and general conditions, so I would maintain, are subject to extensive personal modification.

Let the reader forgive this digression on the part of a spirit that is by nature philosophically inclined and is devoted to observing life less for its ugly and brutal aspects than for its delicate and amiable qualities.

One of the shelves was empty, from which I deduced that one of the eight beds must also be vacant; only I did not know which – to my regret, for I was weary from my journey, and my youth demanded sleep. I had no choice, however, but to await the arrival of my room-mates. For a while I entertained myself by inspecting the washroom, a side door to which stood open. There were five washstands of the commonest sort, with squares of linoleum in front of them, washbowls and pitchers, with slop jars beside them and hand towels hanging on a rack. Mirrors were entirely lacking. In place of them, thumbtacked on door and wall – and in the bedroom, too, so far as space permitted – were all sorts of enticing pictures of women cut out of magazines. Not much comforted, I returned to the bedroom and in order to have something to do I prudently decided to get my nightshirt out of my suitcase. In doing so, however, I came upon the little morocco case that had slipped in so unobtrusively during the customs inspection; happy at seeing it again, I set about investigating it.

Whether curiosity about its contents may not all the time have been at work in the secret recesses of my soul and the notion of getting out my nightshirt had been only an excuse to acquaint myself with the jewel case – on this subject I offer no opinion. Sitting on one of the lower beds, I took it on my knees and began to examine it with the prayerful hope of remaining undisturbed. Its light lock was not fastened, and it was kept shut only by a small hook and eye. I found no fairy-tale treasure inside, but what it did contain was very charming and in part truly remarkable. Right at the top, in a tray that divided the satin-lined interior into two compartments, lay a necklace of several strands of large, graduated, golden topazes in a carved setting, such as I had never seen in any shop window and hardly could have, since it was obviously not of modern design but came from a past century. I may say it was the essence of magnificence, and the sweet, transparent, shimmering honey-gold of the stones enchanted me so completely that for a long time I could not take my eyes off them; it was with considerable reluctance that I lifted the tray to look into the bottom. This was deeper than the upper compartment and less completely filled than the latter had been by the topaz necklace. Nevertheless, charming items laughed up at me, each one of which I retain clearly in memory. A long string of little diamonds set in platinum lay there piled in a glittering heap. There were in addition: a very handsome tortoise-shell comb, ornamented with silver vines set with numerous diamonds, though these, too, were small; a gold double-bar brooch with platinum clasps, ornamented on top with a sapphire the size of a pea surrounded by ten diamonds; a dull-gold brooch delicately formed to represent a little basket filled with grapes; a bracelet in the shape of a bugle, tapering towards the end, with a platinum safety catch, the value of which was enhanced by a noble white pearl, surrounded by diamonds in an *à jour* setting, which was set in the bell; in addition, three or four very attractive rings, one of which contained a grey pearl with two large and two small diamonds, another a dark triangular ruby also set off by diamonds.

I took these precious objects in my hand and let their noble rays flash in the vulgar light of the naked electric bulb. But who can describe the confusion I felt when, plunged in this amusing occupation, I suddenly heard a voice above my head say dryly:

'You have some quite pretty things there.'

Although there is always something disconcerting about believing oneself alone and unobserved and suddenly discovering that this is not so, the present situation redoubled that unpleasantness. No doubt I failed to hide a slight start; nevertheless, I compelled myself to be completely calm, closed the little case without haste, casually put it back in my suitcase, and then and only then got up so that by stepping back a little I could look in the direction from which the voice had come. There, indeed, on the bed above the one I had been sitting on, someone was lying propped up on an elbow looking down at me. My earlier inspection had not been thorough enough to reveal this fellow's presence. Perhaps he had been lying up there with a blanket over his head. He was a young man who could have done with a shave, so dark was his chin. His hair was mussed from lying in bed, he had sideburns, and eyes of a Slavic cast. His face was feverishly red, but although I saw he must be sick, dismay and confusion prompted me to say awkwardly:

'What are you doing up there?'

'I?' he answered. 'It's my privilege to inquire what interesting job you're engaged in down there.'

'Don't speak familiarly to me, please,' I said irritably. 'I am not aware that we are relatives or on terms of intimacy.

He laughed and replied not altogether unreasonably: 'Well, what I saw in your hands is likely to create a certain bond between us. Your dear mother surely did not pack that in your grip for you. Just show me your little hands – what long fingers you have, or how long you can make them!'

'Don't talk nonsense!' I said. 'Do I owe you an explanation of my property simply because you were so rude as to watch me without letting me know you were there? That's very bad form –'

'Yes, you're a fine one to complain about me,' he interrupted. 'Drop this high-flown nonsense. I'm no wild man. Moreover I can tell you that I was asleep until just a little while ago. I have been lying here with influenza for two days and I have a filthy headache. I woke up and quietly said to myself: "What's the pretty boy playing with down there?" For you are pretty; even envy must admit that. Where wouldn't I be today with a phiz like yours!'

'My phiz is no excuse for you to go on saying *du* to me. I'll not speak another word until you stop.'

'By God, prince, I can call you "Your Highness" if you like. But we're colleagues, as I understand it. You're a newcomer?'

'The management had me shown up here,' I replied, 'so that I could choose a free bed. Tomorrow I am to begin my duties in this establishment.'

'As what?'

'That has not yet been decided.'

'Very odd. I work in the kitchen – that is, in the *garde-manger* where the cold dishes are. The bed you were sitting on is taken. The second one above it is free. What's your nationality?'

'I arrived this evening from Frankfurt.'

'I'm a Croat,' he said in German. 'From Agram. I worked in a restaurant kitchen there, too. But I've been in Paris for three years. Do you know your way around in Paris?'

'What do you mean, "know my way around"?'

'You understand very well. I mean, have you any idea where you can sell that stuff of yours at a decent price?'

'Something will turn up.'

'Not by itself. And it's not smart to carry a find like that around with you for long. If I give you a safe address, shall we split fifty-fifty?'

'What are you talking about, fifty-fifty? And for nothing but an address!'

'Something that a greenhorn like you needs just as much as food. I will tell you that the string of diamonds –'

Here we were interrupted. The door opened and a number of young people came in whose working-hours were over: a liftboy in red-braided grey livery; two messengers in high-necked blue jackets with two rows of gold buttons and gold stripes on their trousers; a half-grown youngster in a blue-striped jacket, who was carrying an apron over his arm and was probably employed in the lower kitchen as pot-washer or something of the sort. Before long they were followed by another bellboy of Bob's class and a youth whose white jacket and black trousers showed he might be a busboy or assistant waiter. They said: '*Merde!*' And as there were Germans among them: 'Damnation!' and 'Devil take it!' – imprecations that probably had to do with the day's work, now over. They called up to the man in bed: 'Hello, Stanko, how bad do you feel?' They yawned noisily and at once began to undress. To me they paid very little attention, only saying in jest as though they had expected me: '*Ah, te voilà. Comme nous étions impatients que la boutique deviendrait complète!*' One of them confirmed the fact that the upper bunk that Stanko had pointed out was free. I climbed up, put my bag on the appropriate shelf, undressed sitting on the bed, and almost before my head touched the pillow fell into the deep, sweet sleep of youth.

Chapter Eight

At almost the same instant several alarm clocks shrilled and rattled; it was six o'clock and still dark; those who were out of bed first turned on the ceiling light. Only Stanko paid no attention to this reveille and stayed where he was. As I felt greatly refreshed and much cheered by my sleep, I was not unduly upset by the annoying crowd of untidy young men yawning, stretching, and pulling their nightshirts over their heads in the narrow space between the bunks. Even the battle for the five washstands – five for seven youths much in need of a wash – was something I did not allow to dim my cheerfulness, despite the fact that the water in the jugs was insufficient and we had to rush out naked into the corridor, one after another, to fetch more from the tap. After I had followed the others in soaping and rinsing, I got only a very wet hand-towel that was no longer much use for drying. By way of compensation, however, I was allowed to share the hot water that the liftboy and busboy had warmed over an alcohol stove, and while I guided my razor with practised strokes over my cheeks and chin, I was allowed to join them in peering into a fragment of mirror they had succeeded in fastening to the window catch.

'*Hé, beauté,*' Stanko called to me as I came back into the bedroom, hair

brushed and face washed, to finish dressing and, like everyone else, to make
my bed. 'Hans or Fritz, what's your name?'

'Felix, if that's all right with you,' I replied.

'First-rate. Will you be so kind, Felix, as to bring me a cup of *café au lait*
from the *cantine* when you're through with breakfast? Otherwise I'll
probably get nothing till they bring the gruel up at noon.'

'With pleasure,' I replied. 'I will do it gladly. First I will bring you a cup of
coffee and then I will come back in a very short time.'

I said this for two reasons. First, because of the disquieting fact that
although my suitcase had a lock I did not have the key, and I was far from
happy about leaving Stanko alone with it. Secondly, because I wished to
reopen my conversation of yesterday and get, on more reasonable terms, the
address he had mentioned.

The spacious *cantine des employés* opened off the end of the corridor; it was
warm there and smelt agreeably of coffee, which the man in charge and his
fat and motherly wife were dispensing from two shiny machines behind the
buffet. The sugar was set out ready in bowls, and the woman poured in milk
and gave each of us a brioche as well. There was a great horde of all kinds of
hotel people from the various dormitories, including waiters from the main
dining-room in blue tail-coats with gold buttons. For the most part they ate
and drank standing up, but a few sat at small tables. In accordance with my
promise I asked the motherly lady for a cup '*pour le pauvre malade de numéro
quatre*,' and she handed me one, giving me at the same time the glance and
smile I had come to expect. '*Pas encore équipé?*' she asked, and I explained
my present situation. Then I hurried back to Stanko with the coffee and told
him again that I would drop in to talk with him very shortly. He gave an
amused snort as I turned away, for he thoroughly understood both of my
reasons.

Back in the *cantine*, I served myself, drank my *café au lait*, which tasted
extremely good, for I had had nothing warm for a long time, and ate my
brioche. The room began to empty for it was getting on towards seven
o'clock, and presently I was able to make myself comfortable at one of the
little oilcloth-covered tables in the company of an elderly, frock-coated
commis-de-salle. When he took out a pack of Caporals and lighted one, all I
had to do was smile and give the hint of a wink for him to offer them to me.
Moreover, when he got up to go – after a short conversation in which I told
him about my still uncertain position – he left the still half-filled pack behind
as a present.

The after-breakfast taste of the black, aromatic tobacco was most
agreeable, but I dared not linger over it. Instead, I hurried back to my
patient. He received me in a bad temper, which I easily recognized as
feigned.

'Here again?' he asked crossly. 'What do you want? I have no need of your
company. I have a headache and a sore throat and no inclination whatever
for chit-chat.'

'So you're not feeling any better?' I said. 'I'm sorry. I was just about to
inquire whether you weren't somewhat cheered by the coffee I brought you
out of a natural desire to be of service.'

'I know very well why you brought the coffee. I'm not going to get mixed
up in your miserable affairs. A simpleton like you will just make a mess of
things.'

'It was you,' I replied, 'who started the talk about business. I don't see
why I shouldn't keep you company, and leave business out of it. They're not

going to pay any attention to me right away and I have more time than I know what to do with. Just accept the idea that I'd like to share some of it with you.'

I sat down on the bed under his, but this had the disadvantage of preventing me from seeing him. That was no way to talk, I found, and I was compelled to get up again.

He said: 'It's some progress that you realize you need me and not the other way about.'

'If I understand you right,' I replied, 'you are referring to an offer you made yesterday. It's very friendly of you to come back to it. That reveals, however, that you, too, have a certain interest in it.'

'Damn little. A ninny like you will get done out of his loot. How did you get hold of it anyway?'

'By accident. Actually because a happy moment so decreed.'

'That happens. Besides, you may have been born lucky; there's something about you. But show me your trinkets again so I can make a guess at their value.'

Pleased though I was to find him so much softened, I replied: 'I'd rather not, Stanko. If someone came in, it could easily lead to a misunderstanding.'

'Well, it's not really necessary,' he said. 'I saw it all pretty clearly yesterday. Don't get any mistaken ideas about that topaz necklace. It is –'

There was instant proof of how right I had been to anticipate interruptions. A charwoman with pail, rags, and broom came in to mop up the puddles of water in the washroom and to put things straight. As long as she was there, I sat on the lower bed and we did not say a word. Only after she had gone lumbering off in her clattering clogs did I ask him what he had been about to say.

'I, say?' He started to dissemble again. 'You wanted to hear something,' but there wasn't anything I wanted to say. At most I was going to advise you not to put your hopes in that topaz necklace you looked at so long and so lovingly yesterday. Stuff like that costs a lot if you buy it at Falize's or Tiffany's, but what you get for it is a laugh.'

'What do you call a laugh?'

'A couple of hundred francs.'

'Well, nevertheless.'

'A nincompoop like you says "nevertheless" to everything! That's what makes me sick. If I could only go with you or take charge of this myself!'

'No, Stanko. How could I take the responsibility of that! You have a temperature, after all, and have to stay in bed.'

'Oh, all right. Besides, even I couldn't get a knight's estate for the comb and brooch. Or even the breast pin, in spite of the sapphire. The best is still the necklace, it's easily worth ten thousand francs. And I wouldn't turn up my nose at one or two of the rings, especially when I remember the ruby and the grey pearl. In short, at a quick guess, the whole lot should be worth eighteen thousand francs.'

'That was just about my own estimate.'

'Imagine that! Have you any idea at all about such things?'

'Yes, I have. The jewellers' windows back home in Frankfurt were always my favourite study. But you probably don't mean that I will get the full eighteen thousand?'

'No, my pet, I don't. But if you knew how to look out for your interests a bit and didn't say "nevertheless" to everything and everybody, you should be able to get a good half of it.'

'Nine thousand francs, then.'

'Ten thousand. As much as the string of diamonds is worth by itself. If you're half-way a man, you won't let it go for less.'

'And where do you advise me to take it?'

'Aha! Now my beautiful friend wants me to make him a present. Now I'm to tie my information to the ninny's nose gratis out of pure affection.'

'Who's talking about gratis, Stanko? Naturally I'm prepared to show my appreciation. Only I consider what you said yesterday about fifty-fifty somewhat extreme.'

'Extreme? In such joint enterprises fifty-fifty is the most natural division in the world, the division by the book. You forget that without me you're as helpless as a fish out of water, and besides that I can always tip off the management.'

'Shame on you, Stanko! One doesn't say things like that, let alone do them. You wouldn't dream of doing it either. I am convinced you would prefer a couple of thousand francs to a tip-off from which you would get nothing.'

'You think you can take care of me with a couple of thousand francs?'

'That's what it comes to in round figures if I generously concede you one third of the ten thousand francs which, in your opinion, I will get. Besides, you ought to be proud of me for looking out for my own interests a bit, and that ought to give you confidence in my ability to stand up to the cut-throat.'

'Come here,' he said, and when I approached he said, softly and clearly:

'*Quatre-vingt-douze, rue de l'Échelle au Ciel.*'

'*Quatre-vingt-douze, rue de* –'

'*Echelle au Ciel.* Can't you hear?'

'What an auspicious name!'

'Even though it's been called that for hundreds of years? Go ahead and take it as a good omen! It's a very quiet little street, only it's a long way off, out beyond the Cimetière de Montmartre. Your best way is up to the Sacré-Cœur, which is easy to see, then go through the Jardin between the church and the cemetery and follow the rue Damrémont in the direction of the boulevard Ney. Before Damrémont runs into Championnet, a little street goes off to the left, rue des Vierges Prudentes, and from it your Échelle branches off. You really can't miss it.'

'What's the man's name?'

'It doesn't matter. He calls himself a clock-maker and he is that, too, among other things. Try not to act too much like a sheep. I only told you the address to get rid of you so I could get some rest. As for my money, just remember I can report you any time.'

He turned his back to me.

'I am really grateful to you, Stanko,' I said, 'and you can be sure you will have no reason to complain of me to the management.'

Thereupon I left, silently repeating the address to myself, I went back to the now completely deserted *cantine*, for where else was I to spend my time? I had to wait until the people downstairs remembered me. For a good two hours I sat at one of the little tables without permitting myself the slightest impatience, smoked some more of my Caporals, and devoted myself to thought. It was ten by the wall clock in the *cantine* when I heard a harsh voice in the corridor shouting my name. Before I could get to the door a bellboy appeared there and shouted:

'*L'employé Félix Kroull* – report to the general manager!'

'That's me, dear friend. Take me with you. Even if it were the President of the Republic, I am quite prepared to appear before him.'

'All the better, dear friend,' he answered my genial speech rather pertly, measuring me with his eyes. 'Be so kind as to follow me.'

We walked down a flight of stairs to the fourth floor, where the corridors were much wider and had red carpets. There he rang for one of the guest lifts that came up that high. We had a while to wait.

'How come the Rhinoceros wants to speak to you himself?' he asked.

'You mean Monsieur Stürzli? Connexions. Personal connexions,' I added. 'Tell me, what makes you call him the Rhinoceros?'

'*C'est son sobriquet.* Pardon, I didn't invent it.'

'Not at all, I am grateful for any information,' I replied.

The lift had handsome wainscoting, an electric light, and a red satin banquette. At the controls stood a youth in that sand-coloured livery with red braid. He stopped first too high, then much too low, and let us clamber up over the resulting step.

'*Tu n'apprendras jamais, Eustache,*' said my guide, '*de manier cette gondole.*'

'*Pour toi je m'échaufferais!*' the other replied rudely.

This displeased me and I could not refrain from saying: 'Those who are weak ought not to show their contempt for one another. That does nothing to improve their position in the eyes of the strong.'

'*Tiens,*' said the man I had reprimanded. '*Un philosophe!*'

Now we were down, and as we walked from the lift at one side of the lobby past the reception desk, I could not fail to notice how the bellboy glanced at me repeatedly and curiously out of the corner of his eye. I was always pleased when I made an impression not simply by my attractive appearance but by my intellectual gifts as well.

The private office of the general manager was beyond the reception desk on a corridor that also led, as I saw, to billiard-rooms and reading-rooms. My guide knocked cautiously, was answered by a grunt from inside, and opened the door. With a bow he ushered me in, his cap at his thigh.

Herr Stürzli was a very fat man with a pointed grey beard for which there hardly seemed room on his bulging double chin. He was seated at his desk looking through papers and at first he paid no attention to me. His appearance immediately explained his nickname among the staff, for not only was his back massively arched and his neck larded in fatty folds, but from the end of his nose there actually protruded a horny wart that confirmed his right to the appellation. By contrast, his hands, with which he was sorting the papers into orderly piles of equal size, were astonishingly small and delicate in proportion to his over-all bulk. Despite his size there was nothing awkward about him; on the contrary, as sometimes happens with corpulent people, he possessed a certain elegance of movement.

'So you are the young man,' he said in German with a slight Swiss accent, still busily sorting his papers, 'who was recommended to me by a friend – Krull, if I am not mistaken – *c'est ça* – the young man who wishes to work for us?'

'Exactly as you say, *Herr Generaldirektor,*' I replied, discreetly drawing somewhat closer – and as I did so I observed, not for the first time nor the last, a strange phenomenon. When he looked me in the eye his face was contorted by an expression of revulsion which, as I understood perfectly well, was simply a consequence of my youthful beauty. By this I mean that those men whose interest is wholly concentrated on women, as was no doubt the case with Monsieur Stürzli with his enterprising imperial and his gallant *embonpoint*, when they encounter what is sensually attractive in a person of their own sex often suffer a curious embarrassment at their own impulses. This is due to the fact that the boundary line between the sensual in its most general and in its more specific sense is not easy to draw; constitutionally, however, these men are revolted at any hint of correspondence between this specific sense and their own desires; the result is just this reaction, this grimace of revulsion. Any sort of serious consequence is, of course, out of the question, for the person involved will politely assume the blame for the wavering of this sensual boundary rather than hold it against the innocent who made him conscious of it. He will therefore not attempt to avenge his embarrassment. Nor did Monsieur Stürzli do so in this instance, especially since, confronted by his confusion, I lowered my eyelashes in sincere and decorous modesty. On the contrary, he became very sociable and inquired:

'Well, how are things with my old friend, your uncle Schimmelpreester?'

'Pardon me, *Herr Generaldirektor*,' I replied, 'he is not my uncle, but my godfather, which is perhaps even closer. Thank you for inquiring, everything is going very well with my godfather so far as I know. He enjoys the highest reputation as an artist in the whole Rhineland and even beyond.'

'Yes, yes, a gay old dog, a sly fellow,' he said. 'Really? Is he successful? *Eh bien*, all the better. A gay dog. We had good times together here in the old days.'

'I don't need to say,' I continued, 'how thankful I am to Professor Schimmelpreester for putting in a good word for me with you, *Herr Generaldirektor*.'

'Yes, he did that. What, is he Professor too? How is that? *Mais passons*. He wrote me about you and I did not disregard the matter, because in the old days we had so many larks together. But I must tell you, my friend, there are difficulties. What are we to do with you? You obviously have not the slightest experience in hotel work. You are as yet entirely untrained –'

'Without presumption I think I can say in advance,' I replied, 'that a certain natural adroitness will very quickly make up for my lack of training.'

'Well,' he remarked in a teasing tone, 'your adroitness no doubt shows itself mainly with pretty women.'

In my opinion he said this for three reasons. First of all, the Frenchman – and Herr Stürzli had long been that – loves to pronounce the phrase 'pretty women' for his own gratification as well as that of others. '*Une jolie femme*' is the most popular raillery in that country; with it one can be sure of a gay and sympathetic response. It is much the same as mentioning beer in Munich. There one has only to pronounce the word to produce general high spirits. This in the first place. Secondly, and looking more deeply, in talking about pretty women and joking about my presumed skill with them, Stürzli wanted to subdue the confusion of his instincts, be rid of me in a certain sense, and, as it were, push me towards the female side. This I understood perfectly well. In the third place, however – in opposition, it must be admitted, to the above effort – it was his intention to make me smile, which could only lead to his experiencing that same confusion again. Obviously, in a muddled way, that was just what he wanted. The smile, however restrained, was something I could not refuse him and I accompanied it with the following words:

'Assuredly in this domain, as in every other, I stand far behind you, *Herr Generaldirektor*.'

My pretty speech was wasted. He did not hear it at all, but simply looked at my smile, and his face once more bore a look of revulsion. This is what he had wanted, and there was nothing for me to do but to lower my eyes once more in decorous modesty. And once again he did not make me pay for it.

'That's all very well, young man,' he said, 'the question is what about your rudimentary information? You drop in like this on Paris – do you even know how to speak French?'

This was grist to my mill. I was filled with elation, for now the conversation had taken a turn in my favour. This is the place to insert an observation about my general gift for languages, a gift that was always amazing and mysterious. Universal in my endowments and possessed of every possible potentiality, I did not really need to learn a foreign language, once I had acquired a smattering of it, to give the impression, for a short time at least, of fluent mastery. This was accomplished with such an exaggerated but precise imitation of the characteristic national gestures as bordered on the comic. The imitative, parody element in my performance did not lessen its credibility but actually enhanced it, and with it came a pleasant, almost ecstatic feeling of being possessed by a foreign spirit. Plunged in this or rather taken captive by it, I was in a state of inspiration, in which, to my astonishment (and this in turn increased the daring of my performance) the vocabulary simply flashed into my head, God knows from where.

In the first case, however, my glibness in French had no such supernatural background.

'*Ah, voyons, monsieur le directeur général,*' I gushed with extreme affectation, '*Vous me demandez sérieusement si je parle français? Mille fois pardon, mais cela m'amuse! De fait, c'est plus ou moins ma langue maternelle – ou plutôt paternelle, parce que mon pauvre père – qu'il repose en paix! – nourrissait dans son tendre cœur un amour presque passioné pour Paris et profitait de toute occasion pour s'arrêter dans cette ville magnifique dont les recoins les plus intimes lui étaient familiers. Je vous assure: il connaissait des ruelles aussi perdues comme, disons, la rue de l'Échelle au Ciel, bref, il se sentait chez soi à Paris comme nulle part au monde. La conséquence? Voilà la conséquence. Ma propre éducation fut de bonne part française, et l'idée de la conversation, je l'ai toujours conçue comme l'idée de la conversation française. Causer, c'était pour moi causer en français et la langue française – ah, monsieur, cette langue de l'élégance, de la civilisation, de l'esprit, elle est la langue de la conversation, la conversation elle-même ... Pendant toute mon enfance heureuse j'ai causé avec une charmante demoiselle de Vevey – Vevey en Suisse – qui prenait soin du petit gars de bonne famille, et c'est elle qui m'a enseigné des vers français, vers exquis que je me répète dès que j'en ai le temps et qui littéralement fondent sur ma langue –*'

> *Hirondelles de ma patrie,*
> *De mes amours ne me parlez-vous pas?*'

'Stop!' he interrupted the cascade of my chatter. 'Stop that poetry at once! I can't stand poetry, it upsets my stomach. Here in the lobby at five o'clock in the afternoon we sometimes let French poets appear, if they have anything decent to wear, and recite their verses. The ladies like it, but I keep as far away as possible, it makes the cold sweat break out on me.'

'*Je suis désolé, monsieur le directeur général. Je suis violemment tenté de maudir la poésie.*'

'All right. Do you speak English?'

Yes, did I? I did not, or at most I could act for three minutes or so as though I did – that is, just so long as I could manage with what I had once heard of the accent of the language in Langenschwalbach and in Frankfurt and the bits of vocabulary I had picked up here and there in books. The important thing was to construct out of a total lack of materials something that would be at least momentarily dazzling. And so I said – not in the broad, flat accents that the ignorant tend to associate with English, but pointing my lips instead and whispering, with my nose arrogantly raised in the air:

'I certainly do, sir. Of course, sir, quite naturally I do. Why shouldn't I? I love to, sir. It's a very nice and comfortable language, very much so indeed, sir, very. In my opinion, English is the language of the future, sir. I'll bet you what you like, sir, that in fifty years from now it will be at least the second language of every human being . . .'

'Why do you wave your nose around in the air like that? It's not necessary. Also, your theories are superfluous. I simply asked what you knew. *Parla italiano?*'

Instantly I was in Italian; in place of soft-voiced refinement I became possessed by the fieriest of temperaments. There happily rose up in me all the Italian sounds I had ever heard from my godfather Schimmelpreester, who had enjoyed frequent sojourns in that sunny land. Moving my hand with fingers pressed together in front of my face, I suddenly spread all five fingers wide and carolled and sang:

'*Ma, signore, che cosa mi domanda? Son veramente innamorato di questa bellissima lingua, la più bella del mondo. Ho bisogno s'Itanto d'aprire la mia bocca e involontariamente diventa il fonte di tutta l'armonia di quest'idioma celeste. Sì, caro, signore, per me non c'è dubbio che gli angeli nel cielo parlano italiano. Impossibile d'immaginare che queste beate creature si servano d'una lingua meno musicale –*'

'Stop!' he commanded. 'You're slipping into poetry again and you know that makes me ill. Can't you leave it alone? It's not fitting for an hotel employee. But your accent is not bad, and you have a certain knowledge of languages, as I see. That is more than I had expected. We will try you out, Knoll –'

'Krull, *Herr Generaldirektor.*'

'*Ne me corrigez pas!* So far as I am concerned, you could be called Knall. What's your first name?'

'Felix, *Herr Generaldirektor.*'

'That doesn't suit me at all. Felix – Felix, there's something private and presumptuous about it. You will be called Armand.'

'It gives me the greatest joy, *Herr Generaldirektor*, to change my name.'

'Joy or not, Armand is the name of the liftboy who is quitting his job tonight. You can take his place tomorrow. We will try you out as a liftboy.'

'I venture to promise, *Herr Generaldirektor*, that I will prove quick to learn and that I will do my job even better than Eustache.'

'What's this about Eustache?'

'He stops too high or too low and it makes an awkward step, *Herr Generaldirektor*. Only, of course, when he is carrying his equals. With hotel guests, if I understood him properly, he is more careful. This lack of consistency in carrying out his duties seems to me less than praiseworthy.'

'What business is it of yours to praise things around here? Besides, are you a Socialist?'

'No, indeed, *Herr Generaldirektor*! I find society enchanting just as it is and I am on fire to earn its good opinion. I only meant that when a man knows his business he should never permit himself to make a botch of it even when nothing is at stake.'

'Socialists are something we have no place whatever for in our business.'

'*Ça va sans dire, monsieur le –*'

'Go on now, Knull. Have them give you the proper livery in the storeroom down in the basement. This is supplied by us, but the appropriate shoes are not, and I must call your attention to the fact that yours –'

'That is simply a temporary error, *Herr Generaldirektor*. By tomorrow it will be rectified to your complete satisfaction. I know what I owe the *établissement* and I assure you that my appearance will leave nothing whatever to be desired. I am enormously pleased about the livery, if I may say so. My godfather Schimmelpreester loved to dress me up in the most vivid costumes and always praised me for looking so much at home in each of them, although inborn talent is not really a cause for praise. But I have never yet tried on a liftboy's uniform.'

'It will be no misfortune,' he said, 'if in it you please the pretty women. *Adieu,* your services will not be required here today. Take a look at Paris this afternoon. Tomorrow morning ride up and down a few times with Eustache or one of the others and see how the mechanism works; it's simple and will not exceed your competence.'

'It will be handled with love,' was my reply. 'I will not rest until I no longer make the smallest step. *Du reste, monsieur le directeur général,*' I added and let my eyes melt, '*les paroles me manquent pour exprimer –*'

'*C'est bien, c'est bien,* I've got things to do,' he said and turned away, his face twisting once more in that grimace of distaste. This did not disturb me. Post-haste – for it was important for me to find that clockmaker before noon – I went downstairs to the basement, found the door marked 'Storeroom' without difficulty and knocked. A little old man with eyeglasses was reading the newspaper in a room that looked like a second-hand store or the costume room of a theatre, so crowded was it with colourful servants' liveries. I mentioned my needs, which were promptly met.

'*Et comme ça,*' said the old man, '*tu voudrais t'apprêter, mon petit, pour promener les jolies femmes en haut et en bas?*'

This nation cannot stop doing it. I winked and agreed that this was my wish and duty.

Very briefly he measured me with his eyes, took a sand-coloured livery with red piping, jacket and trousers, from the hanger, and quite simply folded it over my arm.

'Wouldn't it be better for me to try it on?' I asked.

'Not necessary. Not necessary. What I give you will fit. *Dans cet emballage la marchandise attirera l'attention des jolies femmes.*'

The wizened old man was very likely thinking of something else. He spoke quite mechanically, and just as mechanically I winked back at him, called him '*mon oncle*' at parting, and assured him I would owe my *carrière* to him alone.

I took the basement lift to the fifth floor. I was in a hurry, for I was still a little worried as to whether Stanko would leave my suitcase alone in my absence. On the way, the lift made several stops. Guests demanded the services of the lift; as they came in I modestly flattened myself against the wall. A lady entered from the lobby and asked to be taken to the second floor. An English-speaking bride and groom got in at the first floor and asked for the third. The single lady, who had entered first, excited my attention – and here, to be sure, the word 'excited' is appropriate. I observed her with a rapid beating of the heart that was not without sweetness. I knew the lady although she was not wearing a cloche with heron feathers, but another hat instead, a broad-brimmed creation trimmed in satin, over which she had put a white scarf that was tied under her chin and lay on her coat in long streamers. And although this coat was a different one from the one she had worn yesterday, a lighter, brighter one, with big cloth-covered buttons, there could not be the slightest doubt that I had before me my neighbour of the customs shed, the lady with whom I was connected through the possession of the jewel case. I recognized her first of all by a widening of the eyes that she had practised constantly during her argument with the inspector, but that was obviously a habit, for now she kept doing it constantly without cause. There were further signs of nervous tension in her not unlovely face. Otherwise, so far as I could see, there was nothing in the appearance of this forty-year-old brunette that could mar the tender relationship in which I stood to her. A little downy moustache lay not unbecomingly on her upper lip. Moreover her eyes had the golden-brown colour that always pleases me in women. If only she would not keep widening them in such a disturbing way! I had a feeling I ought to talk her out of that compulsive habit.

So we had really alighted here simultaneously – if the word 'alight' can be used in my case. It was only by chance that I had not met her again in front of the blushing gentleman at the reception desk. Her presence in the narrow space of the elevator produced a strange effect on me. Without knowing about me, without ever having seen me, without being aware of me now, she had been carrying me, featureless, in her thoughts ever since the moment yesterday evening or this morning when in unpacking her suitcase she had discovered that the jewel case was missing. I could not bring myself to attribute a hostile intent to her interest, however much this may surprise the solicitous reader. That her concern about me and her questions might have resulted in steps being taken against me (perhaps she was even now returning from taking such steps), these obvious possibilities flitted through my mind, without producing any real conviction; they had small weight against the enchantment of a situation in which the seeker was unwittingly so close to the object of her search. How I regretted, for her as well as for myself, that this proximity was of such short duration, lasting only to the second floor!

As she in whose thoughts I lay stepped out she said to the red-haired liftboy: '*Merci, Armand.*'

It was remarkable, and a proof of her sociability as well, that she, who had so recently arrived, already knew this fellow's name. Perhaps she had been a frequent guest at the Saint James and Albany and had known him for some time. I was even more struck by the name and by the fact that it was Armand who was running the lift. The meeting had been rich in associations.

'Who was that lady?' I asked as we went on.

Like an ignorant boor, the redhead made no reply. Nevertheless, as I got out on the fifth floor I added this question:

'Are you the Armand who is quitting this evening?'

'That's none of your damn business,' he said hoarsely.

'You're wrong,' I replied. 'It is my business. As a matter of fact, I'm Armand now. I'm going to try to cut a less boorish figure than you.'

'*Imbécile!*' he shouted, slamming the lift gate in my face.

Stanko was asleep when I entered *dortoir* number four. Hastily I proceeded as follows: I removed my suitcase from the shelf, carried it into the washroom, took out the little case that the honest Stanko, thank God, had left untouched, and, after removing my jacket and vest, put the charming topaz necklace around my neck and with some difficulty made sure the safety catch was closed behind. I then put my clothing back on, and crammed the rest of the jewellery, which was less bulky, into my right- and left-hand pockets. This done, I put my suitcase back in its place, hung up my livery in the wardrobe beside the hall door, put on my outdoor jacket and a cap and – I think through being disinclined to ride with Armand again – ran down all five flights and was on my way to the rue le l'Echelle au Ciel.

With my pockets full of treasure I still did not have the few sous necessary for a bus. I had to go on foot, and with difficulty, for I had to ask my way and, besides, my pace soon suffered from the weariness of going uphill. It took me a good three-quarters of an hour to reach the Montmartre Cemetery, for which I had been inquiring. From there on, to be sure, Stanko's directions proved completely reliable, and I quickly made my way through the rue Damrémone to the sidestreet of the Wise Virgins. Once there, I was within a few strides of my goal.

A mammoth settlement like Paris consists of many quarters and communities, and very few of these give any hint of the majesty of the whole to which they belong. Behind the magnificent façade the metropolis exhibits to the stranger is hidden the middle-class small town that carries on an independent existence within it. Many of the inhabitants of the street called 'Ladder to Heaven' had probably not seen for years the glitter of the avenue de l'Opéra, or the cosmopolitan hubbub of the boulevard des Italiens. An idyllic provincial scene surrounded me. Children played on the narrow cobbled street. Along the quiet pavements were rows of simple houses, with here and there a shop on the ground floor – a grocer's, a butcher's, a baker's, a saddler's – modestly displaying its wares. There must be a clockmaker here, too. I soon found number 92. '*Pierre Jean-Pierre, Horlogier*' was inscribed on the door of the shop beside the show window, which contained all kinds of timepieces – pocket watches for ladies and gentlemen, tin alarm clocks, and cheap pendulum clocks.

I pressed the latch and stepped in to the accompaniment of a tinkling bell that was set in motion by the opening of the door. The owner, a jeweller's lupe clamped in his eye, sat behind the counter, which was arranged as a showcase and also contained within its glass walls all sorts of watches and chains. He was examining the works of a pocket watch whose owner obviously had reason for complaint. The many-voiced tick-tock of the table clocks and grandfather clocks filled the store.

'Good day, master,' I said. 'Would it surprise you to know that I would like to buy a pocket watch and perhaps a handsome chain to go with it?'

'No one will stop you, my boy,' he replied, taking the lens from his eye. 'Presumably it's not to be a gold one?'

'Not necessarily,' I replied. 'I don't care anything about glitter and show. The inner quality, the precision, that's what I'm interested in.'

'Sound principles. A silver one, then,' he said, opening the inner side of the showcase and taking from among his wares several objects which he laid before me.

He was a haggard little man with stubbly yellow-grey hair and the sort of cheeks that start much too high, directly under the eyes, and hang sallowly where they ought to curve out. A cheerless, depressing picture.

With the silver stem-winder he had recommended in my hand, I asked the price. It was twenty-five francs.

'Incidentally, master,' I said, 'it is not my intention to pay cash for this watch, which I like very much. I prefer to go back to the older way of doing business – barter. Look at this ring!' And I got out the circlet with the grey pearl, which I had kept separate, for just this moment, in the change pocket inside the right-hand pocket of my jacket. 'My idea,' I explained, 'is to sell you this pretty item and to receive from you the difference between its worth and the price of this watch – in other words to pay you for the watch out of my receipts for the ring – or, to put it in still another way, to ask you simply to deduct the price of the watch, to which I entirely agree, from the sum of two thousand francs, let us say, which you will no doubt offer me for the ring. What do you think of that little transaction?'

Sharply, with narrowed eyes, he examined the ring in my hand and then stared in the same fashion into my face, while a slight quiver became noticeable in his malformed cheeks.

'Who are you, and where did you get this ring?' he asked in a tight voice. 'What do you take me for and what kind of deal are you proposing? Get out of here at once! This store belongs to an honest man!'

Dejectedly I hung my head, but after a short pause said with warmth: 'Master Jean-Pierre, you are making a mistake. The mistake of distrust – something I had to reckon with, to be sure, but from which your knowledge of people should have saved you. Look me in the eye . . . Well? Do I look like a – like the sort of person you thought I might be? I don't blame you for your first idea, it is understandable. But your second – I shall be much disappointed if that is not corrected by your personal impressions.'

He continued to peer at the ring and at my face with an abrupt up-and-down motion of his head.

'Where did you hear about my business?' he inquired.

'From a fellow worker and room-mate,' I replied. 'He is not altogether well at the moment; if you like, I will take him your good wishes for a speedy recovery. His name is Stanko.'

He still hesitated, peering up and down at me, his cheeks quivering. But I clearly saw that desire for the ring was gaining the upper hand over his timidity. With a glance at the door he took it out of my hand and quickly seated himself behind the counter to examine it through his watchmaker's lupe.

'It has a flaw,' he said, referring to the pearl.

'Nothing could surprise me more,' I replied.

'I can easily believe that. Only an expert would see it.'

'Well, so well hidden a flaw can't affect the value. And the diamonds, if I may ask?'

'Trash, splinters, roses, chipped-off stuff and simple decoration. A hundred francs,' he said, tossing the ring down between us on the glass top but closer to me.

'I must have misunderstood you!'

'If you think you misunderstood me, my boy, take your loot and be on your way.'

'But then I can't buy the watch.'

'*Je m'en fiche*,' he said. '*Adieu.*'

'Listen to me, Master Jean-Pierre,' I began again. 'With all due regard for your feelings, I can't spare you the reproach of negligence in the way you conduct your business. Through extreme miserliness you are endangering negotiations that have hardly yet begun. You overlook the possibility that this ring, valuable though it is, may not be the hundredth part of what I have to offer. This possibility is, nevertheless, a fact, and you would do well to alter your attitude towards me accordingly.'

He looked at me wide-eyed and the quivering in his misshapen cheeks increased remarkably. Once more he glanced at the door and then, motioning with his head, he muttered between his teeth: 'Come back here.'

He took the ring, led me around the counter, and opened the door to an unaired, windowless back room; there he lighted a brilliant white gas flame in the lamp hanging above a round table with a velvet cover and crocheted doilies. A safe and small desk gave the place an appearance half-way between middle-class living-room and business office.

'Come on! What have you got?' the clockmaker demanded.

'Allow me to remove this,' I replied, taking off my outer jacket. 'There, that's better.' And one by one I took out of my pockets the tortoise-shell comb, the breastpin with the sapphire, the brooch in the form of a little fruit basket, the bracelet with the white pearl, the ruby ring, and, as climax, the string of diamonds, and laid them all, well separated, on the crocheted table cover. Finally, requesting permission, I unbuttoned my vest, took the topaz jewellery from around my neck, and added it to the display on the table.

'What do you think of that?' I asked with a quiet pride.

I saw he could not quite conceal a glitter in his eye and a smacking of his lips. But he gave the appearance of waiting for more and finally inquired in a dry voice: 'Well? Is that all?'

'All?' I repeated. 'Master, you mustn't pretend a collection like this comes your way every day.'

'You'd be happy to get rid of your collection, wouldn't you?'

'Don't over-estimate my eagerness,' I replied. 'If you are asking whether I would like to dispose of it at a reasonable price, I can say yes.'

'Quite so,' he returned. 'Reasonableness is just what you need, my fine fellow.'

Thereupon he drew up one of the plush-covered armchairs that stood around the table and sat down to examine the objects. Without invitation I took a chair, crossed my legs, and watched him. I clearly saw his hand shaking as he took up one piece after another, appraised it, and then abruptly tossed it back on to the table. That was probably to cover up the quiver of greed, as was the repeated shrugging of his shoulders, especially when – this happened twice – he held the string of diamonds in his hands and, blowing on the stones, let them slowly slide between his fingers. And so it sounded all the more ridiculous when he finally said, gesturing at the whole collection:

'Five hundred francs.'

'What for, may I ask?'

'For the whole thing.'

'You're joking.'

'My boy, there's no occasion for either of us to joke. Do you want to leave your loot here for five hundred? Yes or no?'

'No,' I said and got up. 'Very far from it. With your permission I'll take my keepsakes, as I see I am being taken advantage of disgracefully.'

'Dignity,' he said jokingly, 'becomes you. And your strength of character is remarkable, too, for your years. As a tribute to it I'll say six hundred.'

'That's a step that doesn't get you out of the realm of the ridiculous. I look younger, dear sir, than I am, and it won't help at all to treat me as a child. I know the real worth of these things, and although I am not simple-minded enough to think I can insist on getting it, I will not permit the payment to differ to an immoral degree. Finally, I know that in this field of business there are competitors, and I'll be able to find them.'

'You have an oily tongue – along with your other talents. But the idea
hasn't occurred to you that the competitors with whom you threaten me are
very well organized and may have agreed upon common terms.'

'The question is simply this, Master Jean-Pierre, whether *you* want to buy
my things, or whether someone else is to buy them.'

'I am inclined to take them and, as we agreed in advance, at a reasonable
price.'

'And what's that?'

'Seven hundred francs – my last word.'

Silently I began to stow the jewellery in my pockets, first of all the string of
diamonds.

With trembling cheeks he watched me.

'Blockhead,' he said, 'you don't know your own good luck. Think what a
quantity of money that is, seven or eight hundred francs – for me who has to
lay it out and for you who will pocket it! What a lot of things you can buy
yourself for, let us say, eight hundred and fifty francs – pretty women,
clothes, theatre tickets, good dinners. Instead of that, like a fool, you want to
go on carrying the stuff around with you in your pockets. How do you know
the police aren't waiting for you outside? And don't you take my own risk
into account?'

'Have you,' I said at a venture, 'read about these objects anywhere in the
newspapers?'

'Not yet.'

'You see? Despite the fact that we are dealing with a total real value of not
less than eighteen thousand francs. Your risk is absolutely theoretical.
Nevertheless, I will take it into account, as though it were real, since in point
of fact I find myself momentarily short of cash. Give me half their worth,
nine thousand francs, and it's a deal.'

He pretended to roar with laughter, unpleasantly revealing the stumps of
decayed teeth. Squeakingly he repeated over and over the figure I had
named. Finally he said solemnly: 'You're crazy.'

'I take that,' I said, 'as the first thing you've said since the last thing you
said. And you will change that, too.'

'Listen, my young greenhorn, this is certainly the very first transaction of
this sort you have ever tried to carry on?'

'And suppose that were so?' I replied. 'Pay attention to the advent of a new
talent that has just appeared on the scene. Don't reject it through stupid
miserliness. Try rather to win it over to your side through open-handedness,
since it may yet bring you large profits, instead of steering it to another
purchaser with a better nose for luck and more taste for the youthful and
promising!'

Taken aback, he looked at me. Doubtless he was weighing my reasonable words in his shrivelled heart while studying the lips with which I had
spoken them.

Taking advantage of his hesitation, I added: 'There's no point, Master
Jean-Pierre, in our going on with these offers and counter-offers in lump
sums. The collection ought to be examined and evaluated piece by piece. We
must take our time about it.'

'That's all right with me,' he said. 'Let's reckon it up.'

That's where I made a stupid blunder. Of course if we had kept to lump
sums I should never in the world have been able to stick to nine thousand
francs, but the arguing and haggling that now ensued over the price of each
piece, while we sat at the table and the clockmaker noted down on his pad the

miserable valuations he forced on me, beat me down too heart-breakingly. It
lasted a long time, probably three-quarters of an hour or more. In the midst
of it the shop bell rang, and Jean-Pierre went out after commanding in a
whisper: 'Hush! Don't move!'

He came back again, and the haggling continued. I got the string of
diamonds up to two thousand francs, but if that was a victory it was my only
one. In vain I called upon the heavens to witness the beauty of the topaz
jewellery, the rarity of the sapphire that adorned the breastpin, of the white
pearl in the armband, of the ruby and the grey pearl. The rings together
produced fifteen hundred; all the other items except the string of diamonds
were in the range of fifty to three hundred. The sum total was forty-four
hundred and fifty francs, and this villain of mine acted as though he were
horrified by it and were ruining himself and his whole fraternity. He
declared, moreover, that in these circumstances the silver watch that I had to
buy would come to fifty francs instead of twenty-five – as much, that is, as he
was going to pay for the enchanting gold brooch with the grapes. The final
result was, accordingly, forty-four hundred. And Stanko? I thought. Here
was heavy charge against my receipts. Nevertheless there was nothing for
me to do but to say '*Entendu.*' Jean-Pierre opened the iron door of his safe,
bestowed his purchases therein under my regretful leave-taking gaze, and
laid four thousand-franc notes and four hundred-franc notes before me on
the table.

I shook my head.

'Please make these a little smaller,' I said, pushing the thousand franc
notes back to him, and he replied:

'Well, bravo! I was just giving you a little test in discretion. I see that you
don't intend to make too much of a splash when you make your purchases. I
like that. I like you altogether,' he went on as he changed the thousand-franc
notes into hundreds and some gold and silver as well, 'and I should never
have made so inexcusably generous a deal if you had not really inspired me
with confidence. Look, I would like to continue this connexion of ours.
There may really be something special about you. You have a kind of sunny
manner. What's your name anyway?'

'Armand.'

'Well, Armand, prove yourself grateful by coming back! Here's your
watch. I'll make you a present of this chain to go with it.' (It was absolutely
worthless.) '*Adieu*, my boy! Come again! I have fallen a little in love with you
in the course of our business.'

'You certainly controlled your emotions well.'

'Badly, very badly!'

Joking thus, we parted. I took an omnibus to the boulevard Haussman
and found a shoe store in a neighbouring sidestreet where I had myself fitted
with a pair of handsome button shoes, at once solid and flexible. These I kept
on, explaining that I had no further use for the old ones. After that, in the
Printemps department store near by I wandered from department to
department, acquiring first certain useful minor items: three or four collars,
a tie, a silk shirt, a soft hat in place of my cap, which I hid in the inside pocket
of my jacket, an umbrella that fitted inside the shaft of a cane and pleased me
enormously, deer-skin gloves, and a lizard-skin wallet. After that I asked my
way to the ready-made department, where I bought straight off the hanger
an attractive suit of light, warm grey wool that fitted me as though made to
order and, with my turn-down collar and the blue-and-white dotted tie, was
extremely becoming. This, too, I kept on, and asked them to deliver the

clothes I had come in, giving, as a joke, the name: 'Pierre Jean-Pierre, quatre-vingt-douze, rue de l'Échelle au Ciel.'

I was well content as, thus brightened in appearance, I left the Printemps, my umbrella cane hooked over my arm and in my gloved fingers the convenient little wooden handle that was hooked to the red ribbon of my package. Well content, too, when I thought of the woman who bore my featureless image in her mind and, so I believed, was even now searching for a figure more worthy of her and her interest than heretofore. She would certainly have rejoiced with me that I had brought my outer appearance to a polish more in keeping with our relationship. The afternoon was well advanced after these accomplishments and I felt hungry. In a *brasserie* I ordered a strengthening but by no means gluttonous meal, consisting of a fish soup, a good steak with vegetables, cheese, and fruit, and I drank two glasses of beer. Well fed, I decided to allow myself the diversion for which I had envied those engaged in it when I rode by the day before – that is, to sit in front of one of the cafés in the boulevard des Italiens and observe the passing crowd. This I did. Taking a seat at a little table near a warming brazier, I drank my *double* and smoked, glancing alternatively at the colourful and noisy stream of life flowing in front of me and down at my handsome buttoned shoes; I had crossed my legs in order to swing one of them in the air. I must have sat there for an hour, so pleased was I, and I should probably have stayed longer if the creatures creeping round and under my table in search of unregarded trifles had not by degrees become too numerous. I had, to be sure, discreetly slipped a present to a ragged old man and to an equally shabby boy who were picking up my cigarette butts – a franc to the former and ten sous to the latter, to their unspeakable delight – and this had caused an additional contingent of their fellows to come crowding up, before whom I had to flee since I could not possibly succour all the misery in the world. Nevertheless, I have to admit that the impulse to make a gift of this kind, an impulse I had been aware of on the previous evening, had played its part in my desire to visit the café.

It was, incidentally, a financial problem that had occupied me while I sat there, and continued to do so during my further diversions. What about Stanko? In respect to him, I was faced with a difficult choice. I could either admit to him that I had been too maladroit and childish to come anywhere near getting the price for my wares he had so confidently set; in proportion to this shameful failure, I could then settle with him for fifteen hundred francs at most. Or, to my honour and his advantage, I could deceive him and pretend I had at least achieved approximately the stipulated price. In that case I should have to pay out twice as much, and there would remain as my share of all that magnificence a tiny sum, miserably close to Master Jean-Pierre's original shameless offer. Which way would I decide? From the first I suspected that my pride or my vanity would prove stronger than my greed.

As for the diversions after the coffee hour, I entertained myself, for a trivial entrance fee, in looking at a magnificent panorama representing the Battle of Austerlitz with a full sweep of landscape, including burning villages, and teeming with Russian, Austrian, and French troops. It was so admirably executed that one could hardly perceive the division between what was only painted and the actual objects in the foreground, discarded weapons and knapsacks and the puppet figures of fallen warriors. On a hill, surrounded by his staff, the Emperor Napoleon was observing the strategic situation through a spy-glass. Exalted by this sight, I visited still another spectacle, a panopticon, where to your terrified delight you encounter at every turn potentates, famous swindlers, artists crowned by fame, and notorious murderers of women, and expect at every instant to hear them call you by name. The Abbé Liszt, with long white hair and the most natural-looking wart on his face, was sitting at a grand piano, his foot on the pedals, his eyes directed towards Heaven, reaching for the keys with waxen fingers, while near by General Bazaine held a revolver to his temple but did not fire. These were exciting impressions for a young mind, but, despite Liszt and Bazaine, my powers of assimilation were not exhausted. Evening had fallen during my adventures; as she had done the day before, Paris adorned herself with light, with colourful flashing signs, and after a little wandering about I spent an hour and a half in a variety theatre, where sea lions balanced lighted oil lamps on their noses, a magician ground up someone's gold watch in a mortar only to produce it in perfect condition from the back trouser pocket of a completely disinterested spectator sitting well towards the rear of the orchestra, a pale diseuse in long black gloves scattered shady improprieties in a graveyard voice, and a gentleman gave a masterful performance as a ventriloquist. I could not stay for the end of this wonderful programme, for I wanted to get a cup of chocolate and hurry back before the dormitory filled.

By way of the avenue de l'Opéra and the rue des Pyramides I returned to home territory in the rue Saint Honoré. Before entering the hotel I removed my gloves, for, together with the various other improvements in my toilet, they seemed to me possibly a trifle provocative. Nobody paid any attention to me, however, as I rode up to the fifth floor in the lift along with a number of guests. When I entered the room one flight higher, Stanko showed his surprise as he examined me in the light of the hanging bulb.

'*Nom d'un chien!*' he said. 'He has adorned himself. And so the affair went well?'

'Tolerably,' I replied, while I took off my jacket and stepped in front of his bed. 'Quite tolerably, Stanko, I might venture to say, even though all our hopes were not fulfilled. That fellow is by no means the worst of his kind; he's really quite affable if you know how to handle him and if you keep your guard up. I forced him up to nine thousand. Now permit me to pay my debt.' And climbing on to the edge of the lower bed in my button shoes, I counted three thousand francs from my overflowing lizard-skin wallet on to the flannel blanket.

'You swindler!' he said. 'You got twelve thousand.'

'Stanko, I swear to you –'

He burst into laughter.

'My pet, don't excite yourself! I don't believe you got twelve thousand or even nine. At the very most, you got five thousand. Look, I am lying here and my fever has gone down. A fellow gets weak and sentimental from exhaustion after a bout like that. And so I'll admit to you that I myself couldn't have squeezed out more than four or five thousand. Here's a thousand back. We're both honest fellows, aren't we? I'm enchanted by us. *Embrassons-nous! Et bonne nuit!*'

Chapter Nine

There is really nothing easier than running a lift; it can be mastered in almost no time. As I was very pleased with myself in my handsome livery and as many a glance from those members of the beau monde who rode up and down with me showed they were pleased too; as, moreover, I took genuine pleasure in my new name, the work at first was decidedly fun. But child's play though it was in itself, when one had been at it with only short interruptions from seven in the morning until nearly midnight it could become decidedly fatiguing. After such a day one clambered into one's upper bunk rather broken in body and spirit. Sixteen hours at a stretch, it lasted, with time out only during the brief intervals when the staff went to be fed in relays in a room between kitchen and dining-hall. Wretched meals they were, too – little Bob had been only too right about that; stewed up out of all kinds of unappetizing left-overs, they were a constant cause of grumbling. I found these dubious ragouts, hashes, and fricassees, stingily accompanied by a sour *petit vin du pays*, most offensive; in actual fact I have never been so disgustingly fed except in jail. One stood, then, for all that time, without being able to sit down, in an enclosed space, heavy with the perfume of guests, manipulating the controls, glancing at the indicator, stopping where directed, taking in guests, letting them off again, and being amazed by the brainless impatience of the ladies and gentlemen who would stand in the lobby ringing incessantly when anyone ought to know that you could not instantly dash down for them from the fourth floor, but first had to get out, there and on the lower floors, and with a polite bow and your best smile admit those wishing to descend.

I smiled a great deal and said: '*M'sieur et dame –*' and 'Watch your step', which was quite unnecessary, for it was only on the first day that I was occasionally guilty of a slightly uneven landing; after that I was never again responsible for a step that required a warning, or if I was, I immediately rectified it. I gently supported the elbows of elderly women, as though they might have difficulty in getting out, and received in return the slightly bewildered glances of thanks, tinged sometimes with a melancholy coquetry, with which the aged repay the gallantry of youth. Others, to be sure, repressed any sign of pleasure, or had no need to since their hearts were cold and empty of everything except class pride. Moreover, I was equally helpful to young women, and in these cases there was many a delicate blush accompanied by a murmured '*Merci*' for my attentiveness. This sweetened my monotonous day's work, for I really intended these courtesies only for One, and in a sense was simply practising them for her. I was waiting for her who bore me, featureless, in her mind and whom I bore most distinctly in mine, the mistress of the jewel case, the provider of my button shoes, my umbrella-cane, and my Sunday outfit – the woman with whom I lived in sweet secrecy and for whom, unless she had suddenly departed, I should not have long to wait.

It was on the second day towards five in the afternoon – Eustache, too, had just brought his car down – when she appeared in front of the lift bank in the lobby, wearing a scarf over her hat as she had done before. My hopelessly commonplace colleague and I were standing in front of the open gates, and she stopped midway between us, looking at me; she widened her eyes briefly and smiled, swaying slightly, undecided which car to choose. There was no doubt she was drawn to mine, but as Eustache had already stepped aside and invited her into his with a wave of his hand, she probably thought it was his turn. Into his car she stepped and was borne away, but not without an undissembled glance at me over her shoulder and a renewed widening of her eyes.

That was all, for the time being, except that at my next meeting with Eustache downstairs I learned her name. She was Mme Houpflé and came from Strassburg. '*Impudemment riche, tu sais,*' Eustache added, whereupon I answered him with a cool '*Tant mieux pour elle.*'

On the following day at the same hour, when the two other lifts were under way and I was standing alone in front of mine, she appeared again, this time in a very beautiful long-waisted mink jacket and a beret of the same fur. She had been shopping, for she was carrying in her arms several fairly large, elegantly wrapped packages. She nodded in satisfaction at seeing me, smiled at my bow which, accompanied by a deferential 'madame', had some of the quality of an invitation to dance, and let herself be enclosed with me in the bright, suspended room. Meanwhile, there was a ring from the fourth floor.

'*Deuxième, n'est-ce pas, madame?*' I asked, as she had given me no directions.

She had not stepped to the back of the car nor was she standing behind me, but at my side, looking alternately at my hand on the control lever and at my face.

'*Mais oui, deuxième,*' she said. '*Comment savez-vous?*'

'*Je le sais, tout simplement.*'

'Ah? The new Armand, if I am not mistaken.'

'At your service, madame.'

'One might say,' she replied, 'that this change represents an improvement in the personnel.'

'*Trop aimable, madame.*'

Her voice was a very pleasant, nervously vibrant alto. While I was thinking of this she spoke of my own voice.

'I should like to commend you,' she said, 'for your agreeable voice.' The very words of Spiritual Counsellor Chateau!

'*Je serais infiniment content, madame,*' I replied, '*si ma voix n'offenserait pas votre oreille!*'

There was insistent ringing from above. We had arrived at the second floor. She remarked.

'*C'est en effet une oreille musicale et sensible. Du reste, l'ouïe n'est pas le seul de mes sens qui est susceptible.*'

She was astounding! I tenderly held her elbow as she got out, as though there had been any need for that, and said:

'Permit me at least, madame, to relieve you of your burdens and carry them to your room.'

Thereupon I took her packages from her one by one and followed her down the corridor, simply abandoning my lift. It was only twenty paces. She opened number twenty-three on the left and preceded me into her bedroom, from which a door opened into the salon. A luxurious bedroom it was, with a hardwood floor, on which lay a large Persian rug, cherrywood furniture, a glittering array of articles on the toilet table, a wide brass bedstead with satin cover, and a grey silk chaise-longue. On this and on the glass-topped tables I deposited the packages while Madame took off her beret and opened her fur jacket.

'My maid is not here,' she said. 'Her room is on the floor above. Would you make your kindness complete by helping me out of this thing?'

'With great pleasure,' I replied, starting to work. While I was engaged in removing the silk-lined fur, warm from her shoulders, she turned her head. One ringlet of her thick brown hair, whitened before its time, stood out impudently over her forehead; widening her eyes briefly and then narrowing them in a dreamy, swimming look, she spoke these words:

'You are undressing me, darling menial?'

An incredible woman and very articulate!

Taken aback, but full of determination, I managed to reply: 'Would God, madame, that time permitted me to accept that interpretation and go on as long as I liked with this enchanting occupation!'

'You have no time for me?'

'Unhappily not at this moment, madame. My lift is waiting. It stands open while people upstairs and down are ringing for it, and perhaps there's a crowd standing in front of it on this floor. I shall lose my job if I neglect it any longer.'

'But you would have time for me – if you had time for me?'

'An endless amount, madame!'

'*When* will you have time for me?' she asked, alternating the sudden widening of her eyes and the swimming look, and she moved close to me in her blue-grey, tailored suit.

'At eleven o'clock I shall be off duty,' I replied softly.

'I shall wait for you then,' she said in the same tone. 'Here is my pledge!' And before I knew what she was about, my head was between her hands and her mouth on mine in a kiss that went quite far – far enough to make it an unusually binding pledge.

I must certainly have been somewhat pale as I put her fur jacket, which I still had in my hand, on the chaise-longue and withdrew. Three persons were in fact waiting bewilderedly in front of the open lift. I had to make my apologies to them not only for my absence, due to an important errand, but also because, before taking them down, I had first to go to the fourth floor, whence there had been a summons but where now there was no one. Downstairs I had to listen to abuse for interrupting traffic. Against this I defended myself by explaining that I had been compelled to accompany to her room a lady suddenly overcome by faintness.

Mme Houpflé faint! A woman of such boldness! That quality, I reflected, came more easily to her than to me because of her greater age and also because of my subordinate position, to which she had given so oddly a lofty name. 'Darling menial,' she had called me – a woman of poetry! 'You are undressing me, darling menial?' This exciting phrase lay in my mind all evening, the entire six hours that had to be endured until I should have time for her. It wounded me a little, her phrase, and yet at the same time filled me with pride – even for the daring which I had not in the least possessed but which she had simply imputed to me. In any case, I now possessed it in plenty. She had inspired it in me – particularly by that very binding pledge.

At seven o'clock I took her down to dinner: when she entered my car there were other guests already in it. She wore a wonderful silk dress with a short train, laces, and an embroidered tunic; around her waist was a black satin belt, and around her neck a string of flawless, shimmering, milky pearls which, to her good fortune – and the misfortune of Master Jean-Pierre – had not been in the jewel case. The thoroughness with which she disregarded me – and this after so far-reaching a kiss! – nettled me, but I revenged myself, as they got out, by putting my hand not under her elbow but under that of a bedizened, ghost-like old woman. It seemed to me I saw her smile at this charitable gallantry.

At what hour she returned to her room I did not learn. Some time, however, it would have to be eleven, and at that hour service was maintained by one lift only, while the operators of the other two had the rest of the evening off. Tonight I was one of them. To freshen up after my day's labours for the tenderest of rendezvous, I first made my way up to our washroom and then descended afoot to the second floor. The corridor with its red carpet that silenced all footsteps lay already in undisturbed peace. I considered it discreet to knock at the door of Mme Houpflé's salon, number twenty-five, but received no answer, I opened the outside door of number twenty-three, her bedroom, and, inclining my ear, knocked discreetly on the inner one.

An inquiring '*Entrez?*' in a slightly surprised tone answered me. I obeyed, for I felt entitled to disregard the surprise. The room lay in the reddish twilight thrown by a silk-shaded night lamp, which was the only illumination. The daring occupant – it is with justification and pleasure that I return the epithet she had bestowed on me – was discovered by my rapid, inquiring survey in bed under the purple satin cover – in the splendid brass bed that stood with its head against the wall and the chaise-longue at its feet close to the heavily curtained window. My fair traveller lay there, her arms crossed behind her head, in a cambric nightgown with short sleeves and billowing lace-edged décolletage. She had undone the knot of her hair for the night and had wound the braids around her head in a very becoming, loose, tiara-like fashion. Twisted into a curl, the white strand lay back from her brow, which was no longer unfurrowed. Hardly had I shut the door when I heard the bolt – which was controlled from the bed by a wire – fall into place.

She widened her golden eyes for just an instant, as usual, but her face remained slightly disturbed in a kind of nervous deceitfulness as she said:

'Why, what's this? A hotel employee, a domestic, a young man of the people comes into my room at this hour when I have already retired?'

'You expressed the wish, madame,' I replied, approaching the bed.

'The wish? Did I so? You say "the wish" and behave as though you meant the order a lady gives some minor servant, a lift-boy perhaps, but what you really mean in your unheard-of pertness, yes, shamelessness, is the longing, the hot, yearning desire, you mean it quite simply and straightforwardly because you are young and beautiful, so beautiful, so young, so insolent ... "The wish!" Tell me at least, you answer to wishes, dream of my senses, *mignon* in livery, sweet helot, whether you insolently dare to share this wish a little!'

Thereupon she took me by the hand and drew me down to an unsteady perch on the edge of her bed. To keep my balance I had to stretch my arm across her and brace myself against the head of the bed, so that I was bent over her nakedness, so lightly veiled in linen and lace, and enveloped in its fragrant warmth. Slightly offended, I admit, by her repeated insistence on my humble state – what did she expect to gain by that? – instead of answering I bent all the way down to her and pressed my lips against hers. She not only carried this kiss to even greater lengths than the one that afternoon – with no lack of co-operation from me – she also took my hand from its support and guided it inside her décolletage to her breasts, which were very nicely fitted to the hand, moving it about by the wrist in such a way that my manhood, as she could not fail to notice, was most urgently aroused. Touched by this observation, she cooed softly with compassion and delight: 'O lovely youth, far fairer than this body that has the power to inflame you!'

Then she began to tug at the collar of my jacket with both hands, unhooked it, and with incredible speed proceeded to undo the buttons.

'Off, off, away with that and away with that, too,' her words tumbled out. 'Off and away, so that I can see you, can catch sight of the god! Quick, help! *Comment, à ce propos, quand l'heure nous appelle, n'êtes-vous pas encore prêt pour la chapelle? Déshabillez-vous vite! Je compte les instants! La parure de noce!* So I call your divine limbs that I have been thirsting to behold since I first saw you! Ah so, ah there! The holy breast, the shoulders, the sweet arms! Away then finally with this too – oh, la, la, that's what I call gallantry! Come to me, then *bien-aimé!* To me, to me …'

Never was there a more articulate woman! It was poetry she uttered, nothing less. And she continued to express herself when I was with her; it was her habit to put everything into words. In her arms she held the pupil and initiate of that exacting teacher, Rosza. He made her very happy and was privileged to hear about it as he did so:

'Oh, sweetheart! Oh, you angel of love, offspring of desire! Ah, ah, you young devil, naked boy, how you can do it. My husband can do nothing at all, absolutely nothing, you must know. Oh, blessed one, you are killing me! Ecstasy robs me of breath, breaks my heart, I will die of your love!' She bit my lip, my neck. 'Call me *tu!*' she groaned suddenly, near the climax. 'Be familiar with me, degrade me! *J'adore d'être humiliée! Je t'adore! Oh, je t'adore, petit esclave stupide qui me déshonore …*'

She came. We came. I had given my best, had in my enjoyment made proper recompense. But how could I fail to be annoyed that at the very climax she had been stammering about degradation and had called me a stupid little slave? We rested, still united, still in close embrace, but through annoyance at this *'qui me déshonore'* I did not return her kisses of thanks. With her mouth on my body she breathed again:

'Quick, call me *tu!* I have not yet heard this *tu* from you to me. I lie here and make love with a divine and yet quite common servant boy. How delightfully that degrades me! My name is Diane. But you, with your lips, call me whore, explicitly, "You sweet whore!"'

'Sweet Diane!'

'No, say "You whore!" Let me fully savour my degradation in words …'

I freed myself from her. We lay side by side, our hearts still beating high. I said:

'No, Diane, you will hear no such word from me. I refuse. And I must admit I find it very bitter that you think my love degrading.'

'Not yours,' she said, drawing me to her. 'Mine! My love for you, you insignificant boy! Oh, you lovely fool, you don't understand!' Whereupon she took my head and knocked it several times against her own in a kind of tender exasperation. 'I am an author, you must know, a woman of the intellect. Diane Philibert – my husband, his name is Houpflé, *c'est du dernier ridicule* – I write under my maiden name, Diane Philibert, *sous ce nom de plume.* Naturally you have never heard the name – how should you, indeed? – which is on so many books, they are novels, you understand, full of psychological insight, *pleins d'esprit, et des volumes de vers passionés* ... Yes, my poor darling, your Diane, she is *d'une intelligence extrême.* And yet the intellect – oh!' – and once more she knocked our heads together, somewhat harder than before – 'how could you understand that? The intellect longs for the delights of the non-intellect, that which is alive and beautiful *dans sa stupidité*, in love with it, oh, in love with it to the point of idiocy, to the ultimate self-betrayal and self-denial, in love with the beautiful and the divinely stupid, it kneels before it, it prays to it in an ecstasy of self-abnegation, self-degradation, and finds it intoxicating to be degraded by it –'

'Well now, dear child,' thus I finally interrupted her. 'Beauty apart – and if nature made a good job of me, so much the better – you mustn't think me as stupid as all that, even if I haven't read your novels and poems –'

She did not let me go on. I had enchanted her in a quite unintentional way. 'You call me "dear child"?' she cried, embracing me stormily and burying her mouth in my neck. 'Oh, that's delicious! That's much better than "sweet whore"! That's a much deeper delight than anything you've done, you artist in love! A little naked liftboy lies beside me and calls me "dear child", me, Diane Philibert! *C'est exquis, ça me transporte! Armand, chéri*, I didn't mean to offend you. I didn't mean to say that you're especially stupid. All beauty is stupid because it simply exists as an object for glorification by the spirit. Let me see you, see you completely – heaven help me, how beautiful you are! The breast so sweet in its smooth, clear strength, the slim arms, the noble ribs, the narrow hips, and, oh, the Hermes legs –'

'Stop it, Diane, this isn't right. It is I who should be praising you.'

'Nonsense! That's just a male convention. We women are lucky that our curves please you. But the divine, the masterpiece of creation, the model of beauty, that's you, you young, very young men with Hermes legs. Do you know who Hermes is?'

'I must admit at the moment –'

'*Céleste!* Diane Philibert is making love with someone who has never heard of Hermes! What a delicious degradation of the spirit! I will tell you, sweet fool, who Hermes is. He is the suave god of thieves.'

I was taken aback and blushed. I looked at her closely, was suspicious, and then let the suspicion drop. An idea came to me, but I pushed it aside; besides, it was soon drowned in the flood of avowals she was pouring forth, now whispering them into my arm, now lifting her voice, warm and chanting.

'Would you believe, beloved, that I have loved only you, always only you since I was able to feel? That means, of course, not you but the idea of you, the lovely instant you incarnate. Call it perversion if you will, but I detest the grown man full-bearded and woolly-chested, the mature and significant man – *affreux*, dreadful! I am significant myself – that's just what I would consider perverse: *de me coucher avec un homme penseur.* It's only you boys I have loved from the beginning – as a girl of thirteen I was crazy about a boy of fourteen or fifteen. The ideal grew a little as I grew, but it never went above eighteen; my taste, the yearning of my senses never reached beyond that ... How old are you?'

'Twenty,' I replied.

'You look younger, you are practically too old for me.'

'I, too old for you?'

'Come, come! The way you are is right for me, right to the point of heavenly bliss. I will tell you: perhaps my passion is connected with the fact that I was never a mother, never bore a son. I would have loved him with idolatry if he had been only half-way beautiful, which, to be sure, would have been very unlikely if I had got him from Houpflé. Perhaps, I say, this love for you is transferred mother-love, the yearning for a son ... Perversity, do you say? And all of you? What do you want with our breasts that gave you suck, our womb that bore you? Isn't it your wish simply to go back to them, to become sucklings again? Isn't it the mother you illicitly love in the wife? Perversion! Love is perversion through and through, it can't be anything else. Prove it where you will, you will find perversion ... But it's admittedly sad and painful for a woman to be able to love a man only when he is quite, quite young, when he is a boy. *C'est un amour tragique*, inadmissible, not practical, not for life, not for marriage. I, I married Houpflé, a rich businessman, so that in the shelter of his riches I could write my books, *qui sont énormément intelligents*. My husband can do nothing, as I told you, at least with me. *Il me trompe*, as they say, with a theatrical demoiselle. Perhaps he is some good with her – I should rather doubt it. It's a matter of indifference to me – this whole world of men and women and marriage and betrayal is a matter of indifference. I live in my so-called perversion, in the love of my life that lies at the bottom of everything I am, in the happiness and misery of this enthusiasm with its heavy curse that nothing, nothing in the whole visible world equals the enchantment of the youthful male. I live in my love for all of you, you, you image of desire, whose beauty I kiss in complete abnegation of spirit. I kiss your presumptuous lips over the white teeth you show when you smile. I kiss the tender stars of your breast, the little golden hairs on the dark skin of your armpits. And how does that happen? With your blue eyes and blond hair, where do you get this colouring, this tint of light bronze? You are baffling. How baffling! *Le fleur de ta jeunesse remplit mon cœur âgé d'une éternelle ivresse.* This intoxication will never end, I shall die of it, but my spirit will woo you forever with its wiles. You, too, *bien-aimé*, will all too soon grow old and approach the grave, but here are comfort and balm for my heart; ye will endure forever, brief joy of beauty, gracious inconstancy, eternal instant!'

'How strangely you speak!'

'How so? You are surprised that one praises in verse what one so ardently admires? *Tu ne connais pas donc le vers alexandrin – ni le dieu voleur, toi-même si divin?*'

Abashed, like a small boy, I shook my head. She did not on that account cease her endearments, and I must admit that so much praise and adulation, finally even expressed in poetry had greatly excited me. Although my offering in our first embrace had, as was usual with me, been my utmost – she found me once more in manly state – found me so with that combination of compassion and delight that I had noted in her before. We were united again. But did she on that account desist from what she called the self-abnegation of the spirit, from this nonsense about degradation? She did not.

'Armand,' she whispered in my ear, 'be rough with me! I am entirely yours, I am your slave! Treat me as you would the lowest wench! I don't deserve anything else, and it would be heaven for me!'

I paid no attention to this. We expired again. In the ensuing lassitude, however, she brooded and suddenly said:

'Listen, Armand.'

'What is it?'

'How would it be if you beat me? Beat me hard, I mean. Me, Diane Philibert? It would serve me right, I would be thankful to you. There are your braces, take them, beloved, turn me over and whip me till I bleed.'

'I wouldn't think of it, Diane. What do you take me for? I'm not that kind of lover.'

'Oh, what a shame! You have too much respect for this fine lady.'

At that the thought that had slipped away from me returned. I said: 'Listen to me, Diane. I will confess something to you that perhaps will make up in a way for what I have had to refuse you on the grounds of good taste. Tell me this, when you were unpacking your bag, the big one, or having it unpacked, was there perhaps something missing?'

'Missing? No. But yes! How did you know?'

'A little case?'

'A little case, yes! With jewellery. How did you know about that?'

'I took it.'

'Took it? When?'

'At the customs we were standing side by side. You were busy. I took it then.'

'You stole it? You are a thief? *Mais ça c'est suprême!* I am lying in bed with a thief! *C'est une humiliation merveilleuse, tout à fait excitante, un rêve d'humiliation!* Not only a domestic – a common, ordinary thief!'

'I knew it would give you pleasure. But at that time I did not know, and so I must ask your pardon. I could not foresee that we would love each other. Otherwise I would not have inflicted on you the distress and shock of having to get along without your wonderfully beautiful topaz jewellery, the diamonds and all the rest.'

'Distress? Shock? Get along without? Beloved, Juliette, my maid, searched for a while. As for me, I didn't worry about the stuff for two seconds. What does it matter to me? You stole it, sweetheart – so it is yours. Keep it. What are you going to do with it, by the way? Never mind. My husband, who is coming tomorrow to take me away, is so rich! He makes bathroom toilets, I must tell you. Everyone needs them, as you can understand. Strassburg toilets by Houpflé, they are much in demand, they are shipped to the four corners of the earth. He bedecks me with too much jewellery out of sheer bad conscience. He'll present me with things three times as pretty as the ones you stole. Oh, how much more precious to me is the thief than what he took! Hermes! He does not know who it is – and it is he! Hermes, Hermes! ... Armand?'

'What is it?'

'I have a wonderful idea.'

'What's that?'

'Armand, you shall steal from me. Here under my very eyes. That is, I'll shut my eyes and pretend to both of us that I am asleep. But secretly I'll watch you steal. Get up, as you are, thievish god, and steal! You haven't by any means stolen all the things I have with me; for those few days before my husband's arrival I did not deposit anything at the office. There in the upper right-hand drawer of the cupboard is the key to my bureau. In it you will find all sorts of things under the lingerie. There's cash there, too. Prowl around my room on cat feet and catch the mice! You will do this favour for your Diane, won't you?'

'But, dear child – I call you that because you like to hear me say it – dear child, that would not be nice or at all gentlemanly after what we have been to each other.'

'Fool! It will be the most enchanting fulfilment of our love!'

'And tomorrow Monsieur Houpflé comes. What will he –'

'My husband? What has he to say? I'll explain to him, casually and with an expression of complete indifference, that I was robbed on my journey. That happens when rich women are a trifle careless. Gone is gone, and the robber has long ago disappeared. No, just leave my husband to me!'

'But, sweet Diane, under your eyes –'

'Oh, to think that you have no feeling for the charm of my idea! All right, I will not see you. I'll put out the light.' And in fact she turned off the little red-shaded lamp on the night table so that darkness shrouded us. 'I will not see you. I will only listen to the parquet softly creaking under your thief's tread, only hear your breathing as you steal, and the soft clink of the thief's booty in your hands. Go on, steal away from my side, prowl, find, and take! It is my dearest wish.'

And so I obeyed her. Cautiously I left her and took what the room offered – too easy a theft, for right on the night table in a little dish were her rings, and the pearl necklace she had worn at dinner lay on top of the table around which the easy chairs were grouped. Despite the complete darkness I had no trouble in finding the key to the bureau in the corner cupboard. I opened the top drawer almost noiselessly and had only to take out a few items of lingerie to come upon the jewellery, pendants, bracelets, brooches, in addition to some encouragingly large-sized notes. All this I brought to her in the bed, for reasons of propriety, as though I had got it together for her. But she whispered:

'Little fool, what are you doing? This is your booty of love and theft. Put it in your pockets, get dressed, and vanish, as is proper! Hurry and flee! I heard it all, I heard you breathing as you stole. And now I am going to telephone the police. Or would it be better for me not to? What do you think? How far along are you? Finished soon? Have you your livery on again with all your booty of love and theft in it? Surely you didn't steal my button-hook here it is ... *Adieu*, Armand! Farewell, farewell forever, my idol! Do not forget your Diane, for in her you will survive. After years and years when – *le temps t'ai détruit, ce cœur te gardera dans ton moment béni.* Yes, when the grave covers us, me and you too, Armand, *tu vivras dans mes vers et dans mes beaux romans*, every one of which – never breathe this to the world! – has been kissed by your lips. *Adieu, adieu, chéri ...*'

Chapter One

The fact that I have devoted a whole chapter to the foregoing extraordinary episode and have used it as a festive ending to the second book of my confessions will, I trust, seem understandable and even commendable. It was, I can say with assurance, the experience of a lifetime, and its heroine's earnest pleas not to forget her entirely unnecessary. A woman so singular as Diane Houpflé, in every sense of the word, and the amazing circumstances of my meeting with her are not likely to be forgotten ever. This does not mean that the situation in which the reader was privileged to overhear us, considered simply as situation, stands by itself in my career. Ladies travelling alone, particularly older ladies, are not always simply horrified to discover that a young man has found something in their bedrooms to interest him; if their first impulse is to raise an alarm, it is an impulse they sometimes succeed in suppressing. But if I have had such experiences (and I have), they fell far short of that significant and unique night, and at the risk of blunting my reader's interest in the further course of my confessions, I must announce that in the sequel, however high I rose in society, I never again had the experience of being addressed in alexandrines.

For the treasure trove of love and theft which the poetess's bizarre idea had left in my hands I received from Master Pierre Jean-Pierre six thousand francs and innumerable pats on the shoulder. Moreover, as Diane's bureau drawer had provided the thieving god with cash as well – four thousand-franc notes hidden under the lingerie, to be exact – I was now the possessor, all told, of twelve thousand three hundred and fifty francs. Naturally enough, I did not wish to carry such a sum around with me any longer than necessary, and at the first opportunity I deposited it in a bank-account at the Crédit Lyonnais under the name of Armand Kroull, retaining only a couple of hundred francs for pocket money on my afternoons off.

The reader will learn of this step with approval and a feeling of relief. It would be easy to picture a young fop, endowed with such means through the tempting favour of fortune, immediately abandoning his unpaid position, setting himself up in attractive bachelor quarters, and indulging in all the delights that Paris has to offer – until the easily foreseeable day when his treasure was exhausted. I did not think of such a thing, or if I thought of it, I banished the idea with proper decisiveness as soon as it occurred. What could I expect if I acted on it? Where would I be when sooner or later, depending on the liveliness of my dissipations, my windfall was used up? The temptation was easily overcome when I recalled the words of my godfather Schimmelpreester (with whom, now and then, I exchanged short messages on picture postcards) – the words in which he described to me the splendid goals of an hotel career, goals that might be reached by straightforward advancement but also by one or another of the by-paths. I could not show myself ungrateful to him by throwing away the opportunity he had secured for me through his world-wide connexions. To be sure, in holding on to my first position with characteristic tenacity, I gave little or no thought to the 'straightforward advancement' he had mentioned and I did not picture myself as head-waiter, concierge, or even manager. The by-paths were all the more vividly in my mind and I had only to guard against mistaking the first cul-de-sac, such as was offered me now, for a reliable short-cut to happiness.

And so, possessor of a cheque-book though I was, I remained a liftboy at the Hotel Saint James and Albany. There was a certain charm in playing this role against a background of secret wealth, thanks to which my becoming livery took on the quality of a costume my godfather might have had me try on. My secret wealth – for this is how my dream-acquired riches seemed to me – transformed my uniform and my job into a role, a simple extension of my talent for 'dressing up'. Although later on I achieved dazzling success in passing myself off for more than I was, for the time being I passed myself off for less, and it is an open question which deception gave me the greater inner amusement, the greater delight in this fairy-tale magic.

It is true I was ill fed and ill housed in that luxurious and expensive hotel; but in both respects I was at least put to no expense, and if, moreover, I got no salary, I not only could husband my own resources but could increase them modestly through the *pourboires*, or, as I preferred to call them, *douceurs*, which regularly came my way from the travelling public – just as they fell to my colleagues in the lifts. Rather, to be quite accurate, they fell to me in somewhat larger quantities and more readily, a preference revealing people's recognition of finer clay which my more common companions, perceptively enough, never really begrudged me. One franc, two or three, even five, as much as ten francs in special cases of reckless generosity, would be tucked into my never importunate hand by departing guests or, at intervals of a week or fortnight, by grateful permanent residents. They would come from ladies with averted faces or smiling glances – sometimes also from gentlemen who, to be sure, often had to be prompted to it by their ladies. I remember many a little scene between husband and wife, which I was not supposed to see and which I appeared not to, a poke in the ribs accompanied by a murmur: '*Mais donnez donc quelque chose à ce garçon. Give him something, he is nice.*' Whereupon the husband would draw out his wallet murmuring something in reply, only to be rebuked: '*Non, c'est ridicule.* That's not enough, don't be so stingy.' Twelve to fifteen francs per week is what it always amounted to – an agreeable addition to my pocket money for use on the half-day off that the establishment, in its miserly way, granted us every two weeks.

It sometimes happened that I spent those afternoons and evenings with Stanko, who had long ago recovered from his illness and was back at work in the *garde-manger*, perparing his cold dishes and other delicacies for the big buffet. He was fond of me; I liked him well enough and was glad of his company in cafés and places of entertainment, though his presence was hardly distinguished. In ordinary clothes he had a comical, ambiguously exotic appearance, for his taste ran to large checks and bright colours, and no doubt he looked far better in the white apron and high white linen chef's hat of his calling. It is a common mistake: the working class ought never to attempt to be fashionable, at least by bourgeois standards. They do it awkwardly and it damages them in the eyes of the public. More than once I have heard my godfather Schimmelpreester express himself on this subject, and Stanko's appearance reminded me of his words. The abasement of the people, he said, through their acceptance of fashion, which was a result of the standardization of the world through bourgeois taste, was much to be regretted. The holiday attire of the peasantry and the former pomp and circumstance of the artisans' guilds had been far finer spectacles than some plump maid trying to play the lady on Sunday in feathered hat and train, not to mention the party clothes of the factory worker awkwardly striving to be fashionable. Since, however, the time was over and done with when the classes were distinguished from one another by mutual respect, he was for a society in which there were no more classes at all, neither maid nor lady, neither fine gentlemen nor commoner, and all wore the same thing. Golden words, spoken as though out of my own soul. What, I thought, would I have against shirt, breeches, belt, and nothing more? It would become me, and Stanko too would look better thus than in his clumsy approximation of fashion. Almost anything is becoming to a human being except the perverse, the stupid, and the half-baked.

So much by way of marginal comment. It was with Stanko, then, that I visited for a time the cabarets and terrace cafés, including the Café de Madrid, where a colourful and instructive society gathered after the theatres closed. But one special gala evening we spent at the Stoudebecker Circus, which had just opened in Paris for a few weeks' run. A word or two about that – or perhaps more! I should never forgive myself if I passed over such an experience without imparting to it some of the colour it so richly possessed.

This famous institution had pitched its vast round tent on the Square Saint-Jacques near the Théâtre Sarah Bernhardt and the Seine. The attendance was tremendous, since the performance obviously equalled or perhaps excelled the best in this field that had ever been offered the knowledgeable and highly exacting taste of the Parisian public. What an attack on the senses and nerves, what sensuous delight, in fact, lies in the uninterrupted succession of scenes as the fantastic programme unrolls! Exploits that lie at the extreme limits of human ability are achieved with bright smiles and lightly thrown kisses; their basic pattern is the *salto mortale*, for they all involve the fatal risk of a broken neck. Schooled to grace at moments of utmost daring, the performers are accompanied by the flourishes of a music appropriate enough in its commonplaceness to the physical character of the performance but not the extreme heights to which it is raised; it is this that furnishes the breath-taking build-up for the last not-to-be accomplished act – which nevertheless is accomplished.

With a brief nod (for the circus has no use for bows) the artist acknowledges the ecstatic applause of the massed onlookers. This is a unique audience, confusingly and excitingly compounded of the sensation-seeking crowd and the rude elegance of the horsy world. Cavalry officers in the loges, their caps at an angle; young rakes, freshly shaved, wearing monocles, a carnation or a chrysanthemum in the buttonholes of their loose yellow topcoats; cocottes, mingling with inquisitive ladies from the fashionable faubourgs, accompanied by knowledgeable cavaliers in grey frock-coats and grey top hats, their field-glasses slung in sporting fashion around their necks as though at a race at Longchamp. Add to this the excitement of the animals' physical presence, the magnificent, colourful costumes, the glittering spangles, the stable smell extending everywhere, the naked limbs of men and women. Breasts, throats, beauty in its most instantly appreciated form, the savage charm of dangerous deeds performed for the pleasure of the blood-thirsty crowd cater to every taste and enflame every desire. Women riders from the Hungarian steppe spring as though possessed on to wild-eyed, saddleless horses, roused to berserk frenzy by harsh cries. Gymnasts in tight-fitting, flesh-coloured tights; the hairless, bulging arms of athletes, stared at by the ladies with a strange, cold fixity; and charming boys. How forcibly I was struck by a troupe of tumblers and tightrope-walkers distinguished from the fantastic crowd not only by their simple sports clothes, but also by their agreeable trick of consulting briefly before each of their hair-raising performances, as though they first had to come to an agreement. Their star, who was obviously a favourite with everyone, was a boy of fifteen who bounded from a springboard, turned two and a half somersaults in the air, and then landed without so much as a wobble on the shoulders of the man behind him, apparently his elder brother. He was, to be sure, successful in doing this only on his third attempt. Twice he failed, missing his brother's shoulders and falling; his laughter and the way he shook his head at this failure were just as enchanting as the ironic gallantry of the gesture with which his senior summoned him back to the springboard. Possibly it was all intentional, for naturally enough the applause and *bravo*'s of the multitude were all the more tumultuous when on the third attempt he not only completed his *salto mortale* and landed without a quiver but managed to heighten the storm of applause by a gesture of his outspread hands which seemed to say: '*Me voilà!*' It is certain, however, that his calculated or half-intended failures had taken him closer to a broken spine than his triumphant success.

What fabulous creatures these artists are! Are they really human at all? Take the clowns, for example, those basically alien beings, fun-makers, with little red hands, little thin shod feet, red wigs under conical felt hats, their impossible lingo, their hand-stands, their stumbling and falling over everything, their mindless running to and fro and unserviceable attempts to help, the hideously unsuccessful efforts to imitate their serious colleagues – in tightrope-walking, for instance – which brings the crowd to a pitch of mad merriment. Are these ageless, half-grown sons of absurdity, at whom Stanko and I laughed so heartily (I, however, with a thoughtful fellow-feeling), are they human at all? With their chalk-white faces and utterly preposterous painted expressions – triangular eyebrows and deep per-pendicular grooves in their cheeks under the reddened eyes, impossible noses, mouths twisted up at the corners into insane smiles – masks, that is, which stand in inconceivable contrast to the splendour of their costumes – black satin, for example, embroidered with silver butterflies, a child's dream – are they, I repeat, human beings, men that could conceivably find a place in everyday daily life? In my opinion it is pure sentimentality to say that they are 'human too', with the sensibilities of human beings and perhaps even with wives and children. I honour them and defend them against ordinary bad taste when I say no, they are not, they are exceptions, side-splitting monsters of preposterousness, glittering, world-renouncing monks of unreason, cavoring hybrids, part human and part insane art.

Everything must be 'human' for the man in the street, and he thinks himself amazingly tender-hearted and knowledgeable when he penetrates appearances and finds the human beneath the surface. What about Andromache – '*La Fille de l'aire*', as she was called on the lengthy programme? Was she, by chance, human? I still dream of her, and though her person was as far as possible from the sphere of the absurd, it was really she whom I had in mind when I let myself run on about the clowns. She was the star of the circus, the main attraction, and she did an act on the high trapeze that was incomparable. She did it – and this was the sensational novelty, something unique in circus history – without a safety net below her. Her partner, a man of considerable ability who was, nevertheless, not be compared to her, performed with personal restraint, only extending his hand to her at the end of her foolhardy, amazingly executed evolutions in space between the two rapidly swinging trapezes; he really served only to set off her feats. Was she twenty years old, or less, or more? Who can say? Her features were severe and noble. Strangely enough, they were not disfigured but made clearer and more attractive by the elastic cap she pulled on when she set to work, without which her heavy, tightly braided brown hair would have whipped about during her wild, head-over-heels flight. She was more than average size for a woman. Her short pliant silver breast-plate was edged with swansdown, and attached to her shoulder-blades, as though to conform her title of 'daughter of the air', she wore a small pair of white wings. As if they could help her to fly! Her breasts were meagre, her hips narrow, the muscles of her arms, naturally enough, more developed than in other women, and her amazing hands, though not as big as a man's were nevertheless not so small as to rule out the question whether she might not, Heaven forfend, be a boy in disguise. No, the female conformation of her breasts was unmistakable, and so, too, despite her slimness, was the form of her thighs. She barely smiled. Her beautiful lips, far from being compressed, were usually slightly parted, and the nostrils of her pure Grecian nose were dilated. She disdained all flirtatiousness towards the crowd. Pausing after a *tour de force* on the crossbar, one hand resting against the rope, she would just perceptibly stretch out the other in greeting. But her serious eyes, staring straight ahead under even, unruffled, motionless brows, did not join in the greeting.

I worshipped her. She would stand up, set the trapeze in violent motion, leap off and fly past her partner, who would be coming towards her from the opposite trapeze; seize the crossbar with her hands, which were neither male nor female, execute, with body fully extended, a complete giant swing – which few gymnasts can perform – and utilize the tremendous impetus thus attained to fly back, once more passing her partner, and execute another *salto mortale* in mid-career; seize the bar of the swinging trapeze, draw herself up with a barely visible contraction of her arm muscles, and, impassively raising her hand, seat herself on it.

It was incredible, impossible, and nevertheless she did it. A shudder of enthusiasm shook anyone witnessing it and his heart grew cold. The crowd repaid her with awe rather than acclaim, they worshipped her, as I did, in the deathly stillness that followed the cutting off of the music during her daredevil feats. That the most precise calculation was a vital condition of everything she did goes without saying. At exactly the right instant, figured to the fraction of a second, just as she was ready to alight after her giant swing on the opposite trapeze and her *salto* on the way back, the flying trapeze her partner had abandoned must swing towards her, and not on any account start its back swing. If the bar was not there, those magnificent hands would close on emptiness and she would pitch headlong from the element of her art, the air, down to the common ground, which was death. The extreme accuracy these calculations called for made one shudder.

But I repeat my question: was Andromache really human? Was she a human being outside the ring, apart from her professional accomplishments, her almost unnatural – indeed, for a woman, wholly unnatural – achievements? To imagine her as a wife and mother was simply stupid; a wife and mother, or even anyone who could possibly be thought of as one, does not hang head-down from a trapeze, swinging so violently that it almost turns all the way over. She does not let go and fly through the air to her partner, who seizes her by her hands, executes a pendulum motion back and forth, and releases her at the top of the swing so that she returns to her own trapeze to the accompaniment of the famous mid-air *salto*. This was Andromache's way of consorting with a man; any other was unthinkable, for one recognized too well that this disciplined body lavished upon the adventurous accomplishments of her art what others devote to love. She was not a woman; but she was not a man either and therefore not a human being. A solemn angel of daring with parted lips and dilated nostrils, that is what she was, an unapproachable Amazon of the realms of space beneath the canvas, high above the crowd, whose lust for her was transformed into awe.

Andromache! Her vision, painful and uplifting at once, lingered in my mind long after her act was over and others had replaced it. The ringmasters and their attendants formed an avenue through which Director Stoudebecker entered with his twelve black stallions. He was a middle-aged sporting gentleman with a grey moustache, in evening clothes, the ribbon of the Legion of Honour in his buttonhole. In one hand he held a riding-crop and a long whip with an inlaid handle – a gift from the Shah of Persia, as he was careful to explain – which he could crack explosively. Standing in the sand of the ring in his gleaming patent-leather shoes, he addressed quiet, personal directions to one or other of his magnificent pupils, their proud heads decked in white bridles. At his command they went through their paces, knelt and turned and, finally, confronted by his raised crop, executed a magnificent circle of the ring on their hind feet. An impressive sight, but I was thinking of Andromache. Magnificent animal bodies; and it is between animal and angel, so I reflected, that man takes his stand. His place is closer to the animals, that we must admit. But she, my adored one, though all body, was a chaster body, untainted by humanity, and stood much closer to the angels.

Then iron bars were put around the ring and the lion cage was rolled in to offer a spice of danger to the unheroic, gaping crowd. The trainer, Monsieur Mustafa, had gold rings in his ears, was naked to the waist, and wore red trousers and a red hat. He entered through a small door which was quickly opened for him and closed behind him just as fast. Five beasts awaited him inside, their sharp, carnivorous scent mingling with the smell of the stables, They retreated before him and, at his command, one after another crouched reluctantly on the five stools arranged around the cage. They snarled with hideously contorted faces and struck at him with their paws – possibly half in play, but with a large element of rage as well, for they knew that entirely against their inclination and nature they were going to be forced to leap through hoops, and ultimately through fiery ones. A couple of them shook the air with the thunderous roar that had once terrified and scattered the small creatures of the forest. He retorted by shooting his revolver into the air. At this they cringed, snarling, for they realized their nature-given roar was out-trumped by this deafening report. Thereupon Mustafa swaggeringly lighted a cigarette, an action they observed with deep resentment. Then softly but firmly he pronounced a name, Achille or Nero, and with the utmost decisiveness summoned the first of them to his performance. One after another the kingly cats had unwillingly to leave their stools and spring back and forth through hoops held high in the air and finally, as I have said, through a hoop smeared with blazing pitch. Well or ill, they leaped through the flames; it was not hard for them to do, but it was an indignity. Growling, they returned to their stools, which were in themselves an insult, and stared fascinated at the man in red trousers. He kept moving his head lightly and quickly, fixing his dark eyes on the green eyes of each beast in turn – eyes narrowed by fear and by a certain hate and affection. At the slightest sound of disturbance he would swing round instantly and impose quiet with a glance of amazement and a name spoken softly but firmly.

Everyone felt the uncanny and cruel fellowship in which he moved, and this was exactly the titillation for which the rabble sitting in safety had paid. It was perfectly clear that his revolver would be of no use if the five mighty beasts awoke from their illusion of helplessness and decided to tear him to pieces. It was my impression that if he had injured himself in any way and they had seen his blood, it would have been all over with him. I realized, too, that if he went into the cage half naked it was a boon to the crowd, so that their craven joy might be enhanced by the sight of flesh, the flesh into which the great cats – who knows, perhaps it will happen tonight! – might set their terrible claws. Since I, however, continued to think of Andromache, I felt tempted to picture her as Mustafa's beloved; at any rate there was a kind of appropriateness in that. At the mere thought, jealousy pierced my heart like a knife and I actually lost my breath; hastily I banished the image. Comrades in the face of death they might well be, but not a pair of lovers, no, no; besides, it would bode ill to both of them! If he were involved in an affair, the lions would know and would refuse him obedience. And she, the angel of daring, would miss the flying bar, I was sure of it, if she abased herself and became a woman; she would pitch headlong towards the ground into disgrace and death . . .

What more was there, early and late, in the Stoudebecker Circus? A great variety of things, a superfluity of disciplined marvels. There is little to be gained by recalling them all. I do remember that from time to time I glanced sidewise at my friend Stanko, who, like all the people round about, was sunk in passive, blank enjoyment of this never-ending stream of dazzling skill, this colourful cascade of confusing, intoxicating feats and sights. This was not my style at all nor my way of meeting experience. Nothing, to be sure, escaped me; I seized on every detail with passionate attention. This was surrender, but in it there was – how shall I say? – an element of rebellion; I stiffened my back; my soul – how in the world can I express it? – exerted a kind of counter-pressure against the overwhelming flood of impressions. For all my admiration, there was a certain distrust – I am not putting this accurately but only approximately – in my penetrating observation of the tricks and arts and their effects. The crowd around me seethed with joy and merriment – I, however, in some measure shut myself off from their seething and yearning, coolly, like someone who was a member of the profession, who 'belonged' to the performers. Not as a member of the circus profession or a performer of the *salto mortale*, of course; I could not feel myself that, but as a member of a more general profession, as an entertainer and illusionist. That is why I inwardly withdrew from the crowd, which was only the passive victim of entertainment, revelling in self-forgetfulness, and repudiated any idea that I was one of them. They merely enjoyed, and enjoyment is a passive condition that will never satisfy one who feels himself born to act and to achieve.

My neighbour, honest Stanko, had no share in any such thoughts, and so we were dissimilar companions whose friendship could not possibly amount to much. On our walks my delighted attention was held by the spaciousness and spendour of the Parisian scenes; certain glorious perspectives of incredible distinction and magnificence always reminded me of my poor father and the way in which, almost fainting at the memory, he would exclaim '*Magnifique! Magnifique!*' But as I made no ado about my admiration and amazement, my companion hardly noticed any difference in the responsiveness of our souls. On the other hand, he was slowly forced to notice that in some mysterious way our friendship failed to advance, that no real intimacy sprang up between us. This was simply due to my natural inclination towards taciturnity and reserve, to my insistence upon privacy and separateness. I have already mentioned this characteristic, which I consider one of the basic elements of my character, one which I could not have altered even had I wished to.

It is always thus with men who feel, not so much with pride as with acquiescence, that fate has something special in store for them. This feeling creates around them an atmosphere or emanation of coolness which, almost to their own regret, foils and repels all honest offers of friendliness and companionship. Thus it was with Stanko and me. He went to great lengths to confide in me and saw that I was patient rather than receptive. One afternoon, for example, as were drinking wine in a bistro, he told me that before coming to Paris he had spent a year in jail because of a robbery he had been caught at not through any fault of his own but through the stupidity of his accomplice. I received this less than startling news with cheerful sympathy, and in itself it would have done nothing to injure our friendship. Next time, however, he went further and let me see that his confidences had been based on calculation, and this displeased me. He saw in me someone naturally lucky and possessed of childish cunning and skilful fingers, with whom, therefore, it would be useful to work and as he was obtuse enough not to realize that I was not born to be anyone's accomplice he made me a proposal. He had ferreted out a villa in Neuilly where he said a pretty haul could be made quite easily and almost without risk. When I declined with indifference, he became angry and asked me what made me think I was too good for it, adding that he knew all about me. As I have always despised people who thought they knew all about me, I simply shrugged my shoulders and replied that might well be but I was not interested. Whereupon he shouted 'Fool!' or perhaps '*Imbécile!*' and stalked out.

Even this disappointment which I had caused him did not lead to an immediate break in our relations, but they grew less and less close until finally, without actually becoming enemies, we ceased to go out together.

Chapter Two

I continued to be a lift-boy all winter, and in spite of the signs of favour that came my way from the transient public, I soon became bored. I had reason to fear it would go on for ever and I would, so to speak, be forgotten there and grow old and grey in the job. What I heard from Stanko increased my concern. He, for his part, wished to be transferred to the main kitchen, with its two big ranges, four roasting-ovens, grill, and singeing-grate, so that in time he might become, if not actually a chef, then perhaps assistant kitchen-manager, whose duty it is to take the orders from the waiters and divide them among the company of cooks. But in his opinion his chances of such advancement were slight; there was too strong an inclination to keep a man where he happened to be, and he darkly predicted that I would stay tied to the lift for ever, though perhaps not permanently without pay, and would never come to know our cosmopolitan establishment from any point of view, other than my narrow and limited one.

It was just this that worried me. I felt imprisoned in my lift-cage and in the shaft up and down which it moved at my direction. There was no chance, or at best only a fleeting one, for a glance at the scenes of high life in the lobby at five-o'clock teatime, when subdued music filled the air and girls in Greek attire danced for the entertainment of the guests who sat in wicker chairs at their usual small tables, consuming *petits fours* and delicate little sandwiches with their golden drink, and getting rid of the crumbs afterward by a kind of fluttering of their fingers in the air. The grand staircase swept between rows of palms in sculptured urns up to a gallery adorned with potted plants; here, on the carpeted steps, they would pause to chat; their expressions and the movement of their heads betokened wit; they exchanged jokes and indulged in the light laughter of men of the world. How fine it would be to move among them, waiting on them or on the ladies in the card-rooms or, at evening, to attend them in the dining-room, whither I saw tail-coated gentlemen proceeding, and ladies blazing with jewellery. In short, I was restless, longing for my existence to expand, for richer possibilities of contact with the world; and in actual fact kind fortune brought this to pass. My desire to get away from the lift, put on a new uniform, and embark on a new occupation with wider horizons was fulfilled: at Easter I became a waiter. This is how it happened.

The maître d'hôtel, Monsieur Machatschek by name, was a man of great consequence; clad daily in fresh linen, he moved his expansive belly around the dining-room with a vast authority. His clean-shaven moon face beamed. He commanded to perfection those lofty gestures of the lifted arm by which the master of the tables directs from afar the entering guests to their places. His way of dealing with any mistake or awkwardness on the part of the staff – in passing, and out of the corner of his mouth – was both discreet and biting. It was he who summoned me one morning, I must assume on the suggestion of the management, and received me in a small office opening off the magnificent *salle-à-manger*.

'Kroull?' he said. 'Called Armand? *Voyons, voyons. Eh bien,* I have heard of you – not exactly to your discredit and not altogether inaccurately, as would appear at first glance. That may be deceptive, *pourtant.* You realize, of course, that the services you have so far rendered this establishment are child's play and represent a very meagre use of your gifts? *Vous consentez?* It is our intention to make something out of you if possible, here in the restaurant – *si c'est faisable.* Do you feel a certain vocation for the profession of waiter, some *degree* of talent, I say – nothing exceptional and brilliant as you seem to be assuring me, that would mean carrying self-confidence too far, although of course courage doesn't hurt – a certain talent for elegant service and all the subtle attentions that go with it? For a decently skilful attendance on a public like ours? Innate? Of course something of this sort is innate, but the things you seem to consider innate in you would make one's head whirl. However, I can only repeat that healthy self-confidence is no drawback. You have some knowledge of languages? I did not say a comprehensive knowledge, as you claim, but only the most basic. *Bon.* These, of course, are all questions for a later day. In the nature of things, you can hardly expect to start anywhere except at the bottom. First of all, your job will be to scrape food off the plates that come from the dining-room before they go on to the scullery to be washed. You will receive forty francs a month for this employment – an almost exaggeratedly high salary, as your expression seems to indicate. Moreover, it's not customary when conversing with me to smile before I myself smile. I am the one who gives the signal to smile. *Bon.* We will provide the white jacket for your job as a scraper. Are you in a position to acquire a waiter's uniform in case we should need you some day to carry dishes out of the dining-room? You no doubt know this must be done at your own expense. You are *entirely* in a position to do it? Splendid. I see that we will have no difficulties with you. You are also provided with the necessary linen, decent evening shirts? Tell me: have you means of your own, money from your family? Some means? *À la bonne heure.* I believe, Kroull, within the foreseeable future we will be able to increase your salary to fifty or sixty francs. You can get the address of the tailor who makes our uniforms at the office. You may join us whenever you like. We need an assistant, and there are hundreds of applicants for the job of lift-boy. *À bientôt, mon garçon.* We are getting close to the middle of the month, and so you will be paid twenty-five francs this month, for I propose to start you at a salary of six hundred a year. This time your smile is permissible, for I set the example. That is all. You may go.'

Thus Machatschek in his conversation with me. That this momentous interview at first led to a come-down in my status and in what I represented is not to be denied. I had to turn in my lift-boy's uniform at the store and receive a white jacket in exchange. I promptly had to acquire a usable pair of trousers to go with it, since it was out of the question to work in the ones belonging to my Sunday suit. This job of scraping scraps from the dishes into the garbage pail was somewhat degrading in comparison with my former occupation, which had been at any rate loftier, and at first it was not a little repulsive. Moreover, my chores extended into the scullery, where the china passed from hand to hand through a series of washings and ended up with the driers; from time to time I found myself among them attired in a white apron. Thus, in a sense, I stood at the beginning and at the end of this process of restoration.

To submit cheerfully to a position that is beneath one and to remain on cordial terms with those to whom such a situation is appropriate, is not difficult if one can only keep the word 'temporary' in mind. Despite people's insistence on equality, I felt complete confidence in the instinct for what is naturally pre-eminent and the impulse to recognize it. I was therefore convinced that I should not be kept in this position long; indeed, that I had only been put there as a matter of form. And so as soon after my conversation with Monsieur Machatschek as I had the opportunity I ordered a waiter's dress suit *à la* Saint James and Albany at the shop in the rue des Innocents, not far from the hotel, that specialized in uniforms and livery. It meant an investment of seventy-five francs, a special price agreed upon between the firm and the hotel. Employees without means had to pay it out of their wages, in instalments, but I of course paid cash. The livery was extremely pretty, especially if one knew how to wear it. The trousers were black, the tail-coat dark blue with gold buttons and velvet trimming at the collar; there were gold buttons, too, smaller ones on the deep-cut waistcoat. I was thoroughly delighted by this acquisition, which I hung up beside my Sunday clothes in the wardrobe outside the dormitory. I then procured the appropriate white tie and enamelled studs and cuff-links. Thus it came about that I was ready when, after five weeks in the scullery, one of the two tuxedo-clad head-waiters who assisted Monsieur Machatschek told me I would be needed in the dining-room. He instructed me to make the necessary preparations and I was able to inform him that I was completely prepared and could appear at any moment.

Thus at lunchtime the next day I made my début in the dining-room in full glory. It is a magnificent hall, as spacious as a cathedral, with fluted columns whose gilded capitals support the white stucco ceiling. There are wall lights with red shades, billowing draperies at the windows, and countless tables, large and small, covered with white damask and adorned with orchids. Around them stand white lacquer chairs with red upholstered seats, and on the tables rest napkins folded like fans or pyramids, shining silver, delicate glasses, and bottles of wine in gleaming coolers or light wicker baskets – the responsibility of the wine steward, who is identifiable by his chain and cellarman's apron. Long before the first guests appeared I had been on hand, helping to set places and distribute menus at the tables to which I had been assigned as an assistant. I missed no opportunity, when my superior was busy elsewhere, to greet the entering guests with every sign of delight, to push in the ladies' chairs, hand them menus, fill their glasses – in short, to make my presence agreeable to our charges equally without respect to their unequal charms.

At first I had scant right or chance to do this. It was not my place to take orders or serve the courses, but simply to carry out the dishes and silverware after each course and, after the *entremets* and before the dessert was brought in, to remove the crumbs with a brush and flat scoop. The higher duties were the prerogative of my superior, Hector, a rather elderly man with a sleepy expression, whom I instantly recognized as the *commis-de-salle* with whom I had sat in the *cantine* on my first morning and who had given me his cigarettes. He too remembered me with a *'Mais oui, c'est toi'*, accompanied by a weary gesture of resignation, which was to characterize his attitude towards me – an attitude, from the very beginning, of resignation rather than command or reproof. He saw, of course, that the clientele, especially the ladies old and young, were interested in me, motioned to me when they wished some special item – English mustard, Worcestershire sauce, tomato catsup – wishes that in many cases I recognized as simple pretexts for calling me to the table in order to hear my *'Parfaitement, madame'*, *'Tout de suite, madame'*. They would murmur: *'Merci, Armand'* and accompany the words with a dazzling upward glance, hardly justified by the nature of my service. After a few days, while I was at the serving-table helping Hector remove the bones from a sole, he said to me:

'They would much rather be served by you, *au lieu de moi* – they are all crazy about you, *toute la canaille friande!* You'll soon squeeze me out and have these tables to yourself. You're an attraction – *et tu n'as pas l'air de l'ignorer*. The management knows it, too, and they push you ahead. You heard – of course you heard – what Monsieur Cordonnier' (that was the assistant head-waiter who had come to get me) 'said a while ago to the Swedish couple with whom you were chatting so prettily: *"Joli petit charmeur, n'est-ce pas?" Tu iras loin, mon cher – mes meilleurs vœux, ma bénédiction."*'

'You exaggerate, Hector,' I replied. 'I would still have to learn a great deal from you before I could think of ousting you even if I had that in mind.'

This was not exactly my real thought on the matter. On one of the following days at dinnertime Monsieur Machatschek himself, propelling his belly towards my section and standing beside me so that we faced in opposite directions, murmured to me out of the corner of his mouth: 'Not bad, Armand. You don't work too badly. I recommend that you pay close attention to Hector when he is serving – that is, if you are interested in doing the same some time.'

I replied, also sotto voce: 'A thousand thanks, maître, but I know all that already, better than he does. I know, if you will pardon me, by instinct. I will not hurry you into putting me to the proof, but as soon as you decide to do so you will find my words are true.'

'*Blagueur!*' he said and gave a jerk to his stomach and a quick, amused laugh. At the same time, observing that a lady in green with a high, artificially blonde coiffure had observed this little exchange, he winked at her and motioned towards me with his head, before moving on with his remarkably elastic step. As he did so he jerked his stomach again in amusement.

I soon received the additional assignment of serving coffee in the lobby twice a day with a few of my colleagues. This duty was presently extended to include serving tea there in the afternoons. In the meantime Hector had been moved to another part of the dining-room and the group of tables I had first served as an assistant was assigned to me. Thus, I had almost too much to do, and in the evening, towards the end of my varied day's work, I began to feel symptoms of exhaustion. As I handed around coffee and liqueurs, whisky and soda, and *infusion de tilleul* in the lobby after dinner, I felt that the current of sympathy between me and the world was losing vitality, that my zeal to be of service was weakening and my smile had a tendency to stiffen into a mask of pain.

By morning, however, my resilient nature would regain its freshness and gaiety: I could be seen again hurrying between breakfast room, coffee kitchen, and main kitchen, serving such guests as failed to take advantage of room service and have their breakfasts in bed, with tea, porridge, toast, preserves, baked fish, and pancakes with maple syrup; immediately afterwards I could be seen in the dining-hall, assisted by an imbecile of a second, preparing for luncheon, spreading damask cloths over the soft base pads, setting places, and from twelve o'clock on, pencil in hand, taking down the orders of those who had come in. How well I knew how to counsel the indecisive, employing the soft, discreetly reserved tone appropriate to a waiter, and how to avoid any appearance of indifference in arranging and serving the dishes, giving each motion the quality of loving personal service. Bowing, one hand behind my back in the best waiter's tradition, I would proffer the dishes; now and then I would practise the fine art of manipulating fork and spoon with my right hand alone to serve those who preferred me to do it for them. Meanwhile, the object of this attention – whether he or she, but especially if it was she – might take notice with agreeable surprise of my busy hand, which was the hand of no ordinary man.

No wonder, then, considering all this, that they pushed me ahead, that as Hector had said, exploiting the favour I found in the eyes of the over-fed guests of this luxury hotel, they handed me over to the gale of favouritism that beat about me and left it to my ingenuity to whip it up by my melting attentiveness and yet keep it within bounds by the propriety of my conduct.

To keep clear the picture of my character which these memoirs are designed to sketch for the reader, this much must be said to my credit. I have never taken vain or cruel pleasure in the sufferings of those fellow mortals in whom my person has aroused desires that my prudence has forbidden me to gratify. Passions of which one is the unmoved object may fill natures unlike mine with a cold and unlovely vanity or inspire a contemptuous distaste that leads them to trample pitilessly on the feelings of others. How different it is with me! I have always felt compassion for such feelings, have spared them to the best of my ability out of a kind of guilt, and have tried through an attitude of understanding to persuade the victims to a sensible renunciation. As proof I shall cite here, from this period of my life, the double example of little Eleanor Twentyman from Birmingham and Lord Strathbogie, an important member of the Scottish nobility. These simultaneous incidents represented in their different ways temptations to depart prematurely from my chosen career, temptations, in fact, to hasten down one of those by-paths of which my godfather had spoken, and which one cannot too carefully examine in respect to their direction and length.

The Twentymans, father, mother, and daughter, together with a maid, had occupied a suite in the Saint James and Albany for a number of weeks, a fact which in itself indicated a gratifying degree of wealth. This was confirmed and made conspicuous by the magnificent jewellery Mrs Twentyman wore at dinner, which, one must admit, was wasted. For Mrs Twentyman was a joyless woman – joyless for those around her and, probably, for herself as well. Her husband's successful business activities in Birmingham had obviously raised her from some lower-middle-class sphere to a social plane that made her stiff and uncomfortable. Mr Twentyman, his face flushed by his liberal consumption of port, radiated more human kindliness; his joviality, however, was greatly damped by the hardness of hearing which produced an empty, strained expression in his watery blue eyes. He used a black ear trumpet, into which his wife had to speak when, as was seldom the case, she had something to say to him. He extended it to me, too, when I advised him what to order. Eleanor, his daughter, a girl of seventeen or eighteen, sat opposite him at table number eighteen. From time to time he would summon her by a gesture to come and sit beside him for a short conversation through the trumpet.

His fondness for the child was obvious and winning. As to Mrs Twentyman, I will not contest her motherly affection, but instead of expressing it in loving words and glances she concentrated it in a critical supervision of Eleanor's conduct. Each time she raised her tortoiseshell lorgnette to her eyes, Mrs Twentyman would find something to correct in her daughter's coiffure or deportment; she would forbid her to roll bread crumbs into little balls, lift a chicken bone in her fingers or peer inquisitively round the dining-room – and so on. All this supervision indicated a parent's uneasiness and concern and may well have been annoying to Miss Twentyman; the equally annoying experiences I had with her, however, forced me to admit that they were not unjustified.

She was a blonde creature, pretty in the fashion of a young chamois, and when she wore her little silk evening dress with its modest décolletage her collar-bones were the most touching sight in the world. Since I have always had a weakness for the Anglo-Saxon type, of which she was a very notable example, I enjoyed seeing her. Moreover, I saw her constantly, at meal-times, after meals, and at the tea-time musicales where I served and where the Twentymans, at least at first, used to appear. I was kind to my little chamois, surrounded her with the attentions of a devoted brother, set her food before her, passed her the dessert twice, provided her with grenadine, which she loved to drink, and gently draped her embroidered shawl around her thin, snow-white shoulders when she got up from the table. All in all, I did decidedly too much, I thoughtlessly sinned against this too responsive soul by not sufficiently taking into account the magnetism my being exerts, whether I will or no, on all my fellow creatures who are not completely insensitive. The effect would have been the same, I venture to believe, even if my mortal dress, as it is called at the end – my appearance, that is – had been less attractive; for that was only an external symbol of a deeper power – sympathy.

In short, I was very soon forced to realize that the little one had fallen head over heels in love with me, and this realization, naturally, was not mine alone. Peering worriedly through her tortoiseshell lorgnette, Mrs Twentyman had made the same discovery, as I learned at lunch one day from her hisses and whispers behind my back:

'Eleanor! If you don't stop staring at that boy, I'll send you up to your room and you'll have to eat alone till we leave!'

But, alas, the little chamois was lacking in self-control; it never occurred to her to obey or to make the slightest attempt to conceal that she had fallen in love. Her blue eyes clung to me constantly in a dreamy ecstasy; when they met mine she lowered them to her plate and flushed scarlet, but she immediately raised them again, as though under some compulsion, in a glance of complete and glowing surrender. One could understand her mother's watchfulness; no doubt she had been warned by earlier indications that this child of Birmingham respectability was inclined to be irresponsible, inclined, in fact, to an innocent and fierce belief in her right and even her duty to surrender openly to passion. Certainly I did nothing to encourage this, my considerateness bordered on severity, and in my attitude towards her I never went beyond the attentiveness that was part of my duty. I approved the decision, which no doubt was made by her mother and must certainly have seemed cruel to her, when the Twentymans at the beginning of the second week gave up their table with me and moved to the distant part of the hall where Hector served.

But my wild chamois was not without resources. Suddenly at eight o'clock one morning she appeared in the breakfast room for *petit déjeuner*, whereas before that her practice, like her parents', had been to have breakfast in her room. She changed colour on entering and searched for me with reddened eyes. There was no trouble in finding a table in my section, for at that hour the room was almost empty.

'Good morning, Miss Twentyman. Did you rest well?'

'Very little rest, Armand, very little,' she murmured.

I indicated I was sorry to hear it. 'But then,' I said, 'perhaps it would have been wiser to stay in bed a little longer and have your tea and porridge there. I'll get them for you right away, but I can't help thinking you would have enjoyed them more comfortably there. It's so calm and peaceful in the room, in bed ...'

What did this child reply? 'No, I prefer to suffer.'

'But you are making me suffer, too,' I replied softly, indicating to her on the menu the kind of marmalade to order.

'Oh, Armand, then we suffer together!' she said and looked up at me with her tired, tear-stained eyes.

What was to come of it? I wished heartily for their departure, but it was delayed; it was understandable enough that Mr Twentyman was reluctant to have his stay in Paris cut short by his daughter's emotional whims, of which he had no doubt heard through his black trumpet. Miss Twentyman, however, came down every morning while her parents still slept – they used to sleep until ten o'clock, so that Eleanor could pretend, if her mother looked in to see her, that the breakfast dishes had already been taken down by room service – and I had the devil's own time to protect her reputation in the eyes of those around, and conceal her unhappy state, her attempts to press my hand, and other infatuated nonsense. She remained deaf to my warnings that her parents must some day discover the trick she was playing on them, her breakfast secret. No, she replied, Mrs Twentyman slept most soundly in the mornings, and how much better she liked her when she was asleep than when she was supervising her! Mummy did not love her, she was only interested in keeping a sharp eye on her through her lorgnette. Daddy loved her, but did not take her heart seriously; this was something that Mummy did, if only in the worst sense, and Eleanor was inclined to put that down to her credit. 'For I love you!'

For the moment I pretended not to hear her. But when I came back to serve her I said softly and persuasively.

'Miss Eleanor, the words you let fall just now about "love" are pure imagination and simple nonsense. Your Daddy is perfectly right not to take them seriously – although your mother is right, too, in her way, to take them seriously – that is, as nonsense – and to forbid you to indulge in this sort of thing. Please don't take yourself quite so seriously, to your distress and mine, but try instead to see the funny side of this – something I certainly won't do, far from it, but you must try to. For what good is all this? You must see that it is unnatural. Here you are, the daughter of a man like Mr Twentyman, who has reached a pinnacle of wealth and who has brought you with him for a few weeks' stay at the Saint James and Albany, where I am employed as a waiter. For that's all I am, Miss Eleanor, a waiter, a lowly member of our social order, which I regard with reverence, but towards which you behave rebelliously. It's abnormal, too, for you not to ignore me, as would be natural and as your Mummy quite properly demands, but instead to come down secretly to breakfast and talk to me about "love" while your parents are prevented by their peaceful slumbers from coming to the defence of the social order. This "love" of yours is a forbidden love which I cannot approve, and I am forced to dismiss my own pleasure in the fact that you like to see me. It's all right for me to like to see you, if I keep it to myself, that's quite true. But for you, Mr and Mrs Twentyman's daughter, to like to see me, that's impossible, that's contrary to nature. Besides, it's nothing but an optical illusion arising principally from this tail-coat *à la* Saint James and Albany with its velvet trim and gold buttons, which is only an adornment concealing my lowly state; without it I would look like nothing at all, I assure you! What you call "love" is something that happens to people on trips and at the sight of tail-coats like mine. When you have left, as you will very soon, you'll forget it before you get to the next station. Leave the memory of our encounter behind you, leave it to me; then it will be preserved without encumbering you!'

Was that not kindly said? What more could I do for her? But she only wept, so that I was glad the near-by tables were empty; sobbing, she chided me for my cruelty and would hear nothing about the natural social order and the unnaturalness of her infatuation, but every morning insisted that if only we could be entirely alone and undisturbed, untrammelled in word and deed, then everything would work out happily – provided only that I was a little fond of her, a fact I did not dispute, at least to the extent of my being grateful for her partiality. But how were we to contrive a rendezvous where we would be alone and untrammelled in word and deed? She had no more idea than I, but did not on that account cease her pleading; she imposed on me the duty of finding such an opportunity.

In short, I had the very devil of a time with her. And this would have been bad enough if it had happened by itself and not at exactly the same time as the even more serious incident with Lord Strathbogie! No small trial this, since what was at stake was not an infatuated young girl but a personality of great importance whose sensibilities counted for something in the world, so that one could neither invite him to see the funny aspect of the affair nor find anything funny in it oneself. At any rate, I was not the man to do so.

His lordship, who had been staying with us for two weeks and who ate at one of my small single tables, was a man of obvious distinction, about fifty years of age, of moderate height, slender, elegantly dressed; his still thick, carefully brushed hair was iron grey, like the clipped moustache which did not conceal the almost feminine delicacy of his lips. There was nothing delicate or aristocratic about the cut of his too large, almost block-like nose, which jutted straight out of his face to form a high ridge between the somewhat slanting brows beetling above the green-grey eyes. These eyes seemed to meet one as though with a great effort of self-discipline. If his nose was deplorable, his cheeks and chin were quite the reverse, clean-shaven to the ultimate degree of smoothness and well massaged. He used some kind of violet water on his handkerchief, whose perfume had a naturalness and springlike scent I have never encountered since.

There was always a kind of embarrassment in his way of entering the dining-hall, which might have seemed puzzling in so important a gentleman, but which, in my eyes at least, did nothing to detract from his impressiveness. It was completely compensated for by his extreme dignity, and it simply led one to imagine that there was something remarkable about him and that he therefore felt himself singled out and observed. His voice was soft, and I replied to it even more softly, only to discover too late that this was not good for him. His manner was friendly but tinged with melancholy, like that of a man who has suffered a great deal; what person of goodwill would not have reacted to it as I did by a responsive attentiveness in serving him? However, it was not good for him. To be sure, he seldom looked at me during the brief exchanges about the weather or the menu to which our conversation was at first restricted – just as in general he employed his eyes very little, keeping them in reserve and making sparing use of them, as though he were afraid their play might produce unpleasant consequences. It was a week before our relationship became somewhat freer and ceased to be bound completely by the formal and conventional; then I observed with pleasure, which was not unmixed with anxiety, the signs of his personal interest in me. A week – that is probably the minimum time required by a person in daily association with an unfamiliar being to become aware of certain changes, especially when the eyes are so little used.

It was then that he asked me how long I had been in service, where I came from, how old I was, hearing the number of my years with an emotional shrug of the shoulders and the exclamation '*Mon Dieu!*' or 'Good Heavens!' – he spoke English and French interchangeably. Why, he inquired, if I was German by birth did I have the French name of Armand. It was not mine, I replied, I simply answered to it in obedience to instructions from my superiors. My real name was Felix. 'Ah, pretty,' he said. 'If it were within my power, I would give you back your real name.' He added the information that his own Christian name was Nectan, which had been the name of a king of the Picts, the original inhabitants of Scotland. There was something, it seemed to me, inconsistent with his exalted position, something that impressed me as unstable in his saying this. I replied, to be sure, with a show of attentive interest, but I couldn't help wondering what use I was to make of the information that his name was Nectan. It was of no good to me, for I had to call him milord and not Nectan.

Bit by bit I learned that he owned a castle not far from Aberdeen, where he lived alone with an elderly sister, who was unfortunately in delicate health; and he had a summer estate as well on one of the highland lakes in a region where the people still talked Gaelic (he spoke a little himself), a place that was very beautiful and romantic, with rugged and precipitous cliffs and air perfumed by the wild flowers of the heath. Near Aberdeen, too, it was very beautiful, the city afforded every kind of entertainment for those interested in that sort of thing, the air blew in from the North Sea strong and clean. I was further given to understand that he loved music and played the organ. In his country house on the mountain lake it was, to be sure, only a harmonium.

These confidences, which were not made in a single conversation but dropped casually and fragmentarily now and then, could not, with the possible exception of 'Nectan', be considered as evidences of excessive communicativeness on the part of a man travelling alone who had no one to chat with but the waiter. The most favourable opportunity came after lunch, when his lordship, as was his custom at noon, instead of taking his coffee in the lobby, remained at his small table in the almost deserted dining-hall smoking Egyptian cigarettes. He always took several cups of coffee. Before that he would not have drunk anything or eaten much of anything. Indeed, he ate very little, and one was forced to wonder how he could exist on the nourishment he consumed. He made a good start, to be sure, with a soup; strong consommé, mock turtle, or ox-tail soup disappeared completely from his plate. After that, however, whatever delicacies I placed before him were only tasted; he would light another cigarette immediately and let course after course be carried out almost untouched. After a while I could not refrain from commenting on this.

'*Mais vous ne mangez rien*, milord,' I said in distress. '*Le chef se formalisera, si vous dédaignez tous ses plats.*'

'What can I do, I have no appetite,' he replied. 'I never have. The business of nourishment – I have a decided dislike for it. Perhaps it's a symptom of a certain self-repudiation.'

The phrase, which I had never heard before, startled me and called forth my politeness.

'Self-repudiation?' I exclaimed softly. 'Milord, no one can follow you there or agree with you. You will meet with the strongest opposition!'

'Really?' he asked and slowly raised his eyes from his plate to my face. His glance still seemed an act of self-discipline. But this time his eyes showed that the effort was gladly made. His lips smiled with a delicate melancholy. But over them his over-sized nose jutted towards me straight and massive.

How can one, I thought, have so delicate a mouth and such a block of a nose?

'Really!' I assured him in some confusion.

'Perhaps, *mon enfant*,' he said, 'self-repudiation helps one to appreciate someone else.'

At this he got up and went out of the hall. I stayed behind, occupied with a variety of thoughts while I cleared and reset the small table.

There was little doubt that contact with me several times a day was not good for his lordship. But I could neither put an end to it nor could I render it harmless even by excluding all sensitive responsiveness from my conduct and keeping it stiff and formal so that I wounded the very feelings I had inspired. To make merry over them was even more impossible than in the case of little Eleanor. It was equally out of the question to fall in with their intention. This resulted in a difficult conflict, which was to turn into a temptation through the unexpected proposal he made to me – unexpected in its form, though not at all in essence.

It happened towards the end of the second week, while I was serving coffee. As I passed him a second time he asked for a cigar. I brought him two boxes of imported cigars, one with bands, the other without. He looked at it, at the other end of the room, his lordship had chosen a small, isolated table which he had used several times before, and it was here that I served his coffee. As I passed him a second time he asked for a cigar. I brought him two boxes of imported cigars, one with bands, the other without. He looked at them and said:

'Well, then, which shall I take?'

'The dealer,' I replied, 'recommends these,' and I pointed to the banded ones. 'Personally, if I may, I recommend the others.'

I could not resist giving him this chance for a display of courtesy.

He took it. 'I will follow your advice,' he said, but let me stand there holding both boxes while he stared first down at them and then up at me.

'Armand?' he asked softly beneath the music.

'Milord?'

He changed his manner of address. 'Felix?'

'Milord wishes?' I asked, smiling.

'You wouldn't like, would you,' he said without raising his eyes from the cigars, 'to exchange hotel work for a position as a valet?'

There I had it.

'How so, milord?' I asked in apparent incomprehension.

He pretended I had asked 'With whom?' and answered with a slight shrug of the shoulders: 'With me, that's very simple. You will accompany me to Aberdeen and Nectan Hall Castle. You will take off this livery and exchange it for ordinary clothes, distinguished clothes that will indicate your position and set you off from the other servants. There are all sorts of servants there. Your duties would be confined entirely to personal attendance on me. You would be with me all the time, at the castle and at the summer estate in the mountains. Your salary,' he added, 'will be, presumably, two or three times what you make here.'

I was silent, and he did not prompt me to speak by glancing at me. Instead, he took one of the boxes from my hand and compared that brand with the other.

'This requires careful consideration, milord,' I replied finally. 'I need not say that I am greatly honoured by your offer. But it comes so un-expectedly ... I must take time for consideration.'

'There is very little time for consideration,' he replied. 'Today is Friday, I leave on Monday. Come with me! It is my wish.'

He took one of the cigars I had recommended, regarded it thoughtfully from all sides, and passed it under his nose. No observer could have guessed what he was saying as he did so. What he said softly was: 'It is the wish of a lonely heart.'

Who so inhuman as to reproach me for feeling moved? Yet I knew at once I would not choose this by-path.

'I promise your lordship,' I murmured, 'that I will make good use of this period of reflection.' And I withdrew.

He has, I thought, a good cigar to go with his coffee. That combination is highly enjoyable, and enjoyment is, after all, a minor form of happiness. There are circumstances in which one must content oneself with it.

This thought was a tacit temptation to try to help him to help himself. But there now ensued trying days when, at each meal and after tea as well, his lordship would glance at me once and say: 'Well?' I either lowered my eyes and raised my shoulders as though they were heavy-laden, or I replied anxiously: 'I have not yet been able to reach a decision.'

His sensitive mouth became steadily more bitter. But although his ailing sister might have eyes for his happiness alone, had he considered the painful role I would have to play among the numerous servants of whom he had spoken and even among the Gaelic mountaineers? Their contempt, I said to myself, would strike not the great lord but the plaything of his whim. Secretly, despite all my sympathy, I considered him guilty of egotism. If only in addition to this I had not had to keep a close rein on Eleanor Twentyman's demands for untrammelled speech and action!

At dinner on Sunday a lot of champagne was drunk. His lordship, to be sure, drank none, but at the Twentymans' table corks were popping and I thought to myself that this was not good for Eleanor. My concern proved to be justified.

After dinner I served coffee as usual in the lobby. A glass door covered with green silk led from the lobby into a library with leather armchairs and a long table for newspapers. This room was little used; at most, a few people sat there in the morning and read the newly laid-out papers. Guests were really not supposed to remove them from the library, but someone had taken the *Journal des Débats* into the lobby and had left it on the chair beside one of the little tables. In my orderly fashion I rolled it around its staff and carried it back into the empty reading-room. I had just arranged it in its proper place on the long table when Eleanor came in, and it was clear to see that a few glasses of Moët-Chandon had been too much for her. She came straight up to me, quivering and trembling, threw her thin, bare arms around my neck and stammered:

'Armand, I love you so desperately and helplessly, I don't know what to do, I am so deeply, so utterly in love with you that I am lost, lost, lost ... Speak, tell me, do you love me a little bit, too?'

'For heaven's sake, Miss Eleanor, be careful. Somebody might come in. Your mother, for instance. How on earth did you manage to get away from her? Of course I love you, sweet little Eleanor! You have such touching collar-bones, you are such a lovely child in every way ... But now take your arms from around my neck and watch out ... This is extremely dangerous.'

'What do I care about danger? I love you, I love you, Armand, let's run away together, let's die together, but first of all kiss me. Your lips, your lips, I am dying for your lips!'

'No, dear Eleanor,' I said, gently attempting to loosen her embrace, 'we won't begin that. You have been drinking champagne, several glasses, I think, and if I kiss you now, it will be all up, you will be inaccessible to any sensible idea. I have, after all, candidly explained to you how unnatural it is for the daughter of parents like Mr and Mrs Twentyman, raised to a pinnacle of wealth, to become infatuated with the first young waiter who comes along. It is simply an aberration, and even if it corresponded to your nature and temperament, you would nevertheless have to triumph over it out of respect for propriety and the natural laws of society. Now you'll be a good, sensible child, won't you? Let me go, and return to Mummy.'

'Oh, Armand, how can you be so cold and cruel when you have said, after all, that you do love me a little? Go back to Mummy? I hate Mummy and she hates me, but Daddy loves me and will become reconciled to everything if we simply confront him with an accomplished fact. We just have to flee – let's flee tonight on the express, to Spain, for example, to Morocco, that's what I came to propose to you. We will go into hiding there and I will present you with a child that will be the accomplished fact, and Daddy will be reconciled when we throw ourselves at his feet with the child, and he'll give us his money so that we will be rich and happy ... Your lips!'

And the mad child actually behaved as though she wanted to conceive a child by me on the spot.

'That's enough, decidedly enough, dear little Eleanor,' I said finally, removing her arms from about my neck with gentle considerateness. 'These are all preposterous dreams, and I do not intend on their account to abandon my course in life or take this by-path. It's not at all right and doesn't agree with your protestations of love for you to assail me this way with your proposals and try to lead me astray at a time when I have heavy cares of another sort and am faced by a dilemma from a quite different quarter. You're very egotistical, do you know that? But that's the way you all are, and I am not angry at you. Instead, I thank you, and I will never forget little Eleanor. But now let me go about my duties in the lobby.'

She burst into tears. 'No kiss! No child! Poor, unhappy me! Poor little Eleanor, so miserable and disdained!' And with her tiny hand in front of her face she threw herself into one of the leather chairs, sobbing as though her heart would break. I was about to step up to her and pat her comfortingly before leaving. This, however, was reserved for someone else. At that moment a man entered – not just a man, it was Lord Strathbogie of Nectan Hall. In his faultless evening dress, his feet shod not in patent leather but in dull, flexible lambskin, his freshly shaved cheeks gleaming with cream, he advanced, his jutting nose thrust forward. With his head inclined a little towards one shoulder, he stood looking thoughtfully at the weeping girl from under his slanting brows; he approached her chair and sympathetically stroked her cheek with the back of his fingers, With swimming eyes and open mouth she looked up, startled, at the stranger, leaped from her chair, and ran out of the room like a weasel through the door opposite the glass one.

He stared after her thoughtfully as before. Then he turned to me calmly and with a regal demeanour.

'Felix,' he said, 'the last moment has come for your decision. I leave early tomorrow morning. You will have to pack your things tonight if you are going to accompany me to Scotland. What have you decided?'

'Milord,' I replied, 'I thank you most humbly and I beg your indulgence. I do not feel equal to the position you have so kindly offered me and I have come to the conclusion that I had better give up any idea of pursuing this by-path.'

'It's impossible for me,' he said in reply, 'to take seriously your plea of inadequacy. Moreover,' he added, glancing at the door, 'I have the impression that your affairs here have been concluded.'

At this I pulled myself together and replied: 'I must conclude this one as well, and I take the liberty of wishing your lordship a very pleasant journey.'

He bowed his head, and raised it only slowly to look at me in his peculiar fashion, his eyes revealing the effort it cost him.

'Felix!' he said, 'aren't you afraid of making the greatest mistake of your life?'

'That's just what I fear, milord, and hence my decision.'

'Because you don't feel equal to the position I am offering you? I should be much surprised if you do not concur in my feeling that you were born for positions of a quite different kind. My interest in you opens possibilities you do not take into account with your refusal. I am childless and master of my own affairs. There have been cases of adoption ... You might wake up one day as Lord Strathbogie and heir to my possessions.'

That was strong. Indeed, he certainly sprang all his mines at once. Ideas swirled through my mind, but they did not incline me to alter my decision. That would be a suspect lordship, the one he dangled before me because of his interest. Suspect in the eyes of the people and lacking the proper authority. But that was not the main thing. The main thing was that a confident instinct within me rebelled against a form of reality that was simply handed to me and was in addition sloppy – rebelled in favour of free play and dreams, self-created and self-sufficient, dependent, that is, only on imagination. When as a child I had woken up determined to be an eighteen-year-old prince named Karl and had then freely maintained this pure and enchanting conceit for as long as I wished – that had been the right thing for me, not what this man with his jutting nose offered me because of his interest.

I have set down in hasty and condensed form what then flashed through my mind. I said firmly: 'Forgive me, milord, if I confine my answer to a repetition of my best wishes for your journey.'

At this he blanched, and suddenly I saw his chin begin to quiver.

Who would be so inhuman as to blame me for the fact that at this sight my eyes reddened, perhaps even filled – but no, probably they simply reddened? Sympathy is sympathy, only a knave would fail to be grateful for it. I said:

'But, milord, don't take this so much to heart! You met me and have seen me regularly and you took an interest in my youth. I am sincerely grateful for that, but this interest was a matter of accident; it might equally well have fastened upon somebody else. Please – I don't want to wound you or minimize the honour you have paid me, but if someone precisely like me occurs only once – each of us, of course, occurs only once – there are nevertheless millions of young men of my age and general physique, and except for the tiny bit of uniqueness, one is made very much like another. I knew a woman who declared that she was interested in the whole genre without exception – it must be essentially that way with you, too. The genre is present always and everywhere. You are returning to Scotland now – as though it weren't charmingly represented there, and as though you needed me to awaken your interest! There they wear checked jackets and, I understand, go bare-legged, which must be a pleasure to see! So there you can select a brilliant valet from the genre and you can chat with him in Gaelic, and even, in the end, adopt him. Perhaps the transfer of a lordship is not so easy as all that, but ways can be found and at least he will be a countryman of yours. I can see him as so attractive that I am convinced he will drive our accidental encounter completely out of your mind. Leave the remembrance of it to me, I will treasure it. For I promise you that these days during which I have been privileged to serve you and to advise you in the selection of your cigars, these days of your assuredly fleeting interest in me, will be remembered forever with the warmest reverence. And eat more, milord, if I may take the liberty of urging it! As for self-repudiation, no man of heart and intelligence can agree with you there.'

Thus I spoke, and it did him some good despite the fact that he shook his head at my mention of the Highland jackets. He smiled with just the same sensitive and melancholy expression he had worn on the occasion when he had first mentioned self-repudiation. As he did so, he took a very handsome emerald from his finger. I had often admired it on his hand, and I am wearing it now as I write these lines. Not that he put it on my finger, he did not do that, but simply handed it to me and said softly and brokenly:

'Take this ring. It is my wish. I thank you. Farewell.'

Then he turned and left. I cannot too strongly commend to the approval of the public the behaviour of this man.

So much, then, for Eleanor Twentyman and Nectan Lord Strathbogie.

Chapter Three

My basic attitude towards the world and society can only be called contradictory. For all my eagerness to be on affectionate terms with them, I was frequently aware of a considered coolness, a tendency to critical reflection, which astonished me. There was, for example, an idea that occasionally preoccupied me when for a few leisure moments I stood in the lobby or dining-hall, clasping a napkin behind my back and watching the hotel guests being waited and fawned upon by blue-liveried minions. It was the idea of *interchangeability*. With a change of clothes and make-up, the servitors might often just as well have been the masters, and many of those who lounged in the deep wicker chairs, smoking their cigarettes, might have played the waiter. It was pure accident that the reverse was the fact, an accident of wealth; for an aristocracy of money is an accidental and interchangeable aristocracy.

Therefore, my imaginary transpositions sometimes succeeded very well, but not always. For, in the first place, the habit of wealth does, after all, produce at least superficial refinement, which complicated my game, and, in the second place, among the polished riff-raff of hotel society there are always a few persons whose distinction is independent of money, though naturally always accompanied by it. At times I had to select myself – no one else in the corps of waiters would do – if the imaginary substitution was to succeed. This was true in the case of a very engaging young cavalier of airy and carefree manner who did not live in the hotel but made a habit of dining with us once or twice a week, always in my section. On these occasions he would reserve a single table by telephoning to Machatschek, whose good graces he had obviously taken the trouble to acquire. The latter would notify me, his sharp eye on the table setting:

'*Le Marquis de Venosta. Attention!*'

Venosta, who was about my own age, treated me in a cordial, unconstrained, almost friendly fashion. I liked to see him enter in his easy, careless way. I would push in his chair unless Maître Machatschek had done so himself, and would answer his questions about my health with an appropriate tinge of deference.

'*Et vous, monsieur le marquis?*'

'*Comme ci, comme ça.* Is the food any good tonight?'

'*Comme ci, comme ça* – that is, excellent, exactly the way you feel, *monsieur le marquis.*'

'*Farceur!*' he would laugh. 'A lot you know about how I feel!'

He was, in fact, a painter, studying at the Académie des Beaux Arts and fine hands and neat, curly brown hair. His cheeks, however, were fat, red, and childish beneath small roguish eyes. The eyes, however, pleased me and certainly gave the lie to the melancholy he sometimes liked to assume.

'A lot you know about how I feel, *mon cher Armand*, and it's easy for you to talk. Obviously you have a talent for your métier and so you are happy, whereas it seems very doubtful to me that I have any talent for mine.'

He was, in fact, a painter, studying at the Académie des Beaux-Arts and sketching from the nude in his teacher's studio. This and other facts I learned in the course of the fragmentary conversations we carried on while I served him his dinner, conversations that had begun with a friendly inquiry on his part about my home and my circumstances. These questions indicated that I had impressed him as being out of the ordinary, and in answering them I avoided any particulars that might have weakened this impression. During the sporadic exchanges he spoke German and French interchangeably. He knew the former very well because his mother, '*ma pauvre mère*', belonged to the German nobility. His home was in Luxemburg, where his parents, '*mes pauvres parents*', lived not far from the capital in a seventeenth-century family castle surrounded by a park. This, he assured me, looked exactly like the English castles depicted on the plates on which I served him his roast beef and *bombe glacée*. His father was chamberlain to the Grand Duke, 'and all that'. Incidentally, or really not incidentally at all, he had a hand in the steel industry and so was 'pretty rich', as his son Louis naïvely added with a gesture that seemed to say: 'What do you expect him to be? Naturally he is pretty rich.' As though his own way of life, and the thick gold chain he wore around his wrist, the precious stones in his cufflinks, and the pearl in the bosom of his shirt did not clearly reveal it!

Thus when he spoke of his parents as '*mes pauvres parents*' it was a fond affectation, but there was also an overtone of real sympathy, for in his opinion they had a real good-for-nothing for a son. He was supposed to have studied law at the Sorbonne, but had very quickly dropped it out of sheer boredom and, with the pained and grudging acquiescence of his parents, had turned his attention to the arts – not without serious doubts, however, about his gifts in that direction. From his words, it was clear that he regarded himself with a kind of self-complacent concern as a spoiled child, and, without being willing or able to do anything about it, admitted his parents were right in fearing he had no goal in life beyond loafing and leading a rootless bohemian existence. As to the second point, it was soon clear to me that it was not simply a question of his spiritless pursuit of an artistic career but of an unsuitable love affair as well.

From time to time the marquis would come to dinner not alone but in the most charming company. On these occasions he would order a larger table, and Machatschek would see that the flowers on it were especially gay. He would appear about seven o'clock, accompanied by a person who was really extraordinarily pretty – I could not question his taste, although it was a taste for *le beauté de diable* and for what was obviously perishable.

Just then, however, in the bloom of youth, Zaza – so he called her – was the most enchanting creature in the world. She was a shapely brunette, Parisienne by birth, type grisette, but dignified by evening dresses from expensive establishments, which he, of course, ordered for her, and by the rare antique jewellery which was, of course, his gift. Her arms, which were always bare, were remarkably beautiful; her hair was done low on her neck in a bizarre, fluffy coiffure surmounted sometimes by a very becoming turban with silver fringes at the sides and a feather that swept over her forehead; she had a snub nose and her flirtatious glances were accompanied by a continual chatter.

They drank the champagne which was always substituted, when Zaza came, for the half-bottle of Bordeaux Venosta drank when he dined alone, and it was a pleasure to wait on the pair, they took such joy in each other's company. There was no doubt that he was head over heels in love with her – and no wonder – to the point of being completely indifferent to all appearances, captivated by the glimpses of her enticing décolletage, her chatter, the bewitchment of her black eyes. And she, I can well believe, was delighted by his tenderness and happy to respond to it, and tried in every way to inflame it; to her it meant nothing less than first prize in the grand lottery, the basis of her hopes for a glowing future. I was accustomed to address her as 'madame', but once, after her fourth or fifth visit, I ventured to say '*madame la marquise*', which produced a great effect. She blushed in happy terror and threw her friend a questioning and loving glance. He met this with merry eyes, while she, in some embarrassment, lowered her own to the table.

Naturally she flirted with me, too, and the marquis pretended to be jealous, although he certainly could be sure of her faithfulness.

'Zaza, you'll drive me crazy – *tu me feras voir rouge* – if you don't stop ogling Armand. You don't really want to be responsible for a double murder and a suicide, do you? ... Come now, admit you wouldn't mind a bit if he were in a dinner-jacket sitting at the table with you and I were serving you in a blue tail-coat.'

How strange that he should have put into words the preoccupation of my leisure moments, my silent game of exchanging roles! While I held the menu for them both so that they could choose dessert, I was bold enough to answer in Zaza's stead:

'Then you would have the more difficult role, *monsieur le marquis*, for waiting is a trade, but to be a marquis is existence pure and simple.'

'Excellent!' she cried, laughing with the delight of her kind at a well-turned phrase.

'And are you sure,' he inquired, 'that you are more capable of existence pure and simple than I am of a trade?'

'I believe it would be neither courteous nor accurate,' I replied, 'to ascribe to you a special talent as a waiter, *monsieur le marquis*.'

She was much amused. '*Mais il est incomparable, ce gaillard!*'

'Your admiration for him is killing me,' he said with theatrical despair. 'And, besides, he only evaded me.'

I let it go at that and withdrew. The evening dress in which he had pictured me as taking his place actually existed, however; I had acquired it a short time before and kept it, together with some other things, in a little room I had rented in a quiet corner of the central section of the city, not far from the hotel. My purpose was not to sleep there – that seldom happened – but to have a place to keep my personal wardrobe and to change unobserved when I wanted to spend my free evenings in somewhat higher circles than those I had frequented in Stanko's company. The room was in a little *cité*, a covey of old houses enclosed by iron fences and reached through the quiet rue Boissy d'Anglas. There were neither shops nor restaurants there; only a few small hotels and private houses of the sort one can look into from the street through the open door of the porter's loge and see the concierge at her housework and her husband sitting with his bottle of wine, the cat beside him. It was in a house of this sort that I had a short time before become the sub-tenant of a kindly middle-aged widow who occupied a four-room apartment on the third floor. For a moderate monthly rental she turned one of her rooms over to me – a kind of small bed-sitting-room with a cot and a marble fireplace surmounted by a mirror, a pendulum clock on the mantelpiece, rickety upholstered furniture, and sooty silk curtains at the French windows, from which one had a view of a narrow court with glass-roofed kitchens below. Beyond this one looked out on the back windows of the elegant houses of the faubourg Saint-Honoré, where in the evenings one could see the cooks and maids wandering through the service quarters and bedrooms. Moreover, somewhere over there lived the Prince of Monaco and to him belonged this whole peaceful little *cité*, for which he could receive, any time he wanted it, forty-five million francs. Then it would be torn down. But he seemed not to need the money, and so, subject to cancellation, I remained the guest of this monarch and grand croupier, a thought to whose odd charm I was by no means insensible.

The good suit I had bought at the Printemps had its place in the wardrobe outside dormitory number four. My new acquisitions, however – a dinner-jacket, a silk-lined evening cape, in the selection of which I had been unconsciously influenced by my still vivid recollection of Müller-Rosé as attaché and woman-chaser, a silk hat, and a pair of patent-leather shoes – I had not dared exhibit in the hotel; I kept them ready for use in the '*cabinet de toilette*' in my rented room. This was a kind of wall-papered closet where a cretonne curtain protected my clothes. Dress shirts, black silk socks, and bow ties were in the Louis Seize bureau in the room. My dinner-jacket with its satin lapels had not actually been made to order; I had bought it off the hanger and only had it altered a little, but it fitted my figure so perfectly that I would like to have seen the connoisseur who would not have sworn it had been made to measure by an expensive tailor. For what purpose did I keep these and other fineries stored in my quiet private dwelling?

But I have already divulged the answer: from time to time, by way of experiment and practice in living the higher life, I would dine in some elegant restaurant on the rue de Rivoli or the avenue des Champs-Élysées or in some hotel of the same quality as my own, or finer if possible, the Ritz, the Bristol, the Meurice, and would afterwards take a loge seat in some good theatre devoted to the spoken drama or comic opera or even grand opera. This amounted, as one can see, to a kind of dual existence, whose charm lay in the ambiguity as to which figure was the real I and which the masquerade: was I the liveried *commis-de-salle* who waited on and flattered the guests in the Saint James and Albany, or was I the unknown man of distinction who looked as though he must keep a riding horse and who would certainly, once he had finished dinner, call in at various exclusive salons but was meanwhile graciously permitting himself to be served by waiters among whom I found none equal to me in my other role? Thus I masqueraded in both capacities, and the undisguised reality behind the two appearances, the real I, could not be identified because it actually did not exist. Nor am I willing to say that I gave my role as a man of distinction any definite preference over the other. I was too good and successful a waiter to feel appreciably happier when I was the one who was waited on – a part, by the way, that requires as much natural talent as the other. An evening was to come, however, that committed me to this talent, this theatrical gift for playing the master, in a decisive and gratifying, indeed almost intoxicating manner.

Chapter Four

It was a July evening shortly before the national holiday that brings the theatre season to a close, and I was enjoying one of the free nights my employers granted me every fortnight. I had decided to dine, as I had done a few times before, in the attractive roof garden of the Grand Hôtel des Ambassadeurs on the boulevard Saint-Germain. From its lofty heights one has a sweeping view over the flower boxes and across the city in the direction of the Seine, on one side towards the Place de la Concorde and the Madeleine, on the other towards that masterpiece of the World Exposition of 1889, the Eiffel Tower. An elevator takes you up five or six storeys and you find yourself in a refreshing atmosphere, surrounded by the subdued conversation of high society, whose manners forbid curiosity. I fitted in easily and faultlessly. Brightly clad ladies, their hats wide and daring, sat in their wicker chairs at tables lighted by little shaded lamps. The moustached gentlemen escorting them wore correct evening attire, as did I. Some even had on tails. These I did not possess, but my own elegance was more than sufficient, and I felt completely at ease as I took my place at the empty table to which the head waiter escorted me while his assistant removed the second *couvert*. I was looking forward to a delightful evening after an agreeable meal for I had in my pocket a ticket to the Opéra Comique, where *Faust* was to be given that night, my favourite opera, the melodious masterpiece of the late Gounod. I had heard it once before and was looking forward to renewing the charming impressions of that first occasion.

That, however, was not to be. Fate had something quite different and far more significant in store for me that evening.

I had communicated my wishes to the waiter bending over me, menu in hand, and had asked for the wine card. I was allowing my eyes to wander over the assembled company with a casual and purposely weary gaze when they encountered another pair of eyes, merry and alert, the eyes of the young Marquis de Venosta, who, apparelled like me, was sitting at a single table some distance away. Understandably enough, I recognized him before he recognized me. It was obviously easier for me to trust my eyes than for him to believe what he saw. After a brief wrinkling of the brow, a look of merry astonishment appeared on his face; for, though I had hesitated to greet him (I was not sure it would be tactful), the involuntary smile with which I met his glance assured him of my identity – the identity, that is, of the cavalier and the waiter. With a toss of his head and a brief spreading of his hands he indicated his amazement and pleasure, and, laying aside his napkin, made his way over to me between the tables.

'*Mon cher Armand*, is it you or is it not? But forgive my momentary doubt. And forgive me for using your first name out of habit – unfortunately, your family name is unknown to me, or it has escaped my mind. For us you were always just Armand.'

I had risen and was shaking his hand, which of course he had never offered me before.

'Not even the first name,' I said, laughing, 'is exactly right, marquis. Armand is only a *nom de guerre* or *d'affaires*. Actually, my name is Félix – Félix Kroull – enchanted to see you.'

'*Mon cher Kroull*, of course, how could it have slipped my mind? It is I who am enchanted, I assure you! *Comment allez-vous?* Very well indeed, to judge by your appearance, although appearances ... I, too, look well, and yet things are going ill with me. Yes, yes, ill. But none of that. And you – am I to understand that you have quit your delightful activities at the Saint James and Albany?'

'No, indeed, marquis. They go on concurrently. Or this goes on concurrently. I am both here and there.'

'*Très amusant.* You are a magician. But I am inconveniencing you. I shall leave you to – But no, let us join forces. I cannot invite you to my table, it's too small. But I see you have room. I have had my dessert, but if it is agreeable to you, I'll have my coffee here. Or do you yearn for solitude?'

'Not a bit. You are welcome here, marquis,' I replied casually. And, turning to the waiter: 'A chair for this gentleman!' I was at pains not to show that I was flattered or to say anything about the honour he was doing me, but contented myself with calling his proposal a good one. He sat down opposite me and while I finished ordering my dinner and he was served with coffee and a *fine*, he continued to watch me earnestly, bending slightly forward across the table. Obviously my double life fascinated him and he was eager to understand it better.

'My presence doesn't disturb you while you're eating?' he asked. 'I should hate to be a bother. Least of all do I want to appear importunate, which is always a sign of bad upbringing. A cultivated man passes lightly over everything, accepts events without asking questions. That marks a man of the world, such as I ostensibly am. All right, then, such as I am. But on many occasions – the present one, for example – I realize that I am a man of the world without knowledge of the world, without that experience of life which alone justifies us in accepting events of all kinds with the worldly man's light touch. There is no pleasure in playing that role if you are really ignorant ... You will understand that our meeting here strikes me as remarkable as well as pleasant and it makes me eager to understand. Admit that your phrases about "going on concurrently" and "here and there" contain something intriguing – to one who is inexperienced. For God's sake, go on eating and don't say a word! Let me do the talking while I try experimentally to picture the way of life of a contemporary who is obviously far more a man of the world than I am. *Voyons!* You come, as one now sees not for the first time but really always has seen, of a good family – with us members of the nobility, forgive the hard word, one simply says "of family"; only the bourgeois can come of a *good* family. Comical world! A good family, then – and you have chosen a career which will doubtless lead to a goal appropriate to your origin, to attain which it is important that you work your way up from the ranks and temporarily occupy positions which might deceive someone of less penetration into thinking that he was dealing with a person of the lower classes instead, so to speak, of a gentleman in disguise. Am I right? *Àpropos:* it is nice of the English to have spread the word "gentleman" around the world. Thanks to them, we have a designation for a man who is not a nobleman, to be sure, but deserves to be, deserves it more than many a one who is styled *"Hochgeboren"*, whereas the gentleman is only called *"Hochwohlgeboren"* – "only" – and has a *"wohl!"* to make it more explicit ... To *your "Wohl"*! I'll order something to drink at once; that is, if you have emptied your half-bottle, we'll order a whole one together ... The *"Hochgeboren"* and *"Hochwohlgeboren"* make an exact analogy to "family" and *"good* family" ... My, how I chatter! It's just so you may eat in peace and not bother about me. Don't take the goose, it's not well roasted. Take the leg of lamb; my experience confirms what the maître assured me of – it has been soaked in milk for the right length of time ... *Enfin!* What was I saying about you? While your service in the ranks makes you appear to be a member of the lower classes – this must afford you a good deal of amusement, I imagine – you naturally keep a firm inner hold on your position as a gentleman and from time to time return to it outwardly, as you are doing tonight. Very, very nice. But completely new to me and startling – which shows you how little one knows about human life even when one is a man of the world. Technically, if you'll pardon my asking, the "here and there" cannot be entirely easy. You have money of your own. I assume – observe I do not ask, I assume what is perfectly clear. So you are in a position to keep up your wardrobe as a gentleman in addition to your working-livery, and the interesting thing about it is that you appear as much at home in the one as in the other.'

'Clothes make the man, marquis – or perhaps the other way around: the man makes the clothes.'

'And I have sketched your way of life with approximate truth?'

'Very accurately.' And I told him that I did indeed possess some means – oh, very modest ones – and that I kept a small apartment in the city, where I accomplished those changes in my appearance which I now had the pleasure of permitting him to observe.

I was well aware that he was observing my table manners and, without affectation, I preserved a certain well-bred formality, sitting upright with my elbows close to my sides. That my behaviour interested him was betrayed by his casual observations about foreign eating-habits. In America, he remarked, Europeans were recognized by the fact that they raised their forks with their left hands. The American cut his food first, then laid his knife aside and ate with his right hand. 'There's something childish about it, isn't there?' However, he knew this only by hearsay. He had never been over there, nor had he any desire at all to travel – none whatever – not the slightest. Had I seen something of the world?

'My God, no, marquis – and yet in another sense, yes! Nothing except a few attractive Taunus spas and Frankfurt on the Main. But then Paris. And Paris is a great deal.'

'Paris is everything!' he said with emphasis. 'To me it is everything, and I would rather die than leave it, but I shall have to, nevertheless. I shall have to travel, more's the pity, entirely against my wishes and inclinations. The son of the house, dear Kroull. I don't know to what extent you still are that and tied to the apron strings – after all, you only come of a good family, but I, *hélas*, of family ...'

Almost before I had finished my *Pêche Melba* he had ordered the bottle of Lafite that was meant for both of us.

'I'll just begin on this,' he said. 'When you're through with your coffee, join me. If I have too much of a start, we'll order another.'

'Well, marquis, you already have a good start. When you were in my hands at the Saint James and Albany you used to be moderate.'

'Care, sorrow, a breaking heart, dear Kroull! What can you do, there's nothing left but the solace of wine, and you learn to appreciate the gifts of Bacchus. That's his name, isn't it? "Bacchus", not "Bachus", as people usually say for convenience. I call it convenience not to use a harsher word. Are you strong on mythology?'

'Not very, marquis. There is, for instance, the god Hermes. But aside. from him I know very little.'

'Why do you need to? Learning, especially conspicuous learning, is not a gentleman's affair. That's a legacy from the days when a nobleman only needed to have a decent seat on a horse and was taught nothing else, not even reading and writing. The books he left to the priests. There's still a strong tendency in that direction among my fellows. Most of them are elegant loafers, and not even charming. Do you ride? Permit me to fill your glass with this care-killer! Your good fortune again! Oh, my good fortune? There's no point in drinking to that. It's not so easily mended. So you don't ride? I'm convinced you're perfectly suited to it, born for it, in fact; you would put all the cavaliers in the Bois to shame.'

'I admit to you, marquis, I almost think so myself.'

'That's no more than healthy self-confidence, dear Kroull. I call it healthy because I share it, because I myself have confidence in you and not on that point alone ... Let me be frank. I have the impression that you are not really a confiding man or one who opens his heart. You always hold something back. Somehow or other, there's a mystery about you. *Pardon*, I am being indiscreet. My talking this way simply demonstrates my own carefree garrulousness – that is, my confidence in you.'

'For which I am sincerely grateful, dear marquis. May I take the liberty of inquiring after Mademoiselle Zaza's health? I was really surprised to find you here without her.'

'How nice of you to ask after her! You do find her charming, don't you? How could you fail to? I permit you to. I permit the whole world to find her charming. And yet I should really like to withdraw her from the world and have her entirely to myself. The dear child is busy this evening at her little theatre, the Folies Musicales. She is a soubrette; didn't you know? At present she is appearing in *Le Don de la Fée*. But I've seen the thing so often I can't stand being there for every performance. Besides, it makes me a little nervous to see her wearing so little when she sings – the little is becoming, but it is very little indeed, and now I suffer because of it, although at the start that was just what made me fall so madly in love with her. Have you ever been passionately in love?'

'I'm in a very good position to follow you, marquis.'

'I can readily believe you know all about matters of the heart. And yet you seem to me the type who is more loved than loving. Am I wrong? All right, let's put that question aside. Zaza still has to sing in the third act. After that I will take her home and we will have tea together in the little apartment I have furnished for her.'

'My congratulations! But that means we'll have to hurry with our Lafite and end this pleasant meeting before long. For my own part, I have a ticket for the Opéra Comique.'

'Really, I don't like to hurry. Besides, I can telephone the little one to look for me at home a bit later. Would you mind if you didn't get to your box until the second act?'

'Not much. *Faust* is a charming opera, but how could it attract me more than Mademoiselle Zaza attracts you?'

'The thing is, I would like to talk to you more specifically about my problems. You must have realized from a number of things I have said that I am in a dilemma, a serious and painful dilemma of the heart.'

'I did realize it, dear marquis, and I have only been waiting for a signal from you to inquire sympathetically about the nature of your embarrassment. It concerns Mademoiselle Zaza?'

'Whom else? You have heard that I am to take a trip? That I am to be away for a year?'

'A whole year! Why?'

'My dear friend, this is how it is. My poor parents – I have talked to you about them once or twice – know that my liaison with Zaza has been going on for a year or more. There was no need for gossip or an anonymous letter; I myself was childish and trusting enough to let my happiness and my plans appear unmistakably in my letters to them. I wear my heart on my tongue, as you know, and from my tongue to my pen the route is short and easy. The dear old people were quite right in thinking I was serious about the affair and intended to marry the girl – or the "person", as they naturally say – and they have been, as might have been expected, beside themselves. They were here until the day before yesterday – I've had some bad times, a week of uninterrupted argument. My father talked in a very deep voice and my mother in a very high one, vibrating with tears – he in French and she in German. Don't misunderstand me, there were no hard words except the repetition of the word "person", which, to be sure, hurt me more than if they had called me an irresponsible fool and a disgrace to the family. They did not do that; they simply kept on imploring me not to give them or society any grounds for such a description. I assured them in a voice that was both deep and vibrant that I was sincerely sorry to be a source of concern to them. For they really love me and want what is best for me, only they don't understand what that is – in fact, they understand so little that they actually spoke of disinheriting me in case I should carry out my scandalous intentions. They did not use the word, either in French or in German; I have already said that out of love for me they refrained from harsh words. But they indicated the possibility clearly enough – as a consequence and a threat. Now I have always thought, because of my father's position and the hand he has in the Luxemburg steel industry, that at the very least I count on living decently. But being disinherited would be of no help whatever to me or to Zaza. It wouldn't be much fun for her to marry someone who had been disinherited, you can understand that.'

'I pretty well can. At least, I can put myself in Mademoiselle Zaza's place. But now, about the trip?'

'The story about the damned trip is this: my parents want to pry me loose – "You must be pried loose," my father said. Using the German word in the midst of his French discourse – an entirely inappropriate word, whatever they think they have to pry me loose from. For I'm neither stuck fast in the ice like an Arctic explorer – the warmth of Zaza's bed and her sweet body makes that comparison wholly ridiculous – nor am I held by iron chains, but rather by the most delightful chains of roses, whose strength, however, I do not deny. However, I am to break it, at least experimentally, that's the idea, and that's the purpose of the world tour which my parents are generously prepared to finance – their intentions are so good! I am to leave – what's more, for a long time, leave Paris, the Théâtre des Folies Musicales, and Zaza. I am to see foreign lands and people and thereby acquire new ideas and get "these whims out of my head" – "whims", they call it – and return a different person, a different person! Can one wish to be a different person from the one he is? You look uncertain, but I, I do not want it in the least. I want to remain who I am and not to let my heart and head be turned topsy-turvy by this travel cure they prescribe and so become alien to myself and forget Zaza. Of course, that is possible. Long absence, a complete change of scene, and a thousand new experiences might accomplish it. But it's exactly because I consider it theoretically possible that I so thoroughly detest this experiment.'

'Consider, nevertheless,' I said, 'that if you should become another person, you would not feel the lack of your present self or regret it, simply because it would no longer be you.'

'What sort of comfort is that to me now? Who could wish to forget? Forgetting is the most distressing and disagreeable thing in the world.'

'And yet you really know that your dread of the experiment is no proof that it will not succeed.'

'Yes, theoretically. Practically, it's out of the question. For all their love and care, my parents are attempting to murder love. They will be unsuccessful, I am as sure of it as I am of myself.'

'That means something. And may I ask whether your parents are ready to accept this experiment as an experiment, and if the result is negative, accommodate themselves to the proven strength of your desires?'

'I asked them that, too. But I could not get a simple yes. They were concerned with "prying me loose", and they did not think beyond that. That's what's so unfair about it. I had to give them my promise without getting one in return.'

'So you agreed to the trip?'

'What else could I do? After all, I can't expose Zaza to the loss of my inheritance. I told her I had promised to go on the trip and she wept a great deal, partly because of the long separation, partly through her natural fear that the cure my parents propose may work and that I may return a changed man. I understand her fear. At times, after all, I feel it myself. Oh, my dear friend, what a dilemma! I have to travel and I do not want to; I have obligated myself to travel – and cannot do it. What shall I do? Who can help me out of this?'

'Indeed, dear marquis, you are to be pitied,' I said. 'I feel the greatest sympathy for you, but no one can release you from the obligation you have taken upon yourself.'

'No, no one.'

'No one.'

The conversation died away for a few moments. He twisted his glass in his fingers. Suddenly he got up and said: 'I had almost forgotten – I must telephone my little friend. If you will wait a moment ...'

He left. The roof garden was almost empty. Only two other tables were still being served. Most of the waiters were standing idle. I smoked a cigarette to pass the time. When Venosta returned he ordered another bottle of Château Lafite and began again:

'Dear Kroull, I have told you about the conflict with my parents, very painful on both sides. I hope I did not fail in reverence and respect in what I said, or in expressing my gratitude for their loving care – not least for the generous offer which their concern has inspired, even though it may have the appearance of an injunction or even a command. It is only my peculiar situation that makes this invitation to take a trip around the world in total luxury such an unbearable imposition that I scarcely understand how I came to agree to it. For any other man, whether of family or of good family, such an invitation would be a gift from Heaven wrapped in the rainbow hues of novelty and adventure. Even I, in my present situation, sometimes catch myself – it is a kind of disloyalty to Zaza and to our love – picturing in imagination the manifold charms of such a year of travel, the variety of scenes, encounters, experiences, enjoyments that would certainly come with it, if only one were responsive to such things. Just consider – the wide world, the Orient, North and South America, the Far East. In China there are said to be servants in plenty. A European bachelor would have a dozen of them. He would have one to carry his visiting-cards – to run ahead with them. I have heard of a tropical sultan who was thrown from his horse and lost all his teeth; he had new ones made of gold in Paris, with a diamond in the middle of each. His beloved wears the national costume, a precious cloth wrapped around her thighs and tied in front beneath her supple hips, for she is as beautiful as a dream. Around her neck she wears three or four ropes of pearls and below them three or four strands of diamonds of fabulous size.'

'Was it your revered parents who described all this to you?'

'It wasn't exactly my parents. They haven't been there. But isn't it altogether likely and the way you would picture it, especially the hips? What's more, the sultan is said occasionally to relinquish his beloved to favoured guests, guests of distinction. Naturally, I didn't hear that from them either – they have no idea what they are offering me in this trip around the world. But however unresponsive I am, do I not theoretically owe them gratitude for their handsome offer?'

'Unquestionably, marquis. But you are taking over my role. You are, so to speak, talking with my voice. It should be up to me to reconcile you as far as possible to the idea of this trip which you hate so much, especially by pointing out to you the advantages it would offer – it will offer – and while you were telephoning I decided to make exactly that attempt.'

'You would be preaching to deaf ears, even if you were to protest a hundred times how much you envied me – if only on account of the hips.'

'Envy? No, marquis, that's not exactly right. It would not have been envy that inspired me in my well-meant efforts. I am not especially eager to travel. Why does a Parisian need to go abroad in the world? It comes to him. It comes to us here in the hotel, and when I sit on the terrace of the Café de Madrid about the time the theatres close, it is conveniently present right before my eyes. I don't have to tell you about that.'

'No, but in your airy way you have undertaken too much if you think you can make the trip palatable to me.'

'Dear marquis, I shall try, nevertheless. How could I not try to show myself grateful for your confidence? I have already thought of proposing that you take Mademoiselle Zaza with you.'

'Impossible, Kroull. What are you thinking of? I won't mention Zaza's contract with the Folies Musicales. Contracts can be broken. But I cannot travel with Zaza and at the same time keep her hidden. In any case, there are difficulties in taking a woman who is not your wife around the world with you. And I should be seen, my parents have contacts here and there, some of them official, and they would inevitably find out if I defeated the whole purpose of the trip by taking Zaza with me. They would be beside themselves! They would cancel my letter of credit. For instance, I am to make a longish visit at the Argentinian *estancia* of a family whose acquaintance my parents once made at a French watering-place. Shall I leave Zaza alone for weeks at a time in Buenos Aires, exposed to all the dangers of that city? You proposal is unthinkable.'

'I was afraid of that when I made it. I withdraw it.'

'That means you leave me in the lurch. You resign yourself to the fact that I have to travel alone. It's easy enough for you to resign yourself! But I can't. I have to travel and I want to stay here. That means I must attempt the impossible: to travel and to stay here at the same time. That, in turn, means I must become two people, must divide myself in two; one part of Louis Venosta must travel, while the other stays in Paris with his Zaza. It's important to me that the latter should be the real one. In short, the trip must go on concurrently. Louis Venosta must be here and there. Do you follow the convolutions of my thought?'

'I'm trying to, marquis. In other words, it must *look* as though you were travelling, but in reality you will stay at home.'

'Damnably right!'

'Damnably only because no one looks like you.'

'In Argentina no one knows how I look. I have nothing against looking different in different places. As a matter of fact, I'd like it very much if I looked better there than here.'

'So then your name must travel attached to a person who is not you.'

'But who cannot be just anyone.'

'I should think not. One can't be particular enough about that.'

He filled his glass, emptied it in big gulps, and banged it down on the table.

'Kroull,' he said, 'as far as I'm concerned, my choice is made.'

'So soon? With so little consideration?'

'We've been sitting here facing one another for quite a while.'

'We? What are you thinking of?'

'Kroull,' he repeated, 'I call you by your name, the name of a man of good family, a name, naturally, that one would not want to relinquish even temporarily although by doing so one might appear to be a man of family. Would you be willing to help a friend in dire need? You said you were not anxious to travel. But what is the lack of a strong desire to travel compared to my horror at leaving Paris! You said, too – in fact, we agreed about it – that no one could release me from my promise to my parents. How would it be if you released me from it?'

'It seems to me, dear marquis, that you are losing yourself in fantasies.'

'Why? And why do you speak of fantasies as of a realm to which you are a complete stranger? After all, there is something singular about you, Kroull! I called this quality intriguing, I finally even called it mysterious. If I had used the word "fantastic" instead, would you have been angry?'

'No indeed, since you would not have meant it ill.'

'Certainly not! And therefore you can't be angry with me because your appearance suggested the idea to me, because during this meeting my choice – my very particular choice – has fallen on you!'

'On me as the person to bear your name out in the world, represent you, *be* you in the people's eyes, your parents' son, not just a member of your family but you yourself? Have you given this the consideration it requires?'

'I shall remain who I am where I really am.'

'But out in the world you will be another – to wit, me. People will see you in me. In the eyes of the world you will relinquish your personality to me. "Where I really am", you say, but where would you really be? Would that not be a little uncertain, for you as well as for me? And if this uncertainty was all right with me, would it be all right with you, too? Would it not be unpleasant to be yourself only very locally, and in the rest of the world – that is, predominantly – to exist as me, through me, in me?'

'No, Kroull,' he said, warmly extending his hand to me across the table. 'It would not – you would not be – unpleasant to me. It would not be bad at all for Louis Venosta if you changed selves with him and he went about the world in your person, that is, if his name were attached to your person as now, in the world outside, it will be – provided you agree. I have an uncomfortable suspicion that it would not be at all displeasing to certain others if that were the way nature had arranged things. They will just have to put up with reality, about whose vagaries I am not in the least concerned. For I really am where Zaza is. And it is perfectly all right with me for you to be Louis Venosta elsewhere. I should take the greatest pleasure in appearing to people in your person. You are an elegant fellow both here and there, in both roles, as gentleman and as *commis-de-salle*. I could wish many of my fellow noblemen your manners. You know foreign languages, and if the conversation should turn to mythology, which hardly ever happens, you will make out well enough with Hermes. No one demands more from a nobleman – one might even say that you as a bourgeois are obliged to know more. You must take this simplification into account in making your decision. Well, then is it agreed? You will undertake this great act of friendship?'

'My dear marquis,' I said. 'Do you realize that so far we have been moving in mid-air and have not discussed any of the facts or the hundred difficulties that would have to be reckoned with?'

'You're right,' he replied. 'Above all, you're right to remind me that I have to telephone again. I must explain to Zaza that I can't come home right away because I'm involved in a conversation that is vital to our happiness. Excuse me.'

And he left again – to remain away longer than before. Darkness had fallen over Paris, and for some time now the roof garden had been bathed in the white light of the arc lamps. It was completely empty at this hour and would probably not come to life again until the theatres closed. In my pocket I felt the unused opera ticket, without paying much attention to it, although at another time the incident would have pained me. Thoughts whirled through my mind, but reason, I may say, held them in check, imposing a kind of caution and forbidding them to indulge in drunken riot. I was happy to be left alone for a while so that I could appraise the situation and consider in advance a number of points that still had to be discussed. This by-path, this happy digression from the thoroughfare my godfather had opened for me – while pointing out just such a possibility – presented itself so startlingly and in so enticing a form that reason found it tedious to examine it and determine whether it might not be a cul-de-sac that was tempting me. Reason insisted I would be setting forth on a dangerous road, a road that would require cautious treading. Reason repeated this with emphasis and only succeeded in enhancing the charm of the adventure in my eyes, and adventure that would call upon all my talents. It is useless to warn the courageous against some action on the ground that it requires courage. I do not hesitate to admit that long before my companion returned I had decided to embark on the adventure, had indeed so decided at the moment when I told him that *no one* could release him from his promise. And I was less concerned about the practical difficulties we would have to face than about the danger of appearing to him in an ambiguous light because of the skill with which I could meet those difficulties.

Yet he already saw me in a sufficiently ambiguous light; the words he had used to describe my way of life – 'intriguing', 'mysterious', 'fantastic' – proved that. I was under no illusion that he would have made his proposal to any cavalier, and the fact that he had made it to me, though it was an honour, was nevertheless an ambiguous one. And yet I could not forget the warmth of the hand-clasp with which he had assured me that it would be 'not unpleasant' to wander up and down the world in my person; and I said to myself that if we were about to engage in a schoolboy prank, it was he, with his eagerness to deceive his parents, who had the greater stake in it, though I was to play the more active part. As he returned from his telephone conversation I could see quite clearly that he was to a considerable extent excited and enthusiastic about the idea for its own sake – that is, simply as a prank. The colour in his boyish cheeks was high and not from wine alone; there was a sly glitter in his little eyes. No doubt he still heard Zaza's silvery laughter as he outlined our plans to her.

'My dear Kroull,' he said, sitting down again at my table, 'we have always been on good terms, but who would have thought a short while ago that we would come so close – to the point of interchangeability! We have thought out something so amusing now – or, if we haven't quite thought it out, we have at least outlined it – that my heart laughs in my breast. And you? Don't look so solemn! I appeal to your sense of humour, to your taste for a good joke – for a joke so good that it would repay every effort to work it out for its own sake, quite apart from its importance to a pair of lovers. And you, the third person, will you deny that there is profit in it for you, too? There is a lot of profit, the whole joke is profitable to you. Do you deny it?'

'It's not my custom, my dear marquis, to take life as a joke. Frivolity is not my style, especially in the matter of jokes; for certain jokes are pointless if they are not taken seriously. A good joke does not come off unless one approaches it with complete seriousness.'

'Very good. That's what we'll do. You spoke of problems, difficulties. What are the ones you see first off?'

'It would be better, marquis, if you let me put a few questions to you. Where is this prescribed tour to take you?'

'Ah, my good Papa in his concern for me has laid out a very nice itinerary, most attractive for anyone but me: both Americas, the islands of the South Seas and Japan, followed by an interesting voyage to Egypt, Constantinople, Greece, Italy, and so forth. An educational journey by the book; I could not wish anything better for myself if it weren't for Zaza. Now it is you I must congratulate on the trip.'

'Your Papa will pay the expenses?'

'Of course. In his desire for me to travel in proper style he has set aside no less than twenty thousand francs – not including the fare to Lisbon and my ticket to Argentina, where I am to go first. Papa bought those himself and reserved a cabin for me on the *Cap Arcona*. He deposited the twenty thousand francs in the Banque de France, and they are now mine in the form of a so-called circular letter of credit on banks in the principal ports of call on my route.'

I waited.

'I shall, of course, turn the letter of credit over to you,' he added.

I remained silent.

He went on: 'As well as the tickets that have already been bought.'

'And what,' I asked, 'will you live on while I am spending your money in your name?'

'What will I – oh, yes! You put me in a quandary. But you don't ask the question as though it were your intention to leave me in perplexity. Yes, dear Kroull, what shall we do about that? I am really not at all used to thinking about what I shall live on during the coming year.'

'I just wanted to call your attention to the fact that it's not so simple to lend one's personality to someone else. But let's postpone that problem. I don't want to be hurried into solving it, for that would mean presupposing something like cunning in me, and where cunning is concerned, I am quite useless. Cunning is not gentlemanly.'

'I thought it just possible, dear friend, that you might have succeeded in transferring a certain amount of cunning, from your other existence into your life as a gentleman.'

'Something much more respectable links my two existences. It is some little bourgeois savings, a small bank account –'

'Which I can in no circumstances touch!'

'Nevertheless, we'll have to include it in our calculations somehow. By the way, have you anything to write with?'

He quickly felt his pockets. 'Yes, my fountain pen. But no paper.'

'Here's some.' And I tore a page from my notebook. 'It would interest me to see your signature.'

'Why? ... As you like.' With the pen inclined steeply to the left, he wrote his signature and pushed it across to me. Even seen upside down, it was very droll-looking. Dispensing with a flourish at the end, it began with one instead. The artistically elaborated *L* swept off to the right in a wide loop which returned and crossed the stem of the initial from the left; it proceeded from there in a tight back-hand script within the oval thus described as *Louis Marquis de Venosta*. I could not repress a smile, but nodded to him approvingly.

'Inherited or invented?' I asked, taking the fountain pen.

'Inherited,' he said. 'Papa does it just that way. Only not so well,' he added.

'And so you have overreached him.' I spoke mechanically, for I was engaged in my first attempted imitation, which turned out very well. 'Thank goodness I don't have to do it better than you. As a matter of fact that would be a mistake.' Meanwhile I had finished the second copy, less satisfactory than the first. The third, however, was flawless. I struck out the first two and handed the paper to him. He was astounded.

'Incredible!' he cried. 'My writing as though it were photographed! And you pretend to know nothing about cunning! But I am not so lacking in cunning as you think, and I understand perfectly well why you are practising. You will need my signature to draw against the letter of credit.'

'How do you sign yourself when you write to your parents?'

He was taken aback and exclaimed:

'Of course, I'll at least have to send the old folk a few postcards from some of the places where I stay. My friend, you think of everything: I am called Loulou at home because that was what I used to call myself as a child. This is how I do it.'

He did it in the same way as his full name; he drew an ornate *L*, extended it into an oval, crossed the arabesque from the left, and then continued in a stiff back-hand within the loop as *oulou*.

'All right,' I said, 'we can do that. Have you a page of your handwriting with you?'

He said he was sorry he had none.

'Then write this, if you please.' I handed him a fresh piece of paper: 'Write: "*Mon cher Papa*, dearest Mama, from this fascinating city, one of the high points of my journey, I send you my thanks and best wishes. I am brimming with new impressions which drive from my mind much that seemed essential before. Your Loulou." Something like that.'

'No, exactly like that! That's marvellous, Kroull, *vous êtes admirable!* The way you shake these things out of your sleeve –' And he wrote my sentences with his hand twisted to the left, in stiff letters that were just as jammed together as my late father's had been widely spaced, but were not a bit harder to imitate. I put this model in my pocket and inquired about the names of the servants in his castle – the cook, who was called Ferblantier, and the coachman, who was called Klosmann, and the marquis's valet, a shaky man in his late sixties called Radicule, and the marquise's maid, named Adelaide. I even inquired in detail about the domestic animals, the riding-horses, Fripon the wolf-hound, the marquise's Maltese lap-dog, Minime, a creature who suffered a great deal from diarrhoea. Our hilarity increased the longer the meeting lasted, but Loulou's activity of mind and powers of discrimination seemed to diminish with the passage of time. I expressed surprise that he was not going to England, to London. The reason was that he already knew the country, had actually spent two years there in a public school. 'Nevertheless,' he said, 'it would be a very good thing if London were included in the itinerary. How easy it would be for me to trick the old folk and hurry back here to Paris and Zaza in the middle of my tour!'

'But you will be with Zaza all the time!'

'Right you are!' he cried. 'That's the real trick. I was thinking of a false trick that won't compare with the real one. *Pardon.* I hope you will excuse me. The trick is that I shall be brimming with new impressions while I stay with Zaza. You know, I shall have to be on my guard not to inquire about Radicule, Fripon, and Minime when I am writing from here and you are perhaps doing the same from Zanzibar. Those are things, of course, that can't coincide, although a coincidence of persons – even though at a great distance – must take place ... Listen, this situation requires that we stop speaking formally to one another! Do you object? When I speak to myself I don't use a formal manner of address. Is that agreed? Let's drink to it! To your health, Armand – I mean Félix – I mean Loulou. Remember that you must not inquire about Klossmann and Adelaide from Paris, but only from Zanzibar. Besides, so far as I know, I am not going to Zanzibar and neither are you. But no matter – wherever

I happen to be, during the time I stay here I must in any case vanish from Paris. There, you see how clever I am! Zaza and I have to make ourselves scarce, to use a schoolboy's expression. Don't schoolboys say "make yourself scarce"? But how should you, a gentleman and now a young man of family, know about that? I must give notice that I am going to give up my apartment and so must Zaza. We will move together into a suburb, a pretty suburb, either Boulogne or Sèvres, and what's left to me – it will be enough, for it will be with Zaza – would do well perhaps to assume another name – logic seems to me to demand that I should call myself Kroull – to be sure, I would have to learn to imitate your signature, but I hope my cunning is sufficient for that. So there in Versailles or farther out – while I'm on my travels – I'll provide a love-nest for Zaza and me ... But, Armand, I mean *cher Louis*,' and he opened his little eyes as wide as he could, 'answer me this if you can: what are we going to live on?'

I replied that we had solved that problem as soon as it arose. I possessed a bank account of twelve thousand francs, which would stand at his disposal in return for his letter of credit.

He was touched to the point of tears. 'A gentleman!' he exclaimed. 'A nobleman from top to toe! If you do not have the right to send greetings to Minime and Radicule, who should have? Our parents will send back the warmest greetings in their name. A last glass to the gentleman who is us!'

Our meeting had lasted through the quiet theatre hours; as we left, the roof garden was beginning to fill again in the mild night. Over my protest he paid for both dinners and the four bottles of Lafite. He was much confused both by joy and by wine. 'All of it, all of it together!' he instructed the head waiter, who brought the check. 'We are one and the same. Armand de Kroullosta is our name.'

'Very good,' the latter replied with a patient smile which must have come easily to him, for his tip was enormous.

Venosta took me back to my place in a fiacre and let me out there. On the way we agreed to another meeting at which I would transfer my bank account to him and he would give me his letter of credit and the tickets.

'*Bonne nuit, à tantôt, monsieur le marquis,*' he said with drunken *grandezza* as he shook my hand. For the first time I heard from his lips this style of address, and I shivered with joy at the thought of the equality of seeming and being which life was granting me, of the appearance it was now appropriately adding to the substance.

Chapter Five

How inventive life is! Lending substance to airy nothings, it brings our childhood dreams to pass. Had not I in boyhood tasted in imagination those delights of incognito I fully savoured now, as I continued to go about my menial occupations for a while, keeping my new estate as secret as my princedom once had been? Then it had been a merry and delightful game, now it had become reality – at least to this extent: for the space of a year, beyond which period I did not care to look, I had, as it were, a margrave's patent of nobility in my pocket. Awareness of this delicious fact filled my mind from the moment of waking, just as it had before, and accompanied me all day long in the establishment where I played my liveried role, without my associates being a scrap the wiser.

Sympathetic reader! I was very happy. In my own eyes I was priceless, and I loved myself – in the way that is really socially useful, self-love turned outward as amiability. A fool might have been tempted by the secret I possessed into a show of arrogance, into effrontery and disobedience towards those above and uncomradely disdain towards those below. Not I; my courtesy towards the guests in the dining-room had never been more winning, the voice in which I addressed them had never held a gentler deference, my attitude towards those who thought themselves my equals, my fellow waiters and my room-mates in the garret, had never been merrier or more cordial than during those days. My secret was perhaps reflected in the hint of a smile, but this served to hide rather than reveal. Concealment was wise, at any rate at first, for I could not be absolutely sure that the bearer of what was now my real name might not, on the very morning after our meeting, have had sober second thoughts and be preparing to rescind our agreement. I was prudent enough not to resign my livelihood over-night; essentially, however, I was sure of my man. Venosta had been too overjoyed at the solution (which I had hit on before he did), and Zaza's magnetism stood surety for his good faith.

I had not deceived myself. Our great compact had been reached on the evening of July 10, and I would not be free for the next and conclusive meeting until the 24th. On the 17th or 18th, however, I saw him again, for on one of these evenings he dined with us in company with his *petite amie* and on this occasion revealed his own constancy by appealing to mine. '*Nous persistons, n'est-ce pas?*' he whispered to me as I was serving him. To which I replied with a decisive and discreet '*C'est entendu.*' I served him with a deference that was really deference towards myself, and more than once I addressed Zaza, who was indulging in roguish winks and covert glances, as '*madame la marquise*' – a simple tribute of gratitude.

After this there was nothing frivolous in informing Monsieur Machatschek that family circumstances would compel me to leave my post in the Saint James and Albany on August 1. He would not hear of it, he said I had not given the required notice, that I was indispensable, that after this desertion I would never find another job, that he would withhold my salary for the current month, and so forth. He accomplished nothing by this. I simply bowed in pretended compliance and determined to leave the place before the 1st – in fact, at once. For if the time seemed long before I might enter on my new and higher existence, in reality it was all too short to prepare for my travels and to assemble the wardrobe I owed my new position in life. I knew that my ship, the *Cap Arcona*, was to leave Lisbon on August 15th and I thought I ought to be there a week ahead. And so one can see how little time there was for the necessary arrangements and purchases.

I discussed this matter with the stay-at-home traveller on the occasion when I left my private refuge to call on him in his attractive three-room apartment in the rue Croix des Petits Champs, after having withdrawn my funds – that is, after transferring them to him. I had left the hotel silently in the early morning, disdainfully leaving my livery behind and relinquishing my month's salary with indifference. It cost me some effort to give my old, shopworn, and already odious name to the servant who opened the door to me at Venosta's, and I only succeeded by reflecting that I was using it for the last time. Louis received me with excited cordiality and could hardly wait to hand over to me the all-important letter of credit for our journey. It was a double document, one part of it containing the bank's authorization for the traveller to make withdrawals up to the total amount, and the other a list of the correspondent banks in the cities where visits were planned. On the inside of this booklet was a place for the owner's signature as a means of identification, and Loulou had inscribed his there in the manner already so familiar to me. After this he not only handed over the railway ticket to Buenos Aires, but the kind young man presented me with a number of very attractive going-away presents: a flat gold monogrammed watch, a fine platinum chain, a black silk chatelaine for evening wear, also bearing the initials L. de V. in gold, one of those gold chains which run under the waistcoat to the back trouser pocket, and on which in those days men liked to carry their lighters, knives, and pencils, and a thin gold cigarette case. All this was delightful enough, but there was a certain solemnity in the moment when he put on my finger an exact copy of his seal ring which he had wisely had made, a ring with the family coat of arms in malachite – a castle gate flanked by towers and guarded by griffins. This action, which was accompanied by a pantomimed 'Be as I', awakened so many memories of stories heard in childhood, tales of disguise and recognition, that I was filled with strange and profound emotions. Loulou's little laughing eyes, however, were more roguish than ever and clearly revealed that he was determined not to neglect any detail of the hoax and that, quite apart from its purpose, it gave him enormous fun.

We discussed a number of other matters as we sat drinking Benedictine and smoking excellent Egyptian cigarettes. He no longer had the slightest misgivings on the score of my handwriting, but he approved my proposal to send him at his new address (Sèvres, Seine-et-Oise, rue Brancas) the letters I would receive from our parents, so that with his help I could comment, if only belatedly and by way of afterthought, on unforeseeable family or social incidents that would be sure to arise. Something else occurred to him: as he was devoting himself to art, I in his place would, at least on occasion, have to show some competence in that field. *Nom d'un nom*, how was I to manage that! We must not, I said, lose heart about it. And I asked for his sketchbook, which contained some blurred landscapes drawn on rough paper with very soft pencil or chalk, in addition to a number of female portraits and half- and whole-figure studies for which Zaza had obviously sat – or rather lain – as model. The heads were sketched, I may say, with an unjustifiable boldness, but one had to admit a certain resemblance – not much, but some. As for the landscape sketches, they had been lent a shadowy vagueness by the simple process of almost completely obliterating the lines with a stump and blurring them into misty indistinctness. Whether this procedure was artistic or fraudulent I was not called upon to say, but I decided at once that, cheating or no, it was something I could do. I asked for one of his soft pencils and one of the felt-tipped stumps, blackened by much use, with which he bestowed on his productions the consecration of vagueness. After glancing briefly into the air, I drew awkwardly enough a church steeple with storm-tossed trees beside it, meanwhile transmuting the childishness of my work into pure genius by aid of the stump. Louis seemed a little taken aback when I showed him the picture, but he was reassured as well and declared I need have no hesitation in showing my work.

He lamented, if only in the interest of his own reputation, that I should not have time to go to London and order the necessary suits from Paul, a famous tailor whom he patronized. I would require, he pointed out, tails, a frock coat, a cutaway with pin-striped trousers, as well as light, dark, and dark-blue lounge suits. He was all the more pleasantly surprised to discover my exact knowledge of the proper accessories in the way of linen and silk underclothing and various sorts of shoes, hats, and gloves. I still had time to get much of this in Paris – indeed, I would have been able to have had some suits made to order – but I abandoned this formality upon reflecting that any half-way decent suit, when I wore it, would look like the most expensive bespoke work.

The procuring of some things I needed, especially my white tropical wardrobe, was postponed until Lisbon. For my Paris purchases Venosta gave me some hundreds of francs which his parents had presented to him in preparation for the trip, and added to them a few hundred more from the capital I had made over to him. I volunteered to return this money from savings I would make during the trip. He gave me his sketch-book as well, together with some pencils and the helpful stump. Also a box of visiting-cards with our name and his address engraved at the top; he embraced me, laughing uproariously and pounding me on the back, hoped that I would soon be brimming with a flood of new impressions, and thus sent me forth into the wide world.

It was towards that wide world, kind reader, that I was borne, two weeks and a few days later, properly ensconced in a first-class compartment of the Nord-Sud Express. I sat by the window on the grey plush sofa, my arm on the folding arm-rest, my head reclining against the lace runner, my legs crossed; I was wearing a well-pressed suit of English flannel, and light spats over my patent-leather boots. My well-filled steamer trunk had been checked through; my calf-skin and alligator hand-luggage, all stamped with the monogram L. de. V. and the nine-pointed coronet, reposed in the luggage net.

I felt no need for occupation and no desire to read. To sit and be what I was – what better entertainment could there be? My soul was filled with a dream-like ease, but it would be a mistake to think that my satisfaction sprang solely or even predominantly from the fact that I was now so very distinguished a person. No, it was the change and renewal of my worn-out self, the fact that I had been able to put off the old Adam and slip on a new, that gave me such a sense of fulfilment and happiness. I was struck, though, by the fact that in this change of existence there was not simply delightful refreshment but also a sort of emptying out of my inmost being – that is, I had to banish from my soul all memories that belonged to my no longer valid past. As I sat there, I had ceased to have any right to them – which was certainly no loss. My memories! It was no loss whatever that they were no longer mine. Only it was not altogether easy to put others, to which I was now entitled, in their place with any degree of precision. It gave me a strange feeling of faulty memory, of emptiness of memory rather, as I sat there in my luxurious compartment. I became aware that I knew nothing about myself except that I had spent my child-hood and early youth on a nobleman's estate in Luxemburg; there were only a few names like Radicule and Minime to give any degree of precision to my new past. Yes, if I so much as wanted to picture the castle within whose walls I had grown up, I had to call to my aid the representations of English castles on the china from which, in my former lowly existence, I had had to scrape remnants of food – and this, of course, amounted to mixing inadmissible memories with those that alone were appropriate to me now.

Such were the reflections that drifted through my dreaming mind to the rhythmic jolting and hurrying of the train. I do not say for a moment that they were distressing. On the contrary, that inner emptiness, that vagueness and confusion of memory, seemed to me in a kind of melancholy way appropriate to my distinguished position, and I was glad to let my face assume, as I stared straight ahead, a look of quiet, dreamy melancholy combined with a nobleman's helplessness.

The train had left Paris at six o'clock. Twilight fell, the lights went on, and my private abode seemed even more elegant than before. The conductor, a man well advanced in years, knocked softly on the door and raised his hand to the peak of his cap as he entered; returning my ticket, he repeated the salutation. Loyalty and conservatism were to be read in that honest man's face; as he went through the train in the course of his lawful occasions, he came in contact with all strata of society, including the questionable elements, and it was a visible pleasure for him to behold in me wealth and distinction, the fine flower of the social order whose very sight raised and refreshed his spirits. About my well-being, once I had ceased to be his passenger, he assuredly need have no concern. For my part, in place of any kindly questions about his family life, I gave him a gracious smile and a nod *de haut en bas* that assuredly confirmed him in his conservative principles to the point where he would gladly have fought and bled for them.

The man from the dining-car who was handing out reservations for dinner also knocked tentatively at my door. I accepted a number from him; and when, a short time later, the ringing of a gong in the corridor announced the meal, I got out my fitted travelling-case, adjusted my tie in front of the mirror, and then betook myself to the dining-car a few carriages forward. The steward directed me to my place with hospitable gestures and pushed in my chair.

A middly-aged gentleman of fragile appearance was already seated at the little table, busying himself with the hors d'œuvres. His dress was somewhat old-fashioned – I can still see his very high stock. He had a small grey beard, and as I greeted him politely he looked up at me with starlike eyes. I am unable to say in what the starlike quality of his glance consisted. Were the pupils of his eyes especially bright, soft, beaming? They were that, to be sure – but are eyes on that account starlike? 'The light in his eyes' is a common expression, but it refers to something purely physical; it by no means connotes the description that forced itself upon me; something specifically moral has to be involved for bright eyes to be starlike eyes.

They remained fixed on me as I sat down, and only very slowly was the accompanying expression of earnest attentiveness replaced by an assenting, or shall I say approving, smile. Only very tardily, after I was seated and was reaching for the menu, did he answer my greeting. It was exactly as though I had omitted that courtesy myself and the starry-eyed one was setting me an edifying example. And so involuntarily I repeated my 'Bonsoir, monsieur.'

He, however, went on: 'I wish you *bon appetit, monsieur.*' Adding: 'Your youth, I feel sure, will guarantee that.'

Reflecting that a man with starlike eyes was privileged to indulge in unconventional behaviour, I replied with a smile and a bow, already occupied with the plate of sardines, vegetable salad, and celery that the waiter was offering me. As I was thirsty I ordered a bottle of ale, a choice which my grey-bearded companion approved with no sign of fearing that he might be considered guilty of meddling.

'Very sensible,' he said. 'Very sensible to order a strong beer with your evening meal. It is calming and induces sleep, whereas wine usually has a stimulating effect and is prejudicial to sleep, except of course when taken in great quantity.'

'Which would be entirely contrary to my taste.'

'So I assumed. Besides, there is nothing to keep us from sleeping late tomorrow. We will not be in Lisbon until noon. Or is your destination closer?'

'No, I am going to Lisbon. A long trip.'

'No doubt the longest you've ever taken?'

'But a trivial distance,' I said, not answering his question directly, 'in comparison with all that lies before me.'

'Think of that!' he exclaimed, raising his eyebrows and throwing back his head in a gesture of mock astonishment. 'You are off on a serious tour of inspection of this star and its present inhabitants.'

His description of the earth as a star combined with the quality of his eyes made a strange impression on me. Besides, the adjective 'present' which he had applied to the earth's inhabitants immediately aroused in me a feeling of significance and vastness. And yet his manner of speech and the expressions he used were very much like those one uses with a child, a favoured child, to be sure; they held a touch of affectionate teasing. In the consciousness of looking even younger than I was, I took this in good part.

He had refused soup and sat opposite me idly except that from time to time he poured Vichy water into his glass, an action that had to be accomplished with care, for the car was swaying violently. I had simply glanced up from my food in some bewilderment at his words and had not replied. He, however, clearly did not wish the conversation to die, for he went on:

'Well, however long your journey may be, you ought not to neglect its beginning simply because it is a beginning. You are entering a very interesting country of great antiquity, one to which every eager voyager owes a debt of gratitude, since in earlier centuries it opened up so many travel routes. Lisbon, which I hope you will have time enough to see properly, was once the richest city in the world, thanks to the voyages of discovery. Too bad you did not turn up there five hundred years ago – at that time you would have found it wrapped in the rich scent of Eastern spices and you would have seen gold by the bushel. History has brought about a sorry diminution in those fine foreign possessions. But, as you will see, the country and people are still charming. I mention the people because a good part of all longing to travel consists in a yearning for people one has never seen, a lust for the new – to look into strange eyes, strange faces, to rejoice in unknown human types and manners. Or what do you think?'

What was I to think? Probably he was right in attributing part of the love of travel to curiosity, or 'lust for the new'.

'Thus you will find,' he continued, 'in the country you are approaching, a racial mixture that is highly entertaining because of its variety and confusion. The original inhabitants were mixed – Iberians, as of course you know, with a Celtic element. But in the course of two thousand years Venetians, Carthaginians, Romans, Vandals, Suevians, West Goths, and

especially the Arabs, the Moors, have co-operated to produce the type that
awaits you – not to forget a sizeable admixture of Negro blood from the
many dark-skinned slaves that were brought in at the time when Portugal
owned the whole African coast. You must not be surprised at a certain
quality of the hair, certain lips, a certain melancholy animal look in the
eye that appear from time to time. But the Moorish-Berber racial element, as
you will find, is clearly predominant – from the long period of Arab
domination. The net result is a not exactly heroic but decidedly amiable
type: dark-haired, somewhat yellowish in complexion and of delicate build,
with handsome, intelligent brown eyes.'

'I eagerly look forward to making its acquaintance,' I said, adding:
'May I ask, sir, whether you yourself are Portuguese?'

'Why, no,' he replied. 'But I have lived in Portugal for a long time. I
was in Paris this time only on a brief visit – on business. Official business.
I was about to say, if you look about you a bit you will find the Arabic-
Moorish influence everywhere in the architecture of the country. As far
as Lisbon is concerned, I must warn you about the poverty of its historical
buildings. The city, you know, lies on an earthquake fault, and the great
quake of the last century laid two-thirds of it in rubble. However, it has
become a very handsome place again with many sights worth seeing which
I can't too strongly recommend to you. Our botanical garden on the
western heights ought to be your first goal. There is nothing like it in all
Europe, thanks to a climate in which a tropical flora flourishes side by
side with that of the temperate zone. The gardens are crowded with arau-
caria, bamboo, papyrus, yucca, and every kind of palm tree. And there
you will see with your own eyes plants that really do not belong to the
present-day vegetation of our planet, but to an earlier one – I mean the
tree ferns. Go without delay and look at the tree ferns of the Carboniferous period. That's more than short-winded cultural history. That is geological time.'

Again I had the feeling of undefined vastness that his words had aroused
in me before.

'I shall certainly not miss them,' I assured him.

'You must forgive me,' he felt obliged to add, 'for giving you directions
in this way and trying to guide your steps. But do you know what you
remind me of?'

'Please tell me,' I replied smiling.

'A sea lily.'

'That sounds decidedly flattering.'

'Only because it sounds to you like a flower. The sea lily, however, is
not a flower but a sessile small animal of the deep sea, belonging to the
order of echinoderms and constituting probably its oldest species. We have
a quantity of fossils. Such non-mobile animals tend to take on flower-like
forms – that is to say circular symmetry like that of a star or a blossom.
The present-day descendant of the sea lily, the lily-star, is attached to the
ground by a stem only during its youth. After that it frees itself, emancipates
itself, and goes off adventurously swimming and clambering along the
coasts. Forgive me for this association of ideas, but like a modern sea lily
you have freed yourself from your stem and are now off on a tour of
inspection. One is tempted to give advice to this novice at locomotion ...
Allow me: Kuckuck.'

For a moment I thought something was the matter with him, and then
I understood. Although much older than I, he had introduced himself.

'Venosta,' I hastened to reply with an oblique bow, as I was, just then being served fish on my left.

'*Marquis* Venosta?' he asked with a slight raising of the eyebrows.

'At your service,' I replied in a deprecatory tone.

'Of the Luxemburg line, I assume. I have the honour of knowing a Roman aunt of yours, the Contessa Paolina Centurione, born a Venosta of the Italian branch. And that line in turn is related to the Szechényis of Vienna and so to the Esterhazys of Galantha. As you know, you have cousins and connexions everywhere, *monsieur le marquis*. You mustn't be surprised at my knowledge. Family history and the study of descent is my hobby, or rather my profession. Professor Kuckuck,' he completed his introduction. 'Paleontologist and Director of the Museum of Natural History in Lisbon, an as yet insufficiently known institution of which I am the founder.'

He drew out his wallet and handed me his card, which prompted me to offer him mine – that is to say, Loulou's. On his I found his given names, Antonio José, his title, his official position, and his Lisbon address. As to paleontology, his conversation had given me some inkling of his connexion with that subject.

We read the cards with mutual expressions of deference and pleasure. Then we put them in our pockets, exchanging short bows of acknowledgement.

'I feel free to say, *monsieur le professeur*,' I added politely, 'that I have been fortunate in my place at table.'

'The pleasure is altogether mine,' he replied. We had hitherto spoken in French; now he inquired: 'I assume you speak German, Marquis de Venosta? Your good mother, I believe, derives from Gotha – near my own native place – *née* Baroness Plettenberg, if I am not mistaken? You see I really do know my facts. So we can just as well –'

How could Louis possible have failed to inform me that my mother was a Plettenberg! I seized upon this new fact as something with which to enrich my memory.

'But with pleasure,' I replied, changing languages at his suggestion. 'Good Lord, as though I hadn't babbled German all through my childhood, not only with Mama but also with our coachman, Klosmann!'

'And I,' Kuckuck broke in, 'have become almost entirely unaccustomed to my native tongue and am only too happy to seize this opportunity of moving once more within its framework. I am now fifty-seven. It was twenty-five years ago that I came to Portugal. I married a child of the country – *née* da Cruz, since we are speaking of names and families – of ancient Portuguese stock, and if a foreign language is to be spoken, French is far closer to her than German. And our daughter, for all her affection for me, does not share her Papa's taste in tongues, but prefers, after Portuguese, to chatter very prettily in French. A completely enchanting child. Zouzou, we call her.'

'Not Zaza?'

'No, Zouzou. It comes from Susanna. What does Zaza come from?'

'I really can't say. I have encountered it occasionally – in artistic circles.'

'You move in artistic circles?'

'Among others. I'm a bit of an artist myself, a painter and sketcher. I studied under Professor Estompard, Aristide Estompard of the Académie des Beaux-Arts.'

'Oh, an artist in addition to all the rest. Very gratifying.'

'And you, professor, were certainly in Paris on museum business?'

'You have guessed it. The purpose of my trip was to secure from the Paleo-Zoological Institute a few skeletal fragments that are very important to us – the skull, ribs, and shoulder-blade of a long-extinct species of tapir, from which through many evolutionary stages our horse has descended.'

'What's that, our horse descended from the tapir?'

'And from the rhinoceros. Yes, your riding-horse, marquis, has passed through the most varied forms. At one time, when it was already a horse, it was of Lilliputian size. Oh, we have learned names for all its earlier and earliest stages, names that end in *hippos*, "horse", beginning with "eohippos" – the original tapir, that is, which lived in the Eocene.'

'In the Eocene. I assure you, Professor Kuckuck, I will make a note of the name. When do they believe the Eocene was?'

'Recently. It is, geologically speaking, modern times, a few hundred thousand years ago, when the ungulates first appeared. Moreover, it will interest you as an artist to know that we employ specialists, masters of their craft, to reconstruct these extinct animals in highly presentable and lifelike fashion from their skeletal remains, and the men of former times as well.'

'The men!'

'The men as well.'

'The men of Eocene?'

'That is a bit early. We must admit that man's history is to some extent shrouded in darkness. He only emerged late, within the framework of the mammalian order, that much is scientifically well established. As we know him, he is a latecomer here, and the Biblical Book of Genesis is quite right in placing him at the pinnacle of creation. Only it abridges the process rather drastically. Organic life on earth, roughly speaking, has lasted some five hundred and fifty million years. It took some time to get to man.'

'I am extremely thrilled by what you say, professor.'

So I was. I was extremely thrilled – even then, and to an increasing degree henceforth. I listened to this man with such intense, enthralled interest that I almost forgot to eat. Dishes were passed to me, I helped myself and started to eat, but then I would forget to move my jaws as I sat listening to his words, knife and fork idle in my hands, while I stared into his face and into his starlike eyes. I cannot give a name to the thirst with which my soul drank in all he had to say. However, without that concentrated and sustained receptivity, would I, after so many years, be able to repeat that conversation today, at least in its salient points, almost verbatim, indeed, I believe quite literally verbatim? He had spoken of curiosity, of the lust for the new, which makes up a good part of the longing to travel, and as he had done so, I recall, I had found something strangely challenging in what he said, something that impinged sharply upon my emotions. It was just this kind of provocation, this plucking of the inmost strings of one's being, that was to raise his edifying discourse to the height of infinite and intoxicating fascination, although he continued to speak calmly, coolly, in measured tones, at times with a smile on his lips ...

'Whether life has before it,' he went on, 'as long a period as it has behind it, no one can say. Its toughness is, of course, enormous, especially in its lowest forms. Would you believe that the spores of certain bacteria can sustain the uncomfortable temperature of outer space, minus two hundred degrees, for a full six months without perishing?'

'That's amazing.'

'And yet the emergence and continuance of life are limited to certain clearly defined conditions which have not always existed and will not exist forever. The time within which a star is habitable is finite. Life has not always existed and will not always exist. Life is an episode, on the scale of the aeons a very fleeting one.'

'That predisposes me in favour of the same,' I said. I used the phrase 'the same' out of pure excitement and a desire to express myself formally and by the book. 'There's a song,' I added, '"Gather Ye Rosebuds While Ye May".' In it there's a reference to "the glorious lamp of heaven, the sun", and its setting. I heard it when I was very young, and I have always liked it, but what you say now about "a fleeting episode" gives it a much profounder meaning.'

'And how the organic world hurried,' Kuckuck went on, 'to develop its orders and genera, exactly as though it knew the glorious lamp would not shine forever. That applies especially to the earliest phases. In the Cambrian – that's what we call the lowest level, the deepest formation of the Paleozoic period – plant life is, to be sure, meagre: seaweed, algae, and nothing more. Life emerged from salt water, from the warm primeval sea, you must understand. But all of a sudden the animal kingdom is represented not just by the most primitive animals, but by coelenterates, worms, echinoderms, arthropods – that is, by all the phyla except the vertebrates. It seems that less than fifty of the five hundred and fifty millions of years had passed before the first of the vertebrates came out of the water on to land – some of which had emerged by then. And after that, evolution, the development of genera, went on at such a pace that in barely two hundred and fifty million years the whole Noah's Ark, including the reptiles, was present, only the birds and mammals were still missing. And all this thanks to an idea that Nature seized upon in the earliest times and which she has never tired of exploiting up to and including man –'

'Please tell me what that is.'

'Oh, the idea is simple enough, just the cohabitation of cells, just the inspiration not to leave that slimy, glassy bit of primeval life, that elemental organism, by itself, but to construct, at first out of a few and then out of hundreds of millions, living designs of a higher order, multicellular creatures, great individuals – in short to create flesh and blood. What we call "flesh" and what religion deprecates as weak and sinful, as "subject to sin", is nothing but such an assemblage of organically specialized tiny individuals, a multicellular fabric. Nature pursued this precious basic idea of hers with true zeal – sometimes with too much zeal: once or twice she indulged in exaggerations of which she later repented. She was actually busy with mammals when she permitted an exuberance like the blue whale to occur – as big as twenty elephants, a monster not to be sustained or nourished on earth. She sent it into the deep, where that enormous mass of blubber, with vestigial hind legs, fins, and oily eyes, still carries on a rather harried existence, nursing its young in an uncomfortable position, dodging the whalers, and devouring tiny shell-fish. But much earlier than that, at the beginning of earth's middle ages in the Triassic period, long before a bird flew or a tree spread its leaves, we find true horrors, the dinosaurs, the giant reptiles – fellows that occupied more room than is seemly here below. One of those individuals was as high as a room and as long as a railway train, it weighed forty thousand pounds. Its neck was like a palm tree, and its head, compared to its bulk, was ridiculously small. These creatures of exaggerated bodily size must have been dumb as a post. They were, however, good-natured – as often happens with those who are awkward and helpless.'

'So they were not especially sinful, despite all that flesh?'

'Probably not, out of stupidity. What more shall I tell you about the dinosaurs? Perhaps this: they had a tendency to walk upright.'

And as Kuckuck turned his starry eyes on me, I was overcome with something like embarrassment.

'Well,' I said with pretended nonchalance, 'these fellows, for all their upright gait, cannot have been much like Hermes.'

'What makes you think of Hermes?'

'Excuse me, in the course of my education at the castle a good deal of attention was paid to mythology. It was my tutor's personal speciality.'

'Oh, Hermes,' he replied. 'An elegant deity. I won't take coffee,' he said to the waiter. 'Bring me another bottle of Vichy. An elegant deity,' he repeated. 'And the golden mean of human stature, neither too large nor too small. I knew an old master builder who used to say that anyone who wanted to build must first recognize the perfection of the human figure, for in it are contained the profoundest secrets of proportion. Those who find a mystic significance in proportions maintain that man – and so the god in human form as well – occupies the exact middle point in respect of size between the very largest objects in the universe and the very smallest. They say that the largest material body, a red giant star, is exactly as much larger than a man as the tiniest element in an atom, something that would have to be magnified a hundred billion times to become visible, is smaller than he.'

'That shows you how little it helps to walk upright if you don't maintain moderation in size.'

'Highly ingenious, your Hermes must have been,' my companion went on, 'along with his perfect proportions, according to report. The fabric of cells in his brain, if one may speak of such a thing in connexion with a god, must have assumed especially artful forms. But the point is this: if one pictures him as made of flesh and blood and not of marble or plaster or ambrosia, then a lot of natural history survives in him. It is remarkable how primitive, in contrast to the brain, human arms and legs still are. They retain all the bones you find in the most primitive land animals.'

'That is thrilling, professor. It's not the first thrilling piece of information you have given me, but it is among the most thrilling. The bones in human arms and legs are like those in the most primitive land animals! I am not shocked at that; I am thrilled. I won't speak of Hermes' famous legs. But think of a shapely feminine arm, an arm that embraces us if we are lucky, what the deuce are we to make of that?'

'It seems to me, dear marquis, that you make a kind of cult of the extremities. That is perfectly understandable as the expression of a highly evolved creature's rejection of the footless structure of the worm. But as far as the shapely feminine arm is concerned, one should never forget that the limb is simply the hooked wing of the primordial bird and the pectoral fin of the fish.'

'Good, good, I'll remember that in future. I think I can assure you that I'll remember it without bitterness or disenchantment but rather with affection. But the human being comes from the ape, or at least that's what one always hears?'

'Dear marquis, let us rather say he comes from Nature and has his roots there. We should not be too much blinded by his anatomical similarity to the higher apes; too much fuss has been made about that. The pig with its little blue eyes, its eyelashes, and its skin, has more human qualities than any chimpanzee – think how often naked human beings remind us of swine. Our brain, however, in point of structural development, is closest to that of a rat. Echoes of animal physiognomy are to be found among people wherever you look. You see the fish and the fox, the dog, the seal, the hawk, and the sheep. On the other hand, the whole animal world, once we have begun to take notice, strikes us as humanity disguised and bewitched ... Oh, indeed, men and animals are closely related! However, if we want to talk about descent, then we must say that men are descended from animals in just about the same way that the organic is descended from the inorganic. Something was added.'

'Added? What, if I may ask?'

'The same sort of thing that was added when Being arose out of Nothingness. Have you ever heard of spontaneous generation?'

'I'm extremely eager to.'

He glanced about briefly and then began in a confidential tone – obviously for no other reason than because I was the Marquis de Venosta:

'There have been not one but three spontaneous generations: the emergence of Being out of Nothingness, the awakening of Life out of Being, and the birth of Man.'

Kuckuck took a sip of Vichy after this declaration. He held his glass in both hands, since we were careening around a curve. The dining-car was almost empty, and most of the waiters were idle. Having neglected my meal, I now drank cup after cup of coffee, but I do not ascribe to that the ever-increasing excitement that took possession of me. Bending forward, I sat listening to my strange travelling-companion, who spoke to me of Being, of Life, of Man – and of the Nothingness from which all this had been generated and into which it would all return. There was no question, he said, that Life on earth was not only an ephemeral episode, but *Being itself was also* – an interlude between Nothingness and Nothingness. Being had not always existed and would not always exist. It had had a beginning and would have an end, and with it space and time; for they existed only through Being and through it were bound to each other. Space, he said, was nothing but the order of material things and their relationship to one another. Without things to occupy it, there would be no space and no time either, for time was only the ordering of events made possible by the presence of objects; it was the product of motion, of cause and effect, whose sequence gave time its direction and without which there would be no time. Absence of time and space, however, was the definition of Nothingness. This was extensionless in every sense, a changeless eternity, which had only been temporarily interrupted by spatio temporal Being. A greater duration, by aeons, had been vouchsafed to Being than to Life; but some time of a certainty it would end, and with equal certainty the end implied a beginning. When had time, when had events, begun? When had the first quiver of Being emerged from Nothingness in obedience to the words 'Let it be', words that contained within themselves ineluctably those other words 'Let it pass'? Perhaps the 'when' of Being had not been so very long ago and the 'when' of passing was not so very far ahead – possibly only a few billion years this way and that ... Meanwhile, Being celebrated its tumultuous festival in the measureless spaces that were its handiwork and in which it created distances congealed in icy emptiness. And he spoke of the gigantic setting of this festival, the universe, this mortal child of eternal Nothingness, filled with countless material bodies, meteors, moons, comets, nebulae, unnumbered millions of stars that swayed one another, were ordered by the effect of their gravitational fields into groups, clouds, galaxies, and super-systems of galaxies, each with enormous numbers of flaming suns, wheeling planets, masses of attenuated gas, and cold rubbish heaps of ice, stone, and cosmic dust ...

I listened in excitement, knowing well that to receive this information was a mark of distinction, a privilege I owed to one fact: that I was the Marquis de Venosta and that the Contessa Centurione in Rome was my aunt.

Our Milky Way, I learned, was one among billions; almost at its edge, almost like a wallflower, thirty thousand light years from its centre, was our local solar system with its gigantic but relatively insignificant ball of fire called 'the' sun, although it only deserved the indefinite article, and its loyal retainers within its gravitational field, among them the earth, whose joy and labour it was to spin on its axis at the rate of a thousand miles an hour and to circle about the sun at the rate of twenty miles a second, thereby creating its days and years – *its*, be it observed, for there were other quite different ones. The planet Mercury, for example, nearest to the sun, completed its revolution in eighty-eight of our days and in the same period rotated once on its axis, so that for it year and day were the same. There you could see what time amounted to – it had no more general validity than weight. Take, for example, the white companion of Sirius, where matter was in a state of such density that a cubic inch of it would weigh a ton here. Material objects on earth, our mountains or our bodies, were, by comparison, the lightest, fluffiest foam.

While the earth wheeled around its sun, so I was privileged to hear, the earth and its moon wheeled around each other, and at the same time our whole local solar system moved, and at no mean pace, within the framework of a vaster but still very local star group. This gravitating system in turn wheeled with almost vulgar velocity within the Milky Way; the latter, moreover, our Milky Way, was travelling with unimaginable rapidity in respect to its far-away sisters, and they, the most distant existing complexes, were, in addition to all their other velocities, flying away from one another, at a rate that would make an exploding shell seem motionless – flying away in all directions into Nothingness thereby in their headlong career projecting into it space and time.

This interdependent whirling and circling, this convolution of gases into heavenly bodies, this burning, flaming, freezing, exploding, pulverizing, this plunging and speeding, bred out of Nothingness and awaking Nothingness – which would perhaps have preferred to remain asleep and was waiting to fall asleep again – all this was Being, known also as Nature, and everywhere in everything it was one. I was not to doubt that all Being, Nature itself, constituted a unitary system from the simplest inorganic element to Life at its liveliest, to the woman with the shapely arm and to the figure of Hermes. Our human brain, our flesh and bones, these were mosaics made up of the same elementary particles as stars and star dust and the dark clouds hanging in the frigid wastes of interstellar space. Life, which had been called forth from Being just as Being had been from Nothingness – Life, this fine flower of Being – consisted of the same raw material as inanimate Nature. It had nothing new to show that belonged to it alone. One could not even say it was unambiguously distinguishable from simple Being. The boundary line between it and the inanimate world was indistinct. Plant cells aided by sunlight possessed the power of transforming the raw material of the mineral kingdom so that it came to life in them. Thus the spontaneous generative power of the green leaf provided an example of the emergence of the organic from the inorganic. Nor was the opposite process lacking, as in the formation of stones from silicic acid of animal origin. Future cliffs were composed in the depths of the sea out of the skeletons of tiny creatures. In the crystallization of liquids with the illusory appearance of life, Nature was quite evidently playfully crossing the line from one domain into the other. Always when Nature produced the deceptive appearance of the organic in the inorganic – in sulphur flowers, for instance, or ice ferns – she was trying to teach us that she was one.

The organic world itself had no clear divisions within it. The animal kingdom verged on the vegetable when it acquired a stem and circular symmetry like a flower; the vegetable on the animal when it caught animals and ate them instead of deriving its nourishment from the mineral kingdom. Man had emerged from the animal kingdom by descent, as people said, but in truth through the addition of something that was as impossible to define as the essence of Life or the origin of Being. And the point at which he had become a man and was no longer an animal, or no longer simply an animal, was hard to determine. Man retained his animal nature just as Life retained that which was inorganic; for in its ultimate building-blocks, the atoms, it passed into what was no longer organic or not yet organic. Moreover, in its innermost sanctuary, in the invisible atom, matter took refuge in the immaterial, the no longer corporeal; for what was in motion there, the constituent parts of the atom, were almost below Being, since they occupied no definite position in space and did not have a definable mass as any reasonable body should. Being was formed from Not-Yet-Being and passed into Hardly-Still-Being.

Nature in all its forms, from the earliest, simplest, almost immaterial, to the most highly evolved and liveliest, had always remained collective and its forms continued to exist side by side – star cloud, stone, worm, and Man. The fact that many animal species had died out, that there were no more flying saurians and no more mammoths, did not interfere with the fact that contemporaneous with Man the original animal went on existing in unaltered form, the unicellular infusorian, the microbe, with one opening in its cell body for ingestion and another for egestion – no more was required to be an animal, and not much more to be a human being either, in most cases.

This was Kuckuck's jest, a caustic one. He felt he owed a young man of the world a bit of caustic wit, and I laughed, too, as with trembling hand I raised to my lips my sixth – no, probably my eighth – demitasse of sugared mocha. I have said, and I say again, that I was extremely excited, thanks to a feeling of expansion that almost burst the limits of my nature and was the result of my companion's conversation about Being, Life, and Man. Strange as it may sound, this vast expansiveness was closely related to, or rather was identical with, what as a child or half a child I had described in the dream-like phrase 'The Great Joy', a secret formula of my innocence used at first to denote something special, not otherwise nameable, but soon endowed with an intoxicating breadth of significance.

There was progress, Kuckuck said, passing on from his joke; without doubt there was progress, from Pithecanthropus erectus to Newton and Shakespeare had been a long and definitely upward path. But as with the rest of Nature, so too in the world of men everything was always present at the same time, every condition of culture and morality, everything from the earliest to the latest, from the silliest to the wisest, from the most primitive, sodden, barbaric to the highest and most delicately evolved – all this continued to exist side by side in the world, yes, often indeed the finest became tired of itself and infatuated with the primitive and sank drunkenly into barbarism. But no more of that. He would, however, give Man and me, the Marquis de Venosta, our due and not conceal what it was that distinguished Homo sapiens from the rest of Nature, the organic and simple Being both, and which very likely was identical with the thing that had been added when Man emerged from the animal kingdom. It was the knowledge of Beginning and End. I had pronounced what was most characteristically human when I had said that the fact of Life's being only an episode predisposed me in its favour. Transitoriness did not destroy value, far from it, it was exactly what lent all existence its worth, dignity, and charm. Only the episodic, only what possessed a beginning and an end, was interesting and worthy of sympathy because transitoriness had given it a soul. But what was true of everything – the whole of cosmic Being had been given a soul by transitoriness, and the only thing that was eternal, soulless, and therefore unworthy of sympathy, was that Nothingness out of which it had been called forth to labour and to rejoice.

Being was not Well-Being; it was joy and labour, and all Being in space-time, all matter, partook if only in deepest sleep in this joy and this labour, this perception that disposed Man, possessor of the most awakened consciousness, to universal sympathy. 'To universal sympathy,' Kuckuck repeated, bracing his hands on the table as he got up and nodding to me as he looked at me with his starlike eyes.

'Good night, Marquis de Venosta,' he said. 'We are, I observe, the last people in the dining-car. It is time to go to bed. Permit me to hope that I shall see you again in Lisbon. If you like I will be your guide through my museum. Sleep soundly. Dream of Being and of Life. Dream of the whirling galaxies which, since they are there, bear with joy the labour of their existence. Dream of the shapely arm with its ancient armature of bones, and of the flowers of the field that are able, aided by the sun, to break up lifeless matter and incorporate it into their living bodies. And don't forget to dream of stone, of a mossy stone in a mountain brook that has lain for thousands upon thousands of years cooled, bathed, and scoured by foam and flood. Look upon its existence with sympathy. Being at its most alert gazing upon Being in its profoundest sleep, and salute it in the name of Creation! All's well when Being and Well-Being are in some measure reconciled. A very good night!'

Chapter Six

No one will doubt me when I say that despite my innate love of sleep and the ease with which I usually returned to my sweet, refreshing homeland in the unconscious, on that night sleep eluded me almost completely until nearly morning. Not even my well-made berth in the first-class compartment was of any avail. What had possessed me to drink so much coffee before my first night on a train – a train, moreover, that raced, rocked, jolted, stopped, and then jarred into motion again? To have done so was deliberately to rob myself of sleep in a way that my new, unsteady bed could never have done alone. I shall not maintain, although I am as sure of it today as I was then, that six or eight demitasses of mocha could never have accomplished this by themselves if they had not been the purely automatic accompaniment to Professor Kuckuck's thrilling table conversation, which was what had stirred me up so profoundly – I shall not maintain it because a reader of sensibility (and it is for such readers alone that I am setting down my confessions) will have realized it by himself.

Briefly, then, arrayed in silk pyjamas (which protect the person better than a nightshirt against bed linen that may not have been thoroughly washed) I lay awake that night until almost morning, sighing and twisting in an attempt to find a position that would lull me into Morpheus' arms; when slumber finally stole upon me unaware, I had a series of confused dreams such as often accompany shallow, restless sleep. Seated on the skeleton of a tapir, I was riding along the Milky Way, which was easily recognizable because it really consisted of milk or was covered with milk which splashed up around the hoofs of my bony mount. I sat awkwardly and uncomfortably on his backbone, holding on to his ribs with both hands and being badly shaken back and forth by his eccentric gait, which may have been a dream version of the hurrying and jolting of the train. I, however, interpreted it as a reminder that I had not yet learned to ride and must learn to without delay if I was to maintain my position as a young man of family. A brightly dressed crowd streamed towards me, passing to right and left of me, their feet splashing in the Milky Way, small men and women, graceful, of yellowish complexion, with merry brown eyes. They shouted at me in an incomprehensible tongue – representing Portuguese, no doubt. One of them, however, called to me in French: '*Voilà le voyageur curieux!*' Because she spoke French, I recognized that it must be Zouzou, whereas her shapely arms, bare to the shoulder, indicated to me that instead – or rather at the same time – it had to be Zaza. I tugged at my tapir's ribs with all my strength to make him stop and let me dismount, for I longed to join Zouzou or Zaza and begin a conversation about the antiquity of the bony structure in her charming arms. But my mount began to buck fiercely and threw me off into the milk of the Milky Way, at which the dark-haired people, including Zouzou or Zaza, broke into derisive laughter. At this my dream dissolved, only to give place in my sleeping but restless brain to equally silly imaginings. I was, for example, crawling on all fours along a steep chalk cliff above the sea, dragging after me a long liana-like stem, in my heart an anxious doubt as to whether I was animal or plant – a doubt that was not unflattering since it was associated with the name 'sea lily'. And so forth.

At long last, in the morning hours, my sleep deepened to dreamlessness, and it was only a little before our midday arrival in Lisbon that I awoke. Breakfast was not to be thought of, and I had but scant time to wash and avail myself of my beautifully fitted crocodile travelling-case. Professor Kuckuck was not to be seen in the confusion of the station platform or on the square in front of the Moorish-looking station whither I followed my porter. The latter found me an open carriage. The day was bright and sunny, not too warm. The young coachman, who took charge of my steamer trunk and stowed it in the boot, might well have been one of the crowd who had laughed at my fall from the tapir on the Milky Way. He was of delicate build and yellowish complexion, exactly like Kuckuck's description; he had pointed moustaches and slightly Negroid lips, and was smoking a thin cigar; a round cloth cap clung to the side of his head, and his unruly dark hair was long at the temples. The alert expression in his brown eyes was not deceptive, for before I could name the hotel to which I had telegraphed for a reservation, he announced it himself, intelligently assigning me my place: 'Savoy Palace'. That was the sort of establishment where he thought I belonged, and I could only confirm his judgement with the words '*C'est exact.*' This he repeated, laughing, in murderous French as he swung himself into his seat and gave the horse a slap with the reins. '*C'est exact – c'est exact,*' he went on trilling happily during the short ride to the hotel. We had only a few narrow streets to negotiate before a broad, long boulevard opened before us, the Avenida da Liberdade, one of the most magnificent streets I have ever seen, a triple street indeed, with a path for carriages and riding-horses in the centre and well-paved avenues on either side, splendidly adorned with flower beds, statues, and fountains. It was on this magnificent *corso* that my palatial quarters were situated.

How different my advent there from my distressing arrival in the hotel on the rue Saint-Honoré in Paris! Instantly there were three or four liveried grooms and green-aproned porters busy with my baggage, unloading my steamer trunk and bearing hand-bags, coat, and plaid roll ahead of me into the lobby as expeditiously as though I had not a moment to lose. Thus I could stroll in, carrying over my arm only my cane of Spanish bamboo with its ivory handle and silver ferrule, and approach the reception desk, where no one flushed with anger or commanded me to step back, all the way back. Instead, at mention of my name, there were only kind, welcoming smiles, gratified bows, and a deferential request to fill in the required information if it was altogether agreeable to me. A gentleman in a morning coat, warmly interested in whether my trip had been entirely agreeable, escorted me to the second floor and into the apartment I had reserved, a salon and bedroom with a tiled bath. The appearance of these rooms, whose windows opened on the Avenida, enchanted me more than I allowed myself to show. I translated my satisfaction, or rather delight, at this lordly magnificence into a demeanour of casual acceptance and thus I dismissed my guide. Left alone, however, and awaiting the arrival of my luggage, I hurried about, examining my regal living-quarters with more childish joy than I should really have permitted myself.

I took special pride in the walls of the salon, lofty expanses of stucco framed in gilded moulding, such as I have always greatly preferred to the more bourgeois wallpaper. Together with the white-and-gold doors, which were tall, too, and were set in niches, they gave the chamber a decidedly palatial, princely aspect. It was very spacious and divided by an open arch into two unequal parts, the smaller of which could serve, if desired, as a private dining-room. There, as well as in the larger section of the room, hung a crystal chandelier with glittering prisms such as I have always loved. Bright, soft rugs with wide borders lay on the floor, leaving exposed here and there stretches of the highly polished surface. Agreeable paintings hung above the magnificent doors, and on one wall hung a tapestry representing a legendary rape. Beneath it was a cabinet with a pendulum and two Chinese vases. Handsome French arm-chairs stood in comfortable elegance around an oval table with a lace cover and a glass top.

On this, for the guest's refreshment, had been placed a basket of assorted fruits together with fruit knives and grape scissors, a plate of biscuits, and a polished finger-bowl – a courtesy on the part of the hotel management, as the card stuck between two oranges indicated. A cabinet with glass doors containing delightful porcelain figurines of cavaliers contorted into gallant postures, and ladies in crinolines, one of whom had suffered a tear in her dress so that the roundest part of her person was gleamingly revealed, to her great embarrassment as she looked back at it; standing lamps with silk shades, ornamental bronze candelabra on slender standards, a stylish ottoman with cushions and a silk cover completed the furnishings of the room. Its appearance delighted my starved eyes, as did the luxurious blue-and-grey décor of the bedroom, with its four-poster bed and upholstered easy chair, arms spread to invite reflective relaxation before sleep, the soft carpet from wall to wall absorbing all sound, the restful wallpaper, dull blue with long stripes, the tall pier glass, the gas-light in its milky sphere, the toilet table, the wide white closet doors with their glittering brass handles ...

My luggage arrived. I did not as yet have a valet at my disposal, as was occasionally the case later on. I put some necessaries in the drawers of the closet, hung up a few suits, took a bath, and made my toilet in the fashion that has always been peculiar to me. It somewhat resembles an actor's preparations, although the actual use of cosmetics has never tempted me because of the enduring youthfulness of my appearance. Arrayed in fresh linen and wearing a light flannel suit appropriate to the climate, I descended to the dining-room and there hungrily and enthusiastically made up for a dinner missed through listening and a breakfast missed through sleep. My lunch consisted of a ragout *fin*, a charred steak, and an excellent chocolate soufflé. Despite my pleasure in the meal, however, my thoughts still lingered on the conversation of the night before whose cosmic charm had made so deep an impression on my mind. Remembering it gave rise to a superior sort of joy not unrelated to my satisfaction in the distinction of my new existence. What occupied my thoughts more than the meal was wondering whether to get in touch with Kuckuck that very day – perhaps I should simply look him up at his home to make arrangements about visiting the museum and, more particularly, to make Zouzou's acquaintance.

That, however, might appear over-eager and precipitate. I succeeded in forcing myself to postpone my call until the following morning. Still far from rested, I determined to limit my activities for the day to a look around the city, and I set about this after my coffee. In front of the hotel I took a carriage to the Praça do Commércio, where my bank, likewise called Banco do Commércio, was situated; for I intended to make use of the letter of credit in my wallet to withdraw funds for my hotel bill and the various other expenses I would incur. The Praça do Commércio, a dignified and rather quiet square, is open on one side to the harbour, where the River Tagus makes a deep bend; the other three sides are lined with arcades, covered walks from which one enters the Customs House, the main Post Office, various ministries, and the bank for which I was bound. I was received by a black-bearded man of excellent manners and confidence-inspiring aspect, who respectfully examined my documents and set about carrying out my request with alacrity. He made the necessary entries with dexterity and then handed me his pen and a receipt, politely requesting me to sign it. I did not need so much as a glance at Loulou's signature in the document beside me to inscribe, with pleasure and affection, its exact copy, my lovely name, in sharp back-hand letters encircled by the oval loop. 'An original signature,' the clerk could not refrain from saying. I shrugged, smiling. 'A kind of heirloom,' I said apologetically. 'For generations we have signed ourselves that way.' He bowed courteously, and I left the bank, my lizard-skin wallet bulging with milreis.

From there I betook myself to the near-by Post Office, where I dispatched to my home, Castle Monrefuge, the following telegram: 'Arrived safely Savoy Palace and send warmest greetings. Brimming with new impressions of which I hope to write soon. Already observe some alteration in the direction of my thoughts which have not always been what they should be. Your grateful Loulou.' This accomplished, I went through a kind of arch of triumph or monumental gate on the side of the square opposite the harbour and into one of the smartest streets in the city, the Rua Augusta, where I had a social duty to discharge. I thought it would certainly be proper and in accordance with my parents' wishes if I were to pay a formal call at the Luxemburg Embassy, which was situated in the *bel étage* of a stately house. Without inquiring if the diplomatic representative of my native land and his wife were at home, I simply handed the servant who opened the door two of my cards, on one of which I had scribbled my address, with the request that he take them to Monsieur and Mme de Hueon. He was a man already well advanced in years, with stubbly grey hair, rings in his ears, rather broad lips and a kind of melancholy animal expression, which led me to reflect upon the composition of his blood and evoked my sympathetic interest. I nodded to him with special friendliness as I left, for, in a certain sense, he belonged to the period of colonial splendour and the golden world monopoly in spices.

Returning to the Rua Augusta, I followed that busy and crowded thoroughfare towards a square which the porter at my hotel had recommended to me as the most important in the city; it is called Praça de Dom Pedro Quarto, or, familiarly, the 'Rossio'. For purposes of clarity let me say that Lisbon is surrounded by hills, some of them of considerable height, and on these the white houses of the better residential districts rise almost without a break, flanking the straight streets of the new part of town. I knew that Professor Kuckuck's home was located somewhere in those upper regions and so I kept glancing in that direction; indeed, I inquired of a policeman (I have always liked to talk to policemen) more by gesture than by words for the Rua João de Gastilhos, the address I had read on Kuckuck's card. He pointed upward towards a street of villas and added in his tongue, which was as incomprehensible to me as the language I had heard in my dream, something about trams, cable cars, and *mulos*, obviously in reference to means of transportation. I thanked him repeatedly in French for this information, which was not of immediate importance to me, and he raised his hand to the brim of his summer helmet at the end of our brief but animated and pleasant interchange. How agreeable it is to receive such a mark of respect from these simple but smartly uniformed guardians of the public order!

I hope I may be permitted a general observation: that person is fortunate in whose cradle some good fairy has placed the gift of responding to pleasure, a perpetual responsiveness in even the most unlikely circumstances. No doubt this gift involves a heightening of responsiveness in general, the reverse of insensitivity, and therefore brings with it much pain which others are spared. But I cheerfully insist that the increase in joy more than compensates for that disadvantage – if it is one – and it is this gift of responsiveness to the smallest and even the most common-place pleasures that has always made me consider truly appropriate my first and real Christian name, Felix, about which my godfather Schimmel-preester felt so bitter.

How right Kuckuck had been in saying that the principal ingredient in the desire to travel is a vibrant curiosity about as yet unknown human types! With warm interest I studied the people in the busy streets, those black-haired, alert-eyed men and women who accompanied their conversa-tion with rapid southern gestures, and I made a point of getting into personal contact with them. Although I knew the name of the square I was approaching, I stopped a passer-by from time to time to ask the name – children, women, townsmen, sailors – simply to observe the play of ex-pression on their faces while they gave their almost invariably courteous and detailed answers, to listen to their alien speech in their hoarse, exotic tones, and then to part from them with friendly gestures. I placed a gift, the size of which may have been a surprise, in the cup of a blind beggar who sat on the pavement, leaning against the wall of a house, with a card-board sign beside him. To an elderly man who accosted me in a murmur, I gave an even more considerable sum. He was wearing a frock-coat with a medal, but his shoes were broken and he had no collar. He was touched and even wept a little as he bowed his thanks in a way that showed me he had slipped into penury from some higher level of society, whatever his weakness of character may have been.

When I finally, then, reached the Rossio with its two bronze fountains, its memorial columns, and its strangely wavy mosaic paving, there were many more occasions for asking questions of the strollers and the idlers sitting in the sun on the fountain edges – questions about the buildings that loomed so picturesquely in the blue above the houses bordering the square, the Gothic ruins of a church and a newer structure that proved to be the Municipio or City Hall. Below, the façade of a theatre occupied one side of the Praça, while two other sides were lined with shops, cafés, and restaurants. And so when finally, on the pretext of desiring informa-tion, I had had my fun with various children of this alien spring, I sat down at a table in front of one of the cafés to rest and take tea.

Close to me sat a group of three distinguished-looking persons, also enjoying late-afternoon refreshment, and to them my well-bred and un-obtrusive attention was at once attracted. There were two ladies, one con-siderably older than the other – mother and daughter, to all appearances; the third member of the party was a gentleman, just barely middle-aged, with an aquiline nose and spectacles. Below his Panama hat his hair fell in artistic fashion to the collar of his coat. He was hardly old enough to be the husband of the *senhora* and the father of the girl. As he ate his ice he held several neatly tied parcels on his lap, obviously out of courtesy, and two or three similar ones lay on the table in front of the ladies.

While I pretended to be interested in the play of the nearest fountain and in studying the architecture of the ruined church, I glanced sur-reptitiously at the trio. My curiosity and lively interest centred on mother and daughter – for such I considered them – and their disparate charms blended in my mind into an enchanting image of that relationship. This has been a characteristic of my emotional life. Earlier in this book, I reported the feelings with which, as a young pavement loafer, I had drunk in the glimpse of a lovely brother and sister who appeared for a few minutes on the balcony of the Hotel Zum Frankfurter Hof. I remarked explicitly that such excitement could not have been aroused in me by either of the figures alone, either his or hers, but that their lovely brother-and-sister duality was what had moved me so deeply. The connoisseur of humanity will be interested in the way my penchant for twofold enthusiasms, for being enchanted by the double-but-dissimilar was called into play in this case by mother-and-daughter instead of brother-and-sister. At all events, I find it very interesting. I will just add, however, that my fascination was soon enhanced by a sudden suspicion that coincidence was here engaged in an extraordinary game.

At the very first glance the young person – eighteen, as I guessed, and wearing a simple loose summer dress of striped bluish material with a belt of the same stuff – reminded me startlingly of *Zaza*, but at once I am in honour bound to add 'except that'. Another Zaza, except that her beauty, or if that is too exalted a word and more applicable to her mother (this is a subject I shall return to directly) – except that her prettiness, then, was, so to speak, more demonstrable, more authentic, and more naïve than that of Loulou's friend, with whom everything was simply froufrou, a little *feu d'artifice* and an optical illusion not to be examined too closely. Here was dependability – if a word belonging to the moral order can be applied to the world of charm – a childish forthrightness of expression, of which in the sequel I was to receive disconcerting evidence ...

A different Zaza – so different, in fact, that on reflection I asked myself whether any actual similarity existed even though I thought I had seen it with my own eyes. Did I perhaps believe I had seen it only because I *wanted* to see it, because I, strange to say, was in search of Zaza's double? I am not altogether clear in my own mind on this point. Certainly in Paris my emotions had not been in competition with those of the good Loulou; I was not the slightest bit in love with Zaza, however much I liked to flirt with her. Can it have been that as part of my new identity I had assumed the obligation of falling in love with her? Had I fallen in love with her after the event and had I been hoping to meet another Zaza abroad? When I remember my sudden interest at Professor Kuckuck's mention of a daughter with so similar a name, I cannot entirely rule out this hypothesis.

Similarity? Eighteen years and black eyes constitute a similarity, if you like, although these eyes did not dart and flirt, but, narrowed a little by the thick lower lids, stared out with an expression of rather blunt inquiry when they were not sparkling with amused laughter. They were boyish – like the voice whose abrupt exclamations reached my ears a few times, a voice that was by no means silvery but rather brusque and hoarse, without any affectation, honest and direct, like a young boy's. In the nose there was no resemblance whatever: it was not a snub nose like Zaza's, but fine-bridged, although the nostrils were not particularly delicate. In the mouth, to be sure, even today I admit that there was a resemblance; in both instances the lips (whose lively red, in this case, was assuredly the work of Nature alone) were almost always parted, thanks to a habit of pursing the upper one, so that one saw the teeth between. The hollow under them, and the charming line of the chin leading down to the soft throat – these might well remind one of Zaza. Otherwise, everything was different, as memory shows me – transmuted from the Parisian to the exotic and Iberian, thanks especially to the tall tortoise-shell comb with which she held in place her high-piled hair. The hair was drawn back to leave her forehead bare, but at each temple there was a charming curl which again produced a foreign, southern, indeed Spanish effect. She wore her ear-rings – not the long, swaying jet pendants her mother wore, but close-fitting and yet sizeable flat opals surrounded by little pearls which matched the exotic quality of her whole appearance. The southern tint of her ivory skin was something that Zouzou – I called her that immediately – had in common with her mother, whose type and *tenue*, however, were of a quite different order, more imposing, not to say majestic.

Taller than her attractive child, no longer slender but by no means too heavy, this lady in the distinguished simplicity of cream-coloured linen, lace at throat and wrists, and long black gloves, was approaching matronly years without having yet reached them. One would have searched in vain for grey in the dark hair under the wide, flower-trimmed, fashionable hat. A black neckband edged with silver became her well, as did her swaying jet ear-rings, and added a note of dignity to the noble carriage of her head. This quality characterized her whole appearance and was expressed almost to the point of sombreness, almost to severity, in her rather large face with its haughty, compressed lips, flaring nostrils and the two deep creases between her brows. It was the sternness of the south, which many people fail to recognize, obsessed by the mistaken notion that the south is flattering and sweet and soft and that hardness is to be found only in the north, a completely erroneous idea. 'Ancient Iberian stock, presumably,' I thought to myself, 'therefore with a Celtic admixture. And every sort of Phoenician, Carthaginian, Roman, and Arabic strain may be involved. No one to be trifled with.' And I added in my mind that under the protection of such a mother, the daughter would be safer than with any possible male escort.

Nevertheless, it was reassuring that such an escort was present – as was only proper for two women in a public place. The respectable gentleman with the long hair sat nearest me of the three, almost shoulder to shoulder, since he had turned his chair sidewise to the table and his remarkable profile was exposed to me. I have never liked hair that falls to the collar, for, in the long run, it is bound to make the collar greasy. However, I overcame my repugnance and turned to this cavalier, throwing a glance of apology towards the two ladies, and addressed him in these words:

'Forgive, sir, the boldness of a stranger who has just arrived in this country and unfortunately has not yet mastered its language. I cannot converse with the waiter who naturally enough speaks nothing else. Forgive, I repeat' – and once more my glance strayed to the ladies as though barely daring to touch them – 'this unmannerly intrusion. But it is very important for me to gain certain specific information about this neighbourhood. I have the agreeable social duty, and the desire as well, to pay a call at a house in one of the residential streets of the upper city, the Rua João de Castilhos. The house in question – I add this in a sense to identify myself – is that of a famous Lisbon savant, Professor Kuckuck. Would you have the great kindness to tell me what means of transportation I might use for my little excursion?'

What an advantage it is to possess an easy and polished style of address, the gift of good form which that kind fairy thoughtfully laid in my cradle and which is so very necessary for the whole way of life I have adopted! I was satisfied with my speech although towards the end I had become a little disconcerted because the girl, when I named the street and then mentioned Professor Kuckuck, had begun to giggle and had come close to bursting into laughter. This, I say, confused me a little – since it could only confirm the suspicion that had prompted me to speak. The *senhora* glanced at her child, shaking her head in regal reproof at this outburst of merriment – and then could not keep a smile from her own severe lips, of which the upper one was darkened by the faintest shadow of a moustache. The gentleman with long hair was naturally astounded, since he – unlike the ladies, I may say – had not hitherto been aware of my presence. However, he answered very politely:

'Certainly, sir. There are various possibilities – not all to be recommended equally, let me add. You could take a fiacre, but the streets that go up there are very steep, and the passenger usually finds himself obliged to walk beside the carriage at various points. The mule bus is preferable; it gets up the steep places very well. But best of all is the cable car. The entrance is near here in the Rua Augusta, which you certainly already know. It will take you conveniently and directly to the immediate neighbourhood of the Rua João de Castilhos.'

'Splendid,' I replied. 'That's all I need. I can't thank you enough, sir. I shall follow your advice and I am very much obliged.'

Thereupon I settled myself in my chair, indicating clearly that I had no intention of continuing to be a bother. However, the girl – whom I already called Zouzou – seemed not to have been impressed by her mother's admonitory glances and went right on displaying her merriment, until finally the *senhora* was compelled to explain her behaviour.

'Forgive this child's frivolity, sir,' she said in harsh French, her voice an agreeable, husky contralto, 'but I am Madame Kuckuck of the Rua João de Castilhos, this is my daughter, Susanna, and this is Dom Miguel Hurtado, a professional colleague of my husband. I can hardly be mistaken' in assuming that I am addressing Dom Antonio José's travelling-companion, the Marquis de Venosta. My husband told us about his meeting with you when he arrived today.'

'Enchanted, madame,' I replied with sincere pleasure, bowing to her, to the young lady, and to Hurtado. 'This is a charming coincidence! My name is indeed Venosta and I had the pleasure of your husband's company for a time on the train from Paris. I will make bold to say I have never travelled to greater advantage. The professor's conversation is inspiring –'

'You musn't be surprised, *monsieur le marquis*,' young Susanna broke in, 'that your inquiry amused me. You inquire a great deal. I observed you on the square stopping every third person to inquire about something or other. Now you inquire from Dom Miguel about our own home –'

'You are forward, Zouzou,' her mother interrupted her – and it was wonderful to hear her addressed for the first time by the nickname I had long since assigned to her.

'Excuse me, Mama,' the girl retorted, 'but when you are young everything you say is forward, and the marquis, who is still young himself, hardly older than I am, it seems, was just a trifle forward too in beginning a conversation from one table to the next. Moreover, I have not told him what I wanted to say. First of all, I wanted to assure him that Papa did not burst out talking about him the minute he got home, as would almost appear from your words. He told us a great many other things first and then quite incidentally mentioned that he had dined the evening before with a certain de Venosta.'

The lady who had been born da Cruz shook her head reproachfully.

'Even when speaking the truth, my child,' she said, 'one must not be forward.'

'Good God, mademoiselle,' I said, 'it's a truth I never doubted. I did not imagine –'

'That's good. That's good. That you did not imagine!'

The mother: 'Zouzou!'

The girl: 'A young man with a name like that, *chère maman*, who in addition happens to be so good-looking, is in danger of imagining all sorts of things.'

After this there was nothing to do but join in the general merriment. Hurtado joined, too.

I said: 'Mademoiselle Susanna must not overlook the greater danger she herself runs of imagining things because of her own appearance. Added to this there is the natural temptation to pride oneself on such a papa – and such a mama,' bowing towards the *senhora*. Zouzou blushed – partly for her mother, who had not the slightest idea of blushing; but perhaps out of jealousy, too. She rescued herself in disconcerting fashion from this embarrassment by simply disregarding it and remarking with a gesture of the head towards me:

'What pretty teeth he has.'

Never in my life had I encountered such forthrightness. But any awkwardness the speech might have caused was removed when the girl replied to the *senhora's* 'Zouzou, *vous êtes tout à fait impossible!*' with the words:

'But he keeps showing them all the time. Clearly, he wants to have them mentioned. And besides, one ought not to be silent about something like that. Silence is unhealthy. A statement of fact is less harmful to him and to others.'

An extraordinary creature. How extraordinary, how complete a personal exception to all the accepted conventions of her society and country, was to become clear to me only later. Only through experience was I to learn with what almost monstrous forthrightness this girl was capable of acting up to her remarkable principle that silence is unhealthy.

There was a somewhat embarrassed pause in the conversation. Mme Kuckuck-da Cruz drummed lightly on the table with her fingertips. Hurtado adjusted his glasses. I came to the rescue by saying:

'We should probably all do well to profit by Mademoiselle Susanna's pedagogical gift. She was completely right in the first instance in saying it would be ridiculous to assume that her honoured father began his account of his trip by mentioning me. I'll wager he began by the success of his mission, the acquisition in Paris of certain skeletal remains of a very important but unfortunately long-extinct species of tapir that lived in the ancient Eocene.'

'You are entirely right, Marquis,' the *senhora* said. 'That was exactly what Don Antonio spoke of first of all, just as he seems to have spoken of it to you, and here you see someone who is especially pleased by this acquisition since it will mean employment for him. I introduced Monsieur Hurtado to you as my husband's professional colleague. He is, in fact, an admirable animal-sculptor. He has not only created all kinds of contemporary animals for our museum, but he is also able to re-create most convincingly, with the aid of fossils, creatures that have long since vanished.'

That's the reason for wearing his hair down to his coat collar, I thought.

It isn't absolutely necessary. Aloud, I said: 'But, madame – but, Monsieur Hurtado – things couldn't have turned out better! In point of fact, the professor talked to me during the trip about your amazing abilities and now, as good luck will have it, I meet you on my first expedition into the city.'

What did Miss Zouzou say to this? She had the presumption to say: 'How delightful! Why don't you fall on each other's necks? Your acquaintance with us presumably amounts to very little in comparison with this meeting you are rejoicing over. And yet, marquis, you don't look in the least as though you were especially interested in science. Your real interests probably lie more in ballet and horses.'

One might well have disregarded these remarks. I replied, nevertheless: 'Horses? In the first place, mademoiselle, the horse is really related, though at a distance, to the tapir of the Eocene. And even a ballet might prompt one to scientific reflection by awakening recollections of the primitive bony structure of the pretty legs one sees there. Pardon me for mentioning it, but it was you who brought the subject up. Moreover, you are at liberty to take me for an idler with the most banal interests and no feeling for higher things, for the cosmos or the three spontaneous generations of universal sympathy. That is your privilege, as I say, only it is possible you might be doing me an injustice.'

'It's your duty, Zouzou,' her mother said, 'to explain that that was not your intention.'

But Zouzou remained obstinately silent.

Hurtado, on the other hand, was visibly flattered by my enthusiastic greeting and politely took up the conversation.

'Mademoiselle,' he said by way of apology, 'is fond of teasing, *monsieur le marquis*. We men must put up with it, and which of us is not happy to do so? She teases me all the time, calls me the taxidermist because at the beginning that was indeed my occupation: I earned my daily bread by stuffing dead pets, canaries, parrots, and cats and providing them with bright glass eyes. From that, to be sure, I went on to higher things, to plastic reconstruction, from journeyman labour to art, and now I no longer need dead animals to create lifelike models. To do this requires more than manual skill; it requires long observation of nature and long study, that I will not deny. My own abilities in this field have, for a number of years, been at the service of our Natural History Museum – moreover, I am not alone, there are two other artists working in the same department of the Kuckuck Foundation. For the reconstruction of animals of another geological period – the reproduction of archaic life, that is – one naturally requires a sound anatomical basis from which the whole creature can be logically deduced, and it is for this reason that I am so pleased that the professor has succeeded in acquiring in Paris the requisite skeletal remains of this early ungulate. I will be able to proceed from what we have. The animal was no larger than a fox and certainly still had four well-developed toes on the front feet and three on the hind ...'

Hurtado had grown quite warm while talking. I congratulated him heartily on his magnificent assignment, only regretting that I should not be able to see the result of his labours because my ship sailed in a week's time, the ship to Buenos Aires. But I was determined to see as much as possible of his earlier work. Professor Kuckuck had most kindly offered to be my guide through the museum. I had it very much in mind to make an appointment.

That could be done at once, Hurtado said. If I would come to the museum in the Rua do Prata, not far from here, next morning at eleven o'clock, the professor would be there as well as his unworthy self, who would consider it an honour to be allowed to take part in our tour of inspection.

Wonderful! I at once shook hands with him in agreement, and the ladies countenanced the arrangement with varied degrees of good will. The *senhora*'s smile was condescending, Zouzou's mocking. But even she joined with reasonable good grace in the short conversation that followed, although not without a trace of what Monsieur Hurtado had called teasing. I learned that 'Dom Miguel' had gone to meet the professor at the station and had accompanied him home and had taken luncheon with the family. Escorting the ladies afterwards on their shopping-tour, he had finally brought them to this place for refreshment. Without male escort, they would not, according to the customs of the country, have been allowed to appear there. There was talk, too, of my projected trip, the year-long journey around the world to which my dear parents in Luxemburg were treating me – their only son, for whom they happened to have a weakness.

'*C'est le mot,*' Zouzou could not refrain from interjecting. 'That certainly could be called a weakness.'

'I see you are still worried about my modesty, mademoiselle.'

'That would be a lost cause,' she replied.

The mother reproved her: 'My dear child, a girl must learn to distinguish between propriety and prickliness.'

And yet it was just this prickliness that gave me hope that one day – few though my days were – I would be able to kiss those charming, pouting lips.

It was Mme Kuckuck herself who strengthened me in this hope by formally inviting me to lunch next day. Hurtado meanwhile launched into a consideration of the sights I must not fail to see during my limited stay. He recommended the exhilarating view of town and river from the public gardens in the Passeio da Estrella, spoke of an approaching bull-fight, praised in particular the cloister of Belem, a pearl of architectural art, and the castles in Sintra. I, on the other hand, admitted that the object of interest I had heard about that had attracted me most was the botanical garden, where there were said to be plants belonging to the Carboniferous period rather than to the present day, specifically the tree ferns. That interested me more than anything else, and must be my first objective after the Museum of Natural History.

'A walk and nothing more,' the *senhora* declared. It would be pleasant to undertake it. The simplest thing would be for me to have lunch *en famille* after my visit to the museum in the Rua João de Castilhos and to plan to make the botanical promenade in the afternoon either with or without Dom Antonio José.

She made this proposal and issued this invitation majestically; it goes without saying that I accepted it with polite surprise and gratitude. Never, I said, had I looked forward with more joyful anticipation than to the next day's programme. After these arrangements had been made, we got up to go. Hurtado paid the waiter. Not only he, but Mme Kuckuck and Zouzou, too, gave me their hands. Everyone said: '*À demain, à demain*', even Zouzou. But she added mockingly: '*Grâce à l'hospitalité de ma mère.*' And then, dropping her eyes a little: 'I don't like to say what I'm told to say. That's why I postponed telling you that it was not my intention to be unfair to you.'

I was taken aback by this sudden mitigation of her prickliness that I called her Zaza by mistake.

'*Mais, Mademoiselle Zaza –*'

'Zaza!' she repeated, bursting into laughter, and turned her back on me. I had to call after her: '*Zouzou! Zouzou! Excusez ma bévue, je vous en prie!*'

While I made my way back to the hotel past the Moorish railway station and through the narrow Rua do Principe, which connects the Rossio with the Avenida de Liberdade, I scolded myself for that slip of the tongue. Zaza! She had been simply herself, companioned only by her beloved Loulou – not by a proud, ancient Iberian mother – and that, after all, made an enormous difference!

Chapter Seven

The Museum Ciências Naturães of Lisbon, situated in the Rua da Prata, is only a few steps from the Rua Augusta. The façade of the building is unimpressive; there is neither gate nor staircase. One simply walks in, but even before passing through the turnstile next to the cashier's table with its array of photographs and picture postcards, one is amazed by the extent and depth of the entrance hall. The visitor is greeted from afar by a stirring scene from Nature. Approximately in the centre of the room stands a dais, grass-covered, with a background of dark forest thicket, partly painted, partly constructed of real leaves and bushes. On slender legs, hoofs close together, a white stag stands as though just emerging, crowned by antlers with magnificent points and palms. His aspect is both dignified and alert as he cocks his ears forward and surveys approaching visitors with wide-spaced eyes, gleaming, calm yet alert. The ceiling light in the hall fell directly on the grassy plot and the shimmering figure of the proud and wary animal. One feared that if one moved so much as a single step he would disappear at a bound into the darkness of the thicket. And so I lingered, rooted to the spot by the timidity of the lonely creature there, without at once being aware of Senhor Hurtado, who stood waiting at the foot of the dais, his hands behind his back. He came towards me, signalling to the cashier that I was to be admitted without charge, and manipulated the turnstile himself, meanwhile expressing the heartiest welcome.

'I see, *monsieur le marquis*,' he said, 'you are captivated by our receptionist, the white stag. Quite understandable. A good piece. No, I didn't create him. That was done by someone before my time here. The professor is expecting you. May I take the liberty –'

But he had to give me smiling leave to go over to the magnificent animal, which fortunately could not flee, and examine it from close at hand.

'No fallow buck,' Hurtado explained. 'He belongs to the class of noble red deer, which at times are white. However, I am probably talking to an expert. You are a hunter, I assume?'

'Only occasionally, only when it is socially necessary. Here, nothing is further from my thoughts. I believe I would not be able to raise a gun against him. There's something legendary about him. And yet – I am right, am I not, Senhor Hurtado – and yet the deer is a ruminant?'

'Certainly, *monsieur le marquis*. Like his cousins, the reindeer and the elk.'

'And like the ox and cow. You know, one can see it. There is something legendary about him, but one can see it. He is white, by exception, his antlers give him the look of a king of the forest, and his gait is delicate, but his body betrays the family – against which there is nothing to be said. If one examines the rump and hindquarters carefully and thinks about a horse – the horse is nervier, although one knows he is descended from the tapir – then the stag strikes one as a crowned cow.'

'You are a critical observer, *monsieur le marquis.*'

'Critical? Not at all. I have a feeling for the forms and representations of life and Nature, that's all. A feeling for them. A certain enthusiasm. The ruminants have, after all, as I understand it, very remarkable stomachs. There are various compartments in them, and from one they regurgitate what they have eaten. Then they lie and thoroughly chew their cuds once more. You might say it is strange for anyone with such odd family customs to be crowned king of the forest, but I honour Nature in all her inventions and I can quite well put myself in the position of a ruminant! After all, there is such a thing as universal sympathy.'

'No doubt,' Hurtado said, taken aback. He was actually somewhat embarrassed by my exalted manner of speech – as though there were any less exalted way of saying 'universal sympathy'. Because he was stiff and nonplussed from embarrassment, I hastened to remind him that the master of the establishment was waiting for us.

'Very true, marquis. I would be wrong to keep you here any longer. To the left, if you please –'

Kuckuck's office opened off the long corridor. He got up from his desk as we entered, and removed his working-glasses from his star-like eyes, which I recognized as though I had first seen them in a dream. His greeting was cordial. He expressed his pleasure at the accident which had already brought me and his ladies together, and at the arrangements we had made. We sat around his desk for a few minutes while he inquired about my lodgings and my first impressions of Lisbon. Then he said: 'Shall we make our tour of inspection now, marquis?'

This we did. Outside, in front of the stag, there now stood a school-class of ten-year-olds to whom the teacher was lecturing about the animal. They glanced from it to him with equal respect. Then they were led off to inspect the glass cases along the walls which contained collections of beetles and butterflies. We did not linger over them, but at once turned to the right into a series of large and small rooms opening into one another and providing food enough and to spare for anyone with a taste for representations of life such as I had boasted of possessing. Everywhere in the room and hall the receptive eye was caught by forms that had poured uninterruptedly from Nature's womb. Next to the awkward first experiment were the most elaborately evolved, the most perfect of their kind. Behind a glass window was the replica of a patch of sea bottom where the earliest forms of organic life teemed in a kind of furious untidiness of design. Right beside it one saw cross-sections of shells from the lowest strata – of such minute workmanship inside that one could not but wonder at the meticulous artistry Nature had attained in that far bygone day. The soft, headless creatures whose homes these shells had been had mouldered away millions of years ago.

We encountered individual visitors, who had certainly had to pay the modest entrance fee, and were unescorted since their social position gave them no claim to special attention. They were obliged to garner their information from the labels attached to the exhibits which were, of course, written in the language of the country. They gazed at our little group with curiosity, no doubt taking me for a visiting prince for whom the management was doing the honours of the establishment. I will not deny I found this pleasant; and there was the added charm of the contrast between my own fineness and elegance and the primitive crudity of many of the uncanny-looking fossils, the primeval crustaceans, cephalopods, brachiopods, tremendously ancient sponges, and entrail-less lily-stars – Nature's experiments, whose acquaintance I was briefly making.

All this inspired in me the moving reflection that these first beginnings, however absurd and lacking in dignity and usefulness, were preliminary moves in the direction of me – that is, of Man; and it was this that prompted my attitude of courteous self-possession as I was introduced to a marine saurian, a bare-skinned, sharp-jawed creature, represented by a five-metre-long model floating in a glass tank. This friend, who could have attained proportions much greater than those shown, was a reptile but had the shape of a fish and resembled a dolphin, which, however, is a mammal. Hovering thus between the classes, it ogled at me from the side while my own eyes, even as Kuckuck was speaking, wandered ahead to farther distances where there appeared to be a life-sized dinosaur, extending through several rooms and protected by a red velvet cord. That is how it is in museums: they offer too much; the quiet contemplation of one or a few of the objects from their store would certainly be more profitable for the mind and soul; as soon as one steps in front of one, his glance is lured on to another whose attractiveness distracts the attention, and so it goes through the whole series of exhibits. I speak, however, from a single experience, for later I hardly ever visited such places of instruction.

As for the immoderate creature which Nature had abandoned and which was faithfully reproduced here on the basis of fossil remains, no single room in the building could have contained him – he was all in all, God save the mark, forty metres long – and although two rooms connected by an open archway had been set aside for him, it was only through skilful arrangement of his limbs that these met his requirements. We went through one room past the monstrous coils of his tail, his leathery hind legs, and part of his bulging rump; near his upper body, however, a tree trunk – or was it a short stone column? – had been erected and on this the poor creature supported himself with one foot, not without a kind of monstrous grace, while his endless neck and trivial head were bent down towards this foot in troubled meditation – or is meditation possible with a sparrow brain?

I was much touched by the appearance of the dinosaur and addressed it in my mind: 'Don't be sad! It's true you have been cast out and cashiered for lack of moderation, but as you see, we have built a statue to you and we remember you.' And yet not even this, the museum's most famous exhibit, completely held my attention, which was diverted by a simultaneous attraction. Hanging from the ceiling, its leathery wings outspread, was a flying saurian, the primordial bird with reptilian tail and claws on its wing tips. Near by were egg-laying mammals with pouches for their young, and, a little farther on, stupid-looking giant armadillos, whom Nature had considerately protected with a heavy armour of bony plates on back and flanks. But Nature had been just as solicitous of their ravenous boarders, the sabre-tooth tigers, and had provided them with such powerful jaws and rending teeth that they could handle the bony armour and tear great slices of no doubt tasty flesh from the armadillos' bodies. The larger and more heavily armoured the unwilling host became, the more monstrous grew the jaws and teeth of the guest who joyfully leaped upon him at meal-time. One day, however, Kuckuck informed us, climate and vegetation played a prank on the giant armadillos by depriving them of their innocent nourishment, and they became extinct. And there sat the sabre-tooth tiger, after that mighty contest, there he sat with his jaws and his armour-rending teeth and fell rapidly into despondency and gave up the ghost. He had done everything out of regard for the growing armadillo so as not to be left behind but to go on being able to crunch its bones. The latter, in turn, would never have grown so large or so heavily armoured if it had not been for that connoisseur of his flesh. But if Nature wanted to defend him by constantly increasing his coat of mail, why had she, at the same time, steadily strengthened the jaws and sabre-teeth of his enemy? She had been on both sides – and so, of course, on neither – had only been playing with them, and when she had brought them to the pinnacle of their capacities she deserted them. What is Nature thinking of? She is thinking of nothing at all, nor can Man ascribe thoughts to her; he can only admire her busy impartiality when he strolls, as an honoured guest, among the multiplicity of her manifestations, of which such beautiful reproductions, in part the creation of Senhor Hurtado, filled the halls of Kuckuck's museum.

Further introductions were made: the hairy mammoth with its upward-curving tusks, now extinct, and the rhinoceros with its thick, flabby skin which looks extinct but is not. The half-apes gazed down at me from the branches they crouched on, with over-large mirror eyes, and the nocturnal loris won a permanent place in my heart because, quite apart from those eyes, it had such delicate hands and slender arms – which concealed, of course, the same bony armature as that of the most primitive land animals. And the lemur with eyes like teacups and long, thin fingers clasped in front of its breast, and amazingly wide-spaced toes. These faces were like a trick of Nature to make us laugh; I, however, refrained from so much as a smile. For very clearly in the end they all prefigured me, even though disguised as in some sorry jest.

How can I name and praise all the animals the museum had on view, the birds, the nesting white herons, the surly owls, the thin-legged flamingos, the hawks and parrots, the crocodiles, the seals, the frogs, the moles and warty toads – in short, whatever creeps or flies? There was a little fox I shall never forget because of his witty face. I should have liked to pat them all on the head, the foxes, lynxes, sloths, omnivores, yes, even the jaguar in a tree with his slanting eyes green and false, and his look of having been assigned a destructive and bloody role – I should have liked to pat them all, and here and there I did so, although touching exhibits was forbidden. But what freedom might I not allow myself? My guides were entertained to see me shake hands with a bear that was lumbering along on his hind feet, and give an encouraging slap on the back to a chimpanzee that had sunk down on his knuckles.

'But Man, professor!' I said. 'After all, you spoke of Man. Where is he?'

'In the basement,' Kuckuck replied. 'If you have pondered everything here, marquis, we will descend.'

'Ascend, you mean,' I substituted in jest.

There was artificial illumination in the basement. Wherever we went, little theatres were let into the wall behind glass panes, with life-like scenes from the early life of Man. We paused in front of each of them to listen to the commentary of the master of the establishment, and again and again, at my request, returned from a later to an earlier one, however long we might already have stood there. Does the kind reader perhaps recall how in my earlier days I had been at pains to search among the pictures of my forebears for some hint or indication of the source of my own striking physical perfection? Early experiences in life always recur in heightened form, and I now felt myself conpletely reimmersed in that activity as, with probing eyes and beating heart, I saw what had been striving towards me from the grey reaches of antiquity. Good God, what were those small, shaggy creatures squatting together in timid groups as though conferring in some cooing and hissing pre-language about the means of surviving and prospering on an earth already possessed by much better-equipped and more strongly armed creatures? Had the spontaneous generation of which I had been told, the separation from the animal, already taken place or had it not? It had, it had, if anyone asked me. There was proof of it in these shaggy creatures' obvious sense of strangeness and helplessness in a world which had been given to others and in which they had been provided with neither horns nor tusks, fangs nor bony armour nor iron jaws. And yet, it is my conviction that they already knew – and were discussing as they squatted there – that they already knew they were made of finer clay.

A roomy cave housed a group of Neanderthal people tending a fire – bull-necked, thick-set individuals, to be sure – but imagine anyone else, even the lordliest king of the forest, coming along and making a fire and tending it! That required more than a regal demeanour; for that, something had to be added. The head of the clan had an especially thick bull-neck; he was a short man with a moustache and rounded back, his arms too long for his stature; his knee had been bloodily gashed open, one hand grasped the antlers of a deer he had killed and was just dragging into the cave. Short-necked, long-armed, and stooped were they all, these people around the fire, the boy watching the provider and booty-bringer with hero-worship in his eyes, and the woman emerging from the back of the cave with a child at her breast. But look, the child was just like an infant of today, a decidedly modern improvement over the state of the adults, but no doubt in growing he would regress to theirs.

I could not tear myself away from the Neanderthalers, but later I had equal trouble in leaving that eccentric who, many hundreds of thousands of years ago, crouched in his barren cavern and with mysterious diligence covered the walls with pictures of bison, gazelles, and other prey, with pictures of the hunters too. No doubt his companions were actually outside hunting, but he was here painting them with coloured pigments, and the smeary left hand with which he leaned against the rocky wall as he worked had left numerous marks between the pictures. I looked at him for a long time and yet, after we had passed on, I wanted to return once more to that diligent eccentric. 'Here we have someone,' Kuckuck said, 'who is scratching his imaginings in stone as best he can.' And this fellow busily scraping away at his stone was very touching, too. Daring and valiant, however, was the replica of a man attacking a maddened and embattled wild boar with dogs and spear – the boar was daring and valiant, too, but at a subordinate level on Nature's scale. Two dogs – they were of a strange breed, now vanished, which the professor called bog hounds and which had been domesticated in the lake-dwellers' time – lay on the grass ripped open by the boar's tusks. There were others, however, and their master was taking aim with his spear. Since there could be no doubt about the outcome, we passed on, leaving the wild pig to its subordinate fate.

Then came a handsome seascape in which fishermen were carrying on their advanced and bloodless occupation by the shore, hauling in a good catch with their flaxen net. Next to them, however, something was going on quite different from anything else and more significant than the activities of the Neanderthalers, or the wild-boar hunter, or the fishermen hauling their net, or even the diligent eccentric. Stone pillars had been raised, a number of them; they stood unroofed, forming a hall of pillars with only the heavens as ceiling, and on the plain beyond the sun was just rising, flaming red, over the edge of the world. In the roofless hall a powerful-looking man stood with upraised arms presenting a bouquet of flowers to the rising sun! Had anyone ever seen anything like it? The man was not a greybeard and not a child. He was in the prime of life. And it was just the fact of his vigour and strength that lent his action its peculiar delicacy. He and those who, living with him, had for some personal reason chosen him for this office did not yet know how to build and to roof; they could only pile stones on top of one another into pillars, and with these construct a circle wherein to perform ceremonies such as this powerful man was enacting. The burrows of fox or badger, the splendidly constructed nests of birds showed far more art and ingenuity. But they were useful and nothing more – a refuge for themselves and their broods; beyond that, the creatures' thoughts did not go. The circle of piled stone, however, was something else; refuge and brood had nothing to do with it; they were below the attention of one who had freed himself from crude necessity and risen to a nobler need. Just let any other creature in Nature come along and hit on the idea of making a formal gift of flowers to the rising sun!

My head was hot and slightly feverish from my concentrated observations as I pronounced this challenge in my heart, the heart I had so freely bestowed. I heard the professor saying that we had now seen everything and could ascend again and go straight up to the Rua João de Castilhos, where his ladies were awaiting us for luncheon.

'One might almost have forgotten that amid all these sights,' I replied. But I had by no means forgotten it; rather I regarded the tour through the museum as a preparation for my reunion with mother and daughter – exactly as Kuckuck's conversation in the dining-car had been a preparation for this tour of inspection.

'Professor,' I said, wishing to make a short concluding speech, 'I have not, as it happens, seen many museums in my brief life, but that yours is one of the most thrilling is beyond question. City and country owe you a debt of gratitude for establishing it, and I for being my guide. I thank you too most warmly, Senhor Hurtado. How accurately you have reproduced the poor, immoderate dinosaur and the tasty giant armadillo! Now, however, reluctant though I am to leave, we must not on any account keep Senhora Kuckuck and Mademoiselle Zouzou waiting. Mother and daughter – there is something thrilling about that, too. Very often great charm is to be found in brother and sister. But mother and daughter, I feel free to say, even though I may sound a trifle feverish, mother and daughter represent the most enchanting double image on this star.'

Chapter Eight

And so it was that I was introduced into the home of the man whose conversation during the train trip had stirred me so profoundly. Often, peering up from the city, I had tried to search out his domicile, and it had now taken on even greater interest in my eyes through my unexpected encounter with the mother and daughter who lived there. Quickly and comfortably the cable car Hurtado had mentioned bore us upward and deposited us in the immediate vicinity of the Rua João de Castilhos. A few steps brought us to the Villa Kuckuck, a little white house like many others in that quarter. In front of it was a small lawn with a flower bed in the middle. The interior was furnished like the home of a modest scholar and was in such extreme contrast to the magnificence of my own lodgings in the city, both in size and in décor, that I could not forbear a feeling of condescension as I poured out praises of the view and the cosiness of the rooms.

This feeling, however, was quickly moderated to one of timidity by another contrast that forced itself upon me: the appearance, that is, of the lady of the house, Senhora Kuckuck-da Cruz, who greeted us – and me especially – in that small, completely bourgeois living-room with a formality as extreme as though she were in a royal reception hall. The impression this woman had made upon me the day before was now definitely strengthened. She had chosen to appear in a different costume: a dress of very fine white moiré with a close-fitting ruffled coat, narrow ruffled sleeves, and a black silk sash worn high under her bosom. An antique gold necklace with a medallion circled her throat, whose ivory tint seemed several shades darker against the snowy whiteness of her dress. So, too, did her large, severe face framed by the trembling ear-rings. Hatless, today a few threads of silver could after all be seen in the heavy dark hair that fell in curls on her forehead. But how perfectly preserved was that erect figure and how imperiously held the head, as the eyes looked down on you, almost weary with pride. I will not deny that this woman terrified me and, through the self-same qualities, strongly attracted me at the same time. The almost forbidding majesty of her demeanour was hardly justified by her husband's position as a meritorious scholar. There was some property of blood in it, a racial arrogance that had an animal quality about it, and was for that very reason exciting.

Meanwhile, I was on the lookout for Zouzou, who was closer to my own age and interests than Senhora Maria Pia – I heard her given names from the professor, who was pouring port wine for us from a carafe standing on the velvet-covered table in the living-room. I did not have long to wait. We had hardly begun to sip our *apéritif* when Zouzou entered and greeted first her mother, then, in comradely fashion, Hurtado, and last of all me – no doubt for pedagogical reasons, so that I would not begin to imagine anything. She had come from playing tennis with some of her young friends, whose names were something like Cunha, Costa, and Lopes. She pronounced favourable or unfavourable opinions of their individual performances on the courts in a way that showed she regarded herself as an expert. Looking at me over her shoulder, she asked whether I played, and although I had only been a sideline spectator of this diversion of gilded youth and had on a few occasions acted as ball boy on the courts in Frankfurt, I replied lightly that in the old days at Castle Monrefuge I had been a pretty fair player, but since then had got badly out of practice.

She shrugged her shoulders. How happy I was to see again the pretty curls beside her temples, the pouting upper lip, the gleam of her teeth, the enchanting line of chin and neck, the bold inquiring glance! She was wearing a simple white linen dress with a leather belt and short sleeves, which left her sweet arms bare – arms that, curving, gained in enchantment for me as she raised both hands to the slender golden snake she wore as an ornament in her hair. To be sure, Senhora Maria Pia's majesty of race impressed me to the point of terror; but my heart beat for her lovely child, and the idea that this Zouzou was or must become the travelling Loulou Venosta's Zaza implanted itself ever more firmly in my imagination, although I was fully aware of the enormous difficulties in the way of its accomplishment. How could the six or seven days till I took ship suffice, in these most difficult circumstances, for me to place even the first kiss on those lips, on that precious arm – with its primordial bony armature? It was then that the thought thrust itself upon me that I must absolutely prolong my too short stay, alter the programme of my trip, arrange to take another ship, so as to give my relations with Zouzou time to mature.

What fantastic ideas shot through my mind! My *alter ego*, the stay-at-home, was determined to marry, and this now became part of my own thinking. It seemed to me as though I must betray the intentions of my parents in Luxemburg, give up the trip around the world they had prescribed to distract me, woo Professor Kuckuck's enchanting daughter, and stay in Lisbon as her husband – although at the same time it was painfully clear to me that the delicate ambiguity of my existence, its ticklish double aspect, completely ruled out any such excursion into reality. This, as I say, pained me. But how happy I was to be able to meet new friends on a social level corresponding to my own essential fineness!

Meanwhile we went into the dining-room, which was dominated by a walnut sideboard, too large, too heavy, and too ornately carved. The professor sat at the head of the table. My place was beside the lady of the house, opposite Zouzou and Hurtado. The fact that they sat together, combined with my, alas, forbidden dream of marriage, prompted me to observe the behaviour of the pair with a certain uneasiness. The thought that Longhair and the charming child might be destined for each other seemed only too probable, and it worried me. And yet the relationship between them showed such ease and lack of strain that my suspicions gradually evaporated.

An elderly maid with woolly hair brought in the food, which was excellent. There were hors d'œuvres with delicious native sardines, roast mutton, cream kisses for dessert, and afterwards fruit and cheese pastry. A quite strong red wine was served with all this. The ladies diluted it with water and the professor did not touch it at all. The latter saw fit to remark that his house could of course not rival the table at the Savoy Palace, whereupon Zouzou observed tartly, before I could answer, that I had chosen to have lunch here of my own free will and that I certainly could not expect anyone to take particular pains on my account. They *had* taken pains, but I passed over this point and remarked simply that I had no reason whatever to miss the kitchens of the hotel on the Avenida, and that I was enchanted to be lunching in so distinguished and winning a family circle, adding that I kept well in mind to whom I was indebted for this privilege. At this I kissed the *senhora*'s hand, with my eyes fastened on Zouzou.

She encountered my glance sharply, brows somewhat gathered, lips parted, nostrils dilated. I observed with pleasure that the calm which characterized her behaviour towards Dom Miguel was by no means duplicated in her attitude towards me. She hardly took her eyes off me, observed each of my gestures with no attempt at concealment, and listened just as openly, attentive and, as it were, incensed in advance, to each of my remarks, never altering her expression or showing any trace of a smile, but occasionally giving a short, contemptuous snort. In a word, my presence obviously aroused in her a prickly and characteristically combative irritability. Who will blame me for preferring this interest in my person, hostile though it was, to a passive indifference?

The general conversation was carried on in French, while the professor and I occasionally exchanged a few words in German. We talked of my visit to the museum and of the insights I had acquired, which had inspired me with a feeling of universal sympathy, insights, I assured him, that I owed to him. We then discussed the proposed expedition to the botanical gardens and went on to the near-by architectural sights which I must not miss. I expressed my interest, saying that I kept in mind my honoured travelling-companion's advice not to look about Lisbon too hurriedly but to devote enough time to it. But it was just this that worried me; the plan for my trip allowed all too little time, and I was actually beginning to consider how I could lengthen my stay.

Zouzou, who loved to talk of me in the third person over my head, remarked cuttingly that it was wrong to urge thoroughness upon *monsieur le marquis*. In her opinion, this meant a misunderstanding of my habits which were doubtless those of a butterfly, floating from flower to flower, sipping nectar wherever I went. It was charming, I replied, imitating her manner of speech, that Mademoiselle took such an interest in my character, even though she was mistaken about it – and it was especially nice that she did so in such a poetic figure of speech. At this she became even more cutting and said that, confronted by so splendid a personal appearance as mine, it was hard not to be poetic. There was anger in her words along with the conviction she had expressed earlier that one should call things by their right names and that silence is unhealthy. The two gentlemen laughed while the mother rebuked her rebellious child with a shake of her head. As for me, I simply raised my glass in homage to Zouzou, and she, in irritation and confusion, almost raised hers in return. However, she withdrew her hand in time, blushing, and covered her confusion with that short, disparaging snort.

We discussed plans for the rest of my trip, which was to curtail my stay in Lisbon so distressingly, and I mentioned particularly the Argentinian *estanciero* family whose acquaintance my parents had made in Trouville and whose hospitality awaited me. I told all I knew about them on the basis of the information I had received from the stay-at-home. Their name was Meyer, but the children, a son and daughter of Mrs Meyer's by a former marriage, were named Novaro. She had been born, so I related, in Venezuela and at a very early age had been married to an Argentinian in government service, who had been shot in the revolution of 1890. After a year of mourning she had given her hand to the wealthy Consul Meyer. She and the children now stayed with him either in his town house in Buenos Aires or at El Retiro, his large estate in the mountains some distance from the city. It was there that the family spent most of its time. The substantial income Mrs Meyer had inherited from her first husband had gone to the children when she married again, so that they were not only the eventual heirs of the wealthy Meyer but were already independently rich young people. Their ages were about seventeen and eighteen.

'Senhora Meyer is no doubt a beauty?' Zouzou asked.

'I do not know, mademoiselle. But since she found a husband so promptly I assume she is not ugly.'

'One may assume the same of the children, those Novaros. Do you know their first names?'

'I don't remember my parents ever mentioning them.'

'But I'll wager you're impatient to find out.'

'Why?'

'I don't know, you spoke of the pair with unmistakable interest.'

'I was not aware of it,' I said, secretly taken aback. 'As yet, I have no impression of them. But I admit that the combination of brother and sister, when they are attractive, has always held a certain fascination for me.'

'I regret that I have to meet you so single and alone.'

'In the first place,' I replied with a bow, 'what is single can hold fascination enough.'

'And in the second place?'

'Second place? I said "in the first place" quite thoughtlessly. I have no second to offer. At most I might remark in the second place that there are other charming combinations besides that of brother and sister.'

'*Patatípatatá!*'

'We don't say that, Zouzou,' her mother broke in. 'The marquis will commence to wonder about your upbringing.'

I assured her that my high regard for Mlle Zouzou could not be so easily impaired. We rose from the luncheon table and went back to the living-room for coffee. The professor announced that he could not accompany us on our botanical excursion, but would have to return to his office. Accordingly, he simply rode down to the city with us and said good-bye at the Avenida da Liberdade – parting from me with the utmost cordiality, in which I could detect a certain gratitude for the interest I had shown in his museum. He said I had been a most agreeable and valued guest and would be so regarded by him and his at any time during my stay in Lisbon. If I had the desire and the time to take up tennis again, his daughter would count it a pleasure to introduce me into her club.

Zouzou said with enthusiasm that she was quite willing.

With a nod of the head in her direction and a smile that expressed and solicited consideration, he shook hands with me.

From the point where he parted from us it is, in fact, but a pleasant stroll to the heights where lie the famous gardens with their ponds and lakes, grottoes and open slopes. We changed companions as we walked; sometimes Dom Miguel and I were at Senhora Kuckuck's side while Zouzou wandered on ahead. Sometimes I found myself alone beside that proud lady, watching Zouzou strolling ahead with Hurtado. Sometimes it happened, too, that I was paired with the daughter either in front of the *senhora* and the animal-sculptor, or behind. Frequently he joined me to impart information about the landscape and the marvels of the world of plants, and I admit that pleased me most – not because of the 'taxidermist' or his explanations, but because then the 'second place' which I had suppressed got its just due and I could see in front of me the enchanting combination of mother and daughter.

This is a fitting place to remark that Nature, however rare and interesting her guise, gets scant attention from us when we are engrossed with humanity. Despite all her pretensions, she plays no more important role than that of scenery, the background for our emotions, simple decoration. But as that, to be sure, she was worthy of every praise. Conifers of gigantic size claimed our amazed attention, half a hundred metres tall, at a guess. The domain abounded in fan palms and feather palms. In places it had the tangled aspect of a primeval forest. Exotic rushes, bamboos, and papyruses, lined the edges of the ornamental waters on which floated bright-hued bride and mandarin swans. We admired the palm lily with its dark-green tuft of leaves from which springs a great sheaf of white, bell-like blossoms. And everywhere were the geologically ancient fern trees, growing close together in wild and improbable little groves, with their massive trunks and slender stems spreading into crowns of fronds, gigantic leaves, which, as Hurtado explained to us, carry their spore capsules. There were very few places on earth, aside from this one, he observed, where there were still tree ferns. But, he added, primitive man had from time immemorial ascribed magical powers to ferns in general, which have no flowers and really have no seeds, especially in the concoction of love potions.

'*Pfui.*' Zouzou said.

'How do you mean that, mademoiselle?' I asked.

It is startling to encounter so emotional a reaction to a scientific and matter-of-fact term that calls up no specific image. 'Which part of the phrase do you object to?' I inquired. 'To love or to potions?'

She did not reply, but looked angrily at me, actually lowering in a threatening way.

At this point we chanced to be walking alone behind the animal-sculptor and the proud lady.

'Love is itself a potion,' I said. 'What wonder that primitive man, the fern people so to speak, who still exist since everything on earth is contemporaneous and intermixed, were tempted to practise magic with it?'

'That is a disreputable subject,' she said reprovingly.

'Love? How hard you are! One loves beauty. One's eye and soul turn to it like blossoms to the sun. You certainly wouldn't apply your disapproving exclamation to beauty, would you?'

'I find it the height of bad taste to bring the conversation around to beauty when one possesses it oneself.'

To this forthrightness I responded as follows:

'You are unkind, mademoiselle. Should one be penalized for having a passable exterior by being forbidden to admire beauty? Isn't it instead culpable to be ugly? I have always ascribed it to a kind of carelessness. Out of an innate consideration for the world that was awaiting me, I took care while I was being formed that I should not offend its eyes. That is all. I'd call it a kind of self-discipline. Besides, people in glass houses shouldn't throw stones. How beautiful *you* are, Zouzou, how enchanting those ringlets in front of your little ears. I can't look at them enough; in fact, I have made a drawing of them.'

This was true. That morning, while smoking a cigarette after my breakfast in the handsome alcove of my salon, I had supplied Loulou's nude studies of Zaza with Zouzou's ringlets.

'What! You have taken the liberty of drawing me?' she hissed through clenched teeth.

'Yes, I have, with your permission – or without it. Beauty is a freehold of the heart. It cannot prohibit the emotions it inspires, nor can it forbid the temptation of reproducing them.'

'I wish to see that drawing.'

'I don't know whether that's feasible – I mean, whether my drawing could stand your inspection.'

'That's beside the point. I demand that you give me the picture.'

'There are several of them. I will have to think about whether I can lay them before you and also when and where.'

'The when and where must be found. There is no question about the whether. What you have made behind my back is my property, and what you just said about "Freehold" is very, very shameless.'

'It was certainly not intended to be. I would be inconsolable if I had given you reason to question my upbringing. "Freehold of the heart", I said, and is that not right? Beauty is defenceless against our emotions. It may be wholly unmoved and untouched by them, it need not pay the slightest attention to them. But it is defenceless against them.'

'Will you please drop the subject once and for all?'

'The subject? With pleasure! Or, if not with pleasure, at least with alacrity. For example –' I went on in a louder voice and a caricature of a conversational tone: 'May I inquire whether by chance your revered parents are acquainted with Monsieur and Madame von Hueon, the ambassador from Luxemburg and his wife?'

'No, what have we to do with Luxemburg?'

'You are right. I had to call on them. My parents would have expected me to. Now I can probably expect an invitation to luncheon or dinner.'

'Much joy may you have of it!'

'I have a secret motive. It's my wish to be presented by von Hueon to His Majesty the King.'

'Really? So you're a courtier too?'

'If you want to call it that. I have been living for a long time in a bourgeois republic. As soon as it turned out that my trip would take me into a monarchy, I decided to pay my respects to the King. You may think it childish, but it will fulfil a need that I feel and it will give me pleasure to bow as one bows only before a King and to make frequent use of the words "Your Majesty". "Sire, I beg Your Majesty to accept my most humble thanks for the honour Your Majesty –" and so on. I would like even more to secure an audience with the Pope and I will certainly do so some time. There one even bends one's knee, which would give me great satisfaction, and says "Your Holiness".'

'You pretend to talk to me, marquis, of your need for devotion –'

'Not for devotion. For good form.'

'*Patatipatatá!* In point of fact, you simply want to impress me with your acquaintances and your invitation to the Embassy and the fact that you have entrée among the great of the earth.'

'Your mama has forbidden you to say *patatipatatá* to me. Besides –'

'Mama!' she called so that Senhora Maria Pia turned around. 'I must report to you that I have said *"patatipatatá"* to the marquis again.'

'If you go on quarrelling with our young guest,' the Iberian replied in her sonorous husky voice, 'you can't walk with him any more. Come here and let Dom Miguel escort you. Meanwhile, I will try to entertain the marquis.'

'I assure you, madame,' I said after the change had been made, 'that there was nothing resembling a quarrel. Who could fail to be enchanted by Mademoiselle Zouzou's charming forthrightness?'

'I am sure we have left you too long in that child's company, dear marquis,' the regal lady replied, and her jet ear-rings vibrated. 'Youth is generally too young for the young. In the end, association with those who are mature is, if not more welcome, at least more edifying.'

'In any case, it is a greater honour,' I observed, putting a cautious warmth into my words.

'And so,' she went on, 'we'll conclude this excursion together. Have you found it interesting?'

'In the highest degree. I have found it an indescribable pleasure. And I am perfectly certain that this pleasure would not have been half so intense, my responsiveness to the new impressions that Lisbon offers – impressions of things and people, or better, people and things – would not have been half so profound without the preparation which good fortune granted me by allowing me to fall into conversation during my trip with your honoured husband, *senhora* – if one may use the word "conversation" when one's role has been simply that of enthusiastic listener – without, if I may say so, the paleontological loosening-up his discourse produced in the soil of my mind, making it a ready seed-bed for new impressions, racial impressions, for example, such as the experience of seeing the primordial race to which such interesting admixtures have been added at various periods, and which offers eye and heart a majestic image of racial dignity . . .'

I paused to catch my breath. My companion cleared her throat sonorously and drew herself to an even greater height.

'There is no help for it,' I went on, 'I have to keep using the words "primitive" and "primordial". They steal into all my thoughts. This is a result of that paleontological loosening-up I just mentioned. Without it, what would the tree ferns we have just seen have meant to me, even if I had been told that primitive man believed they were useful for love potions? Everything has become so insignificant since then – things and people – I mean, people and things –'

'The real reason for your responsiveness, dear marquis, is probably your youth.'

'How charming it is, *senhora*, to hear the word "youth" on your lips! You pronounce it with the kindliness of maturity. Mademoiselle Zouzou, it appears, finds youth annoying, quite in keeping with your remark that youth is usually too young for the young. In some measure it holds true for me as well. Youth alone could not have produced the enchantment I move in. My advantage is that I can behold beauty in a double image, as child-like blossom and as regal maturity –'

In short, I talked like a book, and my gallantry was not ungraciously received. For as I bade farewell to my companions at the bottom of the cable-car line which would take them back to the Villa Kuckuck, and was about to return to my hotel, the *senhora* casually remarked that she hoped there would be an opportunity of seeing me again before my departure.

Dom Antonio had suggested that, if it pleased me, I should freshen up my neglected tennis with Zouzou's athletic friends. Not a bad idea, perhaps.

Not a bad idea indeed, but a foolhardy one! I questioned Zouzou with my eyes, and when she sketched with her face and shoulders an attitude of neutrality that did not absolutely rule out my assent, an appointment was at once made for the third day following. We would play in the morning and after that I was to lunch with the family once more, a farewell lunch. When I had bowed over Maria Pia's hand and Zouzou's and had exchanged a cordial handshake with Dom Miguel, I went my way, speculating about what form the future would take.

Chapter Nine

Lisbon, 25 August 1895

Dearest Parents, Beloved Mama, Beloved and Revered Papa:

These lines follow so long after the telegram I sent to announce my arrival here that I must fear your displeasure. That will be double – I am, alas, all too sure – because of the above address, which is not at all in accord with your expectation, our agreement, or my own intentions. For ten days now you have pictured me on the high seas, and yet here I am, writing from the capital of Portugal, the first stop on my journey. Dear parents, I shall explain this state of affairs, which I myself could not foresee, together with the reason for my long silence, in a way that will, I hope, nip your displeasure in the bud.

It all began by my meeting on the train a distinguished savant named Professor Kuckuck, whose conversation, I am certain, would have fascinated and inspired you just as it did your son.

German by birth, as his name indicates, and coming from the district of Gotha like you, dear Mama, belonging moreover to a good family, though of course not of family, he is a paleontologist by profession and has been living for a long time in Lisbon, married to a lady of ancient Portuguese family. He is the founder and director of the Natural History Museum here, which I visited under his personal guidance and whose scientific exhibitions both paleozoological and paleo-anthropological (these terms will be familiar to you) made a deep impression on me. It was Kuckuck who first warned me not to take the beginning of my world tour too lightly just because it was a beginning and not to apportion too short a time to my inspection of a city like Lisbon. This made me wonder whether I had not planned too brief a visit properly to see a place that has so impressive a past and so many contemporary wonders – I mention here only the tree ferns in the botanical gardens which really belong to the Carboniferous period.

When in your generosity and wisdom, dear parents, you arranged this trip for me, you probably intended it not only as a distraction from what were, I admit, silly fancies wherein my immaturity had been shared, but also as an educational experience, a kind of grand tour such as is appropriate to a young man of family. Well then, this intention has been promoted by my friendly intercourse with the members of the Kuckuck household. They are three in number – four at times, for one of the professor's professional colleagues, Senhor Hurtado, an animal-sculptor, is there on occasion. To be sure, they contribute to my education in very unequal fashion. I admit I have not succeeded in getting on very well with the ladies of the house. My relations with them have not really seemed to grow cordial in the past weeks nor does this appear likely within the foreseeable future. The *Senhora, née* da Cruz and of ancient Iberian stock, is a woman of terrifying sternness, yes, severity, and of an unconcealed arrogance, the basis of which is, to me at least, by no means clear; the daughter, whose age is perhaps a little less than mine and whose first name I have still not been able to catch, is a young woman one would be inclined to number among the echinoderms, so prickly is her behaviour. Moreover, if in my inexperience I have not misjudged the situation, the above-mentioned Dom Miguel (Hurtado) is probably to be regarded as her presumptive fiancé and husband, although it is an open question in my mind whether he is to be envied on that account.

No, it is the head of the house, Professor K., to whom I am devoted, and his associate as well, who is so deeply versed in the whole world of organic forms and to whose ingenuity the museum owes so much. It is from these two, but principally of course from K. himself, that I receive the enlightenment and information that are so important to my education and that exert a far greater attraction than the study of Lisbon and the architectural delights of its environs. Quite literally they embrace all Being, including the spontaneous generation of Life – everything from stone to Man. These two extraordinary men quite rightly see in me something resembling a sea lily which has freed itself from its stalk – that is, a novice at motion and in need of advice. It is on their account that this prolongation of my stay here contrary to plan – for which, dear parents, I affectionately beg your approval – is especially pleasant and valuable, although it would be going too far to say that they were the authors of it.

The actual reason, rather, was this. I considered it only correct and in accord with your wishes not to go away without leaving cards on our diplomatic representative, Herr von Hueon, and his wife. I was at pains to discharge this formal courtesy on the day of my arrival here, but in view of the time of year I foresaw no further consequences. However, a few days later I received at my hotel an invitation to attend a bachelor party at the Embassy, an event that had obviously been arranged before my arrival. The date was very shortly before I was due to embark. Nevertheless, I was able to follow my inclination and accept without being forced to postpone my departure.

I went, dear parents, and spent a most enjoyable evening in the Embassy on the Rua Augusta, an evening that – I owe it to your love for me not to conceal this – can be put down as a personal triumph.

This, of course, must be attributed to the way you brought me up. The dinner was given in honour of the Roumanian Prince Joan Ferdinand, who is scarcely older than I and happens at the moment to be staying in Lisbon with his military preceptor, Captain Zamfiresku. It was a bachelor gathering because Frau von Hueon was at a watering-place on the Portuguese Riviera, whereas her husband had had to interrupt his vacation and return to the capital for business reasons. The number of guests was small, amounting to hardly more than ten, but the occasion was distinguished by great formality from the very first moment, when we were received by servants in knee-breeches and lace-trimmed coats. In honour of the Prince, dinner clothes and decorations had been stipulated, and I took pleasure in seeing the ribbons and crosses and stars worn by these gentlemen, almost all of whom had the advantage of me in years and *embonpoint* – not, I admit, without a trace of envy at the enchantment of their costumes through these precious baubles. But I can assure you, without flattering you or myself, that from the moment I entered the salon in my unadorned evening dress I won the unanimous favour of the master of the house and his guests not alone because of my name but because of the easy courtesy and social grace that went with it.

At supper, which was served in the panelled dining-room, I felt, to be sure, a trifle bored in that circle of foreign and local diplomats, officers, and big industrialists, among whom an Austrio-Hungarian councillor from the Madrid Embassy, one Count Festetics, stood out picturesquely because of his fur-trimmed Hungarian costume, top boots, and curved sabre. I myself was placed between the rude-mannered captain of a Belgian frigate and a Portuguese wine-exporter, who looked like a roué, and whose imperious behaviour suggested great wealth. For quite a time the conversation turned on political and economic matters I knew nothing about, and so my contribution was necessarily limited to a lively play of expression indicating warm interest. Presently, however, the Prince, who was sitting opposite me – a weary whey-face, by the way, afflicted with both a lisp and a stutter – drew me into conversation about Paris. Who doesn't like to talk about Paris? Soon all had joined in and I, encouraged by the gracious smiles and stuttering lisp of His Highness, allowed myself to take the lead. Well, after dinner, when people were making themselves comfortable in the smoking-room and sampling the liqueurs and coffee, the place beside the distinguished guest fell to me as though automatically; the master of the house sat on his other side. You are undoubtedly familiar with Herr von Hueon's unexceptionable but colourless exterior, his thin hair, watery blue eyes, and long, wispy moustache. Joan Ferdinand hardly turned towards him at all, but allowed himself to be entertained by me. This seemed to be all right with our host. No doubt the prompt invitation I had received had been due to his wish to offer the Prince the society of someone near his own age.

I can venture to say that I amused him very much, and with the simplest of means, which chanced to be just the right ones for him. I told him about my childhood and early youth back home in the castle, about the wobbling of our good old Radicule, my imitation of whom led him to outbursts of childish delight, since it reminded him exactly of the doddering and unprofitable zeal of a valet he had inherited from his father in Bucharest; about the incredible affectations of your Adelaide, dear Mama, whose gossamer swaying and glidings I likewise imitated, floating about the room to his vast amusement; moreover, about the dogs, about Fripon and the chattering of his teeth, induced at regular intervals by the condition of our tiny Minime, and of the latter's unhappy propensity, so inappropriate for a lap dog and on so many occasions so dangerous and damaging to your robe, Mama. In masculine society it was surely permissible for me to speak of this and of the chattering of Fripon's teeth – in elegant turns of phrase, of course; in any case, I found myself justified by the tears of laughter the royal scion kept wiping from his cheeks at descriptions of Minime's delicate condition. There is something touching in seeing a creature, handicapped by both a stammer and a stutter, abandoned to such boundless merriment.

Possibly it will be painful to you, dear Mama, that I exposed to public merriment the delicate constitution of your darling; but the effect I achieved by doing so would have reconciled you to my indiscretion. Everyone became boisterous. The Prince bent double and the Grand Cross, dangling from the collar of his uniform, perforce took part. Everyone joined him in demanding to hear more about Radicule, Adelaide, and Minime, and called for repeated *da capo*'s. The Hungarian in his fur-trimmed uniform kept hitting his thigh so hard it must have hurt, the great wine-dealer, who wore various stars as awards for his wealth, burst a button from his waistcoat, and our ambassador was greatly pleased.

The result of all this was that, at the end of the soirée when I was alone with the ambassador, he proposed that before my departure he should present me to His Majesty the King, Dom Carlos I, who chanced to be in the capital, as the flag of Braganza flying from the castle roof had already informed me. It was in a sense his duty, Herr von Hueon said, to present to His Majesty a son of Luxemburg's nobility who was passing through and who, as he put it, was in addition a young man of agreeable gifts. Moreover, the King's noble spirit – the spirit of an artist, for His Majesty liked to paint in oil, and the spirit of a savant, too, for His Highness was a lover of oceanography, that is, the study of the sea and the creatures that live in it – was depressed by political cares which had begun immediately after his coronation six years before, through the conflict of Portuguese and British interests in Central Africa. At that time his conciliatory attitude had incensed public opinion against him and he had actually been grateful for the British ultimatum that made it possible for his government to give in with a formal protest. Nevertheless, there had been awkward disturbances in the larger cities, and in Lisbon a republican uprising had had to be suppressed. But now it was the sinister deficit in the Portuguese railways, which four years before had precipitated a serious financial crisis and had led to a declaration of state bankruptcy – that is, to a decree reducing government obligations by two-thirds! That had given great impetus to the republican party and had facilitated subversion by the radical elements in the country. His Majesty had not even been spared the repeated and disturbing revelation that conspiracies to assassinate him had been discovered only just in time by the police. In the round of his daily routine audiences my presentation might perhaps have a diverting and refreshing effect upon this great gentleman. If the course of the conversation possibly allowed of it, would I please introduce the subject of Minime, to which poor Prince Joan Ferdinand had reacted so heartily?

You will understand, dear parents, that with my convinced and happy royalist inclinations and my enthusiastic desire (of which perhaps you have not been fully aware) to bow before legitimate royalty, this proposal by the ambassador held a strong attraction for me. What stood in the way of my acceptance was the sad fact that it would take some days, four or five, to arrange the audience and by then the time for my embarkation on the *Cap Arcona* would have passed. What was I to do? My desire to stand before the King, combined with the advice of my learned mentor Kuckuck not to devote too short a time to a city like Lisbon, led to the decision to change my plans at the last minute and take a later ship. A visit to the travel bureau informed me that the next ship of the same line, the *Amphitrite*, which was to leave Lisbon in two weeks, was already heavily booked and would not, in any case, afford me suitable accommodations. The most sensible thing, the clerk said, would be to await the return of the *Cap Arcona* in about six or seven weeks, counting from the 15th of this month, and to re-engage my cabin for the next trip, thus postponing my voyage until the end of September or perhaps the beginning of October.

You know me, dear parents, a man of quick resolves. I agreed to the clerk's proposal, gave the necessary orders, and, I hardly need add, informed your friends, the Meyer-Novaros, of the postponement of my trip, begging them in a courteously worded cable not to expect me until October. In this way, as you see, the period of my stay in this city has been prolonged almost beyond my own wishes. No matter! My lodgings here can without exaggeration be called tolerable, and I shall not lack edifying discourse until the moment I go aboard. So may I count your acquiescence as assured?

Without that, needless to say, my essential happiness would be destroyed. But I believe you will grant it all the more readily when I inform you of the altogether happy, indeed inspiring, course of my audience with His Majesty the King, which has since taken place. Herr von Hueon informed me that it had been graciously granted and came in his carriage to fetch me from my hotel to the royal castle in good time before the specified morning hour. Thanks to his being accredited and to the fact that he was wearing court uniform, we passed the inner and outer guards without formalities and with evidences of respect. We mounted the outer staircase, which is flanked at the bottom by two caryatids in over-strained poses, and came to a suite of reception rooms decorated with busts of former kings, portraits, and crystal chandeliers, and furnished mostly in red silk with period furniture. One makes slow progress from one room to the next. In the second, one of the chamberlain's functionaries desired us to be seated for a while. Aside from the magnificence of the scene, it is not unlike the waiting-room of any popular doctor, who gets further and further behind in his appointments and whose patients have to wait long past the hour of their appointment. The rooms were crowded with all sorts of dignitaries, local and foreign, in uniform and in formal dress; they stood in groups, chatting in low voices, or sat in boredom on the sofas. There were many plumes, epaulettes, and decorations. In each new room we entered, the ambassador exchanged cordial greetings with this or that diplomat of his acquaintance and introduced me, so that through this repeated emphasis upon my station in life – in which I rejoice – the period of waiting passed very rapidly, though it could not have been less than forty minutes.

Finally, an aide-de-camp, wearing a sash and holding a list of names in his hand, asked us to take our places in front of the door leading to the royal study, which was flanked by two lackeys in powdered perukes. Out came an aged gentleman in the uniform of a General of the Guards, who, no doubt, had been paying a visit of thanks for some royal favour. The adjutant entered to announce us. Then the two lackeys opened the gold-panelled leaves of the door.

Although the King is only just over thirty, his hair is already quite thin and he is rather corpulent. He received us standing by his desk, dressed in an olive-green uniform with red facings and wearing on his breast a single star in the middle of which an eagle holds in his talons a sceptre and the imperial orb. His face was flushed from many interviews. His brows are coal-black; his moustache, however, which is bushy but waxed and turned up at the ends, is beginning to turn grey. He acknowledged our deep bows with a practised and gracious wave of the hand and then greeted Herr von Hueon with a wink in which he managed to convey a great deal of flattering intimacy.

'My dear ambassador, it is a real pleasure as always. You're in the city, too? ... I know, I know ... *Ce nouveau traité de commerce ... Mais ça s'arrangera sans aucune difficulté, grâce à votre habileté bien connue ...* And the health of the enchanting Madame de Hueon ... Is excellent. How delighted I am! How truly delighted I am! And so, then – who is this Adonis you bring to see me today?'

Dear parents, you must understand this question as a joke, a courtesy unjustified by fact. A tail-coat, to be sure, is advantageous to my figure, for which I have Papa to thank. At the same time, you know as well as I that with my cheeks like pippins and my little slit eyes, which I never see in the mirror without distaste, there is nothing mythological about me. And so I met this royal jest with an expression of merry resignation; and as though he were hastening to erase it from memory, His Majesty went on most graciously, holding my hand in his:

'My dear marquis, welcome to Lisbon! I don't need to tell you that your name is well known to me and that it gives me pleasure to greet a noble young scion from a country that maintains such cordial and friendly relations with Portugal, thanks by no means to your companion here. Tell me –' and he reflected for an instant what I should tell him '– what brings you here?'

I will not sing my own praises, precious parents, for the engaging dexterity, courtly in the best sense, both serious and easy, with which I entered into conversation with the monarch. I will simply say for your reassurance and satisfaction, that I was not awkward and did not fall on my face. I informed His Majesty of the gift, which I owe to your magnanimity, of a year's educational travel around the world, a trip that had uprooted me from Paris, my place of residence, and brought me on its first stage, to this incomparable city.

'Ah, so Lisbon pleases you then?'

'*Sire, énormément. Je suis tout à fait transporté par la beauté de votre capitale, qui est vraiment digne d'être la résidence d'un grand souverain comme Votre Majesté.* I had the intention of spending only a few days here, but I realized the absurdity of this arrangement and completely changed my plans in order to devote at least a few weeks to a visit that one would like never to have to terminate. What a city, Sire! What avenues, what parks, what promenades and views! Because of personal connexions I became acquainted first of all with Professor Kuckuck's Museum of Natural History – a magnificent institution, Your Majesty, not least interesting to me because of its oceanographic aspect, because so many of its exhibits instructively demonstrate that all forms of life emerged from the waters of the sea. But, then, the marvel of the botanical gardens, Sire, the Avenida-Park, the Campo Grande, the Passeio da Estrella with its incomparable view over city and river ... Is it any wonder that, confronted by all these ideal vistas of a land blessed by Heaven and admirably cultivated by man's hand, tears should come to an eye which is a little – my God, how little! – an artist's eye? In short, I admit that I – very differently from Your Majesty, whose genius in this field is well known – have interested myself a little in Paris in the graphic arts, in drawing and painting, as an eager but, alas, ungifted pupil of Professor Estompard of the Académie des Beaux-Arts. But this is hardly worth mentioning. What must be said is this: in Your Majesty one venerates the ruler of one of the most beautiful lands on earth, probably the most beautiful of all. Where else in the world is there a panorama to compare with the view over Estremadura offered the observer from the lofty royal palaces at Sintra, vaunting its wheat fields, vineyards, and orchards? ...'

Let me remark parenthetically, dear parents, that I had not yet visited the castles of Sintra or the Monastery of Belem, whose delicacy of construction I went on to discuss. I have been prevented from paying those visits as yet because I devote a good deal of my time to tennis at a club for socially eligible young people, to which the Kuckucks introduced me. No matter! To the King I spoke in praise of impressions I had not yet received, and His Majesty was moved to remark that he appreciated my powers of observation.

This encouraged me to launch with all the fluency I possess, or with the fluency that this extraordinary situation inspired in me, on a speech in praise of the country and people of Portugal. One did not visit a nation, I said, on account of the country alone, but rather – and perhaps first of all – on account of the people, out of a love for the new, if I might so express myself, a love for human types never met before, a desire to look into alien eyes and alien faces ... I realized that I was expressing myself badly, but what I meant was a desire to rejoice in unfamiliar customs and attributes. Portugal – *à la bonne heure*. But the Portuguese, His Majesty's subjects, they were exactly what had first captivated my entire attention. This ancient Celtic-Iberian race, to which in historical times admixtures of blood from various sources, Phoenician, Carthaginian, Roman, and Arabic, had been added – what a charming, captivating human type it had little by little brought forth – its demure grace now and again ennobled by a racial pride of an imperious, indeed terrifying kind. 'How warmly is Your Majesty to be congratulated on being the ruler of so fascinating a people!'

'Why, yes, why, yes, very pretty, very polite,' Dom Carlos said. 'Thank you, dear marquis, for the kindly view you take of the country and people of Portugal.' And I had decided that he wished to end the audience with these words when he added, quite to the contrary: 'But shan't we sit down? *Cher ambassadeur*, let's sit down for a while.'

Unquestionably he had originally intended to conduct the audience standing and, as it simply concerned my presentation, to conclude it in a few minutes. If now it was extended and became more intimate, you may attribute that – I say this more to give you pleasure than to feed my own vanity – to the fluency of my speech, which perhaps entertained him, and the agreeableness of my general appearance.

The King, the ambassador, and I sat in leather armchairs in front of a marble fireplace with a screen before it. On the mantel there stood a pendulum clock, candelabra, and Oriental vases. We were in a spacious, handsomely furnished study, with two glass-front bookcases and a Persian rug of gigantic size. Two pictures in heavy gold frames hung on either side of the fireplace, one a mountain landscape, the other a painting of flowery fields. Herr von Hueon directed my attention to the paintings with his eyes, while gesturing towards the King, who was bringing over a silver cigarette-box from a carved smoking-table. I understood.

'Will Your Majesty,' I said, 'most graciously forgive me if I divert my attention momentarily from your person to these masterpieces that irresistibly draw my eyes? May I examine them more closely? Oh, that is painting! That is genius! I can't quite make out the signature, but both of them must be by the first artist of your country.'

'The first?' the King asked, smiling. 'That depends. The pictures are by me. That on the left is a view from the Serra da Estrella, where I have a hunting-lodge, the one on the right is an attempt to reproduce the mood of our marshy lowlands, where I often shoot snipe. You see I have tried to give some idea of the charm of the rock roses that in many places bedeck the plains.'

'One feels as though one could smell their perfume,' I said. 'Good God, before such accomplishment, dilettantism must blush.'

'Dilettantism is just what it is considered,' Dom Miguel replied, shrugging his shoulders, while I, as though by a great effort, tore myself away from his works and resumed my chair. 'People think a king capable of nothing but dilettantism. They at once remember Nero and his *qualis artifex* ambitions.'

'Miserable creatures,' I replied, 'who cannot free themselves from such a prejudice! They should rejoice at a stroke of fortune that unites the highest with the highest, the grace of exalted birth with the gifts of the Muses.'

His Majesty heard this with visible pleasure. He sat comfortably reclining in his chair, while the ambassador and I properly sat bolt upright in ours. The King remarked: 'I take great pleasure, dear marquis, in your responsiveness, in the unconstrained enjoyment with which you observe things, people, the world and its works, the engaging innocence with which you do this and for which you are to be envied. It is perhaps only at the social level which you occupy that this is possible. It is in the depths of society and at its highest pinnacle that one meets the ugliness and bitterness of life. Common man experiences it – and the ruler of a state, who breathes the miasmas of politics.'

'You Majesty's observation,' I replied, 'is full of insight. Only I humbly beg you not to think that my own powers of observation are confined to a mindless enjoyment of surfaces without any attempt to penetrate to what is less agreeable inside. I offered Your Majesty my congratulations on the truly enviable lot of being the ruler of so glorious a country as Portugal. But I am not blind to certain shadows that threaten to dim your happiness and I know about the drops of gall and wormwood that malice has poured into the golden cup of your life. It is not unknown to me that here, too, even here – must I say, especially here? – certain elements are not wanting, elements that call themselves radical, no doubt because, like rats, they gnaw at the roots of society – horrible elements, if I may give moderate expression to my feelings of abhorrence, elements that welcome every embarrassment, every political or financial difficulty of the state, in order to make capital of them through their machinations. They call themselves men of the people, though their only connexion with the people consists in perverting their sound instinct and robbing them, to their own sorrow, of their natural belief in the necessity of a clearly defined social hierarchy. And how? By dinning into them the wholly unnatural notion of equality, which runs counter to the people's interests just because it is unnatural, and by attempting to mislead them through vulgar oratory into a belief in the necessity and desirability – leaving out the possibility – of abolishing the distinctions of birth and blood, the distinctions between rich and poor, nobleman and commoner, distinctions in whose defence Nature and beauty perpetually join hands. By his very existence the beggar, huddled in rags, makes as great a contribution to the colourful picture of the world as the proud gentleman who drops alms in his humbly outstretched hand, carefully avoiding, of course, any contact with it. And, Your Majesty, the beggar knows it; he is aware of the special dignity that the order of the world has allotted to him, and in the depths of his heart he does not wish things otherwise. It takes the instigation to rebellion by men of ill will to make him discontented with his picturesque role and to put into his head the contumacious notion that men must be equal. They are not equal, and they are born realizing that. Man comes into the world with an aristocratic point of view. That, young though I am, has been my experience. Whoever it may be – a minister, a member of the ecclesiastical hierarchy, or that other hierarchy, the Army, some honest noncommissioned officer in his barrackes – he exhibits an infallible eye and instinct to distinguish the common substance from the fine, to recognize the clay of which one is made ... Fine friends of the people indeed, those who take away from the ill-born and lowly their joy in what is above them, in wealth, in the noble manners and customs of the upper strata of society, and who change that joy into envy, greed, and rebellion! They rob the masses of religion, which keeps them within pious and happy bounds, and, in addition, pretend to them that everything can be accomplished by changing the form of the state; the monarchy must fall, and with the establishment of a republic, human nature will be transformed and happiness and equality will appear automatically ... But it is time for me to beg Your Majesty not to take amiss this outpouring that I have allowed myself.'

The King nodded to the ambassador with raised eyebrows, which greatly pleased the latter.

'Dear marquis,' His Majesty then said, 'you give expression to ideas that deserve only praise – ideas, moreover, that are not only appropriate to your origin but, allow me to say, do you personally and individually much credit. Yes, yes, I mean what I say. *À propos*, you mentioned the inflammatory rhetoric of the demagogues, their dangerous glibness. It is an unhappy fact that one encounters skill in speech principally among such people, lawyers, ambitious politicians, apostles of liberalism, and enemies of the established order. That order seldom finds defenders of intelligence and wit. It is a very comforting exception to hear the right side well and winningly presented for once.'

'I cannot say,' I replied, 'how very much honour and happiness the word "comforting" on Your Majesty's lips has given me. However ridiculous it may seem for a simple young nobleman to presume to think he could comfort a King, I confess that just this was my intention. And what prompted me to this attempt? Sympathy, Your Majesty. It is sympathy tinged with awe; if that is audacious, I should like to maintain that there is hardly any profounder combination of emotions than that of awe and sympathy. What I, in my youth, know about Your Majesty's troubles and about the enmity to which the principle you represent and even your exalted person are exposed, touches me deeply and I cannot refrain from wishing you every distraction possible from these troublous concerns and as much happy diversion as can be contrived. No doubt that is what Your Majesty looks for and finds in some measure in painting. Besides, I am happy to learn that you derive enjoyment from hunting.'

'You are right,' he said. 'I am happiest, I admit, when I am far from the capital and its political intrigues, under the open sky in field or on mountain, stalking or standing in a blind with a few tried and true friends. You are a huntsman, marquis?'

'I cannot say that I am, Your Majesty. Beyond question the chase is the most knightly form of diversion, but, on the whole, I am no lover of firearms and participate only infrequently, when invited. The part that gives me the greatest joy is observing the dogs in action. A fine leash of pointers or setters, every muscle tense with excitement, noses to the ground, tails waving – the proud parade step and high-held head with which one of them brings back a bird or rabbit – these are things I delight in watching. I confess, in short, that I am a dog-lover and have associated since childhood with these ancient friends of man. The affection in a dog's eye, his open-mouthed laughter when you joke with him – after all, he's the only animal that can laugh – his awkward tenderness, the elegance of his play, the springy beauty of his gait if he's a thoroughbred – all this warms my heart. In most cases there is hardly any sign left of his descent from wolf and jackal. As little sign, usually, as of the horse's descent from tapir and rhinoceros. Even the bog hounds of the lake-dweller period had ceased to show any similarity. And who would think of a wolf when looking at a spaniel, a dachshund, a poodle, a Scotty, which seems to walk on its belly, or a kindly Saint Bernard? And what variety there is in the species! No other has so much. A pig is a pig, an ox an ox. But would one ever believe that a Great Dane, big as a calf, is a the same animal as a griffon? At the same time,' I chattered on, relaxing my posture now and leaning back in the chair – and the ambassador followed suit, 'at the same time, one has the impression that these creatures are not aware of their proportions, whether gigantic or tiny, and do not take them into account in their relations with one another. Love – Your Majesty, I hope, will forgive me for touching on this subject – obliterates all sense of what is fitting and not fitting. At home in the castle we have a Russian wolfhound called Fripon, a great gentleman reserved in manner and of a sleepy arrogance of demeanour, related, no doubt, to the trivial size of his brain. On the other hand, there is Minime, my Mama's Maltese lap-dog, a little bundle of white silk hardly larger than my fist. One would think that Fripon would not be blind to the fact that in one particular relationship this trembling little princess would be no proper partner for him. However, at the times when her femininity asserts itself, although he is kept far away from her, his teeth commence to chatter from unrealizable love so that he can be heard rooms away.'

The King waxed merry over the chattering teeth.

'Oh, Your Majesty,' I hastened on, 'I must tell you that this precious little creature Minime has a constitution that is very ill-suited to her role as lap-dog.'

And then, dear Mama, I re-enacted, much better and with more ludicrous detail, my performance of the other evening, the portrayal of the, alas, recurrent tragedy in your lap, the cries of alarm, the ringing of bells; I imitated Adelaide's fluttering entrance, her unexampled affectation only augmented by the crisis, her bearing away of the squirming and disgraced favourite, and the doddering attempts of Radicule to come to your assistance with fire shovel and ash bucket. My success was all that had been hoped for, the King held his sides with laughter – and it is really a profound joy to see a crowned head, oppressed by worry over a subversive party in his country, surrender himself to such self-forgetful merriment. I do not know what those waiting in the anteroom may have made of this audience, but it is certain that His Majesty enjoyed to a quite remarkable degree the innocent diversion I offered him. Finally, however, the latter remembered that my name and that of the ambassador (who showed visible signs of pride at having so well served His Majesty's interests by introducing me) were not by any means the last on the list, and gave the signal that the audience was over by rising, meanwhile mopping his eyes. As we were making our deep farewell bows I heard, though apparently I was not intended to, the repeated '*Charmant, charmant!*' with which the monarch expressed his appreciation to Herr von Hueon. And now, dear parents, here is something that will, I hope, make my small sin against piety and my arbitrary prolongation of my stay appear in a more favourable light. Two days later I received from the Court Chamberlain's office a little package that contained the insignia of the Portuguese Order of the Red Lion, second class, which His Majesty had been graciously pleased to bestow on me. This is worn round the neck on a

crimson ribbon, and henceforth on formal occasions I shall not have to
appear in unadorned evening clothes as I did at the ambassador's.

I know very well that one's true worth is not worn in enamel on one's shirt-
front, but deeper in the breast. But people – you have known them longer
and better than I – people like to see the outward show, the symbol, the
decoration worn in full view. I do not criticize them for this, I am full of
kindly understanding of their needs. And it is my sympathy and love for my
fellow men that makes me rejoice at being able to gratify their childish love
of show in the future by wearing the Red Lion, second class.

Nothing further for today, dear parents. Only a fool gives more than he
has. Soon there will be more reports of my experiences and adventures in the
world, all of which I shall owe to your generosity. And if I were to receive a
letter from you at the above address, assuring me of your good health, that
would be the most precious possible addition to the well-being of

Your affectionate and truly obedient son,

LOULOU.

This letter covered a great number of sheets of the Savoy Palace Hotel's best
note-paper. It was composed partly in French and partly in German, in the
carefully imitated stiff back-hand and signed with the oval-encircled
signature. Off it went to my parents in Castle Monrefuge in Luxemburg,. I
had taken pains with it, as my correspondence with this lady and gentleman
who were so close to me was a matter of the deepest importance to me, and I
awaited their answer with a tender curiosity, expecting it to come from the
marquise. I had devoted several days to this little composition, which, by the
way, aside from certain evasions at the start, was an altogether accurate
report of my activities, even in the matter of Herr von Hueon's offering to
present me to the King, thereby anticipating my request. The care I devoted
to this report is all the more laudable because I had to steal time for it from
my association with the Kuckuck family, which I had the greatest difficulty
in keeping within the bounds of discretion. The occasion – who would have
thought it? – was principally tennis, a sport in which I was as completely
unskilled as in every other and which I played with Zouzou and her friends
at the club.

My agreement to appear there was no small act of daring on my part.
Betimes on the morning of the third day, however, I put in an appearance as
agreed, wearing faultless sports attire – white flannels, snow-white shirt
open at the neck, over which I wore a blue blazer, and those noiseless
rubber-soled canvas shoes which give one a dancing movement. The well-
kept double court not far from Zouzou's house was reserved for her and her
friends by the day or hour. My mood was very much the same as when I had
presented myself before the army medical commission: an adventurous
though troubled determination filled my heart. Determination is all.
Reassured by my convincing garb and winged shoes, I promised myself to
play my part brilliantly in this game that I had watched and absorbed but
had in fact never taken part in.

I arrived too early and found myself all alone at the scene. There was a
small building where players could leave their coats and store their
equipment. There I deposited my blazer and selected a racket and some of
the lovely chalk-white balls. I began to practise playfully but self-
confidently with these pretty objects. I bounced the ball on the surface of the
racket, batted it to the ground, and scooped it up from the ground with the
well-known light, shovelling motion. To limber up my arm and experiment

with the force necessary in drives, I sent ball after ball over the net with
forehand or backhand strokes – over the net when I could, that is, for most of
the balls went into the net or far outside the opposite court; indeed, when I
grew too enthusiastic they went straight over the back-stop.

I was thus engaged in a singles match against no one, enjoying the feel of
the handsome racket, when Zouzou Kuckuck came up with two other
people, also dressed in white, a boy and a girl who turned out not to be
brother and sister, but cousins. If his name was not Costa, it was Cunha, and
if her name was not Lopes, it was Camões – I no longer exactly recall. 'Look
at that, the marquis is practising solo. He looks very promising,' Zouzou said
derisively and introduced me to the charming young pair, whose charm,
however, was far less than her own. After this, various other young folk
arrived, members of the club with names like Saldacha, Vicente, de
Menezes, Ferreira, and so forth. There were, all told, probably a dozen
players, including myself, most of whom immediately sat down on the
benches outside the enclosure to look on. Four of us went on to the court,
Zouzou and I on opposite sides of the net. A gangling youngster climbed up
on to the high umpire's seat to keep track of the points and faults, and games
and sets.

Zouzou took up a position close to the net, while I resigned that place to
my partner, a girl with a yellowish complexion and green eyes, and kept to
the back of the court in concentrated alertness. Zouzou's partner, the small
cousin, served first, hard. Springing towards the ball, I managed, with
beginner's luck, to return it with great speed and precision, so that Zouzou
remarked: 'Well, now!' After that I was guilty of a lot of nonsense – energetic
leaping back and forth to conceal my total lack of skill – and this benefited
our opponents; in a spirit of sheer bravado I also made sport of the game,
seeming to take nothing seriously, and played jokes and tricks with the
bouncing ball which aroused as much merriment in the onlookers as my
hopeless errors. All this did not prevent my occasionally performing feats of
pure genius which contrasted bafflingly with my obvious lack of skill and
made the latter look like simple carelessness or an attempt to conceal my true
abilities. Now and then I astonished the gallery by serves of uncanny speed,
by returning a volley, by repeated impossible gets – all of which I owed to the
physical inspiration of Zouzou's presence. I can still see myself receiving a
deep forehand drive, one leg extended, the other knee bent, which must have
made a very handsome picture, for it earned me applause from the gallery; I
see myself leaping incredibly high, to the accompaniment of *bravo*'s and
hand-clapping, to smash back a ball that had gone way over my partner's
head – and there were other wild and inspired triumphs as well.

Zouzou played with skill and calm precision. She neither laughed at my
blunders – as, for example, when I missed the ball I had tossed into the air
when serving – nor at my uncalled-for pranks; on the other hand, she
showed no reaction to my unexpected vituoso feats and the applause they
earned me. These occurred very infrequently and, despite my partner's
solid play, Zouzou's side had won four games after twenty mintues and after
another ten had taken the set. We left the court to other players and sat down
on a bench to cool off.

'The marquis's game is amusing,' said my yellow-and-green partner for
whom I had spoiled so much.

'*Un peu fantastique, pourtant,*' replied Zouzou, who felt responsible for
me because she had introduced me to the club. At the same time, I ventured
to think that the fantastic nature of my play had done nothing to hurt me in

her eyes. I apologized for myself on the ground of beginning over again and expressed the hope that I would quickly regain my lost skill and would then be worthy of such partners and opponents. After some chatter, while we watched the players and applauded their good strokes, a gentleman named Fidelio came over and addressed the two cousins in Portuguese. Presently he took them off for a conference of some kind. Hardly was I alone with Zouzou when she turned on me.

'Well, and what about the drawings, marquis? Where are they? You know that I wish to see them and take possession of them.'

'But, Zouzou,' I replied, 'I couldn't possibly have brought them here. Where would I have left them and how could I have shown them to you? Every instant we would run the risk of being caught at it.'

'What a way to speak – "being caught at it"!'

'Well, yes, these imaginative products of my dreams of you are not for the eyes of a third person – leaving aside the question of your seeing them yourself. By God, I wish that circumstances here and at your house and everywhere else did not make it so hard to share secrets with you.'

'Secrets! Please watch what you say!'

'But you insist upon secrets, which, like everything else, are very hard indeed to arrange.'

'I simply said it was a challenge to your adroitness to find an opportunity of handing over those drawings. You are certainly not lacking in adroitness. You were adroit during the game – fantastic, as I said a moment ago by way of excuse, and often so blundering that one could easily believe you had never played tennis at all. But adroit you certainly were.'

'How happy I am, Zouzou, to hear you say that!'

'How do you happen to be calling me Zouzou?'

'Everyone calls you that, and I love the name very much. I pricked up my ears the first time I heard it and I have clasped it to my heart.'

'How can one clasp a name to one's heart?'

'The name is inseparable from the person who bears it. That's why it makes me so happy, Zouzou, to hear from your lips – how I love to talk about your lips! – a kindly, half-laudatory comment on my poor playing. Believe me, if in its bungling fashion it was in any way passable, that was because I was completely imbued with the consciousness of acting under your dear, bewitching black eyes.'

'Very pretty. What you are practising now, marquis, is called, I believe, paying court to a girl. In this you show less originality than in your fantastic tennis. Most of the young people regard tennis as more or less of a pretext for this disgusting occupation.'

'Disgusting, Zouzou? Why? A short time ago you called love a disreputable theme and said *pfui* to it.'

'I say it again. You young men are all nasty, dirty-minded boys, interested in unseemly behaviour.'

'Oh, if you are going to get up and go away, you deprive me of any chance of defending love.'

'That's just what I intend to do. We have sat here alone too long already. In the first place, it's not proper, and in the second – for when *I* say "in the first place" I am not accustomed to leave out the second – in the second place, you have very little taste for individual persons and wax much more enthusiastic about combinations.'

She is jealous of her mother, I said to myself, not without pleasure, as she threw me an '*Au revoir*' and withdrew. May the queenly Iberian, in turn, be jealous of her daughter! That would dovetail with the jealousy my own devotion to one often provokes in my devotion to the other.

We made our way from the court to the Villa Kuckuck with the young people who had arrived with Zouzou, the two cousins, whose home lay in that direction. At luncheon, which was to have been a farewell meal but had already forfeited that name, there were only four of us, as Hurtado could not attend. It was spiced by Zouzou's scorn and derision for my tennis, in which Dona Maria Pia evinced a certain smiling interest, especially since her daughter prevailed upon herself to mention my occasional glorious feats. I say 'prevailed upon herself' because she spoke with brows knit and teeth clenched as though profoundly annoyed.

I pointed this out, and she replied: 'Annoyed? Of course. You don't play well enough for that. It was unnatural.'

'Say, rather, it was supernatural!' the professor laughed. 'All in all it seems to me that it amounts to this: the marquis was gallant enough to throw the victory your way.'

'Dear Papa,' she replied tartly, 'you know so little about sport that you believe gallantry plays a part in it, and you provide a very kind explanation for the absurd behaviour of your travelling-companion.'

'Papa is always kind,' the *senhora* said, closing the subject.

We did not go for a walk after lunch that day, but I was to enjoy many more luncheons at the Kuckucks' home during the coming weeks, followed by excursions to places outside the city. More about that directly. Here I simply wish to mention the pleasure I derived from a letter from my dear mother which was handed me by the concierge upon my return from such an expedition about two weeks after I had dispatched my letter to her. It was written in German and read as follows:

Victoria Marquise de Venosta *née* Plettenburg
Castle Monrefuge, 3 September 1895

My dear Loulou:

Your letter of the 25th duly reached us, and both Papa and I thank you for its conscientious and undeniably interesting fullness of detail. Your handwriting, my good Loulou, always left much to be desired and is now as ever not unmannered, but your style has decidedly improved in smoothness and polish, a circumstance I attribute, in part, to the atmosphere of Paris, so friendly to word and wit, which you have breathed so long and which is making itself increasingly evident. Moreover, it is probably true that a sense for good and attractive form which has always been yours, since we implanted it in you, is an attribute of the whole man and is not limited to his corporeal deportment, but extends to all the personal manifestations of his life and therefore to the manner of his written and oral expression as well.

Besides, I assume that you did not really speak to His Majesty, King Carlos, in the oratorical and elegant fashion that you report in your letter. That is certainly a letter-writer's fiction. Nevertheless, you have given us pleasure by it, and most of all by the point of view you took the opportunity to express, which represents the sentiments of your father and myself just as accurately as those of the great man. We both completely share your conviction in the God-appointed necessity of distinctions between rich and poor, noble and commoner, on earth, and of the necessity of the beggar caste. Where would the opportunity be for Christian charity and good works if poverty and misery did not exist?

This by way of introduction. I will not conceal from you, and you expected nothing else, that your rather high-handed action in so considerably postponing your journey to Argentina at first troubled us a little. But we have accepted it and are reconciled, for the reasons you advance are sensible and, as you say with justice, the results of your decision have justified it. Naturally, I am thinking first of all of the acquisition of the Order of the Red Lion, which you owe to the grace of the King and to your own engaging behaviour and on which Papa and I send you our hearty congratulations. That is no inconsiderable decoration and is seldom attained by one so young; although it is of the second class, it is by no means to be considered second-class. It does the whole family honour.

This pleasant incident is mentioned, too, in a letter from Frau Irmingard von Hueon, which I received at almost the same time as yours, and in which, on her husband's report, she tells me about your social success. She wished to warm a mother's heart and was completely successful in that purpose. Nevertheless, without wishing to offend you, I must say that her description, or that of the ambassador, was read here with some astonishment. Of course you have always been a prankster, but that you should possess such a talent for parody and such gifts of burlesque that you could set a whole company, including a prince of the blood, to laughing and were even able to move a care-laden monarch to almost unmajestic marriment – this we would never have believed of you. Well and good, Frau von Hueon's letter confirms your own report of the matter, and it must also be admitted here that the result justifies the means. You are to be forgiven, my child, for basing your representation on details of our family life which might better have been kept among us. As I write, Minime lies in my lap and would certainly endorse our attitude if the matter could be brought to her tiny attention. You have allowed yourself exaggeration and grotesque licence in your performance, and, in particular, you have exposed your mother in a ridiculous light, through your description of her lying there in her chair, pathetically dirtied and half unconscious while old Radicule had to come to her assistance with shovel and ash bucket. I know nothing of any ash bucket – it is the product of your zeal to be entertaining. But as this has borne such pleasant fruits in the end, it doesn't greatly matter that you have rather arbitrarily detracted somewhat from my personal dignity.

No doubt it was for a mother's heart, too, that Frau von Hueon assured us that on all sides you are considered as pretty as a picture, a youthful beauty indeed. This announcement has once more caused us a certain degree of bewilderment. You are, to speak frankly, a nice boy, and unquestionably you under-estimate yourself when you talk with engaging self-ridicule of your cheeks like pippins and your slit eyes. That is certainly unjust. But you could never be considered really beautiful or pretty, not that we know of, and compliments of this sort which are paid to me upset me a little, even though as a woman I am well aware that the desire to please can improve the exterior from within, can glorify it and, in short, prove a means *pour corriger la nature*.

But why am I talking about your exterior? Let people call it pretty or passable! The thing of importance is the safety of your soul, your social salvation, for which we at one time had to tremble. And it is this in your letter, as in your telegram, that has brought us a real lightening of the heart when we learned that in this trip we had hit upon the right means to free your soul from the spell of degrading wishes and projects, to cause you to see them in the right light – that is, as impossible and destructive – and to bid them farewell together with the person who, to our concern, inspired them in you!

Wholesome circumstances, according to your letter, have contributed to this result. I cannot help regarding as a providential encounter your meeting with that professor and museum-director whose name, to be sure, sounds so funny, and your visits to his house as useful and conducive to your restoration. Distraction is good; but all the better when it is combined with a gain in education and brilliant information such as is so clearly evident in your letter in the simile of the sea lily (a plant unknown to me) and in your reference to the natural history of the dog and the horse. Such things are an adornment in any social conversation and, if they are woven in without pretension and with good taste, they will not fail to distinguish a young man of attainments from those who have no vocabulary beyond that of sports. Which does not mean that we were not glad to hear, in view of your health, that you have once more taken up the long-neglected game of lawn tennis.

As for your association with the ladies of that household, the mother and daughter, whose description you enliven with a few ironic lights, if this appeals less to you than your conversations with the learned head of the house and his associate, I hardly need warn you – however, I am now doing so – not to allow them to perceive your lower estimation of them and always to treat them with the chivalry that a cavalier owes in all circumstances to the opposite sex.

And now all good wishes, dear Loulou! When you embark in about four weeks, after the return of the *Cap Arcona*, our prayers will rise to Heaven for a smooth crossing that will not unsettle your stomach for so much as a single day. The postponement of your trip means you will arrive in the Argentinian spring and will probably have a taste of summer as well in that region where the seasons are the reverse of ours. You will provide yourself, I trust, with a suitable wardrobe. Light flannel is to be recommended because it is the best protection against chills, which, as is not generally known, are easier to catch in hot weather than in cold. Should the funds at your disposal prove inadequate, be assured that I am the woman to procure a reasonable supplement from your father.

Our kindest greetings to your hosts, Herr and Frau Consul Meyer.
Blessings,
MAMAN.

Chapter Ten

When I recall the extraordinary and elegant equipages that later on were mine for a time – the gleaming victorias, phaetons, and silk-upholstered coupés – I am touched by the childish pleasure I derived, during those weeks in Lisbon, from a barely decent rented carriage. By arrangement with a local livery stable, it was kept constantly at my disposal, so that the concierge of the Savoy Palace had only to telephone for it when occasion arose. Actually it was nothing more than a four-seated droshky with a folding hood, which had probably served as a family carriage before being sold to the stable. The horses and harness were at least presentable, and for a small premium I arranged for the coachman to have an appropriate personal uniform – a hat with rosette, blue coat, and top boots.

It was a pleasure to enter this carriage in front of my hotel with a page holding the door for me and the coachman bending down slightly from the box, as I had taught him, his hand at the brim of his top hat. A conveyance of this sort was an absolute necessity not only for outings and in order to take one's place in the procession of carriages in the parks and along the avenues – which I did for entertainment – but also in order to arrive with a certain elegance at those houses to which I was invited as a result of my evening at the Embassy and, no doubt, also as a result of my audience with the King. Thus, Saldacha, the rich exporter or wines, and his extraordinarily corpulent wife invited me to a garden party at their magnificent estate outside the city; Lisbon society was gradually drifting back from the summer resorts, and many of its representatives were there. These I encountered again, less numerous and with some substitutions, at two dinners, one of which was given by the Greek businessman, Prince Maurocordato and his classically beautiful but astonishingly forward wife, the other by Baron and Baroness Vos von Steenwyck at the Dutch Embassy. On both these occasions I was able to display my Order of the Red Lion and received congratulations on all sides. On the Avenida I was kept busy bowing, for my distinguished acquaintances were increasing in number; nevertheless, all these relationships remained on a superficial and formal footing – or, to be more precise, I kept them so out of indifference, as my true interests were concentrated on the small white house on the hillside and on the double image of mother and daughter.

I need hardly say that these came first rather than last in my list of reasons for securing the carriage. With it, I could invite them to drive to such places of historic interest as, for instance, those whose beauty I had, by way of anticipation, praised to the King; and nothing gave me greater pleasure than to sit, my back to the driver, facing those two: that august representative of her race and her enchanting child. Sometimes Dom Miguel would sit beside me, for he was occasionally free to accompany us, and he liked to serve as our instructor on visits to castle or monastery.

These weekly or biweekly drives and excursions were regularly preceded by tennis and a family luncheon at the Kuckucks'. On the court I sometimes played as Zouzou's partner, sometimes as her opponent, and sometimes with others. My game quickly became more uniform: those sudden spectacular feats came to an end, and with them my laughable exhibitions of ineptitude. I played a decent medium sort of game, though the presence of my beloved gave me the advantage of a sort of physical inspiration – if I may call it that – beyond the average. If only it had been less difficult for us to be alone! The dictates of southern convention were explicitly and disturbingly in our way. To call for Zouzou at her house and accompany her to the courts was not to be thought of; we met there. Nor was there any chance of taking her home alone; it was understood that others must always be present. A *tête-à-tête* in the house before or after lunch, in the drawing-room or anywhere else, was out of the question. Only when we were resting on a bench outside the wire enclosure of the tennis courts was there now and again an opportunity for private conversation. On these occasions she always began by mentioning the portrait sketches and demanding that I show them to her or, rather, that I hand them over to her. Without contesting her stubborn theory that she owned the drawings, I kept evading her demand on the plausible pretext that there was no safe opportunity of submitting them to her. In truth, I doubted whether I would ever risk showing her those daring sketches, and I clung to this doubt as I did to her unsatisfied curiosity – if that is the right word for it – because the unrevealed pictures constituted a secret bond between us which delighted me and which I wished to preserve.

To share a secret with her, to have an understanding of our own – whether she liked it or not – seemed to me to have a sweet significance. And so I made a point of telling her about my social adventures before I recounted them to her family at table – and I also made a point of going into them more thoroughly, more intimately and with more comment so that later on I could look at her and see in her smile the memory of what we had previously discussed. An example of this was my meeting with the Princess Maurocordato, whose divinely noble features and figure made her conduct so unexpected – conduct that was by no means divine but more like that of a soubrette. I had told Zouzou how the lady from Athens had cornered me in her salon, had kept tapping me with her fan, showing the tip of her tongue between her lips, winking, and making the most wanton advances – wholly unmindful of that dignity of deportment which, one might think, the consciousness of classical beauty would naturally inspire in a woman. Sitting on our bench, we discussed for some time this contradiction between appearance and conduct, and we came to the conclusion that either the princess was at odds with her classical appearance, found it boring, and showed her rebellion against it by her behaviour – or that it was a matter of sheer stupidity and lack of awareness of, and respect for, oneself such as, for instance, a poodle might show, emerging snowy-white from its bath only to find a mud puddle and roll in it.

All this I passed over in silence when at luncheon I described my Greek evening and the princess's perfect figure.

'– Which naturally made a profound impression on you,' said Senhora Maria Pia, sitting very straight as always, leaning neither forward nor back, her jet necklace and ear-rings vibrating slightly.

I replied: 'Impressed me, *senhora*? No. On my very first day in Lisbon I was vouchsafed impressions of female beauty which I confess have made me unresponsive to further ones.' At this I kissed her hand, smiling at the same time at Zouzou. That is what I always did. It was dictated by the double image. When I paid the daughter a compliment, I looked at the mother and vice versa. The starry-eyed man of the house, sitting at the head of the small table, observed this by-play with vague benevolence, a testimony to the stellar distances from which he gazed. The reverence I felt for him was not one jot diminished by the realization that in my courtship of the double image consideration for him was wholly superfluous.

'Papa is always kind,' Senhora Maria Pia had accurately declared. I believe that the head of the house would have listened with exactly the same benevolent inattention and absent-minded kindliness to the conversations I carried on with Zouzou at the tennis court or on some excursion when we lingered behind alone – and these were unconventional in the extreme. They were so thanks to her axiom, 'Silence is unhealthy'; to her phenomenal, altogether unconventional forthrightness; and to the subject to which this uneuphemistic bluntness was directed: the theme of love. To this, as we know, she had said: '*Pfui!*' I had trouble enough on that account, for I did indeed love her and let her see it in various ways; she understood it, too, but in what a fashion! This enchanting girl's idea of love was extremely odd and comically distrustful. She appeared to see in it something like the secret behaviour of nasty small boys, professed to ascribe the vice called 'love' entirely to the male sex and to consider that the female sex had nothing to do with it, felt not the slightest natural inclination towards it, and believed that flirtations were begun exclusively by young men for the purpose of enticing girls into unseemly behaviour.

I would hear her say: 'There you go again paying court to me, Louis.' (Yes, it is true, she had begun to call me Louis sometimes when we were alone, just as I called her Zouzou.) 'Murmuring sweet nothings and looking at me imploringly – or shall I say "importunately"? No, I shall say "lovingly", but that is the name for a lie. You look at me with those blue eyes of yours and you know very well that they and your blond hair contrast so very strangely with your dark skin that one can't tell what to make of you. And what do you want? What is the purpose of your melting words and melting glances? Something that is unspeakably laughable and absurd, both childish and repugnant. I say "unspeakably", but of course it is not at all unspeakable, and I shall put it into words. You want me to consent to our embracing, to agree that two creatures whom Nature has carefully and completely separated should embrace each other so that your mouth is pressed upon mine while our nostrils are cross-wise and we breathe each other's breath. That's what you want, isn't it? A repulsive indecency and nothing else, but perverted into a pleasure by sensuality – that's the word for it, as I very well know; and the word means that swamp of impropriety into which all of you want to lure us so that we will go crazy and two civilized beings will behave like cannibals. That's the purpose of your flirtatiousness.'

She stopped speaking and managed to sit quite calm after this outburst of forthrightness, without any quickening of her breath or indication of fatigue. Moreover, it did not seem like an outburst, but rather like simple conformity to the principle of calling things by their right names. I was silent, shocked, touched, and troubled.

'Zouzou,' I said finally, and for a moment I held my hand above hers without touching it, and then completed the gesture in the air, moving my hand above her head and downward, as though to shield her. 'Zouzou, you distress me dreadfully when you use such words – what shall I call them, crude, cruel, exaggeratedly true, and for that very reason only half true, in fact not true at all – when you use such words to tear away the delicate mists in which my admiration for the charms of your person has enwrapped my heart and senses. Don't make fun of "enwrapped"! I purposely, deliberately, and intentionally said "enwrapped" because I must use poetic words to defend the poetry of love against your harsh, distorted version. I beseech you, what a way to talk about love and its purpose! Love has no purpose, it neither wills nor thinks beyond itself, it is entirely itself and entirely inwoven in itself – don't scoff at "inwoven". I have already told you that I am intentionally using poetic words – and that simply means more seemly ones – in the name of love, for love is essentially seemly, and your harsh words far outdistance it in an area that remains alien to love, however familiar it may be with it. I ask you! What a way to talk of a kiss, the tenderest exchange in the world, silent and lovely as a flower! This unforeseen occurrence, happening quite by itself, the mutual discovery of two pairs of lips, beyond which emotion does not even dream of going, because that is in itself the incredibly blessed seal of union with another!'

I pledge my word that is how I spoke. I did so because Zouzou's habit of discrediting love actually seemed to me childish and I regarded poetry as less childish than this girl's crudity. Poetry, moreover, came easily to me in my foundationless existence. It was simple enough for me to say that love has no ulterior object and does not think beyond a kiss at most, because in my unreal state I could not permit myself to come to grips with reality and, for example, to woo Zouzou. At best I could set myself the goal of seducing her, but there were serious obstacles in the way: not circumstances alone, but also her fabulous forthrightness and her exaggeratedly literal notion of the laughable impropriety of love. Just listen to the retort with which she met my poetic sally.

'*Patatipatatá!*' she exclaimed. 'Enwrapped and inwoven and the lovely flowery kiss! All sugar to catch flies, a way of talking us into small-boy nastiness! *Pfui*, the kiss – that tender exchange! It's the beginning, the proper beginning, *mais oui*, or rather, it is the whole thing, *toute la lyre*, and the very worst of it. And why? Because it is the skin that all of you have in mind when you say love, the bare skin of the body. The skin of the lips is tender, you're right there, so tender that the blood is right behind it, and that's the reason for this poetry about the mutual discovery of pairs of lips: they in their tenderness want to go everywhere, and what you have in mind, all of you, is to lie naked with us, skin against skin, and teach us the absurd satisfaction that one miserable creature finds in savouring with lips and hands the moist surface of another. All of you do this without any feeling of shame at the pathetic ludicrousness of your behaviour and without giving thought – for it would spoil your game – to a couplet I once read in a book of spiritual instruction:

> *However fair and smooth the skin,*
> *Stench and corruption lie within.*'

'That's a nasty little verse, Zouzou,' I interrupted with a sad, disapproving shake of my head, 'nasty, however spiritual it pretends to be. I'll accept all your crudity, but that verse you've just recited cries to high heaven. And do you want to know why? Yes, yes, I am sure you do want to know. And I am prepared to tell you. Because this villainous little verse is designed to destroy belief in beauty and form, image and dream, belief in every phenomenon that, because it exists in words, is necessarily appearance and dream. But what would become of life and what would become of joy – without which there can be no life – if appearance and the surface world of the senses no longer counted for anything? I'll tell you something, charming Zouzou: your spiritual verse is more blasphemous than the most sinful lust of the flesh, for it is a spoil-sport, and to spoil the game of life is not only sinful, it is simply and entirely devilish. What do you say now? No, please, I'm not asking that to invite an interruption. I let you talk, however crudely, and now I am talking nobly, and am inspired to do so! If things went according to that altogether malicious verse, then the only thing really and not just apparently admirable would be, at most, the inanimate world, inorganic Being – I say at most, for when you think of it critically there is a question about its soundness, too. One may well ask whether an Alpine sunset or a waterfall is especially admirable, more so than an image or a dream, whether it is as true as it is beautiful – that is, true in itself without us, without our love and admiration. Now some time ago by the mysterious process of spontaneous generation organic life emerged from lifeless, inorganic Being. That its inward processes and essence are not of the cleanest goes without saying. Indeed, a smart aleck might say that all nature is nothing but mildew and corruption on the face of the earth, but that is simply the wisecrack of a smart aleck and never, to the end of time, will it succeed in killing love and joy – the joy in images. It was from a painter that I learned that. He painted the mildew with devotion, and was highly respected for it in the end. He used the human figure, too, as a model, as a model for a Greek god. Once in Paris, in the waiting-room of a dentist who made a small gold inlay for me, I saw a picture book entitled *La Beauté humaine*. It was filled with pictures of the finest reproductions of the human figure painters and sculptors had made throughout the ages with devotion and with joy. And why did it contain so many of these glorious pictures? Because at all times the earth has been full of fellows who paid not the slightest heed to your spiritual rhyme, but saw truth in form and appearance and surface, and made themselves their priests and very often won dignity and fame by doing so.'

I swear that's how I spoke, for I was inspired. And not just once did I speak thus, but repeatedly, whenever opportunity offered and I was alone with Zouzou. Sometimes it was on one of the benches beside the tennis courts, sometimes during a walk when four of us – including Senhor Hurtado, who would join us after luncheon – would stroll along the woody ways of the Campo Grande or between the banana plantings and tropical trees in the Largo do Príncipe Real. There had to be four of us so that I could walk alternately with the august half of the double image and then with her daughter. When I dropped back a little with Zouzou I could always find wise and noble words with which to combat her stupefying forthrightness and her childish notion that love was the unappetizing vice of small boys.

She clung stubbornly to this conception, though once or twice she betrayed by a silent, inquiring, sidewise glance fleetingly directed towards me that she had been struck by my eloquence and partly convinced – in short, that my zealous advocacy of joy and love had not completely missed its mark. There was one such moment, and I shall never forget it, when after many postponements we finally drove out in my carriage to the little village of Sintra. Under Dom Miguel's edifying guidance we had inspected the old castle in the village and then the citadels on the rocky heights with their fair prospects. Finally we drove on to the famous monastery of Belem (that is, Bethlehem), erected by the pious but ostentatious monarch King Emanuel the Happy, in honour and memory of the highly profitable Portuguese voyages of discovery. To be honest, Dom Miguel's lectures on the architectural styles of the castles and monasteries – the Moorish, Gothic, Italian elements, with an unexpected epilogue on Hindu influence – went, as they say, in one ear and out the other. I had other things to think about: to wit, how I could make love comprehensible to the forthright Zouzou. When one is occupied with a human problem, nature and the oddest architectural monuments alike become nothing but decoration, nothing but superficially apprehended background for what is human. Nevertheless, I must admit that this fairyland of stone was not without its effect. The incredible, magic delicacy of the cloister of Belem, belonging to no time and like a child's enchanted dream, with slender towers and delicate columns in the niche-vaults, the lightly patinated white sandstone cut into such fairytale magnificence that it seemed as though the stone could be worked with the slightest of fretsaws to produce these gems of lacy openwork – all this, I say, truly enchanted me, imaginatively exalted my mind, and certainly contributed to the excellence of the words I addressed to Zouzou.

We four had lingered rather a long time in the fabulous cloister, wandering around it repeatedly, and as Dom Miguel had no doubt noticed that we young people were not paying very close attention to his lecture on the King Emanuel style, he stayed with Dona Maria Pia, going ahead, and we followed at a distance that I did all I could to augment.

'Now, Zouzou,' I said, 'I imagine that in respect to this edifice our hearts beat as one. A cloister of this sort is something I have never come across before.' (I had not come across a cloister of any sort before, and it was just chance that my first one was this kind of child's dream.) 'I am very happy to visit it with you. But let's come to an agreement about the right word to describe it. "Beautiful"? No, that does not fit, though, of course, it is anything but unbeautiful. But "beautiful" – the word is too severe and elevated, don't you think? We must take the meaning of "pretty" and "charming" at their best, raise it to the nth degree and then we shall have the right term of praise for this cloister. For that's what it is: prettiness raised to the nth degree.'

'There you go babbling again, marquis. It's not unbeautiful, but it is not beautiful either, but simply extremely pretty. After all, what is extremely pretty is certainly beautiful.'

'No, there is a distinction. How can I make it clear to you? Your Mama, for example –'

'Is a beautiful woman,' Zouzou interrupted me quickly, 'and I am pretty at most; that's what you mean, isn't it? You are going to use us to illustrate your silly distinction, aren't you?'

'You anticipate me,' I replied after a measured pause, 'and you somewhat distort my thought. It does indeed run along the lines you indicate, but not precisely. It delights me to hear you say "we", "we two", of yourself and your mother. But after I have enjoyed the combination, I divide you again and proceed to admire you separately. Dona Maria Pia is perhaps an illustration of the fact that beauty, to be perfect, cannot entirely dispense with prettiness and loveliness. If your mother's face were not so large and stern and such a terrifying example of Iberian racial pride but had instead a little of your loveliness, she would be a completely beautiful woman. As things stand, she is not altogether what she ought to be: a beauty. You on the other hand, Zouzou, are prettiness and charm to perfection, raised to the nth degree. You are like this cloister . . .'

'Oh, thank you! I am a girl in the King Emanuel style, I am a capricious edifice. Many, many thanks. That's what I call gallantry.'

'You're free to make fun of my sincere words, to distort them and to call yourself an edifice. But you mustn't be surprised that this cloister has touched my heart so profoundly that I compare you to it, for you, too, have touched my heart. I am seeing the cloister for the first time. You certainly have seen it often?'

'Yes, a few times.'

'Then you should be happy to see it now in the company of a neophyte to whom it is all completely new. For that allows you to see the familiar with new eyes, the eyes of the neophyte, as though for the first time. One should always try to see everything, even the most commonplace, the most completely matter of fact, with new, astonished eyes as though for the first time. In this way it wins back its power to amaze, which has faded into matter-of-factness, and the world remains fresh. Otherwise, everything fades – life, joy, amazement. Take love, for example –'

'*Fi donc! Taisez-vous!*'

'But why? You, too, have talked of love, repeatedly, in accordance with your probably sound theory that silence is unhealthy. But you have expressed yourself so harshly about it, quoting nasty little spiritual verses, that you make one wonder how it is possible to speak so unlovingly of love. You have so grossly omitted sentiment in talking about the thing called love that what you say is unhealthy in its turn, and one feels obliged to contradict you and, if I may say so, to set you right. When one looks at love with new eyes, as though for the first time, what a touching and altogether amazing spectacle it is! It is nothing more or less than a miracle! In the last analysis, seen in the most comprehensive possible way, all existence is a miracle, but, according to my estimation, love is the greatest. Recently you said that Nature had carefully separated and divided one human being from another. Very apposite and only too true. That's how it is and that's the rule. But in love Nature has made an exception – a very marvellous one if you look at it with new eyes. Notice carefully that it is Nature that admits this astounding exception, or rather, introduces it, and if you take sides in this matter for Nature and against love, Nature will not thank you in the least; it's a *faux pas* on your part, you are taking sides against Nature. I'll explain that, as I've undertaken to set you right. It is true: a man lives separated and divided from others inside his own skin, not only because he does not wish it otherwise. He wants to be as separate as he is because essentially he wants to be alone and cares nothing at all about others. Anyone else, everyone else within a skin of his own, is actually repulsive. His own person is the only thing that is not repulsive. That's a law of Nature, I state it as it is. When he sits meditatively with his elbows on the table, his head in his hands, he may place a couple of fingers against his cheek and one between his lips. All right, it's his finger and his lips, and so what of it? But to have someone else's finger between his lips would be insupportable, it would actually fill him with loathing. Don't you agree? Loathing in actual fact is the essence of his relation to others. When their physical presence becomes oppressive, it is odious to him in the highest degree. He would rather suffocate than open his senses in proximity to alien bodies. Involuntarily he in his own skin takes every precaution, and it is only to spare his own sensibilities that he is considerate of others. Good. Or, at any rate, true. With these words I have sketched the natural over-all state of affairs briefly but accurately, and now I come to a paragraph in the speech I have specially prepared for you.

'For now something enters in through which Nature deviates amazingly from her basic design, something through which man's whole fastidious insistence upon separateness and being alone inside his own skin is annulled; the inflexible law that each is inoffensive only to himself is so completely wiped out that if one were to take the trouble to see it for the first time – and it is one's duty to do so – he might find his orbs overflowing from amazement and emotion. I use the words "orbs" and "overflow" because they are poetic and therefore appropriate to the subject. "To shed tears" seems to me too ordinary in this context. One sheds tears when one gets a cinder in one's eye. But "overflowing orbs" is on a higher plane.

'You must forgive me, Zouzou, if now and again I pause in this speech I have prepared for you and, as it were, begin a new paragraph. I am liable to digress, as here on the subject of orbs, and I must pull myself together again for the task of setting you right. Well, then! What is the digression on Nature's part that, to the astonishment of the universe, wipes out the division between one person and another, between the me and the you. It is love. An everyday affair, but eternally new and, carefully considered, nothing short of miraculous. What happens? Out of their separateness two glances encounter each other as glances never meet at other times. Startled and forgetful of the world, confused and a little shamefaced at their complete difference from all other glances, but not willing to surrender this difference for all the world, they sink into each other – if you wish, I will say "plunge into each other", but "plunge" is not necessary, "sink" is just as good. There is a trace of bad conscience as well – the reason for which I shall not ask. I am a simple nobleman, and no one can demand that I solve the riddles of the universe. In any case, it's the sweetest bad conscience in the world, and with this in their eyes and hearts these two who have suddenly been lifted above all classifications resolutely approach each other. They talk together in ordinary language about this and that, but both this and that are lies, just as the ordinary language is, and for this reason their lips as they speak have a slight mendacious twist and their eyes are full of sweet deceit. They glance at each other's hair and lips and limbs and then the deceitful eyes swiftly drop or wander abroad somewhere in the world where they have no interest and see nothing at all, for these eyes are blind to everything except each other. These glances seek refuge in the world only to return promptly and all the more brightly to the other's hair and lips and limbs, for these, contrary to all usage, have ceased to be alien and worse than indifferent, unpleasant, repulsive because they are not one's own but another's, and have become the object of delight, longing, and a yearning desire to touch – an ecstasy of which the eyes anticipate, steal in advance, all they can.

'That's a paragraph in my speech, Zouzou, and I shall make an indentation. You are listening to me carefully? As though you were hearing about love for the first time? I hope so. Before long there comes the moment when these two privileged beings are sick to death of lies and all the to-do about this and that and the twisted mouths, and they toss all this aside as though they were already tossing aside their clothes, and they pronounce the one true sentence, the only true one for them, in contrast to which everything else has been simply garrulous evasion: the words "I love you". It is a true fulfilment, the boldest and sweetest there is. Thereupon lips sink, or as one might say, plunge into one another in a kiss, an occurrence that is so unique in this world of separateness and isolation that one's orbs might well overflow at it. I ask you, how crudely you talked about the kiss, which is, after all, the pledge of that marvellous release from separateness and from the fastidious refusal to be interested in anything that is not oneself! I admit, I admit with the liveliest sympathy, that it is the beginning of everything that is to follow, for it is the astounding, silent declaration that closeness, ultimate closeness, closeness as complete as possible, just that closeness that otherwise is oppressive to the point of suffocation, has become the essence of all that is desirable. Through lovers, Zouzou, love does everything, exerts itself to the utmost, to make this closeness complete, perfect, to raise it to the actual oneness of two lives, but in this, comically and sadly, it is never successful despite all its efforts. It cannot to this extent triumph over Nature, for Nature, despite the fact that it invented love, sides in principle with separateness. For two to become one is not something that happens to lovers, it happens beyond them, if at all, in a third being, the child, who emerges from their efforts. But I am not talking about the blessings of parenthood and the joys of family life; that goes beyond my theme and I shall not touch on it. I am speaking about love in new and noble words and trying to create new eyes for you, Zouzou, and awaken your understanding to its touching miraculousness, so that you will not again express yourself so crudely about it. I do this by paragraphs because I cannot say it all in one breath, and here I make another indentation in order to say the following as follows:

'Love, Zouzou my love, does not consist simply in the state of being in love where, amazingly, one physically separate body ceases to be unpleasant to another. Everywhere in the world there are delicate signs and intimations of its existence. When a dirty beggar child on a streetcorner looks up at you and you not only give him a few centavos but run your ungloved hand over his hair, though very likely there are lice in it, and you smile into his eyes as you do so, and thereupon walk on happier than you were before – what is that but a delicate sign of love? I will tell you something, Zouzou: stroking that child's louse-infested hair with your bare hand and afterwards being happier than before is perhaps more astounding evidence of love than the fondling of a beloved body. Look about you in the world and look at Man as though you were doing so for the first time. Everywhere you will see signs of love, intimations of it, confessions of it on the part of what is separate and disinclined to have anything to do with another physical body. People shake hands – that is something very ordinary, everyday, and conventional; no one thinks anything about it except those who are in love, and they enjoy this contact because as yet no other is allowed them. Others do it unfeelingly and without considering that it was love that originated the practice; but they do it. Their bodies remain at a measured distance – not too great proximity on any account! But across this space separating two closely guarded individual lives they extend their arms, and the strange hands meet, embrace each other, press each other, and there is nothing in this but what is most ordinary, there is nothing of any special significance, so it seems, so one thinks. In truth, however, carefully examined, it belongs in the domain of the miraculous, and it is no small testimonial to Nature's departure from itself, the denial of the aversion of stranger for stranger, a secret sign of omnipresent love.'

My dear mother in Luxemburg would certainly never have believed that I could possibly have spoken thus and would no doubt have put down my report of it as nothing but a fine fiction. But I swear on my honour that is how I spoke, for it just came to me. Perhaps the fact that I succeeded in making so original a speech is to be attributed in large measure to the extreme prettiness and uniqueness of the Belem cloister through which we were wandering; let that be as it may. In any case that is how I spoke, and when I had finished a very remarkable thing happened. Zouzou gave me her hand! Without looking at me, her head turned away as though she were inspecting the stone fretwork at her side, she put out her right hand – I, of course, was walking on her left. I took it and pressed it, and she responded to the pressure. In the same instant, however, she jerked her hand away and said, with brows gathered stormily:

'And those drawings you took the liberty of making? Where are they? Why don't you finally produce them and hand them over to me?'

'But Zouzou, I have not forgotten. I have no intention of forgetting. Only you know yourself there has been no opportunity –'

'Your lack of imagination in finding an opportunity,' she said, 'is pitiable. I see that I must help out your ineptitude. With a little more circumspection and better powers of observation you would know without my having to tell you that behind our house – in the little garden at the rear, you understand – there is a bench surrounded by oleander bushes, more of a bower really, where I like to sit after luncheon. By this time you might know that, but of course you don't, as I have occasionally said to myself while sitting there. With the slightest degree of imagination and enterprise you would long ago have found an opportunity when lunching with us, after coffee, to act as though you were going away and actually to go a little distance, and then to turn about and come to find me in the bower, so that you could deliver your handiwork to me. Astonishing, isn't it? An idea of genius? Or so it would

seem to you. And so in the near future you will be kind enough to do this –
will you?'

'I most certainly will, Zouzou! It's really as brilliant as it is obvious.
Forgive me for not having noticed the bench under the oleanders. It's so far
at the rear I never paid any attention to it. So you sit there after lunch all
alone among the bushes? Marvellous! I'll do exactly as you say. I will
publicly take my departure, from you too, and appear to be going home;
instead of that, however, I will come to you with the pictures. I give you my
hand on it.'

'Keep your hand to yourself! We can shake hands later on after we have
returned home in your carriage. Meanwhile there's no sense in pressing each
other's hands all the time.'

Chapter Eleven

Happy though this arrangement made me, I was understandably nervous
at the thought of letting Zouzou see the pictures. It would be a rash act,
an impossible act. By adorning Zaza's pretty body, portrayed in various
poses, with Zouzou's highly characteristic cluster of curls I had transferred to it Zouzou's identity. How she would take these impertinent portraits was a disturbing question. Besides, I asked myself why it was necessary
to have luncheon at the Kuckucks' and go through the comedy of leave-
taking before seeking her out in the bower. If it was Zouzou's habit to sit
there alone after the midday meal, I could make my way to the bench
among the oleanders on any convenient day, trusting to the protection of
the siesta hour to escape discovery. If only I dared go to the rendezvous
without those accursed and outrageous drawings!

Whether, through fear of Zouzou's wrath which was unpredictable in
the degree of its violence, I did not in fact so dare, or whether my volatile
soul had been diverted from that desire by a new and thrilling experience
– of which I shall speak directly – suffice it to say that day after day passed
without my obeying Zouzou's command. Something intervened, I repeat,
a distracting experience, a sombre celebration, that altered from one hour
to the next my attitude towards the double image, reversing the emphasis
by revealing one aspect, the mother, in the strongest light, blood-red in
colour, and putting the other, the enchanting daughter, a little in the shade.

Very likely I use the metaphor of light and shade because the contrast
between them plays so important a part in the bull-ring – the contrast, that
is, between the sunny side and the shady side, with the shady side, where
we people of distinction sat, having the preference, of course, while the
small folk are banished into the sun ... But I speak too abruptly of the bull-
ring, as though the reader already knew that this very remarkable ancient
Iberian institution was going to be my subject. Writing is not a conversation with oneself. Orderly development, self-possession, and an unhurried
approach to the subject are indispensable.

To begin with, it must be said that my stay in Lisbon was now gradually
drawing to a close; it was already late September. The return of the *Cap
Arcona* was imminent, and there was barely a week until my departure.
This inspired me with a desire to pay a second and final visit, alone, to the

Museum Ciências Naturães in the Rue da Prata. Before leaving, I wanted to see again the white stag in the entrance hall, the primordial bird, the poor dinosaur, the great armadillo, that delightful nocturnal monkey, the loris, and all the others – not by any means least the worthy Neanderthal family and the Dawn Man presenting his bouquet to the sun. And so I did. One forenoon, my heart flooded with universal sympathy, I wandered without any guide through the halls and galleries on the ground floor and the corridors in the basement of Kuckuck's institution. Nor did I fail to put in a brief appearance in the director's office, for I wanted him to know that I had been drawn back to his museum. As usual, he received me with great cordiality, praised me for my faithfulness to his institution, and then made the following announcement.

That day, Saturday, was the birthday of Prince Luis-Pedro, a brother of the King. In recognition of this, there was to be a *corrida de toiros*, a bull-fight, next day at three in the afternoon, and the great man would be there. It was to be held in the big arena on the Campo Pequeno, and he, Kuckuck, was planning to attend this traditional spectacle with his ladies and Hurtado. He had tickets, seats on the shady side, and he had an extra one for me. For he considered it most opportune, in view of the educational purpose of my tour, that just before my departure I should have this opportunity of seeing a *corrida*. What did I think?

My thoughts were definitely unenthusiastic, and I told him so. The sight of blood made me somewhat queasy, I said, to my own knowledge, I was not the man for quaint national massacres. The horses, for instance – I had been told that the bull often ripped open their stomachs so that the entrails spilled out; I did not at all want to see this, not to mention the bull himself, for whom I should certainly feel sorry. One might suppose that if ladies' nerves were strong enough to stand this spectacle, I ought to be able to endure it if not exactly to enjoy it. But Portuguese ladies were born to these robust traditions, whereas he had in me a somewhat delicate foreigner – and so on, to the same effect.

But Kuckuck reassured me. I ought not to have too grisly an idea of the festival, he said. A *corrida* was, to be sure, a serious occasion, but not horrifying. The Portuguese were animal-lovers and would not permit anything horrible. As far as the horses were concerned, for a long time now they had been provided with protective padding so that hardly anything serious could happen to them, and the bull died a more chivalrous death than in the slaughterhouse. Besides, whenever I liked, I could glance away and turn my attention to the festive crowd and the view of the arena itself which was picturesque and of great ethnic interest.

Very well, I could see that I ought not to scorn this opportunity or his considerateness, for which I thanked him. We agreed that my carriage and I would wait for him and his family at the foot of the cable railway in ample time to ride to the arena together. It would go very slowly, Kuckuck warned; the streets would be crowded. I found this confirmed when next day, to be on the safe side, I left my hotel at two-fifteen. I had never seen the city in such a state, though I had been there on so many Sundays. Obviously, only a *corrida* could get everyone out. The Avenida in all its splendid width was crowded with carriages and people, teams of horses and teams of mules, people riding on asses and people walking, as were also the streets through which I rode to the Rua Augusta, kept to a walking pace by the density of the crowd. From every nook and cranny, from the old city, from the suburbs, from the surrounding villages, streamed city people and country people, mostly in holiday attire brought out only for such occasions. Hence, no doubt, the proud, expectant, and yet dignified, even reverent expression of their faces. Their mood, so it seemed to me, was sedate; there were no shouts or uproar, no quarrelsome collisions, as they moved with one accord in the direction of the Campo Pequino and the amphitheatre.

Whence the strange feeling of oppression, the mixture of awe, sympathy, and excitement tinged with sadness, that constricts the heart at the sight of a crowd exalted by a festival and informed and united by its meaning? There is something inarticulate, primordial, about it that inspires awe and a certain anxiousness as well. The weather was still midsummer's, the bright sun glinted on the copper ferrules of the long staffs the men planted before them like pilgrims. They wore bright-coloured sashes and hats with broad rims. The women's clothes were of snowy cotton, embroidered at breast, sleeve, and hem with gold and silver thread. Many wore high Spanish combs, often with the black or white veil called *mantilha*, which covers head and shoulders. There was nothing surprising about this in the case of farm women out for a holiday, but when Dona Maria Pia came to greet me at the cable-car station, not, to be sure, in the glittering national costume but in an elegant afternoon dress, wearing, however, just such a black *mantilha* over her high comb – I was surprised, yes, startled. She saw no reason for any smile of apology for this ethnic masquerade, and no more did I. Deeply impressed, I bowed with special reverence over her hand. The *mantilha* was particularly becoming to her. Through its fine fabric the sun threw a filigree pattern on her large, pale, stern face.

Zouzou wore no *mantilha*. And in my eyes, at least, the charming cluster of dark curls at her temples was ethnic mark enough. Her dress, however, was even darker than her mother's, a little as though she were going to church. And the gentlemen, the professor as well as Dom Miguel, who had arrived on foot and had joined us as we were exchanging greetings, were in formal attire, black cutaways and bowler hats, whereas I had selected a blue suit with bright stripes. This was somewhat embarrassing, but the ignorance of a stranger might perhaps excuse it.

I ordered my coachman to go by way of the Avenida-Park and the Campo Grande, where it was quieter. The professor and his wife sat on the back seat, Zouzou and I facing them, and Dom Miguel took the seat beside the coachman. The ride passed in silence or with very brief exchanges, due principally to Senhora Maria's extremely dignified, indeed stern, demeanour, which admitted of no chitchat. Once, to be sure, her husband calmly addressed a remark to me, but before answering I involuntarily glanced towards the sombre lady in the Iberian head-dress and replied with reserve. Her black amber ear-rings oscillated, set in motion by the light jolting of the carriage.

At the entrance to the arena, the traffic was dense. Advancing very slowly between the other equipages, we had to wait patiently for our turn to dismount. Then the vast circle of the amphitheatre engulfed us with its barriers, pillared balustrades, and ascending rows of seats, of which only a few were still unoccupied. Beribboned officials directed us to our seats on the shady side at a convenient height above the yellow circle strewn with tanbark and sand. The huge arena filled quickly to the last seat. Kuckuck had not exaggerated the picturesque impressiveness of its appearance. It was a colourful collective portrait of a whole national society, an occasion on which the aristocracy, symbolically at least and somewhat shamefacedly, accommodated itself to the customs of the folk sitting opposite in the blazing sun. Not a few ladies, even foreigners like Frau von Hueon and the Princess Maurocordato, had provided themselves with high combs and *mantilhas*; indeed, some of them had imitated in their dress the gold and silver embroidery of the peasant costume, and the formal attire of the men seemed a mark of respect towards the folk – prompted at least by the popular character of the occasion.

The mood of the enormous circle seemed expectant yet subdued. It differed markedly even on the sunny side, or especially there, from the nasty vulgarity so common among crowds at ordinary sporting-events. Excitement, tension, I felt them myself; but as far as one could see in the thousands of faces staring down at the still empty battleground, whose yellow would soon be stained with pools of blood, these emotions seemed restrained, held in check by a certain air of consecration. The music broke off and changed from a Moorish-Spanish concert piece to the national anthem as the Prince, a lean man with a star on his frock-coat and a chrysanthemum in his buttonhole, entered his loge. With him was his wife, wearing a *mantilha*. Everyone got up and applauded. This was to happen again in honour of a different individual.

These dignitaries had entered at one minute before three. On the stroke of the hour, to a continuing musical accompaniment, the procession moved out of the big centre gate, led by three men bearing swords, epaulettes over their short embroidered jackets, colourful tight trousers extending to the middle of their calves, white stockings, and buckled shoes. Behind them strode the *bandarilleiros*, carrying their pointed, bright-coloured darts, and the *capeadores*, arrayed in similar style, their narrow black cravats dangling over their shirts, their short red capes across their arms. They were followed by a cavalcade of *picadores* armed with lances, their hats strapped beneath their chins, mounted on horses whose padding hung like mattresses on chest and flank. A team of donkeys adorned with flowers and ribbons brought up the rear. The procession moved directly across the yellow circle towards the Prince's box and there dispersed after each member had made a formal bow. I saw some of the *toireadores* cross themselves as they made their way to the protection of the barrier.

All at once the little orchestra again stopped in the middle of a selection. A single very high trumpet note rang out. The ensuing stillness was complete. Through a little gate which I had not noticed before and which had suddenly been thrown open, there breaks – I use the present tense, because the experience is so vivid to me – something elemental, running, the steer, black, heavy, mighty, a visibly irresistible concentration of procreative and murderous force, in which earlier, older peoples certainly saw a god-animal, the animal god, with little, threatening, rolling eyes and horns twisted like drinking-horns affixed to his broad forehead, bending a little upwards at the points, and clearly charged with death. He runs forward, stops with forelegs braced, glares angrily at the red cloth that one of the *capeadores* has spread out on the sand in front of him with the gesture of a servitor, throws himself at it, rams one horn into it, and bores the cloth into the ground. Just as he is about to shift horns, the little human snatches the cloth away, springs behind him, and as this mass of power swings ponderously on itself two *bandarilheiros* plant their bright-coloured darts in the cushion of fat at the back of his neck. There they sit now; barbed, no doubt, they sway but hold fast, standing out at an angle to his body through the rest of the contest. A third man has planted a short feathered lance in the exact middle of his neck, and he carries this decoration, like the spreading wings of a dove, through the remainder of his deadly battle against death.

I sat between Kuckuck and Dona Maria Pia. In a low voice the professor provided me with an occasional commentary on the proceedings. I learned from him the names of the various passes. I heard him say that until that day the bull had led a lordly life in the open fields, cared for and attended with the greatest solicitude and courtesy. My neighbour to the right, the august lady, remained silent. She only took her eyes off the god of procreation and slaughter and what was happening to him long enough to direct a glance of reproof towards her husband when he spoke. Her pale, severe face in the shadow of the *mantilha* was expressionless, but her bosom rose and fell faster and faster and, certain of being unobserved, I watched that face and the ill-controlled surging of that bosom more than I watched the sacrificial animal with the lance in his back, the ridiculously tiny wings, and the blood beginning to streak his sides.

I call him a sacrifice because one would have to be dull indeed not to feel the atmosphere that lay over all, at once oppressive and solemnly joyous, a unique mingling of jest, blood, and dedication, primitive holiday-making combined with the profound ceremonial of death. Later in my carriage when he was at liberty to speak, the professor discoursed about all this, but his erudition added nothing essential to what my alert and subtle intelligence had divined. The jest, combined with rage, burst forth a few minutes later when the bull, obviously having reached the conclusion that things could not possibly turn out well for him, that force and wit were unequally matched, turned round in the direction of the gate through which he had entered with the intention of trotting back to his stall, the ribboned darts still hanging from his neck. There was a storm of outraged, scornful laughter. People sprang to their feet, on the sunny side especially, but on ours as well; there were whistles, shouts, cat-calls, curses. My august companion jumped up, whistled with startling shrillness, made a face at the coward, and emitted a sonorous trill of disdainful laughter. *Picadores* dashed into the bull's path and pushed at him with their blunt lances. New *banderillas* were rammed into his neck and shoulders, some of them equipped with firecrackers to enliven him; they went off with a bang and a hiss against his hide. Under such provocation the brief attack of reason which had so incensed the crowd was quickly transformed into the blind rage appropriate to his might and to this game of death. Once more he played his part and did not fail again. A horse and rider sprawled in the sand. A *capeador* who had stumbled was unhappily lifted on the mighty drinking-horns and hurled into the air. He fell heavily. While the wild beast was being drawn away from the motionless body by exploiting his prejudice against red cloth, the man was lifted and carried out amid honourable applause, which may have been for him or, equally, for the *toiro*. Very likely it was for both. Maria da Cruz joined in, alternately clapping her hands and crossing herself rapidly as she murmured in her own tongue what may have been a prayer for the fallen man.

The professor expressed the opinion that it would amount to no more than a couple of broken ribs and a concussion. 'Here comes Ribeiro,' he added, 'a notable young man.' From the group of actors there now emerged an *espada*, who was greeted with *ah*'s and cheers that testified to his popularity. While all the rest stood back, he occupied the arena alone with the bleeding, maddened bull. Even during the procession I had been struck by him, for my eye automatically selects from among the commonplace whatever is elegant and beautiful. This Ribeiro was eighteen or nineteen

years old and extremely handsome. He wore his black hair smooth and un-
parted, brushed forward over his brow. On his finely chiselled Spanish
face there was the trace of a smile, called forth perhaps by the applause
or perhaps simply by his contempt for death and his awareness of his own
prowess. His narrowed black eyes looked out with quiet earnestness. The
short embroidered jacket with epaulettes and sleeves narrowing at the wrists
became him – ah, it was in just such a costume that my godfather Schimmelpreester had once dressed me – it became him as admirably as it had
me. I saw that he was of slender build, with noble hands. In one hand he
carried a bare bright Damascus blade, which he handled like a cane; in the
other he held a red cape. Reaching the centre of the arena, which was
already torn and blood-flecked, he dropped the sword and gestured with
his cape at the bull standing some distance off shaking the *banderillas.*
Then he stood motionless and watched with that barely perceptible smile
and that earnest expression of the eyes the maddened charge of the frightful martyr, offering himself as a target like a tree standing bare to the
lightning. He stood as though rooted – too long, it was certain; one would
have had to know him well not to be horribly sure that in the next twinkling of an eye he would be hurled to the ground, gored, massacred, trampled
to bits. Instead of that, something extremely graceful occurred, something
casual and expert that produced a magnificent picture. The horns already
had him, they had ripped a bit of embroidery from his jacket, when, with
a single easy gesture of the hand that communicated itself to the cape, he
directed those murderous instruments to where he no longer was, as a
graceful swing of the hips brought him up against the monster's flank, and
the human figure, arm now extended along the black back to where the
horns were plunging into the fluttering cape, blended with the beast in an
inspired design. The crowd leaped up, shouting: 'Ribeiro!' and '*Toiro!*' and
applauding. I did so myself and so did the regal Iberian beside me. Back
and forth I glanced, from her surging breast to the living statue of man
and animal, now rapidly dissolving, for more and more the stern and elemental person of this woman seemed to me one with the game of blood
below.

In his duet with the *toiro* Ribeiro performed various other virtuoso feats
in which he was clearly intent on creating ballet motifs at instants of extreme
danger, and on the plastic mingling of the awesome and the elegant. Once
when the weakened bull, disgusted by the futility of his rage, turned away
and stood brooding dully by himself, his partner was seen to turn his back
and kneel in the sand, very slim and erect with raised arms and bowed
head, spreading the cape behind him. That seemed daring indeed, but
he was no doubt sure of the momentary lethargy of the horned devil. Once,
running in front of the bull, he half fell on one hand while with the other
he let the seductive red cape divert the raging beast to one side. In the
next instant he had sprung to his feet and vaulted lightly over the creature's
back. He never acknowledged the continual applause, for it was obviously
meant for the *toiro* as well, who had no mind for applause or acknowledgement. I half feared the man might consider it unseemly to play such
tricks on a sacrificial creature that had been raised with courtesy on the
open plains. But that was just the point of the jest and, in this ancient folk
ceremonial, was an element in the cult of blood.

To end the game, Ribeiro ran over to the sword he had dropped and
stood, one knee bent, spreading his cape in the usual provocative fashion.
With serious gaze he watched the bull charge at a heavy gallop with horns

levelled. He let him come very close, almost upon him, and in the final instant snatched the sword from the ground and drove the slender, bright steel half way to the hilt in the animal's neck. The bull crumpled, wheeling massively. For a moment he forced one horn into the ground as though it were the red cloth, then he fell on his side and his eyes glazed.

It was indeed the most elegant slaughter. I can still see Ribeiro, his cape under his arm, walking away on tiptoe as though fearful of making a sound, glancing back the while at the fallen creature that moved no more. Before that, during the brief death scene, the public had risen from their seats as one man and given the tribute of their applause to the hero of this game of death, who, but for his early attempt to flee, had conducted himself admirably. The applause lasted until he had been carted off by the colourful mule team and wagon. Ribeiro walked beside him as though to do him a final honour. He did not return. Later, under another name, in a different role, and as part of a double image, he was to reappear in my life. But of that in its proper place.

We saw two more bulls that were not so good as the first, nor were the *espadas*, one of whom drove in the sword so clumsily that the animal haemorrhaged but did not fall. He stood there like someone vomiting, legs braced and neck extended, spewing out thick waves of blood onto the sand, an unpleasant sight. A heavy-set matador of vain deportment and exaggeratedly brilliant dress had to give him the *coup de grâce*, and so the hilts of two swords stuck out of his body. We left. In the carriage, then, Maria Pia's husband provided us with a learned commentary on what we had just seen – I, for the first time. He spoke of a very ancient Roman shrine whose existence testified to a deep descent from the high cult level of Christianity to the service of a deity well disposed towards blood whose worship, through the wide popularity of the rites, almost outstripped that of the Lord Jesus as a world religion. Its converts had been baptized not with water, but with the blood of a bull, who was perhaps the god himself, though the god lived too in the one who spilled his blood. For this teaching contained something that unified its believers irrevocably, joining them in life and in death; and its mystery consisted in the equality and identity of slayer and slain, axe and victim, arrow and target ... I listened to all this with only half an ear, only in so far as it did not interfere with my absorption in the woman whose image and being had been so vastly enhanced by the folk festival, who had, as it were, been truly and completely herself for the first time, ripe for observation. Her bosom was now at rest. I longed to see it surge again.

I will not conceal the fact that Zouzou had gone completely out of my mind during the game of blood. For this reason I was all the more determined to follow her instructions at last and, for God's sake, to show her the pictures that she claimed as her own – those nude studies of Zaza with Zouzou's curls at the temples. I had been invited to the Kuckucks' for lunch the following day. A shower during the night had cooled the air; a light coat was in order, and in the inside pocket I put the roll of drawings. Hurtado, too, was there. At table the conversation turned on yesterday's spectacle, and to please the professor I inquired further about the religion that had been driven from the field, the cult that marked a long step down from Christianity. He could not add much, but answered that those rites had not been so completely driven from the field, for the smoking blood of a victim – the god's blood, that is – had always been a part of the pious, popular ceremonials of mankind, and he sketched a connexion between the sacrament of communion and the festal, fatal drama of the day before. I looked at the lady of the house, curious to see whether or not her bosom was at rest.

After coffee I said farewell to the ladies, planning to pay a final call on my last day. I rode down on the cable car with the gentlemen, who were returning to the museum, and when we arrived I said good-bye to them, with repeated thanks, leaving the question of seeing them again to an indeterminate future. I acted as though I meant to walk back to the Savoy Palace, but turning around and finding the coast clear, I took the next cable car up again.

I knew the gate in the fence in front of the little house would be open. The earlier chill had given place to a mild and sunny autumn day. This was the hour for Dona Maria Pia's siesta. I could be sure of finding Zouzou in the rear garden. With cautious but rapid strides I walked towards it along the gravel path that led around the side of the house. Dahlias and asters were blooming in the middle of the small lawn. The appointed bench stood off to the right, surrounded by a semicircle of oleander bushes. The dear child was sitting there half in shadow, wearing a dress very like the one in which I had seen her first, loose, as she liked a dress to be, blue-striped, with a belt of the same material around the waist and some lacework at the edge of the half-length sleeves. She was reading a book and although she must have heard my cautious approach, she did not look up until I was in front of her. My heart pounded.

'Ah?' she said. Her lips, like the beautiful ivory tint of her skin, seemed somewhat paler than usual. 'Still here?'

'Here again, Zouzou. I have been down to the bottom of the hill. I came back secretly, as we planned, to fulfil my promise.'

'How praiseworthy!' she said. '*Monsieur le marquis* has remembered an obligation – without undue haste. This bench has slowly become a kind of waiting-room –' She had said more than she intended and bit her lip.

'How could you imagine,' I hastened to reply, 'that I would fail to live up to the arrangement we made in the beautiful cloister! May I sit down with you? This bench in the bushes is a good deal more private than the ones at the tennis court. I am afraid I shall have to neglect the game again and forget –'

'Not at all, the Meyer-Novaros across the ocean will certainly have a tennis court.'

'Possibly. But it won't be the same thing. Leaving Lisbon, Zouzou, is very hard for me. I have said good-bye to your esteemed papa. How memorably he talked at luncheon about the pious ceremonials of mankind! The *corrida* yesterday was, after all – I'll say this at least, a curious experience.'

'I did not watch it very closely. Your attention too, seemed to be divided – as you like it to be. But to the point, marquis! Where are my drawings?'

'Here,' I said. 'It was your wish . . . You understand, they are imaginative creations, produced, as it were, involuntarily.'

She held the drawings in her hand and looked at the top one. It was an enamoured sketch of Zaza's body in such-and-such a posture. The flat button ear-rings matched, the cluster of curls matched even more exactly. There was little enough resemblance in the face, but what did the face count for here?

I sat as straight as Dona Maria Pia, prepared for anything, agreeable to anything, and thrilled in advance by whatever might occur. A deep blush suffused her face at the sight of her own sweet nakedness. She sprang up, tore the works of art into tiny pieces, and strewed them fluttering on the breeze. Of course, that was something that had to happen. What did not have to happen and yet did, was this: she stared for an instant with a bewildered expression at the scraps of paper lying on the ground, and the next instant her eyes filled, she sank back on the bench, flung her arm around my neck and buried her glowing face on my breast. She gave little noiseless sighs that were nevertheless clearly perceptible, and at the same time – and this was the most touching of all – she kept up a rhythmic hammering against my shoulder with her little fist, the left one. I kissed the bare arm around my neck, I raised her lips to mine and kissed them. They responded, just as I had dreamed, longed, determined they would when I had first seen her, my Zaza, on the Rossio. Who of you whose eyes peruse these lines will not envy my such sweet instants? Nor envy her as well, however hard the little fist might pound, for her conversion to love? But now what a peripeteia! What a reversal of fortune!

Zouzou suddenly threw back her head and tore herself from our embrace. In front of bush and bench, in front of us, stood her mother.

Silent, as though we had been struck on those lips so recently united, we looked up at the august lady, at her large, pale countenance, jet earrings quivering on either side, at the severe mouth, widened nostrils, and stormy brows. Or rather, I alone looked at her; Zouzou kept her chin lowered on her breast and went on with the rapid-fire pounding of her little fist, striking now against the bench on which we sat. And yet I ask you to believe that I was less cast down by this maternal apparition than one might have thought. However unexpected her appearance, it seemed fitting and necessary, as though she had been summoned, and in my natural confusion there was an element of joy.

'Madame,' I said formally, rising, 'I regret the interruption of your afternoon rest. What has happened has occurred almost accidentally and with complete propriety –'

'Silence!' the lady commanded in her marvellously sonorous, slightly hoarse voice. And turning to Zouzou:

'Susanna, go to your room and remain there until you are called.' Then to me: 'Marquis, I wish to speak to you. Follow me.'

Zouzou rushed off across the lawn, which had obviously deadened the approaching footsteps of the *senhora*. Now she went along the path and, obeying her injunction to follow, I walked not at her side but behind her and a little to one side. Thus we entered the living-room, from which a door led into the dining-room. Behind the opposite door, which was not entirely closed, there seemed to be a room of more intimate character. The austere lady closed that door.

I met her glance. She was not pretty but very beautiful.

'Luiz,' she said, 'the obvious thing would be to ask you whether this is your way of repaying Portuguese hospitality – be silent! I shall spare myself the question and you the answer. I did not summon you here to give you an opportunity for witless apologies. They could not possibly exceed the stupidity of your conduct. That is unsurpassable, and all that is left for you, all you are entitled to, is to be silent and let more mature persons see to your interests and lead you back to the right path from the childish irresponsibility you were youthful enough to engage in. There's seldom more miserable childishness or more wicked nonsense than when youth associates with youth. What were you thinking of? What do you want of this child? With complete ingratitude you bring nonsense and confusion into a home that was hospitably thrown open to you because of your birth and other agreeable attributes, and where order, reason, and intelligent planning prevail. Sooner or later, probably within a short time, Susanna will become the wife of Dom Miguel, the worthy assistant of Dom Antonio José whose unequivocal wish and will this is. You can thus realize what stupidity you were guilty of when, in your need for love, you followed a childish course and formed the capricious notion of turning a child's head. That was not choosing or acting like a man, but like an infant. Mature reason had to intervene before it was too late. Once when we were conversing you spoke to me about the graciousness of maturity and the graciousness with which it speaks of youth. To encounter it successfully requires, of course, a man's courage. If an agreeable youth only showed a man's courage instead of seeking satisfaction in childishness, he would not have to run off like a drenched poodle, uncomforted, into the wide world . . .'

'Maria!' I cried.

And: '*Holé! Heho! Ahé!*' she exclaimed in majestic jubilation. A whirlwind of primordial forces seized and bore me into the realm of ecstasy. And high and stormy, under my ardent caresses, stormier than at the Iberian game of blood, I saw the surging of that queenly bosom.

TITLES IN THIS SERIES:

Eric Ambler
The Mask of Dimitrios Passage of Arms
The Schirmer Inheritance Journey
into Fear The Light of Day

John le Carré
The Spy Who Came in From the Cold
Call for the Dead A Murder of Quality
The Looking-Glass War A Small Town
in Germany

Raymond Chandler★
Farewell My Lovely The Lady in the
Lake Playback The Long Goodbye
The High Window The Big Sleep

Catherine Cookson
The Round Tower The Fifteen Streets
Feathers in the Fire A Grand Man
The Blind Miller

Monica Dickens
One Pair of Hands The Happy
Prisoner Mariana Kate and Emma
One Pair of Feet

F. Scott Fitzgerald★
The Great Gatsby Tender is the Night
This Side of Paradise The Beautiful
and the Damned The Last Tycoon

Ian Fleming
Dr. No Thunderball Goldfinger
On Her Majesty's Secret Service
Moonraker From Russia With Love

C. S. Forester
The Ship Mr. Midshipman Hornblower
The Captain from Connecticut
The General The Earthly Paradise
The African Queen

E. M. Forster
Where Angels Fear to Tread The
Longest Journey A Room with a View
Howards End A Passage to India

John Galsworthy
The Forsyte Saga: The Man of
Property In Chancery To Let
A Modern Comedy: The White Monkey
The Silver Spoon Swan Song

Erle Stanley Gardner
Perry Mason in the Case of the Gilded
Lily The Daring Decoy The Fiery
Fingers The Lucky Loser The Calendar
Girl The Deadly Toy The Mischievous
Doll The Amorous Aunt

Richard Gordon
Doctor in the House Doctor at Sea
Doctor at Large Doctor in Love Doctor
in Clover The Facemaker The Medical
Witness

Graham Greene
The Heart of the Matter Stamboul Train
A Burnt-Out Case The Third Man
Loser Takes All The Quiet American
The Power and the Glory

Ernest Hemingway★
For Whom the Bell Tolls Fiesta The
Snows of Kilimanjaro The Short Happy
Life of Francis Macomber Across the
River and into the Trees The Old Man
and the Sea

Georgette Heyer
These Old Shades Sprig Muslin
Sylvester The Corinthian
The Convenient Marriage

Franz Kafka★
The Trial America In the Penal
Settlement Metamorphosis The Castle
The Great Wall of China Investigations
of a Dog Letter to His Father
The Diaries 1910—1923

Rudyard Kipling
The Just So Stories Stalky and Co.
Puck of Pook's Hill The Jungle Book
The Second Jungle Book

D. H. Lawrence
Sons and Lovers St. Mawr The Fox
The White Peacock Love Among the
Haystacks The Virgin and the Gipsy
Lady Chatterley's Lover

Norah Lofts
Jassy Bless This House Scent of Cloves
How Far to Bethlehem?

Robert Ludlum★
The Scarlatti Inheritance The Matlock
Paper The Osterman Weekend
The Gemini Contenders

Thomas Mann★
Death in Venice Tristan Tonio Kröger
Doctor Faustus Mario and the Magician
A Man and His Dog The Black Swan
Confessions of Felix Krull, Confidence
Man

W. Somerset Maugham
Cakes and Ale The Painted Veil Liza of
Lambeth The Razor's Edge Theatre
The Moon and Sixpence

W. Somerset Maugham
Sixty-five Short Stories

Ed McBain★
Cop Hater Give the Boys a Great Big
Hand Doll Eighty Million Eyes
Hail, Hail, the Gang's All Here! Sadie
When She Died Let's Hear it for the
Deaf Man

James A. Michener★
The Source The Bridges at Toko-Ri
Caravans Sayonara

George Orwell
Animal Farm Burmese Days
A Clergyman's Daughter Coming up for
Air Keep the Aspidistra Flying
Nineteen Eighty-four

Jean Plaidy
St. Thomas's Eve Royal Road to
Fotheringay The Goldsmith's Wife
Perdita's Prince

Nevil Shute
A Town Like Alice Pied Piper
The Far Country The Chequer Board
No Highway

George Simenon
Ten Maigret Stories

Wilbur Smith
When the Lion Feeds The Diamond
Hunters Eagle in the Sky Gold Mine
Shout at the Devil

John Steinbeck★
The Grapes of Wrath The Moon is
Down Cannery Row East of Eden
Of Mice and Men

Mary Stewart
The Crystal Cave The Hollow Hills
Wildfire at Midnight
Airs Above the Ground

Evelyn Waugh
Decline and Fall Black Mischief A
Handful of Dust Scoop Put Out More
Flags Brideshead Revisited

H. G. Wells
The Time Machine The Island of
Dr. Moreau The Invisible Man The
First Men in the Moon The Food of the
Gods In The Days of the Comet
The War of the Worlds

Morris West
The Shoes of the Fisherman
The Second Victory Daughter of Silence
The Salamander The Devil's Advocate

Dennis Wheatley
The Devil Rides Out The Haunting of
Toby Jugg Gateway to Hell
To the Devil—A Daughter

Fourteen Great Plays★

**★ Not currently available in
Canada for copyright reasons**